*The Editor*

PETER SHILLINGSBURG is professor of English at Mississippi State University. He is the author of *Pegasus in Harness: Victorian Publishing and William Makepeace Thackeray* and *Scholarly Editing in the Computer Age.* He is the editor of the Garland Press editions of Thackeray's *Flore et Zéphyr, Yellowplush, Vanity Fair,* and *Pendennis* as well as *Poems of Howell Gwin.* Shillingsburg has been visiting professor at the Australian Defence Force Academy, and was also a Guggenheim Fellow. He is a member and former chairman of the Modern Language Association's Committee on Scholarly Editions.

# VANITY FAIR

AUTHORITATIVE TEXT
BACKGROUNDS AND CONTEXTS
CRITICISM

W. W. NORTON & COMPANY, INC.
*Also Publishes*

THE NORTON ANTHOLOGY OF AFRICAN AMERICAN LITERATURE
*edited by Henry Louis Gates Jr. and Nellie Y. McKay et al.*

THE NORTON ANTHOLOGY OF AMERICAN LITERATURE
*edited by Nina Baym et al.*

THE NORTON ANTHOLOGY OF CONTEMPORARY FICTION
*edited by R. V. Cassill and Joyce Carol Oates*

THE NORTON ANTHOLOGY OF ENGLISH LITERATURE
*edited by M. H. Abrams and Stephen Greenblatt et al.*

THE NORTON ANTHOLOGY OF LITERATURE BY WOMEN
*edited by Sandra M. Gilbert and Susan Gubar*

THE NORTON ANTHOLOGY OF MODERN AND CONTEMPORARY POETRY
*edited by Jahan Ramazani, Richard Ellmann, and Robert O'Clair*

THE NORTON ANTHOLOGY OF POETRY
*edited by Margaret Ferguson, Mary Jo Salter, and Jon Stallworthy*

THE NORTON ANTHOLOGY OF SHORT FICTION
*edited by R. V. Cassill and Richard Bausch*

THE NORTON ANTHOLOGY OF THEORY AND CRITICISM
*edited by Vincent B. Leitch et al.*

THE NORTON ANTHOLOGY OF WORLD LITERATURE
*edited by Sarah Lawall et al.*

THE NORTON FACSIMILE OF THE FIRST FOLIO OF SHAKESPEARE
*prepared by Charlton Hinman*

THE NORTON INTRODUCTION TO LITERATURE
*edited by Jerome Beaty, Alison Booth, J. Paul Hunter, and Kelly J. Mays*

THE NORTON INTRODUCTION TO THE SHORT NOVEL
*edited by Jerome Beaty*

THE NORTON READER
*edited by Linda H. Peterson, John C. Brereton, and Joan E. Hartman*

THE NORTON SAMPLER
*edited by Thomas Cooley*

THE NORTON SHAKESPEARE, BASED ON THE OXFORD EDITION
*edited by Stephen Greenblatt et al.*

For a complete list of Norton Critical Editions, visit
www.wwnorton.com/college/English/nce_home.htm

A NORTON CRITICAL EDITION

WILLIAM MAKEPEACE THACKERAY

# VANITY FAIR

AN AUTHORITATIVE TEXT

BACKGROUNDS AND CONTEXTS

CRITICISM

*Edited by*

PETER SHILLINGSBURG

MISSISSIPPI STATE UNIVERSITY

W • W • NORTON & COMPANY • *New York* • *London*

Printed in the United States of America.

First Edition

The text of this book is composed in Baskerville
with the display set in Bernhard Modern.
Composition by Peter Shillingsburg (the novel) and PennSet, Inc.
Manufacturing by LSC Communications, Crawfordsville.

Library of Congress Cataloging-in-Publication Data
Thackeray, William Makepeace, 1811–1863.
Vanity Fair : authoritative text, backgrounds, criticism / edited
by Peter Shillingsburg.
p. cm.—(A Norton critical edition)
Includes bibliographical references.
1. England—Social life and customs—19th century—Fiction.
2. Thackeray, William Makepeace, 1811–1863. Vanity fair. 3. Women—
England—Fiction. I. Shillingsburg, Peter L.
PR5618.A1 1994
823'.8—dc20 93-48019

W. W. Norton & Company, Inc., 500 Fifth Avenue, New York, N.Y. 10110
http://www.wwnorton.com

W. W. Norton & Company Ltd., Castle House, 15 Carlisle Street, London W1D 3BS
8 9 0

# Contents


Preface ix

**The Text of *Vanity Fair*** xiii

Engraved vignette title page xiv

Appendix: Composition and Revision of Chapter VI 691

**Backgrounds and Contexts** 697

COMPOSITION AND PRODUCTION 699

William Makepeace Thackeray • Selected Letters

To Mrs. Carmichael-Smyth, July 2, 1847 699

To the Duke of Devonshire, May 1, 1848 699

To Miss Smith, June 6, 1848 701

Anne Thackeray Ritchie • [Introduction to *Vanity Vair*] 702

Gordon Ray • [Originals] 703

Edgar F. Harden • The Discipline and Significance of Form in *Vanity Fair* 710

Geoffrey Tillotson • [Philosophy and Narrative Technique] 731

Peter L. Shillingsburg • The "Trade" of Literature 739

RECEPTION 745

Robert A. Colby • [Reception Summary] 745

[Abraham Hayward] • Thackeray's Writings 749

Charlotte Brontë • Selected Letters

To W. S. Williams, March 29, 1848 751

To W. S. Williams, August 14, 1848 751

William Makepeace Thackeray • Letter to George Henry Lews, March 6, 1848 752

[George Henry Lewes] • Review 753

[Robert Bell] • Review 758

William Makepeace Thackeray • Letter to Robert Bell, September 3, 1848 761

Charlotte Brontë • Preface to the Second Edition of *Jane Eyre* 763
[Elizabeth Rigby] • Review 763
CONTEXTS 770
A Pretty Fellow • Wanted a Governess, on Handsome Terms 770
Maria Edgeworth • Female Accomplishments, Etc. 771
Kathleen Tillotson • [Propriety and the Novel] 772
Joan Stevens • *Vanity Fair* and the London Skyline 777
Robert A. Colby • [Victor Cousin and the Foundation for an "Edifice of Humanity"] 798

Criticism 805
William C. Brownell • William Makepeace Thackeray 807
David Cecil • [A Criticism of Life] 811
G. Armour Craig • On the Style of *Vanity Fair* 822
John Loofbourow • Neo-Classical Conventions 830
Peter K. Garrett • [Dialogic Form] 835
Richard Barickman, Susan MacDonald, and Myra Stark • [Politics of Sexuality] 841
Ina Ferris • The Narrator of *Vanity Fair* 856
Catherine Peters • [Didacticism] 857
James Phelan • *Vanity Fair*: Listening as a Rhetorician —and a Feminist 859

CHRONOLOGY 869

SELECTED BIBLIOGRAPHY 873

# Preface

From John Forster and Elizabeth Rigby, among early reviewers, to Percy Lubbock, Jack Rawlins, and Jerome Meckier more recently, readers have objected to *Vanity Fair* because it does not say clearly what is real and what is not, what is good and what is not, because it does not make the moral dilemmas clear, because its author seems to waffle in his stand, because the novel's view of humankind is simultaneously too cynical and too sentimental—in short because the reader cannot be sure what the author or the narrator *really* thinks and, therefore, cannot know whether to agree or disagree. Fiction should not come so close to real life, said Miss Rigby, that the moral imperatives become too complex or obscure.

From Robert Bell and Dr. John Brown, among early reviewers and admirers of the novel, to John Loofbourow, Ina Ferris, and James Phelan in more recent times, readers have delighted in the sleight of hand, the slippery viewpoint, the detached ironic suggestiveness of the novel. These find in the book a challenge to enjoy the impressionist mimicry of the narrative voice as it pretends to give and then withdraws "proper" views of money, sex, and politics as they are manipulated in military, social, and domestic arenas where persons of varying intellectual and moral integrity maneuver and jockey for position and acclaim.

Oddly enough, both groups quote the same passages in support of these opposed interpretations. Both groups are represented, the latter a bit more generously, in the critical materials at the end of this Norton Critical Edition. No one can agree simultaneously with both groups, and each group is filled with internal disagreements about the narrator, the central issues of the novel, its admirable achievements, its flaws. The novel emerged in a century infamous for the easy patriarchal subjugation of women and discrimination against Jews and dark-skinned people; and critical opinion divides on the extent to which Thackeray participated in these insensitivities or questioned the status quo.

A common frustration is the novel's casual but dense references to history, literature, local places, and current events. In every age Thackeray has been praised for the easy lucidity of his prose style, but his frame of reference has with time become steadily less familiar. Critics acknowledge the timelessness of the issues raised, the human relations explored, the politics and morality; but the references to ladies of the opera, generals, harness shops, clubs, country seats, and myriads of other no longer extant concrete items by a narrator who always assumes the reader will recognize what is fact and what is fiction and be able to catch the sly ironic twists—all tend to obscure the text for modern readers. It is to mitigate these difficulties that annotations are provided.

The novel was published in monthly installments from January 1847 to July 1848. With the installments completed, the publisher gathered the unsold parts, printed additional copies, and bound them in single volumes, introducing about 350 changes in the text. In February 1853, while Thackeray was lecturing in America, the publisher brought out a revised edition, called the Cheap Edition, omitting all the illustrations and any text referring to them. Though the revisions are primarily Thackeray's, he was not present to read proofs.

The text of this Norton Critical Edition is closest to that of the one-volume first edition, except that the punctuation of chapters I–VI and VII–XII (those for which the manuscript survives) is in Thackeray's style, not that of the publishers. Thackeray's style was rhetorical—a system not much used today—indicating pauses for reading aloud. A comma is a short pause, a semicolon is about twice as long, a colon three times as long, and a period four times as long. Dashes are significant pauses that usually do not end a sentence; they are frequently used in combination with other points, especially commas. This system is subtle and flexible but takes some getting used to; for by comparison with modern syntactical punctuation, it appears illogical and erratic. Rhetorical punctuation more readily speeds and slows, separating and merging phrases and ideas according to the emotion. These early chapters best reflect the rhetorical cadences of Thackeray's prose.

An enormous debt of gratitude is owed to Edgar F. Harden, Oscar Mendel, John Sutherland, and Geoffrey and Kathleen Tillotson by generations of readers of *Vanity Fair* for their useful annotations.[1] It is impossible to write annotations for *Vanity Fair* as if they had never been done before. Some new notes and additions are offered. In a few instances where I was unable to verify information first provided by others, I have named my source in parentheses in the notes. Even where I have verified and extended explanations, my debt to previous annotators remains significant: the suggestion that a note was required and the suggestion of what the explanation should be.

I am grateful to Professors Robert Colby, Ina Ferris, Judith Fisher, and Edgar Harden for advice about the historical and critical essays at the end of this volume.

The text and textual notes are from the Garland (1989) edition, preparation of which was made possible in part by the National Endowment for the Humanities, an independent federal agency.

1. Edgar F. Harden, ed., *Annotations for the Selected Works of William Makepeace Thackeray*. 2 vols. (New York: Garland, 1990); John Sutherland and Oscar Mandel, *Annotations to Vanity Fair*, 2nd ed. (Lanham, N.Y., and London: University Press of America, 1988); and Geoffrey and Kathleen Tillotson, eds., *Vanity Fair* (Boston: Houghton Mifflin, Riverside Editions, 1963).

### *Symbols*

<word> = canceled, deleted
↑word↓ = interlined, added
«word» = canceled within a deletion
↑↑word↓↓ = interlined within an addition
MS = manuscript

# VANITY FAIR:

PEN AND PENCIL SKETCHES OF ENGLISH SOCIETY.

BY W. M. THACKERAY,

Author of "The Irish Sketch Book:" "Journey from Cornhill to Grand Cairo:" of "Jeames's Diary" and the "Snob Papers" in "Punch:" &c. &c.

LONDON:
PUBLISHED AT THE PUNCH OFFICE, 85, ELEET STREET.
J. MENZIES, EDINBURGH; J. M'LEOD, GLASGOW; J. M'GLASHAN, DUBLIN.
1847.

Cover of original installment

# The Text of VANITY FAIR

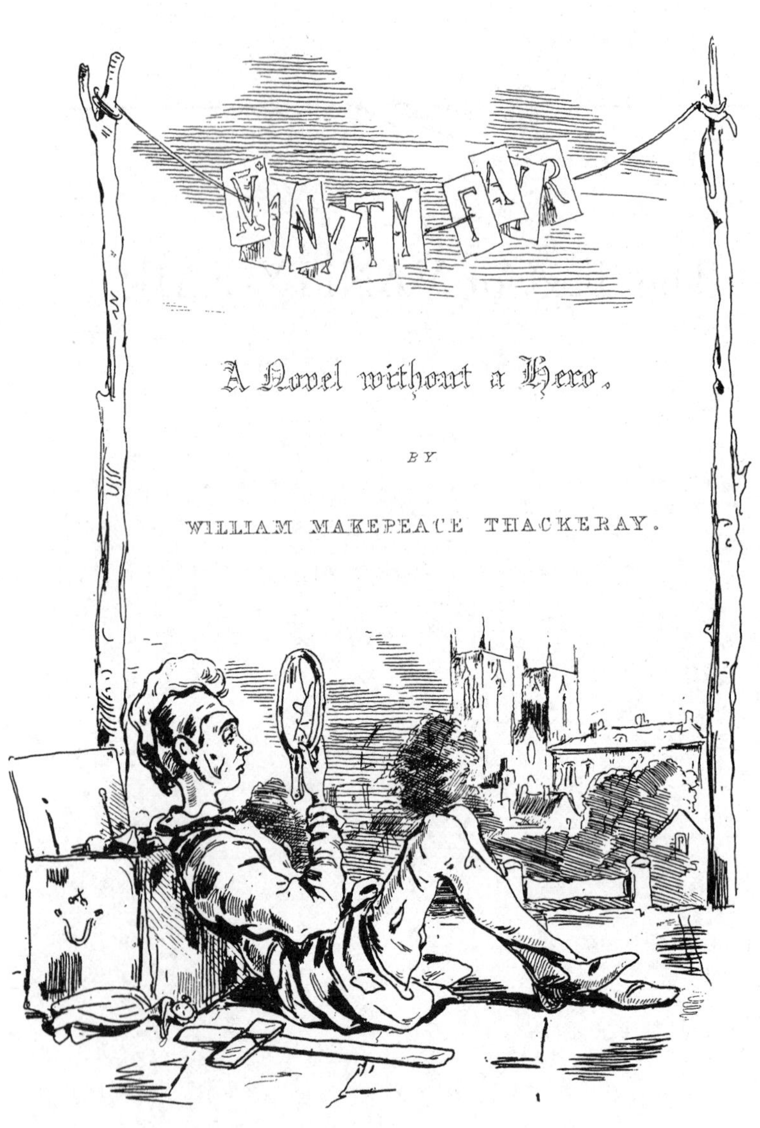


Engraved vignette title page

## *Before the Curtain.*

As the Manager of the Performance sits before the curtain on the boards, and looks into the Fair, a feeling of profound melancholy comes over him in his survey of the bustling place.[1] There is a great quantity of eating and drinking, making love and jilting, laughing and the contrary, smoking, cheating, fighting, dancing, and fiddling: there are bullies pushing about, bucks ogling the women, knaves picking pockets, policemen on the look-out, quacks (*other* quacks, plague take them!) bawling in front of their booths, and yokels looking up at the tinselled dancers and poor old rouged tumblers, while the light-fingered folk are operating upon their pockets behind. Yes, this is VANITY FAIR; not a moral place certainly; nor a merry one, though very noisy. Look at the faces of the actors and buffoons when they come off from their business; and Tom Fool washing the paint off his cheeks before he sits down to dinner with his wife and the little Jack Puddings behind the canvass. The curtain will be up presently, and he will be turning over head and heels, and crying, "How are you?"

A man with a reflective turn of mind, walking through an exhibition of this sort, will not be oppressed, I take it, by his own or other people's hilarity. An episode of humour or kindness touches and amuses him here and there;—a pretty child looking at a gingerbread stall; a pretty girl blushing whilst her lover talks to her and chooses her fairing; poor Tom Fool, yonder behind the waggon, mumbling his bone with the honest family which lives by his tumbling;—but the general impression is one more melancholy than mirthful. When you come home, you sit down, in a sober, contemplative, not uncharitable frame of mind, and apply yourself to your books or your business.

I have no other moral than this to tag to the present story of "Vanity Fair." Some people consider Fairs immoral altogether, and eschew such, with their servants and families: perhaps[2] they are right. But persons who think otherwise and are of a lazy, or a benevolent, or a sarcastic mood, may perhaps like to step in for half an hour and look at the performances. There are scenes of all sorts; some dreadful combats, some grand and lofty horse-riding, some scenes of high life, and some of very middling indeed; some love making for the sentimental, and some light comic business: the whole accompanied by appropriate scenery, and brilliantly illuminated with the Author's own candles.[3]

What more has the Manager of the Performance to say?—To acknowledge the kindness with which it has been received in all the principal towns of England through which the Show has passed, and

1. The first edition was dedicated to Bryan Waller Procter (1787–1874), an attorney and poet, whose wife, Anne, befriended and comforted Thackeray in the tragic illness of his own wife.
2. MS reads: very likely
3. Illustrations. The revised edition (1853) omitted the illustrations and inserted a footnote by way of explanation.

where it has been most favourably noticed by the respected conductors of the Public Press, and by the Nobility and Gentry. He is proud to think that his Puppets have given satisfaction to the very best company in this empire. The famous little Becky Puppet has been pronounced to be uncommonly flexible in the joints and lively on the wire: the Amelia Doll, though it has had a smaller circle of admirers, has yet been carved and dressed with the greatest care by the artist: the Dobbin Figure, though apparently clumsy, yet dances in a very amusing and natural manner: the Little Boys' Dance has been liked by some; and please to remark the richly dressed figure of the Wicked Nobleman, on which no expense has been spared, and which Old Nick will fetch away at the end of this singular performance.

And with this, and a profound bow to his patrons, the Manager retires, and the curtain rises.

LONDON,

*June* 28, 1848.

# VANITY FAIR.

## A NOVEL WITHOUT A HERO.

### *Chapter I.*

#### CHISWICK MALL.

WHILE[1] the present century was in its teens, and on one sun-shiny morning in June, there drove up to the great iron gates of Miss Pinkerton's academy for young ladies on Chiswick Mall,[2] a large family coach with two fat horses in blazing harness, driven by a fat coachman in a three-cornered hat and wig, at the rate of four[3] miles an hour. A black servant who reposed on the box beside the fat coachman, uncurled his bandy legs as soon as the equipage drew up opposite Miss[4] Pinkerton's shining brass plate, and as he pulled the bell, at least a score of young heads were seen peering out of the narrow windows of the stately old brick house,—nay the acute observer might have recognised the little red nose of good-natured Miss Jemima Pinkerton herself, rising over some geranium-pots in the windows of that lady's own drawing room.

"It is Mrs. Sedley's coach, sister," said Miss Jemima. "Sambo, the black servant, has just rung the bell; and the coachman has a new red waistcoat."

"Have you completed all the necessary preparations incident to Miss Sedley's departure, Miss Jemima?" asked Miss Pinkerton herself, that majestic lady: the Semiramis[5] of Hammersmith, the friend of Doctor Johnson, the correspondent of Mrs. Chapone[6] herself.

1. Later events show Thackeray changed the setting to the early teens. MS. reads: Before
2. Chiswick: a country town west of London, now a suburb.
3. MS reads: three
4. MS reads: Mrs.
5. Mythic queen of Babylon, famous for beauty and wisdom. Hammersmith: another small town between London and Chiswick.
6. Samuel Johnson, "The Great Lexicographer," referred to later, compiled a frequently

"The girls were up at four this morning packing her trunks, sister," replied Miss Jemima; "we have made her a bowpot."[7]

"Say a bouquet, sister Jemima, 'tis more genteel."

"Well, a booky as big almost as a hay stack; I have put up two bottles of the gilly flower water[8] for Mrs. Sedley, and the receipt for making it, in Amelia's box."

"And I trust, Miss Jemima, you have made a copy of Miss Sedley's

account—this is it, is it? Very good—ninety three pounds four shillings. Be kind enough to address it to John Sedley, Esquire, and to seal this billet[9] which I have written to his lady."

In Miss Jemima's eyes an autograph letter of her sister, Miss Pinkerton, was an object of as deep veneration as would have been a letter from a sovereign. Only when her pupils quitted the establishment, or when they were about to be married, and once when poor Miss Birch died of the scarlet-fever, was Miss Pinkerton known to write personally to the parents of her pupils; and it was Jemima's opinion that if any thing *could* console Mrs. Birch for her daughter's loss it would be that pious and eloquent composition in which Miss Pinkerton announced the event.

In the present instance Miss Pinkerton's "billet" was to the following effect:—

reprinted *Dictionary of the English Language* (1755). The 1809 edition features an oval portrait of Johnson on the title page, as in the plate illustration. Hester Chapone (1727–1801), a friend of Johnson, authored *Letters on the Improvement of the Mind* (1774).

7. Bough-pot, pot or vase used for flowers; a "vulgar" English word in contrast to "bouquet," of French origin.
8. Clove-scented water.
9. Of French origin, but listed in Johnson's *Dictionary*. Contrasts with "letter" in Jemima's vocabulary.

*"The Mall, Chiswick, June* 15, 18—.

"MADAM,—After her six years' residence at the Mall, I have the honour and happiness of presenting Miss Amelia Sedley to her parents, as a young lady not unworthy to occupy a fitting position in their polished and refined circle. Those virtues which characterise the young English gentlewoman, those accomplishments which become her birth and station,[1] will not be found wanting in the amiable Miss Sedley, whose *industry* and *obedience* have endeared her to her instructors, and whose delightful sweetness of temper has charmed her *aged* and her *youthful* companions.

"In music, in dancing, in orthography, in every variety of embroidery and needle-work she will be found to have realised her friends' *fondest wishes.* In geography there is still much to be desired: and a careful and undeviating use of the backboard for four hours daily during the next three years is recommended as necessary to the acquirement of that dignified *deportment and carriage* so requisite for every young lady of *fashion.*

"In the principles of religion and morality Miss Sedley will be found worthy of an establishment which has been honoured by the presence of *The Great Lexicographer* and the patronage of the admirable Mrs. Chapone. In leaving the Mall Miss Amelia carries with her the hearts of her companions and the affectionate regards of her mistress, who has the honour to subscribe herself,

"Madam,

"Your most obliged humble servant,

"BARBARA PINKERTON."

"P.S. Miss Sharp accompanies Miss Sedley. It is particularly requested that Miss Sharp's stay in Russell Square[2] may not exceed ten days. The family of distinction with whom she is engaged desire to avail themselves of her services as soon as possible."

This letter completed Miss Pinkerton proceeded to write her own name and Miss Sedley's in the fly leaf of a Johnson's Dixonary—the interesting work which she invariably presented to her scholars on their departure from the Mall. On the cover was inserted a copy of "Lines addressed to a young lady on quitting Miss Pinkerton's school at the Mall, by the late revered Doctor Samuel Johnson." In fact, the lexicographer's name was always on the lips of this majestic woman, and a visit he had paid to her was the cause of her reputation and her fortune.

Being commanded by her elder sister to get "the Dictionary" from the cupboard, Miss Jemima had extracted two copies of the book from the receptacle in question. When Miss Pinkerton had finished the inscription in the first, Jemima, with rather a dubious and timid air, handed her the second.

"For whom is this, Miss Jemima?" said Miss Pinkerton with awful coldness.

1. MS reads: become <the person of fashion> ↑her birth and station↓,
2. Newly built in 1804 just west of the City and surrounded primarily by the homes of rich merchants.

"For Becky Sharp," answered Jemima trembling very much and blushing over her withered face[3] and neck, as she turned her back on her sister—"for Becky Sharp: she's going too."

"MISS JEMIMA!" exclaimed Miss Pinkerton in the largest capitals, "are you in your senses? Replace the Dixonary in the closet, and never venture to take such a liberty in future."

"Well, sister, it's only two and ninepence and poor Becky will be miserable if she don't get one."

"Send Miss Sedley instantly to me:" said Miss Pinkerton—and so venturing not to say another word poor Jemima trotted off exceedingly flurried and nervous.

Miss Sedley's papa was a merchant in London and a man of some wealth; whereas Miss Sharp was an articled pupil:[4] for whom Miss Pinkerton had done as she thought quite enough without conferring upon her at parting the high honour of the Dixonary.

Although schoolmistresses' letters are to be trusted no more nor less than churchyard epitaphs; yet as it sometimes happens that a person departs this life, who is really deserving of all the praises the stone-cutter carves over his bones, who *is* a good Christian, a good parent, child, wife or[5] husband, who actually *does* leave a disconsolate family to mourn his loss—so in academies of the male and female sex it occurs every now and then,[6] that the pupil is fully worthy of the praises bestowed by the disinterested instructor. Now Miss Amelia Sedley was a young lady of this singular species: and deserved not only all that Miss Pinkerton said in her praise, but had many charming qualities which that pompous old Minerva[7] of a woman could not see, from the differences of rank and age between her pupil and herself.

For she could not only sing like a lark or a Mrs. Billington and dance like Hillisberg or Parisot:[8] and embroider beautifully, and spell as well as the Dixonary itself, but she had such a kindly, smiling, tender, gentle, generous heart of her own, as won the love of everybody who came near her, from Minerva herself down to the poor girl in the scullery, and the one-eyed tartwoman's daughter who was permitted to vend her wares once a week to the young ladies in the Mall. She had twelve intimate and bosom friends out of the twenty four young ladies: even envious Miss Briggs never spoke ill of her: high and mighty Miss Saltire (Lord Dexter's grand-daughter) allowed that her figure was genteel, and as for Miss Swartz, the rich woolly-haired mulatto from St. Kitts,[9] on the day Amelia went away she was in such a passion of tears, that they were obliged to send for Doctor Floss, and

3. MS reads: withered old face
4. A pupil whose work offset fees. A parlor boarder, by contrast, like Amelia, paid all fees.
5. MS reads: Christian, <mother or daughter or> ↑a good parent, child, wife or↓ husband,
6. MS reads: occurs ↑every now & then,↓ that
7. Roman goddess of wisdom.
8. Elizabeth Billington (1768–1818), a noted singer, performed opera at Covent Garden and Drury Lane Theatres till her retirement in 1811. Hillisberg and Parisot were French dancers frequently performing at the King's Theatre, Haymarket.
9. West Indies island; "Swartz" suggests German "schwarz," for "dark" and is perhaps anti-Semitic.

half tipsify her with salvolatile.[1] Miss Pinkerton's attachment was, as may be supposed from the high position and eminent virtues of that lady, calm and dignified: but Miss Jemima had already blubbered[2] several times at the idea of Amelia's departure, and but for fear of her sister would have gone off in downright hysterics like the heiress (who paid double) of St. Kitts. Such luxury of grief however is only allowed to parlour-boarders. Honest Jemima had all the bills and the washing and the mending and the puddings and the plate and crockery and the servants to superintend—but why speak about her? It is probable that we shall not hear of her again from this moment to the end of time, and that when the great filligree iron gates are once closed on her, she and her awful sister will never issue therefrom into this little[3] world of history.

But as we are to see a great deal of Amelia, there is no harm in saying at the outset of our acquaintance that she was one of the best and dearest creatures that ever lived;[4] and a great mercy it is, both in life and in novels which (and the latter especially) abound in villains of the most sombre sort, that we are to have for a constant companion so guileless and good-natured a person.[5] As she is not a heroine,[6] there is no need to describe her person: indeed I am afraid that her nose was rather short than otherwise, and her cheeks a great deal too round and red for a heroine: but her face blushed with rosy health, and her lips with the freshest of smiles, and she had a pair of eyes which sparkled with the brightest and honestest good humour except indeed when they filled with tears and that was a great deal too often—for the silly thing would cry over a dead canary-bird or over a mouse that the cat haply had seized upon, or over the end of a novel were it ever so stupid—and as for saying an unkind word to her—were any one[7] hard-hearted enough to do so,—why, so much the worse for them. Even Miss Pinkerton, that austere and godlike woman, ceased scolding her after the first time, and though she no more comprehended sensibility[8] than she did Algebra, gave all masters and teachers particular orders to treat Miss Sedley with the utmost gentleness, as harsh treatment was injurious to her.

So that when the day of departure came, between her two customs of laughing and crying Miss Sedley was greatly puzzled how to act. She was glad to go home, and yet most wofully sad at leaving school. For three days before, little Laura Martin the orphan followed her about like a little dog. She had to make and receive at least fourteen presents, to make fourteen solemn promises of writing every week,—"Send my letters under cover to my grand-papa the Earl of Dexter," said Miss Saltire (who by the way was rather shabby): "Never mind the postage but write every day you

1. Smelling salts for fainting fits.
2. Revised edition reads: whimpered
3. MS reads: this <three volume> ↑little↓ world
4. For "one of the . . . ever lived" the revised edition reads: a dear little creature
5. MS reads: creature
6. The novel's subtitle, "A Novel without a Hero," was chosen after this passage was written.
7. MS reads: any persons
8. In its eighteenth-century meaning: sensitivity, emotion. Jane Austen's *Sense and Sensibility* contrasts opposing character traits, using the word in a similar meaning.

dear darling," said the impetuous and woolly-headed, but generous and affectionate Miss Swartz: and little[9] Laura Martin (who was just in round hand)[1] took her friend's[2] hand and said looking up in her face wistfully, "Amelia, when I write to you I shall call

you Mamma."—All which details, I have no doubt JONES[3] who reads this book at his club, will pronounce to be excessively foolish trivial twaddling and ultra-sentimental. Yes, I can see Jones at this minute (rather flushed with his joint of mutton and half-pint of wine,) taking out his pencil and scoring under the words "foolish twaddling" &c., and adding to them his own remark of "*quite true.*" Well he is a lofty man of genius, and admires the great and heroic in life and novels, and so had better take warning and go elsewhere.

Well then—the flowers and the presents, and the trunks and bonnet boxes of Miss Sedley having been arranged by Mr. Sambo in the carriage together with a very small and weatherbeaten old cow's-skin trunk with Miss Sharp's card neatly nailed upon it; the which was delivered by Sambo with a grin and packed by the coachman with a corresponding sneer—the hour for parting came—and the grief of that moment was considerably lessened by the admirable discourse which Miss Pinkerton addressed to her pupil. Not that the parting speech caused Amelia to philosophise, or that it armed her in any way with a calmness the result of argument, but it was intolerably dull pompous and tedious, and having the fear of her schoolmistress greatly before her eyes, Miss Sedley did not venture in her presence to give way to any ebullitions of private grief. A seed-cake and a bottle of wine were produced in the drawing room, as on the solemn occasions of the visit of parents, and these refreshments being partaken of, Miss Sedley was at liberty to depart.

9. Revised edition reads: the orphan, little
1. Style of handwriting with round, full letters, taught in penmanship classes with copybooks.
2. MS reads: patron's
3. Generic name for social club snob, also used thus by Thackeray in *Punch* articles, where an actual George Jones was ridiculed similarly.

"You'll go in and say good bye to Miss Pinkerton, Becky?" said Miss Jemima to a young lady of whom nobody took any notice, and who was coming down stairs with her own band box.

"I suppose I must," said Miss Sharp calmly; and much to the wonder of Miss Jemima, and the latter having knocked at the door, and receiving permission to come in, Miss Sharp advanced in a very unconcerned manner and said in French and with a perfect accent, "Mademoiselle, je viens vous faire mes adieux."[4]

Miss Pinkerton did not understand French, she only directed those who did: but biting her lips and throwing up her venerable and Roman-nosed head, (on the top of which figured a large and solemn turban,) she said, "Miss Sharp, I wish you a good morning." As the Hammersmith Semiramis spoke she waved one hand both by way of adieu, and to give Miss Sharp an opportunity of shaking one of the fingers of the hand which was left out for that purpose.[5]

Miss Sharp only folded her own hands with a very frigid smile and bow, and quite declined to accept the proffered honour: on which Semiramis tossed up her turban more indignantly than ever. In fact it was a little battle between the young lady and the old one, and the latter was worsted. "Heaven bless you, my child," said she, embracing Amelia, and scowling the while over the girl's shoulder at Miss Sharp—"Come away, Becky," said Miss Jemima pulling the young woman away in great alarm, and the drawing-room door closed upon them for ever.

Then came the struggle and parting below. Words refuse to tell it. All the servants were there[6] in the hall—all the dear friends—all the young ladies—the dancing master who had just arrived—and there was such a scuffling and hugging and kissing and crying with the hysterical *yoops* of Miss Swartz the parlour-boarder from her room, as no pen can depict, and as the tender heart would fain pass over. The embracing was over; they parted—that is, Miss Sedley parted from her friends. Miss Sharp had demurely entered the carriage some minutes before—nobody cried for leaving *her.*

Sambo of the bandy legs slammed the carriage door on his young weeping mistress—he sprang up behind the carriage. "Stop!" cried Miss Jemima rushing to the gate with a parcel.

"It's some sandwiches, my dear," said she to Amelia. "You may be hungry you know—and Becky—Becky Sharp—Here's a book for you that my sister—that is I,—Johnson's Dixonary you know—you mustn't leave us without that. Good bye. Drive on, coachman. God bless you!" And the kind creature retreated into the garden overcome with emotions.

But lo, and just as the coach drove off—Miss Sharp put her pale face out of the window—and actually flung the book back into the garden.

4. I have come to bid you goodbye.
5. A patronizing gesture also used by Becky on George Osborne in chapter XIV; see illustration.
6. MS reads: there <sobbing>

Rebecca's Farewell

This almost caused Jemima to faint with terror. "Well I never,"—said she—"what an audacious"—Emotion prevented her from completing either sentence—the carriage rolled away—the great gates were closed—the bell rung for the dancing lesson. The world is before the two young ladies; and so farewell to Chiswick Mall.

## *Chapter II.*

### IN WHICH MISS SHARP AND MISS SEDLEY PREPARE TO OPEN THE CAMPAIGN.

WHEN Miss Sharp had performed the heroical act mentioned in the last chapter, and had seen the Dixonary flying over the pavement of the little garden, fall at length at the feet[1] of the astonished Miss Jemima, the young lady's countenance, which had before worn an almost livid look of hatred, assumed a smile that perhaps was scarcely more agreeable, and she sank back in the carriage in an easy frame of mind saying, "So much for the Dixonary, and thank God I'm out of Chiswick."

Miss Sedley was almost as flurried at the act of defiance as Miss Jemima had been—for consider it was but one minute that she had left school, and the impressions of six years are not got over in that space of time. Nay, with some persons those awes and terrors of youth last for ever and ever. I know for instance an old gentleman of sixty eight, who said to me one morning at breakfast, with a very agitated countenance—"I dreamed last night that I was flogged by Doctor Raine."[2] Fancy had carried him back five and fifty[3] years in the course of that evening. Dr. Raine and his rod were just as awful to him in his heart then at sixty eight as they had been at thirteen. If the Doctor with a large birch had appeared bodily to him even at the age of threescore and eight; and had said in awful voice, "Boy, take

1. MS reads: heels
2. Matthew Raine (1760–1811) was headmaster at Charterhouse School before Thackeray was himself a pupil there.
3. MS reads: back only fifty

down your pant * *" Well, well, Miss Sedley was exceedingly alarmed at this act of insubordination.

"How could you do so, Rebecca?" at last she said after a pause.

"Why, do you think Miss Pinkerton will come out and order me back to the black hole?"[4] said Rebecca laughing.

"No: but——"

"I hate the whole house," continued Miss Sharp in a fury. "I hope I may never set eyes on it again. I wish it were in the bottom of the Thames I do: and if Miss Pinkerton were there I wouldn't pick her out that I wouldn't. O how I should like to see her floating in the water yonder turban and all, with her train streaming after her, and her nose like the beak of a wherry."[5]

"Hush!" cried Miss Sedley.

"Why, will the black footman tell tales?" cried Miss Rebecca laughing. "He may go back and tell Miss Pinkerton that I hate her with all my soul—and I wish he would: and I wish I had a means of proving it too. For two years I have only had insults and outrages from her. I have been treated worse than any servant in the kitchen. I have never had a friend or a kind word except from you; I have been made to tend the little girls in the lower school-room, and to talk French to the Misses until I grew sick of my mother tongue. But that talking French to Miss Pinkerton was capital fun, wasn't it? She doesn't know a word of French, and was too proud to confess it. I believe it was that which made her part with me, and so thank Heaven for French. Vive la France, Vive l'Empereur, *Vive Bonaparte!*"[6]

"O Rebecca, Rebecca, for shame," cried Miss Sedley—for this was the greatest blasphemy Rebecca had as yet uttered—and in those days, in England to say "Long live Bonaparte," was as much as to say "Long live Lucifer." "How can you—how dare you have such wicked, revengeful thoughts?"

"Revenge may be wicked but it's natural," answered Miss Rebecca. "I'm no angel"—and to say the truth she certainly was not.

For it may be remarked in the course of this little conversation, (which took place as the coach rolled along lazily by the river side) that though Miss Rebecca Sharp has twice had occasion to thank Heaven; it has been in the first place for ridding her of some person whom she hated, and secondly for enabling her to bring her enemies to some[7] sort of perplexity or confusion: neither of which are very amiable motives for religious gratitude, or such as would be put forward by persons of a kind and placable disposition. Miss Rebecca was not then in the least kind or placable: all the world used her ill said this young misanthropist (or misogynist—for of the world of men

4. Partly facetious reference to the famous Black Hole of Calcutta episode of 1756, where it was alleged that masses of prisoners died in confinement.
5. Prow of a riverboat.
6. These had become treasonous words when Becky, of French extraction, spoke them; for Napoleon had abandoned the "Republic," declared himself emperor, and was on a campaign to conquer Europe. Becky could hardly have said anything more rebellious. MS reads: "Vive la Republique!" which would indicate a date no later than 1804. According to most dates given later in the book, Becky and Amelia left Chiswick about 1813 or 1814.
7. MS reads: and <for heaping upon> ↑secondly for enabling her to bring↓ her enemies ↑to↓ some

she can be pronounced[8] as yet to have had but little experience),[9] and we may be pretty certain that the persons of either sex whom all the world treats ill, deserve entirely the treatment they get. The world is a looking glass and gives back to every man the reflection of his own face—Frown at it and it will in turn look sourly upon you—laugh at it and with it and it is a jolly kind companion, and so let all young persons take their choice. This is certain that if the world[1] neglected Miss Sharp, she never was known to have done a good action in behalf of anybody: nor can it be expected that twenty four young ladies should all be as amiable as the heroine of this work, Miss Sedley (whom we have selected for the very reason that she was the best-natured of all, otherwise what on earth was to have prevented us from putting up Miss Swartz or Miss Crump or Miss Hopkins as heroine in her place?)—it could not be expected that every one should be of the humble[2] and gentle temper of Miss Amelia Sedley, should take every opportunity to vanquish Rebecca's hard-heartedness, and ill-humour, and by a thousand kind words and offices overcome for once at least her hostility to her kind.

Miss Sharp's father was an artist, and in that quality had given lessons of drawing at Miss Pinkerton's school. He was a clever man: a pleasant companion: a careless student: with[3] a great propensity for running into debt, and a partiality for the tavern. When he was drunk he used to[4] beat his wife and daughter; the next morning with a headache he used to rail at the world for its neglect of his genius: and abuse, with a good[5] deal of cleverness and sometimes with perfect reason, the fools, his brother-painters. As it was with the utmost difficulty that he could keep himself and as he owed money for a mile round Soho[6] where he lived, he thought to better his circumstances by marrying a young woman of the French nation who was by profession an opera-girl. This humble calling of her female parent Miss Sharp never alluded to: but used to state subsequently that the Entrechâts[7] were a noble family of Gascony,[8] and took great pride in her descent from them. And curious it is, that as she advanced in life this young lady's ancestors increased in rank and splendour.[9]

Rebecca's mother had had some education somewhere, and her daughter spoke French with purity and a Parisian accent. It was in those days rather a rare accomplishment, and led to her engagement with the orthodox Miss Pinkerton. For her mother being dead, her father, finding himself not likely to recover after his third attack of

8. MS reads: presumed
9. Revised edition omits the parenthetical passage.
1. MS reads: companion, <always ready to [illegible] your laughter, and welcome your good humour.> ↑and so let all young persons take their choice. This is certain that if the↓ world
2. MS reads: loveable
3. MS and first printing read: had
4. MS reads: he would
5. MS reads: great
6. Bohemian area of west-central London.
7. Ballet dancer's leap in which the feet are repeatedly crossed.
8. French province.
9. Instead of this final sentence, the MS reads: Ill natured persons however say that Rebecca was born before the lawful celebration of her excellent parents' union.

delirium tremens,[1] wrote a manly and pathetic letter to Miss Pinkerton recommending the orphan-child to her protection, and so descended to the grave, after two bailiffs had quarrelled over his corpse. Rebecca was seventeen when she came to Chiswick, and was bound over as an articled-pupil, her duties being to talk French as we have seen, and her privileges to live cost free, and with a few guineas a year, to gather scraps of knowledge from the professors who attended the school.

She was small and slight in person: pale, sandy-haired and with eyes habitually cast down; when they looked up they were very large, odd, and attractive: so attractive that the Reverend Mr. Crisp fresh from Oxford, and curate[2] to the Vicar of Chiswick, the Reverend Mr. Flowerdew, fell in love with Miss Sharp, being shot dead by a glance of her eyes which was fired all the way across Chiswick Church from the school pew to the reading desk. This infatuated young man used sometimes to take tea with Miss Pinkerton to whom he had been presented by his mamma, and actually proposed something like[3] marriage, in an intercepted note which the one-eyed applewoman[4] was charged to deliver. Mrs. Crisp was summoned from Buxton[5] and abruptly carried off her darling boy: but the idea even of such an eagle in the Chiswick dovecot[6] caused a great flutter in the breast of Miss Pinkerton: who would have sent away Miss Sharp but that she was bound to her under a forfeit, and who never would thoroughly believe the young lady's protestations that she had never exchanged a single word with Mr. Crisp, except under her own eyes on the two occasions when she had met him at tea.

By the side of many tall and bouncing young ladies in the establishment Rebecca Sharp looked like a child. But she had the dismal precocity of poverty. Many a dun[7] had she talked to, and turned away from her father's door, many a tradesman had she coaxed and wheedled into good-humour and into the granting of one meal more. She sate commonly with her father who was very proud of her wit—and heard the talk of many of his wild companions—often but ill suited for a girl to hear. But she never had been a girl she said, she had been a woman since she was eight years old. O why[8] did Miss Pinkerton let such a dangerous bird into her cage?

The fact is the old lady thought[9] Rebecca to be the meekest creature in the world, so admirably, on the occasions when her father brought her to Chiswick, used Rebecca to perform the part of the *ingénue*.[1] She thought her a modest and innocent little child, and only[2] a year before the arrangement by which Rebecca had been admitted into her house, and when Rebecca was sixteen years

1. Alcohol-induced hallucinations.
2. Paid assistant to the salaried spiritual leader of an English parish church.
3. MS reads: proposed ↑something like↓ marriage
4. Street vendor, traditional symbol of poverty.
5. City in Derbyshire, northwest of London.
6. Equivalent to "fox in the henhouse." Dovecot is a pen for raising doves.
7. Bill collector.
8. MS reads: old. Why
9. Revised edition reads: believed
1. An innocent.
2. Revised edition reads: *ingénue;* and only

old, Miss Pinkerton majestically and with a little speech made her a present of a doll, which was by the way the confiscated property of Miss Swindle discovered surreptitiously nursing it in school-hours. How the father and daughter laughed as they trudged home together after the evening party! (it was on the occasion of the speeches when all the professors were invited) and how Miss Pinkerton would have raged had she seen the caricature of herself which the little minx, Rebecca, managed to make out of her doll! She[3] used to go through dialogues with it: it formed the delight of Newman Street, Gerard Street,[4] and the artists' quarter: and the young painters when they came to take their gin and water with their lazy, dissolute, clever, jovial senior, used regularly

to ask Rebecca if Miss Pinkerton was at home—she was as well known to them, poor soul, as Mr. Lawrence or President West.[5] Once she had the honour to pass a few days at Chiswick after which she brought back Jemima: and erected another doll as Miss Jemmy; for though that honest creature had given her jelly and cake enough for three children and a seven-shilling piece[6] at parting, the girl's sense of ridicule was far stronger than her gratitude, and she sacrificed Miss Jemmy quite as pitilessly as her sister.

The catastrophe came: and she was brought to the Mall as to her

3. Revised edition reads: doll. Becky
4. Streets in Soho. Sharp's other Soho addresses in Greek and Frith Streets suggest his troubles with landlords.
5. Thomas Lawrence (1738–1830) and Benjamin West (1738–1820) were each president of the Royal Academy of Art.
6. A coin issued from 1806 to 1813—over twice the value of the dictionary Becky flung out the carriage window.

home. The rigid formality of the place suffocated her: the prayers and the meals the lessons and the walks which were arranged with a conventual regularity oppressed her almost beyond endurance; and she looked back to the freedom and the beggary of the old studio in Soho, with so much regret that every body, herself included, fancied she was consumed with grief for her father. She had a little room in the garret where the maids heard her walking and sobbing at night—but it was with rage and not with grief. She had not been much of a dissembler until now, her loneliness taught her to feign. She had never mingled in the society of women: her father, reprobate as he was, was a man of talent; his conversation was a thousand times more agreeable to her than the talk of such of her own sex as she now encountered—the pompous inanity of the old schoolmistress, the foolish good humour of her sister, the silly cackle and scandal of the elder girls and the frigid correctness of the governesses equally annoyed her—and she had no soft maternal heart, this unlucky girl, otherwise the prattle and talk of the younger children with whose care she was chiefly intrusted, might have soothed and interested her: but she lived among them two years and not one was sorry that she went away. The tender-hearted Amelia Sedley was the only person to whom she could attach herself in the least, and who could help attaching herself to Amelia?

The happiness—the superior advantages of the young women round about her gave Rebecca inexpressible pangs of envy. "What airs that girl gives herself because she is an Earl's granddaughter," she said of one—"how they cringe and bow to that Creole because of her hundred thousand pounds! I am a thousand times cleverer and more charming than that creature for all her wealth: I am as well bred as the Earl's granddaughter for all her fine pedigree, and yet every one passes me by here. And yet, when I was at my father's, did not the men give up their gayest balls and parties in order to pass the evening with me?" She determined at any rate to get free from the prison in which she found herself, and now began to act for herself, and for the first time to make connected plans for the future.

She took advantage therefore of the means of study the place offered her: and as she was already a musician and a good linguist, she speedily went through the little course of study which was considered necessary for ladies in those days. Her music she practised incessantly, and one day when the girls were out and she had remained at home, she was overheard to play a piece so well, that Minerva thought wisely she could spare herself the expense of a master for the juniors, and intimated to Miss Sharp that she was to instruct them in music for the future.

The girl refused: and for the first time and to the astonishment of the majestic mistress of the school. "I am here to speak French with the children," Rebecca said abruptly, "not to teach them music, and save money for you. Give me money and I will teach them."

Minerva was obliged to yield and of course disliked her from that day. "For five and thirty years," she said and with great justice, "I never have seen the individual who has dared in my own house to question my authority. I have nourished a viper in my bosom."

"A viper—A fiddlestick," said Miss Sharp to the old lady almost fainting with astonishment. "You took me because I was useful: there is no question of gratitude between us. I hate this place and want to leave it. I will do nothing here but what I am obliged to do."

It was in vain that the old lady asked her if she was aware she was speaking to Miss Pinkerton? Rebecca laughed in her face: with a horrid sarcastic demoniacal laughter that almost sent the schoolmistress into fits. "Give me a sum of money," said the girl, "and get rid of me—or if you like better, get me a good place as governess in a nobleman's family—you can do so if you please." And in their farther disputes she always returned to this point, "Get me a situation—we hate each other, and I am ready to go."

Worthy Miss Pinkerton, although she had a roman nose and a turban and was as tall as a grenadier,[7] and had been up to this time an irresistible Princess, had no will or strength like that of her little apprentice: and in vain did battle against her, and tried to overawe her. Attempting to scold her in public, Rebecca hit upon the beforementioned plan of answering her in French, which quite routed the old woman. In order to maintain authority in her school, it became necessary to remove this rebel, this monster, this serpent, this firebrand—and hearing about this time that Sir Pitt Crawley's family was in want of a governess, she actually recommended Miss Sharp for the situation, firebrand and serpent as she was. "I cannot certainly," she said, "find fault with Miss Sharp's conduct except to myself: and must allow that her talents and accomplishments are of a high order. As far as the head goes at least, she does credit to the Educational system pursued at my Establishment."

And so the schoolmistress reconciled the recommendation to her conscience, and[8] the indentures were cancelled: and the apprentice was free. The battle here described in a few lines of course lasted for some months. And as Miss Sedley being now seventeen years of age[9] was about to leave school, and had a friendship for Miss Sharp ("'tis the only point in Amelia's behaviour," said Minerva, "which has not been satisfactory to her mistress,")—Miss Sharp was invited by her friend to pass a week with her at home, before she entered upon her duties as governess in a private family.

Thus[1] the world began for these two young ladies. For Amelia it was quite a new, fresh, brilliant world with all the bloom upon it. It was not quite a new one for Rebecca—(indeed if the truth must be told with respect to the Crisp affair, the tart-woman hinted to somebody who took an affidavit of the fact to somebody else, that there was a great deal more than was made public regarding Mr. Crisp and Miss Sharp, and that his letter was *in answer* to another letter)—But who can tell you[2] the real truth of the matter? At all events if Rebecca was not beginning the world: she was beginning it[3] over again.

7. Guardsman, originally grenade throwers chosen for their ability to throw great distances; hence, most were tall.
8. The phrase "the schoolmistress . . . conscience and" is interlined in the MS.
9. For "seventeen . . . age" the revised edition reads: in her seventeenth year
1. MS reads: Thus then
2. MS reads: what was
3. MS reads: was <very glad to be> beginning ↑it↓

By the time the young ladies reached Kensington Turnpike[4] Amelia had not forgotten her companions but had dried her tears, and had blushed very much and been delighted at a young officer of the Life Guards[5] who spied her as he was riding by and said, "A dem fine gal, egad!" and before the carriage arrived in Russell Square, a great deal of conversation had taken place about the drawing room, and whether or not young ladies wore powder as well as hoops when presented,[6] and whether she was to have that honour—to the Lord Mayor's Ball she knew she was to go: and when at length home was reached Miss Amelia Sedley skipped out on Sambo's arm, as happy and as handsome a girl as any in the whole big city of London. Both he and Coachman agreed on this point and so did her father and mother, and so did every one of the servants in the house, as they stood bobbing and curtseying and smiling in the hall to welcome their young mistress.

You may be sure that she showed Rebecca over every room of the house, and everything in every one of her drawers; and her books and her piano and her dresses, and all her necklaces, brooches, laces, and gimcracks: she insisted upon Rebecca accepting the white cornelian[7] and the turquoise rings and a sweet sprigged muslin[8] which was too small for her now, though it would fit her friend to a nicety; and she determined in her heart to ask her mother's permission to present her white Cashmere shawl to her friend. Could she not spare it? and had not her brother Joseph just brought her two from India?

When Rebecca saw the two magnificent Cashmere shawls which Joseph Sedley had brought home to his sister, she said with perfect truth that it must be delightful to have a brother, and easily got the pity of the tender-hearted Amelia, for being alone in the world, an orphan without friends or kindred.

"Not alone," said Amelia. "You know, Rebecca, I shall always be your friend, and love you as a sister—indeed I will."

"Ah but to have parents as you have—kind, rich, affectionate parents who give you every thing you ask for, and their love which is more precious than all! My poor papa could give me nothing, and I had but two frocks in all the world! And then to have a brother—a dear brother! oh how you must love him!"

Amelia laughed.

"What! *don't* you love him? you who say you love everybody?"

"Yes of course I do—only . . ."

"Only what?"

"Only Joseph doesn't seem to care much whether I love him or not. He gave me two fingers to shake when he arrived after ten years' absence! he is very kind and good but he scarcely ever speaks to me, I think he loves his pipe a great deal better than his" . . . but here Amelia checked herself, for why should she speak ill of her brother:

4. Tollgate about halfway between Chiswick and Amelia's home in Russell Square.
5. Cavalry regiments of the British army attached to the king's household. First printing reads: Horse Guards
6. It was the aspiration of debutants to meet formally a member of the royal family, especially the sovereign, in the palace drawing room.
7. Semi-precious reddish quartz.
8. Decorated oriental cotton dress.

"he was very kind to me as a child," she added. "I was but five years old when he went away."

"Isn't he very rich?" said Rebecca—"they say all Indian Nabobs[9] are enormously rich."

"I believe he has a very large income."

"And is your sister-in-law a nice pretty woman?"

"La! Joseph is not married," said[1] Amelia laughing again.

Perhaps she had mentioned the fact already to Rebecca, but that young lady did not appear to have remembered it—indeed vowed and protested that she expected to see a number of Amelia's nephews and nieces. She was quite disappointed that Mr. Sedley was not married, she was sure Amelia had said he was, and she doted so on little children.

"I think you must have had enough of them at Chiswick," said Amelia rather wondering at the sudden tenderness on her friend's part—and indeed in later days Miss Sharp would never have committed herself so far as to advance opinions the untruth of which would have been[2] so easily detected. But we must remember that she is but nineteen as yet—unused to the art of deceiving, poor innocent creature! and making her own experience in her own person. The meaning of the above series of queries as translated in the heart of this ingenious young woman was simply this—"If Mr. Joseph Sedley is rich and unmarried, why should I not marry him? I have only a fortnight, to be sure, but there is no harm in[3] trying." And she determined within herself to make this laudable attempt. She redoubled her caresses to Amelia, she kissed the white cornelian necklace as she put it on, and vowed she would never never part with it. When the dinner-bell rung she went down stairs with her arm round her friend's waist, as is the habit of young ladies. She was so agitated at the drawing room door that she could hardly find courage to enter. "Feel my heart how it beats dear!" said she to her friend.

"No it doesn't," said Amelia—"come in, don't be frightened. Papa won't do you any harm."

9. Slang term for Englishmen who had made their fortunes in India.
1. MS reads: married— <I've told you so often and often added> ↑said↓
2. The phrase "the untruth . . . have been" is interlined in the MS.
3. MS omits: in

## *Chapter III.*

REBECCA IS IN PRESENCE OF THE ENEMY.

A VERY stout puffy[1] man, in buckskins and hessian boots[2] with several immense neckcloths that rose almost to his nose, with a red striped waistcoat and an apple green coat with steel buttons almost as large as crown pieces (it was the morning costume of a dandy or blood[3] of those days,) was reading the paper by the fire when the two girls entered—and bounced off his arm-chair, and blushed excessively,[4] and hid his entire face almost in his neckcloths at this apparition.

"It's only your sister, Joseph," said Amelia laughing and shaking the two fingers which he held out; "I've come home *for good* you know, and this is my friend, Miss Sharp, whom you have heard me mention."

"No, never, upon my word," said the head under the neckcloths shaking very much—"that is, yes—what abominably cold weather, Miss"—and herewith he fell to poking the fire with all his might, although it was in the middle of June.

"He's very handsome," whispered Rebecca to Amelia rather loud.

"Do you think so?" said the latter, "I'll tell him."

"Darling! not for worlds," said Miss Sharp starting back as timid as a fawn. She had previously made a respectful virgin-like curtsey to the gentleman, and her modest eyes gazed so perseveringly on the carpets that it was a wonder how she should have found an opportunity to see him.

"Thank you for the beautiful shawls, brother," said Amelia to the fire-poker: "are they not beautiful, Rebecca!"

"O heavenly!" said Miss Sharp, and her eyes went from the carpet straight to the chandelier.

Joseph still continued a huge clattering at the poker and tongues, puffing and blowing the while and turning as red as his yellow face would allow him—"I can't make you such handsome presents, Joseph," continued his sister—"but while I was at school I have embroidered for you a very[5] beautiful pair of braces."

"Good Gad![6] Amelia," cried the brother in serious alarm. "What do you mean?" and plunging with all his might at the bell-rope, that article of furniture came away in his hand and increased the honest fellow's confusion. "For heaven's sake see if my buggy's at the door. I *can't* wait. I must go. D— that groom of mine. I must go."

1. MS reads: handsome.
2. Leather breeches extending to just below the knees. The change from "top boots" (MS) to "hessian boots" may emphasize Joseph's propensity to cultivate a martial appearance. The attire was made famous by England's most elegant dandy, George Brummell.
3. Slang for fast young man.
4. MS omits: excessively,
5. MS reads: most
6. MS reads: God

At this minute the father of the family walked in rattling his seals like a true British merchant. "What's the matter, Emmy?" says he.

"Joseph wants me to see if his—his *buggy* is at the door. What is a buggy, papa?"

"It is a one horse palanquin,"[7] said the old gentleman, who was a wag in his way.

Joseph at this burst out into a wild fit of laughter—in which encountering the eye of Miss Sharp—he stopped all of a sudden as if he had been shot.

"This young lady is your friend? Miss Sharp, I am very happy to see you. Have you and Emmy been quarreling already with Jos, that he wants to be off."

"I promised Bonamy of our service,[8] Sir," said Joseph, "to dine with him."

"O fie! didn't you tell your Mother you would dine here?"

"But in this dress it's impossible."

"Look at him, isn't he handsome enough to dine anywhere, Miss Sharp."

On which of course Miss Sharp looked at her friend and they both set off in a fit of laughter highly agreeable to the old gentleman.

"Did you ever see a pair of buckskins like those at Miss Pinkerton's?" continued he following up his advantage.[9]

"Gracious Heavens! Father," cried Joseph.

"There now—I have hurt his feelings. Mrs. Sedley my dear, I have hurt your son's feelings. I have alluded to his buckskins. Ask Miss Sharp if I haven't? Come, Joseph, be friends with Miss Sharp, and let us all go to dinner."

"There's a pillau,[1] Joseph, just as you like it: and Papa has brought home the best turbot in Billingsgate."[2]

"Come, come, Sir, walk down stairs with Miss Sharp, and I will follow with these two young women," said the Father, and he took an arm of wife, and daughter and walked merrily off.

If Miss Rebecca Sharp had determined in her heart upon making the conquest of this big beau, I don't think, ladies, we have any right to blame her; for though the task of husband-hunting is generally, and with becoming modesty, intrusted by young persons to their Mammas, recollect that Miss Sharp had no kind parent to arrange these delicate matters for her, and that if she did not get a husband for herself there was no one else in the wide world who would take the trouble off her hands. What causes young people to "come *out*"[3] but the noble ambition of matrimony? What sends them trooping to watering places, what keeps them dancing till five o'clock in the morning through a whole mortal season, what causes them to labour at[4] piano-forte sonatas, and to learn four songs from a fashionable

7. A one-person litter (wheel-less vehicle) carried by four to six men. For buggy, see this chapter's tailpiece.
8. The East India Company's civil service. For "Bonamy" MS reads: Mulligatawny
9. The phrase "continued . . . advantage" is interlined in the MS.
1. Pilau or pilaf; an oriental dish of spiced rice boiled with fowl, meat, or fish.
2. The main London fishmarket, famous, too, for foul language.
3. To be formally presented to society. For "people" the MS reads: women
4. MS reads: to <learn> ↑labour at↓

master at a guinea a lesson, and to play the harp if they have handsome arms and neat elbows, and to wear Lincoln Green Toxophilite[5] hats and feathers, but that they may bring down some "desirable" young man with those killing bows and arrows of theirs? What causes respectable parents to take up their carpets, set their houses topsy-turvy, and spend a fifth of their year's income in ball-suppers and iced champagne—is it sheer love of their species, and an unadulterated wish to see young people happy and dancing? Psha! they want to marry their daughters; and as honest Mrs. Sedley has[6] in the depths of her kind heart already arranged[7] a score of little schemes for the settlement of her Amelia; so also had our beloved but unprotected Rebecca, determined to do her very best to secure the husband, who was even more necessary for her than for her friend. She had a vivid imagination, she had besides, read the "Arabian Nights" and "Guthrie's Geography,"[8] and it is a fact that while she was dressing for dinner and after she had asked Amelia whether her brother was very rich, she had built for herself a most magnificent castle in the air of which she was mistress, with a husband somewhere in the back-ground (she had not seen him as yet, and his figure would not therefore be very distinct). She had arrayed herself in an infinity of shawls, turbans, and diamond-necklaces, and had mounted upon an elephant to the sound of the March in Bluebeard,[9] in order to pay a visit of ceremony to the Grand Mogul.[1] Charming Alnaschar visions![2] it is the happy privilege of youth to construct you, and many a fanciful young creature besides Rebecca Sharp has indulged in these delightful day-dreams ere now!

Joseph Sedley was twelve years older than his sister Amelia. He was in the East India Company's civil service,[3] and his name appeared at the period of which we write in the Bengal division of the East India Register as Collector of Boggley wollah[4]—an honourable and lucrative post as everybody knows—in order to know to what higher posts Joseph rose in the service, the reader is referred to the same periodical.[5]

Boggley wollah is situated in a fine, lonely, marshy, jungly district famous for snipe shooting and where not unfrequently you may flush a tiger. Ramgunge where there is a magistrate is only forty miles off,

5. England's most famous toxophilite, or lover of archery, was Robin Hood, who favored lincoln green clothing.
6. MS reads: had
7. MS reads: heart ↑already↓ arranged
8. *Arabian Nights Entertainments*, Arabic stories best known in Europe through the French translation by Antoine Galland, but available in English since 1713. By 1800 there were many competing English editions. William Guthrie's *New Geographical Historical and Commercial Grammar* (1770) was slightly outdated by 1813 but revised and enlarged in 1843, hence probably familiar to Thackeray's first audience.
9. *Bluebeard*, the play by George Colman, made into a musical in 1798.
1. Emperor of Delhi, ruler of Hindustan.
2. In the *Arabian Nights* Alnaschar, in order to make enough money to marry the vizir's daughter, spends all he has on a basket of glassware to resell at a profit. But in a dream quarrel he kicks and breaks the ware. Hence, an unfulfilled dream.
3. Though a private trading company, the East India Company controlled all trade between England and India. In addition, it exercised civil control in India, collecting taxes and administering courts for civil justice.
4. Boggley wollah and Ramgunge are fictitious places. "Whollah" is an Anglo-Indian adjectival suffix meaning "pertaining to." Gunge is dung.
5. MS reads: <authority> ↑periodical↓

and there is a cavalry-station about thirty miles farther—so Joseph wrote home to his parents when he took possession of his collectorship. He had lived for about eight years of his life quite alone at this charming place, scarcely seeing a Christian face except twice a year when the detachment arrived to carry off revenues which he had collected to Calcutta.[6]

Luckily at this time he caught a liver complaint for the cure of which he returned to Europe; and which was the source of great comfort and amusement to him in his native country. He did not live with his family while in London, but had lodgings of his own like a gay young bachelor. Before he went to India he was too young to partake of the delightful pleasures of a man about town; and plunged into them on his return with considerable assiduity. He drove his horses in the Park,[7] he dined at the fashionable taverns (for the Oriental Club[8] was not as yet invented), he frequented the theatres as the mode was in those days, or made his appearance at the opera laboriously attired in tights and a cocked hat.

On returning to India, and ever after he used to talk of the pleasures of this period of his existence with great enthusiasm and give you to understand that he and Brummel[9] were the leading bucks of the day. But he was as lonely here as in his jungle at Boggley wollah. He scarcely knew a single soul in the metropolis: and were it not for his Doctor and the society of his blue pill[1] and his liver-complaint[2] he must have died of loneliness. He was lazy, peevish, and a *bon-vivant;*[3] the appearance of a lady frightened him beyond measure—hence it was but seldom that he joined the paternal circle in Russell Square, where there was plenty of gaiety, and where the jokes of his good-natured old father frightened his *amour-propre.*[4] His bulk caused Joseph much anxious thought and alarm—now and then he would make a desperate attempt to get rid of his superabundant fat, but his indolence and love of good living speedily got the better of these endeavours at reform, and he found himself again at his three meals a day. He never was well dressed: but he took the hugest pains to adorn his big person: and passed many hours daily in that occupation. His valet made a fortune out of his wardrobe. His toilet-table was covered with as many pomatums[5] and essences as ever were employed by an old beauty: he had tried, in order to give himself a waist, every girth, stay, and waist-band then invented. Like most fat men he *would* have his clothes made too tight and took care they should be of the most brilliant colours and youthful cut. When dressed at length in the afternoon he would issue forth to take a drive with nobody in the park: and then would come back in order to dress again and go and dine with nobody at the Piazza Coffee

6. Administrative center for Bengal, founded and built by the East India Company.
7. Hyde Park, west-central London.
8. Opened in Hanover Square in 1824; Joseph joined when he retired in 1827 (chapter LX).
9. George "Beau" Brummel (1778–1840) typified the concept of Regency dandy.
1. Standard patent medicine for liver ailments.
2. This suggests that in his loneliness, Joseph drank too much.
3. One who enjoys life.
4. Vanity, self-love.
5. Scented ointments.

House.[6] He was as vain as a girl: and perhaps his extreme shyness was one of the results of his extreme vanity. If Miss Rebecca can get the better of *him,* and at her first entrance into life, she is a young person of no ordinary cleverness.

The first move showed considerable skill. When she called Sedley a very handsome man, she knew that Amelia would tell her mother, who would probably tell Joseph, or who at any rate would be pleased by the compliment paid to her son. All mothers are. If you had told Sicorax that her son Caliban[7] was as handsome as Apollo,[8] she would have been pleased, witch as she was. Perhaps too Joseph Sedley would overhear the compliment: Rebecca spoke loud enough: and he *did* hear and (thinking in his heart that he was a very fine man) the praise thrilled through every fiber of his big body, and made it tingle with pleasure. Then however came a recoil. "Is the girl making fun of me?" he thought, and straightway he bounced towards the bell and was for retreating as we have seen, when his father's jokes and his mother's entreaties caused him to pause and stay where he was. He conducted the young lady down to dinner in a dubious and agitated frame of mind—"does she really think I am handsome," thought he, "or is she only making game of me?" We have talked of Joseph Sedley being as vain as a girl—Heaven help us! the girls have only to turn the tables and say of one of their own sex, "She is as vain as a man," and they will have perfect reason. The bearded creatures are quite as eager for praise, quite as finikin over their toilettes, quite as proud of their personal advantages, quite as conscious of their powers of fascination as any coquette in the world.

Down stairs then they went—Joseph very red and blushing, Rebecca very modest and holding her green eyes downwards. She was dressed in white, with bare shoulders as white as snow—the picture of gentle unprotected innocence, and humble virgin simplicity. "I must be very quiet," thought Rebecca, "and very much interested about India."

Now we have heard how Mrs. Sedley had prepared a fine curry for her son just as he liked it: and in the course of dinner a portion of this dish was offered to Rebecca. "What is it?" said she turning an appealing look to Mr. Joseph.

"Capital," said he—his mouth was full of it: his face quite red with the delightful exercise of gobbling. "Mother, it's as good as my own curries in India."

"O I must try some if it is an Indian dish," said Miss Rebecca. "I am sure every thing must be good that comes from *there.*"[9]

"Give Miss Sharp some curry, my dear," said Mr. Sedley laughing.

Rebecca had never tasted the dish before.

"Do you find it as good as every thing else from India?" said Mr. Sedley.

6. Possibly modeled on the fashionable Bedford Coffee House, at the Piazza, Covent Garden. George looks for Joseph at the Bedford in chapter VI.
7. Caliban is a deformed creature only partly human; Sycorax is his witch mother (Shakespeare, *The Tempest*).
8. Greek god of the sun, youth, beauty, music, and poetry.
9. MS adds: <Why? said Mr. Sedley—the flattery had gone rather too far>

"O excellent!" said Rebecca, who was suffering tortures with the cayenne-pepper.

"Try a chili with it, Miss Sharp," said Joseph really interested.

"A chili," said Rebecca gasping—"o yes!"—she thought a chili was something cool, as its name imported, and was served with some. "How fresh and green they look!" she said, and put one into her mouth. It was hotter than the curry, flesh and blood could bear it no longer. She laid down her fork. "Water for Heaven's sake water!" she cried. Mr. Sedley burst out laughing, (he was a coarse man from the Stock Exchange where they love all sorts of practical jokes). "They are real Indian, I assure you," said he. "Sambo, give Miss Sharp some water."

The paternal laugh was echoed by Joseph who thought the joke capital. The ladies only smiled a little. They thought poor Rebecca suffered too much. She would have liked to choke old Sedley, but she swallowed her mortification as well as she had the abominable curry before it, and as soon as she could speak, said with a comical good-humoured air—

"I ought to have remembered the pepper which the Princess of Persia puts in the cream-tarts in the Arabian Nights.[1] Do you put cayenne into your cream-tarts in India, Sir?"

Old Sedley began to laugh, and thought Rebecca was a good-humoured girl. Joseph simply said—"Cream-tarts, Miss?—our cream is very bad in Bengal. We generally use goats' milk, and, gad! do you know I've got to prefer it?"

"You won't like *everything* from India now, Miss Sharp," said the old gentleman. And when the ladies had retired after dinner,[2] the wily old fellow said to his son, "Have a care, Joe, that girl is setting her cap at you."

"Pooh nonsense," said Joe, highly flattered. "I recollect, Sir, there was a girl at Dumdum a daughter of Cutler of the artillery, and afterward married to Lance the surgeon: who made a dead set at me in the year '4—at me and Mulligatawney whom I mentioned to you before dinner—a dev'lish good fellow Mulligatawney—he's a magistrate at Budgebudge[3] and sure to be in council in five years. Well sir—the artillery gave a ball, and Quintin of the King's 14th. said to me, 'Sedley,' said he, 'I bet you thirteen to ten, that Sophy Cutler hooks either you or Mulligatawney before the rains.' 'Done,' says I, and egad Sir—this claret's very good—Adamson's or Carbonell's?"[4]
* * *

1. Becky is "remembering" Sir Walter Scott's *Heart of Midlothian* (1818) in which Effie Dean was "near discovering herself to Mary Hetley by betraying her acquaintance with the celebrated receipt for Dunlop cheese, that she compared herself to Bedreddin Hassan, whom the vizier his father-in-law discovered by his superlative skill in composing cream-tarts with pepper in them." In "The Story of Noureddin Ali and Bedreddin Hassan," in *The Arabian Nights* Bedreddin is charged with making cheese-cakes (not cream-tarts) without (not with) peppers and it was not the vizier but his mother who made the discovery. Becky compounds Scott's "errors" by making Bedreddin, or his mother (a vizier's widow) who taught him to make cheese-cake, a Princess of Persia, whereas they were of Balsora, not Persia.
2. The custom was for women and children to withdraw to the drawing room after dinner, leaving the men to smoke, drink, and engage in "man talk" for a short while before joining the ladies for coffee.
3. Mulligatawney is actually the name of a spicy soup. Dumdum and Budgebudge: villages near Calcutta. "Council" is the Indian legislative council.
4. London wine merchants.

A slight snore was the only reply: the honest stock-broker was asleep and so the rest of Joseph's story was lost for that day.[5] But he is[6] always exceedingly communicative in a man's party, and has told this delightful tale many scores of times to his apothecary, Dr. Gollop, when he came to enquire about the liver and the blue pill.

Being an invalid Joseph Sedley contented himself with a bottle of claret besides his madeira at dinner. And he managed a couple of plates-full of strawberries and cream, and twenty four little rout cakes that were lying neglected in a plate near him—and certainly (for novelists have the privilege of knowing every thing) he thought a great deal about the girl up stairs. "A nice, gay, merry young creature," thought he to himself—"how she looked at me when I picked up her handkerchief at dinner! She dropped it twice. Who's that singing in the drawing-room? Gad! shall I go up and see?"

But his modesty came rushing upon him with uncontrollable force. His father was asleep. His hat was in the hall—there was a hackney-coach[7] stand hard by in Southampton Row. "I'll go and see the *Forty Thieves,*" said he, "and Miss DeCamp's dance,"[8] and he slipped away gently on the pointed toes of his boots, and disappeared without waking his worthy parent.

"There goes Joseph," said Amelia who was looking from the open windows of the drawing-room, while Rebecca was singing at the piano.

"Miss Sharp has frightened him away," said Mrs. Sedley. "Poor Joe why *will* he be so shy?"[9]

5. MS reads: for ever.
6. Revised edition reads: was
7. Equivalent of a taxi; a coach seating six, drawn by two horses (hacks).
8. Adelaide De Camp danced in the musical play at Drury Lane.
9. Tailpiece: Joseph in a "buggy," not a hackney coach.

*Chapter IV.*

THE GREEN SILK PURSE.

OOR Joe's[1] panic lasted for two or three days: during which he did not visit the house, nor during that period did Miss Rebecca ever mention his name. She was all respectful gratitude to[2] Mrs. Sedley—delighted beyond measure at the Bazaars, and in a whirl of wonder at the theatre whither the good-natured lady took her. One day Amelia had a headache and could not go upon some party of pleasure to which the two young people were invited:—nothing would induce her friend to go without her. "What! you who have shown the poor orphan what happiness and love are for the first time in her life—quit *you?* never!" and the green eyes looked up to heaven and filled with tears: and Mrs. Sedley could not but own that her daughter's friend had a charming kind heart of her own.

As for Mr. Sedley's jokes, Rebecca laughed at them with a cordiality and perseverance which not a little pleased and softened that good-natured gentleman. Nor was it with the chiefs of the family alone that Miss Sharp found favour. She interested Mrs. Blenkinsop by evincing the deepest sympathy in the raspberry-jam preserving, which operation was then going on in the Housekeeper's room; she persisted in calling Sambo "Sir," and "Mr. Sambo," to the delight of that attendant; and she apologised to the lady's maid for giving her trouble in venturing to ring the bell, with such sweetness and humility, that the Servants' Hall was almost as charmed with her as the Drawing Room.[3]

Once in looking over some drawings which Amelia had sent from school, Rebecca suddenly came upon one which caused her to burst into tears and leave the room. It was on the day when Joe Sedley made his second appearance.

Amelia hastened after her friend to know the cause of this display of feeling, and the good-natured girl came back without her companion, rather affected too. "You know her father was our drawing-master, Mamma, at Chiswick and used to do all the best parts of our drawings."

"My love! I'm sure I always heard Miss Pinkerton say that he did not touch them—he only *mounted* them."

"It was called mounting, Mamma. Rebecca remembers the drawing and her father working at[4] it, and the thought of it came upon her rather suddenly—and so you know she . . ."

1. MS reads: His
2. MS reads: for
3. This paragraph was added in proof stage.
4. MS reads: on

"The poor child is all heart," said Mrs. Sedley.

"I wish she could stay with us another week," said Amelia.

"She's dev'lish like Miss Cutler that I used to meet at Dumdum, only fairer. She's married now to Lance the artillery surgeon. Do you know Ma'am that once Quintin of the 14th bet me . . ."

"O Joseph, we know that story," said Amelia laughing. "Never mind about telling that; but persuade Mamma to write to Sir Something Crawley."

"Had he a son in the King's[5] Light-Dragoons in India?"

"Well will you write to him for[6] leave of absence for poor dear Rebecca—here she comes her eyes red with weeping."

"I'm better now," said the girl with the sweetest smile possible, taking good-natured Mrs. Sedley's extended hand and kissing it respectfully. "How kind you all are to me!—all," added she with a laugh, "except you, Mr. Joseph."

"Me," said Joseph meditating an instant departure. "Gracious Heavens. Good Gad—Miss Sharp."

"Yes, how could you be so[7] cruel as to make me eat that horrid pepper dish at dinner the first day I ever saw you? You are not so good to me as dear Amelia."

"He doesn't know you so well," cried Amelia.

"I defy any body not to be good to you, my dear," said her mother.

"The curry was capital indeed it was," said Joe quite gravely. "Perhaps there was *not* enough citron juice in it—no there was *not*."

"And the chilis?"

"By Jove how they made you cry out," said Joe, caught by the ridicule of the circumstance, and exploding in a fit of laughter which ended quite suddenly as usual.[8]

"I shall take care how I let *you* choose for me another time," said Rebecca as they went down again to dinner. "I didn't think men were fond of putting poor harmless girls to pain."

"By Gad Miss Rebecca I wouldn't hurt you for the world."

"No," said she, "I *know* you wouldn't," and then she gave him ever so gentle a pressure with her little hand, and drew it back quite frightened and looked just for one instant in his face, and then down at the carpet-rods, and I am not prepared to say that Joe's heart did not thump at this little involuntary, timid, gentle motion of regard on the part of the simple girl.

It was an advance and as such perhaps some ladies of indisputable correctness and gentility will condemn the action as[9] immodest—but you see poor dear Rebecca had all this work to do for herself. If a person is too poor to keep a servant, though ever so elegant, he must sweep his[1] own rooms: if a dear girl has no dear mamma to settle matters with the young man, she must do it for herself. And oh what a mercy it is that these women do not exercise their power[2]

5. "King's" is interlined in the MS.
6. Revised edition reads: Something Crawley, for
7. MS reads: as
8. The phrase "exploding . . . as usual." is interlined in the MS.
9. The phrase "as such perhaps . . . action as" is interlined in the MS.
1. MS reads: out his
2. MS reads: own power

oftener! We can't resist them if they do. Let them show ever so little inclination and men go down on their knees at once, old or ugly it is all the same. And this I set down as a positive truth.[3] A woman with fair opportunities and without an absolute hump, may marry WHOM SHE LIKES. Only let us be thankful that the darlings are like the beasts of the field, and don't know their own power. They would overcome us entirely if they did.

"Egad," thought[4] Joseph entering the dining room, "I exactly begin to feel as I did at Dumdum with Miss Cutler." Many sweet little appeals, half tender half jocular did Miss Sharp make to him about the dishes at dinner, for by this time she was on a footing of considerable familiarity with the family; and as for the girls they loved each other like sisters. Young unmarried girls always do if they are in a house together for ten days.

As if bent upon advancing Rebecca's plans in every way—what must Amelia do but remind her brother of a promise made last Easter holidays—"when I was a girl at school," said she laughing—a promise that he, Joseph, would take her to Vauxhall. "Now," she said, "that Rebecca is with us, will be the very time."

"O delightful," said Rebecca, going to clap her hands, but she recollected herself and paused like a modest creature as she was.

"To-night is not the night," said Joe.

"Well tomorrow."

"Tomorrow your Papa and I dine out," said Mrs. Sedley.

"You don't suppose that *I*'m going, Mrs. Sed?" said her husband, "and that a woman of your years and size is to catch cold, in such an abominable damp place?"

"The[5] children must have some one with them," cried Mrs. Sedley.

"Let Joe go," said his father laughing. "He's *big* enough." At which speech even Mr. Sambo at the side-board burst out laughing, and poor fat Joe felt inclined to become a parricide almost.

"Undo his stays," continued the pitiless old gentleman. "Fling some water in his face, Miss Sharp, or carry him up stairs—the dear creature's fainting. Poor victim! carry him up; he's as light as a feather."

"If I stand this, Sir, I'm d——!" roared Joseph.

"Order Mr. Jos's elephant, Sambo," cried the father. "Send to Exeter Change,[6] Sambo"—but seeing Jos ready almost to cry with vexation, the old joker stopped his laughter, and said, holding out his hand to his son, "It's all fair on the Stock-Exchange, Jos—and Sambo, never mind the elephant but give me and Mr. Jos a glass of Champagne—Boney[7] himself hasn't got such in his cellars, my boy."

A goblet of Champagne restored Joseph's equanimity, and before the bottle was emptied of which as an invalid he took two thirds he had agreed to take the young ladies to Vauxhall.

3. This sentence is interlined in the MS.
4. MS reads: said
5. MS reads:—Sir the
6. A collection of small shops built about 1679 in the Strand but known principally in the years before 1829 for Edward Cross's menagerie and its star attraction, the Indian elephant Chunee, put down in 1826. Not to be confused with the Stock Exchange, also referred to as "Change."
7. Derogatory name for Napoleon Bonaparte.

"The girls must have a gentleman apiece," said the old gentleman. "Jos will be sure to leave Emmy in the crowd he will be so taken up with Miss Sharp here. Send to 96[8] and ask George Osborne if he'll come."

At this I don't know in the least for what reason, Mrs. Sedley looked at her husband and laughed. Mr. Sedley's eyes twinkled in a manner indescribably roguish, and he looked at Amelia, and Amelia hanging down her head, blushed as only young ladies of seventeen know how to blush, and as Miss Rebecca Sharp never blushed in her life—at least not since she was eight years old and when she was caught stealing jam out of a cupboard by her godmother. "Amelia had better write a note," said her father: "and let George Osborne see what a beautiful handwriting we have brought back from Miss Pinkerton's—do you remember when you wrote to him to come on Twelfth night,[9] Emmy, and spelt twelfth without the f?"

"That was years ago," said Amelia.

"It seems like yesterday don't it, John?" said Mrs. Sedley to her husband; and that night in a conversation which took place in a front room in the second-floor, in a sort of tent hung round with chintz of a rich and fantastic India pattern, and *doublé*[1] with calico of a tender rose colour, in the interior of which species of marquee was a featherbed on which were two pillows on which were two round red faces, one in a laced night-cap, and one in a simple cotton one ending in a tassel—in *a curtain lecture*[2] I say Mrs. Sedley took her husband to task for his cruel conduct to poor Joe.

"It was quite wicked of you, Mr. Sedley," said she, "to torment the poor boy so."

"My dear," said the cotton-tassel in defence of his conduct, "Jos is a great deal vainer than you ever were in your life, and that's saying a good deal—though some thirty years ago in the year seventeen hundred and eighty—what was it?—perhaps you had a right to be vain. I don't say no. But I've no patience with Jos and his dandyfied modesty—It is out Josephing Joseph,[3] my dear, and all the while the boy[4] is only thinking of himself and what a fine fellow he is. I doubt,[5] Ma'am, we shall have some trouble with him yet. Here is Emmy's little friend making love to him as hard as she can, that's quite clear—and if she does not catch him some other will. That man is destined to be a prey to woman as I am to go on Change every day. It's a mercy he did not bring us over a black daughter in law, my dear—but mark my words the first woman who fishes for him hooks him."

"She shall go off tomorrow, the little artful creature,"[6] said Mrs.

8. The Osborne residence, 96 Russell Square. MS reads: 26
9. Last night of the Christmas season, January 6.
1. Lined.
2. This phrase had recently been revived in Douglas Jerrold's *Mrs. Caudle's Curtain Lectures*, in *Punch* (1845), featuring the bedtime nagging of a husband by his wife. The curtains are on the four-poster bed.
3. Jos outdoes the biblical Joseph, wearing his coat of many colors and dreaming of his superiority to his brothers (Genesis 37).
4. MS reads: <fellow> ↑boy↓
5. I half expect.
6. MS reads: little <odious wretch> ↑artful creature↓

Sedley with great energy.[7]

"Why not she as well as another, Mrs. Sed?—The girl's a white face at any rate. *I* don't care who marries him. Let Jos please himself"—and presently the voices of the two speakers were hushed, or were replaced by the gentle but unromantic music of the nose—and save when the churchbells tolled the hour and the watchman called it all was silent in the house of John Sedley, Esquire, of Russell Square and the Stock Exchange.

When morning came the good-natured Mrs. Sedley no longer thought of executing her threats with regard to Miss Sharp; for though nothing is more keen, nor more common, nor more justifiable than maternal jealousy, yet she could not bring herself to suppose that the little humble grateful gentle governess, would dare to look up to such a magnificent personage as the Collector of Boggley wollah. The petition too for an extension of the young lady's leave of absence had already been dispatched, and it would be difficult to find a pretext for abruptly dismissing her.

And as if all things conspired in favour of the gentle Rebecca, the very elements (although she was not inclined at first to acknowledge their action in her behalf) interposed to aid her. For on the evening appointed for the Vauxhall party, George Osborne having come to dinner, and the elders of the house having departed according to invitation to dine with Alderman Balls[8] at Highbury Barn, there came on such a thunder-storm as only happens on Vauxhall nights, and as obliged the young people perforce to remain at home. Mr. Osborne did not seem in the least disappointed at this occurrence. He and Joseph Sedley drank a fitting quantity of port-wine *tête-à-tête*[9] in the dining room, during the drinking of which Sedley told a number of his best Indian stories, for he was extremely talkative in man's society, and afterwards Miss Amelia Sedley did the honours of the drawing room, and these four young persons passed such a comfortable evening together, that they declared they were rather glad of the thunder-storm than otherwise which had caused them to put off their visit to Vauxhall.

Osborne was Sedley's godson, and had been one of the family any time these three and twenty years. At six weeks old he had received from John Sedley a present of a silver cup, at six months old a coral with a gold[1] whistle and bells, from his youth upwards he was "tipped"[2] regularly by the old gentleman at Christmas and on going back to school, he remembered perfectly well being thrashed by Joseph Sedley when the latter was a big, swaggering hobbldyhoy and George an impudent urchin of ten years old—in a word George was as familiar with the family as such daily acts of kindness and intercourse could make him.

"Do you remember, Sedley, what a fury you were in when I cut off the tassels of your Hessian boots—and how Miss—hem!—how Amelia

7. The phrase "with great energy" was added in proof.
8. Fictitious name and place. MS reads: Gollop
9. By themselves; literally, "face to face."
1. The phrase "coral with a gold" is interlined in the MS.
2. Given a small coin.

rescued me from a beating, by falling down on her knees and crying out to her brother Dos[3] not to beat little George?"

Jos remembered this remarkable circumstance perfectly well, but vowed that he had totally forgotten it.

"Well, do you remember coming down in a gig[4] to Dr. Swishtail's to see me before you went to India, and giving me half a guinea and a pat on[5] the head? I always had an idea that you were at least seven feet high, and was quite astonished at your return from India to find you no taller than myself."

"How good of Mr. Sedley to go to your school and give you the money!" exclaimed Rebecca in accents of extreme delight.

"Yes and after I had cut the tassels off his boots too. Boys never forget those tips at school nor the givers."

"I delight in Hessian boots," said Rebecca. Jos Sedley who admired his own legs prodigiously and always wore this ornamental *chaussure,*[6] was extremely pleased at this remark, though he drew his legs under his chair as it was made.

"Miss Sharp," said George Osborne, "you who are so clever an artist, you must make a grand historical picture of the scene of the boots. Sedley shall be represented in buckskins and holding one of the injured boots in one hand—by the other he shall have hold of my shirt frill. Amelia shall be kneeling near him with her little hands up: and the picture shall have a grand allegorical title as the frontispieces have in the Medulla and the spelling book."[7]

"I shan't have time to do it here," said Rebecca. "I'll do it where—when I am[8] gone." And she dropped her voice and looked so sad and piteous, that everybody felt how cruel her lot was and how sorry they would be to part with her.

"O that you could stay longer, dear Rebecca," said Amelia.

"Why?" answered the other still more sadly. "That I may be only the more unhap—unwilling to lose you?" and she turned away her head. Amelia began[9] to give way to that natural infirmity of tears which we have said was one of the defects of this silly little thing; George Osborne looked at the two young women[1] with a touched curiosity, and Joseph Sedley heaved something very like a sigh out of his big chest, as he cast his eyes down towards his favourite Hessian boots.

"Let us have some music, Miss Sedley—Amelia," said George, who felt at that moment an extraordinary, almost irresistible, impulse to seize the above-mentioned young woman in his arms, and to kiss her in the face of the company—and she looked at him for a moment, and if I should say that they fell in love with each other at that single

3. First edition "corrects" Amelia's childish lisp to: Jos
4. Light two-wheeled, one-horse carriage, like the buggy of chapter III.
5. MS reads: of
6. Footware.
7. William Howell's *Medulla Historiae Anglicanae* has an appropriate "grand allegorical" frontispiece in the twelfth edition, 1766. Some editions of Dilworth's *Spelling Book* evidently contained an allegorical frontispiece of "Education leading up Youth to the temple of Industry" (Tillotson).
8. Revised edition reads: I'm
9. MS reads: <felt inclined> ↑began↓
1. MS reads: <pair> ↑two young women↓

instant of time I should perhaps be telling an untruth: for the fact is that these two young people had been bred up by their parents for this very purpose, and their banns had as it were been read in their[2] respective families any time these ten years. They went off to the piano which was situated as pianos usually are in the back drawing room; and as it was rather dark, Miss Amelia in the most unaffected way in the world put her hand into Mr. Osborne's, who of course could see the way among the chairs and ottomans a great deal better than she could. But this arrangement left Mr. Joseph Sedley *tête-à-tête* with Rebecca at the drawing-room table where the latter was occupied in netting a green silk purse.

"There is no need to ask family secrets," said Miss Sharp. "Those two have told theirs."

"As soon as he gets his company,"[3] said Joseph, "I believe the affair is settled. George Osborne is as good a fellow as ever breathed."[4]

"And your sister the dearest creature in the world," said Rebecca. "Happy the man who wins her." With this Miss Sharp gave a great sigh.

When two unmarried persons get together, and talk upon such delicate subjects as the present a great deal of confidence and intimacy is presently established between them. There is no need of giving a special report of the conversation which now took place between Mr. Sedley and the young lady: for the conversation as may be judged from the foregoing specimen was not especially witty or eloquent—it seldom is in private societies or any where except in very high-flown and ingenious novels. As there was music in the next room, the talk was carried on of course in a low and becoming tone, though for the matter of that, the couple in the next apartment would not have been disturbed had the talking been ever so loud, so occupied were they with their own pursuits.

Almost for the first time in his life Mr. Sedley found himself talking without the least timidity or hesitation to a person of the other sex. Miss Rebecca asked him a great number of questions about India which gave him an opportunity of narrating many interesting anecdotes about that country and himself. He described the balls at Government House,[5] and the manner in which they kept themselves cool in the hot weather with punkahs, tatties,[6] and other contrivances, and he was very witty regarding the number of Scotchmen whom Lord Minto, the governor-general,[7] patronised, and then he described a tiger-hunt, and the manner in which the mahout[8] of his elephant had been pulled off his seat by one of the infuriated animals. How delighted Miss Rebecca was at the Government balls, and how she laughed at the stories of the Scotch *aides-de-camp*,[9] and called Mr.

2. MS reads: these
3. I.e., becomes captain of a company.
4. For "as good . . . breathed" the revised edition reads: a capital fellow
5. Official residence of the governor-general.
6. Large fans and moistened mats or screens to cool the air.
7. Sir Gilbert Elliot (1715–1814), a Scotsman, became governor-general of India in 1806; he was made first earl of Minto in 1813.
8. Elephant driver.
9. Officers assisting a general.

Sedley a sad wicked satirical creature! and how frightened she was at the story of the elephant! "For your mother's sake, dear Mr. Sedley," she said, "for the sake of all your friends, promise *never* to go on one of those horrid expeditions."

"Pooh, pooh, Miss Sharp," said he pulling up his shirt collars[1]—"the danger makes the sport only the pleasanter." He had never been but once at a tiger hunt when the accident in question occurred and when he was half killed—not by the tiger but by the fright. And as he talked on he grew quite bold and actually had the audacity to ask Miss Rebecca for whom she was knitting the green silk purse? He was quite surprised and delighted at his own graceful familiar manners.

"For any one who wants a purse," replied Miss Rebecca looking at him in the most gentle winning way. Sedley was going to make one of the most eloquent speeches possible—and had begun, "O Miss Sharp, how . . . " when some song which was performed in the other room came to an end, and caused him to hear his own voice so distinctly that he stopped, blushed, and blew his nose in great agitation.

"Did you ever hear anything like your brother's eloquence?" whispered Mr. Osborne to Amelia, "why, your friend has worked miracles!"

"The more the better," said Miss Amelia: who like almost all women who are worth a pin was a match-maker in her heart: and would have been delighted that Joseph should carry back a wife to India. She had too in the course of this few days' constant intercourse warmed into a most tender friendship for Rebecca, and discovered a million of virtues and amiable qualities in her, which she had not perceived when they were at Chiswick together. For the affection of young ladies is of as rapid growth as Jack's bean stalk and reaches[2] up to the sky in a night. It is no blame to them that after marriage this *Sehnsucht nach der Liebe*[3] subsides: it is what sentimentalists who deal in *very* big words call a yearning after the Ideal: and simply means that women are commonly not satisfied until they have husbands and children on whom they may centre affections, which are spent elsewhere as it were in small change.

Having expended her little store of songs, or having staid long enough in the back drawing-room it now appeared proper to Miss Amelia to ask her friend to sing. "You would not have listened to me," she said to Mr. Osborne (though she knew she was telling a fib) "had you heard Rebecca first."

"I give Miss Sharp warning though," said Osborne; "that right or wrong I consider Miss Amelia Sedley the first singer in the world."

"You shall hear," said Amelia; and Joseph Sedley was actually polite enough to carry the candles to the piano. Osborne hinted that he should like quite as well to sit in the dark; but Miss Sedley laughing declined to bear him company any farther, and the two accordingly followed Mr. Joseph. Rebecca sang far better than her friend—(though of course Osborne was free to keep his opinions) and exerted

1. The phrase "pulling . . . collars" is interlined in the MS.
2. MS reads: <grows> ↑reaches↓
3. Longing after love.

herself to the utmost and indeed to the wonder of Amelia who had never known her perform so well. She sang a French song, which Joseph did not understand in the least, and which George confessed he did not understand: and then a number of those simple ballads which were the fashion forty years ago, and in which British tars, our king, poor Susan, blue eyed Mary, and the like were the principal themes.[4] They are not, it is said, very brilliant in a musical point of view, but contain numberless good-natured simple appeals to the affections which people understood better than the milk-and-water *lagrime, sospiri,* and *felicità,* of the eternal Donizettian music[5] with which we are favoured now a days.

Conversation of a sentimental sort befitting the subject was carried on between the songs to which Sambo after he had brought the tea,

the delighted cook[6] and even Mrs. Blenkinsop the housekeeper condescended to listen on the landing place.[7]

Among these ditties was one, the last of the concert, and to the following effect:—

Ah! bleak and barren was the moor,
  Ah! loud and piercing was the storm,
The cottage roof was shelter'd sure,
  The cottage hearth was bright and warm—
An orphan boy the lattice pass'd,
  And, as he mark'd its cheerful glow,

4. Among popular songs recorded by Geoffrey and Kathleen Tillotson are "The Britsh Tars," John Gay's "Black-Eyed Susan, or All in the Downs," "Blue-Eyed Mary" and "I Am a Jolly Sailor Bold."
5. Tears, sighs, and happiness—words frequent in the operas of Gaetano Donizetti (1797–1848).
6. MS adds: and the housemaid—
7. Revised edition omits this paragraph and, of course, the illustration.

Felt doubly keen the midnight blast,
And doubly cold the fallen snow.

They mark'd him as he onward prest,
With fainting heart and weary limb;
Kind voices bade him turn and rest,
And gentle faces welcomed him.
The dawn is up—the guest is gone,
The cottage hearth is blazing still;
Heaven pity all poor wanderers lone!
Hark to the wind upon the hill![8]

It was the sentiment of the before mentioned words, "When I'm gone," over again. As she came to the last words Miss Sharp's "deep-toned voice faltered."[9] Every body felt the allusion to her departure and to her hapless orphan state. Joseph Sedley who was fond of music and soft hearted was in a state of ravishment during the performance of the song, and profoundly touched at its conclusion. If he had had the courage: if George and Miss Sedley had remained according to the former's proposal in the farther room, Joseph Sedley's bachelorhood would have been at an end and this work would never have been written. But at[1] the close of the ditty Rebecca quitted the piano and giving her hand to Amelia walked away into the front drawing room twilight, and at this moment Mr. Sambo made his appearance with a tray containing sandwiches, jellies, and some glittering glasses and decanters, on which Joseph Sedley's attention was immediately fixed. When the parents of the house of Sedley returned from their dinner-party they found the young people so busy in talking that they had not heard the arrival of the carriage and Mr. Joseph was in the act of saying, "My dear Miss Sharp, one little tea-spoonful of jelly to recruit you after your immense—your—your *delightful* exertions."[2]

"Bravo, Jos!" said Mr. Sedley—on hearing the bantering of which well-known voice Jos instantly relapsed into an alarmed silence, and quickly took his departure. He did not lie awake all night thinking whether or not he was in love with Miss Sharp—the passion of love never interfered with the appetite or the slumber of Mr. Joseph Sedley—but he thought to himself how delightful it would be to hear such songs as those after cutcherry.[3] What a *distinguée* girl she was, how she could speak French better than the Governor General's lady herself, and what a sensation she would make at the Calcutta balls. "It's evident the poor devil's[4] in love with me," thought he. "She is just as rich as most of the girls who come out to India. I might go farther and fare worse, egad," and in these meditations he fell asleep.

8. An original composition by Thackeray, reprinted in his *Ballads*.
9. From "We met—'twas in a crowd" by Thomas Haynes Bayly (1797–1839): "He spoke—his words were cold, and his smile was unalter'd: / I knew how much he *felt*, for his deep-toned voice falterd."
1. MS reads: But <his modesty interfered> <↑he could not pop questions↓> at
2. The phrase "immense—your—your" is interlined in the MS.
3. Administrative office hours in India.
4. MS reads: devil is

How Miss Sharp lay awake thinking will he come or not tomorrow? need not be told here. Tomorrow came and as sure as fate, Mr. Joseph Sedley made his appearance before luncheon. He had never been known before to confer such an honour on[5] Russell Square.[6] George Osborne was somehow there already (sadly "putting out" Amelia, who was writing to her twelve dearest friends at Chiswick Mall), and Rebecca was employed upon her yesterday's work. As Joe's buggy drove up, and while, after his usual thundering knock and pompous bustle at the door, the Collector[7] of Boggley wollah laboured up stairs to the drawing-room, knowing glances were telegraphed between Osborne and Miss Sedley, and the pair, smiling archly, looked at Rebecca, who actually blushed as she bent her fair ringlets over her netting. How her heart beat as Joseph appeared,—Joseph, puffing from the staircase in shining creaking boots,—Joseph, in a new waistcoat, red with heat and nervousness, and blushing behind his wadded neckcloth. It was a nervous moment for all; and as for Amelia, I think she was more frightened than even the people most concerned.

Sambo, who flung open the door and announced Mr. Joseph, followed grinning, in the Collector's rear, and bearing two handsome nosegays of flowers, which the monster had actually had the gallantry to purchase in Covent Garden Market[8] that morning—they were not as big as the hay-stacks which ladies carry about with them now-a-days, in cones of filagree paper; but the young women were delighted with the gift, as Joseph presented one to each, with an exceedingly solemn and clumsy bow.

"Bravo, Jos!" cried Osborne.

"Thank you, dear Joseph," said Amelia, quite ready to kiss her brother, if he were so minded. (And I think for a kiss from such a dear creature as Amelia, I would purchase all Mr. Lee's conservatories[9] out of hand.)

"O heavenly, heavenly flowers!" exclaimed Miss Sharp, and smelt them delicately, and held them to her bosom, and cast up her eyes to the ceiling, in an ecstasy of admiration. Perhaps she just looked first into the bouquet, to see whether there was a *billet-doux*[1] hidden among the flowers; but there was no letter.

"Do they talk the language of flowers at Boggley wollah, Sedley?" asked Osborne, laughing.

"Language of fiddlestick!"[2] replied the sentimental youth. "Bought 'em at Nathan's;[3] very glad you like 'em; and eh, Amelia, my dear, I bought a pine-apple at the same time, which I gave to Sambo. Let's have it for tiffin;[4] very cool and nice this hot weather." Rebecca said

5. For "before . . . honour on" the MS reads: to confer such an honour before on the house in
6. The rest of the chapter was apparently added in proof. The MS has two more sentences here, followed by what is now chapter VI: When was the party fixed for Vauxhall[?] That was the great question which brought him. The matter had not been fully arranged the night previous.
7. Revised edition reads: ex-Collector
8. Wholesale London fruit, vegetable, and flower market.
9. Famous nurseries in Hammersmith.
1. Love note.
2. Revised edition reads: Pooh, nonsense
3. Untraced.
4. Light lunch.

she had never tasted a pine, and longed beyond everything to taste one.

So the conversation went on. I don't know on what pretext Osborne left the room, or why, presently, Amelia went away, perhaps to superintend the slicing of the pine-apple; but Jos was left alone with Rebecca, who had resumed her work, and the green silk and the shining needles were quivering rapidly under her white slender fingers.

"What a beautiful, *byoo-ootiful* song that was you sang last night, dear Miss Sharp," said the Collector. "It made me cry almost; 'pon my honour it did."

"Because you have a kind heart, Mr. Joseph: all the Sedleys have, I think."

"It kept me awake last night, and I was trying to hum it this morning, in bed; I was, upon my honour. Gollop, my doctor, came in at eleven (for I'm a sad invalid, you know, and see Gollop every day), and, 'gad! there I was, singing away like—a robin."

"O you droll creature! Do let me hear you sing it."

"Me? No, you, Miss Sharp; my dear Miss Sharp, do sing it."

"Not now, Mr. Sedley," said Rebecca, with a sigh. "My spirits are not equal to it: besides, I must finish the purse. Will you help me, Mr. Sedley?" And before he had time to ask how, Mr. Joseph Sedley, of the East India Company's service, was actually seated *tête-à-tête* with a young lady, looking at her with a most killing expression; his arms stretched out before her in an imploring attitude, and his hands bound in a web of green silk, which she was unwinding.

* * * * * *

In this romantic position Osborne and Amelia found the interesting pair, when they entered to announce that tiffin was ready. The skein of silk was just wound round the card; but Mr. Jos had never spoken.

"I am sure he will to-night, dear," Amelia said, as she pressed Rebecca's hand; and Sedley, too, had communed with his soul, and said to himself, " 'Gad, I'll pop the question at Vauxhall."

Mr. Joseph entangled

*Number 2* *Feb. 1847*

## *Chapter V.*

### DOBBIN OF OURS.[1]

UFF'S fight with Dobbin[2] and the unexpected issue of that contest will long be remembered by every man who was educated at Dr. Swishtail's famous school.[3] The latter youth (who used to be called Heigh ho Dobbin Gee ho Dobbin, and by many other names indicative of puerile contempt) was the quietest, the clumsiest, and as it seemed the dullest of[4] all Dr. Swishtail's young gentlemen. His parent was a grocer in the city:[5] and it was bruited abroad that he was admitted into Dr. Swishtail's academy upon what are called 'mutual principles'—that is to say the expences of his board and schooling were defrayed by his father in goods not in money—and he stood there—almost at the bottom of the school in his scraggy corduroys and jacket through the seams of which his great big bones were bursting—as the representative of so many pounds of tea, candles, sugar, mottled-soap, plums (of which a very mild proportion was supplied for the puddings of the establishment), and other commodities. A dreadful day it was for young Dobbin when one of the youngsters of the school, having run into the town upon a poaching excursion for hardbake and polonies,[6] espied the cart of Dobbin & Rudge Grocers & Oilmen Thames St. London at the Doctor's door discharging a cargo of the wares in which the firm dealt.

Young Dobbin had no peace after that. The jokes were frightful and merciless against him.[7] "Hullo, Dobbin," one wag would say, "here's good news in the paper. Sugars is ris', my boy." Another would set a sum. "If a pound of mutton-candles cost sevenpence halfpenny, how much must Dobbin cost?" and a roar would follow

1. I.e., of our regiment.
2. Cuff was originally named Phipps in the MS. Although the date of Cuff's fight with Dobbin had to be about 1804, the paper hat in the vignette is made of the *Daily News*, started in 1845. This humorous anachronism would have been obvious to most early readers.
3. A thinly veiled allusion to Charterhouse School, which Thackeray attended and hated, in part because of the headmaster's frequent recourse to corporal punishment.
4. MS reads: dullest <youth><↑boy↓><in the whole seminary. He was «always sho» the object of scorn> of
5. Within the walls of the original City of London, now east-central London, the center of commerce.
6. Almond toffee and pork sausages.
7. MS reads: him <as they frequently are in our admirable Country>.

from all the circle of young knaves, usher[8] and all, who rightly considered that the selling of goods by retail is a shameful and infamous practice meriting the contempt and scorn of all real gentlemen.

"Your father's only a merchant,[9] Osborne," Dobbin said in private to the little boy who had brought down this storm upon him—on which the latter replied haughtily, "My father's a gentleman and keeps his carriage," and Mr. William Dobbin retired to a remote out-house in the play-ground where he passed a half-holiday in the bitterest sadness and wo. Who amongst us is there that does not recollect similar hours of bitter, bitter childish grief? Who feels injustice; who shrinks before a slight; who has a sense of wrong so acute, and so glowing a gratitude for kindness as a generous boy? and how many of those gentle souls do you degrade, estrange, torture, for the sake of a little loose arithmetic and miserable dog-latin?[1]

Now William Dobbin—from an incapacity to acquire the rudiments of the above language as they are propounded in that wonderful book the Eton Latin Grammar[2]—was compelled to remain among the very last of Doctor Swishtail's scholars and was 'taken down' continually by little fellows with pink faces and pinafores when he marched up with the lower-form,[3] a giant amongst them, with his downcast stupified look, his dogs-eared primer and his tight corduroys. High and low, all made fun of him. They sowed up those corduroys tight as they were. They cut his bed-strings.[4] They upset buckets and benches so that he might break his shins over them which he never failed to do. They sent him parcels which when opened were found to contain the paternal soap and candles. There was no little fellow but had his jeer and joke at Dobbin—and he bore everything quite patiently and was entirely dumb and miserable.

Cuff on the contrary was the great chief and dandy of the Swishtail Seminary. He smuggled wine in. He fought the town-boys. Poneys used to come for him to ride home on Saturdays. He had his top-boots in his room, in which he used to hunt in the holidays. He had a gold repeater: and took snuff like the Doctor.[5] He had been to the Opera, and knew the merits of the principal actors preferring Mr. Kean to Mr. Kemble.[6] He could knock you off forty Latin verses in an hour. He could make French poetry. What else didn't he know, or couldn't he do?—They said even the Doctor himself was afraid of him.[7]

8. Schoolmaster's assistant.
9. For "Your ... merchant" the MS reads: Your <father> ↑grandfather↓ was in the same business
1. The phrase "loose ... dog-latin" is interlined in the MS above canceled: miserable as in prosenti or a few acquirements so contemptible mean & trivial
2. *An Introduction to the Latin Tongue* (1758), a standard school text.
3. The beginner's class.
4. Ropes upon which the mattress rested.
5. This sentence is interlined in the MS. Repeater: a watch that sounded the hour again at the touch of a spring.
6. An anachronism, since Edmund Kean began his acting career ten years after the events of this chapter. John Kemble was an actor Cuff could have seen. Kemble's and Kean's careers overlapped from 1814 to 1817.
7. This sentence is interlined in the MS.

Cuff the unquestioned king of the school ruled over his subjects and bullied them with splendid superiority. This one blacked his shoes: that toasted his bread—others would fag out and give him balls[8] at cricket during whole summer-afternoons. 'Figs' was the fellow whom he despised most and with whom though always abusing him and sneering at him he scarcely ever condescended to hold personal communication.

One day in private these two young gentlemen had had a difference. Figs alone in the school-room was blundering over a home-letter; when Cuff entering bade him go upon some message[9] of which tarts were probably the subject.

"I can't," says Dobbin; "I want to finish my letter."

"You *can't*?" says Mr. Cuff laying hold of that document (in which many words were scratched out, many were misspelt, on which had been spent I don't know how much thought and labour and tears, for the poor fellow was writing to his mother who was fond of him although she was a grocer's wife and lived in a back parlor in Thames St.), "You *can't*?" says Mr. Cuff: "I should like to know why, pray? Can't you write to old Mother Figs tomorrow."

"Don't call names," Dobbin said getting up off the bench very nervous.

"Well, sir, will you go?" crowed the Cock of the School.

"Put down the letter," Dobbin replied, "no gentleman readth letterth."

"Well *now* will you go," says the other.

"No I won't—Don't strike—or I'll *thmash* you," roars out Dobbin, springing to a leaden inkstand and looking so wicked that Mr. Cuff paused, turned down his coat sleeves again, put his hands into his pockets and walked away with a sneer. But he never meddled personally with the grocer's boy after that, though we must do him the justice to say he always spoke of Mr. Dobbin with contempt behind his back.

Some time after this interview, it happened[1] that Mr. Cuff on a sunshiny afternoon[2] was in the neighbourhood of poor William Dobbin who was lying under a tree[3] in the play ground, spelling over a favourite copy of the Arabian Nights which he had, apart from the rest of the school who were pursuing their various sports,—quite lonely and almost happy. If people would but leave children to themselves; if teachers would cease to bully them; if parents would not insist upon directing their thoughts and dominating their feelings—those feelings and thoughts which are a mystery to us all (for how much do you and I know of each other, of our children, of our

8. To field balls and bowl batsman's practice.
9. MS reads:<errand>↑message↓
1. MS reads: <chanced>↑happened↓
2. MS reads: half-holiday <happened to be>
3. MS reads: under <the wall> ↑a tree↓

fathers, of our neighbour? and how far more beautiful and sacred are the thoughts of the poor lad or girl whom you govern likely to be, than those of the dull and world-corrupted person[4] who rules him?) if, I say, parents and masters[5] would leave their children alone a little more,—small harm would accrue although a less quantity of *as in præsenti*[6] might be acquired.

Well, William Dobbin had for once forgotten the world, and was away with Sindbad the Sailor in the Valley of Diamonds, or with Prince Whatdyecallem and the Fairy Peribanou in that delightful cavern where the Prince found her,[7] and whither we should all like to make a tour—when shrill cries as of a little fellow weeping woke up his pleasant reverie; and, looking up, he saw Cuff before him belabouring a little boy.

It was the lad who had peached[8] upon him about the grocer's cart: but he bore little malice:—not at least towards the young and small. "How dare you, Sir, break the bottle?" says Cuff to the little urchin, swinging a yellow cricket-stump[9] over him.

The boy had been instructed to get over the play-ground wall (at a selected spot where the broken-glass had been removed from the

4. MS reads: world<ly minded being>↑-corrupted person↓
5. The phrase "and masters" is interlined in the MS.
6. From *Eton Latin Grammar*'s section on the past perfect tense of verbs of the first conjugation.
7. References to two famous episodes in the *Arabian Nights*: Sindbad and the giant bird, Roc, and the marriage of Prince Ahmed and the Fairy Peribanou.
8. Tattled.
9. One of three sticks about eighteen inches long that form part of a wicket.

top, and niches made convenient in the brick)—to run a quarter of a mile—to purchase a pint of rum-shrub[1] on credit—to brave all the Doctor's outlying spies—and to clamber back into the playground again; during the performance of which feat, his foot had slipt, and the bottle was broken, and the shrub had been spilt, and his pantaloons had been damaged, and he appeared before his employer a perfectly guilty and trembling, though harmless wretch.

"How dare you, Sir, break it?" says Cuff. "You blundering little thief. You drank the shrub, and now you pretend to have broken the bottle. Hold out your hand, Sir."

Down came the stump with a great heavy thump on the child's hand. A moan followed. Dobbin looked up. The Princess Peribanou had fled into the inmost cavern with Prince Ahmed: the Roc had whisked away Sindbad the Sailor out of the Valley of Diamonds out of sight far into the clouds:—and there was every-day life before honest William, and a big boy beating a little one without cause.

"Hold out your other hand, Sir," roars Cuff to his little schoolfellow whose face was distorted with pain. Dobbin quivered and gathered himself up in his narrow old clothes.

"Take that, you little devil!" cried Mr. Cuff, and down came the wicket again on the child's hand.—Don't be horrified, ladies, every boy at a public school has done it. Your children will so do and be done by in all probability.—Down came the wicket again; and Dobbin started up.

I can't tell what his motive was. Torture in a public school[2] is as much licensed as the knout[3] in Russia. It would be ungentlemanlike (in a manner) to resist it. Perhaps Dobbin's foolish soul revolted against that exercise of tyranny: or perhaps he had a hankering feeling of revenge in his mind and longed to measure himself against that splendid bully and tyrant who had all the glory, pride, pomp, circumstance, banners flying, drums beating, guards saluting, in the place. Whatever may have been his incentive however up he sprang and screamed out, "Hold off, Cuff—don't bully that child any more: or I'll——"

"Or you'll what?" Cuff asked in amazement at this interruption. "Hold out your hand, you little beast."

"I'll give you the worst thrashing you ever had in your life," Dobbin said, in reply to the first part of Cuff's sentence—and little Osborne, gasping and in tears, looked up with wonder and incredulity at seeing this amazing champion put up suddenly to defend him: while Cuff's astonishment was scarcely less. Fancy our late monarch George III[4] when he heard of the revolt of the North American Colonies: fancy brazen Goliah when little David[5] stepped forward and claimed a meeting; and you have the feelings of Mr. Reginald

1. Rum, sugar, and citrus juice.
2. A select boarding school like Eton or Thackeray's own Charterhouse.
3. A wooden and rawhide lash whose use often led to death. Abolished from use in 1845.
4. In the MS "our late monarch" is interlined. George III reigned 1780–1820.
5. Goliath, the giant Philistine hero, challenged any hero of Israel and was met and killed by David, a shepherd boy, with a sling (I Samuel 17.40–48).

Cuff when this rencontre[6] was proposed to him.

"After school," says he of course, after a pause and a look as much as to say, 'Make your will and communicate your last wishes to your friends between this time and that.'

"As you please," Dobbin said. "You must be my bottle-holder, Osborne."

"Well—if you like," little Osborne replied; for you see his Papa kept a carriage and he was rather ashamed of his champion.

Yes, when the hour of battle[7] came he was almost ashamed to say 'Go it, Figs'—and not a single other boy in the place uttered that cry for the first two or three rounds of this famous combat—at the commencement of which the scientific Cuff with a contemptuous smile on his face, and as light and as gay as if he was at a ball—planted his blows upon his adversary, and floored that unlucky champion three times running. At each fall there was a cheer, and every body was anxious to have the honour of offering the conqueror a knee.[8]

'What a licking[9] I shall get when it's over,' young Osborne thought picking up his man. "You'd best give in," he said to Dobbin. "It's only a thrashing, Figs, and you know I'm used to it"—but Figs, all whose limbs were in a quiver and whose nostrils were breathing rage, put his little bottleholder aside, and went in for a fourth time.

As he did not in the least know how to parry the blows that were aimed at himself, and Cuff had begun the attack on the three preceding occasions without ever allowing his enemy to strike, Figs now determined that he would commence the engagement by a charge on his own part—and accordingly being a left-handed man, brought that arm into action and hit out a couple of times[1] with all his might—once on Mr. Cuff's left eye, and once on his beautiful Roman nose.

Cuff went down this time to the astonishment of the assembly. "Well hit, by Jove," says little Osborne with the air of a connoisseur clapping his man on the back. "Give it him with the left, Figs, my boy."

Figs's left made terrific play during all the rest of the combat. Cuff went down every time. At the sixth round, there were almost as many fellows shouting out, "Go it, Figs," as there were youths exclaiming, "Go it, Cuff." At the twelfth round the latter champion was all abroad as the saying is, and had lost all presence of mind and power of attack or defence. Figs on the contrary was as calm as a Quaker. His face being quite pale, his eyes shining open,[2] and a great cut on his under lip bleeding profusely, gave this young fellow a fierce and ghastly air, which perhaps struck terror into many spectators. Nevertheless his intrepid adversary[3] prepared to close for the thirteenth time.

6. Meeting for conflict.
7. MS reads: <combat> ↑battle↓
8. This sentence is interlined in the MS.
9. MS reads: <thrashing> ↑licking↓
1. MS reads: <straight blows> ↑times↓
2. The phrase "his eyes shining open" is interlined in the MS.
3. MS reads: <warrior> <↑enemy↓> ↑adversary↓

If I had the pen of a Napier or a Bell's Life,[4] I should like to describe this combat properly. It was the last charge of the Guard (that is *it would* have been, only Waterloo had not yet taken place.) It was Ney's column breasting[5] the hill of La Haye Sainte,[6] bristling with ten thousand bayonets and crowned with twenty eagles—It was the shout of the beef-eating British, as leaping down the hill they rushed to hug the enemy in[7] the savage arms of Battle—in other words, Cuff coming up full of pluck but quite reeling and groggy, the Fig merchant put in his left as usual on his adversary's nose and sent him down for the last time.

"I think *that* will do for him," Figs said as his opponent dropped as neatly on the green as I have seen Jack Spot's ball plump into the pocket at billiards—and the fact is, when Time was called Mr. Reginald Cuff was not able or did not choose to stand up again.

And now all the boys set up such a shout for Figs as would make you think he had been their darling champion through the whole battle; and as absolutely brought Dr. Swishtail out of his study curious to know the cause of the uproar. He threatened to flog Figs violently, of course: but Cuff who had come to himself by this time and was washing his wounds, stood up and said, "It's my fault, Sir—not Figs'—not Dobbin's. I was bullying a little boy and he served me right." By which magnanimous speech he not only saved his conqueror a whipping, but got back all his ascendancy over the boys which his defeat had nearly cost him.

Young Osborne wrote home to his parents an account of the transaction.

*"Sugarcane House, Richmond, March,* 18—.

"DEAR MAMA. I hope you are quite well. I should be much obliged to you to send me a cake and five shillings. There has been a fight here between Cuff & Dobbin. Cuff, you know was the Cock of the School. They fought thirteen rounds and Dobbin licked. So Cuff is now Only Second Cock. The fight was about me. Cuff was licking me for breaking a bottle of milk and figs wouldn't stand it. We call him figs because his father is a Grocer—Figs & Rudge, Thames St., City—I think as he fought for me you ought to buy your Tea & Sugar at his father's. Cuff goes Home every Saturday but can't this because he has 2 Black Eyes. He has a white Poney to come and fetch him, and a groom in livery on a bay mare. I wish my Papa would let me have a Poney and I am

"Your dutiful Son,

"GEORGE SEDLEY OSBORNE.

4. Sir William Napier (1785–1860) was a general and historian of the war against Napoleon's force in Spain and Portugal, 1808–14. *Bell's Life in London,* a weekly sporting journal (1824–59), covered boxing matches.
5. MS reads: <cresting> ↑breasting↓
6. Marshal Michel Ney, in one of the final successful actions of Napoleon's forces, captured La Haye Sainte. Napoleon's final charge ensued, and he was defeated in the Battle of Waterloo several days later.
7. MS reads: <they closed «upon» ↑with↓ the enemy—and rushed> ↑they rushed to hug the enemy↓ in<to>

"P.S. Give my love to little Emmy. I am cutting her out a Coach in card board."

In consequence of Dobbin's victory, his character rose prodigiously in the estimation of all his schoolfellows and the name of Figs which had been a byword and reproach became as respectable and popular a nickname as any other in use in the school.[8] "After all it's not his fault that his father's a grocer," George Osborne said, who though a little chap had a very high popularity among the Swishtail youth; and this opinion was received with great applause.[9] It was voted low to sneer at Dobbin about this accident of birth. 'Old Figs' grew to be a name of kindness and endearment: and the sneak of an Usher jeered at him no longer.

And Dobbin's spirit rose with his altered circumstances. He made wonderful advances in scholastic learning. The superb Cuff himself, at whose condescension Dobbin could only blush and wonder, helped him on with his Latin verses; 'coached' him in play-hours; carried him triumphantly out of the little-boy class, into the middle-sized form; and even there got a fair place for him. It was discovered that although dull at classical learning, at mathematics he was uncommonly quick. To the contentment of all he passed third in Algebra, and got a French prize book at the Public Midsummer examination. You should have seen his Mother's face when Telemaque[1] (that delicious romance) was presented to him by the Doctor in the face of the whole school and the parents and company,[2] with an inscription to Gulielmo[3] Dobbin. All the boys clapped hands in token of applause and sympathy. His blushes, his stumbles, his awkwardness, and the number of feet which he crushed as he went back to his place who shall describe or calculate? Old Dobbin, his father, who now respected him for the first time[4] gave him two guineas publicly; most of which he spent in a general tuck out[5] for the school, and he came back in a tail-coat after the holidays.

Dobbin was much too modest a young fellow to suppose that this happy change in all his circumstances arose from his own generous and manly disposition: he chose from some perverseness to attribute his good fortune[6] to the sole agency and benevolence of little George Osborne, to whom henceforth he vowed such a love and affection as is only felt by children—such an affection as we read in the charming fairy-book Uncouth Orson had for splendid young Valentine his conqueror. He flung himself down at little Osborne's feet and loved him.

8. MS adds two canceled phrases: <Old Figs never broke out into combativeness again,> <the sneak of an Usher sneered at him no longer>
9. The phrase "and this . . . applause" is interlined in the MS.
1. A French mythological romance about Ulysses's son, it was a popular schoolbook throughout the century.
2. The phrase "and the parents and company" is interlined in the MS.
3. Latin: William.
4. The phrase "who now . . . time" is interlined in the MS.
5. Treats for all.
6. MS reads:<This ↑happy↓ change in all his circumstances Dobbin did not in the least attribute to> ↑Dobbin was much too modest a young fellow to <attribute> ↑↑suppose that↓↓ this happy change in all his circumstances arose from↓ his own generous and manly disposition: <but ↑arose from↓> ↑he chose from some perverseness to attribute his good fortune↓

Even before they were acquainted, he had admired Osborne in secret. Now he was his valet, his dog, his man-Friday.[7] He believed Osborne to be the possessor of every perfection, to be the handsomest, the bravest, the most active, the cleverest, the most generous of created boys. He shared his money with him: bought him uncountable presents of knives, pencil-cases, gold seals, toffy, Little-Warblers[8] and romantic books with large coloured pictures of knights and robbers, in many of which latter you might read inscriptions to George Sedley Osborne, Esquire, from his attached friend William Dobbin—the which tokens of homage George received very graciously, as became his superior merit.

So that when Lieutenant Osborne coming to Russell Square on the day of the Vauxhall party said to the ladies, "Mrs. Sedley, Ma'am, I hope you have room, I've asked Dobbin of ours to come and dine here, and go with us to Vauxhall. He's almost as modest as Jos."

"Modesty—pooh," said the stout gentleman casting a *vainqueur* look[9] at Miss Sharp.

"He is—but you are incomparably more graceful, Sedley," Osborne added laughing. "I met him at the Bedford[1] where I went to look for you—and I told him that Miss Amelia was come home, and that we were all bent on going out for a night's pleasuring: and that Mrs. Sedley had forgiven his breaking the punch-bowl at the child's party. Don't you remember the catastrophe, Ma'am, seven years ago?"

"Over Mrs. Flamingo's crimson silk gown," said good-natured Mrs. Sedley —"What a gawky it was! and his sisters are not much more graceful—Lady Dobbin was at Highbury last night with three of them—Such figures, my dears!"

"The Alderman's very rich isn't he?" Osborne said archly, "don't you think one of the daughters would be a good spec for me, Ma'am?"

"You foolish creature, who would take *you* I should like to know with your yellow face?—and what can Alderman Dobbin leave amongst fourteen?"

"Mine a yellow face? Stop till you see Dobbin. Why, he had the yellow fever three times; twice at Nassau, and once at St. Kitts."[2]

"Well well, yours is quite yellow enough for us. Isn't it Emmy?" Mrs. Sedley said, at which speech Miss Amelia only made a smile and a blush; and looking at Mr. George Osborne's pale interesting countenance, and those beautiful black, curling, shining whiskers which the young gentleman himself regarded with no ordinary complacency, she thought in her little heart that in his Majesty's army or in the wide world there never was such a face or such a hero. "I don't care

7. In the French romance *Valentine and Orson*, Orson is raised by a bear; his brother, Valentine, captures and educates him. Friday is Robinson Crusoe's servant in the novel by Daniel Defoe.
8. A child's songbook.
9. Look of a conqueror.
1. Bedford Coffee House, Covent Garden, central London. See note on the Piazza Coffee House, chapter III.
2. West Indian military postings, undesirable because of pestilent climates.

about Captain Dobbin's complexion," she said, "or about his awkwardness. *I* shall always like him I know"—her little reason being that he was the friend and champion of George.

"There's not a finer fellow in the service," Osborne said, "nor a better officer though he is not an Adonis[3] certainly." And he looked towards the glass himself with much *naïveté,* and in so doing caught Miss Sharp's eye fixed keenly upon him, on which he blushed a little, and Rebecca thought in her heart, '*Ah, mon beau Monsieur,*[4] I think I have *your* gage'—the little artful minx!

That evening when Amelia came tripping[5] into the drawing room in a white muslin frock prepared for conquest at Vauxhall, singing like a lark, and as fresh as a rose; a very tall ungainly gentleman with large hands and feet and large ears set off by a closely cropped head of black hair, and in the hideous military frogged coat[6] and cocked-hat of those times, advanced to meet her and made her one of the clumsiest bows that was ever performed by a mortal—

This was no other than Captain William Dobbin of his Majesty's — Regiment of Foot, returned from yellow fever in the West Indies, to which the fortune of the service had ordered his regiment, whilst so many of his gallant comrades were reaping glory in the Peninsula.[7]

He had arrived with a knock so very timid and quiet, that it was inaudible to the ladies upstairs: otherwise you may be sure Miss Amelia

3. Renowned in Greek myth for male beauty.
4. Ah, handsome sir.
5. MS reads: <down stairs> ↑tripping in↓to
6. A frogged or frocked coat has braided button loops.
7. The Iberian Peninsula, fighting the French.

would never have been so bold as to[8] come singing into the room. As it was, the sweet fresh little voice went right into the Captain's heart and nestled there. When she held out her hand for him to shake, before he envelloped it in his own, he paused, and thought—"Well—is it possible—are you the little maid I remember in the pink frock such a short time ago—the night I upset the punchbowl just after I was gazetted. Are you the little girl that George Osborne said should marry him? What a blooming young creature you seem, and what a prize the rogue has got . . ." All this he thought, before he took Amelia's hand into his own, and as he let his cocked hat fall.[9]

His history since he left school until this very moment when we have the pleasure of meeting him again, although not fully narrated, has yet I think been indicated sufficiently for an ingenious reader by the conversation in the last page. Dobbin the despised grocer was Alderman Dobbin. Alderman Dobbin was Colonel of the City Light-Horse then burning with military ardour to resist the French invasion.[1] Colonel Dobbin's corps in which old Mr. Osborne himself was but an indifferent Corporal had been reviewed by the Sovereign and the Duke of York; and the Colonel and Alderman had been knighted. His son had entered the army: and young Osborne followed presently in the same regiment. They had served in the West Indies and in Canada. Their regiment had just come home and the attachment of Dobbin to George Osborne was as warm and generous now as it had been, when the two were schoolboys.[2]

So these worthy people sate down to dinner presently. They talked about war and glory and Boney and Lord Wellington[3] and the last Gazette.[4] In those famous days every gazette had a victory in it, and the two gallant young men longed to see their own names in the glorious list, and cursed their unlucky fate to belong to a regiment which had been away from the chances of honour. Miss Sharp kindled with this exciting talk but Miss Sedley trembled and grew quite faint as she heard it. Mr. Jos told several of his tiger-hunting stories, finished the one about Miss Cutler and Lance the surgeon: helped Rebecca to everything on the table and himself gobbled and drank a great deal.

He sprang to open[5] the door for the ladies when they retired, with the most killing grace—and coming back to the table filled himself bumper after bumper of Claret which he swallowed with nervous rapidity.

"He's priming himself"—Osborne whispered to Dobbin and at length the hour and the carriage arrived for Vauxhall.

8. The phrase "been . . . as to" is interlined in the MS.
9. In the MS this final phrase originally preceded the record of Dobbins's thoughts.
1. Militias, formed in anticipation of a Napoleonic invasion of England, were reviewed in Hyde Park by George III and his brother the duke of York.
2. Originally these two sentences read: same regiment, and the attachment of the elder to him was just as warm now. . . . The cancelations and additions were made in the MS.
3. Arthur Wellesley (1769–1852), first duke of Wellington.
4. Listed in one of the official gazettes as having a commission in the army.
5. MS reads: ↑sprang to↓ open<ed>

## *Chapter VI.*

VAUXHALL.

KNOW[1] that the tune which I am piping is a very mild one,—(although there are some terrific chapters coming presently)—and must beg the good-natured reader to remember that we are only discoursing at present about a stock-broker's family in Russell Square, who are taking walks or luncheon or dinner, or talking and making love as people do in common life, and without a single passionate and wonderful incident to mark the progress of their loves. The argument stands thus—Osborne in love with Amelia has asked an old friend to dinner and to Vauxhall—Jos Sedley is in love with Rebecca. Will he marry her? That is the great subject now in hand.

We might have treated this subject in the genteel or in the romantic or in the facetious manner.[2] Suppose we had laid the scene in Grosvenor Square[3] with the very same adventures—would not some people have listened? Suppose we had shown how Lord Joseph Sedley fell in love, and the Marquis of Osborne became attached to Lady Amelia with the full consent of the Duke her noble father; or instead of the supremely genteel suppose we had resorted to the entirely low and described what was going on in Mr. Sedley's kitchen—how black Sambo was in love with the Cook, (as indeed he was) and how he fought a battle with the coachman in her behalf; how the knife boy was caught stealing a cold shoulder of mutton, and Miss Sedley's new *femme de chambre*[4] refused to go to bed without a wax candle; such incidents might be made to provoke much delightful laughter, and be supposed to represent scenes of 'life.' Or if on the contrary we had taken a fancy for the terrible and made the lover of the new *femme de chambre* a professional burglar, who bursts into the house with his band, slaughters black Sambo at the feet of his master and carries off Amelia in her night-dress not to be let loose again till the third volume[5]—we should easily have constructed a tale of thrilling interest through the fiery chapters of which the reader should hurry panting.[6] Fancy this chapter having been headed

THE NIGHT ATTACK.

1. Two manuscripts and a revised edition present widely varying versions of this chapter. See Appendix, "Composition and Revision of chapter VI." Manuscript alterations are not shown in footnotes for this chapter.
2. References to types of fashionable fiction that Thackeray was currently parodying in *Punch* magazine in a series called "Punch's Prize Novelists."
3. Upscale residential area.
4. Chambermaid.
5. A standard form of publishing fiction was in three volumes, known as three-deckers. Subscription libraries lent the volumes one at a time.
6. Following this sentence, the revised edition canceled two and one-half pages, through "that it scarcely would have deserved" on page 52. Revised edition reads: But my readers must hope for no such romance, only a homely story, and must be content with a chapter about Vauxhall, which is so short that it scarce deserves

The night was dark and wild—the clouds black—black—ink-black. The wild wind tore the chimney-pots[7] from the roofs of the old houses, and sent the tiles whirling and crashing through desolate streets. No soul braved that tempest—the watchmen shrank into their boxes whither the searching rain followed them—where the crashing thunderbolt fell and destroyed them—one had so been slain opposite The Foundling[8]—a scorched gaberdine[9] a shivered lantern a staff rent in twain by the flash were all that remained of stout Will Steadfast. A hackney coachman had been blown off his coach box in Southampton Row—and whither? But the whirlwind tells no tidings of its victim save his parting scream as he is borne onwards! Horrible night! it was dark pitch dark—no moon, No, no, no moon—Not a star: Not a little feeble twinkling solitary star. There had been one at early evening but he showed his face shuddering for a moment in the black heaven, and then retreated back.

One two three! It is the signal that Black Vizard had agreed on.

"Mofy! is that your snum?" said a voice from the area. "I'll gully the dag and bimbole the clicky in a snuffkin."[1]

"Nuffle your clod and beladle your glumbanions,"[2] said Vizard with a dreadful oath. "This way, men—if they screak, out with your snickers and slick! Look to the pewter room, Blowser—You, Mark, to the old gaff's mopus box[3]—and I," added he in a lower but more horrible voice, "I will look to Amelia!"

There was a dead silence. "Ha!" said Vizard—"was that the click of a pistol?"

* * * * * *

Or suppose we adopted the genteel rose-water style—The Marquis

7. Earthware pipes capping chimney shafts.
8. Foundling Hospital in Guildford Street (see chapter XII).
9. Heavy cloth coat.
1. Captain, is that your voice? I'll light the candle and open the door in a minute. (Thackeray's note, omitted from all printed editions.)
2. Hold your tongue, and stir your stumps. (Thackeray's note, omitted from all printed editions.)
3. Nonsense parody of thieves' jargon; mopus, the only real slang, means "money."

of Osborne has just dispatched his *petit tigre* with a *billet doux*[4] to the Ladye Amelia.

The dear creature has received it from the hands of her *femme de chambre,* Mademoiselle Anastasie.

Dear Marquis! What amiable politeness! His lordship's note contains the wished for invitation to D— House![5]

"Who is that monstrous fine girl," said the *Semillant*[6] Prince G—rge of C—mbr—dge at a mansion in Piccadilly the same evening (having just arrived from the omnibus at the opera.) "My dear Sedley, in the name of all the Cupids introduce me to her!"

"Her name, *Monseigneur,*" said Lord Joseph bowing gravely, "is Sedley."

*"Vous avez alors un bien beau nom,"*[7] said the young Prince turning on his heel rather disappointed and treading on the foot of an old gentleman who stood behind in deep admiration of the beautiful Lady Amelia.

*"Trente mille tonnerres!"*[8] shouted the victim writhing under the *ag-*

4. Little tiger, i.e., liveried boy acting as messenger; with a love letter.
5. Imposing house in Piccadilly. MS reads: Devonshire House.
6. Brilliant.
7. You have, then, a very pretty name.
8. Thirty thousand thunderbolts.

*onie du moment.*

"I beg a thousand pardons of your Grace," said the young *étourdi*[9] blushing and bending low his fair curls. He had trodden on the toe of the great Captain of the age![1]

"O D——!" cried the young Prince to a tall and good-natured nobleman, whose features proclaimed him of the blood of the Cavendishes.[2] "A word with you!—Have you still a mind to part with your diamond necklace?"

"I have sold it for two hundred and fifty thousand pounds to Prince Esterhazy[3] here."

*"Und das war gar nicht theuer, potztausend!"*[4] exclaimed the princely Hungarian &c &c &c.

* * * * *

Thus you see, ladies, how this story *might* have been written, if the author had but a mind—for to tell the truth he is just as familiar with Newgate[5] as with the palaces of our revered aristocracy and has seen the outside of both. But as I don't understand the language or manners of the Rookery,[6] nor that polyglot[7] conversation which according to the fashionable novelists is spoken by the leaders of *ton*[8]—we must if you please preserve our middle course modestly amidst those scenes and personages with which we are most us familiar. In a word this chapter about Vauxhall would have been so exceedingly short but for the above little disquisition, that it scarcely would have deserved to be called a chapter at all. And yet it is a chapter and a very important one too. Are not there little chapters in every body's life, that seem to be nothing and yet affect all the rest of the history?

Let us then step into the coach with the Russell Square party and be off to the Gardens. There is barely room between Jos and Miss Sharp who are on the front seat—Mr. Osborne sitting bodkin[9] opposite between Captain Dobbin and Amelia.

Every soul in the coach agreed that on that night Jos would propose to make Rebecca Sharp Mrs. Sedley. The parents at home had acquiesced in the arrangement: though between ourselves, old Mr. Sedley had a feeling very much akin to contempt for his son. He said he was vain selfish lazy and effeminate. He could not endure his airs as a man of fashion, and laughed heartily at his pompous braggadocio stories. "I shall leave the fellow half my property," he said; "and he will have besides plenty of his own: but as I am perfectly sure that if you and I and his sister were to die tomorrow, he would say 'Good Gad!' and eat his dinner just as well as usual, I am not going to make myself anxious about him. Let him marry whom he likes. It's no affair of mine."

9. Scatterbrain.
1. Wellington.
2. Family name of the duke of Devonshire.
3. Pal Antal (1786–1866), Prince Esterhazy, Austrian diplomat.
4. And that was not at all dear, by heavens!
5. Prison on Newgate Street.
6. Flocking place for jailbirds—a slum area. Rooks are blackbirds.
7. Mixture of languages.
8. Fashion.
9. Wedged between two others.

Amelia on the other hand, as became a young woman of her prudence and temperament was quite enthusiastic for the match. Once or twice Jos had been on the point of saying something very important to her, to which she was most willing to lend an ear, but the fat fellow could not be brought to unbosom himself of his great secret, and very much to his sister's disappointment he only rid himself of a large sigh and turned away.

This mystery served to keep Amelia's gentle bosom in a perpetual flutter of excitement. If she did not speak with Rebecca on the tender subject, she compensated herself with long and intimate conversations with Mrs. Blenkinsop the housekeeper, who dropped some hints to the lady's maid, who may have cursorily mentioned it to the Cook, who carried the news I have no doubt to all the tradesmen, so that Mr. Jos's marriage was now talked of by a very considerable number of persons in the Russell Square world.

It was of course Mrs. Sedley's opinion that her son would demean himself by a marriage with an artist's daughter. "But, lor', Ma'am," ejaculated Mrs. Blenkinsop, "we was only grocers when we married Mr. S. who was a stock-broker's clerk, and we hadn't five hundred pound among us and we're rich enough now." And Amelia was entirely of this opinion, to which gradually the good-natured Mrs. Sedley was brought.

Mr. Sedley was neutral. "Let Jos marry whom he likes," he says; "it's no affair of mine. This girl has no fortune, no more had Mrs. Sed. She seems good-humoured and clever and will keep him in order perhaps. Better she, my dear, than a black Mrs. Sedley and a dozen of mahogany grandchildren."

So that everything seemed to smile upon Rebecca's fortunes. She took Jos's arm as a matter of course on going to dinner; she had sate by him on the box of his open carriage (a most tremendous 'buck' he was, as he sate there serene in state, driving his greys) and though nobody said a word on the subject of the marriage every body seemed to understand it. All she wanted was the proposal, and ah! how Rebecca now felt the want of a mother!—a dear tender mother who would have managed the business in ten minutes, and in the course of a little delicate confidential conversation would have extracted the interesting avowal from the bashful lips of the young man!

Such was the state of affairs as the carriage crossed Westminster bridge.

The party was landed at the Royal Gardens[1] in due time. As the majestic Jos stepped out of the creaking vehicle the crowd gave a cheer for the fat gentleman, who blushed and looked very big and mighty, as he walked away with Rebecca under his arm. George, of course, took charge of Amelia. She looked as happy as a rose-tree in sunshine.

"I say, Dobbin," says George, "just look to the shawls and things there's a good fellow." And so while he paired off with Miss Sedley: and Jos squeezed through the gate into the Gardens with Rebecca at

1. Vauxhall Gardens, though not actually called the Royal Gardens until 1822, were the best-known public gardens of Europe. Frequented by all classes, the gardens regularly entertained a thousand visitors a night.

his side; honest Dobbin contented himself by giving an arm to the shawls and by paying at the door for the whole party.

He walked very modestly behind them. He was not willing to spoil sport. About Rebecca and Jos he did not care a fig. But he thought Amelia worthy even of the brilliant George Osborne and as he saw that good looking couple, threading the walks to the girl's delight and wonder, he watched her artless happiness with a sort of fatherly pleasure. Perhaps he felt that he would have liked to have something on his own arm besides a shawl; (the people laughed at seeing the gawky young officer carrying this female burthen) but William Dobbin was very little addicted to selfish calculations at all: and so long as his friend was enjoying himself; how should he be discontented? And the truth is that of all the delights of the Gardens—of the hundred thousand *extra* lamps[2] which were always lighted, the fiddlers in cocked hats who played ravishing melodies under the gilded cockle shell[3] in the midst of the gardens, the singers both of comic and sentimental ballads who charmed the ears there, the country dances formed by bouncing cockneys and cockneyesses and executed amidst jumping thumping and laughter, the signal which announced that Madame Saqui[4] was about to mount skyward on a slack rope ascending to the stars, the hermit that always sat in the illuminated hermitage, the dark walks so favourable to the interviews of young lovers, the pots of stout handed about by the people in the shabby old liveries, and the twinkling boxes in which the happy feasters made believe to eat slices of almost invisible ham;—of all these things, and of the gentle Simpson,[5] that kind smiling idiot, who I daresay presided even then over the place—Captain William Dobbin did not take the slightest notice.

He carried about Amelia's white cashmere shawl, and having attended under the gilt cockle-shell while Mrs. Salmon[6] performed the Battle of Borodino (a savage cantata against the Corsican Upstart, who had lately met with his Russian reverses)—Mr. Dobbin tried to hum it as he walked away, and found he was humming—the tune which Amelia Sedley sang on the stairs as she came down to dinner.

He burst out laughing at himself; for the truth is he could sing no better than an owl.

It is to be understood as a matter of course that our young people being in parties of two and two made the most solemn promises to keep together during the evening, and separated in ten minutes afterwards. Parties at Vauxhall always did separate, but 'twas only to meet again at supper-time, when they could talk of their mutual adventures in the interval.

What were the adventures of Mr. Osborne and Miss Amelia? That is a secret. But be sure of this—they were perfectly happy, and correct in their behaviour, and as they had been in the habit of being

2. An exaggeration, referring satirically to the eight thousand extra lamps added at the prince regent's birthday gala in 1811 and increased at subsequent galas.
3. Shell-shaped shelter for the musicians.
4. Another anachronism; this tightrope walker first appeared at Vauxhall in 1816.
5. Simpson was already emcee in 1813, and still there in 1848.
6. Eliza Salmon (1787–1849), a singer.

together any time these fifteen years, their *tête-à-tête* offered no particular novelty.

But when Miss Rebecca Sharp and her stout companion lost themselves in a solitary walk similarly straying, they both felt that the situation was extremely tender and critical and now or never was the moment Miss Sharp thought to provoke that declaration which was trembling on the timid lips of Mr. Sedley. They had previously been to the panorama of Moscow where a rude fellow treading on Miss Sharp's foot caused her to fall back with a little shriek into the arms of Mr. Sedley, and this little incident increased the tenderness and confidence of that gentleman to such a degree, that he told her several of his favourite Indian stories over again for at least the sixth time.

"How I should like to see India," said Rebecca.

"*Should* you?" said Joseph with a most killing tenderness; and was no doubt about to follow up this artful interrogatory by a question still more tender (for he puffed and panted a great deal and Rebecca's hand which was placed near his heart could count the feverish pulsa-

tions of that organ)—when oh provoking!—the bell rang for the fireworks and a great scuffling and running taking place, these interesting lovers were obliged to follow in the stream of people.

Captain Dobbin had some thoughts of joining the party at supper: as in truth he found the Vauxhall amusement not particularly lively—but he paraded twice before the box where the now united couples were met and nobody took any notice of him. Covers were laid for four.[7] The mated pairs were prattling away quite happily, and Dobbin knew he was as clean forgotten as if he had never existed in this world.

'I should only be *de trop,*' said the Captain looking at them rather wistfully. 'I'd best go and talk to the hermit'—and so he strolled off out of the hum of men, and noise and clatter of the banquet, into the dark walk at the end of which lived that well-known pasteboard Solitary. It wasn't very good fun for Dobbin—and indeed to be alone at Vauxhall, I have found from my own experience to be one of the most dismal sports ever entered into by a bachelor.

The two couples were perfectly happy then in their box: where the most delightful and intimate conversation took place. Jos was in his glory ordering about the waiters with great majesty. He made the salad; and uncorked the Champagne; and carved the chickens; and ate and drank the greater part of the refreshments on the tables. Finally he insisted upon having a bowl of rack punch:[8] every body had rack punch at Vauxhall. "Waiter, Rack Punch."

That bowl of rack punch was the cause of all this history. And why not a bowl of rack punch as well as any other cause? Was not a bowl of Prussic acid the cause of fair Rosamond's retiring from the world? Was not a bowl of wine the cause of the demise of Alexander the Great,[9] or at least does not Dr. Lempriere[1] say so?—so did this bowl of rack punch influence the fates of all the principal characters in this Novel without a hero, which we are now relating. It influenced their life although most of them did not taste a drop of it.

The young ladies did not drink it; Osborne did not like it; and the consequence was that Jos that fat gourmand[2] drank up the whole contents of the bowl. And the consequence of his drinking up the whole contents of the bowl, was a liveliness which at first was astonishing and then became almost painful; for he talked and laughed so loud as to bring scores of listeners round the box much to the confusion of the innocent party within it, and volunteering to sing a song (which he did in that maudlin high key peculiar to gentlemen in an inebriated state) he almost drew away the audience who were gathered round the musicians in the gilt scollop-shell, and received from his hearers a great deal of applause.

"Brayvo, Fat un!" said one; "Angcore, Daniel Lambert!"[3] said another; "What a figure for the tight-rope!" exclaimed another wag, to the inexpressible alarm of the ladies, and the great anger of Mr. Osborne.

"For Heaven's sake, Jos, let us get up and go," cried that gentleman, and the young women rose.

"Stop, my dearest diddle-diddle-darling," shouted Jos, now as bold as a lion, and clasping Miss Rebecca round the waist. Rebecca

7. Place settings for four—that is, not for five.
8. Probably "arrack"—a sweet alcoholic drink made variously from dates, coco-palm, or rice.
9. According to legend, Rosamund, mistress to King Henry II, was poisoned by the king's wife. Alexander the Great is supposed to have drunk himself to death in boredom.
1. John Lempriere's *Biblioteca Classica* (1788).
2. A connoisseur of fine food or merely a glutton.
3. Lambert (1771–1809) was a celebrated fat man memorialized on numerous inn signs.

Mr. Joseph in a state of excitement

started, but she could not get away her hand. The laughter outside redoubled. Jos continued to drink, to make love, and to sing; and, winking and waving his glass gracefully to his audience, challenged all or any to come in and take a share of his punch.

Mr. Osborne was just on the point of knocking down a gentleman in top-boots, who proposed to take advantage of this invitation, and a commotion seemed to be inevitable, when by the greatest good luck a gentleman of the name of Dobbin who had been walking about the gardens stepped up to the box. "Be off, you fools!" said this gentleman—shouldering off a great number of the crowd, who vanished presently before his cocked hat and fierce appearance—and he entered the box in a most agitated state.

"Good Heavens, Dobbin, where *have* you been?" Osborne said seizing the white cashmere shawl from his friend's arm, and huddling up Amelia in it. "Make yourself useful, and take charge of Jos here whilst I take the ladies to the carriage."

Jos was for rising to interfere—but a single push from Osborne's finger sent him puffing back into his seat again and the Lieutenant was enabled to remove the ladies in safety—Jos kissed his hand to them as they retreated and hiccupped out Bless you. Bless you. Then seizing Captain Dobbin's hand, and weeping in the most pitiful way, he confided to that gentleman the secret of his loves. He adored that girl who had just gone out; he had broken her heart he knew he had by his conduct—he would marry her next morning at Saint George's, Hanover Square[4]—he'd knock up the Archbishop of Canterbury at Lambeth,[5] he would by Jove, and have him in readiness—and acting on this hint Captain Dobbin shrewdly induced him to leave the gardens and hasten to Lambeth Palace, and when once out of the gates, easily conveyed Mr. Jos Sedley into a hackney-coach, which deposited him safely at his lodgings.

George Osborne conducted the girls home in safety: and when the door was closed upon them and as he walked across Russell Square laughed so as to astonish the watchman. Amelia looked very ruefully at her friend as they went up stairs, and kissed her, and went to bed without any more talking.

"He must propose tomorrow," thought Rebecca. "He called me his soul's darling four times; he squeezed my hand in Amelia's presence. He must propose tomorrow." And so thought Amelia, too. And I dare say she thought of the dress she was to wear as bride's-maid, and of the presents which she should make to her nice little sister-in-law, and of a subsequent ceremony in which she herself might play a principal part, &c., and &c., and &c., and &c.

O ignorant young creatures! how little do you know the effect of rack punch! What is the rack in the punch at night to the rack in the head of a morning? To this truth I can vouch as a man—there is no head-ache in the world like that caused by Vauxhall punch. Through the lapse of twenty years I can remember the consequence of two

4. Church in west-central London.
5. I.e., he would knock at the door and awaken the archbishop at his London residence, Lambeth Palace.

wine glasses, two glasses—but two upon the honour of a gentleman, and Joseph Sedley, who had a liver complaint had swallowed at least a quart of the abominable mixture.

That next morning which Rebecca thought was to dawn upon her fortune, found Sedley groaning in agonies which the pen refuses to

describe. Soda water was not invented yet. Small beer, will it be believed? was the only drink with which unhappy gentlemen soothed the fever of their previous night's potation! With this mild beverage before him, George Osborne found the ex-collector of Boggley wollah groaning on the sofa at his lodgings. Dobbin was already in the room, good-naturedly tending his patient of the night before. The two officers looking at the prostrate Bacchanalian, and askance at each other, exchanged the most frightful sympathetic grins. Even Sedley's valet, the most solemn and correct of gentlemen, with the muteness and gravity of an undertaker, could hardly keep his countenance in order, as he looked at his unfortunate master.

"Mr. Sedley was uncommon wild last night, sir," he whispered in confidence to Osborne, as the latter mounted the stair. "He wanted to fight the 'ackney-coachman, sir. The Capting was obliged to bring him up stairs in his harms like a babby." A momentary smile flickered over Mr. Brush's features as he spoke; instantly, however, they relapsed into their usual unfathomable calm, as he flung open the drawing-room door, and announced "Mr. Hosbin."

"How are you, Sedley?" that young wag began, after surveying his victim. "No bones broke? There's a hackney-coachman down stairs with a black eye, and a tied up head, vowing he'll have the law of you."

"What do you mean,—law?" Sedley faintly asked.

"For thrashing him last night—didn't he, Dobbin? You hit out, sir, like Molyneux.[6] The watchman says he never saw a fellow go down so straight. Ask Dobbin."

6. Tom Cribb (1781–1848) twice defeated the black American fighter Tom Molineaux in 1810 and 1811—the latter witnessed by 20,000 spectators. Cribb was never defeated after 1805 and was champion of England for life. He died just as *Vanity Fair* was completing publication. See chapter XXXIV.

"You *did* have a round with the coachman," Captain Dobbin said, "and showed plenty of fight too."

"And that fellow with the white coat at Vauxhall! How Jos drove at him! How the women screamed! By Jove, sir, it did my heart good to see you. I thought you civilians had no pluck; but *I'll* never get in your way when you are in your cups, Jos."

"I believe I'm very terrible, when I'm roused," ejaculated Jos from the sofa, and made a grimace so dreary and ludicrous, that the Captain's politeness could restrain him no longer, and he and Osborne fired off a ringing volley of laughter.

Osborne pursued his advantage pitilessly. He thought Jos a milksop. He had been revolving in his mind the marriage-question pending between Jos and Rebecca, and was not over-well pleased that a member of a family into which he, George Osborne, of the —th, was going to marry, should make a *mésalliance* with a little nobody—a little upstart governess. "You hit, you poor old fellow?" said Osborne. "You terrible? Why, man, you couldn't stand—you made everybody laugh in the Gardens, though you were crying yourself. You were maudlin, Jos. Don't you remember singing a song?"

"A what?" Jos asked.

"A sentimental song, and calling Rosa, Rebecca, what's her name, Amelia's little friend—your dearest diddle, diddle, darling?" And this ruthless young fellow, seizing hold of Dobbin's hand, acted over the scene, to the horror of the original performer, and in spite of Dobbin's good-natured entreaties to him to have mercy.

"Why should I spare him?" Osborne said to his friend's remonstrances, when they quitted the invalid, leaving him under the hands of Doctor Gollop. "What the deuce right has he to give himself his patronising airs, and make fools of us at Vauxhall? Who's this little school-girl that is ogling and making love to him? Hang it, the family's low enough already, without *her.* A governess is all very well, but I'd rather have a lady for my sister-in-law. I'm a liberal man; but I've proper pride, and know my own station: let her know hers. And I'll take down that great hectoring Nabob, and prevent him from being made a greater fool than he is. That's why I told him to look out, lest she brought an action against him."

"I suppose you know best," Dobbin said, though rather dubiously. "You always were a Tory, and your family's one of the oldest in England. But,"——

"Come and see the girls, and make love to Miss Sharp yourself," the lieutenant here interrupted his friend; but Captain Dobbin declined to join Osborne in his daily visit to the young ladies in Russell Square.

As he walked down Southampton Row, from Holborn, he laughed as he saw, at the Sedley Mansion, in two different stories, two heads on the look-out.

The fact is, Miss Amelia, in the drawing-room balcony, was looking very eagerly towards the opposite side of the Square, where Mr. Osborne dwelt, on the watch for the lieutenant himself; and Miss Sharp, from her little bed-room on the second-floor, was in observation until Mr. Joseph's great form should heave in sight.

"Sister Anne is on the watch-tower,"[7] said he to Amelia, "but there's nobody coming;" and laughing and enjoying the joke hugely, he described in the most ludicrous terms to Miss Sedley, the dismal condition of her brother.

"I think it's very cruel of you to laugh, George," she said, looking particularly unhappy; but George only laughed the more at her piteous and discomfited mien, persisted in thinking the joke a most diverting one, and when Miss Sharp came down stairs, bantered her with a great deal of liveliness upon the effect of her charms on the fat civilian.

"O Miss Sharp! if you could but see him this morning," he said—"moaning in his flowered dressing-gown—writhing on his sofa; if you could but have seen him lolling out his tongue to Gollop the apothecary."

"See whom?" said Miss Sharp.

"Whom? O whom? Captain Dobbin, of course, to whom we were all so attentive, by the way, last night."

"We were very unkind to him," Emmy said, blushing very much. "I—I quite forgot him."

"Of course you did," cried Osborne, still on the laugh. "One can't be *always* thinking about Dobbin, you know, Amelia. Can one, Miss Sharp?"

"Except when he overset the glass of wine at dinner," Miss Sharp said, with a haughty air and a toss of the head, "I never gave the existence of Captain Dobbin one single moment's consideration."

"Very good, Miss Sharp, I'll tell him," Osborne said; and as he spoke Miss Sharp began to have a feeling of distrust and hatred towards this young officer, which he was quite unconscious of having inspired. "*He* is to make fun of me, is he?" thought Rebecca. "Has he been laughing about me to Joseph? Has he frightened him? Perhaps he won't come."—A film passed over her eyes, and her heart beat quite quick.

"You're always joking," said she, smiling as innocently as she could. "Joke away, Mr. George; there's nobody to defend *me*." And George Osborne, as she walked away—and Amelia looked reprovingly at him—felt some little manly compunction for having inflicted any unnecessary unkindness upon this helpless creature. "My dearest Amelia," said he, "you are too good—too kind. You don't know the world. I do. And your little friend Miss Sharp must learn her station."

"Don't you think Jos will—"

"Upon my word, my dear, I don't know. He may, or may not. I'm not his master. I only know he is a very foolish vain fellow, and put my dear little girl into a very painful and awkward position last night. My dearest diddle—diddle—darling!" He was off laughing again; and he did it so drolly that Emmy laughed too.

All that day Jos never came. But Amelia had no fear about this; for the little schemer had actually sent away the page, Mr. Sambo's

7. In the story of Bluebeard, Fatima's sister Anne watches from a tower in Bluebeard's house for her brothers coming to the rescue.

aide-de-camp, to Mr. Joseph's lodgings, to ask for some book he had promised, and how he was; and the reply through Jos's man, Mr. Brush, was, that his master was ill in bed, and had just had the doctor with him. He must come to-morrow, she thought, but she never had the courage to speak a word on the subject to Rebecca; nor did that young woman herself allude to it in any way during the whole evening after the night at Vauxhall.

The next day, however, as the two young ladies sate on the sofa, pretending to work, or to write letters, or to read novels, Sambo came into the room with his usual engaging grin, with a packet under his arm, and a note on a tray. "Note from Mr. Jos, Miss," says Sambo.

How Amelia trembled as she opened it!

So it ran:—

"DEAR AMELIA,—I send you the Orphan of the Forest.[8] I was too ill to come yesterday. I leave town to-day for Cheltenham.[9] Pray excuse me, if you can, to the amiable Miss Sharp, for my conduct at Vauxhall, and entreat her to pardon and forget every word I may have uttered when excited by that fatal supper. As soon as I have recovered, for my health is very much shaken, I shall go to Scotland for some months, and am

"Truly yours,

"JOS. SEDLEY."

8. Perhaps William Dimond's play *The Foundling of the Forest*, or an invented title.
9. A spa town with curative waters west of London.

It was the death-warrant. All was over. Amelia did not dare to look at Rebecca's pale face and burning eyes, but she dropt the letter into her friend's lap; and got up, and went upstairs to her room, and cried her little heart out.

Blenkinsop, the housekeeper, there sought her presently with consolation; on whose shoulder Amelia wept confidentially, and relieved herself a good deal. "Don't take on, Miss. I didn't like to tell you. But none of us in the house have liked her except at fust. I sor her with my own eyes reading your Ma's letters. Pinner says she's always about your trinket-box and drawers, and everybody's drawers, and she's sure she's put your white ribbing into her box."

"I gave it her, I gave it her," Amelia said.

But this did not alter Mrs. Blenkinsop's opinion of Miss Sharp. "I don't trust them governesses, Pinner," she remarked to the maid. "They give themselves the hairs and hupstarts of ladies, and their wages is no better than you nor me."

It now became clear to every soul in the house, except poor Amelia, that Rebecca should take her departure, and high and low (always with the one exception) agreed that that event should take place as speedily as possible. Our good child ransacked all her drawers, cupboards, reticules, and gimcrack boxes—passed in review all her gowns, fichus, tags, bobbins, laces, silk stockings, and fallals[1]—selecting this thing and that and the other, to make a little heap for Rebecca. And going to her Papa, that generous British merchant, who had promised to give her as many guineas as she was years old—she begged the old gentleman to give the money to dear Rebecca, who must want it, while she lacked for nothing.

She even made George Osborne contribute, and nothing loth (for he was as free-handed a young fellow as any in the army), he went to Bond Street,[2] and bought the best hat and spencer[3] that money could buy.

"That's George's present to you, Rebecca, dear," said Amelia, quite proud of the bandbox conveying these gifts.[4] "What a taste he has! There's nobody like him."

"Nobody," Rebecca answered. "How thankful I am to him!" She was thinking in her heart, "It was George Osborne who prevented my marriage.—And she loved George Osborne accordingly.

She made her preparations for departure with great equanimity; and accepted all the kind little Amelia's presents, after just the proper degree of hesitation and reluctance. She vowed eternal gratitude to Mrs. Sedley, of course; but did not intrude herself upon that good lady too much, who was embarrassed, and evidently wishing to avoid her. She kissed Mr. Sedley's hand, when he presented her with the purse; and asked permission to consider him for the future as her kind, kind friend and protector. Her behaviour was so affecting that he was going to write her a checque for twenty pounds more; but

1. Reticules, net bags; fichus, shawls; bobbins, fine cords; and fallals, finery.
2. The most luxuriant shopping area of London.
3. A short, double-breasted jacket named for the second Earl Spencer (1758–1834).
4. It was the author's intention, faithful to history, to depict all the characters of this tale in their proper costumes, as they wore them at the commencement of the century. But when I

he restrained his feelings: the carriage was in waiting to take him to dinner: so he tripped away with a "God bless you, my dear. Always come here when you come to town, you know.—Drive to the Mansion House,[5] James."

Finally came the parting with Miss Amelia, over which picture I intend to throw a veil. But after a scene in which one person was in earnest and the other a perfect performer—after the tenderest caresses, the most pathetic tears, the smelling-bottle, and some of the very best feelings of the heart, had been called into requisition—Rebecca and Amelia parted, the former vowing to love her friend for ever and ever and ever.

remember the appearance of people those days, and that an officer and lady were actually habited like this—

I have not the heart to disfigure my heroes and heroines by costumes so hideous; and have, on the contrary, engaged a model of rank dressed according to the present fashion (Thackeray's note).

5. Official residence of the lord mayor of London.

## *Chapter VII.*

CRAWLEY OF QUEEN'S CRAWLEY.

MONG the most respected of the names beginning in C, which the Court-Guide contained, in the year 18—, was that of Crawley, Sir Pitt, Baronet, Great Gaunt Street,[1] and Queen's Crawley, Hants.[2] This honourable name had figured constantly also in the Parliamentary list for many years, in conjunction with that of a number of other worthy gentlemen who sat in turns for the borough.

It is related, with regard to the borough of Queen's Crawley, that Queen Elizabeth[3] in one of her progresses,[4] stopping at Crawley to breakfast, was so delighted with some remarkably fine Hampshire beer which was then presented to her by the Crawley of the day (a handsome gentleman with a trim beard and a good leg), that she forthwith erected Crawley into a borough to send two members to Parliament; and the place, from the day of that illustrious visit, took the name of Queen's Crawley, which it holds up to the present moment. And though by the lapse of time, and those mutations which ages produce in empires, cities, and boroughs, Queen's Crawley was no longer so populous a place as it had been in Queen Bess's time—nay, was come down to that condition of borough which used to be denominated rotten[5]—yet, as Sir Pitt Crawley would say with perfect justice in his elegant way, "Rotten! be hanged—it produces me a good fifteen hundred a year."

Sir Pitt Crawley (named after the great Commoner),[6] was the son of Walpole Crawley, first Baronet, of the Tape and Sealing-Wax Office in the reign of George II., when he was impeached for pecula-

1. Gaunt Street and Gaunt Square are fictitious locations.
2. Hampshire County.
3. Elizabeth I ruled from 1558 to 1603.
4. The queen's royal trip honoring the nobility by visiting overnight.
5. Rotten because before reform in 1832, sparsely populated boroughs like Queen's Crawley had guaranteed representation in Parliament, while newer large cities were under-represented.
6. William Pitt (1708–78), a younger son without wealth, rose to power on the strength of his oratorical skills and his integrity and popularity with the poeple. In the 1750s he reached the peak of his power and became known as the Great Commoner, a "title" he lost in 1766 when he accepted a peerage, becoming first earl of Chatham.

tion,[7] as were a great number of other honest gentlemen of those days; and Walpole Crawley was, as need scarcely be said, son of John Churchill Crawley, named after the celebrated military commander of the reign of Queen Anne. The family tree (which hangs up at Queen's Crawley), furthermore mentions Charles Stuart, afterwards called Barebones Crawley, son of the Crawley of James the First's time, and finally, Queen Elizabeth's Crawley, who is represented as the foreground of the picture in his forked beard and armour. Out of his waistcoat, as usual, grows a tree, on the main branches of which the above illustrious names are inscribed. Close by the name of Sir Pitt Crawley, Baronet (the subject of the present memoir), are written that of his brother, the Reverend Bute Crawley (the great Commoner was in disgrace when the reverend gentleman was born), rector of Crawley-cum-Snailby, and of various other male and female members of the Crawley family.[8]

Sir Pitt was first married to Grizzel, sixth daughter of Mungo Binkie, Lord Binkie, and cousin, in consequence of Mr. Dundas.[9] She brought him two sons: Pitt, named not so much after his father as after the heaven-born minister;[1] and Rawdon Crawley, from the Prince of Wales's friend, whom his Majesty George IV. forgot so completely.[2] Many years after her ladyship's demise, Sir Pitt led to the altar Rose, daughter of Mr. T. Dawson of Mudbury, by whom he had two daughters, for whose benefit Miss Rebecca Sharp was now engaged as governess. It will be seen that the young lady was come into a family of very genteel connexions, and was about to move in a much more distinguished circle than that humble one which she had just quitted in Russell Square.

She had received her orders to join her pupils, in a note which was written upon an old envelope, and which contained the following words:—

7. Embezzlement.
8. Queen Anne I ruled from 1702 to 1714; James I ruled from 1603 to 1625. The Crawleys' changing political allegiances are recorded in the names taken from the succession of political and military leaders. The older Pitt Crawley was named for William Pitt, whose heydays were 1756–61. Bute is named for John Stuart, third earl of Bute (1713–92), who shared power with Pitt in 1761 but gradually outshone him. Their father, Walpole Crawley, was named for Robert Walpole, who flourished in the 1720s and 1730s and who was opposed in his later years by William Pitt. Walpole's father, John Churchill Crawley, was named for the great general Marlborough, and Charles Stuart Crawley was named for the royal family Marlborough served. His change of name to Barebones signals a typical Crawley change of allegiance after the execution of Charles I. The names indicate a history of shifting and ill-timed allegiances to whoever was in power or, as in the naming of the brothers Pitt and Rawdon, aligning with both sides at once. Rawdon was originally named Petty in the manuscript. William Petty (1737–1805), earl of Shelbourne (by which name he is best known) and marquis of Landowne, was a political ally of Pitt the younger. Though he enjoyed a brief period of popularity in 1780, following a duel with Lieutenant Colonel William Fullarton, thought to be an "instrument of the government," he was one of the most unpopular statesmen of his time.
9. Grizzel and Binkie are fictional family names with no real relation to Henry Dundas, first Viscount Melville, a political ally of William Pitt the younger.
1. The younger William Pitt (1759–1806), though arguing against Dundas' position on the American colonies, found in Dundas a friend and ally during his years as prime minister. The duke of Chandos called him "the heaven born minister" in 1789.
2. Francis Rawdon-Hastings (1754–1826), first marquis of Hastings and second earl of Moira, governor-general of Bengal (1812–21), was a miltary man involved in at least one duel and politically opposed to both Pitt and Dundas. His support for the prince of Wales went largely unrequited when the prince became regent.

"Sir Pitt Crawley begs Miss Sharp and baggidge may be hear on Tuesday, as I leaf for Queen's Crawley to-morrow morning *erly*.

"Great Gaunt Street."

Rebecca had never seen a Baronet, as far as she knew, and as soon as she had taken leave of Amelia, and counted the guineas which good-natured Mr. Sedley had put into a purse for her, and as soon as she had done wiping her eyes with her handkerchief (which operation she concluded the very moment the carriage had turned the corner of the street), she began to depict in her own mind what a baronet must be. "I wonder, does he wear a star?" thought she, "or is it only lords that wear stars? But he will be very handsomely dressed in a court suit, with ruffles and his hair a little powdered, like Mr. Wroughton at Covent Garden.[3] I suppose he will be awfully proud, and that I shall be treated most contemptuously. Still I must bear my hard lot as well as I can—at least, I shall be amongst *gentlefolks,* and not with vulgar city people:" and she fell to thinking of her Russell Square friends with that very same philosophical bitterness with which, in a certain apologue, the fox is represented as speaking of the grapes.

Having passed through Gaunt Square[4] into Great Gaunt Street, the carriage at length stopped at a tall gloomy house between two other tall gloomy houses, each with a hatchment[5] over the middle drawing-room window; as is the custom of houses in Great Gaunt Street, in which gloomy locality death seems to reign perpetual. The shutters of the first floor windows of Sir Pitt's mansion were closed—those of the dining-room were partially open, and the blinds neatly covered up in old newspapers.

John, the groom, who had driven the carriage alone, did not care to descend to ring the bell; and so prayed a passing milk-boy to perform that office for him. When the bell was rung, a head appeared between the interstices of the dining-room shutters, and the door was opened by a man in drab breeches and gaiters, with a dirty old coat, a foul old neckcloth lashed round his bristly neck, a shining bald head, a leering red face, a pair of twinkling grey eyes, and a mouth perpetually on the grin.

"This Sir Pitt Crawley's?" says John, from the box.

"Ees," says the man at the door, with a nod.

"Hand down these 'ere trunks then," said John.

"Hand 'n down yourself," said the porter.

"Don't you see I can't leave my hosses? Come, bear a hand, my fine feller, and Miss will give you some beer," said John, with a horse-laugh, for he was no longer respectful to Miss Sharp, as her connexion with the family was broken off, and as she had given nothing to the servants on coming away.

3. Becky would more likely have known of the actor Richard Wroughton (1748–1822) for his performances at Drury Lane Theatre, for he moved from Covent Garden in 1786 or 1787.
4. First printing reads: Shiverly Square
5. The tablet displayed on the front of a house during mourning, bearing the heraldic symbols of the deceased.

Rebecca makes acquaintance with a live Baronet

The bald-headed man, taking his hands out of his breeches pockets, advanced on this summons, and throwing Miss Sharp's trunk over his shoulder, carried it into the house.

"Take this basket and shawl, if you please, and open the door," said Miss Sharp, and descended from the carriage in much indignation. "I shall write to Mr. Sedley and inform him of your conduct," said she to the groom.

"Don't," replied that functionary. "I hope you've forgot nothink? Miss 'Melia's gownds—have you got them—as the lady's-maid was to have 'ad? I hope they'll fit you. Shut the door, Jim, you'll get no good out of *'er,*" continued John, pointing with his thumb towards Miss Sharp: "a bad lot, I tell you, a bad lot," and so saying, Mr. Sedley's groom drove away. The truth is, he was attached to the lady's-maid in question, and indignant that she should have been robbed of her perquisites.

On entering the dining-room, by the orders of the individual in gaiters, Rebecca found that apartment not more cheerful than such rooms usually are, when genteel families are out of town. The faithful chambers seem, as it were, to mourn the absence of their masters. The turkey carpet[6] has rolled itself up, and retired sulkily under the sideboard: the pictures have hidden their faces behind old sheets of brown paper: the ceiling lamp is muffled up in a dismal sack of brown holland:[7] the window-curtains have disappeared under all sorts of shabby envelopes: the marble bust of Sir Walpole Crawley is looking from its black corner at the bare boards and the oiled fire-irons, and the empty card-racks over the mantel-piece: the cellaret[8] has lurked away behind the carpet: the chairs are turned up heads and tails along the walls: and in the dark corner opposite the statue, is an old-fashioned crabbed knife-box, locked and sitting on a dumb waiter.[9]

Two kitchen chairs, and a round table, and an attenuated old poker and tongs were, however, gathered round the fire-place, as was a saucepan over a feeble sputtering fire. There was a bit of cheese and bread, and a tin candlestick on the table, and a little black porter in a pint-pot.

"Had your dinner? I suppose. It is not too warm for you? Like a drop of beer?"

"Where is Sir Pitt Crawley?" said Miss Sharp majestically.

"He, he! *I*'m[1] Sir Pitt Crawley. Reklect you owe me a pint for bringing down your luggage. He, he! Ask Tinker if I aynt.[2] Mrs. Tinker, Miss Sharp; Miss Governess, Mrs. Charwoman. Ho, ho!"

The lady addressed as Mrs. Tinker, at this moment made her appearance with a pipe and a paper of tobacco, for which she had been despatched a minute before Miss Sharp's arrival; and she handed the articles over to Sir Pitt, who had taken his seat by the fire.

6. Oriental rug.
7. Unbleached linen.
8. Wine cabinet.
9. Not an elevator; more like a lazy Susan.
1. First printing reads: *I* be
2. First printing reads: baynt

"Where's the farden?"[3] said he. "I gave you three halfpence. Where's the change? old Tinker."

"There!" replied Mrs. Tinker, flinging down the coin; "it's only baronets as cares about farthings."

"A farthing a day is seven shillings a year," answered the M.P.;[4] "seven shillings a year is the interest of seven guineas. Take care of your farthings, old Tinker, and your guineas will come quite nat'ral."

"You may be sure it's Sir Pitt Crawley, young woman," said Mrs. Tinker, surlily; "because he looks to his farthings. You'll know him better afore long."

"And like me none the worse, Miss Sharp," said the old gentleman, with an air almost of politeness. "I must be just before I'm generous."[5]

"He never gave away a farthing in his life," growled Tinker.

"Never, and never will: it's against my principle. Go and get another chair from the kitchen, Tinker, if you want to sit down; and then we'll have a bit of supper."

Presently the baronet plunged a fork into the saucepan on the fire, and withdrew from the pot a piece of tripe and an onion, which he divided into pretty equal portions, and of which he partook with Mrs. Tinker. "You see, Miss Sharp, when I'm not here Tinker's on board wages:[6] when I'm in town she dines with the family. Haw! haw! I'm

3. Farthing, one-fourth of a penny.
4. Member of Parliament.
5. Sir Pitt seems to be quoting Machiavelli's *The Prince*.
6. Wages for servants to keep themselves in food and drink in their master's absence.

glad Miss Sharp's not hungry, ain't you, Tink?" And they fell to upon their frugal supper.

After supper Sir Pitt Crawley began to smoke his pipe; and when it became quite dark, he lighted the rushlight in the tin candlestick, and producing from an interminable pocket a huge mass of papers, began reading them, and putting them in order.

"I'm here on law business, my dear, and that's how it happens that I shall have the pleasure of such a pretty travelling companion to-morrow."

"He's always at law business," said Mrs. Tinker, taking up the pot of porter.

"Drink and drink about," said the Baronet. "Yes, my dear, Tinker is quite right: I've lost and won more lawsuits than any man in England. Look here at Crawley, Bart. v. Snaffle. I'll throw him over, or my name's not Pitt Crawley. Podder and another versus Crawley, Bart. Overseers of Snaily parish against Crawley, Bart. They can't prove it's common: I'll defy 'em; the land's mine. It no more belongs to the parish than it does to you or Tinker here. I'll beat 'em, if it cost me a thousand guineas. Look over the papers; you may if you like, my dear. Do you write a good hand? I'll make you useful when we're at Queen's Crawley, depend on it Miss Sharp. Now the dowager's dead I want some one."

"She was as bad as he," said Tinker. "She took the law of every one of her tradesmen; and turned away forty-eight footmen in four year."

"She was close—very close," said the baronet,[7] simply; "but she was a valyble woman to me, and saved me a steward."—And in this confidential strain, and much to the amusement of the new-comer, the conversation continued for a considerable time. Whatever Sir Pitt Crawley's qualities might be, good or bad, he did not make the least disguise of them. He talked of himself incessantly, sometimes in the coarsest and vulgarest Hampshire accent; sometimes adopting the tone of a man of the world. And so, with injunctions to Miss Sharp to be ready at five in the morning, he bade her good night. "You'll sleep with Tinker to-night," he said; "It's a big bed, and there's room for two. Lady Crawley died in it. Good night."

Sir Pitt went off after this benediction, and the solemn Tinker, rushlight in hand, led the way up the great bleak stone stairs, past the great dreary drawing-room doors, with the handles muffled up in paper, into the great front bed-room, where Lady Crawley had slept her last. The bed and chamber were so funereal and gloomy, you might have fancied, not only that Lady Crawley died in the room, but that her ghost inhabited it. Rebecca sprang about the apartment, however, with the greatest liveliness, and had peeped into the huge wardrobes, and the closets, and the cupboards, and tried the drawers which were locked, and examined the dreary pictures and toilette appointments, while the old charwoman was saying her prayers. "I shouldn't like to sleep in this yeer bed without a good conscience, Miss," said the old woman. "There's room for us and a half-dozen of

7. First printing reads: orphan

ghosts in it," says Rebecca. "Tell me all about Lady Crawley and Sir Pitt Crawley, and everybody, my *dear* Mrs. Tinker."

But old Tinker was not to be pumped by this little cross-questioner; and signifying to her that bed was a place for sleeping, not conversation, set up in her corner of the bed such a snore as only the nose of innocence can produce. Rebecca lay awake for a long, long time, thinking of the morrow, and of the new world into which she was going, and of her chances of success there. The rushlight flickered in the basin. The mantel-piece cast up a great black shadow, over half of a mouldy old sampler, which her defunct ladyship had worked, no doubt, and over two little family pictures of young lads, one in a college gown, and the other in a red jacket like a soldier. When she went to sleep, Rebecca chose that one to dream about.

At four o'clock, on such a roseate summer's morning as even made Great Gaunt Street look cheerful, the faithful Tinker, having wakened her bedfellow, and bid her prepare for departure, unbarred and unbolted the great hall door, (the clanging and clapping whereof startled the sleeping echoes in the street), and taking her way into Oxford Street,[8] summoned a coach from a stand there. It is needless to particularise the number of the vehicle, or to state that the driver was stationed thus early in the neighbourhood of Swallow Street,[9] in hopes that some young buck, reeling homeward from the tavern, might need the aid of his vehicle, and pay him with the generosity of intoxication.

It is likewise needless to say, that the driver, if he had any such hopes as those above stated, was grossly disappointed; and that the worthy Baronet whom he drove to the City did not give him one single penny more than his fare. It was in vain that Jehu[1] appealed and stormed; that he flung down Miss Sharp's bandboxes in the gutter at the 'Necks,[2] and swore he would take the law of his fare.

"You'd better not," said one of the ostlers; "it's Sir Pitt Crawley."

"So it is, Joe," cried the Baronet, approvingly; "and I'd like to see the man can do me."

"So should oi," said Joe, grinning sulkily, and mounting the baronet's baggage on the roof of the coach.

"Keep the box[3] for me, Leader," exclaims the Member of Parliament to the coachman; who replied, "Yes, Sir Pitt," with a touch of his hat, and rage in his soul, (for he had promised the box to a young gentleman from Cambridge, who would have given a crown to a certainty), and Miss Sharp was accommodated with a back seat inside the carriage, which may be said to be carrying her into the wide world.

How the young man from Cambridge sulkily put his five great coats in front; but was reconciled when little Miss Sharp was made to quit the carriage, and mount up beside him—when he covered her up in one of his Benjamins,[4] and became perfectly good-

8. Main thoroughfare from Hyde Park, at the Marble Arch, to Tottenham Court Road.
9. Now Regent Street, a main street connecting Oxford Street and Piccadilly.
1. "The driving is like the driving of Jehu . . . for he driveth furiously" (2 Kings 9.30).
2. Tavern in Lad Lane called The Swan with Two Necks (two *nicks* indicated the bird belonged to the Vinters' Company) from which the coach left for Queen's Crawley.
3. Coachman's seat.
4. Overcoats.

humoured—how the asthmatic gentleman, the prim lady, who declared upon her sacred honour she had never travelled in a public carriage before, (there is always such a lady in a coach,—Alas! was; for the coaches, where are they?), and the fat widow with the brandy-bottle, took their places inside—how the porter asked

them all for money, and got sixpence from the gentleman and five greasy halfpence from the fat widow—and how the carriage at length drove away—now, threading the dark lanes of Aldersgate,[5] anon clattering by the Blue Cupola of Paul's, gingling rapidly by the strangers' entry of Fleet-Market, which, with Exeter 'Change, has now departed to the world of shadows—how they passed the White Bear in Piccadilly,[6] and saw the dew rising up from the market-gardens of Knightsbridge—how Turnham-green, Brentford, Bagshot,[7] were passed—need not be told here. But the writer of these pages, who has pursued in former days, and in the same bright weather, the same remarkable journey, cannot but think of it with a sweet and tender regret. Where[8] is the road now, and its merry incidents of life? Is there no Chelsea or Greenwich[9] for the old honest pimple-nosed coach-

5. From Lad Lane, the coach entered Aldersgate, passing St. Paul's Cathedral.
6. Entry for out-of-town suppliers at Fleet Market on Farringdon Street. The market and Exeter 'Change (see chapter IV) were both removed in 1829. The White Bear Inn still stood in 1848.
7. Villages west of London.
8. First printing reads: What
9. Chelsea Hospital for veteran soldiers and the Royal Naval College at Greenwich for disabled sailors.

men? I wonder where are they, those good fellows? Is old Weller[1] alive or dead? and the waiters, yea, and the inns at which they waited, and the cold-rounds-of-beef inside, and the stunted ostler, with his blue nose and clinking pail, where is he, and where is his generation? To those great geniuses now in petticoats, who shall write novels for the beloved reader's children, these men and things will be as much legend and history as Nineveh, or Cœur de Lion, or Jack Sheppard.[2] For them stage-coaches will have become romances—a team of four bays as fabulous as Bucephalus or Black Bess.[3] Ah, how their coats shone, as the stable-men pulled their clothes off, and away they went—ah, how their tails shook, as with smoking sides at the stage's end they demurely walked away into the inn-yard. Alas! we shall never hear the horn sing at midnight, or see the pike-gates fly open any more. Whither, however, is the light four-inside Trafalgar coach[4] carrying us? Let us be set down at Queen's Crawley without further divagation, and see how Miss Rebecca Sharp speeds there.

1. Sam Weller's coach-driving father in Charles Dickens' *Pickwick Papers* (1837).
2. Though Austen Henry Layard's expeditions to record the history of Nineveh were undertaken in 1845–47, while *Vanity Fair* was being written, his famous books on the subject did not appear until 1849. Thackeray probably is referring to the biblical account of Jonah's prophecies of the destruction of Nineveh. Richard the Lion-Hearted was king of England from 1189 to 1199. Jack Sheppard, an actual prisoner hanged in 1724, was made famous by W. H. Ainsworth's popular Newgate novel *Jack Sheppard* (1839).
3. Alexander the Great's horse and Dick Turpin's horse in Ainsworth's novel *Rookwood* (1834).
4. Stagecoach named after the British victory at Trafalgar, 1805.

## *Chapter VIII.*

### PRIVATE AND CONFIDENTIAL.

*Miss Rebecca Sharp to Miss Amelia Sedley, Russell Square, London.*
(Free.[1]—Pitt Crawley.)

"MY DEAREST, SWEETEST AMELIA,

"With what mingled joy and sorrow do I take up the pen to write to my dearest friend! Oh, what[2] a change between to day and yesterday!—*now* I am friendless and alone—yesterday I was at home in the sweet company of a sister whom I shall ever *ever* cherish!

"I will not tell you in what tears and sadness I passed the fatal night in which I separated from you. *You* went on Tuesday to joy and happiness, with your mother and *your devoted young soldier* by your side, and I thought of you all night, dancing at the Perkins's,[3] the prettiest I am sure of all the young ladies at the Ball. I was brought by the groom in the old carriage to Sir Pitt Crawley's town-house,

1. As an M.P. Sir Pitt has franking privileges (i.e., can send letters postage free).
2. MS reads: friend!—What
3. An allusion to Thackeray's 1846 Christmas book *Mrs. Perkins's Ball* (dated 1847).

where after John the groom had behaved most rudely and insolently to me (alas 'twas safe to insult poverty and misfortune!) I was given over to Sir P's care and made to pass the night in an old gloomy bed and by the side of a horrid gloomy[4] old charwoman,[5] who keeps the house. I did not sleep one single wink the whole night.

"Sir Pitt is not what we silly girls when we used to read Cecilia at Chiswick, imagined a baronet must have been, anything indeed less like Lord Orville[6] cannot be imagined. Fancy an old, stumpy, short, vulgar, and very dirty man, in old clothes and shabby old gaiters[7] who smokes a horrid pipe, and cooks his own horrid supper in a saucepan. He speaks with a country accent, and swore a great deal, at the old charwoman, at the hackney coachman who drove us to the inn[8] where the coach went from, and on which I made the journey *outside for the greater part of the way.*

"I was wakened at day break by the charwoman, and having arrived at the inn was at first placed inside the coach. But when we got to a place called Leakington, where the rain began to fall very heavily, will you believe it? I was forced to come outside, for Sir Pitt is a proprietor of the coach, and as a passenger came at Leakington who wanted an inside place, I was obliged to go outside in the rain, where however a young gentleman from Cambridge College sheltered me very kindly in one of his *several* great coats.

"This gentleman and the guard seemed to know Sir Pitt very well; and laughed at him a great deal. They both agreed in calling him an *old screw* which means a very stingy, avaricious person. He never gives any money to any body they said (and this meanness I hate) and the young gentleman made me remark that we drove very slow for the last two stages on the road, because Sir Pitt was on the box, and because he is proprietor of the horses for this part of the journey. 'But won't I flog 'em on to Squashmore when I take the ribbons,' said the young *Cantab*[9]—'And sarve em right, Master Jack,' said the guard. When I comprehended the meaning of their phrase, and that Master Jack intended to drive the rest of the way,—and revenge himself on Sir Pitt's horses, of course I laughed too.[1]

"A carriage and four splendid horses covered with armorial bearings however awaited us at Mudbury, four miles from Queen's Crawley, and we made our entrance to the baronet's park in state. There is a fine avenue of a mile long leading to the house, and the woman at the lodge-gate (over the pillars of which are a Serpent and a Dove the supporters of the Crawley arms) made us a number of curtsies as she flung open the old iron carved doors,[2] which are something like

4. MS reads: horrid & gloomy
5. MS has Becky throughout this letter spelling this word: chairwoman
6. *Cecilia, or Memoirs of an Heiress* (1782) and *Evelina, or A Young Lady's Entrance into the World* (1778), by Fanny Burney. Lord Orville is hero of the latter. In each novel a girl overcomes adversity and evil to marry happily.
7. Cloth or leather ankle coverings.
8. MS reads: drove with him
9. Student at Cambridge University.
1. The final phrase, from the dash, is interlined in the MS above the canceled phrase: of course I intervened for the poor animals
2. MS reads: old worn iron doors,

those at odious Chiswick.

" 'There's an avenue,' said Sir Pitt, 'a mile long. There's six thousand pound of timber in them there trees. Do you call that nothing?' He pronounces avenue *evenue* and nothing *nothink*. So droll—and he had a Mr. Hodson his hind from Mudbury into the carriage with him, and they talked about distraining and selling up and draining and sub-soiling[3] and a great deal about tenants and farming—much more than I could understand. Sam Miles had been caught poaching, and Peter Bailey had gone to the workhouse at last. 'Serve him right,' said Sir Pitt, 'him and his fam'ly has been cheating me on that farm these hundred and fifty years.' Some old tenant I suppose who could not pay his rent. Sir Pitt might have said '*he* and his family' to be sure: but rich[4] baronets do not need to be careful about grammar, as poor governesses must be.

"As we passed I remarked a beautiful church-spire rising above some old elms in the park: and before them in the midst of a lawn and some outhouses an old red house with tall chimnies covered with ivy, and the windows shining in the sun. 'Is that your Church, Sir?' I said.

" 'Yes hang it,' (said Sir Pitt, only he used, dear, *a much wickeder word*); 'how's Buty, Hodson?—Buty's my brother Buty, my dear, my brother the parson. Buty and the Beast I call him, ha, ha!'

"Hodson laughed too, and then looking more grave and nodding his head said—'I'm afraid he's better, Sir Pitt. He was out on his poney yesterday, looking at our corn.'

" 'Looking after his tithes hang 'un' (only he used the same wicked word). 'Will brandy and water never kill him? He's as tough as old whatdyecallum—old Methusalem.'[5]

"Mr. Hodson laughed again. 'The young men is home from college. They've whopped John Scroggins till he's well nigh dead.'

" 'Whop my second keeper,'[6] roared out Sir Pitt.

" 'He was on the parson's ground, Sir,' replied Mr. Hodson. And Sir Pitt in a fury swore that if ever he caught 'em poaching on his ground he'd transport 'em by the Lord he would. However, he said, 'I've sold the presentation of the living,[7] Hodson; none of that breed shall get it *I* war'nt'—and Mr. Hodson said he was quite right: and I have no doubt from this that the two brothers are at variance—as brothers often are and sisters too. Don't you remember the two Miss Scratchleys at Chiswick how they used always to fight and quarrel?—and Mary Box how she was always thumping Louisa?

"Presently seeing two little boys gathering sticks in the wood, Mr. Hodson jumped out of the carriage at Sir Pitt's orders, and rushed

3. Distraining: forced sale of possessions to pay debt. Selling up: disposing of a bankrupt person's entire property by auction. Subsoiling: deep plowing.
4. The word "rich" is interlined in the MS.
5. Methuselah, oldest man in the Bible (Genesis 5.27).
6. Gamekeeper
7. Transport: banish to a penal colony. Presentation of the living: Sir Pitt, as baronet and squire, had the right to recommend a candidate for a vacant church post (living) in his parish, but he had sold the right for cash.

upon them with his whip. 'Pitch into 'em Hodson,' roared the Baronet; 'flog their little souls out, and bring 'em up to the House the vagabonds, I'll commit[8] 'em as sure as my name's Pitt.' And presently we heard Mr. Hodson's whip clacking on the shoulders of the poor little blubbering wretches, and Sir Pitt seeing that the malefactors were in custody drove on to the Hall.

"All the servants were ready to meet us and

* * * * * * *

"Here, my dear, I was interrupted last night by a dreadful thumping at my door: and who do you think it was? Sir Pitt Crawley in his night-cap and dressing gown, such a figure! As I shrunk away from such a visitor—he came forward and seized my candle—'No candles after eleven o'clock, Miss Becky,' said he—'Go to bed in the dark you pretty little hussey' (that is what he called me) 'and unless you wish me to come for the candle every night, mind and be in bed at eleven.' And with this he and Mr. Horrocks the Butler went off laughing. You may be sure I shall not encourage any more of their visits. They let loose two immense blood-hounds at night, which all last night were yelling and howling at the moon. 'I call the dog Gorer,' said Sir Pitt—'he's killed a man that dog has, and is master of a bull, and the mother I used to call Flora—but now I calls her Aroarer[9] for she's too old to bite. Haw Haw.'[1]

"Before the house of Queen's Crawley, which is an odious old fashioned red brick mansion with tall chimnies and gables of the style of Queen Bess,[2] there is a terrace flanked by the family dove and serpent and on which the great hall door opens. And oh my dear the great hall I am sure is as big and as glum as the great hall in the dear Castle of Udolpho.[3] It has a large fire-place, in which we might put half Miss Pinkerton's school and the grate is big enough to roast an ox at the very least. Round the room hang I don't know how many generations of Crawleys, some with beards and ruffs, some with huge wigs and toes turned out; some dressed in long straight stays[4] and gowns that look as stiff as towers, and some with long ringlets and oh my dear, scarcely any stays at all: At one end of the hall is the great stair case all in black oak as dismal as may be, and on either side are tall doors with stags' heads over them, leading to the billiard-room and the library and the great yellow saloon and the morning-rooms. I think there are at least twenty bed rooms on the first floor; one of them has the bed in which Queen Elizabeth slept, and I have been taken by my new pupils through all these fine apartments this morning: they are not rendered less gloomy I

8. Imprison.
9. Flora, Roman goddess of fertility and flowers, and Aurora, Roman goddess of the dawn.
1. The next paragraph was begun and abandoned twice in the MS: <But to resume the history of the family I must begin as in duty bound with my lady Crawley> <The first room you enter at Queens Crawley>
2. Elizabeth I.
3. In *The Mysteries of Udolpho* (1794) by Ann Radcliffe, Emily is kidnapped and taken to the horrific Castle of Udolpho—the only "dear" thing about it is Emily's escape and marriage in the end to the hero. The word "dear" is interlined in the MS.
4. Corsets. MS reads: <waist> ↑stays↓

promise you by having the shutters always shut, and there is scarce one of the apartments, but when the light was let into it, I expected to see a ghost in the room. We have a school-room on the second floor, with my bed room leading into it on one side and that of the young ladies on the other. Then there are Mr. Pitt's apartments—Mr. Crawley he is called—the eldest son, and Mr. Rawdon Crawley's rooms—he is an officer like *somebody* and away with his regiment. There is no want of room I assure you. You might lodge all the people in Russell Square in the house I think: and have space to spare.

"Half an hour after our arrival—the great dinner bell was rung and I came down with my two pupils (they are very thin insignificant little chits of ten and eight years old)—I came down in your *dear* muslin gown (about which that odious Mrs. Pinner was so rude because you gave it me) for I am to be treated as one of the family, except on company days; when the young ladies and I are to dine up stairs.[5]

"Well the great dinner-bell rung, and we all assembled in the little drawing room where my Lady Crawley sits. She is the second Lady Crawley and mother of the young ladies. She was an ironmonger's daughter and her marriage was thought a great match. She looks as if she had been handsome once, and her eyes are always weeping for the loss of her beauty. She is pale and meagre and high-shouldered: and has not a word to say for herself evidently. Her step son, Mr. Crawley, was likewise in the room. He was in full dress as pompous as an undertaker. He is pale, thin, ugly, silent; he has thin legs, no chest, hay-coloured whiskers and straw-coloured hair. He is the very picture of his sainted mother over the mantel-piece. Griselda[6] of the noble house of Binkie.

" 'This is the new governess, Mr. Crawley,' said Lady Crawley, coming forward and taking my hand—'Miss Sharp.'

" 'O!' said Mr. Crawley and pushed his head once forward and began again to read a great pamphlet with which he was busy.

" 'I hope you will be kind to my girls,' said Lady Crawley—with her pink eyes always full of tears.

" 'Law Ma, of course she will,' said the eldest: and I saw at a glance that I need not be afraid of *that* woman.

5. In the MS two canceled paragraphs follow here. Parts were rewritten for use later: <Well, the grand dinner bell rung—and we all assembled in the little grim room where Lady Crawley always sits. She is a «tall snuffy pompous old lady in grey silk» ↑poor pale sickly looking body, gentle and with weak eyes.↓—just like a schoolmistress «in a word.» With her was her «son» ↑step son↓ Mr. Crawley in full dress though his clothes look very old. He is a pale thin ugly silent young man with hay-coloured whiskers, and pink eyes and staw-coloured hair. Mr. Crawley said his mamma of whom he is the very picture—this is the governess of your sisters Miss Sharp. [New paragraph] O said Mr. Crawley: and pushed out his head a little way by way of bowing. Miss Sharp continued my lady, you will be treated as one of the family of Queen's Crawley, and I hope that you will find everything conducive to your comfort and that we shall have every cause for mutual satisfaction.'—This lady is a speech maker like horrid old Miss Pinkerton. I hate speech makers but of course I made a pretty speech in reply.>

6. A generic name for long-suffering wife, from Boccaccio's *Decameron.* MS originally read: Jemima

" 'My lady is served,' says the Butler in black and an immense white shirt-frill that looked as if it had been one of the Queen Elizabeth ruffs depicted in the hall; and so taking Mr. Crawley's arm she led the way to the dining room, whither I followed with my little pupils in each hand.

"Sir Pitt was already in the room with a silver jug. He had just been to the cellar: and was in full dress too, that is he had taken his gaiters off, and showed his little dumpy legs in black worsted stockings. The side-board was covered with glistening old plate—old cups both gold and silver, old salvers and cruet stands like Rundell and Bridge's Shop.[7] Every thing on the table was in silver too, and two footmen with red hair and canary coloured liveries stood on either side of the side-board.

"Mr. Crawley said a long grace, and Sir Pitt said amen—and the great silver dish-covers were removed.

" 'What have we for dinner, Betsy,' said the Baronet.

" 'Mutton broth I believe, Sir Pitt,' answered Lady Crawley.[8]

7. Salvers and cruet stands are trays and condiment holders. Rundell and Bridge's was an actual goldsmith's shop in east-central London.

8. MS here contains the following canceled passage: <The black Hampshire Sir Pitt said the butler and as fine a beast as ever I stuck a knife into. There was a roast leg of pork on the silver dish before Sir Pitt; black-puddings before me, another entrée of pig's fry before the young ladies, a silver dish of cabbages and another of potatoes on the other side of the table. We had all silver tankards and the butler came round frequently saying Ale or Water. [New paragraph] Will you take some mock-turtle soup Miss Ah— Miss Blunt says Mr. Crawley. My dear it was pig again!—a sort of pig's head broth; and so we made our first dinner at Queen's Crawley. ↑In a note↓ We have had pig for three days since; and yesterday we killed a sheep!>

" '*Mouton aux navets,*' added the Butler gravely (pronounce if you please moutongonavvy) 'and the soup is *potage de mouton à l'Écossaise.* The side dishes contain *pommes de terre au naturel,* and *choufleur à l'Eau.*'[9]

" 'Mutton's mutton,' said the Baronet, 'and a devilish good thing— What *ship* was it, Horrocks—and when did you kill?'

" 'One of the black faced Scotch, Sir Pitt: we killed on Thursday.'

" 'Who took any?'

" 'Steel of Mudbury took the saddle and two legs, Sir Pitt: but he says the last was too young and confounded woolly, Sir Pitt.'

" 'Will you take some *potage?* Miss Ah—Miss Blunt,' said Mr. Crawley.

" 'Capital Scotch broth, my dear,' said Sir Pitt, 'though they call it by a French name.'

" 'I believe it is the custom, Sir, in decent society,' said Mr. Crawley haughtily, 'to call the dish as I have called it:' and it was served to us on silver soup-plates by the footmen in the canary coats with the *mouton aux navets.*[1] The 'ale and water' was brought, and was served to us young ladies in wine glasses. I am not a judge of ale, but I can say with a clear conscience I prefer water.

"While we were enjoying our repast, Sir Pitt took occasion to ask what had become of the shoulders of the mutton.

" 'I believe they were eaten in the servants' hall,' said my lady humbly.[2]

" 'They was, my lady,' said Horrocks, 'and precious little else we get there neither.'

"Sir Pitt burst into a hoarse laugh; and continued his conversation with Mr. Horrocks. 'That there little black pig of the Kent sow's breed must be uncommon fat now.'

" 'It's not quite busting, Sir Pitt,' said the butler with the gravest air; at which Sir Pitt and with him the young ladies this time began to laugh violently.

" 'Miss Crawley, Miss Rose Crawley,' said Mr. Crawley; 'your laughter strikes me as being exceedingly out of place.'

" 'Never mind my Lord, girls,' said the Baronet—'We'll try the porker on Saturday. Kill un on Saturday morning, John Horrocks. Miss Sharp adores pork don't you, Miss Sharp?'

"And I think this is all the conversation that I remember at dinner. When the repast was concluded a jug of hot water was placed before Sir Pitt, with a case bottle[3] containing I believe rum. Mr. Horrocks served myself and my pupils with three little glasses of wine, and a bumper[4] was poured out for my lady. When we retired, she took from her work drawer an enormous interminable piece of knitting; the young ladies began to play at cribbage with a dirty pack of cards. We had but one candle lighted, but it was in a magnificent old silver

9. Mutton and turnips; mutton soup in the Scottish manner; boiled potatoes; boiled cauliflower.
1. MS added and canceled: <My lady as a great invalid had a little private silver dish containing mutton cutlets. The rest of the family dined upon the mouton aux mavets.>
2. For "believe" and "humbly" the MS originally read "presume" and "loftily"
3. A square bottle in a sleeve.
4. Brim-full glass of wine.

candlestick, and after a very few questions from my lady I had my choice of amusement between a volume of sermons, and a pamphlet on the corn-laws[5] which Mr. Crawley had been reading before dinner.

"So we sate for an hour until steps were heard. 'Put away the cards, girls,' cried my lady in a great tremor—'put down Mr. Crawley's books, Miss Sharp'—and these orders had been scarcely obeyed when Mr. Crawley entered the room.

" 'We will resume yesterday's discourse, young ladies,' said he—'and you shall each read a page by turns—so that Miss a—Miss Short may have an opportunity of hearing you.' And the poor girls began to spell a long dismal sermon delivered at Bethesda Chapel Liverpool in behalf of the mission for the Chickasaw Indians.[6] Was it not a charming evening?

"At ten the servants were told to call Sir Pitt and the household to prayers. Sir Pitt came in first very much flushed and rather unsteady in his gait—[7] and after him the butler, the canaries, Mr. Crawley's man, three other men smelling very much of the stable, and four women one of whom I remarked was very much overdressed, and who flung me a look of great scorn as she plumped down on her knees.

"After Mr. Crawley had done haranguing and expounding,[8] we received our candles and then we went to bed and then I was disturbed in my writing as I have described to my dearest sweetest Amelia.

" 'Good night, a thousand thousand thousand kisses!'

"*Saturday.* This morning at five I heard the shrieking of the little black pig. Rose[9] and Violet introduced me to it yesterday: and to the stables, and to the kennel, and to the gardener, who was picking fruit to send to market, and from whom they begged hard a bunch of hot-house grapes, but he said that Sir Pitt had numbered every 'Man Jack' of them and it would be as much as his place was worth to give any away. The darling girls caught a colt in a paddock and asked me if I would ride, and began to ride themselves when the groom coming with horrid oaths drove them away.

"Lady Crawley is always knitting the worsted. Sir Pitt is always tipsy every night and I believe sits with Horrocks the butler—Mr. Crawley always reads sermons in the evening; and in the morning is locked up in his study or else rides to Mudbury on county business or to Squashmore where he preaches on Wednesdays and Fridays to the tenants there.[1]

5. Tariffs to protect English landowners' profits from cheap imported grain, particularly wheat. The laws were repealed in 1846.

6. The term "chapel" denotes "nonconformist" (i.e., not Church of England). This one is named for the healing pool in John 5.2–4. Chickasaw Indians lived in Mississippi and Tennessee.

7. MS added and canceled:<and do you know the horrid man poked ↑pushed↓ me once or twice in the side at wh. the girls began to giggle. [New paragraph] <<Papa'th poking Mith Crawley in the wibth>> ↑Papas pinching Miss Sharp↓! roared out Miss Rosa at wh. ↑I blushed &↓ Mr. Crawley looked as black as thunder, and Lady Crawley blushed too as well as her tallowy face would let her. Sir Pitt was evidently tipsy, and was beginning to break out in some frightful oaths when the door opened and the servants came in>

8. For the phrase "After Mr. Crawley . . . expounding," the MS reads: Mr. Crawley delivered an extempore prayer which lasted twenty minutes and then expounded on a chapter of Habakkuk. ↑Sir Pitt hiccupped all the time in the drollest way,↓ and then

9. MS, inconsistent with its usual spelling, reads: Rosa

1. The MS contains a paragraph omitted from the first edition. The omission corresponds to

"A hundred thousand grateful loves to your dear papa and mamma. Is your poor brother recovered of his rack-punch? O dear, O dear, how men should beware of wicked punch!

"Ever and Ever thine own,

"REBECCA."

Everything considered, I think it is quite as well for our dear Amelia Sedley in Russell Square, that Miss Sharp[2] and she are parted. Rebecca is a droll funny creature to be sure: and those descriptions of the poor lady weeping for the loss of her beauty, and the gentleman "with hay-coloured whiskers and straw-coloured hair" are very smart doubtless and show a great[3] knowledge of the world. That she might when on her knees have been thinking of something better than Miss Horrocks's ribbons has possibly struck both of us—But my kind reader will please to remember that these histories in their gaudy yellow covers,[4] have 'Vanity Fair' for a title and that Vanity Fair is a very vain, wicked, foolish place, full of all sorts of humbugs and falsenesses and pretentions.[5] And while the moralist who is holding forth on the cover,[6] (an accurate portrait of your humble servant) professes to wear neither gown nor bands, but only the very same long-eared livery, in which his congregation is arrayed:[7] yet, look you, one is bound to speak the truth as far as one knows it, whether one mounts a cap and bells or a shovel-hat,[8] and a deal of disagreeable matter must come out in the course of such an undertaking.[9]

I have heard a brother of the story-telling trade at Naples,[1] preaching to a pack of good for nothing honest lazy fellows by the sea-shore; work himself up into such a rage and passion with some of the villains whose wicked deeds he was describing and inventing, that the audience could not resist it, and they and the poet together would burst out into a roar of oaths and execrations against the fictitious monster of the tale, so that the hat went round and the bajocchi[2]

the deletion from the manuscript of another passage, near the beginning of Ch. X, describing Miss Horrocks. Here the MS reads: The odious pert ↑ogling↓ creature with the red cheeks and the flaunting ribbons in her cap is Horrocks's daughter and *I very much fear* Sir Pitt is,—but hush! What would Miss Pinkerton say at such stories? My dear I will tell them to Mrs. George Osborne.

2. MS reads: <this young person whose> ↑Miss Sharp↓
3. MS reads: great deal of
4. This, and other references to the form of original publication, were altered in various ways for republication in other formats.
5. In the following passage, added and canceled and partially recopied in the MS, the Greek means: "As is the generation of leaves, so is that of man": <You see too by the picture outside; that the moralist who is holding forth ↑on the cover↓ is dressed in the very same long eared livery wh. his audience sports: and professes to be no better than they. 'Οιηπερ φυλλων γενεη τοιηδε και ανδρων.'> ↑And while the moralist↓ who is
6. MS added and canceled: <fraternizes with his audience>
7. Gown and bands: clergy's official robe and collar. Long- eared livery: donkey-eared clown's cap. See cover illustration.
8. Cap and bells: clown suit. Shovel-hat: clergyman's hat.
9. MS added and canceled a paragraph here. William Beauford (dates not known) and Alexander Bridport Becher (1796–1876) were cartographers and authors of travel narratives.: <When Captain Beauford & Captain Becher make charts at the Admiralty they set down the rocks creeks bays quicksands in their proper places—or the deuce would be in it and the unwary mariner would find himself «perched» ↑↑striking↓↓ on a «reef» ↑bar↓ or floundering in a quicksand: where he had been led to expect a clear channel and deep water.>

1. Thackeray was quarantined for a week in Naples in 1844.
2. Copper coins.

tumbled into it in the midst of a perfect storm of sympathy.

At the little Paris Theatres on the other hand you will not only hear the people yelling out *'Ah gredin, ah monstre!'* and cursing the tyrant of the play from the boxes, but the actors themselves positively refuse to play the wicked parts such as those of *infâmes Anglais,*[3] brutal Cossacks, and what not, and prefer to appear, at a smaller salary, in their real character as loyal Frenchmen. I set the two stories, one against the other, so that you may see that it is not from mere mercenary motives, that the present performer is desirous to show up and trounce his villains—but because he has a sincere hatred of them which he cannot keep down, and which must find a vent in suitable abuse and bad language.

I warn 'my kyind friends'[4] then, that I am going to tell a story of harrowing villainy and complicated but as I trust intensely interesting crime. My rascals are no milk and water rascals I promise you—When we come to the proper places we won't spare fine language—no no! But when we are going over the quiet country we must perforce be calm. A tempest[5] in a slop basin is absurd. We will reserve that sort of thing for the mighty ocean and the lonely midnight—The present number will be very mild—others—but we will not anticipate *those*.

And as we bring our characters forward, I will ask leave as a man and a brother[6] not only to introduce them, but occasionally to step down from the platform and talk about them. If they are good and kindly, to love them and shake them by the hand: if they are silly, to laugh at them confidentially in the reader's sleeve: if they are wicked and heartless, to abuse them in the strongest terms which politeness admits of.

Otherwise you might fancy it was I who was sneering at the practice of devotion, which Miss Sharp finds so ridiculous; that it was I who laughed good-humouredly at the reeling old Silenus[7] of a baronet—whereas the laughter comes from one who has no reverence except for prosperity and no eye for anything beyond success. Such people there are living and flourishing in the world—Faithless, Hopeless, Charityless[8]—let us have at them, dear friends, with might and main. Some there are, and very successful too; mere quacks and fools: and it[9] was to combat and expose such as those no doubt, that Laughter was made.[1]

3. *Gredin*: rascal. *Infâmes Anglais*: vile Englishmen.
4. Alfred Bunn (1796–1860), theatrical manager, typically greeted audiences at Drury Lane with these words. See Thackeray's *Snobs* in *Punch*, February 20, 1847.
5. MS reads: tornado
6. Allusion to the abolitionist slogan, "Am I not a man and a brother?"
7. In Greek myth, an old drunk.
8. "Now these three remain: faith, hope and charity. But the greatest of these is charity" (I Corinthians 13.13).
9. MS reads: fools—it
1. MS added and canceled a paragraph: <Miss Sharp's opinion with regard to the two young ladies whom she was to instruct was made with her usual intelligence and fine feeling. They had been educated by servants hitherto, the coachman ≪giving≫ ↑imparted↓ them instructions in the stable, the cook giving lectures ex cathedrâ in the kitchen, the house maids and gardeners ≪let≫ completing the rest of their education.>

## *Chapter IX.*

### FAMILY PORTRAITS.

SIR PITT CRAWLEY was a philosopher with a taste for what is called low life. His first marriage with the daughter of the noble Binkie[1] had been made under the auspices of his parents, and as he often told Lady Crawley in her life time 'she was such a confounded quarrelsome high-bred jade that when she died, he was hanged[2] if he would ever take another of her sort,' and on her ladyship's demise, he kept his promise, and selected for a second wife Miss Rose Dawson, daughter of Mr. John Thomas Dawson ironmonger[3] of Mudbury. What a happy woman was Rose to be my Lady Crawley!

Let us set down the items of her happiness. In the first place she gave up Peter Butt, a young man who kept company with her, and in consequence of his disappointment in love, took to smuggling, poaching, and a thousand other bad courses. Then she quarreled as in duty bound with all the friends and intimates of her youth who of course could not be received by my Lady at Queen's Crawley—nor did she find in her new rank and abode any persons who were willing to welcome her. Who ever did? Sir Huddleston Fuddleston had three daughters who all hoped[4] to be Lady Crawley. Sir Giles Wapshot's family were insulted that one of the Wapshot girls had not the preference in the marriage, and the remaining baronets of the county were indignant at their comrade's mésalliance—Never mind the commoners whom we will leave to grumble anonymously.[5]

Sir Pitt did not care as he said a brass farden for any one of them. He had his pretty Rose and what more need[6] a man require than to please himself? So he used to get drunk every night: to beat his pretty Rose sometimes: to leave her in Hampshire when he went to London for the parliamentary session, without a single friend in the wide world. Even[7] Mrs. Bute Crawley the rector's wife refused to visit[8] her as she said she would never give the *pas*[9] to a tradesman's daughter.

As the only endowments with which nature had gifted Lady Crawley were those of pink cheeks and a white skin, and as she had no sort of character, nor talents, nor opinions, nor occupations, nor amuse-

1. Fictitious name.
2. MS reads: d—
3. Interlined in MS over: <gardener>
4. MS reads: looked
5. The clause "Never mind . . . anonymously" is interlined in MS.
6. MS reads: must
7. Interlined in MS.
8. MS reads: enter the same room with
9. Give precedence or courtesy.

ments, nor that vigour of soul and ferocity of temper which often falls to the lot of entirely foolish women, her hold upon Sir Pitt's affections was not very great—the roses faded out of her cheeks and the pretty freshness left her figure after the birth of a couple of children, and she became a mere machine in her husband's house of no more use than the late Lady Crawley's grand piano. Being a light complexioned woman she wore light clothes as most blondes will and appeared by preference[1] in draggled sea green or slatternly sky blue. She worked that worsted day and night or other pieces like it—She had counterpanes in the course of a few years to all the beds in Crawley. She had a small flower garden for which she had rather an affection but beyond this no other liking or disliking. When her husband was rude to her she was apathetic: whenever he struck her she cried. She had not character enough to take to drinking—and moaned about slip-shod and in curl-papers all day. O Vanity Fair, Vanity Fair!—this might have been but for you a cheery lass:—Peter Butt and Rose a happy man and wife, in a snug farm with a hearty family, and an honest portion of pleasures, cares, hopes, and struggles. But a title and a coach and four[2] are toys more precious than happiness in Vanity Fair: and if Harry the Eighth or Bluebeard[3] were alive now, and wanted a tenth wife, do you suppose he could not get the prettiest girl that shall be presented this Season?

The languid dullness of their mamma did not, as it may be supposed, awaken much affection in her little daughters but they were very happy in the servants' hall: and in the stables; and the Scotch gardner having luckily a good wife and some good children they got a little wholesome society and instruction in his lodge, which was the only education bestowed upon them until Miss Sharp came.

Her engagement was owing to the remonstrances of Mr. Pitt Crawley—the only friend or protector Lady Crawley ever had; and the only person besides her children[4] for whom she entertained a little feeble attachment. Mr. Pitt took after the noble Binkies from whom he was descended; and was a very polite and proper gentleman. When he grew to man's estate[5] and came back from Christchurch he began to reform the slackened discipline of the hall; in spite of his father who stood in awe of him. He was a man of such rigid refinement, that he would have starved rather than have dined without a white neck-cloth. Once when just from college, and when Horrocks the butler brought him a letter without placing it previously on a tray, he gave that domestic a look and administered to him a speech so cutting, that Horrocks ever after trembled before him; the whole household bowed to him. Lady Crawley's curl-papers

1. The phrase "by preference" is interlined in MS.
2. Title of nobility and coach drawn by four horses.
3. Henry VIII (1491–1547) had six wives several of whom were executed. Bluebeard, from the French *La Barbe Bleue*, kept the bodies of his former wives stacked in a locked room of his castle.
4. The phrase "besides her children" is interlined in MS.
5. The clown's closing song in Shakespeare's *Twelfth Night*, V.i.393. Christchurch: a college at Oxford.

came off earlier when he was at home: Sir Pitt's muddy gaiters disappeared;[6] and if that incorrigible old man still adhered to other[7] old habits, he never fuddled himself with rum and water in his son's presence, and only talked to his servants in a very reserved and polite manner. And those persons remarked that Sir Pitt never swore at Lady Crawley while his son was in the room.

It was he who taught the butler to say 'My lady is served' and who insisted on handing her ladyship into dinner. He seldom spoke to her but when he did it was with the most powerful respect: and he never let her quit the apartment, without rising in the most stately manner to open the door, and making an elegant bow at her egress.

At Eton he was called Miss Crawley; and there I am sorry to say his younger brother Rawdon used to lick him violently. But though his parts were not brilliant he made up for his lack of talent by meritorious industry and was never known during eight years at school to be subject to that punishment, which it is generally thought none but a Cherub can escape.

At College his career was of course highly creditable. And here he prepared himself for public life into which he was to be introduced by the patronage of his grandfather, Lord Binkie, by studying the ancient and modern orators with great assiduity and by speaking unceasingly at the debating societies. But though he had a fine flux of words and delivered his little voice with great pomposity and pleasure to himself, and never advanced any sentiment or opinion which was not perfectly trite and stale and supported by a Latin quotation—yet he[8] failed somehow in spite of a mediocrity which ought to have insured any man a success. He did not even get the prize-poem which all his friends said he was sure of.[9]

After leaving College he became private Secretary to Lord Binkie, and was then appointed attaché to the Legation at Pumpernickel which post he filled with perfect honour, and brought home despatches consisting of Strasburg-pie[1] to the foreign minister of the day. After remaining ten years attaché (several years after the lamented Lord Binkie's demise), and finding the advancement slow, he at length gave up the diplomatic service in some disgust and began to turn country gentleman.[2]

He wrote a pamphlet on Malt on returning to England (for he was an ambitious man and always liked to be before the public) and took a strong part in the negro emancipation question. Then he became

6. MS adds: before him
7. MS reads: his
8. MS adds: was called Nightcap Crawley and
9. MS added and canceled two paragraphs: <On quitting Christchurch—without a debt «without» and with the sincere regards of the Dean—he became> <a stingy fellow who never could be got to owe them a halfpenny. Petty ↑Rawdon↓ Crawley's disposition was very different as we shall hear when we come to discuss that gentleman's character. [New paragraph] The tipsy old boor of a baronet had a great respect for his eldest Son, who by his constantly frigid and haughty demeanour obtained great influence over him. «He was of course»>
1. Literally goose-liver paté, but probably a metaphorical reference to the goose sillyness of Pitt's despatches.
2. MS added and canceled: <And here again it may be said that his misfortunate star pursued him, for he was such a fool and so solemn that it is a wonder Government did not see his merit and look to his rapid advancement.>

a friend of Mr. Wilberforce's whose politics he admired, and had that famous correspondence with the Reverend Silas Hornblower on the Ashantee Mission.[3] He was in London if not for the Parliament session, at least in May for the religious meetings. In the country he was a magistrate, and an active visitor and speaker among those destitute of religious instruction. He was said to be paying his addresses to Lady Jane Sheepshanks, Lord Muttondown's third daughter: and whose sister, Lady Emily, wrote those sweet tracts, "The Sailor's True Binnacle,"[4] and "The Applewoman of Finchley Common."

Miss Sharp's account of his employments at Queen's Crawley was not a caricature. He subjected the servants there to the devotional exercises before mentioned: in which he (and so much the better) brought[5] his father to join.[6] He patronised an independent meeting house[7] in Crawley parish, much to the indignation of his uncle the Rector and to the consequent delight of Sir Pitt, who was induced to go himself once or twice, which occasioned some violent sermons at Crawley Parish Church directed point-blank at[8] the Baronet's old Gothic pew there. Honest Sir Pitt, however,[9] did not feel the force of these discourses, as he always took his nap during sermon-time.

Mr. Crawley was very earnest, for the good of the nation and of the Christian world, that the old gentleman should yield him up his place in parliament: but this the elder constantly refused to do. Both were of course too prudent to give up the fifteen hundred a year which was brought in by the second seat, (at this period filled by Mr. Quadroon with carte-blanche on the Slave Question).[1] Indeed the family estate was much embarrassed, and the income drawn[2] from the borough was of great use to the house of Queen's Crawley.

It had never recovered the heavy fine imposed upon Walpole Crawley, first Baronet, for peculation in the Tape and Sealing Wax Office.[3] Sir Walpole was a jolly fellow eager to seize and to spend money (*alieni appetens sui profusus,*[4] Mr. Crawley would remark with a sigh,) and in his day beloved by all the county for the constant drunkenness and hospitality which was maintained at Queen's Crawley. The cellars were filled with Burgundy then, the kennels with hounds and the stables with gallant hunters; now such horses as Queen's Crawley possessed went to plough or ran in the Trafalgar Coach, and

3. William Wilberforce (1759–1833), the evangelical political leader and ally of William Pitt, for whom Pitt Crawley was named, was an antislavery philanthropist. Hornblower is fictitious. Ashantee is a region in west Africa.
4. A binnacle is housing for the compass on a ship.
5. MS reads: devotional services before mentioned: in which after some time he brought
6. The rest of this paragraph was inserted in the MS in revision.
7. Place of worship for protestant groups dissenting from the Church of England.
8. MS reads: against
9. MS placed "however" after "feel"
1. Sir Pitt, a sitting member of Parliament, controlled the election for the second seat in his rotten borough, but he had sold control to Mr. Quadroon, a mulatto, who probably was as antislavery as Pitt's hero, Wilberforce.
2. MS reads: derivable
3. MS reads: affair
4. "Covetous of another's possessions, prodigal of his own," from the Roman historian Sallust (86–35 B.C.).

it was with a team of these very horses on an off day, that Miss Sharp[5] was brought to the Hall:[6] for boor as he was Sir Pitt was a stickler for his dignity while at home, and seldom drove out but with four horses, and though he dined off boiled mutton had always three footmen to serve it.

If mere parsimony would have made a man rich Sir Pitt Crawley might have become very wealthy—if he had been an attorney in a country town, with no capital but his brains it is very possible that he would have turned them to good account, and might have atchieved for himself a very considerable influence and competency. But he was unluckily endowed[7] with a good name and a large though encumbered estate, both of which went rather to injure than to advance him. He had a taste for law which cost him many thousands yearly, and being a great deal too clever to be robbed as he said by any single agent, allowed his affairs to be mismanaged by a dozen, whom he all equally mistrusted. He was such a sharp landlord that he could hardly find any but bankrupt tenants: and such a close farmer as to grudge almost the seed to the ground, whereupon revengeful nature grudged him the crops which she granted to more liberal husbandmen. He speculated in every possible way; he worked mines; bought canal-shares, horsed coaches, took government contracts, and was the busiest man and magistrate of his County. As he would not pay honest agents at his granite quarry, he had the satisfaction of finding that four overseers ran away and took fortunes with them to America. For want of proper precautions his coal-mines filled with water. The government flung his contract of damaged beef upon his hands, and for his coach-horses every mail-proprietor in the kingdom knew that he lost more horses than any man in the county from under-feeding and buying cheap. In disposition he was sociable and far from being proud: nay he rather preferred the society of a farmer or a horse-dealer to that of a gentleman like My Lord, his son. He was fond of drink, of swearing, of joking with the farmers' daughters; he was never known to give away a shilling or to do a good action but was of a pleasant, sly, laughing mood, and would cut his joke and drink his glass with a tenant and 'sell him up' the next day, or have his laugh with the poacher he was transporting with equal good humour. His politeness for the fair-sex has already been hinted at by Miss Rebecca Sharp—in a word, the whole Baronetage, Peerage, Commonage of England did not contain a more cunning, mean, selfish, foolish, disreputable old man. That blood-red hand[8] of Sir Pitt Crawley's would be in anybody's pocket except his own; and it is with grief and pain that as admirers of the British aristocracy we find ourselves obliged to admit the

5. MS adds: our heroine or the heroine of this chapter at least
6. For "the Hall" MS reads "Queen's Crawley"; the rest of this paragraph was inserted in the MS in revision.
7. MS reads: unluckily born to both: and was endowed by luck
8. Double meaning: (a) criminal hand and (b) all baronets had or could have in their coats of arms the heraldic device of the red hand of Ulster, commemorating the fact that in creating the baronetage, James I required each new baronet to pay £1,000 for the benefit of Ulster (Chambers' *Book of Days*).

existence of[9] so many ill qualities in a person whose name is in Debrett.[1]

The great cause why Mr. Crawley had such a hold over the affections of his father resulted from money arrangements. The Baronet owed his son a sum of money out of the jointure of his mother, which he did not find it convenient to pay:[2]—indeed he had an almost invincible repugnance to paying anybody, and could only be brought by force to discharge his debts. Miss Sharp calculated, for she became as we shall hear, speedily inducted into most of the secrets of the family, that the mere payment of his creditors cost the honourable baronet several hundreds yearly: but this was a delight he could not forego, he had a savage pleasure in making the poor wretches wait and in shifting from court to court and from term to term the period of satisfaction. What's the good of being in parliament, he said, if you must pay your debts?[3] Hence indeed his position as a senator was not a little useful to him.

O Vanity Fair Vanity Fair!—Here was a man, who could not spell, and did not care to read—who had the habits[4] and the cunning of a boor: whose aim in life was pettifogging: who never had a taste or emotion or enjoyment but what was sordid and foul: and yet he had rank and honours and power somehow and was a dignitary of the land and a pillar of the state. He was high sheriff[5] and rode in a golden coach, great ministers[6] and statesmen courted him: and in Vanity Fair he had a higher place than the most brilliant genius or spotless virtue.

Sir Pitt had an unmarried half-sister who inherited her mother's large fortune, and though the Baronet proposed to borrow this money of her on mortgage, Miss Crawley declined the offer and preferred the security of the funds.[7] She had signified however her intention of leaving her inheritance[8] between Sir Pitt's second son and the family at the Rectory, and had once or twice paid the debts of Rawdon Crawley, in his career at college and in the army. Miss Crawley was in consequence an object of great respect when she came to Queen's Crawley, for she had a balance at her banker's which would have made her beloved anywhere.

What a dignity it gives an old lady, that balance at the banker's! How tenderly we look at her faults if she is a relative (and may every reader have a score of such)! What a kind good-natured old creature we find her! How the junior partner of Hobbs and Dobbs leads her

9. MS reads: <confess> ↑admit the existence of↓
1. *The Peerage of England* (1802), a regularly updated guide to English noble families.
2. Sir Pitt's first wife left her own money to her husband and her son. Sir Pitt has yet to pay his son's share
3. M.P.s could not be arrested for debt.
4. MS reads: <tastes> ↑habits↓
5. A county official with a variety of duties, including presiding over elections.
6. MS reads: somehow <and quite gravely governed his country: and «despised» had the most utter & hearty contempt for all beneath him> ↑& was . . . ministers↓
7. Public funds: stock of the national debt, held as investment.
8. MS and first printing read: fortune equally

smiling to the carriage with the lozenge[9] upon it and the fat wheezy coachman! How, when she comes to pay us a visit, we generally find an opportunity to let our friends know her station in the world! We say (and with perfect truth!) I wish I had Miss MacWhirter's signature to a cheque for five thousand pounds—She wouldn't miss it, says your wife. She is my aunt, say you, in an easy careless way when your friend asks if Miss MacWhirter is any relation? Your wife is perpetually sending her little testimonies of affection, your little girls work endless worsted baskets, cushions and footstools for her. What a good fire there is in her room when she comes to pay you a visit! although your wife laces her stays without one—The house during her stay assumes a festive, neat, warm, jovial, snug appearance not visible at other seasons. You yourself, dear Sir, forget to go to sleep after dinner and find yourself all of a sudden (though you invariably lose) very fond of a rubber.[1] What good dinners you have, game every day, Malmsey-Madeira[2] and no end of fish from London. Even the servants in the kitchen share in the general prosperity, and somehow during the stay of Miss MacWhirter's fat coachman the beer is grown much stronger, and the consumption of tea and sugar in the nursery (where her maid takes her meals) is not regarded in the least. Is it so or is it not so? I appeal to the middle classes—ah Gracious powers! I wish you would send me[3] an old aunt—a maiden aunt—an aunt with a lozenge on her carriage, and a front of light coffee-coloured hair—how my children should work workbags for her, and my Julia and I would make her comfortable!—Sweet sweet vision! foolish foolish dream.[4]

9. A heraldic device indicating the nobility of the carriage owner.
1. In any game, including cards, backgammon, etc., a rubber is the determining game in a set (i.e., two of three, three of five).
2. Wine from Spain or the Azores and the Madeira Islands.
3. MS reads: <I wish I had an old aunt> ↑I wish you would send me↓
4. The tailpiece illustration is a self-portrait of Thackeray. The MS added and canceled: <Twice a year a big carriage drawn by fat horses driven by a fat coachman (the establishment of maiden-ladies is always fat) used to drive up the avenue to Queen's Crawley House in to the abode of the worthy rector of that parish.>

## *Chapter X.*

### MISS SHARP BEGINS TO MAKE FRIENDS.

ND now being received as a member of the amiable family whose portraits we have sketched in the foregoing pages, it became naturally Rebecca's duty to make herself, as she said, agreeable to her benefactors, and to gain their confidence to the utmost of her power. Who can but admire this quality of gratitude in an unprotected orphan; and, if there entered some degree of selfishness into her calculations, who can say but that her prudence was perfectly justifiable?—'I am alone in the world,' said the friendless girl—'I have nothing to look for but what my own labour can bring me; and while that little pink faced chit Amelia with not half my sense, has ten[1] thousand pounds and an establishment secure, poor Rebecca (and my figure is far better than her's) has only herself and her own wits to trust to. Well let us see if my wits cannot provide me with an honourable maintenance, and if some day or the other I cannot show Miss Amelia my real superiority over her. Not that I dislike poor Amelia, who can dislike such a harmless, good-natured creature?—only it will be a fine day when I can take my place above her in the world, as why indeed should I not?' Thus it was that our little romantic friend formed visions of the future for herself—nor must we be scandalised, that in all her castles in the air a husband was the principal inhabitant. Of what else have young ladies to think but husbands? Of what else do their dear Mammas think? 'I must be my own Mamma,' said Rebecca, not without a tingling consciousness of defeat as she thought over her little misadventure with Jos Sedley.

So she wisely determined to render her position with the Queen's Crawley family comfortable and secure: and to this end resolved to make friends of every one around her who could at all interfere with her comfort.

As my Lady Crawley was not one of these personages, and a woman, moreover, so indolent and void of character as not to be of the least consequence in her own house, Rebecca soon found that it was not at all necessary to cultivate her good will—indeed impossible to gain it. She used to talk to her pupils about their 'poor Mamma': and though she treated that lady with every demonstration of cool respect, it was to the rest of the family that she wisely directed the chief part of her attentions.

With the young people whose applause[2] she thoroughly gained: her method was pretty simple. She did not pester their young brains

1. MS reads: <two> ↑ten↓
2. MS reads: ↑good-↓will

with too much learning—but on the contrary let them have their own way in regard to educating themselves: for what instruction is more effectual than self-instruction? The eldest was rather fond of books; and as there was in the old library at Queen's Crawley a considerable provision of works of light literature of the last century both in the French and English languages (they had been purchased by the Secretary of the Tape and Sealing Wax Office at the period of his disgrace) and as nobody ever troubled the book shelves but herself Rebecca was enabled agreeably and as it were in playing to impart a great deal of instruction to Miss Rose Crawley.

She and Miss Rose thus read together many delightful French and English works—among which may be mentioned those of the learned Dr. Smollett, of the ingenious Mr. Henry Fielding, of the graceful and fantastic Monsieur Crébillon the younger whom our immortal poet Gray so much admired, and of the universal Monsieur de Voltaire.[3] Once when Mr. Crawley asked what the young people were reading—the governess replied "Smollett." "O Smollett," said Mr. Crawley, quite satisfied, "his history is more dull but by no means so dangerous as that of Mr. Hume—It is history you are reading?" "Yes," said Miss Rose, without however adding that it was the history of Mr. Humphrey Clinker. On another occasion he was rather scandalised at finding his sister with a book of French plays, but as the Governess remarked that it was for the purpose of acquiring the French idiom in conversation, he was fain to be content. Mr. Crawley as a diplomatist was exceedingly proud of his own skill in speaking the French language, (for he was of the world still)—and not a little pleased with[4] the compliments which the governess continually paid him upon his proficiency.

Miss Violet's tastes were on the contrary more rude and boisterous than those of her sister. She knew the banks whereon[5] the strawberries grew. She knew the sequestered spots where the hens layed their eggs. She could climb a tree to rob the nests of the feathered songsters of their speckled spoils. She was the favourite of her father and of the stable-men and her pleasure was to ride the young colts and to scour the plains like Camilla.[6] She was the darling and withal the terror of the cook, for she discovered the haunts of the jam-pots and would attack them when they were within her reach. She and her sister were engaged in constant battles.[7] Any of which peccadilloes if Miss Sharp discovered she did not tell them to Lady Crawley who

3. Tobias Smollett (1721–71), author of *History of England* and novels such as *The History of Humphery Clinker* (1771); Fielding (1707–54), political satirist and author of *The Adventures of Joseph Andrews* (1742) and *The History of Tom Jones* (1749); Claude de Crébillon (1707–77), racy French writer; Thomas Gray (1716–71), poet who praised the romances of Marivaux and Crébillon; François Voltaire (1694–1778), whose philosophical writings were upsetting to moral conservatives; David Hume (1711–76), mentioned in the next sentence, Scottish philosopher and historian.
4. MS reads: at
5. MS added and canceled the following allusion to *A Midsummer Night's Dream*, II.i.249: <not the wild thyme, but>
6. "Not so, when swift Camilla scours the plain, / Flies o'er the unbending corn, and skims along the main" Alexander Pope, *An Essay on Criticism* (1711). The phrase "and her pleasure . . . Camilla" is interlined in the MS.
7. This sentence was added in proof.

Miss Sharp in her School-room

would have told them to the father or, worse, to[8] Mr. Crawley, but promised not to tell if Miss Violet would be a good girl and love her governess.[9]

With Mr. Crawley Miss Sharp was respectful and obedient. She used to consult him on passages of French which she could not understand though her mother was a Frenchwoman, and which he would construe to her satisfaction: and besides giving her his aid in profane literature he was kind enough to select for her books of a more serious tendency, and address to her much of his conversation. She admired beyond measure his speech at the Quashimaboo Aid Society; took an interest in his pamphlet on malt; was often affected even to tears by his discourses of an evening, and would say—"O thank you, Sir," with a sigh and a look up to heaven, that made him occasionally condescend to shake hands with her. "Blood is everything after all," would that aristocratic religionist say—"How Miss Sharp is awakened by my words when not one of the people here is touched. I am too fine for them: too delicate: I must familiarise my style—but she understands it. Her mother was a Montmorency."

Indeed it was from this famous family, as it appears, that Miss Sharp by the mother's side was descended. Of course she did not say that her mother had been on the stage; it would have shocked Mr. Crawley's religious scruples.[1] How many noble *emigrées*[2] had the horrid revolution plunged in poverty! She had several stories about her ancestors ere she had been many months in the house: some of which Mr. Crawley happened to find in D'Hozier's dictionary[3] which was in the library and which strengthened his belief in their truth, and in the high-breeding of Rebecca. Are we to suppose from this curiosity and prying into dictionaries,—could our heroine suppose that Mr. Crawley was interested in her?—no, only in a friendly way: Have we not stated that he was attached to Lady Jane Sheepshanks?

He took Rebecca to task once or twice about the propriety of playing at back-gammon with Sir Pitt—saying that it was a godless

8. The phrase "worse, to" was added in proof.

9. MS added and canceled: <A certain housemaid has been mentioned with red cheeks and a very fine ribbon to her cap the daughter of the butler Mr. Horrocks, who took a great dislike to Miss ≪Crawley≫ ↑Sharp↓ on her first arrival at Queen's Crawley and did not scruple (for she was a free-spoken wench to whom somehow, any liberty of speech or action was permitted) to declare her animosity. Towards ≪Martha≫ ↑Sarah↓ Horrocks far from showing any sign of ill-feeling Rebeccas conduct was on the other hand, extremely conciliatory. She bore her jealousy with infinite good humour, and though by no means of a ↑lavish or what is called↓ generous disposition tried to overcome her anger with presents as well as kind words. O ≪Martha≫ ↑Sarah↓ she would say how I wish I had that lovely black hair of yours' and how these ribbons would become it! Also and at various intervals she gave ≪Martha≫ ↑Sarah↓ a worked collar, a satin slip, and a coral necklace all of wh. by the way were presents from Miss Sedley. Lady Crawley could not abide this↑, as the phrase is,↓ ≪Martha≫ ↑Sarah↓ Rebecca in her conversation with the young woman, did not give herself any trouble to disguise her contempt for her Ladyship and many a laugh did they have together mimicking her ways. It was strange that some of Rebecca's jokes regarding Lady Crawley, ↑(jokes↓ founded chiefly on the profession of the ironmonger her father) ≪were≫ and only mentioned to Martha, found their way to Sir Pitt who loved a joke and took them very good naturedly. At last one evening ≪when≫ walking in the Park alone, Miss Sharp found Miss Martha engaged in earnest conversation with Mr Stock the second keeper, and from that day the two ladies were perfect friends, or to all outward seeming appeared so to be.>

1. MS added and canceled: <Mr. Crawley hoped she had not died a Catholic>

2. French exiles.

3. Guide to the French nobility.

amusement, and that she would be much better engaged in reading 'Thrump's Legacy,' or 'The Blind Washerwoman of Moorfields,'[4] or any work of a more serious nature: but Miss Sharp said her dear mother used often to play the same game with the old Count de Trictrac and the venerable Abbé du Cornet[5] and so found an excuse for this and other worldly amusements.

But it was not only by playing at backgammon with the Baronet, that the little governess rendered herself agreeable to her employer. She found many different ways of being useful to him. She read over with indefatigable patience all those law papers with which before she came to Queen's Crawley he had promised to entertain her. She volunteered to copy many of his letters, and adroitly altered the spelling of them so as to suit the usages of the present day. She became interested in everything appertaining to the estate, to the farm, the park, the garden, and the stables: and so delightful a companion was she that the Baronet would seldom take his after breakfast walk without her (and the children of course) when she would give her advice as to the trees which were to be lopped in the shrubberies, the garden-beds to be dug, the crops which were to be cut, the horses which were to go to cart or plough. Before she had been a year at Queen's Crawley she had quite won the Baronet's confidence; and the conversation at the dinner table which before used to be held between him and Mr. Horrocks the Butler was now almost exclusively between Sir Pitt and Miss Sharp. She was almost mistress of the house when Mr. Crawley was absent, but conducted herself in her new and exalted situation with such circumspection and modesty as not to offend the authorities of the kitchen and stables, among whom her behaviour was always exceedingly modest and affable. She was quite a different person from the haughty, sly, dissatisfied little girl whom we have known previously, and this change of temper proved[6] great prudence, a sincere desire of amendment or at any rate great moral courage on her part. Whether it was the heart which dictated this new system of complaisance and humility adopted by our Rebecca is to be proved by her after history—A system of hypocrisy which lasts through whole years is one seldom satisfactorily practised by a person of one and twenty—however our readers will recollect that though young in years our heroine was old in life and experience, and we have written to no purpose if they have not discovered that she was a very clever woman.

The elder and younger son of the house of Crawley were, like the gentleman and lady in the weather-box, never at home together—they hated each other cordially—indeed Rawdon Crawley the dragoon[7] had a great contempt for the establishment altogether and seldom came thither except when his aunt paid her annual visit.

The great good quality of this old lady has been mentioned. She possessed seventy thousand pounds and had almost adopted Raw-

4. Moorfields is associated with open-air evangelical preaching and with the Moorfields eye hospital. These pamphlet titles are probably fictitious.
5. Trictrac: backgammon. Cornet: dice box.
6. MS reads: <argued> ↑proved↓
7. Cavalryman.

don. She disliked her elder nephew exceedingly, and despised him as a milksop.[8] In return he did not hesitate to state that her soul was irretrievably lost, and was of opinion that his brother's chance in the next world was not a whit better. "She is a godless woman of the world," would Mr. Crawley say. "She lives with atheists and Frenchmen. My mind shudders when I think of her awful awful situation, and that near as she is to the grave, she should be so given up to vanity, licentiousness, profaneness, and folly."

In fact the old lady declined altogether to hear his hour's lecture of an evening: and when she came to Queen's Crawley alone, he was obliged to pretermit his usual devotional exercises.

"Shut up your sarmons, Pitt, when Miss Crawley comes down," said his father. "She has written to say that she won't stand the preachifying."

"O Sir, consider the servants."

"The servants be hanged,"[9] said Sir Pitt; and his son thought even worse would happen were they[1] deprived of the benefit of his instruction.

"Why, hang it, Pitt," said the father to his remonstrance. "You wouldn't be such a flat[2] as to let three thousand a year go out of the family?"

"What is money compared to our souls, Sir?" continued Crawley.[3]

"You mean that the old lady won't leave the money to you"—and who knows but it *was* Mr. Crawley's meaning?[4]

Old Miss Crawley was certainly one of the reprobate. She had a snug little house in Park Lane,[5] and as she ate and drank a great deal too much during the season[6] in London, she went to Harrogate or Cheltenham for the summer.[7] She was the most hospitable and jovial of old vestals: and had been a beauty in her day, she said,—(all old women were beauties once we very well know.) She was a *bel esprit,*[8] and a dreadful Radical for those days. She had been in France (where Saint Just they say inspired her with an unfortunate passion) and loved ever after French novels, French cookery, and French wines. She read Voltaire and had Rousseau by heart;[9] talked very lightly about Divorce and most energetically of the rights

8. MS added and canceled: <She was a jolly old lady>
9. For "hanged" MS reads: —
1. For "even . . . they" MS reads: they would be: when
2. Simpleton.
3. MS reads: soul's fslashsalvationbslash Sir? continued Crawley <↑who knew he was not to inherit a shilling of his aunt's money↓>
4. Italics were added in proof. In the MS this last phrase is interlined over the following canceled passage: <this was «the» in fact the meaning of Mr. Crawley. No man for his own interest could accommodate himself to circumstances more. In London he would let a great man talk and laugh and be as wicked as he liked: but as he could get no good from Miss Crawley's money why compromise his conscience?. This was another reason why he should hate «Petty» ↑Rawdon↓ Crawley. He thought his brother robbed him. Elder brothers often do think so; and curse the conspiracy of the younger «Sons» ↑children↓ wh. unjustly deprives them of their fortune.>
5. Off Hyde Park.
6. In spring, wealthy Londoners came to their townhouses for rounds of dinners, parties, bazaars, races, etc. The season and the sitting of Parliament broke up together in late July.
7. Spa towns north and west of London.
8. A wit.
9. Louis de Saint-Just (1767–94) was a revolutionist guillotined at the end of the Reign of Terror. Jean Jacques Rousseau (1712–78) and Voltaire were French liberal writers.

of women. She had pictures of Mr. Fox in every room in the house,—when that Statesman was in opposition, I am not sure that she had not flung a main[1] with him—and when he came into office she took great credit for bringing over to him Sir Pitt and his colleague for Queen's Crawley[2]—although Sir Pitt would have come over himself without any trouble on the honest lady's part. It is needless to say that Sir Pitt was brought to change his views after[3] the death of the great Whig Statesman.

This worthy old lady took a fancy to Rawdon Crawley when a boy, sent him to Cambridge (in opposition to his brother at Oxford) and when the young man was requested by the authorities of the first named University to quit after a residence of two years, she bought him his commissions in the Life Guards Green.[4]

A perfect and celebrated 'blood' or dandy about town was this young officer. Boxing, rat-hunting, the fives' court, and four-in-hand[5] driving were then the fashion of our British aristocracy: and he was an Adept in all these noble sciences. And though he belonged to the household troops, who as it was their duty to rally round the Prince Regent[6] had not shown their valour in foreign service yet, Rawdon Crawley had already (apropos[7] of play of which he was immoderately fond) fought three bloody duels in which he gave ample proofs[8] of his contempt for death.

"And for what follows after death," would Mr. Crawley observe, throwing his gooseberry-coloured eyes up to the ceiling. He was always thinking of his brother's soul or of the souls of those who differed with him in opinion—it is a sort of comfort which many of the serious give themselves.

Silly romantic Miss Crawley far from being horrified at the courage of her favourite always used to pay his debts after his duels, and would not listen to a word that was whispered against his morality. "He will sow his wild-oats," she would say, "and is worth far more than that puling hypocrite of a brother of his."

1. Played at dice. Charles James Fox (1749–1806), originally a wealthy Tory, gambled away his fortune and joined the Whigs in opposing the American Revolution. He was in and out of the administration, always maintaining his reputation for dissipation, but he was indefatigable in Parliament.
2. The two members for Queen's Crawley; Sir Pitt, of course, regularly switched allegiance according to the party in power.
3. MS reads: upon
4. One of the actual historical royal escort troupes was called Royal Horse Guards Blue. First edition substituted "the Life Guards Green" in the second printing for "as Cornet and Lieutenant Crawley" in the first printing. MS reads: she <purchased his> ↑bought him his↓ commission ↑as Cornet & Lieutenant Crawley↓ <for him, and though it was war time had interest enough to keep him at home. His ≪cour≫ ↑reputation↓ for courage did not suffer for to do him justice he was as brave as a Lion, and had already, apropos of play of wh. he was immoderately fond, fought three bloody duels in wh. he gave ample proofs>.
5. Rat hunting was with feists or ferrets. Fives' court: a form of handball. Four-in-hand: a carriage with four horses.
6. The prince of Wales was named regent in 1811 when his father, George III, became irretrievably mad.
7. MS reads: *àpropos*
8. This paragraph, to this point, is interlined in the MS above the cancelation from the previous paragraph.

## *Chapter XI.*

### ARCADIAN[1] SIMPLICITY.

BESIDES these honest folks at the Hall whose simplicity[2] and sweet rural purity surely show the advantage of a country life over a town one—we must introduce the reader to their relatives and neighbours at the Rectory, Bute Crawley and his wife.[3]

The Reverend Bute Crawley was a[4] tall, stately, jolly, shovel-hatted man, far more popular in his county than the Baronet his brother. At college he pulled stroke oar[5] in the Christ-Church boat, and had thrashed all the best bruisers of the 'town.' He carried his taste for boxing and athletic exercise into private life: there was not a fight within twenty miles at which he was not present; nor a race: nor a coursing match[6] nor a regatta nor a ball nor an election nor a visitation-dinner[7] nor indeed a good dinner in the whole county but he found means to attend it. You might see his bay-mare and gig-lamps[8] a score of miles away from his Rectory House whenever there was any dinner-party at Fuddleston or at Roxby or at Wapshot Hall, or at the great lords of the county, with all of whom he was intimate. He had a fine voice, sung 'A southerly wind and a cloudy sky'[9] and gave the 'whoop' in chorus with general applause. He rode to hounds in a pepper and salt frock and was one of the best fishermen in the county.

Mrs. Crawley, the rector's wife, was a smart little body who wrote this worthy divine's sermons. Being of a domestic turn, and keeping the house a great deal with her daughters, she ruled absolutely within the rectory, wisely giving her husband full liberty without. He was welcome to come and go, and dine abroad as many days as his fancy dictated, for Mrs. Crawley was a saving woman and knew the price of port-wine.

1. Ideal pastoral existence.
2. The MS, which has no chapter title, reads: Arcadian simplicity
3. MS reads: wife, who had no little influence in the end on Miss Rebecca Sharp's history.
4. MS reads: was of a sort of ecclesiastics who are becoming daily more rare in the country, but of whom most country districts contain a few specimens still. Bute was a
5. Stern oarsman in a racing shell; sets the stroke pattern.
6. Hunt with greyhounds.
7. Ecclesiastical visit to review the diocese or parish.
8. Carriage lights.
9. Popular hunting song, "The Fox Chase" (Sutherland).

Ever since Mrs. Bute carried off the young rector of Queen's Crawley (she was of a good family, daughter of the late Lt. Colonel Hector MacTavish, and she and her mother played for Bute and won him at Harrogate) she had been a prudent and thrifty wife to him. In spite of her care however, he was always in debt. It took him at least ten years to pay off his college-bills contracted during his father's lifetime. In the year 179— when he was just clear of these incumbrances he gave the odds of 100 to 1 (in twenties) against Kangaroo who won the Derby.[1] The rector was obliged to take up the money at a ruinous interest and had been struggling ever since. His sister helped him with a hundred now and then: but, of course, his great hope was in her death—when 'hang it' (as he would say), 'Matilda *must* leave me half her money.'

So that the Baronet and his brother had every reason which two brothers possibly can have for being by the ears.[2] Sir Pitt had had the better of Bute in innumerable family transactions. Young Pitt not only did not hunt: but set up a meeting house[3] under his Uncle's very nose. Rawdon, it was known, was to come in for the bulk of Miss Crawley's property.—These money transactions, these speculations in[4] life and death—these silent battles for reversionary spoil—make brothers very loving towards each other in Vanity Fair. I, for my part, have known a five-pound note to interpose and knock up a half century's attachment between two brethren: and can't but admire as I think what a fine and durable thing Love is among worldly people.

It cannot be supposed that the arrival of such a personage as Rebecca at Queen's Crawley and her gradual establishment in the good graces of all people there could be unremarked by Mrs. Bute Crawley. Mrs. Bute who knew how many days the sirloin of beef lasted at the Hall: how much linen was got ready at the great wash: how many peaches were on the South Wall: how many doses her Ladyship took when she was ill—for such points are matters of intense interest to certain persons in the Country—Mrs. Bute, I say, could not pass over the Hall governess without making every enquiry respecting her history and character. There was always the best understanding between the servants at the Rectory and the Hall—there was always a good glass of ale in the kitchen of the former place for the Hall people whose ordinary drink was very small, (and indeed the Rector's Lady knew exactly how much malt went to every barrel of Hall beer)—ties of relationship existed between the Hall and Rectory domestics as between their masters, and through these channels each family was perfectly well acquainted with the doings of the other.—That by the way may be set down as a general remark. When you and your brother are friends his doings are indifferent to you[5]—when you have quarrelled, you know all his outgoings and incomings

1. Annual horse race at Epsom Downs; Kangaroo, not traced, is fictitious.
2. MS reads: <hating each other.> ↑being by the ears.↓
3. MS reads: <dissenting shop> ↑meeting house↓
4. First edition "in" suggests "investments"; the MS "on" suggests ruminations.
5. MS reads: <you don't care about him> ↑his doings are indifferent to you↓

as if you were his spy.[6]

Very soon then after[7] her arrival Rebecca began to take a regular place in Mrs. Crawley's Bulletin from the Hall. It was to this effect:— "The black porker's killed—weighed *x* stone—salted the sides—pig's pudding and leg of pork for dinner. Mr. Cramp from Mudbury over with Sir Pitt about putting John Blackmore in gaol—Mr. Pitt at meeting (with all the names of the people who attended) my lady as usual. The young ladies with the governess."

Then the report would come—The new governess be a rare manager—Sir Pitt be very sweet on her—Mr. Crawley too. He be reading tracts to her—"What an abandoned wretch!" said little, eager, active, black-faced Mrs. Bute Crawley.

Finally the reports were that the Governess had 'come round' everybody, wrote Sir Pitt's letters, did his business, managed his accounts—had the upper hand of the whole house, my lady, Mr. Crawley, the girls and all—At which Mrs. Crawley declared she was an artful hussey and had some dreadful designs in view.—Thus the doings at the Hall were the great food for conversation at the Rectory and Mrs. Bute's bright eyes spied out everything that took place in the enemy's camp—every thing and a great deal besides.

"MRS. BUTE CRAWLEY TO MISS PINKERTON, THE MALL, CHISWICK.

*"Rectory, Queen's Crawley, December —.*

"MY DEAR MADAM,—Although it is so *many* years since I profited by your *delightful and invaluable* instruction, yet I have *ever* retained the *fondest* and *most reverential* regard for Miss Pinkerton and *dear* Chiswick. I hope your health is *good.* The world and *the cause of education* cannot afford to lose Miss Pinkerton for *many many years.* When my friend, Lady Fuddleston, mentioned that her dear girls required an instructress (I am *too poor* to engage a governess for mine, but was I not educated at Chiswick?)—'Who,' I exclaimed, 'can we consult but the excellent, the incomparable Miss Pinkerton?'

"In a word, have you, dear Madam, any ladies on your list, whose services might be made available to my kind friend and neighbour? I assure you she will take no governess *but of your choosing.*

"My dear husband is pleased to say that he likes *everything which comes from Miss Pinkerton's School.* How I wish I could present him and my beloved girls, to the friend of my youth, and the *admired* of the great lexicographer of our country! If you ever travel into Hampshire, Mr. Crawley begs me to say, he hopes you will adorn our *rural rectory* with your presence. 'Tis the humble but happy home of

"Your affectionate

"MARTHA CRAWLEY."

"P.S. Mr. Crawley's brother the baronet, with whom we are not alas! upon those terms of *unity* in which it *becomes brethren to dwell*—has a

6. The phrase "all his . . . his spy" is interlined in the MS over canceled: <everything becomes prodigiously interesting> ; MS then added and canceled a paragraph: <Mrs. Bute Crawley very soon found that the new governess had been educated at Miss Pinkerton's Academy Chiswick Mall, where she herself had received her accomplishments: and of course she soon had a pretext for writing to her old Instructress (Sir Huddleston Fuddleston had 2>

7. MS reads: soon after

governess for his little girls, who I am told had the good fortune to be educated at Chiswick. I hear various reports of her: and as I have the tenderest interest in my dearest little nieces, whom I wish in spite of family differences to see among my own children—and as I long to be attentive to *any pupil of yours*—do, my dear Miss Pinkerton, tell me *the history* of this young lady, whom for *your sake* I am most anxious to befriend. M. C."

"MISS PINKERTON TO MRS. BUTE CRAWLEY.

"*Johnson House, Chiswick, Dec.* 18—.

"DEAR MADAM,—I have the honor to acknowledge your polite communication, to which I promptly reply. 'Tis most gratifying to one in my most arduous position to find that my maternal cares have elicited a responsive affection—and to recognise in the amiable Mrs. Bute Crawley, my excellent pupil of former years, *the sprightly and accomplished* Miss Martha MacTavish—I am happy to have under my charge now, the daughters of many of those who were your contemporaries at my establishment—what pleasure it would give me if your own beloved young ladies had need of my instructive superintendence!

"Presenting my respectful compliments to Lady Fuddleston I have the honour (epistolarily) to introduce to her Ladyship my two friends, Miss Tuffin and Miss Hawky.[8]

"Either of these young ladies is *perfectly qualified* to instruct in Greek, Latin, and the rudiments of Hebrew[9]—in mathematics and history, in Spanish, French, Italian and geography—in music, vocal and instrumental, in dancing, without the aid of a master, and in the elements of the natural sciences. In the use of the globes both are proficients. In addition to these Miss Tuffin (who is daughter of the late Reverend Thomas Tuffin, Fellow of Corpus College, Cambridge) can instruct in the Syriac language and the elements of Constitutional law. But as she is only eighteen years of age and of exceedingly pleasing personal appearance, perhaps this young lady[1] may be objectionable in Sir Huddleston Fuddleston's family.

"Miss Lætitia Hawky on the other hand is not personally well favour'd. She is twenty-nine; her face is much pitted with the small pox. She has a halt in her gait, red hair, and a trifling obliquity of vision.[2] Both ladies are endowed with *every moral and religious virtue*. Their terms of course are such as their accomplishments merit.

"With my most grateful respects to the Reverend Bute Crawley I have the honour to be

"Dear Madam,

"Your most faithful and obedient Servt,

"BARBARA PINKERTON."

"P.S. The Miss Sharp whom you mention as governess to Sir Pitt

8. MS here and ten lines later reads: Hawks
9. MS added and canceled: <acquired under her ↑late↓ father the Revd Thomas Tuffin, of Corpus College Cambridge>
1. MS added and deleted: <will be better placed in a family where there are no young men.>
2. MS reads: gait and a trifling obliguity of vision and red hair.

Crawley, Bart., M.P., was a pupil of mine—and I have nothing to say in her disfavour. Though her appearance is disagreeable, we cannot control the operations[3] of nature: and though her parents were disreputable (her father being a painter, several times bankrupt, and her mother as I have since learned with horror a dancer at the opera); yet her talents are considerable and I cannot regret that I received her *out of charity*. My dread is, lest the principles of the mother who was represented to me as a French Countess forced to emigrate in the late revolutionary horrors, but who as I have since found was a person of the *very lowest order and morals*—should at any time prove to be *hereditary* in the unhappy young woman whom I took as *an outcast*. But her principles have *hitherto* been correct (I believe): and I am sure nothing will occur to injure them in the elegant and refined circle of the eminent Sir Pitt Crawley."

"MISS REBECCA SHARP TO MISS AMELIA SEDLEY.

"I have not written to my beloved Amelia for these many weeks[4] past, for what news was there to tell of the sayings and doings at Humdrum Hall as I have christened it—and what do you care whether the turnip crop is good or bad, whether the fat pig weighed thirteen stone or fourteen,[5] and whether the beasts thrive well upon mangel-wurzel?[6] Every day since I last wrote has been like its neighbour. Before[7] breakfast a walk with Sir Pitt and his spud;[8] after breakfast, studies (such as they are) in the school-room; after school-room, reading and writing about lawyers, leases, coal mines, canals, with Sir Pitt (whose Secretary I am become); after dinner Mr. Crawley's discourses or the baronet's backgammon: during both of which amusements my lady looks on with equal placidity. She has become rather more interesting by being ailing of late which has brought a new visitor to the Hall in the person of a young doctor. Well, my dear, young women need never despair. The young Doctor gave a certain friend of yours to understand that if she chose to be Mrs. Glauber,[9] she was welcome to ornament the Surgery!—I told his impudence that the gilt pestle and mortar was quite ornament enough—as if *I* was born indeed to be a Country Surgeon's wife! Mr. Glauber went home seriously indisposed at his rebuff, took a cooling draught, and is now quite cured. Sir Pitt applauded my resolution highly, he would be sorry to lose his little Secretary I think, and I believe the old wretch likes me as much as it is in his nature to like any one. Marry indeed!—and with a country apothecary, after—no no, one cannot so soon forget old associations, about which I will talk no more—Let us return to Humdrum Hall.

3. For "disagreeable . . . operations" the MS originally read: unfavorable to her we cannot <prevent the varieties> ↑rebuke the↓ works
4. MS reads: <months> ↑weeks↓
5. A stone is fourteen pounds.
6. A hybrid beet or potato.
7. MS reads: <After> ↑Before↓
8. Digging or weeding implement.
9. Glauber's salts was a popular patent medicine.

"For some time past it is Humdrum Hall no longer. My dear Miss Crawley has arrived with her fat horses, fat servants, fat spaniel. The great rich Miss Crawley with seventy thousand pounds in the five per cents whom, or I had better say *which,* her two brothers adore. She looks very apoplectic, the dear soul, no wonder her brothers are anxious about her.[1] You should see them struggling to settle her cushions or to hand her coffee!—'When I come into the country,' she says (for she has a great deal of humour), 'I leave my toady, Miss Briggs, at home—My brothers are my toadies here, my dear'—and a pretty pair they are![2]

"When she comes into the county our Hall is thrown open, and for a month at least you would fancy old Sir Walpole was come to life again. We have dinner parties and drive out in the coach and four—the footmen put on their newest canary-coloured liveries, we drink Claret and Champagne as if we were accustomed to it every day. We have wax candles in the Schoolroom and fires to warm ourselves with. Lady Crawley is made to put on the brightest pea-green in her wardrobe, and my pupils leave off their thick shoes and tight old tartan pelisses[3] and wear silk stockings and muslin frocks[4] as fashionable baronets' daughters should. Rose came in yesterday in a sad plight. The Wiltshire sow (an enormous pet of hers) ran her down and destroyed a most lovely flowered lilac silk dress by dancing over it,[5]—had this happened a week ago—Sir Pitt would have sworn frightfully, have boxed the poor wretch's ears, and put her upon bread and water for a month—All he said was, 'I'll zerve you out, Miss, when your Aunt's gone,' and laughed off the accident as quite trivial. Let us hope his wrath will have passed away before Miss Crawley's departure. I hope so for Miss Rose's sake I am sure. What a charming reconciler and peace maker money is!

"Another admirable effect of Miss Crawley and her seventy thousand pounds is to be seen in the conduct of the two brothers Crawley. I mean the baronet and the Rector, not *our* brothers—but the former who hate each other all the year round become quite loving at Xmas.[6] I wrote to you last year how the abominable horse-racing[7] Rector was in the habit of preaching clumsy sermons at us at church, and how Sir Pitt snored in answer—when Miss Crawley arrives there is no such thing as quarreling heard of—The Hall visits the rectory and *vice-versâ.* The parson and the Baronet talk about the pigs and the poachers and the County-business in the most affable manner,[8] and without quarreling in their cups I believe—indeed Miss Crawley won't hear of their quarreling and vows that she will leave her money

1. The remainder of this paragraph is interlined in the MS.
2. First edition moves the closing single quotation mark from "dear" to "are!" changing the speaker of the last remark.
3. Mantles or shifts worn by children over their other clothes.
4. MS reads: silk gowns
5. The phrase "by dancing over it" is interlined in the MS.
6. First edition expands to "Christmas," but this abbreviation may be Becky's in her letter to Amelia, rather than Thackeray's in the manuscript for the compositor.
7. The adjectives are interlined in the MS, as is "clumsy" in the next line.
8. MS added and canceled: <both are fond of getting tipsy>

Miss Crawley's affectionate relatives

to the Shropshire Crawleys if they offend her—If they were clever people, those Shropshire Crawleys, they might have it all I think—but the Shropshire Crawley is a clergyman like his Hampshire cousin, and mortally offended Miss Crawley (who had fled thither in a fit of rage against her impracticable brethren) by some straight laced notions of morality. He would have prayers in the house I believe.

"Our sermon-books are shut up when Miss Crawley arrives; and Mr. Pitt whom she abominates finds it convenient to go to town—On the other hand the young dandy, *'blood'* I believe is the term, Captain Crawley makes his appearance, and I suppose you would like to know what sort of a person he is.

"Well—he is a very large young dandy. He is six feet high and speaks with a great voice: and swears a great deal—and orders about the servants who all adore him nevertheless; for he is very generous of his money; and the domestics will do anything for him—Last week the keepers almost killed a bailiff[9] and his man who came down from London to arrest the Captain, and who were found lurking about the Park Wall. They beat them, ducked them, and were going to shoot them for poachers but the Baronet interfered.

"The Captain has a hearty contempt for his father, I can see, and calls him an old *put,* an old *snob,* an old *chaw-bacon*[1] and numberless other pretty names. He has a *dreadful reputation* among the ladies.[2] He brings his hunters[3] home with him, lives with the Squires of the County, asks whom he pleases to dinner, and Sir Pitt dares not say no: for fear of offending Miss Crawley and missing his legacy when she dies of her apoplexy. Shall I tell you a compliment the Captain paid me? I must, it is so pretty. One evening we actually had a dance. There was Sir Huddleston Fuddleston and his family, Sir Giles Wapshot and his young ladies and I don't know how many more—Well I heard him say—'By Jove she's a neat little filly'—meaning your humble servant—and he did me the honour to dance two country-dances with me. He gets on pretty gaily with the young Squires with whom he drinks, bets, rides and talks about hunting and shooting—but he says the country girls are *bores*—indeed I don't think he is far wrong. You should see the contempt with which they look down on poor me! When they dance I sit and play the piano very demurely—but the other night coming in rather flushed from the dining-room and seeing me employed in this way, he swore out loud that I was the best dancer in the room and took a great oath that he would have the fiddlers from Mudbury.

"'I'll go and play a country-dance,' said Mrs. Bute Crawley, very readily (she is a little black-faced old woman in a turban, rather crooked, and with very twinkling eyes)—and after the Captain and your poor little Rebecca had performed a dance together, do[4] you

9. Arresting officer; sheriff's assistant.
1. A blockhead, a vulgar person, a country bumpkin. Thackeray's very different use of the word "snob" (in *The Book of Snobs*) changed it to its present meaning, "stuck-up."
2. This sentence is interlined in the MS.
3. Dogs, horses.
4. "After the Captain . . . together, do" is interlined in the MS with an indication to add the woodcut.

know she actually did me the honour to compliment me upon

my steps! Such a thing was never heard of before—the proud Mrs. Bute Crawley, first cousin to the Earl of Tiptoff, who won't condescend to visit Lady Crawley except when her sister is in the County—Poor Lady Crawley! during most part of these gaieties she is upstairs taking pills.

"Mrs. Bute has all of a sudden taken a great fancy to me. 'My dear Miss Sharp,' she says, 'why not bring over your girls to the Rectory?—their cousins will be so happy to see them'—I know what she means. Signor Clementi did not teach us the piano for nothing—at which price Mrs. Bute hopes to get a professor for her children. I can see through her schemes, as though she told them to me: but I shall go, as I am determined to make myself agreeable—is it not a poor governess's duty who has not a friend or protector in the world. The Rector's wife paid me a score of compliments about the progress my pupils made, and thought no doubt to touch my heart—poor, simple, country soul—as if I cared a fig about my pupils!

"Your India muslin and your pink silk, dearest Amelia, are said to become me very well—They are a good deal worn now, you know we poor girls can't afford *des fraîches toilettes*.[5] Happy, happy you, who

5. New outfits.

have but to drive to St. James's Street[6] and a dear mother who will give you anything you ask. Farewell, dearest girl.

"Your affectionate

"REBECCA.

"P.S. I wish you could have seen the faces of the Miss Blackbrooks (Admiral Blackbrook's daughters, my dear): fine young ladies, with dresses from London, when Captain Rawdon selected poor me for a partner!

"Here they are. 'Tis the very image of them. Adieu, adieu!"[7]

When Mrs. Bute Crawley (whose artifices our ingenious Rebecca had so soon discovered) had procured from Miss Sharp the promise of a visit, she induced the all-powerful Miss Crawley to make the necessary application to Sir Pitt; and the good-natured old lady who loved to be gay herself, as to see[8] every one gay and happy round about her, was quite charmed and ready to establish a reconciliation and intimacy between her two brothers. It was therefore agreed that

6. Fasionable shops were to be found on this street in west-central London.
7. The entire postscript was added at proof stage and is not in the manuscript. The effect was to extend the installment to the required thirty-two-page length. The drawing and the second paragraph were dropped from the unillustrated revised edition of 1853.
8. In the MS notice that the word "to" was originally on the line and must serve both before and after the insertion. There was no caret to indicate where the insertion was to go. MS reads: loved to ↑be gay herself, as↓ see

the young people of both families should visit each other frequently for the future, and the friendship of course lasted as long as the jovial old mediatrix was there to keep the peace.

"Why did you ask that scoundrel, Rawdon Crawley, to dine," said the Rector to his lady as they were walking home through the park. "*I* don't want the fellow. He looks down upon us country people as so many blackamoors[9]—He's never content unless he gets my yellow-sealed wine which costs me ten shillings a bottle, hang him!—besides he's such an infernal character—he's a gambler, he's a drunkard, he's a profligate in every way. He's killed[1] a man in a duel—he's over head and ears in debt, and he's robbed me and mine of the best part of Miss Crawley's fortune. Waxy says she has him down in her will for fifty thousand—him"—here the Rector shook his fist at the moon with something very like an oath, and added in a melancholious tone[2]—"and there won't be above thirty to divide."

"I think she's going," said the Rector's wife. "She was very red in the face when we left dinner. I was obliged to unlace her."

"She drank seven glasses of Champagne," said the Reverend Gentleman in a low voice—"and filthy Champagne it is too that my brother poisons us with—but you women never know what's what."

"We know nothing," said Mrs. Bute Crawley.

"She drank cherry-brandy after dinner," continued his Reverence, "and took Curaçao[3] with her coffee. *I* wouldn't take a glass for a five pound note: it kills me with heart burn. She can't stand it, Mrs. Crawley, she must go—flesh and blood won't bear it, and I lay five to two Matilda drops in a year."

Indulging in these solemn speculations, and thinking about his debts, and his son Jim at college, and Frank at Woolwich,[4] and the four girls who were no beauties poor things and would not have a penny but what they got from the aunt's expected legacy—the Rector and his lady walked on for a while.

"Pitt can't be such an infernal villain as to sell the reversion of the living,[5] and that Methodist milksop of an eldest[6] son looks to parliament," continued Mr. Crawley after a pause.

"Sir Pitt Crawley will do anything," said the Rector's wife. "We must get Miss Crawley to make him promise it to James."

"Pitt will promise any thing," replied the brother. "He promised he'd pay my college bills when my father died—he promised he'd build the new wing to the rectory—he promised he'd let me have Jibb's field and the six-acre meadow—and much he executed his promises! And it's to this man's son, this scoundrel, gambler, swindler, murderer of a Rawdon Crawley that Matilda leaves the bulk of

9. Negroes.
1. Revised edition reads: shot
2. The phrase "him—here . . . tone" is interlined in the MS.
3. Sweet, orange-flavored liqueur. MS reads: <Marachino> ↑Curacao↓
4. I.e., at a royal military academy east of London. MS reads: <the naval school ↑Sandwich↓> ↑Woolwich↓
5. The right of nominating the successor on the death of a beneficed clergyman.
6. MS reads: oldest

her money. I say it's unchristian—by Jove it is. The infamous dog has got every vice except hypocrisy and that belongs to his brother."

"Hush, my dearest love we're in Sir Pitt's grounds," interposed his wife.

"I say he *has* got every vice, Mrs. Crawley, don't, Ma'am, bully *me*. Didn't he shoot Captain Firebrace?[7] Didn't he rob young Lord Dovedale at the Cocoa-Tree[8]—didn't he cross the fight between Bill Soames and the Cheshire Trump,[9] by which I lost forty pound? You know he did—and as for the women why you heard[1] that before me in my own magistrate's room—"[2]

"For Heaven's sake, Mr. Crawley," said the lady, "spare me the details."[3]

"And you ask this villain into your house," continued the exasperated rector—"you the mother of a young family—the wife of a Clergyman of the Church of England by Jove—"

"Bute Crawley, you are a fool," said the Rector's wife, scornfully.

"Well Ma'am, fool or not—and I don't say, Martha, I'm so clever as *you* are, I never did. But I won't meet Rawdon Crawley that's flat. I'll go over, that I will, to Huddleston. And I'll see his black greyhound, Mrs. Crawley—and I'll run Lancelot against him for fifty, by Jove I will, or against any dog in England. But I won't meet that beast Rawdon Crawley."

"Mr. Crawley, you are intoxicated as usual," replied his wife: and the next morning when the Rector woke and called for small beer, she put him in mind of his promise to visit Sir Huddleston Fuddleston, and on Saturday and as he knew he should have a *'wet night'*[4] it was agreed that he might gallop back again in time for church on Sunday morning. Thus it will be seen that the parishioners of Crawley were equally happy in their Squire, and in their rector.

Miss Crawley had not long been established at the Hall, before Rebecca's fascinations had won the heart of that good-natured London rake, as they had of the country innocents whom we have been describing. Taking her accustomed drive one day she thought fit to order that 'that little governess' should accompany her to Mudbury: before they had returned Rebecca had made a conquest of her; having made her laugh four times and amused her during the whole of the little journey.

"Not let Miss Sharp dine at table!" said she to Sir Pitt who had arranged a dinner of ceremony and asked all the neighbouring baronets. "My dear creature, do you suppose I can talk about the nursery with Lady Fuddleston, or discuss justices' business with that goose, old Sir Giles Wapshot?—I insist upon Miss Sharp appearing.

7. Revised edition reads: Marker?
8. Cocoa Tree Chocolate House, turned private club and gambling dive, was in St. James's Street till 1835.
9. Not traced.
1. MS reads: know
2. MS reads: room <Susan Rowdy and Betsy Tufnots swore x x x>↑—↓
3. MS reads: details <of Susan Rowdy>.
4. The phrase "on Saturday . . . *night*'" is interlined in the MS.

Let Lady Crawley remain up stairs if there is no room—but little Miss Sharp, why she's the only person fit to talk to in the County!"

Of course after such a peremptory order as this, Miss Sharp the governess received commands to dine with the illustrious company below stairs: and when Sir Huddleston had with great pomp and ceremony handed Miss Crawley into dinner and was preparing 'to take his place by her side,' the old lady cried out in a shrill voice—"Becky Sharp! Miss Sharp! come you and sit by me and amuse me, and let Sir Huddleston sit by Lady Wapshot."

When the parties were over, and the carriages had rolled away, the insatiable Miss Crawley would say, "Come to my dressing room, Becky, and let us abuse the company,"—which, between them this pair of friends did perfectly—Old Sir Huddleston wheezed a great deal at dinner: Sir Giles Wapshot had a particularly noisy manner of imbibing his soup, and her Ladyship a wink of the left eye; all of which Becky caricatured to admiration; as well as the particulars of the night's conversation—the politics; the war;[5] the quarter-sessions;[6] the famous run with the H. H.,[7] and those heavy and dreary themes about which country gentlemen converse. As for the Misses Wapshot's toilettes and Lady Fuddleston's famous yellow hat, Miss Sharp tore them to tatters,[8] to the infinite amusement of her audience.

"My dear, you are a perfect *trouvaille,*"[9] Miss Crawley would say. "I wish you could come to me in London but I couldn't make a butt of you as I do of poor Briggs—no no you little sly creature; you are too clever—Isn't she, Firkin?"[1]

Mrs. Firkin (who was dressing the very small remnant of hair which remained on Miss Crawley's pate)—flung up her head and said, "I think Miss *is* very clever," with the most killing sarcastic air. In fact Mrs. Firkin had that natural jealousy which is one of the main principles of every honest woman.

After rebuffing Sir Huddleston Fuddleston, Miss Crawley ordered that Rawdon Crawley should lead her into dinner every day, and that Becky should follow with her cushion—or else she would have Becky's arm and Rawdon with the pillow—"We must sit together," she said. "We're the only three Christians in the county, my love"—in which case it must be confessed that religion[2] was at a very low ebb in the County of Hants.

Besides being such a fine religionist, Miss Crawley was as we have said an ultra-liberal in opinions and always took occasion to express these in the most candid manner.

"What is birth, my dear," she would say to Rebecca—"Look at my brother Pitt; look at the Huddlestons who have been here since

5. The words "the war;" are interlined in the MS.
6. Local court held quarterly by the justice of the peace.
7. Hampshire hounds.
8. MS reads: <off their backs> ↑to tatters,↓
9. Lucky find.
1. A firkin is a small cask holding fish, liquids, butter, etc., commonly applied humorously to persons.
2. MS read: <Christi> religion

Henry II,[3] look at poor Bute at the parsonage—are any one of them equal to you in intelligence or breeding? Equal to *you*—they are not even equal to poor dear Briggs, my companion, or Bowls, my butler. You, my love, are a little paragon—positively a little jewel—You have more brains than half the shire—If merit had its reward you ought to be a Duchess—no, there ought to be no Duchesses at all—but you ought to have no superior and I consider you, my love, as my equal in every respect; and—will you put some coals on the fire, my dear; and will you unpick this dress of mine and alter it, you who can do it so well." So this old philanthropist used to make her equal run of her errands, execute her millinery, and read her to sleep with French novels every night.

At this time as some old old readers may recollect the genteel world had been thrown into a considerable state of excitement, by two events, which as the papers say might give employment to gentlemen[4] of the long robe. Ensign Shafton had run away with Lady Barbara Fitzurse, the Earl of Bruin's daughter and heiress, and poor Vere Vane, a gentleman who up to forty had maintained a most respectable character and reared a numerous family, suddenly and outrageously left his home for the sake of Mrs. Rougemont,[5] the actress, who was sixty five years of age.

"That was the most beautiful part of dear Lord Nelson's character," Miss Crawley said. "He went to the deuce for a woman.[6] There *must* be good in a man who will do that. I adore all imprudent matches. What I like best is for a nobleman to marry a miller's daughter as Lord Flowerdale did—it makes all the women so angry—I wish some great man would run away[7] with *you*, my dear; I'm sure you're pretty enough."

"Two post boys[8]—o, it would be delightful!" Rebecca owned.

"And what I like next best is for a poor fellow to run away with a rich girl. I have set my heart on Rawdon running away with some one."

"A rich some one, or a poor some one?"

"Why you goose; Rawdon has not a shilling but what I give him. He is *criblé de dettes;*[9] he must repair his fortunes and succeed in the world."

"Is he very clever?" Rebecca asked.

"Clever, my love? not an idea in the world beyond his horses and his regiment and his hunting and his play: but he must succeed, he's so delightfully wicked. Don't you know he has killed[1] a man: and shot an injured father through the hat only? He's adored in his

3. Ruled 1154–89.
4. Revised edition reads: the gentlemen
5. Shafton—Rougemont: all fictitious characters. MS originally read: suddenly left home and carried off Mrs. Rougemont
6. Horatio Nelson (1785–1805), naval hero of Trafalgar, had a notorious affair with Lady Emma Hamilton.
7. MS reads: <marry> ↑run away↓
8. Normally a carriage and four horses has one post boy riding a lead horse; two post boys suggests a grander arrangement.
9. Riddled with debts.
1. Revised edition reads: hit

regiment, and all the young men at Wattier's and the Cocoa Tree swear by him.[2]

When Miss Rebecca Sharp wrote to her beloved friend the account of the little ball at Queen's Crawley; and the manner in which for the first time Captain Crawley had distinguished her; she did not, strange to relate, give an altogether accurate account of the transaction. The Captain had distinguished her a great number of times before. The Captain had met her in a half score of walks. The Captain had lighted upon her in a half hundred of corridors and passages. The Captain had hung over her piano twenty times of an evening as she sang—(My Lady was now up stairs, being ill, and nobody heeded her).[3] The Captain had written her notes (the best that the great blundering dragoon could devise[4] and spell, but dullness gets on as well as any other quality with women). But when he put the first of the notes into the leaves of the song she was singing—the little governess rising and looking him steadily in the face, took up the triangular missive daintily and waved it about as if it were a cocked hat and she advancing to the enemy—and popped the note into the fire, and made him a very low curtsey and went back to her place, and began to sing away again more merrily than ever.

"What's that?" said Miss Crawley, interrupted in her after-dinner doze by the stoppage of the music.

"It's a false note," Miss Sharp said with a laugh: and Rawdon Crawley fumed[5] with rage and mortification.

Seeing the evident partiality of Miss Crawley for the new governess; how good it was of Mrs. Bute Crawley not to be jealous; and to welcome the young lady to the Rectory—and not only her but Rawdon Crawley, her husband's rival in the Old Maid's five per cents!—They became very fond of each other's society, Mrs. Crawley and her Nephew. He gave up hunting: he declined entertainments at Fuddleston: he would not dine with the Mess of the Depot at Mudbury: his great pleasure was to stroll over to Crawley Parsonage—whither Miss Crawley came too, and as their Mamma was ill, why not the children with Miss Sharp? So the children (little dears!) came with Miss Sharp; and of an evening some of the party would walk back together.[6] Not Miss Crawley—she preferred

2. If any body considers this is an overdrawn picture of a noble and influential class of persons—I refer them to contemporaneous histories such as Byron's Memoirs for instance —in which popular illustration of Vanity Fair, you have the morals of Richelieu and the elegance of Dutch Sam (Thackeray's note).

   Wattier's and the Cocoa Tree were private clubs well-known for good food and gambling. Thackeray considered Lord Byron (1788–1824) immoral though brilliant. The reference is to *The Letters and Journals of Lord Byron, with Notices of his Life by Thomas Moore* (1832–33). Cardinal Richelieu (1585–1642) was scrupleless and effective in serving Louis XIII of France. Dutch Sam (actually Samuel Elias) was a boxer active in the ring from 1801 to 1814—see also chapter XXXIV. Thackeray's footnote was deleted in the revised edition.
3. Parenthetical remark is interlined in the MS.
4. MS reads: <coin> ↑devise↓
5. MS reads: <burst> ↑fumed↓
6. MS added and canceled: <[New paragraph] Take care of that scoundrel my Son—whispered Sir Pitt, in his elegant way, to his governess. Take care on um, you little zilly thing. [New paragraph] I can «defend myself» ↑take care a↓ against the son & the father Sir, said she with a toss of her head. And so she could, that's the truth.>

her carriage—but the walk over the Rectory fields, and in at the little park wicket, and through the dark plantation, and up the checkered avenue to Queen's Crawley was charming in the moonlight[7] to two such lovers of the picturesque as the Captain and Miss Rebecca.

"O those stars those stars!" Miss Rebecca would say turning her twinkling green eyes up towards them. "I feel myself almost a spirit when I gaze upon them—"

"O—ah—Gad—yes so do I exactly, Miss Sharp," the other enthusiast replied. "You don't mind my cigar do you, Miss Sharp?" Miss Sharp loved the smell of[8] a cigar out of doors beyond everything in the world—and she just tasted one too, in the prettiest way possible, and gave a little puff, and a little scream, and a little giggle, and restored the delicacy to the Captain; who twirled his moustache and straightway puffed it into a blaze that glowed quite red in the dark plantations—and swore—"Jove—aw—Gad—aw—it's the finest segaw I ever smoked in the wald aw"—For his intellect and conversation were alike brilliant and becoming to a heavy young dragoon.

Old Sir Pitt who was taking his pipe and beer and talking to John Horrocks about a 'ship' that was to be killed, espied the pair so occupied from his study window, and with dreadful oaths swore that if it wasn't for Miss Crawley, he'd take Rawdon and bundle un out of doors like a rogue as he was.

"He *be* a bad'n sure enough," Mr. Horrocks remarked—"and his man Flethers is wuss, and have made such a row in the Housekeeper's Room about the dinners and hale, as no lord would make—but—I think Miss Sharp's a match for'n, Sir Pitt," he added, after a pause.

And so in truth she was—for father and son too.

7. The passage "Not Miss Crawley . . . the moonlight" is interlined in the MS.
8. The phrase "the smell of" is interlined in the MS.

*Number 4* *April 1847*

## *Chapter XII.*

### QUITE A SENTIMENTAL CHAPTER.

E must now take leave of Arcadia, and those amiable people practising the rural virtues there, and travel back to London to enquire what has become of[1] Miss Amelia.

'We don't care a fig for her,' writes some unknown correspondent with a pretty little hand-writing and a pink seal to her note—'she is *fade* and insipid,' and adds some more kind remarks in this strain which I should never have repeated at all, but that they are in truth prodigiously complimentary to the young lady whom they concern.

Has the beloved reader in his experience of society never heard similar remarks by good-natured female friends, who always wonder what you *can* see in Miss Smith that is so fascinating; or what *could* induce Major Jones to propose for that silly insignificant simpering Miss Thompson, who has nothing but her wax-doll face to recommend her? What is there in a pair of pink cheeks and blue eyes forsooth? these dear Moralists ask, and hint wisely that the gifts of genius, the accomplishments of the mind, the mastery of Mangnall's questions and a ladylike knowledge of botany and geology,[2] the knack[3] of making poetry, the power[4] of rattling sonatas in the Herz manner, and so forth are far more valuable endowments for a female, than those fugitive charms which a few years will inevitably tarnish.[5] It is quite edifying to hear women speculate upon the worthlessness and the duration of beauty.

But though virtue is a much finer thing; and those hapless creatures who suffer under the misfortune of good looks ought to be continually put in mind of the fate which awaits them; and though very likely the Heroic Female character which ladies admire is a more glorious and beautiful object than the kind, fresh, smiling, artless, tender little domestic goddess, whom men are inclined to worship—yet the latter and inferior sort of women must have this consolation—that the men *do* admire them after all:—and—that, in spite of all our

1. These opening lines are interlined in the MS above two canceled openings: <And now, while these things are befalling in the country, we must travel back to London by «the» Sir Pitts Coach, or that still more rapid conveyance the Fancy, and have a little Chapter about> [New paragraph] ↑<It becomes our duty now to quit>
2. The phrases "the mastery . . . geology" and, later in the sentence, "in the Herz manner" are interlined in the MS.
3. MS reads: power ] First edition, first printing reads: gift ] Second printing reads: knack
4. MS reads: performance
5. Richmal Mangnall, *Historical and Miscellaneous Questions for Young People* (1800); Henri Herz (1806–88), minor composer and author of instructional books on the piano.

kind friends' warnings and protests, we go on in our desperate error and folly, and shall to the end of the chapter. Indeed for my own part though I have been repeatedly told by persons for whom I have the greatest respect that Miss Brown is an insignificant chit[6] and Mrs. White has nothing but her *petit minois chiffonné*,[7] and Mrs. Black has not a word to say for herself,—yet I know that I have had the most delightful conversations with Mrs. Black (of course, my dear Madam, they are inviolable): I see all the men in a cluster round Mrs. White's chair;—all the young fellows battling to dance with Miss Brown—and so I am tempted to think that to be despised by her sex is a very great compliment to a woman.

The young ladies in Amelia's society did this for her very satisfactorily. For instance there was scarcely any point upon which the Miss Osbornes, George's sisters, and the Mesdemoiselles Dobbin agreed so well as in their estimate of her very trifling[8] merits: and their wonder that their brothers could find any charms in her. "We are kind to her," the Misses Osborne said—a pair of fine black-browed young ladies who had had the best of governesses, masters, and milliners; and they treated her with such extreme kindness and condescension, and patronised her so insufferably, that the poor little thing *was* in fact perfectly dumb in their presence, and to all outward appearance as stupid as they thought her. She made efforts to like them as in duty bound, and as sisters of her future husband. She passed 'long mornings' with them—the most dreary and serious of forenoons. She drove out solemnly in their great family coach with them and Miss Wirt their governess, that raw-boned Vestal.[9] They took her to the Ancient Concerts by way of a treat, and to the Oratorio; and to St. Paul's to see the Charity-Children[1]—where, in such terror was she of her friends, she almost did not dare be affected by the hymn the children sang. Their house was comfortable: their Papa's table rich and handsome: their society solemn and genteel: their self-respect prodigious. They had the best pew at the Foundling:[2] all their habits were pompous and orderly: and all their amusements intolerably dull and decorous. After every one of her visits (and o how glad she was when they were over!) Miss Osborne and Miss Maria Osborne and Miss Wirt the Vestal Governess, asked each other with increased wonder, 'What *could* George find in that creature?'

How is this? some carping reader exclaims—How is it that Amelia who had such a number of friends at school, and was so beloved there comes out into the world and is spurned by her discriminating sex?[3]

6. MS added and canceled: <and Mrs. Black has no brains>
7. Pretty little odd face.
8. MS reads: <notions regarding her> ↑estimate of her very trifling↓
9. Confirmed spinster; in Roman culture, a virgin tending the fire in the Temple of Vesta.
1. The children, as many as 8,000 sometimes, from London's charity schools sang an oratorio (semidramatic musical performance) annually in St. Paul's Cathedral throughout the eighteenth and nineteenth centuries.
2. The chapel at the Foundling Hospital, an orphanage, held regular services attended by fashionable supporters. George Frederick Handel (1685–1759) performed there to raise money for the project. His oratorios would still have been performed there in the Osbornes' days.
3. MS reads: <makes no effect there> ↑is <quite friendless> spurned by her discriminating sex?"↓

My dear Sir, there were no men at Miss Pinkerton's establishment except the old dancing-master: and you would not have had the girls fall out about *him*? When George, their handsome brother, ran off directly after breakfast, and dined from home half a dozen times a week—no wonder the neglected sisters felt a little vexation. When young Bullock (of the firm of Hulker, Bullock & Co., Bankers, Lombard St.[4]) who had been making up to Miss Maria the last two seasons, actually asked Amelia to dance the Cotillon—could you expect that the former young lady should be pleased?—And yet she said she was, like an artless forgiving creature: "I'm so delighted you like dear Amelia," she said quite eagerly to Mr. Bullock after the dance—"She's engaged to my brother George—there's not much in her, but she's the best-natured and[5] most unaffected young creature: at home we're all *so* fond of her." Dear girl! Who can calculate the depth of affection expressed in that enthusiastic *so*?

Miss Wirt and these two affectionate young women so earnestly and frequently impressed upon George Osborne's mind the enormity of the sacrifice he was making, and his romantic generosity in throwing himself away upon Amelia, that I'm not sure but that he really thought he was one of the most deserving characters in the British army, and gave himself up to be loved with a good deal of easy resignation.

Somehow although he left home every morning as was stated and dined abroad six days in the week when his sisters believed the infatuated youth to be at Miss Sedley's apron-strings: he was *not* always with Amelia whilst the world supposed him at her feet. Certain it is that on more occasions than one when[6] Captain Dobbin called to look for his friend, Miss Osborne (who was very attentive to the Captain and anxious to hear his military stories and to know about the health of his dear Mamma)—Miss Osborne would laughingly point to the opposite side of the square and say, "O, you must go to the Sedleys' to ask for George, *we* never see him from morning till night." At which kind of speech the Captain would laugh in rather an absurd constrained manner, and turn off the conversation like a consummate man of the world, to some topic of general interest such as the Opera, the Prince's last ball at Carlton House,[7] or the weather—that blessing to society.

"What an innocent it is, that pet of yours," Miss Maria would then say to Miss Jane upon the Captain's departure—"Did you see how he blushed at the mention of poor George on duty?"

"It's a pity Frederic Bullock hadn't some of his modesty, Maria," replies the elder sister, with a toss of her head.[8]

"Modesty!—Awkwardness you mean, Jane. I don't want Frederic to trample a hole in my muslin frock, as Captain Dobbin did

4. London's banking center.
5. The word "and" is not in the MS.
6. MS adds: the faithful
7. One of the prince regent's homes where he entertained, but which he abandoned when he became king.
8. The phrase "replies . . . head" is interlined in the MS. So is "Modesty!" in the next line.

in your's[9] at Mrs. Perkins'."

"In *your* frock, he he! How could he, wasn't he dancing with Amelia?"

The fact is when Captain Dobbin blushed so and looked so awkward he remembered a circumstance of which he did not think it was necessary to inform the[1] young ladies—viz. that he had been calling at Mr. Sedley's house already—on the pretense of seeing George of course—and George wasn't there—only poor little Amelia with rather a sad wistful face seated near the drawing-room window, who after some very trifling stupid talk—ventured to ask, Was there any truth in the report that the regiment was soon to be ordered abroad and—had Captain Dobbin seen Mr. Osborne that day?

The regiment was not ordered abroad as yet—and Captain Dobbin had not seen George—"He was with his sisters most likely," the Captain said. Should he go and fetch the truant? So she gave him her hand kindly and gratefully: and he crossed the Square; and she waited and waited, but George never came.

Poor little tender heart! and so it goes on hoping and beating and longing and trusting. You see it is[2] not much of a life to describe. There is[3] not much of what you call incident in it. Only one feeling all day, When will he come? only one thought to sleep and wake upon. I believe George was playing billiards with Captain Cannon in Swallow Street at the time when Amelia was asking Captain Dobbin about him:[4]—for he[5] was a jolly sociable fellow and excelled in all games of skill.

Once after three days of absence Miss Amelia put on her bonnet and actually invaded the Osborne house. "What, leave our brother to come to us?" said the young ladies. "Have you had a quarrel, Amelia? Do tell us!"—No indeed there had been no quarrel; "who *could* quarrel with him," says she, with her eyes filled with tears. She only came over to—to see her dear friends. They had not met for so long.—And this day she was so perfectly stupid and awkward that the Miss Osbornes and their governess, who stared after her as she went sadly away wondered more than ever what George could see in poor little Amelia.

Of course they did. How was she to bare that timid little heart for the inspection of those young ladies with their bold black eyes?[6] It was best that it should shrink and hide itself. I know the Miss Osbornes were excellent critics of a cashmere shawl or a pink satin slip: and when Miss Turner had her's died purple and made into a spencer; and when Miss Pickford had her ermine tippet twisted[7]

9. Thackeray infrequently but accurately uses this and other archaic forms, like "her's."
1. MS reads: these
2. MS reads: it's
3. MS reads: There's
4. The phrase "at the time . . . about him" is interlined in the MS over the canceled "& trying his new horse"
5. Revised edition reads: George
6. MS originally read: "How was that timid little heart to bare itself for the inspection of those young ladies with the big black eyes?" The first edition changed "the bold" to "their bold." The MS version fits much better with the next sentence.
7. Spencer: jacket, see chapter VI. Tippet: cape. MS reads: <chopped> ↑twisted↓

into a muff and trimmings, I warrant you the changes did not

escape the two intelligent young women before mentioned.[8] But there are things, look you, of a finer texture than fur or[9] satin, and all Solomon's glories, and all the wardrobe of the Queen of Sheba;[1]—things whereof the beauty escapes the eyes of many Connoisseurs—And there are sweet modest little souls on which you light, fragrant and blooming tenderly in quiet shady places—and there are garden-ornaments, as big as brass warming-pans,[2] that are fit to stare the sun itself out of countenance—Miss Sedley was not of the sun flower sort; and I say it is out of the rules of all proportion to draw a violet of the size of a double-dahlia.

No indeed; the life of a good young girl who is in the paternal

8. The phrase "the two . . . mentioned." is interlined over canceled "them."
9. MS reads: and
1. Of lilies, Jesus said, "Even Solomon in all his glory was not arrayed like one of these" (Matthew 6.28–29). The Queen of Sheba (Ethiopia) visited Solomon because of his reputed wealth and wisdom (1 Kings 10.1–13).
2. Long-handled metal containers for hot coals used to warm beds. The phrase "And there are sweet . . . fragrant and blooming" is interlined above another, canceled, interlineation: "You may see a Sun-flower any day, of wh. you can only surprize the beauty, by looking"

nest as yet, can't have many of those thrilling incidents, to which the heroine of romance commonly lays claim. Snares or shot may take off the old birds foraging without—hawks may be abroad from which they escape or by whom they suffer; but the young ones in the nest have a pretty comfortable unromantic sort of existence in the down and the straw, till it comes to their turn too to get on the wing. While Becky Sharp was on her own wing in the Country hopping on all sorts of twigs and amid a multiplicity of traps, and pecking up her food quite harmless and successful, Amelia lay snug in her home of Russell Square; if she went into the world it was under the guidance of the elders, nor did it seem that any evil could befal her or that opulent cheery comfortable home[3] in which she was affectionately sheltered. Mamma had her morning duties, and her daily drive and that delightful round of visits and shopping which forms the amusement or the profession as you may call it of the rich London lady. Papa conducted his mysterious operations in the City—a stirring place in those days, when war was raging[4] all over Europe, and Empires were being staked—when the "Courier" newspaper had tens of thousands of subscribers—when one day brought you a Battle of Vittoria, another a Burning of Moscow, or a newsman's horn blowing down Russell Square about dinner time announced such a fact as 'Battle of Leipsic, six hundred thousand men engaged, total defeat of the French, two hundred thousand killed.'[5] Old Sedley once or twice came home with a very grave face: and no wonder when such news as this was agitating all the hearts and all the Stocks of Europe.

Meanwhile matters went on in Russell Square, Bloomsbury, just as if matters in Europe were not in the least disorganised. The retreat from Leipsic made no difference in the number of meals Mr. Sambo took in the Servant's Hall—the allies poured into France and the dinner bell rang at five o'clock just as usual—I don't think poor Amelia cared anything about Brienne and Montmirail,[6] or was fairly interested in the war until the abdication of the Emperor[7]; when she clapped her hands and said prayers, o how grateful, and flung herself into George Osborne's arms with all her soul to the astonishment of every body who witnessed that ebullition of sentiment—The fact is peace was declared, Europe was going to be at rest: The Corsican was overthrown,—and Lieutenant Osborne's regiment would not be ordered on service. That was the way in which Miss Amelia reasoned. The fate of Europe was Lieutenant George Osborne to her—His dangers being over she sang Te Deum.[8] He was her Europe: her Emperor: her allied Monarchs[9] and august Prince Regent:

3. MS originally read: house
4. MS reads: <battles were being fought> ↑war was raging↓
5. The French were defeated at Vittoria, Spain, June 21, and at Leipzig, Saxony (now Germany), October 16–19, 1813. The Russians themselves burned Moscow in September to prevent Napoleon from winning it.
6. Short-lived French victories in January and February 1814.
7. Napoleon Bonaparte, variously called Boney or the Corsican.
8. Hymn of thanksgiving: "Thee God we praise."
9. Of Russia, Austria, and Prussia.

he was her Sun and Moon, and I believe she thought the[1] Grand Illumination and Ball at the Mansion House given to the sovereigns, were especially in honour of George Osborne.

We have talked of Shift, Self and Poverty, as those dismal instructors under whom poor Miss Becky Sharp got her education—Now Love was Miss Amelia Sedley's last tutoress, and it was amazing what a progress our young lady made under that popular teacher. In the course of fifteen or eighteen months' daily and constant attention to this eminent Finishing Governess, what a deal of secrets Amelia learned which Miss Wirt and the black eyed young ladies over the way, which old Miss Pinkerton of Chiswick herself, had no cognizance of!—As indeed how should any of those prim and reputable virgins? With Misses P and W the tender passion is out of the question: I would not dare to breathe such an idea regarding them—Miss Maria Osborne it is true was 'attached' to Mr. Frederic Augustus Bullock, of the firm of Hulker, Bullock, & Bullock, but her's was a most respectable attachment and she would have taken Bullock Senior just the same—her mind being fixed, as that of a well-bred young woman should be, upon a house in Park Lane, a country house at Wimbledon, a handsome chariot,[2] and two prodigious tall horses and footmen, and a fourth of the annual profits of the eminent firm of Hulker & Bullock, all of which advantages were represented in the person of Frederic Augustus. Had orange blossoms been invented then, (those touching emblems of female purity imported by us from France where people's daughters are universally sold in marriage,[3]) Miss Maria I say would have assumed the spotless wreath, and stepped into the travelling carriage by the side of gouty old bald-headed bottle-nosed Bullock Senior; and devoted her beautiful existence to his happiness with perfect modesty,[4]—only the old gentleman was married already—so she bestowed her young affections on the junior[5] partner. Sweet blooming orange flowers! The other day I saw Miss Trotter (that was) arrayed in them, trip into the travelling carriage at St. George's Hanover Square,[6] and Lord Methuselah hobbled in after—With what an engaging modesty she pulled down the blinds of the chariot—the dear innocent!—there were half the carriages of Vanity Fair at the wedding.

This was not the sort of Love that finished Amelia's education, and in the course of a year turned a good young girl into a good young woman, to be a good wife presently when the happy time should come. This young person (perhaps it was very imprudent in her parents to encourage her and abet her in such idolatry and silly romantic ideas) loved with all her heart the young officer in his Majesty's service with whom we have made a brief acquaintance. She thought about him the very first moment on waking: and his was the very last

1. MS reads: <He was her> ↑and I believe she thought the↓
2. MS reads: handsome yellow chariot,
3. The custom of brides wearing orange blossoms was introduced to England around 1820. The blossoms conventionally signified marriage, purity, and love.
4. MS adds and cancels: & devotion
5. MS reads: <proposed to devote herself to> ↑bestowed her young affections on↓ the <younger> ↑junior↓
6. Church famous for its weddings; see chapter VI.

name mentioned in her prayers. She never had seen a man so beautiful or so clever: such a figure on horseback: such a dancer: such a hero in general—Talk of the Prince's bow! What was it to George's? She had seen Mr. Brummell whom every body praised so—compare such a person as that to her George!—Not amongst all the Beaux at the Opera (and there were Beaux in those days with actual opera hats) was there any one[7] to equal him—He was only good enough to be a Fairy Prince; and o what magnanimity to stoop to such a humble Cinderella! Miss Pinkerton would have tried to check this blind devotion very likely had she been Amelia's confidante—but not with much success, depend upon it. It is in the nature and instinct of some women.[8] Some are made to scheme, and some to love—and I wish any respected bachelor that reads this may take the sort that best likes him.

While under this overpowering impression Miss Amelia neglected her twelve dear friends at Chiswick most cruelly as such selfish people commonly will do—She had but this subject of course to think about, and Miss Saltire was too cold for a confidante: and[9] she couldn't bring her mind to[1] tell Miss Swartz the woolly-haired young heiress from Saint Kitt's. She had little Laura Martin home for the holidays; and my belief is she made a Confidante of her, and promised that Laura should come and live with her when she was married, and gave Laura a great deal of information regarding the passion of love, which must have been singularly useful and novel to that little person. Alas, Alas, I fear she[2] had not a well regulated mind.

What were her parents doing, not to keep this little heart from beating so fast? Old Sedley did not seem much to notice matters—He was graver of late and his City affairs absorbed him. Mrs. Sedley was of so easy and uninquisitive a nature, that she wasn't even jealous. Mr. Jos was away being besieged by an Irish widow at Cheltenham. Amelia had the house to herself—ah! too much to herself sometimes—not that she ever doubted; for to be sure George must be at the Horseguards; and he can't always get leave from Chatham;[3] and he must see his friends and sisters and mingle in society when in town (he such an ornament to every society!)—and when he is with the regiment he is too tired to write long letters. I know where she kept that packet she had—and can steal in and out of her chamber like Iachimo,—like Iachimo? No—that's a bad part—I will only act Moonshine and peep harmless into the bed where faith and beauty and innocence lie dreaming.[4]

But if Osborne's were short and soldierlike letters, it must be confessed that were Miss Sedley's letters to Mr. Osborne to be published we should have to extend this novel to[5] such a multiplicity of volumes

7. MS reads: anything
8. This sentence is interlined in the MS.
9. MS reads: <—> ↑for a confidante: &↓
1. The phrase "bring her mind to" is interlined in the MS.
2. Revised edition reads: poor Emmy.
3. Naval dockyard southeast of London.
4. Iachimo, in Shakespeare's *Cymbeline*, steals a bracelet from Imogen's bedroom and claims she was unfaithful to her husband. Moonshine, the tailor in *A Midsummer Night's Dream*, spies on the lovers Pyramus and Thisbe.
5. MS originally read: But it must be confessed that if Miss Sedley's letters to Mr. Osborne

as not the most sentimental reader could support; that she not only filled sheets of large paper but crossed them[6] with the most astonishing perverseness; that she wrote whole pages out of poetry-books without the least pity—that she underlined words and passages with quite a frantic emphasis: and in fine gave the usual tokens of her condition. She wasn't a heroine. Her letters *were* full of repetition—She wrote rather doubtful grammar sometimes: and in her verses took all sorts of liberties with the metre—but oh Mesdames, if you are not allowed to touch the heart sometimes in spite of syntax, and are not to be loved until you all know the difference between trimeter and tetrameter, may all Poetry go to the deuce, and every Schoolmaster perish miserably!

## *Chapter XIII.*

### SENTIMENTAL AND OTHERWISE.

I FEAR the gentleman to whom Miss Amelia's letters were addressed was rather an obdurate critic. Such a number of notes followed Lieutenant Osborne about the Country, that he became almost ashamed of the jokes of his mess room companions regarding them—and ordered his servant never to deliver them except at his private apartment. He was seen lighting his cigar with one to the horror of Captain Dobbin, who it is my belief would have given a bank note for the document.[1]

For some time George strove to keep the liaison a secret. There *was* a woman in the case, that he admitted—"And not the first either," said Ensign Spooney to Ensign Stubbles—"That Osborne's a devil of a fellow—There was a Judge's daughter at Demerara went almost mad about him; then there was that beautiful quadroon girl, Miss Pye, at St. Vincent's[2] you know; and since he's been home they say he's a regular Don Giovanni[3] by Jove."

Stubbles and Spooney thought that to be 'a regular Don Giovanni by Jove' was one of the finest qualities a man could possess: and Osborne's reputation was prodigious amongst the young men of the regiment. He was famous in field sports, famous at a song, famous on parade, free with his money, which was bountifully supplied[4] by

were to be published there would be

6. Saved paper by turning the written sheet half round and writing crossways over the original writing.

1. The last sentence is interlined in the MS.
2. Demerara: Georgetown, British Guyana. St. Vincent's: British island in the West Indies.
3. The Don Juan of Mozart's opera (1787).
4. MS originally read: song, famous over the bottle, liberal with his purse always bountifully filled

his father. His coats were better made than any man's in the regiment and he had more of them. He was adored by the men: he could drink more than any officer of the whole mess including old Heavytop the Colonel. He could spar better than Knuckles the private (who would have been a corporal but for his drunkenness, and who had[5] been in the Prize-ring), and was the best batter and bowler, out and out, of the regimental club. He rode his own horse, Greased Lightning, and won the Garrison-cup at Quebec races. There were other people besides Amelia who worshipped him. Stubbles and Spooney thought him a sort of Apollo. Dobbin took him to be an Admirable Crichton:[6] and[7] Mrs. Major O'Dowd acknowledged he was an elegant young fellow and put her in mind of Fitzjurld Fogarty, Lord Castlefogarty's second son.

Well, Stubbles and Spooney and the rest indulged in most romantic conjectures regarding this female correspondent[8] of Osborne's,—opining that it was a Duchess in London who was in love with him—or that it was a General's daughter who was engaged to somebody else and madly attached to him—or that it was a member of Parliament's lady who proposed four horses and an elopement—or that it was some other victim of a passion delightfully exciting, romantic, and disgraceful to all parties—on none of which conjectures would Osborne throw the least light, leaving his young admirers and friends to invent and arrange their whole history.

And the real state of the case would never have been known at all in the regiment but for Captain Dobbin's indiscretion.—The Captain was eating his breakfast one day in the mess-room,[9] while Cackle the assistant surgeon and the two above-named[1] worthies were speculating upon Osborne's intrigue—Stubbles holding out that the Lady was a Duchess about Queen Charlotte's Court[2] and Cackle vowing she was an opera singer of the worst reputation. At this idea Dobbin became so moved that though his mouth was full of egg and bread and butter at the time and though he ought not to have spoken at all—yet he couldn't help blurting out, "Cackle, you're a thtupid[3] fool, you're always talking nonsense and scandal. Othborne is not going to run off with a Duchess or ruin a milliner; Miss Sedley is[4] one of the most charming young women that ever lived—he's been engaged to her ever so long—and the man who calls her names had better not do so in my hearing"—With which, turning exceedingly red, Dobbin ceased speaking, and almost choked himself with a cup of tea. The story was over the regiment in half an hour and that very evening Mrs. Major O'Dowd wrote off to her sister Glorvina at O'Dowdstown

5. MS omits "who"
6. James Crichton, sixteenth-century Scottish adventurer, poet, and scholar, was killed in a brawl at about age twenty-five. He was the subject of a novel by W. H. Ainsworth, *The Admirable Crichton* (1837).
7. MS reads: even
8. MS reads: correspondence
9. For "in the mess-room," MS reads: at mess:
1. MS adds: young
2. The wife of George III was queen from 1761 to 1818.
3. In addition to this lisped word, the MS has Dobbin say, "alwayth talking nonthenth and thcandal. Othborne ith"; the revised edition changed "thtupid" to "stupid"
4. MS reads: <he's engaged to be married to> ↑Miss Sedley is↓

not to hurry from Dublin, young Osborne being prematurely engaged already.

She complimented the Lieutenant, in an appropriate speech over a glass of whisky-toddy that evening, and he went home perfectly furious to quarrel with Dobbin, (who had declined Mrs. Major O'Dowd's party and sate in his own room playing the flute and I believe writing poetry in a very melancholy manner)—to quarrel with Dobbin for betraying his secret.

"Who the devil asked you to talk about my affairs," Osborne shouted indignantly. "Why the deuce[5] is all the regiment to know that I am going to be married? Why is that tattling old harridan, Peggy O'Dowd, to make free with my name over her d—d supper table and advertise my engagement over the three kingdoms? After all what right have you to say I *am* engaged or to meddle in my business at all, Dobbin."

"It seems to me,"—Captain Dobbin began.

"Seems be hanged, Dobbin," his junior interrupted him. "I am under obligations to you—I know it a d—d deal too well too—but I won't be always sermonised by you because you're five years my senior. I'm hanged if I'll stand your airs of superiority and infernal pity and patronage—pity and patronage! I should like to know in what I'm your inferior?"

"Are you engaged?" Captain Dobbin interposed.

"What the devil's that to you or any one here if I am?"

"Are you ashamed of it?" Dobbin resumed.

"What right have you to ask me that question, Sir? I should like to know," George said.

"Good God you don't mean to say you want to break off?" asked Dobbin starting up.

"In other words you ask me if I'm a man of honour," said Osborne fiercely: "is that what you mean? You've adopted such a tone regarding me lately that I'm —— if I'll bear it any more."

"What have I done? I've told you you were neglecting a sweet girl, George. I've told you that when you go to town you ought to go to her and not to the gambling-houses about St. James's."

"You want your money back I suppose," said George with a sneer.

"Of course I do—I always did didn't I?" says Dobbin—"You speak like a generous fellow."

"No hang it, William, I beg your pardon"—here George interposed in a fit of remorse. "You *have* been my friend in a hundred ways Heaven knows.[6] You've got me out of a score of scrapes: when Crawley of the Guards won that sum of money of me I should have been done but for you. I know I should. But you shouldn't deal so hardly with me—You shouldn't be always catechising me. I *am* very fond of Amelia; I adore her and that sort of thing—Don't look angry. She's faultless, I know she is. But you see there's no fun in winning a thing unless you play for it. Hang it: the regiment's just back from the West Indies: I must have a little fling: and then when I'm married I'll reform—I will upon my honour now.—And—I say—Dob—don't

5. MS reads: devil
6. MS added and canceled: and I've no <more> right to rebuke you.

be angry with me, and I'll give you a hundred next month, when I know my father will stand something handsome—and I'll ask Heavytop for leave: and I'll go to town and see Amelia tomorrow—there now, will *that* satisfy you?"

"It's impossible to be long angry with you, George," said the good-natured Captain—"And as for the money, old boy: you know if I wanted it you'd share your last shilling with me."

"That I would by Jove, Dobbin," George said with the greatest generosity though by the way he never had any money to spare.

"Only I wish you had sown those wild oats of yours, George. If you could have seen poor little Miss Emmy's face when she asked me[7] about you the other day you would have pitched those billiard balls to the deuce. Go and comfort her, you rascal. Go and write her a long letter. Do something to make her happy. A very little will."

"I believe she is[8] d—d fond of me," the lieutenant said with a self-satisfied air: and went off to finish the evening with some jolly fellows in the mess-room.

Amelia meanwhile in Russell Square, was looking at the moon which was shining upon that peaceful spot as well as upon the square

of the Chatham barracks where Lieutenant Osborne was quartered: and thinking to herself how her hero was employed—perhaps he is visiting the sentries, thought she: perhaps he is bivouacking: perhaps he is attending the couch of a wounded comrade; or studying

7. MS omits: me
8. MS reads: she's

the art of war up in his own desolate chamber: And her kind thoughts sped away, as if they were angels and had wings, and flying down the river to Chatham and Rochester[9] strove to peep into the barracks where George was.

All things considered, I think it[1] was as well the gates were shut and the sentry allowed no one to pass—so that the poor little white-robed Angel could not hear the songs those young fellows were roaring over the whiskey-punch.

The day after the little conversation at Chatham barracks, young Osborne to show that he would be as good as his word prepared to go to town, thereby incurring Captain Dobbin's applause. "I should have liked to make her a little present," Osborne said to his friend in confidence,[2] "only I am[3] quite out of cash until my father tips up"—but Dobbin would not allow this good nature and generosity to be balked: and so accommodated Mr. Osborne with a few pound-notes, which the latter took after a little faint scruple.

And I daresay he would have bought something very handsome for Amelia; only, getting off the coach in Fleet Street,[4] he was attracted by a handsome shirt-pin in a jeweller's window which he could not resist, and having paid for that had very little money to spare for indulging in any farther exercise of kindness. Never mind: you may be sure it was not his presents Amelia wanted. When he came to Russell Square, her face lighted up as if he had been Sunshine. The little cares, fears, tears, timid misgivings, sleepless fancies of I don't know how many days and nights were forgotten under one moment's influence[5] of that familiar irresistible smile. He beamed on her from the drawing room door—magnificent—with ambrosial whiskers—like a god—Sambo whose face as he announced Captain Osbin (having conferred a brevet rank[6] on that young officer) blazed with a sympathetic grin, saw the little girl start and flush and jump up from her watching place in the window—and Sambo retreated: and as soon as the door was shut, she went fluttering to Lieutenant George Osborne's heart as if it was the only natural home for her to nestle in. O thou poor panting little soul! The very finest tree in the whole forest, with the straightest stem and the strongest arms and the thickest foliage wherein you choose to build and coo, may be marked for what you know and may be down with a crash ere long. What an old old simile that is between man and timber!

In the meanwhile George kissed her very kindly on her forehead and glistening eyes; and was very gracious and good: and she thought his diamond shirt pin (which she had not known him to wear[7] before,) the prettiest ornament ever seen.

9. Chatham: where George's unit was stationed. Rochester: a nearby town on the Medway River.
1. MS reads: George was.—It ] First edition added the paragraph break and the phrase: All things considered, I think it ] Revised edition changed "was." to "was. . . . " and suppressed the paragraph break.
2. The phrase "to his friend in confidence" is interlined in the MS.
3. MS reads: I'm
4. A main thoroughfare of central London.
5. MS reads: influences
6. A nominal or honorary rank.
7. The word "new" is canceled in the MS before "diamond" and "known him to wear" is interlined over canceled "seen"

The observant reader, who has marked our young Lieutenant's previous behaviour, and has perused our report of the brief conversation which he has just had with Captain Dobbin, has possibly come to certain conclusions regarding the character of Mr. Osborne. Some cynical Frenchman[8] has said that there are two parties to a Love-transaction: the one who loves and the other who condescends to be so treated. Perhaps the love is occasionally on the man's side: perhaps on the lady's. Perhaps some infatuated swain has ere this mistaken insensibility for modesty, dullness for maiden-reserve, mere vacuity for sweet bashfulness and a goose in a word for a swan—Perhaps some beloved female subscriber has arrayed an ass in the splendour and glory of her imagination; admired his dullness as manly simplicity; worshipped his selfishness as manly superiority, treated his stupidity as majestic gravity and used him as the brilliant Fairy Titania did a certain Weaver of Athens.[9] I think I have seen such comedies of errors going on in the world. But this is certain that Amelia believed her lover[1] to be one of the most gallant and brilliant men in the empire: and it is possible[2] Lieutenant Osborne thought so too.

He was a little wild, how many young men are; and don't girls like a rake better than a milksop? He hadn't sown his wild oats as yet but he would soon: and quit the army now that Peace was proclaimed; the Corsican monster locked up at Elba;[3] promotion by consequence over; and no chance left for the display of his undoubted military talents and valour: and his allowance, with Amelia's settlement,[4] would enable them to take a snug place in the country somewhere, in a good sporting neighbourhood; and he would hunt a little and farm a little; and they would be very happy. As for remaining in the army as a married man that was impossible. Fancy Mrs. George Osborne in lodgings in a Country town or worse still in the East or West Indies—with a society of officers—and patronised by Mrs. Major O'Dowd! Amelia died with laughing at Osborne's stories about Mrs. Major O'Dowd. He loved her much too fondly to subject her to that horrid woman and her vulgarities and the rough treatment of a soldier's wife. He didn't care for himself, not he—but his dear little girl should take the place in society to which as his wife she was entitled: and to these proposals you may be sure she acceded as she would to any other from the same author.

Holding this kind of conversation and building numberless castles in the air, (which Amelia adorned with all sorts of flower-gardens, rustic walks, country churches, Sunday-schools and the like; while George had his mind's eye directed to the stables, the kennel, and

8. Not identified; possibly Michel de Montaigne (1533–1592) or François de la Rochefoucauld (1613–1680), whose *Maxim* #371 reads, "It is almost always the fault of the one in love not to realize that the other one no longer is."
9. In Shakespeare's *A Midsummer Night's Dream* Titania loves Bottom the Weaver, though he wears an ass's head.
1. MS reads: hero
2. MS reads: <world> ↑empire↓: and ↑it is possible↓
3. In April 1814, Napoleon was restricted to Elba, not literally locked up. The victors deliberated at the Congress of Vienna; no one anticipated the escape and return of Napoleon in March 1815.
4. Marriage settlement or dowry provided by her father. Married women had no legal standing outside their husbands, but marriage settlements provided them some security.

the cellar) this young pair passed away a couple of hours very pleasantly; and as the Lieutenant had only that single day in town and a great deal of most important business to transact; it was proposed that Miss Emmy should dine with her future sisters-in-law. This invitation was accepted joyfully. He conducted her to his sisters; where he left her talking and prattling in a way that astonished those ladies, who thought that George might make something of her; and then[5] went off to transact his business.

In a word, he went out and ate ices at a pastry-cook's shop in Charing Cross, tried a new coat in Pall Mall,—dropped in at the Old Slaughter's[6] and called for Captain Cannon; played eleven games at billiards with the Captain, of which he won eight, and returned to Russell Square half an hour late for dinner, but in very good humour.

It was not so with old Mr. Osborne. When that gentleman came from the City, and was welcomed in the drawing room by his daughters and the elegant Miss Wirt, they saw at once by his face, which was puffy, solemn, and yellow at the best of times, and by the scowl and twitching of his black eye brows, that the heart within his large white waistcoat was disturbed and uneasy. When Amelia stepped forward to salute him which she always did with great trembling and timidity, he gave a surly grunt of recognition, and dropped the little hand out of his great hirsute paw without any attempt to hold it there—He looked round gloomily at his eldest daughter, who comprehending the meaning of his look, which asked unmistakeably 'Why the devil is *she* here?' said at once:—

"George is in town, Papa, and has gone to the Horse Guards and will be back to dinner."

"O he is, is he? I won't have the dinner kept waiting for *him*, Jane:"[7] with which this worthy man lapsed into his particular chair, and there was an utter silence[8] in his genteel well-furnished drawing room only interrupted by the alarmed ticking of the great French clock.

When that Chronometer which was surmounted by a cheerful brass group of the sacrifice of Iphigenia tolled five in a heavy cathedral tone,[9] Mr. Osborne pulled the bell at his right hand violently, and the butler rushed up.

"Dinner," roared Mr. Osborne.

"Mr. George isn't come in, Sir," interposed the man.

5. Revised edition reads: and he then
6. Charing Cross: the hub of London activity where the Strand, Whitehall, and Cockspur Street meet. Pall Mall: broad avenue celebrated for shops, coffee houses, and clubs. Old Slaughters' Coffee House or Chop House on St. Martin's Lane: famous for food and gaming, a hangout for actors, writers, and painters.
7. MS, mistakenly, reads: Maria. Thackeray confused the two girls again nine paragraphs later and in chapter XXIII. Jane is the house manager in charge of servants and is the perpetual spinster; Maria marries Bullock.
8. First edition seems to be a patchwork misreading of the manuscript. First edition reads: and then the utter silence ] MS, not clear, appears to read: and then in the utter silence
9. Agamemnon sacrified his daughter, Iphigenia, to Artemis to gain favorable winds for Troy. The canceled passage refers to the Old Testament figure Jephthah, who sacrificed his daughter to Jehovah as a result of a rash vow. MS reads: Chronometer <tolled five in a heavy Cathedral tone> <it had> ↑wh. was surmounted by↓ a cheerful brass group of the sacrifice of <Jepththah sacrificing his daughter> ↑of Iphigenia tolled five in a heavy Cathedral tone↓

Mr. Osborne's welcome to Amelia

"Damn Mr. George, Sir—am I Master of the house? DINNER!" Mr. Osborne scowled.[1] Amelia trembled—A telegraphic communication of eyes passed between the other three ladies—The obedient bell in the lower regions[2] began ringing the announcement of the meal.—The tolling over, the head of the family thrust his hands into the great tail pockets of his great blue coat and brass-buttons, and without waiting for a farther announcement strode down stairs alone, scowling over his shoulder at the four females.

"What's the matter now, my dear?" asked one of the other as they rose and tripped gingerly[3] behind the Sire.

"I suppose the funds are falling," whispered Miss Wirt; and so, trembling and in silence this hushed female company followed their dark leader. They took their places in silence. He growled out a blessing which sounded as gruffly as a curse.[4] The great silver dish-covers were removed.—Amelia trembled in her place, for she was next to the awful Osborne, and alone on her side of the table—the gap being occasioned by the absence of George.

"Soup?" says Mr. Osborne clutching the ladle, fixing his eyes on her, in a sepulchral tone[5]—and having helped her and the rest, did not speak for a while.—

"Take Miss Sedley's plate away"—at last he said—"She can't eat the soup—no more can I. It's beastly. Take away the soup, Hicks, and tomorrow turn the cook out of the house, Jane."[6]

Having concluded his observations[7] upon the soup, Mr. Osborne made a few curt remarks respecting the fish[8]—also of a savage and satirical tendency, and cursed Billingsgate with an emphasis quite worthy of the place.[9] Then he lapsed into silence and swallowed sundry glasses of wine, looking more and more terrible, till a brisk knock at the door told of George's arrival when everybody began to rally—

He could not come before, General Daguilet had kept him waiting at the Horse Guards—never mind soup or fish—give him any thing—he didn't care what—capital mutton—capital everything—His good humour contrasted with his father's severity, and he rattled on unceasingly during dinner to the delight of all—of one especially who need not be mentioned.

As soon as the young ladies had discussed the orange and the glass of wine which formed the ordinary conclusion of the dismal banquets at Mr. Osborne's house, the signal to make sail for the drawing-room

1. MS reads: howled.
2. MS reads: <down stairs> ↑lower regions↓
3. MS reads: they tripped <silently> ↑gingerly↓
4. This sentence is interlined in the MS.
5. MS added and canceled: but whether she took any or not does not matter for the purpose of this history
6. The manuscript has old Osborne address his remarks to Maria, but Jane is the house manager. MS reads: Hicks <roared the Master. At this moment came a brisk knock at the door. Succour had arrived and every body began to rally.> ↑and tomorrow turn the cook out of the House Maria.↓
7. MS reads: <remarks> ↑observations↓
8. MS reads: <commenced a series of observations regarding the fish> ↑made a few curt remarks respecting the fish↓
9. Billingsgate, the fish-market, was famous for foul language; "Billingsgate" means foul language.

was given and they all arose and departed. Amelia hoped George would soon join them there—She began playing some of his favourite waltzes (then newly imported)[1]—at the great carved-legged, leather-cased grand piano in the drawing-room over head—This little artifice did not bring him. He was deaf to the waltzes; they grew fainter and fainter; the discomfited performer left the huge instrument presently; and though her three friends performed some of the loudest and most brilliant new pieces of their *répertoire*;[2] she did not hear a single note, but sate thinking, and boding evil. Old Osborne's scowl, terrific always, had never before looked so deadly to her. His eyes followed her out of the room as if she had been guilty of something. When they brought her coffee, she started as though it were a cup of poison which[3] Mr. Hicks the butler wished to propose to her. What mystery was there lurking? O those women! They nurse and cuddle their presentiments: and make darlings of their ugliest thoughts as they do of their deformed children.[4]

The gloom on the paternal countenance had also impressed George Osborne with anxiety. With such eyebrows and a look so decidedly bilious, how was he to extract that[5] money from the governor, of which George was consumedly in want? He began praising his father's wine. That was generally a successful means of cajoling the old gentleman.

"We never got such Madeira[6] in the West Indies, Sir, as yours—Colonel Heavytop took off three bottles of that you sent me down, under his belt the other day."

"Did he?" said the old gentleman. "It stands me in eight shillings a bottle."

"Will you take six guineas a dozen for it, Sir?" said George with a laugh—"There's one of the greatest men in the kingdom wants some."

"Does he?" growled the senior—"wish he may get it."

"When General Daguilet was at Chatham, Sir, Heavytop gave him a breakfast, and asked me for some of the wine—The general liked it just as well—wanted a pipe[7] for the Commander in Chief[8]—He's His Royal Highness's right hand man."

"It *is* devilish fine wine:" said the Eyebrows and they looked more good-humoured—and George was going to take advantage of this complacency and bring the supply question on the mahogany; when the father relapsing into solemnity though rather cordial in manner, bade him ring the bell for Claret. "And we'll see if that's as good as the Madeira, George, to which His Royal Highness is welcome I'm

1. Though waltz music was known in England before the turn of the century, the dance was introduced in 1812, and even Byron expressed shock at "hands which may freely range in public sight."
2. MS reads: <rattling pieces> ↑of the loudest and most brilliant new pieces of their repertoire↓
3. MS omits: which
4. MS originally read: and they prefer their ugly thoughts to the pleasant ones, <like t> as mothers of their deformed children.
5. MS reads: <get some> ↑extract that↓
6. MS reads: good Madeira
7. A cask holding 126 gallons.
8. The prince regent's brother, Frederick Augustus, duke of York.

sure—and as we are drinking it, I'll talk to you about a matter of importance."

Amelia heard the claret-bell ringing as she sate nervously up stairs. She thought somehow it was a mysterious and presentimental bell. Of the presentiments which some people are always having, *some* surely must come right.

"What I want to know, George," the old gentleman said, after slowly smacking his first bumper—"What I want to know is—how you and—ah—that little thing up stairs are carrying on?"

"I think, Sir, it's not hard to see"—George said, with a self satisfied grin—"pretty clear, Sir. What capital wine!"

"How diyou mean, pretty clear, Sir?"

"Why, hang it, Sir—don't push me too hard. I'm a modest man. I—ah—I don't set up to be a lady-killer—but I do own that she's as devilish fond of me as she can be. Any body can see that with half an eye."

"And you yourself?"

"Why Sir—didn't you order me to marry her and ain't I a good boy? Haven't our Papas settled it ever so long?"

"A pretty boy indeed. Haven't I heard of your doings, Sir, with Lord Tarquin,[9] Captain Crawley of the Guards, the Honorable Mr. Deuceace and that set—Have a care, Sir, have a care."

The old gentleman pronounced these aristocratic names with the greatest gusto. Whenever he met a great man he grovelled before him, and mylorded him as only a free-born Briton can do. He came home and looked out his history in the Peerage: he introduced his name into his daily conversation: he bragged about his Lordship to his daughters. He fell down prostrate and basked in him as a Neapolitan beggar does in the Sun. George was alarmed when he heard the names—he feared his father might have been informed of certain transactions at play. But the old moralist eased him by saying serenely,

"Well well, young men will be young men—And the comfort to me is, George, that living in the best society in England, as I hope you do: as I think you do: as my means will allow you to do" . . .

"Thank you, Sir," says George making his point at once—"one can't live with these great folks for nothing—and my purse, Sir—Look at it"—and he held up a little token which had been netted by Amelia and contained the very last of Dobbin's pound notes.

"You shan't want, Sir—The British Merchant's Son shan't want, Sir. My guineas are as good as their's George, my boy: and I dont grudge 'em. Call on Mr. Chopper as you go through the city to-morrow, he'll have something for you—I dont grudge money when I know you're in good society: because I know that good society can never go wrong—There's no pride in me. I was a humbly born man—but you have had advantages. Make a good use of 'em. Mix with the young nobility—There's many of 'em who can't spend a dollar to your guinea,[1] my boy—And as for the pink-bonnets (here from

9. Named for the legendary Etruscan family famous for tyranny, arrogance, and the rape of Lucrece.
1. From 1760 to 1816 few British coins were minted. Spanish pieces of eight were restamped

under the heavy eyebrows there came a knowing and not very pleasing leer) why boys will be boys. Only there's one thing I order you to avoid—which if you do I'll[2] cut you off with a shilling by Jove; and that's gambling, Sir."

"O of course, Sir," said George.

"But to return to the other business—about Amelia—Why shouldn't you marry higher than a Stock-broker's daughter, George—that's what I want to know."

"It's a family business, Sir," says George cracking filberts—"You and Mr. Sedley made the match a hundred years ago."

"I don't deny it: but people's positions alter, Sir. I don't deny that Sedley made my fortune—or rather put me in the way of acquiring by my own talents and genius that proud position,[3] which I may say I occupy in the tallow-trade and the City of London—I've shown my gratitude to Sedley: and he's tried it of late, Sir, as my check-book can show. George! I tell you in confidence I don't like the looks of Mr. Sedley's affairs—My chief clerk, Mr. Chopper, does not like the looks of 'em and he's an old file[4] and knows Change[5] as well as any man in London. Hulker & Bullock are looking shy at him. He's been dabbling on his own account I fear. They say the Jeune Amelie was his, which was taken by the Yankee Privateer Molasses[6]—And that's flat—unless I see Amelia's ten thousand down, you don't marry her. I'll have no lame duck's daughter in my family—Pass the wine, Sir—or ring for coffee."

With which Mr. Osborne spread out the Evening-paper and George knew from this signal that the colloquy was ended and that his Papa was about to take a nap.

He hurried up stairs to Amelia in the highest spirits. What was it that made him more attentive to her on this night than he had been for a long long time—more eager to amuse her, more tender, more brilliant in talk? Was it that his generous heart warmed to her at the prospect of misfortune: or that the idea of losing the dear little prize made him value it more?

She lived upon the recollections of that happy evening for many days afterwards, remembering his words; his looks; the song he sang: his attitudes as he leant over her or looked at her from a distance—As it seemed to her,[7] no night ever passed so quickly at Mr. Osborne's house before; and for once this young person was almost provoked to be angry by the premature arrival of Mr. Sambo with her shawl.

and issued as thalers or dollars worth less than a pound (twenty shillings). A guinea was worth a pound and one shilling.

2. First edition reads: do not, I'll ] The MS reading is ambiguous: if you do avoid or if you do gamble. The first edition is clearer but seems uncharacteristically complex, verbally, for old Osborne.
3. MS originally read: acquiring that position
4. Shrewd man of experience.
5. The Stock Exchange in Chapel Court; not to be confused with Exeter Change or the Royal Exchange, which were collections of shops and commercial meeting centers. Osborne and Sedley were licensed stockbrokers. It was illegal for a broker to trade on his own behalf.
6. Jeune Amelie: the name of a ship—the Young Amelia. From 1812 to 1814 England and the United States were at war; the American naval fleet consisted in large part of private ships with government commissions.
7. The phrase "As it seemed to her," is interlined in the MS.

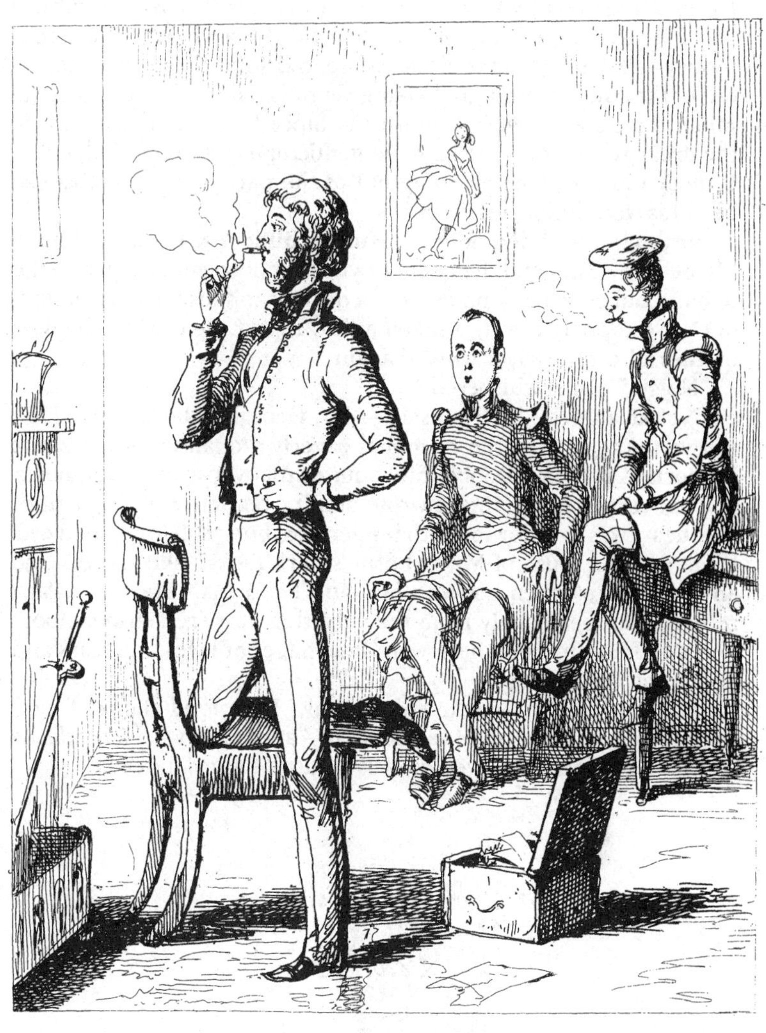

Lieutenant Osborne and his ardent love letters

George came and took a tender leave of her the next morning: and then hurried off to the City where he visited Mr. Chopper, his father's head man, and received from that gentleman a document which he exchanged at Hulker & Bullock's for a whole pocket-full of money—As George entered the house; old John Sedley was passing out of the banker's parlour, looking very dismal. But his Godson was much too elated to mark the worthy Stock-broker's depression, or the dreary eyes which the kind old gentleman cast upon him. Young Bullock did not come grinning out of the parlour with him as had been his wont in former years.[8]

And as the swinging doors of Hulker, Bullock & Co. closed upon Mr. Sedley—Mr. Quill the cashier (whose benevolent occupation it is to hand out crisp bank notes from a drawer and dispense sovereigns out[9] of a copper-shovel), winked at Mr. Driver the clerk at the desk on his right. Mr. Driver winked again.

"No go," Mr. D whispered.[1]

"Not at no price," Mr. Q said—"Mr. George Osborne, Sir. How will you take it?" George crammed eagerly a quantity of notes into his pockets and paid Dobbin fifty pounds that very evening at mess.[2]

That very evening Amelia wrote him the tenderest of long letters. Her heart was overflowing with tenderness, but it still foreboded evil. What was the cause of Mr. Osborne's dark looks? she asked. Had any difference arisen between him and her Papa? Her poor Papa returned so melancholy from the City, that all were alarmed about him at home—in fine, there were four pages of loves and fears and hopes and forebodings.

"Poor little Emmy—dear little Emmy. How fond she is of me," George said, as he perused the missive—"and, Gad, what a headache that mixed punch has given me!" Poor little Emmy, indeed.

8. This sentence is interlined in the MS.
9. MS originally read: (whose happy occupation it is to dispense guineas out
1. MS originally read: That cock won't fight Mr. D said
2. MS added and canceled the following paragraph, which was used in chapter XII: <Poor little tender heart! and so it goes on hoping & throbbing and longing and trusting. You see—it's not much of a life to describe— There's not much of what you call incident in it—Only one feeling for all the day; and one thought to sleep and wake upon. When will he come? Why didn't he come? he promised> [Manuscript ends].

## *Chapter XIV.*

### MISS CRAWLEY AT HOME.

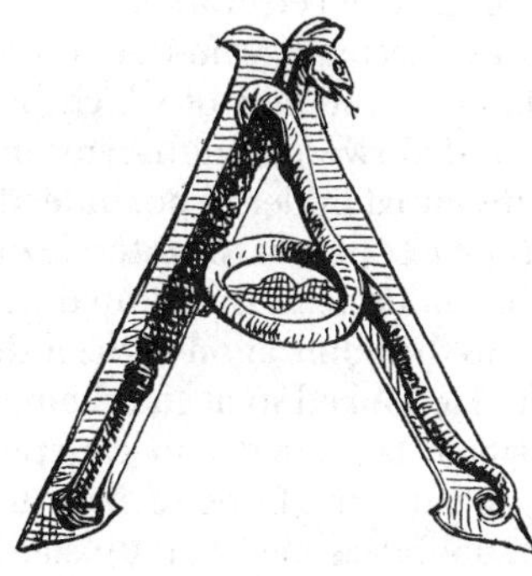

BOUT[1] this time there drove up to an exceedingly snug and well appointed house in Park Lane, a travelling chariot with a lozenge on the panels, a discontented female in a green veil and crimped curls on the rumble,[2] and a large and confidential man on the box. It was the equipage of our friend Miss Crawley, returning from Hants. The windows of the carriage[3] were shut: the fat spaniel, whose head and tongue ordinarily lolled out of one of them, reposed on the lap of the discontented female. When the vehicle stopped, a large round bundle of shawls was taken out of the carriage by the aid of various domestics and a young lady who accompanied the heap of cloaks. That bundle contained Miss Crawley, who was conveyed up-stairs forthwith, and put into a bed and chamber warmed properly as for the reception of an invalid. Messengers went off for her physician and medical man. They came, consulted, prescribed, vanished. The young companion of Miss Crawley, at the conclusion of their interview, came in to receive their instructions, and administered those antiphlogistic medicines[4] which the eminent men ordered.

Captain Crawley of the Life Guards rode up from Knightsbridge Barracks the next day: his black charger pawed the straw before his invalid aunt's door. He was most affectionate in his inquiries regarding that amiable relative. There seemed to be much source of apprehension. He found Miss Crawley's maid (the discontented female) unusually sulky and despondent: he found Miss Briggs, her dame de compagnie,[5] in tears alone in the drawing-room. She had hastened home, hearing of her beloved friend's illness. She wished to fly to her couch, that couch which she, Briggs, had so often smoothed in the hour of sickness. She was denied admission to Miss Crawley's apartment. A stranger was administering her medicines—a stranger from the country—an odious Miss . . . tears choked the utterance of the dame de compagnie, and she buried her crushed affections and her poor old red nose in her pocket handkerchief.

Rawdon Crawley sent up his name by the sulky femme de chambre,[6] and Miss Crawley's new companion, coming tripping down from the sick-room, put a little hand into his as he stepped for-

1. The initial vignette depicts the serpent and file from Aesop's fable, where the file says, "It's my business to take from all and give to none."
2. In the rumble seat at the back of the carriage.
3. Revised edition reads: The carriage-windows
4. For inflammation.
5. Employed female companion.
6. Chambermaid.

ward eagerly to meet her, gave a glance of great scorn at the bewildered Briggs, and, beckoning the young Guardsman out of the back drawing-room, led him down stairs into that now desolate dining-parlour, where so many a good dinner had been celebrated.

Here these two talked for ten minutes, discussing, no doubt, the symptoms of the old invalid above stairs; at the end of which period the parlour-bell was rung briskly, and answered on that instant by Mr. Bowls, Miss Crawley's large confidential butler (who, indeed, happened to be at the keyhole during the most part of the interview); and the Captain coming out, curling his moustachios, mounted the black charger pawing among the straw[7] to the admiration of the little blackguard boys collected in the street. He looked in at the dining-room window, managing his horse, which curvetted and capered beautifully—for one instant the young person might be seen at the window, then her figure vanished, and, doubtless, she went up-stairs again to resume the affecting duties of benevolence.

Who could this young woman be, I wonder? That evening a little dinner for two persons was laid in the dining-room—when Mrs. Firkin, the lady's maid, pushed into her mistress's apartment, and bustled about there during the vacancy occasioned by the departure of the new nurse—and the latter and Miss Briggs sat down to the neat little meal.

Briggs was so much choked by emotion that she could hardly take a morsel of meat. The young person carved a fowl with the utmost delicacy, and asked so distinctly for egg-sauce, that poor Briggs, before whom that delicious condiment was placed, started, made a great clattering with the ladle, and once more fell back in the most gushing hysterical state.

"Had you not better give Miss Briggs a glass of wine?" said the person to Mr. Bowls, the large confidential man. He did so. Briggs seized it mechanically, gasped it down convulsively, moaned a little, and began to play with the chicken on her plate.

"I think we shall be able to help each other," said the person with great suavity: "and shall have no need of Mr. Bowls's kind services. Mr. Bowls, if you please, we will ring when we want you." He went down stairs, where, by the way, he vented the most horrid curses upon the unoffending footman, his subordinate.

"It is a pity you take on so, Miss Briggs," the young lady said, with a cool, slightly sarcastic, air.

"My dearest friend is so ill, and wo—o—o—on't see me," gurgled out Briggs in an agony of renewed grief.

"She's not very ill any more. Console yourself, dear Miss Briggs. She has only overeaten herself—that is all. She is greatly better. She will soon be quite restored again. She is weak from being cupped[8] and from medical treatment, but she will rally immediately. Pray console yourself, and take a little more wine."

7. It was common to spread straw in front of a house facing much-used streets to deaden traffic noise. See also chapter XIX.

8. For centuries it was believed that bad blood needed to be removed from the ill. To cup is to use a glass vessel and partial vacuum for the operation.

"But why, why won't she see me again?" Miss Briggs bleated out. "Oh, Matilda, Matilda, after three-and-twenty years' tenderness! is this the return to your poor, poor Arabella?"

"Don't cry too much, poor Arabella," the other said (with ever so little of a grin); "she only won't see you, because she says you don't nurse her as well as I do. It's no pleasure to me to sit up all night. I wish you might do it instead."

"Have I not tended that dear couch for years?" Arabella said, "and now—"

"Now she prefers somebody else. Well, sick people have these fancies, and must be humoured. When she's well I shall go."

"Never, never," Arabella exclaimed, madly inhaling her salts-bottle.[9]

"Never be well or never go? Miss Briggs," the other said, with the same provoking good nature. "Pooh—she will be well in a fortnight, when I shall go back to my little pupils at Queen's Crawley, and to their mother, who is a great deal more sick than our friend. You need not be jealous about me, my dear Miss Briggs. I am a poor little girl without any friends, or any harm in me. I don't want to supplant you in Miss Crawley's good graces. She will forget me a week after I am gone: and her affection for you has been the work of years. Give me a little wine if you please, my dear Miss Briggs, and let us be friends. I'm sure I want friends."

The placable and soft-hearted Briggs speechlessly pushed out her hand at this appeal; but she felt the desertion most keenly for all that, and bitterly, bitterly moaned the fickleness of her Matilda. At the end of half an hour, the meal over, Miss Rebecca Sharp (for such, astonishing to state, is the name of her who has been described ingeniously as the person hitherto), went up-stairs again to her patient's rooms, from which, with the most engaging politeness, she eliminated poor Firkin. "Thank you, Mrs. Firkin, that will quite do; how nicely you make it! I will ring when anything is wanted." "Thank you;" and Firkin came down stairs in a tempest of jealousy, only the more dangerous because she was forced to confine it in her own bosom.

Could it be the tempest which, as she passed the landing of the first floor, blew open the drawing-room door? No; it was stealthily opened by the hand of Briggs. Briggs had been on the watch. Briggs too well heard the creaking Firkin descend the stairs, and the clink of the spoon and gruel-basin the neglected female carried.

"Well, Firkin?" says she, as the other entered the apartment. "Well, Jane?"

"Wuss and wuss, Miss B.," Firkin said, wagging her head.

"Is she not better then?"

"She never spoke but once, and I asked her if she felt a little more easy, and she told me to hold my stupid tongue. Oh, Miss B., I never thought to have seen *this* day!" And the water-works again began to play.

9. Bottle of smelling salts to relieve fainting spells.

"What sort of a person is this Miss Sharp, Firkin? I little thought, while enjoying my Christmas revels in the elegant home of my firm friends, the Reverend Lionel Delamere and his amiable lady, to find a stranger had taken my place in the affections of my dearest, my still dearest Matilda!" Miss Briggs, it will be seen by her language, was of a literary and sentimental turn, and had once published a volume of poems—"Trills of the Nightingale"—by subscription.

"Miss B., they are all infatyated about that young woman," Firkin replied. "Sir Pitt wouldn't have let her go, but he daredn't refuse Miss Crawley anythink. Mrs. Bute at the Rectory jist as bad—never happy out of her sight. The Capting quite wild about her. Mr. Crawley mortial jealous. Since Miss C. was took ill, she won't have nobody near her but Miss Sharp, I can't tell for where nor for why; and I think somethink has bewidged everybody."

Rebecca passed that night in constant watching upon Miss Crawley; the next night the old lady slept so comfortably, that Rebecca had time for several hours' comfortable repose herself on the sofa, at the foot of her patroness's bed; very soon, Miss Crawley was so well that she sat up and laughed heartily at a perfect imitation of Miss Briggs and her grief, which Rebecca described to her. Briggs' weeping snuffle, and her manner of using the handkerchief, were so completely rendered, that Miss Crawley became quite cheerful, to the admiration of the doctors when they visited her, who usually found this worthy woman of the world, when the least sickness attacked her, under the most abject depression and terror of death.

Captain Crawley came every day, and received bulletins from Miss Rebecca respecting his aunt's health. This improved so rapidly, that poor Briggs was allowed to see her patroness; and persons with tender hearts may imagine the smothered emotions of that sentimental female, and the affecting nature of the interview.

Miss Crawley liked to have Briggs in a good deal soon. Rebecca used to mimic her to her face with the most admirable gravity, thereby rendering the imitation doubly picquante to her worthy patroness.

The causes which had led to the deplorable illness of Miss Crawley, and her departure from her brother's house in the country, were of such an unromantic nature that they are hardly fit to be explained in this genteel and sentimental novel. For how is it possible to hint of a delicate female, living in good society, that she ate and drank too much, and that a hot supper of lobsters profusely enjoyed at the Rectory was the reason of an indisposition which Miss Crawley herself persisted was solely attributable to the dampness of the weather? The attack was so sharp that Matilda—as his Reverence expressed it—was very nearly "off the hooks;"[1] all the family was in a fever of expectation regarding the will, and Rawdon Crawley was making sure of at least forty thousand pounds before the commencement of the London season. Mr. Crawley sent over a choice parcel of tracts, to prepare her for the change from Vanity Fair and Park Lane for

1. To drop off the hooks is slang for "to die."

another world; but a good doctor from Southampton[2] being called in in time, vanquished the lobster which was so nearly fatal to her, and gave her sufficient strength to enable her to return to London. The baronet did not disguise his exceeding mortification at the turn which affairs took.

While everybody was attending on Miss Crawley, and messengers every hour from the Rectory were carrying news of her health to the affectionate folks there, there was a lady in another part of the house, being exceedingly ill, of whom no one took any notice at all; and this was the lady of Crawley herself. The good doctor shook his head after seeing her; to which visit Sir Pitt consented, as it could be paid without a fee;[3] and she was left fading away in her lonely chamber, with no more heed paid to her than to a weed in the park.

The young ladies, too, lost much of the inestimable benefit of their governess's instruction. So affectionate a nurse was Miss Sharp, that Miss Crawley would take her medicines from no other hand. Firkin had been deposed long before her mistress's departure from the country. That faithful attendant found a gloomy consolation on returning to London, in seeing Miss Briggs suffer the same pangs of jealousy and undergo the same faithless treatment to which she herself had been subject.

Captain Rawdon got an extension of leave on his aunt's illness, and remained dutifully at home. He was always in her antechamber. (She lay sick in the state bed-room, into which you entered by the little blue saloon.) His father was always meeting him there; or if he came down the corridor ever so quietly, his father's door was sure to open, and the hyæna face of the old gentleman to glare out. What was it set one to watch the other so? A generous rivalry, no doubt, as to which should be most attentive to the dear sufferer in the state bedroom. Rebecca used to come out and comfort both of them; or one or the other of them rather. Both of these worthy gentlemen were most anxious to have news of the invalid from her little confidential messenger.

At dinner—to which meal she descended for half an hour—she kept the peace between them: after which she disappeared for the night; when Rawdon would ride over to the depôt of the 150th at Mudbury, leaving his Papa to the society of Mr. Horrocks and his rum and water. She passed as weary a fortnight as ever mortal spent in Miss Crawley's sick room; but her little nerves seemed to be of iron, and she was quite unshaken by the duty and the tedium of the sick-chamber.

She never told until long afterwards how painful that duty was; how peevish a patient was the jovial old lady; how angry; how sleepless; in what horrors of death; during what long nights she lay moaning, and in almost delirious agonies respecting that future world which she quite ignored when she was in good health.—Picture to yourself, oh fair young reader, a worldly, selfish, graceless, thankless,

2. Seaport and resort town in Hampshire on the south coast.
3. The doctor was paid for the house call, not the number of patients treated.

religionless old woman, writhing in pain and fear, and without her wig. Picture her to yourself, and ere you be old, learn to love and pray!

Sharp watched this graceless bedside with indomitable patience. Nothing escaped her; and, like a prudent steward, she found a use for everything. She told many a good story about Miss Crawley's illness in after days,—stories which made the lady blush through her artificial carnations. During the illness she was never out of temper; always alert; she slept light, having a perfectly clear conscience; and could take that refreshment at almost any minute's warning. And so you saw few traces of fatigue in her appearance. Her face might be a trifle paler, and the circles round her eyes a little blacker than usual; but whenever she came out from the sick-room she was always smiling, fresh, and neat, and looked as trim in her little dressing-gown and cap, as in her smartest evening suit.

The Captain thought so, and raved about her in uncouth convulsions. The barbed shaft of love had penetrated his dull hide. Six weeks—appropinquity—opportunity—had victimised him completely. He made a confidante of his aunt at the Rectory, of all persons in the world. She rallied him about it; she had perceived his folly; she warned him; she finished by owning that little Sharp was the most clever, droll, odd, good-natured, simple, kindly creature in England. Rawdon must not trifle with her affections, though—dear Miss Crawley would never pardon him for that; for she, too, was quite overcome by the little governess, and loved Sharp like a daughter. Rawdon must go away—go back to his regiment and naughty London, and not play with a poor artless girl's feelings.

Many and many a time this good-natured lady, compassionating the forlorn life-guardsman's condition, gave him an opportunity of seeing Miss Sharp at the Rectory, and of walking home with her, as we have seen. When men of a certain sort, ladies, are in love, though they see the hook and the string, and the whole apparatus with which they are to be taken, they gorge the bait nevertheless—they must come to it—they must swallow it—and are presently struck and landed gasping. Rawdon saw there was a manifest intention on Mrs. Bute's part to captivate him with Rebecca. He was not very wise; but he was a man about town, and had seen several seasons. A light dawned upon his dusky soul, as he thought, through a speech of Mrs. Bute's.

"Mark my words, Rawdon," she said. "You will have Miss Sharp one day for your relation."

"What relation,—my cousin, hey, Mrs. Bute? James sweet on her, hey?" inquired the waggish officer.

"More than that," Mrs. Bute said, with a flash from her black eyes.

"Not Pitt?—He sha'n't have her. The sneak a'n't worthy of her. He's booked to Lady Jane Sheepshanks."

"You men perceive nothing. You silly, blind creature—if anything happens to Lady Crawley, Miss Sharp will be your mother-in-law; and *that's* what will happen."

Rawdon Crawley, Esquire, gave vent to a prodigious whistle, in token of astonishment at this announcement. He couldn't deny it. His father's evident liking for Miss Sharp had not escaped him. He knew the old gentleman's character well; and a more unscrupulous old—whyou—he did not conclude the sentence, but walked home, curling his moustachios, and convinced he had found a clue to Mrs. Bute's mystery.

"By Jove, it's too bad," thought Rawdon, "too bad, by Jove! I do believe the woman wants the poor girl to be ruined, in order that she shouldn't come into the family as Lady Crawley."

When he saw Rebecca alone, he rallied her about his father's attachment in his graceful way. She flung up her head scornfully, looked him full in the face, and said,—

"Well, suppose he *is* fond of me. I know he is, and others too. You don't think I am afraid of him, Captain Crawley? You don't suppose I can't defend my own honour," said the little woman, looking as stately as a queen.

"O, ah, why—give you fair warning—look out, you know—that's all," said the moustachio-twiddler.

"You hint at something not honourable, then?" said she, flashing out.

"O—Gad—really—Miss Rebecca," the heavy dragoon interposed.

"Do you suppose I have no feeling of self-respect, because I am poor and friendless, and because rich people have none? Do you think, because I am a governess, I have not as much sense, and feeling, and good breeding as you gentle-folks in Hampshire? I'm a Montmorency. Do you suppose a Montmorency is not as good as a Crawley?"

When Miss Sharp was agitated, and alluded to her maternal relatives, she spoke with ever so slight a foreign accent, which gave a great charm to her clear ringing voice. "No," she continued, kindling as she spoke to the Captain; "I can endure poverty, but not shame—neglect, but not insult; and insult from—from *you.*"

Her feelings gave way, and she burst into tears.

"Hang it, Miss Sharp—Rebecca—by Jove—upon my soul, I wouldn't for a thousand pounds. Stop, Rebecca!"

She was gone. She drove out with Miss Crawley that day. It was before the latter's illness. At dinner she was unusually brilliant and lively; but she would take no notice of the hints, or the nods, or the clumsy expostulations of the humiliated, infatuated guardsman. Skirmishes of this sort passed perpetually during the little campaign—tedious to relate, and similar in result. The Crawley heavy cavalry was maddened by defeat, and routed every day.

If the baronet of Queen's Crawley had not had the fear of losing his sister's legacy before his eyes, he never would have permitted his dear girls to lose the educational blessings which their invaluable governess was conferring upon them. The old house at home seemed a desert without her, so useful and pleasant had Rebecca made herself there. Sir Pitt's letters were not copied and corrected; his books not made up; his household business and manifold schemes neglected, now that his little secretary was away. And it was easy to see how necessary such an amanuensis was to him, by the tenor and spelling of the numerous letters which he sent to her, entreating her and commanding her to return. Almost every day brought a frank from the baronet, enclosing the most urgent prayers to Becky for her return, or conveying pathetic statements to Miss Crawley, regarding the neglected state of his daughters' education; of which documents Miss Crawley took very little heed.

Miss Briggs was not formally dismissed, but her place as companion was a sinecure and a derision; and her company was the fat spaniel in the drawing-room, or occasionally the discontented Firkin in the housekeeper's closet. Nor, though the old lady would by no means hear of Rebecca's departure, was the latter regularly installed in office in Park Lane. Like many wealthy people, it was Miss Crawley's habit to accept as much service as she could get from her inferiors; and good-naturedly to take leave of them when she no longer found them useful. Gratitude amongst certain rich folks is scarcely natural or to be thought of. They take needy people's services as their due. Nor have you, O poor parasite and humble hanger-on, much reason to complain! Your friendship for Dives[4] is about as sincere as the return which it usually gets. It is money you love, and not the man; and were Crœsus[5] and his footman to change places, you know, you poor rogue, who would have the benefit of your allegiance.

And I am not sure, that, in spite of Rebecca's simplicity and activity, and gentleness and untiring good humour, the shrewd old London lady, upon whom these treasures of friendship were lavished, had not a lurking suspicion all the while of her affectionate nurse and friend. It must have often crossed Miss Crawley's mind that nobody does anything for nothing. If she measured her own feeling towards the world, she must have been pretty well able to gauge those of the world towards herself; and perhaps she reflected, that it is the ordinary lot of people to have no friends if they themselves care for nobody.

Well, meanwhile Becky was the greatest comfort and convenience to her, and she gave her a couple of new gowns, and an old necklace and shawl, and shewed her friendship by abusing all her intimate acquaintances to her new confidante (than which there can't be a more touching proof of regard), and meditated vaguely some great future benefit—to marry her perhaps to Clump, the apothecary, or to settle her in some advantageous way of life; or, at any rate, to send her back to Queen's Crawley when she had done with her, and the full London season had begun.

When Miss Crawley was convalescent and descended to the drawing-room, Becky sang to her, and otherwise amused her; when she was well enough to drive out, Becky accompanied her. And amongst the drives which they took, whither, of all places in the world, did Miss Crawley's admirable good nature and friendship actually induce her to penetrate, but to Russell Square, Bloomsbury, and the house of John Sedley, Esquire.

4. Rich man; an allusion to the parable of the rich man and Lazarus (Luke 16).
5. Symbol of unlimited wealth, Crœsus was king of Lydia (560–c. 546 B.C.).

Ere that event, many notes had passed, as may be imagined, between the two dear friends. During the months of Rebecca's stay in Hampshire, the eternal friendship had (must it be owned?) suffered considerable diminution, and grown so decrepit and feeble with old age as to threaten demise altogether. The fact is, both girls had their own real affairs to think of: Rebecca her advance with her employers—Amelia her own absorbing topic. When the two girls met, and flew into each other's arms with that impetuosity which distinguishes the behaviour of young ladies towards each other, Rebecca performed her part of the embrace with the most perfect briskness and energy. Poor little Amelia blushed as she kissed her friend, and thought she had been guilty of something very like coldness towards her.

Their first interview was but a very short one. Amelia was just ready to go out for a walk. Miss Crawley was waiting in her carriage below, her people wondering at the locality in which they found themselves, and gazing upon honest Sambo, the black footman of Bloomsbury, as one of the queer natives of the place. But when Amelia came down with her kind smiling looks (Rebecca must introduce her to her friend, Miss Crawley was longing to see her, and was too ill to leave her carriage)—when, I say, Amelia came down, the Park Lane shoulder-knot aristocracy[6] wondered more and more that such a thing could come out of Bloomsbury; and Miss Crawley was fairly captivated by the sweet blushing face of the young lady who came forward so timidly and so gracefully to pay her respects to the protector of her friend.

"What a complexion, my dear. What a sweet voice!" Miss Crawley said, as they drove away westward after the little interview. "My dear Sharp, your young friend is charming. Send for her to Park Lane, do you hear?" Miss Crawley had a good taste. She liked natural manners—a little timidity only set them off. She liked pretty faces near her; as she liked pretty pictures, and nice china. She talked of Amelia with rapture half-a-dozen times that day. She mentioned her to Rawdon Crawley, who came dutifully to partake of his aunt's chicken.

Of course, on this Rebecca instantly stated, that Amelia was engaged to be married—to a Lieutenant Osborne—a very old flame.

"Is he a man in a line-regiment?"[7] Captain Crawley asked, remembering after an effort, as became a guardsman, the number of the regiment, the —th.

Rebecca thought that was the regiment. "The Captain's name," she said, "was Captain Dobbin."

"A lanky, gawky fellow," said Crawley, "tumbles over everybody. I know him; and Osborne's a goodish-looking fellow, with large black whiskers?"

"Enormous," Miss Rebecca Sharp said, "and enormously proud of them, I assure you."

6. In the seventeenth and eighteenth centuries, fashionable men and their liveried (uniformed) servants often wore ribbons with the family colors.
7. Member of regular troops. Rawdon belonged to a more fashionable guard unit.

Captain Rawdon Crawley burst into a hoarse laugh by way of reply; and being pressed by the ladies to explain, did so when the explosion of hilarity was over. "He fancies he can play at billiards," said he. "I won two hundred of him at the Cocoa Tree. *He* play, the young flat! He'd have played for anything that day, but his friend Captain Dobbin carried him off, hang him!"

"Rawdon, Rawdon, don't be so wicked," Miss Crawley remarked, highly pleased.

"Why, ma'am, of all the young fellows I've seen out of the line, I think this fellow's the greenest. Tarquin and Deuceace get what money they like out of him. He'd go to the deuce to be seen with a Lord. He pays their dinners at Greenwich, and they invite the company."

"And very pretty company too, I dare say."

"Quite right, Miss Sharp. Right, as usual, Miss Sharp. Uncommon pretty company,—haw, haw!" and the Captain laughed more and more, thinking he had made a good joke.

"Rawdon, don't be naughty!" his aunt exclaimed.

"Well, his father's a city man—immensely rich, they say. Hang those city fellows, they must bleed; and I've not done with him yet, I can tell you. Haw, haw!"

"Fie, Captain Crawley; I shall warn Amelia. A gambling husband!"

"Horrid, ain't he, hey?" the Captain said with great solemnity; and then added, a sudden thought having struck him:—"Gad, I say, ma'am, we'll have him here."

"Is he a presentable sort of a person?" the aunt inquired.

"Presentable?—oh, very well. You wouldn't see any difference," Captain Crawley answered. "Do let's have him, when you begin to see a few people; and his whatdyecallem—his inamorato—eh, Miss Sharp; that's what you call it—comes. Gad, I'll write him a note, and have him; and I'll try if he can play picquet[8] as well as billiards. Where does he live, Miss Sharp?"

Miss Sharp told Crawley the Lieutenant's town address; and a few days after this conversation, Lieutenant Osborne received a letter, in Captain Rawdon's school-boy hand, and enclosing a note of invitation from Miss Crawley.

Rebecca despatched also an invitation to her darling Amelia, who, you may be sure, was ready enough to accept it when she heard that George was to be of the party. It was arranged that Amelia was to spend the morning with the ladies of Park Lane, where all were very kind to her. Rebecca patronised her with calm superiority: she was so much the cleverer of the two, and her friend so gentle and unassuming, that she always yielded when anybody chose to command, and so took Rebecca's orders with perfect meekness and good humour. Miss Crawley's graciousness was also remarkable. She continued her raptures about little Amelia, talked about her before her face as if she were a doll, or a servant, or a picture, and admired her with the most benevolent wonder possible. I admire that admiration which

8. Card game.

the genteel world sometimes extends to the commonalty. There is no more agreeable object in life than to see May Fair[9] folks condescending. Miss Crawley's prodigious benevolence rather fatigued poor little Amelia, and I am not sure that of the three ladies in Park Lane she did not find honest Miss Briggs the most agreeable. She sympathised with Briggs as with all neglected or gentle people: she wasn't what you call a woman of spirit.

George came to dinner—a repast *en garçon*[1] with Captain Crawley.

The great family coach of the Osbornes transported him to Park Lane from Russell Square; where the young ladies, who were not themselves invited, and professed the greatest indifference at that slight, nevertheless looked at Sir Pitt Crawley's name in the baronetage; and learned everything which that work had to teach about the Crawley family and their pedigree, and the Binkies, their relatives, &c., &c. Rawdon Crawley received George Osborne with great frankness and graciousness: praised his play at billiards: asked him when he would have his revenge: was interested about Osborne's regiment: and would have proposed picquet to him that very evening, but Miss Crawley absolutely forbade any gambling in her house; so that the young Lieutenant's purse was not lightened by his gallant patron, for that day at least. However, they made an engagement for the next, somewhere: to look at a horse that Crawley had to sell, and to try him in the Park; and to dine together, and to pass the evening with some jolly fellows. "That is, if you're not on duty to that pretty Miss Sedley," Crawley said, with a knowing wink. "Monstrous nice girl, 'pon my honour, though, Osborne," he was good enough to add. "Lots of tin,[2] I suppose, eh?"

Osborne wasn't on duty; he would join Crawley with pleasure: and the latter, when they met the next day, praised his new friend's horsemanship—as he might with perfect honesty—and introduced him to three or four young men of the first fashion, whose acquaintance immensely elated the simple young officer.

"How's little Miss Sharp, by-the-bye," Osborne inquired of his friend over their wine, with a dandified air. "Good-natured little girl that. Does she suit you well at Queen's Crawley? Miss Sedley liked her a good deal last year."

Captain Crawley looked savagely at the Lieutenant out of his little blue eyes, and watched him when he went up to resume his acquaintance with the fair governess. Her conduct must have relieved Crawley if there was any jealousy in the bosom of that life-guardsman.

When the young men went up stairs, and after Osborne's introduction to Miss Crawley, he walked up to Rebecca with a patronising, easy swagger. He was going to be kind to her and protect her. He would even shake hands with her, as a friend of Amelia's; and saying, "Ah, Miss Sharp! how-dy-doo?" held out his left hand towards her, expecting that she would be quite confounded at the honour.

9. Among the most elegant districts of London.
1. For males only.
2. Wealth.

Miss Sharp put out her right fore-finger[3]—

And gave him a little nod, so cool and killing, that Rawdon Crawley, watching the operations from the other room, could hardly restrain his laughter as he saw the Lieutenant's entire discomfiture; the start he gave, the pause, and the perfect clumsiness with which he at length condescended to take the finger which was offered for his embrace.

"She'd beat the devil, by Jove!" the Captain said, in a rapture; and the Lieutenant, by way of beginning the conversation, agreeably asked Rebecca how she liked her new place.

"My place?" said Miss Sharp, coolly, "how kind of you to remind me of it! It's a tolerably good place: the wages are pretty good—not so good as Miss Wirt's, I believe, with your sisters in Russell Square. How are those young ladies?—not that I ought to ask."

"Why not?" Mr. Osborne said, amazed.

"Why, they never condescended to speak to me, or to ask me into their house, whilst I was staying with Amelia; but we poor governesses, you know, are used to slights of this sort."

"My dear Miss Sharp!" Osborne ejaculated.

"At least in some families," Rebecca continued. "You can't think what a difference there is though. We are not so wealthy in Hampshire as you lucky folks of the city. But then I am in a gentleman's family—good old English stock. I suppose you know Sir Pitt's father

3. An insulting gesture of condescension also used by Mrs. Pinkerton on Becky in chapter I.

refused a peerage. And you see how I am treated. I am pretty comfortable. Indeed, it is rather a good place. But how *very* good of you to inquire!"

Osborne was quite savage. The little Governess patronised him and *persifflèd*[4] him until this young British Lion felt quite uneasy; nor could he muster sufficient presence of mind to find a pretext for backing out of this most delectable conversation.

"I thought you liked the City families pretty well," he said haughtily.

"Last year you mean, when I was fresh from that horrid vulgar school? Of course I did. Doesn't every girl like to come home for the holidays? And how was I to know any better? But oh, Mr. Osborne, what a difference eighteen months' experience makes!—eighteen months spent, pardon me for saying so, with gentlemen. As for dear Amelia, she, I grant you, is a pearl, and would be charming anywhere. There now, I see you are beginning to be in a good humour; but oh these queer odd City people! And Mr. Jos.—how is that wonderful Mr. Joseph?"

"It seems to me you didn't dislike that wonderful Mr. Joseph last year," Osborne said kindly.

"How severe of you! Well, *entre nous,*[5] I didn't break my heart about him; yet if he had asked me to do what you mean by your looks (and very expressive and kind they are, too), I wouldn't have said no."

Mr. Osborne gave a look as much as to say, "Indeed, how very obliging!"

"What an honour to have had you for a brother-in-law, you are thinking? To be sister-in-law to George Osborne, Esquire, son of John Osborne, Esquire, son of—what was your grandpapa, Mr. Osborne? Well, don't be angry. You can't help your pedigree, and I quite agree with you that I would have married Mr. Joe Sedley; for could a poor penniless girl do better? Now you know the whole secret. *I'm* frank and open; and, considering all things, it was very kind of you to allude to the circumstance—very kind and polite. Amelia dear, Mr. Osborne and I were talking about your poor brother Joseph. How is he?"

Thus was George utterly routed. Not that Rebecca was in the right; but she had managed most successfully to put him in the wrong. And he now shamefully fled, feeling if he stayed another minute, that he would have been made to look foolish in the presence of Amelia.

Though Rebecca had had the better of him, George was above the meanness of tale-bearing or revenge upon a lady,—only he could not help cleverly confiding to Captain Crawley, next day, some notions of his regarding Miss Rebecca—that she was a sharp one, a dangerous one, a desperate flirt, &c.; in all of which opinions Crawley agreed laughingly, and with every one of which Miss Rebecca was made acquainted before twenty-four hours were over. They added to her original regard for Mr. Osborne. Her woman's instinct had told her,

4. Bantered or toyed with.
5. Confidentially.

that it was George who had interrupted the success of her first love-passage, and she esteemed him accordingly.

"I only just warn you," he said to Rawdon Crawley, with a knowing look—he had bought the horse, and lost some score of guineas after dinner, "I just warn you—I know women, and counsel you to be on the look-out."

"Thank you, my boy," said Crawley, with a look of peculiar gratitude. "You're wide awake, I see." And George went off, thinking Crawley was quite right.

He told Amelia of what he had done, and how he had counselled Rawdon Crawley—a devilish good, straight-forward fellow—to be on his guard against that little sly, scheming Rebecca.

"Against *whom?*" Amelia cried.

"Your friend the Governess.—Don't look so astonished."

"O George, what *have* you done?" Amelia said. For her woman's eyes, which Love had made sharp-sighted, had in one instant discovered a secret which was invisible to Miss Crawley, to poor virgin Briggs, and, above all, to the stupid peepers of that young whiskered prig, Lieutenant Osborne.

For as Rebecca was shawling her in an upper apartment, where these two friends had an opportunity for a little of that secret talking and conspiring which forms the delight of female life, Amelia, coming up to Rebecca, and taking her two little hands in hers, said, "Rebecca, I see it all."

Rebecca kissed her.

And regarding this delightful secret, not one syllable more was said by either of the young women. But it was destined to come out before long.

Some short period after the above events, and Miss Rebecca Sharp still remaining at her patroness's house in Park Lane, one more hatchment might have been seen in Great Gaunt Street, figuring amongst the many which usually ornament that dismal quarter. It was over Sir Pitt Crawley's house; but it did not indicate the worthy baronet's demise. It was a feminine hatchment, and indeed a few years back had served as a funeral compliment to Sir Pitt's old mother, the late dowager lady Crawley. Its period of service over, the hatchment had come down from the front of the house, and lived in retirement somewhere in the back premises of Sir Pitt's mansion. It re-appeared now for poor Rose Dawson. Sir Pitt was a widower again. The arms quartered on the shield along with his own were not, to be sure, poor Rose's. She had no arms. But the cherubs painted on the scutcheon answered as well for her as for Sir Pitt's mother, and *Resurgam*[6] was written under the coat, flanked by the Crawley Dove and Serpent. Arms and Hatchments, Resurgam.—Here is an opportunity for moralising!

Mr. Crawley had tended that otherwise friendless bed-side. She went out of the world strengthened by such words and comfort as he could give her. For many years his was the only kindness she ever knew; the only friendship that solaced in any way that feeble, lonely

6. I shall arise.

soul. Her heart was dead long before her body. She had sold it to become Sir Pitt Crawley's wife. Mothers and daughters are making the same bargain every day in Vanity Fair.

When the demise took place, her husband was in London attending to some of his innumerable schemes, and busy with his endless lawyers. He had found time, nevertheless, to call often in Park Lane, and to despatch many notes to Rebecca, entreating her, enjoining her, commanding her to return to her young pupils in the country, who were now utterly without companionship during their mother's illness. But Miss Crawley would not hear of her departure; for though there was no lady of fashion in London who would desert her friends more complacently as soon as she was tired of their society, and though few tired of them sooner, yet as long as her *engoûment*[7] lasted her attachment was prodigious, and she clung still with the greatest energy to Rebecca.

The news of Lady Crawley's death provoked no more grief or comment than might have been expected in Miss Crawley's family circle. "I suppose I must put off my party for the 3rd," Miss Crawley said; and added, after a pause, "I hope my brother will have the decency not to marry again." "What a confounded rage Pitt will be in if he does," Rawdon remarked, with his usual regard for his elder brother. Rebecca said nothing. She seemed by far the gravest and most impressed of the family. She left the room before Rawdon went away that day; but they met by chance below, as he was going away after taking leave, and had a parley together.

On the morrow, as Rebecca was gazing from the window, she startled Miss Crawley, who was placidly occupied with a French novel, by crying out in an alarmed tone, "Here's Sir Pitt, Ma'am!" and the baronet's knock followed this announcement.

"My dear, I can't see him. I won't see him. Tell Bowls not at home, or go down stairs and say I'm too ill to receive any one. My nerves really won't bear my brother at this moment;" cried out Miss Crawley, and resumed the novel.

"She's too ill to see you, Sir," Rebecca said, tripping down to Sir Pitt, who was preparing to ascend.

"So much the better," Sir Pitt answered. "I want to see *you,* Miss Becky. Come along a me into the parlour," and they entered that apartment together.

"I wawnt you back at Queen's Crawley, Miss," the baronet said, fixing his eyes upon her, and taking off his black gloves and his hat with its great crape hat-band. His eyes had such a strange look, and fixed upon her so stedfastly, that Rebecca Sharp began almost to tremble.

"I hope to come soon," she said in a low voice, "as soon as Miss Crawley is better—and return to—to the dear children."

"You've said so these three months, Becky," replied Sir Pitt, "and still you go hanging on to my sister, who'll fling you off like an old shoe, when she's wore you out. I tell you I *want* you. I'm going back to the Vuneral. Will you come back? Yes or no."

7. Infatuation.

"I daren't—I don't think—it would be right—to be alone—with you, Sir," Becky said, seemingly in great agitation.

"I say agin, I want you," Sir Pitt said, thumping the table. "I can't git on without you. I didn't see what it was till you went away. The house all goes wrong. It's not the same place. All my accounts has got muddled agin. You *must* come back. Do come back. Dear Becky, do come."

"Come—as what, Sir?" Rebecca gasped out.

"Come as Lady Crawley, if you like," the baronet said, grasping his crape hat. "There! will that zatusfy you? Come back and be my wife. Your vit vor't. Birth be hanged. You're as good a lady as ever I see. You've got more brains in your little vinger than any baronet's wife in the county. Will you come? Yes or no?"

"Oh, Sir Pitt!" Rebecca said, very much moved.

"Say yes, Becky," Sir Pitt continued. "I'm an old man, but a good'n. I'm good for twenty years. I'll make you happy, zee if I don't. You shall do what you like; spend what you like; and 'av it all your own way. I'll make you a zettlement.[8] I'll do everything reglar. Look year!" and the old man fell down on his knees and leered at her like a satyr.

Rebecca started back a picture of consternation. In the course of this history we have never seen her lose her presence of mind; but she did now, and wept some of the most genuine tears that ever fell from her eyes.

"Oh, Sir Pitt!" she said. "Oh, Sir—I—I'm *married already.*"

8. Settlement, i.e., a legal financial security for a wife. Married women without a settlement had no legal standing.

*Number 5* *May 1847*

## *Chapter XV.*

### IN WHICH REBECCA'S HUSBAND APPEARS FOR A SHORT TIME.

VERY reader of a sentimental turn (and we desire no other) must have been pleased with the *tableau* with which the last act of our little drama concluded; for what can be prettier than an image of Love on his knees before Beauty?

But when Love heard that awful confession from Beauty that she was married already, he bounced up from his attitude of humility on the carpet, uttering exclamations which caused poor little Beauty to be more frightened than she was when she made her avowal. "Married! you're joking," the Baronet cried, after the first explosion of rage and wonder. "You're making vun of me, Becky. Who'd ever go to marry you without a shilling to your vortune?"

"Married! married!" Rebecca said, in an agony of tears—her voice choking with emotion, her handkerchief up to her ready eyes, fainting against the mantel-piece—a figure of woe fit to melt the most obdurate heart. "O Sir Pitt, dear Sir Pitt, do not think me ungrateful for all your goodness to me. It is only your generosity that has extorted my secret."

"Generosity be hanged!" Sir Pitt roared out. "Who is it tu, then, you're married? Where was it?"

"Let me come back with you to the country, sir! Let me watch over you as faithfully as ever! Don't, don't separate me from dear Queen's Crawley!"

"The feller has left you, has he?" the Baronet said, beginning, as he fancied, to comprehend. "Well, Becky—come back if you like. You can't eat your cake and have it. Any ways I made you a vair offer. Coom back as governess—you shall have it all your own way." She held out one hand. She cried fit to break her heart; her ringlets fell over her face, and over the marble mantel-piece where she laid it.

"So the rascal ran off, eh?" Sir Pitt said, with a hideous attempt at consolation. "Never mind, Becky, *I'll* take care of 'ee."

"O Sir! it would be the pride of my life to go back to Queen's Crawley, and take care of the children, and of you as formerly, when you said you were pleased with the services of your little Rebecca. When I think of what you have just offered me, my heart fills with gratitude—indeed it does. I can't be your wife, sir; let me—let me be your daughter!"

Saying which, Rebecca went down on *her* knees in a most tragical way, and, taking Sir Pitt's horny black hand between her own two (which were very pretty and white, and as soft as satin), looked up in his face with an expression of exquisite pathos and confidence, when—when the door opened, and Miss Crawley sailed in.

Mrs. Firkin and Miss Briggs, who happened by chance to be at the

parlour-door soon after the Baronet and Rebecca entered the apartment, had also seen accidentally, through the key-hole, the old gentleman prostrate before the governess, and had heard the generous proposal which he made her. It was scarcely out of his mouth, when Mrs. Firkin and Miss Briggs had streamed up the stairs, had rushed into the drawing-room where Miss Crawley was reading the French novel, and had given that old lady the astounding intelligence that Sir Pitt was on his knees, proposing to Miss Sharp. And if you calculate the time for the above dialogue to take place—the time for Briggs and Firkin to fly to the drawing-room—the time for Miss Crawley to be astonished, and to drop her volume of Pigault le Brun[1]—and the time for her to come down stairs—you will see how exactly accurate this history is, and how Miss Crawley *must* have appeared at the very instant when Rebecca had assumed the attitude of humility.

"It is the lady on the ground, and not the gentleman," Miss Crawley said, with a look and voice of great scorn. "They told me that *you* were on your knees, Sir Pitt: do kneel once more, and let me see this pretty couple!"

"I have thanked Sir Pitt Crawley, ma'am," Rebecca said, rising, "and have told him that—that I never can become Lady Crawley."

1. Popular French risqué novelist (1753–1835).

"Refused him!" Miss Crawley said, more bewildered than ever.

Briggs and Firkin at the door opened the eyes of astonishment and the lips of wonder.

"Yes—refused," Rebecca continued, with a sad, tearful voice.

"And am I to credit my ears that you absolutely proposed to her, Sir Pitt?" the old lady asked.

"Ees," said the Baronet, "I did."

"And she refused you as she says?"

"Ees," Sir Pitt said, his features on a broad grin.

"It does not seem to break your heart at any rate," Miss Crawley remarked.

"Nawt a bit," answered Sir Pitt, with a coolness[2] and good-humour which set Miss Crawley almost mad with bewilderment. That an old gentleman of station should fall on his knees to a penniless governess, and burst out laughing because she refused to marry him,—that a penniless governess should refuse a Baronet with four thousand a year,—these were mysteries which Miss Crawley could never comprehend. It surpassed any complications of intrigue in her favourite Pigault le Brun.

"I'm glad you think it good sport, brother," she continued, groping wildly through this amazement.

"Vamous," said Sir Pitt. "Who'd ha' thought it! what a sly little devil! what a little fox it waws!" he muttered to himself, chuckling with pleasure.

"Who'd have thought what?" cries Miss Crawley, stamping with her foot. "Pray, Miss Sharp, are you waiting for the Prince Regent's divorce,[3] that you don't think our family good enough for you?"

"My attitude," Rebecca said, "when you came in, Ma'am, did not look as if I despised such an honour as this good—this noble man has deigned to offer me. Do you think I have no heart? Have you all loved me, and been so kind to the poor orphan—deserted—girl, and am *I* to feel nothing? O my friends! O my benefactors! may not my love, my life, my duty, try to repay the confidence you have shown me? Do you grudge me even gratitude, Miss Crawley? It is too much—my heart is too full;" and she sank down in a chair so pathetically, that most of the audience present were perfectly melted with her sadness.

"Whether you marry me or not, you're a good little girl, Becky, and I'm your vriend, mind," said Sir Pitt, and putting on his crape-bound hat, he walked away—greatly to Rebecca's relief; for it was evident that her secret was unrevealed to Miss Crawley, and she had the advantage of a brief reprieve.

Putting her handkerchief to her eyes, and nodding away honest Briggs, who would have followed her up-stairs, she went up to her apartment; while Briggs and Miss Crawley, in a high state of excitement, remained to discuss the strange event, and Firkin, not less moved, dived down into the kitchen regions, and talked of it with all the male and female company there. And so impressed was Mrs.

2. Revised edition reads: coldness
3. The open conflict between the prince and his wife Caroline was public knowledge by 1813, though divorce proceedings were not initiated until 1820 when George IV was king.

Firkin with the news, that she thought proper to write off by that very night's post, "with her humble duty to Mrs. Bute Crawley and the famly at the Rectory, and Sir Pitt has been and proposed for to marry Miss Sharp, wherein she has refused him to the wonder of all."

The two ladies in the dining-room (where worthy Miss Briggs was delighted to be admitted once more to a confidential conversation with her patroness) wondered to their hearts' content at Sir Pitt's offer, and Rebecca's refusal; Briggs very acutely suggesting that there must have been some obstacle in the shape of a previous attachment, otherwise no young woman in her senses would ever have refused so advantageous a proposal.

"You would have accepted it yourself, wouldn't you, Briggs?" Miss Crawley said, kindly.

"Would it not be a privilege to be Miss Crawley's sister?" Briggs replied, with meek evasion.

"Well, Becky would have made a good Lady Crawley, after all," Miss Crawley remarked, (who was mollified by the girl's refusal, and very liberal and generous now there was no call for her sacrifices). "She has brains in plenty (much more wit in her little finger than you have my poor dear Briggs in all your head). Her manners are excellent now I have formed her. She is a Montmorency, Briggs, and blood *is* something, though I despise it for my part; and she would have held her own amongst those pompous stupid Hampshire people much better than that unfortunate ironmonger's daughter."

Briggs coincided as usual, and the "previous attachment" was then discussed in conjectures. "You poor friendless creatures are always having some foolish *tendre*,"[4] Miss Crawley said. "You yourself, you know, were in love with a writing master (don't cry, Briggs—you're always crying, and it won't bring him to life again), and I suppose this unfortunate Becky has been silly and sentimental too—some apothecary, or house-steward, or painter, or young curate, or something of that sort."

"Poor thing, poor thing!" says Briggs (who was thinking of twenty-four years back, and that hectic[5] young writing master whose lock of yellow hair, and whose letters, beautiful in their illegibility, she cherished in her old desk up stairs.) "Poor thing, poor thing!" says Briggs. Once more she was a fresh-cheeked lass of eighteen; she was at evening church and the hectic writing master and she were quavering out of the same psalm-book.

"After such conduct on Rebecca's part," Miss Crawley said enthusiastically, "our family should do something. Find out who is the *objet*, Briggs. I'll set him up in a shop; or order my portrait of him, you know; or speak to my cousin the Bishop—and I'll *doter*[6] Becky, and we'll have a wedding, Briggs, and you shall make the breakfast, and be a brides' maid."

Briggs declared that it would be delightful, and vowed that her dear Miss Crawley was always kind and generous, and went up to Rebecca's bed-room to console her and prattle about the offer, and

4. Tenderness.
5. Consumptive.
6. Give a dowry to.

the refusal, and the cause thereof; and to hint at the generous intentions of Miss Crawley, and to find out who was the gentleman that had the mastery of Miss Sharp's heart.

Rebecca was very kind, very affectionate and affected—responded to Briggs' offers of tenderness with grateful fervour—owned there was a secret attachment—a delicious mystery—what a pity Miss Briggs had not remained half a minute longer at the key-hole! Rebecca might, perhaps, have told more: but five minutes after Miss Briggs' arrival in Rebecca's apartment, Miss Crawley actually made her appearance there—an unheard of honour;—her impatience had overcome her; she could not wait for the tardy operations of her ambassadress: so she came in person, and ordered Briggs out of the room. And expressing her approval of Rebecca's conduct, she asked particulars of the interview and the previous transactions which had brought about the astonishing offer of Sir Pitt.

Rebecca said she had long had some notion of the partiality with which Sir Pitt honoured her, (for he was in the habit of making his feelings known in a very frank and unreserved manner) but, not to mention private reasons with which she would not for the present trouble Miss Crawley, Sir Pitt's age, station, and habits were such as to render a marriage quite impossible; and could a woman with any feeling of self-respect and any decency listen to proposals at such a moment, when the funeral of the lover's deceased wife had not actually taken place?

"Nonsense, my dear, you would never have refused him had there not been some one else in the case," Miss Crawley said, coming to her point at once. "Tell me the private reasons; what are the private reasons? There *is* some one; who is it that has touched your heart?"

Rebecca cast down her eyes, and owned there was. "You have guessed right, dear Lady," she said with a sweet simple faltering voice. "You wonder at one so poor and friendless having an attachment, don't you? I have never heard that poverty was any safeguard against it. I wish it were."

"My poor dear child," cried Miss Crawley, who was always quite ready to be sentimental, "Is our passion unrequited, then? Are we pining in secret? Tell me all, and let me console you."

"I wish you could, dear Madam," Rebecca said in the same tearful tone. "Indeed, indeed I need it." And she laid her head upon Miss Crawley's shoulder and wept there so naturally that the old lady, surprised into sympathy, embraced her with an almost maternal kindness, uttered many soothing protests of regard and affection for her, vowed that she loved her as a daughter, and would do everything in her power to serve her. "And now who is it, my dear? Is it that pretty Miss Sedley's brother? You said something about an affair with him. I'll ask him here, my dear. And you shall have him: indeed you shall."

"Don't ask me now," Rebecca said. "You shall know all soon. Indeed you shall. Dear kind Miss Crawley—Dear friend, may I say so?"

"That you may, my child," the old lady replied, kissing her.

"I can't tell you now," sobbed out Rebecca, "I am very miserable. But O! love me always—promise you will love me always." And in the midst of mutual tears—for the emotions of the younger woman had awakened the sympathies of the elder—this promise was solemnly given by Miss Crawley, who left her little protégée, blessing and admiring her as a dear, artless, tender-hearted, affectionate, incomprehensible creature.

And now she was left alone to think over the sudden and wonderful events of the day, and of what had been and what might have been. What think you were the private feelings of Miss, no, (begging her pardon) of Mrs. Rebecca? If, a few pages back, the present writer claimed the privilege of peeping into Miss Amelia Sedley's bed-room, and understanding with the omniscience of the novelist all the gentle pains and passions which were tossing upon that innocent pillow, why should he not declare himself to be Rebecca's confidante too, master of her secrets, and seal-keeper of that young woman's conscience?

Well then, in the first place, Rebecca gave way to some very sincere and touching regrets that a piece of marvellous good fortune should have been so near her, and she actually obliged to decline it. In this natural emotion every properly regulated mind will certainly share. What good mother is there that would not commiserate a penniless spinster, who might have been my lady, and have shared four thousand a year? What well-bred young person is there in all Vanity Fair, who will not feel for a hard-working, ingenious, meritorious girl, who gets such an honourable, advantageous, provoking offer, just at the very moment when it is out of her power to accept it? I am sure our friend Becky's disappointment deserves and will command every sympathy.

I remember one night being in the Fair myself, at an evening party. I observed old Miss Toady there also present, single out for her special attentions and flattery little Mrs. Briefless,[7] the barrister's wife, who is of a good family certainly, but, as we all know, is as poor as poor can be.

What, I asked in my own mind, can cause this obsequiousness on the part of Miss Toady; has Briefless got a county court, or has his wife had a fortune left her? Miss Toady explained presently, with that simplicity which distinguishes all her conduct. 'You know,' she said, 'Mrs. Briefless is granddaughter of Sir John Redhand, who is so ill at Cheltenham that he can't last six months. Mrs. Briefless's papa, succeeds; so you see she *will* be a baronet's daughter.' And Toady asked Briefless and his wife to dinner the very next week.

If the mere chance of becoming a baronet's daughter can procure a lady such homage in the world, surely, surely we may respect the agonies of a young woman who has lost the opportunity of becoming a baronet's wife. Who would have dreamed of Lady Crawley dying so soon? She was one of those sickly women that might have lasted these ten years—Rebecca thought to herself, in all the woes of repentance—and I might have been my lady! I might have led that old man whither I would. I might have thanked Mrs. Bute for her patronage, and Mr. Pitt for his insufferable condescension. I would have had the town-house newly furnished and decorated. I would have had the handsomest carriage in London, and a box at

7. A brief is legal counsel's summary of arguments for a case at law.

the Opera; and I would have been presented next season. All this *might* have been; but[8] now—now all was doubt and mystery.

But Rebecca was a young lady of too much resolution and energy of character to permit herself much useless and unseemly sorrow for the irrevocable past; so, having devoted only the proper portion of regret to it, she wisely turned her whole attention towards the future, which was now vastly more important to her. And she surveyed her position, and its hopes, doubts, and chances.

In the first place, she was *married;*—that was a great fact. Sir Pitt knew it. She was not so much surprised into the avowal, as induced to make it by a sudden calculation. It must have come some day; and why not now as at a later period? He who would have married her himself must at least be silent with regard to her marriage. But how[9] Miss Crawley would bear the news—was the great question. Misgivings Rebecca had; but she remembered all Miss Crawley had said; the old lady's avowed contempt for birth; her daring liberal opinions; her general romantic propensities; her almost doting attachment to her nephew, and her repeatedly-expressed fondness for Rebecca herself. She is so fond of him, Rebecca thought, that she will forgive him anything: she is so used to me that I don't think she could be comfortable without me: when the *éclaircissement*[1] comes there will be a scene, and hysterics, and a great quarrel, and then a great reconciliation. At all events, what use was there in delaying? the die was thrown, and now or to-morrow the issue must be the same. And so, resolved that Miss Crawley should have the news, the young person debated in her mind as to the best means of conveying it to her; and whether she should face the storm that must come, or fly and avoid it until its first fury was blown over. In this state of meditation she wrote the following letter:—

Dearest Friend,—The great crisis which we have debated about so often is *come.* Half of my secret is known, and I have thought and thought, until I am quite sure that now is the time to reveal *the whole of the mystery.* Sir Pitt came to me this morning, and made—what do you think?—*a declaration in form.* Think of that! Poor little me. I might have been lady Crawley. How pleased Mrs. Bute would have been; and *ma tante*[2] if I had taken precedence of her! I might have been somebody's mamma, instead of—O, I tremble, I tremble, when I think how soon we must tell all!—

Sir Pitt knows I am married, and not knowing to whom, is not very much displeased as yet. Ma tante is *actually angry* that I should have refused him. But she is all kindness and graciousness. She condescends to say I would have made him a good wife; and vows that she will be a mother to your little Rebecca. She will be shaken when she first hears the news. But need we fear anything beyond a momentary anger? I think not: *I am sure* not. She dotes upon you so (you naughty, good-for-nothing man), that she would pardon you

8. Revised edition reads: and
9. "But how" was altered to "How" in the revised edition.
1. Explanation.
2. Aunt.

*anything:* and, indeed, I believe, the next place in her heart is mine: and that she would be miserable without me. Dearest! something *tells me* we shall conquer. You shall leave that odious regiment: quit gaming, racing, and *be a good boy;* and we shall all live in Park Lane: and *ma tante* shall leave us all her money.

I shall try and walk to-morrow at 3 in the usual place. If Miss B. accompanies me, you must come to dinner, and bring an answer, and put it in the third volume of Porteus's Sermons.[3] But, at all events, come to your own.

R.

To Miss Eliza Styles,
At Mr. Barnet's, Saddler, Knightsbridge.[4]

And I trust there is no reader of this little story who has not discernment enough to perceive that the Miss Eliza Styles (an old schoolfellow, Rebecca said, with whom she had resumed an active correspondence of late) and who used to fetch these letters from the saddler's, wore brass spurs, and large curling mustachios, and was indeed no other than Captain Rawdon Crawley.

3. Beilby Porteus (1731–1808), bishop of London.
4. A stable and tack shop on the south side of Hyde Park near Knightsbridge Barracks.

## *Chapter XVI.*

### THE LETTER ON THE PINCUSHION.

ow they were married is not of the slightest consequence to any body. What is to hinder a Captain who is a major, and a young lady who is of age, from purchasing a license, and uniting themselves at any church in this town? Who needs to be told, that if a woman has a will, she will assuredly find a way?—My belief is, that one day, when Miss Sharp had gone to pass the forenoon with her dear friend Miss Amelia Sedley, in Russell-square, a lady very like her might have been seen entering a church in the city, in company with a gentleman with dyed mustachoes, who, after a quarter of an hour's interval, escorted her back to the hackney-coach in waiting, and that this was a quiet bridal party. And who on earth, after the daily experience we have, can question the probability of a gentleman marrying any body? How many of the wise and learned have married their cooks? Did not Lord Eldon[1] himself, the most prudent of men, make a run-away match? Were not Achilles and Ajax both in love with their servant maids?[2] And are we to expect a heavy dragoon with strong desires and small brains, who had never controlled a passion in his life, to become prudent all of a sudden, and to refuse to pay any price for an indulgence to which he had a mind? If people only made prudent marriages, what a stop to population there would be!

It seems to me, for my part, that Mr. Rawdon's marriage was one of the honestest actions which we shall have to record in any portion of that gentleman's biography which has to do with the present history. No one will say it is unmanly to be captivated by a woman, or, being captivated, to marry her; and the admiration, the delight, the passion, the wonder, the unbounded confidence, and frantic adoration with which, by degrees, this big warrior got to regard the little Rebecca, were feelings which the ladies at least will pronounce were not altogether discreditable to him. When she sang, every note thrilled in his dull soul, and tingled through his huge frame. When she spoke, he brought all the force of his brains to listen and wonder. If she was jocular, he used to revolve her jokes in his mind, and ex-

1. John Scott, first earl of Eldon (1751–1838), of a merchant family, was lord chancellor from 1801 to 1827. He eloped in 1772 with the wealthy Elizabeth Surtees.
2. Greek heroes in the *Iliad* who had slave concubines of noble birth.

plode over them half an hour afterwards in the street, to the surprise of the groom in the tilbury by his side, or the comrade riding with him in Rotten Row.[3] Her words were oracles to him, her smallest actions marked by an infallible grace and wisdom. "How she sings,—how she paints," thought he. "How she rode that kicking mare at Queen's Crawley!" And he would say to her in confidential moments, "By Jove, Beck, you're fit to be Commander-in-Chief, or Archbishop of Canterbury, by Jove." Is his case a rare one? and don't we see every day in the world many an honest Hercules at the apron-strings of Omphale, and great whiskered Samsons prostrate in Delilah's lap?[4]

When, then, Becky told him that the great crisis was near, and the time for action had arrived, Rawdon expressed himself as ready to act under her orders, as he would be to charge with his troop at the command of his colonel. There was no need for him to put his letter into the third volume of Porteus. Rebecca easily found a means to get rid of Briggs, her companion, and met her faithful friend in "the usual place" on the next day. She had thought over matters at night, and communicated to Rawdon the result of her determinations. He agreed, of course, to every thing; was quite sure that it was all right; that what she proposed was best; that Miss Crawley would infallibly relent, or "come round," as he said, after a time. Had Rebecca's resolutions been entirely different, he would have followed them as implicitly. "You have head enough for both of us, Beck," said he. "You're sure to get us out of the scrape. I never saw your equal, and I've met with some clippers[5] in my time too." And with this simple confession of faith, the love-stricken dragoon left her to execute his part of the project which she had formed for the pair.

It consisted simply in the hiring of quiet lodgings at Brompton,[6] or in the neighbourhood of the barracks, for Captain and Mrs. Crawley. For Rebecca had determined, and very prudently, we think, to fly. Rawdon was only too happy at her resolve; he had been entreating her to take this measure any time for weeks past. He pranced off to engage the lodgings with all the impetuosity of love. He agreed to pay two guineas a week so readily, that the landlady regretted she had asked him so little. He ordered in a piano, and half a nursery house full of flowers, and a heap of good things. As for shawls, kid gloves, silk stockings, gold French watches, bracelets and perfumery, he sent them in with the profusion of blind love and unbounded credit. And having relieved his mind by this outpouring of generosity, he went and dined nervously at the club, waiting until the great moment of his life should come.

The occurrences of the previous day; the admirable conduct of Rebecca in refusing an offer so advantageous to her, the secret un-

3. Tilbury: two-wheeled open carriage. Rotten Row: a circular road reserved for horse riding in Hyde Park.
4. Because of a murder, Hercules became the slave of Omphale, queen of Lydia, doing woman's work for a year. Samson, the strong man of Israel, lost his hair and his strength sleeping in Delilah's lap.
5. At best an ambiguous compliment, for the clippers Rawdon thinks might get the best of him are cheats (the word refers to one who clipped coins).
6. A residential suburb west of Kensington.

happiness preying upon her, the sweetness and silence with which she bore her affliction, made Miss Crawley much more tender than usual. An event of this nature, a marriage, or a refusal, or a proposal, thrills through a whole houseful of women, and sets all their hysterical sympathies at work. As an observer of human nature, I regularly frequent St. George's, Hanover Square,[7] during the genteel marriage season; and though I have never seen the bridegroom's male friends give way to tears, or the beadles and officiating clergy any way affected, yet it is not at all uncommon to see women who are not in the least concerned in the operations going on—old ladies who are long past marrying, stout middle-aged females with plenty of sons and daughters, let alone pretty young creatures in pink bonnets, who are on their promotion,[8] and may naturally take an interest in the ceremony,—I say it is quite common to see the women present piping, sobbing, sniffling, hiding their little faces in their little useless pocket-handkerchiefs, and heaving old and young with emotion.[9] When my friend, the fashionable John Pimlico, married the lovely Lady Belgravia Green Parker,[1] the emotion was so general, that even the little snuffy old pew-opener who let me into the seat, was in tears. And wherefore? I enquired of my own soul: *she* was not going to be married.

Miss Crawley and Briggs in a word, after the affair of Sir Pitt, indulged in the utmost luxury of sentiment, and Rebecca became an object of the most tender interest to them. In her absence Miss Crawley solaced herself with the most sentimental of the novels in her library. Little Sharp, with her secret griefs, was the heroine of the day.

That night Rebecca sang more sweetly and talked more pleasantly than she had ever been heard to do in Park Lane. She twined herself round the heart of Miss Crawley. She spoke lightly and laughingly of Sir Pitt's proposal, ridiculed it as the foolish fancy of an old man; and her eyes filled with tears, and Briggs's heart with unutterable pangs of defeat, as she said she desired no other lot than to remain for ever with her dear benefactress. "My dear little creature," the old lady said, "I don't intend to let you stir for years, that you may depend upon. As for going back to that odious brother of mine after what has passed, it is out of the question. Here you stay with me and Briggs. Briggs wants to go to see her relations very often. Briggs, you may go when you like. But as for you, my dear, you must stay and take care of the old woman."

If Rawdon Crawley had been then and there present, instead of being at the club nervously drinking claret, the pair might have gone down on their knees before the old spinster, avowed all, and been forgiven in a twinkling. But that good chance was denied to the young couple, doubtless in order that this story might be written, in which numbers of their wonderful adventures are narrated—adventures which could never have occurred to them if they had been housed

7. Frequently mentioned in connection with weddings; a church in May Fair.
8. Hoping to be noticed.
9. Revised edition reads: excitement
1. The names are made up of references to the most elegant parts of London.

and sheltered under the comfortable uninteresting forgiveness of Miss Crawley.

Under Mrs. Firkin's orders, in the Park Lane establishment, was a young woman from Hampshire, whose business it was, among other duties, to knock at Miss Sharp's door with that jug of hot water, which Firkin would rather have perished than have presented to the intruder. This girl, bred on the family estate, had a brother in Captain Crawley's troop, and if the truth were known, I daresay it would come out that she was aware of certain arrangements, which have a great deal to do with this history. At any rate she purchased a yellow shawl, a pair of green boots, and a light blue hat with a red feather, with three guineas which Rebecca gave her, and as little Sharp was by no means too liberal with her money, no doubt it was for services rendered that Betty Martin was so bribed.

On the second day after Sir Pitt Crawley's offer to Miss Sharp, the sun rose as usual, and at the usual hour Betty Martin, the upstairs maid, knocked at the door of the governess's bed-chamber.

No answer was returned, and she knocked again. Silence was still uninterrupted; and Betty, with the hot water, opened the door and entered the chamber.

The little white dimity bed was as smooth and trim as on the day previous when Betty's own hands had helped to make it. Two little trunks were corded in one end of the room; and on the table before the window—on the pincushion—the great fat pincushion lined with pink inside, and twilled like a lady's nightcap—lay a letter. It had been reposing there probably all night.

Betty advanced towards it on tiptoe, as if she were afraid to awake it—looked at it, and round the room with an air of great wonder and satisfaction, took up the letter, and grinned intensely as she turned it round and over, and finally carried it in to Miss Briggs's room below.

How could Betty tell that the letter was for Miss Briggs, I should like to know? All the schooling Betty had was at Mrs. Bute Crawley's Sunday School, and she could no more read writing than Hebrew.

"La, Miss Briggs," the girl exclaimed, "O, Miss, something must have happened—there's nobody in Miss Sharp's room; the bed aint been slep in, and she've run away, and left this letter for you, Miss."

*"What!"* cries Briggs, dropping her comb, the thin wisp of faded hair falling over her shoulders; "an elopement! Miss Sharp a fugitive! What, what is this?" and she eagerly broke the neat seal, and, as they say, "devoured the contents" of the letter addressed to her.

"Dear Miss Briggs," the refugee wrote, "the kindest heart in the world as yours is, will pity and sympathise with me and excuse me. With tears, and prayers, and blessings, I leave the home where the poor orphan has ever met with kindness and affection. Claims even superior to those of my benefactress call me hence. I go to my duty—to my *husband.* Yes, I am married. My husband *commands* me to seek the *humble home* which we call ours. Dearest Miss Briggs, break the news as your delicate sympathy will know how to do it—to my dear, my beloved friend and benefactress. Tell her, ere I went, I shed

The Note on the Pincushion

tears on her dear pillow—that pillow that I have so often soothed in sickness—that I long *again* to watch—Oh, with what joy shall I return to dear Park Lane! How I tremble for the answer which is to *seal my fate!* When Sir Pitt deigned to offer me his hand, an honour of which my beloved Miss Crawley said I was *deserving,* (my blessings go with her for judging the poor orphan worthy to be *her sister!*), I told Sir Pitt that I was *already a wife.* Even he forgave me. But my courage failed me, when I should have told him all—that I could not be his wife, for I *was his daughter!* I am wedded to the best and most generous of men—Miss Crawley's Rawdon is *my* Rawdon. At his *command* I open my lips, and follow him to our humble home, as I would *through the world.* O, my excellent and kind friend, intercede with my Rawdon's beloved aunt for him and the poor girl to whom all *his noble race* have shown such *unparalleled affection.* Ask Miss Crawley to receive *her children.* I can say no more, but blessings, blessings on all in the dear house I leave, prays

"Your affectionate and *grateful,*

"Midnight." "REBECCA CRAWLEY."

Just as Briggs had finished reading this affecting and interesting document, which reinstated her in her position as first confidante of Miss Crawley, Mrs. Firkin entered the room. "Here's Mrs. Bute Crawley just arrived by the mail[2] from Hampshire, and wants some tea, will you come down and make breakfast, Miss?"

And to the surprise of Firkin, clasping her dressing-gown around her, the wisp of hair floating dishevelled behind her, the little curl-papers still sticking in bunches round her forehead, Briggs sailed down to Mrs. Bute with the letter in her hand containing the wonderful news.

"Oh, Mrs. Firkin," gasped Betty, "sech a business. Miss Sharp have a gone and run away with the Capting, and they're off to Gretny Green!"[3] We would devote a chapter to describe the emotions of Mrs. Firkin, did not the passions of her mistresses occupy our genteeler muse.

When Mrs. Bute Crawley, numbed with midnight travelling, and warming herself at the newly crackling parlour fire, heard from Miss Briggs the intelligence of the clandestine marriage, she declared it was quite providential that she should have arrived at such a time to assist poor dear Miss Crawley in supporting the shock—that Rebecca was an artful little hussy of whom she had always had her suspicions; and that as for Rawdon Crawley, she never could account for his aunt's infatuation regarding him, and had long considered him a profligate, lost, and abandoned being. And this awful conduct, Mrs. Bute said, will have at least *this* good effect, it will open poor dear Miss Crawley's eyes to the real character of this wicked man. Then Mrs. Bute had a comfortable hot toast and tea; and as there was a vacant room in the house now, there was no need for her to remain

2. The mail coach carried passengers.
3. A Scottish town famous for runaway English weddings; Scottish marriage laws did not require waiting time or published banns.

at the Gloster Coffee House[4] where the Portsmouth mail had set her down, and whence she ordered Mr. Bowls's aide-de-camp the footman to bring away her trunks.

Miss Crawley, be it known, did not leave her room until near noon—taking chocolate in bed in the morning, while Becky Sharp read the Morning Post[5] to her, or otherwise amusing herself or dawdling. The conspirators below agreed that they would spare the dear lady's feelings until she appeared in her drawing-room: meanwhile it was announced to her, that Mrs. Bute Crawley had come up from Hampshire by the mail, was staying at the Gloster, sent her love to Miss Crawley, and asked for breakfast with Miss Briggs. The arrival of Mrs. Bute, which would not have caused any extreme delight at another period, was hailed with pleasure now; Miss Crawley being pleased at the notion of a gossip with her sister-in-law regarding the late Lady Crawley, the funeral arrangements pending, and Sir Pitt's abrupt proposals to Rebecca.

It was not until the old lady was fairly ensconced in her usual arm-chair in the drawing-room, and the preliminary embraces and inquiries had taken place between the ladies, that the conspirators thought it advisable to submit her to the operation. Who has not admired the artifices and delicate approaches with which women "prepare" their friends for bad news? Miss Crawley's two friends made such an apparatus of mystery before they broke the intelligence to her, that they worked her up to the necessary degree of doubt and alarm.

"And she refused Sir Pitt, my dear dear Miss Crawley, prepare yourself for it," Mrs. Bute said, "because—because she couldn't help herself."

"Of course there was a reason," Miss Crawley answered. "She liked somebody else. I told Briggs so yesterday."

"*Likes* somebody else!" Briggs gasped. "O my dear friend, she is married already."

"Married already," Mrs. Bute chimed in; and both sate with clasped hands looking from each other at their victim.

"Send her to me, the instant she comes in. The little sly wretch: how dared she not tell me?" cried out Miss Crawley.

"She won't come in soon. Prepare yourself, dear friend—she's gone out for a long time—she's—she's gone altogether."

"Gracious goodness, and who's to make my chocolate? Send for her and have her back; I desire that she come back," the old lady said.

"She decamped last night, Ma'am," cried Mrs. Bute.

"She left a letter for me," Briggs exclaimed. "She's married to—"

"Prepare her, for heaven's sake. Don't torture her, my dear Miss Briggs."

"She's married to whom?" cries the spinster in a nervous fury.

"To—to a relation of——".

4. The Old Gloucester Coffee House on the corner of Piccadilly and Berkeley Street served the west England coaches. Its name was changed first to St. James Hotel and then to Berkeley Hotel.
5. Prominent daily paper devoting significant space to socialite news.

"She refused Sir Pitt," cried the victim. "Speak at once. Don't drive me mad."

"O Ma'am—prepare her, Miss Briggs—she's married to Rawdon Crawley."

"Rawdon married—Rebecca—governess—nobod—Get out of my house, you fool, you idiot—you stupid old Briggs—how dare you? You're in the plot—you made him marry, thinking that I'd leave my money from him—you did, Martha," the poor old lady screamed in hysteric sentences.

"I, Ma'am, ask a member of this family to marry a drawing-master's daughter?"

"Her mother was a Montmorency," cried out the old lady, pulling at the bell with all her might.

"Her mother was an opera girl, and she has been on the stage or worse herself," said Mrs. Bute.

Miss Crawley gave a final scream, and fell back in a faint. They were forced to take her back to the room which she had just quitted. One fit of hysterics succeeded another. The doctor was sent for—the apothecary arrived. Mrs. Bute took up the post of nurse by her bedside. "Her relations ought to be round about her," that amiable woman said.

She had scarcely been carried up to her room, when a new person arrived to whom it was also necessary to break the news. This was Sir Pitt. "Where's Becky?" he said, coming in. "Where's her traps? She's coming with me to Queen's Crawley."

"Have you not heard the astonishing intelligence regarding her surreptitious union?" Briggs asked.

"What's that to me?" Sir Pitt asked. "I know she's married. That makes no odds. Tell her to come down at once, and not keep me."

"Are you not aware, Sir," Miss Briggs asked, "that she has left our roof, to the dismay of Miss Crawley, who is nearly killed by the intelligence of Captain Rawdon's union with her?"

When Sir Pitt Crawley heard that Rebecca was married to his son, he broke out into a fury of language, which it would do no good to repeat in this place, as indeed it sent poor Briggs shuddering out of the room; and with her we will shut the door upon the figure of the frenzied old man, wild with hatred and insane with baffled desire.

One day after he went to Queen's Crawley, he burst like a madman into the room she had used when there—dashed open her boxes with his foot, and flung about her papers, clothes, and other relics. Miss Horrocks, the butler's daughter, took some of them. The children dressed themselves and acted plays in the others. It was but a few days after the poor mother had gone to her lonely burying-place; and was laid, unwept and disregarded, in a vault full of strangers.

"Suppose the old lady doesn't come to," Rawdon said to his little wife, as they sate together in the snug little Brompton lodgings. She had been trying the new piano all the morning. The new gloves fitted her to a nicety; the new shawls became her wonderfully; the new rings glittered on her little hands, and the new watch ticked at her waist; "suppose she don't come round, eh, Becky?"

*"I'll* make your fortune," she said; and Delilah patted Samson's cheek.

"You can do anything," he said, kissing the little hand. "By Jove, you can; and we'll drive down to the Star and Garter,[6] and dine, by Jove."

## *Chapter XVII.*

### HOW CAPTAIN DOBBIN BOUGHT A PIANO.

IF there is any exhibition in all Vanity Fair which Satire and Sentiment can visit arm in arm together; where you light on the strangest contrasts laughable and tearful: where you may be gentle and pathetic, or savage and cynical with perfect propriety: it is at one of those public assemblies, a crowd of which are advertised every day in the last page of the Times newspaper, and over which the late Mr. George Robins[1] used to preside with so much dignity. There are very few London people, as I fancy, who have not attended at these meetings, and all with a taste for moralising must have thought, with a sensation and interest not a little startling and queer, of the day when their turn shall come too, and Mr. Hammerdown will sell by the orders of Diogenes's assignees, or will be instructed by the executors, to offer to public competition, the library, furniture, plate, wardrobe, and choice cellar of wines of Epicurus deceased.[2]

Even with the most selfish disposition, the Vanity-fairian, as he witnesses this sordid part of the obsequies of a departed friend, can't but feel some sympathies and regret. My Lord Dives's remains are in the family vault: the statuaries are cutting an inscription veraciously commemorating his virtues, and the sorrows of his heir, who is disposing of his goods. What guest at Dives's table can pass the familiar house without a sigh?—the familiar house of which the lights used to shine so cheerfully at seven o'clock, of which the hall-doors opened so readily, of which the obsequious servants, as you passed up the comfortable stair, sounded your name from landing to landing, until it reached the apartment where jolly old Dives welcomed his friends! What a number of them he had; and what a noble way of entertaining them. How witty people used to be here who were morose when they got out of the door; and how courteous and friendly men who slandered and hated each other every where else! He was pompous,

6. Expensive tavern and club meeting-place patronized by the prince regent and aristocracy.
1. A famous, very successful auctioneer (1778–1847), probably the original for the hypothetical gentleman auctioneer described by Thackeray in Fitzboodle's "Being Appeals to the Unemployed Younger Sons of the Nobility: First Profession."
2. Diogenes and Epicurus were Greek philosophers whose views are now taken as synonymous with asceticism and hedonism.

An Elephant for Sale

but with such a cook what would one not swallow? he was rather dull, perhaps, but would not such wine make any conversation pleasant? We must get some of his Burgundy at any price, the mourners cry at his club. "I got this box at old Dives's sale," Pincher says, handing it round, "one of Louis XV.'s mistresses—pretty thing, is it not—sweet miniature," and they talk of the way in which young Dives is dissipating his fortune.[3]

How changed the house is, though! The front is patched over with bills, setting forth the particulars of the furniture in staring capitals. They have hung a shred of carpet out of an upstairs window—a half dozen of porters are lounging on the dirty steps—the hall swarms with dingy guests of oriental countenance, who thrust printed cards into your hand, and offer to bid. Old women and amateurs have invaded the upper apartments, pinching the bed curtains, poking into the feathers, shampooing[4] the mattresses, and clapping the wardrobe drawers to and fro. Enterprising young housekeepers are measuring the looking glasses and hangings to see if they will suit the new ménage.[5]—(Snob will brag for years that he has purchased this or that at Dives's sale,) and Mr. Hammerdown is sitting on the great mahogany dining-tables, in the dining-room below, waving the ivory hammer, and employing all the artifices of eloquence, enthusiasm, entreaty, reason, despair; shouting to his people; satirising Mr. Davids for his sluggishness; inspiriting Mrs. Moss into action; imploring, commanding, bellowing, until down comes the hammer like fate, and we pass to the next lot. O Dives, who would ever have thought, as we sat round the broad table sparkling with plate and spotless linen, to have seen such a dish at the head of it as that roaring auctioneer?

It was rather late in the sale. The excellent drawing-room furniture by the best makers; the rare and famous wines selected, regardless of cost, and with the well known taste of the purchaser; the rich and complete set of family plate had been sold on the previous days. Certain of the best wines (which all had a great character among amateurs in the neighbourhood) had been purchased for his master, who knew them very well, by the butler of our friend John Osborne, Esquire, of Russell Square. A small portion of the most useful articles of the plate had been bought by some young stock-brokers from the city. And now the public being invited to the purchase of minor objects, it happened that the orator on the table was expatiating on the merits of a picture, which he sought to recommend to his audience: it was by no means so select or numerous a company as had attended the previous days of the auction.

"No. 369," roared Mr. Hammerdown. "Portrait of a gentleman on an elephant. Who'll bid for the gentleman on the elephant? Lift up the picture, Blowman, and let the company examine this lot." A long, pale, military-looking gentleman, seated demurely at the mahogany table, could not help grinning as this valuable lot was shown by Mr. Blowman. "Turn the elephant to the Captain, Blowman. What shall

3. The name is taken from the story of the rich man (Dives) and Lazarus (Luke 16). Louis XV was king of France from 1715 to 1774.
4. Massaging.
5. Household.

we say, sir, for the elephant?" but the Captain, blushing in a very hurried and discomfited manner, turned away his head, and the auctioneer respected his discomposure.[6]

"Shall we say twenty guineas for this work of art?—fifteen, five, name your own price. The gentleman without the elephant is worth five pound."

"I wonder it aint come down with him," said a professional wag, "he's any how a precious big one;" at which (for the elephant-rider was represented as of a very stout figure) there was a general giggle in the room.

"Don't be trying to deprecate the value of the lot, Mr. Moss," Mr. Hammerdown said; "let the company examine it as a work of art—the attitude of the gallant animal quite according to natur'; the gentleman in a nankeen-jacket,[7] his gun in his hand is going to the chace; in the distance a banyhann-tree and a pagody, most likely resemblances of some interesting spot in our famous Eastern possessions. How much for this lot? Come, gentlemen, don't keep me here all day."

Some one bid five shillings, at which the military gentleman looked towards the quarter from which this splendid offer had come; and there saw another officer with a young lady on his arm, who both appeared to be highly amused with the scene, and to whom, finally,

this lot was knocked down for half-a-guinea. He at the table looked more surprised and discomposed than ever when he spied this pair, and his head sank into his military collar, and he turned his back upon them, so as to avoid them altogether.

Of all the other articles which Mr. Hammerdown had the honour to offer for public competition that day it is not our purpose to make mention, save of one only; this was a[8] little square piano which came down from the upper regions of the house (the state grand piano having been disposed of previously); this the young lady tried with

6. There is no manuscript to refer to here. The first edition reads: and the auctioneer repeated his discomposure. The emendation to "respected" was first suggested in 1908 by George Saintsbury. Many earlier editions stop the paragraph at "head."

7. Naturally yellow Chinese cotton.

8. Revised edition reads: only, a

a rapid and skilful hand, (making the officer blush and start again), and for it, when its turn came, her agent began to bid.

But there was an opposition here. The Hebrew aide-de-camp in the service of the officer at the table bid against the Hebrew gentleman employed by the elephant purchasers, and a brisk battle ensued over this little piano, the combatants being greatly encouraged by Mr. Hammerdown.

At last, when the competition had been prolonged for some time, the elephant captain and lady desisted from the race; and the hammer coming down, the auctioneer said:—"Mr. Lewis, twenty-five," and Mr. Lewis's chief thus became the proprietor of the little square piano. Having effected the purchase, he sate up as if he was greatly relieved, and the unsuccessful competitors catching a glimpse of him at this moment, the lady said to her friend,

"Why, Rawdon, it's Captain Dobbin."

I suppose Becky was discontented with the new piano her husband had hired for her, or perhaps the proprietors of that instrument had fetched it away, declining farther credit, or perhaps she had a particular attachment for the one which she had first tried to purchase, recollecting it in old days, when she used to play upon it, in the little sitting-room of our dear Amelia Sedley.

The sale was at the old house in Russell Square, where we passed some evenings together at the beginning of this story. Good old John Sedley was a ruined man. His name had been proclaimed as a defaulter on the Stock Exchange, and his bankruptcy and commercial extermination had followed. Mr. Osborne's butler came to buy some of the famous port wine to transfer to the cellars over the way. As for one dozen well-manufactured silver spoons and forks at per oz., and one dozen dessert ditto ditto, there were three young stockbrokers (Messrs. Dale, Spiggot, and Dale, of Threadneedle street,[9] indeed), who having had dealings with the old man, and kindnesses from him in days when he was kind to every body with whom he dealt, sent this little spar out of the wreck with their love to good Mrs. Sedley; and with respect to the piano, as it had been Amelia's, and as she might miss it and want one now, and as Captain William Dobbin could no more play upon it, than he could dance on the tight-rope, it is probable that he did not purchase it[1] for his own use.

In a word, it arrived that evening, at a wonderful small cottage in a street leading from the Fulham Road—one of those streets which have the finest romantic names—(this was called St. Adelaide Villas, Anna-Maria Road, West),[2] where the houses look like baby-houses; where the people looking out of the first-floor windows, must infallibly, as you think, sit with their feet in the parlours; where the shrubs in the little gardens in front, bloom with a perennial display of little

9. Banking and commercial establishments, including the Royal Exchange and Stock Exchange, bordered this street.
1. Revised edition reads: the instrument
2. Fulham Road was the coaching road to Portsmouth and points west of London; it went through the growing suburb of Brompton, which had street names similar to those given in parentheses.

children's pinafores, little red socks, caps, &c. (polyandria polygynia);[3] whence you hear the sound of jingling spinets and women singing; where little porter pots[4] hang on the railings sunning themselves; whither of evenings you see city clerks padding wearily: here it was that Mr. Clapp, the clerk of Mr. Sedley, had his domicile, and in this asylum the good old gentleman hid his head with his wife and daughter when the crash came.

Jos Sedley had acted as a man of his disposition would, when the announcement of the family-misfortune reached him. He did not come to London, but he wrote to his mother to draw upon his agents for whatever money was wanted, so that his kind broken-spirited old parents had no present poverty to fear. This done, Jos went on at the boarding-house at Cheltenham pretty much as before. He drove his curricle;[5] he drank his claret; he played his rubber; he told his Indian stories, and the Irish widow consoled and flattered him as usual. His present of money, needful as it was, made little impression on his parents; and I have heard Amelia say, that the first day on which she saw her father lift up his head after the failure, was on the receipt of the packet of forks and spoons with the young stockbroker's love, over which he burst out, crying like a child, being greatly more affected than even his wife, to whom the present was addressed. Edward Dale, the junior of the house, who purchased the spoons for the firm, was, in fact, very sweet upon Amelia, and offered for her in spite of all. He married Miss Louisa Cutts (daughter of Higham and Cutts, the eminent corn-factors),[6] with a handsome fortune in 1820; and is now living in splendour, and with a numerous family, at his elegant villa, Muswell Hill.[7] But we must not let the recollections of this good fellow cause us to diverge from the plain and[8] principal history.

I hope the reader has much too good an opinion of Captain and Mrs. Crawley to suppose that they ever would have dreamed of paying a visit to so remote a district as Bloomsbury, if they thought the family whom they proposed to honour with a visit were not merely out of fashion, but out of money, and could be serviceable to them in no possible manner. Rebecca was entirely surprised at the sight of the comfortable old house where she had met with no small kindness, ransacked by brokers and bargainers, and its quiet family treasures given up to public desecration and plunder. A month after her flight, she had bethought her of Amelia, and Rawdon, with a horse laugh, had expressed a perfect willingness to see young George Osborne again. "He's a very agreeable acquaintance, Beck," the wag added. "I'd like to sell him another horse, Beck. I'd like to play a few more games at billiards with him. He'd be what I call *useful* just now, Mrs. C.—ha, ha!" by which sort of speech it is not to be supposed

3. Greek for "many men and women"—a playful stab at botanical names for laundry blooming (drying) on the shrubs.
4. Beer mugs.
5. Two-wheeled carriage drawn by a pair of horses.
6. Grain dealers.
7. A village north of London.
8. Revised edition omits: plain and

that Rawdon Crawley had a deliberate desire to cheat Mr. Osborne at play, but only wished to take that fair advantage of him which almost every sporting gentleman in Vanity Fair considers to be his due from his neighbour.

The old Aunt was long in "coming-to." A month had elapsed. Rawdon was denied the door by Mr. Bowls; his servants could not get a lodgement in the house at Park Lane; his letters were sent back unopened. Miss Crawley never stirred out—she was unwell—and Mrs. Bute remained still and never left her. Crawley and his wife both of them augured evil from the continued presence of Mrs. Bute.

"Gad, I begin to perceive now why she was always bringing us together at Queen's Crawley," Rawdon said.

"What an artful little woman!" ejaculated Rebecca.

"Well, *I* don't regret it, if you don't," the Captain cried, still in an amorous rapture with his wife, who rewarded him with a kiss by way of reply, and was indeed not a little gratified by the generous confidence of her husband.

"If he had but a little more brains," she thought to herself, "I might make something of him;" but she never let him perceive the opinion she had of him; listened with indefatigable complacency to his stories of the stable and the mess; laughed at all his jokes; felt the greatest interest in Jack Spatterdash, whose cab-horse had come down, and Bob Martingale, who had been taken up in a gambling-house, and Tom Cinqbars, who was going to ride the steeple-chase.[9] When he came home she was alert and happy: when he went out she pressed him to go: when he stayed at home, she played and sang for him, made him good drinks, superintended his dinner, warmed his slippers, and steeped his soul in comfort. The best of women (I have heard my grandmother say) are hypocrites. We don't know how much they hide from us: how watchful they are when they seem most artless and confidential: how often those frank smiles which they wear so easily, are traps to cajole or elude or disarm—I don't mean in your mere coquettes, but your domestic models, and paragons of female virtue. Who has not seen a woman hide the dulness of a stupid husband, or coax the fury of a savage one? We accept this amiable slavishness, and praise a woman for it: we call this pretty treachery truth. A good housewife is of necessity a humbug; and Cornelia's husband was hoodwinked, as Potiphar was—only in a different way.[1]

By these attentions, that veteran rake, Rawdon Crawley, found himself converted into a very happy and submissive married man. His former haunts knew him not. They asked about him once or twice at his clubs, but did not miss him much: in those booths of Vanity Fair people seldom do miss each other. His secluded wife ever smiling and cheerful, his little comfortable lodgings, snug meals, and homely evenings, had all the charms of novelty and secrecy. The marriage was not yet declared to the world, or published in the Morning Post. All his creditors would have come rushing on him in a

9. In gambling, to martingale is to double the stake after each loss; a single win recoups all. To be taken up is to be arrested. Cinqbars' name alludes to a five-barred gate in steeplechase.

1. Cornelia, legendary for faithfulness, was wife of Tiberius Sempronius Gracchus. Potiphar's wife failed to seduce Joseph and charged him with attempted rape (Genesis 39).

body, had they known that he was united to a woman without fortune. "My relations won't cry fie upon me," Becky said, with rather a bitter laugh; and she was quite contented to wait until the old aunt should be reconciled, before she claimed her place in society. So she lived at Brompton, and meanwhile saw no one, or only those few of her husband's male companions who were admitted into her little dining- room. These were all charmed with her. The little dinners, the laughing and chatting, the music afterwards, delighted all who participated in these enjoyments. Major Martingale never thought about asking to see the marriage license. Captain Cinqbars was perfectly enchanted with her skill in making punch. And young Lieutenant[2] Spatterdash (who was fond of piquet, and whom Crawley would often invite) was evidently and quickly smitten by Mrs. Crawley; but her own circumspection and modesty never forsook her for a moment, and Crawley's reputation as a fire-eating and jealous warrior, was a further and complete defence to his little wife.

There are gentlemen of very good blood and fashion in this city, who never have entered a lady's drawing-room; so that though Rawdon Crawley's marriage might be talked about in his county, where, of course, Mrs. Bute had spread the news, in London it was doubted, or not heeded, or not talked about at all. He lived comfortably on credit. He had a large capital of debts, which laid out judiciously, will carry a man along for many years, and on which certain men about town contrive to live a hundred times better than even men with ready money can do. Indeed who is there that walks London streets, but can point out a half-dozen of men riding by him splendidly, while he is on foot, courted by fashion, bowed into their carriages by tradesmen, denying themselves nothing, and living on who knows what? We see Jack Thriftless prancing in the park, or darting in his brougham[3] down Pall Mall: we eat his dinners served on his miraculous plate, "How did this begin, we say, or where will it end?" "My dear fellow," I heard Jack once say, "I owe money in every capital in Europe." The end must come some day, but in the mean time Jack thrives as much as ever; people are glad enough to shake him by the hand, ignore the little dark stories that are whispered every now and then against him, and pronounce him a good-natured, jovial, reckless fellow.

Truth obliges us to confess that Rebecca had married a gentleman of this order. Everything was plentiful in his house but ready money, of which their *ménage* pretty early felt the want; and reading the Gazette one day, and coming upon the announcement of "Lieutenant G. Osborne to be Captain by purchase, vice Smith, who exchanges,"[4] Rawdon uttered that sentiment regarding Amelia's lover, which ended in the visit to Russell Square.

When Rawdon and his wife wished to communicate with Captain Dobbin at the sale, and to know particulars of the catastrophe which

2. First edition, first printing, reads: Young cornet and Lieutenant
3. Pronounced "broom"—a one-horse, closed carriage for two to four persons, named for Henry Peter Brougham (1778–1868).
4. Osborne's commission was purchased, according to established regulations, from Smith, who retired or advanced to a higher rank.

had befallen Rebecca's old acquaintances, the Captain had vanished; and such information as they got, was from a stray porter or broker at the auction.

"Look at them with their hooked beaks," Becky said, getting into the buggy, her picture under her arm in great glee. "They're like vultures after a battle."

"Don't know. Never was in action, my dear. Ask Martingale, he was in Spain, aide-de-camp to General Blazes."

"He was a very kind old man, Mr. Sedley," Rebecca said; "I'm really sorry he's gone wrong."

"O stockbrokers—bankrupts—used to it, you know," Rawdon replied, cutting a fly off the horse's ear.

"I wish we could have afforded some of the plate, Rawdon," the wife continued sentimentally. "Five-and-twenty guineas was monstrously dear for that little piano. We chose it at Broadwood's[5] for Amelia, when she came from school. It only cost five-and-thirty then."

"What d'ye-call'em 'Osborne,' will cry off now, I suppose, since the family is smashed. How cut up your pretty little friend will be; hey, Becky?"

"I daresay she'll recover it;" Becky said, with a smile—and they drove on and talked about something else.

## *Chapter XVIII.*

### WHO PLAYED ON THE PIANO CAPTAIN DOBBIN BOUGHT?

UR[1] surprised story now finds itself for a moment among very famous events and personages, and hanging on to the skirts of history. When the eagles of Napoleon Bonaparte, the Corsican upstart, were flying from Provence, where they had perched after a brief sojourn in Elba, and from steeple to steeple until they reached the towers of Notre Dame, I wonder whether the Imperial birds had any eye for a little corner of the parish of Bloomsbury, London, which you might have thought so quiet, that even the whirring and flapping of those mighty wings would pass unobserved there?[2]

5. John Broadwood, one of London's largest harpsichord and piano makers, was producing 1,400 instruments a year by 1820.
1. Initial: Napoleon and a clown.
2. Napoleon's ensignia consisted of eagles, the "Imperial birds." On his escape from Elba in

"Napoleon has landed at Cannes." Such news might create a panic at Vienna, and cause Russia to drop his cards, and take Prussia into a corner, and Talleyrand and Metternich to wag their heads together, while Prince Hardenberg, and even the present Marquis of Londonderry, were puzzled;[3] but how was this intelligence to affect a young lady in Russell Square, before whose door the watchman sang the hours when she was asleep: who, if she strolled in the square, was guarded there by the railings and the beadle:[4] who, if she walked ever so short a distance to buy a ribbon in Southampton Row, was followed by black Sambo with an enormous cane: who was always cared for, dressed, put to bed, and watched over by ever so many guardian angels, with and without wages. Bon Dieu, I say, is it not hard that the fateful rush of the great Imperial struggle can't take place without affecting a poor little harmless girl of eighteen, who is occupied in billing and cooing, or working muslin collars in Russell Square? You, too, kindly, homely flower!—is the great roaring war tempest coming to sweep you down, here, although cowering under the shelter of Holborn?[5] Yes; Napoleon is flinging his last stake, and poor little Emmy Sedley's happiness forms, somehow, part of it.

In the first place, her father's fortune was swept down with that fatal news. All his speculations had of late gone wrong with the luckless old gentleman. Ventures had failed: merchants had broken: funds had risen when he calculated they would fall. What need to particularise? If success is rare and slow, everybody knows how quick and easy ruin is. Old Sedley had kept his own sad counsel. Everything seemed to go on as usual in the quiet, opulent house: the good-natured mistress pursuing, quite unsuspiciously, her bustling idleness, and daily easy avocations; the daughter absorbed still in one selfish, tender thought, and quite regardless of all the world besides, when that final crash came under which this worthy family fell.

One night Mrs. Sedley was writing cards for a party; the Osbornes had given one, and she must not be behindhand; John Sedley, who had come home very late from the city, sate silent at the chimney side, while his wife was prattling to him; Emmy had gone up to her room ailing and low-spirited. "She's not happy," the mother went on. "George Osborne neglects her. I've no patience with the airs of those people. The girls have not been in the house these three weeks; and George has been twice in town without coming. Edward Dale saw him at the Opera. Edward would marry her I'm sure; and there's Captain Dobbin who, I think, would—only I hate all army men. Such a dandy as George has become. With his military airs, indeed! We must show some folks that we're as good as they. Only give Edward Dale any encouragement, and you'll see. We must have a party, Mr. S. Why don't you speak, John? Shall I say Tuesday fortnight? Why don't you answer? Good God, John, what has happened?"

March 1819, Napoleon landed at Cannes in Provence, on the south coast of France. He proceeded to Notre Dame Cathedral in Paris.

3. Talleyrand of France, Metternich of Austria, Hardenberg of Prussia, and Londonderry of England were all at the Congress of Vienna, discussiong post-Napoleonic alliances, when Napoleon escaped from Elba to begin the war again.
4. Caretaker or park attendant.
5. The district containing Russell Square.

John Sedley sprang up out of his chair to meet his wife, who ran to him. He seized her in his arms, and said with a hasty voice, "We're ruined, Mary. We've got the world to begin over again, dear. It's best that you should know all, and at once." As he spoke, he trembled in every limb, and almost fell. He thought the news would have overpowered his wife—his wife, to whom he had never said a hard word. But it was he that was the most moved, sudden as the shock was to her. When he sank back into his seat, it was the wife that took the office of consoler. She took his trembling[6] hand, and kissed it, and put it round her neck: she called him her John—her dear John—her old man—her kind old man: she poured out a hundred words of incoherent love and tenderness; her faithful voice and simple caresses wrought this sad heart[7] up to an inexpressible delight and anguish, and cheered and solaced his overburdened soul.

Only once in the course of the long night as they sate together, and poor Sedley opened his pent-up soul, and told the story of his losses and embarrassments—the treason of some of his oldest friends, the manly kindness of some from whom he never could have expected it—in a general confession—only once did the faithful wife give way to emotion.

"My God, my God, it will break Emmy's heart," she said.

The father had forgotten the poor girl. She was lying, awake and unhappy, overhead. In the midst of friends, home, and kind parents, she was alone. To how many people can any one tell all? Who will be open where there is no sympathy, or has call to speak to those who never can understand? Our gentle Amelia was thus solitary. She had no confidante, so to speak, ever since she had anything to confide. She could not tell the old mother[8] her doubts and cares: the would-be sisters seemed every day more strange to her. And she had misgivings and fears which she dared not acknowledge to herself, though she was always secretly brooding over them.

Her heart tried to persist in asserting that George Osborne was worthy and faithful to her, though she knew otherwise. How many a thing had she said, and got no echo from him. How many suspicions of selfishness and indifference had she to encounter and obstinately overcome. To whom could the poor little martyr tell these daily struggles and tortures? Her hero himself only half understood her. She did not dare to own that the man she loved was her inferior; or to feel that she had given her heart away too soon. Given once, the pure bashful maiden was too modest, too tender, too trustful, too weak, too much woman to recal it. We are Turks with the affections of our women; and have made them subscribe to our doctrine too. We let their bodies go abroad liberally enough, with smiles and ringlets and pink bonnets to disguise them instead of veils and yakmaks.[9] But their souls must be seen by only one man, and they obey not unwillingly, and consent to remain at home as our slaves—ministering to us and doing drudgery for us.

6. First printing reads: honest, kind
7. First printing reads: kind heart
8. First printing reads: good mother
9. Yashmaks, veils worn to cover the face of Islamic women.

So imprisoned and tortured was this gentle little heart, when in the month of March, Anno Domini 1815, Napoleon landed at Cannes, and Louis XVIII. fled,[1] and all Europe was in alarm, and the funds fell, and old John[2] Sedley was ruined.

We are not going to follow the worthy old stockbroker through those last pangs and agonies of ruin through which he passed before his commercial demise befel. They declared him[3] at the Stock Exchange; he was absent from his house of business: his bills were protested:[4] his act of bankruptcy formal. The house and furniture of Russell Square were seized and sold up, and he and his family were thrust away, as we have seen, to hide their heads where they might.

John Sedley had not the heart to review the domestic establishment who have appeared now and anon in our pages, and of whom he was now forced by poverty to take leave. The wages of those worthy people were discharged with that punctuality which men frequently show who only owe in great sums—they were sorry to leave good places—but they did not break their hearts at parting from their adored master and mistress. Amelia's maid was profuse in condolences, but went off quite resigned to better herself in a genteeler quarter of the town. Black Sambo, with the infatuation of his profession, determined on setting up a public-house. Honest old Mrs. Blenkinsop indeed, who had seen the birth of Jos and Amelia, and the wooing of John Sedley and his wife, was for staying by them without wages, having amassed a considerable sum in their service: and she accompanied the fallen people into their new and humble place of refuge, where she tended them and grumbled against them for a while.

Of all Sedley's opponents in his debates with his creditors which now ensued, and harassed the feelings of the humiliated old[5] gentleman so severely, that in six weeks he oldened more than he had done for fifteen years before—the most determined and obstinate seemed to be John Osborne, his old friend and neighbour—John Osborne, whom he had set up in life—who was under a hundred obligations to him—and whose son was to marry Sedley's daughter. Any one of these circumstances would account for the bitterness of Osborne's opposition.

When one man has been under very remarkable obligations to another, with whom he subsequently quarrels, a common sense of decency, as it were, makes of the former a much severer enemy than a mere stranger would be. To account for your own hardheartedness and ingratitude in such a case, you are bound to prove the other party's crime. It is not that you are selfish, brutal, and angry at the failure of a speculation—no, no—it is that your partner has led you into it by the basest treachery and with the most sinister motives. From a mere sense of consistency, a persecutor is bound to shew that

1. Louis XVIII (1755–1824), weak, timid, and henpecked king of France, retreated to Ghent in Belgium.
2. First printing reads: good old John
3. Statement of formal legal action.
4. I.e., formally rejected.
5. First printing reads: the good kindly old

the fallen man is a villain—otherwise he the persecutor is a wretch himself.

And as a general rule, which may make all creditors who are inclined to be severe, pretty comfortable in their minds, no men embarrassed are altogether honest, very likely. They conceal something; they exaggerate chances of good-luck, hide away the real state of affairs, say that things are flourishing when they are hopeless: keep a smiling face (a dreary smile it is) upon the verge of bankruptcy—are ready to lay hold of any pretext for delay, or of any money, so as to stave off the inevitable ruin a few days longer. "Down with such dishonesty," says the creditor in triumph, and reviles his sinking enemy. "You fool, why do you catch at a straw?" calm good sense says to the man that is drowning. "You villain, why do you shrink from plunging into the irretrievable Gazette?"[6] says prosperity to the poor devil battling in that black gulf. Who has not remarked the readiness with which the closest of friends and honestest of men suspect and accuse each other of cheating when they fall out on money matters. Everybody does it. Everybody is right, I suppose, and the world is a rogue.

Then Osborne had the intolerable sense of former benefits to goad and irritate him: these are always a cause of hostility aggravated. Finally, he had to break off the match between Sedley's daughter and his son; and as it had gone very far indeed, and as the poor girl's happiness and perhaps character were compromised, it was necessary to show the strongest reasons for the rupture, and for John Osborne to prove John Sedley to be a very bad character indeed.

At the meetings of creditors, then, he comported himself with a savageness and scorn towards Sedley, which almost succeeded in breaking the heart of that ruined bankrupt man. On George's intercourse with Amelia he put an instant veto—menacing the youth with maledictions if he broke his commands, and vilipending the poor innocent girl as the basest and most artful of vixens. One of the great conditions of anger and hatred is, that you must tell and believe lies against the hated object, in order, as we said, to be consistent.

When the great crash came—the announcement of ruin, and the departure from Russell Square, and the declaration that all was over between her and George—all over between her and love, her and happiness, her and faith in the world—a brutal letter from John Osborne told her in a few curt lines that her father's conduct had been of such a nature that all engagements between the families were at an end—when the final award came, it did not shock her so much as her parents, as her mother rather expected (for John Sedley himself was entirely prostrate in the ruins of his own affairs and shattered honour). Amelia took the news very palely and calmly. It was only the confirmation of the dark presages which had long gone before. It was the mere reading of the sentence—of the crime she had long ago been guilty—the crime of loving wrongly, too violently, against reason. She told no more of her thoughts now than she had before. She seemed scarcely more unhappy now when convinced all hope

6. Declaring bankruptcy and being listed in the Gazette, a newspaper column of official announcements.

was over, than before when she felt but dared not confess that it was gone. So she changed from the large house to the small one without any mark or difference; remained in her little room for the most part; pined silently; and died away day by day. I do not mean to say that all females are so. My dear Miss Bullock, I do not think *your* heart would break in this way. You are a strong-minded young woman with proper principles. I do not venture to say that mine would; it has suffered, and, it must be confessed, survived. But there are some souls thus gently constituted, thus frail, and delicate, and tender.

Whenever old John Sedley thought of the affair between George and Amelia, or alluded to it, it was with bitterness almost as great as Mr. Osborne himself had shown. He cursed Osborne and his family as heartless, wicked, and ungrateful. No power on earth, he swore, would induce him to marry his daughter to the son of such a villain, and he ordered Emmy to banish George from her mind, and to return all the presents and letters which she had ever had from him.

She promised acquiescence, and tried to obey. She put up the two or three trinkets; and, as for the letters, she drew them out of the place where she kept them; and read them over—as if she did not know them by heart already: but she could not part with them. That effort was too much for her; she placed them back in her bosom again—as you have seen a woman nurse a child that is dead. Young Amelia felt that she would die or lose her senses outright, if torn away from this last consolation. How she used to blush and lighten up when those letters came! How she used to trip away with a beating heart, so that she might read unseen. If they were cold, yet how perversely this fond little soul interpreted them into warmth. If they were short or selfish, what excuses she found for the writer!

It was over these few worthless papers that she brooded and brooded. She lived in her past life—every letter seemed to recall some circumstance of it. How well she remembered them all! His looks and tones, his dress, what he said and how—these relics and remembrances of dead affection were all that were left her in the world, and the business of her life, to[7] watch the corpse of Love.

To death she looked with inexpressible longing. Then, she thought, I shall always be able to follow him. I am not praising her conduct or setting her up as a model for Miss Bullock to imitate. Miss B. knows how to regulate her feelings better than this poor little creature. Miss B. would never have committed herself as that imprudent Amelia had done; pledged her love irretrievably; confessed her heart away, and got back nothing—only a brittle promise which was snapt and worthless in a moment. A long engagement is a partnership which one party is free to keep or to break, but which involves all the capital of the other.

Be cautious then, young ladies; be wary how you engage. Be shy of loving frankly; never tell all you feel, or (a better way still) feel very little. See the consequences of being prematurely honest and confiding, and mistrust yourselves and everybody. Get yourselves married as they do in France, where the lawyers are the bridesmaids and confidantes. At any rate, never have any feelings which may

7. Revised edition reads: life, was—to

make you uncomfortable, or make any promises which you cannot at any required moment command and withdraw. That is the way to get on, and be respected, and have a virtuous character in Vanity Fair.

If Amelia could have heard the comments regarding her which were made in the circle from which her father's ruin had just driven her, she would have seen what her own crimes were, and how entirely her character was jeopardied. Such criminal imprudence Mrs. Smith never knew of; such horrid familiarities Mrs. Brown had always condemned, and the end might be a warning to *her* daughters. "Captain Osborne, of course, could not marry a bankrupt's daughter," the Miss Dobbins said. "It was quite enough to have been swindled by the father. As for that little Amelia, her folly had really passed all—"

"All what?" Captain Dobbin roared out. "Haven't they been engaged ever since they were children? Wasn't it as good as a marriage? Dare any soul on earth breathe a word against the sweetest, the purest, the tenderest, the most angelical of young women?"

"La, William, don't be so highty tighty with *us*. We're not men. We can't fight you," Miss Jane said. "We've said nothing against Miss Sedley: but that her conduct throughout was *most imprudent*, not to call it by any worse name; and that her parents are people who certainly merit their misfortunes."

"Hadn't you better, now that Miss Sedley is free, propose for her yourself, William?" Miss Ann asked sarcastically. "It would be a most eligible family connexion. He! he!"

"I marry her!" Dobbin said, blushing very much and talking quick. "If you are so ready, young ladies, to chop and change,[8] do you suppose that *she* is? Laugh and sneer at that angel. She can't hear it; and she's miserable and unfortunate, and deserves to be laughed at. Go on joking, Ann. You're the wit of the family, and the others like to hear it."

"I must tell you again we're not in a barrack, William," Miss Ann remarked.

"In a barrack, by Jove—I wish anybody in a barrack would say what you do," cried out this uproused British lion. "I should like to hear a man breathe a word against her, by Jupiter. But men don't talk in this way, Ann: it's only women, who get together, and hiss, and shriek, and cackle. There, get away—don't begin to cry. I only said you were a couple of geese," Will Dobbin said, perceiving Miss Ann's pink eyes were beginning to moisten as usual. "Well, you're not geese, you're swans—anything you like, only do, do leave Miss Sedley alone."

Anything like William's infatuation about that silly little flirting, ogling thing was never known, the mamma and sisters agreed together in thinking: and they trembled lest, her engagement being off with Osborne, she should take up immediately her other admirer and Captain. In which forebodings these worthy young women no doubt judged according to the best of their experience; or rather (for as yet they had had no opportunities of marrying or of jilting) according to their own notions of right and wrong.

8. To bargain and exchange.

"It is a mercy, Mamma, that the regiment is ordered abroad," the girls said. "*This* danger, at any rate, is spared our brother."

Such, indeed, was the fact; and so it is that the French Emperor comes in to perform a part in this domestic comedy of Vanity Fair which we are now playing, and which would never have been enacted without the intervention of this august mute personage. It was he that ruined the Bourbons[9] and Mr. John Sedley. It was he whose arrival in his capital called up all France in arms to defend him there; and all Europe to oust him. While the French nation and army were swearing fidelity round the eagles in the Champ de Mai,[1] four mighty European hosts were getting in motion for the great *chasse à l'aigle;*[2] and one of these was a British army, of which two heroes of ours, Captain Dobbin and Captain Osborne, formed a portion.

The news of Napoleon's escape and landing was received by the gallant —th with a fiery delight and enthusiasm, which everybody can understand who knows that famous corps. From the colonel to the smallest drummer in the regiment, all were filled with hope and ambition and patriotic fury; and thanked the French Emperor as for a personal kindness in coming to disturb the peace of Europe. Now was the time the —th had so long panted for, to show their comrades in arms that they could fight as well as the Peninsular veterans, and that all the pluck and valour of the —th had not been killed by the West Indies and the yellow fever. Stubble and Spooney looked to get their companies without purchase. Before the end of the campaign (which she resolved to share), Mrs. Major O'Dowd hoped to write herself Mrs. Colonel O'Dowd, C.B.[3] Our two friends (Dobbin and Osborne) were quite as much excited as the rest: and each in his way—Mr. Dobbin very quietly, Mr. Osborne very loudly and energetically—was bent upon doing his duty, and gaining his share of honour and distinction.

The agitation thrilling through the country and army in consequence of this news was so great, that private matters were little heeded: and hence probably George Osborne, just gazetted to his company, busy with preparations for the march, which must come inevitably, and panting for further promotion—was not so much affected by other incidents which would have interested him at a more quiet period. He was not, it must be confessed, very much cast down by good old Mr. Sedley's catastrophe. He tried his new uniform, which became him very handsomely, on the day when the first meeting of the creditors of the unfortunate gentleman took place. His father told him of the wicked, rascally, shameful conduct of the bankrupt, reminded him of what he had said about Amelia, and that their connexion was broken off for ever; and gave him that evening a good sum of money to pay for the new clothes and epaulets in which he looked so well. Money was always useful to this free-handed young fellow, and he took it without many words. The bills were

9. The ruling family of France temporarily deposed by Napoleon.
1. Napoleon commissioned his troupes and made empty gestures toward a democratic future for France at a huge "town meeting" held under the emblem of eagles on the Champ de Mai, in Paris, on June 1, 1815. His final defeat came eighteen days later. The four mighty hosts were the Allies: Russians, Prussians, Austrians, and English.
2. Eagle hunt.
3. The lowest of three Orders of the Bath.

up in the Sedley house, where he had passed so many, many happy hours. He could see them as he walked from home that night (to the Old Slaughters', where he put up when in town) shining white in the moon. That comfortable home was shut, then, upon Amelia and her parents: where had they taken refuge? The thought of their ruin affected him not a little. He was very melancholy that night in the coffee-room at the Slaughters'; and drank a good deal, as his comrades remarked there.

Dobbin came in presently, cautioned him about the drink, which he only took, he said, because he was deuced low; but when his friend began to put to him clumsy inquiries, and asked him for news in a significant manner, Osborne declined entering into conversation with him; avowing, however, that he was devilish disturbed and unhappy.

Three days afterwards, Dobbin found Osborne in his room at the barracks:—his head on the table, a number of papers about, the young Captain evidently in a state of great despondency. "She's—she's sent me back some things I gave her—some damned trinkets. Look here!" There was a little packet directed in the well-known hand to Captain George Osborne, and some things lying about—a ring, a silver knife he had bought, as a boy, for her at a fair; a gold chain, and a locket with hair in it. "It's all over," said he, with a groan of sickening remorse. "Look, Will, you may read it if you like."

There was a little letter of a few lines, to which he pointed, which said:

"My papa has ordered me to return to you these presents, which you made in happier days to me; and I am to write to you for the last time. I think, I know you feel as much as I do the blow which has come upon us. It is I that absolve you from an engagement which is impossible in our present misery. I am sure you had no share in it, or in the cruel suspicions of Mr. Osborne, which are the hardest of all our griefs to bear. Farewell. Farewell. I pray God to strengthen me to bear this and other calamities, and to bless you always. A.

"I shall often play upon the piano—your piano. It was like you to send it."

Dobbin was very soft-hearted. The sight of women and children in pain always used to melt him. The idea of Amelia broken-hearted and lonely, tore that good-natured soul with anguish. And he broke out into an emotion, which anybody who likes may consider unmanly. He swore that Amelia was an angel, to which Osborne said aye with all his heart. He, too, had been reviewing the history of their lives,—and had seen her from her childhood to her present age, so sweet, so innocent, so charmingly simple, and artlessly fond and tender.

What a pang it was to lose all that: to have had it and not prized it! A thousand homely scenes and recollections crowded on him—in which he always saw her good and beautiful. And for himself, he blushed with remorse and shame, as the remembrance of his own selfishness and indifference contrasted with that perfect purity. For a while, glory, war, everything was forgotten, and the pair of friends talked about her only.

"Where are they?" Osborne asked, after a long talk, and a long pause,—and, in truth, with no little shame at thinking that he had taken no steps to follow her. "Where are they? There's no address to the note."

Dobbin knew. He had not merely sent the piano; but had written a note to Mrs. Sedley, and asked permission to come and see her,—and he had seen her, and Amelia too, yesterday, before he came down to Chatham; and, what is more, he had brought that farewell letter and packet which had so moved them.

The good-natured fellow had found Mrs. Sedley only too willing to receive him, and greatly agitated by the arrival of the piano, which, as she conjectured, *must* have come from George, and was a signal of amity on his part. Captain Dobbin did not correct this error of the worthy lady, but listened to all her story of complaints and misfortunes with great sympathy—condoled with her losses and privations, and agreed in reprehending the cruel conduct of Mr. Osborne towards his first benefactor. When she had eased her overflowing bosom somewhat, and poured forth many of her sorrows, he had the courage to ask actually to see Amelia, who was above in her room as usual, and whom her mother led trembling down stairs.

Her appearance was so ghastly, and her look of despair so pathetic, that honest William Dobbin was frightened as he beheld it; and read the most fatal forebodings in that pale fixed face. After sitting in his company a minute or two, she put the packet into his hand, and said, "Take this to Captain Osborne, if you please, and—and I hope he's quite well—and it was very kind of you to come and see us—and we like our new house very much. And I—I think I'll go upstairs, Mamma, for I'm not very strong." And with this, and a curtsey and a smile, the poor child went her way. The mother, as she led her up, cast back looks of anguish towards Dobbin. The good fellow wanted no such appeal. He loved her himself too fondly for that. Inexpressible grief, and pity, and terror pursued him, and he came away as if he was a criminal after seeing her.

When Osborne heard that his friend had found her, he made hot and anxious inquiries regarding the poor child. How was she? How did she look? What did she say? His comrade took his hand, and looked him in the face.

"George, she's dying," William Dobbin said,—and could speak no more.

There was a buxom Irish servant-girl, who performed all the duties of the little house where the Sedley family had found refuge; and this girl had in vain, on many previous days, striven to give Amelia aid or consolation. Emmy was much too sad to answer her,[4] or even to be aware of the attempts the other was making in her favour.

Four hours after the talk between Dobbin and Osborne, this servant-maid came into Amelia's room, where she sate as usual, brooding silently over her letters—her little treasures. The girl, smiling, and looking arch and happy, made many trials to attract poor Emmy's attention, who, however, took no heed of her.

"Miss Emmy!" said the girl.

4. Revised edition omits: her

"I'm coming," Emmy said, not looking round.

"There's a message," the maid went on. "There's something—somebody—sure, here's a new letter for you—don't be reading them old ones any more." And she gave her a letter, which Emmy took, and read.

"I must see you," the letter said. "Dearest Emmy—dearest love—dearest wife, come to me."

George and her mother were outside, waiting until she had read the letter.

*Number 6* *June 1847*

## *Chapter XIX.*

### MISS CRAWLEY AT NURSE.

E have seen how Mrs. Firkin, the lady's maid, as soon as any event of importance to the Crawley family came to her knowledge, felt bound to communicate it to Mrs. Bute Crawley, at the Rectory; and have before mentioned how particularly kind and attentive that good-natured lady was to Miss Crawley's confidential servant. She had been a gracious friend to Miss Briggs, the companion, also; and had secured the latter's good will by a number of those attentions and promises, which cost so little in the making, and are yet so valuable and agreeable to the recipient. Indeed every good economist and manager of a household must know how cheap and yet how amiable these professions are, and what a flavour they give to the most homely dish in life. Who was the blundering idiot who said that "fine words butter no parsnips?" Half the parsnips of society are served and rendered palatable with no other sauce. As the immortal Alexis Soyer[1] can make more delicious soup for a halfpenny than an ignorant cook can concoct with pounds of vegetables and meat, so a skilful artist will make a few simple and pleasing phrases go farther than ever so much substantial benefit-stock in the hands of a mere bungler. Nay, we know that substantial benefits often sicken some stomachs; whereas,

1. Soyer (1808–58), renowned chef to various aristocratic families and then at the Reform Club, conducted communal kitchens in Ireland in 1847 and authored *Soyer's Charitable Cookery, or The Poor Man's Regenerator* (1847).

most will digest any amount of fine words, and be always eager for more of the same food. Mrs. Bute had told Briggs and Firkin so often of the depth of her affection for them; and what *she* would do if she had Miss Crawley's fortune for friends so excellent and attached, that the ladies in question had the deepest regard for her; and felt as much gratitude and confidence as if Mrs. Bute had loaded them with the most expensive favours.

Rawdon Crawley, on the other hand, like a selfish heavy dragoon as he was, never took the least trouble to conciliate his aunt's aides-de-camp, showed his contempt for the pair with entire frankness—made Firkin pull off his boots on one occasion—sent her out in the rain on ignominious messages—and if he gave her a guinea, flung it to her as if it were a box on the ear. As his Aunt, too, made a butt of Briggs, the Captain followed the example and levelled his jokes at her—jokes about as delicate as a kick from his charger. Whereas, Mrs. Bute consulted her in matters of taste or difficulty, admired her poetry, and by a thousand acts of kindness and politeness, showed her appreciation of Briggs; and if she made Firkin a twopenny-halfpenny present, accompanied it with so many compliments, that the twopence-halfpenny was transmuted into gold in the heart of the grateful waiting-maid, who, besides, was looking forwards quite contentedly to some prodigious benefit which must happen to her on the day when Mrs. Bute came in to her fortune.

The different conduct of these two people is pointed out respectfully to the attention of persons commencing the world. Praise everybody, I say to such: never be squeamish, but speak out your compliment both point-blank in a man's face, and behind his back, when you know there is a reasonable chance of his hearing it again. Never lose a chance of saying a kind word. As Collingwood[2] never saw a vacant place in his estate but he took an acorn out of his pocket and popped it in; so deal with your compliments through life. An acorn costs nothing; but it may sprout into a prodigious bit of timber.

In a word, during Rawdon Crawley's prosperity, he was only obeyed with sulky acquiescence; when his disgrace came, there was nobody to help or pity him. Whereas, when Mrs. Bute took the command at Miss Crawley's house, the garrison there were charmed to act under such a leader, expecting all sorts of promotion from her promises, her generosity, and her kind words.

That he would consider himself beaten, after one defeat, and make no attempt to regain the position he had lost, Mrs. Bute Crawley never allowed herself to suppose. She knew Rebecca to be too clever and spirited, and desperate a woman to submit without a struggle; and felt that she must prepare for that combat, and be incessantly watchful against assault, or mine, or surprise.

In the first place, though she held the town, was she sure of the principal inhabitant? Would Miss Crawley herself hold out; and had she not a secret longing to welcome back the ousted adversary? The old lady liked Rawdon, and Rebecca, who amused her. Mrs. Bute could not disguise from herself the fact that none of her party could so contribute to the pleasures of the town-bred lady. "My girls'

2. Vice-Admiral Lord Collingwood (1750–1810).

singing, after that little odious governess's, I know is unbearable," the candid rector's wife owned to herself. "She always used to go to sleep when Martha and Louisa played their duets. Jim's stiff college manners and poor dear Bute's talk about his dogs and horses always annoyed her. If I took her to the Rectory, she would grow angry with us all, and fly, I know she would; and might fall into that horrid Rawdon's clutches again, and be the victim of that little viper of a Sharp. Meanwhile, it is clear to me that she is exceedingly unwell, and cannot move for some weeks, at any rate; during which we must think of some plan to protect her from the arts of those unprincipled people."

In the very best of moments, if anybody told Miss Crawley that she was, or looked ill, the trembling old lady sent off for her doctor; and I daresay she *was* very unwell after the sudden family event, which might serve to shake stronger nerves than hers. At least, Mrs. Bute thought it was her duty to inform the physician, and the apothecary, and the dame-de-compagnie, and the domestics, that Miss Crawley was in a most critical state, and that they were to act accordingly. She had the street laid knee-deep with straw; and the knocker put by with Mr. Bowls's plate.[3] She insisted that the Doctor should call twice a day; and deluged her patient with draughts every two hours. When anybody entered the room, she uttered a *shshshsh* so sibilant and ominous, that it frightened the poor old lady in her bed, from which she could not look without seeing Mrs. Bute's beady eyes eagerly fixed on her, as the latter sat steadfast in the arm-chair by the bed-side. They seemed to lighten in the dark (for she kept the

curtains closed) as she moved about the room on velvet paws like a cat. There Miss Crawley lay for days—ever so many days—Mrs. Bute reading books of devotion to her: for nights, long nights, during

3. The straw deadened traffic noise (see chapter XIV); the door knocker and the butler's tray (for visitors' cards) were retired from use.

which she had to hear the watchman sing, the night-light sputter; visited at midnight, the last thing, by the stealthy apothecary; and then left to look at Mrs. Bute's twinkling eyes, or the flicks of yellow that the rushlight threw on the dreary darkened ceiling. Hygeia[4] herself would have fallen sick under such a regimen; and how much more this poor old nervous victim? It has been said that when she was in health and good spirits, this venerable inhabitant of Vanity Fair had as free notions about religion and morals as Monsieur de Voltaire himself could desire, but when illness overtook her, it was aggravated by the most dreadful terrors of death, and an utter cowardice took possession of the prostrate old sinner.

Sick-bed homilies and pious reflections are, to be sure, out of place in mere story-books, and we are not going (after the fashion of some novelists of the present day) to cajole the public into a sermon, when it is only a comedy that the reader pays his money to witness. But, without preaching, the truth may surely be borne in mind, that the bustle, and triumph, and laughter, and gaiety which Vanity Fair exhibits in public, do not always pursue the performer into private life, and that the most dreary depression of spirits and dismal repentances sometimes overcome him. Recollection of the best ordained banquets will scarcely cheer sick epicures. Reminiscences of the most becoming dresses and brilliant ball triumphs will go very little way to console faded beauties. Perhaps statesmen, at a particular period of existence, are not much gratified at thinking over the most triumphant divisions;[5] and the success or the pleasure of yesterday become of very small account when a certain (albeit uncertain) morrow is in view, about which all of us must some day or other be speculating. O brother wearers of motley! Are there not moments when one grows sick of grinning and tumbling, and the jingling of cap and bells? This, dear friends and companions, is my amiable object—to walk with you through the Fair, to examine the shops and the shows there; and that we should all come home after the flare, and the noise, and the gaiety, and be perfectly miserable in private.

"If that poor man of mine had a head on his shoulders," Mrs. Bute Crawley thought to herself, "how useful he might be, under present circumstances, to this unhappy old lady! He might make her repent of her shocking free-thinking ways; he might urge her to do her duty, and cast off that odious reprobate who has disgraced himself and his family; and he might induce her to do justice to my dear girls and the two boys, who require and deserve, I am sure, every assistance which their relatives can give them."

And, as the hatred of vice is always a progress towards virtue, Mrs. Bute Crawley endeavoured to instil into her sister-in-law a proper abhorrence for all Rawdon Crawley's manifold sins: of which his uncle's wife brought forward such a catalogue as indeed would have served to condemn a whole regiment of young officers. If a man has committed wrong in life, I don't know any moralist more anxious to point his errors out to the world than his own relations; so Mrs. Bute showed

4. Greek goddess of health.
5. Members of Parliament registered their votes by entering separate lobbies.

a perfect family interest and knowledge of Rawdon's history. She had all the particulars of that ugly quarrel with Captain Firebrace,[6] in which Rawdon, wrong from the beginning, ended in shooting the Captain. She knew how the unhappy Lord Dovedale, whose mamma had taken a house at Oxford, so that he might be educated there, and who had never touched a card in his life till he came to London, was perverted by Rawdon at the Cocoa Tree, made helplessly tipsy by this abominable seducer and perverter of youth, and fleeced of four thousand pounds. She described with the most vivid minuteness the agonies of the country families whom he had ruined—the sons whom he had plunged into dishonour and poverty—the daughters whom he had inveigled into perdition. She knew the poor tradesmen who were bankrupt by his extravagance—the mean shifts and rogueries with which he had ministered to it—the astounding falsehoods by which he had imposed upon the most generous of aunts, and the ingratitude and ridicule by which he had repaid her sacrifices. She imparted these stories gradually to Miss Crawley; gave her the whole benefit of them; felt it to be her bounden duty as a Christian woman and mother of a family to do so; had not the smallest remorse or compunction for the victim whom her tongue was immolating; nay, very likely thought her act was quite meritorious, and plumed herself upon her resolute manner of performing it. Yes, if a man's character is to be abused, say what you will, there's nobody like a relation to do the business. And one is bound to own, regarding this unfortunate wretch of a Rawdon Crawley, that the mere truth was enough to condemn him, and that all inventions of scandal were quite superfluous pains on his friends' parts.

Rebecca, too, being now a relative, came in for the fullest share of Mrs. Bute's kind inquiries. This indefatigable pursuer of truth (having given strict orders that the door was to be denied to all emissaries or letters from Rawdon), took Miss Crawley's carriage, and drove to her old friend Miss Pinkerton, at Minerva House, Chiswick Mall, to whom she announced the dreadful intelligence of Captain Rawdon's seduction by Miss Sharp, and from whom she got sundry strange particulars[7] regarding the ex-governess's birth and early history. The friend of the Lexicographer had plenty of information to give. Miss Jemima was made to fetch the drawing-master's receipts and letters. This one was from a spunging-house:[8] that entreated an advance: another was full of gratitude for Rebecca's reception by the ladies of Chiswick: and the last document from the unlucky artist's pen was that in which, from his dying bed, he recommended his orphan child to Miss Pinkerton's protection. There were juvenile letters and petitions from Rebecca, too, in the collection, imploring aid for her father, or declaring her own gratitude. Perhaps in Vanity Fair there are no better satires than letters. Take a bundle of your dear friend's of ten years back—your dear friend whom you hate now. Look at a file of your sister's: how you clung to each other till you quarrelled about the twenty pound legacy! Get down the round-hand scrawls of

6. Revised edition reads: Marker,
7. First printing reads: got all the particulars she could
8. A bailiff's house for debtors; if in a few days arrangements were not made to pay, the debtor was moved to a prison.

your son who has half broken your heart with selfish undutifulness since; or a parcel of your own, breathing endless ardour and love eternal, which were sent back by your mistress when she married the Nabob—your mistress for whom you now care no more than for Queen Elizabeth. Vows, love, promises, confidences, gratitude, how queerly they read after a while! There ought to be a law in Vanity Fair ordering the destruction of every written document (except receipted tradesmen's bills) after a certain brief and proper interval. Those quacks and misanthropes who advertise indelible Japan ink, should be made to perish along with their wicked discoveries. The best ink for Vanity Fair use would be one that faded utterly in a couple of days, and left the paper clean and blank, so that you might write on it to somebody else.

From Miss Pinkerton's the indefatigable Mrs. Bute followed the track of Sharp and his daughter back to the lodgings in Greek Street, which the defunct painter had occupied; and where portraits of the landlady in white satin, and of the husband in brass buttons, done by Sharp in lieu of a quarter's rent, still decorated the parlour walls. Mrs. Stokes was a communicative person, and quickly told all she knew about Mr. Sharp; how dissolute and poor he was; how good-natured and amusing; how he was always hunted by bailiffs and duns; how, to the landlady's horror, though she never could abide the woman, he did not marry his wife till a short time before her death; and what a queer little wild vixen his daughter was; how she kept them all laughing with her fun and mimicry; how she used to fetch the gin from the public-house, and was known in all the studios in the quarter—in brief, Mrs. Bute got such a full account of her new niece's parentage, education, and behaviour as would scarcely have pleased Rebecca, had the latter known that such inquiries were being made concerning her.

Of all these industrious researches Miss Crawley had the full benefit. Mrs. Rawdon Crawley was the daughter of an opera girl. She had danced herself. She had been a model to the painters. She was brought up as became her mother's daughter. She drank gin with her father, &c. &c. It was a lost woman who was married to a lost man; and the moral to be inferred from Mrs. Bute's tale was, that the knavery of the pair was irremediable, and that no properly-conducted person should ever notice them again.

These were the materials which prudent Mrs. Bute gathered together in Park Lane, the provisions and ammunition as it were with which she fortified the house against the siege which she knew that Rawdon and his wife would lay to Miss Crawley.

But if a fault may be found with her arrangements, it is this, that she was too eager: she managed rather too well; undoubtedly she made Miss Crawley more ill than was necessary; and though the old invalid succumbed to her authority, it was so harassing and severe, that the victim would be inclined to escape at the very first chance which fell in her way. Managing women, the ornaments of their sex,—women who order everything for everybody, and know so much better than any person concerned what is good for their neighbours, don't sometimes speculate upon the possibility of a domestic revolt, or upon other extreme consequences resulting from their overstrained authority.

Thus for instance Mrs. Bute, with the best intentions no doubt in the world, and wearing herself to death as she did by foregoing sleep, dinner, fresh air, for the sake of her invalid sister-in-law, carried her conviction of the old lady's illness so far that she almost managed her into her coffin. She pointed out her sacrifices and their results one day to the constant apothecary, Mr. Clump.

"I am sure, my dear Mr. Clump," she said, "no efforts of mine have been wanting to restore our dear invalid, whom the ingratitude of her nephew has laid on the bed of sickness. *I* never shrink from personal discomfort: *I* never refuse to sacrifice myself."

"Your devotion, it must be confessed, is admirable," Mr. Clump says, with a low bow; "but—"

"I have scarcely closed my eyes since my arrival: I give up sleep, health, every comfort, to my sense of duty. When my poor James was in the small-pox, did I allow any hireling to nurse him? No."

"You did what became an excellent mother, my dear Madam—the best of mothers; but—"

"As the mother of a family and the wife of an English clergyman, I humbly trust that my principles are good," Mrs. Bute said, with a happy solemnity of conviction; "and, as long as Nature supports me, never, never, Mr. Clump, will I desert the post of duty. Others may bring that gray head with sorrow to the bed of sickness," (here Mrs. Bute, waving her hand, pointed to one of old Miss Crawley's coffee-coloured fronts,[9] which was perched on a stand in the dressing-room,) "but *I* will never quit it. Ah, Mr. Clump! I fear, I know that that couch needs spiritual as well as medical consolation."

"What I was going to observe, my dear Madam,"—here the resolute Clump once more interposed with a bland air—"what I was going to observe when you gave utterance to sentiments which do you so much honour, was that I think you alarm yourself needlessly about our kind friend, and sacrifice your own health too prodigally in her favour."

"I would lay down my life for my duty, or for any member of my husband's family," Mrs. Bute interposed.

"Yes, Madam, if need were; but we don't want Mrs. Bute Crawley to be a martyr," Clump said gallantly. "Dr. Squills and myself[1] have both considered Miss Crawley's case with every anxiety and care, as you may suppose. We see her low-spirited and nervous; family events have agitated her."

"Her nephew will come to perdition," Mrs. Crawley cried.

"Have agitated her: and you arrived like a guardian angel, my dear Madam, a positive guardian angel, I assure you, to soothe her under the pressure of calamity. But Dr. Squills and I were thinking that our amiable friend is not in such a state as renders confinement to her bed necessary. She is depressed, but this confinement perhaps adds to her depression. She should have change, fresh air, gaiety; the most delightful remedies in the pharmacopœia,"[2] Mr. Clump said,

9. Locks of false hair.
1. Clump is an apothecary, Squills a physician.
2. Stock of drugs; also, a listing of drugs and directions for compounding them.

grinning and showing his handsome teeth. "Persuade her to rise, dear Madam; drag her from her couch and her low spirits; insist upon her taking little drives. They will restore the roses too to *your* cheeks, if I may so speak to Mrs. Bute Crawley."

"The sight of her horrid nephew casually in the Park, where I am told the wretch drives with the brazen partner of his crimes," Mrs. Bute said, (letting the cat of selfishness out of the bag of secrecy,) "would cause her such a shock, that we should have to bring her back to bed again. She must not go out, Mr. Clump. She shall not go out as long as I remain to watch over her. And as for *my* health, what matters it? I give it cheerfully, Sir. I sacrifice it at the altar of my duty."

"Upon my word, Madam," Mr. Clump now said bluntly, "I won't answer for her life if she remains locked up in that dark room. She is so nervous that we may lose her any day; and if you wish Captain Crawley to be her heir, I warn you frankly, Madam, that you are doing your very best to serve him."

"Gracious mercy! is her life in danger?" Mrs. Bute cried. "Why, why, Mr. Clump, did you not inform me sooner?"

The night before, Mr. Clump and Dr. Squills had had a consultation (over a bottle of wine at the house of Sir Lapin Warren,[3] whose lady was about to present him with a thirteenth blessing), regarding Miss Crawley and her case.

"What a little harpy that woman from Hampshire is, Clump," Squills remarked, "that has seized upon old Tilly Crawley. Devilish good Madeira."

"What a fool Rawdon Crawley has been," Clump replied, "to go and marry a governess! There was something about the girl, too."

"Green eyes, fair skin, pretty figure, famous frontal development," Squills remarked. "There *is* something about her; and Crawley *was* a fool, Clump."

"A d—— fool—always was," the apothecary replied.

"Of course the old girl will fling him over," said the physician, and after a pause added, "She'll cut up well,[4] I suppose."

"Cut up," says Clump with a grin; "I wouldn't have her cut up for two hundred a year."

"That Hampshire woman will kill her in two months, Clump, my boy, if she stops about her," Dr. Squills said. "Old woman; full feeder; nervous subject; palpitation of the heart; pressure on the brain; apoplexy; off she goes. Get her up, Clump; get her out: or I wouldn't give many weeks' purchase for your two hundred a year." And it was acting upon this hint that the worthy apothecary spoke with so much candour to Mrs. Bute Crawley.

Having the old lady under her hand; in bed; with nobody near, Mrs. Bute had made more than one assault upon her, to induce her to alter her will. But Miss Crawley's usual terrors regarding death increased greatly when such dismal propositions were made to her, and Mrs. Bute saw that she must get her patient into cheerful spirits and health before she could hope to attain the pious object which she

3. The name means "rabbit warren."
4. Her wealth will divide up well when she is dead.

had in view. Whither to take her was the next puzzle. The only place where she is not likely to meet those odious Rawdons is at church, and that won't amuse her, Mrs. Bute justly felt. "We must go and visit our beautiful suburbs of London," she then thought. "I hear they are the most picturesque in the world;" and so she had a sudden interest for Hampstead, and Hornsey, and found that Dulwich[5] had great charms for her, and getting her victim into her carriage, drove her to those rustic spots, beguiling the little journeys with conversations about Rawdon and his wife, and telling every story to the old lady which could add to her indignation against this pair of reprobates.

Perhaps Mrs. Bute pulled the string unnecessarily tight. For though she worked up Miss Crawley to a proper dislike of her disobedient nephew, the invalid had a great hatred and secret terror of her victimiser, and panted to escape from her. After a brief space, she rebelled against Highgate and Hornsey utterly. She would go into the Park. Mrs. Bute knew they would meet the abominable Rawdon there, and she was right. One day in the ring, Rawdon's stanhope[6] came in sight; Rebecca was seated by him. In the enemy's equipage Miss Crawley occupied her usual place, with Mrs. Bute on her left, the poodle and Miss Briggs on the back seat. It was a nervous moment, and Rebecca's heart beat quick as she recognised the carriage; and as the two vehicles crossed each other in the line, she clasped her hands, and looked towards the spinster with a face of agonised attachment and devotion. Rawdon himself trembled, and his face grew purple behind his dyed mustachios. Only old Briggs was moved in the other carriage, and cast her great eyes nervously towards her old friends. Miss Crawley's bonnet was resolutely turned towards the Serpentine.[7] Mrs. Bute happened to be in ecstacies with the poodle, and was calling him a little darling, and a sweet little zoggy, and a pretty pet. The carriages moved on, each in his line.

"Done, by Jove," Rawdon said to his wife.

"Try once more, Rawdon," Rebecca answered. "Could not you lock your wheels into theirs, dearest?"

Rawdon had not the heart for that manœuvre. When the carriages met again, he stood up in his stanhope; he raised his hand ready to doff his hat; he looked with all his eyes. But this time Miss Crawley's face was not turned away; she and Mrs. Bute looked him full in the face, and cut their nephew pitilessly. He sank back in his seat with an oath, and striking out of the ring, dashed away desperately homewards.

It was a gallant and decided triumph for Mrs. Bute. But she felt the danger of many such meetings, as she saw the evident nervousness of Miss Crawley; and she determined that it was most necessary for her dear friend's health, that they should leave town for a while, and recommended Brighton[8] very strongly.

5. Outlying suburbs of London.
6. An open one-seated, four-wheeled carriage, drawn by one horse.
7. Hyde Park's lake.
8. Seaside resort on the south coast.

## *Chapter XX.*

### IN WHICH CAPTAIN DOBBIN ACTS AS THE MESSENGER OF HYMEN.[1]

WITHOUT knowing how, Captain William Dobbin found himself the great promoter, arranger, and manager of the match between George Osborne and Amelia. But for him it never would have taken place: he could not but confess as much to himself, and smiled rather bitterly as he thought that he of all men in the world should be the person upon whom the care of this marriage had fallen. But though indeed the conducting of this negotiation was about as painful a task as could be set to him, yet when he had a duty to perform, Captain Dobbin was accustomed to go through it without many words or much hesitation; and, having made up his mind completely, that if Miss Sedley was balked of her husband she would die of the disappointment, he was determined to use all his best endeavours to keep her alive.

I forbear to enter into minute particulars of the interview between George and Amelia, when the former was brought back to the feet (or should we venture to say the arms?) of his young mistress by the intervention of his friend honest William. A much harder heart than George's would have melted at the sight of that sweet face so sadly ravaged by grief and despair, and at the simple tender accents in which she told her little broken-hearted story: but as she did not faint when her mother, trembling, brought Osborne to her; and as she only gave relief to her overcharged grief, by laying her head on her lover's shoulder and there weeping for a while the most tender, copious, and refreshing tears—old Mrs. Sedley, too greatly relieved, thought it was best to leave the young persons to themselves; and so quitted Emmy crying over George's hand, and kissing it humbly, as if it[2] were her supreme chief and master, and as if she were quite a guilty and unworthy person needing every favour and grace from him.

This prostration and sweet unrepining obedience exquisitely touched and flattered George Osborne. He saw a slave before him in that simple yielding faithful creature, and his soul within him thrilled secretly somehow at the knowledge of his power. He would be generous-minded, Sultan as he was, and raise up this kneeling Esther[3] and make a queen of her: besides, her sadness and beauty

1. The personification of marriage in Greek and Roman myths.
2. Revised edition reads: as if he
3. The Persian king Ahasuerus chose the humble Jewess Esther to be his queen.

touched him as much as her submission, and so he cheered her, and raised her up and forgave her, so to speak. All her hopes and feelings, which were dying and withering, this her sun having been removed from her, bloomed again and at once, its light being restored. You would scarcely have recognised the beaming little face upon Amelia's pillow that night as the one that was laid there the night before, so wan, so lifeless, so careless of all round about. The honest Irish maid-servant, delighted with the change, asked leave to kiss the face that had grown all of a sudden so rosy. Amelia put her arms round the girl's neck and kissed her with all her heart, like a child. She was little more. She had that night a sweet refreshing sleep, like one—and what a spring of inexpressible happiness as she woke in the morning sunshine!

"He will be here again to-day," Amelia thought. "He is the greatest and best of men." And the fact is, that George thought he was one of the generousest creatures alive: and that he was making a tremendous sacrifice in marrying this young creature.

While she and Osborne were having their delightful *tête-à-tête*[4] above stairs, old Mrs. Sedley and Captain Dobbin were conversing below upon the state of the affairs, and the chances and future arrangements of the young people. Mrs. Sedley having brought the two lovers together and left them embracing each other with all their might, like a true woman, was of opinion that no power on earth would induce Mr. Sedley to consent to the match between his daughter and the son of a man who had so shamefully, wickedly, and monstrously treated him. And she told a long story about happier days and their earlier splendours, when Osborne lived in a very humble way in the New Road,[5] and his wife was *too glad* to receive some of Jos's little baby things, with which Mrs. Sedley accommodated her at the birth of one of Osborne's own children. The fiendish ingratitude of that man, she was sure, had broken Mr. S.'s heart: and as for a marriage, he would never, never, never, *never* consent.

"They must run away together, Ma'am," Dobbin said, laughing, "and follow the example of Captain Rawdon Crawley, and Miss Emmy's friend the little governess." Was it possible? Well she never! Mrs. Sedley was all excitement about this news. She wished that Blenkinsop were here to hear it: Blenkinsop always mistrusted that Miss Sharp.—What an escape Jos had had! and she described the already well-known love-passages between Rebecca and the Collector of Boggley wollah.

It was not, however, Mr. Sedley's wrath which Dobbin feared, so much as that of the other parent concerned, and he owned that he had a very considerable doubt and anxiety respecting the behaviour of the black-browed old tyrant of a Russia merchant[6] in Russell Square. He has forbidden the match peremptorily Dobbin thought. He knew what a savage determined man Osborne was, and

4. Private talk.
5. Called New Road until 1857, it is the present Marylebone Road, from Paddington to Islington.
6. Russia's main exports were grains, but included furs, tallow, and seed oils; England and Germany were its chief trading partners.

how he stuck by his word. "The only chance George has of reconcilement," argued his friend, "is by distinguishing himself in the coming campaign. If he dies they both go together. If he fails in distinction—what then? He has some money from his mother, I have heard—enough to purchase his majority—or he must sell out and go and dig in Canada or rough it in a cottage in the country." With such a partner Dobbin thought he would not mind Siberia—and, strange to say, this absurd and utterly imprudent young fellow never for a moment considered that the want of means to keep a nice carriage and horses, and of an income which should enable its possessors to entertain their friends genteelly, ought to operate as bars to the union of George and Miss Sedley.

It was these weighty considerations which made him think too that the marriage should take place as quickly as possible. Was he anxious himself, I wonder, to have it over?—as people, when death has occurred, like to press forward the funeral, or when a parting is resolved upon, hasten it. It is certain that Mr. Dobbin, having taken the matter in hand, was most extraordinarily eager in the conduct of it. He urged on George the necessity of immediate action: he showed the chances of reconciliation with his father, which a favourable mention of his name in the Gazette must bring about. If need were he would go himself and brave both the fathers in the business. At all events, he besought George to go through with it before the orders came, which everybody expected, for the departure of the regiment from England on foreign service.

Bent upon these hymeneal projects, and with the applause and consent of Mrs. Sedley, who did not care to break the matter personally to her husband, Mr. Dobbin went to seek John Sedley at his house of call in the City, the Tapioca Coffee-house, where, since his own offices were shut up, and fate had overtaken him, the poor broken-down old gentleman used to betake himself daily, and write letters and receive them, and tie them up into mysterious bundles, several of which he carried in the flaps of his coat. I don't know anything more dismal than that business and bustle and mystery of a ruined man: those letters from the wealthy which he shows you: those worn greasy documents promising support and offering condolence which he places wistfully before you, and on which he builds his hopes of restoration and future fortune. My beloved reader has no doubt in the course of his experience been waylaid by many such a luckless companion. He takes you into the corner; he has his bundle of papers out of his gaping coat pocket; and the tape off, and the string in his mouth, and the favourite letters selected and laid before you; and who does not know the sad eager half-crazy look which he fixes on you with his hopeless eyes?

Changed into a man of this sort, Dobbin found the once florid, jovial, and prosperous John Sedley. His coat, that used to be so glossy and trim, was white at the seams, and the buttons showed the copper. His face had fallen in, and was unshorn; his frill and neckcloth hung limp under his bagging waistcoat. When he used to treat the boys in old days at a coffee-house, he would shout and laugh louder than anybody there, and have all the waiters skipping

Mr. Sedley at the Coffee House

round him; it was quite painful to see how humble and civil he was to John of the Tapioca, a blear-eyed old attendant in dingy stockings and cracked pumps, whose business it was to serve glasses of wafers,[7] and bumpers of ink in pewter, and slices of paper to the frequenters of this dreary house of entertainment, where nothing else seemed to be consumed. As for William Dobbin, whom he had tipped repeatedly in his youth, and who had been the old gentleman's butt on a thousand occasions, old Sedley gave his hand to him in a very hesitating humble manner now, and called him "Sir." A feeling of shame and remorse took possession of William Dobbin as the broken old man so received and addressed him, as if he himself had been somehow guilty of the misfortunes which had brought Sedley so low.

"I am very glad to see you, Captain Dobbin, Sir," says he, after a skulking look or two at his visitor (whose lanky figure and military appearance caused some excitement likewise to twinkle in the blear eyes of the waiter in the cracked dancing pumps, and awakened the old lady in black, who dozed among the mouldy old coffee-cups in the bar). "How is the worthy alderman, and my lady, your excellent mother, Sir?" He looked round at the waiter as he said, "My lady," as much as to say, "Hark ye, John, I have friends still, and persons of rank and reputation, too." "Are you come to do anything in my way, sir? My young friends Dale and Spiggot do all my business for me now, until my new offices are ready; for I'm only here temporarily, you know, Captain. What can we do for you, sir? Will you like to take anything?"

Dobbin, with a great deal of hesitation and stuttering, protested that he was not in the least hungry or thirsty; that he had no business to transact; that he only came to ask if Mr. Sedley was well, and to shake hands with an old friend; and, he added, with a desperate perversion of truth, "My mother is very well—that is, she's been very unwell, and is only waiting for the first fine day to go out and call upon Mrs. Sedley. How is Mrs. Sedley, Sir? I hope she's quite well." And here he paused, reflecting on his own consummate hypocrisy; for the day was as fine, and the sunshine as bright as it ever is in Coffin Court, where the Tapioca Coffee-house is situated; and Mr. Dobbin remembered that he had seen Mrs. Sedley himself only an hour before, having driven Osborne down to Fulham in his gig, and left him there *tête-à-tête* with Miss Amelia.

"My wife will be very happy to see her ladyship," Sedley replied, pulling out his papers. "I've a very kind letter here from your father, Sir, and beg my respectful compliments to him. Lady D. will find us in rather a smaller house than we were accustomed to receive our friends in; but it's snug, and the change of air does good to my daughter, who was suffering in town rather—you remember little Emmy, Sir?—yes, suffering a good deal." The old gentleman's eyes were wandering as he spoke, and he was thinking of something else, as he sate thrumming on his papers and fumbling at the worn red tape.

7. Wax for sealing envelopes.

"You're a military man," he went on; "I ask you, Bill Dobbin, could any man ever have speculated upon the return of that Corsican scoundrel from Elba? When the allied sovereigns were here last year, and we gave 'em that dinner in the City, Sir, and we saw the Temple of Concord, and the fireworks, and the Chinese bridge in St. James's Park, could any sensible man suppose that peace wasn't really concluded, after we'd actually sung *Te Deum* for it, Sir? I ask you, William, could I suppose that the Emperor of Austria was a damned traitor—a traitor, and nothing more? I don't mince words—a double-faced infernal traitor and schemer, who meant to have his son-in-law back all along. And I say that the escape of Boney from Elba was a damned imposition and plot, Sir, in which half the powers of Europe were concerned, to bring the funds down, and to ruin this country. That's why I'm here, William. That's why my name's[8] in the Gazette. Why, Sir?—because I trusted the Emperor of Russia and the Prince Regent. Look here. Look at my papers. Look what the funds were on the 1st of March—what the French fives were when I bought for the account. And what they're at now. There was collusion, Sir, or that villain never would have escaped. Where was the English Commissioner who allowed him to get away? He ought to be shot, Sir—brought to a court-martial, and shot, by Jove."[9]

"We're going to hunt Boney out, Sir," Dobbin said, rather alarmed at the fury of the old man, the veins of whose forehead began to swell, and who sate drumming his papers with his clenched fist. "We are going to hunt him out, Sir—the Duke's in Belgium already, and we expect marching orders every day."[1]

"Give him no quarter. Bring back the villain's head, Sir. Shoot the coward down, Sir," Sedley roared. "I'd enlist myself, by ——; but I'm a broken old man—ruined by that damned scoundrel—and by a parcel of swindling thieves in this country whom I made, Sir, and who are rolling in their carriages now," he added, with a break in his voice.

Dobbin was not a little affected by the sight of this once kind old friend, crazed almost with misfortune and raving with senile anger. Pity the fallen gentleman: you to whom money and fair repute are the chiefest good; and so, surely, are they in Vanity Fair.

"Yes," he continued, "there are some vipers that you warm, and they sting you afterwards. There are some beggars that you put on horseback, and they're the first to ride you down. You know whom

8. Revised edition reads: name is
9. Following Napoleon's exile to Elba in April 1814, the emperor of Russia and the king of Prussia visited England in June for celebrations. Oxford conferred honorary LL.D.s upon them. On August 1, the Grand Jubilee in London was celebrated with fireworks, a nearly fatal balloon assent, a Chinese pagoda (which burned, killing two people), a Chinese bridge in St. James's Park, and a Temple of Concord in Green Park. All these activities celebrated the victory, the revival of trade, the rollback of taxes, family reunions, and, for John Sedley, investments in French stocks, consols, or mutual funds, and the French 5 percent shares. But Napoleon escaped the confinement of Colonel Neil Campbell, English commissioner (who was acquitted of any blame). Napoleon's invasion of France on March 1, 1815, was not reflected in that day's financial news, on which John Sedley had relied. Having divorced Josephine in 1809, Napoleon married Maria Louisa, daughter of the king of Austria—who denied having anything to do with Napoleon's sudden return.
1. The duke of Wellington, who had attended the Congress of Vienna, took command of Allied armies in Belgium in April 1815.

I mean, William Dobbin, my boy. I mean a purse-proud villain in Russell Square, whom I knew without a shilling, and whom I pray and hope to see a beggar as he was when I befriended him."

"I have heard something of this, Sir, from my friend George," Dobbin said, anxious to come to his point. "The quarrel between you and his father has cut him up a great deal, Sir. Indeed, I'm the bearer of a message from him."

"O, *that's* your errand, is it?" cried the old man, jumping up. "What! perhaps he condoles with me, does he? Very kind of him, the stiff-backed prig with his dandified airs and West-end swagger.[2] He's hankering about my house, is he still? If my son had the courage of a man, he'd shoot him. He's as big a villain as his father. I won't have his name mentioned in my house. I curse the day that ever I let him into it; and I'd rather see my daughter dead at my feet than married to him."

"His father's harshness is not George's fault, Sir. Your daughter's love for him is as much your doing as his. Who are you, that you are to play with two young people's affections and break their hearts at your will?"

"Recollect it's not his father that breaks the match off," old Sedley cried out. "It's I that forbid it. That family and mine are separated for ever. I'm fallen low, but not so low as that: no, no. And so you may tell the whole race—son, and father, and sisters, and all."

"It's my belief, Sir, that you have not the power or the right to separate those two," Dobbin answered in a low voice; "and that if you don't give your daughter your consent, it will be her duty to marry without it. There's no reason she should die or live miserably because you are wrong-headed. To my thinking she's just as much married as if the banns had been read in all the churches in London. And what better answer can there be to Osborne's charges against you, as charges there are, than that his son claims to enter your family and marry your daughter?"

A light of something like satisfaction seemed to break over old Sedley as this point was put to him: but he still persisted that with his consent the marriage between Amelia and George should never take place.

"We must do it without," Dobbin said, smiling, and told Mr. Sedley, as he had told Mrs. Sedley in the day, before, the story of Rebecca's elopement with Captain Crawley. It evidently amused the old gentleman. "You're terrible fellows, you Captains," said he, tying up his papers; and his face wore something like a smile upon it, to the astonishment of the blear-eyed waiter who now entered, and had never seen such an expression upon Sedley's countenance since he had used the dismal coffee-house.

The idea of hitting his enemy Osborne such a blow soothed, perhaps, the old gentleman: and, their colloquy presently ending, he and Dobbin parted pretty good friends.

---

2. George's gait is that of a west London dandy, not an east London merchant.

"My sisters say she has diamonds as big as pigeons' eggs," George said laughing. "How they must set off her complexion! A perfect illumination it must be when her jewels are on her neck. Her jet-black hair is as curly as Sambo's. I dare say she wore a nose-ring when she went to court; and with a plume of feathers in her top-knot she would look a perfect Belle Sauvage."[3]

George, in conversation with Amelia, was rallying the appearance of a young lady of whom his father and sisters had lately made the acquaintance, and who was an object of vast respect to the Russell Square family. She was reported to have I don't know how many plantations in the West Indies; a deal of money in the funds; and three stars to her name[4] in the East India stockholders' list. She had a mansion in Surrey, and a house in Portland Place.[5] The name of the rich West India heiress had been mentioned with applause in the Morning Post. Mrs. Haggistoun, Colonel Haggistoun's widow, her relative, "chaperoned" her, and kept her house. She was just from school, where she had completed her education, and George and his sisters had met her at an evening party at old Hulker's house, Devonshire Place[6] (Hulker, Bullock, & Co. were long the correspondents of her house in the West Indies), and the girls had made the most cordial advances to her, which the heiress had received with great good humour. An orphan in her position—with her money—so interesting! the Misses Osborne said. They were full of their new friend when they returned from the Hulker ball to Miss Wirt, their companion: they had made arrangements for continually meeting,

3. The reference is to Miss Swartz, but the allusion is complex. The Belle Sauvage Inn, from which coaches left for Cambridge, was originally Savage's Inn and then The Bell. Pocahontas, the American Indian princess, was a guest there, after which the final name change took place. But at the Exeter Exchange, from 1810 to 1815, there was, on exhibit as a freak show, a South African Hottentot woman, a Belle Sauvage whom George calls a Hottentot Venus in chapter XXI.
4. Each star represents stock holdings of 2,000 pounds (Harden).
5. One of the grandest streets of London.
6. Another nearby street of the same vintage and class as Portland Place.

and had the carriage and drove to see her the very next day. Mrs. Haggistoun, Colonel Haggistoun's widow, a relation of Lord Binkie, and always talking of him, struck the dear unsophisticated girls as rather haughty, and too much inclined to talk about her great relations: but Rhoda was everything they could wish—the frankest, kindest, most agreeable creature—wanting a little polish, but so good-natured. The girls Christian-named each other at once.

"You should have seen her dress for court, Emmy," Osborne cried, laughing. "She came to my sisters to show it off, before she was presented in state by my Lady Binkie, the Haggistoun's kinswoman. She's related to every one, that Haggistoun. Her diamonds blazed out like Vauxhall on the night we were there. (Do you remember Vauxhall, Emmy, and Jos singing to his dearest diddle iddle arling?) Diamonds and mahogany, my dear! think what an advantageous contrast—and the white feathers in her hair—I mean in her wool. She had ear-rings like chandeliers; you might have lighted 'em up, by Jove—and a yellow satin train that streeled[7] after her like the tail of a comet."

"How old is she?" asked Emmy, to whom George was rattling away regarding this dark paragon, on the morning of their re-union—rattling away as no other man in the world surely could.

"Why, the Black Princess, though she has only just left school, must be two or three and twenty. And you should see the hand she writes! Mrs. Colonel Haggistoun usually writes her letters, but in a moment of confidence, she put pen to paper for my sisters; she spelt satin satting, and Saint James's, Saint Jams."

"Why, surely it must be Miss Swartz, the parlour boarder,"[8] Emmy said, remembering that good-natured young Mulatto girl, who had been so hysterically affected when Amelia left Miss Pinkerton's academy.

"The very name," George said. "Her father was a German Jew—a slave-owner they say—connected with the Cannibal Islands in some way or other. He died last year, and Miss Pinkerton has finished her education. She can play two pieces on the piano; she knows three songs; she can write when Mrs. Haggistoun is by to spell for her; and Jane and Maria already have got to love her as a sister."

"I wish they would have loved me," said Emmy, wistfully. "They were always very cold to me."

"My dear child, they would have loved you if you had had two hundred thousand pounds," George replied. "That is the way in which they have been brought up. Ours is a ready-money society. We live among bankers and city big-wigs, and be hanged to them, and every man, as he talks to you, is jingling his guineas in his pocket. There is that jackass Fred Bullock, is going to marry Maria—there's Goldmore, the East India Director, there's Dipley, in the tallow trade—*our* trade," George said, with an uneasy laugh and a blush. "Curse the whole pack of money-grubbing vulgarians! I fall asleep at their great heavy dinners. I feel ashamed in my father's great stupid parties.

7. Trailed.
8. One who paid extra to live in and with the host's family.

I've been accustomed to live with gentlemen, and men of the world and fashion, Emmy, not with a parcel of turtle-fed[9] tradesmen. Dear little woman, you are the only person of our set who ever looked, or thought, or spoke like a lady: and you do it because you're an angel and can't help it. Don't remonstrate. You *are* the only lady. Didn't Miss Crawley remark it, who has lived in the best company in Europe? And as for Crawley, of the Life Guards, hang it, he's a fine fellow: and I like him for marrying the girl he had chosen."

Amelia admired Mr. Crawley very much, too, for this; and trusted Rebecca would be happy with him, and hoped (with a laugh) Jos would be consoled. And so the pair went on prattling, as in quite early days. Amelia's confidence being perfectly restored to her, though she expressed a great deal of pretty jealousy about Miss Swartz, and professed to be dreadfully frightened—like a hypocrite as she was—lest George should forget her for the heiress and her money and her estates in Saint Kitt's. But the fact is, she was a great deal too happy to have fears or doubts or misgivings of any sort: and having George at her side again, was not afraid of any heiress or beauty, or indeed of any sort of danger.

When Captain Dobbin came back in the afternoon to these people—which he did with a great deal of sympathy for them—it did his heart good to see how Amelia had grown young again—how she laughed, and chirped, and sang familiar old songs at the piano, which were only interrupted by the bell from without proclaiming Mr. Sedley's return from the City, before whom George received a signal to retreat.

Beyond the first smile of recognition—and even that was an hypocrisy, for she thought his arrival rather provoking—Miss Sedley did not once notice Dobbin during his visit. But he was content, so that he saw her happy; and thankful to have been the means of making her so.

9. Turtle soup was a symbol of ostentatious living.

## *Chapter XXI.*

### A QUARREL ABOUT AN HEIRESS.

LOVE may be felt for any young lady endowed with such qualities as Miss Swartz possessed; and a great dream of ambition entered into old Mr. Osborne's soul, which she was to realise. He encouraged, with the utmost enthusiasm and friendliness, his daughters' amiable attachment to the young heiress, and protested that it gave him the sincerest pleasure as a father to see the love of his girls so well disposed.

"You won't find," he would say to Miss Rhoda, "that splendour and rank to which you are accustomed at the West End, my dear Miss, at our humble mansion in Russell Square. My daughters are plain, disinterested girls, but their hearts are in the right place, and they've conceived an attachment for you which does them honour—I say, which does them honour. I'm a plain, simple, humble British merchant—an honest one, as my respected friends Hulker & Bullock will vouch, who were the correspondents of your late lamented father. You'll find us a united, simple, happy, and I think I may say respected, family—a plain table, a plain people, but a warm welcome, my dear Miss Rhoda—Rhoda, let me say, for my heart warms to you, it does really. I'm a frank man, and I like you. A glass of Champagne! Hicks, Champagne to Miss Swartz."

There is little doubt that old Osborne believed all he said, and that the girls were quite earnest in their protestations of affection for Miss Swartz. People in Vanity Fair fasten on to rich folks quite naturally. If the simplest people are disposed to look not a little kindly on great Prosperity, (for I defy any member of the British public to say that the notion of Wealth has not something awful and pleasing to him; and you, if you are told that the man next you at dinner has got half a million, not to look at him with a certain interest;)—if the simple look benevolently on money, how much more do your old worldlings regard it! Their affections rush out to meet and welcome money. Their kind sentiments awaken spontaneously towards the interesting possessors of it. I know some respectable people who don't consider themselves at liberty to indulge in friendship for any individual who has not a certain competency, or place in society. They give a loose to their feelings on proper occasions. And the proof is, that the major part of the Osborne family, who had not, in fifteen years, been able to get up a hearty regard for Amelia Sedley, became as fond of Miss Swartz in the course of a single evening as the most romantic advocate of friendship at first-sight could desire.

What a match for George she'd be (the sisters and Miss Wirt agreed), and how much better than that insignificant little Amelia! Such a dashing young fellow as he is, with his good looks, rank, and accomplishments, would be the very husband for her. Visions of balls in Portland Place, presentations at Court, and introductions to half the peerage, filled the minds of the young ladies; who talked of nothing but George and his grand acquaintances to their beloved new friend.

Old Osborne thought she would be a great match, too, for his son. He should leave the army; he should go into Parliament; he should cut a figure in the fashion and in the state. His blood boiled with honest British exultation, as he saw the name of Osborne ennobled in the person of his son, and thought that he might be the progenitor of a glorious line of baronets. He worked in the City and on 'Change, until he knew everything relating to the fortune of the heiress, how her money was placed, and where her estates lay. Young Fred Bullock, one of his chief informants, would have liked to make a bid for her himself (it was so the young banker expressed it), only he was booked to Maria Osborne. But not being able to secure her as a wife, the disinterested Fred quite approved of her as a sister-in-law. "Let George cut in directly and win her," was his advice. "Strike while the iron's hot, you know—while she's fresh to the town; in a few weeks some d—— fellow from the West End will come in with a title and a rotten rent-roll[1] and cut all us City men out, as Lord Fitzrufus did last year with Miss Grogram, who was actually engaged to Podder, of Podder & Brown's. The sooner it is done the better, Mr. Osborne; them's my sentiments," the wag said; though, when Osborne had left the bank parlour, Mr. Bullock remembered Amelia, and what a pretty girl she was, and how attached to George Osborne; and he gave up at least ten seconds of his valuable time to regretting the misfortune which had befallen that unlucky young woman.

While thus George Osborne's good feelings, and his good friend and genius, Dobbin, were carrying back the truant to Amelia's feet, George's parent and sisters were arranging this splendid match for him, which they never dreamed he would resist.

When the elder Osborne gave what he called "a hint," there was no possibility for the most obtuse to mistake his meaning. He called kicking a footman down stairs, a hint to the latter to leave his service. With his usual frankness and delicacy, he told Mrs. Haggistoun that he would give her a check for ten[2] thousand pounds on the day his son was married to her ward; and called that proposal a hint, and considered it a very dexterous piece of diplomacy. He gave George finally such another hint regarding the heiress; and ordered him to marry her out of hand, as he would have ordered his butler to draw a cork, or his clerk to write a letter.

This imperative hint disturbed George a good deal. He was in the very first enthusiasm and delight of his second courtship of Amelia, which was inexpressibly sweet to him. The contrast of her manners and appearance with those of the heiress, made the idea of a union

1. A man with a title of nobility and lands, even if unoccupied, might nevertheless win an heiress without a title away from a rising merchant's son.
2. Revised edition reads: five

with the latter appear doubly ludicrous and odious. Carriages and opera-boxes, thought he; fancy being seen in them by the side of such a Mahogany Charmer as that! Add to all, that the Junior Osborne was quite as obstinate as the Senior: when he wanted a thing, quite as firm in his resolution to get it; and quite as violent when angered, as his father in his most stern moments.

On the first day when his father formally gave him the hint that he was to place his affections at Miss Swartz's feet, George temporised with the old gentleman. "You should have thought of the matter sooner, Sir," he said. "It can't be done now, when we're expecting every day to go on foreign service. Wait till my return, if I do return;" and then he represented, that the time when the regiment was daily expecting to quit England, was exceedingly ill-chosen: that the few days or week during which they were still to remain at home, must be devoted to business and not to love-making: time enough for that when he came home with his majority; "for, I promise you," said he, with a satisfied air, "that one way or other you shall read the name of George Osborne in the Gazette."

The father's reply to this was founded upon the information which he had got in the City: that the West End chaps would infallibly catch hold of the heiress if any delay took place: that if he didn't marry Miss S., he might at least have an engagement in writing, to come into effect when he returned to England; and that a man who could get ten thousand a year by staying at home, was a fool to risk his life abroad.

"So that you would have me shown up as a coward, Sir, and our name dishonoured for the sake of Miss Swartz's money," George interposed.

This remark staggered the old gentleman; but as he had to reply to it, and as his mind was nevertheless made up, he said, "You will dine here to-morrow, Sir, and every day Miss Swartz comes, you will be here to pay your respects to her. If you want for money, call upon Mr. Chopper." Thus a new obstacle was in George's way, to interfere with his plans regarding Amelia; and about which he and Dobbin had more than one confidential consultation. His friend's opinion respecting the line of conduct which he ought to pursue, we know already. And as for Osborne, when he was once bent on a thing, a fresh obstacle or two only rendered him the more resolute.

The dark object of the conspiracy into which the chiefs of the Osborne family had entered, was quite ignorant of all their plans regarding her (which, strange to say, her friend and chaperon did not divulge), and, taking all the young ladies' flattery for genuine sentiment, and being, as we have before had occasion to show, of a very warm and impetuous nature, responded to their affection with quite a tropical ardour. And if the truth may be told, I dare say that she too had some selfish attraction in the Russell Square house; and in a word, thought George Osborne a very nice young man. His whiskers had made an impression upon her, on the very first night she beheld them at the ball at Messrs. Hulkers; and, as we know, she was not the first woman who had been charmed by them. George had an air at once swaggering and melancholy, languid and fierce. He looked like a man who had passions, secrets, and private harrowing griefs and adventures. His voice was rich and deep. He would say it was a warm evening, or ask his partner to take an ice, with a tone as sad and confidential as if he were breaking her mother's death to her, or preluding a declaration of love. He trampled over all the young bucks of his father's circle, and was the hero among those third-rate men. Some few sneered at him and hated him. Some, like Dobbin, fanatically admired him. And his whiskers had began to do their work, and to curl themselves round the affections of Miss Swartz.

Whenever there was a chance of meeting him in Russell Square, that simple and good-natured young woman was quite in a flurry to see her dear Miss Osbornes. She went to great expenses in new gowns, and bracelets, and bonnets, and in prodigious feathers. She adorned her person with her utmost skill to please the Conqueror, and exhibited all her simple accomplishments to win his favour. The girls would ask her, with the greatest gravity, for a little music, and she would sing her three songs and play her two little pieces as often as ever they asked, and with an always increasing pleasure to herself. During these delectable entertainments, Miss Wirt and the chaperon sate by, and conned over the peerage, and talked about the nobility.

The day after George had his hint from his father, and a short time before the hour of dinner, he was lolling upon a sofa in the drawing-room in a very becoming and perfectly natural attitude of melancholy. He had been, at his father's request, to Mr. Chopper in the city, (the old gentleman, though he gave great sums to his son, would never specify any fixed allowance for him, and rewarded him only as he was in the humour). He had then been to pass three hours with Amelia, his dear little Amelia, at Fulham; and he came home to find his sisters spread in starched muslin in the drawing-room, the dowagers cackling in the back-ground, and honest Swartz in her favourite amber-coloured satin, with turquoise-bracelets, countless rings, flowers, feathers, and all sorts of tags and gimcracks, about as elegantly decorated as a she chimney-sweep on May day.[3]

The girls, after vain attempts to engage him in conversation, talked about fashions and the last drawing-room until he was perfectly sick of their chatter. He contrasted their behaviour with little Emmy's,—their shrill cracked[4] voices with her tender ringing tones; their attitudes and their elbows and their starch, with her humble soft movements and modest graces. Poor Swartz was seated in a place where Emmy had been accustomed to sit. Her bejewelled hands lay sprawling in her amber satin lap. Her tags and ear-rings twinkled, and her big eyes rolled about. She was doing nothing with perfect contentment, and thinking herself charming. Anything so becoming as the satin the sisters had never seen.

"Dammy," George said to a confidential friend, "she looked like a China doll, which has nothing to do all day but to grin and wag its head. By Jove, Will, it was all I could do to prevent myself from throwing the sofa cushion at her." He restrained that exhibition of sentiment, however.

3. May Day parades and celebrations brought out all types of working-class people in holiday dress.
4. Revised edition omits: cracked

Miss Swartz rehearsing for the Drawing Room

The sisters began to play the Battle of Prague. "Stop that d—— thing," George howled out in a fury from the sofa. "It makes me mad. *You* play us something, Miss Swartz, do. Sing something, anything but the Battle of Prague."

"Shall I sing Blue Eyed Mary, or the air from the Cabinet?" Miss Swartz asked.

"That sweet thing from the Cabinet," the sisters said.

"We've had that," replied the misanthrope on the sofa.

"I can sing Fluvy du Tajy,"[5] Swartz said, in a meek voice, "if I had the words." It was the last of the worthy young woman's collection.

"O, Fleuve du Tage," Miss Maria cried; "we have the song," and went to fetch the book in which it was.

Now it happened that this song, then in the height of the fashion, had been given to the young ladies by a young friend of theirs, whose name was on the title, and Miss Swartz, having concluded the ditty with George's applause, (for he remembered that it was a favourite of Amelia's,) was hoping for an encore perhaps, and fiddling with the leaves of the music, when her eye fell upon the title, and she saw "Amelia Sedley" written in the corner.

"Lor!" cried Miss Swartz, spinning swiftly round on the music-

stool, "is it *my* Amelia? Amelia that was at Miss P.'s at Hammersmith? I know it is. It's her, and—Tell me about her—where is she?"

5. "The Battle of Prague," piano sonata by F. Kotzvara. "Blue-Eyed Mary," one of many popular ballads of the time. *The Cabinet*, a comic opera by T. J. Dibdin. "Fleuve du Tage," from *Le Troubadour du Tage*, by B. Pollet, which was adapted as a beginner's piece for piano.

"Don't mention her," Miss Maria Osborne said hastily. "Her family has disgraced itself. Her father cheated papa, and as for her, she is never to be mentioned *here.*" This was Miss Maria's return for George's rudeness about the Battle of Prague.

"Are you a friend of Amelia's?" George said, bouncing up. "God bless you for it, Miss Swartz. Don't believe what the girls say. *She's* not to blame at any rate. She's the best—"

"You know you're not to speak about her, George," cried Jane. "Papa forbids it."

"Who's to prevent me?" George cried out. "I *will* speak of her. I say she's the best, the kindest, the gentlest, the sweetest girl in England; and that, bankrupt or no, my sisters are not fit to hold candles to her. If you like her, go and see her, Miss Swartz; she wants friends now; and I say, God bless everybody who befriends her. Anybody who speaks kindly of her is my friend; anybody who speaks against her is my enemy. Thank you, Miss Swartz;" and he went up and wrung her hand.

"George! George!" one of the sisters cried imploringly.

"I say," George said fiercely, "I thank everybody who loves Amelia Sed—". He stopped. Old Osborne was in the room with a face livid with rage, and eyes like hot coals.

Though George had stopped in his sentence, yet, his blood being up, he was not to be cowed by all the generations of Osborne; rallying instantly, he replied to the bullying look of his father, with another so indicative of resolution and defiance, that the elder man quailed in his turn, and looked away. He felt that the tussle was coming. "Mrs. Haggistoun, let me take you down to dinner," he said. "Give your arm to Miss Swartz, George," and they marched.

"Miss Swartz, I love Amelia, and we've been engaged almost all our lives," Osborne said to his partner; and during all the dinner, George rattled on with a volubility which surprised himself, and made his father doubly nervous, for the fight which was to take place as soon as the ladies were gone.

The difference between the pair was, that while the father was violent and a bully, the son had thrice the nerve and courage of the parent, and could not merely make an attack, but resist it; and finding that the moment was now come when the contest between him and his father was to be decided, he took his dinner with perfect coolness and appetite before the engagement began. Old Osborne, on the contrary, was nervous, and drank much. He floundered in his conversation with the ladies, his neighbours; George's coolness only rendering him more angry. It made him half mad to see the calm way in which George, flapping his napkin, and with a swaggering bow, opened the door for the ladies to leave the room; and filling himself a glass of wine, smacked it, and looked his father full in the face, as if to say, "Gentlemen of the Guard, fire first."[6] The old man also took a supply of ammunition, but his decanter clinked against the glass as he tried to fill it.

6. At the Battle of Fontenay in 1745, the English and French politely offered each other the opportunity of opening fire, according to Voltaire in *Le Siècle de Louis XV* (Harden).

After giving a great heave, and with a purple choking face, he then began. "How dare you, Sir, mention that person's name before Miss Swartz to-day, in my drawing-room? I ask you, Sir, how dare you do it?"

"Stop, Sir," says George, "don't say dare, Sir. Dare isn't a word to be used to a Captain in the British Army."

"I shall say what I like to my son, Sir. I can cut him off with a shilling if I like. I can make him a beggar if I like. I *will* say what I like," the elder said.

"I'm a gentleman though I *am* your son, Sir," George answered haughtily. "Any communications which you have to make to me, or any orders which you may please to give, I beg may be couched in that kind of language which I am accustomed to hear."

Whenever the lad assumed his haughty manner, it always created either great awe or great irritation in the parent. Old Osborne stood in secret terror of his son as a better gentleman than himself; and perhaps my readers may have remarked in their experience of this Vanity Fair of ours, that there is no character which a low-minded man so much mistrusts, as that of a gentleman.

"My father didn't give me the education you have had, nor the advantages you have had, nor the money you have had. If I had kept the company *some folks* have had through *my means,* perhaps my son wouldn't have any reason to brag, Sir, of his *superiority* and *West End airs*" (these words were uttered in the elder Osborne's most sarcastic tones). "But it wasn't considered the part of a gentleman, in *my* time, for a man to insult his father. If I'd done any such thing, mine would have kicked me down stairs, Sir."

"I never insulted you, Sir. I said I begged you to remember your son was a gentleman as well as yourself. I know very well that you give me plenty of money," said George (fingering a bundle of notes which he had got in the morning from Mr. Chopper). "You tell it me often enough, Sir. There's no fear of my forgetting it."

"I wish you'd remember other things as well, Sir," the sire answered. "I wish you'd remember that in this house—so long as you choose to *honour* it with your *company,* Captain—I'm the master, and that name, and that that—that you—that I say—"

"That what, Sir?" George asked, with scarcely a sneer, filling another glass of claret.

"——!" burst out his father with a screaming oath—"that the name of those Sedleys never be mentioned here, Sir—not one of the whole damned lot of 'em, Sir."

"It wasn't I, Sir, that introduced Miss Sedley's name. It was my sisters who spoke ill of her to Miss Swartz; and by Jove I'll defend her wherever I go. Nobody shall speak lightly of that name in my presence. Our family has done her quite enough injury already, I think, and may leave off reviling her now she's down. I'll shoot any man but you who says a word against her."

"Go on, Sir, go on," the old gentleman said, his eyes starting out of his head.

"Go on about what, Sir? about the way in which we've treated that angel of a girl? Who told me to love her? It was your doing. I might have chosen elsewhere, and looked higher, perhaps, than your society: but I obeyed you. And now that her heart's mine you give me orders to fling it away, and punish her, kill her perhaps—for the faults of other people. It's a shame, by Heavens," said George, working himself up into passion and enthusiasm as he proceeded, "to play at fast and loose with a young girl's affections—and with such an angel as that—one so superior to the people amongst whom she lived that she might have excited envy, only she was so good and gentle, that it's a wonder anybody dared to hate her. If I desert her, Sir, do you suppose she forgets me?"

"I ain't going to have any of this dam sentimental nonsense and humbug here, Sir," the father cried out. "There shall be no beggar-marriages in my family. If you choose to fling away eight thousand a-year which you may have for the asking you may do it: but by Jove you take your pack and walk out of this house, Sir. Will you do as I tell you, once for all, Sir, or will you not?"

"Marry that mulatto woman?" George said, pulling up his shirt-collars. "I don't like the colour, sir. Ask the black that sweeps opposite Fleet Market, Sir. *I'm* not going to marry a Hottentot Venus."

Mr. Osborne pulled frantically at the cord by which he was accustomed to summon the butler when he wanted wine—and, almost black in the face, ordered that functionary to call a coach for Captain Osborne.

"I've done it," said George, coming into the Slaughters' an hour afterwards, looking very pale.

"What, my boy?" says Dobbin.

George told what had passed between his father and himself.

"I'll marry her to-morrow," he said with an oath. "I love her more every day, Dobbin."

## *Chapter XXII.*

### A MARRIAGE AND PART OF A HONEYMOON.

NEMIES[1] the most obstinate and courageous can't hold out against starvation: so the elder Osborne felt himself pretty easy about his adversary in the encounter we have just described; and as soon as George's supplies fell short, confidently expected his unconditional submission. It was unlucky, to be sure, that the lad should have secured a stock of provisions on the very day when the first encounter took place; but this relief was only temporary, old Osborne thought, and would but delay George's surrender. No communication passed between father and son for some days. The former was sulky at this silence, but not disquieted; for, as he said, he knew where he could put the screw upon George, and only waited the result of that operation. He told the sisters the upshot of the dispute between them, but ordered them to take no notice of the matter, and welcome George on his return as if nothing had happened. His cover was laid as usual every day, and perhaps the old gentleman rather anxiously expected him; but he never came. Some one inquired at the Slaughters' regarding him, where it was said that he and his friend Captain Dobbin had left town.

One gusty, raw day at the end of April,—the rain whipping the pavement of that ancient street where the old Slaughters' Coffee-house was once situated,—George Osborne came into the coffee-room, looking very haggard and pale; although dressed rather smartly in a blue coat and brass buttons, and a neat buff waistcoat of the fashion of those days. Here was his friend Captain Dobbin, in blue and brass too, having abandoned the military frock and French-grey trowsers, which were the usual coverings of his lanky person.

Dobbin had been in the coffee-room for an hour or more. He had tried all the papers, but could not read them. He had looked at the clock many scores of times; and at the street, where the rain was pattering down, and the people as they clinked by in pattens, left long reflections on the shining stones: he tattooed at the table: he bit his nails most completely, and nearly to the quick (he was accustomed to ornament his great big hands in this way): he balanced the tea-spoon dexterously on the milk jug: upset it, &c. &c.; and in fact showed those signs of disquietude, and practised those desperate attempts at amusement, which men are accustomed to employ when very anxious, and expectant, and perturbed in mind.

Some of his comrades, gentlemen who used the room, joked him about the splendour of his costume and his agitation of manner. One

1. Initial vignette: Cupid with Alpha and Omega banner—Love conquers all.

asked him if he was going to be married? Dobbin laughed, and said he would send his acquaintance (Major Wagstaff, of the Engineers) a piece of cake, when that event took place. At length Captain Osborne made his appearance, very smartly dressed, but very pale and agitated, as we have said. He wiped his pale face with a large yellow bandanna pocket-handkerchief that was prodigiously scented. He shook hands with Dobbin, looked at the clock, and told John, the waiter, to bring him some curaçoa. Of this cordial he swallowed off a couple of glasses with nervous eagerness. His friend asked with some interest about his health.

"Couldn't get a wink of sleep till daylight, Dob," said he. "Infernal headache and fever. Got up at nine, and went down to the Hummums[2] for a bath. I say, Dob, I feel just as I did on the morning I went out[3] with Rocket at Quebec."

"So do I," William responded. "I was a deuced deal more nervous than you were that morning. You made a famous breakfast, I remember. Eat something now."

"You're a good old fellow, Will. I'll drink your health, old boy, and farewell to—"

"No, no; two glasses are enough," Dobbin interrupted him. "Here, take away the liqueurs, John. Have some cayenne-pepper with your fowl. Make haste though, for it is time we were there."

It was about half-an-hour from twelve when this brief meeting and colloquy took place between the two captains. A coach, into which Captain Osborne's servant put his master's desk and dressing-case, had been in waiting for some time; and into this the two gentlemen hurried under an umbrella, and the valet mounted on the box, cursing the rain and the dampness of the coachman who was steaming beside him. "We shall find a better trap than this at the chutch-door," says he; "that's a comfort." And the carriage drove on, taking the road down Piccadilly, where Apsley House and St. George's Hospital wore red jackets still;[4] where there were oil-lamps; where Achilles was not yet born; nor the Pimlico arch raised; nor the hideous equestrian monster which pervades it and the neighbourhood;—and so they drove down by Brompton to a certain chapel near the Fulham road there.

A chariot was in waiting with four horses; likewise a coach of the kind called glass coaches.[5] Only a very few idlers were collected on account of the dismal dismal rain.

"Hang it!" said George, "I said only a pair."

2. A Turkish bath. Though many baths in Covent Garden were also brothels in the eighteenth century, the character of the area was already on the mend by 1813.
3. Dueled with (Harden).
4. Apsley House, home of the duke of Wellington, and St. George's Hospital, both on Park Lane opposite Hyde Park, were originally red brick. In 1827–29 the first was veneered in gray stone and the other was reconstructed. A statue of Achilles (1822), an arch (1825), and an equestrian statue (1846) were erected in Wellington's honor in sight of his house. The equestrian statue was much satirized in the press the year before this chapter was written. See "*Vanity Fair* and the London Skyline" at the end of this volume. Though gas lighted parts of the city, Hyde Park had oil lamps until 1825. Link boys, or lamp carriers, were still required for much of the city, which was unlighted.
5. Hackney coaches usually had curtain windows, but special glazed-window coaches were available for private hire.

"My master would have four," said Mr. Joseph Sedley's servant, who was in waiting; and he and Mr. Osborne's man agreed as they followed George and William into the church, that it was a "reg'lar shabby turn hout; and with scarce so much as a breakfast or a wedding faviour."

"Here you are," said our old friend, Jos Sedley, coming forward. "You're five minutes late, George, my boy. What a day, eh? Demmy, it's like the commencement of the rainy season in Bengal. But you'll find my carriage is water-tight. Come along, my mother and Emmy are in the vestry."

Jos Sedley was splendid. He was fatter than ever. His shirt collars were higher; his face was redder; his shirt-frill flaunted gorgeously out of his variegated waistcoat. Varnished boots were not invented as yet; but the Hessians on his beautiful legs shone so, that they must have been the identical pair in which the gentleman in the old picture used to shave himself;[6] and on his light green coat there bloomed a fine wedding favour, like a great white spreading magnolia.

In a word, George had thrown the great cast. He was going to be married. Hence his pallor and nervousness—his sleepless night and agitation in the morning. I have heard people who have gone through the same thing own to the same emotion. After three or four ceremonies, you get accustomed to it, no doubt; but the first dip, every body allows, is awful.

The bride was dressed in a brown silk pelisse, (as Captain Dobbin has since informed me), and wore a straw bonnet with a pink ribbon: over the bonnet she had a veil of white Chantilly lace, a gift from Mr. Joseph Sedley, her brother. Captain Dobbin himself had asked leave to present her with a gold chain and watch, which she sported on this occasion; and her mother gave her her diamond brooch; almost the only trinket which was left to the old lady. As the service went on, Mrs. Sedley sat and whimpered a great deal in a pew, consoled by the Irish maid servant and Mrs. Clapp from the lodgings. Old Sedley would not be present. Jos acted for his father, giving away the bride, whilst Captain Dobbin stepped up as groom's-man to his friend George.

There was nobody in the church besides the officiating persons and the small marriage party and their attendants. The two valets sat aloof superciliously. The rain came rattling down on the windows. In the intervals of the service you heard it, and the sobbing of old Mrs. Sedley in the pew. The parson's tones echoed sadly through the empty walls. Osborne's "I will" was sounded in very deep base. Emmy's response came fluttering up to her lips from her heart, but was scarcely heard by anybody except Captain Dobbin.

When the service was completed, Jos Sedley came forward and kissed his sister, the bride, for the first time for many months—George's look of gloom had gone, and he seemed quite proud and radiant. "It's your turn, William," says he, putting his hand fondly

6. George Cruikshank's woodcut advertisements for Warren's Blacking include one showing a man shaving with his face reflected in a well-polished boot; it appeared regularly in, for example, the *National Omnibus* for 1832 (Tillotson).

upon Dobbin's shoulder; and Dobbin went up and touched Amelia on the cheek.

Then they went into the vestry and signed the register. "God bless you, Old Dobbin," George said, grasping him by the hand, with something very like moisture glistening in his eyes. William replied only by nodding his head. His heart was too full to say much.

"Write directly, and come down as soon as you can, you know," Osborne said. After Mrs. Sedley had taken an hysterical adieu of her daughter, the pair went off to the carriage. "Get out of the way, you little devils," George cried to a small crowd of damp urchins, that were hanging about the chapel-door. The rain drove into the bride and bridegroom's faces as they passed to the chariot. The postillions' favours draggled on their dripping jackets. The few children made a dismal cheer, as the carriage, splashing mud, drove away.

William Dobbin stood in the church-porch, looking at it, a queer figure. The small crew of spectators jeered him. He was not thinking about them or their laughter.

"Come home and have some tiffin, Dobbin," a voice cried behind him; as a pudgy hand was laid on his shoulder, and the honest fellow's reverie was interrupted. But the Captain had no heart to go a feasting with Jos Sedley. He put the weeping old lady and her attendants into the carriage along with Jos, and left them without any farther words passing. This carriage, too, drove away, and the urchins gave another sarcastical cheer.

"Here, you little beggars," Dobbin said, giving some sixpences amongst them, and then went off by himself through the rain. It was all over. They were married, and happy, he prayed God. Never since he was a boy had he felt so miserable and so lonely. He longed with a heart-sick yearning for the first few days to be over, that he might see her again.

Some ten days after the above ceremony, three young men of our acquaintance were enjoying that beautiful prospect of bow windows on the one side and blue sea on the other, which Brighton affords to the traveller. Sometimes it is towards the ocean—smiling with countless dimples, speckled with white sails, with a hundred bathing-machines[7] kissing the skirt of his blue garment—that the Londoner looks enraptured: sometimes, on the contrary, a lover of human nature rather than of prospects of any kind, it is towards the bow windows that he turns, and that swarm of human life which they exhibit. From one issue the notes of a piano, which a young lady in ringlets practises six hours daily, to the delight of the fellow-lodgers: at another, lovely Polly, the nursemaid, may be seen dandling Master Omnium in her arms: whilst Jacob, his papa, is beheld eating prawns, and devouring the Times for breakfast, at the window below.[8] Yonder are the Misses Leery, who are looking out for the young officers of the heavies, who are pretty sure to be pacing the cliff; or again it is a City man, with a nautical turn, and a telescope, the

7. Closets on wheels, in which bathers protected their modesty, were pushed into the sea.
8. Jacob Omnium was the pseudonym of Matthew Higgins (1810–68), a friend of Thackeray's. Omnium had a family, though Higgins was unmarried at the time of writing.

size of a six-pounder, who has his instrument pointed seawards, so as to command every pleasure-boat, herring-boat, or bathing-machine that comes to, or quits, the shore, &c., &c. But have we any leisure for a description of Brighton?—for Brighton, a clean Naples with genteel lazzaroni[9]—for Brighton, that always looks brisk, gay, and gaudy, like a harlequin's jacket—for Brighton, which used to be seven hours' distant from London at the time of our story; which is now only a hundred minutes off; and which may approach who knows how much nearer, unless Joinville[1] comes and untimely bombards it?

"What a monstrous fine girl that is in the lodgings over the milliners," one of these three promenaders remarked to the other; "Gad, Crawley, did you see what a wink she gave me as I passed?"

"Don't break her heart, Jos, you rascal," said another. "Don't trifle with her affections, you Don Juan!"[2]

"Get away," said Jos Sedley, quite pleased, and leering up at the maid-servant in question with a most killing ogle. Jos was even more splendid at Brighton than he had been at his sister's marriage. He had brilliant under-waistcoats, any one of which would have set up a moderate buck. He sported a military frock-coat, ornamented with frogs, knobs, black buttons, and meandering embroidery. He had affected a military appearance and habits of late; and he walked with his two friends, who were of that profession, clinking his boot-spurs, swaggering prodigiously, and shooting death-glances at all the servant girls who were worthy to be slain.

"What shall we do, boys, till the ladies return?" the buck asked. The ladies were out to Rottingdean[3] in his carriage, on a drive. "Let's have a game at billiards," one of his friends said—the tall one, with lacquered mustachios.

"No, dammy; no, Captain," Jos replied, rather alarmed. "No billiards to-day, Crawley, my boy; yesterday was enough."

"You play very well," said Crawley, laughing. "Don't he, Osborne? How well he made that five stroke,[4] eh?"

"Famous," Osborne said. "Jos is a devil of a fellow at billiards, and at everything else, too. I wish there were any tiger-hunting about here; we might go and kill a few before dinner. (There goes a fine girl! what an ancle, eh Jos?) Tell us that story about the tiger-hunt, and the way you did for him in the jungle—it's a wonderful story that, Crawley." Here George Osborne gave a yawn. "It's rather slow work," said he, "down here; what *shall* we do?"

"Shall we go and look at some horses that Snaffler's[5] just brought from Lewes[6] fair?" Crawley said.

"Suppose we go and have some jellies at Dutton's," said the rogue Jos, willing to kill two birds with one stone. "Devilish fine gal at Dutton's."

9. Naples' beggars.
1. François Joinville, duke of Orleans (1818–1900), proposed a steam-driven French navy, which Thackeray satirized in *Punch*, June 1 and 15, 1844.
2. A lothario, a womanizer.
3. A small spa town just east of Brighton.
4. A stroke in billiards by which five points are scored: sinking the red ball scores three points, and striking the other white one, two more.
5. A snaffle is a bridle bit.
6. A country town near Brighton.

"Suppose we go and see the Lightning come in, it's just about time?" George said. This advice prevailing over the stables and the jelly, they turned towards the coach-office to witness the Lightning's arrival.[7]

As they passed, they met the carriage—Jos Sedley's open carriage, with its magnificent armorial bearings—that splendid conveyance in which he used to drive about at Cheltenham, majestic and solitary, with his arms folded, and his hat cocked; or, more happy, with ladies by his side.

Two were in the carriage now: one a little person, with light hair, and dressed in the height of the fashion; the other in a brown silk pelisse, and a straw bonnet with pink ribbons, with a rosy, round, happy face, that did you good to behold. She checked the carriage as it neared the three gentlemen, after which exercise of authority she looked rather nervous, and then began to blush most absurdly. "We have had a delightful drive, George," she said, "and—and we're so glad to come back; and Joseph, don't let him be late."

"Don't be leading our husbands into mischief, Mr. Sedley, you wicked, wicked man you," Rebecca said, shaking at Jos a pretty little finger covered with the neatest French kid glove. "No billiards, no smoking, no naughtiness!"

"My dear Mrs. Crawley—Ah now! upon my honour!" was all Jos could ejaculate by way of reply; but he managed to fall into a tolerable attitude, with his head lying on his shoulder, grinning upwards at his victim, with one hand at his back, which he supported on his cane, and the other hand (the one with the diamond ring) fumbling in his shirt-frill and among his under-waistcoats. As the carriage drove off he kissed the diamond hand to the fair ladies within. He wished all Cheltenham, all Chowringhee,[8] all Calcutta, could see him in that position, waving his hand to such a beauty, and in company with such a famous buck as Rawdon Crawley of the Guards.

Our young bride and bridegroom had chosen Brighton as the place where they would pass the first few days after their marriage. And having engaged apartments at the Ship Inn,[9] enjoyed themselves there in great comfort and quietude, until Jos presently joined them. Nor was he the only companion they found there. As they were coming into the Hotel from a sea-side walk one afternoon, on whom should they light but Rebecca and her husband. The recognition was immediate. Rebecca flew into the arms of her dearest friend. Crawley and Osborne shook hands together cordially enough: and Becky, in the course of a very few hours, found means to make the latter forget that little unpleasant passage of words which had happened between them. "Do you remember the last time we met at Miss Crawley's, when I was so rude to you, dear Captain Osborne? I thought you seemed careless about dear Amelia. It was that made me angry: and so pert: and so unkind: and so ungrateful. Do forgive me!" Rebecca said, and she held out her hand with so frank

7. Stagecoaches and their schedules were known by names like Eclipse, Comet, Dart, etc. "Lightning" has not been verified as an actual coach name for the London-to-Brighton run.
8. A fashionable street in Calcutta (Harden).
9. There was a hotel named The Ship Tavern and, later, The Old Ship, but it did not overlook the sea. See illustration, chapter XXV (Sutherland).

and winning a grace, that Osborne could not but take it. By humbly and frankly acknowledging yourself to be in the wrong, there is no knowing, my son, what good you may do. I knew once a gentleman, and very worthy practitioner in Vanity Fair, who used to do little wrongs to his neighbours on purpose, and in order to apologise for them in an open and manly way afterwards—and what ensued? My friend Crocky Doyle was liked everywhere, and deemed to be rather impetuous—but the honestest fellow. Becky's humility passed for sincerity with George Osborne.

These two young couples had plenty of tales to relate to each other. The marriages of either were discussed; and their prospects in life canvassed with the greatest frankness and interest on both sides. George's marriage was to be made known to his father by his friend Captain Dobbin; and young Osborne trembled rather for the result of that communication. Miss Crawley, on whom all Rawdon's hopes depended, still held out. Unable to make an entry into her house in Park Lane, her affectionate nephew and niece had followed her to Brighton, where they had emissaries continually planted at her door.

"I wish you could see some of Rawdon's friends who are always about *our* door," Rebecca said, laughing. "Did you ever see a dun, my dear; or a bailiff and his man? Two of the abominable wretches watched all last week at the greengrocer's opposite, and we could not get away until Sunday. If aunty does not relent, what *shall* we do?"

Rawdon, with roars of laughter, related a dozen amusing anecdotes of his duns, and Rebecca's adroit treatment of them. He vowed with a great oath, that there was no woman in Europe who could talk a creditor over as she could. Almost immediately after their marriage, her practice had begun, and her husband found the immense value of such a wife. They had credit in plenty, but they had bills also in abundance, and laboured under a scarcity of ready money. Did these debt-difficulties affect Rawdon's good spirits? No. Everybody in Vanity Fair must have remarked how well those live who are comfortably and thoroughly in debt: how they deny themselves nothing; how jolly and easy they are in their minds. Rawdon and his wife had the very best apartments at the inn at Brighton; the landlord, as he brought in the first dish, bowed before them as to his greatest customers: and Rawdon abused the dinners and wine with an audacity which no grandee in the land could surpass. Long custom, a manly appearance, faultless boots and clothes, and a happy fierceness of manner, will often help a man as much as a great balance at the banker's.

The two wedding parties met constantly in each other's apartments. After two or three nights the gentlemen of an evening had a little picquet, as their wives sate and chatted apart. This pastime, and the arrival of Jos Sedley, who made his appearance in his grand open carriage, and who played a few games at billiards with Captain Crawley, replenished Rawdon's purse somewhat, and gave him the benefit of that ready money for which the greatest spirits are sometimes at a stand-still.

So the three gentlemen walked down to see the Lightning coach come in. Punctual to the minute, the coach crowded inside and out, the guard blowing his accustomed tune on the horn—the Lightning came tearing down the street, and pulled up at the coach-office.

"Hullo! there's old Dobbin," George cried, quite delighted to see his old friend perched on the roof; and whose promised visit to Brighton had been delayed until now. "How are you, old fellow? Glad you're come down. Emmy'll be delighted to see you," Osborne said, shaking his comrade warmly by the hand as soon as his descent from the vehicle was effected—and then he added, in a lower and agitated voice, "What's the news. Have you been in Russell Square? What does the governor say? Tell me everything."

Dobbin looked very pale and grave. "I've seen your father," said he. "How's Amelia—Mrs. George? I'll tell you all the news presently: but I've brought the great news of all: and that is—"

"Out with it, old fellow," George said.

"We're ordered to Belgium. All the army goes—Guards and all. Heavytop's got the gout, and is mad at not being able to move. O'Dowd goes in command, and we embark from Chatham next week."

This news of war could not but come with a shock upon our lovers, and caused all these gentlemen to look very serious.

*Number 7* *July 1847*

## *Chapter XXIII.*

### CAPTAIN DOBBIN PROCEEDS ON HIS CANVASS.[1]

HAT is the secret mesmerism which friendship possesses, and under the operation of which a person ordinarily sluggish, or cold, or timid, becomes wise, active, and resolute, in another's behalf? As Alexis, after a few passes from Dr. Elliotson, despises pain, reads with the back of his head, sees miles off, looks into next week, and performs other wonders, of which, in his own private normal condition, he is quite incapable;[2] so you see, in the affairs of the world and under the magnetism of friendship, the modest man become bold, the shy confident, the lazy active, or the impetuous prudent and peaceful. What is it, on the other hand, that makes the lawyer eschew his own cause, and

1. To examine all options and solicit support.
2. John Elliotson (1791–1868), physician, phrenologist, mesmerist, and a personal acquaintance of Thackeray's, published accounts of his subject, Alexis, who became clairvoyant under hypnosis. Elliotson also conducted séances.

call in his learned brother as an adviser? And what causes the doctor, when ailing, to send for his rival, and not sit down and examine his own tongue in the chimney glass,[3] or write his own prescription at his study table? I throw out these queries for intelligent readers to answer, who know, at once, how credulous we are, and how sceptical, how soft and how obstinate, how firm for others and how diffident about ourselves: meanwhile it is certain that our friend William Dobbin, who was personally of so complying a disposition that if his parents had pressed him much, it is probable he would have stepped down into the kitchen and married the cook, and who, to further his own interests, would have found the most insuperable difficulty in walking across the street, found himself as busy and eager in the conduct of George Osborne's affairs, as the most selfish tactician could be in the pursuit of his own.

Whilst our friend George and his young wife were enjoying the first blushing days of the honeymoon at Brighton, honest William was left as George's plenipotentiary in London, to transact all the business part of the marriage. His duty it was to call upon old Sedley and his wife, and to keep the former in good humour: to draw Jos and his brother-in-law nearer together, so that Jos's position and dignity, as collector of Boggley wollah, might compensate for his father's loss of station, and tend to reconcile old Osborne to the alliance: and finally, to communicate it to the latter in such a way as should least irritate the old gentleman.

Now, before he faced the head of the Osborne house with the news which it was his duty to tell, Dobbin bethought him that it would be politic to make friends of the rest of the family, and, if possible, have the ladies on his side. They can't be angry in their hearts, thought he. No woman ever was really angry at a romantic marriage. A little crying out, and they must come round to their brother; when the three of us will lay siege to old Mr. Osborne. So this Machiavellian[4] captain of infantry cast about him for some happy means or stratagem by which he could gently and gradually bring the Miss Osbornes to a knowledge of their brother's secret.

By a little inquiry regarding his mother's engagements, he was pretty soon able to find out by whom of her ladyship's friends parties were given at that season; where he would be likely to meet Osborne's sisters; and, though he had that abhorrence of routs and evening parties, which many sensible men, alas, entertain, he soon found one where the Miss Osbornes were to be present. Making his appearance at the ball, where he danced a couple of sets with both of them, and was prodigiously polite, he actually had the courage to ask Miss Osborne for a few minutes' conversation at an early hour the next day, when he had, he said, to communicate to her news of the very greatest interest.

What was it that made her start back, and gaze upon him for a moment, and then on the ground at her feet, and make as if she would faint on his arm, had he not by opportunely treading on her toes, brought the young lady back to self-control? Why was she so

3. Mirror.
4. Cunning, practical, following the advice of Niccolò Machiavelli (1469–1527) in *The Prince*.

violently agitated at Dobbin's request? This can never be known. But when he came the next day, Maria was not in the drawing-room with her sister, and Miss Wirt went off for the purpose of fetching the latter, and the Captain and Miss Osborne were left together. They were both so silent that the tick-tock of the Sacrifice of Iphigenia[5] clock on the mantel-piece became quite rudely audible.

"What a nice party it was last night," Miss Osborne at length began, encouragingly; "and—and how you're improved in your dancing, Captain Dobbin. Surely somebody has taught you," she added, with amiable archness.

"You should see me dance a reel with Mrs. Major O'Dowd of ours; and a jig—did you ever see a jig? But I think anybody could dance with *you,* Miss Osborne, who dance so well."

"Is the Major's lady young and beautiful, Captain?" the fair questioner continued. "Ah, what a terrible thing it must be to be a soldier's wife! I wonder they have any spirits to dance, and in these dreadful times of war too! O Captain Dobbin, I tremble sometimes when I think of our dearest George, and the dangers of the poor soldier. Are there many married officers of the —th, Captain Dobbin?"

"Upon my word, she's playing her hand rather too openly," Miss Wirt thought; but this observation is merely parenthetic, and was not heard through the crevice of the door at which the governess uttered it.

"One of our young men is just married," Dobbin said, now coming to the point. "It was a very old attachment, and the young couple are as poor as church mice."

"O, how delightful! O, how romantic!" Miss Osborne cried, as the Captain said "old attachment" and "poor." Her sympathy encouraged him.

"The finest young fellow in the regiment," he continued. "Not a braver or handsomer officer in the army; and such a charming wife! How you would like her; how you *will* like her when you know her, Miss Osborne." The young lady thought the actual moment had arrived, and that Dobbin's nervousness which now came on and was visible in many twitchings of his face, in his manner of beating the ground with his great feet, in the rapid buttoning and unbuttoning of his frock-coat, &c.—Miss Osborne, I say, thought that when he had given himself a little air, he would unbosom himself entirely, and prepared eagerly to listen. And the clock, in the altar on which Iphigenia was situated, beginning, after a preparatory convulsion, to toll twelve, the mere tolling seemed as if it would last until one—so prolonged was the knell to the anxious spinster.

"But it's not about marriage that I came to speak—that is that marriage—that is—no, I mean—my dear Miss Osborne, it's about our dear friend George," Dobbin said.

"About George?" she said in a tone so discomfited that Maria and Miss Wirt laughed at the other side of the door, and even that abandoned wretch of a Dobbin felt inclined to smile himself; for he was not altogether unconscious of the state of affairs; George having of-

5. Daughter of Agamemnon, who sacrificed her to Artemis in order to gain favorable winds in the journey to Troy. See also chapters XV, XLII, and LI.

ten bantered him gracefully and said, "Hang it, Will, why don't you take old Jane?[6] She'll have you if you ask her. I'll bet you five to two she will."

"Yes, about George, then," he continued. "There has been a difference between him and Mr. Osborne. And I regard him so much—for you know we have been like brothers—that I hope and pray the quarrel may be settled. We must go abroad, Miss Osborne. We may be ordered off at a day's warning. Who knows what may happen in the campaign? Don't be agitated, dear Miss Osborne; and those two at least should part friends."

"There has been no quarrel, Captain Dobbin, except a little usual scene with papa," the lady said. "We are expecting George back daily. What papa wanted was only for his good. He has but to come back, and I'm sure all will be well; and dear Rhoda, who went away from here in sad sad anger, I know will forgive him. Woman forgives but too readily, Captain."

"Such an angel as *you* I am sure would," Mr. Dobbin said, with atrocious astuteness. "And no man can pardon himself for giving a woman pain. What would you feel, if a man were faithless to you?"

"I should perish—I should throw myself out of window—I should take poison—I should pine and die. I know I should," Miss cried, who had nevertheless gone through one or two affairs of the heart without any idea of suicide.

"And there are others," Dobbin continued, "as true and as kind-hearted as yourself. I'm not speaking about the West India heiress, Miss Osborne, but about a poor girl whom George once loved, and who was bred from her childhood to think of nobody but him. I've seen her in her poverty uncomplaining, broken-hearted, without a fault. It is of Miss Sedley I speak. Dear Miss Osborne, can your generous heart quarrel with your brother for being faithful to her? Could his own conscience ever forgive him if he deserted her? Be her friend—she always loved you—and—and I am come here charged by George to tell you that he holds his engagement to her as the most sacred duty he has; and to entreat *you,* at least, to be on his side."

When any strong emotion took possession of Mr. Dobbin, and after the first word or two of hesitation, he could speak with perfect fluency, and it was evident that his eloquence on this occasion made some impression upon the lady whom he addressed.

"Well," said she, "this is—most surprising—most painful—most extraordinary—what will Papa say?—that George should fling away such a superb establishment as was offered to him,—but at any rate he has found a very brave champion in you, Captain Dobbin. It is of no use, however," she continued, after a pause, "I feel for poor Miss Sedley, most certainly—most sincerely you know. We never thought the match a good one, though we were always very kind to her here—very. But Papa will never consent, I am sure. And a well brought up young woman you know,—with a well regulated mind must—George must give her up, dear Captain Dobbin, indeed he must."

"Ought a man to give up the woman he loved, just when misfortune befel her?" Dobbin said, holding out his hand. "Dear Miss Os-

6. The first edition erroneously reads "old Polly" (a diminutive for Mary, who is outside with Miss Wirt).

borne! is this the counsel I hear from *you*? My dear young lady! you must befriend her. He can't give her up. He must not give her up. Would a man, think you, give *you* up if you were poor?"

This adroit question touched the heart of Miss Jane Osborne not a little. "I don't know whether we poor girls ought to believe what you men say, Captain," she said. "There is that in woman's tenderness which induces her to believe too easily. I'm afraid you are cruel cruel deceivers,"—and Dobbin certainly thought he felt a pressure of the hand which Miss Osborne had extended to him.

He dropped it in some alarm. "Deceivers!" said he. "No, dear Miss Osborne, all men are not; your brother is not; George has loved Amelia Sedley ever since they were children; no wealth would make him marry any but her. Ought he to forsake her? Would you counsel him to do so?"

What could Miss Jane say to such a question, and with her own peculiar views? She could not answer it, so she parried it by saying, "Well, if you are not a deceiver, at least you are *very* romantic;" and Captain William let this observation pass without challenge.

At length when, by the help of farther polite speeches, he deemed that Miss Osborne was sufficiently prepared to receive the whole news, he poured it into her ear. "George could not give up Amelia—George was married to her"—and then he related the circumstances of the marriage as we know them already, how the poor girl would have died had not her lover kept his faith: how Old Sedley had refused all consent to the match, and a licence had been got: and Jos Sedley had come from Cheltenham to give away the bride: how they had gone to Brighton in Jos's chariot-and-four to pass the honeymoon: and how George counted on his dear kind sisters to befriend him with their father, as women—so true and tender as they were—assuredly would do. And so, asking permission (readily granted) to see her again, and rightly conjecturing that the news he had brought would be told in the next five minutes to the other ladies, Captain Dobbin made his bow and took his leave.

He was scarcely out of the house, when Miss Maria and Miss Wirt rushed in to Miss Osborne, and the whole wonderful secret was imparted to them by that lady. To do them justice, neither of the sisters were very much displeased. There is something about a runaway match with which few ladies can be seriously angry, and Amelia rather rose in their estimation, from the spirit which she had displayed in consenting to the union. As they debated the story, and prattled about it, and wondered what Papa would do and say, came a loud knock, as of an avenging thunder-clap, at the door, which made these conspirators start. It must be Papa, they thought. But it was not he. It was only Mr. Frederic Bullock, who had come from the city according to appointment, to conduct the ladies to a flower-show.

This gentleman, as may be imagined, was not kept long in ignorance of the secret. But his face, when he heard it, showed an amazement which was very different to that look of sentimental wonder which the countenances of the sisters wore. Mr. Bullock was a man of the world, and a junior partner of a wealthy firm. He knew what money was, and the value of it: and a delightful throb of expectation lighted up his little eyes, and caused him to smile on his Maria, as he thought that by this piece of folly of Mr. George's she might be worth thirty thousand pounds more than he had ever hoped to get with her.

"Gad! Jane," said he, surveying even the elder sister with some interest, "Eels will be sorry he cried off.[7] You may be a fifty thousand pounder yet."

The sisters had never thought of the money question up to that moment, but Fred Bullock bantered them with graceful gaiety about it during their forenoon's excursion; and they had risen not a little in their own esteem by the time when, the morning amusement over, they drove back to dinner. And do not let my respected reader exclaim against this selfishness as unnatural. It was but this present morning, as he rode on the omnibus from Richmond;[8] while it changed horses, this present chronicler, being on the roof, marked three little children playing in a puddle below, very dirty and friendly and happy. To these three presently came another little one. *"Polly,"* says she, *"your sister's got a penny."* At which the children got up from the puddle instantly, and ran off to pay their court to Peggy. And as the omnibus drove off I saw Peggy with the infantine procession at her tail, marching with great dignity towards the stall of a neighbouring lollipop-woman.

## *Chapter XXIV.*

### IN WHICH MR. OSBORNE TAKES DOWN THE FAMILY BIBLE.

So[1] having prepared the sisters, Dobbin hastened away to the City to perform the rest and more difficult part of the task which he had undertaken. The idea of facing old Osborne rendered him not a little nervous, and more than once he thought of leaving the young ladies to communicate the secret, which, as he was aware, they could not long retain. But he had promised to report to George upon the manner in which the elder Osborne bore the intelligence; so going into the City to the paternal counting-house in Thames Street, he despatched thence a note to Mr. Osborne begging for a half-hour's conversation relative to the affairs of his son George. Dobbin's messenger returned from Mr. Osborne's house of business, with the compliments of the latter, who would be

7. Broke off his courtship.
8. Another anachronism, since omnibuses were not introduced until the late 1820s; see also the initial vignette, chapter XLI.
1. Initial vignette: St. George, patron saint of England, slaying the dragon.

very happy to see the Captain immediately, and away accordingly Dobbin went to confront him.

The Captain, with a half-guilty secret to confess, and with the prospect of a painful and stormy interview before him, entered Mr. Osborne's offices with a most dismal countenance and abashed gait, and, passing through the outer room where Mr. Chopper presided, was greeted by that functionary from his desk with a waggish air which farther discomfited him. Mr. Chopper winked and nodded and pointed his pen towards his patron's door, and said, "You'll find the governor all right," with the most provoking good humour.

Osborne rose too, and shook him heartily by the hand, and said, "How do, my dear boy?" with a cordiality that made poor George's ambassador feel doubly guilty. His hand lay as if dead in the old gentleman's grasp. He felt that he, Dobbin, was more or less the cause of all that had happened. It was he had brought back George to Amelia; it was he had applauded, encouraged, transacted almost the marriage which he was come to reveal to George's father: and the latter was receiving him with smiles of welcome; patting him on the shoulder, and calling him "Dobbin, my dear boy." The envoy had indeed good reason to hang his head.

Osborne fully believed that Dobbin had come to announce his son's surrender. Mr. Chopper and his principal were talking over the matter between George and his father, at the very moment when Dobbin's messenger arrived. Both agreed that George was sending in his submission. Both had been expecting it for some days—and "Lord! Chopper, what a marriage we'll have," Mr. Osborne said to his clerk, snapping his big fingers, and jingling all the guineas and shillings in his great pockets as he eyed his subordinate with a look of triumph.

With similar operations conducted in both pockets, and a knowing jolly air, Osborne from his chair regarded Dobbin seated blank and silent opposite to him. "What a bumpkin he is for a Captain in the army," old Osborne thought. "I wonder George hasn't taught him better manners."

At last Dobbin summoned courage to begin. "Sir," said he, "I've brought you some very grave news. I have been at the Horse Guards[2] this morning, and there's no doubt that our regiment will be ordered abroad, and on its way to Belgium before the week is over. And you know, Sir, that we sha'n't be home again before a tussle which may be fatal to many of us."

Osborne looked grave. "My s——, the regiment will do its duty, Sir, I daresay," he said.

"The French are very strong, Sir," Dobbin went on. "The Russians and Austrians will be a long time before they can bring their troops down. We shall have the first of the fight, Sir; and depend on it Boney will take care that it shall be a hard one."

"What are you driving at, Dobbin," his interlocutor said, uneasy and with a scowl. "I suppose no Briton's afraid of any d—— Frenchman, hay?"

2. The headquarters of the general staff of the army.

"I only mean, that before we go, and considering the great and certain risk that hangs over every one of us—if there are any differences between you and George—it would be as well, Sir, that—that you should shake hands: wouldn't it? Should anything happen to him, I think you would never forgive yourself if you hadn't parted in charity."

As he said this, poor William Dobbin blushed crimson, and felt and owned that he himself was a traitor. But for him, perhaps, this severance need never have taken place. Why had not George's marriage been delayed? What call was there to press it on so eagerly? He felt that George would have parted from Amelia at any rate without a mortal pang. Amelia, too, *might* have recovered the shock of losing him. It was his counsel had brought about this marriage, and all that was to ensue from it. And why was it? Because he loved her so much that he could not bear to see her unhappy: or because his own sufferings of suspense were so unendurable that he was glad to crush them at once—as we hasten a funeral after a death, or, when a separation from those we love is imminent, cannot rest until the parting be over.

"You are a good fellow, William," said Mr. Osborne in a softened voice; "and me and George shouldn't part in anger, that is true. Look here. I've done for him as much as any father ever did. He's had three times as much money from me, as I warrant your father ever gave you. But I don't brag about that. How I've toiled for him, and worked and employed my talents and energy, *I* won't say. Ask Chopper. Ask himself. Ask the City of London. Well, I propose to him such a marriage as any nobleman in the land might be proud of—the only thing in life I ever asked him—and he refuses me. Am *I* wrong? Is the quarrel of *my* making? What do I seek but his good, for which I've been toiling like a convict ever since he was born? Nobody can say there's anything selfish in *me*. Let him come back. I say, here's my hand. I say, forget and forgive. As for marrying now, it's out of the question. Let him and Miss S. make it up, and make out the marriage afterwards, when he comes back a Colonel; for he shall be a Colonel, by G—— he shall, if money can do it. I'm glad you've brought him round. I know it's you Dobbin. You've took him out of many a scrape before. Let him come. *I* shan't be hard. Come along, and dine in Russell Square to-day: both of you. The old shop, the old hour. You'll find a neck of venison, and no questions asked."

This praise and confidence smote Dobbin's heart very keenly. Every moment the colloquy continued in this tone, he felt more and more guilty. "Sir," said he, "I fear you deceive yourself. I am sure you do. George is much too high-minded a man ever to marry for money. A threat on your part that you would disinherit him in case of disobedience would only be followed by resistance on his."

"Why, hang it, man, you don't call offering him eight or ten thousand a year, threatening him?" Mr. Osborne said, with still provoking good humour. "'Gad, if Miss S. will have me, I'm her man. *I* aint particular about a shade or so of tawny." And the old gentleman gave his knowing grin, and coarse laugh.

"You forget, Sir, previous engagements into which Captain Osborne had entered," the ambassador said, gravely.

"What engagements? What the devil do you mean? You don't mean," Mr. Osborne continued, gathering wrath and astonishment as the thought now first came upon him—"you don't mean that he's such a d—— fool as to be still hankering after that swindling old bankrupt's daughter? You've not come here for to make me suppose that he wants to marry *her?* Marry *her,* that *is* a good one. My son and heir marry a beggar's girl out of a gutter. D—— him, if he does, let him buy a broom and sweep a crossing. She was always dangling and ogling after him, I recollect now; and I've no doubt she was put on by her old sharper of a father."

"Mr. Sedley was your very good friend, Sir," Dobbin interposed, almost pleased at finding himself growing angry. "Time was you called him better names than rogue and swindler. The match was of your making. George had no right to play fast and loose———."

"Fast and loose!" howled out old Osborne. "Fast and loose! Why, hang me, those are the very words my gentleman used himself when he gave himself airs, last Thursday was a fortnight, and talked about the British army to his father who made him. What, it's you who have been a setting of him up—is it? and my service to you, *Captain.* It's you who want to introduce beggars into my family. Thank you for nothing, Captain. Marry *her* indeed—he, he! why should he? I warrant you she'd go to him fast enough without."

"Sir," said Dobbin, starting up in undisguised anger; "no man shall abuse that lady in my hearing, and you least of all."

"O, you're a going to call me out, are you? Stop, let me ring the bell for pistols for two. Mr. George sent you here to insult his father, did he?" Osborne said, pulling at the bell-cord.

"Mr. Osborne," said Dobbin, with a faltering voice, "it's you who are insulting the best creature in the world. You had best spare her, Sir, for she's your son's wife."

And with this, feeling that he could say no more, Dobbin went away, Osborne sinking back in his chair, and looking wildly after him. A clerk came in, obedient to the bell; and the Captain was scarcely out of the court where Mr. Osborne's offices were, when Mr. Chopper the chief clerk came rushing hatless after him.

"For God's sake, what is it?" Mr. Chopper said, catching the Captain by the skirt. "The governor's in a fit. What has Mr. George been doing?"

"He married Miss Sedley five days ago," Dobbin replied. "I was his groomsman, Mr. Chopper, and you must stand his friend."

The old clerk shook his head. "If that's your news, Captain, it's bad. The governor will never forgive him."

Dobbin begged Chopper to report progress to him at the hotel where he was stopping, and walked off moodily westwards, greatly perturbed as to the past and the future.

When the Russell Square family came to dinner that evening, they found the father of the house seated in his usual place, but with that air of gloom on his face, which, whenever it appeared there, kept the whole circle silent. The ladies and Mr. Bullock who dined with them, felt that the news had been communicated to Mr. Osborne. His dark looks affected Mr. Bullock so far as to render him still and quiet: but he was unusually bland and attentive to Miss Maria, by whom he sat, and to her sister presiding at the head of the table.

Miss Wirt, by consequence, was alone on her side of the board, a gap being left between her and Miss Jane Osborne. Now this was George's place when he dined at home; and his cover, as we said, was laid for him in expectation of that truant's return. Nothing occurred during dinner-time except smiling Mr. Frederic's flagging confidential whispers, and the clinking of plate and china, to interrupt the silence of the repast. The servants went about stealthily doing their duty. Mutes at funerals could not look more glum than the domestics of Mr. Osborne. The neck of venison of which he had invited Dobbin to partake, was carved by him in perfect silence; but his own share went away almost untasted, though he drank much, and the butler assiduously filled his glass.

At last, just at the end of the dinner, his eyes, which had been staring at everybody in turn, fixed themselves for a while upon the plate laid for George. He pointed to it presently with his left hand. His daughters looked at him and did not comprehend, or choose to comprehend, the signal; nor did the servants at first understand it.

"Take that plate away," at last he said, getting up with an oath—and with this pushing his chair back, he walked into his own room.

Behind Mr. Osborne's dining-room was the usual apartment which went in his house by the name of the study; and was sacred to the master of the house. Hither Mr. Osborne would retire of a Sunday forenoon when not minded to go to church; and here pass the morning in his crimson leather chair, reading the paper. A couple of glazed book-cases were here, containing standard works in stout gilt bindings. The "Annual Register," the "Gentleman's Magazine," "Blair's Sermons," and "Hume and Smollet."[3] From year's end to year's end he never took one of these volumes from the shelf; but there was no member of the family that would dare for his life to touch one of the books, except upon those rare Sunday evenings when there was no dinner party, and when the great scarlet Bible and Prayer-book were taken out from the corner where they stood beside his copy of the Peerage, and the servants being rung up to the dining parlour, Osborne read the evening service to his family in a loud grating pompous voice. No member of the household, child or domestic, ever entered that room without a certain terror. Here he checked the housekeeper's accounts, and overhauled the butler's cellar-book.[4] Hence he could command, across the clean gravel court-yard, the back entrance of the stables with which one of his bells communicated, and into this yard the coachman issued from his premises as into a dock,[5] and Osborne swore at him from

3. *The Annual Register*: begun in 1758, an annual summary of noteworthy events and political, military, and official news. *Gentleman's Magazine*: a monthly magazine that ran from 1731 to 1907. The Reverend Hugh Blair (d. 1800), a Scottish clergyman and professor of literature. David Hume (1711–76), a philosopher and historian. Tobias Smollett (1721–71), a novelist and historian.
4. Record of wine and other provisions.
5. In a courtroom, the designated place for the accused.

the study window. Four times a year Miss Wirt entered this apartment to get her salary; and his daughters to receive their quarterly allowance. George as a boy had been horsewhipped in this room many times; his mother sitting sick on the stair listening to the cuts of the whip. The boy was scarcely ever known to cry under the punishment; the poor woman used to fondle and kiss him secretly, and give him money to soothe him when he came out.

There was a picture of the family over the mantel-piece, removed thither from the front room after Mrs. Osborne's death—George was on a poney, the elder sister holding him up a bunch of flowers; the younger led by her mother's hand; all with red cheeks and large red mouths, simpering on each other in the approved family-portrait manner. The mother lay under ground now, long since forgotten—the sisters and brother had a hundred different interests of their own, and, familiar still, were utterly estranged from each other. Some few score of years afterwards, when all the parties represented are grown old, what bitter satire there is in those flaunting childish family-portraits, with their farce of sentiment and smiling lies, and innocence so self-conscious and self-satisfied. Osborne's own state portrait, with that of his great silver inkstand and arm-chair, had taken the place of honour in the dining-room, vacated by the family-piece.

To this study old Osborne retired then, greatly to the relief of the small party whom he left. When the servants had withdrawn, they began to talk for a while volubly but very low; then they went up stairs quietly, Mr. Bullock accompanying them stealthily on his creaking shoes. He had no heart to sit alone drinking wine, and so close to the terrible old gentleman in the study hard at hand.

An hour at least after dark, the butler, not having received any summons, ventured to tap at his door and take him in wax candles and tea. The master of the house sate in his chair, pretending to read the paper, and when the servant, placing the lights and refreshment on the table by him, retired, Mr. Osborne got up and locked the door after him. This time there was no mistaking the matter; all the household knew that some great catastrophe was going to happen which was likely direly to affect Master George.

In the large shining mahogany escrutoire[6] Mr. Osborne had a drawer especially devoted to his son's affairs and papers. Here he kept all the documents relating to him ever since he had been a boy: here were his prize copy-books and drawing-books, all bearing George's hand, and that of the master: here were his first letters in large round hand sending his love to papa and mama, and conveying his petitions for a cake. His dear godpapa Sedley was more than once mentioned in them. Curses quivered on old Osborne's livid lips, and horrid hatred and disappointment writhed in his heart, as looking through some of these papers he came on that name. They were all marked and docketed, and tied with red tape. It was—"From Georgy, requesting 5*s*., April 23, 18—; answered, April

6. Writing desk.

25,"—or "Georgy about a poney, October 13,"—and so forth. In another packet were "Dr. S.'s accounts"—"G.'s tailor's bills and outfit, drafts on me by G. Osborne, jun." &c.,—his letters from the West Indies—his agent's letters, and the newspapers containing his commissions: here was a whip he had when a boy, and in a paper a locket containing his hair, which his mother used to wear.

Turning one over after another, and musing over these memorials, the unhappy man passed many hours. His dearest vanities, ambitions, hopes, had all been here. What pride he had in his boy! He was the handsomest child ever seen. Everybody said he was like a nobleman's son. A royal princess had remarked him, and kissed him, and asked his name in Kew Gardens.[7] What city-man could show such another? Could a prince have been better cared for? Anything that money could buy had been his son's. He used to go down on speech-days with four horses and new liveries, and scatter new shillings among the boys at the school where George was: when he went with George to the depôt of his regiment, before the boy embarked for Canada, he gave the officers such a dinner as the Duke of York might have sat down to. Had he ever refused a bill when George drew one? There they were—paid without a word. Many a general in the army couldn't ride the horses he had! He had the child before his eyes, on a hundred different days when he remembered George—after dinner, when he used to come in as bold as a lord and drink off his glass by his father's side, at the head of the table—on the poney at Brighton, when he cleared the hedge and kept up with the huntsman—on the day when he was presented to the Prince Regent at the levee, when all Saint James's couldn't produce a finer young fellow.[8] And this, this was the end of all!—to marry a bankrupt and fly in the face of duty and fortune! What humiliation and fury: what pangs of sickening rage, balked ambition and love; what wounds of outraged vanity, tenderness even, had this old worldling now to suffer under!

Having examined these papers, and pondered over this one and the other, in that bitterest of all helpless woe, with which miserable men think of happy past times[9]—George's father took the whole of the documents out of the drawer in which he had kept them so long, and locked them into a writing-box, which he tied and sealed with his seal. Then he opened the book-case, and took down the great red Bible we have spoken of—a pompous book, seldom looked at, and shining all over with gold. There was a frontispiece to the volume, representing Abraham sacrificing Isaac.[1] Here, according to custom, Osborne had recorded on the fly-leaf, and in his large clerk-like hand, the dates of his marriage and his wife's death, and the births and Christian names of his children. Jane came first, then George

7. Royal botanical gardens located in Kew, west of London on the Thames River.
8. The prince regent formally received visitors in the levee room of St. James's Palace. The surrounding residential area, also known as St. James's, was very expensive.
9. Compare Francesca's speech in Dante's *Inferno,* V. 121–23: "There is no greater pain than to recall a happy time in misery" (Harden).
1. The contrast between Old Osborne, sacrificing George, and Abraham, sacrificing Isaac by God's command, could hardly be sharper (Genesis 22).

Sedley Osborne, then Maria Frances, and the days of the christening of each. Taking a pen, he carefully obliterated George's names from the page; and when the leaf was quite dry, restored the volume to the place from which he had moved it. Then he took a document out of another drawer, where his own private papers were kept; and having read it, crumpled it up and lighted it at one of the candles, and saw it burn entirely away in the grate. It was his will; which being burned, he sate down and wrote off a letter, and rang for his servant, whom he charged to deliver it in the morning. It was morning already: as he went up to bed, the whole house was alight with the sunshine: and the birds were singing among the fresh green leaves in Russell Square.

Anxious to keep all Mr. Osborne's family and dependants in good humour, and to make as many friends as possible for George in his hour of adversity, William Dobbin, who knew the effect which good dinners and good wines have upon the soul of man, wrote off immediately on his return to his inn, the most hospitable of invitations to Thomas Chopper, Esquire, begging that gentleman to dine with him at the Slaughters' next day. The note reached Mr. Chopper before he left the City, and the instant reply was, that "Mr. Chopper presents his respectful compliments, and will have the honour and pleasure of waiting on Captain D." The invitation and the rough draft of the answer were shown to Mrs. Chopper and her daughters on his return to Somers' Town[2] that evening, and they talked about military gents and West End men with great exultation as the family sate and partook of tea. When the girls had gone to rest, Mr. and Mrs. C. discoursed upon the strange events which were occurring in the governor's family. Never had the clerk seen his principal so moved. When he went in to Mr. Osborne, after Captain Dobbin's departure, Mr. Chopper found his chief black in the face, and all but in a fit: some dreadful quarrel, he was certain, had occurred between Mr. O. and the young Captain. Chopper had been instructed to make out an account of all sums paid to Captain Osborne within the last three years. "And a precious lot of money he has had too," the chief clerk said, and respected his old and young master the more, for the liberal way in which the guineas had been flung about. The dispute was something about Miss Sedley. Mrs. Chopper vowed and declared, she pitied that poor young lady to lose such a handsome young fellow as the Capting. As the daughter of an unlucky speculator, who had paid a very shabby dividend, Mr. Chopper had no great regard for Miss Sedley. He respected the house of Osborne before all others in the city of London: and his hope and wish was, that Captain George should marry a nobleman's daughter. The clerk slept a great deal sounder than his principal that night; and, cuddling his children after breakfast, of which he partook with a very hearty appetite (though his modest cup of life was only sweetened with brown sugar), he set off in his best Sunday suit and frilled shirt for business, promising his admiring wife not to punish Captain D.'s port too severely that evening.

2. Working-class neighborhood in north London.

Mr. Osborne's countenance, when he arrived in the City at his usual time, struck those dependants who were accustomed, for good reasons, to watch its expression, as peculiarly ghastly and worn. At twelve o'clock Mr. Higgs (of the firm of Higgs & Blatherwick, solicitors, Bedford Row,)[3] called by appointment, and was ushered into the governor's private room, and closeted there for more than an hour. At about one Mr. Chopper received a note brought by Captain Dobbin's man, and containing an inclosure for Mr. Osborne, which the clerk went in and delivered. A short time afterwards Mr. Chopper and Mr. Birch, the next clerk, were summoned, and requested to witness a paper. "I've been making a new will," Mr. Osborne said, to which these gentlemen appended their names accordingly. No conversation passed. Mr. Higgs looked exceedingly grave as he came into the outer rooms, and very hard in Mr. Chopper's face; but there were not any explanations. It was remarked that Mr. Osborne was particularly quiet and gentle all day, to the surprise of those who had augured ill from his darkling demeanour. He called no man names that day, and was not heard to swear once. He left business early; and before going away, summoned his chief clerk once more, and having given him general instructions, asked him, after some seeming hesitation and reluctance to speak, if he knew whether Captain Dobbin was in town?

Chopper said he believed he was. Indeed both of them knew the fact perfectly.

Osborne took a letter directed to that officer, and, giving it to the clerk, requested the latter to deliver it into Dobbin's own hands immediately.

3. Area of law offices near Gray's Inn.

"And now Chopper," says he, taking his hat, and with a strange look, "my mind will be easy." Exactly as the clock struck two, (there was no doubt an appointment between the pair,) Mr. Frederic Bullock called, and he and Mr. Osborne walked away together.

The Colonel of the —th regiment, in which Messieurs Dobbin and Osborne had companies, was an old general who had made his first campaign under Wolf at Quebec,[4] and was long since quite too old and feeble for command; but he took some interest in the regiment of which he was the nominal head, and made certain of his young officers' welcome at his table, a kind of hospitality which I believe is not altogether common amongst his brethren of the present day.[5] Captain Dobbin was an especial favourite of this old General. Dobbin was versed in the literature of his profession, and could talk about the great Frederick and the Empress Queen[6] and their wars almost as well as the General himself, who was indifferent to the triumphs of the present day, and whose heart was with the tacticians of fifty years back. This officer sent a summons to Dobbin to come and breakfast with him, on the morning when Mr. Osborne altered his will and Mr. Chopper put on his best shirt frill, and then informed his young favourite, a couple of days in advance, of that which they were all expecting—a marching order to go to Belgium. The order for the regiment to hold itself in readiness would leave the Horse Guards in a day or two; and as transports were in plenty, they would get their route before the week was over. Recruits had come in during the stay of the regiment at Chatham;[7] and the old General hoped that the regiment which had helped to beat Montcalm in Canada, and to rout Mr. Washington on Long Island,[8] would prove itself worthy of its historical reputation on the oft-trodden battle-grounds of the Low Countries. "And so my good friend, if you have any *affaire là*,"[9] said the old General, taking a pinch of snuff with his trembling white old hand, and then pointing to the spot of his *robe de chambre*[1] under which his heart was still feebly beating, "if you have any Phillis[2] to console, or to bid farewell to papa and mama, or any will to make, I recommend you to set about your business without delay." With which the General gave his young friend a finger to shake, and a good-natured nod of his powdered and pig-tailed head; and the door being closed upon Dobbin, sate down to pen a *poulet*[3] (he was exceedingly vain of his French) to Mademoiselle Aménaide of His Majesty's Theatre.[4]

4. Major General James Wolfe died in the taking of Quebec, September 12, 1759.
5. Revised edition reads: not now common amongst his brethren.
6. Fredrick II, king of Prussia from 1740 to 1786. The Empress Queen could be Catherine II, queen of Russia from 1762 to 1796, or Maria Theresa, queen of Hungary and Bohemia from 1740 to 1780, who ruled through the weak titular king, her husband.
7. British naval station on the Thames estuary.
8. Wolfe defeated the French Marquis de Montcalm at Quebec; General Sir William Howe (1729–1814) defeated American troops under George Washington, capturing the city of New York in August 1776.
9. Affair here.
1. Dressing gown.
2. A conventional name (sometimes "Phyllis") for a country maiden or arcadian lover.
3. Love letter.
4. The actress is untraced; the theater is in the Haymarket.

Ensign Stubble practising the art of War

This news made Dobbin grave, and he thought of our friends at Brighton, and then he was ashamed of himself that Amelia was always the first thing in his thoughts, (always before anybody—before father and mother, sisters and duty—always at waking and sleeping indeed, and all day long); and returning to his hotel, he sent off a brief note to Mr. Osborne acquainting him with the information which he had received, and which might tend farther, he hoped, to bring about a reconciliation with George.

This note, dispatched by the same messenger who had carried the invitation to Chopper on the previous day, alarmed the worthy clerk not a little. It was inclosed to him, and as he opened the letter he trembled lest the dinner should be put off on which he was calculating. His mind was inexpressibly relieved when he found that the envelope was only a reminder for himself. ("I shall expect you at half-past five," Captain Dobbin wrote). He was very much interested about his employer's family; but, *que voulez vous?*[5] a grand dinner was of more concern to him than the affairs of any other mortal.

Dobbin was quite justified in repeating the General's information to any officers of the regiment whom he should see in the course of his peregrinations;[6] accordingly he imparted it to Ensign Stubble, whom he met at the agent's, and who, such was his military ardour, went off instantly to purchase a new sword at the accoutrement-maker's. Here this young fellow, who though only seventeen years of age, and about sixty-five inches high, with a constitution naturally rickety and much impaired by premature brandy and water, had an undoubted courage and a lion's heart, poised, tried, bent, and balanced a weapon such as he thought would do execution amongst Frenchmen. Shouting "Ha, ha," and stamping his little feet with tremendous energy, he delivered the point twice or thrice at Captain Dobbin, who parried the thrust laughingly with his bamboo walking-stick.

Mr. Stubble, as may be supposed from his size and slenderness, was of the Light Bobs. Ensign Spooney, on the contrary, was a tall youth, and belonged to (Captain Dobbin's) the Grenadier Company,[7] and he tried on a new bear-skin cap, under which he looked savage beyond his years. Then these two lads went off to the Slaughters', and having ordered a famous dinner, sate down and wrote off letters to the kind anxious parents at home—letters full of love and heartiness, and pluck and bad spelling. Ah! there were many anxious hearts beating through England at that time; and mothers' prayers and tears flowing in many homesteads.

Seeing young Stubble engaged in composition at one of the coffee-room tables at the Slaughters', and the tears trickling down his nose on to the paper, (for the youngster was thinking of his mama, and that he might never see her again,) Dobbin, who was going to write off a letter to George Osborne, relented, and locked up his desk. "Why should I?" said he. "Let her have this night happy. I'll go and see

5. What do you expect?
6. Wanderings.
7. Light Bobs: light infantry. Grenadier Company: a troop of tall, strong soldiers—traditionally, grenade throwers.

my parents early in the morning, and go down to Brighton myself to-morrow."

So he went up and laid his big hand on young Stubble's shoulder, and backed up that young champion, and told him if he would leave off brandy and water he would be a good soldier, as he always was a gentlemanly good-hearted fellow. Young Stubble's eyes brightened up at this, for Dobbin was greatly respected in the regiment, as the best officer and the cleverest man in it.

"Thank you, Dobbin," he said, rubbing his eyes with his knuckles, "I was just—just telling her I would. And, O Sir, she's so *dam* kind to me." The water pumps were at work again, and I am not sure that the soft-hearted Captain's eyes did not also twinkle.

The two ensigns, the captain and Mr. Chopper, dined together in the same box.[8] Chopper brought the letter from Mr. Osborne in which the latter briefly presented his compliments to Captain Dobbin, and requested him to forward the inclosed to Captain George Osborne. Chopper knew nothing further; he described Mr. Osborne's appearance, it is true, and his interview with his lawyer, wondered how the governor had sworn at nobody, and, especially as the wine circled round, abounded in speculations and conjectures. But these grew more vague with every glass, and at length became perfectly unintelligible. At a late hour Captain Dobbin put his guest into a hackney coach, in a hiccupping state, and swearing that he would be the kick—the kick—captain's friend for ever and ever.

When Captain Dobbin took leave of Miss Osborne we have said that he asked leave to come and pay her another visit, and the spinster expected him for some hours the next day, when, perhaps, had he come, and had he asked her that question which she was prepared to answer, she would have declared herself as her brother's friend,

8. Booth or compartment in a coffee house.

and a reconciliation might have been effected between George and his angry father. But though she waited at home the captain never came. He had his own affairs to pursue; his own parents to visit and console; and at an early hour of the day to take his place on the Lightning coach, and go down to his friends at Brighton. In the course of the day Miss Osborne heard her father give orders that that meddling scoundrel, Captain Dobbin, should never be admitted within his doors again, and any hopes in which she may have indulged privately, were thus abruptly brought to an end. Mr. Frederic Bullock came, and was particularly affectionate to Maria, and attentive to the broken-spirited old gentleman. For though he said his mind would be easy, the means which he had taken to secure quiet did not seem to have succeeded as yet, and the events of the past two days had visibly shattered him.

## *Chapter XXV.*

### IN WHICH ALL THE PRINCIPAL PERSONAGES THINK FIT TO LEAVE BRIGHTON.

ONDUCTED to the ladies, at the Ship Inn, Dobbin assumed a jovial and rattling manner, which proved that this young officer was becoming a more consummate hypocrite every day of his life. He was trying to hide his own private feelings, first upon seeing Mrs. George Osborne in her new condition, and secondly to mask the apprehensions he entertained as to the effect which the dismal news brought down by him would certainly have upon her.

"It is my opinion, George," he said, "that the French Emperor will be upon us, horse and foot, before three weeks are over, and will give the Duke such a dance as shall make the Peninsula appear mere child's play. But you need not say that to Mrs. Osborne, you know. There mayn't be any fighting on our side after all, and our business in Belgium may turn out to be a mere military occupation. Many persons think so; and Brussels is full of fine people and ladies of fashion." So it was agreed to represent the duty of the British army in Belgium in this harmless light to Amelia.

This plot being arranged, the hypocritical Dobbin saluted Mrs. George Osborne quite gaily, tried to pay her one or two compliments relative to her new position as a bride (which compliments, it must be confessed, were exceedingly clumsy and hung fire wofully), and then fell to talking about Brighton, and the sea-air, and the gaieties of the place, and the beauties of the road and the merits of the "Lightning" coach and horses,—all in a manner quite incomprehensible to Amelia, and very amusing to Rebecca, who was watching the Captain, as indeed she watched every one near whom she came.

Little Amelia, it must be owned, had rather a mean opinion of her husband's friend, Captain Dobbin. He lisped—he was very plain and homely-looking: and exceedingly awkward and ungainly. She liked him for his attachment to her husband, (to be sure there was very little merit in that), and she thought George was most generous and kind in extending his friendship to his brother officer. George had mimicked Dobbin's lisp and queer manners many times to her, though to do him justice, he always spoke most highly of his friend's good qualities. In her little day of triumph, and not knowing him intimately as yet, she made light of honest William—and he knew her opinions of him quite well, and acquiesced in them very humbly. A time came when she knew him better, and changed her notions regarding him: but that was distant as yet.

As for Rebecca, Captain Dobbin had not been two hours in the ladies' company, before she understood his secret perfectly. She did not like him, and feared him privately; nor was he very much prepossessed in her favour. He was so honest, that her arts and cajoleries did not affect him, and he shrank from her with instinctive repulsion. And, as she was by no means so far superior to her sex as to be above jealousy, she disliked him the more for his adoration of Amelia. Nevertheless, she was very respectful and cordial in her manner towards him. A friend to the Osbornes! a friend to her dearest benefactors! She vowed she should always love him sincerely: she remembered him quite well on the Vauxhall night, as she told Amelia archly, and she made a little fun of him when the two ladies went to dress for dinner. Rawdon Crawley paid scarcely any attention to Dobbin, looking upon him as a good-natured nincompoop, and under-bred city man. Jos patronised him with much dignity.

When George and Dobbin were alone in the latter's room, to which George had followed him, Dobbin took from his desk the letter which he had been charged by Mr. Osborne to deliver to his son. "It's not in my father's hand-writing," said George, looking rather alarmed; nor was it: the letter was from Mr. Osborne's lawyer, and to the following effect:—

"BEDFORD ROW, *May* 7, 1815.

"SIR,

"I am commissioned by Mr. Osborne to inform you, that he abides by the determination which he before expressed to you, and that in consequence of the marriage which you have been pleased to contract, he ceases to consider you henceforth as a member of his family. This determination is final and irrevocable.

"Although the monies expended upon you in your minority, and the bills which you have drawn upon him so unsparingly of late years, far exceed in amount the sum to which you are entitled in your own right, (being the third part of the fortune of your mother, the late Mrs. Osborne, and which reverted to you at her decease, and to Miss Jane Osborne and Miss Maria Frances Osborne;) yet I am instructed by Mr. Osborne to say, that he waives all claim upon your estate, and that the sum of £2000, 4 per cent. annuities, at the value of the day (being your one-third share of the sum of £6000,) shall be paid over to yourself or your agents upon your receipt for the same, by

"Your obedient Servt.,

"S. HIGGS."

"P.S.—Mr. Osborne desires me to say, once for all, that he declines to receive any messages, letters, or communications from you on this or any other subject."

"A pretty way you have managed the affair," said George, looking savagely at William Dobbin. "Look there, Dobbin," and he flung over to the latter his parent's letter. "A beggar, by Jove, and all in consequence of my d—d sentimentality. Why couldn't we have waited? A ball might have done for me in the course of the war, and may still, and how will Emmy be bettered by being left a beggar's widow? It was all your doing. You were never easy until you had got me married and ruined. What the deuce am I to do with two thousand pounds? Such a sum won't last two years. I've lost a hundred and forty to Crawley at cards and billiards since I've been down here. A pretty manager of a man's matters *you* are, forsooth."

"There's no denying that the position is a hard one," Dobbin replied, after reading over the letter with a blank countenance; "and, as you say, it is partly of my making. There are some men that wouldn't mind changing with you," he added, with a bitter smile. "How many Captains in the regiment have two thousand pounds to the fore, think you? You must live on your pay till your father relents, and if you die, you leave your wife a hundred a year."

"Do you suppose a man of my habits can live on his pay and a hundred a year?" George cried out in great anger. "You must be a fool to talk so, Dobbin. How the deuce am I to keep up my position in the world upon such a pitiful pittance? I can't change my habits. I *must* have my comforts. *I* wasn't brought up on porridge like MacWhirter, or on potatoes, like old O'Dowd. Do you expect my wife to take in soldiers' washing, or ride after the regiment in a baggage waggon?"

"Well, well," said Dobbin, still good-naturedly, "we'll get her a better conveyance. But try and remember that you are only a dethroned prince now, George, my boy; and be quiet whilst the tempest lasts. It won't be for long. Let your name be mentioned in the Gazette, and I'll engage the old father relents towards you."

"Mentioned in the Gazette!" George answered. "And in what part of it? Among the killed and wounded returns, and at the top of the list, very likely."

"Psha! It will be time enough to cry out when we are hurt," Dobbin said. "And if anything happens, you know, George, I have got a little, and I am not a marrying man, and I shall not forget my godson in my will," he added, with a smile. Whereupon the dispute ended,—as many scores of such conversations between Osborne and his friend had concluded previously—by the former declaring there was no possibility of being angry with Dobbin long, and forgiving him very generously after abusing him without cause.

"I say, Becky," cried Rawdon Crawley out of his dressing-room, to his lady, who was attiring herself for dinner in her own chamber.

"What?" said Becky's shrill voice. She was looking over her shoulder in the glass. She had put on the neatest and freshest white frock imaginable, and with bare shoulders and a little necklace, and a light blue sash, she looked the image of youthful innocence and girlish happiness.

"I say, what'll Mrs. O. do, when O. goes out with the regiment?" Crawley said coming into the room, performing a duet on his head with two huge hair-brushes, and looking out from under his hair with admiration on his pretty little wife.

"I suppose she'll cry her eyes out," Becky answered. "She has been whimpering half-a-dozen of times at the very notion of it, already to me."

"*You* don't care, I suppose," Rawdon said, half angry at his wife's want of feeling.

"You wretch! don't you know that I intend to go with you," Becky replied. "Besides, you're different. You go as General Tufto's aide-de-camp. *We* don't belong to the line,"[1] Mrs. Crawley said, throwing up her head with an air that so enchanted her husband that he stooped down and kissed it.

"Rawdon, dear—don't you think—you'd better get that—money from Cupid, before he goes?" Becky continued, fixing on a killing bow. She called George Osborne, Cupid. She had flattered him about

his good looks a score of times already. She watched over him kindly

1. As a member of Tufto's staff and of the Horse Guards, Rawdon would not be a front-line soldier and thus not in great danger.

A Family Party at Brighton

at écarté[2] of a night when he would drop in to Rawdon's quarters for a half-hour before bed-time.

She had often called him a horrid dissipated wretch, and threatened to tell Emmy of his wicked ways and naughty extravagant habits. She brought his cigar and lighted it for him; she knew the effect of that manœuvre, having practised it in former days upon Rawdon Crawley. He thought her gay, brisk, arch, distinguée, delightful. In their little drives and dinners Becky, of course, quite outshone poor Emmy, who remained very mute and timid while Mrs. Crawley and her husband rattled away together, and Captain Crawley (and Jos after he joined the young married people) gobbled in silence.

Emmy's mind somehow misgave her about her friend. Rebecca's wit, spirits, and accomplishments troubled her with a rueful disquiet. They were only a week married, and here was George already suffering ennui and eager for others' society! She trembled for the future. How shall I be a companion for him, she thought,—so clever and so brilliant, and I such a humble foolish creature? How noble it was of him to marry me—to give up everything and stoop down to me. I ought to have refused him, only I had not the heart. I ought to have stopped at home and taken care of poor papa. And her neglect of her parents (and indeed there was some foundation for this charge which the poor child's uneasy conscience brought against her) was now remembered for the first time, and caused her to blush with humiliation. Oh! thought she, I have been very wicked and selfish—selfish in forgetting them in their sorrows—selfish in forcing George to marry me. I know I'm not worthy of him—I know he would have been happy without me—and yet—I tried, I tried to give him up.

It is hard when, before seven days of marriage are over, such thoughts and confessions as these force themselves on a little bride's mind. But so it was, and the night before Dobbin came to join these young people—on a fine brilliant moonlight night of May—so warm and balmy that the windows were flung open to the balcony, from which George and Mrs. Crawley were gazing upon the calm ocean spread shining before them, while Rawdon and Jos were engaged at back gammon within—Amelia couched in a great chair quite neglected, and watching both these parties, felt a despair and remorse such as were bitter companions for that tender lonely soul. Scarce a week was past, and it was come to this! The future, had she regarded it, offered a dismal prospect; but Emmy was too shy, so to speak, to look to that, and embark alone on that wide sea, and unfit to navigate it without a guide and protector. I know Miss Smith has a mean opinion of her. But how many, my dear Madam, are endowed with your prodigious strength of mind?

"Gad, what a fine night, and how bright the moon is!" George said, with a puff of his cigar, which went soaring up skywards.

"How delicious they smell in the open air! I adore them. Who'd think the moon was two hundred and thirty-six thousand eight hundred and forty-seven miles off?" she added, gazing at that orb with

2. A card game for two. The text and illustration suggest collusion between Becky and Rawdon, as Becky can see George's cards.

a smile. "Isn't it clever of me to remember that? Pooh! we learned it all at Miss Pinkerton's! How calm the sea is, and how clear everything. I declare I can almost see the coast of France?" and her bright green eyes streamed out, and shot into the night as if they *could* see through it.

"Do you know what I intend to do one morning?" she said; "I find I can swim beautifully, and some day, when my Aunt Crawley's companion—old Briggs, you know—you remember her—that hook-nosed woman, with the long wisps of hair—when Briggs goes out to bathe, I intend to dive under her awning, and insist on a reconciliation in the water. Isn't that a stratagem?"

George burst out laughing at the idea of this aquatic meeting. "What's the row there, you two?" Rawdon shouted out, rattling the box. Amelia was making a fool of herself in an absurd hysterical manner, and retired to her own room to whimper in private.

Our history is destined in this Chapter to go backwards and forwards in a very irresolute manner seemingly, and having conducted our story to to-morrow presently, we shall immediately again have occasion to step back to yesterday, so that the whole of the tale may get a hearing. As you behold at her Majesty's drawing-room, the ambassadors' and high dignitaries' carriages whisk off from a private door, while Captain Jones's ladies are waiting for their fly:[3] as you see in the Secretary of the Treasury's antechamber, a half-dozen of petitioners waiting patiently for their audience, and called out one by one, when suddenly an Irish member or some eminent personage enters the apartment, and instantly walks into Mr. Under-Secretary over the heads of all the people present: so in the conduct of a tale, the romancer is obliged to exercise this most partial sort of justice. Although all the little incidents must be heard, yet they must be put off when the great events make their appearance; and surely such a circumstance as that which brought Dobbin to Brighton, viz. the ordering out of the Guards and the line to Belgium, and the mustering of the allied armies in that country under the command of his Grace the Duke of Wellington—such a dignified circumstance as that I say—was entitled to the *pas*[4] over all minor occurrences whereof this history is composed mainly, and hence a little trifling disarrangement and disorder was excusable and becoming. We have only now advanced in time so far beyond Chapter XXII. as to have got our various characters up into their dressing-rooms before the dinner, which took place as usual on the day of Dobbin's arrival.

George was too humane or too much occupied with the tie of his neckcloth to convey at once all the news to Amelia which his comrade had brought with him from London. He came into her room, however, holding the attorney's letter in his hand, and with so solemn and important an air that his wife, always ingeniously on the watch for calamity, thought the worst was about to befal, and running up to her husband, besought her dearest George to tell her everything—he

3. A one-horse covered carriage.
4. Literally "the step," to take precedence.

was ordered abroad; there would be a battle next week—she knew there would.

Dearest George parried the question about foreign service, and with a melancholy shake of the head said, "No, Emmy; it isn't that: it's not myself I care about: it's you. I have had bad news from my father. He refuses any communication with me; he has flung us off; and leaves us to poverty. *I* can rough it well enough; but you, my dear, how will you bear it? read here." And he handed her over the letter.

Amelia, with a look of tender alarm in her eyes, listened to her noble hero as he uttered the above generous sentiments, and sitting down on the bed, read the letter which George gave her with such a pompous martyr-like air. Her face cleared up as she read the document, however. The idea of sharing poverty and privation in company with the beloved object, is, as we have before said, far from being disagreeable to a warm-hearted woman. The notion was actually pleasant to little Amelia. Then, as usual, she was ashamed of herself for feeling happy at such an indecorous moment, and checked her pleasure, saying demurely, "O, George, how your poor heart must bleed at the idea of being separated from your papa."

"It does," said George, with an agonised countenance.

"But he can't be angry with you long," she continued. "Nobody could, I'm sure. He must forgive you, my dearest, kindest husband. O, I shall never forgive myself if he does not."

"What vexes me, my poor Emmy, is not *my* misfortune, but yours," George said. "I don't care for a little poverty; and I think, without vanity, I've talents enough to make my own way."

"That you have," interposed his wife, who thought that war should cease, and her husband should be made a general instantly.

"Yes, I shall make my way as well as another," Osborne went on; "but you, my dear girl, how can I bear your being deprived of the comforts and station in society which my wife had a right to expect? My dearest girl in barracks; the wife of a soldier in a marching regiment; subject to all sorts of annoyance and privation! It makes me miserable."

Emmy, quite at ease, as this was her husband's only cause of disquiet, took his hand, and with a radiant face and smile began to warble that stanza from the favourite song of "Wapping Old Stairs," in which the heroine, after rebuking her Tom for inattention, promises "his trowsers to mend, and his grog too to make," if he will be constant and kind, and not forsake her.[5] "Besides," she said, after a pause, during which she looked as pretty and happy as any young woman need, "isn't two thousand pounds an immense deal of money, George?"

5. A popular ballad (music by Jn. Percy, words by Arley), which Thackeray had quoted at length in "Our Annual Execution," *Fraser's Magazine*, January 1839:

> In silence I stood your unkindness to hear,
> And only upbraided my Tom with a tear.
> Why should Sal or should Susan than me be more prized?
> For the heart that is true it should ne'er be despised.
> Then be constant and kind, nor your Molly forsake;
> Still your trousers I'll wash, and your grog too I'll make.

George laughed at her naïveté; and finally they went down to dinner, Amelia clinging on George's arm, still warbling the tune of "Wapping Old Stairs," and more pleased and light of mind than she had been for some days past.

Thus the repast, which at length came off, instead of being dismal, was an exceedingly brisk and merry one. The excitement of the campaign counteracted in George's mind the depression occasioned by the disinheriting letter. Dobbin still kept up his character of rattle. He amused the company with accounts of the army in Belgium, where nothing but fêtes and gaiety and fashion were going on. Then, having a particular end in view, this dexterous captain proceeded to describe Mrs. Major O'Dowd, packing her own and her Major's wardrobe, and how his best epaulets had been stowed into a tea canister, whilst her own famous yellow turban, with the bird of paradise[6] wrapped in brown paper, was locked up in the Major's tin cocked-hat case, and wondered what effect it would have at the French king's court at Ghent, or the great military balls at Brussels.[7]

"Ghent! Brussels!" cried out Amelia with a sudden shock and start. "Is the regiment ordered away, George,—is it ordered away?" A look of terror came over the sweet smiling face, and she clung to George as by an instinct.

"Don't be afraid, dear," he said good-naturedly; "it is but a twelve hour's passage. It won't hurt you. You shall go, too, Emmy."

"*I* intend to go,"[8] said Becky, "I'm on the staff. General Tufto is a great flirt of mine. Isn't he, Rawdon?"

Rawdon laughed out with his usual roar. William Dobbin flushed up quite red. "She can't go," he said; "think of the—of the danger," he was going to add; but had not all his conversation during dinner-time tended to prove there was none? He became very confused and silent.

"I must and will go," Amelia cried with the greatest spirit; and George, applauding her resolution, patted her under the chin, and asked all the persons present if they ever saw such a termagant of a wife, and agreed that the lady should bear him company. "We'll have Mrs. O'Dowd to chaperon you," he said. What cared she so long as her husband was near her? Thus somehow the bitterness of a parting was juggled away. Though war and danger were in store, war and danger might not befal for months to come. There was a respite at any rate, which made the timid little Amelia almost as happy as a full reprieve would have done, and which even Dobbin owned in his heart was very welcome. For, to be permitted to see her was now the greatest privilege and hope of his life, and he thought with himself secretly how he would watch and protect her. I wouldn't have let her

6. A bird of New Guinea remarkable for colorful plumage, often used to decorate women's hats.
7. Louis XVIII, who became king upon Napoleon's defeat in 1814, retreated to Ghent, in Belgium, upon Napoleon's return from Elba in March 1815. Brussels is the capital of Belgium.
8. R. Gleig's *Story of the Battle of Waterloo* (1847), which served Thackeray as a source, indicated that many family members and other noncombatants were taken very near the front in the belief that this would not be a defensive war. See Amelia's declaration to go, a few pages later.

go if I had been married to her, he thought. But George was the master, and his friend did not think fit to remonstrate.

Putting her arm round her friend's waist, Rebecca at length carried Amelia off from the dinner-table where so much business of importance had been discussed, and left the gentlemen in a highly exhilarated state, drinking and talking very gaily.

In the course of the evening Rawdon got a little family-note from his wife, which although he crumpled it up and burnt it instantly in the candle, we had the good luck to read over Rebecca's shoulder. "Great news," she wrote. "Mrs. Bute is gone. Get the money from Cupid to-night, as he'll be off to-morrow most likely. Mind this.—R." So when the little company was about adjourning to coffee in the women's apartment, Rawdon touched Osborne on the elbow, and said gracefully, "I say, Osborne, my boy, if quite convenient, I'll trouble you for that 'ere small trifle." It was not quite convenient, but nevertheless George gave him a considerable present instalment in bank notes from his pocket-book, and a bill on his agents at a week's date, for the remaining sum.

This matter arranged, George, and Jos, and Dobbin, held a council of war over their cigars, and agreed that a general move should be made for London in Jos's open carriage the next day. Jos, I think, would have preferred staying until Rawdon Crawley quitted Brighton, but Dobbin and George overruled him, and he agreed to carry the party to town, and ordered four horses, as became his dignity. With these they set off in state, after breakfast, the next day. Amelia had risen very early in the morning, and packed her little trunks with the greatest alacrity, while Osborne lay in bed deploring that she had not a maid to help her. She was only too glad, however, to perform this office for herself. A dim uneasy sentiment about Rebecca filled her mind already; and although they kissed each other most tenderly at parting, yet we know what jealousy is; and Mrs. Amelia possessed that among other virtues of her sex.

Besides these characters who are coming and going away, we must remember that there were some other old friends of ours at Brighton; Miss Crawley, namely, and the suite in attendance upon her. Now, although Rebecca and her husband were but at a few stones' throw of the lodgings which the invalid Miss Crawley occupied, the old lady's door remained as pitilessly closed to them as it had been heretofore in London. As long as she remained by the side of her sister-in-law, Mrs. Bute Crawley took care that her beloved Matilda should not be agitated by a meeting with her nephew. When the spinster took her drive, the faithful Mrs. Bute sate beside her in the carriage. When Miss Crawley took the air in a chair, Mrs. Bute marched on one side of the vehicle, whilst honest Briggs occupied the other wing. And if they met Rawdon and his wife by chance—although the former constantly and obsequiously took off his hat, the Miss-Crawley party passed him by with such a frigid and killing indifference, that Rawdon began to despair.

"We might as well be in London as here," Captain Rawdon often said, with a downcast air.

"A comfortable inn in Brighton is better than a spunging-house in Chancery Lane,"[9] his wife answered, who was of a more cheerful temperament. "Think of those two aides-de-camp of Mr. Moses, the

sheriff's-officer, who watched our lodging for a week. Our friends here are very stupid, but Mr. Jos and Captain Cupid are better companions than Mr. Moses's men, Rawdon, my love."

"I wonder the writs[1] haven't followed me down here," Rawdon continued, still desponding.

"When they do, we'll find means to give them the slip," said dauntless little Becky, and further pointed out to her husband the great comfort and advantage of meeting Jos and Osborne, whose acquaintance had brought to Rawdon Crawley a most timely little supply of ready money.

"It will hardly be enough to pay the inn bill," grumbled the Guardsman.

"Why need we pay it?" said the lady, who had an answer for everything.

Through Rawdon's valet, who still kept up a trifling acquaintance with the male inhabitants of Miss Crawley's servants' hall, and was instructed to treat the coachman to drink whenever they met, old Miss Crawley's movements were pretty well known by our young couple; and Rebecca luckily bethought herself of being unwell, and of calling in the same apothecary who was in attendance upon the spinster,

9. A private, but secure, halfway house presided over by a bailiff or sheriff where debtors were taken and held while they cleared their debts. If they could not, they were put in debtor's prison.

1. Formal court orders.

so that their information was on the whole tolerably complete. Nor was Miss Briggs, although forced to adopt a hostile attitude, secretly inimical to Rawdon and his wife. She was naturally of a kindly and forgiving disposition. Now that the cause of jealousy was removed, her dislike for Rebecca disappeared also, and she remembered the latter's invariable good words and good humour. And, indeed, she and Mrs. Firkin, the lady's-maid, and the whole of Miss Crawley's household, secretly[2] groaned under the tyranny of the triumphant Mrs. Bute.

As often will be the case, that good but imperious woman pushed her advantages too far, and her successes quite unmercifully. She had in the course of a few weeks brought the invalid to such a state of helpless docility, that the poor soul yielded herself entirely to her sister's orders, and did not even dare to complain of her slavery to Briggs or Firkin. Mrs. Bute measured out the glasses of wine which Miss Crawley was daily allowed to take with irresistible accuracy, greatly to the annoyance of Firkin and the butler, who found themselves deprived of control over even the Sherry-bottle. She apportioned the sweet-breads, jellies, chickens; their quantity and order. Night and noon and morning she brought the abominable drinks ordained by the Doctor, and made her patient swallow them with so affecting an obedience, that Firkin said my poor Missus du take her physic like a lamb. She prescribed the drive in the carriage or the ride in the chair, and, in a word, ground down the old lady in her convalescence in such a way as only belongs to your proper-managing, motherly, moral woman. If ever the patient faintly resisted, and pleaded for a little bit more dinner or a little drop less medicine, the nurse threatened her with instantaneous death, when Miss Crawley instantly gave in. "She's no spirit left in her," Firkin remarked to Briggs; "she aint ave called me a fool these three weeks." Finally, Mrs. Bute had made up her mind to dismiss the aforesaid honest lady's-maid, Mr. Bowls the large confidential man, and Briggs herself, and to send for her daughters from the Rectory, previous to removing the dear invalid bodily to Queen's Crawley, when an odious accident happened which called her away from duties so pleasing. The Reverend Bute Crawley her husband, riding home one night, fell with his horse and broke his collar-bone. Fever and inflammatory symptoms set in, and Mrs. Bute was forced to leave Sussex for Hampshire. As soon as ever Bute was restored she promised to return to her dearest friend, and departed, leaving the strongest injunctions with the household regarding their behaviour to their mistress; and as soon as she got into the Southampton coach, there was such a jubilee and sense of relief in all Miss Crawley's house, as the company of persons assembled there had not experienced for many a week before. That very day Miss Crawley left off her afternoon dose of medicine: that afternoon Bowls opened an independent bottle of Sherry for himself and Mrs. Firkin: that night Miss Crawley and Miss Briggs indulged in a game of picquet instead of one of Porteus's sermons. It was as in the old

2. Revised edition omits: secretly

nursery-story, when the stick forgot to beat the dog,[3] and the whole course of events underwent a peaceful and happy revolution.

At a very early hour in the morning, twice or thrice a week, Miss Briggs used to betake herself to a bathing-machine, and disport in the water in a flannel gown, and an oilskin cap. Rebecca, as we have seen, was aware of this circumstance, and though she did not attempt to storm Briggs as she had threatened, and actually dive into that lady's presence and surprise her under the sacredness of the awning, Mrs. Rawdon determined to attack Briggs as she came away from her bath, refreshed and invigorated by her dip, and likely to be in good humour.

So, getting up very early the next morning, Becky brought the telescope in their sitting-room, which faced the sea, to bear upon the bathing-machines on the beach; saw Briggs arrive, enter her box, and put out to sea; and was on the shore just as the nymph of whom she came in quest stepped out of the little caravan on to the shingles.[4] It was a pretty picture: the beach; the bathing-women's faces; the long line of rocks and building were blushing and bright in the sunshine. Rebecca wore a kind, tender smile on her face, and was holding out her pretty white hand as Briggs emerged from the box. What could Briggs do but accept the salutation?

"Miss Sh—, Mrs. Crawley," she said.

Mrs. Crawley seized her hand, pressed it to her heart, and with a sudden impulse, flinging her arms round Briggs, kissed her affectionately. "Dear, dear friend!" she said, with a touch of such natural feeling, that Miss Briggs of course at once began to melt, and even the bathing-woman was mollified.

Rebecca found no difficulty in engaging Briggs in a long, intimate, and delightful conversation. Every thing that had passed since the morning of Becky's sudden departure from Miss Crawley's house in Park Lane up to the present day, and Mrs. Bute's happy retreat, was discussed and described by Briggs. All Miss Crawley's symptoms, and the particulars of her illness and medical treatment, were narrated by the confidante with that fulness and accuracy which women delight in. About their complaints and their doctors do ladies ever tire of talking to each other? Briggs did not on this occasion; nor did Rebecca weary of listening. She was thankful, truly thankful, that the dear kind Briggs, that the faithful, the invaluable Firkin, had been permitted to remain with their benefactress through her illness. Heaven bless her! though she, Rebecca, had seemed to act undutifully towards Miss Crawley; yet was not her fault a natural and excusable one? Could she help giving her hand to the man who had won her heart? Briggs, the sentimental, could only turn up her eyes to heaven at this appeal, and heave a sympathetic sigh, and think that she, too, had given away her affections long years ago, and own that Rebecca was no very great criminal.

"Can I ever forget her who so befriended the friendless orphan? No, though she has cast me off," the latter said, "I shall never cease to

3. Untraced. It could refer to "The Old Woman and Her Pig," in which the stick refuses to beat the dog until threatened with fire.
4. A pebble beach, not sand.

love her, and I would devote my life to her service. As my own benefactress, as my beloved Rawdon's adored relative, I love and admire Miss Crawley, dear Miss Briggs, beyond any woman in the world, and next to her I love all those who are faithful to her. *I* would never have treated Miss Crawley's faithful friends as that odious designing Mrs. Bute had done. Rawdon, who was all heart," Rebecca continued, "although his outward manners might seem rough and careless, had said a hundred times, with tears in his eyes, that he blessed Heaven for sending his dearest Aunty two such admirable nurses as her attached Firkin and her admirable Miss Briggs. Should the machinations of the horrible Mrs. Bute end, as she too much feared they would, in banishing everybody that Miss Crawley loved from her side, and leaving that poor lady a victim to those harpies[5] at the Rectory, Rebecca besought her (Miss Briggs) to remember, that her own home, humble as it was, was always open to receive Briggs. Dear friend," she exclaimed, in a transport of enthusiasm, "*some* hearts can *never* forget benefits; *all* women are not Bute Crawleys! Though why should I complain of her," Rebecca added; "though I have been her tool and the victim to her arts, do I not owe my dearest Rawdon to her?" And Rebecca unfolded to Briggs all Mrs. Bute's conduct at Queen's Crawley, which, though unintelligible to her then, was clearly enough explained by the events now,—now that the attachment had sprung up which Mrs. Bute had encouraged by a thousand artifices,—now that two innocent people had fallen into the snares which she had laid for them, and loved and married and been ruined through her schemes.

It was all very true. Briggs saw the stratagems as clearly as possible. Mrs. Bute had made the match between Rawdon and Rebecca. Yet, though the latter was a perfectly innocent victim, Miss Briggs could not disguise from her friend her fear that Miss Crawley's affections were hopelessly estranged from Rebecca, and that the old lady would never forgive her nephew for making so imprudent a marriage.

On this point Rebecca had her own opinion, and still kept up a good heart. If Miss Crawley did not forgive them at present, she might at least relent on a future day. Even now, there was only that puling, sickly Pitt Crawley between Rawdon and a baronetcy; and should anything happen to the former, all would be well. At all events, to have Mrs. Bute's designs exposed, and herself well abused, was a satisfaction, and might be advantageous to Rawdon's interest; and Rebecca, after an hour's chat with her recovered friend, left her with the most tender demonstrations of regard, and quite assured that the conversation they had had together would be reported to Miss Crawley before many hours were over.

This interview ended, it became full time for Rebecca to return to her inn, where all the party of the previous day were assembled at a farewell breakfast. Rebecca took such a tender leave of Amelia as became two women who loved each other as sisters; and having used her handkerchief plentifully, and hung on her friend's neck as if they were parting for ever, and waved the handkerchief (which was

5. In myth, vultures with women's heads; i.e., predatory persons.

quite dry, by the way) out of window, as the carriage drove off; she came back to the breakfast-table, and ate some prawns with a good deal of appetite, considering her emotion; and while she was munching these delicacies, explained to Rawdon what had occurred in her morning walk between herself and Briggs. Her hopes were very high: she made her husband share them. She generally succeeded in making her husband share all her opinions, whether melancholy or cheerful.

"You will now, if you please, my dear, sit down at the writing-table and pen me a pretty little letter to Miss Crawley, in which you'll say that you are a good boy, and that sort of thing." So Rawdon sate down, and wrote off, "Brighton, Thursday," and "My dear Aunt," with great rapidity: but there the gallant officer's imagination failed him. He mumbled the end of his pen, and looked up in his wife's face. She could not help laughing at his rueful countenance, and, marching up and down the room with her hands behind her, the little woman began to dictate a letter, which he took down.

"Before quitting the country and commencing a campaign, which very possibly may be fatal,"

"What?" said Rawdon, rather surprised, but took the humour of the phrase, and presently wrote it down with a grin.

"Which very possibly may be fatal, I have come hither—"

"Why not say come here; Becky, come here's grammar," the dragoon interposed.

"I have come hither," Rebecca insisted with a stamp of her foot, "to say farewell to my dearest and earliest friend. I beseech you before I go, not perhaps to return, once more to let me press the hand from which I have received nothing but kindnesses all my life."

"Kindnesses all my life," echoed Rawdon, scratching down the words, and quite amazed at his own facility of composition.

"I ask nothing from you but that we should part not in anger. I have the pride of my family on some points, though not on all. I married a painter's daughter, and am not ashamed of the union."

"No, run me through the body if I am!" Rawdon ejaculated.

"You old booby," Rebecca said, pinching his ear and looking over to see that he made no mistakes in spelling—"beseech is not spelt with an *a*, and earliest is." So he altered these words, bowing to the superior knowledge of his little Missis.

"I thought that you were aware of the progress of my attachment," Rebecca continued: "I knew that Mrs. Bute Crawley confirmed and encouraged it. But I make no reproaches. I married a poor woman, and am content to abide by what I have done. Leave your property, dear Aunt, as you will. *I* shall never complain of the way in which you dispose of it. I would have you believe that I love you for yourself, and not for money's sake. I want to be reconciled to you ere I leave England. Let me, let me see you before I go. A few weeks or months hence it may be too late, and I cannot bear the notion of quitting the country without a kind word of farewell from you."

"She won't recognise my style in *that,*" said Becky. "I made the sentences short and brisk on purpose." And this authentic missive was dispatched under cover to Miss Briggs.

Old Miss Crawley laughed when Briggs with great mystery handed her over this candid and simple statement. "We may read it now Mrs. Bute is away," she said. "Read it to me, Briggs."

When Briggs had read the epistle out, her patroness laughed more. "Don't you see, you goose," she said to Briggs, who professed to be much touched by the honest affection which pervaded the composition, "Don't you see that Rawdon never wrote a word of it. He never wrote to me without asking for money in his life, and all his letters are full of bad spelling, and dashes, and bad grammar. It is that little serpent of a governess who rules him." They are all alike, Miss Crawley thought in her heart. They all want me dead, and are hankering for my money.

"I don't mind seeing Rawdon," she added, after a pause, and in a tone of perfect indifference. "I had just as soon shake hands with him as not. Provided there is no scene, why shouldn't we meet? I don't mind. But human patience has its limits; and mind, my dear, I respectfully decline to receive Mrs. Rawdon—I can't support *that* quite"—and Miss Briggs was fain to be content with this half-message of conciliation; and thought that the best method of bringing the old lady and her nephew together, was to warn Rawdon to be in waiting on the Cliff, when Miss Crawley went out for her air in her chair.

There they met. I don't know whether Miss Crawley had any private feeling of regard, or emotion upon seeing her old favourite; but she held out a couple of fingers to him with as smiling and good-humoured an air, as if they had met only the day before. And as for Rawdon, he turned as red as scarlet, and wrung off Briggs's hand, so great was his rapture and his confusion at the meeting. Perhaps it was interest that moved him: or perhaps affection: perhaps he was touched by the change which the illness of the last weeks had wrought in his aunt.

"The old girl has always acted like a trump to me," he said to his wife, as he narrated the interview, "and I felt, you know, rather queer, and that sort of thing. I walked by the side of the what-dy'e-call-'em, you know, and to her own door, where Bowls came to help her in. And I wanted to go in very much, only—"

"*You didn't go in,* Rawdon!" screamed his wife.

"No, my dear, I'm hanged if I wasn't afraid when it came to the point."

"You fool! you ought to have gone in, and never come out again," Rebecca said.

"Don't call me names," said the big guardsman, sulkily. "Perhaps I *was* a fool, Becky, but you shouldn't say so;" and he gave his wife a look, such as his countenance could wear when angered, and such as was not pleasant to face.

"Well, dearest, to-morrow you must be on the look-out, and go and see her, mind, whether she asks you or no," Rebecca said, trying to soothe her angry yoke-mate. On which he replied, that he would do exactly as he liked, and would just thank her to keep a civil tongue in her head—and the wounded husband went away, and passed the forenoon at the billiard-room, sulky, silent, and suspicious.

But before the night was over he was compelled to give in, and own, as usual, to his wife's superior prudence and foresight, by the most melancholy confirmation of the presentiments which she had regarding the consequences of the mistake which he had made. Miss Crawley *must* have had some emotion upon seeing him and shaking hands with him after so long a rupture. She mused upon the meeting a considerable time. "Rawdon is getting very fat and old, Briggs," she said to her companion. "His nose has become red, and he is exceedingly coarse in appearance. His marriage to that woman has hopelessly vulgarised him. Mrs. Bute always said they drank together; and I have no doubt they do. Yes: he smelt of gin abominably. I remarked it. Didn't you?"

In vain Briggs interposed, that Mrs. Bute spoke ill of everybody: and, as far as a person in *her* humble position could judge, was an—

"An artful designing woman? Yes, so she is, and she does speak ill of every one,—but I am certain that woman has made Rawdon drink. All those low people do—"

"He was very much affected at seeing you, Ma'am," the companion said; "and I am sure, when you remember that he is going to the field of danger—"

"How much money has he promised you, Briggs?" the old spinster cried out, working herself into a nervous rage—"there now, of course you begin to cry. I hate scenes. Why am I always to be worried? Go and cry up in your own room, and send Firkin to me,—no, stop, sit down and blow your nose, and leave off crying, and write a letter to Captain Crawley." Poor Briggs went and placed herself obediently at the writing-book. Its leaves were blotted all over with relics of the firm, strong, rapid handwriting of the spinster's late amanuensis, Mrs. Bute Crawley.

"Begin 'My dear sir,' or 'Dear sir,' that will be better, and say you are desired by Mrs. Crawley—no, by Miss Crawley's medical man, by Mr. Creamer, to state, that my health is such that all strong emotions would be dangerous in my present delicate condition—and that I must decline any family discussions or interviews whatever. And thank him for coming to Brighton, and so forth, and beg him not to stay any longer on my account. And, Miss Briggs, you may add that I wish him a *bon voyage,* and that if he will take the trouble to call upon my lawyer's in Gray's Inn Square,[6] he will find there a communication for him. Yes, that will do; and that will make him leave Brighton." The benevolent Briggs penned this sentence with the utmost satisfaction.

"To seize upon me the very day after Mrs. Bute was gone," the old lady prattled on; "it was too indecent. Briggs, my dear, write to Mrs. Crawley, and say *she* needn't come back. No—she needn't—and she shan't—and I won't be a slave in my own house—and I won't be starved and choked with poison. They all want to kill me—all—all"—and with this the lonely old woman burst into a scream of hysterical tears.

6. Gray's Inn, one of the Inns of Court, provides living space, offices, and libraries for the legal profession.

The last scene of her dismal Vanity Fair comedy was fast approaching; the tawdry lamps were going out one by one; and the dark curtain was almost ready to descend.

That final paragraph, which referred Rawdon to Miss Crawley's solicitor in London, and which Briggs had written so good-naturedly, consoled the dragoon and his wife somewhat, after their first blank disappointment, on reading the spinster's refusal of a reconciliation. And it effected the purpose for which the old lady had caused it to be written, by making Rawdon very eager to get to London.

Out of Jos's losings and George Osborne's bank-notes, he paid his bill at the inn, the landlord whereof does not probably know to this day how doubtfully his account once stood. For, as a general sends his baggage to the rear before an action, Rebecca had wisely packed up all their chief valuables and sent them off under care of George's servant, who went in charge of the trunks on the coach back to London. Rawdon and his wife returned by the same conveyance next day.

"I should have liked to see the old girl before we went," Rawdon said. "She looks so cut up and altered that I'm sure she can't last long. I wonder what sort of a cheque I shall have at Waxy's. Two hundred—it can't be less than two hundred,—hey Becky?"

In consequence of the repeated visits of the gentlemen whose portraits have been taken in a preceding page,[7] Rawdon and his wife did not go back to their lodgings at Brompton, but put up at an inn. Early the next morning, Rebecca had an opportunity of seeing them as she skirted that suburb on her road to old Mrs. Sedley's house at Fulham, whither she went to look for her dear Amelia and her Brighton friends. They were all off to Chatham, thence to Harwich, to take shipping for Belgium with the regiment[8]—kind old Mrs. Sedley very much depressed and tearful, solitary. Returning from this visit, Rebecca found her husband, who had been off to Gray's Inn, and learnt his fate. He came back furious.

"By Jove, Becky," says he, "she's only given me twenty pounds!"

Though it told against themselves, the joke was too good, and Becky burst out laughing at Rawdon's discomfiture.

7. Revised edition reads: visits of the aides-de-camp of the Sheriff of Middlesex,

8. They traveled from London to Chatham by land and then by sea up the coast to Harwich, a seaport directly across the English Channel from Ostend, Belgium. Margate, just east and south of Chatham, was another important point of departure for Belgium (see chapter XXVI).

*Number 8* *Aug. 1847*

## *Chapter XXVI.*

### BETWEEN LONDON AND CHATHAM.

In quitting Brighton, our friend George as became a person of rank and fashion travelling in a barouche[1] with four horses, drove in state to a fine hotel in Cavendish Square,[2] where a suite of splendid rooms, and a table magnificently furnished with plate and surrounded by a half-dozen of black and silent waiters, was ready to receive the young gentleman and his bride. George did the honours of the place with a princely air to Jos and Dobbin; and Amelia, for the first time, and with exceeding shyness and timidity, presided at what George called her own table.

George pooh-poohed the wine and bullied the waiters royally, and Jos gobbled the turtle with immense satisfaction. Dobbin helped him to it; for the lady of the house, before whom the tureen was placed, was so ignorant of the contents, that she was going to help Mr. Sedley without bestowing upon him either calipash or calipee.[3]

The splendour of the entertainment, and the apartments in which it was given, alarmed Mr. Dobbin, who remonstrated after dinner, when Jos was asleep in the great chair. But, in vain he cried out against the enormity of turtle and champagne that was fit for an archbishop. "I've always been accustomed to travel like a gentleman," George said, "and, damme, my wife shall travel like a lady. As long as there's a shot in the locker,[4] *she* shall want for nothing," said the generous fellow, quite pleased with himself for his magnificence of spirit. Nor did Dobbin try and convince him that Amelia's happiness was not centred in turtle-soup.

A while after dinner, Amelia timidly expressed a wish to go and see her mamma, at Fulham: which permission George granted her with some grumbling. And she tripped away to her enormous bedroom, in the centre of which stood the enormous funereal bed, 'that the Emperor Halixander's sister[5] slep in when the allied sufferings was here,' and put on her little bonnet and shawl with the utmost eagerness and pleasure. George was still drinking claret when she returned to the dining-room, and made no signs of moving. "Ar'n't you coming with me, dearest?" she asked him. No; the 'dearest' had 'business' that night. His man should get her a coach and go with her.

1. A four-wheeled carriage with a convertible hood, seating four and a driver.
2. Aristocratic, upscale neighborhood in the West End.
3. Turtle delicacies.
4. A mixed metaphor: a shot is a bill or payment; a shot locker on a ship holds cannonballs.
5. Tzar Alexander and his sister the grand duchess of Oldenburgh, the sovereigns (sufferings) of Russia, visited London for the summer celebrations of victory over Napoleon in 1814, but they actually stayed at a different hotel.

And the coach being at the door of the hotel, Amelia made George a little disappointed curtsey after looking vainly into his face once or twice, and went sadly down the great staircase, Captain Dobbin after, who handed her into the vehicle, and saw it drive away to its destination. The very valet was ashamed of mentioning the address to the hackney-coachman before the hotel-waiters, and promised to instruct him when they got further on.

Dobbin walked home to his old quarters at the Slaughters', thinking very likely that it would be delightful to be in that hackney-coach, along with Mrs. Osborne. George was evidently of quite a different taste; for when he had taken wine enough, he went off to half-price at the play, to see Mr. Kean perform in Shylock.[6] Captain Osborne was a great lover of the drama, and had himself performed high-comedy characters with great distinction in several garrison theatrical entertainments. Jos slept on until long after dark, when he woke up with a start at the motions of his servant, who was removing and emptying the decanters on the table; and the hackney-coach stand was again put into requisition for a carriage to convey this stout hero to his lodgings and bed.

Mrs. Sedley, you may be sure, clasped her daughter to her heart with all maternal eagerness and affection, running out of the door as the carriage drew up before the little garden-gate, to welcome the weeping, trembling, young bride. Old Mr. Clapp, who was in his shirt-sleeves, trimming the garden-plot, shrank back alarmed. The Irish servant-lass rushed up from the kitchen and smiled a 'God bless you.' Amelia could hardly walk along the flags and up the steps into the parlour.

How the floodgates were opened and mother and daughter wept, when they were together embracing each other in this sanctuary, may readily be imagined by every reader who possesses the least sentimental turn. When don't ladies weep? At what occasion of joy, sorrow, or other business of life? and, after such an event as a marriage, mother and daughter were surely at liberty to give way to a sensibility which is as tender as it is refreshing. About a question of marriage I have seen women who hate each other kiss and cry together quite fondly. How much more do they feel when they love! Good mothers are married over again at their daughters' weddings: and as for subsequent events, who does not know how ultra-maternal grandmothers are?—in fact a woman, until she is a grandmother, does not often really know what to be a mother is. Let us respect Amelia and her mamma whispering and whimpering and laughing and crying in the parlour and the twilight. Old Mr. Sedley did. *He* had not divined who was in the carriage when it drove up. He had not flown out to meet his daughter, though he kissed her very warmly when she entered the room (where he was occupied, as usual, with his papers and tapes and statements of accounts), and after sitting with the mother

6. After 8:00 P.M. one could enter for half price. Edmund Kean (d. 1833), virtually destitute and unknown, became famous overnight in January 1814 for his Drury Lane Theater performance of Shylock in *The Merchant of Venice*. He repeated it periodically; George would have seen him in the spring of 1815.

and daughter for a short time, he very wisely left the little apartment in their possession.

George's valet was looking on in a very supercilious manner at Mr. Clapp in his shirt-sleeves, watering his rose-bushes. He took off his hat, however, with much condescension to Mr. Sedley, who asked news about his son-in-law, and about Jos's carriage, and whether his horses had been down to Brighton, and about that infernal traitor Bonaparty, and the war; until the Irish maid-servant came with a plate and a bottle of wine, from which the old gentleman insisted

upon helping the valet. He gave him a half-guinea too, which the servant pocketed with a mixture of wonder and contempt. "To the health of your master and mistress, Trotter," Mr. Sedley said, "and here's something to drink your health when you get home, Trotter."

There were but nine days past since Amelia had left that little cottage and home—and yet how far off the time seemed since she had bidden it farewell. What a gulf lay between her and that past life. She could look back to it from her present standing-place, and contemplate, almost as another being, the young unmarried girl absorbed in her love, having no eyes but for one special object, receiving parental affection if not ungratefully, at least indifferently, and as if it were her due—her whole heart and thoughts bent on the accomplishment of one desire. The review of those days, so lately gone yet so far away, touched her with shame; and the aspect of the kind parents[7] filled her with tender remorse. Was the prize gained—the heaven of life—and the winner still doubtful and unsatisfied? As his hero and heroine pass the matrimonial barrier, the novelist generally drops the curtain, as if the drama were over then: the doubts and struggles of life ended: as if, once landed in the marriage country, all were green and pleasant there: and wife and husband had nothing but to link

7. First and second printings read: mother

each other's arms together, and wander gently downwards towards old age in happy and perfect fruition. But our little Amelia was just on the bank of her new country, and was already looking anxiously back towards the sad friendly figures waving farewell to her across the stream, from the other distant shore.

In honour of the young bride's arrival, her mother thought it necessary to prepare I don't know what festive entertainment, and after the first ebullition of talk, took leave of Mrs. George Osborne for a while, and dived down to the lower regions of the house to a sort of kitchen-parlour (occupied by Mr. and Mrs. Clapp, and in the evening, when her dishes were washed and her curl-papers removed, by Miss Flanagan the Irish servant), there to take measures for the preparing of a magnificent ornamented tea. All people have their ways of expressing kindness, and it seemed to Mrs. Sedley that a muffin and a quantity of orange marmalade spread out in a little cut-glass saucer would be peculiarly agreeable refreshments to Amelia in her most interesting situation.

While these delicacies were being transacted below, Amelia, leaving the drawing-room, walked up stairs and found herself, she scarce knew how, in the little room which she had occupied before her marriage, and in that very chair in which she had passed so many bitter hours. She sank back in its arms as if it were an old friend; and fell to thinking over the past week, and the life beyond it. Already to be looking sadly and vaguely back: always to be pining for something which, when obtained, brought doubt and sadness rather than pleasure: here was the lot of our poor little creature, and harmless lost wanderer in the great struggling crowds of Vanity Fair.

Here she sate, and recalled to herself fondly that image of George

to which she had knelt before marriage. Did she own to herself how different the real man was from that superb young hero whom she had worshipped? It requires many many years—and a man must be very bad indeed—before a woman's pride and vanity will let her own to such a confession. Then Rebecca's twinkling green eyes and baleful smile lighted upon her, and filled her with dismay. And so she sate for awhile indulging in her usual mood of selfish brooding, in that very listless melancholy attitude in which the honest maid-servant had found her, on the day when she brought up the letter in which George renewed his offer of marriage.

She looked at the little white bed, which had been hers a few days before, and thought she would like to sleep in it that night, and wake, as formerly, with her mother smiling over her in the morning. Then she thought with terror of the great funereal damask pavilion in the vast and dingy state bed-room, which was awaiting her at the grand hotel in Cavendish Square. Dear little white bed! how many a long night had she wept on its pillow! How she had despaired and hoped to die there; and now were not all her wishes accomplished, and the lover of whom she had despaired her own for ever? Kind mother! how patiently and tenderly she had watched round that bed! She went and knelt down by the bed-side; and there this wounded and timorous, but gentle and loving soul, sought for consolation, where as yet, it must be owned, our little girl had but seldom looked for it. Love had been her faith hitherto; and the sad, bleeding, disappointed heart, began to feel the want of another consoler.

Have we a right to repeat or to overhear her prayers? These, brother, are secrets, and out of the domain of Vanity Fair, in which our story lies.

But this may be said, that when the tea was finally announced, our young lady came down stairs a great deal more cheerful; that she did not despond, or deplore her fate, or think about George's coldness, or Rebecca's eyes, as she had been wont to do of late. She went down stairs, and kissed her father and mother, and talked to the old gentleman, and made him more merry than he had been for many a day. She sate down at the piano which Dobbin had bought for her, and sang over all her father's favourite old songs. She pronounced the tea to be excellent, and praised the exquisite taste in which the marmalade was arranged in the saucers. And in determining to make everybody else happy, she found herself so; and was sound asleep in the great funereal pavilion, and only woke up with a smile when George arrived from the theatre.

For the next day, George had more important 'business' to transact than that which took him to see Mr. Kean in Shylock. Immediately on his arrival in London he had written off to his father's solicitors, signifying his royal pleasure that an interview should take place between them on the morrow. His hotel losses at billiards and cards to Captain Crawley had almost drained the young man's purse, which wanted replenishing before he set out on his travels, and he had no resource but to infringe upon the two thousand pounds which the attorneys were commissioned to pay over to him. He had a perfect belief in his own mind that his father would relent before very long. How could any parent be obdurate for a length of time against such a paragon as he was? If his mere past and personal merits did not succeed in mollifying the father, George determined that he would distinguish himself so prodigiously in the ensuing campaign that the old gentleman must give in to him. And if not? Bah! the world was before him. His luck might change at cards, and there was a deal of spending in two thousand pounds.

So he sent off Amelia once more in a carriage to her mamma, with strict orders and carte blanche to the two ladies to purchase everything requisite for a lady of Mrs. George Osborne's fashion, who was going on a foreign tour. They had but one day to complete the outfit, and it may be imagined that their business therefore occupied them pretty fully. In a carriage once more, bustling about from milliner to linendraper, escorted back to the carriage by obsequious shopmen or polite owners, Mrs. Sedley was herself again almost, and sincerely happy for the first time since their misfortunes. Nor was Mrs. Amelia at all above the pleasure of shopping, and bargaining, and seeing and buying pretty things. (Would any man, the most philosophic, give twopence for a woman who was?) She gave herself a little treat, obedient to her husband's orders, and purchased a quantity of lady's gear, showing a great deal of taste and elegant discernment, as all the shopfolks said.

And about the war that was ensuing, Mrs. Osborne was not much alarmed; Bonaparty was to be crushed almost without a struggle. Margate packets[8] were sailing every day, filled with men of fashion and ladies of note, on their way to Brussels and Ghent. People were going not so much to a war as to a fashionable tour. The newspapers laughed the wretched upstart and swindler to scorn. Such a Corsican wretch as that withstand the armies of Europe and the genius of the immortal Wellington! Amelia held him in utter contempt; for it needs not to be said that this soft and gentle creature took her opinions from those people who surrounded her, such fidelity being much too humble-minded to think for itself. Well, in a word, she and her mother performed a great day's shopping, and she acquitted herself with considerable liveliness and credit on this her first appearance in the genteel world of London.

George meanwhile, with his hat on one side, his elbows squared, and his swaggering martial air, made for Bedford Row, and stalked into the attorney's offices as if he was lord of every pale-faced clerk who was scribbling there. He ordered somebody to inform Mr. Higgs that Captain Osborne was waiting, in a fierce and patronising way, as if the *pékin*[9] of an attorney, who had thrice his brains, fifty times his money, and a thousand times his experience, was a wretched underling who should instantly leave all his business in life to attend on the Captain's pleasure. He did not see the sneer of contempt which passed all round the room, from the first clerk to the articled gents,[1]

8. Boats for Belgium from Margate, a port east of Chatham.
9. Name originally given by Napoleon's soldiers to civilians; also adopted by the English.
1. Apprentices.

from the articled gents to the ragged writers and white-faced runners, in clothes too tight for them, as he sate there tapping his boot with his cane, and thinking what a parcel of miserable poor devils these were. The miserable poor devils knew all about his affairs. They talked about them over their pints of beer at their public-house clubs to other clerks of a night. Ye Gods, what do not attorneys and attorneys' clerks know in London! Nothing is hidden from their inquisition, and their familiars mutely rule our city.

Perhaps George expected, when he entered Mr. Higgs's apartment, to find that gentleman commissioned to give him some message of compromise or conciliation from his father; perhaps his haughty and cold demeanour was adopted as a sign of his spirit and resolution: but if so, his fierceness was met by a chilling coolness and indifference on the attorney's part, that rendered swaggering absurd. He pretended to be writing at a paper, when the Captain entered. "Pray, sit down, Sir," said he, "and I will attend to your little affair in a moment. Mr. Poe, get the release papers, if you please;" and then he fell to writing again.

Poe having produced those papers, his chief calculated the amount of two thousand pounds stock at the rate of the day; and asked Captain Osborne whether he would take the sum in a cheque upon the bankers, or whether he should direct the latter to purchase stock to that amount. "One of the late Mrs. Osborne's trustees is out of town," he said indifferently, "but my client wishes to meet your wishes, and have done with the business as quick as possible."

"Give me a cheque, Sir," said the Captain very surlily. "Damn the shillings and halfpence, Sir," he added, as the lawyer was making out the amount of the draft; and, flattering himself that by this stroke of magnanimity he had put the old quiz[2] to the blush, he stalked out of his office with the paper in his pocket.

"That chap will be in gaol in two years," Mr. Higgs said to Mr. Poe.

"Won't O. come round, Sir, don't you think?"

"Won't the monument[3] come round," Mr. Higgs replied.

"He's going it pretty fast," said the clerk. "He's only married a week, and I saw him and some other military chaps handing Mrs. Highflyer to her carriage after the play." And then another case was called, and Mr. George Osborne thenceforth dismissed from these worthy gentlemen's memory.

The draft was upon our friends Hulker & Bullock of Lombard Street, to whose house, still thinking he was doing business, George bent his way, and from whom he received his money. Frederic Bullock, Esq., whose yellow face was over a ledger, at which sate a demure clerk, happened to be in the banking-room when George entered. His yellow face turned to a more deadly colour when he saw the Captain, and he slunk back guiltily into the inmost parlour. George was too busy gloating over the money (for he had never had such a sum before), to mark the countenance or flight of the cadaverous suitor of his sister.

2. Fool.
3. A pillar known simply as the monument, erected in 1671 in Monument Street, where the Great Fire of London is supposed to have started in 1666.

Fred. Bullock told old Osborne of his son's appearance and conduct. "He came in as bold as brass," said Frederic. "He has drawn out every shilling. How long will a few hundred pounds last such a chap as that?" Osborne swore with a great oath that he little cared when or how soon he spent it. Fred. dined every day in Russell Square now. But altogether, George was highly pleased with his day's business. All his own baggage and outfit was put into a state of speedy preparation, and he paid Amelia's purchases with cheques on his agents, and with the splendour of a lord.

## *Chapter XXVII.*

### IN WHICH AMELIA JOINS HER REGIMENT.

HEN Jos's fine carriage drove up to the inn door at Chatham, the first face which Amelia recognised was the friendly countenance of Captain Dobbin, who had been pacing the street for an hour past in expectation of his friends' arrival. The Captain, with shells[1] on his frock-coat, and a crimson sash and sabre, presented a military appearance, which made Jos quite proud to be able to claim such an acquaintance, and the stout civilian hailed him with a cordiality very different from the reception which Jos vouchsafed to his friend in Brighton and Bond Street.

Along with the Captain was Ensign Stubble; who, as the barouche neared the inn, burst out with an exclamation of "By Jove! what a pretty girl!" highly applauding Osborne's choice. Indeed, Amelia dressed in her wedding-pelisse and pink ribbons, with a flush in her face, occasioned by rapid travel through the open air, looked so fresh and pretty, as fully to justify the Ensign's compliment. Dobbin liked him for making it. As he stepped forward to help the lady out of the carriage, Stubble saw what a pretty little hand she gave him, and what a sweet pretty little foot came tripping down the step. He blushed profusely, and made the very best bow of which he was capable; to which Amelia, seeing the number of the —th regiment embroidered on the Ensign's cap, replied with a blushing smile, and a curtsey on her part; which finished the young Ensign on the spot. Dobbin took most kindly to Mr. Stubble from that day, and encouraged him to talk about Amelia in their private walks, and at each other's quarters. It became the fashion indeed among all the honest young fellows of the —th to adore and admire Mrs. Osborne. Her simple artless

1. Epaulettes or metal substitutes called scales.

behaviour, and modest kindness of demeanour, won all their unsophisticated hearts; all which simplicity and sweetness are quite impossible to describe in print. But who has not beheld these among women, and recognised the presence of all sorts of qualities in them, even though they say no more to you than that they are engaged to dance the next quadrille,[2] or that it is very hot weather? George, always the champion of his regiment, rose immensely in the opinion of the youth of the corps, by his gallantry in marrying this portionless young creature, and by his choice of such a pretty kind partner.

In the sitting-room which was awaiting the travellers, Amelia, to her surprise, found a letter addressed to Mrs. Captain Osborne. It was a triangular billet, on pink paper, and sealed with a dove and an olive branch, and a profusion of light-blue sealing wax, and it was written in a very large, though undecided female hand.

"It's Peggy O'Dowd's fist," said George, laughing. "I know it by the kisses on the seal." And in fact, it was a note from Mrs. Major O'Dowd, requesting the pleasure of Mrs. Osborne's company that very evening to a small friendly party. "You must go," George said. "You will make acquaintance with the regiment there. O'Dowd goes in command of the regiment, and Peggy goes in command of O'Dowd."

But they had not been for many minutes in the enjoyment of Mrs. O'Dowd's letter, when the door was flung open, and a stout jolly lady, in a riding-habit, followed by a couple of officers of Ours, entered the

2. French square dance for four couples.

room. "Sure, I couldn't stop till tay-time. Present me, Garge, my dear fellow, to your lady. Madam, I'm deloighted to see ye; and to present to you me husband, Meejor O'Dowd;" and with this, the jolly lady in the riding-habit grasped Amelia's hand very warmly, and the latter knew at once that the lady was before her whom her husband had so often laughed at. "You've often heard of me from that husband of yours," said the lady with great vivacity.

"You've often heard of her," echoed her husband, the Major.

Amelia answered, smiling, "that she had."

"And small good he's told you of me," Mrs. O'Dowd replied; adding that "George was a wicked divvle."

"That I'll go bail for," said the Major, trying to look knowing, at which George laughed; and Mrs. O'Dowd, with a tap of her whip, told the Major to be quite;[3] and then requested to be presented in form to Mrs. Captain Osborne.

"This, my dear," said George with great gravity, "is my very good, kind, and excellent friend, Auralia Margaretta, otherwise called Peggy."

"Faith, you're right," interposed the Major.

"Otherwise called Peggy, lady of Major Michael O'Dowd of our regiment, and daughter of Fitzjurld Ber'sford de Burgo Malony of Glenmalony, County Kildare."[4]

"And Muryan Squeer,[5] Doblin," said the lady with calm superiority.

"And Muryan Square, sure enough," the Major whispered.

"'Twas there ye coorted me, Meejor, dear," the lady said; and the Major assented to this as to every other proposition which was made generally in company.

Major O'Dowd, who had served his sovereign in every quarter of the world, and had paid for every step[6] in his profession by some more than equivalent act of daring and gallantry, was the most modest, silent, sheep-faced and meek of little men, and as obedient to his wife as if he had been her tay-boy. At the mess-table he sate silently, and drank a great deal. When full of liquor, he reeled silently home. When he spoke, it was to agree with everybody on every conceivable point; and he passed through life in perfect ease and good humour. The hottest suns of India never heated his temper; and the Walcheren ague never shook it.[7] He walked up to a battery with just as much indifference as to a dinner-table; had dined on horse-flesh and turtle with equal relish and appetite; and had an old mother, Mrs. O'Dowd of O'Dowdstown indeed, whom he had never disobeyed but when he ran away and enlisted, and when he persisted in marrying that odious Peggy Malony.

Peggy was one of five sisters, and eleven children of the noble house of Glenmalony; but her husband, though her own cousin, was of the mother's side, and so had not the inestimable advantage of

3. The spelling, though in indirect speech, represents Mrs. O'Dowd's dialect.
4. In Ireland. Beresford and Malone are well-known Irish family names—General William Beresford was a firey but not well-liked commander under Wellington at Waterloo.
5. Merrion Square, in Dublin.
6. Promotion.
7. Ague, also called the shakes. Walcheren: a swampy, pestiferous island on the southern coast of the Netherlands from which in 1809 British forces failed to take Antwerp.

being allied to the Malonies, whom she believed to be the most famous family in the world. Having tried nine seasons at Dublin and two at Bath and Cheltenham, and not finding a partner for life, Miss Malony ordered her cousin Mick to marry her when she was about thirty-three years of age; and the honest fellow obeying, carried her off to the West Indies to preside over the ladies of the —th regiment, into which he had just exchanged.

Before Mrs. O'Dowd was half an hour in Amelia's (or indeed in anybody else's) company, this amiable lady told all her birth and pedigree to her new friend. "My dear," said she, good-naturedly, "it was my intention that Garge should be a brother of my own, and my sister Glorvina would have suited him entirely. But as bygones are bygones, and he was engaged to yourself, why, I'm determined to take you as a sister instead, and to look upon you as such, and to love you as one of the family. Faith, you've got such a nice good-natured face and way widg you, that I'm sure we'll agree; and that you'll be an addition to our family anyway."

"'Deed and she will," said O'Dowd with an approving air, and Amelia felt herself not a little amused and grateful to be thus suddenly introduced to so large a party of relations.

"We're all good fellows here," the Major's lady continued. "There's not a regiment in the service where you'll find a more united society nor a more agreeable mess-room. There's no quarrelling, bickering, slandthering, nor small talk amongst *us*. We all love each other."

"Especially Mrs. Magenis," said George, laughing.

"Mrs. Captain Magenis and me has made up, though her treatment of me would bring me gray hairs with sorrow to the grave."

"And you with such a beautiful front of black, Peggy my dear," the Major cried.

"Hould your tongue, Mick, you booby. Them husbands are always in the way, Mrs. Osborne, my dear; and as for my Mick, I often tell him he should never open his mouth but to give the word of command, or to put meat and drink into it. I'll tell you about the regiment, and warn you when we're alone. Introduce me to your brother now; sure he's a mighty fine man, and reminds me of me cousin Dan Malony (Malony of Ballymalony, my dear, you know, who mar'ied Ophalia Scully, of Oystherstown, own cousin to Lord Poldoody). Mr. Sedley, Sir, I'm deloighted to be made known te ye. I suppose you'll dine at the mess to-day. (Mind that divvle of a docther, Mick, and whatever ye du, keep yourself sober for me party this evening.)"

"It's the 150th gives us a farewell dinner, my love," interposed the Major, "but we'll easy get a card for Mr. Sedley."

"Run Simple. (Ensign Simple, of Ours, my dear Amelia. I forgot to introjuice him to ye.) Run in a hurry, with Mrs. Major O'Dowd's compliments to Colonel Tavish, and Captain Osborne has brought his brothernlaw down, and will bring him to the 150th mess at five o'clock sharp—when you and I, my dear, will take a snack here, if you like." Before Mrs. O'Dowd's speech was concluded, the young Ensign was trotting down stairs on his commission.

"Obedience is the soul of the army. We will go to our duty while

Mrs. O'Dowd will stay and enlighten you, Emmy," Captain Osborne said; and the two Captains, taking each a wing of the Major, walked out with that officer, grinning at each other over his head.

And, now having her new friend to herself, the impetuous Mrs. O'Dowd proceeded to pour out such a quantity of information as no poor little woman's memory could ever tax itself to bear. She told Amelia a thousand particulars relative to the very numerous family of which the amazed young lady found herself a member. "Mrs. Heavytop, the Colonel's wife, died in Jamaica of the yellow faver and a broken heart comboined, for the horrud old Colonel, with a head as bald as a cannon-ball, was making sheep's eyes at a half-caste girl there. Mrs. Magenis, though without education, was a good woman, but she had the divvle's tongue, and would cheat her own mother at whist. Mrs. Captain Kirk must turn up her lobster eyes forsooth at the idea of an honest round game, (wherein me fawther, as pious a man as ever went to church, me uncle Dane Malony, and our cousin the Bishop, took a hand at loo, or whist,[8] every night of their lives). Nayther of 'em's goin with the regiment this time," Mrs. O'Dowd added. "Fanny Magenis stops with her mother, who sells small coal and potatoes, most likely, in Islington-town,[9] hard by London, though she's always bragging of her father's ships, and pointing them out to us as they go up the river: and Mrs. Kirk and her children will stop here in Bethesda Place, to be nigh to her favourite preacher, Dr. Ramshorn. Mrs. Bunny's in an interesting situation—faith, and she always is, then—and has given the Lieutenant seven already. And Ensign Posky's wife, who joined two months before you, my dear, has quarl'd with Tom Posky a score of times, till you can hear 'em all over the bar'ck, (they say they're come to broken pleets, and Tom never accounted for his black oi,) and she'll go back to her mother, who keeps a ladies' siminary at Richmond,—bad luck to her for running away from it! Where did ye get your finishing, my dear? I had moin, and no expince spared,[1] at Madame Flanahan's, at Ilyssus Grove, Booterstown, near Dublin, wid a Marchioness to teach us the true Parisian pronunciation, and a retired Major-General of the French service to put us through the exercise."

Of this incongruous family our astonished Amelia found herself all of a sudden a member: with Mrs. O'Dowd as an elder sister. She was presented to her other female relations at tea-time, on whom, as she was quiet, good-natured, and not too handsome, she made rather an agreeable impression until the arrival of the gentlemen from the mess of the 150th, who all admired her so, that her sisters began, of course, to find fault with her.

"I hope Osborne has sown his wild oats," said Mrs. Magenis to Mrs. Bunny. "If a reformed rake makes a good husband, sure it's she will have the fine chance with Garge," Mrs. O'Dowd remarked to Posky, who had lost her position as bride in the regiment, and was quite angry with the usurper. And, as for Mrs. Kirk; the disciple of Dr. Ramshorn put one or two leading professional questions to

8. Card games.
9. Lower-class suburb of north London.
1. Revised edition reads: speered,

Amelia, to see whether she was awakened, whether she was a professing Christian and so forth, and finding from the simplicity of Mrs. Osborne's replies that she was yet in utter darkness, put into her hands three little penny books with pictures, viz. the "Howling Wilderness," the "Washerwoman of Wandsworth Common," and the "British Soldier's best Bayonet," which, bent upon awakening her before she slept, Mrs. Kirk begged Amelia to read that night ere she went to bed.

But all the men, like good fellows as they were, rallied round their comrade's pretty wife, and paid her their court with soldierly gallantry. She had a little triumph, which flushed her spirits and made her eyes sparkle. George was proud of her popularity, and pleased with the manner (which was very gay and graceful though naïve and a little timid) with which she received the gentlemen's attentions, and answered their compliments. And he in his uniform—how much handsomer he was than any man in the room! She felt that he was affectionately watching her, and glowed with pleasure at his kindness. "I will make all his friends welcome," she resolved in her heart. "I will love all who love him.[2] I will always try and be gay and good-humoured and make his home happy."

The regiment indeed adopted her with acclamation. The Captains approved, the Lieutenants applauded, the Ensigns admired. Old Cutler the Doctor made one or two jokes, which, being professional, need not be repeated; and Cackle, the Assistant M.D. of Edinburgh, condescended to examine her upon leeterature, and tried her with his three best French quotations. Young Stubble went about from man to man whispering, "Jove, isn't she a pretty gal?" and never took his eyes off her except when the negus[3] came in.

As for Captain Dobbin, he never so much as spoke to her during the whole evening. But he and Captain Porter of the 150th took home Jos to the hotel, who was in a very maudlin state, and had told his tiger-hunt story with great effect, both at the mess-table; and at the *soirée,*[4] to Mrs. O'Dowd in her turban and bird of paradise. Having put the Collector into the hands of his servant, Dobbin loitered about, smoking his cigar before the inn door. George had meanwhile very carefully shawled his wife, and brought her away from Mrs. O'Dowd's after a general hand-shaking from the young officers, who accompanied her to the fly, and cheered that vehicle as it drove off. So Amelia gave Dobbin her little hand as she got out of the carriage, and rebuked him smilingly for not having taken any notice of her all night.

The Captain continued that deleterious amusement of smoking, long after the inn and the street were gone to bed. He watched the lights vanish from George's sitting-room windows, and shine out in the bed-room close at hand. It was almost morning when he returned to his own quarters. He could hear the cheering from the ships in

2. This sentence is dropped out of the New York edition; it is changed in some nonauthorial editions, ambiguously, to: I will love all as I love him.
3. Hot drink of sweetened and spiced wine, water, and lemon.
4. Evening party.

the river, where the transports were already taking in their cargoes preparatory to dropping down the Thames.

## *Chapter XXVIII.*

### IN WHICH AMELIA INVADES THE LOW COUNTRIES.

THE regiment with its officers was to be transported in ships provided by His Majesty's government for the occasion: and in two days after the festive assembly at Mrs. O'Dowd's apartments, in the midst of cheering from all the East India ships in the river, and the military on shore, the band playing 'God save the King,' the officers waving their hats, and the crews hurrahing gallantly, the transports went down the river and proceeded under convoy to Ostend.[1] Meanwhile the gallant Jos had agreed to escort his sister and the Major's wife, the bulk of whose goods and chattels, including the famous bird of paradise and turban, were with the regimental baggage: so that our two heroines drove pretty much unencumbered to Ramsgate,[2] where there were plenty of packets plying, in one of which they had a speedy passage to Ostend.

That period of Jos's life which now ensued was so full of incident, that it served him for conversation for many years after, and even the tiger-hunt story was put aside for more stirring narratives which he had to tell about the great campaign of Waterloo. As soon as he had agreed to escort his sister abroad, it was remarked that he ceased shaving his upper lip. At Chatham he followed the parades and drills with great assiduity. He listened with the utmost attention to the conversation of his brother officers, (as he called them in after days sometimes,) and learned as many military names as he could. In these studies the excellent Mrs. O'Dowd was of great assistance to him; and on the day finally when they embarked on board the Lovely Rose[3] which was to carry them to their destination, he made his ap-

1. Belgian seaport.
2. English seaport south of Margate.
3. Also the name of a poem by Edmund Waller (1606–87), which ends:

   Then die, that she  
The common fate of all things rare  
   May read in thee;  
How small a part of time they share,  
   That are so wondrous sweet and fair. (Harden)

pearance in a braided frock-coat and duck trowsers, with a foraging cap ornamented with a smart gold band. Having his carriage with him, and informing everybody on board confidentially that he was going to join the Duke of Wellington's army, folks mistook him for a great personage, a commissary-general, or a government courier at the very least.

He suffered hugely on the voyage, during which the ladies were likewise prostrate; but Amelia was brought to life again as the packet made Ostend, by the sight of the transports conveying her regiment, which entered the harbour almost at the same time with the Lovely Rose. Jos went in a collapsed state to an inn, while Captain Dobbin escorted the ladies, and then busied himself in freeing Jos's carriage and luggage from the ship and the customhouse, for Mr. Jos was at present without a servant, Osborne's man and his own pampered menial having conspired together at Chatham, and refused point-blank to cross the water. This revolt, which came very suddenly, and on the last day, so alarmed Mr. Sedley, junior, that he was on the point of giving up the expedition, but Captain Dobbin (who made himself immensely officious in the business, Jos said), rated him and laughed at him soundly: the mustachios were grown in advance, and Jos finally was persuaded to embark. In place of the well-bred and well-fed London domestics, who could only speak English, Dobbin procured for Jos's party a swarthy little Belgian servant who could speak no language at all; but who by his bustling behaviour, and by invariably addressing Mr. Sedley as "My lord," speedily acquired that gentleman's favour. Times are altered at Ostend now; of the Britons who go thither, very few look like lords, or act like those members of our hereditary aristocracy. They seem for the most part shabby in attire, dingy of linen, lovers of billiards and brandy, and cigars and greasy ordinaries.[4]

But it may be said as a rule, that every Englishman in the Duke of Wellington's army paid his way. The remembrance of such a fact surely becomes a nation of shopkeepers.[5] It was a blessing for a commerce-loving country to be overrun by such an army of customers: and to have such creditable warriors to feed. And the country which they came to protect is not military. For a long period of history they have let other people fight there. When the present writer went to survey with eagle glance the field of Waterloo, we asked the conductor of the diligence,[6] a portly warlike-looking veteran, whether he had been at the battle. "*Pas si bête*"[7]—such an answer and sentiment as no Frenchman would own to—was his reply. But on the other hand, the postilion[8] who drove us was a *Viscount*, a son of some bankrupt Imperial General, who accepted a pennyworth of beer on the road. The moral is surely a good one.

4. Eating establishments.
5. Adam Smith referred to the English as a nation of shopkeepers in *The Wealth of Nations* (1776), from which, apparently, Napoleon picked up the expression and repeated it (Harden).
6. Stagecoach.
7. Not so foolish.
8. The post boy riding one of several horses drawing the coach.

This flat, flourishing, easy country never could have looked more rich and prosperous, than in that opening summer of 1815, when its green fields and quiet cities were enlivened by multiplied red-coats: when its wide *chaussées*[9] swarmed with brilliant English equipages: when its great canal-boats, gliding by rich pastures and pleasant quaint old villages, by old chateaux lying amongst old trees, were all crowded with well-to-do English travellers: when the soldier who drank at the village inn, not only drank, but paid his score; and Donald the Highlander, billeted in the Flemish farm-house, rocked the baby's cradle, while Jean and Jeannette were out getting in the hay.[1] As our painters are bent on military subjects just now, I throw out this as a good subject for the pencil, to illustrate the principle of an honest English war.[2] All looked as brilliant and harmless as a Hyde Park review. Meanwhile, Napoleon screened behind his curtain of frontier-fortresses, was preparing for the outbreak which was to drive all these orderly people into fury and blood; and lay so many of them low.

Everybody had such a perfect feeling of confidence in the leader (for the resolute faith which the Duke of Wellington had inspired in the whole English nation was as intense, as that more frantic enthusiasm with which at one time the French regarded Napoleon), the country seemed in so perfect a state of orderly defence, and the help at hand in case of need so near and overwhelming, that alarm was unknown, and that our travellers, among whom two were naturally of a very timid sort, were, like all the other multiplied English tourists, entirely at ease. The famous regiment, with so many of whose officers we have made acquaintance, was drafted in canal-boats to Bruges[3] and Ghent, thence to march to Brussels. Jos accompanied the ladies in the public boats; the which all old travellers in Flanders must remember for the luxury and accommodation they afforded. So prodigiously good was the eating and drinking on board these sluggish but most comfortable vessels, that there are legends extant of an English traveller who coming to Belgium for a week, and travelling in one of these boats, was so delighted with the fare there that he went backwards and forwards from Ghent to Bruges perpetually until the railroads were invented, when he drowned himself on the last trip of the passage-boat. Jos's death was not to be of this sort, but his comfort was exceeding, and Mrs. O'Dowd insisted that he only wanted her sister Glorvina to make his happiness complete. He sate on the roof of the cabin all day drinking Flemish beer, shouting for Isidor his servant, and talking gallantly to the ladies.

9. Roads.
1. This incident is mentioned in Mr. Gleig's recently published "Story of the Battle of Waterloo" (Thackeray's note). Gleig says: "It is recorded of the Highland regiments in particular, that so completely had they become domesticated with the people on whom they were billeted, that it was no unusual thing to find a kilted warrior rocking the cradle." In the reference to Gleig's book, the revised edition omits: recently published
2. On July 10, 1847, in *Punch* magazine Thackeray wrote a facetious review of a competitive exhibition at Westminster Hall, in which he objected to violence in military art. It is not clear how tongue-in-cheek is his remark, but the suggestion here is in keeping with it.
3. The trip from Ostend through Bruges to Ghent was made by canal boats pulled by draught animals.

His courage was prodigious. "Boney attack *us!*" he cried. "My dear creature, my poor Emmy, don't be frightened. There's no danger. The allies will be in Paris in two months, I tell you: when I'll take you to dine in the Palais Royal, by Jove. There are three hundred thousand Rooshians, I tell you, now entering France by Mayence[4] and the Rhine—three hundred thousand under Wittgenstein and Barclay de Tolly,[5] my poor love. You don't know military affairs, my dear. I do, and I tell you there's no infantry in France can stand against Rooshian infantry, and no general of Boney's that's fit to hold a candle to Wittgenstein. Then there are the Austrians, they are five hundred thousand if a man, and they are within ten marches of the frontier by this time under Schwartzenberg and Prince Charles.[6] Then there are the Prooshians under the gallant Prince Marshal.[7] Show me a cavalry chief like him now that Murat is gone. Hey, Mrs. O'Dowd? Do you think our little girl here need be afraid. Is there any cause for fear, Isidor? Hey, Sir? Get some more beer."

Mrs. O'Dowd said that her "Glorvina was not afraid of any man alive let alone a Frenchman," and tossed off a glass of beer with a wink which expressed her liking for the beverage.

Having frequently been in presence of the enemy, or, in other words, faced the ladies at Cheltenham and Bath, our friend, the Collector, had lost a great deal of his pristine timidity, and was now, especially when fortified with liquor, as talkative as might be. He was rather a favourite with the regiment, treating the young officers with sumptuosity, and amusing them by his military airs. And as there

4. Mainz: German city on the Rhine.
5. Russian commanders.
6. Jos is not as knowledgeable as he pretends, for Prince Charles *is* Schwartzenberg: Prince Karl Philipp von Schwarzenberg (1771–1820), Austrian commander.
7. The Prussian field marshal was prince of Wahlstadt, Gebhard Leberecht von Blücher (1742–1819). Joachim Murat, the brilliant French general, made king of Naples by Napoleon, briefly supported and then abandoned the Allied forces in 1815.

is one well-known regiment of the army which travels with a goat heading the column, whilst another is led by a deer, George said with respect to his brother-in-law, that his regiment marched with an elephant.[8]

Since Amelia's introduction to the regiment, George began to be rather ashamed of some of the company to which he had been forced to present her; and determined, as he told Dobbin (with what satisfaction to the latter it need not be said), to exchange into some better regiment soon, and to get his wife away from these[9] damned vulgar women. But this vulgarity of being ashamed of one's society is much more common among men than women; (except very great ladies of fashion, who, to be sure, indulge in it;) and Mrs. Amelia, a natural and unaffected person, had none of that artificial shamefacedness which her husband mistook for delicacy on his own part. Thus Mrs. O'Dowd had a cock's plume in her hat, and a very large "repayther"[1] on her stomach, which she used to ring on all occasions, narrating how it had been presented to her by her fawther, as she stipt into the car'ge after her mar'ge; and these ornaments, with other outward peculiarities of the Major's wife, gave excruciating agonies to Captain Osborne, when his wife and the Major's came in contact; whereas Amelia was only amused by the honest lady's eccentricities, and not in the least ashamed of her company.

As they made that well-known journey, which almost every Englishman of middle rank has travelled since, there might have been more instructive, but few more entertaining companions than Mrs. Major O'Dowd. "Talk about kenal boats, my dear. Ye should see the kenal boats between Dublin and Ballinasloe.[2] It's there the rapid travelling is; and the beautiful cattle. Sure me fawther got a goold medal (and his Excellency himself eat a slice of it, and said never was finer mate in his loif) for a four-year-old heifer, the like of which ye never saw in *this* country any day." And Jos owned with a sigh, "that for good streaky beef, really mingled with fat and lean, there was no country like England."

"Except Ireland, where all your best mate comes from," said the Major's lady; proceeding, as is not unusual with patriots of her nation, to make comparisons greatly in favour of her own country. The idea of comparing the market at Bruges with those of Dublin, although she had suggested it herself, caused immense scorn and derision on her part. "I'll thank ye to tell me what they mean by that old gazabo on the top of the market-place," said she, in a burst of ridicule fit to have brought the old tower down. The place was full of English soldiery as they passed. English bugles woke them in the morning: at night-fall they went to bed to the note of the British fife and drum: all the country and Europe was in arms, and the greatest event of history pending; and honest Peggy O'Dowd, whom it concerned as well as another, went on prattling about Ballinafad, and the

8. The goat and deer were emblems for the Royal Welsh Fusiliers and the Warwickshire regiments; Jos's regiment is, of course, nonexistent.
9. Revised edition reads: those
1. Repeater: a timepiece that repeated the sound of the hour at the touch of a button.
2. The Grand Canal connects Ballinasloe in the west of Ireland to Dublin on the east coast. Thackeray once made that trip in person but went by coach, not by canal.

Mrs. O'Dowd at the Flower Market

horses in the stables at Glenmalony, and the clar't drunk there; and Jos Sedley interposed about curry and rice at Dumdum; and Amelia thought about her husband, and how best she should show her love for him; as if these were the great topics of the world.

Those who like to lay down the History-book, and to speculate upon what *might* have happened in the world, but for the fatal occurrence of what actually did take place (a most puzzling, amusing, ingenious, and profitable kind of meditation) have no doubt often thought to themselves what a specially bad time Napoleon took to come back from Elba, and to let loose his eagle from Gulf San Juan to Notre Dame.[3] The historians on our side tell us that the armies of the allied powers were all providentially on a war-footing, and ready to bear down at a moment's notice upon the Elban Emperor. The august jobbers assembled at Vienna, and carving out the kingdoms of Europe according to their wisdom,[4] had such causes of quarrel among themselves as might have set the armies which had overcome Napoleon to fight against each other, but for the return of the object of unanimous hatred and fear. This monarch had an army in full force because he had jobbed to himself Poland, and was determined to keep it: another had robbed half Saxony, and was bent upon maintaining his acquisition: Italy was the object of a third's solicitude. Each was protesting against the rapacity of the other; and could the Corsican but have waited in his prison until all these parties were by the ears, he might have returned and reigned unmolested. But what would have become of our story and all our friends, then? If all the drops in it were dried up, what would become of the sea?

In the meanwhile the business of life and living and the pursuits of pleasure, especially, went on as if no end were to be expected to them, and no enemy in front. When our travellers arrived at Brussels, in which their regiment was quartered, a great piece of good fortune, as all said, they found themselves in one of the gayest and most brilliant little capitals in Europe, and where all the Vanity Fair booths were laid out with the most tempting liveliness and splendour. Gambling was here in profusion, and dancing in plenty: feasting was there to fill with delight that great gourmand of a Jos: there was a theatre where a miraculous Catalani[5] was delighting all hearers; beautiful rides, all enlivened with martial splendour; a rare old city, with strange costumes and wonderful architecture, to delight the eyes of little Amelia, who had never before seen a foreign country, and fill her with charming surprises: so that now and for a few weeks' space, in a fine handsome lodging, whereof the expenses were borne by Jos and Osborne, who was flush of money and full of kind attentions to his wife—for about a fortnight I say, during which her honeymoon

3. I.e., from the south coast of France to Paris.
4. The Congress of Vienna was the meeting of Russia, Prussia, Austria, Britain, France, and a few lesser countries to redraw the map of Europe. A contemporary cartoon shows Napoleon, back from Elba, throwing into confusion the party cutting up a cake in the shape of Europe.
5. Angélique Catalani (1780–1849), opera singer noted for her mechanical mastery and financial management, of whom Stendhal remarked that she had a silver throat and heart of stone.

ended, Mrs. Amelia was as pleased and happy as any little bride out of England.

Every day during this happy time there was novelty and amusement for all parties. There was a church to see, or a picture gallery—there was a ride, or an opera. The bands of the regiments were making music at all hours. The greatest folks of England walked in the Park—there was a perpetual military festival. George taking out his wife to a new jaunt or junket every night, was quite pleased with himself as usual, and swore he was becoming quite a domestic character. And a jaunt or a junket with *him!* Was it not enough to set this little heart beating with joy? Her letters home to her mother were filled with delight and gratitude at this season. Her husband bade her buy laces, millinery, jewels, and gimcracks of all sorts. Oh, he was the kindest, best, and most generous of men!

The sight of the very great company of lords and ladies and fashionable persons who thronged the town and appeared in every public place, filled George's truly British soul with intense delight. They flung off that happy frigidity and insolence of demeanour which occasionally characterises the great at home, and appearing in numberless public places, condescended to mingle with the rest of the company whom they met there. One night at a party given by the general of the division to which George's regiment belonged, he had the honour of dancing with Lady Blanche Thistlewood, Lord Bareacres' daughter; he bustled for ices and refreshments for the two noble ladies; he pushed and squeezed for Lady Bareacres' carriage; he bragged about the Countess when he got home, in a way which his own father could not have surpassed. He called upon the ladies the next day; he rode by their side in the Park; he asked their party to a great dinner at a restaurateur's, and was quite wild with exultation when they agreed to come. Old Bareacres, who had not much pride and a large appetite, would go for a dinner anywhere.

"I hope there will be no women besides our own party," Lady Bareacres said, after reflecting upon the invitation which had been made, and accepted with too much precipitancy.

"Gracious Heaven, Mamma—you don't suppose the man would bring his wife," shrieked Lady Blanche, who had been languishing in George's arms in the newly-imported waltz for hours the night before. "The men are bearable, but their women—"

"Wife, just married, dev'lish pretty woman, I hear," the old Earl said.

"Well, my dear Blanche," said the mother, "I suppose as Papa wants to go, we must go: but we needn't know them in England, you know." And so, determined to cut their new acquaintance in Bond Street, these great folks went to eat his dinner at Brussels, and condescending to make him pay for their pleasure, showed their dignity by making his wife uncomfortable, and carefully excluding her from the conversation. This is a species of dignity in which the high-bred British female reigns supreme. To watch the behaviour of a fine lady to other and humbler women is a very good sport for a philosophical frequenter of Vanity Fair.

This festival, on which honest George spent a great deal of money, was the very dismallest of all the entertainments which Amelia had in her honey-moon. She wrote the most piteous accounts of the feast home to her mamma: how the Countess of Bareacres would not answer when spoken to; how Lady Blanche stared at her with her eyeglass; and what a rage Captain Dobbin was in at their behaviour; and how my lord as they came away from the feast, asked to see the bill, and pronounced it a d— bad dinner, and d— dear. But though Amelia told all these stories, and wrote home regarding her guests' rudeness, and her own discomfiture; old Mrs. Sedley was mightily pleased nevertheless, and talked about Emmy's friend, the Countess of Bareacres, with such assiduity that the news how his son was entertaining Peers and Peeresses actually came to Osborne's ears in the City.

Those who know the present Lieutenant-General Sir George Tufto, K.C.B.,[6] and have seen him, as they may on most days in the season, padded and in stays, strutting down Pall-Mall with a ricketty swagger on his high-heeled lacquered boots, leering under the bonnets of passers by, or riding a showy chestnut, and ogling Broughams in the Parks—those who know the present Sir George Tufto would hardly recognise the daring Peninsula and Waterloo officer. He has thick curling brown hair and black eyebrows now, and his whiskers are of the deepest purple. He was light-haired and bald in 1815, and stouter in the person and in the limbs, which especially have shrunk very much of late. When he was about seventy years of age (he is now nearly eighty), his hair, which was very scarce and quite white, suddenly grew thick, and brown, and curly, and his whiskers and eyebrows took their present colour. Ill-natured people say that his chest is all wool, and that his hair, because it never grows, is a wig. Tom Tufto, with whose father he quarrelled ever so many years ago, declares that Mademoiselle de Jaisey,[7] of the French theatre, pulled his grandpapa's hair off in the green-room;[8] but Tom is notoriously spiteful and jealous; and the General's wig has nothing to do with our story.

One day, as some of our friends of the —th were sauntering in the flower-market of Brussels, having been to see the Hotel de Ville,[9] which Mrs. Major O'Dowd declared was not near so large or handsome as her fawther's mansion of Glenmalony, an officer of rank with an orderly behind him, rode up to the market, and descending from his horse, came amongst the flowers, and selected the very finest bouquet which money could buy. The beautiful bundle being tied up in a paper, the officer remounted, giving the nosegay into the charge of his military groom, who carried it with a grin, following his chief who rode away in great state and self-satisfaction.

"You should see the flowers at Glenmalony," Mrs. O'Dowd was remarking. "Me fawther has three Scotch garners with nine helpers. We have an acre of hot-houses, and pines as common as pays in the sayson. Our greeps weighs six pounds every bunch of 'em, and upon

6. Knight commander of the Bath, the middle of three orders of the Bath. See chapter XVIII.
7. A play on (English) Jasey, a wig made of worsted.
8. Actor's lounge.
9. City hall.

me honour and conscience I think our magnolias is as big as taykettles."

Dobbin, who never used to 'draw out' Mrs. O'Dowd as that wicked Osborne delighted in doing, (much to Amelia's terror, who implored him to spare her,) fell back in the crowd, crowing and sputtering until he reached a safe distance, when he exploded amongst the astonished market-people with shrieks of yelling laughter.

"Hwhat's that gawky guggling about?" said Mrs. O'Dowd. "Is it his nose bleedn? He always used to say 'twas his nose bleedn, till he must have pomped all the blood out of um. An't the magnolias at Glenmalony as big as taykettles, O'Dowd?"

"Deed then they are, and bigger, Peggy," the Major said. When the conversation was interrupted in the manner stated by the arrival of the officer who purchased the bouquet.

"Devlish fine horse,—who is it?" George asked.

"You should see me brother Molloy Malony's horse, Molasses, that won the cop at the Curragh,"[1] the Major's wife was exclaiming, and was continuing the family history, when her husband interrupted her by saying—

"It's General Tufto, who commands the —— cavalry division;" adding quietly, "he and I were both shot in the same leg at Talavera."[2]

"Where you got your step,"[3] said George with a laugh. "General Tufto! Then my dear the Crawleys are come."

Amelia's heart fell,—she knew not why. The sun did not seem to shine so bright. The tall old roofs and gables looked less picturesque all of a sudden, though it was a brilliant sunset, and one of the brightest and most beautiful days at the end of May.

1. Racecourse southwest of Dublin.
2. A battle in July 1809 in Spain where the British defeated the French.
3. "Step" means "promotion" as well as "gait."

## *Chapter XXIX.*

### BRUSSELS.

R. Jos had hired a pair of horses for his open carriage, with which cattle, and the smart London vehicle, he made a very tolerable figure in the drives about Brussels. George purchased a horse for his private riding, and he and Captain Dobbin would often accompany the carriage in which Jos and his sister took daily excursions of pleasure. They went out that day in the park for their accustomed diversion, and there, sure enough, George's remark with regard to the arrival of Rawdon Crawley and his wife proved to be correct. In the midst of a little troop of horsemen, consisting of some of the very greatest persons in Brussels, Rebecca was seen in the prettiest and tightest of riding-habits, mounted on a beautiful little Arab, which she rode to perfection (having acquired the art at Queen's Crawley, where the Baronet, Mr. Pitt, and Rawdon himself had given her many lessons), and by the side of the gallant General Tufto.

"Sure, it's the Juke himself," cried Mrs. Major O'Dowd to Jos, who began to blush violently; "and that's Lord Uxbridge[1] on the bay. How elegant he looks! Me brother, Molloy Malony,[2] is as like him as two peas."

Rebecca did not make for the carriage; but as soon as she perceived her old acquaintance Amelia seated in it, acknowledged her presence by a gracious word and smile, and by kissing and shaking her fingers playfully in the direction of the vehicle. Then she resumed her conversation with General Tufto, who asked "who the fat officer was in the gold-laced cap?" on which Becky replied, "that he was an officer in the East Indian service." But Rawdon Crawley rode out of the ranks of his company, and came up and shook hands heartily with Amelia, and said to Jos, "Well, old boy, how are you?" and stared in Mrs. O'Dowd's face and black cock's feathers until she began to think she had made a conquest of him.

George, who had been delayed behind, rode up almost immediately with Dobbin, and they touched their caps to the august personages, among whom Osborne at once perceived Mrs. Crawley. He was delighted to see Rawdon leaning over his carriage familiarly and talking to Amelia, and met the aide-de-camp's cordial greeting with

1. Juke: duke of Wellington. Lord Uxbridge: Henry William Paget (1768–1854), earl of Uxbridge, second in command.
2. This name appears variously as Maloney, Moloney, Maloneys, Malonies, and Malonys, but Malony and Malonies are the most frequent spellings and have been standarized.

more than corresponding warmth. The nods between Rawdon and Dobbin were of the very faintest specimens of politeness.

Crawley told George where they were stopping with General Tufto at the Hotel du Parc, and George made his friend promise to come speedily to Osborne's own residence. "Sorry I hadn't seen you three days ago," George said. "Had a dinner at the Restaurateur's—rather a nice thing. Lord Bareacres, and the Countess, and Lady Blanche, were good enough to dine with us—wish we'd had you." Having thus let his friend know his claims to be a man of fashion, Osborne parted from Rawdon, who followed the august squadron down an alley into which they cantered, while George and Dobbin resumed their places, one on each side of Amelia's carriage.

"How well the Juke looked," Mrs. O'Dowd remarked. "The Wellesleys and Malonies[3] are related; but, of course, poor *I* would never dream of introjuicing myself unless his Grace thought proper to remember our family-tie."

"He's a great soldier," Jos said, much more at ease now the great man was gone. "Was there ever a battle won like Salamanca?[4] Hey, Dobbin? But where was it he learnt his art? In India, my boy! The jungle's the school for a general, mark me that. I knew him myself, too, Mrs. O'Dowd: we both of us danced the same evening with Miss Cutler, daughter of Cutler of the Artillery, and a devilish fine girl, at Dumdum."[5]

The apparition of the great personages held them all in talk during the drive; and at dinner; and until the hour came when they were all to go to the Opera.

It was almost like Old England. The house was filled with familiar British faces, and those toilettes for which the British female has long been celebrated. Mrs. O'Dowd's was not the least splendid amongst these, and she had a curl on her forehead, and a set of Irish diamonds and Cairngorms,[6] which outshone all the decorations in the house, in her notion. Her presence used to excruciate Osborne; but go she would upon all parties of pleasure on which she heard her young friends were bent. It never entered into her thought but that they must be charmed with her company.

"She's been useful to you, my dear," George said to his wife, whom he could leave alone with less scruple when she had this society.[7] "But what a comfort it is that Rebecca's come: you will have her for a friend, and we may get rid now of this damn'd Irishwoman." To this Amelia did not answer, yes or no: and how do we know what her thoughts were?

The *coup d'œil*[8] of the Brussels opera-house did not strike Mrs. O'Dowd as being so fine as the theatre in Fishamble Street, Dublin, nor was French music at all equal in her opinion to the melodies of

3. The duke of Wellington (Arthur Welleseley) did have Irish family through his mother, but the Malonies are fictional.
4. On July 22, 1812, Wellingon defeated the French at Salamanca, a Spanish city northwest of Madrid.
5. Wellington served in India from 1797 to 1805.
6. Yellow or wine-colored rock crystals.
7. First and second printings read: company.
8. First impression.

her native country. She favoured her friends with these and other opinions in a very loud tone of voice, and tossed about a great clattering fan she sported, with the most splendid complacency.

"Who is that wonderful woman with Amelia, Rawdon, love?" said a lady in an opposite box (who, almost always civil to her husband in private, was more fond than ever of him in company). "Don't you see that creature with a yellow thing in her turban, and a red satin gown, and a great watch?"

"Near the pretty little woman in white?" asked a middle-aged gentleman seated by the querist's side, with orders in his button, and several under-waistcoats, and a great, choky, white stock.[9]

"That pretty woman in white is Amelia, General: you are remarking all the pretty women, you naughty man."

"Only one, begad, in the warld!" said the General, delighted, and the lady gave him a tap with a large bouquet which she had.

"Bedad it's him," said Mrs. O'Dowd; "and that's the very bokay he bought in the Marshy aux Flures!"[1] and when Rebecca, having caught her friend's eye, performed the little hand-kissing operation once more, Mrs. Major O'D., taking the compliment to herself, returned the salute with a gracious smile, which sent that unfortunate Dobbin shrieking out of the box again.

At the end of the act, George was out of the box in a moment, and

9. Neck cloth.
1. *Marché aux fleurs*: flower market.

he was even going to pay his respects to Rebecca in her *loge.*[2] He met Crawley in the lobby, however, where they exchanged a few sentences upon the occurrences of the last fortnight.

"You found my cheque all right at the agent's?" George said, with a knowing air.

"All right, my boy," Rawdon answered. "Happy to give you your revenge. Governor come round?"

"Not yet," said George, "but he will; and you know I've some private fortune through my mother. Has Aunty relented?"

"Sent me twenty pound, damned old screw. When shall we have a meet? The General dines out on Tuesday. Can't you come Tuesday? I say, make Sedley cut off his moustache. What the devil does a civilian mean with a moustache and those infernal frogs to his coat. By-bye. Try and come on Tuesday;" and Rawdon was going off with two brilliant young gentlemen of fashion, who were, like himself, on the staff of a general officer.

George was only half pleased to be asked to dinner on that particular day when the General was *not* to dine. "I will go in and pay my respects to your wife," said he; at which Rawdon said, "Hm, as you please," looking very glum, and at which the two young officers exchanged knowing glances. George parted from them, and strutted down the lobby to the General's box, the number of which he had carefully counted.

"*Entrez,*"[3] said a clear little voice, and our friend found himself in Rebecca's presence; who jumped up, clapped her hands together, and held out both of them to George, so charmed was she to see him. The General, with the orders in his button, stared at the new comer with a sulky scowl, as much as to say, who the devil are you?

"My dear Captain George!" cried little Rebecca in an ecstacy. "How good of you to come. The General and I were moping together *tête-à-tête.* General, this is my Captain George of whom you heard me talk."

"Indeed," said the General, with a very small bow, "of what regiment is Captain George?"

George mentioned the —th: how he wished he could have said it was a crack cavalry corps.

"Come home lately from the West Indies, I believe. Not seen much service in the late war. Quartered here, Captain George?"—the General went on with killing haughtiness.

"Not Captain George, you stupid man; Captain Osborne," Rebecca said. The General all the while was looking savagely from one to the other.

"Captain Osborne, indeed! Any relation to the L— Osbornes?"

"We bear the same arms," George said, as indeed was the fact; Mr. Osborne having consulted with a herald in Long Acre, and picked the L— arms out of the peerage, when he set up his carriage fifteen years before.[4] The General made no reply to this announcement; but took

2. Mezzanine box.
3. Enter.
4. George Frederick Osborne, sixth duke of Leeds (1775–1838), was no relation to George Osborne. The herald in Long Acre had set up shop in the coach-building district.

up his opera-glass—the double-barrelled lorgnon was not invented in those days—and pretended to examine the house; but Rebecca saw that his disengaged eye was working round in her direction, and shooting out blood-shot glances at her and George.

She redoubled in cordiality. "How is dearest Amelia? But I needn't ask: how pretty she looks! And who is that nice good-natured looking creature with her—a flame of yours? O, you wicked men! And there is Mr. Sedley eating ices, I declare: how he seems to enjoy it! General, why have we not had any ices?"

"Shall I go and fetch you some?" said the General, bursting with wrath.

"Let *me* go, I entreat you," George said.

"No, I will go to Amelia's box. Dear, sweet girl! Give me your arm, Captain George;" and so saying, and with a nod to the General, she tripped into the lobby. She gave George the queerest, knowingest look, when they were together, a look which might have been interpreted, "Don't you see the state of affairs, and what a fool I'm making of him?" But he did not perceive it. He was thinking of his own plans, and lost in pompous admiration of his own irresistible powers of pleasing.

The curses to which the General gave a low utterance, as soon as Rebecca and her conqueror had quitted him, were so deep, that I am sure no compositor in Messrs. Bradbury and Evans's establishment[5] would venture to print them were they written down. They came from the General's heart; and a wonderful thing it is to think that the human heart is capable of generating such produce, and can throw out, as occasion demands, such a supply of lust and fury, rage and hatred.

Amelia's gentle eyes, too, had been fixed anxiously on the pair, whose conduct had so chafed the jealous General; but when Rebecca entered her box, she flew to her friend with an affectionate rapture which showed itself, in spite of the publicity of the place; for she embraced her dearest friend in the presence of the whole house, at least in full view of the General's glass, now brought to bear upon the Osborne party. Mrs. Rawdon saluted Jos, too, with the kindliest greeting: she admired Mrs. O'Dowd's large Cairngorm brooch and superb Irish diamonds, and wouldn't believe that they were not from Golconda[6] direct. She bustled, she chattered, she turned and twisted, and smiled upon one, and smirked on another, all in full view of the jealous opera-glass opposite. And when the time for the ballet came (in which there was no dancer that went through her grimaces or performed her comedy of action better), she skipped back to her own box, leaning on Captain Dobbin's arm this time. No, she would not have George's: he must stay and talk to his dearest, best, little Amelia.

"What a humbug that woman is," honest old Dobbin mumbled to George, when he came back from Rebecca's box, whither he had conducted her in perfect silence, and with a countenance as glum as

5. Original typesetters and publishers of *Vanity Fair*.
6. Formerly a center of diamond trade in India.

an undertaker's. "She writhes and twists about like a snake. All the time she was here, didn't you see, George, how she was acting at the General over the way?"

"Humbug—acting? Hang it, she's the nicest little woman in England," George replied, showing his white teeth, and giving his ambrosial whiskers a twirl. "You ain't a man of the world, Dobbin. Dammy, look at her now, she's talked over Tufto in no time. Look how he's laughing! Gad, what a shoulder she has! Emmy, why didn't you have a bouquet? Everybody has a bouquet."

"Faith, then, why didn't you *boy* one?" Mrs. O'Dowd said; and both Amelia and William Dobbin thanked her for this timely observation. But beyond this neither of the ladies rallied. Amelia was overpowered by the flash and the dazzle and the fashionable talk of her worldly rival. Even the O'Dowd was silent and subdued after Becky's brilliant apparition, and scarcely said a word more about Glenmalony all the evening.

"When do you intend to give up play, George, as you have promised me any time these hundred years?" Dobbin said to his friend a few days after the night at the Opera. "When do you intend to give up sermonising?" was the other's reply. "What the deuce, man, are you alarmed about? We play low; I won last night. You don't suppose Crawley cheats? With fair play it comes to pretty much the same thing at the year's end."

"But I don't think he could pay if he lost," Dobbin said; and his advice met with the success which advice usually commands. Osborne and Crawley were repeatedly together now. General Tufto dined abroad almost constantly. George was always welcome in the apartments (very close indeed to those of the General), which the Aide-de-camp and his wife occupied in the hotel.

Amelia's manners were such when she and George visited Crawley and his wife at these quarters, that they had very nearly come to their first quarrel; that is, George scolded his wife violently for her evident unwillingness to go, and the high and mighty manner in which she comported herself towards Mrs. Crawley, her old friend; and Amelia did not say one single word in reply; but with her husband's eye upon her, and Rebecca scanning her as she felt, was, if possible, more bashful and awkward on the second visit which she paid to Mrs. Rawdon, than on her first call.

Rebecca was doubly affectionate, of course, and would not take notice, in the least, of her friend's coolness. "I think Emmy has become prouder since her father's name was in the —, since Mr. Sedley's *misfortunes*," Rebecca said, softening the phrase charitably for George's ear.

"Upon my word, I thought when we were at Brighton she was doing me the honour to be jealous of me; and now I suppose she is scandalised because Rawdon, and I, and the General live together. Why, my dear creature, how could we, with our means, live at all, but for a friend to share expenses? And do you suppose that Rawdon is not big enough to take care of my honour? But I'm very much obliged to Emmy, very," Mrs. Rawdon said.

"Pooh, jealousy!" answered George, "all women are jealous."

"And all men too. Weren't you jealous of General Tufto, and the General of you, on the night of the Opera? Why, he was ready to eat me for going with you to visit that foolish little wife of your's; as if I care a pin for either of you," Crawley's wife said, with a pert toss of her head. "Will you dine here? The dragon dines with the Commander-in-Chief. Great news is stirring. They say the French have crossed the frontier. We shall have a quiet dinner."

George accepted the invitation, although his wife was a little ailing. They were now not quite six weeks married. Another woman was laughing or sneering at her expense, and he not angry. He was not even angry with himself, this good-natured fellow. It is a shame, he owned to himself; but hang it, if a pretty woman *will* throw herself into your way, why, what can a fellow do, you know? I *am* rather free about women, he had often said, smiling and nodding knowingly to Stubble and Spooney, and other comrades of the mess-table; and they rather respected him than otherwise for this prowess. Next to conquering in war, conquering in love has been a source of pride, time out of mind, amongst men in Vanity Fair, or how should schoolboys brag of their amours, or Don Juan be popular?

So Mr. Osborne, having a firm conviction in his own mind that he was a woman-killer and destined to conquer, did not run counter to his fate, but yielded himself up to it quite complacently. And as Emmy did not say much or plague him with her jealousy, but merely became unhappy and pined over it miserably in secret, he chose to fancy that she was not suspicious of what all his acquaintance were perfectly aware—namely, that he was carrying on a desperate flirtation with Mrs. Crawley. He rode with her whenever she was free. He pretended regimental business to Amelia, (by which falsehood she was not in the least deceived) and consigning his wife to solitude or her brother's society, passed his evenings in the Crawleys' company; losing money to the husband and flattering himself that the wife was dying in love for him. It is very likely that this worthy couple never absolutely conspired, and agreed together in so many words: the one to cajole the young gentleman, whilst the other won his money at cards: but they understood each other perfectly well, and Rawdon let Osborne come and go with entire good-humour.

George was so occupied with his new acquaintances that he and William Dobbin were by no means so much together as formerly. George avoided him in public and in the regiment, and, as we see, did not like those sermons which his senior was disposed to inflict upon him. If some parts of his conduct made Captain Dobbin exceedingly grave and cool; of what use was it to tell George that though his whiskers were large, and his own opinion of his knowingness great, he was as green as a schoolboy? that Rawdon was making a victim of him as he had done of many before, and as soon as he had used him would fling him off with scorn? He would not listen: and so, as Dobbin upon those days when he visited the Osborne house, seldom had the advantage of meeting his old friend, much painful and unavailing talk between them was spared. Our friend George was in the full career of the pleasures of Vanity Fair.

There never was, since the days of Darius,[7] such a brilliant train of camp-followers as hung round the train of the Duke of Wellington's army in the Low Countries, in 1815; and led it dancing and feasting, as it were, up to the very brink of battle. A certain ball which a noble Duchess gave at Brussels on the 15th of June in the above-named year is historical.[8] All Brussels had been in a state of excitement about it, and I have heard from ladies who were in that town at the period, that the talk and interest of persons of their own sex regarding the ball was much greater even than in respect of the enemy in their front. The struggles, intrigues, and prayers to get tickets were such as only English ladies will employ, in order to gain admission to the society of the great of their own nation.

Jos and Mrs. O'Dowd, who were panting to be asked, strove in vain to procure tickets; but others of our friends were more lucky. For instance, through the interest of my Lord Bareacres, and as a set-off for the dinner at the restaurateur's, George got a card for Captain and Mrs. Osborne; which circumstance greatly elated him. Dobbin, who was a friend of the General commanding the division in which their regiment was, came laughing one day to Mrs. Osborne, and displayed a similar invitation, which made Jos envious, and George wonder how the deuce *he* should be getting into society. Mr. and Mrs. Rawdon, finally, were of course invited; as became the friends of a General commanding a cavalry brigade.

On the appointed night, George, having commanded new dresses and ornaments of all sorts for Amelia, drove to the famous ball, where his wife did not know a single soul. After looking about for Lady Bareacres, who cut him, thinking the card was quite enough—and after placing Amelia on a bench, he left her to her own cogitations there, thinking, on his own part, that he had behaved very handsomely in getting her new clothes, and bringing her to the ball, where she was free to amuse herself as she liked. Her thoughts were not of the pleasantest, and nobody except honest Dobbin came to disturb them.

Whilst her appearance was an utter failure (as her husband felt with a sort of rage), Mrs. Rawdon Crawley's *début* was, on the contrary, very brilliant. She arrived very late. Her face was radiant; her dress perfection. In the midst of the great persons assembled, and the eye-glasses directed to her,[9] Rebecca seemed to be as cool and collected as when she used to marshal Miss Pinkerton's little girls to church. Numbers of the men she knew already, and the dandies thronged round her. As for the ladies, it was whispered among them that Rawdon had run away with her from out of a convent, and that she was a relation of the Montmorency family. She spoke French so perfectly that there might be some truth in this report, and it was agreed that her manners were fine, and her air *distingué*. Fifty would-be partners thronged round her at once, and pressed to have the

7. Persian ruler (521–486 B.C.) defeated by the Greeks at Marathon.
8. Charlotte, duchess of Richmond (d. 1842), hosted this famous ball, which features in Byron's *Childe Harold*, Canto III.
9. The first edition reads: perfection, in the midst of the great persons assembled, and the eye-glasses directed to her.

honour to dance with her. But she said she was engaged, and only going to dance very little; and made her way at once to the place where Emmy sate quite unnoticed, and dismally unhappy. And so, to finish the poor child at once, Mrs. Rawdon ran and greeted affectionately her dearest Amelia, and began forthwith to patronise her. She found fault with her friend's dress, and her hair-dresser, and wondered how she could be so *chaussée,*[1] and vowed that she must send her *corsetière*[2] the next morning. She vowed that it was a delightful ball; that there was everybody that every one knew, and only a *very* few nobodies in the whole room. It is a fact, that in a fortnight, and after three dinners in general society, this young woman had got up the genteel jargon so well, that a native could not speak it better; and it was only from her French being so good, that you could know she was not a born woman of fashion.

George, who had left Emmy on her bench on entering the ball-room, very soon found his way back when Rebecca was by her dear friend's side. Becky was just lecturing Mrs. Osborne upon the follies which her husband was committing. "For God's sake, stop him from gambling, my dear," she said, "or he will ruin himself. He and Rawdon are playing at cards every night, and you know he is very poor, and Rawdon will win every shilling from him if he does not take care. Why don't you prevent him, you little careless creature? Why don't you come to us of an evening, instead of moping at home with that Captain Dobbin? I dare say he is *très-aimable;*[3] but how could one love a man with feet of such size? Your husband's feet are darlings—Here he comes. Where have you been, wretch? Here is Emmy crying her eyes out for you. Are you coming to fetch me for the quadrille?" And she left her bouquet and shawl by Amelia's side, and tripped off with George to dance. Women only know how to wound so. There is a poison on the tips of their little shafts, which stings a thousand times more than a man's blunter weapon. Our poor Emmy, who had never hated, never sneered all her life, was powerless in the hands of her remorseless little enemy.

George danced with Rebecca twice or thrice—how many times Amelia scarcely knew. She sate quite unnoticed in her corner, except when Rawdon came up with some words of clumsy conversation: and later in the evening, when Captain Dobbin made so bold as to bring her refreshments and sit beside her. He did not like to ask her why she was so sad; but as a pretext for the tears which were filling in her eyes, she told him that Mrs. Crawley had alarmed her by telling her that George would go on playing.

"It is curious, when a man is bent upon play, by what clumsy rogues he will allow himself to be cheated," Dobbin said; and Emmy said, "Indeed." She was thinking of something else. It was not the loss of the money that grieved her.

At last George came back for Rebecca's shawl and flowers. She was going away. She did not even condescend to come back and say good bye to Amelia. The poor girl let her husband come and go

1. Shod.
2. Corset maker.
3. Very agreeable.

without saying a word, and her head fell on her breast. Dobbin had been called away, and was whispering deep in conversation with the general of the division, his friend, and had not seen this last parting. George went away then with the bouquet; but when he gave it to the owner, there lay a note, coiled like a snake among the flowers. Rebecca's eye caught it at once. She had been used to deal with notes in early life. She put out her hand and took the nosegay. He saw by her eyes as they met, that she was aware what she should find there. Her husband hurried her away, still too intent upon his own thoughts, seemingly, to take note of any marks of recognition which might pass between his friend and his wife. These were, however, but trifling. Rebecca gave George her hand with one of her usual quick knowing glances, and made a curtsey and walked away. George bowed over the hand, said nothing in reply to a remark of Crawley's, did not hear it even, his brain was so throbbing with triumph and excitement, and allowed them to go away without a word.

His wife saw the one part at least of the bouquet-scene. It was quite natural that George should come at Rebecca's request to get her her scarf and flowers: it was no more than he had done twenty times before in the course of the last few days; but now it was too much for her. "William," she said, suddenly clinging to Dobbin, who was near her, "you've always been very kind to me—I'm—I'm not well. Take me home." She did not know she called him by his Christian name, as George was accustomed to do. He went away with her quickly. Her lodgings were hard by; and they threaded through the crowd without, where everything seemed to be more astir than even in the ball-room within.

George had been angry twice or thrice at finding his wife up on his return from the parties which he frequented: so she went straight to bed now; but although she did not sleep, and although the din and clatter and the galloping of horsemen was incessant, she never heard any of these noises, having quite other disturbances to keep her awake.

Osborne meanwhile, wild with elation, went off to a play-table, and began to bet frantically. He won repeatedly. "Everything succeeds with me to-night," he said. But his luck at play even did not cure him of his restlessness, and he started up after awhile, pocketing his winnings, and went to a buffet, where he drank off many bumpers of wine.

Here, as he was rattling away to the people around, laughing loudly and wild with spirits, Dobbin found him. He had been to the card-tables to look there for his friend. Dobbin looked as pale and grave as his comrade was flushed and jovial.

"Hullo, Dob! Come and drink, old Dob! The Duke's wine is famous. Give me some more, you Sir;" and he held out a trembling glass for the liquor.

"Come out, George," said Dobbin, still gravely; "don't drink."

"Drink! there's nothing like it. Drink yourself, and light up your lantern jaws, old boy. Here's to you."

Dobbin went up and whispered something to him, at which George, giving a start and a wild hurray, tossed off his glass, clapped

Mrs. Osborne's carriage stopping the way

it on the table, and walked away speedily on his friend's arm. "The enemy has passed the Sambre,"[4] William said, "and our left is already engaged. Come away. We are to march in three hours."

Away went George, his nerves quivering with excitement at the news so long looked for, so sudden when it came. What were love and intrigue now? He thought about a thousand things but these in his rapid walk to his quarters—his past life and future chances—the fate which might be before him—the wife, the child perhaps, from whom unseen he might be about to part. Oh, how he wished that night's work undone! and that with a clear conscience at least he might say farewell to the tender and guileless being by whose love he had set such little store!

He thought over his brief married life. In those few weeks he had frightfully dissipated his little capital. How wild and reckless he had been! Should any mischance befal him: what was then left for her? How unworthy he was of her. Why had he married her? He was not fit for marriage. Why had he disobeyed his father, who had been always so generous to him? Hope, remorse, ambition, tenderness, and selfish regret filled his heart. He sate down and wrote to his father, remembering what he had said once before, when he was engaged to fight a duel. Dawn faintly streaked the sky as he closed this farewell letter. He sealed it, and kissed the superscription. He thought how he had deserted that generous father, and of the thousand kindnesses which the stern old man had done him.

He had looked into Amelia's bed-room when he entered; she lay quiet, and her eyes seemed closed, and he was glad that she was asleep. On arriving at his quarters from the ball, he had found his regimental servant already making preparations for his departure: the man had understood his signal to be still, and these arrangements were very quickly and silently made. Should he go in and wake Amelia, he thought, or leave a note for her brother to break the news of departure to her? He went in to look at her once again.

She had been awake when he first entered her room, but had kept her eyes closed, so that even her wakefulness should not seem to reproach him. But when he had returned, so soon after herself, too, this timid little heart had felt more at ease, and turning towards him as he stept softly out of the room, she had fallen into a light sleep. George came in and looked at her again, entering still more softly. By the pale night-lamp he could see her sweet, pale face—the purple eyelids were fringed and closed, and one round arm, smooth and white, lay outside of the coverlet. Good God! how pure she was; how gentle, how tender, and how friendless! and he, how selfish, brutal, and black with crime! Heart-stained, and shame-stricken, he stood at the bed's foot, and looked at the sleeping girl. How dared he—who was he, to pray for one so spotless! God bless her! God bless her! He came to the bed-side, and looked at the hand, the little soft hand, lying asleep; and he bent over the pillow noiselessly towards the gentle pale face.

4. River in Belgium southwest of Brussels.

Two fair arms closed tenderly round his neck as he stooped down. "I am awake, George," the poor child said, with a sob fit to break the little heart that nestled so closely by his own. She was awake, poor soul, and to what? At that moment a bugle from the Place of Arms began sounding clearly, and was taken up through the town; and amidst the drums of the infantry, and the shrill pipes of the Scotch, the whole city awoke.

*Number 9* *Sept. 1847*

## *Chapter XXX.*

### "THE GIRL I LEFT BEHIND ME."

WE do not claim to rank among the military novelists. Our place is with the non-combatants. When the decks are cleared for action we go below and wait meekly. We should only be in the way of the manœuvres that the gallant fellows are performing over head. We shall go no farther with the —th than to the city gate: and leaving Major O'Dowd to his duty, come back to the Major's wife, and the ladies and the baggage.

Now, the Major and his lady, who had not been invited to the ball at which in our last chapter other of our friends figured, had much more time to take their wholesome natural rest in bed, than was accorded to people who wished to enjoy pleasure as well as to do duty. "It's my belief, Peggy, my dear," said he, as he placidly pulled his night-cap over his ears, "that there will be such a ball danced in a day or two as some of 'em has never heard the chune of;" and he was much more happy to retire to rest after partaking of a quiet tumbler, than to figure at any other sort of amusement. Peggy, for her part, would have liked to have shown her turban and bird of paradise at the ball, but for the information which her husband had given her, and which made her very grave.

"I'd like ye wake me about half an hour before the assembly beats," the Major said to his lady. "Call me at half-past one, Peggy, dear, and see me things is ready. May be I'll not come back to breakfast, Mrs. O'D." With which words, which signified his opinion that the regiment would march the next morning, the Major ceased talking, and fell asleep.

Mrs. O'Dowd, the good housewife, arrayed in curl-papers and a camisole, felt that her duty was to act, and not to sleep, at this juncture. "Time enough for that," she said, "when Mick's gone;" and so she packed his travelling-valise ready for the march, brushed his cloak, his cap, and other warlike habiliments, set them out in order

Venus preparing the armour of Mars

for him; and stowed away in the cloak-pockets a light package of portable refreshments, and a wicker-covered flask or pocket-pistol, containing near a pint of a remarkably sound Cognac brandy, of which she and the Major approved very much, and as soon as the hands of the "repayther" pointed to half-past one, and its interior arrangements (it had a tone quite aqual to a cathaydral, its fair owner considered) knelled forth that fatal hour, Mrs. O'Dowd woke up her Major, and had as comfortable a cup of coffee prepared for him as any made that morning in Brussels. And who is there will deny that this worthy lady's preparations betokened affection as much as the fits of tears and hysterics by which more sensitive females exhibited their love, and that their partaking of this coffee, which they drank together while the bugles were sounding the turn-out and the drums beating in the various quarters of the town, was not more useful and to the purpose than the outpouring of any mere sentiment could be? The consequence was, that the Major appeared on parade quite trim, fresh, and alert, his well-shaved rosy countenance, as he sate on horseback, giving cheerfulness and confidence to the whole corps. All the officers saluted her when the regiment marched by the balcony on which this brave woman stood, and waved them a cheer as they passed; and I daresay it was not from want of courage, but from a sense of female delicacy and propriety, that she refrained from leading the gallant —th personally into action.

On Sundays, and at periods of a solemn nature, Mrs. O'Dowd used to read with great gravity out of a large volume of her uncle the Dean's sermons. It had been of great comfort to her on board the transport as they were coming home, and were very nearly wrecked on their return from the West Indies. After the regiment's departure she betook herself to this volume for meditation; perhaps she did not understand much of what she was reading, and her thoughts were elsewhere: but the sleep project, with poor Mick's nightcap there on the pillow, was quite a vain one. So it is in the world. Jack or Donald marches away to glory with his knapsack on his shoulder, stepping out briskly to the tune of "The Girl I left behind me." It is she who remains and suffers,—and has the leisure to think, and brood, and remember.

Knowing how useless regrets are, and how the indulgence of sentiment only serves to make people more miserable, Mrs. Rebecca wisely determined to give way to no vain feelings of sorrow, and bore the parting from her husband with quite a Spartan equanimity. Indeed Captain Rawdon himself was much more affected at the leave-taking than the resolute little woman to whom he bade farewell. She had mastered this rude coarse nature; and he loved and worshipped her with all his faculties of regard and admiration. In all his life he had never been so happy, as, during the past few months, his wife had made him. All former delights of turf, mess, hunting-field, and gambling-table; all previous loves and courtships of milliners, opera-dancers, and the like easy triumphs of the clumsy military Adonis, were quite insipid when compared to the lawful matrimonial pleasures which of late he had enjoyed. She had known perpetually how to divert him; and he had found his house and her society a thousand times more pleasant than any place or company which he had ever frequented from his childhood until now. And he cursed his past follies and extravagances, and bemoaned his vast outlying debts above all, which must remain for ever as obstacles to prevent his wife's advancement in the world. He had often groaned over these in midnight conversations with Rebecca, although as a bachelor they had never given him any disquiet. He himself was struck with this phenomenon. "Hang it," he would say (or perhaps use a still stronger expression out of his simple vocabulary) "before I was married I didn't care what bills I put my name to, and so long as Moses would wait or Levy would renew for three months, I kept on never minding. But since I'm married, except renewing of course, I give you my honour I've not touched a bit of stamped paper."[1]

Rebecca always knew how to conjure away these moods of melancholy. "Why, my stupid love," she would say, "we have not done with your aunt yet. If she fails us, isn't there what you call the Gazette? or, stop, when your uncle Bute's life drops, I have another scheme. The living has always belonged to the younger brother, and why shouldn't you sell out and go into the Church?" The idea of this conversion set Rawdon into roars of laughter: you might have heard the explosion through the hotel at midnight, and the haw-haws of the great dragoon's voice. General Tufto heard him from his quarters on the first floor above them; and Rebecca acted the scene with great spirit, and preached Rawdon's first sermon, to the immense delight of the General at breakfast.

But these were mere by-gone days and talk. When the final news arrived that the campaign was opened, and the troops were to march, Rawdon's gravity became such that Becky rallied him about it in a manner which rather hurt the feelings of the Guardsman. "You don't suppose I'm afraid, Becky, I should think," he said, with a tremor in his voice. "But I'm a pretty good mark for a shot, and you see if it brings me down, why I leave one and perhaps two behind me whom I should wish to provide for, as I brought 'em into the scrape. It is no laughing matter *that,* Mrs. C., anyways."

Rebecca by a hundred caresses and kind words tried to soothe the feelings of the wounded lover. It was only when her vivacity and sense of humour got the better of this sprightly creature (as they would do under most circumstances of life indeed,) that she would break out with her satire, but she could soon put on a demure face. "Dearest love," she said, "do you suppose I feel nothing?" and, hastily dashing something from her eyes, she looked up in her husband's face with a smile.

"Look here," said he. "If I drop let us see what there is for you. I have had a pretty good run of luck here, and here's two hundred and thirty pounds. I have got ten Napoleons[2] in my pocket. That is as much as I shall want; for the General pays everything like a prince; and if I'm hit, why you know I cost nothing. Don't cry, little woman; I may live to vex you yet. Well, I shan't take either of my

1. Promissory notes required a stamp (tax) to be official.
2. Twenty-franc gold coins.

horses, but shall ride the General's grey charger: it's cheaper, and I told him mine was lame. If I'm done, those two ought to fetch you something. Grigg offered ninety for the mare yesterday, before this confounded news came, and like a fool I wouldn't let her go under the two 0's. Bulfinch will fetch his price any day, only you'd better sell him in this country, because the dealers have so many bills of mine, and so I'd rather he shouldn't go back to England. Your little mare the General gave you will fetch something, and there's no d—d livery stable bills here as there are in London," Rawdon added, with a laugh. "There's that dressing-case cost me two hundred,—that is, I owe two for it; and the gold tops and bottles must be worth thirty or forty. Please to put *that* up the spout,[3] ma'am, with my pins, and rings, and watch and chain, and things. They cost a precious lot of money. Miss Crawley, I know, paid a hundred down for the chain and ticker. Gold tops and bottles, indeed! dammy, I'm sorry I didn't take more now. Edwards pressed on me a silver-gilt boot-jack, and I might have had a dressing-case fitted up with a silver warming-pan, and a service of plate. But we must make the best of what we've got, Becky, you know."

And so, making his last dispositions, Captain Crawley, who had seldom thought about anything but himself, until the last few months of his life, when Love had obtained the mastery over the dragoon, went through the various items of his little catalogue of effects, striving to see how they might be turned into money for his wife's benefit, in case any accident should befal him. He pleased himself by noting down with a pencil, in his big school-boy handwriting, the various items of his portable property which might be sold for his widow's advantage—as for example, "My double-barril by Manton, say 40 guineas; my driving cloak, lined with sable fur, £50; my duelling pistols in rosewood case, (same which I shot Captain Marker), £20; my regulation saddle-holsters and housings; my Laurie ditto,"[4] and so forth, over all of which articles he made Rebecca the mistress.

Faithful to his plan of economy, the Captain dressed himself in his oldest and shabbiest uniform and epaulets, leaving the newest behind, under his wife's (or it might be his widow's) guardianship. And this famous dandy of Windsor[5] and Hyde Park went off on his campaign with a kit as modest as that of a serjeant, and with something like a prayer on his lips for the woman he was leaving. He took her up from the ground, and held her in his arms for a minute, tight pressed against his strong-beating heart. His face was purple and his eyes dim, as he put her down and left her. He rode by his General's side, and smoked his cigar in silence as they hastened after the troops of the General's brigade, which preceded them; and it was not until they were some miles on their way that he left off twirling his moustache and broke silence.

And Rebecca, as we have said, wisely determined not to give way to unavailing sentimentality on her husband's departure. She waved

3. Pawnshops had lifts, called spouts, for raising pawned objects into storage.
4. Manton: double barreled shotgun made by the London gunsmith Joseph Manton. Laurie: saddle made by Peter and John Laurie (Harden).
5. Villiage and royal residence west of London.

him an adieu from the window, and stood there for a moment looking out after he was gone. The cathedral towers and the full gables of the quaint old houses were just beginning to blush in the sunrise. There had been no rest for her that night. She was still in her pretty ball-dress, her fair hair hanging somewhat out of curl on her neck, and the circles round her eyes dark with watching. "What a fright I seem," she said, examining herself in the glass, "and how pale this pink makes one look!" So she divested herself of this pink raiment; in doing which a note fell out from her corsage, which she picked up with a smile, and locked into her dressing-box. And then she put her bouquet of the ball into a glass of water, and went to bed, and slept very comfortably.

The town was quite quiet when she woke up at ten o'clock, and partook of coffee, very requisite and comfortable after the exhaustion and grief of the morning's occurrences.

This meal over, she resumed honest Rawdon's calculations of the night previous, and surveyed her position. Should the worst befal, all things considered, she was pretty well to do. There were her own trinkets and trousseau, in addition to those which her husband had left behind. Rawdon's generosity, when they were first married, has already been described and lauded. Besides these, and the little mare, the General, her slave and worshipper, had made her many very handsome presents in the shape of cashmere shawls bought at the auction of a bankrupt French general's lady, and numerous tributes from the jewellers' shops, all of which betokened her admirer's taste and wealth. As for "tickers," as poor Rawdon called watches, her apartments were alive with their clicking. For, happening to mention one night that hers, which Rawdon had given to her, was of English workmanship, and went ill, on the very next morning there came to her a little bijou marked Leroy,[6] with a chain and cover charmingly set with turquoises, and another signed Breguet, which was covered with pearls, and yet scarcely bigger than a half-crown. General Tufto had bought one, and Captain Osborne had gallantly presented the

6. Delicately ornamented jewelry by Leroy, French watchmakers. Abraham Louis Bréguet (1747–1823) was another French watchmaker (Harden).

other. Mrs. Osborne had no watch, though, to do George justice, she might have had one for the asking, and the Honourable Mrs. Tufto in England had an old instrument of her mother's that might have served for the plate warming-pan which Rawdon talked about. If Messrs. Howell and James[7] were to publish a list of the purchasers of all the trinkets which they sell, how surprised would some families be; and if all these ornaments went to gentlemen's lawful wives and daughters, what a profusion of jewellery there would be exhibited in the genteelest homes of Vanity Fair!

Every calculation made of these valuables Mrs. Rebecca found, not without a pungent feeling of triumph and self-satisfaction, that should circumstances occur, she might reckon on six or seven hundred pounds at the very least, to begin the world with: and she passed the morning disposing, ordering, looking out, and locking up her properties in the most agreeable manner. Among the notes in Rawdon's pocket-book, was a draft for twenty pounds on Osborne's banker. This made her think about Mrs. Osborne. "I will go and get the draft cashed," she said, "and pay a visit afterwards to poor little Emmy." If this is a novel without a hero, at least let us lay claim to a heroine. No man in the British army which has marched away, not the great duke himself, could be more cool or collected in the presence of doubts and difficulties, than the indomitable little aide-de-camp's wife.

And there was another of our acquaintances who was also to be left behind, a non-combatant, and whose emotions and behaviour we have therefore a right to know. This was our friend the ex-collector of Boggley wollah, whose rest was broken, like other people's, by the sounding of the bugles in the early morning. Being a great sleeper, and fond of his bed, it is possible he would have snoozed on until his usual hour of rising in the forenoon, in spite of all the drums, bugles, and bagpipes in the British army, but for an interruption, which did not come from George Osborne, who shared Jos's quarters with him, and was as usual occupied too much with his own affairs, or with grief at parting with his wife, to think of taking leave of his slumbering brother-in-law—it was not George, we say, who interposed between Jos Sedley and sleep, but Captain Dobbin, who came and roused him up, insisting on shaking hands with him before his departure.

"Very kind of you," said Jos, yawning, and wishing the Captain at the deuce.

"I—I didn't like to go off without saying good-bye, you know," Dobbin said in a very incoherent manner; "because you know some of us mayn't come back again, and I like to see you all well and—and that sort of thing, you know."

"What do you mean?" Jos asked, rubbing his eyes. The Captain did not in the least hear him or look at the stout gentleman in the night-cap, about whom he professed to have such a tender interest. The hypocrite was looking and listening with all his might in the direction of George's apartments, striding about the room, upsetting

7. Shop in Regent Street.

the chairs, beating the tattoo, biting his nails, and showing other signs of great inward emotion.

Jos had always had rather a mean opinion of the Captain, and now began to think his courage was somewhat equivocal. "What is it I can do for you, Dobbin?" he said in a sarcastic tone.

"I tell you what you can do," the Captain replied, coming up to the bed; "we march in a quarter of an hour, Sedley, and neither George nor I may ever come back. Mind you, you are not to stir from this town until you ascertain how things go. You are to stay here and watch over your sister, and comfort her, and see that no harm comes to her. If anything happens to George, remember she has no one but you in the world to look to. If it goes wrong with the army, you'll see her safe back to England; and you will promise me on your word that you will never desert her. I know you won't: as far as money goes you were always free enough with that. Do you want any? I mean, have you enough gold to take you back to England in case of a misfortune?"

"Sir," said Jos, majestically, "when I want money, I know where to ask for it. And as for my sister, *you* needn't tell me how I ought to behave to her."

"You speak like a man of spirit, Jos," the other answered good-naturedly, "and I am glad that George can leave her in such good hands. So I may give him your word of honour, may I, that in case of extremity you will stand by her?"

"Of course, of course," answered Mr. Jos, whose generosity in money matters Dobbin estimated quite correctly.

"And you'll see her safe out of Brussels in the event of a defeat?"

"A defeat! D— it, Sir, it's impossible. Don't try and frighten *me*," the hero cried from his bed; and Dobbin's mind was thus perfectly set at ease now that Jos had spoken out so resolutely respecting his conduct to his sister. "At least," thought the Captain, "there will be a retreat secured for her in case the worst should ensue."

If Captain Dobbin expected to get any personal comfort and satisfaction from having one more view of Amelia before the regiment marched away, his selfishness was punished just as such odious egotism deserved to be. The door of Jos's bed-room opened into the sitting-room which was common to the family party, and opposite this door was that of Amelia's chamber. The bugles had wakened everybody: there was no use in concealment now. George's servant was packing in this room: Osborne coming in and out of the contiguous bed-room, flinging to the man such articles as he thought fit to carry on the campaign. And presently Dobbin had the opportunity which his heart coveted, and he got sight of Amelia's face once more. But what a face it was! So white, so wild and despair-stricken, that the remembrance of it haunted him afterwards like a crime, and the sight smote him with inexpressible pangs of longing and pity.

She was wrapped in a white morning dress, her hair falling on her shoulders, and her large eyes fixed and without light. By way of helping on the preparations for the departure, and showing that she too could be useful at a moment so critical, this poor soul had taken up a sash of George's from the drawers whereon it lay, and followed him to and fro with the sash in her hand, looking on mutely as his packing proceeded. She came out and stood, leaning at the wall, holding this sash against her bosom, from which the heavy net of crimson dropped like a large stain of blood. Our gentle-hearted Captain felt a guilty shock as he looked at her. "Good God," thought he, "and is it grief like this I dared to pry into?" And there was no help: no means to soothe and comfort this helpless, speechless misery. He stood for a moment and looked at her, powerless and torn with pity, as a parent regards an infant in pain.

At last, George took Emmy's hand, and led her back into the bedroom, from whence he came out alone. The parting had taken place in that moment, and he was gone.

"Thank Heaven that is over," George thought, bounding down the stair, his sword under his arm, and as he ran swiftly to the alarm-ground, where the regiment was mustered, and whither trooped men and officers hurrying from their billets, his pulse was throbbing and his cheeks flushed: the great game of war was going to be played, and he one of the players. What a fierce excitement of doubt, hope, and pleasure! What tremendous hazards of loss or gain! What were all the games of chance he had ever played compared to this one? Into all contests requiring athletic skill and courage, the young man, from his boyhood upwards, had flung himself with all his might. The champion of his school and his regiment, the bravos of his companions had followed him everywhere; from the boys' cricket-match to the garrison-races, he had won a hundred of triumphs; and wherever he went, women and men had admired and envied him. What qualities are there for which a man gets so speedy a return of applause, as those of bodily superiority, activity, and valour? Time out of mind strength and courage have been the theme of bards and romances; and from the story of Troy down to to-day, poetry has always chosen a soldier for a hero. I wonder is it because men are cowards in heart that they admire bravery so much, and place military valour so far beyond every other quality for reward and worship?

So, at the sound of that stirring call to battle, George jumped away from the gentle arms in which he had been dallying; not without a feeling of shame (although his wife's hold on him had been but feeble), that he should have been detained there so long. The same feeling of eagerness and excitement was amongst all those friends of his of whom we have had occasional glimpses, from the stout senior Major, who led the regiment into action, to little Stubble, the Ensign, who was to bear its colours on that day.

The sun was just rising as the march began—it was a gallant sight—the band led the column, playing the regimental march—then came the Major in command, riding upon Pyramus,[8] his stout charger—then marched the grenadiers, their captain at their head; in the centre were the colours, borne by the senior and junior Ensigns—then George came marching at the head of his company. He looked up, and smiled at Amelia, and passed on; and even the sound of the music died away.

8. Named after the tragic lover of Thisbe in Ovid's *Metamorphoses* and Shakespeare's *A Midsummer Night's Dream*.

## *Chapter XXXI.*

IN WHICH JOS SEDLEY TAKES CARE OF HIS SISTER.

THUS all the superior officers being summoned on duty elsewhere, Jos Sedley was left in command of the little colony at Brussels, with Amelia invalided, Isidor his Belgian servant, and the *bonne,* who was maid-of-all-work for the establishment, as a garrison under him. Though he was disturbed in spirit, and his rest destroyed by Dobbin's interruption and the occurrences of the morning, Jos nevertheless remained for many hours in bed, wakeful and rolling about there until his usual hour of rising had arrived. The sun was high in the heavens, and our gallant friends of the —th miles on their march, before the civilian appeared in his flowered dressing-gown at breakfast.

About George's absence, his brother-in-law was very easy in mind. Perhaps Jos was rather pleased in his heart that Osborne was gone, for during George's presence, the other had played but a very secondary part in the household, and Osborne did not scruple to show his contempt for the stout civilian. But Emmy had always been good and attentive to him. It was she who ministered to his comforts, who superintended the dishes that he liked, who walked or rode with him (as she had many, too many, opportunities of doing, for where was George?) and who interposed her sweet kind face[1] between his anger and her husband's scorn. Many timid remonstrances had she uttered to George in behalf of her brother. But the former in his trenchant way cut these entreaties short. "I'm an honest man," he said, "and if I have a feeling I show it, as an honest man will. How the deuce, my dear, would you have me behave respectfully to such a fool as your brother?" So Jos was pleased with George's absence. His plain hat and gloves on a sideboard, and the idea that the owner was away, caused Jos I don't know what secret thrill of pleasure. "*He* won't be troubling me this morning," Jos thought, "with his dandified airs and his impudence."

"Put the Captain's hat into the ante-room," he said to Isidor the servant.

"Perhaps he won't want it again," replied the lackey, looking knowingly at his master. He hated George too, whose insolence towards him was quite of the English sort.

"And ask if Madam is coming to breakfast," Mr. Sedley said with great majesty, ashamed to enter with a servant upon the subject of his dislike for George. The truth is, he had abused his brother to the valet a score of times before.

1. Revised edition reads: sweet face

Alas! Madam could not come to breakfast, and cut the *tartines*[2] that Mr. Jos liked. Madam was a great deal too ill, and had been in a frightful state ever since her husband's departure, so her *bonne* said. Jos showed his sympathy, by pouring her out a large cup of tea. It was his way of exhibiting kindness: and he improved on this; he not only sent her breakfast, but he bethought him what delicacies she would most like for dinner.

Isidor, the valet, had looked on very sulkily, while Osborne's servant was disposing of his master's baggage previous to the Captain's departure: for in the first place he hated Mr. Osborne, whose conduct to him, and to all inferiors, was generally overbearing, (nor does the continental domestic like to be treated with insolence as our own better-tempered servants do;) and secondly, he was angry that so many valuables should be removed from under his hands, to fall into other people's possession when the English discomfiture should arrive. Of this defeat he and a vast number of other persons in Brussels and Belgium did not make the slightest doubt. The almost universal belief was, that the Emperor would divide the Prussian and English armies, annihilate one after the other, and march into Brussels before three days were over; when all the moveables of his present masters, who would be killed, or fugitives, or prisoners, would lawfully become the property of Monsieur Isidor.

As he helped Jos through his toilsome and complicated daily toilette, this faithful servant would calculate what he should do with the very articles with which he was decorating his master's person. He would make a present of the silver essence-bottles and toilet knicknacks to a young lady of whom he was fond; and keep the English cutlery and the large ruby pin for himself. It would look very smart upon one of the fine frilled shirts, which, with the gold-laced cap and the frogged frock coat, that might easily be cut down to suit his shape, and the Captain's gold-headed cane, and the great double ring with the rubies, which he would have made into a pair of beautiful earrings, he calculated would make a perfect Adonis of himself, and render Mademoiselle Reine an easy prey. "How those sleeve-buttons will suit me," thought he, as he fixed a pair on the fat pudgy wrists of Mr. Sedley. "I long for sleeve-buttons; and the Captain's boots with brass spurs, in the next room, *corbleu*[3] what an effect they will make in the Allée-Verte!" So while Monsieur Isidor with bodily fingers was holding on to his master's nose, and shaving the lower part of Jos's face, his imagination was rambling along the Green Avenue, dressed out in a frogged coat and lace, and in company with Mademoiselle Reine; he was loitering in spirit on the banks, and examining the barges sailing slowly under the cool shadows of the trees by the canal, or refreshing himself with a mug of Faro[4] at the bench of a beer-house on the road to Laeken.

But Mr. Joseph Sedley, luckily for his own peace, no more knew what was passing in his domestic's mind than the respected reader

2. Slices of buttered bread.
3. By God!
4. Belgian beer. Laeken is near Brussels.

and I suspect what John or Mary, whose wages we pay, think of ourselves. What our servants think of us!—Did we know what our intimates and dear relations thought of us, we should live in a world that we should be glad to quit, and in a frame of mind and a constant terror, that would be perfectly unbearable. So Jos's man was marking his victim down, as you see one of Mr. Paynter's assistants in Leadenhall-street ornament an unconscious turtle with a placard on which is written, "Soup to-morrow."[5]

Amelia's attendant was much less selfishly disposed. Few dependants could come near that kind and gentle creature without paying their usual tribute of loyalty and affection to her sweet and affectionate nature. And it is a fact that Pauline, the cook, consoled her mistress more than anybody whom she saw on this wretched morning; for when she found how Amelia remained for hours, silent, motionless, and haggard, by the windows in which she had placed herself to watch the last bayonets of the column as it marched away, the honest girl took the lady's hand, and said, *Tenez, Madame, est-ce qu'il n'est pas aussi à l'armée, mon homme à moi?*[6] with which she burst into tears, and Amelia falling into her arms, did likewise, and so each pitied and soothed the other.

Several times during the forenoon Mr. Jos's Isidor went from his lodgings into the town, and to the gates of the hotels and lodging-houses round about the Parc, where the English were congregated, and there mingling with other valets, couriers, and lackeys, gathered such news as was abroad, and brought back bulletins for his master's information. Almost all these gentlemen were in heart partisans of the Emperor, and had their opinions about the speedy end of the campaign. The Emperor's proclamation from Avesnes had been distributed everywhere plentifully in Brussels. "Soldiers!" it said, "this is the anniversary of Marengo and Friedland, by which the destinies of Europe were twice decided. Then, as after Austerlitz, as after Wagram, we were too generous. We believed in the oaths and promises of princes whom we suffered to remain upon their thrones. Let us march once more to meet them. We and they, are we not still the same men? Soldiers! these same Prussians who are so arrogant to-day, were three to one against you at Jena, and six to one at Montmirail. Those among you who were prisoners in England can tell their comrades what frightful torments they suffered on board the English hulks. Madmen! a moment of prosperity has blinded them, and if they enter into France it will be to find a grave there!"[7] But the partisans of the French prophesied a more speedy extermination of the Emperor's enemies than this; and it was agreed on all hands that Prussians and British would never return except as prisoners in the rear of the conquering army.

5. George Painter ran the Ship and Turtle tavern in Leadenhall Street in London.
6. Well, Madam, isn't my man in the army too?
7. Napoleon's proclamation at Avesnes, just south of the Belgian border, on June 14 (the day before the duchess of Richmond's ball) alludes to various French victories from as many as fifteen years earlier. The Battle of Montmirail, February 14, 1814, was Napoleon's last victory before his first capture and exile to Elba. Hulks are old ships converted into prisons.

These opinions in the course of the day were brought to operate upon Mr. Sedley. He was told that the Duke of Wellington had gone to try and rally his army, the advance of which had been utterly crushed the night before.

"Crushed, psha!" said Jos, whose heart was pretty stout at breakfast-time. "The Duke has gone to beat the Emperor as he has beaten all his generals before."

"His papers are burned, his effects are removed, and his quarters are being got ready for the Duke of Dalmatia,"[8] Jos's informant replied. "I had it from his own *maître d'hôtel.* Milor Duc de Richemont's people are packing up everything. His Grace has fled already, and the Duchess is only waiting to see the plate packed to join the King of France at Ostend."

"The King of France is at Ghent, fellow," replied Jos, affecting incredulity.

"He fled last night to Bruges, and embarks to-day from Ostend. The Duke de Berri is taken prisoner.[9] Those who wish to be safe had better go soon, for the dykes will be open to-morrow, and who can fly when the whole country is under water?"

"Nonsense, Sir, we are three to one, Sir, against any force Bony can bring in the field," Mr. Sedley objected; "the Austrians and the Russians are on their march. He must, he shall be crushed," Jos said, slapping his hand on the table.

"The Prussians were three to one at Jena, and he took their army and kingdom in a week. They were six to one at Montmirail, and he scattered them like sheep. The Austrian army *is* coming, but with the Empress and the King of Rome[1] at its head; and the Russians, bah! the Russians will withdraw. No quarter is to be given to the English, on account of their cruelty to our braves on board the infamous pontoons. Look here, here it is in black and white. Here's the proclamation of his Majesty the Emperor and King," said the now declared partisan of Napoleon, and taking the document from his pocket, Isidor sternly thrust it into his master's face, and already looked upon the frogged coat and valuables as his own spoil.

Jos was, if not seriously alarmed as yet, at least considerably disturbed in mind. "Give me my coat and cap, Sir," said he, "and follow me. I will go myself and learn the truth of these reports." Isidor was furious as Jos put on the braided frock. "Milor had better not wear that military coat," said he; "the Frenchmen have sworn not to give quarter to a single British soldier."

"Silence, Sirrah!" said Jos, with a resolute countenance still, and thrust his arm into the sleeve with indomitable resolution, in the performance of which heroic act he was found by Mrs. Rawdon Crawley, who at this juncture came up to visit Amelia, and entered without ringing at the antechamber door.

8. Marshal of France, Major General Nicholas Jean de Dieu Soult (1769–1851), duke of Dalmatia.
9. Charles Ferdinand de Bourbon (1778–1820), Duc de Berry, was at Ghent with King Louis XVIII, his uncle.
1. Napoleon's wife, Marie Louise, daughter of the king of Prussia, and her son, François Charles Joseph, whom Napoleon had named king of Rome.

Rebecca was dressed very neatly and smartly, as usual; her quiet sleep after Rawdon's departure had refreshed her, and her pink smiling cheeks were quite pleasant to look at, in a town and on a day when everybody else's countenance wore the appearance of the deepest anxiety and gloom. She laughed at the attitude in which Jos was discovered, and the struggles and convulsions with which the stout gentleman thrust himself into the braided coat.

"Are you preparing to join the army, Mr. Joseph?" she said. "Is there to be nobody left in Brussels to protect us poor women?" Jos

succeeded in plunging into the coat, and came forward blushing and stuttering out excuses to his fair visitor. "How was she after the events of the morning—after the fatigues of the ball the night before?" Monsieur Isidor disappeared into his master's adjacent bed-room, bearing off the flowered dressing-gown.

"How good of you to ask," said she, pressing one of his hands in both her own. "How cool and collected you look when everybody else is frightened! How is our dear little Emmy? It must have been an awful, awful parting."

"Tremendous," Jos said.

"You men can bear anything," replied the lady. "Parting or danger are nothing to you. Own now that you were going to join the army, and leave us to our fate. I know you were—something tells me you were. I was so frightened, when the thought came into my head (for I do sometimes think of you when I am[2] alone, Mr. Joseph!), that I

2. Revised edition reads: I'm

ran off immediately to beg and entreat you not to fly from us."

This speech might be interpreted, "My dear Sir, should an accident befal the army, and a retreat be necessary, you have a very comfortable carriage, in which I propose to take a seat." I don't know whether Jos understood the words in this sense. But he was profoundly mortified by the lady's inattention to him, during their stay at Brussels. He had never been presented to any of Rawdon Crawley's great acquaintances: he had scarcely been invited to Rebecca's parties; for he was too timid to play much, and his presence bored George and Rawdon equally, who neither of them, perhaps, liked to have a witness of the amusements in which the pair chose to indulge. "Ah!" thought Jos, "now she wants me she comes to me. When there is nobody else in the way she can think about old Joseph Sedley!" But besides these doubts he felt flattered at the idea Rebecca expressed of his courage.

He blushed a good deal, and put on an air of importance. "I should like to see the action," he said. "Every man of any spirit would, you know. I've seen a little service in India, but nothing on this grand scale."

"You men would sacrifice anything for a pleasure," Rebecca answered. "Captain Crawley left me this morning as gay as if he was[3] going to a hunting party. What does he care! What do any of you care for the agonies and tortures of a poor forsaken woman? (I wonder whether he *could* really have been going to the troops, this great lazy gourmand?) Oh! dear Mr. Sedley, I have come to you for comfort—for consolation. I have been on my knees all the morning. I tremble at the frightful danger into which our husbands, our friends, our brave troops and allies, are rushing. And I come here for shelter, and find another of my friends—the last remaining to me—bent upon plunging into the dreadful scene!"

"My dear Madam," Jos replied, now beginning to be quite soothed. "Don't be alarmed. I only said I should like to go—what Briton would not? But my duty keeps me here: I can't leave that poor creature in the next room." And he pointed with his finger to the door of the chamber in which Amelia was.

"Good noble brother!" Rebecca said, putting her handkerchief to her eyes, and smelling the eau-de-cologne with which it was scented. "I have done you injustice: you have got a heart. I thought you had not."

"O, upon my honour!" Jos said, making a motion as if he would lay his hand upon the spot in question. "You do me injustice, indeed you do—my dear Mrs. Crawley."

"I do, now your heart is true to your sister. But I remember two years ago—when it was false to me!" Rebecca said, fixing her eyes upon him for an instant, and then turning away into the window.

Jos blushed violently. That organ which he was accused by Rebecca of not possessing began to thump tumultuously. He recalled the days when he had fled from her, and the passion which had once inflamed him—the days when he had driven her in his curricle: when she had

3. Revised edition reads: were

knit the green purse for him: when he had sate enraptured gazing at her white arms, and bright eyes.

"I know you think me ungrateful," Rebecca continued, coming out of the window, and once more looking at him and addressing him in a low tremulous voice. "Your coldness, your averted looks, your manner when we have met of late—when I came in just now, all proved it to me. But were there no reasons why I should avoid you? Let your own heart answer that question. Do you think my husband was too much inclined to welcome you? The only unkind words I have ever had from him (I will do Captain Crawley that justice) have been about you—and most cruel, cruel words they were."

"Good gracious! what have I done?" asked Jos in a flurry of pleasure and perplexity; "what have I done—to—to—?"

"Is jealousy nothing?" said Rebecca. "He makes me miserable about you. And whatever it might have been once—my heart is all his. I am innocent now. Am I not, Mr. Sedley?"

All Jos's blood tingled with delight, as he surveyed this victim to his attractions. A few adroit words, one or two knowing tender glances of the eyes, and his heart was inflamed again and his doubts and suspicions forgotten. From Solomon downwards, have not wiser men than he been cajoled and befooled by women? "If the worst comes to the worst," Becky thought, "my retreat is secure; and I have a right-hand seat in the barouche."

There is no knowing into what declarations of love and ardour the tumultous passions of Mr. Joseph might have led him, if Isidor the valet had not made his re-appearance at this minute, and begun to busy himself about the domestic affairs. Jos, who was just going to gasp out an avowal, choked almost with the emotion that he was obliged to restrain. Rebecca too bethought her that it was time she should go in and comfort her dearest Amelia. "*Au revoir,*" she said, kissing her hand to Mr. Joseph, and tapped gently at the door of his sister's apartment. As she entered and closed the door on herself, he sank down in a chair, and gazed and sighed and puffed portentously. "That coat is very tight for Milor," Isidor said, still having his eye on the frogs; but his master heard him not: his thoughts were elsewhere: now glowing, maddening, upon the contemplation of the enchanting Rebecca: anon shrinking guiltily before the vision of the jealous Rawdon Crawley, with his curling, fierce mustachios, and his terrible duelling pistols loaded and cocked.

Rebecca's appearance struck Amelia with terror, and made her shrink back. It recalled her to the world and the remembrance of yesterday. In the overpowering fears about to-morrow she had forgotten Rebecca,—jealousy—everything except that her husband was gone and was in danger. Until this dauntless worldling came in and broke the spell, and lifted the latch, we too have forborne to enter into that sad chamber. How long had that poor girl been on her knees! what hours of speechless prayer and bitter prostration had she passed there! The war-chroniclers who write brilliant stories of fight and triumph scarcely tell us of these. These are too mean parts of the pageant: and you don't hear widows' cries or mothers' sobs in the midst of the shouts and jubilation in the great Chorus of Victory. And yet when was the time, that such have not cried out: heart-broken, humble Protestants, unheard in the uproar of the triumph!

After the first movement of terror in Amelia's mind—when Rebecca's green eyes lighted upon her, and rustling in her fresh silks and brilliant ornaments, the latter tripped up with extended arms to embrace her—a feeling of anger succeeded, and from being deadly pale before, her face flushed up red, and she returned Rebecca's look after a moment with a steadiness which surprised and somewhat abashed her rival.

"Dearest Amelia, you are very unwell," the visitor said, putting forth her hand to take Amelia's. "What is it? I could not rest until I knew how you were."

Amelia drew back her hand—never since her life began had that gentle soul refused to believe or to answer any demonstration of good-will or affection. But she drew back her hand, and trembled all over. "Why are *you* here, Rebecca?" she said, still looking at her solemnly with her large eyes. These glances troubled her visitor.

"She must have seen him give me the letter at the ball," Rebecca thought. "Don't be agitated, dear Amelia," she said, looking down. "I came but to see if I could—if you were well."

"Are you well?" said Amelia. "I dare say you are. You don't love your husband. You would not be here if you did. Tell me, Rebecca, did I ever do you anything but kindness?"

"Indeed, Amelia, no," the other said, still hanging down her head.

"When you were quite poor, who was it that befriended you? Was I not a sister to you? You saw us all in happier days before he married me. I was all in all then to him; or would he have given up his fortune, his family, as he nobly did to make me happy? Why did you come between my love and me? Who sent you to separate those whom God joined, and take my darling's heart from me—my own husband? Do you think you could love him as I did? His love was everything to me. You knew it, and wanted to rob me of it. For shame, Rebecca; bad and wicked woman—false friend and false wife."

"Amelia, I protest before God, I have done my husband no wrong," Rebecca said, turning from her.

"Have you done *me* no wrong, Rebecca? You did not succeed, but you tried. Ask your heart if you did not?"

She knows nothing, Rebecca thought.

"He came back to me. I knew he would. I knew that no falsehood, no flattery, could keep him from me long. I knew he would come. I prayed so that he should."

The poor girl spoke these words with a spirit and volubility which Rebecca had never before seen in her, and before which the latter was quite dumb. "But what have I done to you," she continued in a more pitiful tone, "that you should try and take him from me? I had him but for six weeks. You might have spared me those, Rebecca. And yet, from the very first day of our wedding, you came and blighted it. Now he is gone, are you come to see how unhappy I am?" She continued, "You made me wretched enough for the past fortnight: you might have spared me to-day."

"I—I never came here," interposed Rebecca, with unlucky truth.

"No. You didn't come. You took him away. Are you come to fetch him from me?" she continued in a wilder tone. "He was here, but he is gone now. There on that very sofa he sate. Don't touch it. We sate and talked there. I was on his knee, and my arms were round his neck, and we said 'Our Father.' Yes, he was here: and they came and took him away, but he promised me to come back."

"He will come back, my dear," said Rebecca, touched in spite of herself.

"Look," said Amelia, "this is his sash—isn't it a pretty colour?" and she took up the fringe and kissed it. She had tied it round her waist at some part of the day. She had forgotten her anger, her jealousy, the very presence of her rival seemingly. For she walked silently and almost with a smile on her face, towards the bed, and began to smooth down George's pillow.

Rebecca walked, too, silently away. "How is Amelia?" asked Jos, who still held his position in the chair.

"There should be somebody with her," said Rebecca. "I think she is very unwell;" and she went away with a very grave face, refusing Mr. Sedley's entreaties that she would stay and partake of the early dinner which he had ordered.

Rebecca was of a good-natured and obliging disposition; and she liked Amelia rather than otherwise. Even her hard words, reproachful as they were, were complimentary—the groans of a person stinging under defeat. Meeting Mrs. O'Dowd, whom the Dean's sermons had by no means comforted, and who was walking very disconsolately in the Parc, Rebecca accosted the latter, rather to the surprise of the Major's wife, who was not accustomed to such marks of politeness from Mrs. Rawdon Crawley, and informing her that poor little Mrs. Osborne was in a desperate condition, and almost mad with grief, sent off the good-natured Irishwoman straight to see if she could console her young favourite.

"I've cares of my own enough," Mrs. O'Dowd said, gravely, "and I thought poor Amelia would be little wanting for company this day. But if she's so bad as you say, and you can't attend to her, who used to be so fond of her, faith I'll see if I can be of service. And so good marning to ye, Madam;" with which speech and a toss of her head, the lady of the repayther took a farewell of Mrs. Crawley, whose company she by no means courted.

Becky watched her marching off, with a smile on her lip. She had the keenest sense of humour, and the Parthian[4] look which the retreating Mrs. O'Dowd flung over her shoulder almost upset Mrs. Crawley's gravity. "My service to ye, me fine Madam, and I'm glad to see ye so cheerful," thought Peggy. "It's not *you* that will cry your eyes out with grief, any way." And with this she passed on, and speedily found her way to Mrs. Osborne's lodgings.

The poor soul was still at the bedside, where Rebecca had left her, and stood almost crazy with grief. The Major's wife, a stronger minded woman, endeavoured her best to comfort her young friend.

4. Ancient Parthian soldiers were famous for firing while in retreat.

"You must bear up, Amelia, dear," she said kindly, "for he mustn't find you ill when he sends for you after the victory. It's not you are the only woman that are in the hands of God this day."

"I know that. I am very wicked, very weak," Amelia said. She knew her own weakness well enough. The presence of the more resolute friend checked it, however: and she was the better of this control and company. They went on till two o'clock; their hearts were with the column as it marched farther and farther away. Dreadful doubt and anguish—prayers and fears and griefs unspeakable—followed the regiment. It was the women's tribute to the war. It taxes both alike, and takes the blood of the men, and the tears of the women.

At half-past two an event occurred of daily importance to Mr. Joseph: the dinner hour arrived. Warriors may fight and perish, but he must dine. He came into Amelia's room to see if he could coax her to share that meal. "Try," said he; "the soup is very good. Do try, Emmy," and he kissed her hand. Except when she was married, he had not done so much for years before. "You are very good and kind, Joseph," she said. "Everybody is, but, if you please, I will stay in my room to-day."

The savour of the soup, however, was agreeable to Mrs. O'Dowd's nostrils: and she thought she would bear Mr. Jos company. So the two sate down to their meal. "God bless the meat," said the Major's wife, solemnly: she was thinking of her honest Mick, riding at the head of his regiment: "'Tis but a bad dinner those poor boys will get to-day," she said, with a sigh, and then, like a philosopher, fell to.

Jos's spirits rose with his meal. He would drink the regiment's health; or, indeed, take any other excuse to indulge in a glass of champagne. "We'll drink to O'Dowd and the brave —th," said he, bowing gallantly to his guest. "Hey, Mrs. O'Dowd. Fill Mrs. O'Dowd's glass, Isidor."

But all of a sudden, Isidor started, and the Major's wife laid down her knife and fork. The windows of the room were open, and looked southward, and a dull distant sound came over the sun-lighted roofs from that direction. "What is it?" said Jos. "Why don't you pour, you rascal?"

*"C'est le feu,"*[5] said Isidor, running to the balcony.

"God defend us; it's cannon!" Mrs. O'Dowd cried, starting up, and followed too to the window. A thousand pale and anxious faces might have been seen looking from other casements. And presently it seemed as if the whole population of the city rushed into the streets.

5. It's firing.

## *Chapter XXXII.*

IN WHICH JOS TAKES FLIGHT, AND THE WAR IS BROUGHT TO A CLOSE.

WE of peaceful London City, have never beheld—and please God never shall witness—such a scene of hurry and alarm, as that which Brussels presented. Crowds rushed to the Namur gate,[1] from which direction the noise proceeded, and many rode along the level *chaussée,*[2] to be in advance of any intelligence from the army. Each man asked his neighbour for news; and even great English lords and ladies condescended to speak to persons whom they did not know. The friends of the French went abroad, wild with excitement, and prophecying the triumph of their Emperor. The merchants closed their shops, and came out to swell the general chorus of alarm and clamour. Women rushed to the churches, and crowded the chapels, and knelt and prayed on the flags and steps. The dull sound of the cannon went on rolling, rolling. Presently carriages with travellers began to leave the town, galloping away by the Ghent barrier.[3] The prophecies of the French partisans began to pass for facts. "He has cut the armies in two," it was said. "He is marching straight on Brussels. He will overpower the English, and be here to-night." "He will overpower the English," shrieked Isidor to his master, "and will be here to-night." The man bounded in and out from the lodgings to the street, always returning with some fresh particulars of disaster. Jos's face grew paler and paler. Alarm began to take entire possession of the stout civilian. All the champagne he drank brought no courage to him. Before sunset he was worked up to such a pitch of nervousness as gratified his friend Isidor to behold, who now counted surely upon the spoils of the owner of the laced coat.

The women were away all this time. After hearing the firing for a moment, the stout Major's wife bethought her of her friend in the next chamber, and ran in to watch, and if possible to console, Amelia. The idea that she had that helpless and gentle creature to protect, gave additional strength to the natural courage of the honest Irishwoman. She passed five hours by her friend's side, sometimes in remonstrance, sometimes talking cheerfully, oftener in silence, and terrified mental supplication. "I never let go her hand once," said the stout lady afterwards, "until after sunset, when the firing was over." Pauline, the *bonne,* was on her knees at church hard by, praying for

1. Exit from Brussels south toward Namur and Waterloo.
2. Road.
3. Exit from Brussels northwest toward the coast and England.

*son homme à elle.*[4]

When the noise of the cannonading was over, Mrs. O'Dowd issued out of Amelia's room into the parlour adjoining, where Jos sate with two emptied flasks, and courage entirely gone. Once or twice he had ventured into his sister's bed-room, looking very much alarmed, and as if he would say something. But the Major's wife kept her place, and he went away without disburthening himself of his speech. He was ashamed to tell her that he wanted to fly.

But when she made her appearance in the dining-room, where he sate in the twilight in the cheerless company of his empty champagne-bottles, he began to open his mind to her.

"Mrs. O'Dowd," he said, "hadn't you better get Amelia ready?"

"Are you going to take her out for a walk?" said the Major's lady; "sure she's too weak to stir."

"I—I've ordered the carriage," he said, "and—and post-horses; Isidor is gone for them," Jos continued.

"What do you want with driving to-night?" answered the lady. "Isn't she better on her bed? I've just got her to lie down."

"Get her up," said Jos; "she must get up, I say:" and he stamped his foot energetically. "I say the horses are ordered—yes, the horses are ordered. It's all over, and—"

"And what?" asked Mrs. O'Dowd.

"I'm off for Ghent," Jos answered. "Everybody is going; there's a place for you! We shall start in half-an-hour."

The Major's wife looked at him with infinite scorn. "I don't move till O'Dowd gives me the route," said she. "You may go if you like, Mr. Sedley; but, faith, Amelia and I stop here."

"She *shall* go," said Jos, with another stamp of his foot. Mrs. O'Dowd put herself with arms akimbo before the bed-room door.

"Is it her mother you're going to take her to?" she said; "or do you want to go to Mamma yourself, Mr. Sedley? Good marning—a pleasant journey to ye, sir. *Bon voyage,* as they say, and take my counsel, and shave off them mustachios, or they'll bring you into mischief."

"D—n!" yelled out Jos, wild with fear, rage, and mortification; and Isidor came in at this juncture, swearing in his turn. *"Pas de chevaux, sacrebleu!"*[5] hissed out the furious domestic. All the horses were gone. Jos was not the only man in Brussels seized with panic that day.

But Jos's fears, great and cruel as they were already, were destined to increase to an almost frantic pitch before the night was over. It has been mentioned how Pauline, the *bonne,* had *son homme à elle,* also in the ranks of the army that had gone out to meet the Emperor Napoleon. This lover was a native of Brussels, and a Belgian hussar. The troops of his nation signalised themselves in this war for anything but courage, and young Van Cutsum, Pauline's admirer, was too good a soldier to disobey his Colonel's orders to run away. Whilst in garrison at Brussels young Regulus[6] (he had been born in the revolutionary times) found his great comfort, and passed almost all his leisure moments in Pauline's kitchen; and it was with pock-

4. Her man.
5. No horses, damn it!
6. Named for Marcus Atilius Regulus, a third-century B.C. Roman who did not save himself but deliberately sacrificed himself for honor and country.

ets and holsters crammed full of good things from her larder, that he had taken leave of his weeping sweetheart, to proceed upon the campaign a few days before.

As far as his regiment was concerned, this campaign was over now. They had formed a part of the division under the command of his Sovereign apparent, the Prince of Orange,[7] and as respected length of swords and mustachios, and the richness of uniform and equipments, Regulus and his comrades looked to be as gallant a body of men as ever trumpets sounded for.

When Ney[8] dashed upon the advance of the allied troops, carrying one position after the other, until the arrival of the great body of the British army from Brussels changed the aspect of the combat of Quatre Bras, the squadrons among which Regulus rode showed the greatest activity in retreating before the French, and were dislodged from one post and another which they occupied with perfect alacrity on their part.[9] Their movements were only checked by the advance of the British in their rear. Thus forced to halt, the enemy's cavalry (whose bloodthirsty obstinacy cannot be too severely reprehended) had at length an opportunity of coming to close quarters with the brave Belgians before them; who preferred to encounter the British rather than the French, and at once turning tail rode through the English regiments that were behind them, and scattered in all directions. The regiment in fact did not exist any more. It was nowhere. It had no head quarters. Regulus found himself galloping many miles from the field of action, entirely alone; and whither should he fly for refuge so naturally as to that kitchen and those faithful arms in which Pauline had so often welcomed him?

At some ten o'clock the clinking of a sabre might have been heard up the stair of the house where the Osbornes occupied a storey in the continental fashion. A knock might have been heard at the kitchen door; and poor Pauline, come back from church, fainted almost with terror as she opened it and saw before her her haggard hussar. He looked as pale as the midnight dragoon who came to disturb Leonora.[1] Pauline would have screamed, but that her cry would have called her masters, and discovered her friend. She stifled her scream, then, and leading her hero into the kitchen, gave him beer, and the choice bits from the dinner, which Jos had not had the heart to taste. The hussar showed he was no ghost by the prodigious quantity of flesh and beer which he devoured—and during the mouthfuls he told his tale of disaster.

His regiment had performed prodigies of courage, and had withstood for a while the onset of the whole French army. But they were

7. To the chagrin of many Belgians, the Congress of Vienna had united the Netherlands and Belgium under William I, who was proclaimed king of the united countries in March 1815. His son, William Frederick (1792–1849), commanded Dutch troops at Waterloo; he became king in 1840.

8. Marshal Michel Ney (1769–1815), one of Europe's best generals, served the Bourbons briefly in 1814, but returned to Napoleon in March 1815, leading some temporary advances in the days before Waterloo. He was court-martialed and shot in December 1815.

9. Wellington defeated the French at Quatre Bras (twenty miles from Brussels), but reverses in other localities, somewhat exaggerated in Thackeray's account, moved the field of action to Waterloo, twelve miles away.

1. *Lenore* (1774) by Gottfried August Bürger, translated by J. C. Mangan as *Leonore*, is the story of a girl carried away by the ghost of her slain lover.

overwhelmed at last, as was the whole British army by this time. Ney destroyed each regiment as it came up. The Belgians in vain interposed to prevent the butchery of the English. The Brunswickers were routed and had fled—their Duke[2] was killed. It was a general *debâcle.* He sought to drown his sorrow for the defeat in floods of beer.

Isidor, who had come into the kitchen, heard the conversation, and rushed out to inform his master. "It is all over," he shrieked to Jos. "Milor Duke is a prisoner; the Duke of Brunswick is killed; the British army is in full flight; there is only one man escaped, and he is in the kitchen now—come and hear him." So Jos tottered into that apartment where Regulus still sate on the kitchen-table, and clung

fast to his flagon of beer. In the best French which he could muster, and which was in sooth of a very ungrammatical sort, Jos besought the hussar to tell his tale. The disasters deepened as Regulus spoke. He was the only man of his regiment not slain on the field. He had seen the Duke of Brunswick fall, the black hussars fly, the Ecossais[3] pounded down by the cannon.

"And the —th?" gasped Jos.

"Cut in pieces," said the hussar—upon which Pauline crying out, "O my mistress, *ma bonne petite dame,*" went off fairly into hysterics, and filled the house with her screams.

Wild with terror, Mr. Sedley knew not how or where to seek for safety. He rushed from the kitchen back to the sitting-room, and cast an appealing look at Amelia's door, which Mrs. O'Dowd had closed and locked in his face; but he remembered how scornfully the latter had received him, and after pausing and listening for a brief space

2. Friedrich Wilhelm (1771–1815), duke of Brunswick-Oels, was in fact killed at Quatre Bras.
3. Black Hussars, also known as Death Hussars or Black Brunswickers, were famous for neither giving nor asking quarter, but those put to flight that day were raw recuits. Ecossais: Scots.

at the door, he left it, and resolved to go into the street, for the first time that day. So, seizing a candle, he looked about for his gold-laced cap, and found it lying in its usual place, on a console-table,[4] in the ante-room, placed before a mirror at which Jos used to coquet, always giving his side-locks a twirl, and his cap the proper cock over his eye, before he went forth to make appearance in public. Such is the force of habit, that even in the midst of his terror he began mechanically to twiddle with his hair, and arrange the cock of his hat. Then he looked amazed at the pale face in the glass before him, and especially at his mustachios, which had attained a rich growth in the course of near seven weeks, since they had come into the world. They *will* mistake me for a military man, thought he, remembering Isidor's warning, as to the massacre with which all the defeated British army was threatened; and staggering back to his bed-chamber, he began wildly pulling the bell which summoned his valet.

Isidor answered that summons. Jos had sunk in a chair—he had torn off his neckcloths, and turned down his collars, and was sitting with both his hands lifted to his throat.

"*Coupez-moi,* Isidor," shouted he; "*vite! Coupez-moi!*"[5]

Isidor thought for a moment he had gone mad, and that he wished his valet to cut his throat.

4. Two-legged table attached to a wall.
5. Cut me, hurry, cut me!

Mr. Jos shaves off his mustachios

*"Les moustaches,"* gasped Jos; *"les moustaches—coupy, rasy, vite!"*[6]—his French was of this sort—voluble, as we have said, but not remarkable for grammar.

Isidor swept off the mustachios in no time with the razor, and heard with inexpressible delight his master's orders that he should fetch a hat and a plain coat. *"Ne porty ploo—habit militair—bonny—donny a voo, prenny dehors"*[7]—were Jos's words,—the coat and cap were at last his property.

This gift being made, Jos selected a plain black coat and waistcoat from his stock, and put on a large white neckcloth, and a plain beaver. If he could have got a shovel-hat he would have worn it. As it was, you would have fancied he was a flourishing, large parson of the Church of England.

*"Venny maintenong,"* he continued, *"sweevy—ally—party—dong la roo."*[8] And so having said, he plunged swiftly down the stairs of the house, and passed into the street.

Although Regulus had vowed that he was the only man of his regiment or of the allied army, almost, who had escaped being cut to pieces by Ney, it appeared that his statement was incorrect, and that a good number more of the supposed victims had survived the massacre. Many scores of Regulus's comrades had found their way back to Brussels, and—all agreeing that they had run away—filled the whole town with an idea of the defeat of the allies. The arrival of the French was expected hourly; the panic continued, and preparations for flight went on everywhere. No horses! thought Jos, in terror. He made Isidor inquire of scores of persons, whether they had any to lend or sell, and his heart sank within him, at the negative answers returned everywhere. Should he take the journey on foot? Even fear could not render that ponderous body so active.

Almost all the hotels occupied by the English in Brussels face the Parc, and Jos wandered irresolutely about in this quarter, with crowds of other people, oppressed as he was by fear and curiosity. Some families he saw more happy than himself, having discovered a team of horses, and rattling through the streets in retreat; others again there were whose case was like his own, and who could not for any bribes or entreaties procure the necessary means of flight. Amongst these would-be fugitives, Jos remarked the Lady Bareacres and her daughter, who sate in their carriage[9] in the *porte-cochère*[1] of their hotel, all their imperials[2] packed, and the only drawback to whose flight was the same want of motive power which kept Jos stationary.

Rebecca Crawley occupied apartments in this hotel; and had before this period had sundry hostile meetings with the ladies of the Bareacres family. My Lady Bareacres cut Mrs. Crawley on the stairs when they met by chance; and in all places where the latter's name was mentioned, spoke perseveringly ill of her neighbour. The Countess was shocked at the familiarity of General Tufto with the aide-de-

6. My moustaches, cut, shave off, quickly!
7. Fractured French: No longer wear—military clothes—cap—give to you, take away.
8. Fractured French: Come now, follow—go—leave—into the street.
9. First and second printings read: her carriage
1. Coach door.
2. Trunks designed to fit a coach roof.

camp's wife. The Lady Blanche avoided her as if she had been an infectious disease. Only the Earl himself kept up a sly occasional acquaintance with her, when out of the jurisdiction of his ladies.

Rebecca had her revenge now upon these insolent enemies. It became known in the hotel that Captain Crawley's horses had[3] been left behind, and when the panic began, Lady Bareacres condescended to send her maid to the Captain's wife with her Ladyship's compliments, and a desire to know the price of Mrs. Crawley's horses. Mrs. Crawley returned a note with her compliments, and an intimation that it was not her custom to transact bargains with ladies' maids.

This curt reply brought the Earl in person to Becky's apartment; but he could get no more success than the first ambassador. "Send a lady's maid to *me!*" Mrs. Crawley cried in great anger; "why didn't my Lady Bareacres tell me to go and saddle the horses! Is it her Ladyship that wants to escape, or her Ladyship's *femme de chambre?*" And this was all the answer that the Earl bore back to his Countess.

What will not necessity do? The Countess herself actually came to wait upon Mrs. Crawley on the failure of her second envoy. She entreated her to name her own price; she even offered to invite Becky to Bareacres House, if the latter would but give her the means of returning to that residence. Mrs. Crawley sneered at her.

"I don't want to be waited on by bailiffs in livery," she said; "you will never get back though most probably—at least, not you and your diamonds together. The French will have those. They will be here in two hours, and I shall be half way to Ghent by that time. I would not sell you my horses, no, not for the two largest diamonds that your Ladyship wore at the ball." Lady Bareacres trembled with rage and terror. The diamonds were sewed into her habit, and secreted in my Lord's padding and boots. "Woman, the diamonds are at the banker's, and I *will* have the horses," she said. Rebecca laughed in her face. The infuriate Countess went below, and sate in her carriage; her maid, her courier, and her husband were sent once more through the town, each to look for cattle; and wo betide those who came last! Her Ladyship was resolved on departing the very instant the horses arrived from any quarter—with her husband or without him.

Rebecca had the pleasure of seeing her Ladyship in the horseless carriage, and keeping her eyes fixed upon her, and bewailing, in the loudest tone of voice, the Countess's perplexities. "Not to be able to get horses!" she said, "and to have all those diamonds sewed in to the carriage cushions! What a prize it will be for the French when they come!—the carriage and the diamonds I mean; not the lady!" She gave this information to the landlord, to the servants, to the guests, and the innumerable stragglers about the court-yard. Lady Bareacres could have shot her from the carriage-window.

It was while enjoying the humiliation of her enemy that Rebecca caught sight of Jos, who made towards her directly he perceived her.

That altered, frightened, fat face, told his secret well enough. He too wanted to fly, and was on the look-out for the means of escape. "*He* shall buy my horses," thought Rebecca, "and I'll ride the mare."

3. First printing reads: Captain Crawley had

Jos walked up to his friend, and put the question for the hundredth time during the past hour, "Did she know where horses were to be had?"

"What, *you* fly?" said Rebecca, with a laugh. "I thought you were the champion of all the ladies, Mr. Sedley."

"I—I'm not a military man," gasped he.

"And Amelia?—Who is to protect that poor little sister of yours," asked Rebecca. "You surely would not desert her?"

"What good can I do her, suppose—suppose the enemy arrive?" Jos answered. "They'll spare the women; but my man tells me that they have taken an oath to give no quarter to the men—the dastardly cowards."

"Horrid!" cried Rebecca, enjoying his perplexity.

"Besides, I don't want to desert her," cried the brother. "She *shan't* be deserted. There is a seat for her in my carriage, and one for you, dear Mrs. Crawley, if you will come; and if we can get horses—" sighed he—

"I have two to sell," the lady said. Jos could have flung himself into her arms at the news. "Get the carriage, Isidor," he cried; "we've found them—we have found them."

"My horses never were in harness," added the lady. "Bulfinch would kick the carriage to pieces, if you put him in the traces."

"But he is quiet to ride?" asked the civilian.

"As quiet as a lamb, and as fast as a hare," answered Rebecca.

"Do you think he is up to my weight?" Jos said. He was already on his back, in imagination, without ever so much as a thought for poor Amelia. What person who loved a horse-speculation could resist such a temptation?

In reply, Rebecca asked him to come into her room, whither he followed her quite breathless to conclude the bargain. Jos seldom spent a half hour in his life which cost him so much money. Rebecca measuring the value of the goods which she had for sale by Jos's eagerness to purchase, as well as by the scarcity of the article, put upon her horses a price so prodigious as to make even the civilian draw back. "She would sell both or neither," she said, resolutely. Rawdon had ordered her not to part with them for a price less than that which she specified. Lord Bareacres below would give her the same money—and with all her love and regard for the Sedley family, her dear Mr. Joseph must conceive that poor people must live—nobody, in a word, could be more affectionate, but more firm about the matter of business.

Jos ended by agreeing, as might be supposed of him. The sum he had to give her was so large that he was obliged to ask for time; so large as to be a little fortune to Rebecca, who rapidly calculated that with this sum, and the sale of the residue of Rawdon's effects, and her pension as a widow should he fall, she would now be absolutely independent of the world, and might look her weeds steadily in the face.

Once or twice in the day she certainly had herself thought about flying. But her reason gave her better counsel. "Suppose the French do come," thought Becky, "what can they do to a poor officer's widow? Bah! the times of sacks and sieges are over. We shall be let to go home quietly, or I may live pleasantly abroad with a snug little income."

Meanwhile Jos and Isidor went off to the stables to inspect the newly-purchased cattle. Jos bade his man saddle the horses at once. He would ride away that very night, that very hour. And he left the valet busy in getting the horses ready, and went homewards himself to prepare for his departure. It must be secret. He would go to his chamber by the back entrance. He did not care to face Mrs. O'Dowd and Amelia, and own to them that he was about to run.

By the time Jos's bargain with Rebecca was completed, and his horses had been visited and examined, it was almost morning once more. But though midnight was long passed, there was no rest for the city; the people were up, the lights in the houses flamed, crowds were still about the doors, and the streets were busy. Rumours of various natures went still from mouth to mouth: one report averred that the Prussians had been utterly defeated; another that it was the English who had been attacked and conquered; a third that the latter had held their ground. This last rumour gradually got strength. No Frenchmen had made their appearance. Stragglers had come in from the army bringing reports more and more favourable: at last an aide-de-camp actually reached Brussels with despatches for the Commandant of the place, who placarded presently through the town an official announcement of the success of the allies at Quatre Bras, and the entire repulse of the French under Ney after a six hours' battle. The aide-de-camp must have arrived sometime while Jos and Rebecca were making their bargain together, or the latter was inspecting his purchase. When he reached his own hotel, he found a score of its numerous inhabitants on the threshold discoursing of the news; there was no doubt as to its truth. And he went up to communicate it to the ladies under his charge. He did not think it was necessary to tell them how he had intended to take leave of them, how he had bought horses, and what a price he had paid for them.

But success or defeat was a minor matter to them, who had only thought for the safety of those they loved. Amelia, at the news of the victory, became still more agitated even than before. She was for going that moment to the army. She besought her brother with tears to conduct her thither. Her doubts and terrors reached their paroxysm; and the poor girl, who for many hours had been plunged into stupor, raved and ran hither and thither in hysteric insanity—a piteous sight. No man writhing in pain on the hard-fought field fifteen miles off, where lay, after their struggles, so many of the brave—no man suffered more keenly than this poor harmless victim of the war. Jos could not bear the sight of her pain. He left his sister in the charge of her stouter female companion, and descended once more to the threshold of the hotel, where everybody still lingered, and talked, and waited for more news.

It grew to be broad daylight as they stood here, and fresh news began to arrive from the war, brought by men who had been actors in the scene. Waggons and long country carts laden with wounded came rolling into the town; ghastly groans came from within them, and haggard faces looked up sadly from out of the straw. Jos Sedley was looking at one of these carriages with a painful curiosity—the moans of the people within were frightful—the wearied horses could hardly pull the cart. Stop! stop! a feeble voice cried from the straw, and the carriage stopped opposite Mr. Sedley's hotel.

"It is George, I know it is!" cried Amelia, rushing in a moment to the balcony, with a pallid face and loose flowing hair. It was not George, however, but it was the next best thing: it was news of him.

It was poor Tom Stubble, who had marched out of Brussels so gallantly twenty-four hours before, bearing the colours of the regiment, which he had defended very gallantly upon the field. A French lancer had speared the young ensign in the leg, who fell, still bravely holding to his flag. At the conclusion of the engagement, a place had been found for the poor boy in a cart, and he had been brought back to Brussels.

"Mr. Sedley, Mr. Sedley!" cried the boy faintly, and Jos came up almost frightened at the appeal. He had not at first distinguished who it was that called him.

Little Tom Stubble held out his hot and feeble hand. "I'm to be taken in here," he said. "Osborne—and—and Dobbin said I was; and you are to give the man two Napoleons: my mother will pay you." This young fellow's thoughts, during the long feverish hours passed in the cart, had been wandering to his father's parsonage which he had quitted only a few months before, and he had sometimes forgotten his pain in that delirium.

The hotel was large, and the people kind, and all the inmates of the cart were taken in and placed on various couches. The young ensign was conveyed up-stairs to Osborne's quarters. Amelia and the Major's wife had rushed down to him, when the latter had recognised him from the balcony. You may fancy the feelings of these women when they were told that the day was over, and both their husbands were safe; in what mute rapture Amelia fell on her good friend's neck, and embraced her; in what a grateful passion of prayers she fell on her knees, and thanked the Power which had saved her husband.

Our young lady, in her fevered and nervous condition, could have had no more salutary medicine prescribed for her by any physician than that which chance put in her way. She and Mrs. O'Dowd watched incessantly by the wounded lad, whose pains were very severe, and in the duty thus forced upon her, Amelia had not time to brood over her personal anxieties, or to give herself up to her own fears and forebodings after her wont. The young patient told in his simple fashion the events of the day, and the actions of our friends of the gallant —th. They had suffered severely. They had lost very many officers and men. The Major's horse had been shot under him as the regiment charged, and they all thought that O'Dowd was gone, and that Dobbin had got his majority, until on their return from the charge to their old ground, the Major was discovered seated on Pyramus's carcase, refreshing himself from a case-bottle. It was Captain Osborne that cut down the French lancer who had speared the ensign. Amelia turned so pale at the notion, that Mrs. O'Dowd stopped the young ensign in this story. And it was Captain Dobbin who at the end of the day, though wounded himself, took up the lad in his arms and carried him to the surgeon, and thence to the cart which was to bring him back to Brussels. And it was he who promised the driver two louis[4] if he would make his way to Mr. Sedley's hotel in the city; and tell Mrs. Captain Osborne that the action was over, and that her husband was unhurt and well.

"Indeed, but he has a good heart that William Dobbin," Mrs. O'Dowd said, "though he is always laughing at me."

Young Stubble vowed there was not such another officer in the army, and never ceased his praises of the senior captain, his modesty, his kindness, and his admirable coolness in the field. To these parts of the conversation, Amelia lent a very distracted attention: it was only when George was spoken of that she listened, and when he was not mentioned, she thought about him.

In tending her patient, and in thinking of the wonderful escapes of the day before, her second day passed away not too slowly with Amelia. There was only one man in the army for her: and as long as he was well, it must be owned that its movements interested her little. All the reports which Jos brought from the streets fell very vaguely on her ears; though they were sufficient to give that timorous gentleman, and many other people then in Brussels, every disquiet. The French had been repulsed certainly, but it was after a severe and doubtful struggle, and with only a division of the French army. The Emperor, with the main body, was away at Ligny,[5] where he had utterly annihilated the Prussians, and was now free to bring his whole force to bear upon the allies. The Duke of Wellington was retreating upon the capital, and a great battle must be fought under its walls probably, of which the chances were more than doubtful. The Duke of Wellington had but twenty thousand British troops on whom he could rely, for the Germans were raw militia, the Belgians disaffected; and with this handful his Grace had to resist a hundred and fifty thousand men that had broken into Belgium under Napoleon. Under Napoleon! What warrior was there, however famous and skilful, that could fight at odds with him?

Jos thought of all these things, and trembled. So did all the rest of Brussels—where people felt that the fight of the day before was but the prelude to the greater combat which was imminent. One of the armies opposed to the Emperor was scattered to the winds already. The few English that could be brought to resist him would perish at their posts, and the conqueror would pass over their bodies into the city. Woe be to those whom he found there! Addresses were prepared, public functionaries assembled and debated secretly, apartments were got ready, and tricoloured banners and triumphal emblems manufactured, to welcome the arrival of His Majesty the Emperor and King.

The emigration still continued, and wherever families could find means of departure, they fled. When Jos, on the afternoon of the 17th of June, went to Rebecca's hotel, he found that the great Bareacres' carriage had at length rolled away from the *porte-cochère*. The Earl had procured a pair of horses somehow, in spite of Mrs. Crawley, and was rolling on the road to Ghent. Louis the Desired[6]

4. Coin of same value as a Napoleon, twenty francs.
5. Battle six miles from Quatre Bras.
6. Louis XVIII.

was getting ready his portmanteau in that city, too. It seemed as if Misfortune was never tired of worrying into motion that unwieldy exile.

Jos felt that the delay of yesterday had been only a respite, and that his dearly bought horses must of a surety be put into requisition. His agonies were very severe all this day. As long as there was an English army between Brussels and Napoleon, there was no need of immediate flight; but he had his horses brought from their distant stables, to the stables in the court-yard of the hotel where he lived; so that they might be under his own eyes, and beyond the risk of violent abduction. Isidor watched the stable-door constantly, and had the horses saddled, to be ready for the start. He longed intensely for that event.

After the reception of the previous day, Rebecca did not care to come near her dear Amelia. She clipped the bouquet which George had brought her, and gave fresh water to the flowers, and read over the letter which he had sent her. "Poor wretch," she said, twirling round the little bit of paper in her fingers, "how I could crush her with this!—and it is for a thing like this that she must break her heart forsooth—for a man who is stupid—a coxcomb—and who does not care for her. My poor good Rawdon is worth ten of this creature." And then she fell to thinking what she should do if—if anything happened to poor good Rawdon, and what a great piece of luck it was that he had left his horses behind.

In the course of this day too, Mrs. Crawley, who saw not without anger the Bareacres party drive off, bethought her of the precaution which the countess had taken, and did a little needlework for her own advantage; she stitched away the major part of her trinkets, bills, and bank-notes about her person, and so prepared, was ready for any event—to fly if she thought fit, or to stay and welcome the conqueror, were he Englishman or Frenchman. And I am not sure that she did not dream that night of becoming a duchess and Madame la Maréchale,[7] while Rawdon wrapped in his cloak, and making his bivouac under the rain at Mount Saint John,[8] was thinking, with all the force of his heart, about the little wife whom he had left behind him.

The next day was a Sunday. And Mrs. Major O'Dowd had the satisfaction of seeing both her patients refreshed in health and spirits by some rest which they had taken during the night. She herself had slept on a great chair in Amelia's room, ready to wait upon her poor friend or the ensign, should either need her nursing. When morning came, this robust woman went back to the house where she and her Major had their billet; and here performed an elaborate and splendid toilette, befitting the day. And it is very possible that whilst alone in that chamber, which her husband had inhabited, and where his cap still lay on the pillow, and his cane stood in the corner, one prayer at least was sent up to Heaven for the welfare of the brave soldier, Michael O'Dowd.

7. Maréchal Ney's allegiances were as flexible as Becky's.
8. A hill between Waterloo and the battleground at La Haye Sainte.

When she returned she brought her prayer-book with her, and her uncle the Dean's famous book of sermons, out of which she never failed to read every Sabbath: not understanding all, haply, not pronouncing many of the words aright, which were long and abstruse—for the Dean was a learned man, and loved long Latin words—but with great gravity, vast emphasis, and with tolerable correctness in the main. How often has my Mick listened to these sermons, she thought, and me reading in the cabin of a calm! She proposed to resume this exercise on the present day, with Amelia and the wounded ensign for a congregation. The same service was read on that day in twenty thousand churches at the same hour; and millions of British men and women, on their knees, implored protection of the Father of all.

They did not hear the noise which disturbed our little congregation at Brussels. Much louder than that which had interrupted them two days previously, as Mrs. O'Dowd was reading the service in her best voice, the cannon of Waterloo began to roar.[9]

When Jos heard that dreadful sound, he made up his mind that he would bear this perpetual recurrence of terrors no longer, and would fly at once. He rushed into the sick man's room, where our three friends had paused in their prayers, and further interrupted them by a passionate appeal to Amelia.

"I can't stand it any more, Emmy," he said; "I won't stand it; and you must come with me. I have bought a horse for you—never mind at what price—and you must dress and come with me, and ride behind Isidor."

"God forgive me, Mr. Sedley, but you are no better than a coward," Mrs. O'Dowd said, laying down the book.

"I say come, Amelia," the civilian went on; "never mind what she says; why are we to stop here and be butchered by the Frenchmen?"

"You forget the —th, my boy," said the little Stubble, the wounded hero, from his bed—"and—and you won't leave me, will you, Mrs. O'Dowd?"

"No, my dear fellow," said she, going up and kissing the boy. "No harm shall come to you while *I* stand by. I don't budge till I get the word from Mick. A pretty figure I'd be, wouldn't I, stuck behind that chap on a pillion?"

This image made[1] the young patient to burst out laughing in his bed, and even made Amelia smile. "I don't ask her," Jos shouted out—"I don't ask that—that Irishwoman, but you, Amelia; once for all, will you come?"

"Without my husband, Joseph?" Amelia said with a look of wonder, and gave her hand to the Major's wife. Jos's patience was exhausted.

"Good bye, then," he said, shaking his fist in a rage, and slamming the door by which he retreated. And this time he really gave his order for march: and mounted in the court-yard. Mrs. O'Dowd heard the clattering hoofs of the horses as they issued from the gate; and looking on, made many scornful remarks on poor Joseph as he rode down the street with Isidor after him in the laced cap. The horses,

9. Noon, June 18, 1815.
1. Revised edition reads: caused

which had not been exercised for some days, were lively, and sprang about the street. Jos, a clumsy and timid horseman, did not look to advantage in the saddle. "Look at him, Amelia, dear, driving into the parlour window. Such a bull in a china-shop *I* never saw." And presently the pair of riders disappeared at a canter down the street leading in the direction of the Ghent road. Mrs. O'Dowd pursuing them with a fire of sarcasm so long as they were in sight.

All that day from morning until past sunset, the cannon never ceased to roar. It was dark when the cannonading stopped all of a sudden.[2]

All of us have read of what occurred during that interval. The tale is in every Englishman's mouth; and you and I, who were children when the great battle was won and lost, are never tired of hearing and recounting the history of that famous action. Its remembrance rankles still in the bosoms of millions of the countrymen of those brave men who lost the day. They pant for an opportunity of revenging that humiliation; and if a contest, ending in a victory on their part, should ensue, elating them in their turn, and leaving its cursed legacy of hatred and rage behind to us, there is no end to the so-called glory and shame, and to the alternations of successful and unsuccessful murder, in which two high-spirited nations might engage. Centuries hence, we Frenchmen and Englishmen might be boasting and killing each other still, carrying out bravely the Devil's code of honour.

All our friends took their share and fought like men in the great field. All day long, whilst the women were praying ten miles away, the lines of the dauntless English infantry were receiving and repelling the furious charges of the French horsemen. Guns which were heard at Brussels were ploughing up their ranks, and comrades falling, and the resolute survivors closing in. Towards evening, the attack of the French, repeated and resisted so bravely, slackened in its fury. They had other foes besides the British to engage, or were preparing for a final onset. It came at last: the columns of the Imperial Guard marched up the hill of Saint Jean, at length and at once to sweep the English from the height which they had maintained all day, and spite of all: unscared by the thunder of the artillery, which hurled death from the English line—the dark rolling column pressed on and up the hill. It seemed almost to crest the eminence, when it began to wave and falter. Then it stopped, still facing the shot. Then at last the English troops rushed from the post from which no enemy had been able to dislodge them, and the Guard turned and fled.

No more firing was heard at Brussels—the pursuit rolled miles away. The darkness[3] came down on the field and city, and Amelia was praying for George, who was lying on his face, dead, with a bullet through his heart.

---

2. The battle ended about 8:00 P.M. with 40,000 French and 22,000 Allied soldiers dead.
3. Revised edition reads: Darkness

*Number 10* *Oct. 1847*

## *Chapter XXXIII.*

### IN WHICH MISS CRAWLEY'S RELATIONS ARE VERY ANXIOUS ABOUT HER.

THE kind reader must please to remember—while the army is marching from Flanders, and, after its heroic actions there, is advancing to take the fortifications on the frontiers of France, previous to an occupation of that country,—that there are a number of persons living peaceably in England who have to do with the history at present in hand, and must come in for their share of the chronicle. During the time of these battles and dangers, old Miss Crawley was living at Brighton, very moderately moved by the great events that were going on. The great events rendered the newspapers rather interesting, to be sure, and Briggs read out the Gazette, in which Rawdon Crawley's gallantry was mentioned with honour, and his promotion to be Lieutenant-Colonel was[1] presently recorded.

"What a pity that young man has taken such an irretrievable step in the world," his aunt said; "with his rank and distinction he might have married a brewer's daughter with a quarter of a million—like Miss Grains; or have looked to ally himself with the best families in England. He would have had my money some day or other; or his children would—for I'm not in a hurry to go, Miss Briggs, although you may be in a hurry to be rid of me; and instead of that, he is a doomed pauper, with a dancing-girl for a wife."

"Will my dear Miss Crawley not cast an eye of compassion upon the heroic soldier, whose name is inscribed in the annals of his country's glory?" said Miss Briggs, who was greatly excited by the Waterloo proceedings, and loved speaking romantically when there was an occasion. "Has not the Captain—or the Colonel as I may now style him—done deeds which make the name of Crawley illustrious?"

"Briggs, you are a fool," said Miss Crawley: "Colonel Crawley has dragged the name of Crawley through the mud, Miss Briggs. Marry a drawing-master's daughter, indeed!—marry a *dame de compagnie*[2]—for she was no better, Briggs; no, she was just what you are—only younger, and a great deal prettier and cleverer. Were you an accomplice of that abandoned wretch, I wonder, of whose vile arts he became a victim, and of whom you used to be such an admirer? Yes, I daresay you were an accomplice. But you will find yourself disappointed in my will, I can tell you: and you will have the goodness to write to Mr. Waxy, and say that I desire to see him immediately."

1. First and second printings read: promotion to be Captain and Lieutenant-Colonel was ] Revised edition reads: promotion was
2. Paid companion.

Miss Crawley was now in the habit of writing to Mr. Waxy her solicitor almost every day in the week, for her arrangements respecting her property were all revoked, and her perplexity was great as to the future disposition of her money.

The spinster had, however, rallied considerably; as was proved by the increased vigour and frequency of her sarcasms upon Miss Briggs, all which attacks the poor companion bore with meekness, with cowardice, with a resignation that was half generous, and half hypocritical—with the slavish submission, in a word, that women of her disposition and station are compelled to show. Who has not seen how women bully women? What tortures have men to endure, comparable to those daily-repeated shafts of scorn and cruelty with which poor women are riddled by the tyrants of their sex? Poor victims! But we are starting from our proposition, which is, that Miss Crawley was always particularly annoying and savage when she was rallying from illness—as they say wounds tingle most when they are about to heal.

While thus approaching, as all hoped, to convalescence, Miss Briggs was the only victim admitted into the presence of the invalid; yet Miss Crawley's relatives afar off did not forget their beloved kinswoman, and by a number of tokens, presents, and kind affectionate messages, strove to keep themselves alive in her recollection.

In the first place, let us mention her nephew, Rawdon Crawley. A few weeks after the famous fight of Waterloo, and after the Gazette had made known to her the promotion and gallantry of that distinguished officer, the Dieppe packet brought over to Miss Crawley at Brighton, a box containing presents, and a dutiful letter, from the Colonel her nephew. In the box were a pair of French epaulets, a Cross of the Legion of Honour, and the hilt of a sword—relics from the field of battle: and the letter described with a good deal of humour how the latter belonged to a commanding-officer of the Guard, who having sworn that "the Guard died, but never surrendered,"[3] was taken prisoner the next minute by a private soldier, who broke the Frenchman's sword with the butt of his musket, when Rawdon made himself master of the shattered weapon. As for the cross and epaulets, they came from a Colonel of French cavalry, who had fallen under the aide-de-camp's arm in the battle: and Rawdon Crawley did not know what better to do with the spoils than to send them to his kindest and most affectionate old friend. Should he continue to write to her from Paris, whither the army was marching? He might be able to give her interesting news from that capital, and of some of Miss Crawley's old friends of the emigration, to whom she had shown so much kindness during their distress.

The spinster caused Briggs to write back to the Colonel a gracious and complimentary letter, encouraging him to continue his correspondence. His first letter was so excessively lively and amusing that she should look with pleasure for its successors.—"Of course I know," she explained to Miss Briggs, "that Rawdon could not write such a good letter any more than you could, my poor Briggs, and that it is that clever little wretch of a Rebecca, who dictates every word to him;

3. Baron Pierre Jacques Étienne Cambronne (1770–1842) commanded the Imperial Guard at Waterloo. His tomb records that his response to a call to surrender was "The Guard dies but never surrenders"; however, in life he claimed to have said merely, "Merde."

but that is no reason why my nephew should not amuse me; and so I wish to let him understand that I am in high good-humour."

I wonder whether she knew that it was not only Becky who wrote the letters, but that Mrs. Rawdon actually took and sent home the trophies—which she bought for a few francs, from one of the innumerable pedlars, who immediately began to deal in relics of the war. The novelist, who knows everything, knows this also. Be this, however, as it may, Miss Crawley's gracious reply greatly encouraged our young friends Rawdon and his lady, who hoped for the best from their aunt's evidently pacified humour: and they took care to entertain her with many delightful letters from Paris, whither, as Rawdon said, they had the good luck to go in the track of the conquering army.

To the rector's lady, who went off to tend her husband's broken collar-bone at the Rectory at Queen's Crawley, the spinster's communications were by no means so gracious. Mrs. Bute, that brisk, managing, lively, imperious woman, had committed the most fatal of all errors with regard to her sister-in-law. She had not merely oppressed her and her household—she had bored Miss Crawley: and if poor Miss Briggs had been a woman of any spirit, she might have been made happy by the commission which her principal gave her, to write a letter to Mrs. Bute Crawley, saying that Miss Crawley's health was greatly improved since Mrs. Bute had left her, and begging the latter on no account to put herself to trouble, or quit her family for Miss Crawley's sake. This triumph over a lady who had been very haughty and cruel in her behaviour to Miss Briggs, would have rejoiced most women; but the truth is, Briggs was a woman of no spirit at all, and the moment her enemy was discomfited she began to feel compassion in her favour.

"How silly I was," Mrs. Bute thought, and with reason, "ever to hint that I was coming, as I did, in that foolish letter when we sent Miss Crawley the guinea-fowls. I ought to have gone without a word to the poor dear doting old creature, and taken her out of the hands of that ninny Briggs, and that harpy of a *femme de chambre*. Oh! Bute, Bute, why did you break your collar-bone?"

Why, indeed? We have seen how Mrs. Bute, having the game in her hands, had really played her cards too well. She had ruled over Miss Crawley's household utterly and completely, to be utterly and completely routed when a favourable opportunity for rebellion came. She and her household, however, considered that she had been the victim of horrible selfishness and treason, and that her sacrifices in Miss Crawley's behalf had met with the most savage ingratitude. Rawdon's promotion, and the honourable mention made of his name in the Gazette, filled this good Christian lady also with alarm. Would his aunt relent towards him now that he was a Colonel[4] and a C.B.? and would that odious Rebecca once more get into favour? The rector's wife wrote a sermon for her husband about the vanity of military glory and the prosperity of the wicked, which the worthy parson read in his best voice and without understanding one syllable of it. He had Pitt Crawley for one of his auditors—Pitt, who had

4. Revised edition reads: Lieutenant-Colonel

come with his two half-sisters to church, which the old Baronet could now by no means be brought to frequent.

Since the departure of Becky Sharp, that old wretch had given himself up entirely to his bad courses, to the great scandal of the county and the mute horror of his son. The ribbons in Miss Horrocks's cap became more splendid than ever. The polite families fled the hall and its owner in terror. Sir Pitt went about tippling at his tenants' houses; and drank rum-and-water with the farmers at Mudbury and the neighbouring places on market-days. He drove the family coach-and-four to Southampton with Miss Horrocks inside: and the county people expected, every week, as his son did in speechless agony, that his marriage with her would be announced in the provincial paper. It was indeed a rude burthen for Mr. Crawley to bear. His eloquence was palsied at the missionary meetings, and other religious assemblies in the neighbourhood, where he had been in the habit of presiding, and of speaking for hours; for he felt, when he rose, that the audience said, "That is the son of the old reprobate Sir Pitt, who is very likely drinking at the public-house at this very moment." And once when he was speaking of the benighted condition of the king of Timbuctoo, and the number of his wives who were likewise in darkness, some tipsy miscreant from the crowd asked, "How many is there at Queen's Crawley, Young Squaretoes?"[5] to the surprise of the platform, and the ruin of Mr. Pitt's speech. And the two daughters of the house of Queen's Crawley would have been allowed to run utterly wild (for Sir Pitt swore that no governess should ever enter into his doors again), had not Mr. Crawley, by threatening the old gentleman, forced the latter to send them to school.

Meanwhile, as we have said, whatever individual differences there might be between them all, Miss Crawley's dear nephews and nieces were unanimous in loving her and sending her tokens of affection. Thus Mrs. Bute sent guinea-fowls, and some remarkably fine cauliflowers, and a pretty purse or pincushion worked by her darling girls, who begged to keep a *little* place in the recollection of their dear aunt, while Mr. Pitt sent peaches and grapes and venison from the Hall. The Southampton coach used to carry these tokens of affection to Miss Crawley at Brighton: it used sometimes to convey Mr. Pitt thither too: for his differences with Sir Pitt caused Mr. Crawley to absent himself a good deal from home now: and besides, he had an attraction at Brighton in the person of the Lady Jane Sheepshanks whose engagement to Mr. Crawley has been formerly mentioned in this history. Her Ladyship and her sisters lived at Brighton with their mamma, the Countess Southdown, that strong-minded woman so favourably known in the serious world.

A few words ought to be said regarding her Ladyship and her noble family, who are bound by ties of present and future relationship to the house of Crawley. Respecting the chief of the Southdown family, Clement William, fourth Earl of Southdown, little need be told, except that his Lordship came into Parliament (as Lord Wolsey), under the auspices of Mr. Wilberforce,[6] and for a time was a credit to his

5. Though generally the word means "old-fashioned" or "conservative," it also was slang for "preacher."
6. See chapter IX.

political sponsor, and decidedly a serious young man. But words cannot describe the feelings of his admirable mother, when she learned, very shortly after her noble husband's demise, that her son was a member of several worldly clubs, had lost largely at play at Wattiers and the Cocoa Tree; that he had raised money on post-obits,[7] and encumbered the family estate; that he drove four-in-hand, and patronised the ring; and that he actually had an opera-box, where he entertained the most dangerous bachelor company. His name was only mentioned with groans in the dowager's circle.

The Lady Emily was her brother's senior by many years; and took considerable rank in the serious world as author of some of the delightful tracts before mentioned, and of many hymns and spiritual pieces. A mature spinster, and having but faint[8] ideas of marriage, her love for the blacks occupied almost all her feelings. It is to her, I believe, we owe that beautiful poem,—

> "Lead us to some sunny isle,
> Yonder in the western deep;
> Where the skies for ever smile,
> And the blacks for ever weep," &c.[9]

She had correspondences with clerical gentlemen in most of our East and West India possessions; and was secretly attached[1] to the Reverend Silas Hornblower, who was tattooed in the South Sea Islands.

As for the Lady Jane, on whom, as it has been said, Mr. Pitt Crawley's affection had been placed, she was gentle, blushing, silent, and timid. In spite of his falling away, she wept for her brother, and was quite ashamed of loving him still. Even yet she used to send him little hurried smuggled notes, and pop them in the post in private. The one dreadful secret which weighed upon her life was, that she and the old housekeeper had been to pay Southdown a furtive visit at his chambers in the Albany;[2] and found him—O the naughty dear abandoned wretch! smoking a cigar with a bottle of Curaçoa before him. She admired her sister, she adored her mother, she thought Mr. Crawley the most delightful and accomplished of men, after Southdown, that fallen angel: and her mamma and sister, who were ladies of the most superior sort, managed everything for her, and regarded her with that amiable pity, of which your really superior woman always has such a share to give away. Her mamma ordered her dresses, her books, her bonnets, and her ideas for her. She was made to take pony-riding, or piano-exercise, or any other sort of bodily medicament, according as my lady Southdown saw meet; and her ladyship would have kept her daughter in pinafores up to her present age of six-and-twenty, but that they were thrown off when Lady Jane was presented to Queen Charlotte.

7. Wattiers, the Cocoa Tree: clubs in Piccadilly and St. James's Street. See chapter XI. Post-obits: Money borrowed against an expected inheritance.
8. First and second printings read: having given up all
9. Quoted, probably from memory, from "Go! ye messengers of God," in *A Selection of Hymns Used in Trinity Church, Lower Gardiner-street, Dublin* (1841). In *The Irish Sketch Book*, chapter XXIV, Thackeray called it "nonsensical false twaddle."
1. First and second printings read: and report says was once attached
2. A mansion in Piccadilly converted to bachelor quarters for which the list of tenants reads like a "Who's Who."

When these ladies first came to their house at Brighton, it was to them alone that Mr. Crawley paid his personal visits, contenting himself by leaving a card at his aunt's house, and making a modest inquiry of Mr. Bowls or his assistant footman, with respect to the health of the invalid. When he met Miss Briggs coming home from the library with a cargo of novels under her arm, Mr. Crawley blushed in a manner quite unusual to him, as he stepped forward and shook Miss Crawley's companion by the hand. He introduced Miss Briggs to the lady with whom he happened to be walking, the Lady Jane Sheepshanks, saying, "Lady Jane, permit me to introduce to you my aunt's kindest friend and most affectionate companion, Miss Briggs, whom you know under another title, as authoress of the delightful 'Lyrics of the Heart,' of which you are so fond." Lady Jane blushed too as she held out a kind little hand to Miss Briggs, and said something very civil and incoherent about mamma, and proposing to call on Miss Crawley, and being glad to be made known to the friends and relatives of Mr. Crawley; and with soft dove-like eyes saluted Miss Briggs as they separated, while Pitt Crawley treated her to a profound courtly bow, such

as he had used to H.H. the Duchess[3] of Pumpernickel, when he was

3. First and second printings read: to the Grand Duchess

attaché at that court. The artful diplomatist and disciple of the Machiavellian Binkie! It was he who had given Lady Jane that copy of poor Briggs's early poems, which he remembered to have seen at Queen's Crawley, with a dedication from the poetess to his father's late wife; and he brought the volume with him to Brighton, reading it in the Southampton coach, and marking it with his own pencil, before he presented it to the gentle Lady Jane.

It was he, too, who laid before Lady Southdown the great advantages which might occur from an intimacy between her family and Miss Crawley,—advantages both worldly and spiritual, he said: for Miss Crawley was now quite alone; the monstrous dissipation and alliance of his brother Rawdon, had estranged her affections from that reprobate young man; the greedy tyranny and avarice of Mrs. Bute Crawley had caused the old lady to revolt against the exorbitant pretensions of that part of the family; and though he himself had held off all his life from cultivating Miss Crawley's friendship, with perhaps an improper pride, he thought now that every becoming means should be taken, both to save her soul from perdition, and to secure her fortune to himself as the head of the house of Crawley.

The strong-minded Lady Southdown quite agreed in both proposals of her son-in-law, and was for converting Miss Crawley off hand. At her own home, both at Southdown and at Trottermore Castle, this tall and awful missionary of the truth rode about the country in her barouche with outriders,[4] launched packets of tracts among the cottagers and tenants, and would order Gaffer Jones to be converted, as she would order Goody Hicks[5] to take a James's powder, without appeal, resistance, or benefit of clergy.[6] My Lord Southdown, her late husband, an epileptic and simple-minded nobleman, was in the habit of approving of everything which his Matilda did and thought. So that whatever changes her own belief might undergo (and it accommodated itself to a prodigious variety of opinion, taken from all sorts of doctors among the Dissenters)[7] she had not the least scruple in ordering all her tenants and inferiors to follow and believe after her. Thus whether she received the Reverend Saunders McNitre the Scotch divine; or the Reverend Luke Waters the mild Wesleyan; or the Reverend Giles Jowls the illuminated Cobbler who dubbed himself Reverend as Napoleon crowned himself Emperor—the household, children, tenantry of my Lady Southdown were expected to go down on their knees with her Ladyship, and say Amen to the prayers of either Doctor. During these exercises old Southdown, on account of his invalid condition, was allowed to sit in his own room, and have negus and the paper read to him. Lady Jane was the old Earl's favourite daughter, and tended him and loved him sincerely: as for Lady Emily, the authoress of the "Washerwoman of Finchley Common," her denunciations of future punishment (at this period, for her opinions modified afterwards) were so awful that they used to

4. Attendants on horseback accompanying the carriage.
5. Gaffer and Goody were terms of respect in lower and rural classes. James's powder was a patented fever medicine introduced by Dr. Robert James (1705–76) and still popular in the early nineteenth century.
6. The clergy was immune from trial in secular courts until 1827.
7. Protestants who did not conform to the Church of England.

frighten the timid old gentleman her father, and the physicians declared his fits always occurred after one of her Ladyship's sermons.

"I will certainly call," said Lady Southdown then, in reply to the exhortation of her daughter's *prétendu,*[8] Mr. Pitt Crawley—"Who is Miss Crawley's medical man?"

Mr. Crawley mentioned the name of Mr. Creamer.

"A most dangerous and ignorant practitioner, my dear Pitt. I have providentially been the means of removing him from several houses: though in one or two instances I did not arrive in time. I could not save poor dear General Glanders, who was dying under the hands of that ignorant man—dying. He rallied a little under the Podger's pills which I administered to him; but alas! it was too late. His death was delightful, however; and his change was only for the better: Creamer, my dear Pitt, must leave your aunt."

Pitt expressed his perfect acquiescence. He too had been carried along by the energy of his noble kinswoman, and future mother-in-law. He had been made to accept Saunders McNitre, Luke Waters, Giles Jowls, Podger's Pills, Rodger's Pills, Pokey's Elixir, every one of her Ladyship's remedies spiritual or temporal. He never left her house without carrying respectfully away with him piles of her quack theology and medicine. O my dear brethren and fellow-sojourners in Vanity Fair, which among you does not know and suffer under such benevolent despots? It is in vain you say to them, "Dear Madam, I took Podger's specific at your orders last year, and believe in it. Why, why, am I to recant and accept the Rodger's articles now?" There is no help for it; the faithful proselytiser, if she cannot convince by argument, bursts into tears, and the recusant finds himself, at the end of the contest, taking down the bolus,[9] and saying, "Well, well, Rodger's be it."

"And as for her spiritual state," continued the Lady, "that of course must be looked to immediately; with Creamer about her, she may go off any day: and in what a condition, my dear Pitt, in what a dreadful condition! I will send the Reverend Mr. Irons to her instantly. Jane, write a line to the Reverend Bartholomew Irons, in the third person, and say that I desire the pleasure of his company this evening at tea at half past six. He is an awakening man; he ought to see Miss Crawley before she rests this night. And Emily, my love, get ready a packet of books for Miss Crawley. Put up 'A Voice from the Flames,' 'A Trumpet-warning to Jericho,' and the 'Fleshpots Broken; or, the Converted Cannibal.'"

"And the 'Washerwoman of Finchley Common,' Mamma," said Lady Emily. "It is as well to begin soothingly at first."

"Stop, my dear ladies," said Pitt the diplomatist. "With every deference to the opinion of my beloved and respected Lady Southdown, I think it would be quite unadvisable to commence so early upon serious topics with Miss Crawley. Remember her delicate condition, and how little, how *very* little accustomed she has hitherto been to considerations connected with her immortal welfare."

8. Intended, fiancé.
9. Large pill.

"Can we then begin too early, Pitt?" said Lady Emily, rising with six little books already in her hand.

"If you begin abruptly, you will frighten her altogether. I know my aunt's worldly nature so well as to be sure that any abrupt attempt at conversion will be the very worst means that can be employed for the welfare of that unfortunate lady. You will only frighten and annoy her. She will very likely fling the books away, and refuse all acquaintance with the givers."

"You are as worldly as Miss Crawley, Pitt," said Lady Emily, tossing out of the room, her books in her hand.

"And I need not tell you, my dear Lady Southdown," Pitt continued, in a low voice, and without heeding the interruption, "how fatal a little want of gentleness and caution may be to any hopes which we may entertain with regard to the worldly possessions of my aunt. Remember she has seventy thousand pounds; think of her age, and her highly nervous and delicate condition: I know that she has destroyed the will which was made in my brother's (Colonel Crawley's) favour: it is by soothing that wounded spirit that we must lead it into the right path, and not by frightening it; and so I think you will agree with me that—that"—

"Of course, of course," Lady Southdown remarked. "Jane, my love, you need not send that note to Mr. Irons. If her health is such that discussions fatigue her, we will wait her amendment. I will call upon Miss Crawley to-morrow."

"And if I might suggest, my sweet lady," Pitt said in a bland tone, "it would be as well not to take our precious Emily, who is too enthusiastic; but rather that you should be accompanied by our sweet and dear Lady Jane."

"Most certainly, Emily would ruin everything," Lady Southdown said; and this time agreed to forego her usual practice, which was, as we have said, before she bore down personally upon any individual whom she proposed to subjugate, to fire in a quantity of tracts upon the menaced party; (as a charge of the French was always preceded by a furious cannonade). Lady Southdown, we say, for the sake of the invalid's health, or for the sake of her soul's ultimate welfare, or for the sake of her money, agreed to temporise.

The next day the great Southdown female family carriage, with the Earl's coronet and the lozenge (upon which the three lambs trottant argent upon the field vert of the Southdowns, were quartered with sable on a bend or, three snuff-mulls gules, the cognizance[1] of the house of Binkie), drove up in state to Miss Crawley's door, and the tall serious footman handed in to Mr. Bowls her Ladyship's cards for Miss Crawley, and one likewise for Miss Briggs. By way of compromise, Lady Emily sent in a packet in the evening for the latter lady, containing copies of the "Washerwoman," and other mild and favourite tracts for Miss B.'s own perusal; and a few for the servants' hall, viz.: "Crumbs from the Pantry;" "The Frying Pan and the Fire," and "The Livery of Sin," of a much stronger kind.

1. Lambs trottant argent: silver or white lambs in trotting stance. Vert: green. Sable: black. Bend or: gold diagonal. Snuff-mulls gules: red snuff grinders. Cognizance: emblem, heraldic shield.

## *Chapter XXXIV.*

### JAMES CRAWLEY'S PIPE IS PUT OUT.

HE amiable behaviour of Mr. Crawley and Lady Jane's kind reception of her, highly flattered Miss Briggs, who was enabled to speak a good word for the latter, after the cards of the Southdown family had been presented to Miss Crawley. A Countess's card left personally too for her, Briggs, was not a little pleasing to the poor friendless companion. "What could Lady Southdown mean by leaving a card upon *you,* I wonder, Miss Briggs?" said the republican Miss Crawley; upon which the companion meekly said "that she hoped there could be no harm in a lady of rank taking notice of a poor gentlewoman," and she put away this card in her work-box amongst her most cherished personal treasures. Furthermore, Miss Briggs explained how she had met Mr. Crawley walking with his cousin and long-affianced bride the day before: and she told how kind and gentle-looking the lady was, and what a plain, not to say common, dress she had, all the articles of which, from the bonnet down to the boots, she described and estimated with female accuracy.

Miss Crawley allowed Briggs to prattle on without interrupting her too much. As she got well, she was pining for society. Mr. Creamer, her medical man, would not hear of her returning to her old haunts and dissipation in London. The old spinster was too glad to find any companionship at Brighton, and not only were the cards acknowledged the very next day, but Pitt Crawley was graciously invited to come and see his aunt. He came, bringing with him Lady Southdown and her daughter. The dowager did not say a word about the state of Miss Crawley's soul; but talked with much discretion about the weather: about the war and the downfall of the monster Bonaparte: and above all, about doctors, quacks, and the particular merits of Dr. Podgers, whom she then patronised.

During their interview Pitt Crawley made a great stroke, and one which showed that, had his diplomatic career not been blighted by early neglect, he might have risen to a high rank in his profession. When the Countess Dowager of Southdown fell foul of the Corsican upstart, as the fashion was in those days, and showed that he was a monster stained with every conceivable crime, a coward and a tyrant not fit to live, one whose fall was predicted, &c., Pitt Crawley suddenly took up the cudgels in favour of the man of Destiny. He described the First Consul as he saw him at Paris at the Peace of Amiens;[1] when he, Pitt Crawley, had the gratification of making the acquaintance of

1. Napoleon, as first consul, signed the short-lived treaty at Amiens, which was to end the French Revolution. Napoleon's wars of expansion began the next year.

the great and good Mr. Fox, a statesman whom, however much he might differ with him, it was impossible not to admire fervently—a statesman who had always had the highest opinion of the Emperor Napoleon.[2] And he spoke in terms of the strongest indignation of the faithless conduct of the allies towards this dethroned monarch, who, after giving himself generously up to their mercy, was consigned to an ignoble and cruel banishment, while a bigotted Popish rabble was tyrannising over France in his stead.[3]

This orthodox horror of Romish superstition saved Pitt Crawley in Lady Southdown's opinion, whilst his admiration for Fox and Napoleon raised him immeasurably in Miss Crawley's eyes. Her friendship with that defunct British statesman was mentioned when we first introduced her in this history. A true Whig, Miss Crawley had been in opposition all through the war, and though, to be sure, the downfall of the Emperor did not very much agitate the old lady, or his ill-treatment tend to shorten her life or natural rest, yet Pitt spoke to her heart when he lauded both her idols; and by that single speech made immense progress in her favour.

"And what do you think, my dear?" Miss Crawley said to the young lady, for whom she had taken a liking at first sight, as she always did for pretty and modest young people; though it must be owned her affections cooled as rapidly as they rose.

Lady Jane blushed very much, and said "that she did not understand politics, which she left to wiser heads than her's; but though Mamma was, no doubt, correct, Mr. Crawley had spoken beautifully." And when the ladies were retiring at the conclusion of their visit, Miss Crawley hoped "Lady Southdown would be so kind as to send her Lady Jane sometimes, if she could be spared to come down and console a poor sick lonely old woman." This promise was graciously accorded, and they separated upon great terms of amity.

"Don't let Lady Southdown come again, Pitt," said the old lady. "She is stupid and pompous like all your mother's family, whom I never could endure. But bring that nice good-natured little Lady Jane as often as ever you please." Pitt promised that he would do so. He did not tell the Countess of Southdown what opinion his aunt had formed of her Ladyship, who, on the contrary, thought that she had made a most delightful and majestic impression on Miss Crawley.

And so, nothing loth to comfort a sick lady, and perhaps not sorry in her heart to be freed now and again from the dreary spouting of the Reverend Bartholomew Irons, and the serious toadies who gathered round the footstool of the pompous Countess, her mamma, Lady Jane became a pretty constant visitor to Miss Crawley, accompanied her in her drives, and solaced many of her evenings. She was so naturally good and soft, that even Firkin was not jealous of her; and the gentle Briggs thought her friend was less cruel to her, when kind Lady Jane was by. Towards her Ladyship Miss Crawley's manners were charming. The old spinster told her a thousand anecdotes about her youth, talking to her in a very different strain from

2. Charles James Fox (1749–1806), Whig statesman and a favorite of Miss Crawley. See chapter X.
3. Napoleon had surrendered to the British navy in hopes of safe passage to America but was imprisoned on St. Helena. The Bourbons, hardly rabble, were Catholic and tyrannical.

that in which she had been accustomed to converse with the godless little Rebecca; for there was that in Lady Jane's innocence which rendered light talking impertinence before her, and Miss Crawley was too much of a gentlewoman to offend such purity. The young lady herself had never received kindness except from this old spinster, and her brother and father: and she repaid Miss Crawley's *engoûment*[4] by artless sweetness and friendship.

In the autumn evenings (when Rebecca was flaunting at Paris, the gayest among the gay conquerors there, and our Amelia, our dear wounded Amelia, ah! where was she?) Lady Jane would be sitting in Miss Crawley's drawing-room singing sweetly to her, in the twilight, her little simple songs and hymns, while the sun was setting and the sea was roaring on the beach. The old spinster used to wake up when these ditties ceased, and ask for more. As for Briggs, and the quantity of tears of happiness which she now shed as she pretended to knit, and looked out at the splendid ocean darkling before the windows, and the lamps of heaven beginning more brightly to shine—who, I say, can measure the happiness and sensibility of Briggs?

Pitt meanwhile in the dining-room, with a pamphlet of the Corn Laws[5] or a Missionary Register by his side, took that kind of recreation which suits romantic and unromantic men after dinner. He sipt Madeira: built castles in the air: thought himself a fine fellow: felt himself much more in love with Jane than he had been any time these seven years, during which their *liaison* had lasted without the slightest impatience on Pitt's part—and slept a good deal. When the time for coffee came, Mr. Bowls used to enter in a noisy manner, and summon Squire Pitt, who would be found in the dark very busy with his pamphlet.

"I wish, my love, I could get somebody to play picquet with me," Miss Crawley said, one night, when this functionary made his appearance with the candles and the coffee. "Poor Briggs can no more play than an owl, she is so stupid" (the spinster always took an opportunity of abusing Briggs before the servants); "and I think I should sleep better if I had my game."

At this Lady Jane blushed to the tips of her little ears, and down to the ends of her pretty fingers; and when Mr. Bowls had quitted the room, and the door was quite shut, she said:

"Miss Crawley, I can play a little. I used to—to play a little with poor dear papa."

"Come and kiss me. Come and kiss me this instant, you dear good little soul," cried Miss Crawley in an ecstacy; and in this picturesque and friendly occupation Mr. Pitt found the old lady and the young one, when he came up-stairs with his pamphlet in his hand. How she did blush all the evening, that poor Lady Jane!

It must not be imagined that Mr. Pitt Crawley's artifices escaped the attention of his dear relations at the Rectory at Queen's Crawley. Hampshire and Sussex lie very close together, and Mrs. Bute had friends in the latter county who took care to inform her of all,

4. Infatuation.
5. Tariffs on imported grain, passed in 1815, repealed in 1846.

and a great deal more than all, that passed at Miss Crawley's house at Brighton. Pitt was there more and more. He did not come for months together to the Hall, where his abominable old father abandoned himself completely to rum and water, and the odious society of the Horrocks family. Pitt's success rendered the Rector's family furious, and Mrs. Bute regretted more (though she confessed less) than ever her monstrous fault in so insulting Miss Briggs, and in being so haughty and parsimonious to Bowls and Firkin, that she had not a single person left in Miss Crawley's household to give her information of what took place there. "It was all Bute's collar-bone," she persisted in saying; "if that had not broke, I never would have left her. I am a martyr to duty and to your odious unclerical habit of hunting, Bute."

"Hunting; nonsense! It was you that frightened her, Barbara," the divine interposed. "You're a clever woman, but you've got a devil of a temper; and you're a screw with your money, Barbara."

"You'd have been screwed in gaol, Bute, if I had not kept your money."

"I know I would, my dear," said the Rector, good-naturedly. "You *are* a clever woman, but you manage too well, you know:" and the pious man consoled himself with a big glass of port.

"What the deuce can she find in that spoony of a Pitt Crawley?" he continued. "The fellow has not pluck enough to say Bo to a goose. I remember when Rawdon, who *is* a man and be hanged to him, used to flog him round the stables as if he was a whipping-top: and Pitt would go howling home to his ma—ha, ha! Why, either of my boys would wap him with one hand. Jim says he's remembered at Oxford as Miss Crawley still—the spooney."

"I say, Barbara," his reverence continued, after a pause.

"What!" said Barbara, who was biting her nails, and drubbing the table.

"I say, why not send Jim over to Brighton to see if he can do any thing with the old lady. He's very near getting his degree, you know. He's only been plucked[6] twice—so was I—but he's had the advantages of Oxford and a university education. He knows some of the best chaps there. He pulls stroke in the Boniface boat. He's a handsome feller. D— it, ma'am, let's put him on the old woman, hey; and tell him to thrash Pitt if he says any think. Ha, ha, ha!"

"Jim might go down and see her, certainly," the housewife said; adding, with a sigh, "If we could but get one of the girls into the house; but she could never endure them, because they are not pretty!" Those unfortunate and well-educated women made themselves heard from the neighbouring drawing-room, where they were thrumming away, with hard fingers, an elaborate music-piece on the piano-forte, as their mother spoke; and indeed they were at music, or at backboard, or at geography, or at history, the whole day long. But what avail all these accomplishments, in Vanity Fair, to girls who are short, poor, plain, and have a bad complexion? Mrs. Bute could think of nobody but the Curate to take one of them off her hands; and Jim coming in from the stable at this minute, through the par-

6. Failed at the university.

lour window, with a short pipe stuck in his oil-skin cap, he and his father fell to talking about odds on the St. Leger,[7] and the colloquy between the Rector and his wife ended.

Mrs. Bute did not augur much good to the cause from the sending of her son James as an ambassador, and saw him depart in rather a despairing mood. Nor did the young fellow himself, when told what his mission was to be, expect much pleasure or benefit from it; but he was consoled by the thought that possibly the old lady would give him some handsome remembrance of her, which would pay a few of his most pressing bills at the commencement of the ensuing Oxford term, and so took his place by the coach from Southampton, and was safely landed at Brighton on the same evening, with his portmanteau, his favourite bull-dog Towzer, and an immense basket of farm and garden produce, from the dear Rectory folks to the dear Miss Crawley. Considering it was too late to disturb the invalid lady on the first night of his arrival, he put up at an inn, and did not wait upon Miss Crawley until a late hour in the noon of next day.

James Crawley, when his aunt had last beheld him, was a gawky lad, at that uncomfortable age when the voice varies between an unearthly treble and a preternatural base; when the face not uncommonly blooms out with appearances for which Rowland's Kalydor[8] is said to act as a cure; when boys are seen to shave furtively with their sister's scissors, and the sight of other young women produces intolerable sensations of terror in them; when the great hands and ankles protrude a long way from garments which have grown too tight for them; when their presence after dinner is at once frightful to the ladies, who are whispering in the twilight in the drawing room, and inexpressibly odious to the gentlemen over the mahogany,[9] who are restrained from freedom of intercourse and delightful interchange of wit by the presence of that gawky innocence; when, at the conclusion of the second glass, papas say, "Jack, my boy, go out and see if the evening holds up," and the youth, willing to be free, yet hurt at not being yet a man, quits the incomplete banquet. James, then a hobbadehoy,[1] was now become a young man, having had the benefits of a university education, and acquired the inestimable polish, which is gained by living in a fast set at a small college, and contracting debts, and being rusticated,[2] and being plucked.

He was a handsome lad, however, when he came to present himself to his aunt at Brighton, and good looks were always a title to the fickle old lady's favour. Nor did his blushes and awkwardness take away from it: she was pleased with these healthy tokens of the young gentleman's ingenuousness.

He said "he had come down for a couple of days to see a man of his college, and—and to pay my respects to you, Ma'am, and my father's and mother's, who hope you are well."

7. A September horse race for three-year-olds run at Doncaster, Yorkshire.
8. Rowland marketed a number of patent medicines; Kalydor was for acne.
9. Dinner over, the ladies by custom ascended to the drawing room, leaving the men at the table for drink and talk.
1. Youth at an awkward stage.
2. Suspended from the university.

Pitt was in the room with Miss Crawley when the lad was announced, and looked very blank when his name was mentioned. The old lady had plenty of humour, and enjoyed her correct nephew's perplexity. She asked after all the people at the Rectory with great interest; and said she was thinking of paying them a visit. She praised the lad to his face, and said he was well-grown and very much improved, and that it was a pity his sisters had not some of his good looks; and finding, on inquiry, that he had taken up his quarters at an hotel, would not hear of his stopping there, but bade Mr. Bowls send for Mr. James Crawley's things instantly; "and hark ye, Bowls," she added, with great graciousness, "you will have the goodness to pay Mr. James's bill."

She flung Pitt a look of arch triumph, which caused that diplomatist almost to choke with envy. Much as he had ingratiated himself with his aunt, she had never yet invited him to stay under her roof, and here was a young whipper-snapper, who at first sight was made welcome there.

"I beg your pardon, Sir," says Bowls, advancing with a profound bow; "what otel, Sir, shall Thomas fetch the luggage from?"

"O, dam," said young James, starting up, as if in some alarm, "I'll go."

"What!" said Miss Crawley.

"The Tom Cribb's Arms,"[3] said James, blushing deeply.

Miss Crawley burst out laughing at this title. Mr. Bowls gave one abrupt guffaw, as a confidential servant of the family, but choked the rest of the volley; the diplomatist only smiled.

"I—I didn't know any better," said James, looking down. "I've never been here before; it was the coachman told me." The young story-teller! The fact is, that on the Southampton coach, the day previous, James Crawley had met the Tutbury Pet, who was coming to Brighton to make a match with the Rottingdean Fibber;[4] and enchanted by the Pet's conversation, had passed the evening in company with that scientific man and his friends, at the inn in question.

"I—I'd best go and settle the score," James continued. "Couldn't think of asking you, Ma'am," he added, generously.

This delicacy made his aunt laugh the more.

"Go and settle the bill, Bowls," she said, with a wave of her hand, "and bring it to me."

Poor lady, she did not know what she had done! "There—there's a little *dawg*," said James, looking frightfully guilty. "I'd best go for him. He bites footmen's calves."

All the party cried out with laughing at this description; even Briggs and Lady Jane, who was sitting mute during the interview between Miss Crawley and her nephew; and Bowls, without a word, quitted the room.

Still, by way of punishing her elder nephew, Miss Crawley persisted in being gracious to the young Oxonian. There were no limits to her kindness or her compliments when they once began. She told

3. Many taverns were named for this boxing champion (see chapter VI), who retired into innkeeping himself, though never at one that bore his name.

4. Tutbury Pet: identified by Thackeray in *The Snobs of England*, chapter XIV, as William Ramm. The Fibber is untraced (Harden).

Pitt he might come to dinner, and insisted that James should accompany her in her drive, and paraded him solemnly up and down the cliff, on the back seat of the barouche. During all this excursion, she condescended to say civil things to him: she quoted Italian and French poetry to the poor bewildered lad, and persisted that he was a fine scholar, and was perfectly sure he would gain a gold medal, and be a Senior Wrangler.[5]

"Haw, haw," laughed James, encouraged by these compliments; "Senior Wrangler, indeed; that's at the other shop."

"What is the other shop, my dear child?" said the lady.

"Senior Wrangler's at Cambridge, not Oxford," said the scholar, with a knowing air; and would probably have been more confidential, but that suddenly there appeared on the cliff in a tax-cart,[6] drawn by a bang-up pony, dressed in white flannel coats, with mother-of-pearl buttons, his friends the Tutbury Pet and the Rottingdean Fibber, with three other gentlemen of their acquaintance, who all saluted poor James there in the carriage as he sate. This incident damped the ingenuous youth's spirits, and no word of yea or nay could he be induced to utter during the rest of the drive.

On his return he found his room prepared, and his portmanteau ready, and might have remarked that Mr. Bowls's countenance, when the latter conducted him to his apartment,[7] wore a look of gravity, wonder, and compassion. But the thought of Mr. Bowls did not enter his head. He was deploring the dreadful predicament in which he found himself, in a house full of old women, jabbering French and Italian, and talking poetry to him. "Reglarly up a tree, by jingo!" exclaimed the modest boy, who could not face the gentlest of her sex—not even Briggs—when she began to talk to him; whereas, put him at Iffley Lock,[8] and he could out-slang the boldest bargeman.

At dinner, James appeared choking in a white neckcloth, and had the honour of handing my Lady Jane down stairs, while Briggs and Mr. Crawley followed afterwards, conducting the old lady, with her apparatus of bundles, and shawls, and cushions. Half of Briggs's time at dinner was spent in superintending the invalid's comfort, and in cutting up chicken for her fat spaniel. James did not talk much, but he made a point of asking all the ladies to drink wine, and accepted Mr. Crawley's challenge, and consumed the greater part of a bottle of champagne which Mr. Bowls was ordered to produce in his honour. The ladies having withdrawn, and the two cousins being left together, Pitt, the ex-diplomatist, became very communicative and friendly. He asked after James's career at college—what his prospects in life were—hoped heartily he would get on; and, in a word, was frank and amiable. James's tongue unloosed with the Port, and he told his cousin his life, his prospects, his debts, his troubles at the little-go,[9] and his rows with the proctors, filling rapidly from the bottles before him, and flying from Port to Madeira with joyous activity.

5. Top honors in mathematics.
6. Open farm cart.
7. Revised edition reads: apartments,
8. Two miles southeast of Oxford on the Thames.
9. First examination for the B.A. degree.

"The chief pleasure which my aunt has," said Mr. Crawley, filling his glass, "is that people should do as they like in her house. This is Liberty Hall, James, and you can't do Miss Crawley a greater kindness than to do as you please, and ask for what you will.[1] I know you have all sneered at me in the country for being a Tory. Miss Crawley is liberal enough to suit any fancy. She is a Republican in principle, and despises everything like rank or title."

"Why are you going to marry an Earl's daughter?" said James.

"My dear friend, remember it is not poor Lady Jane's fault that she is well born," Pitt replied with a courtly air. "She cannot help being a lady. Besides, I am a Tory, you know."

"O as for that," said Jim, "there's nothing like old blood; no, dammy, nothing like it. I'm none of your radicals. I know what it is to be a gentleman, dammy. See the chaps in a boat-race; look at the fellers in a fight; aye, look at a dawg killing rats,—which is it wins? the good blooded ones. Get some more port, Bowls, old boy, whilst I buzz[2] this bottle here. What was I a saying?"

"I think you were speaking of dogs killing rats," Pitt remarked mildly, handing his cousin the decanter to buzz.

"Killing rats was I? Well, Pitt, are you a sporting man? Do you want to see a dawg as *can* kill a rat? If you do, come down with me to Tom Corduroy's, in Castle Street Mews, and I'll show you such a bull-terrier as—

"Pooh! gammon," cried James, bursting out laughing at his own absurdity,—"*you* don't care about a dawg or a rat; it's all nonsense. I'm blest if I think you know the difference between a dog and a duck."

"No; by the way," Pitt continued with increased blandness, "it was about blood you were talking, and the personal advantages which people derive from patrician birth. Here's the fresh bottle."

"Blood's the word," said James, gulping the ruby fluid down. "Nothing like blood, Sir, in hosses, dawgs, *and* men. Why only last term, just before I was rusticated, that is, I mean just before I had the measles, ha, ha,—there was me and Ringwood of Christchurch, Bob Ringwood, Lord Cinqbar's son, having our beer at the Bell at Blenheim, when the Banbury bargeman offered to fight either of us for a bowl of punch. I couldn't. My arm was in a sling; couldn't even take the drag down,—a brute of a mare of mine had fell with me only two days before, out with the Abingdon,[3] and I thought my arm was broke. Well, Sir, I couldn't finish him, but Bob had his coat off at once—he stood up to the Banbury man for three minutes, and polished him off in four rounds easy. Gad, how he did drop, Sir, and what was it? Blood, Sir, all blood."

"You don't drink, James," the ex-attaché continued. "In my time, at Oxford, the men passed round the bottle a little quicker than you young fellows seem to do."

1. In Oliver Goldsmith's *She Stoops to Conquer* (1773), Hardcastle welcomes young Marlow and Hastings, who have mistaken the place for an inn, saying, "This is Liberty Hall, gentlemen. You may do just as you please here." See chapter XLIX.
2. Finish to the last drop.
3. Bell at Blenheim: an inn at a village near Oxford and the palace of the duke of Marlborough. A drag is a carriage with two horses. The Abingdon: a fox hunt near Oxford.

"Come, come," said James, putting his hand to his nose and winking at his cousin with a pair of vinous eyes, "no jokes, old boy; no trying it on on me. You want to trot me out, but it's no go. In vino veritas, old boy. Mars, Bacchus, Apollo virorum,[4] hay? I wish my aunt would send down some of this to the governor; it's a precious good tap."

"You had better ask her," Machiavel continued, "or make the best of your time now. What says the bard, 'Nunc vino pellite curas Cras ingens iterabimus æquor,'"[5] and the Bacchanalian quoting the above with a House of Commons air, tossed off nearly a thimblefull of wine with an immense flourish of his glass.

At the Rectory, when the bottle of port wine was opened after dinner, the young ladies had each a glass from a bottle of currant wine. Mrs. Bute took one glass of port, honest James had a couple commonly, but as his father grew very sulky if he made further inroads on the bottle, the good lad generally refrained from trying for more, and subsided either into the currant wine, or to some private gin-and-water in the stables, which he enjoyed in the company of the coachman and his pipe. At Oxford, the quantity of wine was unlimited, but the quality was inferior: but when quantity and quality united, as at his aunt's house, James showed that he could appreciate them indeed; and hardly needed any of his cousin's encouragement in draining off the second bottle supplied by Mr. Bowls.

When the time for coffee came, however, and for a return to the ladies, of whom he stood in awe, the young gentleman's agreeable frankness left him, and he relapsed into his usual surly timidity: contenting himself by saying yes and no, by scowling at Lady Jane, and by upsetting one cup of coffee during the evening.

If he did not speak he yawned in a pitiable manner, and his presence threw a damp upon the modest proceedings of the evening, for Miss Crawley and Lady Jane at their piquet, and Miss Briggs at her work, felt that his eyes were wildly fixed on them, and were uneasy under that maudlin look.

"He seems a very silent, awkward, bashful lad," said Miss Crawley to Mr. Pitt.

"He is more communicative in men's society than with ladies," Machiavel dryly replied: perhaps rather disappointed that the port wine had not made Jim speak more.

He had spent the early part of the next morning in writing home to his mother a most flourishing account of his reception by Miss Crawley. But ah! he little knew what evils the day was bringing for him, and how short his reign of favour was destined to be. A circumstance which Jim had forgotten—a trivial but fatal circumstance—had taken place at the Cribb's Arms on the night before he had come to his aunt's house. It was no other than this—Jim, who was always of a generous disposition, and when in his cups especially hospitable, had in the course of the night treated the Tutbury champion and the

4. In vino veritas: truth in wine. "Ut sunt Divorum; Mars, Bacchus, Apollo: Virorum": Of men as they are of gods—Mars, Bacchus, Apollo. James is quoting from memory from the Eton *Latin Grammar*.
5. Now banish care with wine; tomorrow we will again take our course upon the mighty sea. Horace, *Odes*.

Rottingdean man, and their friends, twice or thrice to the refreshment of gin-and-water—so that no less than eighteen glasses of that fluid at eight-pence per glass were charged in Mr. James Crawley's bill. It was not the amount of eight-pences, but the quantity of gin which told fatally against poor James's character, when his aunt's butler, Mr. Bowls, went down at his mistress's request to pay the young gentleman's bill. The landlord, fearing lest the account should be refused altogether, swore solemnly that the young gent had consumed personally every farthing's worth of the liquor: and Bowls paid the bill finally, and showed it on his return home to Mrs. Firkin, who was shocked at the frightful prodigality of gin; and took the bill to Miss Briggs as accountant-general; who thought it her duty to mention the circumstance to her principal, Miss Crawley.

Had he drunk a dozen bottles of claret the old spinster could have pardoned him. Mr. Fox and Mr. Sheridan drank claret.[6] Gentlemen drank claret. But eighteen glasses of gin consumed among boxers in an ignoble pot-house[7]—it was an odious crime and not to be pardoned readily. Everything went against the lad: he came home perfumed from the stables, whither he had been to pay his dog Towzer a visit—and whence he was going to take his friend out for an airing, when he met Miss Crawley and her wheezy Blenheim spaniel, which Towzer would have eaten up had not the Blenheim fled squealing to the protection of Miss Briggs, while the atrocious master of the bull-dog stood laughing at the horrible persecution.

This day too the unlucky boy's modesty had likewise forsaken him. He was lively and facetious at dinner. During the repast he levelled one or two jokes against Pitt Crawley: he drank as much wine as upon the previous day: and going quite unsuspiciously to the drawing-room began to entertain the ladies there with some choice Oxford stories. He described the different pugilistic qualities of Molyneux and Dutch Sam, offered playfully to give Lady Jane the odds upon the Tutbury Pet against the Rottingdean man, or take them, as her Ladyship chose: and crowned the pleasantry by proposing to back himself against his cousin Pitt Crawley, either with or without the gloves. "And that's a fair offer, my buck," he said, with a loud laugh, slapping Pitt on the shoulder, "and my father told me to make it too, and he'll go halves in the bet, ha ha!" So saying, the engaging youth nodded knowingly at poor Miss Briggs, and pointed his thumb over his shoulder at Pitt Crawley in a jocular and exulting manner.

Pitt was not pleased altogether perhaps, but still not unhappy in the main. Poor Jim had his laugh out: and staggered across the room with his aunt's candle, when the old lady moved to retire, and offered to salute her with the blandest tipsy smile: and he took his own leave and went up-stairs to his bed-room perfectly satisfied with himself, and with a pleased notion that his aunt's money would be left to him in preference to his father and all the rest of his family.[8]

6. Fox was a large, athletic, hard-working, hard-playing man—a copious but not heavy drinker. Richard Brinsley Sheridan (1751–1816), playwright, theater manager, member of Parliament, and a political ally of Fox, had a well-known preference for claret.
7. Beer joint.
8. Revised edition reads: of the family.

Mr. James's pipe put out

Once up in the bed-room, one would have thought he could not make matters worse; and yet this unlucky boy did. The moon was shining very pleasantly out on the sea, and Jim, attracted to the window by the romantic appearance of the ocean and the heavens, thought he would farther enjoy them while smoking. Nobody would smell the tobacco, he thought, if he cunningly opened the window and kept his head and pipe in the fresh air. This he did: but being in an excited state, poor Jim had forgotten that his door was open all this time, so that the breeze blowing inwards and a fine thorough draft being established, the clouds of tobacco were carried down-stairs, and arrived with quite undiminished fragrance to Miss Crawley and Miss Briggs.

That pipe of tobacco finished the business: and the Bute-Crawleys never knew how many thousand pounds it cost them. Firkin rushed down-stairs to Bowls who was reading out the "Fire and the Frying

Pan" to his aide-de-camp in a loud and ghostly voice. The dreadful secret was told to him by Firkin with so frightened a look, that for the first moment Mr. Bowls and his young man thought that robbers were in the house; the legs of whom had probably been discovered by the woman under Miss Crawley's bed. When made aware of the fact however—to rush up-stairs at three steps at a time—to enter the unconscious James's apartment, calling out, "Mr. James," in a voice stifled with alarm, and to cry "For Gawd's sake, Sir, stop that 'are pipe," was the work of a minute with Mr. Bowls. "O, Mr. James, what *'ave* you done," he said in a voice of the deepest pathos, as he threw the implement out of the window. "What 'ave you done, Sir; Misses can't abide 'em."

"Missis needn't smoke," said James with a frantic misplaced laugh, and thought the whole matter an excellent joke. But his feelings were very different in the morning, when Mr. Bowls's young man, who operated upon Mr. James's boots, and brought him his hot water to shave that beard which he was so anxiously expecting, handed a note into Mr. James in bed, in the handwriting of Miss Briggs.

"Dear Sir," it said, "Miss Crawley has passed an exceedingly disturbed night, owing to the shocking manner in which the house has been polluted by tobacco; Miss Crawley bids me say she regrets that she is too unwell to see you before you go—and above all, that she ever induced you to remove from the ale-house, where she is sure you will be much more comfortable during the rest of your stay at Brighton."

And herewith honest James's career as a candidate for his aunt's favour ended. He *had* in fact, and without knowing it, done what he menaced to do. He had fought his cousin Pitt with the gloves.

Where meanwhile was he who had been once first favourite for this race for money? Becky and Rawdon, as we have seen, were come together after Waterloo, and were passing the winter of 1815 at Paris in great splendour and gaiety. Rebecca was a good economist, and the price poor Jos Sedley had paid for her two horses was in itself sufficient to keep their little establishment afloat for a year, at the least; there was no occasion to turn into money "my pistols, the same which I shot Captain Marker," or the gold dressing-case, or the cloak lined with sable. Becky had it made into a pelisse for herself, in which she rode in the Bois de Boulogne[9] to the admiration of all: and you should have seen the scene between her and her delighted husband, whom she rejoined after the army had entered Cambray,[1] and when she unsewed herself, and let out of her dress all those watches, knick-knacks, bank-notes, checks, and valuables, which she had secreted in the wadding, previous to her meditated flight from Brussels! Tufto was charmed, and Rawdon roared with delightful laughter, and swore that she was better than any play he ever saw, by Jove. And the way in which she jockied Jos, and which she described with infinite fun, carried up his delight to a pitch of quite insane enthusiasm. He believed in his wife as much as the French soldiers in Napoleon.

Her success in Paris was remarkable. All the French ladies voted her charming. She spoke their language admirably. She adopted at once their grace, their liveliness, their manner. Her husband was stupid certainly—all English are stupid—and, besides, a dull husband at Paris is always a point in a lady's favour. He was the heir

9. Forest in west Paris, a favorite place for the gentry to ride and drive.
1. In northern France.

of the rich and *spirituelle*[2] Miss Crawley, whose house had been open to so many of the French noblesse during the emigration. They received the Colonel's wife in their own hotels—"Why," wrote a great lady to Miss Crawley, who had bought her lace and trinkets at the Duchess's own price, and given her many a dinner during the pinching times after the Revolution—"Why does not our dear Miss come to her nephew and niece, and her attached friends in Paris? All the world *raffoles* of the charming Mistress and her *espiègle* beauty.[3] Yes, we see in her the grace, the charm, the wit of our dear friend Miss Crawley! The King took notice of her yesterday at the Tuilleries,[4] and we are all jealous of the attention which Monsieur[5] pays her. If you could have seen the spite of a certain stupid Miladi Bareacres, (whose eagle-beak and toque[6] and feathers may be seen peering over the heads of all assemblies) when Madame, the Duchess of Angoulême, the august daughter and companion of kings,[7] desired especially to be presented to Mrs. Crawley, as your dear daughter and *protégée,* and thanked her in the name of France, for all your benevolence towards our unfortunates during their exile! She is of all the societies, of all the balls—of the balls—yes—of the dances, no; and yet how interesting and pretty this fair creature looks surrounded by the homage of the men, and so soon to be a mother! To hear her speak of you, her protectress, her mother, would bring tears to the eyes of ogres. How she loves you! how we all love our admirable, our respectable Miss Crawley!"

It is to be feared that this letter of the Parisian great lady did not by any means advance Mrs. Becky's interest with her admirable, her respectable, relative. On the contrary, the fury of the old spinster was beyond bounds, when she found what was Rebecca's situation, and how audaciously she had made use of Miss Crawley's name, to get an *entrée* into Parisian society. Too much shaken in mind and body to compose a letter in the French language in reply to that of her correspondent, she dictated to Briggs a furious answer in her own native tongue, repudiating Mrs. Rawdon Crawley altogether, and warning the public to beware of her as a most artful and dangerous person. But as Madame the Duchess of X— had only been twenty years in England, she did not understand a single word of the language, and contented herself by informing Mrs. Rawdon Crawley at their next meeting, that she had received a charming letter from that *chère Mees,* and that it was full of benevolent things for Mrs. Crawley, who began seriously to have hopes that the spinster would relent.

Meanwhile, she was the gayest and most admired of Englishwomen: and had a little European congress on her reception-night—Prussians and Cossacks, Spaniards and English—all the world was at Paris during this famous winter: to have seen the stars and cor-

2. Witty.
3. *Raffole*: dotes upon, is wild over. *Espiègle*: roguish.
4. Louis XVIII, whose 1814–24 reign was interrupted by Napoleon's return from Elba. Tuilleries: royal palace.
5. Title of the younger brother of the king of France.
6. Nose and bonnet.
7. Marie-Thérèse (1778–1851), daughter of Louis XVI, wife of Louis-Antoine de Bourbon, the son of Charles X. Her brothers became Louis XVII and Louis XVIII.

dons in Rebecca's humble saloon would have made all Baker Street[8] pale with envy. Famous warriors rode by her carriage in the Bois, or crowded her modest little box at the Opera. Rawdon was in the highest spirits. There were no duns in Paris as yet: there were parties every day at Véry's or Beauvilliers'[9]; play was plentiful and his luck good. Tufto perhaps was sulky. Mrs. Tufto had come over to Paris at her own invitation, and besides this *contretemps,*[1] there were a score of generals now round Becky's chair, and she might take her choice of a dozen bouquets when she went to the play. Lady Bareacres and the chiefs of the English society, stupid and irreproachable females, writhed with anguish at the success of the little upstart Becky, whose poisoned jokes quivered and rankled in their chaste breasts. But she had all the men on her side. She fought the women with indomitable courage, and they could not talk scandal in any tongue but their own.

So in *fêtes,* pleasures, and prosperity, the winter of 1815-16 passed away with Mrs. Rawdon Crawley, who accommodated herself to polite life as if her ancestors had been people of fashion for centuries past—and who from her wit, talent, and energy, indeed merited a place of honour in Vanity Fair. In the early spring of 1816, Galignani's Journal[2] contained the following announcement in an interesting corner of the paper: "On the 26th of March—the Lady of Lieutenant-Colonel Crawley, of — Life Guards Green—of a son and heir."

This event was copied into the London papers, out of which Miss Briggs read the statement to Miss Crawley, at breakfast, at Brighton. The intelligence, expected as it might have been, caused a crisis in the affairs of the Crawley family. The spinster's rage rose to its height, and sending instantly for Pitt, her nephew, and for the Lady Southdown, from Brunswick Square,[3] she requested an immediate celebration of the marriage which had been so long pending between the two families. And she announced that it was her intention to allow the young couple a thousand a year during her lifetime, at the expiration of which the bulk of her property would be settled upon her nephew and her dear niece, Lady Jane Crawley. Waxy came down to ratify the deeds—Lord Southdown gave away his sister—she was married by a Bishop, and not by the Rev. Bartholomew Irons—to the disappointment of the irregular prelate.

When they were married—Pitt would have liked to take a hymeneal tour with his bride, as became people of their condition. But the affection of the old lady towards Lady Jane had grown so strong, that she fairly owned she could not part with her favourite. Pitt and his wife came therefore, and lived with Miss Crawley: and (greatly to the annoyance of poor Pitt, who conceived himself a most injured character—being subject to the humours of his aunt on one side and

8. Upper-middle-class neighborhood where William Pitt had lived; its renovation left it, in Thackeray's opinion, worse than it had been. See chapter LI.
9. Restaurants in Paris: Véry's was in the Palais Royal, the other by the Bois de Boulogne.
1. Hindrance.
2. *Galignani's Messenger*, an English-language newspaper, began publication in 1814. Thackeray worked for this paper in 1835.
3. Upper-class residential area next to the Foundling Hospital. See chapter XII.

of his mother-in-law on the other,) Lady Southdown, from her neighbouring house, reigned over the whole family—Pitt, Lady Jane, Miss Crawley, Briggs, Bowls, Firkin, and all. She pitilessly dosed them with her tracts and her medicine: she dismissed Creamer, she installed Rodgers, and soon stripped Miss Crawley of even the semblance of authority. The poor soul grew so timid that she actually left off bullying Briggs any more, and clung to her niece, more fond and more terrified every day. Peace to thee, kind and selfish, vain and generous old heathen!—We shall see thee no more. Let us hope that Lady Jane supported her kindly, and led her with gentle hand out of the busy struggle of Vanity Fair.

## *Chapter XXXV.*

### WIDOW AND MOTHER.

HE[1] news of the great fights of Quatre Bras and Waterloo reached England at the same time. The Gazette first published the result of the two battles; at which glorious intelligence all England thrilled with triumph and fear. Particulars then followed; and after the announcement of the victories came the list of the wounded and the slain. Who can tell the dread with which that catalogue was opened and read! Fancy, at every village and homestead almost through the three kingdoms, the great news coming of the battles of Flanders, and the feelings of exultation and gratitude, bereavement and sickening dismay, when the lists of the regimental losses were gone through, and it became known whether the dear friend and relative had escaped or had fallen. Anybody who will take the trouble of looking back to a file of the newspapers of the time, must, even now, feel at second-hand this breathless pause of expectation. The lists of casualties are carried on from day to day: you stop in the midst as in a story which is to be continued in our next. Think what the feelings must have been as those papers followed each other fresh from the press; and if such an interest could be felt in our country, and about a battle where but twenty thousand of our people were engaged, think of the condition of Europe for twenty years before, where people were fighting,

1. The chapter initial shows George Osborne's memorial on the church wall, described in paragraphs nine and ten.

not by thousands, but by millions; each one of whom as he struck his enemy wounded horribly some other innocent heart far away.

The news which that famous Gazette brought to the Osbornes gave a dreadful shock to the family and its chief. The girls indulged unrestrained in their grief. The gloom-stricken old father was still more borne down by his fate and sorrow. He strove to think that a judgment was on the boy for his disobedience. He dared not own that the severity of the sentence frightened him, and that its fulfilment had come too soon upon his curses. Sometimes a shuddering terror struck him, as if he had been the author of the doom which he had called down on his son. There was a chance before of reconciliation. The boy's wife might have died; or he might have come back and said, Father I have sinned.[2] But there was no hope now. He stood on the other side of the gulf impassable, haunting his parent with sad eyes. He remembered them once before so in a fever, when every one thought the lad was dying, and he lay on his bed speechless, and gazing with a dreadful gloom. Good God! how the father clung to the doctor then; and with what a sickening anxiety he followed him: what a weight of grief was off his mind when, after the crisis of the fever, the lad recovered, and looked at his father once more with eyes that recognised him. But now there was no help or cure, or chance of reconcilement: above all, there were no humble words to soothe vanity outraged and furious, or bring to its natural flow the poisoned, angry blood. And it is hard to say which pang it was tore the proud father's heart most keenly—that his son should have gone out of the reach of his forgiveness, or that the apology which his own pride expected should have escaped him.

Whatever his sensations might have been, however, the stern old man would have no confidant. He never mentioned his son's name to his daughters; but ordered the elder to place all the females of the establishment in mourning; and desired that the male servants should be similarly attired in deep black. All parties and entertainments, of course, were to be put off. No communications were made to his future son-in-law, whose marriage-day had been fixed; but there was enough in Mr. Osborne's appearance to prevent Mr. Bullock from making any inquiries, or in any way pressing forward that ceremony. He and the ladies whispered about it under their voices in the drawing-room sometimes, whither the father never came. He remained constantly in his own study; the whole front part of the house being closed until some time after the completion of the general mourning.

About three weeks after the 18th of June, Mr. Osborne's acquaintance, Sir William Dobbin, called at Mr. Osborne's house in Russell Square, with a very pale and agitated face, and insisted upon seeing that gentleman. Ushered into his room, and after a few words, which neither the speaker nor the host understood, the former produced from an inclosure a letter sealed with a large red seal. "My son, Major Dobbin," the Alderman said, with some hesitation, "dispatched me a letter by an officer of the —th, who arrived in town to-day. My

2. First words of the prodigal son on his return home. Luke 16.18, 21.

son's letter contains one for you, Osborne." The Alderman placed the letter on the table, and Osborne stared at him for a moment or two in silence. His looks frightened the ambassador, who, after looking guiltily for a little time at the grief-stricken man, hurried away without a farther word.

The letter was in George's well-known bold hand-writing. It was that one which he had written before day-break on the 16th of June, and just before he took leave of Amelia. The great red seal was emblazoned with the sham coat of arms which Osborne had assumed from the Peerage, with "Pax in bello"[3] for a motto; that of the ducal house with which the vain old man tried to fancy himself connected. The hand that signed it would never hold pen or sword more. The very seal that sealed it had been robbed from George's dead body as it lay on the field of battle. The father knew nothing of this, but sat and looked at the letter in terrified vacancy. He almost fell when he went to open it.

Have you ever had a difference with a dear friend? How his letters, written in the period of love and confidence, sicken and rebuke you! What a dreary mourning it is to dwell upon those vehement protests of dead affection! What lying epitaphs they make over the corpse of love! What dark, cruel comments upon Life and Vanities! Most of us have got or written drawers full of them. They are closet-skeletons which we keep and shun. Osborne trembled long, before the letter from his dead son.

The poor boy's letter did not say much. He had been too proud to acknowledge the tenderness which his heart felt. He only said, that on the eve of a great battle, he wished to bid his father farewell, and solemnly to implore his good offices for the wife—it might be for the child—whom he left behind him. He owned with contrition that his irregularities and extravagance had already wasted a large part of his mother's little fortune. He thanked his father for his former generous conduct; and he promised him, that if he fell on the field or survived it, he would act in a manner worthy of the name of George Osborne.

His English habit, pride, awkwardness perhaps, had prevented him from saying more. His father could not see the kiss George had placed on the superscription of his letter. Mr. Osborne dropped it with the bitterest, deadliest pang of balked affection and revenge. His son was still beloved and unforgiven.

About two months afterwards however, as the young ladies of the family went to church with their father, they remarked how he took a different seat from that which he usually occupied when he chose to attend divine worship; and that from his cushion opposite, he looked up at the wall over their heads. This caused the young women likewise to gaze in the direction towards which the father's gloomy eyes pointed: and they saw an elaborate monument upon the wall, where Britannia was represented weeping over an urn, and a broken sword, and a couchant lion, indicated that the piece of sculpture had been

3. Peace in war. The motto was appropriated along with the coat of arms from the Osbornes from Leeds. See chapter XXIX.

erected in honour of a deceased warrior. The sculptors of those days had stocks of such funereal emblems in hand; as you may see still on the walls of St. Paul's, which are covered with hundreds of these braggart heathen allegories. There was a constant demand for them during the first fifteen years of the present century.

Under the memorial in question were emblazoned the well known and pompous Osborne arms; and the inscription said, that the monument was "Sacred to the memory of George Osborne, Junior, Esq., late a Captain in his Majesty's —th regiment of foot, who fell on the 18th of June, 1815, aged 28 years, while fighting for his king and country in the glorious victory of Waterloo. *Dulce et decorum est pro patriâ mori.*"[4]

The sight of that stone agitated the nerves of the sisters so much, that Miss Maria was compelled to leave the church. The congregation made way respectfully for those sobbing girls clothed in deep black, and pitied the stern old father seated opposite the memorial of the dead soldier. "Will he forgive Mrs. George?" the girls said to themselves as soon as their ebullition of grief was over. Much conversation passed too among the acquaintances of the Osborne family, who knew of the rupture between the son and father caused by the former's marriage, as to the chance of a reconciliation with the young widow. There were bets among the gentlemen both about Russell Square and in the City.

If the sisters had any anxiety regarding the possible recognition of Amelia as a daughter of the family, it was increased presently, and towards the end of the autumn, by their father's announcement that he was going abroad. He did not say whither, but they knew at once that his steps would be turned towards Belgium, and were aware that George's widow was still in Brussels. They had pretty accurate news indeed of poor Amelia from Lady Dobbin and her daughters. Our honest Captain had been promoted in consequence of the death of the second Major of the regiment on the field; and the brave O'Dowd, who had distinguished himself greatly here as upon all occasions where he had a chance to show his coolness and valour, was a Colonel and Companion of the Bath.

Very many of the brave —th, who had suffered severely upon both days of action, were still at Brussels in the autumn, recovering of their wounds. The city was a vast military hospital for months after the great battles; and as men and officers began to rally from their hurts, the gardens and places of public resort swarmed with maimed warriors old and young, who, just rescued out of death, fell to gambling, and gaiety, and love-making, as people of Vanity Fair will do. Mr. Osborne found out some of the —th easily. He knew their uniform quite well, and had been used to follow all the promotions and exchanges in the regiment, and loved to talk about it and its officers as if he had been one of the number. On the day after his arrival at Brussels, and as he issued from his hotel, which faced the park, he saw a soldier in the well-known facings, reposing on a stone-bench

4. It is sweet and fitting to die for one's country. Horace, *Odes*.

in the garden, and went and sate down trembling by the wounded convalescent man.

"Were you in Captain Osborne's company?" he said, and added, after a pause, "he was my son, Sir."

The man was not of the Captain's company, but he lifted up his unwounded arm and touched his cap sadly and respectfully to the haggard broken-spirited gentleman who questioned him. "The whole army didn't contain a finer or a better officer," the soldier said. "The sergeant of the Captain's company (Captain Raymond had it now), was in town though, and was just well of a shot in the shoulder. His honour might see him if he liked, who could tell him anything he wanted to know about—about the —'s actions. But his honour had seen Major Dobbin no doubt, the brave Captain's great friend; and Mrs. Osborne, who was here too, and had been very bad, he heard everybody say. They say she was out of her mind like for six weeks or more. But your honour knows all about that—and asking your pardon"—the man added.

Osborne put a guinea into the soldier's hand, and told him he should have another if he would bring the sergeant to the Hotel du Parc; a promise which very soon brought the desired officer to Mr. Osborne's presence. And the first soldier went away; and after telling a comrade or two how Captain Osborne's father was arrived, and what a free-handed generous gentleman he was, they went and made good cheer with drink and feasting, as long as the guineas lasted which had come from the proud purse of the mourning old father.

In the Sergeant's company, who was also just convalescent, Osborne made the journey of Waterloo and Quatre Bras, a journey which thousands of his countrymen were then taking. He took the Sergeant with him in his carriage, and went through both fields under his guidance. He saw the point of the road where the regiment marched into action on the 16th, and the slope down which they drove the French cavalry who were pressing on the retreating Belgians. There was the spot where the noble Captain cut down the French officer who was grappling with the young Ensign for the colours, the Colour-Sergeants having been shot down. Along this road they retreated on the next day, and here was the bank at which the regiment bivouacked under the rain of the night of the seventeenth. Further on was the position which they took and held during the day, forming time after time to receive the charge of the enemy's horsemen, and lying down under shelter of the bank from the furious French cannonade. And it was at this declivity when at evening the whole English line received the order to advance, as the enemy fell back after his last charge, that the Captain hurraying and rushing down the hill waving his sword, received a shot and fell dead. "It was Major Dobbin who took back the Captain's body to Brussels," the Sergeant said, in a low voice, "and had him buried, as your Honour knows." The peasants and relic-hunters about the place were screaming round the pair, as the soldier told his story, offering for sale all sorts of mementoes of the fight, crosses, and epaulets, and shattered cuirasses, and eagles.

Osborne gave a sumptuous reward to the Sergeant when he parted with him, after having visited the scenes of his son's last exploits. His burial place he had already seen. Indeed he had driven thither immediately after his arrival at Brussels. George's body lay in the pretty burial-ground of Lacken, near the city; in which place, having once visited it on a party of pleasure, he had lightly expressed a wish to have his grave made. And there the young officer was laid by his friend, in the unconsecrated corner of the garden, separated by a little hedge from the temples and towns[5] and plantations of flowers and shrubs, under which the Roman Catholic dead repose. It seemed a humiliation to old Osborne to think that his son, an English gentleman, a Captain in the famous British army, should not be found worthy to lie in ground where mere foreigners were buried. Which of us is there can tell how much vanity lurks in our warmest regard for others, and how selfish our love is? Old Osborne did not speculate much upon the mingled nature of his feelings, and how his instinct and selfishness were combating together. He firmly believed that everything he did was right, that he ought on all occasions to have his own way—and like the sting of a wasp or serpent his hatred rushed out armed and poisonous against anything like opposition. He was proud of his hatred as of everything else. Always to be right, always to trample forward, and never to doubt, are not these the great qualities with which dullness takes the lead in the world?

As after the drive to Waterloo, Mr. Osborne's carriage was nearing the gates of the city at sunset, they met another open barouche, in which were a couple of ladies and a gentleman, and by the side of which an officer was riding. Osborne gave a start back, and the Sergeant, seated with him cast a look of surprise at his neighbour, as he touched his cap to the officer, who mechanically returned his salute.[6] It was Amelia, with the lame young Ensign by her side, and opposite to her her faithful friend Mrs. O'Dowd. It was Amelia, but how changed from the fresh and comely girl Osborne knew. Her face was white and thin. Her pretty brown hair was parted under a widow's cap—the poor child. Her eyes were fixed, and looking nowhere. They stared blank in the face of Osborne, as the carriages crossed each other, but she did not know him; nor did he recognise her, until looking up, he saw Dobbin riding by her, and then he knew who it was. He hated her. He did not know how much until he saw her there. When her carriage had passed on, he turned and stared at the Sergeant, with a curse and defiance in his eye, cast at his companion, who could not help looking at him—as much as to say. "How dare *you* look at me? Damn you: I *do* hate her. It is she who has tumbled my hopes and all my pride down." "Tell the scoundrel to drive on quick," he shouted with an oath, to the lackey on the box. A minute afterwards, a horse came clattering over the pavement behind Osborne's carriage, and Dobbin rode up. His thoughts had been elsewhere as the carriages passed each other, and it was not until he had ridden some paces forward that he remembered it was Osborne who had just passed him. Then he turned to examine if the sight of her father-in-law had made any impression on Amelia,

5. Some nonauthoritative editions read: towers
6. Revised edition reads: the salute.

but the poor girl did not know who had passed. Then William, who daily used to accompany her in her drives, taking out his watch, made some excuse about an engagement which he suddenly recollected, and so rode off. She did not remark that either: but sate looking before her, over the homely landscape towards the woods in the distance, by which George marched away.

"Mr. Osborne, Mr. Osborne!" cried Dobbin, as he rode up and held out his hand. Osborne made no motion to take it, but shouted out once more and with another curse to his servant to drive on.

Dobbin laid his hand on the carriage side. "I will see you, Sir," he said. "I have a message for you."

"From that woman?" said Osborne, fiercely.

"No," replied the other, "from your son;" at which Osborne fell back into the corner of his carriage, and Dobbin allowing it to pass on, rode close behind it, and so through the town until they reached Mr. Osborne's hotel, and without a word. There he followed Osborne up to his apartments. George had often been in the rooms; they were the lodgings which the Crawleys had occupied during their stay in Brussels.

"Pray, have you any commands for me, Captain Dobbin, or, I beg your pardon, I should say *Major* Dobbin, since better men than you are dead, and you step into their *shoes,*" said Mr. Osborne, in that sarcastic tone which he sometimes was pleased to assume.

"Better men *are* dead," Dobbin replied. "I want to speak to you about one."

"Make it short, Sir," said the other with an oath, scowling at his visitor.

"I am here as his closest friend," the Major resumed, "and the executor of his will. He made it before we went into action. Are you aware how small his means are, and of the straitened circumstances of his widow?"

"I don't know his widow, Sir," Osborne said. "Let her go back to her father." But the gentleman whom he addressed was determined to remain in good temper, and went on without heeding the interruption.

"Do you know, Sir, Mrs. Osborne's condition? Her life and her reason almost have been shaken by the blow which has fallen on her. It is very doubtful whether she will rally. There is a chance left for her however, and it is about this I came to speak to you. She will be a mother soon. Will you visit the parent's offence upon the child's head?[7] or will you forgive the child for poor George's sake?"

Osborne broke out into a rhapsody of self-praise and imprecations. By the first, excusing himself to his own conscience for his conduct; by the second, exaggerating the undutifulness of George. No father in all England could have behaved more generously to a son, who had rebelled against him wickedly. He had died without even so much as confessing he was wrong. Let him take the consequences of his undutifulness and folly. As for himself, Mr. Osborne, he was a man of

7. The second commandment forbids worship of graven images, "for I the Lord thy God am a jealous God, visiting the iniquity of the fathers upon the children" (Exodus 20.5; Deuteronomy 5.9).

his word. He had sworn never to speak to that woman or to recognise her as his son's wife. "And that's what you may tell her," he concluded with an oath; "and that's what I will stick to to the last day of my life."

There was no hope from that quarter then. The widow must live on her slender pittance, or on such aid as Jos could give her. "I might tell her, and she would not heed it," thought Dobbin sadly: for the poor girl's thoughts were not here at all since her catastrophe, and stupified under the pressure of her sorrow, good and evil were alike indifferent to her. So, indeed, were even friendship and kindness. She received them both uncomplainingly, and having accepted them, relapsed into her grief.

Suppose some twelve months after the above conversation took place to have passed in the life of our poor Amelia. She has spent the first portion of that time in a sorrow so profound and pitiable, that we who have been watching and describing some of the emotions of that weak and tender heart, must draw back in the presence of the cruel grief under which it is bleeding. Tread silently round the hapless couch of the poor prostrate soul. Shut gently the door of the dark chamber, wherein she suffers, as those kind people did who nursed her through the first months of her pain, and never left her until heaven had sent her consolation. A day came—of almost terrified delight and wonder—when the poor widowed girl pressed a child upon her breast,—a child, with the eyes of George who was gone—a little boy, as beautiful as a cherub. What a miracle it was to hear its first cry! How she laughed and wept over it—how love, and hope, and prayer woke again in her bosom as the baby nestled there. She was safe. The doctors who attended her, and had feared for her life or for her brain, had waited anxiously for this crisis before they could pronounce that either was secure. It was worth the long months of doubt and dread which the persons, who had constantly been with her, had passed, to see her eyes once more beaming tenderly upon them.

Our friend Dobbin was one of them. It was he who brought her back to England and to her mother's house; when Mrs. O'Dowd, receiving a peremptory summons from her Colonel, had been forced to quit her patient. To see Dobbin holding the infant, and to hear Amelia's laugh of triumph as she watched him, would have done any man good who had a sense of humour. William was the godfather of the child, and exerted his ingenuity in the purchase of cups, spoons, pap-boats, and corals[8] for this little Christian.

How his mother nursed him, and dressed him, and lived upon him; how she drove away all nurses, and would scarce allow any hand but her own to touch him; how she considered that the greatest favour she could confer upon his godfather, Major Dobbin, was to allow the Major occasionally to dandle him, need not be told here. This child was her being. Her existence was a maternal caress. She enveloped the feeble and unconscious creature with love and worship. It was her life which the baby drank in from her bosom. Of

8. Pap-boats: infant feeding dishes. Corals: teething toys.

Major Sugarplums

nights, and when alone, she had stealthy and intense raptures of motherly love, such as God's marvellous care has awarded to the female instinct—joys how far higher and lower than reason—blind beautiful devotions which only women's hearts know. It was William Dobbin's task to muse upon these movements of Amelia's, and to watch her heart; and if his love made him divine almost all the feelings which agitated it, alas! he could see with a fatal perspicuity that there was no place there for him. And so, gently, he bore his fate, knowing it, and content to bear it.

I suppose Amelia's father and mother[9] saw through the intentions of the Major, and were not ill-disposed to encourage him; for Dobbin visited their house daily, and stayed for hours with them, or with Amelia, or with the honest landlord, Mr. Clapp, and his family. He brought, on one pretext or another, presents to everybody, and almost every day; and went with the landlord's little girl who was rather a favourite with Amelia, by the name of Major Sugarplums. It was this little child who commonly acted as mistress of the ceremonies to introduce him to Mrs. Osborne. She laughed one day when Major Sugarplums' cab drove up to Fulham, and he descended from it, bringing out a wooden horse, a drum, a trumpet, and other warlike toys, for little Georgy, who was scarcely six months old, and for whom the articles in question were entirely premature.

The child was asleep. "Hush," said Amelia, annoyed, perhaps, at the creaking of the Major's boots; and she held out her hand; smiling because William could not take it until he had rid himself of his cargo of toys. "Go down stairs, little Mary," said he presently to the child, "I want to speak to Mrs. Osborne." She looked up rather astonished, and laid down the infant on its bed.

"I am come to say good-bye, Amelia," said he, taking her slender little white hand gently.

"Good-bye? and where are you going?" she said, with a smile.

"Send the letters to the agents," he said; "they will forward them; for you will write to me, won't you? I shall be away a long time."

"I'll write to you about Georgy," she said. "Dear William, how good you have been to him and to me. Look at him! Isn't he like an angel?"

The little pink hands of the child closed mechanically round the honest soldier's finger, and Amelia looked up in his face with bright maternal pleasure. The cruellest looks could not have wounded him more than that glance of hopeless kindness. He bent over the child and mother. He could not speak for a moment. And it was with all his strength that he could force himself to say a God bless you. "God bless you," said Amelia, and held up her face and kissed him.

"Hush! Dont wake Georgy!" she added, as William Dobbin went to the door with heavy steps. She did not hear the noise of his cab-wheels as he drove away: she was looking at the child, who was laughing in his sleep.

9. The New York edition, which is rarely interesting in its deviations from the first edition, reads: Amelia's parents

## *Chapter XXXVI.*

### HOW TO LIVE WELL ON NOTHING A-YEAR.

I SUPPOSE there is no man in this Vanity Fair of ours so little observant as not to think sometimes about the worldly affairs of his acquaintances, or so extremely charitable as not to wonder how his neighbour Jones, or his neighbour Smith, can make both ends meet at the end of the year. With the utmost regard for the family for instance, (for I dine with them twice or thrice in a season,)[1] I cannot but own that the appearance of the Jenkinses in the Park,[2] in the large barouche with the grenadier-footmen, will surprise and mystify me to my dying day: for though I know the equipage is only jobbed,[3] and all the Jenkins people are on board-wages, yet those three men and the carriage must represent an expense of six hundred a-year at the very least—and then there are the splendid dinners, the two boys at Eton,[4] the prize governess and masters for the girls, the trip abroad, or to Eastbourne or Worthing[5] in the autumn, the annual ball with a supper from Gunter's (who, by the way, supplies most of the *first-rate* dinners which J. gives, as I know very well, having been invited to one of them to fill a vacant place, when I saw at once that these repasts are very superior to the *common* run of entertainments for which the *humbler* sort of J.'s acquaintances get cards)—who, I say, with the most good-natured feelings in the world can help wondering how the Jenkinses make out matters? What *is* Jenkins?—we all know—Commissioner of the Tape and Sealing Wax Office, with £1200 a-year for a salary. Had his wife a private fortune? Pooh!—Miss Flint—one of eleven children of a small squire in Buckinghamshire. All she ever gets from her family is a turkey at Christmas, in exchange for which she has to board two or three of her sisters in the off season; and lodge and feed her brothers when they come to town. How does Jenkins balance his income? I say, as every friend of his must say, How is it that he has not been outlawed

1. Revised edition reads: thrice a season,)
2. The Jenkinses were a standing joke in *Punch* magazine for toadies and social climbers.
3. Hired.
4. Expensive private school, called a public school in England.
5. Resort towns on the south coast on either side of Brighton. Gunter's Tea Shop, in Berkeley Square, caterers and confectioners.

long since: and that he ever came back (as he did to the surprise of everybody) last year from Boulogne?[6]

"I" is here[7] introduced to personify the world in general—the Mrs. Grundy[8] of each respected reader's private circle—every one of whom can point to some families of his acquaintance who live nobody knows how. Many a glass of wine have we all of us drunk, I have very little doubt, hob-and-nobbing with the hospitable giver, and wondering how the deuce he paid for it.

Some three or four years after his stay in Paris, when Rawdon Crawley and his wife were established in a very small comfortable house in Curzon Street, Mayfair, there was scarcely one of the numerous friends whom they entertained at dinner that did not ask the above question regarding them. The novelist, it has been said before, knows everything, and as I am in a situation to be able to tell the public how Crawley and his wife lived without any income, may I entreat the public newspapers which are in the habit of extracting portions of the various periodical works now published, *not* to reprint the following exact narrative and calculations—of which I ought, as the discoverer, (and at some expense, too,) to have the benefit. My son,—I would say, were I blessed with a child—you may by deep inquiry and constant intercourse with him, learn how a man lives comfortably on nothing a-year. But it is best not to be intimate with gentlemen of this profession, and to take the calculations at second-hand, as you do logarithms, for to work them yourself, depend upon it, will cost you something considerable.

On nothing per annum then, and during a course of some two or three years, of which we can afford to give but a very brief history, Crawley and his wife lived very happily and comfortably at Paris. It was in this period that he quitted the Guards, and sold out of the army. When we find him again, his mustachios and the title of Colonel on his card are the only relics of his military profession.

It has been mentioned that Rebecca, soon after her arrival in Paris, took a very smart and leading position in the society of that capital, and was welcomed at some of the most distinguished houses of the restored French nobility. The English men of fashion in Paris courted her, too, to the disgust of the ladies their wives, who could not bear the parvenue.[9] For some months the salons of the Faubourg St. Germain,[1] in which her place was secured, and the splendours of the new Court, where she was received with much distinction, delighted, and perhaps a little intoxicated Mrs. Crawley, who may have been disposed during this period of elation to slight the people—honest young military men mostly,—who formed her husband's chief society.

But the Colonel yawned sadly among the duchesses and great ladies of the Court. The old women who played *écarté* made such a noise about a five-franc piece, that it was not worth Colonel Crawley's while to sit down at a card-table. The wit of their conversation

6. French seaport, a safe haven for Englishmen who, at home, would be imprisoned for debt.
7. Revised edition reads: here is
8. A character who never actually appears onstage in Thomas Morton's *Speed the Plough* (1798), but is frequently referred to in the phrase "I wonder what Mrs. Grundy would think?" Hence, a censoring influence.
9. Upstart newcomer.
1. Fashionable Left Bank, Paris.

he could not appreciate, being ignorant of their language. And what good could his wife get, he urged, by making curtsies every night to a whole circle of Princesses? He left Rebecca presently to frequent these parties alone; resuming his own simple pursuits and amusements amongst the amiable friends of his own choice.

The truth is, when we say of a gentleman that he lives elegantly on nothing a-year, we use the word "nothing," to signify something unknown; meaning, simply, that we don't know how the gentleman in question defrays the expenses of his establishment. Now, our friend the Colonel had a great aptitude for all games of chance: and exercising himself, as he continually did, with the cards, the dice-box, or the cue, it is natural to suppose that he attained a much greater skill in the use of these articles than men can possess who only occasionally handle them. To use a cue at billiards well is like using a pencil, or a German flute, or a small-sword—you cannot master any one of these implements at first, and it is only by repeated study and perseverance, joined to a natural taste, that a man can excel in the handling of either. Now Crawley, from being only a brilliant amateur had grown to be a consummate master of billiards. Like a great general, his genius used to rise with the danger, and when the luck had been unfavourable to him for a whole game, and the bets were consequently against him, he would, with consummate skill and boldness, make some prodigious hits which would restore the battle, and come in a victor at the end, to the astonishment of everybody—of everybody, that is, who was a stranger to his play. Those who were accustomed to see it were cautious how they staked their money against a man of such sudden resources, and brilliant, and overpowering skill.

At games of cards he was equally skilful; for though he would constantly lose money at the commencement of an evening, playing so carelessly and making such blunders, that new comers were often inclined to think meanly of his talent; yet when roused to action, and awakened to caution by repeated small losses, it was remarked that Crawley's play became quite different, and that he was pretty sure of beating his enemy thoroughly before the night was over. Indeed, very few men could say that they ever had the better of him.

His successes were so repeated that no wonder the envious and the vanquished spoke sometimes with bitterness regarding them. And as the French say of the Duke of Wellington, who never suffered a defeat, that only an astonishing series of lucky accidents enabled him to be an invariable winner; yet even they allow that he cheated at Waterloo, and was enabled to win the last great trick:—so it was hinted at head-quarters in England, that some foul play must have taken place in order to account for the continuous successes of Colonel Crawley.

Though Frascati's and the Salon[2] were open at that time in Paris, the mania for play was so widely spread, that the public gambling-rooms did not suffice for the general ardour, and gambling went on in private houses as much as if there had been no public means for gratifying the passion. At Crawley's charming little *réunions* of an evening this fatal amusement commonly was practised—much to good-natured little Mrs. Crawley's annoyance. She spoke about her husband's passion for dice with the deepest grief; she bewailed it to everybody who came to her house. She besought the young fellows never, never to touch a box; and when young Green, of the Rifles, lost a very considerable sum of money, Rebecca passed a whole night in tears, as the servant told the unfortunate young gentleman, and actually went on her knees to her husband to beseech him to remit the debt, and burn the acknowledgment. How could he? He had lost just as much himself to Blackstone of the Hussars, and Count Punter of the Hanoverian Cavalry. Green might have any decent time; but pay?—of course he must pay;—to talk of burning I O U's was child's-play.

Other officers, chiefly young—for the young fellows gathered round Mrs. Crawley—came from her parties with long faces, having dropped more or less money at her fatal card-tables. Her house began to have an unfortunate reputation. The old hands warned the less experienced of their danger. Colonel O'Dowd, of the —th regiment, one of those occupying in Paris, warned Lieutenant Spooney of that corps. A loud and violent fracas took place between the infantry-colonel and his lady, who were dining at the Café de Paris,[3] and Colonel and Mrs. Crawley, who were also taking their meal there. The ladies engaged on both sides. Mrs. O'Dowd snapped her fingers in Mrs. Crawley's face, and called her husband "no betther than a black-leg."[4] Colonel Crawley challenged Colonel O'Dowd, C.B. The Commander-in-Chief hearing of the dispute sent for Colonel Crawley, who was getting ready the same pistols, 'which he shot Captain

2. Two of many fashionable gambling houses in Paris. All were closed in 1838.
3. Restaurant on the Avenue de l'Opéra, Paris.
4. A cheat.

Marker,' and had such a conversation with him that no duel took place. If Rebecca had not gone on her knees to General Tufto, Crawley would have been sent back to England; and he did not play, except with civilians, for some weeks after.

But in spite of Rawdon's undoubted skill and constant successes, it became evident to Rebecca, considering these things, that their position was but a precarious one, and that even, although they paid scarcely anybody, their little capital would end one day by dwindling into zero. "Gambling," she would say, "dear, is good to help your income, but not as an income itself. Some day people may be tired of play, and then where are we?" Rawdon acquiesced in the justice of her opinion; and in truth he had remarked that after a few nights of his little suppers, &c., gentlemen *were* tired of play with him, and, in spite of Rebecca's charms, did not present themselves very eagerly.

Easy and pleasant as their life at Paris was, it was after all only an idle dalliance and amiable trifling; and Rebecca saw that she must push Rawdon's fortune in their own country. She must get him a place or appointment at home or in the colonies; and she determined to make a move upon England as soon as the way could be cleared for her. As a first step she had made Crawley sell out of the Guards, and go on half-pay. His function as aide-de-camp to General Tufto had ceased previously. Rebecca laughed in all companies at that officer, at his toupee (which he mounted on coming to Paris), at his waistband, at his false teeth, at his pretensions to be a lady-killer above all, and his absurd vanity in fancying every woman whom he came near was in love with him. It was to Mrs. Brent, the beetle-browed wife of Mr. Commissary Brent, to whom the General transferred his attentions now—his bouquets, his dinners at the restaurateurs, his opera-boxes, and his knick-knacks. Poor Mrs. Tufto was no more happy than before, and had still to pass long evenings alone with her daughters, knowing that her General was gone off scented and curled to stand behind Mrs. Brent's chair at the play. Becky had a dozen admirers in his place to be sure; and could cut her rival to pieces with her wit. But as we have said, she was growing tired of this idle social life: opera-boxes and restaurateur-dinners palled upon her: nosegays could not be laid by as a provision for future years: and she could not live upon knick-knacks, laced handkerchiefs, and kid gloves. She felt the frivolity of pleasure, and longed for more substantial benefits.

At this juncture news arrived which was spread among the many creditors of the Colonel at Paris, and which caused them great satisfaction. Miss Crawley, the rich aunt from whom he expected his immense inheritance, was dying; the Colonel must haste to her bedside. Mrs. Crawley and her child would remain behind until he came to reclaim them. He departed for Calais, and having reached that place in safety, it might have been supposed that he went to Dover; but instead he took the Diligence to Dunkirk,[5] and thence travelled to Brussels, for which place he had a former predilection. The fact is, he owed more money at London than at Paris; and he preferred the quiet little Belgian city to either of the more noisy capitals.

5. Calais and Dunkirk are French coastal towns; Dover, in England, is directly across the channel from Calais.

Her aunt was dead. Mrs. Crawley ordered the most intense mourning for herself and little Rawdon. The Colonel was busy arranging the affairs of the inheritance. They could take the premier now, instead of the little entresol[6] of the hotel which they occupied. Mrs. Crawley and the landlord had a consultation about the new hangings, an amicable wrangle about the carpets, and a final adjustment of everything except the bill. She went off in one of his carriages; her French *bonne* with her; the child by her side; the admirable landlord and landlady smiling farewell to her from the gate. General Tufto was furious when he heard she was gone, and Mrs. Brent furious with him for being furious; Lieutenant Spooney was cut to the heart; and the landlord got ready his best apartments previous to the return of the fascinating little woman and her husband. He *serréd*[7] the trunks which she left in his charge with the greatest care. They had been especially recommended to him by Madame Crawley. They were not, however, found to be particularly valuable when opened some time after.

But before she went to join her husband in the Belgic capital, Mrs. Crawley made an expedition into England, leaving behind her her little son upon the continent, under the care of her French maid.

The parting between Rebecca and the little Rawdon did not cause either party much pain. She had not, to say truth, seen much of the young gentleman since his birth. After the amiable fashion of French mothers, she had placed him out at nurse in a village in the neighbourhood of Paris, where little Rawdon passed the first months of his

6. Premier: first floor (second floor in American parlance). Entresol: mezzanine.
7. Anglicized French: put in safe storage.

Mrs. Rawdon's departure from Paris

life, not unhappily, with a numerous family of foster-brothers in wooden shoes. His father would ride over many a time to see him here, and the elder Rawdon's paternal heart glowed to see him rosy and dirty, shouting lustily, and happy in the making of mud-pies under the superintendence of the gardener's wife, his nurse.

Rebecca did not care much to go and see the son and heir. Once he spoiled a new dove-coloured pelisse of hers. He preferred his nurse's caresses to his mamma's, and when finally he quitted that jolly nurse and almost parent, he cried loudly for hours. He was only consoled by his mother's promise that he should return to his nurse the next day; indeed the nurse herself, who probably would have been pained at the parting too, was told that the child would immediately be restored to her, and for some time awaited quite anxiously his return.

In fact, our friends may be said to have been among the first of that brood of hardy English adventurers who have subsequently invaded the Continent, and swindled in all the capitals of Europe. The respect in those happy days of 1817–18, was very great for the wealth and honour of Britons. They had not then learned, as I am told, to haggle for bargains with the pertinacity which now distinguishes them. The great cities of Europe had not been as yet open to the enterprise of our rascals. And whereas, there is now hardly a town of France or Italy in which you shall not see some noble countryman of our own, with that happy swagger and insolence of demeanour which we carry everywhere, swindling inn-landlords, passing fictitious cheques upon credulous bankers, robbing coachmakers of their carriages, goldsmiths of their trinkets, easy travellers of their money at cards,—even public libraries of their books;—thirty years ago you needed but to be a Milor Anglais, travelling in a private carriage, and credit was at your hand wherever you chose to seek it, and gentlemen, instead of cheating, were cheated. It was not for some weeks after the Crawleys' departure that the landlord of the hotel which they occupied during their residence at Paris, found out the losses which he had sustained: not until Madame Marabou[8] the milliner made repeated visits with her little bill for articles supplied to Madame Crawley: not until Monsieur Didelot from the Boule d'Or in the Palais Royal had asked half-a-dozen times whether cette charmante Miladi[9] who had bought watches and bracelets of him was de retour.[1] It is a fact that even the poor gardener's wife, who had nursed Madame's child, was never paid after the first six months for that supply of the milk of human kindness with which she had furnished the lusty and healthy little Rawdon. No, not even the nurse was paid—the Crawleys were in too great a hurry to remember their trifling debt to her. As for the landlord of the hotel, his curses against the English nation were violent for the rest of his natural life. He asked all travellers whether they knew a certain Colonel Lor Crawley—avec sa femme—une petite dame, très spirituelle. *"Ah, Monsieur!"* he would add—*"ils*

8. Named for an African stork, feathers from which were much used in decorating women's clothing.
9. That charming woman.
1. Returned.

*m'ont affreusement volé.*"[2] It was melancholy to hear his accents as he spoke of that catastrophe.

Rebecca's object in her journey to London was to effect a kind of compromise with her husband's numerous creditors, and by offering them a dividend of ninepence or a shilling in the pound, to secure a return for him into his own country. It does not become us to trace the steps which she took in the conduct of this most difficult negotiation; but, having shown them to their satisfaction, that the sum which she was empowered to offer was all her husband's available capital, and having convinced them that Colonel Crawley would prefer a perpetual retirement on the continent to a residence in this country with his debts unsettled; having proved to them that there was no possibility of money accruing to him from other quarters, and no earthly chance of their getting a larger dividend than that which she was empowered to offer, she brought the Colonel's creditors unanimously to accept her proposals, and purchased with fifteen hundred pounds of ready money, more than ten times that amount of debts.

Mrs. Crawley employed no lawyer in the transaction. The matter was so simple, to have or to leave, as she justly observed, that she made the lawyers of the creditors themselves do the business. And Mr. Lewis representing Mr. Davids of Red Lion Square, and Mr. Moss acting for Mr. Manasseh of Cursitor Street,[3] (chief creditors of the Colonel's,) complimented his lady upon the brilliant way in which she did business, and declared that there was no professional man who could beat her.

Rebecca received their congratulations with perfect modesty; ordered a bottle of sherry and a bread cake to the little dingy lodgings where she dwelt, while conducting the business, to treat the enemy's lawyers; shook hands with them at parting, in excellent good humour, and returned straightway to the continent, to rejoin her husband and son, and acquaint the former with the glad news of his entire liberation. As for the latter, he had been considerably neglected during his mother's absence by Mademoiselle Genevieve, her French maid; for that young woman, contracting an attachment for a soldier in the garrison of Calais, forgot her charge in the society of this *militaire,* and little Rawdon very narrowly escaped drowning on Calais sands at this period, where the absent Genevieve had left and lost him.[4]

And so, Colonel[5] and Mrs. Crawley came to London: and it is at their house in Curzon Street, May Fair, that they really showed the skill which must be possessed by those who would live on the resources above named.

2. With his wife, a small woman, very witty, "Ah, Sir, they have fearfully robbed me."
3. Red Lion Square, next to Gray's Inn, had many law firms. On Cursitor Street, nearby, there were money lenders and sponging houses. Davids, Moss, and Manasseh all imply Jewish origins.
4. First printing contained an extra paragraph here: After a stay at Brussels, where they lived in good fashion, with carriages and horses, and giving pretty little dinners at their hotel, the Colonel and his lady again quitted that city, from which slander pursued them as it did from Paris, and where it is said they left a vast amount of debt behind them. Indeed, this is the way in which gentlemen who live upon nothing a-year, make both ends meet.
5. First printing reads: From Brussels, Colonel

## *Chapter XXXVII.*

THE SUBJECT CONTINUED.

N the first place, and as a matter of the greatest necessity, we are bound to describe how a house may be got for nothing a-year. These mansions are to be had either unfurnished, where, if you have credit with Messrs. Gillows or Bantings,[1] you can get them splendidly arranged[2] and decorated entirely according to your own fancy; or they are to be let furnished; a less troublesome and complicated arrangement to most parties. It was so that Crawley and his wife preferred to hire their house.

Before Mr. Bowls came to preside over Miss Crawley's house and cellar in Park Lane, that lady had had for a butler, a Mr. Raggles, who was born on the family estate of Queen's Crawley, and indeed was a younger son of a gardener there. By good conduct, a handsome person and calves, and a grave demeanour, Raggles rose from the knife-board to the foot-board of the carriage; from the foot-board to the butler's pantry. When he had been a certain number of years at the head of Miss Crawley's establishment, where he had had good wages, fat perquisites, and plenty of opportunities of saving, he announced that he was about to contract a matrimonial alliance with a late cook of Miss Crawley's, who had subsisted in an honourable manner by the exercise of a mangle, and the keeping of a small green shop[3] in the neighbourhood. The truth is, that the ceremony had been clandestinely performed some years back; although the news of Mr. Raggles' marriage was first brought to Miss Crawley by a little boy and girl of seven and eight years of age, whose continual presence in the kitchen had attracted the attention of Miss Briggs.

Mr. Raggles then retired and personally undertook the superintendence of the small shop and the greens. He added milk and cream, eggs and country fed pork to his stores, contenting himself, whilst other retired butlers were vending spirits in public houses, by dealing in the simplest country produce. And having a good connection amongst the butlers in the neighbourhood, and a snug back parlour where he and Mrs. Raggles received them, his milk, cream, and eggs got to be adopted by many of the fraternity, and his profits increased every year. Year after year he quietly and modestly amassed money, and when at length that snug and complete bachelor's residence at No. 201, Curzon Street, May Fair, lately the residence of the Honourable Frederick Deuceace, gone abroad, with its rich and appropriate furniture by the first makers, was brought to the ham-

1. Furniture dealers in the West End, London.
2. Revised edition reads: *montées*
3. Greengrocer's.

mer,[4] who should go in and purchase the lease and furniture of the house but Charles Raggles? A part of the money he borrowed, it is true, and at rather a high interest, from a brother butler, but the chief part he paid down, and it was with no small pride that Mrs. Raggles found herself sleeping in a bed of carved mahogany, with silk curtains, with a prodigious cheval glass[5] opposite to her, and a wardrobe which would contain her, and Raggles, and all the family.

Of course, they did not intend to occupy permanently an apartment so splendid. It was in order to let the house again that Raggles purchased it. As soon as a tenant was found, he subsided into the greengrocer's shop once more; but a happy thing it was for him to walk out of that tenement and into Curzon Street, and there survey his house—his own house—with geraniums in the window and a carved bronze knocker. The footman occasionally lounging at the area railing, treated him with respect; the cook took her green stuff at his house and called him Mr. Landlord; and there was not one thing the tenants did, or one dish which they had for dinner, that Raggles might not know of, if he liked.

He was a good man; good and happy. The house brought him in so handsome a yearly income, that he was determined to send his children to good schools, and accordingly, regardless of expense, Charles was sent to boarding at Dr. Swishtail's, Sugar-cane Lodge, and little Matilda to Miss Peckover's, Laurentinum House, Clapham.

Raggles loved and adored the Crawley family as the author of all his prosperity in life. He had a silhouette of his mistress in his back shop, and a drawing of the Porter's Lodge at Queen's Crawley, done by that spinster herself in India ink—and the only addition he made to the decorations of the Curzon Street House was a print of Queen's Crawley in Hampshire, the Seat of Sir Walpole Crawley, Baronet, who was represented in a gilded car drawn by six white horses, and passing by a lake covered with swans, and barges containing ladies in hoops, and musicians with flags and periwigs. Indeed, Raggles thought there was no such palace in all the world, and no such august family.

As luck would have it, Raggles' house in Curzon Street was to let when Rawdon and his wife returned to London. The Colonel knew it and its owner quite well; the latter's connexion with the Crawley family had been kept up constantly, for Raggles helped Mr. Bowls whenever Miss Crawley received friends. And the old man not only let his house to the Colonel, but officiated as his butler whenever he had company; Mrs. Raggles operating in the kitchen below, and sending up dinners of which old Miss Crawley herself might have approved. This was the way, then, Crawley got his house for nothing: for though Raggles had to pay taxes and rates, and the interest of the mortgage to the brother butler; and the insurance of his life; and the charges for his children at school; and the value of the meat and drink which his own family—and for a time that of Colonel Crawley too—consumed; and though the poor wretch was utterly ruined by

4. Gone abroad, i.e., avoided arrest, leaving his goods to the auctioneer's hammer for his debts.
5. Full-length mirror on a tilting frame.

the transaction, his children being flung on the streets, and himself driven into the Fleet Prison; yet somebody must pay even for gentlemen who live for nothing a-year—and so it was this unlucky Raggles was made the representative of Colonel Crawley's defective capital.

I wonder how many families are driven to roguery and to ruin by great practitioners in Crawley's way?—how many great noblemen rob their petty tradesmen, condescend to swindle their poor retainers out of wretched little sums, and cheat for a few shillings? When we read that a noble nobleman has left for the continent, or that another noble nobleman has an execution[6] in his house—and that one or other owe six or seven millions, the defeat seems glorious even, and we respect the victim in the vastness of his ruin. But who pities a poor barber who can't get his money for powdering the footmen's heads; or a poor carpenter who has ruined himself by fixing up ornaments and pavilions for my lady's *déjeuné;*[7] or the poor devil of a tailor whom the steward patronises, and who has pledged all he is worth, and more, to get the liveries ready, which my lord has done him the honour to bespeak?—When the great house tumbles down, these miserable wretches fall under it unnoticed: as they say in the old legends, before a man goes to the devil himself, he sends plenty of other souls thither.

Rawdon and his wife generously gave their patronage to all such of Miss Crawley's tradesmen and purveyors as chose to serve them. Some were willing enough, especially the poor ones. It was wonderful to see the pertinacity with which the washerwoman from Tooting[8] brought the cart every Saturday, and her bills week after week. Mr. Raggles himself had to supply the green-groceries. The bill for servants' porter at the Fortune of War public house is a curiosity in the chronicles of beer. Every servant also was owed the greater part of his wages, and thus kept up perforce an interest in the house. Nobody in fact was paid. Not the blacksmith who opened the lock; nor the glazier who mended the pane; nor the jobber who let the carriage; nor the groom who drove it; nor the butcher who provided the leg of mutton; nor the coals which roasted it; nor the cook who basted it; nor the servants who eat it: and this I am given to understand is not unfrequently the way in which people live elegantly on nothing a-year.

In a little town such things cannot be done without remark. We know there the quantity of milk our neighbour takes, and espy the joint or the fowls which are going in for his dinner. So, probably, 200 and 202 in Curzon Street might know what was going on in the house between them, the servants communicating through the area-railings; but Crawley and his wife and his friends did not know 200 and 202. When you came to 201 there was a hearty welcome, a kind smile, a good dinner, and a jolly shake of the hand from the host and hostess there, just for all the world, as if they had been undisputed masters of three or four thousand a year—and so they were, not in money, but in produce and labour—if they did not pay for the mutton, they had it: if they did not give bullion in exchange for their

6. Enforcement of a court judgment for debt.
7. Luncheon.
8. Five miles south of London.

wine, how should we know? Never was better claret at any man's table than at honest Rawdon's; dinners more gay and neatly served. His drawing rooms were the prettiest, little, modest salons conceivable: they were decorated with the greatest taste, and a thousand knick-knacks from Paris, by Rebecca: and when she sate at her piano trilling songs with a lightsome heart, the stranger voted himself in a little paradise of domestic comfort, and agreed that if the husband was rather stupid, the wife was charming, and the dinners the pleasantest in the world.

Rebecca's wit, cleverness, and flippancy, made her speedily the vogue in London among a certain class. You saw demure chariots at her door, out of which stepped very great people. You beheld her carriage in the park, surrounded by dandies of note. The little box in the third tier of the Opera was crowded with heads constantly changing; but it must be confessed that the ladies held aloof from her, and that their doors were shut to our little adventurer.

With regard to the world of female fashion and its customs, the present writer of course can only speak at second hand. A man can no more penetrate or understand those mysteries than he can know what the ladies talk about when they go up stairs after dinner. It is only by inquiry and perseverance, that one sometimes gets hints of those secrets; and by a similar diligence every person who treads the Pall Mall pavement and frequents the clubs of this metropolis, knows, either through his own experience or through some acquaintance with whom he plays at billiards or shares the joint, something about the genteel world of London, and how, as there are men (such as Rawdon Crawley, whose position we mentioned before), who cut a good figure to the eyes of the ignorant world and to the apprentices in the Park, who behold them consorting with the most notorious dandies there, so there are ladies, who may be called men's women, being welcomed entirely by all the gentlemen, and cut or slighted by all their wives. Mrs. Firebrace is of this sort; the lady with the beautiful fair ringlets whom you see every day in Hyde Park, surrounded by the greatest and most famous dandies of this empire. Mrs. Rockwood is another, whose parties are announced laboriously in the fashionable newspapers, and with whom you see that all sorts of ambassadors and great noblemen dine; and many more might be mentioned had they to do with the history at present in hand. But while simple folks who are out of the world, or country people with a taste for the genteel, behold these ladies in their seeming glory in public places, or envy them from afar off, persons who are better instructed could inform them that these envied ladies have no more chance of establishing themselves in "society," than the benighted squire's wife in Somersetshire, who reads of their doings in the *Morning Post.* Men living about London are aware of these awful truths. You hear how pitilessly many ladies of seeming rank and wealth are excluded from this "society." The frantic efforts which they make to enter this circle, the meannesses to which they submit, the insults which they undergo, are matters of wonder to those who take human or womankind for a study; and the pursuit of fashion under difficulties would be a fine theme for any very great person who had the wit, the leisure, and the knowledge of the English language necessary for the compiling of such a history.[9]

Now the few female acquaintances whom Mrs. Crawley had known abroad, not only declined to visit her when she came to this side of the channel, but cut her severely when they met in public places. It was curious to see how the great ladies forgot her, and no doubt not altogether a pleasant study to Rebecca. When Lady Bareacres met her in the waiting-room at the Opera, she gathered her daughters about her as if they would be contaminated by a touch of Becky, and retreating a step or two, placed herself in front of them, and stared at her little enemy. To stare Becky out of countenance required a severer glance than even the frigid old Bareacres could shoot out of her dismal eyes. When Lady de la Mole, who had ridden a score of times by Becky's side at Brussels, met Mrs. Crawley's open carriage in Hyde Park, her Ladyship was quite blind, and could not in the least recognise her former friend. Even Mrs. Blenkinsop, the banker's wife, cut her at church. Becky went regularly to church now; it was edifying to see her enter there with Rawdon by her side, carrying a couple of large gilt prayer-books, and afterwards going through the ceremony with the gravest resignation.

Rawdon at first felt very acutely the slights which were passed upon his wife, and was inclined to be gloomy and savage. He talked of calling out the husbands or brothers of every one of the insolent women who did not pay a proper respect to his wife; and it was only by the strongest commands and entreaties on her part, that he was brought into keeping a decent behaviour. "You can't shoot me into society," she said good-naturedly. "Remember, my dear, that I was but a governess, and you, you poor silly old man, have the worst reputation for debt, and dice, and all sorts of wickedness. We shall get quite as many friends as we want by and by, and in the mean while you must be a good boy, and obey your schoolmistress in every thing she tells you to do. When we heard that your aunt had left almost everything to Pitt and his wife, do you remember what a rage you were in? You would have told all Paris, if I had not made you keep your temper, and where would you have been now?—in prison at Ste. Pélagie[1] for debt, and not established in London in a handsome house, with every comfort about you—you were in such a fury you were ready to murder your brother, you wicked Cain you, and what good would have come of remaining angry? All the rage in the world won't get us your aunt's money; and it is much better that we should be friends with your brother's family than enemies, as those foolish Butes are. When your father dies, Queen's Crawley will be a pleasant house for you and me to pass the winter in. If we are ruined, you can carve and take charge of the stable, and I can be a governess to Lady Jane's children. Ruined! fiddlededee! I will get you a good place before that; or Pitt and his little boy will die, and we will be Sir Rawdon and my lady. While there is life, there is hope, my dear, and I intend to make a man of you yet. Who sold your horses for you? Who paid your

9. George Lillie Craik's *The Pursuit of Learning under Difficulties* (1830) was a well-known and very serious description of the "industrious apprentice" (Colby).

1. Paris debtor's prison.

debts for you?" Rawdon was obliged to confess that he owed all these benefits to his wife, and to trust himself to her guidance for the future..

Indeed, when Miss Crawley quitted the world, and that money for which all her relatives had been fighting so eagerly was finally left to Pitt, Bute Crawley, who found that only five thousand pounds had been left to him instead of the twenty upon which he calculated, was in such a fury at his disappointment, that he vented it in savage abuse upon his nephew; and the quarrel always rankling between them ended in an utter breach of intercourse. Rawdon Crawley's conduct, on the other hand, who got but a hundred pounds, was such as to astonish his brother and delight his sister-in-law, who was disposed to look kindly upon all the members of her husband's family. He wrote to his brother a very frank, manly, good-humoured letter from Paris. He was aware, he said, that by his own marriage he had forfeited his aunt's favour; and though he did not disguise his disappointment that she should have been so entirely relentless towards him, he was glad that the money was still kept in their branch of the family, and heartily congratulated his brother on his good fortune. He sent his affectionate remembrances to his sister, and hoped to have her good-will for Mrs. Crawley;[2] and the letter concluded with a postscript to Pitt in the latter lady's own hand-writing. She, too, begged to join in her husband's congratulations. She should ever remember Mr. Crawley's kindness to her in early days when she was a friendless orphan, the instructress of his little sisters, in whose welfare she still took the tenderest interest. She wished him every happiness in his married life, and, asking his permission to offer her remembrances to Lady Jane (of whose goodness all the world informed her), she hoped that one day she might be allowed to present her little boy to his uncle and aunt, and begged to bespeak for him their good-will and protection.

Pitt Crawley received this letter[3] very graciously—more graciously than Miss Crawley had received some of Rebecca's previous compositions in Rawdon's hand-writing; and as for Lady Jane, she was so charmed with the letter, that she expected her husband would instantly divide her aunt's legacy into two equal portions, and send off one-half to his brother at Paris.

To her ladyship's surprise, however, Pitt declined to accommodate his brother with a check for thirty thousand pounds. But he made Rawdon a handsome offer of his hand whenever the latter should come to England and choose to take it; and, thanking Mrs. Crawley for her good opinion of himself and Lady Jane, he graciously pronounced his willingness to take any opportunity to serve her little boy.

Thus an almost reconciliation was brought about between the brothers. When Rebecca came to town Pitt and his wife were not in London. Many a time she drove by the old door in Park Lane to see whether they had taken possession of Miss Crawley's house there.

2. Rawdon's "sister" is Lady Jane, who is Mrs. Pitt Crawley, but there can be little doubt here that Mrs. Crawley is Rawdon's wife, Becky. Mrs. Bute Crawley is a third Mrs. Crawley. Revised edition reads: Mrs. Rawdon;
3. Revised edition reads: communication

But the new family did not make its appearance; it was only through Raggles that she heard of their movements—how Miss Crawley's domestics had been dismissed with decent gratuities, and how Mr. Pitt had only once made his appearance in London, when he stopped for a few days at the house, did business with his lawyers there, and sold off all Miss Crawley's French novels to a bookseller out of Bond Street. Becky had reasons of her own which caused her to long for the arrival of her new relation. "When Lady Jane comes," thought she, "she shall be my sponsor in London society; and as for the women! bah!—the women will ask me when they find the men want to see me."

An article as necessary to a lady in this position as her Brougham or her bouquet, is her companion. I have always admired the way in which the tender creatures, who cannot exist without sympathy, hire an exceedingly plain friend of their own sex from whom they are almost inseparable. The sight of that inevitable woman in her faded gown seated behind her dear friend in the opera-box, or occupying the back seat of the barouche, is always a wholesome and moral one to me, as jolly a reminder as that of the Death's-head which figured in the repasts of Egyptian *bon-vivants,* a strange sardonic memorial of Vanity Fair.[4] What?—even battered, brazen, beautiful, conscienceless, heartless, Mrs. Firebrace, whose father died of her shame: even lovely, daring, Mrs. Mantrap, who will ride at any fence which any man in England will take, and who drives her greys in the Park, while her mother keeps a huxter's stall in Bath still;—even those who are so bold, one might fancy they could face anything, dare not face the world without a female friend. They must have somebody to cling to, the affectionate creatures! And you will hardly see them in any public place without a shabby companion in a dyed silk, sitting somewhere in the shade close behind them.

"Rawdon," said Becky, very late one night as a party of gentlemen were seated round her crackling drawing-room fire; (for the men came to her house to finish the night; and she had ice and coffee for them, the best in London): "I must have a sheep-dog."

"A what?" said Rawdon, looking up from an *écarté* table.

"A sheep-dog," said young Lord Southdown. "My dear Mrs. Crawley, what a fancy! Why not have a Danish dog? I know of one as big as a camel-leopard,[5] by Jove. It would almost pull your Brougham. Or a Persian grey-hound, eh? (I propose, if you please); or a little pug that would go into one of Lord Steyne's snuff-boxes? There's a man at Bayswater[6] got one with such a nose that you might,—I mark the king and play,—that you might hang your hat on it."

"I mark the trick," Rawdon gravely said. He attended to his game commonly, and didn't much meddle with the conversation except when it was about horses and betting.

"What *can* you want with a shepherd's dog?" the lively little Southdown continued.

4. The memento mori served ambiguously to remind one of the seriousness and temporariness of life, or as encouragement to enjoy the moment while it lasted.
5. Giraffe.
6. A west London suburb.

"I mean a *moral* shepherd's dog," said Becky, laughing, and looking up at Lord Steyne.

"What the devil's that?" said his Lordship.

"A dog to keep the wolves off me," Rebecca continued. "A companion."

"Dear little innocent lamb, you want one," said the Marquis; and his jaw thrust out, and he began to grin hideously, his little eyes leering towards Rebecca.

The great Lord of Steyne was standing by the fire sipping coffee. The fire crackled and blazed pleasantly. There was a score of candles sparkling round the mantelpiece, in all sorts of quaint sconces, of gilt and bronze and porcelain. They lighted up Rebecca's figure to admiration, as she sate on a sofa covered with a pattern of gaudy flowers. She was in a pink dress, that looked as fresh as a rose; her dazzling white arms and shoulders were half covered with a thin hazy scarf through which they sparkled; her hair hung in curls round her neck; one of her little feet peeped out from the fresh crisp folds of the silk; the prettiest little foot in the prettiest little sandal in the finest silk stocking in the world.[7]

7. The following illustration disappeared from the third printing of the first edition, probably because the woodblock was damaged. Some have speculated that it was suppressed because it too closely resembled the living marquis of Hertford, but other illustrations of Lord Steyne remain, and it is disputed which marquis of Hertford the illustration resembled.

The candles lighted up Lord Steyne's shining bald head, which was fringed with red hair. He had thick bushy eyebrows, with little twinkling bloodshot eyes, surrounded by a thousand wrinkles. His jaw was underhung, and when he laughed, two white buck-teeth protruded themselves and glistened savagely in the midst of the grin. He had been dining with royal personages, and wore his garter and ribbon.[8] A short man was his Lordship, broad-chested, and bow-legged, but proud of the fineness of his foot and ancle, and always caressing his garter-knee.

"And so the Shepherd is not enough," said he, "to defend his lambkin?"

"The Shepherd is too fond of playing at cards and going to his clubs," answered Becky, laughing.

"'Gad, what a debauched Corydon!" said my lord—"what a mouth for a pipe!"

"I take your three to two;" here said Rawdon, at the card-table.

"Hark at Melibœus,"[9] snarled the noble Marquis; "he's pastorally occupied too; he's shearing a Southdown. What an innocent mutton, hey? Damme, what a snowy fleece!"

Rebecca's eyes shot out gleams of scornful humour. "My lord," she said, "you are a knight of the Order." He had the collar round his neck, indeed—a gift of the restored Princes of Spain.[1]

Lord Steyne in early life had been notorious for his daring and his success at play. He had sat up two days and two nights with Mr. Fox at hazard. He had won money of the most august personages of the realm: he had won his marquisate, it was said, at the gaming-table; but he did not like an allusion to those by-gone *fredaines*.[2] Rebecca saw the scowl gathering over his heavy brow.

She rose up from her sofa, and went and took his coffee cup out of his hand, with a little curtsey. "Yes," she said, "I must get a watch-dog. But he won't bark at *you*." And, going into the other drawing-room, she sate down to the piano, and began to sing little French songs in such a charming, thrilling voice, that the mollified nobleman speedily followed her into that chamber, and might be seen nodding his head and bowing time over her.

Rawdon and his friend meanwhile played *écarté* until they had enough. The Colonel won; but, say that he won ever so much and often, nights like these, which occurred many times in the week—his wife having all the talk and all the admiration, and he sitting silent without the circle, not comprehending a word of the jokes, the allusions, the mystical language within—must have been rather wearisome to the ex-dragoon.

"How is Mrs. Crawley's husband," Lord Steyne used to say to him by way of a good day when they met: and indeed that was now his

8. A dark blue ribbon and motto from the badge of the Order of the Garter, the highest order of English knighthood.

9. Corydon and Melibœus are common pastoral names; Melibœus, in *The Canterbury Tales*, discusses with his wife the best way to deal with enemies.

1. Becky's elliptical reference to "the Order" makes Steyne a knight of the order of fleecers (like Rawdon, who is taking Southdown's money) as well as knight of the Spanish Order of the Golden Fleece, the emblem of which is on a ribbon round Steyne's neck. Napoleon had deposed the royal house of Spain, which was restored at his first capture in 1814.

2. Episodes, pranks.

avocation in life. He was Colonel Crawley no more. He was Mrs. Crawley's husband.

About the little Rawdon, if nothing has been said all this while, it is because he is hidden up-stairs in a garret somewhere, or has crawled below into the kitchen for companionship. His mother scarcely ever took notice of him. He passed the days with his French *bonne* as long as that domestic remained in Mr. Crawley's family, and when the Frenchwoman went away, the little fellow, howling in the loneliness of the night, had compassion taken on him by a housemaid, who took him out of his solitary nursery into her bed in the garret hard by, and comforted him.

Rebecca, my Lord Steyne, and one or two more were in the drawing-room taking tea after the Opera, when this shouting was heard overhead. "It's my cherub crying for his nurse," she said. She did not offer to move to go and see the child. "Don't agitate your feelings by going to look for him," said Lord Steyne sardonically. "Bah!" replied the other, with a sort of blush, "he'll cry himself to sleep;" and they fell to talking about the Opera.

Rawdon had stolen off though, to look after his son and heir; and came back to the company when he found that honest Dolly was consoling the child. The Colonel's dressing-room was in those upper regions. He used to see the boy there in private. They had interviews together every morning when he shaved; Rawdon minor sitting on a box by his father's side and watching the operation with never ceasing pleasure. He and the sire were great friends. The father would bring him sweet-meats from the dessert, and hide them in a certain old epaulet box, where the child went to seek them, and laughed with joy on discovering the treasure: laughed, but not too loud; for mamma was below asleep and must not be disturbed. She did not go to rest till very late, and seldom rose till after noon.

Rawdon bought the boy plenty of picture-books, and crammed his nursery with toys. Its walls were covered with pictures pasted up by the father's own hand, and purchased by him for ready money. When he was off duty with Mrs. Rawdon in the Park, he would sit up here, passing hours with the boy; who rode on his chest, who pulled his great mustachios as if they were driving-reins, and spent days with him in indefatigable gambols. The room was a low room, and once, when the child was not five years old, his father, who was tossing him wildly up in his arms, hit the poor little chap's skull so violently against the ceiling that he almost dropped the child, so terrified was he at the disaster.

Rawdon Minor had made up his face for a tremendous howl—the severity of the blow indeed authorised that indulgence: but just as he was going to begin, the father interposed.

"For God's sake, Rawdy, don't wake mamma," he cried. And the child looking in a very hard and piteous way at his Father, bit his lips, clenched his hands, and didn't cry a bit. Rawdon told that story at the clubs, at the mess, to everybody in town. "By Gad, Sir," he explained to the public in general, "what a good plucked[3] one that boy of mine is—what a trump he is! I half sent his head through the ceiling, by Gad, and he wouldn't cry for fear of disturbing his mother."

Sometimes—once or twice in a week—that lady visited the upper regions in which the child lived. She came like[4] a vivified figure out of the *Magasin des Modes*[5]—blandly smiling in the most beautiful new clothes and little gloves and boots. Wonderful scarfs, laces, and jewels glittered about her. She had always a new bonnet on: and flowers bloomed perpetually in it: or else magnificent curling ostrich feathers, soft and snowy as Camellias. She nodded twice or thrice patronisingly to the little boy, who looked up from his dinner or from the pictures of soldiers he was painting. When she left the room, an odour of rose, or some other magical fragrance, lingered about the nursery. She was an unearthly being in his eyes, superior to his father—to all the world: to be worshipped and admired at a distance. To drive with that lady in the carriage was an awful rite: he sate up in the back seat, and did not dare to speak: he gazed with all his eyes at the beautifully dressed princess opposite to him. Gentlemen on splendid prancing horses came up, and smiled and talked with her. How her eyes beamed upon all of them! Her hand used to quiver and wave gracefully as they passed. When he went out with her he had his new red dress on. His old brown holland was good enough when he staid at home. Sometimes, when she was away, and Dolly his maid was making her bed, he came into his mother's room. It was as the abode of a fairy to him—a mystic chamber of splendour and delights. There in the wardrobe hung those wonderful robes—pink, and blue, and many-tinted. There was the jewel-case, silver-clasped: and the mystic[6] bronze hand on the dressing-table, glistening all over with a hundred rings. There was the cheval-glass, that miracle of art, in which he could just see his own wondering head, and the reflection of Dolly (queerly distorted, and as if up in the ceiling), plumping and patting the pillows of the bed. O, thou poor lonely little benighted boy! Mother is the name for God in the lips and hearts of little children; and here was one who was worshipping a stone!

Now Rawdon Crawley, rascal as the Colonel was, had certain manly tendencies of affection in his heart, and could love a child and a woman still. For Rawdon Minor he had a great secret tenderness then, which did not escape Rebecca, though she did not talk about it to her husband. It did not annoy her: she was too good-natured. It only increased her scorn for him. He felt somehow ashamed of this paternal softness, and hid it from his wife—only indulging in it when alone with the boy.

He used to take him out of mornings, when they would go to the stables together and to the Park. Little Lord Southdown, the best-natured of men, who would make you a present of the hat from his head, and whose main occupation in life was to buy knick-knacks that he might give them away afterwards, bought the little chap a pony not

3. One with pluck, spirited.
4. Revised edition reads: came in like
5. Paris shop of that name, or a reference to any of several fashion journals with fashion plates.
6. Revised edition reads: wondrous

much bigger than a large rat, the donor said, and on this little black Shetland pigmy young Rawdon's great father was pleased to mount the boy, and to walk by his side in the Park. It pleased him to see his old quarters, and his old fellow-guardsmen at Knightsbridge: he had begun to think of his bachelorhood with something like regret. The old troopers were glad to recognise their ancient officer, and dandle the little Colonel. Colonel Crawley found dining at mess and with his brother-officers very pleasant. "Hang it, I ain't clever enough for her—I know it. She won't miss me," he used to say: and he was right: his wife did not miss him.

Rebecca was fond of her husband. She was always perfectly good-humoured and kind to him. She did not even show her scorn much for him; perhaps she liked him the better for being a fool. He was her upper servant and *maître d' hôtel.*[7] He went on her errands: obeyed her orders without question: drove in the carriage in the ring with her without repining; took her to the Opera-box; solaced himself at his club during the performance, and came punctually back to fetch her when due. He would have liked her to be a little fonder of the boy: but even to that he reconciled himself. "Hang it, you know she's so clever," he said, "and I'm not literary and that, you know." For, as we have said before, it requires no great wisdom to be able to win at cards and billiards, and Rawdon made no pretensions to any other sort of skill.

When the companion came, his domestic duties became very light. His wife encouraged him to dine abroad: she would let him off duty at the Opera. "Don't stay and stupify yourself at home to night, my dear," she would say. "Some men are coming who will only bore you. I would not ask them, but you know it's for your good, and now I have a sheep-dog, I need not be afraid to be alone."

"A sheep-dog—a companion! Becky Sharp with a companion! Isn't it good fun?" thought Mrs. Crawley to herself. The notion tickled hugely her sense of humour.

One Sunday morning, as Rawdon Crawley, his little son, and the pony were taking their accustomed walk in the Park, they passed by an old acquaintance of the Colonel's, Corporal Clink, of the regiment, who was in conversation with a friend, an old gentleman, who held a boy in his arms about the age of little Rawdon. This other youngster had seized hold of the Waterloo medal which the Corporal wore, and was examining it with delight.

"Good morning, your Honour," said Clink, in reply to the "How-do, Clink?" of the Colonel. "This ere young gentleman is about the little Colonel's age, Sir," continued the Corporal.

"His father was a Waterloo man, too," said the old gentleman, who carried the boy. "Wasn't he, Georgy?"

"Yes," said Georgy. He and the little chap on the pony were looking at each other with all their might—solemnly scanning each other as children do.

"In a line regiment," Clink said, with a patronising air.

7. Butler, house manager.

Georgy makes acquaintance with a Waterloo Man

"He was a Captain in the —th regiment," said the old gentleman rather pompously. "Captain George Osborne, Sir—perhaps you knew him. He died the death of a hero, Sir, fighting against the Corsican tyrant."

Colonel Crawley blushed quite red. "I knew him very well, Sir," he said, "and his wife, his dear little wife, Sir—how is she?"

"She is my daughter, Sir," said the old gentleman, putting down the boy, and taking out a card with great solemnity, which he handed to the Colonel. On it was written—

Mr. Sedley, Sole Agent for the Black Diamond and Anti-Cinder Coal Association, Bunker's Wharf, Thames Street, and Anna-Maria Cottages, Fulham Road West.

Little Georgy went up and looked at the Shetland pony.

"Should you like to have a ride?" said Rawdon Minor from the saddle.

"Yes," said Georgy. The Colonel, who had been looking at him with some interest, took up the child and put him on the pony behind Rawdon Minor.

"Take hold of him, Georgy," he said—"take my little boy round the waist—his name is Rawdon." And both the children began to laugh.

"You won't see a prettier pair, I think, *this* summer's day, Sir," said the good-natured Corporal; and the Colonel, the Corporal, and old Mr. Sedley with his umbrella, walked by the side of the children.

## *Chapter XXXVIII.*

### A FAMILY IN A VERY SMALL WAY.

E must suppose little George Osborne has ridden from Knightsbridge towards Fulham, and will stop and make inquiries at that village regarding some friends whom we have left there. How is Mrs. Amelia after the storm of Waterloo? Is she living and thriving? What has come of Major Dobbin, whose cab was always hankering about her premises? and are there any news of the Collector of Boggley wollah? The facts concerning the latter are briefly these:

Our worthy fat friend Joseph Sedley returned to India not long after his escape from Brussels. Either his furlough was up, or he dreaded to meet any witnesses of his Waterloo flight. However it might be, he went back to his duties in

Bengal, very soon after Napoleon had taken up his residence at Saint Helena, where Jos saw the ex-emperor.[1]

To hear Mr. Sedley talk on board ship you would have supposed that it was not the first time he and the Corsican had met, and that the civilian had bearded the French General at Mount St. John. He had a thousand anecdotes about the famous battles; he knew the position of every regiment, and the loss which each had incurred. He did not deny that he had been concerned in those victories—that he had been with the army, and carried dispatches for the Duke of Wellington. And he described what the Duke did and said on every conceivable moment of the day of Waterloo, with such an accurate knowledge of his Grace's sentiments and proceedings, that it was clear he must have been by the conqueror's side throughout the day; though, as a non-combatant, his name was not mentioned in the public documents relative to the battle. Perhaps he actually worked himself up to believe that he had been engaged with the army; certain it is that he made a prodigious sensation for some time at Calcutta, and was called Waterloo Sedley during the whole of his subsequent stay in Bengal.

The bills which Jos had given for the purchase of those unlucky horses were paid without question by him and his agents. He never was heard to allude to the bargain, and nobody knows for a certainty what became of the horses, or how he got rid of them, or of Isidor, his Belgian servant, who sold a grey horse, very like the one which Jos rode, at Valenciennes[2] sometime during the autumn of 1815.

Jos's London agents had orders to pay one hundred and twenty pounds yearly to his parents at Fulham. It was the chief support of the old couple; for Mr. Sedley's speculations in life subsequent to his bankruptcy did not by any means retrieve the broken old gentleman's fortune. He tried to be a wine-merchant, a coal-merchant, a commission-lottery agent, &c., &c. He sent round prospectuses to his friends whenever he took a new trade, and ordered a new brass plate for the door, and talked pompously about making his fortune still. But Fortune never came back to the feeble and stricken old man. One by one his friends dropped off, and were weary of buying dear coals and bad wine from him; and there was only his wife in all the world who fancied, when he tottered off to the city of a morning, that he was still doing any business there. At evening he crawled slowly back; and he used to go of nights to a little club at a tavern, where he disposed of the finances of the nation. It was wonderful to hear him talk about millions, and agios, and discounts, and what Rothschild was doing, and Baring Brothers.[3] He talked of such vast sums that the gentlemen of the club (the apothecary, the undertaker, the great carpenter and builder, the parish clerk, who was allowed to come stealthily, and Mr. Clapp, our old acquaintance)

1. Island in south Atlantic to which Napoleon was exiled. Thackeray at age six, in 1817, stopped four days in St. Helena on his way from India to England. He saw Napoleon in a garden.
2. In northern France.
3. Agios: currency conversion fees. Nathan Mayer Rothschild (1777–1836), banker, financier, and "foremost capitalist of the world." Francis Thornhill Baring (1796–1866), lord of the Treasury and chancellor of the exchequer, and Thomas Baring (1800–73), M.P. and head of Baring and Company, Bankers.

respected the old gentleman. "I was better off once, Sir," he did not fail to tell everybody who 'used the room.' "My son, Sir, is at this minute chief magistrate of Ramgunge in the Presidency of Bengal, and touching his four thousand rupees per mensem.[4] My daughter might be a Colonel's lady if she liked. I might draw upon my son, the first magistrate, Sir, for two thousand pound to-morrow, and Alexander[5] would cash my bill, down Sir, down on the counter, Sir. But the Sedleys were always a proud family." You and I, my dear reader, may drop into this condition one day: for have not many of our friends attained it? Our luck may fail: our powers forsake us: our place on the boards be taken by better and younger mimes—the chance of life roll away and leave us shattered and stranded. Then men will walk across the road when they meet you—or, worse still, hold you out a couple of fingers and patronise you in a pitying way—then you will know, as soon as your back is turned, that your friend begins with a "Poor devil, what imprudences he has committed, what chances *that* chap has thrown away!" Well, well—a carriage and three thousand a-year is not the summit of the reward nor the end of God's judgment of men. If quacks prosper as often as they go to the wall—if zanies succeed and knaves arrive at fortune, and, *vice versâ,* sharing ill luck and prosperity for all the world like the ablest and most honest amongst us—I say, brother, the gifts and pleasures of Vanity Fair cannot be held of any great account, and that it is probable . . . but we are wandering out of the domain of the story.

Had Mrs. Sedley been a woman of energy, she would have exerted it after her husband's ruin, and, occupying a large house, would have taken in boarders. The broken Sedley would have acted well as the boarding-house landlady's husband; the Munoz of private life;[6] the titular lord and master: the carver, house-steward, and humble husband of the occupier of the dingy throne. I have seen men of good brains and breeding, and of good hopes and vigour once, who feasted squires and kept hunters in their youth, meekly cutting up legs of mutton for rancorous old harridans, and pretending to preside over their dreary tables—but Mrs. Sedley, we say, had not spirit enough to bustle about for "a few select inmates to join a cheerful musical family," such as one reads of in the *Times.*[7] She was content to lie on the shore where fortune had stranded her—and you could see that the career of this old couple was over.

I don't think they were unhappy. Perhaps they were a little prouder in their downfall than in their prosperity. Mrs. Sedley was always a great person for her landlady, Mrs. Clapp, when she descended and passed many hours with her in the basement or ornamented kitchen. The Irish maid Betty Flanagan's bonnets and rib-

4. Per month.
5. Alexander's Discount Company, established in 1810, was one of the largest known in London. A bill was an order to a bank to pay a certain amount at a future date. Discount companies would pay a lesser amount of cash at an earlier date and hold the bill to maturity for the full amount.
6. Fernando Muñoz (1808–73), an officer who secretly (1833) and publicly (1844) married Maria Cristina (1806–78), queen of Spain, but had no claim to title or property through the marriage.
7. On Thursday, September 2, 1847, for example, there were fifteen such ads in the *Times*; on Saturday, September 4, there were forty. See chapter XL.

bons, her sauciness, her idleness, her reckless prodigality of kitchen candles, her consumption of tea and sugar, and so forth, occupied and amused the old lady almost as much as the doings of her former household, when she had Sambo and the coachman, and a groom and a footboy, and a housekeeper with a regiment of female domestics—her former household, about which the good lady talked a hundred times a-day. And besides Betty Flanagan, Mrs. Sedley had all the maids-of-all-work in the street to superintend. She knew how each tenant of the cottages paid or owed his little rent. She stepped aside when Mrs. Rougemont the actress passed with her dubious family. She flung up her head when Mrs. Pestler, the apothecary's lady, drove by in her husband's professional one-horse chaise. She had colloquies with the green-grocer about the pennorth of turnips which Mr. Sedley loved: she kept an eye upon the milkman, and the baker's boy: and made visitations to the butcher, who sold hundreds of oxen very likely with less ado than was made about Mrs. Sedley's loin of mutton: and she counted the potatoes under the joint on Sundays, on which days, drest in her best, she went to church twice and read Blair's Sermons in the evening.

On that day, for "business" prevented him on week days from taking such a pleasure, it was old Sedley's delight to take out his little grandson Georgy to the neighbouring Parks or Kensington Gardens, to see the soldiers, or to feed the ducks. Georgy loved the red-coats, and his grandpapa told him how his father had been a famous soldier, and introduced him to many sergeants and others with Waterloo medals on their breasts, to whom the old grandfather pompously presented the child as the son of Captain Osborne of the —th, who died gloriously on the glorious eighteenth. He has been known to treat some of these non-commissioned gentlemen to a glass of porter, and, indeed, in their first Sunday walks was disposed to spoil little Georgy, sadly gorging the boy with apples and parliament,[8] to the detriment of his health—until Amelia declared that George should never go out with his grandpapa, unless the latter promised solemnly, and on his honour, not to give the child any cakes, lollipops, or stall produce whatever.

Between Mrs. Sedley and her daughter there was a sort of coolness about this boy, and a secret jealousy—for one evening, in George's very early days, Amelia, who had been seated at work in their little parlour scarcely remarking that the old lady had quitted the room, ran up stairs instinctively to the nursery at the cries of the child, who had been asleep until that moment—and there found Mrs. Sedley in the act of surreptitiously administering Daffy's Elixir[9] to the infant. Amelia, the gentlest and sweetest of every-day mortals, when she found this meddling with her maternal authority, thrilled and trembled all over with anger. Her cheeks, ordinarily pale, now flushed up, until they were as red as they used to be when she was a child of twelve years old. She seized the baby out of her mother's arms, and then grasped at the bottle, leaving the old lady gaping at her, furious, and holding the guilty tea-spoon.

8. Gingerbread cake.
9. *Elixir salutis*, invented by Thomas Daffy (d. 1680), a clergyman.

Amelia flung the bottle crashing into the fire-place. "I will *not* have baby poisoned, Mamma," cried Emmy, rocking the infant about violently with both her arms round him, and turning with flashing eyes at her mother.

"Poisoned, Amelia!" said the old lady; "this language to me?"

"He shall not have any medicine but that which Mr. Pestler sends for him. He told me that Daffy's Elixir was poison."

"Very good: you think I'm a murderess, then," replied Mrs. Sedley. "This is the language you use to your mother. I have met with misfortunes: I have sunk low in life: I have kept my carriage, and now walk on foot: but I did not know I was a murderess before, and thank you for the *news*."

"Mamma," said the poor girl, who was always ready for tears—"you shouldn't be hard upon me. I—I didn't mean—I mean, I did not wish to say you would do any wrong to this dear child; only—"

"O, no, my love—only that I was a murderess; in which case, I had better go to the Old Bailey.[1] Though I didn't poison *you,* when you were a child; but gave you the best of education, and the most expensive masters money could procure. Yes; I've nursed five children, and buried three; and the one I loved the best of all, and tended through croup, and teething, and measles, and hooping-cough, and brought up with foreign masters, regardless of expense, and with accomplishments at Minerva House—which I never had when I was a girl—when I was too glad to honour my father and mother, that I

1. Next door to Newgate Prison, the Old Bailey Sessions House was the criminal justice court for London.

might live long in the land, and to be useful, and not to mope all day in my room and act the fine lady—says I'm a murderess. Ah, Mrs. Osborne! may *you* never nourish a viper in your bosom, that's *my* prayer."

"Mamma, Mamma!" cried the bewildered girl: and the child in her arms set up a frantic chorus of shouts.

"A murderess, indeed! Go down on your knees and pray to God to cleanse your wicked ungrateful heart, Amelia, and may He forgive you as I do;" and Mrs. Sedley tossed out of the room, hissing out the word poison, once more, and so ending her charitable benediction.

Till the termination of her natural life, this breach between Mrs. Sedley and her daughter was never thoroughly mended. The quarrel gave the elder lady numberless advantages which she did not fail to turn to account with female ingenuity and perseverance. For instance, she scarcely spoke to Amelia for many weeks afterwards. She warned the domestics not to touch the child, as Mrs. Osborne might be offended. She asked her daughter to see and satisfy herself that there was no poison prepared in the little daily messes that were concocted for Georgy. When neighbours asked after the boy's health, she referred them pointedly to Mrs. Osborne. *She* never ventured to ask whether the baby was well or not. *She* would not touch the child although he was her grandson, and own precious darling, for she was not *used* to children, and might kill it. And whenever Mr. Pestler came upon his healing inquisition, she received the Doctor with such a sarcastic and scornful demeanour, as made the surgeon declare that not Lady Thistlewood herself, whom he had the honour of attending professionally, could give herself greater airs than old Mrs. Sedley, from whom he never took a fee. And very likely Emmy was jealous too, upon her own part, as what mother is not, of those who would manage her children for her, or become candidates for the first place in their affections? It is certain that when anybody nursed the child, she was uneasy, and that she would no more allow Mrs. Clapp or the domestic to dress or tend him, than she would have let them wash her husband's miniature which hung up over her little bed;—the same little bed from which the poor girl had gone to his; and to which she retired now for many long, silent, tearful, but happy years.

In this room was all Amelia's heart and treasure. Here it was that she tended her boy, and watched him through the many ills of childhood, with a constant passion of love. The elder George returned in him somehow, only improved, and as if come back from heaven. In a hundred little tones, looks, and movements, the child was so like his father, that the widow's heart thrilled as she held him to it; and he would often ask the cause of her tears. It was because of his likeness to his father, she did not scruple to tell him. She talked constantly to him about this dead father, and spoke of her love for George to the innocent and wondering child; much more than she ever had done to George himself, or to any confidante of her youth. To her parents she never talked about this matter: shrinking from baring her heart to them. Little George very likely could understand no better than they; but into his ears she poured her sentimental secrets unreservedly, and into his only. The very joy of this woman was a sort of grief, or so tender, at least, that its expression was tears. Her sensibilities were so weak and tremulous, that perhaps they ought not to be talked about in a book. I was told by Dr. Pestler, (now a most flourishing lady's physician, with a sumptuous dark-green carriage, a prospect of speedy knighthood, and a house in Manchester Square,)[2] that her grief at weaning the child was a sight that would have unmanned a Herod.[3] He was very soft-hearted many years ago, and his wife was mortally jealous of Mrs. Amelia, then and long afterwards.

Perhaps the Doctor's lady had good reason for her jealousy: most women shared it, of those who formed the small circle of Amelia's acquaintance, and were quite angry at the enthusiasm with which the other sex regarded her. For almost all men who came near her loved her; though no doubt they would be at a loss to tell you why. She was not brilliant, nor witty, nor wise overmuch, nor extraordinarily handsome. But wherever she went she touched and charmed every one of the male sex, as invariably as she awakened the scorn and incredulity of her own sisterhood. I think it was her weakness which was her principal charm:—a kind of sweet submission and softness, which seemed to appeal to each man she met for his sympathy and protection. We have seen how in the regiment, though she spoke but to few of George's comrades there, all the swords of the young fellows at the mess-table would have leapt from their scabbards to fight round her:[4] and so it was in the little narrow lodging-house and circle of Fulham, she interested and pleased everybody. If she had been Mrs. Mango herself, of the great house of Mango, Plantain, and Co.,[5] Crutched Friars,[6] and the magnificent proprietress of the Pineries,[7] Fulham, who gave summer *déjeûnés* frequented by Dukes and Earls, and drove about the parish with magnificent yellow liveries and bay horses, such as the royal stables at Kensington themselves could not turn out—I say had she been Mrs. Mango herself, or her son's wife, Lady Mary Mango, (daughter of the Earl of Castlemouldy, who condescended to marry the head of the firm,) the tradesmen of the neighbourhood could not pay her more honour than they invariably showed to the gentle young widow, when she passed by their doors, or made her humble purchases at their shops.

Thus it was not only Mr. Pestler, the medical man, but Mr. Linton, the young assistant, who doctored the servant maids and small tradesmen, and might be seen any day reading the *Times* in the surgery, who openly declared himself the slave of Mrs. Osborne. He was a personable young gentleman, more welcome at Mrs. Sedley's lodgings than his principal; and if anything went wrong with Georgy, he would drop in twice or thrice in the day, to see the little chap,

2. A small square where Manchester House is located, home of the marquess of Hertford, purported by some to be the prototype of Lord Steyne.
3. Roman-appointed king in Jerusalem who ordered the slaughter of all Jewish boys in Bethlehem under two years old in an attempt to kill the "new born king of the Jews." Matthew 2.16.
4. Edmund Burke, in *Reflections on the Revolution in France* (1790), says of Marie Antoinette: "I thought ten thousand swords must have leaped from their scabbards to avenge even a look that threatened her with insult."
5. Revised edition reads: & Co.,
6. Near the Tower of London.
7. Pines are pineapples; a pinery is a hothouse for growing them; mangos, plantains, and tamarinds are other tropical fruits used as names in this passage.

and without so much as the thought of a fee. He would abstract lozenges, tamarinds, and other produce from the surgery-drawers for little Georgy's benefit, and compounded draughts and mixtures for him of miraculous sweetness, so that it was quite a pleasure to the child to be ailing. He and Pestler, his chief, sate up two whole nights by the boy in that momentous and awful week when Georgy had the measles; and when you would have thought, from the mother's terror, that there had never been measles in the world before. Would they have done as much for other people? Did they sit up for the folks at the Pineries, when Ralph Plantagenet,[8] and Gwendoline, and Guinever Mango had the same juvenile complaint? Did they sit up for little Mary Clapp, the landlord's daughter, who actually caught the disease of little Georgy? Truth compels one to say, no. They slept quite undisturbed, at least as far as she was concerned—pronounced hers to be a slight case, which would almost cure itself, sent her in a draught or two, and threw in bark[9] when the child rallied, with perfect indifference, and just for form's sake.

Again, there was the little French chevalier opposite, who gave lessons in his native tongue at various schools in the neighbourhood, and who might be heard in his apartment of nights playing tremulous old gavottes[1] and minuets, on a wheezy old fiddle. Whenever this powdered and courteous old man, who never missed a Sunday at the convent chapel at Hammersmith, and who was in all respects, thoughts, conduct, and bearing, utterly unlike the bearded savages of his nation, who curse perfidious Albion, and scowl at you from over their cigars, in the Quadrant arcades[2] at the present day,—whenever the old Chevalier de Talonrouge spoke of Mistress Osborne, he would first finish his pinch of snuff, flick away the remaining particles of dust with a graceful wave of his hand, gather up his fingers again into a bunch, and, bringing them up to his mouth, blow them open with a kiss, exclaiming, *Ah, la divine créature!* He vowed and protested that when Amelia walked in the Brompton Lanes flowers grew in profusion under her feet. He called little Georgy Cupid, and asked him news of Venus, his mamma; and told the astonished Betty Flanagan that she was one of the Graces, and the favourite attendant of the *Reine des Amours.*[3]

Instances might be multiplied of this easily gained and unconscious popularity. Did not Mr. Binny, the mild and genteel curate of the district chapel, which the family attended, call assiduously upon the widow, dandle the little boy on his knee, and offer to teach him Latin, to the anger of the elderly virgin, his sister, who kept house for him? "There is nothing in her, Beilby," the latter lady would say. "When she comes to tea here she does not speak a word during the whole evening. She is but a poor lackadaisical creature, and it is my belief has no heart at all. It is only her pretty face which all you gentlemen admire so. Miss Grits, who has five thousand pounds and

8. Name of English rulers before 1399.
9. Quinine.
1. French peasant dances.
2. The curved stretch of Regent Street, known as the Quadrant, had a covered walkway, which was removed one year after this passage was written.
3. Queen of Loves.

expectations besides, has twice as much character, and is a thousand times more agreeable to *my* taste; and if she were good-looking I know that you would think her perfection."

Very likely Miss Binny was right to a great extent. It *is* the pretty face which creates sympathy in the hearts of men, those wicked rogues. A woman may possess the wisdom and chastity of Minerva, and we give no heed to her, if she has a plain face. What folly will not a pair of bright eyes make pardonable? What dullness may not red lips and sweet accents render pleasant? And so, with their usual sense of justice, ladies argue that because a woman is handsome, therefore she is a fool. Oh ladies, ladies! some there are[4] of you who are neither handsome nor wise.

These are but trivial incidents to recount in the life of our heroine. Her tale does not deal in wonders, as the gentle reader has already no doubt perceived; and if a journal had been kept of her proceedings during the seven years after the birth of her son, there would be found few incidents more remarkable in it than that of the measles, recorded in the foregoing page. Yes, one day, and greatly to her wonder, the Reverend Mr. Binny, just mentioned, asked her to change her name of Osborne for his own; when, with deep blushes, and tears in her eyes and voice, she thanked him for his regard for her, expressed gratitude for his attentions to her and to her poor little boy, but said that she never, never could think of any but—but the husband whom she had lost.

On the twenty-fifth of April, and the eighteenth of June, the days of her marriage and widowhood, she kept her room entirely, conse-

4. Revised edition reads: there are some

crating them (and we do not know how many hours of solitary night-thought, her little boy sleeping in his crib by her bed-side) to the memory of that departed friend. During the day she was more active. She had to teach George to read and to write, and a little to draw. She read books, in order that she might tell him stories from them. As his eyes opened, and his mind expanded, under the influence of the outward nature round about him, she taught the child, to the best of her humble power, to acknowledge the Maker of all; and every night and every morning he and she—(in that awful and touching communion which I think must bring a thrill to the heart of every man who witnesses or who remembers it)—the mother and the little boy—prayed to Our Father together, the mother pleading with all her gentle heart, the child lisping after[5] as she spoke. And each time they prayed to God to bless dear papa, as if he were alive and in the room with them.

To wash and dress this young gentleman—to take him for a run of the mornings, before breakfast, and the retreat of grandpapa for "business"—to make for him the most wonderful and ingenious dresses, for which end the thrifty widow cut up and altered every available little bit of finery which she possessed out of her wardrobe during her marriage—for Mrs. Osborne herself, (greatly to her mother's vexation, who preferred fine clothes, especially since her misfortunes) always wore a black gown, and a straw bonnet with a black ribbon—occupied her many hours of the day. Others she had to spare, at the service of her mother and her old father. She had taken the pains to learn, and used to play cribbage with this gentleman on the nights when he did not go to his club. She sang for him when he was so minded, and it was a good sign, for he invariably fell into a comfortable sleep during the music. She wrote out his numerous memorials, letters, prospectuses, and projects. It was in her hand-writing that most of the old gentleman's former acquaintances were informed that he had become an agent for the Black Diamond and Anti-Cinder Coal Company, and could supply his friends and the public with the best coals at —*s.* per chaldron. All he did was to sign the circulars with his flourish and signature, and direct them in a shaky, clerk-like hand. One of these papers was sent to Major Dobbin,—Regt., care of Messrs. Cox and Greenwood; but the Major being in Madras at the time, had no particular call for coals.[6] He knew, though, the hand which had written the prospectus. Good God! what would he not have given to hold it in his own! A second prospectus came out, informing the Major that J. Sedley and Company, having established agencies at Oporto, Bordeaux, and St. Mary's,[7] were enabled to offer to their friends and the public generally, the finest and most celebrated growths of ports, sherries, and claret wines at reasonable prices, and under extraordinary advantages. Acting upon this hint, Dobbin furiously canvassed the governor, the commander-in-chief, the judges, the regiments, and every-

5. Revised edition reads: after her
6. Possibly Cox & Company, a firm that by 1815 was serving as agent and banker for many army regiments. Madras is in southeastern India.
7. Seaports in wine regions of Portugal, France, and the Azores, respectively.

body whom he knew in the Presidency, and sent home to Sedley and Co. orders for wine which perfectly astonished Mr. Sedley and Mr. Clapp, who was the Co. in the business. But no more orders came after that first burst of good fortune, on which poor old Sedley was about to build a house in the city, a regiment of clerks, a dock to himself, and correspondents all over the world. The old gentleman's former taste in wine had gone: the curses of the mess-room assailed Major Dobbin for the vile drinks he had been the means of introducing there; and he bought back a great quantity of the wine, and sold it at public outcry, at an enormous loss to himself. As for Jos, who was by this time promoted to a seat at the Revenue Board at Calcutta, he was wild with rage when the post brought him out a bundle of these Bacchanalian prospectuses, with a private note from his father, telling Jos that his senior counted upon him in this enterprise, and had consigned a quantity of select wines to him, as per invoice, drawing bills upon him for the amount of the same. Jos, who would no more have it supposed that his father, Jos Sedley's father, of the Board of Revenue, was a wine merchant asking for orders, than that he was Jack Ketch,[8] refused the bills with scorn, wrote back contumeliously to the old gentleman, bidding him to mind his own affairs; and the protested paper coming back, Sedley and Co. had to take it up[9] with the profits which they had made out of the Madras venture, and with a little portion of Emmy's savings.

Besides her pension of fifty pounds a-year, there had been five hundred pounds, as her husband's executor stated, left in the agent's hands at the time of Osborne's demise, which sum, as George's guardian, Dobbin proposed to put out at 8 per cent. in an Indian house of agency. Mr. Sedley, who thought the Major had some roguish intentions of his own about the money, was strongly against this plan; and he went to the agents to protest personally against the employment of the money in question, when he learned, to his surprise, that there had been no such sum in their hands, that all the late Captain's assets did not amount to a hundred pounds, and that the five hundred pounds in question must be a separate sum, of which Major Dobbin knew the particulars. More than ever convinced that there was some roguery, old Sedley pursued the Major. As his daughter's nearest friend, he demanded, with a high hand, a statement of the late Captain's accounts. Dobbin's stammering, blushing, and awkwardness added to the other's convictions that he had a rogue to deal with; and in a majestic tone he told that officer a piece of his mind, as he called it, simply stating his belief that the Major was unlawfully detaining his late son-in-law's money.

Dobbin at this lost all patience, and if his accuser had not been so old and so broken, a quarrel might have ensued between them at the Slaughters' Coffee-house, in a box of which place of entertainment the gentlemen had their colloquy. "Come up stairs, Sir," lisped out the Major. "I insist on your coming up the[1] stairs, and I will show

8. Ketch (d. 1696) was a notorious executioner, whose name became generic for that profession.
9. Protested paper: the bill that the bankers would not honor. Take it up: pay.
1. Revised edition omits: the

which is the injured party, poor George or I;" and, dragging the old gentleman up to his bed-room, he produced from his desk Osborne's accounts, and a bundle of I O U's which the latter had given, who, to do him justice, was always ready to give an I O U. "He paid his bills in England," Dobbin added, "but he had not a hundred pounds in the world when he fell. I and one or two of his brother-officers made up the little sum, which was all that we could spare, and you dare to[2] tell us that we are trying to cheat the widow and orphan."[3] Sedley was very contrite and humbled, though the fact is, that William Dobbin had told a great falsehood to the old gentleman; having himself given every shilling of the money, having buried his friend and paid all the fees and charges incident upon the calamity and removal of poor Amelia.

About these expenses old Osborne had never given himself any trouble to think, nor any other relative of Amelia, nor Amelia herself indeed. She trusted to Major Dobbin as an accountant, took his somewhat confused calculations for granted: and never once suspected how much she was in his debt.

Twice or thrice in the year according to her promise she wrote him letters to Madras—letters all about little Georgy. How he treasured those papers! Whenever Amelia wrote he answered, and not until then. But he sent over endless remembrances of himself to his godson and to her. He ordered and sent a box of scarfs and a grand ivory set of chessmen from China. The pawns were little green and white men with real swords and shields, the knights were on horseback the castles were on the backs of elephants. "Mrs. Mango's own set at the Pineries was not so fine," Mr. Pestler remarked. These chessmen were the delight of Georgy's life who printed his first letter in acknowledgment of this gift of his godpapa. He sent over preserves and pickles, which latter the young gentleman tried surreptitiously in the sideboard and half-killed himself with eating. He thought it was a judgment upon him for stealing, they were so hot. Emmy wrote a comical little account of this mishap to the Major. It pleased him to think that her spirits were rallying and that she could be merry sometimes now. He sent over a pair of shawls, a white one for her and a black one with palm-leaves for her mother, and a pair of red scarfs as winter wrappers for old Mr. Sedley and George. The shawls were worth fifty guineas a piece at the very least as Mrs. Sedley knew. She wore her's in state at Church at Brompton, and was congratulated by her female friends upon the splendid acquisition. Emmy's too became prettily her modest black gown. "What a pity it is she won't think of him!" Mrs. Sedley remarked to Mrs. Clapp, and to all her friends of Brompton. "Jos never sent us such presents I am sure and grudges us everything. It is evident that the Major is over head and ears in love with her: and yet whenever I so much as hint it she turns red and begins to cry, and goes and sits up stairs with her miniature—I'm sick of that miniature. I wish we had never seen those odious purse-proud Osbornes."

2. Revised edition omits: to
3. Revised edition reads: and the orphan."

Amidst such humble scenes and associates George's early youth was passed, and the boy grew up delicate, sensitive, imperious, woman-bred—domineering the gentle mother whom he loved with passionate affection. He ruled all the rest of the little world round about him. As he grew, the elders were amazed at his haughty manner and his constant likeness to his father. He asked questions about everything, as inquiring youth will do. The profundity of his remarks and interrogatories astonished his old grandfather, who perfectly bored the club at the tavern with stories about the little lad's learning and genius. He suffered his grandmother with a good-humoured indifference. The small circle round about him believed that the equal of the boy did not exist upon the earth. Georgy inherited his father's pride, and perhaps thought they were not wrong.

When he grew to be about six years old, Dobbin began to write to him very much. The Major wanted to hear that Georgy was going to a school, and hoped he would acquit himself with credit there: or would he have a good tutor at home? it was time that he should begin to learn; and his godfather and guardian hinted that he hoped to be allowed to defray the charges of the boy's education, which would fall heavily upon his mother's straitened income. The Major, in a word, was always thinking about Amelia and her little boy, and by orders to his agents kept the latter provided with picture-books, paint-boxes, desks, and all conceivable implements of amusement and instruction. Three days before George's sixth birth-day, a gentleman in a gig, accompanied by a servant, drove up to Mr. Sedley's house, and asked to see Master George Osborne: it was Mr. Woolsey, military tailor, of Conduit Street,[4] who came at the Major's order to measure the young gentleman for a suit of cloth clothes. He had had the honour of making for the Captain, the young gentleman's father.

Sometimes too, and by the Major's desire no doubt, his sisters, the Misses Dobbin, would call in the family carriage to take Amelia and the little boy a drive if they were so inclined. The patronage and kindness of these ladies was very uncomfortable to Amelia, but she bore it meekly enough, for her nature was to yield; and, besides, the carriage and its splendours gave little Georgy immense pleasure. The ladies begged occasionally that the child might pass a day with them, and he was always glad to go to that fine garden-house at Denmark Hill,[5] where they lived, and where there were such fine grapes in the hot-houses and peaches on the walls.

One day they kindly came over to Amelia with news which they were *sure* would delight her—something *very* interesting about their dear William.

"What was it: was he coming home?" she asked with pleasure beaming in her eyes.

"Oh, no—not the least—but they had very good reason to believe that dear William was about to be married—and to a relation of a very dear friend of Amelia's—to Miss Glorvina O'Dowd, Sir Michael O'Dowd's sister, who had gone out to join Lady O'Dowd at Madras—a very beautiful and accomplished girl, everybody said."

4. Connecting New Bond and Regent Streets, an area still known for tailors.
5. A semirural suburb of London.

Amelia said "Oh!" Amelia was very *very* happy indeed. But she supposed Glorvina could not be like her old acquaintance, who was most kind—but—but she was very happy indeed. And by some impulse, of which I cannot explain the meaning, she took George in her arms and kissed him with an extraordinary tenderness. Her eyes were quite moist when she put the child down; and she scarcely spoke a word during the whole of the drive—though she was so very happy indeed.

*Number 12* *Dec. 1847*

## *Chapter XXXIX.*

### A CYNICAL CHAPTER.

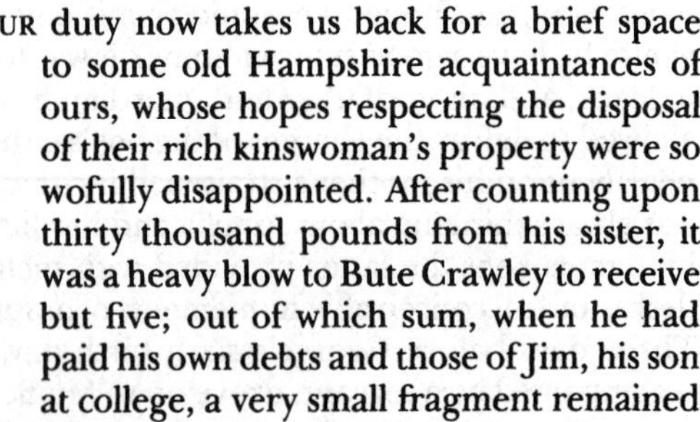

UR duty now takes us back for a brief space to some old Hampshire acquaintances of ours, whose hopes respecting the disposal of their rich kinswoman's property were so wofully disappointed. After counting upon thirty thousand pounds from his sister, it was a heavy blow to Bute Crawley to receive but five; out of which sum, when he had paid his own debts and those of Jim, his son at college, a very small fragment remained to portion off his four plain daughters. Mrs. Bute never knew, or at least never acknowledged, how far her own tyrannous behaviour had tended to ruin her husband. All that woman could do, she vowed and protested she had done. Was it her fault if she did not possess those sycophantic arts which her hypocritical nephew, Pitt Crawley, practised? She wished him all the happiness which he merited out of his ill-gotten gains. "At least the money will remain in the family," she said, charitably. "Pitt will never spend it, my dear, that is quite certain; for a greater miser does not exist in England, and he is as odious, though in a different way, as his spendthrift brother, the abandoned Rawdon."

So Mrs. Bute, after the first shock of rage and disappointment, began to accommodate herself as best she could to her altered fortunes, and to save and retrench with all her might. She instructed her daughters how to bear poverty cheerfully, and invented a thousand notable methods to conceal or evade it. She took them about to balls and public places in the neighbourhood, with praiseworthy energy; nay, she entertained her friends in a hospitable comfortable manner at the Rectory, and much more frequently than before dear Miss Crawley's legacy had fallen in. From her outward bearing nobody would have supposed that the family had been disappointed in their expectations: or have guessed from her frequent appearance in public how she pinched and starved at home. Her girls had more milliner's furniture than they had ever enjoyed before. They appeared perseveringly at the Winchester and Southampton assemblies; they penetrated to Cowes[1] for the race-balls and regatta-gaieties there; and their carriage, with the horses taken from the plough, was at work perpetually, until it began almost to be believed that the four sisters had had fortunes left them by their aunt, whose name the family never mentioned in public but with the most tender gratitude and regard. I know no sort of lying which is more frequent in Vanity Fair than this; and it may be remarked how people who practise it take credit to themselves for their hypocrisy, and fancy that they are exceedingly virtuous and praiseworthy, because they are able to deceive the world with regard to the extent of their means.

Mrs. Bute certainly thought herself one of the most virtuous women in England, and the sight of her happy family was an edifying one to strangers. They were so cheerful, so loving, so well-educated, so simple! Martha painted flowers exquisitely, and furnished half the charity-bazaars in the county. Emma was a regular County Bulbul,[2] and her verses in the "Hampshire Telegraph" were the glory of its Poet's Corner. Fanny and Matilda sang duets together, mamma playing the piano, and the other two sisters sitting with their arms round each other's waists, and listening affectionately. Nobody saw the poor girls drumming at the duets in private. No one saw mamma drilling them rigidly hour after hour. In a word, Mrs. Bute put a good face against fortune, and kept up appearances in the most virtuous manner.

Every thing that a good and respectable mother could do Mrs. Bute did. She got over yachting men from Southampton, parsons from the Cathedral Close at Winchester, and officers from the barracks there. She tried to inveigle the young barristers at assizes, and encouraged Jim to bring home friends with whom he went out hunting with the H. H.[3] What will not a mother do for the benefit of her beloved ones?

Between such a woman and her brother-in-law, the odious Baronet at the Hall, it is manifest that there could be very little in common. The rupture between Bute and his brother Sir Pitt was complete; indeed, between Sir Pitt and the whole county, to which the old man was a scandal. His dislike for respectable society increased with age, and the lodge-gates had not opened to a gentleman's carriage-wheels since Pitt and Lady Jane came to pay their visit of duty after their marriage.

That was an awful and unfortunate visit, never to be thought of by the family without horror. Pitt begged his wife, with a ghastly countenance, never to speak of it; and it was only through Mrs. Bute herself, who still knew everything which took place at the Hall, that the circumstances of Sir Bute's reception of his son and daughter-in-law were ever known at all.

As they drove up the avenue of the Park in their neat and well-appointed carriage, Pitt remarked with dismay and wrath great gaps among the trees—his trees,—which the old Baronet was felling en-

1. Winchester is a cathedral town inland from the seaport and resort at Southampton, which is just across the harbor from Cowes, a yacht-racing center on the Isle of Wight.
2. Persian songbird.
3. Assizes: periodic county court sessions, which coincided with social events. H. H.: Hampton Hounds, fox hunting.

tirely without license. The park wore an aspect of utter dreariness and ruin. The drives were ill kept, and the neat carriage splashed and foundered in muddy pools along the road. The great sweep in front of the terrace and entrance stair was black and covered with mosses; the once trim flower-beds rank and weedy. Shutters were up along almost the whole line of the house; the great hall-door was unbarred after much ringing of the bell; an individual in ribbons was seen flitting up the black oak stair, as Horrocks at length admitted the heir of Queen's Crawley and his bride into the halls of their fathers. He led the way into Sir Pitt's "Library," as it was called, the fumes of tobacco growing stronger as Pitt and Lady Jane approached that apartment. "Sir Pitt ain't very well," Horrocks remarked apologetically, and hinted that his master was afflicted with lumbago.

The library looked out on the front walk and park. Sir Pitt had opened one of the windows, and was bawling out thence to the postillion and Pitt's servant, who seemed to be about to take the baggage down.

"Don't move none of them trunks," he cried, pointing with a pipe which he held in his hand. "It's only a morning visit, Tucker, you fool. Lor, what cracks that off hoss has in his heels! Ain't there no one at the King's Head to rub 'em a little? How do, Pitt? How do, my dear? Come to see the old man, hay? 'Gad—you've a pretty face, too. You ain't like that old horse-godmother, your mother. Come and give old Pitt a kiss, like a good little gal."

The embrace disconcerted the daughter-in-law somewhat, as the caresses of old gentlemen[4] unshorn and perfumed with tobacco might well do. But she remembered that her brother Southdown had mustachios, and smoked cigars, and submitted to the Baronet with a tolerable grace.

"Pitt has got vat," said the Baronet, after this mark of affection. "Does he read ee very long zermons, my dear? Hundredth Psalm, Evening Hymn, hay Pitt? Go and get a glass of Malmsey[5] and a cake for my Lady Jane, Horrocks, you great big booby, and don't stand stearing there like a fat pig. I won't ask you to stop, my dear; you'll find it too stoopid, and so should I too along a Pitt. I'm an old man now, and like my own ways, and my pipe and backgammon of a night."

"I can play at backgammon, Sir," said Lady Jane, laughing. "I used to play with Papa and Miss Crawley, didn't I, Mr. Crawley?"

"Lady Jane can play, Sir, at the game to which you state that you are so partial," Pitt said, haughtily.

"But she wawn't stop for all that. Naw naw, goo back to Mudbury and give Mrs. Rincer a benefit: or drive down to the Rectory, and ask Buty for a dinner. He'll be charmed to see you, you know; he's so much obliged to you for gittin the old woman's money. Ha, ha. Some of it will do to patch up the Hall when I'm gone."

"I perceive, Sir," said Pitt, with a heightened voice, "that your people will cut down the timber."

"Yees, yees, very fine weather, and seasonable for the time of year,"

4. Revised edition reads: of the old gentleman,
5. Sweet wine.

Sir Pitt answered, who had suddenly grown deaf. "But I'm gittin old, Pitt, now. Law bless you, you ain't far from fifty yourself. But he wears well, my pretty Lady Jane, don't he? It's all godliness, sobriety, and a moral life. Look at me, I'm not very fur from fowr-score—he, he;" and he laughed, and took snuff, and leered at her, and pinched her hand.

Pitt once more brought the conversation back to the timber; but the Baronet was deaf again in an instant.

"I'm gittin very old, and have been cruel bad this year with the lumbago. I shan't be here now for long; but I'm glad ee've come, daughter-in-law. I like your face, Lady Jane: it's got none of the damned high-boned Binkie look in it; and I'll give ee something pretty, my dear, to go to Court in." And he shuffled across the room to a cupboard, from which he took a little old case containing jewels of some value. "Take that," said he, "my dear; it belonged to my mother, and afterwards to the first Lady Binkie. Pretty pearls—never gave 'em the ironmonger's daughter. No, no. Take 'em and put 'em up quick," said he, thrusting the case into his daughter's hand, and clapping the door of the cabinet too, as Horrocks entered with a salver and refreshments.

"What have you a been and given Pitt's wife?" said the individual in ribbons, when Pitt and Lady Jane had taken leave of the old gentleman. It was Miss Horrocks, the butler's daughter—the cause of the scandal throughout the country—the lady who reigned now almost supreme at Queen's Crawley.

The rise and progress of those Ribbons had been marked with dismay by the county and family. The Ribbons opened an account at the Mudbury Branch Savings Bank; the Ribbons drove to Church, monopolising the pony-chaise,[6] which was for the use of the servants at the Hall. The domestics were dismissed at her pleasure. The Scotch gardener, who still lingered on the premises, taking a pride in his walls and hothouses, and indeed making a pretty good livelihood by the garden, which he farmed, and of which he sold the produce at Southampton, found the Ribbons eating peaches in a sunshiny morning at the south-wall, and had his ears boxed, when he remonstrated about this attack on his property. He and his Scotch wife and his Scotch children, the only respectable inhabitants of Queen's Crawley, were forced to migrate, with their goods and their chattels, and left the stately comfortable gardens to go to waste, and the flower-beds to run to seed. Poor Lady Crawley's rose-garden became the dreariest wilderness. Only two or three domestics shuddered in the bleak old servants' hall. The stables and offices were vacant, and shut up, and half ruined. Sir Pitt lived in private, and boozed nightly with Horrocks, his butler or house-steward (as he now began to be called), and the abandoned Ribbons. The times were very much changed since the period when she drove to Mudbury in the spring-cart,[7] and called the small tradesmen "Sir." It may have been shame, or it may have been dislike of his neighbours, but the old Cynic of Queen's Crawley hardly issued from his park-gates at all now. He quarrelled with his

6. Open, one-horse carriage for two.
7. A light two-wheeled cart with springs.

agents, and screwed his tenants by letter. His days were past in conducting his own correspondence; the lawyers and farm-bailiffs, who had to do business with him, could not reach him but through the Ribbons, who received them at the door of the housekeeper's room, which commanded the back entrance by which they were admitted; and so the Baronet's daily perplexities increased, and his embarrassments multiplied round him.

The horror of Pitt Crawley may be imagined, as these reports of his father's dotage reached the most exemplary and correct of gentlemen. He trembled daily lest he should hear that the Ribbons was proclaimed his second legal mother-in-law. After that first and last visit, his father's name was never mentioned in Pitt's polite and genteel establishment. It was the skeleton in his house, and all the family walked by it in terror and silence. The Countess Southdown kept on dropping per coach at the lodge-gate the most exciting tracts, tracts which ought to frighten the hair off your head. Mrs. Bute at the parsonage nightly looked out to see if the sky was red over the elms behind which the Hall stood, and the mansion was on fire. Sir G. Wapshot and Sir H. Fuddlestone, old friends of the house, wouldn't sit on the bench with Sir Pitt at Quarter Sessions,[8] and cut him dead in the High-street of Southampton, where the reprobate stood offering his dirty old hands to them. Nothing had any effect upon him; he put his hands into his pockets, and burst out laughing, as he scrambled into his carriage and four; he used to burst out laughing at Lady Southdown's tracts; and he laughed at his sons, and at the world, and at the Ribbons when she was angry, which was not seldom.

Miss Horrocks was installed as housekeeper at Queen's Crawley, and ruled all the domestics there with great majesty and rigour. All the servants were instructed to address her as "Mum," or "Madam"—and there was one little maid, on her promotion, who persisted in calling her "My Lady," without any rebuke on the part of the housekeeper. "There has been better ladies, and there has been worser, Hester," was Miss Horrocks' reply to this compliment of her inferior: so she ruled, having supreme power over all except her father, whom, however, she treated with considerable haughtiness, warning him not to be too familiar in his behaviour to one "as was to be a Baronet's lady." Indeed, she rehearsed that exalted part in life with great satisfaction to herself, and to the amusement of old Sir Pitt, who chuckled at her airs and graces, and would laugh by the hour together at her assumptions of dignity and imitations of genteel life. He swore it was as good as a play to see her in the character of a fine dame, and he made her put on one of the first Lady Crawley's court-dresses, swearing, (entirely to Miss Horrocks' own concurrence,) that the dress became her prodigiously, and threatening to drive her off that very instant to Court in a coach-and-four. She had the ransacking of the wardrobes of the two defunct ladies, and cut and hacked their posthumous finery so as to suit her own tastes and figure. And she would have liked to take possession of their jewels and trinkets too; but the old Baronet had locked them away in his private cabinet, nor could she coax or wheedle him out of the keys. And it is a fact,

8. Local civil and criminal courts held by justices of the peace.

that some time after she left Queen's Crawley a copy-book belonging to this lady was discovered, which showed that she had taken great pains in private to learn the art of writing in general, and especially of writing her own name as Lady Crawley, Lady Betsy Horrocks, Lady Elizabeth Crawley, &c.

Though the good people of the Parsonage never went to the Hall, and shunned the horrid old dotard its owner, yet they kept a strict knowledge of all that happened there, and were looking out every day for the catastrophe, for which Miss Horrocks was also eager. But Fate intervened enviously, and prevented her from receiving the reward due to such immaculate love and virtue.

One day the Baronet surprised "her ladyship," as he jocularly called her, seated at that old and tuneless piano in the drawing-room, which had scarcely been touched since Becky Sharp played quadrilles upon it. Seated at the piano with the utmost gravity, and squalling to the best of her power in imitation of the music which she had sometimes heard. The little kitchen-maid on her promotion was standing at her mistress's side, quite delighted during the operation, and wagging her head up and down, and crying "Lor, Mum, 'tis bittiful,"—just like a genteel sycophant in a real drawing-room.

This incident made the old Baronet roar with laughter, as usual. He narrated the circumstance a dozen times to Horrocks in the course of the evening, and greatly to the discomfiture of Miss Horrocks. He thrummed on the table as if it had been a musical instrument and squalled in imitation of her manner of singing. He vowed that such a beautiful voice ought to be cultivated, and declared she ought to have singing-masters, in which proposals she saw nothing ridiculous. He was in great spirits that night; and drank with his friend and butler an extraordinary quantity of rum-and-water—at a very late hour the faithful friend and domestic conducted his master to his bed-room.

Half an hour afterwards there was a great hurry and bustle in the house. Lights went about from window to window in the lonely desolate old Hall, whereof but two or three rooms were ordinarily occupied by its owner. Presently, a boy on a pony went galloping off to Mudbury, to the Doctor's house there. And in another hour (by which fact we ascertain how carefully the excellent Mrs. Bute Crawley had always kept up an understanding with the great house), that lady in her clogs and calash,[9] the Reverend Bute Crawley, and James Crawley, her son, had walked over from the Rectory through the park, and had entered the mansion by the open hall-door.

They passed through the hall and the small oak parlour, on the table of which stood the three tumblers and the empty rum-bottle which had served for Sir Pitt's carouse, and through that apartment into Sir Pitt's study, where they found Miss Horrocks, of the guilty ribbons, with a wild air, trying at the presses and escritoires[1] with a bunch of keys. She dropped them with a scream of terror, as little Mrs. Bute's eyes flashed out at her from under her black calash.

"Look at that, James and Mr. Crawley," cried Mrs. Bute, pointing at the scared figure of the black-eyed, guilty wench.

"He gave 'em me; he gave 'em me!" she cried.

"Gave them you, you abandoned creature!" screamed Mrs. Bute. "Bear witness, Mr. Crawley, we found this good-for-nothing woman in the act of stealing your brother's property; and she will be hanged, as I always said she would."

Betsy Horrocks quite daunted, flung herself down on her knees, bursting into tears. But those who know a really good woman are aware that she is not in a hurry to forgive, and that the humiliation of an enemy is triumph[2] to her soul.

"Ring the bell, James," Mrs. Bute said. "Go on ringing it till the people come." The three or four domestics resident in the deserted old house came presently at that jangling and continued summons.

"Put that woman in the strong-room," she said. "We caught her in the act of robbing Sir Pitt. Mr. Crawley, you'll make out her committal—and, Beddoes, you'll drive her over in the spring-cart, in the morning, to Southampton Gaol."

"My dear," interposed the Magistrate and Rector—"she's only—"

"Are there no handcuffs?" Mrs. Bute continued, stamping in her clogs. "There used to be handcuffs. Where's the creature's abominable father?"

9. Wooden-soled shoes and a hooped hood or shawl. See illustration: "The Ribbons discovered in the fact."
1. Wardrobes and desks.
2. Revised edition reads: is a triumph

The Ribbons discovered in the fact

"He *did* give 'em me," still cried poor Betsy; "didn't he, Hester? You saw Sir Pitt—you know you did—give 'em me, ever so long ago—the day after Mudbury fair: not that I want 'em. Take 'em if you think they ain't mine." And here the unhappy wretch pulled out from her pocket a large pair of paste shoe-buckles which had excited her admiration, and which she had just appropriated out of one of the bookcases in the study, where they had lain.

"Law, Betsy, how could you go for to tell such a wicked story!" said Hester, the little kitchen-maid late on her promotion—"and to Madam Crawley, so good and kind, and his Rev'rince (with a curtsey) and you may search all *my* boxes, Mum, I'm sure, and here's my keys as I'm an honest girl though of pore parents and workhouse bred—and if you find so much as a beggarly bit of lace or a silk stocking out of all the gownds as *you've* had the picking of may I never go to church agin."

"Give up your keys, you hardened hussey," hissed out the virtuous little lady in the calash.

"And here's a candle, Mum, and if you please, Mum, I can show you her room, Mum, and the prees in the housekeeper's room, Mum, where she keeps heaps and heaps of things, Mum," cried out the eager little Hester with a profusion of curtseys.

"Hold your tongue, if you please. I know the room which the creature occupies perfectly well. Mrs. Brown, have the goodness to come with me, and Beddoes don't you lose sight of that woman," said Mrs. Bute, seizing the candle.—"Mr. Crawley you had better go up stairs, and see that they are not murdering your unfortunate brother"—and the calash, escorted by Mrs. Brown, walked away to the apartment which, as she said truly, she knew perfectly well.

Bute went up stairs, and found the Doctor from Mudbury, with the frightened Horrocks over his master in a chair. They were trying to bleed Sir Pitt Crawley.

With the early morning an express was sent off to Mr. Pitt Crawley by the Rector's lady, who assumed the command of everything, and had watched the old Baronet through the night. He had been brought back to a sort of life; he could not speak, but seemed to recognise people. Mrs. Bute kept resolutely by his bed-side. She never seemed to want to sleep, that little woman, and did not close her fiery black eyes once, though the Doctor snored in the arm-chair. Horrocks made some wild efforts to assert his authority and assist his master: but Mrs. Bute called him a tipsy old wretch, and bade him never show his face again in that house or he should be transported[3] like his abominable daughter.

Terrified by her manner he slunk down to the oak parlour where Mr. James was, who, having tried the bottle standing there and found no liquor in it, ordered Mr. Horrocks to get another bottle of rum, which he fetched with clean glasses, and to which the Rector and his son sate down: ordering Horrocks to put down the keys at that instant and never to show his face again.

3. Deported to a penal colony.

Cowed by this behaviour Horrocks gave up the keys: and he and his daughter slunk off silently through the night, and gave up possession of the house of Queen's Crawley.

## *Chapter XL.*

### IN WHICH BECKY IS RECOGNISED BY THE FAMILY.

THE[1] heir of Crawley arrived at home, in due time, after this catastrophe, and henceforth may be said to have reigned in Queen's Crawley. For though the old Baronet survived many months, he never recovered the use of his intellect or his speech completely, and the government of the estate devolved upon his elder son. In a strange condition Pitt found it. Sir Pitt was always buying and mortgaging: he had twenty men of business, and quarrels with each; quarrels with all his tenants, and lawsuits with them; lawsuits with the lawyers; lawsuits with the Mining and Dock Companies in which he was proprietor; and with every person with whom he had business. To unravel these difficulties, and set[2] the estate clear, was a task worthy of the orderly and persevering diplomatist of Pumpernickel: and he set himself to work with prodigious assiduity. His whole family, of course, was transported to Queen's Crawley, whither Lady Southdown, of course, came too; and she set about converting the parish under the Rector's nose, and brought down her irregular clergy to the dismay of the angry Mrs. Bute. Sir Pitt had concluded no bargain for the sale of the living of Queen's Crawley; when it should drop, her Ladyship proposed to take the patronage into her own hands, and present a young protégé to the Rectory; on which subject the diplomatic Pitt said nothing.

Mrs. Bute's intentions with regard to Miss Betsy Horrocks were not carried into effect: and she paid no visit to Southampton Gaol. She and her father left the Hall, when the latter took possession of the Crawley Arms in the village, of which he had got a lease from Sir Pitt. The ex-butler had obtained a small freehold[3] there likewise, which gave him a vote for the borough. The Rector had another

1. Initial vignette of funeral procession in clown caps.
2. Revised edition reads: and to set
3. Owned, as opposed to leased, property, which gave the ex-butler the right to vote in the "rotten borough" of Queens Crawley, where six voters elected two members to Parliament.

of these votes, and these and four others formed the representative body which returned the two members for Queen's Crawley.

There was a show of courtesy kept up between the Rectory and the Hall ladies, between the younger ones at least, for Mrs. Bute and Lady Southdown never could meet without battles, and gradually ceased seeing each other. Her Ladyship kept her room when the ladies from the Rectory visited their cousins at the Hall. Perhaps Mr. Pitt was not very much displeased at these occasional absences of his mamma-in-law. He believed the Binkie family to be the greatest and wisest, and most interesting in the world, and her Ladyship and his aunt had long held ascendancy over him; but sometimes he felt that she commanded him too much. To be considered young was complimentary doubtless; but at six-and-forty to be treated as a boy was sometimes mortifying. Lady Jane yielded up every thing, however, to her mother. She was only fond of her children in private; and it was lucky for her that Lady Southdown's multifarious business, her conferences with ministers, and her correspondence with all the missionaries of Africa, Asia, and Australasia, &c. occupied the venerable Countess a great deal, so that she had but little time to devote to her granddaughter, the little Matilda, and her grandson, Master Pitt Crawley. The latter was a feeble child: and it was only by prodigious quantities of calomel[4] that Lady Southdown was able to keep him in life at all.

As for Sir Pitt he retired into those very apartments where Lady Crawley had been previously extinguished, and here was tended by Miss Hester, the girl upon her promotion, with constant care and assiduity. What love, what fidelity, what constancy is there equal to that of a nurse with good wages? They smooth pillows: and make arrow-root:[5] they get up at nights: they bear complaints and querulousness: they see the sun shining out of doors and don't want to go abroad: they sleep on arm-chairs, and eat their meals in solitude: they pass long long evenings doing nothing, watching the embers, and the patient's drink simmering in the jug: they read the weekly paper the whole week through; and Law's Serious Call or the Whole Duty of Man[6] suffices them for literature for the year—and we quarrel with them because, when their relations come to see them once a week, a little gin is smuggled in in their linen-basket. Ladies, what man's love is there that would stand a year's nursing of the object of his affection? Whereas a nurse will stand by you for ten pounds a quarter, and we think her too highly paid. At least Mr. Crawley grumbled a good deal about paying half as much to Miss Hester for her constant attendance upon the Baronet his father.

Of sunshiny days this old gentleman was taken out in a chair on the terrace—the very chair which Miss Crawley had had at Brighton, and which had been transported thence with a number of Lady Southdown's effects to Queen's Crawley. Lady Jane always walked by the old man: and was an evident favourite with him. He used to nod

4. A purgative.
5. A starchy food from the arrow-root plant of tropical America.
6. *A Serious Call to a Devout and Holy Life* (1728) by William Law and *The Whole Duty of Man* (1658) by Richard Allestree.

Sir Pitt's last Stage

many times to her and smile when she came in, and utter inarticulate deprecatory moans when she was going away. When the door shut upon her he would cry and sob—whereupon Hester's face and manner, which was always exceedingly bland and gentle while her lady was present, would change at once and she would make faces at him, and clench her fist, and scream out "Hold your tongue, you stoopid old fool," and twirl away his chair from the fire which he loved to look at—at which he would cry more. For this was all that was left after more than seventy years of cunning and struggling, and drinking and scheming, and sin and selfishness—a whimpering old idiot put in and out of bed and cleaned and fed like a baby!

At last a day came when the nurse's occupation was over. Early one morning as Pitt Crawley was at his steward's and bailiff's books in the study, a knock came to the door, and Hester presented herself dropping a curtsey, and said,

"If you please, Sir Pitt, Sir Pitt died this morning, Sir Pitt. I was a-making of his toast, Sir Pitt, for his gruel, Sir Pitt, which he took every morning reglar at six, Sir Pitt, and—I thought I heard a moan-like, Sir Pitt—and—and—and—". She dropped another curtsey.

What was it that made Pitt's pale face flush quite red? Was it because he was Sir Pitt at last with a seat in Parliament, and perhaps future honours in prospect? "I'll clear the estate now with the ready money," he thought, and rapidly calculated its incumbrances and the improvements which he would make. He would not use his aunt's money previously, lest Sir Pitt should recover, and his outlay be in vain.

All the blinds were pulled down at the Hall and Rectory: the church bell was tolled, and the chancel[7] hung in black; and Bute Crawley didn't go to a coursing meeting, but went and dined quietly at Fuddlestone, where they talked about his deceased brother and young Sir Pitt over their port. Miss Betsy, who was by this time married to a saddler at Mudbury, cried a good deal. The family surgeon[8] rode over and paid his respectful compliments, and inquiries for the health of their ladyships. The death was talked about at Mudbury and at the Crawley Arms; the landlord whereof had become reconciled with the Rector of late, who was occasionally known to step into the parlour and taste Mr. Horrocks' mild beer.

"Shall I write to your brother—or will you?" asked Lady Jane of her husband, Sir Pitt.

"I will write, of course," Sir Pitt said, "and invite him to the funeral: it will be but becoming."

"And—and—Mrs. Rawdon," said Lady Jane, timidly.

"Jane!" said Lady Southdown, "how can you think of such a thing?"

"Mrs. Rawdon must of course be asked," said Sir Pitt, resolutely.

"Not whilst *I* am in the house!" said Lady Southdown.

"Your Ladyship will be pleased to recollect that I am the head of this family," Sir Pitt replied. "If you please, Lady Jane, you will write a letter to Mrs. Rawdon Crawley, requesting her presence upon this melancholy occasion."

7. Altar, pulpit and choir area of a church.
8. First printing reads: Mr. Glauber, the surgeon,

"Jane, I forbid you to put pen to paper!" cried the Countess.

"I believe I am the head of this family," Sir Pitt repeated; "and however much I may regret any circumstance which may lead to your Ladyship quitting this house, must, if you please, continue to govern it as I see fit."

Lady Southdown rose up as magnificent as Mrs. Siddons in Lady Macbeth,[9] and ordered that horses might be put to her carriage. If her son and daughter turned her out of their house, she would hide her sorrows somewhere in loneliness and pray for their conversion to better thoughts.

"We don't turn you out of our house, Mamma," said the timid Lady Jane imploringly.

"You invite such company to it as no Christian lady should meet, and I will have my horses to-morrow morning."

"Have the goodness to write, Jane, under my dictation," said Sir Pitt rising and throwing himself into an attitude of command like the Portrait of a Gentleman in the Exhibition,[1] "and begin. 'Queen's Crawley, September 14, 1822.—My dear brother—' "

Hearing these decisive and terrible words, Lady Macbeth, who had been waiting for a sign of weakness or vacillation on the part of her son-in-law, rose, and with a scared look, left the library. Lady Jane looked up to her husband as if she would fain follow and soothe her mamma; but Pitt forbade his wife to move.

"She won't go away," he said. "She has let her house at Brighton, and has spent her last half-year's dividends. A Countess living at an inn is a ruined woman. I have been waiting long for an opportunity to take this—this decisive step, my love; for, as you must perceive, it is impossible that there should be two chiefs in a family: and now, if you please, we will resume the dictation. 'My dear brother, the melancholy intelligence which it is my duty to convey to my family must have long been anticipated by,' " &c.

In a word, Pitt having come to his kingdom, and having by good luck, or desert rather, as he considered, assumed almost all the fortune which his other relatives had expected, was determined to treat his family kindly and respectably, and make a house of Queen's Crawley once more. It pleased him to think that he should be its chief. He proposed to use the vast influence that his commanding talents and position must speedily acquire for him in the county to get his brother placed and his cousins decently provided for, and perhaps had a little sting of repentance as he thought that he was the proprietor of all that they had hoped for. In the course of three or four days' reign his bearing was changed, and his plans quite fixed: he determined to rule justly and honestly, to depose Lady Southdown, and to be on the friendliest possible terms with all the relations of his blood.

So he dictated a letter to his brother Rawdon—a solemn and elaborate letter, containing the profoundest observations, couched in the longest words, and filling with wonder the simple little secretary, who wrote under her husband's order. "What an orator this will be,"

9. Sarah Siddons (1755–1831), who played hundreds of roles, was especially noted for a few outstanding ones, including Lady Macbeth, which she played in 1812 as her farewell to the stage.

1. Annual Royal Academy exhibition; the particular picture alluded to, if any, is unidentified.

thought she, "when he enters the House of Commons" (on which point, and on the tyranny of Lady Southdown, Pitt had sometimes dropped hints to his wife in bed); "how wise and good, and what a genius my husband is! I fancied him a little cold; but how good, and what a genius!"

The fact is, Pitt Crawley had got every word of the letter by heart, and had studied it, with diplomatic secrecy, deeply and perfectly, long before he thought fit to communicate it to his astonished wife.

This letter, with a huge black border and seal, was accordingly dispatched by Sir Pitt Crawley, to his brother the Colonel, in London. Rawdon Crawley was but half-pleased at the receipt of it. "What's the use of going down to that stupid place?" thought he. "I can't stand being alone with Pitt after dinner, and horses there and back will cost us twenty pound."

He carried the letter, as he did all difficulties, to Becky, upstairs in her bed-room—with her chocolate, which he always made and took to her of a morning.

He put the tray with the breakfast and the letter on the dressing-table, before which Becky sate combing her yellow hair. She took up the black-edged missive, and having read it, she jumped up from the chair, crying "Hurray!" and waving the note round her head.

"Hurray?" said Rawdon, wondering at the little figure capering about in a streaming flannel dressing-gown, with tawny locks dishevelled. "He's not left us anything, Becky. I had my share when I came of age."

"You'll never be of age, you silly old man," Becky replied. "Run out now to Madam Brunoy's,[2] for I must have some mourning: and get a crape on your hat, and a black waistcoat—I don't think you've got one; order it to be brought home to-morrow, so that we may be able to start on Thursday."

"You don't mean to go?" Rawdon interposed.

"Of course I mean to go. I mean that Lady Jane shall present me at Court next year. I mean that your brother shall give you a seat in Parliament, you stupid old creature. I mean that Lord Steyne shall have your vote and his, my dear, old, silly man; and that you shall be an Irish Secretary, or a West Indian Governor: or a Treasurer, or a Consul, or some such thing."

"Posting will cost a dooce of a lot of money," grumbled Rawdon.

"We might take Southdown's carriage, which ought to be present at the funeral, as he is a relation of the family: but, no—I intend that we shall go by the coach. They'll like it better. It seems more humble—"

"Rawdy goes of course?" the Colonel asked.

"No such thing; why pay an extra place? He's too big to travel bodkin between you and me. Let him stay here in the nursery, and Briggs can make him a black frock. Go you: and do as I bid you. And you had best tell Sparks, your man, that old Sir Pitt is dead, and that you will come in for something considerable when the affairs are arranged. He'll tell this to Raggles, who has been pressing for money, and it will console poor Raggles." And so Becky began sipping her chocolate.

When the faithful Lord Steyne arrived in the evening, he found Becky and her companion, who was no other than our friend Briggs, busy culling, ripping, snipping, and tearing all sorts of black stuffs available for the melancholy occasion.

"Miss Briggs and I are plunged in grief and despondency for the death of our Papa," Rebecca said. "Sir Pitt Crawley is dead, my lord. We have been tearing our hair all the morning, and now we are tearing up our old clothes."

"Oh, Rebecca, how can you—" was all that Briggs could say as she turned up her eyes.

"Oh, Rebecca, how can you—" echoed my Lord. "So that old scoundrel's dead, is he? He might have been a Peer if he had played his cards better. Mr. Pitt had very nearly made him; but he ratted always at the wrong time. What an old Silenus it was."[3]

"I might have been Silenus's widow," said Rebecca. "Don't you remember, Miss Briggs, how you peeped in at the door, and saw old

2. There is a Paris suburb named Brunoy, which may have suggested the name of this as yet unidentified milliner.
3. Sir Pitt was a baronet, the lowest hereditary English title and one that took precedence over all knights except those of the Order of the Garter. The next rank up, baron, was the lowest title of the peerage. Sir Pitt's periodic switchings of political allegiances were ill-timed, or William Pitt might have arranged a peerage for him. Silenus: a drunken satyr.

Sir Pitt on his knees to me?" Miss Briggs, our old friend, blushed very much at this reminiscence; and was glad when Lord Steyne ordered her to go down stairs and make him a cup of tea.

Briggs was the house-dog whom Rebecca had provided as guardian of her innocence and reputation. Miss Crawley had left her a little annuity. She would have been content to remain in the Crawley family with Lady Jane, who was good to her and to everybody; but Lady Southdown dismissed poor Briggs as quickly as decency permitted; and Mr. Pitt (who thought himself much injured by the uncalled-for generosity of his deceased relative towards a lady who had only been Miss Crawley's faithful retainer a score of years) made no objections to that exercise of the dowager's authority. Bowls and Firkin likewise received their legacies, and their dismissals; and married and set up a lodging-house, according to the custom of their kind.

Briggs tried to live with her relations in the country, but found that attempt was vain after the better society to which she had been accustomed. Those persons,[4] small tradesmen in a country town, quarrelled over Miss Briggs's forty pounds a-year, as eagerly and more openly than Miss Crawley's kinsfolk had for that lady's inheritance. Briggs's brother, a radical hatter and grocer, called his sister a purse-proud aristocrat, because she would not advance a part of her capital to stock his shop: and she would have done it[5] most likely, but that their sister, a dissenting shoemaker's lady, at variance with the hatter and grocer who went to another chapel, showed how their brother was on the verge of bankruptcy, and took possession of Briggs for a while. The dissenting shoemaker wanted Miss Briggs to send his son to college, and make a gentleman of him. Between them the two families got a great portion of her private savings out of her: and finally she fled to London followed by the anathemas of both, and determined to seek for servitude again as infinitely less onerous than liberty. And advertising in the papers that a "Gentlewoman of agreeable manners, and accustomed to the best society was anxious to," &c., she took up her residence with Mr. Bowls in Half Moon Street, and waited the result of the advertisement.[6]

So it was that she fell in with Rebecca. Mrs. Rawdon's dashing little carriage and ponies was whirling down the street one day, just as Miss Briggs, fatigued, had reached Mr. Bowls's door, after a weary walk to the Times Office in the City, to insert her advertisement for the sixth time. Rebecca was driving, and at once recognised the gentlewoman with agreeable manners, and being a perfectly good-humoured woman, as we have seen, and having a regard for Briggs, she pulled up the ponies at the door-steps, gave the reins to the groom, and jumping out had hold of both Briggs's hands, before she of the agreeable manners had recovered from the shock of seeing an old friend.

4. Revised edition reads: Briggs's friends,
5. Revised edition reads: so
6. See chapter XXXVIII on ads in the *Times* for accommodation within families. Ads for lodgings to let were, of course, far more numerous.

Briggs cried, and Becky laughed a great deal, and kissed the gentlewoman as soon as they got into the passage; and thence into Mrs. Bowls's front parlour, with the red moreen[7] curtains, and the round looking-glass, with the chained eagle above, gazing upon the back of the ticket in the window which announced "Apartments to Let."

Briggs told all her history amidst those perfectly uncalled-for sobs and ejaculations of wonder with which women of her soft nature salute an old acquaintance, or regard a rencontre[8] in the street; for though people meet other people every day, yet some there are who insist upon discovering miracles; and women, even though they have disliked each other, begin to cry when they meet, deploring and remembering the time when they last quarrelled. So, in a word, Briggs told all her history, and Becky gave a narrative of her own life, with her usual artlessness and candour.

Mrs. Bowls, late Firkin, came and listened grimly in the passage to the hysterical sniffling and giggling which went on in the front parlour. Becky had never been a favourite of her's. Since the establishment of the married couple in London they had frequented their former friends of the house of Raggles, and did not like the latter's account of the Colonel's *ménage.*[9] "*I* wouldn't trust him, Ragg, my boy," Bowls remarked: and his wife, when Mrs. Rawdon issued from the parlour, only saluted the lady with a very sour curtsey; and her fingers were like so many sausages, cold and lifeless, when she held them out in deference to Mrs. Rawdon, who persisted in shaking hands with the retired lady's maid. She whirled away into Piccadilly, nodding, with the sweetest of smiles towards Miss Briggs, who hung nodding at the window close under the advertisement-card, and at the next moment was in the Park with a half dozen of dandies cantering after her carriage.

When she found how her friend was situated, and how having a snug legacy from Miss Crawley, salary was no object to our gentlewoman, Becky instantly formed some benevolent little domestic plans concerning her. This was just such a companion as would suit her establishment, and she invited Briggs to come to dinner with her that very evening, when she would show her[1] dear little darling Rawdon.

Mrs. Bowls cautioned her lodger against venturing into the lion's den, "wherein you will rue it, Miss B., mark my words, and as sure as my name is Bowls." And Briggs promised to be very cautious. The upshot of which caution was that she went to live with Mrs. Rawdon the next week, and had lent Rawdon Crawley six hundred pounds upon annuity[2] before six more months were over.

7. Ribbed upholstery fabric.
8. Meeting.
9. Household.
1. Revised edition reads: she should see Becky's
2. In exchange for annual payments.

## *Chapter XLI.*

IN WHICH BECKY REVISITS THE HALLS OF HER ANCESTORS.

So the mourning being ready, and Sir Pitt Crawley warned of their arrival, Colonel Crawley and his wife took a couple of places in the same old High-flyer coach, by which Rebecca had travelled in the defunct Baronet's company, and[1] on her first journey into the world some nine years before. How well she remembered the Inn Yard, and the ostler to whom she refused money, and the insinuating Cambridge lad who wrapped her in his coat on the journey. Rawdon took his place outside, and would have liked to drive, but his grief forbade him. He sate by the coachman, and talked about horses and the road the whole way; and who kept the inns, and who horsed the coach by which he had travelled so many a time, when he and Pitt were boys going to Eton. At Mudbury a carriage and a pair of horses received them, with a coachman in black. "It's the old drag, Rawdon," Rebecca said, as they got in. "The worms have eaten the cloth a good deal—there's the stain which Sir Pitt—ha! I see Dawson the Ironmonger has his shutters up[2]—which Sir Pitt made such a noise about. It was a bottle of cherry brandy he broke which we went to fetch for your aunt from Southampton. How time flies, to be sure! that can't be Polly Talboys, that bouncing girl standing by her mother at the cottage there. I remember her a mangy little urchin picking weeds in the garden."

"Fine gal," said Rawdon, returning the salute which the cottage gave him, by two fingers applied to his crape hat-band. Becky bowed and saluted, and recognised people here and there graciously. Their[3] recognitions were inexpressibly pleasant to her. It seemed as if she was not an impostor any more, and was coming to the home of her ancestors. Rawdon was rather abashed, and cast down on the other hand. What recollections of boyhood and innocence might have been flitting across his brain? What pangs of dim remorse and doubt and shame?

"Your sisters must be young women now," Rebecca said, thinking of those girls for the first time perhaps since she had left them.

"Don't know, I'm shaw," replied the Colonel. "Hullo! here's old Mother Lock. How-dy-do, Mrs. Lock. Remember me, don't you?

1. Revised edition omits: and
2. In spite of his deceased daughter's miserable life as the second Lady Crawley, Dawson displays his connection with the baronet by indicating mourning.
3. Revised edition reads: These

Master Rawdon, hey? Dammy how those old women last; she was a hundred when I was a boy."

They were going through the lodge-gates kept by old Mrs. Lock, whose hand Rebecca insisted upon shaking, as she flung open the creaking old iron gate, and the carriage passed between the two moss-grown pillars surmounted by the dove and serpent.

"The governor has cut into the timber," Rawdon said, looking about, and then was silent—so was Becky. Both of them were rather agitated, and thinking of old times. He about Eton, and his mother, whom he remembered, a frigid demure woman, and a sister who died, of whom he had been passionately fond; and how he used to thrash Pitt; and about little Rawdy at home. And Rebecca thought about her own youth, and the dark secrets of those early tainted days; and of her entrance into life by yonder gates; and of Miss Pinkerton, and Joe, and Amelia.

The gravel walk and terrace had been scraped quite clean. A grand painted hatchment was already over the great entrance, and two very solemn and tall personages in black flung open each a leaf of the door as the carriage pulled up at the familiar steps. Rawdon turned red, and Becky somewhat pale, as they passed through the old hall, arm in arm. She pinched her husband's arm as they entered the oak parlour, where Sir Pitt and his wife were ready to receive them. Sir Pitt in black, Lady Jane in black, and my Lady Southdown with a large black head-piece of bugles[4] and feathers, which waved on her Ladyship's head like an undertaker's tray.

Sir Pitt had judged correctly, that she would not quit the premises. She contented herself by preserving a solemn and stony silence, when in company of Pitt and his rebellious wife, and by frightening the children in the nursery by the ghastly gloom of her demeanour. Only a very faint bending of the head-dress and plumes welcomed Rawdon and his wife, as those prodigals returned to their family.

To say the truth, they were not affected very much one way or other by this coolness. Her Ladyship, strange to say, was a person only of secondary consideration in their minds just then—they were intent upon the reception which the reigning brother and sister would afford them.

Pitt with rather a heightened colour went up and shook his brother by the hand; and saluted Rebecca with a hand-shake and a very low bow. But Lady Jane took both the hands of her sister-in-law and kissed her affectionately. The embrace somehow brought tears into the eyes of the little adventuress—which ornaments, as we know, she wore very seldom. The artless mark of kindness and confidence touched and pleased her; and Rawdon, encouraged by this demonstration on his sister's part, twirled up his mustachios, and took leave to salute Lady Jane with a kiss, which caused her Ladyship to blush exceedingly.

"Dev'lish nice little woman, Lady Jane," was his verdict, when he and his wife were together again. "Pitt's got fat too, and is doing the thing handsomely." "He can afford it," said Rebecca, and agreed in

4. Glass beads.

her husband's farther opinion, "that the mother-in-law was a tremendous old Guy[5]—and that the sisters were rather well-looking young women."

They, too, had been summoned from school to attend the funeral ceremonies. It seemed Sir Pitt Crawley, for the dignity of the house and family, had thought right to have about the place as many persons in black as could possibly be assembled. All the men and maids of the house, the old women of the Alms House, whom the elder Sir Pitt had cheated out of a great portion of their due, the Parish clerk's family, and the special retainers of both Hall and Rectory were habited in sable; added to these, the undertaker's men, at least a score, with crapes and hat-bands, and who made a goodly show when the great burying show took place—but these are mute personages in our drama, and having nothing to do or say need occupy a very little space here.

With regard to her sisters-in-law Rebecca did not attempt to forget her former position of Governess towards them, but recalled it frankly and kindly, and asked them about their studies with great gravity, and told them that she had thought of them many and many a day, and longed to know of their welfare. In fact you would have supposed that ever since she had left them she had not ceased to keep them uppermost in her thoughts, and to take the tenderest interest in their welfare. So supposed Lady Crawley herself and her young sisters.

"She's hardly changed since eight years," said Miss Rosalind to Miss Violet, as they were preparing for dinner.

"Those red-haired women look wonderfully well," replied the other.

"Her's is much darker than it was; I think she must dye it," Miss Rosalind added. "She is stouter, too, and altogether improved," continued Miss Rosalind, who was disposed to be very fat.

"At least she gives herself no airs, and remembers that she was our Governess once," Miss Violet said, intimating that it befitted all governesses to keep their proper place, and forgetting altogether that she was granddaughter not only of Sir Walpole Crawley, but of Mr. Dawson of Mudbury, and so had a coal-scuttle in her scutcheon. There are other very well-meaning people whom one meets every day in Vanity Fair, who are surely equally oblivious.

"It can't be true what the girls at the Rectory said, that her mother was an opera-dancer—"

"A person can't help their birth," Rosalind replied with great liberality. "And I agree with our brother, that as she is in the family, of course we are bound to notice her. I am sure Aunt Bute need not talk: she wants to marry Kate to young Hooper, the wine-merchant, and absolutely asked him to come to the Rectory for orders."

"I wonder whether Lady Southdown will go away, she looked very glum upon Mrs. Rawdon," the other said.

"I wish she would. *I* won't read the 'Washerwoman of Finchley Common,'" vowed Violet; and so saying, and avoiding a passage at

5. Grotesque, like Guy Fawkes, who was burned in effigy every November 5.

the end of which a certain coffin was placed with a couple of watchers, and lights perpetually burning in the closed room, these young women came down to the family dinner, for which the bell rang as usual.

But before this, Lady Jane conducted Rebecca to the apartments prepared for her, which with the rest of the house had assumed a very much improved appearance of order and comfort during Pitt's regency, and here beholding that Mrs. Rawdon's modest little trunks had arrived, and were placed in the bed-room and dressing-room adjoining, helped her to take off her neat black bonnet and cloak, and asked her sister-in-law in what more she could be useful.

"What I should like best," said Rebecca, "would be to go to the nursery; and see your dear little children:" On which the two ladies looked very kindly at each other, and went to that apartment hand in hand.

Becky admired little Matilda, who was not quite four years old, as the most charming little love in the world; and the boy, a little fellow of two years—pale, heavy-eyed, and large-headed, she pronounced to be a perfect prodigy in point of size, intelligence, and beauty.

"I wish Mamma would not insist on giving him so much medicine," Lady Jane said, with a sigh. "I often think we should all be better without it." And then Lady Jane and her new-found friend had one of those confidential medical conversations about the children, which all mothers, and most women, as I am given to understand, delight in. Fifty years ago, and when the present writer, being an interesting little boy, was ordered out of the room with the ladies after dinner, I remember quite well that their talk was chiefly about their ailments; and putting this question directly to two or three since, I have always got from them the acknowledgment that times are not changed. Let my fair readers remark for themselves this very evening when they quit the dessert-table, and assemble to celebrate the drawing-room mysteries. Well—in half-an-hour Becky and Lady Jane were close and intimate friends—and in the course of the evening her Ladyship informed Sir Pitt that she thought her new sister-in-law was a kind, frank, unaffected, and affectionate young woman.

And so having easily won the daughter's good-will, the indefatigable little woman bent herself to conciliate the august Lady Southdown. As soon as she found her Ladyship alone, Rebecca attacked her on the nursery question at once, and said that her own little boy was saved, actually saved, by calomel, freely administered, when all the physicians in Paris had given the dear child up. And then she mentioned how often she had heard of Lady Southdown from that excellent man the Reverend Lawrence Grills, Minister of the chapel in May Fair, which she frequented; and how her views were very much changed by circumstances and misfortunes; and how she hoped that a past life spent in worldliness and error might not incapacitate her from *more serious* thought for the future. She described how in former days she had been indebted to Mr. Crawley for religious instruction, touched upon the "Washerwoman of Finchley Common," which she had read with the greatest profit, and asked about Lady Emily, its gifted author, now Lady Emily Hornblower, at Cape Town, where her husband had strong hopes of becoming Bishop of Caffraria.[6]

But she crowned all, and confirmed herself in Lady Southdown's favour, by feeling very much agitated and unwell after the funeral, and requesting her Ladyship's medical advice, which the Dowager not only gave, but, wrapped up in a bed-gown, and looking more like Lady Macbeth than ever, came privately in the night to Becky's room, with a parcel of favourite tracts, and a medicine of her own composition, which she insisted that Mrs. Rawdon should take.

Becky first accepted the tracts, and began to examine them with great interest, engaging the Dowager in a conversation concerning them and the welfare of her soul, by which means she hoped that her body might escape medication. But after the religious topics were exhausted, Lady Macbeth would not quit Becky's chamber until her cup of night-drink was emptied too; and poor Mrs. Rawdon was compelled actually to assume a look of gratitude, and to swallow the medicine under the unyielding old Dowager's nose, who left her victim finally with a benediction.

It did not much comfort Mrs. Rawdon; her countenance was very queer when Rawdon came in and heard what had happened; and

6. A forlorn hope, for Kaffraria, at the east end of the Cape Colony in South Africa, was still, in the early 1820s, a wild frontier area that by 1848 was barely opened for settlement. It had no bishop.

his explosions of laughter were as loud as usual, when Becky, with a fun which she could not disguise, even though it was at her own expense, described the occurrence, and how she had been victimised by Lady Southdown. Lord Steyne, and her son in London, had many a laugh over the story, when Rawdon and his wife returned to their quarters in May Fair. Becky acted the whole scene for them. She put on a night-cap and gown. She preached a great sermon in the true serious manner: she lectured on the virtue of the medicine which she pretended to administer, with a gravity of imitation so perfect, that you would have thought it was the Countess's own Roman nose through which she snuffled. "Give us Lady Southdown and the black dose,"[7] was a constant cry amongst the folks in Becky's little drawing-room in May Fair. And for the first time in her life the Dowager Countess of Southdown was made amusing.

Sir Pitt remembered the testimonies of respect and veneration which Rebecca had paid personally to himself in early days, and was tolerably well disposed towards her. The marriage, ill-advised as it was, had improved Rawdon very much—that was clear from the Colonel's altered habits and demeanour—and had it not been a lucky union as regarded Pitt himself? The cunning diplomatist smiled inwardly as he owned that he owed his fortune to it, and acknowledged that he at least ought not to cry out against it. His satisfaction was not removed by Rebecca's own statements, behaviour, and conversation.

She doubled the deference which before had charmed him, calling out his conversational powers in such a manner as quite to surprise Pitt himself, who, always inclined to respect his own talents, admired them the more when Rebecca pointed them out to him. With her sister-in-law, Rebecca was satisfactorily able to prove, that it was Mrs. Bute Crawley who brought about the marriage which she afterwards so calumniated: that it was Mrs. Bute's avarice—who hoped to gain all Miss Crawley's fortune, and deprive Rawdon of his aunt's favour—which caused and invented all the wicked reports against Rebecca. "She succeeded in making us poor," Rebecca said, with an air of angelical patience; "but how can I be angry with a woman who has given me one of the best husbands in the world? And has not her own avarice been sufficiently punished by the ruin of her own hopes, and the loss of the property by which she set so much store? Poor!" she cried. "Dear Lady Jane, what care we for poverty? I am used to it from childhood, and I am often thankful that Miss Crawley's money has gone to restore the splendour of the noble old family of which I am so proud to be a member. I am sure Sir Pitt will make a much better use of it than Rawdon would."

All these speeches were reported to Sir Pitt by the most faithful of wives, and increased the favourable impression which Rebecca made; so much so, that when on the third day after the funeral the family party were at dinner, Sir Pitt Crawley, carving fowls at the head of the table, actually said to Mrs. Rawdon, "Ahem! *Rebecca,* may I give you a wing?"—a speech which made the little woman's eyes sparkle with pleasure.

7. A medicine containing opium, also known as black drop and black draught.

While Rebecca was prosecuting the above schemes and hopes, and Pitt Crawley arranging the funeral ceremonial and other matters connected with his future progress and dignity, and Lady Jane busy with her nursery, as far as her mother would let her, and the sun rising and setting, and the clock-tower bell of the Hall ringing to dinner and to prayers as usual, the body of the late owner of Queen's Crawley lay in the apartment which he had occupied, watched unceasingly by the professional attendants who were engaged for that rite. A woman or two, and three or four undertaker's men, the best whom Southampton could furnish, dressed in black, and of a proper stealthy and tragical demeanour, had charge of the remains which they watched turn about, having the housekeeper's room for their place of rendezvous when off duty, where they played at cards in privacy and drank their beer.

The members of the family and servants of the house kept away from the gloomy spot, where the bones of the descendant of an ancient line of knights and gentlemen lay awaiting their final consignment to the family crypt. No regrets attended them, save those of the poor woman who had hoped to be Sir Pitt's wife and widow, and who had fled in disgrace from the Hall over which she had so nearly been a ruler. Beyond her and a favourite old pointer he had, and between whom and himself an attachment subsisted during the period of his imbecility, the old man had not a single friend to mourn him, having indeed, during the whole course of his life, never taken the least pains to secure one. Could the best and kindest of us who depart from the earth, have an opportunity of revisiting it, I suppose he or she (assuming that any Vanity Fair feelings subsist in the sphere whither we are bound) would have a pang of mortification at finding how soon our survivors were consoled. And so Sir Pitt was forgotten—like the kindest and best of us—only a few weeks sooner.

Those who will may follow his remains to the grave, whither they were borne on the appointed day, in the most becoming manner, the family in black coaches, with their handkerchiefs up to their noses, ready for the tears which did not come: the undertaker and his gentlemen in deep tribulation: the select tenantry mourning out of compliment to the new landlord: the neighbouring gentry's carriages at three miles an hour, empty, and in profound affliction: the parson speaking out the formula about "our dear brother departed." As long as we have a man's body, we play our Vanities upon it, surrounding it with humbug and ceremonies, laying it in state, and packing it up in gilt nails and velvet; and we finish our duty by placing over it a stone, written all over with lies. Bute's curate, a smart young fellow from Oxford, and Sir Pitt Crawley, composed between them an appropriate Latin epitaph for the late lamented Baronet: and the former preached a classical sermon, exhorting the survivors not to give way to grief, and informing them in the most respectful terms that they also would be one day called upon to pass that gloomy and mysterious portal which had just closed upon the remains of their lamented brother. Then the tenantry mounted on horseback again, or stayed and refreshed themselves at the Crawley Arms. Then, after a lunch in the servants' hall at Queen's Crawley, the gentry's carriages wheeled off to their different destinations: then the undertaker's men, taking the ropes, palls, velvets, ostrich feathers, and other mortuary properties, clambered up on the roof of the hearse, and rode off to Southampton. Their faces relapsed into a natural expression as the horses, clearing the lodge-gates, got into a brisker trot on the open road; and squads of them might have been seen, speckling with black the public-house entrances, with pewter-pots flashing in the sunshine. Sir Pitt's invalid-chair was wheeled away into a tool-house in the garden: the old pointer used to howl sometimes at first, but these were the only accents of grief which were heard in the Hall of which Sir Pitt Crawley, Baronet, had been master for some three-score years.

As the birds were pretty plentiful, and partridge-shooting is as it were the duty of an English gentleman of statesman-like propensities, Sir Pitt Crawley, the first shock of grief over, went out a little and partook of that diversion in a white hat with a crape round it. The sight of those fields of stubble and turnips, now his own, gave him many secret joys. Sometimes, and with an exquisite humility, he took no gun, but went out with a peaceful bamboo cane; Rawdon, his big brother, and the keepers blazing away at his side. Pitt's money and acres had a great effect upon his brother. The penniless Colonel became quite obsequious and respectful to the head of his house, and despised the milk-sop Pitt no longer. Rawdon listened with sympathy to his senior's prospects of planting and draining: gave his advice about the stables and cattle, rode over to Mudbury to look at a mare which he thought would carry Lady Jane, and offered to break her: &c: the[8] rebellious dragoon was quite humbled and subdued, and became a most creditable younger brother. He had constant bulletins from Miss Briggs in London respecting little Rawdon, who was left behind there: who sent messages of his own. "I am very well," he wrote. "I hope you are very well. I hope Mamma is very well. The pony is very well. Grey takes me to ride in the Park. I can canter. I met the little boy who rode before. He cried when he cantered. I do not cry." Rawdon read these letters to his brother, and Lady Jane, who was delighted with them. The Baronet promised to take charge of the lad at school; and his kind-hearted wife gave Rebecca a bank-note, begging her to buy a present with it for her little nephew.

One day followed another, and the ladies of the house passed their life in those calm pursuits and amusements which satisfy country ladies. Bells rang to meals, and to prayers. The young ladies took exercise on the piano-forte every morning after breakfast, Rebecca giving them the benefit of her instruction. Then they put on thick shoes and walked in the park and[9] shrubberies, or beyond the palings into the village, descending upon the cottages, with Lady Southdown's medicine and tracts for the sick people there. Lady Southdown drove out in a pony-chaise, when Rebecca would take her place by the Dowager's side, and listen to her solemn talk with the utmost

8. First printing reads: her. The ] Revised edition reads: her, &c.; the
9. Revised edition reads: or

interest. She sang Handel and Haydn[1] to the family of evenings, and engaged in a large piece of worsted work, as if she had been born to the business, and as if this kind of life was to continue with her until she should sink to the grave in a polite old age, leaving regrets and a great quantity of consols[2] behind her—as if there were not cares and duns, schemes, shifts, and poverty, waiting outside the Park gates, to pounce upon her when she issued into the world again.

"It isn't difficult to be a country gentleman's wife," Rebecca thought. "I think I could be a good woman if I had five thousand a year. I could dawdle about in the nursery, and count the apricots on the wall. I could water plants in a green-house, and pick off dead leaves from the geraniums. I could ask old women about their rheumatisms, and order half-a-crown's worth of soup for the poor. I shouldn't miss it much, out of five thousand a year. I could even drive out ten miles to dine at a neighbour's, and dress in the fashions of the year before last. I could go to church and keep awake in the great family pew: or go to sleep behind the curtains, and[3] with my veil down, if I only had practice. I could pay everybody, if I had but the money. This is what the conjurors here pride themselves upon doing. They look down with pity upon us miserable sinners who have none. They think themselves generous if they give our children a five-pound note, and us contemptible if we are without one." And who knows but Rebecca was right in her speculations—and that it was only a question of money and fortune which made the difference between her and an honest woman? If you take temptations into account, who is to say that he is better than his neighbour? A comfortable career of prosperity, if it does not make people honest, at least keeps them so. An alderman coming from a turtle feast will not step out of his carriage to steal a leg of mutton; but put him to starve, and see if he will not purloin a loaf. Becky consoled herself by so balancing the chances and equalising the distribution of good and evil in the world.

The old haunts, the old fields and woods, the copses, ponds and gardens, the rooms of the old[4] house where she had spent a couple of years seven years ago, were all carefully revisited by her. She had been young there or comparatively so, for she forgot the time when she ever *was* young—but she remembered her thoughts and feelings seven years back, and contrasted them with those which she had at present, now that she had seen the world and lived with great people, and raised herself far beyond her original humble station.

"I have passed beyond it because I have brains," Becky thought, "and almost all the rest of the world are fools. I could not go back, and consort with those people now, whom I used to meet in my father's studio. Lords come up to my door with stars and garters instead of poor artists with screws of tobacco in their pockets. I have a gentleman for my husband, and an Earl's daughter for my sister in the very

1. George Frederick Handel (1685–1759) and Franz Joseph Haydn (1732–1809), German and Austrian composers who both spent significant time living in England.
2. Consolidated annuities, investment in government stocks paying 3 percent per annum.
3. Revised edition omits: and
4. Revised edition reads: whole

house where I was little better than a servant a few years ago. But am I much better to do now in the world than I was when I was the poor painter's daughter, and wheedled the grocer round the corner for sugar and tea? Suppose I had married Francis who was so fond of me—I couldn't have been much poorer than I am now. Heigho! I wish I could exchange my position in society, and all my relations for a snug sum in the Three per Cent. Consols;" for so it was that Becky felt the Vanity of human affairs, and it was in those securities that she would have liked to cast anchor.

It may, perhaps, have struck her that to have been honest and humble, to have done her duty, and to have marched straightforward on her way, would have brought her as near happiness as that path by which she was striving to attain it. But,—just as the children at Queen's Crawley went round the room, where the body of their father lay;—if ever Becky had these thoughts, she was accustomed to walk round them, and not look in. She eluded them, and despised them—or at least she was committed to the other path from which retreat was now impossible. And for my part I believe that remorse is the least active of all a man's moral senses—the very easiest to be deadened when wakened: and in some never wakened at all. We grieve at being found out, and at the idea of shame or punishment; but the mere sense of wrong makes very few people unhappy in Vanity Fair.

So Rebecca, during her stay at Queen's Crawley, made as many friends of the Mammon of Unrighteousness[5] as she could possibly bring under control. Lady Jane and her husband bade her farewell with the warmest demonstrations of good will. They looked forward with pleasure to the time when, the family-house in Gaunt Street being repaired and beautified, they were to meet again in London. Lady Southdown made her up a packet of medicine, and sent a letter by her to the Rev. Lawrence Grills, exhorting that gentleman to save the brand who "honoured" the letter from the burning.[6] Pitt accompanied them with four horses in the carriage to Mudbury, having sent on their baggage in a cart previously, accompanied with loads of game.

"How happy you will be to see your darling little boy again," Lady Crawley said, taking leave of her kinswoman.

"O so happy!" said Rebecca, throwing up the green eyes. She was immensely happy to be free of the place, and yet loth to go. Queen's Crawley was abominably stupid; and yet the air there was somehow purer than that which she had been accustomed to breathe. Everybody had been dull, but had been kind in their way. "It is all the influence of a long course of Three per Cents," Becky said to herself, and was right very likely.

However, the London lamps flashed joyfully as the stage rolled

5. Mammon is wealth. Jesus, after telling the story of the shrewd servant, gave ironic advice: "Make to yourselves friends of the mammon of unrighteousness; that, when ye fail, they may receive you into everlasting habitations." Luke 16.9. Becky takes it as straight advice.

6. The prophet Amos, preaching against the empty and prideful fulfillment of rituals (honoring the letter of the law), complains that though you "were as a firebrand plucked out of the burning," you still did not return to God.

into Piccadilly, and Briggs had made a beautiful fire in Curzon Street, and little Rawdon was up to welcome back his papa and mamma.

## *Chapter XLII.*

### WHICH TREATS OF THE OSBORNE FAMILY.

CONSIDERABLE time has elapsed since we have seen our respectable friend, old Mr. Osborne of Russell Square. He has not been the happiest of mortals since last we met him. Events have occurred which have not improved his temper, and in more instances than one he has not been allowed to have his own way. To be thwarted in this reasonable desire was always very injurious to the old gentleman; and resistance became doubly exasperating when gout, age, loneliness, and the force of many disappointments combined to weigh him down. His stiff black hair began to grow quite white soon after his son's death; his face grew redder; his hands trembled more and more as he poured out his glass of port wine. He led his clerks a dire life in the city: his family at home were not much happier. I doubt if Rebecca, whom we have seen piously praying for Consols, would have exchanged her poverty and the dare-devil excitement and chances of her life, for Osborne's money and the humdrum gloom which enveloped him. He had proposed for Miss Swartz, but had been rejected scornfully by the partizans of that lady, who married her to a young sprig of Scotch nobility. He was a man to have married a woman out of low life, and bullied her dreadfully afterwards: but no person presented herself suitable to his taste; and instead, he tyrannised over his unmarried daughter at home. She had a fine carriage and fine horses, and sate at the head of a table loaded with the grandest plate. She had a cheque-book, a prize footman to follow her when she walked, unlimited credit, and bows and compliments from all the tradesmen, and all the appurtenances of an heiress; but she spent a woful time. The little charity-girls at the Foundling, the sweeperess at the crossing, the poorest under-kitchen-maid in the servants' hall, was happy compared to that unfortunate and now middle-aged young lady.

Frederic Bullock, Esq., of the house of Bullock, Hulker, & Bullock, had married Maria Osborne, not without a great deal of difficulty and grumbling on Mr. Bullock's part. George being dead and cut out of his father's will, Frederic insisted that the half of the old gentleman's property should be settled upon his Maria, and indeed, for a long time, refused "to come to the scratch" (it was Mr. Frederic's own expression) on any other terms. Osborne said Fred had agreed to take his daughter with twenty thousand, and he should bind himself to no more. "Fred might take it, and welcome, or leave it, and go and be hanged." Fred, whose hopes had been raised when George had been disinherited, thought himself infamously swindled by the old merchant, and for some time made as if he would break off the match altogether. Osborne withdrew his account from Bullock and Hulker's, went on Change with a horsewhip which he swore he would lay across the back of a certain scoundrel that should be nameless, and demeaned himself in his usual violent manner. Jane Osborne condoled with her sister Maria during this family feud. "I always told you, Maria, that it was your money he loved, and not you," she said soothingly.

"He selected *me* and my money at any rate: he didn't choose you and yours," replied Maria, tossing up her head.

The rupture was, however, only temporary. Fred's father and senior partners counselled him to take Maria, even with the twenty thousand settled, half down, and half at the death of Mr. Osborne, with the chances of the further division of the property. So he "knuckled down," again to use his own phrase; and sent old Hulker with peaceable overtures to Osborne. It was his father, he said, who would not hear of the match, and had made the difficulties; he was most anxious to keep the engagement. The excuse was sulkily accepted by Mr. Osborne. Hulker & Bullock were a high family of the city aristocracy, and connected with the "nobs" at the West End. It was something for the old man to be able to say "My son, Sir, of the house of Hulker, Bullock, & Co., Sir; my daughter's cousin, Lady Mary Mango, Sir, daughter of the Right Hon. the Earl of Castlemouldy." In his imagination he saw his house peopled by the "nobs." So he forgave young Bullock, and consented that the marriage should take place.

It was a grand affair—the bridegroom's relatives giving the breakfast, their habitations being near St. George's Hanover Square, where the business took place. The "nobs of the West End," were invited, and many of them signed the book. Mr. Mango and Lady Mary Mango were there, with the dear young Gwendoline and Gwinever Mango as bridesmaids; Colonel Bludyer of the Dragoon Guards (eldest son of the house of Bludyer Brothers, Mincing Lane),[1] another cousin of the bridegroom, and the Honourable Mrs. Bludyer; the Honourable George Boulter, Lord Levant's son, and his lady, Miss Mango that was; Lord Viscount Castletoddy; Honourable James McMull and Mrs. McMull (formerly Miss Swartz), and a host of fashionables, who have all married into Lombard Street, and done a great deal to ennoble Cornhill.[2]

The young couple had a house near Berkeley Square, and a small villa at Roehampton,[3] among the banking colony there. Fred was considered to have made rather a *mésalliance* by the ladies of his family, whose grandfather had been in a Charity School, and who were allied through the husbands with some of the best blood in England.[4] And Maria was bound, by superior pride and great care in the com-

1. Near the Tower of London.
2. A street with a history of pillories and prisons was developing as a street of reputable trades, printers, publishers, and bankers.
3. Fashionable residential area in town and in a southwest suburb.
4. *Mésalliance*: mismatched marriage, particularly between social classes. Charity schools were for the poor. Fred's sisters, like Maria, have married above themselves.

position of her visiting-book, to make up for the defects of birth; and felt it her duty to see her father and sister as little as possible.

That she should utterly break with the old man, who had still so many scores of thousand pounds to give away, is absurd to suppose. Fred Bullock would never allow her to do that. But she was still young and incapable of hiding her feelings: and by inviting her papa and sister to her third-rate parties, and behaving very coldly to them when they came, and by avoiding Russell Square, and indiscreetly begging her father to quit that odious vulgar place; she did more harm than all Frederic's diplomacy could repair, and perilled her chance of her inheritance like a giddy heedless creature as she was.

"So Russell Square is not good enough for Mrs. Maria, hay?" said the old gentleman, rattling up the carriage-windows, as he and his daughter drove away one night from Mrs. Frederic Bullock's, after dinner. "So she invites her father and sister to a second day's dinner (if those sides, or *ontrys*,[5] as she calls 'em, weren't served yesterday, I'm d—d), and to meet City folks and littery men, and keeps the Earls, and the Ladies, and the Honourables to herself. Honourables? Damn Honourables. I am a plain British merchant I am: and could buy the beggarly hounds over and over. Lords, indeed!—why, at one of her *swarreys*[6] I saw one of 'em speak to a dam fiddler—a fellar I despise. And they won't come to Russell Square, won't they? Why, I'll lay my life I've got a better glass of wine, and pay a better figure for it, and can show a handsomer service of silver, and can lay a better dinner on my mahogany, than ever they see on theirs—the cringing, sneaking, stuck-up fools. Drive on quick, James; I want to get back to Russell Square—ha, ha!" and he sank back into the corner with a furious laugh. With such reflections on his own superior merits, it was the custom of the old gentleman not unfrequently to console himself.

Jane Osborne could not but concur in these opinions respecting her sister's conduct; and when Mrs. Frederic's first-born, Frederic Augustus Howard Stanley Devereux Bullock,[7] was born, old Osborne, who was invited to the christening and to be godfather, contented himself with sending the child a gold cup, with twenty guineas inside it for the nurse. "That's more than any of your Lords will give, *I'll* warrant," he said, and refused to attend at the ceremony.

The splendour of the gift, however, caused great satisfaction to the house of Bullock. Maria thought that her father was very much pleased with her, and Frederic augured the best for his little son and heir.

One can fancy the pangs with which Miss Osborne in her solitude in Russell Square read the "Morning Post," where her sister's name occurred every now and then, in the articles headed "Fashionable Réunions," and where she had an opportunity of reading a descrip-

5. *Entrées*: main courses.
6. *Soirées*: evening parties.
7. The names are taken from actual noble families, but in addition, Devereux would have been recognized by most original readers as the hero of one of Edward Bulwer Lytton's novels.

tion of Mrs. F. Bullock's costume, when presented at the drawing-room by Lady Frederica Bullock. Jane's own life, as we have said, admitted of no such grandeur. It was an awful existence. She had to get up of black winter's mornings to make breakfast for her scowling old father, who would have turned the whole house out of doors if his tea had not been ready at half-past eight. She remained silent opposite to him, listening to the urn hissing, and sitting in tremor while the parent read his paper, and consumed his accustomed portion of muffins and tea. At half-past nine he rose and went to the City, and she was almost free till dinner-time, to make visitations in the kitchen and to scold the servants: to drive abroad and descend upon the tradesmen, who were prodigiously respectful: to leave her cards and her papa's at the great glum respectable houses of their City friends; or to sit alone in the large drawing-room, expecting visitors; and working at a huge piece of worsted by the fire, on the sofa, hard by the great Iphigenia clock, which ticked and tolled with mournful loudness in the dreary room. The great glass over the mantel-piece, faced by the other great console glass at the opposite end of the room, increased and multiplied between them the brown Holland bag in which the chandelier hung; until you saw these brown Holland bags fading away in endless perspectives, and this apartment of Miss Osborne's seemed the centre of a system of drawing-rooms. When she removed the cordovan leather from the grand piano, and ventured to play a few notes on it, it sounded with a mournful sadness, startling the dismal echoes of the house. George's picture was gone, and laid up-stairs in a lumber-room in the garret; and though there was a consciousness of him, and father and daughter often instinctively knew that they were thinking of him, no mention was ever made of the brave and once darling son.

At five o'clock Mr. Osborne came back to his dinner, which he and his daughter took in silence (seldom broken, except when he swore and was savage, if the cooking was not to his liking), or which they shared twice in a month with a party of dismal friends of Osborne's rank and age. Old Dr. Gulp and his lady from Bloomsbury Square: old Mr. Frowser, the attorney, from Bedford Row, a very great man, and from his business, hand-in-glove with the "nobs at the West End:" old Colonel Livermore, of the Bombay Army, and Mrs. Livermore, from Upper Bedford Place: old Serjeant Toffy and Mrs. Toffy; and sometimes old Sir Thomas Coffin and Lady Coffin, from Bedford Square.[8] Sir Thomas was celebrated as a hanging judge, and the particular tawny port was produced when he dined with Mr. Osborne.

These people and their like gave the pompous Russell Square merchant pompous dinners back again. They had solemn rubbers of whist, when they went up-stairs after drinking, and their carriages were called at half-past ten. Many rich people, whom we poor devils are in the habit of envying, lead contentedly an existence like that above described. Jane Osborne scarcely ever met a man under sixty, and almost the only bachelor who appeared in their society was Mr. Smirk, the celebrated Lady's doctor.

8. Bedford Place connects Bloomsbury and Bedford Squares.

I can't say that nothing had occurred to disturb the monotony of this awful existence: the fact is, there had been a secret in poor Jane's life which had made her father more savage and morose than even nature, pride, and over-feeding had made him. This secret was connected with Miss Wirt, who had a cousin an artist, Mr. Smee, very celebrated since as a portrait-painter and R.A.,[9] but who once was glad enough to give drawing-lessons to ladies of fashion. Mr. Smee has forgotten where Russell Square is now, but he was glad enough to visit it in the year 1818, when Miss Osborne had instruction from him.

Smee (formerly a pupil of Sharpe of Frith Street,[1] a dissolute, irregular, and unsuccessful man, but a man with great knowledge of his art) being the cousin of Miss Wirt, we say, and introduced by her to Miss Osborne, whose hand and heart were still free after various incomplete love affairs, felt a great attachment for this lady, and it is believed inspired one in her bosom. Miss Wirt was the confidante of this intrigue. I know not whether she used to leave the room where the master and his pupil were painting, in order to give them an opportunity for exchanging those vows and sentiments which cannot be uttered advantageously in the presence of a third party: I know not whether she hoped that should her cousin succeed in carrying off the rich merchant's daughter, he would give Miss Wirt a portion of the wealth, which she had enabled him to win—all that is certain is, that Mr. Osborne got some hint of the transaction, came back from the City abruptly, and entered the drawing-room with his bamboo cane; found the painter, the pupil, and the companion all looking exceedingly pale there; turned the former out of doors with menaces that he would break every bone in his skin, and half-an-hour afterwards dismissed Miss Wirt likewise, kicking her trunks down the stairs, trampling on her band-boxes, and shaking his fist at her hackney coach, as it bore her away.

Jane Osborne kept her bed-room for many days. She was not allowed to have a companion afterwards. Her father swore to her that she should not have a shilling of his money if she made any match without his concurrence; and as he wanted a woman to keep his house, he did not choose that she should marry: so that she was obliged to give up all projects with which Cupid had any share. During her papa's life, then, she resigned herself to the manner of existence here described, and was content to be an Old Maid. Her sister, meanwhile, was having children with finer names every year—and the intercourse between the two grew fainter continually. "Jane and I do not move in the same sphere of life," Mrs. Bullock said. "I regard her as a sister, of course"—which means—what does it mean when a lady says that she regards Jane as a sister?

It has been described how the Misses Dobbin lived with their father at a fine villa at Denmark Hill, where there were beautiful graperies and peach-trees which delighted little Georgy Osborne. The Misses

9. Royal Academician. Smee reappears as a portrait painter in *The Newcomes*.

1. In the Soho district with a history of artists, sculptors, and actors in residence. Sharpe is Becky's father.

Dobbin, who drove often to Brompton to see our dear Amelia, came sometimes to Russell Square too, to pay a visit to their old acquaintance Miss Osborne. I believe it was in consequence of the commands of their brother the Major in India (for whom their papa had a prodigious respect), that they payed attention to Mrs. George; for the Major, the godfather and guardian of Amelia's little boy, still hoped that the child's grandfather might be induced to relent towards him, and acknowledge him for the sake of his son. The Miss Dobbins kept Miss Osborne acquainted with the state of Amelia's affairs; how she was living with her father and mother: how poor they were: how they wondered what men, and such men as their brother and dear Captain Osborne, could find in such an insignificant little chit: how she was still, as heretofore, a namby-pamby milk-and-water affected creature—but how the boy was really the noblest little boy ever seen—for the hearts of all women warm towards young children, and the sourest spinster is kind to them.

One day, after great entreaties, on the part of the Misses Dobbin, Amelia allowed little George to go and pass a day with them at Denmark Hill—a part of which day she spent herself in writing to the Major in India. She congratulated him on the happy news which his sisters had just conveyed to her. She prayed for his prosperity, and that of the bride he had chosen. She thanked him for a thousand thousand kind offices and proofs of stedfast friendship to her in her affliction. She told him the last news about little Georgy, and how he was gone to spend that very day with his sisters in the country. She underlined the letter a great deal, and she signed herself affectionately his friend, Amelia Osborne. She forgot to send any message of kindness to Lady O'Dowd, as her wont was—and did not mention Glorvina by name, and only in italics, as the Major's *bride,* for whom she begged *blessings.* But the news of the marriage removed the reserve which she had kept up towards him. She was glad to be able to own and feel how warmly and gratefully she regarded him—and as for the idea of being jealous of Glorvina, (Glorvina, indeed!) Amelia would have scouted it, if an angel from heaven had hinted it to her.

That night, when Georgy came back in the pony-carriage in which he rejoiced, and in which he was driven by Sir Wm. Dobbin's old coachman, he had round his neck a fine gold chain and watch. He said an old lady, not pretty, had given it him, who cried and kissed him a great deal. But he didn't like her. He liked grapes very much. And he only liked his mamma. Amelia shrunk and started: the timid soul felt a presentiment of terror when she heard that the relations of the child's father had seen him.

Miss Osborne came back to give her father his dinner. He had made a good speculation in the City, and was rather in a good humour that day, and chanced to remark the agitation under which she laboured. "What's the matter, Miss Osborne?" he deigned to say.

The woman burst into tears. "O, Sir," she said, "I've seen little George. He is as beautiful as an angel—and so like him!" The old man opposite to her did not say a word, but flushed up, and began to tremble in every limb.

## *Chapter XLIII.*

### IN WHICH THE READER HAS TO DOUBLE THE CAPE.[1]

THE astonished reader must be called upon to transport himself ten thousand miles to the military station of Bundlegunge, in the Madras division of our Indian empire, where our gallant old friends of the —th regiment are quartered under the command of the brave Colonel, Sir Michael O'Dowd. Time has dealt kindly with that stout officer, as it does ordinarily with men who have good stomachs and good tempers, and are not perplexed over much by fatigue of the brain. The Colonel plays a good knife and fork at tiffin, and resumes those weapons with great success at dinner. He smokes his hookah[2] after both meals, and puffs away[3] as quietly while his wife scolds him, as he did under the fire of the French at Waterloo. Age and heat have not diminished the activity or the eloquence of the descendant of the Malonies and the Molloys. Her ladyship, our old acquaintance, is as much at home at Madras as at Brussels, in the cantonment as under the tents. On the march you saw her at the head of the regiment seated on a royal elephant, a noble sight. Mounted on that beast, she has been into action with tigers in the jungle: she has been received by native princes, who have welcomed her and Glorvina into the recesses of their zenanas[4] and offered her shawls and jewels which it went to her heart to refuse. The sentries of all arms salute her wherever she makes her appearance: and she touches her hat gravely to their salutation. Lady O'Dowd is one of the greatest ladies in the Presidency of Madras—her quarrel with Lady Smith, wife of Sir Minos Smith the puisne judge,[5] is still remembered by some at Madras, when the Colonel's lady snapped her fingers in the Judge's lady's face, and said *she'd* never stir a foot be-

1. To sail round the southern tip of Africa.
2. Water-cooled smoking pipe.
3. First printing reads "meals, puffs away"; a correction in the stereotyped plate for a second printing reads "meals, puffs and" (which is clearly an error); revised edition corrects to "meals, and puffs", but the only reason the original was not corrected by simply inserting the required "and" before "puffs" is that in the stereotyped plate, the correction had to occupy the same space as the error. The present edition merely inserts the "and".
4. Women's quarters.
5. Minos (pronounced "minus"): in myth, a judge of the underworld. Puisne (pronounced "puny"): an inferior or associate judge.

fore[6] ever a beggarly civilian. Even now, though it is five-and-twenty years ago, people remember Lady O'Dowd dancing[7] a jig at Government House, where she danced down two Aides-de-Camp, a Major of Madras cavalry and two gentlemen of the Civil Service; and, persuaded by Major Dobbin, C.B., second in command of the —th, to retire to the supper room, *lassata nondum satiata recessit.*[8]

Peggy O'Dowd is indeed the same as ever: kind in act and thought: impetuous in temper; eager to command: a tyrant over her Michael: a dragon amongst all the ladies of the regiment: a mother to all the young men, whom she tends in their sickness, defends in all their scrapes, and with whom Lady Peggy is immensely popular. But the Subalterns'[9] and Captains' ladies (the Major is unmarried) cabal against her a good deal. They say that Glorvina gives herself airs, and that Peggy herself is intolerably domineering. She interfered with a little congregation which Mrs. Kirk had got up, and laughed the young men away from her sermons, stating that a soldier's wife had no business to be a parson: that Mrs. Kirk would be much better mending her husband's clothes: and, if the regiment wanted sermons, that she had the finest in the world, those of her uncle, the Dean. She abruptly put a termination to a flirtation which Lieutenant Stubble of the regiment had commenced with the Surgeon's wife, threatening to come down upon Stubble for the money which he had borrowed from her (for the young fellow was still of an extravagant turn) unless he broke off at once and went to the Cape, on sick leave. On the other hand, she housed and sheltered Mrs. Posky who fled from her bungalow one night, pursued by her infuriate husband, wielding his second brandy bottle, and actually carried Posky through the delirium tremens, and broke him of the habit of drinking, which had grown upon that officer as all evil habits will grow upon men. In a word, in adversity she was the best of comforters, in good fortune the most troublesome of friends; having a perfectly good opinion of herself always, and an indomitable resolution to have her own way.

Among other points, she had made up her mind that Glorvina should marry our old friend Dobbin. Mrs. O'Dowd knew the Major's expectations and appreciated his good qualities, and the high character which he enjoyed in his profession. Glorvina, a very handsome, fresh-coloured, black-haired, blue-eyed young lady, who could ride a horse, or play a sonata with any girl out of the County Cark, seemed to be the very person destined to insure Dobbin's happiness—much more than that poor good little weak-spur'ted Amelia, about whom he used to take on so.—"Look at Glorvina enter a room," Mrs. O'Dowd would say, "and compare her with that poor Mrs. Osborne, who couldn't say bo to a goose. She'd be worthy of you, Major—you're a quiet man yourself, and want some one to talk for ye. And though she does not come of such good blood as the Malonies or

6. Revised edition reads: never walk behind
7. Revised edition reads: performing
8. Wearied but unsatisfied, she withdrew (Juvenal, *Satires*, vi.130); said of the empress Messalina (d. 48 A.D.) leaving a brothel.
9. Officers of ranks below captain.

Glorvina tries her fascinations on the Major

Molloys, let me tell ye, she's of an ancient family that any nobleman might be proud to marry into."

But before she had come to such a resolution, and determined to subjugate Major Dobbin by her endearments, it must be owned that Glorvina had practised them a good deal elsewhere. She had had a season in Dublin, and who knows how many in Cork, Killarney, and Mallow?[1] She had flirted with all the marriageable officers whom the depôts of her country afforded, and all the bachelor squires who seemed eligible. She had been engaged to be married a half score times in Ireland, besides the clergyman at Bath who used her so ill. She had flirted all the way to Madras with the Captain and chief-mate of the Ramchunder East Indiaman,[2] and had a season at the Presidency with her brother and Mrs. O'Dowd who was staying there, while the Major of the regiment was in command at the station. Everybody admired her there: everybody danced with her: but no one proposed who was worth the marrying; one or two exceedingly young subalterns sighed after her, and a beardless civilian or two; but she rejected these as beneath her pretensions; and other and younger virgins than Glorvina were married before her. There are women, and handsome women too, who have this fortune in life. They fall in love with the utmost generosity; they ride and walk with half the Army-list, though they draw near to forty, and yet the Miss O'Gradys are Miss O'Gradys still: Glorvina persisted that but for Lady O'Dowd's unlucky quarrel with the Judge's lady, she would have made a good match at Madras, where old Mr. Chutney, who was at the head of the civil service, (and who afterwards married Miss Dolby, a young lady, only thirteen years of age, who had just arrived from school in Europe,) was just at the point of proposing to her.

Well, although Lady O'Dowd and Glorvina quarrelled a great number of times every day, and upon almost every conceivable subject—indeed, if Mick O'Dowd had not possessed the temper of an angel, two such women constantly about his ears would have driven him out of his senses—yet they agreed between themselves on this point, that Glorvina should marry Major Dobbin, and were determined that the Major should have no rest until the arrangement was brought about. Undismayed by forty or fifty previous defeats, Glorvina laid siege to him. She sang Irish Melodies at him unceasingly. She asked him so frequently and pathetically, will ye come to the bower? that it is a wonder how any man of feeling could have resisted the invitation. She was never tired of inquiring, if Sorrow had his young days faded; and was ready to listen and weep like Desdemona at the stories of his dangers and his campaigns.[3] It has been said that our honest and dear old friend used to perform on the flute in private: Glorvina insisted upon having duets with him, and Lady O'Dowd would rise and artlessly quit the room, when the young couple were

1. Irish towns.
2. Ship in the service of the East India Company. See chapter III.
3. *Irish Melodies* (1821) by Thomas Moore includes "Has Sorrow Thy Young Days Shaded?" "Will Ye Come to the Bower I Have Shaded for You?" though not in that collection, is also probably by Moore. Desdemona fell in love with Othello while he recounted his life's adventures.

so engaged. Glorvina forced the Major to ride with her of mornings. The whole cantonment saw them set out and return. She was constantly writing notes over to him at his house, borrowing his books, and scoring with her great pencil-marks such passages of sentiment or humour as awakened her sympathy. She borrowed his horses, his servants, his spoons, and palankin;[4]—no wonder that public rumour assigned her to him, and that the Major's sisters in England should fancy they were about to have a sister-in-law.

Dobbin, who was thus vigorously besieged, was in the meanwhile in a state of the most odious tranquillity. He used to laugh when the young fellows of the regiment joked him about Glorvina's manifest attentions to him. "Bah!" said he, "she is only keeping her hand in—she practises upon me as she does upon Mrs. Tozer's piano, because it's the most handy instrument in the station. I am much too battered and old for such a fine young lady as Glorvina." And so he went on riding with her, and copying music and verses into her albums, and playing at chess with her very submissively; for it is with these simple amusements that some officers in India are accustomed to while away their leisure moments; while others of a less domestic turn hunt hogs, and shoot snipes,[5] or gamble and smoke cheroots, and betake themselves to brandy-and-water. As for Sir Michael O'Dowd, though his Lady and her sister both urged him to call upon the Major to explain himself, and not keep on torturing a poor innocent girl in that shameful way; the old soldier refused point-blank to have anything to do with the conspiracy—"'Faith, the Major's big enough to choose for himself," Sir Michael said; "he'll ask ye when he wants ye;"—or else he would turn the matter off jocularly, declaring that "Dobbin was too young to keep house, and had written home to ask lave of his mamma." Nay, he went farther, and in private communications with his Major, would caution and rally him—crying, "Mind your oi, Dob, my boy, them girls is bent on mischief—me Lady has just got a box of gowns from Europe, and there's a pink satin for Glorvina, which will finish ye, Dob, if it's in the power of woman or satin to move ye."

But the truth is, neither beauty nor fashion could conquer him. Our honest friend had but one idea of a woman in his head, and that one did not in the least resemble Miss Glorvina O'Dowd in pink satin. A gentle little woman in black, with large eyes and brown hair, seldom speaking, save when spoken to, and then in a voice not the least resembling Miss Glorvina's—a soft young mother tending an infant and beckoning the Major up with a smile to look at him—a rosy-cheeked lass coming singing into the room in Russell Square or hanging on George Osborne's arm happy and loving—there was but this image that filled our honest Major's mind by day and by night and reigned over it always. Very likely Amelia was not like the portrait the Major had formed of her: there was a figure in a book of fashions which his sisters had in England, and with which William had made away privately, pasting it into the lid of his desk,

4. Palanquin or palankeen, an enclosed litter carried by four men.
5. Marsh birds.

and fancying he saw some resemblance to Mrs. Osborne in the print, whereas I have seen it, and can vouch that it is but the picture of a high-waisted gown with an impossible doll's face simpering over it—and, perhaps, Mr. Dobbin's sentimental Amelia was no more like the real one than this absurd little print which he cherished. But what man in love, of us, is better informed?—or is he much happier when he sees and owns his delusion? Dobbin was under this spell. He did not bother his friends and the public much about his feelings, or indeed lose his natural zest or appetite on account of them. His head has grizzled since we saw him last; and a line or two of silver may be seen in the soft brown hair likewise. But his feelings are not in the least changed or oldened; and his love remains as fresh, as a man's recollections of boyhood are.

We have said how the two Miss Dobbins and Amelia, the Major's correspondents in Europe, wrote him letters from England; Mrs. Osborne congratulating him with great candour and cordiality upon his approaching nuptials with Miss O'Dowd.

"Your sister has just kindly visited me," Amelia wrote in her letter, "and informed me of an *interesting event,* upon which I beg to offer my *most sincere congratulations.* I hope the young lady to whom I hear you are to be *united* will in every respect prove worthy of one who is himself all kindness and goodness. The poor widow has only her prayers to offer, and her cordial cordial wishes for *your prosperity!* Georgy sends his love to *his dear godpapa,* and hopes that you will not forget him. I tell him that you are about to form *other ties,* with one who I am sure merits *all your affection,* but that although such ties must of course be the strongest and most sacred, and supersede *all others,* yet that I am sure the widow and the child whom you have ever protected and loved will always *have a corner in your heart.*" The letter which has been before alluded to, went on in this strain, protesting throughout as to the extreme satisfaction of the writer.

This letter, which arrived by the very same ship which brought out Lady O'Dowd's box of millinery from London, (and which you may be sure Dobbin opened before any one of the other packets which the mail brought him), put the receiver into such a state of mind that Glorvina, and her pink satin, and everything belonging to her became perfectly odious to him. The Major cursed the talk of women: and the sex in general. Everything annoyed him that day—the parade was insufferably hot and wearisome. Good heavens! was a man of intellect to waste his life, day after day, inspecting cross-belts, and putting fools through their manœuvres? The senseless chatter of the young men at mess was more than ever jarring. What cared he, a man on the high road to forty, to know how many snipes Lieutenant Smith had shot, or what were the performances of Ensign Brown's mare? The jokes about the table filled him with shame. He was too old to listen to the banter of the assistant-surgeon and the slang of the youngsters, at which old O'Dowd, with his bald head and red face, laughed quite easily. The old man had listened to those jokes any time these thirty years—Dobbin himself had been fifteen years hearing them. And after the boisterous dullness of the mess-table, the quarrels and scandal of the ladies of the regiment! It was unbearable, shameful. "O Amelia, Amelia," he thought, "you to whom I have been so faithful,—you reproach me! It is because you cannot feel for me, that I drag on this wearisome life. And you reward me after years of devotion by giving me your blessing upon my marriage, forsooth, with this flaunting Irish girl!" Sick and sorry felt poor William: more than ever wretched and lonely. He would like to have done with life and its vanity altogether—so bootless and unsatisfactory the struggle, so cheerless and dreary the prospect, seemed to him. He lay all that night sleepless, and yearning to go home. Amelia's letter had fallen as a blank upon him. No fidelity, no constant truth and passion, could move her into warmth. She would not see that he loved her. Tossing in his bed, he spoke out to her. "Good God, Amelia!" he said, "don't you know that I only love you in the world—you, who are a stone to me—you, whom I tended through months and months of illness and grief, and who bade me farewell with a smile on your face, and forgot me before the door shut between us!" The native servants lying outside his verandahs beheld with wonder the Major, so cold and quiet ordinarily, at present so passionately moved and cast down. Would she have pitied him had she seen him? He read over and over all the letters which he ever had from her—letters of business relative to the little property which he had made her believe her husband had left to her—brief notes of invitation—every scrap of writing that she had ever sent to him—how cold, how kind, how hopeless, how selfish, they were!

Had there been some kind gentle soul near at hand who could

read and appreciate this silent generous heart, who knows but that the reign of Amelia might have been over, and that friend William's love might have flowed into a kinder channel? But there was only Glorvina of the jetty ringlets with whom his intercourse was familiar, and this dashing young woman was not bent upon loving the Major, but rather on making the Major admire *her*—a most vain and hopeless task too, at least considering the means that the poor girl possessed to carry it out. She curled her hair and showed her shoulders at him, as much as to say, did ye ever see such jet ringlets and such a complexion? She grinned at him so that he might see that every tooth in her head was sound—and he never heeded all these charms. Very soon after the arrival of the box of millinery, and perhaps indeed in honour of it, Lady O'Dowd and the ladies of the King's Regiment gave a ball to the Company's Regiments and the civilians at the station. Glorvina sported the killing pink frock, and the Major, who attended the party and walked very ruefully up and down the rooms, never so much as perceived the pink garment. Glorvina danced past him in a fury with all the young subalterns of the station, and the Major was not in the least jealous of her performance, or angry because Captain Bangles of the Cavalry handed her to supper. It was not jealousy, or frocks or shoulders, that could move him, and Glorvina had nothing more.

So these two were each exemplifying the Vanity of this life, and each longing for what he or she could not get. Glorvina cried with rage at the failure. She had set her mind on the Major "more than on any of the others," she owned, sobbing. "He'll break my heart, he will, Peggy," she would whimper to her sister-in-law when they were good friends; "sure every one of me frocks must be taken in—it's such a skeleton I'm growing." Fat or thin, laughing or melancholy, on horseback or the music-stool, it was all the same to the Major. And the Colonel, puffing his pipe and listening to these complaints, would suggest that Glory should have some black frocks out in the next box from London, and told a mysterious story of a lady in Ireland who died of grief for the loss of her husband before she got ere a one.

While the Major was going on in this tantalising way, not proposing, and declining to fall in love, there came another ship from Europe bringing letters on board, and amongst them some more for the heartless man. These were home letters bearing an earlier post mark than that of the former packets, and as Major Dobbin recognised among his, the handwriting of his sister, who always crossed and recrossed her letters to her brother,—gathered together all the possible bad news which she could collect, abused him and read him lectures with sisterly frankness, and always left him miserable for the day after "dearest William" had achieved the perusal of one of her epistles—the truth must be told that, "dearest William" did not hurry himself to break the seal of Miss Dobbin's letter, but waited for a particularly favourable day and mood for doing so. A fortnight before, moreover, he had written to scold her for telling those absurd stories to Mrs. Osborne, and had despatched a letter in reply to that lady, undeceiving her with respect to the reports concerning him, and assuring her that "he had no sort of present intention of altering his condition."

Two or three nights after the arrival of the second package of letters, the Major had passed the evening pretty cheerfully at Lady O'Dowd's house, where Glorvina thought that he listened with rather more attention than usual to the Meeting of the Wathers, the Minsthrel Boy,[6] and one or two other specimens of song with which she favoured him, (the truth is, he was no more listening to Glorvina than to the howling of the jackalls in the moonlight outside, and the delusion was her's as usual,) and having played his game at chess with her, (cribbage with the surgeon was Lady O'Dowd's favourite evening pastime,) Major Dobbin took leave of the Colonel's family at his usual hour, and retired to his own house.

There on his table, his sister's letter lay reproaching him. He took it up, ashamed rather of his negligence regarding it, and prepared himself for a disagreeable hour's communing with that crabbed-handed absent relative . . . . . It may have been an hour after the Major's departure from the Colonel's house—Sir Michael was sleeping the sleep of the just; Glorvina had arranged her black ringlets in the innumerable little bits of paper, in which it was her habit to confine them; Lady O'Dowd, too, had gone to her bed in the nuptial chamber, on the ground-floor, and had tucked her musquito curtains round her fair form, when the guard at the gates of the Commanding-officer's compound, beheld Major Dobbin, in the moonlight, rushing towards the house with a swift step and a very agitated countenance, and he passed the sentinel and went up to the windows of the Colonel's bed-chamber.

"O'Dowd—Colonel!" said Dobbin, and kept up a great shouting.

"Heavens, Meejor!" said Glorvina of the curl-papers, putting out her head too, from her window.

"What is it, Dob, me boy?" said the Colonel, expecting there was a fire in the station, or that the route had come from head-quarters.

"I—I must have leave of absence. I must go to England—on the most urgent private affairs," Dobbin said.

"Good heavens, what has happened!" thought Glorvina, trembling with all the papillotes.[7]

"I want to be off—now—to-night," Dobbin continued; and the Colonel getting up, came out to parley with him.

In the postscript of Miss Dobbin's cross-letter—the Major had just come upon a paragraph, to the following effect:—"I drove yesterday to see your old *acquaintance*, Mrs. Osborne. The wretched place they live at, since they were bankrupts, you know—Mr. S., to judge from a *brass plate* on the door of his hut (it is little better) is a coal-merchant. The little boy, your godson, is certainly a fine child, though forward, and inclined to be saucy and self-willed. But we have taken notice of him as you wish it, and have introduced him to his aunt, Miss O., who was rather pleased with him. Perhaps his grandpapa, not the bankrupt one, who is almost doting, but Mr. Osborne, of Russell Square, may be induced to relent towards the child of your friend,

6. Two more songs from *Irish Melodies*, one about being with friends "the belov'd of my bosom," the other about the captive minstrel boy who would not sing in slavery.
7. Curl papers.

*his erring and self-willed son.* And Amelia will not be ill-disposed to give him up. The widow is *consoled,* and is about to marry a reverend gentleman, the Rev. Mr. Binney, one of the curates of Brompton. A poor match. But Mrs. O. is getting old, and I saw a great deal of gray in her hair—she was in very good spirits: and your little godson overate himself at our house. Mamma sends her love with that of your affectionate, Ann Dobbin."

## *Chapter XLIV.*

### A ROUND-ABOUT CHAPTER BETWEEN LONDON AND HAMPSHIRE.

UR old friends the Crawleys' family house,[1] in Great Gaunt Street, still bore over its front the hatchment which had been placed there as a token of mourning for Sir Pitt Crawley's demise, yet this heraldic emblem was in itself a very splendid and gaudy piece of furniture, and all the rest of the mansion became more brilliant than it had ever been during the late baronet's reign. The black outer-coating of the bricks was removed and they appeared with a cheerful blushing face streaked with white: the old bronze lions of the knocker were gilt handsomely, the railings painted, and the dismallest house in Great Gaunt Street, became the smartest in the whole quarter, before the green leaves in Hampshire had replaced those yellowing ones which were on the trees in Queen's Crawley avenue when old Sir Pitt Crawley passed under them for the last time.

A little woman, with a carriage to correspond, was perpetually seen about this mansion; an elderly spinster, accompanied by a little boy, also might be remarked coming thither daily. It was Miss Briggs and little Rawdon, whose business it was to see to the inward renovation of Sir Pitt's house, to superintend the female band engaged in stitching the blinds and hangings, to poke and rummage in the drawers and cupboards crammed with the dirty relics and congregated trumperies of a couple of generations of Lady Crawleys, and to take inventories of the china, the glass, and other properties in the closets and store-rooms.

Mrs. Rawdon Crawley was general-in-chief over these arrangements, with full orders from Sir Pitt to sell, barter, confiscate, or purchase furniture: and she enjoyed herself not a little in an occupation which gave full scope to her taste and ingenuity. The renovation of the house was determined upon when Sir Pitt came to town in

1. Initial illustration: in Greek myth, sirens lured sailors to destruction. Revised edition omits all illustrations and reads: The family house of our old friends the Crawleys,

November to see his lawyers, and when he passed nearly a week in Curzon Street, under the roof of his affectionate brother and sister.

He had put up at an hotel at first; but, Becky as soon as she heard of the Baronet's arrival, went off alone to greet him, and returned in an hour to Curzon Street with Sir Pitt in the carriage by her side. It was impossible sometimes to resist this artless little creature's hospitalities, so kindly were they pressed, so frankly and amiably offered. Becky seized Pitt's hand in a transport of gratitude when he agreed to come. "Thank you," she said, squeezing it, and looking into the Baronet's eyes, who blushed a good deal; "how happy this will make Rawdon." She bustled up about to Pitt's bed-room, leading on the servants, who were carrying his trunks thither. She came in herself laughing, with a coal-scuttle out of her own room.

A fire was blazing already in Sir Pitt's apartment, (it was Miss Briggs' room, by the way, who was sent up stairs to sleep with the maid.) "I knew I should bring you," she said, with pleasure beaming in her glance. Indeed, she was really and sincerely happy at having him for a guest.

Becky made Rawdon dine out once or twice on business, while Pitt stayed with them, and the Baronet passed the happy evening alone with her and Briggs. She went down stairs to the kitchen and actually cooked little dishes for him. "Isn't it a good salmi?"[2] she said; "I made it for you. I can make you better dishes than that: and will when you come to see me."

2. A ragout of partly roasted game stewed with wine, bread, and condiments.

"Everything you do, you do well," said the Baronet gallantly. "The salmi is excellent indeed."

"A poor man's wife," Rebecca replied gaily, "must make herself useful, you know:" on which her brother-in-law vowed that "she was fit to be the wife of an Emperor, and that to be skilful in domestic duties was surely one of the most charming of woman's qualities." And Sir Pitt thought with something like mortification of Lady Jane at home, and of a certain pie which she had insisted upon[3] making, and serving to him at dinner—a most abominable pie.

Besides the salmi, which was made of Lord Steyne's pheasants from his lordship's cottage of Stillbrook, Becky gave her brother-in-law a bottle of white wine, some that Rawdon had brought with him from France, and had picked up for nothing, the little story-teller said; whereas the liquor was, in truth, some White Hermitage[4] from the Marquis of Steyne's famous cellars, which brought fire into the Baronet's pallid cheeks and a glow into his feeble frame.

Then, when he had drunk up the bottle of *petit vin blanc* she gave him her hand and took him up to the drawing-room, and made him snug on the sofa by the fire, and let him talk as she listened with the tenderest kindly interest, sitting by him, and hemming a shirt for her dear little boy. Whenever Mrs. Rawdon wished to be particularly humble and virtuous, this little shirt used to come out of her work-box. It had got to be too small for Rawdon long before it was finished, though.

Well, Rebecca listened to him,[5] she talked to him, she sang to him, she coaxed him, and cuddled him, so that he found himself more and more glad every day to get back from the lawyer's at Gray's Inn,[6] to the blazing fire in Curzon Street—a gladness in which the men of law likewise participated, for Pitt's harangues were of the longest—and so that when he went away he felt quite a pang at departing. How pretty she looked kissing her hand to him from the carriage and waving her handkerchief when he had taken his place in the mail! She put the handkerchief to her eyes once. He pulled his sealskin cap over his, as the coach drove away, and, sinking back, he thought to himself how she respected him and how he deserved it, and how Rawdon was a foolish dull fellow who didn't half appreciate his wife: and how mum and stupid his own wife was compared to that brilliant little Becky. Becky had hinted every one of these things herself, perhaps, but so delicately and gently, that you hardly knew when or where. And, before they parted, it was agreed that the house in London should be redecorated for the next season, and that the brothers' families should meet again in the country at Christmas.

"I wish you could have got a little money out of him," Rawdon said to his wife moodily when the Baronet was gone. "I should like to give something to old Raggles, hanged if I shouldn't. It ain't right, you know, that the old fellow should be kept out of all his money. It may be inconvenient, and he might let to somebody else besides us, you know."

3. Revised edition reads: on
4. White wine from the Ermitage district, France.
5. Revised edition reads: Pitt,
6. One of the Inns of Court with residences, offices, and libraries for lawyers and legal societies.

"Tell him," said Becky, "that as soon as Sir Pitt's affairs are settled, everybody will be paid, and give him a little something on account. Here's a check that Pitt left for the boy," and she took from her bag and gave her husband a paper which his brother had handed over to her, on behalf of the little son and heir of the younger branch of the Crawleys.

The truth is, she had tried personally the ground on which her husband expressed a wish that she should venture—tried it ever so delicately, and found it unsafe. Even at a hint about embarrassments, Sir Pitt Crawley was off and alarmed. And he began a long speech, explaining how straitened he himself was in money matters; how the tenants would not pay; how his father's affairs, and the expenses attendant upon the demise of the old gentleman, had involved him; how he wanted to pay off incumbrances; and how the bankers and agents were overdrawn; and Pitt Crawley ended by making a compromise with his sister-in-law, and giving her a very small sum for the benefit of her little boy.

Pitt knew how poor his brother and his brother's family must be. It could not have escaped the notice of such a cool and experienced old diplomatist, that Rawdon's family had nothing to live upon, and that houses and carriages are not to be kept for nothing. He knew very well that he was the proprietor or appropriator of the money, which, according to all proper calculation, ought to have fallen to his younger brother, and he had, we may be sure, some secret pangs of remorse within him, which warned him that he ought to perform some act of justice, or, let us say, compensation, towards these disappointed relations. A just, decent man, not without brains, who said his prayers, and knew his catechism, and did his duty outwardly through life, he could not be otherwise than aware that something was due to his brother at his hands, and that morally he was Rawdon's debtor.

But, as one reads in the columns of the *Times* newspaper every now and then, queer announcements from the Chancellor of the Exchequer, acknowledging the receipt of £50 from A. B., or £10 from W. T., as conscience-money, on account of taxes due by the said A. B. or W. T., which payments the penitents beg the Right Honourable gentleman to acknowledge through the medium of the public press;—so is the Chancellor no doubt, and the reader likewise, always perfectly sure that the above-named A. B. and W. T. are only paying a very small instalment of what they really owe, and that the man who sends up a twenty pound-note has very likely hundreds or thousands more for which he ought to account. Such, at least, are my feelings, when I see A. B. or W. T.'s insufficient acts of repentance. And I have no doubt that Pitt Crawley's contrition, or kindness if you will, towards his younger brother, by whom he had so much profited, was only a very small dividend upon the capital sum in which he was indebted to Rawdon. Not everybody is willing to pay even so much. To part with money is a sacrifice beyond almost all men endowed with a sense of order. There is scarcely any man alive who does not think himself meritorious for giving his neighbour five pounds. Thriftless gives, not from a beneficent pleasure in giving, but from a lazy delight in spending. He would not deny himself one enjoyment; not his opera-stall, not his horse, not his dinner, not even the pleasure of giving Lazarus[7] the five pounds. Thrifty, who is good, wise, just, and owes no man a penny, turns from a beggar, haggles with a hackney-coachman, or denies a poor relation, and I doubt which is the most selfish of the two. Money has only a different value in the eyes of each.

So, in a word, Pitt Crawley thought he would do something for his brother, and then thought that he would think about it some other time.

And with regard to Becky, she was not a woman who expected too much from the generosity of her neighbours, and so was quite content with all that Pitt Crawley had done for her. She was acknowledged by the head of the family. If Pitt would not give her anything, he would get something for her some day. If she got no money from her brother-in-law, she got what was as good as money,—credit. Raggles was made rather easy in his mind by the spectacle of the union between the brothers, by a small payment on the spot, and by the promise of a much larger sum speedily to be assigned to him. And Rebecca told Miss Briggs, whose Christmas dividend upon the little sum lent by her, Becky paid with an air of candid joy, and as if her exchequer was brimming over with gold—Rebecca, we say, told Miss Briggs, in strict confidence, that she had conferred with Sir Pitt, who was famous as a financier, on Briggs's special behalf, as to the most profitable investment of Miss B.'s remaining capital; that Sir Pitt, after much consideration, had thought of a most safe and advantageous way in which Briggs could lay out her money; that, being especially interested in her as an attached friend of the late Miss Crawley, and of the whole family, and that long before he left town, he had recommended that she should be ready with the money at a moment's notice, so as to purchase at the most favourable opportunity the shares which Sir Pitt had in his eye. Poor Miss Briggs was very grateful for this mark of Sir Pitt's attention—it came so unsolicited, she said, for she never should have thought of removing the money from the funds—and the delicacy enhanced the kindness of the office; and she promised to see her man of business immediately, and be ready with her little cash at the proper hour.

And this worthy woman was so grateful for the kindness of Rebecca in the matter, and for that of her generous benefactor, the Colonel, that she went out and spent a great part of her half year's dividend in the purchase of a black velvet coat for little Rawdon, who by the way was grown almost too big for black velvet now, and was of a size and age befitting him for the assumption of the virile jacket and pantaloons.

He was a fine open faced boy, with blue eyes and waving flaxen hair, sturdy in limb, but generous and soft in heart: fondly attaching himself to all who were good to him—to the pony—to Lord Southdown, who gave him the horse—(he used to blush and glow all over when he saw that kind young nobleman)—to the groom who had charge of the pony—to Molly, the cook, who crammed him with ghost stories at night, and with good things from the dinner—to Briggs,

7. Beggar who ate crumbs from the table of Dives. Luke 16.19–31.

whom he plagued and laughed at—and to his father especially, whose attachment towards the lad was curious too to witness. Here, as he grew to be about eight years old, his attachments may be said to have ended. The beautiful mother-vision had faded away after a while. During near two years she had scarcely spoken to the child. She disliked him. He had the measles and the hooping-cough. He bored her. One day when he was standing at the landing-place, having crept down from the upper regions, attracted by the sound of his mother's voice, who was singing to Lord Steyne, the drawing-room door opening suddenly, discovered the little spy, who but a moment before had been rapt in delight, and listening to the music.

His mother came out and struck him violently a couple of boxes on the ear. He heard a laugh from the Marquis in the inner room, (who was amused by this free and artless exhibition of Becky's temper,) and fled down below to his friends of the kitchen, bursting in an agony of grief.

"It is not because it hurts me," little Rawdon gasped out—"only—only"—sobs and tears wound up the sentence in a storm. It was the little boy's heart that was bleeding. "Why mayn't I hear her singing? Why don't she ever sing to me—as she does to that bald-headed man with the large teeth?" He gasped out at various intervals these exclamations of rage and grief. The cook looked at the housemaid: the housemaid looked knowingly at the footman—the awful kitchen inquisition which sits in judgment in every house, and knows everything,—sate on Rebecca at that moment.

After this incident, the mother's dislike increased to hatred; the consciousness that the child was in the house was a reproach and a pain to her. His very sight annoyed her. Fear, doubt, and resistance sprang up, too, in the boy's own bosom. They were separated from that day of the boxes on the ear.

Lord Steyne also heartily misliked the boy. When they met by mischance, he made sarcastic bows or remarks to the child, or glared at him with savage-looking eyes. Rawdon used to stare him in the face, and double his little fists in return. He knew his enemy; and this gentleman, of all who came to the house, was the one who angered him most. One day the footman found him squaring his fists at Lord Steyne's hat in the hall. The footman told the circumstance as a good joke to Lord Steyne's coachman; that officer imparted it to Lord Steyne's gentleman, and to the servants' hall in general. And very soon afterwards, when Mrs. Rawdon Crawley made her appearance at Gaunt House, the porter who unbarred the gates, the servants of all uniforms in the hall, the functionaries in white waistcoats, who bawled out from landing to landing the names of Colonel and Mrs. Rawdon Crawley, knew about her, or fancied they did. The man who brought her refreshment and stood behind her chair, had talked her character over with the large gentleman in motley-coloured clothes at his side. Bon Dieu! it is awful, that servants' inquisition! You see a woman in a great party in a splendid saloon, surrounded by faithful admirers, distributing sparkling glances, dressed to perfection, curled, rouged, smiling and happy:—Discovery walks respectfully up to her, in the shape of a huge powdered man with large calves and a tray of ices—with Calumny (which is as fatal as truth)—behind him, in the shape of the hulking fellow carrying the wafer-biscuits. Madam, your secret will be talked over by those men at their club at the public-house to night. Jeames will tell Chawls his notions about you over their pipes and pewter beer-pots. Some people ought to have mutes for servants in Vanity Fair—mutes who could not write. If you are guilty: tremble. That fellow behind your chair may be a Janissary with a bow-string[8] in his plush breeches pocket. If you are not guilty have a care of appearances: which are as ruinous as guilt.

"Was Rebecca guilty or not?" the Vehmgericht[9] of the servants' hall had pronounced against her.

And, I shame to say, she would not have got credit had they not believed her to be guilty. It was the sight of the Marquis of Steyne's carriage-lamps at her door, contemplated by Raggles, burning in the blackness of midnight, "that kep him up," as he afterwards said; that, even more than Rebecca's arts and coaxings.

And so—guiltless very likely—she was writhing and pushing onward towards what they call "a position in society," and the servants were pointing at her as lost and ruined. So you see Molly the housemaid of a morning, watching a spider in the door-post lay his thread and laboriously crawl up it, until, tired of the sport, she raises her broom and sweeps away the thread and the artificer.

A day or two before Christmas, Becky, her husband and her son made ready and went to pass the holydays at the seat of their ancestors at Queen's Crawley. Becky would have liked to leave the little brat behind, and would but[1] for Lady Jane's urgent invitations to the youngster; and the symptoms of revolt and discontent which Rawdon manifested at her neglect of her son. "He's the finest boy in England," the father said, in a tone of reproach to her, "and you don't seem to care for him, Becky, as much as you do for your spaniel. He shan't bother you much: at home he will be away from you in the nursery, and he shall go outside on the coach with me."

"Where you go yourself because you want to smoke those filthy cigars," replied Mrs. Rawdon.

"I remember when you liked 'em though," answered the husband.

Becky laughed: she was almost always good-humoured. "That was when I was on my promotion, Goosey," she said. "Take Rawdon outside with you, and give him a cigar too if you like."

Rawdon did not warm his little son for the winter's journey in this way, but he and Briggs wrapped up the child in shawls and comforters, and he was hoisted respectfully on to the roof of the coach in the dark morning, under the lamps of the White Horse Cellar:[2] and with no small delight he watched the dawn rise, and made his first journey to the place which his father still called home. It was a journey of infinite pleasure to the boy, to whom the incidents of the road afforded endless interest; his father answering to him all questions connected with it, and telling him who lived in the great white house

8. A sultan's bodyguard prepared to punish on the spot.
9. Secret tribunals in medieval Westphalia (Germany) described in Sir Walter Scott's *Anne of Geierstein* (1829).
1. Revised edition reads: would have done so but
2. No. 90, Fetter Street, starting place for coaches to the west.

The arrival at Queen's Crawley

to the right, and whom the park belonged to. His mother, inside the vehicle with her maid and her furs, her wrappers, and her scent bottles, made such a to-do that you would have thought she never had been in a stage coach before—much less, that she had been turned out of this very one to make room for a paying passenger on a certain journey performed some half-score years ago.

It was dark again when little Rawdon was wakened up to enter his uncle's carriage at Mudbury, and he sate and looked out of it wondering as the great iron gates flew open, and at the white trunks of the limes as they swept by, until they stopped, at length, before the light windows of the Hall, which were blazing and comfortable with Christmas welcome. The hall-door was flung open—a big fire was burning in the great old fire-place—a carpet was down over the chequered black flags—"It's the old Turkey one that used to be in the Ladies' Gallery," thought Rebecca, and the next instant was kissing Lady Jane.

She and Sir Pitt performed the same salute with great gravity: but Rawdon having been smoking, hung back rather from his sister-in-law, whose two children came up to their cousin; and, while Matilda held out her hand and kissed him, Pitt Binkie Southdown, the son and heir, stood aloof rather, and examined him as a little dog does a big dog.

Then the kind hostess conducted her guests to the snug apartments blazing with cheerful fires. Then the young ladies came and knocked at Mrs. Rawdon's door, under the pretence that they were desirous to be useful, but in reality to have the pleasure of inspecting the contents of her band and bonnet-boxes, and her dresses which, though black, were of the newest London fashion. And they told her how much the Hall was changed for the better, and how old Lady Southdown was gone, and how Pitt was taking his station in the country, as became a Crawley in fact. Then the great dinner-bell having rung, the family assembled at dinner, at which meal Rawdon Junior was placed by his aunt, the good-natured lady of the house; Sir Pitt being uncommonly attentive to his sister-in-law at his own right hand.

Little Rawdon exhibited a fine appetite, and showed a gentleman-like behaviour.

"I like to dine here," he said to his aunt when he had completed his meal, at the conclusion of which, and after a decent grace by Sir Pitt, the young son and heir was introduced, and was perched on a high chair by the baronet's side, while the daughter took possession of the place and the little wine-glass prepared for her near her mother. "I like to dine here," said Rawdon Minor, looking up at his relation's kind face.

"Why?" said the good Lady Jane.

"I dine in the kitchen when I am at home," replied Rawdon Minor, "or else with Briggs." But Becky was so engaged with the baronet, her host, pouring out a flood of compliments and delights and raptures, and admiring young Pitt Binkie, whom she declared to be the most beautiful, intelligent, noble looking little creature, and so like his father, that she did not hear the remarks of her own flesh and blood at the other end of the broad shining table.

As a guest, and it being the first night of his arrival, Rawdon the Second was allowed to sit up until the hour when tea being over, and a great gilt book being laid on the table before Sir Pitt, all the domestics of the family streamed in, and Sir Pitt read prayers. It was the first time the poor little boy had ever witnessed or heard of such a ceremonial.

The house had been much improved even since the Baronet's brief reign, and was pronounced by Becky to be perfect, charming, delightful, when she surveyed it in his company. As for little Rawdon, who examined it with the children for his guides, it seemed to him a perfect palace of enchantment and wonder. There were long galleries, and ancient state-bedrooms, there were pictures and old china, and armour. There were the rooms in which Grandpapa died, and by which the children walked with terrified looks. "Who was Grandpapa?" he asked; and they told him how he used to be very old, and used to be wheeled about in a garden-chair, and they showed him the garden-chair one day rotting in the outhouse in which it had lain since the old gentleman had been wheeled away yonder to the church, of which the spire was glittering over the park elms.

The brothers had good occupation for several mornings in examining the improvements which had been effected by Sir Pitt's genius and economy. And as they walked or rode, and looked at them, they could talk without too much boring each other. And Pitt took care to tell Rawdon what a heavy outlay of money these improvements had occasioned; and that a man of landed and funded property was often very hard pressed for twenty pounds. "There is that new lodge gate," said Pitt, pointing to it humbly with the bamboo cane, "I can no more pay for it before the dividends in January than I can fly."

"I can lend you, Pitt, till then," Rawdon answered rather ruefully; and they went in and looked at the restored lodge, where the family arms were just new scraped in stone; and where old Mrs. Lock, for the first time these many long years, had tight doors, sound roofs, and whole windows.

## *Chapter XLV.*

### BETWEEN HAMPSHIRE AND LONDON.

SIR PITT CRAWLEY had done more than repair fences and restore dilapidated lodges on the Queen's Crawley estate. Like a wise man he had set to work to rebuild the injured popularity of his house, and stop up the gaps and ruins in which his name had been left by his disreputable and thriftless old predecessor. He was elected for the borough speedily after his father's demise; a magistrate, a member of parliament, a county magnate and representative of an ancient family, he made it his duty to show himself before the Hampshire public, subscribed handsomely to the county charities, called assiduously upon all the county folks, and laid himself out in a word to take that position in Hampshire, and in the Empire afterwards, to which he thought his prodigious talents justly entitled him. Lady Jane was instructed to be friendly with the Fuddlestones, and the Wapshots, and the other famous baronets, their neighbours. Their carriages might frequently be seen in the Queen's Crawley avenue now; they dined pretty frequently at the Hall (where the cookery was so good, that it was clear Lady Jane very seldom had a hand in it), and in return Pitt and his wife most energetically dined out in all sorts of weather, and at all sorts of distances. For though Pitt did not care for joviality, being a frigid man of poor health and appetite, yet he considered that to be hospitable and condescending was quite incumbent on his station, and every time that he got a headache from too long an after-dinner sitting, he felt that he was a martyr to duty. He talked about crops, corn-laws, politics, with the best country gentlemen. He (who had been formerly inclined to be a sad freethinker on these points) entered into poaching and game preserving with ardour. He didn't hunt: he wasn't a hunting man: he was a man of books and peaceful habits: but he thought that the breed of horses must be kept up in the country, and that the breed of foxes must therefore be looked to, and for his part, if his friend, Sir Huddlestone Fuddlestone liked to draw his country,[1] and meet as of old the F. hounds used to do at Queen's Crawley, he should be happy to see him there, and the gentlemen of the Fuddlestone hunt. And to Lady Southdown's dismay too he became orthodox in his tendencies every day: gave up preaching in public and attending meeting-houses; went stoutly to Church: called on the Bishop, and all the Clergy at Winchester; and made no objection when the Venerable Archdeacon Trumper asked for a game of whist. What pangs must have been those of Lady Southdown, and what an utter cast-away she must have thought her son-in-law for permitting such

1. To hunt.

a godless diversion! and when, on the return of the family from an oratorio at Winchester, the Baronet announced to the young ladies that he should next year very probably take them to the county balls. They worshipped him for his kindness. Lady Jane was only too obedient, and perhaps glad herself to go. The Dowager wrote off the direst descriptions of her daughter's worldly behaviour to the authoress of the "Washerwoman of Finchley Common" at the Cape; and her house in Brighton being about this time unoccupied, returned to that watering-place, her absence being not very much deplored by her children. We may suppose, too, that Rebecca, on paying a second visit to Queen's Crawley, did not feel particularly grieved at the absence of the lady of the medicine-chest; though she wrote a Christmas letter to her ladyship, in which she respectfully recalled herself to Lady Southdown's recollection, spoke with gratitude of the delight which her ladyship's conversation had given her on the former visit, dilated on the kindness with which her ladyship had treated her in sickness, and declared that everything at Queen's Crawley reminded her of her absent friend.

A great part of the altered demeanour and popularity of Sir Pitt Crawley might have been traced to the counsels of that astute little lady of Curzon Street. "*You* remain a baronet—you consent to be a mere country gentleman," she said to him, while he had been her guest in London. "No, Sir Pitt Crawley, I know you better. I know your talents and your ambition. You fancy you hide them both: but you can conceal neither from me. I showed Lord Steyne your pamphlet on malt. He was familiar with it: and said it was in the opinion of the whole Cabinet the most masterly thing that had appeared on the subject. The Ministry has its eye upon you, and I know what you want. You want to distinguish yourself in Parliament; every one says you are the finest speaker in England (for your speeches at Oxford are still remembered). You want to be Member for the County, where with your own vote and your borough at your back, you can command anything. And you want to be Baron Crawley of Queen's Crawley,[2] and will be before you die. I saw it all. I could read your heart, Sir Pitt. If I had a husband who possessed your intellect as he does your name, I sometimes think I should not be unworthy of him—but—but I am your kinswoman now," she added with a laugh. "Poor little penniless I have got a little interest—and who knows, perhaps the mouse may be able to aid the lion."[3]

Pitt Crawley was amazed and enraptured with her speech. "How that woman comprehends me!" he said. "I never could get Jane to read three pages of the malt-pamphlet. *She* has no idea that I have commanding talents or secret ambition. So they remember my speaking at Oxford, do they? The rascals! now that I represent my borough and may sit for the county, they begin to recollect me! Why, Lord Steyne cut me at the levee last year: they are beginning to find out that Pitt Crawley is some one at last. Yes, the man was always the same whom these people neglected: it was only the opportunity that

2. An advance to the next rank of English nobility would make him eligible for the House of Lords.
3. As in Aesop's fable in which the mouse released the lion from a net.

was wanting, and I will show them now that I can speak and act as well as write. Achilles did not declare himself until they gave him the sword.[4] I hold it now, and the world shall yet hear of Pitt Crawley."

Therefore it was that this roguish diplomatist had grown so hospitable; that he was so civil to oratorios and hospitals; so kind to Deans and Chapters;[5] so generous in giving and accepting dinners; so uncommonly gracious to farmers on market-days; and so much interested about county business; and that the Christmas at the Hall was the gayest which had been known there for many a long day.

On Christmas day a great family gathering took place. All the Crawleys from the Rectory came to dine. Rebecca was as frank and fond of Mrs. Bute, as if the other had never been her enemy,[6] affectionately interested in the dear girls, and surprised at the progress which they had made in music since her time: and insisted upon encoring one of the duets out of the great song-books which Jim, grumbling, had been forced to bring under his arm from the Rectory. Mrs. Bute, perforce, was obliged to adopt a decent demeanour towards the little adventuress—of course being free to discourse with her daughters afterwards about the absurd respect with which Sir Pitt treated his sister-in-law. But Jim, who had sate next to her at dinner, declared she was a trump: and one and all of the Rector's family agreed that the little Rawdon was a fine boy. They respected a possible baronet in the boy, between whom and the title there was only the little sickly pale Pitt Binkie.

The children were very good friends. Pitt Binkie was too little a dog for such a big dog as Rawdon to play with: and Matilda being only a girl, of course not fit companion for a young gentleman who was near eight years old, and going into jackets very soon. He took the command of this small party at once—the little girl and the little boy following him about with great reverence at such times as he condescended to sport with them. His happiness and pleasure in the country were extreme. The kitchen-garden pleased him hugely, the flowers moderately, but the pigeons and the poultry, and the stables when he was allowed to visit them, were delightful objects to him. He resisted being kissed by the Miss Crawleys: but he allowed Lady Jane sometimes to embrace him: and it was by her side that he liked to sit when the signal to retire to the drawing-room being given, the ladies left the gentlemen to their claret—by her side rather than by his mother. For Rebecca seeing that tenderness was the fashion, called Rawdon to her one evening, and stooped down and kissed him in the presence of all the ladies.

He looked her full in the face after the operation, trembling and turning very red, as his wont was when moved. "You never kiss me at home, Mamma," he said; at which there was a general silence and consternation, and a by no means pleasant look in Becky's eyes.

4. To declare in the sense of revealing himself. Achilles, disguised as a girl among the daughters of Lycomedes to avoid going to war, revealed himself by preferring arms to jewels when they were offered by Ulysses, who was disguised as a merchant.
5. In a collegiate or cathedral church, the dean is the head of a chapter, a group of churchmen (canons) living at the church.
6. Revised edition reads: enemy: she was

Rawdon was fond of his sister-in-law, for her regard for his son. Lady Jane and Becky did not get on *quite* so well at this visit as on occasion of the former one, when the Colonel's wife was bent upon pleasing. Those two speeches of the child struck rather a chill. Perhaps Sir Pitt was rather too attentive to her.

But Rawdon, as became his age and size, was fonder of the society of the men than of the women; and never wearied of accompanying his sire to the stables, whither the Colonel retired to smoke his cigar—Jim, the Rector's son, sometimes joining his cousin in that and other amusements. He and the Baronet's keeper were very close friends, their mutual taste for "dawgs" bringing them much together. On one day, Mr. James, the Colonel, and Horn, the keeper, went and shot pheasants, taking little Rawdon with them. On another most blissful morning, these four gentlemen partook of the amusement of rat-hunting in a barn, than which sport Rawdon as yet had never seen anything so[7] noble. They stopped up the ends of certain drains in the barn, into the other openings of which ferrets were inserted; and then stood silently aloof with uplifted stakes in their hands, and an anxious little terrier (Mr. James's celebrated "dawg" Forceps, indeed,) scarcely breathing from excitement, listening motionless on three legs, to the faint squeaking of the rats below. Desperately bold at last, the persecuted animals bolted[8] above-ground: the terrier accounted for one, the keeper for another, Rawdon, from flurry and excitement missed his rat, but on the other hand he half-murdered a ferret.

But the greatest day of all was that on which Sir Huddlestone Fuddlestone's hounds met upon the lawn at Queen's Crawley.

That was a famous sight for little Rawdon. At half-past ten, Tom Moody, Sir Huddlestone Fuddlestone's huntsman, is[9] seen trotting up the avenue, followed by the noble pack of hounds in a compact body—the rear being brought up by the two whips clad in stained scarlet frocks—light hard-featured lads on well-bred lean horses, possessing marvellous dexterity in casting the points of their long heavy whips at the thinnest part of any dog's skin who dares to straggle from the main body, or to take the slightest notice, or even so much as wink at the hares and rabbits starting under their noses.

Next comes boy Jack, Tom Moody's son, who weighs five stone,[1] measures eight-and-forty inches, and will never be any bigger. He is perched on a large raw-boned hunter, half-covered by a capacious saddle. This animal is Sir Huddlestone Fuddlestone's favourite horse—the Nob. Other horses, ridden by other small boys, arrive from time to time, awaiting their masters, who will come cantering on anon.

7. Revised edition reads: more
8. First printing reads: sneaked
9. In a copy of the first edition exhibited at "A *Punch* 150th Anniversary Exhibition" in 1991, there are penciled in several suggested corrections, including "bolted" for "sneaked" two paragraphs above, and "Many" for the sentence about the arrival of hunters three paragraphs below, both adopted in the second printing. Among other suggestions, not adopted, is one here: "is seen" to "was seen". The suggested corrections are in an unknown hand.
1. A stone is fourteen pounds.

Tom Moody rides up to the door of the Hall, where he is welcomed by the butler, who offers him drink, which he declines. He and his pack then draw off into a sheltered corner of the lawn, where the dogs roll on the grass, and play or growl angrily at one another, ever and anon breaking out into furious fight speedily to be quelled by Tom's voice, unmatched at rating, or the snaky thongs of the whips.

Many[2] young gentlemen canter up on thorough-bred hacks spatterdashed to the knee,[3] and enter the house to drink cherry-brandy and pay their respects to the ladies, or more modest and sportsmanlike, divest themselves of their mud-boots, exchange their hacks for their hunters, and warm their blood by a preliminary gallop round the lawn. Then they collect round the pack in the corner, and talk with Tom Moody of past sport and the merits of Sniveller and Diamond, and of the state of the country and of the wretched breed of foxes.

Sir Huddlestone presently appears mounted on a clever cob,[4] and rides up to the Hall, where he enters and does the civil thing by the ladies, after which, being a man of few words, he proceeds to business. The hounds are drawn up to the Hall-door and little Rawdon descends amongst them, excited yet half alarmed by the caresses which they bestow upon him, at the thumps he receives from their waving tails, and at their canine bickerings, scarcely restrained by Tom Moody's tongue and lash.

Meanwhile, Sir Huddlestone has hoisted himself unwieldily on the Nob: "Let's try Sowster's Spinney, Tom," says the Baronet, "Farmer Mangle tells me there are two foxes in it." Tom blows his horn and trots off, followed by the pack, by the whips, by the young gents from Winchester, by the farmers of the neighbourhood, by the labourers of the parish on foot, with whom the day is a great holiday; Sir Huddlestone bringing up the rear with Colonel Crawley, and the whole cortège[5] disappears down the avenue.

The Reverend Bute Crawley (who has been too modest to appear at the public meet before his nephew's windows), and whom Tom Moody remembers forty years back a slender divine riding the wildest horses, jumping the widest brooks, and larking over the newest gates in the country,—his Reverence, we say, happens to trot out from the Rectory Lane on his powerful black horse, just as Sir Huddlestone passes; he joins the worthy baronet. Hounds and horsemen disappear, and little Rawdon remains on the door-steps, wondering and happy.

During the progress of this memorable holiday, little Rawdon, if he had got no special liking for his uncle, always awful and cold, and locked up in his study plunged in justice-business and surrounded by bailiffs and farmers—has gained the good graces of his married and maiden aunts, of the two little folks of the Hall, and of Jim of the Rectory, whom Sir Pitt is encouraging to pay his addresses to one

2. First printing reads: Hunters arrived, from time to time, in charge of boys of the boy Jack species—the
3. Wearing protective spats or leg coverings. Hunters are the horses for hunting. Hacks are riding horses.
4. Short, stocky horse.
5. Procession.

of the young ladies, with an understanding doubtless that he shall be presented to the living when it shall be vacated by his fox-hunting old sire. Jim has given up that sport himself and confines himself to a little harmless duck or snipe shooting, or a little quiet trifling with the rats during the Christmas holidays, after which he will return to the University and try and not be plucked, once more. He has already eschewed green coats, red neckcloths, and other worldly ornaments, and is preparing himself for a change in his condition. In this cheap and thrifty way Sir Pitt tries to pay off his debt to his family.

Also before this merry Christmas was over, the Baronet had screwed up courage enough to give his brother another draft on his bankers and for no less a sum than a hundred pounds, an act which caused Sir Pitt cruel pangs at first, but which made him glow afterwards to think himself one of the most generous of men. Rawdon and his son went away with the utmost heaviness of heart. Becky and the ladies parted with some alacrity, however: and our friend returned to London to commence those avocations with which we find her occupied when this chapter begins. Under her care the Crawley House in Great Gaunt Street was quite rejuvenescent, and ready for the reception of Sir Pitt and his family, when the Baronet came to London to attend his duties in Parliament, and to assume that position in the country for which his vast genius fitted him.

For the first session, this profound dissembler hid his projects and never opened his lips but to present a petition from Mudbury. But he attended assiduously in his place, and learned thoroughly the routine and business of the house. At home he gave himself up to the perusal of Blue Books,[6] to the alarm and wonder of Lady Jane, who thought he was killing himself by late hours and intense application. And he made acquaintance with the ministers, and the chiefs of his party, determining to rank as one of them before many years were over.

Lady Jane's sweetness and kindness had inspired Rebecca with such a contempt for her ladyship as the little woman found no small difficulty in concealing. That sort of goodness and simplicity which Lady Jane possessed, annoyed our friend Becky, and it was impossible for her at times not to show, or to let the other divine her scorn. Her presence, too, rendered Lady Jane uneasy. Her husband talked constantly with Becky. Signs of intelligence seemed to pass between them: and Pitt spoke with her on subjects on which he never thought of discoursing with Lady Jane. The latter did not understand them to be sure, but it was mortifying to remain silent; still more mortifying to know that you had nothing to say, and hear that little audacious Mrs. Rawdon dashing on from subject to subject, with a word for every man, and a joke always pat; and to sit in one's own house alone, by the fireside, and watching all the men round your rival.

In the country, when Lady Jane was telling stories to the children, who clustered about her knees, (little Rawdon into the bargain, who was very fond of her)—and Becky came into the room, sneering, with green scornful eyes, poor Lady Jane grew silent under those baleful

6. Official reports of Parliament and the Privy Council, so-called for their invariable paper covers.

glances. Her simple little fancies shrank away tremulously, as fairies in the story-books, before a superior bad angel. She could not go on, although Rebecca, with the smallest inflection of sarcasm in her voice, besought her to continue that charming story. And on her side, gentle thoughts and simple pleasures were odious to Mrs. Becky, they discorded with her; she hated people for liking them; she spurned children and children-lovers. "I have no taste for bread and butter," she would say, when caricaturing Lady Jane and her ways to my Lord Steyne.

"No more has a certain person for holy water," his lordship replied with a bow and a grin, and a great jarring laugh afterwards.

So these two ladies did not see much of each other except upon those occasions, when the younger brother's wife, having an object to gain from the other, frequented her. They my-loved and my-deared each other assiduously, but kept apart generally: whereas Sir Pitt, in the midst of his multiplied avocations, found daily time to see his sister-in-law.

On the occasion of his first Speaker's dinner, Sir Pitt took the opportunity of appearing before his sister-in-law in his uniform—that old diplomatic suit which he had worn when attaché to the Pumpernickel legation.

Becky complimented him upon that dress, and admired him almost as much as his own wife and children, to whom he displayed himself before he set out. She said that it was only the thorough-bred gentleman that[7] could wear the Court suit with advantage: it was only your men of ancient race whom the *culotte courte*[8] became. Pitt looked down with complacency at his legs, which had not, in truth, much more symmetry or swell than the lean Court sword which dangled by his side: looked down at his legs and thought in his heart that he was killing.

When he was gone, Mrs. Becky made a caricature of his figure, which she showed to Lord Steyne when he arrived. His lordship carried off the sketch, delighted with the accuracy of the resemblance. He had done Sir Pitt Crawley the honour to meet him at Mrs. Becky's house, and had been most gracious to the new baronet and member. Pitt was struck too by the deference with which the great Peer treated his sister-in-law, by her ease and sprightliness in the conversation, and by the delight with which the other men of the party listened to her talk. Lord Steyne made no doubt but that the baronet had only commenced his career in public life, and expected rather anxiously to hear him as an orator; as they were neighbours (for Great Gaunt Street leads into Gaunt Square, whereof Gaunt House, as everybody knows, forms one side) my lord hoped that as soon as Lady Steyne arrived in London she would have the honour of making the acquaintance of Lady Crawley. He left a card upon his neighbour in the course of a day or two: his neighbour whom he had, as his predecessor, never thought fit to notice[9] though they had lived near each other for near a century past.

In the midst of these intrigues and fine parties and wise and brilliant personages Rawdon felt himself more and more isolated every day. He was allowed to go to the club more: to dine abroad with bachelor friends: to come and go when he liked, without any questions being asked. And he and Rawdon the younger many a time would walk to Gaunt Street, and sit with the lady and the children there while Sir Pitt was closeted with Rebecca, on his way to the House, or on his return from it.

The ex-Colonel would sit for hours in his brother's house very silent, and thinking and doing as little as possible. He was glad to be employed of an errand: to go and make inquiries about a horse or a servant: or to carve the roast mutton for the dinner of the children. He was beat and cowed into laziness and submission. Dalilah[1] had imprisoned him and cut his hair off, too.[2] The bold and reckless young blood of ten years back was subjugated, and was turned into a torpid, submissive, middle-aged, stout gentleman.

7. Revised edition reads: who
8. Knee breeches.
9. This passage appears to mean that neither Steyne nor his predecessor in the past century had ever thought to call on his neighbor. The revision in 1853 is worse; it seems to mean that Steyne had never thought of calling on the former Sir Pitt, though they had been neighbors for nearly a century. Revised edition reads: two; having never thought fit to notice his predecessor
1. First printing reads: submission, and Dalilah
2. When Delilah cut Samson's hair, the symbol of his vow, he lost his strength and was blinded and imprisoned by the Philistines. Judges 16.

And poor Lady Jane was aware that Rebecca had captivated her husband: although she and Mrs. Rawdon my-deared and my-loved each other every day they met.

## *Chapter XLVI.*

### STRUGGLES AND TRIALS.

UR friends at Brompton were meanwhile passing their Christmas after their fashion, and in a manner by no means too cheerful.

Out of the hundred pounds a year, which was about the amount of her income, the widow Osborne had been in the habit of giving up nearly three-fourths to her father and mother, for the expenses of herself and her little boy. With £120 more, supplied by Jos., this family of four people, attended by a single Irish servant who also did for Clapp and his wife, might manage to live in decent comfort through the year, and hold up their heads yet, and be able to give a friend a dish of tea still, after the storms and disappointments of their early life. Sedley still maintained his ascendancy over the family of Mr. Clapp, his ex-clerk. Clapp remembered the time when, sitting on the edge of the chair, he tossed off a bumper to the health of 'Mrs. S——, Miss Emmy, and Mr. Joseph in India,' at the merchant's rich table in Russell Square. Time magnified the splendour of those recollections in the honest clerk's bosom. Every time he[1] came up from the kitchen-parlour to the drawing-room, and partook of tea or gin-and-water with Mr. Sedley, he would say, "This was not what you was accustomed to once, Sir," and as gravely and reverentially drink the health of the ladies as he had done in the days of their utmost prosperity. He thought Miss 'Melia's playing the divinest music ever performed, and her the finest lady. He never would sit down before Sedley at the club even, nor would he have[2] that gentleman's character abused by any member of the society. He had seen the first men in London shaking hands with Mr. S——; he said, "He'd known him in times when Rothschild might be seen on Change with him any day, and he owed him personally everythink."

1. Revised edition reads: Whenever he
2. Revised edition reads: hear

Clapp, with the best of characters and hand-writings, had been able very soon after his master's disaster to find other employment for himself. "Such a little fish as me can swim in any bucket," he used to remark, and a member of the house from which old Sedley had seceded was very glad to make use of Mr. Clapp's services, and to reward them with a comfortable salary. In fine, all Sedley's wealthy friends had dropped off one by one, and this poor ex-dependent still remained faithfully attached to him.

Out of the small residue of her income, which Amelia kept back for herself, the widow had need of all the thrift and care possible in order to enable her to keep her darling boy dressed in such a manner as became George Osborne's son, and to defray the expenses of the little school to which, after much misgiving and reluctance, and many secret pangs and fears on her own part, she had been induced to send the lad. She had sate up of nights conning lessons and spelling over crabbed grammars and geography books in order to teach them to Georgy. She had worked even at the Latin accidence,[3] fondly hoping that she might be capable of instructing him in that language. To part with him all day: to send him out to the mercy of a schoolmaster's cane and his schoolfellows' roughness, was almost like weaning him over again, to that weak mother, so tremulous and full of sensibility. He, for his part, rushed off to the school with the utmost happiness. He was longing for the change. That childish gladness wounded his mother, who was herself so grieved to part with him. She would rather have had him more sorry, she thought: and then was deeply repentant within herself, for daring to be so selfish as to wish her own son to be unhappy.

Georgy made great progress in the school, which was kept by a friend of his mother's constant admirer, the Rev. Mr. Binney. He brought home numberless prizes and testimonials of ability. He told his mother countless stories every night about his school-companions: and what a fine fellow Lyons was, and what a sneak Sniffin was: and how Steel's father actually supplied the meat for the establishment, whereas Golding's mother came in a carriage to fetch him every Saturday: and how Neat had straps to his trowsers,—might he have straps? and how Bull Major was so strong (though only in Eutropius)[4] that it was believed he could lick the Usher, Mr. Ward himself. So Amelia learned to know every one of the boys in that school as well as Georgy himself: and of nights she used to help him in his exercises and puzzle her little head over his lessons as eagerly as if she was herself going in the morning into the presence of the master. Once, after a certain combat with Master Smith, George came home to his mother with a black eye, and bragged prodigiously to his parent and his delighted old grandfather about his valour in the fight, in which, if the truth was known, he did not behave with particular heroism, and in which he decidedly had the worst. But Amelia has never forgiven that Smith to this day, though he is now a peaceful apothecary near Leicester Square.

3. Accents, inflections.
4. Flavius Eutropius (fourth century A.D.), author of *Epitome of Roman History*, a standard school textbook. It marks Bull Major's stage in school.

In these quiet labours and harmless cares the gentle widow's life was passing away, a silver hair or two marking the progress of time on her head, and a line deepening ever so little on her fair forehead. She used to smile at these marks of time. "What matters it," she asked, "for an old woman like me?" All she hoped for was to live to see her son great, famous, and glorious, as he deserved to be. She kept his copy-books, his drawings, and compositions, and showed them about in her little circle, as if they were miracles of genius. She confided some of these specimens to Miss Dobbin: to show them to Miss Osborne, George's aunt, to show them to Mr. Osborne himself—to make that old man repent of his cruelty and ill-feeling towards him who was gone. All her husband's faults and foibles she had buried in the grave with him: she only remembered the lover, who had married her at all sacrifices: the noble husband so brave and beautiful, in whose arms she had hung on the morning when he had gone away to fight, and die gloriously for his king. From heaven the hero must be smiling down upon that paragon of a boy whom he had left to comfort and console her.

We have seen how one of George's grandfathers (Mr. Osborne), in his easy chair in Russell Square, daily grew more violent and moody, and how his daughter, with her fine carriage, and her fine horses, and her name on half the public charity-lists of the town, was a lonely, miserable, persecuted old maid. She thought again and again of the beautiful little boy, her brother's son, whom she had seen. She longed to be allowed to drive in the fine carriage to the house in which he lived: and she used to look out day after day as she took her solitary drive in the Park, in hopes that she might see him. Her sister, the banker's lady, occasionally condescended to pay her old home and companion a visit in Russell Square. She brought a couple of sickly children attended by a prim nurse, and in a faint genteel giggling tone cackled to her sister about her fine acquaintance, and how her little Frederic was the image of Lord Claud Lollypop, and her sweet Maria had been noticed by the Baroness as they were driving in their donkey-chaise at Roehampton. She urged her to make her papa do something for the darlings. Frederic she had determined should go into the Guards; and if they made an elder son of him (and Mr. Bullock was positively ruining and pinching himself to death to buy land), how was the darling girl to be provided for? "I expect *you,* dear," Mrs. Bullock would say, "for, of course my share of our Papa's property must go to the head of the house, you know. Dear Rhoda Macmull will disengage[5] the whole of the Castletoddy property as soon as poor dear Lord Castletoddy dies, who is quite epileptic; and little Macduff Macmull will be Viscount Castletoddy. Both the Mr. Bludyers of Mincing Lane have settled their fortunes on Fanny Bludyer's little boy. My darling Frederic must positively be an eldest son; and—and do ask Papa to bring us back his account in Lombard Street, will you, dear? It doesn't look well, his going to Stumpy and Rowdy's."[6] After which kind of speeches, in which

5. To free from financial obligation.
6. Both words are puns. To stump is to pay and to render penniless; rowdy indicates money and disrepute.

fashion and the main chance were blended together, and after a kiss, which was like the contact of an oyster—Mrs. Frederic Bullock would gather her starched nurslings, and simper back into her carriage.

Every visit which this leader of *ton*[7] paid to her family was more unlucky for her. Her father paid more money into Stumpy and Rowdy's. Her patronage became more and more insufferable. The poor widow in the little cottage at Brompton, guarding her treasure there, little knew how eagerly some people coveted it.

On that night when Jane Osborne had told her father that she had seen his grandson, the old man had made her no reply: but he had shown no anger—and had bade her good night on going himself to his room in rather a kindly voice. And he must have meditated on what she said, and have made some inquiries of the Dobbin family regarding her visit; for a fortnight after it took place, he asked her where was her little French watch and chain she used to wear?

"I bought it with my money, Sir," she said in a great fright.

"Go and order another like it, or a better if you can get it," said the old gentleman, and lapsed again into silence.

Of late, the Miss Dobbins more than once repeated their entreaties to Amelia, to allow George to visit them. His aunt had shown her inclination; perhaps his grandfather himself, they hinted, might be disposed to be reconciled to him. Surely, Amelia could not refuse such advantageous chances for the boy. Nor could she: but she acceded to their overtures with a very heavy and suspicious heart, was always uneasy during the child's absence from her, and welcomed him back as if he was rescued out of some danger. He brought back money and toys, at which the widow looked with alarm and jealousy: she asked him always if he had seen any gentleman—"Only old Sir William, who drove him about in the four-wheeled chaise, and Mr. Dobbin, who arrived on the beautiful bay horse in the afternoon—in the green coat and pink neck-cloth, with the gold-headed whip, who promised to show him the Tower of London, and take him out with the Surrey hounds." At last, he said, "There *was* an old gentleman, with thick eye-brows and a broad hat, and large chain and seals. He came one day as the coachman was lunging Georgy round the lawn on the gray pony. He looked at me very much. He shook very much. I said 'My name is Norval'[8] after dinner. My aunt began to cry. She is always crying." Such was George's report on that night.

Then Amelia knew that the boy had seen his grandfather: and looked out feverishly for a proposal which she was sure would follow, and which came, in fact, in a few days afterwards. Mr. Osborne formally offered to take the boy, and make him heir to the fortune which he had intended that his father should inherit. He would make Mrs. George Osborne an allowance, such as to assure her a decent competency. If Mrs. George Osborne proposed to marry again, as Mr. O. heard was her intention, he would not withdraw that allowance. But it must be understood, that the child would live entirely with his grandfather in Russell Square, or at whatever other place Mr. O.

7. Fashion.
8. From John Home's romantic tragedy *Douglas* (1756), a common recitation piece. Norval's father's "constant cares were to increase his store / And keep his only son at home."

should select; and that he would be occasionally permitted to see Mrs. George Osborne at her own residence. This message was brought or read to her in a letter one day, when her mother was from home, and her father absent as usual, in the City.

She was never seen angry but twice or thrice in her life, and it was in one of these moods that Mr. Osborne's attorney had the fortune to behold her. She rose up trembling and flushing very much as soon as, after reading the letter, Mr. Poe handed it to her, and she tore the paper into a hundred fragments, which she trod on. "I marry again!—I take money to part from my child! Who dares insult me by proposing such a thing? Tell Mr. Osborne it is a cowardly letter, Sir—a cowardly letter—I will not answer it. I wish you good morning, Sir—and she bowed me out of the room like a tragedy Queen," said the lawyer who told the story.

Her parents never remarked her agitation on that day, and she never told them of the interview. They had their own affairs to interest them, affairs which deeply interested this innocent and unconscious lady. The old gentleman, her father, was always dabbling in speculation. We have seen how the Wine Company and the Coal Company had failed him. But, prowling about the City always eagerly and restlessly still, he lighted upon some other scheme, of which he thought so well that he embarked in it in spite of the remonstrances of Mr. Clapp, to whom indeed he never dared to tell how far he had engaged himself in it. And as it was always Mr. Sedley's maxim not to talk about money matters before women, they had no inkling of the misfortunes that were in store for them until the unhappy old gentleman was forced to make gradual confessions.

The bills of the little household, which had been settled weekly, first fell into arrear. The remittances had not arrived from India, Mr. Sedley told his wife with a disturbed face. As she had paid her bills very regularly hitherto, one or two of the tradesmen to whom the poor lady was obliged to go round asking for time were very angry at a delay, to which they were perfectly used from more irregular customers. Emmy's contribution, paid over cheerfully without any questions, kept the little company in half rations however. And the first six months passed away pretty easily: old Sedley still keeping up with the notion that his shares must rise, and that all would be well.

No sixty pounds, however, came to help the household at the end of the half year; and it fell deeper and deeper into trouble—Mrs. Sedley, who was growing infirm and was much shaken, remained silent or wept a great deal with Mrs. Clapp in the kitchen. The butcher was particularly surly: the grocer insolent—once or twice little Georgy had grumbled about the dinners: and Amelia, who still would have been satisfied with a slice of bread for her own dinner, could not but perceive that her son was neglected, and purchased little things out of her private purse to keep the boy in health.

At last they told her, or told her such a garbled story as people in difficulties tell. One day, her own money having been received, and Amelia about to pay it over: she who had kept an account of the moneys expended by her, proposed to keep a certain portion back out of her dividend, having contracted engagements for a new suit for Georgy.

Then it came out that Jos's remittances were not paid; that the house was in difficulties which Amelia ought to have seen before, her mother said, but she cared for nothing or nobody except Georgy. At this she passed all of her money across the table without a word to her mother, and returned to her room to cry her eyes out. She had a great access of sensibility too that day, when obliged to go and countermand the clothes, the darling clothes on which she had set her heart for Christmas day, and the cut and fashion of which she had arranged in many conversations with a small milliner, her friend.

Hardest of all, she had to break the matter to Georgy, who made a loud outcry. Every body had new clothes at Christmas. The others would laugh at him. He *would* have new clothes. She had promised them to him. The poor widow had only kisses to give him. She darned the old suit in tears. She cast about among her little ornaments to see could she sell any thing to procure the desired novelties? There was her India shawl that Dobbin had sent her. She remembered in former days going with her mother to a fine India shop on Ludgate Hill, where the ladies had all sorts of dealings and bargains in these articles. Her cheeks flushed and her eyes shone with pleasure as she thought of this resource, and she kissed away George to school in the morning, smiling brightly after him. The boy felt there was good news in her look.

Packing up her shawl in a handkerchief, (another of the gifts of the good Major,) she hid them under her cloak, and walked flushed and eager all the way to Ludgate Hill, tripping along by the Park wall, and running over the crossings, so that many a man turned as she hurried by him, and looked after her rosy pretty face.[9] She calculated how she should spend the proceeds of her shawl: how, besides the clothes, she would buy the books that he longed for, and pay his half-year's schooling; and how she would buy a cloak for her father instead of that old great-coat which he wore. She was not mistaken as to the value of the Major's gift. It was a very fine and beautiful web: and the merchant made a very good bargain when he gave her twenty guineas for her shawl.

She ran on amazed and flurried with her riches to Darton's shop in St. Paul's Church Yard, and there purchased the "Parent's Assistant," and the "Sandford and Merton"[1] Georgy longed for, and got into the coach there with her parcel, and went home exulting. And she pleased herself by writing in the fly-leaf in her neatest little hand, "George Osborne, A Christmas gift from his affectionate mother." The books are extant to this day, with the fair delicate superscription.

She was going from her own room with the books in her hand to place them on George's table, where he might find them on his return from school; when in the passage, she and her mother met.

9. The Sedleys' cottage in Fulham Road, south and west of Hyde Park, is over three miles from Ludgate Hill leading up to St. Paul's Cathedral.

1. The first, by Maria Edgeworth, is a six-volume collection of stories for children; the second, by Thomas Day, is a tale contrasting the rich and objectionable Merton with the poor and virtuous Sandford.

The gilt bindings of the seven handsome little volumes caught the old lady's eye.

"What are those?" she said.

"Some books for Georgy," Amelia replied, blushing[2]—"I—I promised them to him at Christmas."

"Books!" cried the elder lady indignantly, "Books, when the whole house wants bread! Books, when to keep you and your son in luxury, and your dear father out of gaol, I've sold every trinket I had, the India shawl from my back—even down to the very spoons, that our tradesmen mightn't insult us, and that Mr. Clapp, which indeed he is justly entitled, being not a hard landlord, and a civil man, and a father, might have his rent. O Amelia! you break my heart with your books, and that boy of yours, whom you are ruining, though part with him you will not. O Amelia, may God send you a more dutiful child than I have had. There's Jos deserts his father in his old age: and there's George, who might be provided for, and who might be rich, going to school like a lord, with a gold watch and chain round his neck—while my dear, dear old man is without a sh—shilling." Hysteric sobs and cries ended Mrs. Sedley's speech—it echoed through every room in the small house, whereof the other female inmates heard every word of the colloquy.

"O mother, mother!" cried the poor Amelia in reply. "You told me nothing—I—I promised him the books. I—I only sold my shawl this morning. Take the money—take everything"—and with quivering hands she took out her silver, and her sovereigns—her precious golden sovereigns, which she thrust into the hands of her mother, whence they overflowed and tumbled, rolling down the stairs.

And then she went into her room, and sank down in despair and utter misery. She saw it all now. Her selfishness was sacrificing the boy. But for her he might have wealth, station, education, and his father's place, which the elder George had forfeited for her sake. She had but to speak the words, and her father was restored to competency: and the boy raised to fortune. O what a conviction it was to that tender and stricken heart!

2. Revised edition omits: blushing

*Number 14* *Feb. 1848*

## *Chapter XLVII.*

### GAUNT HOUSE.

LL the world knows that Lord Steyne's town palace stands in Gaunt-square, out of which Great Gaunt-street leads, whither we first conducted Rebecca, in the time of the departed Sir Pitt Crawley. Peering over the railings and through the black trees into the garden of the Square, you see a few miserable governesses with wan-faced pupils wandering round and round it, and round the dreary grass-plot in the centre of which rises the statue of Lord Gaunt, who fought at Minden,[1] in a three-tailed wig, and otherwise habited like a Roman Emperor. Gaunt House occupies nearly a side of the Square. The remaining three sides are composed of mansions that have passed away into Dowagerism;—tall, dark houses, with window-frames of stone, or picked out of a lighter red. Little light seems to be behind those lean, comfortless casements now: and hospitality to have passed away from those doors as much as the laced lacqueys and link-boys of old times, who used to put out their torches in the blank iron extinguishers that still flank the lamps over the steps. Brass plates have penetrated into the Square—Doctors, the Diddlesex bank Western Branch—the English and European Reunion, &c.—it has a dreary look—nor is my Lord Steyne's palace less dreary. All I have ever seen of it is the vast wall in front, with the rustic columns at the great gate, through which an old porter peers sometimes with a fat and gloomy red face—and over the wall the garret and bed-room windows, and the chimneys, out of which there seldom comes any smoke now. For the present Lord Steyne lives at Naples, preferring the view of the Bay and Capri and Vesuvius, to the dreary aspect of the wall in Gaunt-square.

A few score of yards down New Gaunt-street, and leading into Gaunt-mews indeed, is a little modest back door, which you would not remark from that of any of the other stables. But many a little close carriage has stopped at that door, as my informant (little Tom Eaves, who knows everything, and who showed me the place) told me. "The Prince and Perdita have been in and out of that door, Sir," he has often told me; "Marianne Clarke has entered it with the Duke of ——.[2] It conducts to the famous *petits appartements*[3] of Lord Steyne—one, Sir, fitted up all in ivory and white satin, another in

1. A battle in Germany, August 1759, where the British defeated the French.
2. The Prince and Perdita: the prince regent and Mary Robinson, an actress who was his mistress briefly in 1789. Her nickname derives from her role as Perdita in Shakespeare's *The Winter's Tale*. Mary Anne Clarke was mistress of Frederick, duke of York, George's brother.
3. Private rooms.

ebony and black velvet; there is a little banqueting-room taken from Sallust's house at Pompeii, and painted by Cosway[4]—a little private kitchen, in which every saucepan was silver, and all the spits were gold. It was there that Egalité Orleans[5] roasted partridges on the night when he and the Marquis of Steyne won a hundred thousand from a great personage at Hombre. Half of the money went to the French Revolution, half to purchase Lord Gaunt's Marquisate and Garter—and the remainder—" but it forms no part of our scheme to tell what became of the remainder, for every shilling of which, and a great deal more, little Tom Eaves, who knows everybody's affairs, is ready to account.

Besides his town palace, the Marquis had castles and palaces in various quarters of the three kingdoms, whereof the descriptions may be found in the Road-books[6]—Castle Strongbow, with its woods, on the Shannon shore; Gaunt Castle, in Carmarthenshire, where Richard II. was taken prisoner[7]—Gauntly Hall in Yorkshire, where I have been informed there were two hundred silver teapots for the breakfasts of the guests of the house, with everything to correspond in splendour; and Stillbrook in Hampshire, which was my lord's farm, a humble place of residence, of which we all remember the wonderful furniture which was sold at my lord's demise by a late celebrated auctioneer.

The Marchioness of Steyne was of the renowned and ancient family of the Caerlyons, Marquises of Camelot, who have preserved the old faith ever since the conversion of the venerable Druid, their first ancestor, and whose pedigree goes far beyond the date of the arrival of King Brute in these islands. Pendragon is the title of the eldest son of the house. The sons have been called Arthurs, Uthers, and Caradocs, from immemorial time.[8] Their heads have fallen in many a loyal conspiracy. Elizabeth chopped off the head of the Arthur of her day, who had been Chamberlain to Philip and Mary, and carried letters between the Queen of Scots and her uncles the Guises.[9] A cadet of the house was an officer of the great Duke, and distinguished in the famous Saint Bartholomew conspiracy.[1] During the

4. Gaius Sallustius Crispus (86–35 B.C.), Roman historian and senator whose house Thackeray described in a lecture as a place of worldly pleasures. Richard Cosway (1740–1821), popular painter of miniatures for the aristocracy. His wife, Maria Haddfield, also a painter and musician, conducted many fashionable parties in her home.

5. Philippe Egalité, duke of Orléans (father of Louis Philippe, who later became king of France), visited England in 1789–90, spending time with the prince of Wales. He supported the French Revolution and abdicated his title in 1792, but he was beheaded in 1793.

6. Descriptions of the roads of a district or county and of local sights and coach schedules.

7. Actually Richard was captured (1399) at Flint Castle on the northern coast of Wales; Carmarthenshire is on the south coast; Gaunt Castle is fictional.

8. This fictional family tree evokes Carleon, where King Arthur was crowned; Uther Pendragon, Arthur's father; Caradoc, king of West Britain who was taken to Rome in 51 A.D. King Brute was the ledengary founder and namer of Britain.

9. Philip II of Spain (1556–98) revived the Spanish Inquisition and married Mary Tudor, who ruled England from 1553 to 1558 as Mary I, known as Bloody Mary. Elizabeth I, a Protestant, ruled from 1858 to 1603, reversing Mary I's laws concerning religion. The queen of Scots, Mary Stuart, was married to Francis II, briefly king of France, whose power was wielded by Mary's uncles, Lieutenant General Francis, second duke de Guise (the great duke), and his brothers Cardinal Louis and Cardinal Charles de Lorraine. Mary herself sought refuge in England in 1568; she was confined there until 1587, when she was beheaded.

1. Catherine de Medici (1519–89), apparently supported by Charles IX, king of France (ruled

whole of Mary's confinement, the house of Camelot conspired in her behalf. It was as much injured by its charges in fitting out an armament against the Spaniards, during the time of the Armada,[2] as by the fines and confiscations levied on it by Elizabeth for harbouring of priests, obstinate recusancy,[3] and Popish misdoings. A recreant of James's time was momentarily perverted from his religion by the arguments of that great theologian,[4] and the fortunes of the family somewhat restored by his timely weakness. But the Earl of Camelot, of the reign of Charles, returned to the old creed of his family, and they continued to fight for it, and ruin themselves for it, as long as there was a Stuart left to head or to instigate a rebellion.[5]

Lady Mary Caerlyon was brought up at a Parisian convent, the Dauphiness Marie Antoinette[6] was her godmother. In the pride of her beauty she had been married—sold, it was said—to Lord Gaunt, then at Paris, who won vast sums from the lady's brother at some of Philip of Orleans's banquets. The Earl of Gaunt's famous duel with the Count de la Marche,[7] of the Grey Musqueteers, was attributed by common report to the pretensions of that officer (who had been a page, and remained a favourite of the Queen) to the hand of the beautiful Lady Mary Caerlyon. She was married to Lord Gaunt while the Count lay ill of his wound, and came to dwell at Gaunt House, and to figure for a short time in the splendid Court of the Prince of Wales. Fox had toasted her. Morris and Sheridan had written songs about her. Malmsbury had made her his best bow; Walpole had pronounced her charming; Devonshire[8] had been almost jealous of her; but she was scared by the wild pleasures and gaieties of the society into which she was flung, and after she had borne a couple of sons, shrank away into a life of devout seclusion. No wonder that my Lord Steyne, who liked pleasure and cheerfulness, was not often seen after their marriage, by the side of this trembling, silent, superstitious, unhappy lady.

The before-mentioned Tom Eaves, (who has no part in this history, except that he knew all the great folks in London, and the stories and mysteries of each family,) had further information regarding my lady Steyne, which may or may not be true. "The humiliations," Tom used to say, "which that woman has been made to undergo, in

1560–74), lured the Huguenots into a massacre on the eve of St. Barholomew's Day, August 23, 1572.

2. Philip II's failed naval assault on England in 1588.
3. Refers to the refusal of Roman Catholics to attend Church of England services during the reigns of Henry VIII and Elizabeth I.
4. James I, who ruled after Elizabeth, sponsored the King James Bible.
5. Charles I ruled 1625–49. He was beheaded in the Puritan Revolution. James II, the last reigning Stuart, abdicated in 1688. James Francis and Charles Edward, styled Pretenders, attempted to regain the throne for the Stuarts until 1746.
6. Marie Antoinette (1755–93) was married to the dauphin, heir apparent to the French throne, who became Louis XVI in 1774.
7. Fictional character who reappears disguised as a priest on the next page.
8. Fox: see chapter X. Charles Morris, a soldier, authored many political and other songs and was patronized by the prince regent. Like Sheridan (see chapter XXXIV), Morris was a political ally of Fox. James Harris, first earl of Malmsbury, was a famous and courtly diplomat. Horace Walpole, fourth earl of Orford, was a politician, wit, and author of *The Castle of Otronto*. Georgiana, wife of the fifth duke of Devonshire, was said to have purchased votes for Fox by allowing electorates to kiss her.

her own house, have been frightful; Lord Steyne has made her sit down to table with women with whom I would rather die than allow Mrs. Eaves to associate—with Lady Crackenbury, with Mrs. Chippenham, with Madame de la Cruchecassée, the French secretary's wife," (from every one of which ladies Tom Eaves—who would have sacrificed his wife for knowing them—was too glad to get a bow or a dinner), "with the *reigning favourite,* in a word. And do you suppose that that woman, of that family, who are as proud as the Bourbons, and to whom the Steynes are but lackeys, mushrooms of yesterday (for after all, they are *not* of the old Gaunts,[9] but of a minor and doubtful branch of the house); do you suppose, I say," (the reader must bear in mind that it is always Tom Eaves who speaks,) "that the Marchioness of Steyne, the haughtiest woman in England, would bend down to her husband so submissively, if there were not some cause? Pooh! I tell you there are *secret reasons.* I tell you, that in the emigration,[1] the Abbé de la Marche who was here and was employed in the Quiberoon business with Puisaye and Tinteniac,[2] was the same Colonel of Mousquetaires Gris with whom Steyne fought in the year '86—that he and the Marchioness met again: that it was after the Reverend Colonel was shot in Brittany, that Lady Steyne took to those extreme practices of devotion which she carries on now: for she is closeted with her director every day—she is at service at Spanish-place,[3] every morning, I've watched her there—that is, I've happened to be passing there—and depend on it there's a mystery in her case. People are not so unhappy unless they have something to repent of," added Tom Eaves with a knowing wag of his head; "and depend on it, that woman would not be so submissive as she is, if the Marquis had not some sword to hold over her."

So, if Mr. Eaves's information be correct, it is very likely that this lady in her high station, had to submit to many a private indignity, and to hide many secret griefs under a calm face. And let us, my brethren, who have not our names in the Red Book,[4] console ourselves by thinking comfortably how miserable our betters may be, and that Damocles, who sits on satin cushions, and is served on gold plate, has an awful sword hanging over his head in the shape of a bailiff, or an hereditary disease, or a family secret, which peeps out every now and then from the embroidered arras in a ghastly manner, and will be sure to drop one day or the other in the right place.[5]

In comparing, too, the poor man's situation with that of the great, there is (always according to Mr. Eaves) another great[6] source of comfort for the former. You who have little or no patrimony to bequeath

9. John of Gaunt, duke of Lancaster, father of Henry IV—the Prince Hal of Shakespeare's play; see two paragraphs below.
1. The aristocracy fled France in the Revolution of 1789.
2. Royalist leaders landed in Brittany at the swampy island of Quiberoon in a failed attempt to restore the monarchy in 1795.
3. At the Catholic chapel in the Spanish Embassy.
4. *Webster's Royal Red Book* (1847) listed the British nobility.
5. When Damocles envied his wealth and status, Dionysius of Syracuse placed him in the seat of honor under a sword dangling by a hair to give him a real sense of the position he envied.
6. Revised edition omits: great

or to inherit, may be on good terms with your father or your son, whereas the heir of a great prince, such as my Lord Steyne, must naturally be angry at being kept out of his kingdom, and eye the occupant of it with no very agreeable glances. "Take it as a rule," this sardonic old Eaves would say, "the fathers and elder sons of all great families hate each other. The Crown Prince is always in opposition to the crown or hankering after it. Shakspeare knew the world, my good Sir, and when he describes Prince Hal (from whose family the Gaunts pretend to be descended, though they are no more related to John of Gaunt than you are,) trying on his father's coronet, he gives you a natural description of all heirs-apparent. If you were heir to a dukedom and a thousand pounds a day, do you mean to say you would not wish for possession? Pooh! And it stands to reason that every great man, having experienced this feeling towards his father, must be aware that his son entertains it towards himself; and so they can't but be suspicious and hostile.

"Then again, as to the feeling of elder towards younger sons. My dear Sir, you ought to know that every elder brother looks upon the cadets of the house as his natural enemies who deprive him of so much ready money which ought to be his by right. I have often heard George Mac Turk, Lord Bajazet's[7] eldest son, say that if he had his will, when he came to the title, he would do what the sultans do, and clear the estate by chopping off all his younger brothers' heads at once; and so the case is, more or less, with them all. I tell you they are all Turks in their hearts. Pooh! Sir, they know the world." And here, haply, a great man coming up, Tom Eaves's hat would drop off his head, and he would rush forward with a bow and a grin, which showed that he knew the world too—in the Tomeavesian way, that is. And having laid out every shilling of his fortune on an annuity,[8] Tom could afford to bear no malice to his nephews and nieces, and to have no other feeling with regard to his betters, but a constant and generous desire to dine with them.

Between the Marchioness and the natural and tender regard of mother for children, there was that cruel barrier placed of difference of faith. The very love which she might feel for her sons, only served to render the timid and pious lady more fearful and unhappy. The gulph which separated them was fatal and impassable. She could not stretch her weak arms across it, or draw her children over to that side away from which her belief told her there was no safety. During the youth of his sons, Lord Steyne, who was a good scholar and amateur casuist, had no better sport in the evening after dinner in the country than in setting the boys' tutor, the Reverend Mr. Trail, (now my Lord Bishop of Ealing,)[9] on her ladyship's director, Father Mole, over their wine, and in putting Oxford

7. The name is taken from a fourteenth-century Ottoman sultan.
8. Probably a life annuity, where in exchange for an investment, a fixed sum is paid annually for life with no remainder—i.e., he will leave no inheritance.
9. Ealing has no bishop, but it used to belong to the grounds of the Palace of Fulham, the seat of the bishop of London.

against St. Acheul. He cried "Bravo, Latimer! Well said, Loyola!"[1] alternately; he promised Mole a bishopric if he would come over; and vowed he would use all his influence to get Trail a cardinal's hat if he would secede. Neither divine allowed himself to be conquered; and though the fond mother hoped that her youngest and favourite son would be reconciled to her church—his mother church—a sad and awful disappointment awaited the devout lady—a disappointment which seemed to be a judgment upon her for the sin of her marriage.

My Lord Gaunt married, as every person who frequents the Peerage knows, the Lady Blanche Thistlewood, a daughter of the noble house of Bareacres, before mentioned in this veracious history. A wing of Gaunt House was assigned to this couple; for the head of the family chose to govern it, and while he reigned to reign supreme: his son and heir, however, living little at home, disagreeing with his wife, borrowing upon post-obits such monies as he required beyond the very moderate sums which his father was disposed to allow him. The marquis knew every shilling of his son's debts. At his lamented

1. The prime function of Oxford was to produce ministers for the Church of England; St. Acheul is a Jesuit seminary in France. Hugh Latimer led English reform theology under Henry VIII and was burned at the stake under Mary I. St. Ignatius Loyola founded the Jesuit Order.

demise, he was found himself to be possessor of many of his heir's bonds, purchased for their benefit, and devised by his Lordship to the children of his younger son.

As, to my Lord Gaunt's dismay, and the chuckling delight of his natural enemy and father, the Lady Gaunt had no children—the Lord George Gaunt was desired to return from Vienna, where he was engaged in waltzing and diplomacy, and to contract a matrimonial alliance with the Honourable Joan, only daughter of John Johnes, First Baron Helvellyn, and head of the firm of Jones, Brown, and Robinson,[2] of Threadneedle Street, Bankers; from which union sprang several sons and daughters, whose doings do not appertain to this story.

The marriage at first was a happy and prosperous one. My Lord George Gaunt could not only read, but write pretty correctly. He spoke French with considerable fluency; and was one of the finest waltzers in Europe. With these talents, and his interest[3] at home, there was little doubt that his lordship would rise to the highest dignities in his profession. The lady, his wife, felt that courts were her sphere; and her wealth enabled her to receive splendidly in those continental towns whither her husband's diplomatic duties led him. There was talk of appointing him minister, and bets were laid at the Travellers'[4] that he would be ambassador ere long, when of a sudden, rumours arrived of the secretary's extraordinary behaviour. At a grand diplomatic dinner given by his chief, he had started up, and declared that a *pâté de foie gras* was poisoned. He went to a ball at the hotel of the Bavarian envoy, the Count de Springbock-Hohenlaufen, with his head shaved, and dressed as a Capuchin friar.[5] It was not a masked ball, as some folks wanted to persuade you. It was something queer, people whispered. His grandfather was so. It was in the family.

His wife and family returned to this country, and took up their abode at Gaunt House. Lord George gave up his post on the European continent, and was gazetted to Brazil. But people knew better; he never returned from that Brazil expedition—never died there—never lived there—never was there at all. He was nowhere: he was gone out altogether. "Brazil," said one gossip to another, with a grin—"Brazil is St. John's Wood.[6] Rio Janeiro is a cottage surrounded by four walls; and George Gaunt is accredited to a keeper, who has invested him with the order of the Straight Waistcoat." These are the kinds of epitaphs which men pass over one another in Vanity Fair.

2. The name evokes the same group suggested by Tom, Dick, and Harry. Douglas Jerrold wrote "The Lives of Brown, Jones, and Robinson" for *The New Monthly Magazine* (Sept.–Nov. 1837). Richard Doyle, who later illustrated Thackeray's *The Newcomes*, wrote an illustrated series for *Punch* in the 1840s titled "Brown, Jones, and Robinson." The Royal Exchange, Stock Exchange, and the Bank of England all faced Threadneedle Street.
3. Revised edition reads: interests
4. Club in Pall Mall, precurser to the Royal Geographical Society; membership was restricted to those who had been at least 500 miles from the British Isles.
5. Springbock-Hohenlaufen: literally, high-running antelope. Capuchin: a very strict order of Franciscans.
6. A still largely rural residential area of London west of Regent's Park, where, apparently, Steyne had a walled house and garden within which George was kept.

Twice or thrice in a week, in the earliest morning, the poor mother went for her sins and saw the poor invalid. Sometimes he laughed at her, (and his laughter was more pitiful than to hear him cry); sometimes she found the brilliant dandy diplomatist of the Congress of Vienna dragging about a child's toy, or nursing the keeper's baby's doll. Sometimes he knew her and Father Mole, her director and companion: oftener he forgot her, as he had done wife, children, love, ambition, vanity. But he remembered his dinner-hour, and used to cry if his wine-and-water was not strong enough.

It was the mysterious taint of the blood: the poor mother had brought it from her own ancient race. The evil had broken out once or twice in the father's family, long before Lady Steyne's sins had begun, or her fasts and tears and penances had been offered in their expiation. The pride of the race was struck down as the firstborn of Pharaoh.[7] The dark mark of fate and doom was on the threshold,—the tall old threshold surmounted by coronets and carved heraldry.

The absent lord's children meanwhile prattled and grew on quite unconscious that the doom was over them too.[8] First they talked of

7. In the last and worst of the ten plagues on Egypt before Moses led the Israelites into the wilderness, the firstborn son of all who did not observe the Passover by marking the lintel over the threshold was striken dead. Exodus 12.29.
8. The illustration is suggestive of the sword of Damocles.

their father, and devised plans against his return. Then the name of the living dead man was less frequently in their mouths—then not mentioned at all. But the stricken old grandmother trembled to think that these too were the inheritors of their father's shame as well as of his honours: and watched sickening for the day when the awful ancestral curse should come down on them.

This dark presentiment also haunted Lord Steyne. He tried to lay the horrid bed-side ghost in Red Seas of wine and jollity, and lost sight of it sometimes in the crowd and rout of his pleasures. But it always came back to him when alone, and seemed to grow more threatening with years. "I have taken your son," it said, "why not you? I may shut you up in a prison some day like your son George. I may tap you on the head to-morrow, and away go pleasure and honours, feasts and beauty, friends, flatterers, French cooks, fine horses and houses—in exchange for a prison, a keeper, and a straw mattrass like George Gaunt's." And then my lord would defy the ghost which threatened him: for he knew of a remedy by which he could baulk his enemy.

So there was splendour and wealth, but no great happiness perchance behind the tall carved portals of Gaunt House with its smoky coronets and ciphers.[9] The feasts there were of the grandest in London, but there was not over-much content therewith, except among the guests who sate at my lord's table. Had he not been so great a Prince very few possibly would have visited him: but in Vanity Fair the sins of very great personages are looked at indulgently. *"Nous régardons a deux fois"*[1] (as the French lady said) before we condemn a person of my lord's undoubted quality. Some notorious carpers and squeamish moralists might be sulky with Lord Steyne, but they were glad enough to come when he asked them.

"Lord Steyne is really too bad," Lady Slingstone said, "but everybody goes, and of course I shall see that my girls come to no harm." "His lordship is a man to whom I owe much, everything in life," said the Right Reverend Doctor Trail, thinking that the Archbishop was rather shaky; and Mrs. Trail and the young ladies would as soon have missed going to church as to one of his lordship's parties. "His morals are bad," said little Lord Southdown to his sister, who meekly expostulated, having heard terrific legends from her mamma with respect to the doings at Gaunt House; "but hang it, he's got the best dry Sillery[2] in Europe!" And as for Sir Pitt Crawley, Bart.—Sir Pitt that pattern of decorum, Sir Pitt who had led off at missionary meetings,—he never for one moment thought of not going too. "Where you see such persons as the Bishop of Ealing and the Countess of Slingstone, you may be pretty sure, Jane," the Baronet would say, "that *we* cannot be wrong. The great rank and station of Lord Steyne put him in a position to command people in our station in life. The Lord Lieutenant of a County, my dear, is a respectable man. Besides George Gaunt and I were intimate in early life: he was my junior when we were attachés at Pumpernickel together."

9. The shape of the coronet indicates rank; ciphers are monograms.
1. We consider twice.
2. Wine from the Sillery region in France.

In a word everybody went to wait upon this great man—everybody who was asked: as you the reader (do not say nay) or I the writer hereof would go if we had an invitation.

## *Chapter XLVIII.*

### IN WHICH THE READER IS INTRODUCED TO THE VERY BEST OF COMPANY.

AT[1] last Becky's kindness and attention to the chief of her husband's family, were destined to meet with an exceeding great reward; a reward which, though certainly somewhat unsubstantial, the little woman coveted with greater eagerness than more positive benefits. If she did not wish to lead a virtuous life, at least she desired to enjoy a character for virtue, and we know that no lady in the genteel world can possess this desideratum, until she has put on a train and feathers, and has been presented to her Sovereign at Court. From that august interview they come out stamped as honest women. The Lord Chamberlain gives them a certificate of virtue. And as dubious goods or letters are passed through an oven at quarantine, sprinkled with aromatic vinegar, and then pronounced clean—many a lady whose reputation would be doubtful otherwise and liable to give infection, passes through the wholesome ordeal of the Royal presence, and issues from it free from all taint.

It might be very well for my Lady Bareacres, my Lady Tufto, Mrs. Bute Crawley in the country, and other ladies who had come into contact with Mrs. Rawdon Crawley, to cry fie at the idea of the odious little adventuress making her curtsey before the Sovereign, and to declare, that if dear good Queen Charlotte[2] had been alive, *she* never would have admitted such an extremely ill-regulated personage into Her chaste drawing-room. But when we consider, that it was the First Gentleman in Europe in whose high presence Mrs. Rawdon passed her examination, and as it were, took her degree in reputation, it surely must be flat disloyalty to doubt any more about her

1. The initial depicts a statue of George IV, who became king in 1820. In this chapter he is referred to as Sovereign, the First Gentleman in Europe, the Premier Gentilhomme of his Kingdom, and the Star of Brunswick.
2. George IV's mother, wife of George III.

virtue. I, for my part, look back with love and awe to that Great Character in history. Ah, what a high and noble appreciation of Gentlemanhood there must have been in Vanity Fair, when that revered and august being was invested, by the universal acclaim of the refined and educated portion of this empire, with the title of Premier Gentilhomme of his Kingdom. Do you remember, dear M——, oh friend of my youth, how one blissful night five-and-twenty years since, the Hypocrite being acted, Elliston being manager, Dowton and Liston performers, two boys had leave from their loyal masters to go out from Slaughter House School[3] where they were educated, and to appear on Drury Lane stage, amongst a crowd which assembled there to greet the king. THE KING? There he was. Beef-eaters[4] were before the august box: the Marquis of Steyne (Lord of the Powder Closet,) and other great officers of state were behind the chair on which he sate, *He* sate—florid of face, portly of person, covered with orders, and in a rich curling head of hair—How we sang God save him! How the house rocked and shouted with that magnificent music. How they cheered, and cried, and waved handkerchiefs. Ladies wept: mothers clasped their children: some fainted with emotion. People were suffocated in the pit, shrieks and groans rising up amidst the writhing and shouting mass there of his people who were, and indeed showed themselves almost to be, ready to die for him. Yes, we saw him. Fate cannot deprive us of *that*. Others have seen Napoleon. Some few still exist who have beheld Frederick the Great, Doctor Johnson, Marie Antoinette,[5] &c.—be it our reasonable boast to our children, that we saw George the Good, the Magnificent, the Great.[6]

Well, there came a happy day in Mrs. Rawdon Crawley's existence when this angel was admitted into the paradise of a Court which she coveted: her sister-in-law acting as her god-mother. On the appointed day, Sir Pitt and his lady in their great family carriage (just newly built, and ready for the baronet's assumption of the office of High Sheriff of his county) drove up to the little house in Curzon Street, to the edification of Raggles who was watching from his greengrocer's shop, and saw fine plumes within, and enormous bunches of flowers in the breasts of the new livery-coats of the footmen.

Sir Pitt, in a glittering uniform, descended and went into Curzon Street, his sword between his legs. Little Rawdon stood with his face against the parlour window panes, smiling and nodding with all his might to his aunt in the carriage within; and presently Sir Pitt issued forth from the house again, leading forth a lady with grand feathers, covered in a white shawl, and holding up daintily a train of magnificent brocade. She stepped into the vehicle as if she were a princess and accustomed all her life to go to Court, smiling graciously on the

3. Isaac Bickerstaffe's *The Hypocrite* (1768) was performed before King George on December 1, 1823 (Tillotson). Robert Elliston, theater manager, William Dowton and John Liston, actors. "Slaughter House" was one of several nicknames for Thackeray's own school, Charterhouse.
4. Members of the sovereign's personal guard.
5. Frederick (of Prussia) died in 1786, Samuel Johnson in 1784, Marie Antoinette (wife of Louis XVI) in 1793.
6. These appellations for George IV are real, not Thackeray's satiric inventions.

footman at the door, and on Sir Pitt, who followed her into the carriage.

Then Rawdon followed in his old Guards' uniform, which had grown wofully shabby, and was much too tight. He was to have followed the procession, and waited upon his sovereign in a cab; but that his good-natured sister-in-law insisted that they should be a family party. The coach was large, the ladies not very big, they would hold their trains in their laps—finally, the four went fraternally together; and their carriage presently joined the line of loyal equipages which was making its way down Piccadilly and St. James's Street, towards the old brick palace,[7] where the Star of Brunswick[8] was in waiting to receive his nobles and gentlefolks.

Becky felt as if she could bless the people out of the carriage windows, so elated was she in spirit, and so strong a sense had she of the dignified position which she had at last attained in life. Even our Becky had her weaknesses, and as one often sees how men pride themselves upon excellencies which others are slow to perceive: how, for instance, Comus[9] firmly believes that he is the greatest tragic actor in England; how Brown, the famous novelist, longs to be considered, not a man of genius, but a man of fashion; while Robinson, the great lawyer, does not in the least care about his reputation in Westminster Hall,[1] but believes himself incomparable across country, and at a five-barred gate—so, to be, and to be thought, a respectable woman was Becky's aim in life, and she got up the genteel with amazing assiduity, readiness, and success. We have said, there were times when she believed herself to be a fine lady, and forgot that there was no money in the chest at home—duns round the gate, tradesmen to coax and wheedle—no ground to walk upon, in a word. And as she went to court in the carriage, the family carriage, she adopted a demeanour so grand, self-satisfied, deliberate, and imposing, that it made even Lady Jane laugh. She walked into the royal apartments with a toss of the head which would have befitted an empress, and I have no doubt had she been one, she would have become the character perfectly.

We are authorised to state that Mrs. Rawdon Crawley's *costume de cour*[2] on the occasion of her presentation to the Sovereign was of the most elegant and brilliant description. Some ladies we may have seen, we, who wear stars and cordons, and attend the St. James's assemblies, or we, who, in muddy boots, dawdle up and down Pall Mall, and peep into the coaches as they drive up with the great folks in their feathers—some ladies of fashion, I say, we may have seen, about two o'clock of the forenoon of a levee day, as the laced-jacketed band of the Life Guards are blowing triumphal marches seated on those prancing music-stools, their cream-coloured chargers—who are by no means lovely and enticing objects at that early period of noon.

7. St. James's Palace, no longer the Royal Mansion but still used for formal presentations, was made of brick with blue diapered decoration.
8. From 1815 to 1823, George IV, as prince regent and king, was also regent of the Duchy of Brunswick until Karl Brunswick-Oels reached his majority.
9. The name means "revelry."
1. Standing next to the Parliament Houses, it was the principal court in England until 1882.
2. Court dress.

A stout countess of sixty, *décolletée,*[3] painted, wrinkled, with rouge up to her drooping eyelids, and diamonds twinkling in her wig, is a wholesome and edifying, but not a pleasant sight. She has the faded look of a St. James's Street illumination, as it may be seen of an early morning, when half the lamps are out, and the others are blinking wanly, as if they were about to vanish like ghosts before the dawn. Such charms, as those of which we catch glimpses while her ladyship's carriage passes, should appear abroad at night alone. If even Cynthia[4] looks haggard of an afternoon as we may see her sometimes in the present winter season, with Phœbus[5] staring her out of countenance from the opposite side of the heavens, how much more can old Lady Castlemouldy keep her head up when the sun is shining full upon it through the chariot windows, and showing all the chinks and crannies with which time has marked her face? No. Drawing-rooms should be announced for November, or the first foggy day: or the elderly sultanas of our Vanity Fair should drive up in closed litters, descend in a covered way, and make their curtsey to the Sovereign under the protection of lamplight.

Our beloved Rebecca had no need, however, of any such a friendly halo to set off her beauty. Her complexion could bear any sunshine as yet; and her dress, though if you were to see it now, any present lady of Vanity Fair would pronounce it to be the most foolish and preposterous attire ever worn, was as handsome in her eyes and those of the public, some five-and-twenty years since, as the most brilliant costume of the most famous beauty of the present season. A score of years hence that, too, that milliner's wonder, will have passed into the domain of the absurd, along with all previous vanities. But we are wandering too much. Mrs. Rawdon's dress was pronounced to be charmante on the eventful day of her presentation. Even good little Lady Jane was forced to acknowledge this effect, as she looked at her kinswoman; and owned sorrowfully to herself that she was quite inferior in taste to Mrs. Becky.

She did not know how much care, thought, and genius Mrs. Rawdon had bestowed upon that garment. Rebecca had as good taste as any milliner in Europe, and such a clever way of doing things as Lady Jane little understood. The latter quickly spied out the magnificence of the brocade of Becky's train, and the splendour of the lace on her dress.

The brocade was an old remnant, Becky said; and as for the lace, it was a great bargain. She had had it these hundred years.

"My dear Mrs. Crawley, it must have cost a little fortune," Lady Jane said, looking down at her own lace, which was not nearly so good; and then examining the quality of the ancient brocade, which formed the material of Mrs. Rawdon's court dress, she felt inclined to say that she could not afford such fine clothing, but checked that speech, with an effort, as one uncharitable to her kinswoman.

And yet if Lady Jane had known all, I think even her kindly temper would have failed her. The fact is, when she was putting Sir Pitt's

3. Low-cut dress.
4. The moon.
5. The sun.

house in order, Mrs. Rawdon had found the lace and the brocade in old wardrobes, the property of the former ladies of the house, and had quietly carried the goods home, and had suited them to her own little person. Briggs saw her take them, asked no questions, told no stories; but I believe quite sympathised with her on this matter, and so would many another honest woman.

And the diamonds—"Where the doose did you get the diamonds, Becky?" said her husband, admiring some jewels which he had never seen before, and which sparkled in her ears and on her neck with brilliance and profusion.

Becky blushed a little, and looked at him hard for a moment. Pitt Crawley blushed a little too, and looked out of window. The fact is, he had given her a very small portion of the brilliants; a pretty diamond clasp, which confined a pearl necklace which she wore; and the Baronet had omitted to mention the circumstance to his lady.

Becky looked at her husband, and then at Sir Pitt, with an air of saucy triumph—as much as to say, "Shall I betray you?"

"Guess!" she said to her husband. "Why, you silly man," she continued, "where do you suppose I got them—all except the little clasp, which a dear friend of mine gave me long ago. I hired them, to be sure. I hired them at Mr. Polonius's, in Coventry-street.[6] You don't suppose that all the diamonds which go to Court belong to the owners; like those beautiful stones which Lady Jane has, and which are much handsomer than any which I have, I am certain."

"They are family jewels," said Sir Pitt, again looking uneasy. And in this family conversation the carriage rolled down the street, until its cargo was finally discharged at the gates of the palace where the Sovereign was sitting in state.

The diamonds, which had created Rawdon's admiration, never went back to Mr. Polonius, of Coventry-street, and that gentleman never applied for their restoration; but they retired into a little private repository, in an old desk, which Amelia Sedley had given her years and years ago, and in which Becky kept a number of useful and, perhaps, valuable things, about which her husband knew nothing. To know nothing, or little, is in the nature of some husbands. To hide, in the nature of how many women? O ladies! how many of you have surreptitious milliners' bills? How many of you have gowns and bracelets, which you daren't show, or which you wear trembling?—trembling, and coaxing with smiles the husband by your side, who does not know the new velvet gown from the old one, or the new bracelet from last year's, or has any notion that the ragged-looking yellow lace scarf cost forty guineas, and that Madame Bobinot is writing dunning letters every week for the money!

Thus Rawdon knew nothing about the brilliant diamond earrings, or the superb brilliant ornament which decorated the fair bosom of his lady; but Lord Steyne, who was in his place at court, as Lord of the Powder Closet, and one of the great dignitaries and illustrious defences of the throne of England, and came up with all his stars, garters, collars, and cordons, and paid particular attention to

6. A street of shops and entertainments from Piccadilly to Leicester Square.

the little woman, knew whence the jewels came, and who paid for them.

As he bowed over her he smiled, and quoted the hackneyed and beautiful lines, from the Rape of the Lock, about Belinda's diamonds, "which Jews might kiss and infidels adore."[7]

"But I hope your lordship is orthodox," said the little lady, with a toss of her head. And many ladies round about whispered and talked, and many gentlemen nodded and whispered, as they saw what marked attention the great nobleman was paying to the little adventuress.

What were the circumstances of the interview between Rebecca Crawley, née Sharp, and her Imperial Master, it does not become such a feeble and inexperienced pen as mine to attempt to relate. The dazzled eyes close before that Magnificent Idea. Loyal respect and decency tell even the imagination not to look too keenly and audaciously about the sacred audience-chamber, but to back away rapidly, silently, and respectfully, making profound bows out of the August Presence.

This may be said, that in all London there was no more loyal heart than Becky's after this interview. The name of her king was always on her lips, and he was proclaimed by her to be the most charming of men. She went to Colnaghi's[8] and ordered the finest portrait of him that art had produced, and credit would[9] supply. She chose that famous one in which the best of monarchs is represented in a frock-coat with a fur collar, and breeches and silk stockings, simpering on a sofa from under his curly brown wig. She had him painted in a brooch and wore it—indeed she amused and somewhat pestered her acquaintance with her perpetual talk about his urbanity and beauty. Who knows? Perhaps the little woman thought she might play the part of a Maintenon or a Pompadour.[1]

But the finest sport of all after her presentation was to hear her talk virtuously. She had a few female acquaintances, not, it must be owned, of the very highest reputation in Vanity Fair. But being made an honest woman of, so to speak, Becky would not consort any longer with these dubious ones, and cut Lady Crackenbury, when the latter nodded to her from her opera-box; and gave Mrs. Washington White the go-by in the Ring. "One must, my dear, show one is somebody;" she said. "One musn't be seen with doubtful people. I pity Lady Crackenbury from my heart; and Mrs. Washington White may be a very good-natured person. *You* may go and dine with them, as you like your rubber. But *I* mustn't, and won't; and you will have the goodness to tell Smith to say I am not at home when either of them calls."

The particulars of Becky's costume were in the newspapers—feathers, lappets,[2] superb diamonds, and all the rest. Mrs. Crackenbury read the paragraph in bitterness of spirit, and discoursed to

7. Canto II, line 8, of Alexander Pope's 1717 poem.
8. Print dealers. The print is from a portrait by Sir Thomas Lawrence, P.R.A., in the Wallace Collection.
9. Revised edition reads: could
1. Mistresses, respectively, of Louis XIV and Louis XV.
2. Headdress streamers.

her followers about the airs which that woman was giving herself. Mrs. Bute Crawley and her young ladies in the country had a copy of the Morning Post from town; and gave a vent to their honest indignation. "If you had been sandy-haired, green-eyed, and a French rope-dancer's daughter," Mrs. Bute said to her eldest girl (who, on the contrary, was a very swarthy, short, and snub-nosed young lady), "you might have had superb diamonds forsooth, and have been presented at court, by your cousin, the Lady Jane. But you're only a gentlewoman, my poor dear child. You have only some of the best blood in England in your veins, and good principles and piety for your portion. I, myself, the wife of a Baronet's younger brother, too, never thought of such a thing as going to court—nor would other people, if good Queen Charlotte had been alive." In this way the worthy Rectoress consoled herself; and her daughters sighed, and sate over the Peerage all night.

A few days after the famous presentation, another great and exceeding honour was vouchsafed to the virtuous Becky. Lady Steyne's carriage drove up to Mr. Rawdon Crawley's door, and the footman, instead of driving down the front of the house, as by his tremendous knocking he appeared to be inclined to do, relented, and only delivered in a couple of cards, on which were engraven the names of the Marchioness of Steyne and the Countess of Gaunt. If these bits of pasteboard had been beautiful pictures, or had had a hundred yards of Malines lace[3] rolled round them, worth twice the number of guineas, Becky could not have regarded them with more pleasure. You may be sure they occupied a conspicuous place in the china bowl on the drawing-room table, where Becky kept the cards of her visitors. Lord! lord! how poor Mrs. Washington White's card and Lady Crackenbury's card, which our little friend had been glad enough to get a few months back, and of which the silly little creature was rather proud once—Lord! lord! I say, how soon at the appearance of these grand court cards, did those poor little neglected deuces sink down to the bottom of the pack. Steyne! Bareacres, Johnes of Helvellyn! and Caerlyon of Camelot! we may be sure that Becky and Briggs looked out those august names in the Peerage, and followed the noble races up through all the ramifications of the family tree.

My Lord Steyne coming to call a couple of hours afterwards, and looking about him, and observing everything as was his wont, found his lady's cards already ranged as the trumps of Becky's hand, and grinned, as this old cynic always did at any naïve display of human weakness. Becky came down to him presently: whenever the dear girl expected his lordship, her toilette was prepared, her hair in perfect order, her mouchoirs,[4] aprons, scarfs, little morocco slippers, and other female gimcracks arranged, and she seated in some artless and agreeable posture ready to receive him—whenever she was surprised, of course, she had to fly to her apartment to take a rapid survey of matters in the glass, and to trip down again to wait upon the great peer.

3. Lace from Malines in Belgium.
4. Handkerchiefs.

She found him grinning over the bowl. She was discovered, and she blushed a little. "Thank you, Monseigneur," she said. "You see your ladies have been here. How good of you! I couldn't come before—I was in the kitchen making a pudding."

"I know you were, I saw you through the area-railings as I drove up," replied the old gentleman.

"You see everything," she replied.

"A few things, but not that, my pretty lady," he said good-naturedly. "You silly little fibster! I heard you in the room over head, where I have no doubt you were putting a little rouge on; you must give some of yours to my Lady Gaunt, whose complexion is quite preposterous; and I heard the bed-room door open, and then you came down stairs."

"Is it a crime to try and look my best when *you* come here?" answered Mrs. Rawdon plaintively, and she rubbed her cheek with her handkerchief as if to show there was no rouge at all, only genuine blushes and modesty in her case. About this who can tell? I know there is some rouge that won't come off on a pocket-handkerchief; and some so good that even tears will not disturb it.

"Well," said the old gentleman, twiddling round his wife's card, "you are bent upon becoming a fine lady. You pester my poor old life out to get you into the world. You won't be able to hold your own there, you silly little fool. You've got no money."

"You will get us a place," interposed Becky, as quick as possible.

"You've got no money, and you want to compete with those who have. You poor little earthenware pipkin, you want to swim down the stream along with the great copper kettles.[5] All women are alike. Everybody is striving for what is not worth the having! Gad! I dined with the King yesterday and we had neck of mutton and turnips. A dinner of herbs is better than a stalled ox very often.[6] You will go to Gaunt House. You give an old fellow no rest until you get there. It's not half so nice as here. You'll be bored there. I am. My wife is as gay as Lady Macbeth, and my daughters as cheerful as Regan and Goneril.[7] I daren't sleep in what they call my bed-room. The bed is like the baldaquin of St. Peter's,[8] and the pictures frighten me. I have a little brass bed in a dressing-room: and a little hair mattrass like an anchorite. I am an anchorite. Ho! ho! You'll be asked to dinner next week. And *gare aux femmes,*[9] look out and hold your own! How the women will bully you!" This was a very long speech for a man of few words like my Lord Steyne; nor was it the first which he had uttered for Becky's benefit on that day.

Briggs looked up from the work table at which she was seated in the farther room and gave a deep sigh as she heard the great Marquis speak so lightly of her sex.

5. In Aesop's fable, the earthenware pot refuses the company of the brass pot as they floated in the flood, for any contact would break and sink the earthen pot.
6. "Better is a dinner of herbs where love is, than a stalled ox and hatred therewith." Proverbs 15.17.
7. Greedy, ambitious daughters of King Lear.
8. The Bernini canopy on columns over the central altar in St. Peter's Basilica in Rome.
9. Look out for women.

"If you don't turn off that abominable sheep-dog,"[1] said Lord Steyne with a savage look over his shoulder at her, "I will have her poisoned."[2]

"I always give my dog dinner from my own plate," said Rebecca laughing mischievously; and having enjoyed for some time the discomfiture of my lord who hated poor Briggs for interrupting his tête-à-tête with the fair Colonel's wife—Mrs. Rawdon at length had pity upon her admirer, and calling to Briggs, praised the fineness of the weather to her, and bade her to take out the child for a walk.

"I can't send her away," Becky said presently after a pause, and in a very sad voice—Her eyes filled with tears as she spoke and she turned away her head.

"You owe her her wages? I suppose," said the Peer.

"Worse than that," said Becky still casting down her eyes—"I have ruined her—"

"Ruined her?—then why don't you turn her out?" the gentleman asked.

"Men do that," Becky answered bitterly. "Women are[3] not so bad as you. Last year when we were reduced to our last guinea she gave us every thing. She shall never leave me, until we are ruined utterly ourselves, which does not seem far off, or until[4] I can pay her the uttermost farthing."

"—— it how much is it?" said the Peer with an oath. And Becky, reflecting on the largeness of his means, mentioned not only the sum which she had borrowed from Miss Briggs but one of nearly double the amount.

This caused the Lord Steyne to break out in another brief and energetic expression of anger, at which Rebecca held down her head the more, and cried bitterly. "I could not help it. It was my only chance. I dare not tell my husband. He would kill me if I told him what I have done. I have kept it a secret from every body but you—and you forced it from me. Ah, what shall I do, Lord Steyne? for I am very, very unhappy!"

Lord Steyne made no reply except by beating the devil's tattoo,[5] and biting his nails. At last he clapt his hat on his head, and flung out of the room. Rebecca did not rise from her attitude of misery until the door slammed upon him, and his carriage whirled away. Then she rose up with the queerest expression of victorious mischief glittering in her green eyes. She burst out laughing once or twice to herself, as she sate at work; and sitting down to the piano, she rattled away a triumphant voluntary on the keys, which made the people pause under her window to listen to her brilliant music.

That night, there came two notes from Gaunt House for the little woman, the one containing a card of invitation from Lord and Lady Steyne to a dinner at Gaunt House next Friday: while the other en-

1. MS reads: <house> ↑sheep↓ dog
2. MS originally read: I will poison her.
3. MS originally read: answered sadly. I am
4. "we are ruined . . . or until" is interlined in the MS.
5. Drumming his fingers on the table.

Becky in Lombard Street

closed a slip of gray paper bearing Lord Steyne's signature and the address of Messrs. Jones, Brown, and Robinson, Lombard Street.

Rawdon heard Becky laughing in the night once or twice. It was only her delight at going to Gaunt House and facing the ladies there, she said, which amused her so. But the truth was, that she was occupied with a great number of other thoughts. Should she pay off old Briggs and give her her congé?[6] Should she astonish Raggles by settling his account? She turned over all these thoughts on her pillow and on the next day when Rawdon went out to pay his morning visit to the Club Mrs. Crawley (in a modest dress with a veil on)[7] whipped off in a hackney coach to the City: and being landed at Messrs. Jones & Robinson's bank, presented a document there to the authority at the desk, who in reply asked her "how she would take it?"

She gently[8] said she would take a hundred and fifty pounds in small notes and the remainder in one note: and passing through St. Paul's Church Yard stopped there and bought the handsomest black silk gown for Briggs which money could buy; and which with a kiss and the kindest speeches she presented to the simple old spinster.

Then she walked to Mr. Raggles, inquired about his children affectionately, and gave him fifty pounds on account. Then she went to the livery man from whom she jobbed her carriages and gratified him with a similar sum. "And I hope this will be a lesson to you, Spavin," she said, "and that on the next drawing room day my brother, Sir Pitt, will not be inconvenienced by being obliged to take four of us in his carriage to wait upon His Majesty, because my *own* carriage is not forthcoming." It appears there had been a difference on the last drawing room day. Hence the degradation which the Colonel had almost suffered, of being obliged to enter the presence of his Sovereign in a hack cab.

These arrangements concluded, Becky paid a visit up stairs to the before-mentioned desk which Amelia Sedley had given her years and years ago and which contained a number of useful and valuable little things: in which private museum she placed the one note which Messrs. Jones & Robinson's cashier had given her.

6. Dismissal.
7. The parenthetical remark is interlined in the MS, and for "modest" the MS reads: black
8. MS reads: modestly

## *Chapter XLIX.*

### IN WHICH WE ENJOY THREE COURSES AND A DESSERT.

When the ladies of Gaunt House[1] were at breakfast that morning, Lord Steyne (who took his chocolate in private, and seldom disturbed the females of his household, or saw them except upon public days, or when they crossed each other in the hall, or when from his pit-box at the Opera he surveyed them in their box on the grand tier)—His lordship, we say, appeared among the ladies and the children who were assembled over the tea and toast, and a battle royal ensued apropos of Rebecca.

"My Lady Steyne," he said, "I want to see the list for your dinner on Friday; and I want you, if you please, to write a card for Colonel and Mrs. Crawley."

"Blanche writes them," Lady Steyne said in a flutter. "Lady Gaunt writes them."

"I will not write to that person," Lady Gaunt said, a tall and stately lady, who looked up for an instant and then down again after she had spoken. It was not good to meet Lord Steyne's eyes for those who had offended him.

"Send the children out of the room. Go!" said he, pulling at the bell-rope. The urchins, always frightened before him, retired: their mother would have followed too. "Not you," he said. "You stop."

"My Lady Steyne," he said, "once more will you have the goodness to go to the desk, and write that card for your dinner on Friday?"

"My Lord, I will not be present at it," Lady Gaunt said; "I will go home."

"I wish you would, and stay there. You will find the bailiffs at Bareacres very pleasant company, and I shall be freed from lending money to your relations, and from your own damned tragedy airs. Who are you to give orders here? You have no money. You've got no brains. You were here to have children, and you have not had any. Gaunt's tired of you; and George's wife is the only person in the family who doesn't wish you were dead. Gaunt would marry again if you were."

1. Steyne's wife and two daughters-in-law. The elder is childless and is daughter of the Bareacres, who are totally mortgaged and in hock; the second brought money into the family and has children, though her husband is insane.

"I wish I were," her Ladyship answered, with tears and rage in her eyes.

"You, forsooth, must give yourself airs of virtue; while my wife, who is an immaculate saint, as everybody knows, and never did wrong in her life, has no objection to meet my young friend, Mrs. Crawley. My Lady Steyne knows that appearances are sometimes against the best of women; that lies are often told about the most innocent of them. Pray, Madam, shall I tell you some little anecdotes about my Lady Bareacres, your mamma?"

"You may strike me if you like, Sir, or hit any cruel blow," Lady Gaunt said. To see his wife and daughter suffering always put his Lordship into a good humour.

"My sweet Blanche," he said, "I am a gentleman, and never lay my hand upon a woman, save in the way of kindness. I only wish to correct little faults in your character. You women are too proud, and sadly lack humility, as Father Mole, I'm sure, would tell my Lady Steyne if he were here. You mustn't give yourselves airs: you must be meek and humble, my blessings. For all Lady Steyne knows, this calumniated, simple, good-humoured Mrs. Crawley, is quite innocent—even more innocent than herself. Her husband's character is not good, but it is as good as Bareacres', who has played a little and not payed a great deal, who cheated you out of the only legacy you ever had, and left you a pauper on my hands. And Mrs. Crawley is not very well born; but she is not worse than Fanny's illustrious ancestor, the first de la Jones."

"The money which I brought into the family, Sir," Lady George cried out——

"You purchased a contingent reversion[2] with it," the Marquis said, darkly. "If Gaunt dies, your husband may come to his honours; your little boys may inherit them, and who knows what besides? In the meanwhile, ladies, be as proud and virtuous as you like abroad, but don't give *me* any airs. As for Mrs. Crawley's character, I shan't demean myself, or that most spotless and perfectly irreproachable lady, by even hinting that it requires a defence. You will be pleased to receive her with the utmost cordiality, as you will receive all persons whom I present in this house. This house?" He broke out with a laugh. "Who is the master of it? and what is it? This Temple of Virtue belongs to me. And if I invite all Newgate or all Bedlam[3] here, by —— they shall be welcome."

After this vigorous allocution, to one of which sort Lord Steyne treated his "Hareem," whenever symptoms of insubordination appeared in his household, the crest-fallen women had nothing for it but to obey. Lady Gaunt wrote the invitation which his Lordship required, and she and her mother-in-law drove in person, and with bitter and humiliated hearts, to leave the cards on Mrs. Rawdon, the reception of which caused that innocent woman so much pleasure.

There were families in London who would have sacrificed a year's income to receive such an honour at the hands of those great ladies.

2. I.e., the chance that Lord Gaunt would die childless.
3. Newgate prison; Bethlehem Royal Hospital for the insane.

Mrs. Frederic Bullock, for instance, would have gone on her knees from Mayfair to Lombard Street, if Lady Steyne and Lady Gaunt had been waiting in the City to raise her up, and say, "Come to us next Friday,"—not to one of the great crushes, and grand balls of Gaunt House, whither everybody went, but to the sacred, unapproachable, mysterious, delicious entertainments, to be admitted to one of which was a privilege, and an honour, and a blessing indeed.

Severe, spotless, and beautiful, Lady Gaunt held the very highest rank in Vanity Fair. The distinguished courtesy with which Lord Steyne treated her, charmed everybody who witnessed his behaviour, caused the severest critics to admit how perfect a gentleman he was, and to own that his Lordship's heart at least was in the right place.

The Ladies of Gaunt House called Lady Bareacres into their aid, in order to repulse the common enemy. One of Lady Gaunt's carriages went to Hill Street for her Ladyship's mother, all whose equipages were in the hands of the bailiffs, whose very jewels and wardrobe, it was said, had been seized by those inexorable Israelites. Bareacres Castle was theirs, too, with all its costly pictures, furniture, and articles of vertù[4]—the magnificent Vandykes; the noble Reynolds' pictures; the Lawrence portraits, tawdry and beautiful, and, thirty years ago, deemed as precious as works of real genius; the matchless Dancing Nymph of Canova,[5] for which Lady Bareacres had sate in her youth—Lady Bareacres splendid then, and radiant in wealth, rank, and beauty—a toothless, bald, old woman now—a mere rag of a former robe of state. Her Lord, painted at the same time by Lawrence, as waving his sabre in front of Bareacres Castle, and clothed in his uniform of[6] Colonel of the Thistlewood Yeomanry, was a withered, old, lean man in a great coat and a Brutus wig:[7] slinking about Gray's Inn of mornings chiefly, and dining alone at clubs. He did not like to dine with Steyne now. They had run races of pleasure together in youth when Bareacres was the winner. But Steyne had more bottom than he, and had lasted him out. The Marquis was ten times a greater man now than the young Lord Gaunt of '85; and Bareacres nowhere in the race—old, beaten, bankrupt, and broken down. He had borrowed too much money of Steyne to find it pleasant to meet his old comrade often. The latter, whenever he wished to be merry, used jeeringly to ask Lady Gaunt, why her father had not come to see her? "He has not been here for four months," Lord Steyne would say. "I can always tell by my cheque-book afterwards, when I get a visit from Bareacres. What a comfort it is, my Ladies, I bank with one of my sons' fathers-in-law, and the other banks with me!"

Of the other illustrious persons whom Becky had the honour to encounter on this her first presentation to the grand world, it does

4. Antiques and art objects. Van Dyck, Reynolds, and Lawrence were, in succession, the greatest portrait painters in seventeenth- and eighteenth-century England. Van Dyck was Flemish but lived his last ten years in England.
5. Described as the "greatest sculptor of his age" when he died in 1822, Antonio Canova had made statues of Napoleon, Washington, and other heads of state.
6. Revised edition reads: as
7. The rough-cut, disorderly hairstyle, supposedly like that of the Roman Brutus, was popular in the late 1780s and 1790s, hence comically old-fashioned in the 1820s.

not become the present historian to say much. There was his Excellency the Prince of Peterwaradin,[8] with his Princess; a nobleman tightly girthed, with a large military chest, on which the *plaque* of his order shone magnificently, and wearing the red collar of the Golden Fleece round his neck. He was the owner of countless flocks. "Look at his face. I think he must be descended from a sheep," Becky whispered to Lord Steyne. Indeed, his Excellency's countenance, long, solemn, and white, with the ornament round his neck, bore some resemblance to that of a venerable bell-wether.

There was Mr. John Paul Jefferson Jones, titularly attached to the American Embassy, and correspondent of the New York Demagogue; who, by way of making himself agreeable to the company, asked Lady Steyne, during a pause in the conversation at dinner, how his dear friend, George Gaunt, liked the Brazils?—He and George had been most intimate at Naples, and had gone up Vesuvius together. Mr. Jones wrote a full and particular account of the dinner, which appeared duly in the Demagogue. He mentioned the names and titles of all the guests, giving biographical sketches of the principal people. He described the persons of the ladies with great eloquence; the service of the table: the size and costume of the servants: enumerated the dishes and wines served: the ornaments of the side-board, and the probable value of the plate. Such a dinner he calculated could not be dished up under fifteen or eighteen dollars per head. And he was in the habit, until very lately, of sending over *protégés,* with letters of recommendation to the present Marquis of Steyne, encouraged to do so by the intimate terms on which he had lived with his dear friend, the late lord. He was most indignant that a young and insignificant aristocrat, the Earl of Southdown, should have taken the *pas* of him in their procession to the dining room. "Just as I was stepping up to offer my hand to a very pleasing and witty fashionable, the brilliant and exclusive Mrs. Rawdon Crawley"—he wrote—"the young patrician interposed between me and the lady, and whisked my Helen off without a word of apology. I was fain to bring up the rear with the Colonel, the lady's husband, a stout red-faced warrior who distinguished himself at Waterloo, where he had better luck than befel some of his brother red-coats at New Orleans."[9]

The Colonel's countenance on coming into this polite society wore as many blushes as the face of a boy of sixteen assumes when he is confronted with his sister's schoolfellows. It has been told before that honest Rawdon had not been much used at any period of his life to ladies' company. With the men at the Club or the Mess-room, he was well enough; and could ride, bet, smoke, or play at billiards with the boldest of them. He had had his time for female friendships too: but that was twenty years ago, and the ladies were of the rank of those with whom Young Marlow in the comedy is represented as having been familiar before he became abashed in the presence of

8. Town on the Danube River.
9. The 1815 Battle of New Orleans, where Americans under Andrew Jackson defeated the British.

Miss Hardcastle.[1] The times are such that one scarcely dares to allude to that kind of company which thousands of our young men in Vanity Fair are frequenting every day, which nightly fills casinos and dancing-rooms, which is known to exist as well as the Ring in Hyde Park or the Congregation at St. James's—but which the most squeamish if not the most moral of societies is determined to ignore. In a word, although Colonel Crawley was now five-and-forty years of age, it had not been his lot in life to meet with a half dozen good women, besides his paragon of a wife. All except her and his kind sister Lady Jane, whose gentle nature had tamed and won him, scared the worthy Colonel: and on occasion of his first dinner at Gaunt House he was not heard to make a single remark except to state that the weather was very hot. Indeed Becky would have left him at home, but that virtue ordained that her husband should be by her side to protect the timid and fluttering little creature on her first appearance in polite society.

On her first appearance Lord Steyne stepped forward, taking her hand, and greeting her with great courtesy, and presenting her to Lady Steyne and their ladyships, her daughters. Their ladyships made three stately curtsies, and the elder lady to be sure gave her hand to the new comer, but it was as cold and lifeless as marble.

Becky took it, however, with grateful humility; and performing a reverence which would have done credit to the best dancing master, put herself at Lady Steyne's feet, as it were, by saying that his Lordship had been her father's earliest friend and patron, and that she, Becky, had learned to honour and respect the Steyne family from the days of her childhood. The fact is, that Lord Steyne had once purchased a couple of pictures of the late Sharp, and the affectionate orphan could never forget her gratitude for that favour.

The Lady Bareacres then came under Becky's cognizance—to whom the Colonel's lady made also a most respectful obeisance: it was returned with severe dignity by the exalted person in question.

"I had the pleasure of making your Ladyship's acquaintance at Brussels, ten years ago," Becky said, in the most winning manner. "I had the good fortune to meet Lady Bareacres, at the Duchess of Richmond's ball, the night before the Battle of Waterloo. And I recollect your Ladyship, and my Lady Blanche, your daughter, sitting in the carriage in the porte-cochère at the Inn, waiting for horses. I hope your Ladyship's diamonds are safe."

Everybody's eyes looked into their neighbour's. The famous diamonds had undergone a famous seizure, it appears, about which Becky, of course, knew nothing. Rawdon Crawley retreated with Lord Southdown into a window, where the latter was heard to laugh immoderately, as Rawdon told him the story of Lady Bareacres wanting horses, and 'knuckling down by Jove,' to Mrs. Crawley. "I think I needn't be afraid of *that* woman," Becky thought. Indeed, Lady Bareacres exchanged terrified and angry looks with her daughter; and retreated to a table, where she began to look at pictures with great energy.

1. In Oliver Goldsmith's *She Stoops to Conquer* (1773), young Marlow is forward enough with Miss Hardcastle as long as he believes her to be a country servant girl.

When the Potentate from the Danube made his appearance, the conversation was carried on in the French language, and the Lady Bareacres and the younger ladies found, to their farther mortification, that Mrs. Crawley was much better acquainted with that tongue, and spoke it with a much better accent than they. Becky had met other Hungarian magnates with the army in France, in 1816–17. She asked after her friends with great interest. The foreign personages thought that she was a lady of great distinction; and the Prince and the Princess asked severally of Lord Steyne and the Marchioness, whom they conducted to dinner, who was that petite dame who spoke so well?

Finally, the procession being formed in the order described by the American diplomatist, they marched into the apartment where the

banquet was served: and which, as I have promised the reader he shall enjoy it, he shall have the liberty of ordering himself so as to suit his fancy.

But it was when the ladies were alone that Becky knew the tug of war would come. And then indeed the little woman found herself in such a situation, as made her acknowledge the correctness of Lord Steyne's caution to her to beware of the society of ladies above her own sphere. As they say the persons who hate Irishmen most are

Irishmen; so, assuredly, the greatest tyrants over women are women. When poor little Becky, alone with the ladies, went up to the fire-place whither the great ladies had repaired, the great ladies marched away and took possession of a table of drawings. When Becky followed them to the table of drawings, they dropped off one by one to the fire again. She tried to speak to one of the children (of whom she was commonly fond in public places,) but Master George Gaunt was called away by his mamma; and the stranger was treated with such cruelty finally, that even Lady Steyne herself pitied her, and went up to speak to the friendless little woman.

"Lord Steyne," said her Ladyship, as her wan cheeks glowed with a blush, "says you sing and play very beautifully, Mrs. Crawley—I wish you would do me the kindness to sing to me."

"I will do anything that may give pleasure to my Lord Steyne or to you," said Rebecca, sincerely grateful, and seating herself at the piano, began to sing.

She sang religious songs of Mozart, which had been early favourites of Lady Steyne, and with such sweetness and tenderness that the lady lingering round the piano, sate down by its side, and listened until the tears rolled down her eyes. It is true that the opposition ladies at the other end of the room kept up a loud and ceaseless buzzing and talking: but the Lady Steyne did not hear those rumours. She was a child again—and had wandered back through a forty years' wilderness to her Convent Garden. The chapel organ had pealed the same tones, the organist, the sister whom she loved best of the community, had taught them to her in those early happy days. She was a girl once more, and the brief period of her happiness bloomed out again for an hour—she started when the jarring doors were flung open and with a loud laugh from Lord Steyne, the men of the party entered full of gaiety.

He saw at a glance what had happened in his absence: and was grateful to his wife for once. He went and spoke to her, and called her by her Christian name, so as again to bring blushes to her pale face—"My wife says you have been singing like an angel," he said to Becky. Now there are angels of two kinds, and both sorts, it is said, are charming in their way.

Whatever the previous portion of the evening had been, the rest of that night was a great triumph for Becky. She sang her very best and it was so good that every one of the men came and crowded round the piano.[2] The women her enemies were left quite alone. And Mr. Paul Jefferson Jones thought he had made a conquest of Lady Gaunt by going up to her Ladyship and praising her delightful friend's first-rate singing.

2. MS added and canceled: Even the American diplomatist forgot his business wh. was to

## *Chapter L.*

### CONTAINS A VULGAR INCIDENT.

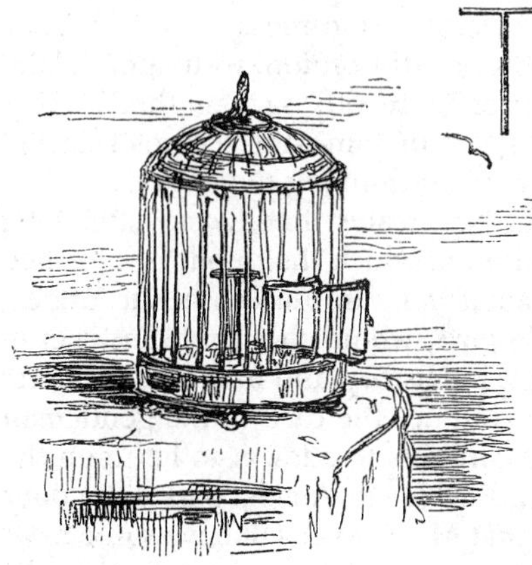

THE Muse, whoever she be, who presides over this Comic History must now descend from the genteel heights in which she has been soaring, and have the goodness to drop down upon the lowly roof of John Sedley at Brompton, and describe what events are taking place there. Here too, in this humble tenement, live care, and distrust, and dismay. Mrs. Clapp in the kitchen is grumbling in secret to her husband about the rent, and urging the good fellow to rebel against his old friend and patron and his present lodger. Mrs. Sedley has ceased to visit her landlady in the lower regions now, and indeed is in a position to patronise Mrs. Clapp no longer. How can one be condescending to a lady to whom one owes a matter of forty pound, and who is perpetually throwing out hints for the money? The Irish maidservant has not altered in the least in her kind and respectful behaviour; but Mrs. Sedley fancies that she is growing insolent and ungrateful, and, as the guilty thief who fears each bush an officer, sees threatening innuendoes and hints of capture in all the girl's speeches and answers. Miss Clapp, grown quite a young woman now, is declared by the soured old lady to be an unbearable and impudent little minx. Why Amelia can be so fond of her, or have her in her room so much, or walk out with her so constantly, Mrs. Sedley cannot conceive. The bitterness of poverty has poisoned the life of the once cheerful and kindly woman. She is thankless for Amelia's constant and gentle bearing towards her; carps at her for her efforts at kindness or service; rails at her for her silly pride in her child, and her neglect of her parents. Georgy's house is not a very lively one since uncle Jos's annuity has been withdrawn, and the little family are almost upon famine diet.

Amelia thinks, and thinks, and racks her brain, to find some means of increasing the small pittance upon which the household is starving. Can she give lessons in anything? paint card-racks? do fine work? She finds that women are working hard, and better than she can, for twopence a-day. She buys a couple of begilt Bristol boards at the Fancy Stationer's, and paints her very best upon them—a shepherd with a red waistcoat on one, and a pink face smiling in the midst of a pencil landscape—a shepherdess on the other, crossing a little bridge, with a little dog, nicely shaded. The man of the Fancy Repository and Brompton Emporium of Fine Arts, (of whom she bought the screens, vainly hoping that he would re-purchase them when ornamented by her hand,) can hardly hide the sneer with which he examines these feeble works of art. He looks askance at the lady who waits in the shop, and ties up the cards again in their envelope of whitey-brown paper, and hands them to the poor widow and Miss Clapp, who had never seen such beautiful things in her life, and had been quite confident that the man must give at least two guineas for the screens. They try at other shops in the interior of London, with faint sickening hopes. "Don't want 'em," says one. "Be off," says another fiercely. Three and sixpence have been spent in vain—the screens retire to Miss Clapp's bed-room, who persists in thinking them lovely.

She writes out a little card in her neatest hand, and after long thought and labour of composition; in which the public is informed that "A Lady who has some time at her disposal, wishes to undertake the education of some little girls, whom she would instruct in English, in French, in Geography, in History, and in Music—address A. O., at Mr. Brown's;" and she confides the card to the gentleman of the Fine Art Repository, who consents to allow it to lie upon the counter, where it grows dingy and flyblown. Amelia passes the door wistfully many a time, in hopes that Mr. Brown will have some news to give her; but he never beckons her in. When she goes to make little purchases, there is no news for her. Poor simple lady, tender and weak—how are you to battle with the struggling, violent world?

She grows daily more care-worn and sad: fixing upon her child alarmed eyes, whereof the little boy cannot interpret the expression. She starts up of a night and peeps into his room stealthily, to see that he is sleeping and not stolen away. She sleeps but little now. A constant thought and terror is haunting her. How she weeps and prays in the long silent nights,—how she tries to hide from herself the thought which will return to her, that she ought to part with the boy,—that she is the only barrier between him and prosperity. She can't, she can't! Not now, at least. Some other day. Oh! it is too hard to think of and to bear.

A thought comes over her which makes her blush and turn from herself,—her parents might keep the annuity—the curate would marry her and give a home to her and the boy. But George's picture and dearest memory are there to rebuke her. Shame and love say no to the sacrifice. She shrinks from it as from something unholy; and such thoughts never found a resting-place in that pure and gentle bosom.

The combat, which we describe in a sentence or two, lasted for many weeks in poor Amelia's heart: during which, she had no confidante: indeed, she could have none: as she would not allow to herself the possibility of yielding: though she was giving way daily before the enemy with whom she had to battle. One truth after another was marshalling itself silently against her, and keeping its ground. Poverty and misery for all, want and degradation for her parents, injustice to the boy—one by one the outworks of the little citadel were taken, in which the poor soul passionately guarded her only love and treasure.

At the beginning of the struggle, she had written off a letter of tender supplication to her brother at Calcutta, imploring him not to withdraw the support which he had granted to their parents, and painting in terms of artless pathos their lonely and hapless condition. She did not know the truth of the matter. The payment of Jos's annuity was still regular: but it was a money-lender in the city who was receiving it: old Sedley had sold it for a sum of money wherewith to prosecute his bootless schemes. Emmy was calculating eagerly the time that would elapse before the letter would arrive and be answered. She had written down the date in her pocket-book of the day when she dispatched it. To her son's guardian, the good Major at Madras, she had not communicated any of her griefs and perplexities. She had not written to him since she wrote to congratulate him on his approaching marriage. She thought with sickening despondency, that that friend,—the only one, the one who had felt such a regard for her,—was fallen away.

One day, when things had come to a very bad pass—when the creditors were pressing, the mother in hysteric grief, the father in more than usual gloom, the inmates of the family avoiding each other, each secretly oppressed with his private unhappiness and notion of wrong—the father and daughter happened to be left alone together; and Amelia thought to comfort her father, by telling him what she had done. She had written to Joseph—an answer must come in three or four months. He was always generous, though careless. He could not refuse, when he knew how straitened the circumstances of his parents.

Then the poor old gentleman revealed the whole truth to her—that his son was still paying the annuity, which his own imprudence had flung away. He had not dared to tell it sooner. He thought Amelia's ghastly and terrified look, when, with a trembling, miserable voice he made the confession, conveyed reproaches to him for his concealment. "Ah!" said he, with quivering lips and turning away, "you despise your old father now."

"O Papa! it is not that," Amelia cried out, falling on his neck, and kissing him many times. "You are always good and kind. You did it for the best. It is not for the money—it is—O my God! my God! have mercy upon me, and give me strength to bear this trial;" and she kissed him again wildly, and went away.

Still the father did not know what that explanation meant, and the burst of anguish with which the poor girl left him. It was that she was conquered. The sentence was passed. The child must go from her—to others—to forget her. Her heart and her treasure—her joy, hope, love, worship—her God, almost! She must give him up; and then—and then she would go to George; and they would watch over the child, and wait for him until he came to them in Heaven.

She put on her bonnet, scarcely knowing what she did, and went out to walk in the lanes by which George used to come back from school, and where she was in the habit of going on his return to meet the boy. It was May, a half holiday. The leaves were all coming out, the weather was brilliant: the boy came running to her, flushed with health, singing, his bundle of school-books hanging by a thong. There he was. Both her arms were round him. No, it was impossible. They could not be going to part. "What is the matter, mother?" said he; "you look very pale."

"Nothing, my child," she said, and stooped down and kissed him.

That night Amelia made the boy read the story of Samuel to her, and how Hannah, his mother, having weaned him, brought him to Eli the High Priest to minister before the Lord. And he read the song of gratitude which Hannah sang: and which says, Who it is who maketh poor and maketh rich, and bringeth low and exalteth—how the poor shall be raised up out of the dust, and how, in his own might, no man shall be strong. Then he read how Samuel's mother made him a little coat, and brought it to him from year to year when she came up to offer the yearly sacrifice.[1] And then, in her sweet simple way, George's mother made commentaries to the boy upon this affecting story. How Hannah, though she loved her son so much, yet gave him up because of her vow. And how she must always have thought of him as she sate at home, far away, making the little coat: and Samuel, she was sure, never forgot his mother: and how happy she must have been as the time came (and the years pass away very quick) when she should see her boy, and how good and wise he had grown. This little sermon she spoke with a gentle solemn voice, and dry eyes, until she came to the account of their meeting—then the discourse broke off suddenly, the tender heart overflowed, and taking the boy to her breast, she rocked him in her arms, and wept silently over him in a sainted agony of tears.

Her mind being made up, the widow began to take such measures as seemed right to her for advancing the end which she proposed. One day, Miss Osborne, in Russell Square, (Amelia had not written the name or number of the house for ten years—her youth, her early story came back to her as she wrote the superscription)—one day Miss Osborne got a letter from Amelia, which made her blush very much and look towards her father, sitting glooming in his place at the other end of the table.

In simple terms, Amelia told her the reasons which had induced her to change her mind respecting her boy. Her father had met with fresh misfortunes, which had entirely ruined him. Her own pittance was so small that it would barely enable her to support her parents, and would not suffice to give George the advantages which were his due. Great as her sufferings would be at parting with him, she would, by God's help, endure them for the boy's sake. She knew that those to whom he was going, would do all in their power to make him happy. She described his disposition, such as she fancied it; quick and impatient of control or harshness; easily to be moved by love and kindness. In a postscript, she stipulated that she should have a written agreement, that she should see the child as often as she wished,—she could not part with him under any other terms.

"What? Mrs. Pride has come down, has she?" old Osborne said, when with a tremulous eager voice Miss Osborne read him the letter—"Reg'lar starved out, hey? ha, ha! I knew she would." He tried to keep his dignity and to read his paper as usual,—but he could not follow it. He chuckled and swore to himself behind the sheet.

1. Hannah, to fulfill a vow, dedicated her only son, Samuel, sending him to live with Eli the priest, where she visited him once a year. I Samuel 1–2.

At last he flung it down: and scowling at his daughter, as his wont was, went out of the room into his study adjoining, from whence he presently returned with a key. He flung it to Miss Osborne.

"Get the room over mine—his room that was—ready," he said. "Yes, sir," his daughter replied in a tremble. It was George's room. It had not been opened for more than ten years. Some of his clothes, papers, handkerchiefs, whips and caps, fishing-rods and sporting gear, were still there. An army list of 1814, with his name written on the cover; a little dictionary he was wont to use in writing; and the Bible his mother had given him, were on the mantel-piece; with a pair of spurs, and a dried inkstand covered with the dust of ten years. Ah! since that ink was wet, what days and people had passed away! The writing-book still on the table, was blotted with his hand.

Miss Osborne was much affected when she first entered this room with the servants under her. She sank quite pale on the little bed. "This is blessed news, mam—indeed, mam," the housekeeper said; "and the good old times is returning, mam. The dear little feller, to be sure, mam; how happy he will be! But some folks in May Fair, mam, will owe him a grudge, mam;" and she clicked back the bolt which held the window-sash, and let the air into the chamber.

"You had better send that woman some money," Mr. Osborne said, before he went out. "She shan't want for nothing. Send her a hundred pound."

"And I'll go and see her to-morrow?" Miss Osborne asked.

"That's your look out. She don't come in here, mind. No, by —, not for all the money in London. But she mustn't want now. So look out, and get things right." With which brief speeches Mr. Osborne took leave of his daughter, and went on his accustomed way into the City.

"Here, Papa, is some money," Amelia said that night, kissing the old man, her father, and putting a bill for a hundred pounds into his hands. "And—and, Mamma, don't be harsh with Georgy. He—he is not going to stop with us long." She could say nothing more, and walked away silently to her room. Let us close it upon her prayers and her sorrow. I think we had best speak little about so much love and grief.

Miss Osborne came the next day, according to the promise contained in her note, and saw Amelia. The meeting between them was friendly. A look and a few words from Miss Osborne showed the poor widow, that, with regard to this woman at least, there need be no fear lest she should take the first place in her son's affection. She was cold, sensible, not unkind. The mother had not been so well pleased, perhaps, had the rival been better looking, younger, more affectionate, warmer-hearted. Miss Osborne, on the other hand, thought of old times and memories, and could not but be touched with the poor mother's pitiful situation. She was conquered, and, laying down her arms as it were: she humbly submitted. That day they arranged together the preliminaries of the treaty of capitulation.

George was kept from school the next day, and saw his aunt. Amelia left them alone together, and went to her room. She was trying the separation:—as that poor gentle Lady Jane Grey felt the edge of the axe that was to come down and sever her slender life.[2] Days were passed in parleys, visits, preparations. The widow broke the matter to Georgy with great caution; she looked to see him very much affected by the intelligence. He was rather elated than otherwise, and the poor woman turned sadly away. He bragged about the news that day to the boys at school; told them how he was going to live with his grandpapa, his father's father, not the one who comes here sometimes; and that he would be very rich, and have a carriage, and a poney, and go to a much finer school, and when he was rich he would buy Leader's pencil-case, and pay the tart woman. The boy was the image of his father, as his fond mother thought.

Indeed I have no heart, on account of our dear Amelia's sake, to go through the story of George's last days at home.

At last the day came, the carriage drove up, the little humble packets containing tokens of love and remembrance were ready and disposed in the hall long since—George was in his new suit, for which the tailor had come previously to measure him. He had sprung up with the sun and put on the new clothes, his mother hearing him from the room close by, in which she had been lying, in speechless grief and watching. Days before she had been making preparations for the end: purchasing little stores for the boy's use; marking his books and linen; talking with him and preparing him for the change—fondly fancying that he needed preparation.

So that he had change, what cared he? He was longing for it. By a thousand eager declarations as to what he would do, when he went to live with his grandfather, he had shown the poor widow how little the idea of parting had cast him down. "He would come and see his mamma often on the poney," he said: "he would come and fetch her in the carriage; they would drive in the Park, and she should have everything she wanted." The poor mother was fain to content herself with these selfish demonstrations of attachment, and tried to convince herself how sincerely her son loved her. He must love her. All children were so: a little anxious for novelty, and—no, not selfish, but self-willed. Her child must have his enjoyments and ambition in the world. She herself, by her own selfishness and imprudent love for him, had denied him his just rights and pleasures hitherto.

I know few things more affecting than that timorous debasement and self-humiliation of a woman. How she owns that it is she and not the man who is guilty: how she takes all the faults on her side: how she courts in a manner punishment for the wrongs which she has not committed, and persists in shielding the real culprit! It is those who injure women who get the most kindness from them—they are born timid and tyrants, and maltreat those who are humblest before them.

So poor Amelia had been getting ready in silent misery for her son's departure, and had passed many and many a long solitary hour in making preparations for the end. George stood by his mother,

2. Lady Jane, at age seventeen, was for nine days the reluctant queen of England, the pawn of her unscrupulous and ambitious father-in-law. She was deposed in favor of Mary Tudor. The legendary scene referred to here is not recorded in any traced history, play, or novel of her life. It could have occurred in stage action, not recorded in the text, of Nicholas Rowe's *Lady Jane Grey* or Thomas Dekker's *Sir Thomas Wyatt*, both of which have a scene with the axe man and Jane, though in each the beheading takes place offstage.

watching her arrangements without the least concern. Tears had fallen into his boxes; passages had been scored in his favourite books: old toys, relics, treasures had been hoarded away for him, and packed with strange neatness and care,—and of all these things the boy took no note. The child goes away smiling as the mother breaks her heart. By heavens it is pitiful, the bootless love of women for children in Vanity Fair.

A few days are past: and the great event of Amelia's life is consummated. No angel has intervened.[3] The child is sacrificed and offered up to fate: and the widow is quite alone.

The boy comes to see her often, to be sure. He rides on a poney with the coachman behind him, to the delight of his old grandfather, Sedley, who walks proudly down the lane by his side. She sees him, but he is not her boy any more. Why, he rides to see the boys at the little school, too, and to show off before them his new wealth and splendour. In two days he has adopted a slight imperious air and patronising manner. He was born to command, his mother thinks, as his father was before him.

It is fine weather now. Of evenings on the days when he does not

3. When Abraham offers to sacrifice Isaac, an angel appears, substituting a ram. Genesis 22.11–12.

come, she takes a long walk into London—yes, as far as Russell Square, and rests on the stone by the railing of the garden opposite Mr. Osborne's house. It is so pleasant and cool. She can look up and see the drawing-room windows illuminated, and, at about nine o'clock, the chamber in the upper story where Georgy sleeps. She knows—He has told her. She prays there as the light goes out, prays with a humble humble heart, and walks home shrinking and silent. She is very tired when she comes home. Perhaps she will sleep the better for that long weary walk; and she may dream about Georgy.

One Sunday she happened to be walking in Russell Square, at some distance from Mr. Osborne's house (she could see it from a distance though) when all the bells of Sabbath were ringing, and George and his aunt came out to go to church; a little sweep asked for charity, and the footman, who carried the books, tried to drive him away; but Georgy stopped and gave him money. May God's blessing be on the boy! Emmy ran round the square, and coming up to the sweep, gave him her mite too. All the bells of Sabbath were ringing, and she followed them until she came to the Foundling Church, into which she went. There she sat in a place whence she could see the head of the boy under his father's tombstone. Many hundred fresh children's voices rose up there and sang hymns to the Father Beneficent; and little George's soul thrilled with delight at the burst of glorious psalmody. His mother could not see him for awhile, through the mist that dimmed her eyes.

Georgy goes to church genteelly

# *Chapter LI.*

## IN WHICH A CHARADE IS ACTED WHICH MAY OR MAY NOT PUZZLE THE READER.

FTER[1] Becky's appearance at my Lord Steyne's private and select parties the claims of that estimable woman as regards fashion, were settled; and some of the very greatest and tallest doors in the metropolis were speedily opened to her—doors so great and tall that the beloved reader and writer hereof may hope in vain to enter at them. Dear brethren, let us tremble before those august portals. I fancy them guarded by grooms of the chamber with flaming silver forks with which they prong all those who have not the right of the *entrée.* They say the honest newspaper-fellow who sits in the hall and takes down the names of the great ones who are admitted to the feasts, dies after a little time. He can't survive the glare of fashion long. It scorches him up, as the presence of Jupiter in full dress wasted that poor imprudent Semele—a giddy moth of a creature who ruined herself by venturing out of her natural atmosphere.[2] Her myth ought to be taken to heart amongst the Tyburnians, the Belgravians,—her story, and perhaps Becky's too. Ah, ladies!—ask the Reverend Mr. Thurifer[3] if Belgravia is not a sounding brass, and Tyburnia a tinkling cymbal.[4] These are vanities. Even these will pass away. And some day or other (but it will be after our time, thank goodness,) Hyde Park Gardens will be no better known than the celebrated horticultural outskirts of Babylon; and Belgrave Square will be as desolate as Baker Street, or Tadmor in the wilderness.[5]

Ladies, are you aware that the great Pitt lived in Baker Street? What would not your grandmothers have given to be asked to Lady

1. Initial illustration may represent the fallen statue of Memnon, referred to in the charades, or the sleeping Gulliver at Lilliput, a land with an endless bureaucratic aristocracy.
2. The mortal Semele, at Juno's cunningly jealous instigation, asked to see her lover, Jupiter, in all his glory; she was destroyed by it.
3. Tyburnia and Belgravia were fashionable to aristocratic residential areas of London. A thurifer is one who carries a censer in an ecclesiastical rite.
4. Uselessness of accomplishments without charity. I Corinthians 13.1.
5. The Hanging Gardens of Babylon were among the wonders of the ancient world; Tadmor was one of Solomon's rebuilt cities in the desert, thought to be the ruins at Palmyra.

Hester's parties in that now decayed mansion?[6] I have dined in it—*moi qui vous parle.*[7] I peopled the chamber with ghosts of the mighty dead. As we sate soberly drinking claret there with men of to-day, the spirits of the departed came in and took their places round the darksome board. The pilot who weathered the storm tossed off great bumpers of spiritual port: the shade of Dundas did not leave the ghost of a heeltap.—Addington sate bowing and smirking in a ghastly manner, and would not be behindhand when the noiseless bottle went round; Scott, from under bushy eyebrows winked at the apparition of a beeswing; Wilberforce's eyes went up to the ceiling, so that he did not seem to know how his glass went up full to his mouth and came down empty;—up to the ceiling which was above us only yesterday, and which the great of the past days have all looked at.[8] They let the house as a furnished lodging now. Yes, Lady Hester once lived in Baker Street, and lies asleepin the wilderness. Eothen saw her there—not in Baker Street: but in the other solitude.[9]

It is all vanity to be sure: but who will not own to liking a little of it? I should like to know what well-constituted mind, merely because it is transitory, dislikes roast-beef? That is a vanity; but may every man who reads this, have a wholesome portion of it through life, I beg: aye, though my readers were five hundred thousand. Sit down, gentlemen, and fall to, with a good hearty appetite; the fat, the lean, the gravy, the horse-radish as you like it—don't spare it. Another glass of wine, Jones, my boy—a little bit of the Sunday side. Yes, let us eat our fill of the vain thing, and be thankful therefor. And let us make the best of Becky's aristocratic pleasures likewise—for these too, like all other mortal delights, were but transitory.

The upshot of her visit to Lord Steyne was, that his Highness the Prince of Peterwaradin took occasion to renew his acquaintance with Colonel Crawley, when they met on the next day at the Club, and to compliment Mrs. Crawley in the Ring of Hyde Park with a profound salute of the hat. She and her husband were invited immediately to one of the Prince's small parties at Levant House, then occupied by his Highness during the temporary absence from England of its noble proprietor. She sang after dinner to a very little *comité.*[1] The Marquis of Steyne was present, paternally superintending the progress of his pupil.

At Levant House Becky met one of the finest gentlemen and greatest ministers that Europe has produced—the Duc de la Jabotière,

6. William Pitt the younger (d. 1806), Whig prime minister, lived in Baker Street, where his niece Lady Hester Stanhope (d. 1839) kept house for him.
7. I who speak with you.
8. "When our perils are past, shall our gratitude sleep? / No—here's to the pilot who weathered the storm." Lines by George Canning (d. 1827) written for William Pitt's birthday in 1802, the year Henry Addington (d. 1844) briefly and without distinction replaced Pitt as prime minister. Henry Dundas (d. 1811), statesman (see chapter VII). Sir Walter Scott (d. 1832), who repeated Canning's line in "Health to Lord Melville" (1806). William Wilberforce (d. 1833), politician, abolitionist, philanthropist, friend and political ally of Pitt (see chapter IX).
9. After Pitt died, his niece, Lady Hester, left England for a life of adventure in Spain and then the Middle East, where she "went native" and lived like an Eastern princess till her death. Alexander W. Kinglake (1809–91), author of *Eothen*, visited Lady Hester in Lebanon.
1. *En petit comité*: a select few.

then Ambassador from the Most Christian King, and subsequently Minister to that monarch.[2] I declare I swell with pride as these august names are transcribed by my pen; and I think in what brilliant company my dear Becky is moving. She became a constant guest at the French Embassy, where no party was considered to be complete without the presence of the charming Madame Ravdonn Cravley.

Messieurs de Truffigny (of the Périgord family)[3] and Champignac, both attachés of the Embassy, were straightway smitten by the charms of the fair Colonel's wife: and both declared, according to the wont of their nation, (for who ever yet met a Frenchman, come out of England, that has not left half a dozen families miserable, and brought away as many hearts in his pocket-book?) both, I say, declared that they were *au mieux*[4] with the charming Madame Ravdonn.

But I doubt the correctness of the assertion. Champignac was very fond of écarté, and made many *parties* with the Colonel of evenings, while Becky was singing to Lord Steyne in the other room; and as for Truffigny, it is a well-known fact that he dared not go to the Travellers', where he owed money to the waiters, and if he had not had the Embassy as a dining-place, the worthy young gentleman must have starved. I doubt, I say, that Becky would have selected either of these young men as a person on whom she would bestow her special regard. They ran of her messages, purchased her gloves and flowers, went in debt for opera-boxes for her, and made themselves amiable in a thousand ways. And they talked English with adorable simplicity, and to the constant amusement of Becky and my Lord Steyne. She would mimic one or other to his face, and compliment him on his advance in the English language with a gravity which never failed to tickle the Marquis, her sardonic old patron. Truffigny gave Briggs a shawl by way of winning over Becky's confidante, and asked her to take charge of a letter which the simple spinster handed over in public to the person to whom it was addressed; and the composition of which amused everybody who read it greatly. Lord Steyne read it: everybody, but honest Rawdon; to whom it was not necessary to tell everything that passed in the little house in May Fair.

Here, before long, Becky received not only "the best" foreigners (as the phrase is in our noble and admirable society slang), but some of the best English people too. I don't mean the most virtuous, or indeed the least virtuous, or the cleverest, or the stupidest, or the richest, or the best born, but "the best,"—in a word, people about whom there is no question—such as the great Lady Fitz-Willis, that Patron Saint of Almack's,[5] the great Lady Slowbore, the great Lady Grizzel Macbeth, (she was Lady G. Glowry, daughter of Lord Grey of Glowry,) and the like. When the Countess of Fitz-Willis (her ladyship is of the Kingstreet family, see Debrett and Burke,)[6] takes up a person, he or she is safe. There is no question about them any more.

2. Charles X of France; the ambassador's name derives from *jabot*, or shirt frills.
3. The names of the new aristocracy are derived from varieties of mushrooms.
4. On the best of terms.
5. Assembly rooms in St. James, where weekly balls with exclusive guest lists (presided over by a committee of grand dams) and strict dress codes made entry very selective.
6. Two guides to British nobility.

Not that my Lady Fitz-Willis is any better than anybody else, being, on the contrary, a faded person, fifty-seven years of age, and neither handsome, nor wealthy, nor entertaining; but it is agreed on all sides that she is of the "best people." Those who go to her are of the best: and from an old grudge probably to Lady Steyne (for whose coronet her ladyship, then the youthful Georgina Frederica, daughter of the Prince of Wales's favourite, the Earl of Portansherry, had once tried), this great and famous leader of the fashion chose to acknowledge Mrs. Rawdon Crawley: made her a most marked curtsey at the assembly over which she presided: and not only encouraged her son, St. Kitts (his lordship got his place through Lord Steyne's interest), to frequent Mrs. Crawley's house, but asked her to her own mansion, and spoke to her twice in the most public and condescending manner during dinner. The important fact was known all over London that night. People who had been crying fie about Mrs. Crawley, were silent. Wenham, the wit and lawyer, Lord Steyne's right-hand man, went about everywhere praising her: some who had hesitated, came forward at once and welcomed her: little Tom Toady, who had warned Southdown about visiting such an abandoned woman, now besought to be introduced to her. In a word, she was admitted to be among the "best" people. Ah, my beloved readers and brethren, do not envy poor Becky prematurely—glory like this is said to be fugitive. It is currently reported that even in the very inmost circles, they are no happier than the poor wanderers outside the zone; and Becky, who penetrated into the very centre of fashion, and saw the great George IV. face to face, has owned since that there too was Vanity.

We must be brief in descanting upon this part of her career. As I cannot describe the mysteries of freemasonry, although I have a shrewd idea that it is a humbug: so an uninitiated man cannot take upon himself to pourtray the great world accurately, and had best keep his opinions to himself whatever they are.

Becky has often spoken in subsequent years of this season of her life, when she moved among the very greatest circles of the London fashion. Her success excited, elated, and then bored her. At first no occupation was more pleasant than to invent and procure (the latter a work of no small trouble and ingenuity, by the way, in a person of Mrs. Rawdon Crawley's very narrow means)—to procure, we say, the prettiest new dresses and ornaments; to drive to fine dinner parties, where she was welcomed by great people; and from the fine dinner parties to fine assemblies, whither the same people came with whom she had been dining, whom she had met the night before, and would see on the morrow—the young men faultlessly appointed, handsomely cravatted, with the neatest glossy boots and white gloves—the elders portly, brass-buttoned, noble-looking, polite, and prosy—the young ladies blonde, timid, and in pink—the mothers grand, beautiful, sumptuous, solemn, and in diamonds. They talked in English, not in bad French, as they do in the novels. They talked about each others' houses, and characters, and families: just as the Joneses do about the Smiths. Becky's former acquaintances hated and envied her: the poor woman herself was yawning in spirit. "I wish I were out of it," she said to herself. "I would rather be a parson's wife, and teach a Sunday School than this; or a sergeant's lady and ride in the regimental waggon; or, O how much gayer it would be to wear spangles and trowsers, and dance before a booth at a fair."

"You would do it very well," said Lord Steyne, laughing. She used to tell the great man her *ennuis*[7] and perplexities in her artless way—they amused him.

"Rawdon would make a very good Écuyer[8]—Master of the Ceremonies—what do you call him—the man in the large boots and the uniform, who goes round the ring cracking the whip? He is large, heavy, and of a military figure. I recollect," Becky continued, pensively, "my father took me to see a show at Brookgreen Fair[9] when I was a child; and when we came home I made myself a pair of stilts, and danced in the studio to the wonder of all the pupils."

"I should have liked to see it," said Lord Steyne.

"I should like to do it now," Becky continued. "How Lady Blinkey would open her eyes, and Lady Grizzel Macbeth would stare! Hush! silence! there is Pasta[1] beginning to sing." Becky always made a point of being conspicuously polite to the professional ladies and gentlemen who attended at these aristocratic parties—of following them into the corners where they sate in silence, and shaking hands with them, and smiling in the view of all persons. She was an artist herself, as she said very truly: there was a frankness and humility in the manner in which she acknowledged her origin, which provoked, or disarmed, or amused lookers-on, as the case might be. "How cool that woman is," said one; "what airs of independence she assumes, where she ought to sit still and be thankful if anybody speaks to her." "What an honest and good-natured soul she is," said another. "What an artful little minx," said a third. They were all right very likely; but Becky went her own way, and so fascinated the professional personages, that they would leave off their sore throats in order to sing at her parties, and give her lessons for nothing.

Yes, she gave parties in the little house in Curzon Street. Many scores of carriages, with blazing lamps, blocked up the street, to the disgust of No. 100, who could not rest for the thunder of the knocking, and of 102, who could not sleep for envy. The gigantic footmen who accompanied the vehicles, were too big to be contained in Becky's little hall, and were billeted off in the neighbouring public-houses, whence, when they were wanted, call-boys summoned them from their beer. Some[2] of the great dandies of London squeezed and trod on each other on the little stairs, laughing to find themselves there; and many spotless and severe ladies of *ton*[3] were seated in the little drawing-room, listening to the professional singers, who were singing according to their wont, and as if they wished to blow the windows down. And the day after, there appeared among the fash-

7. Trials.
8. Equerry, master of horses.
9. In Hammersmith, between London and Chiswick.
1. Guidetta Pasta (1798–1865), Italian soprano.
2. Revised edition reads: Scores
3. High society, tone setters.

ionable *réunions* in the "Morning Post," a paragraph to the following effect:—

"Yesterday, Colonel and Mrs. Crawley entertained a select party at dinner at their house in May Fair. Their Excellencies the Prince and Princess of Peterwaradin, H. E. Papoosh Pasha, the Turkish Ambassador (attended by Kibob Bey, dragoman[4] of the mission), the Marquis of Steyne, Earl of Southdown, Mr. Pitt[5] and Lady Jane Crawley, Mr. Wagg, &c. After dinner Mrs. Crawley had an assembly which was attended by the Duchess (Dowager) of Stilton,[6] Duc de la Gruyère, Marchioness of Cheshire, Marchese Alessandro Strachino, Comte de Brie, Baron Schapzuger, Chevalier Tosti, Countess of Slingstone, and Lady F. Macadam, Major-General and Lady G. Macbeth, and (2) Miss Macbeths; Viscount Paddington, Sir Horace Fogey, Hon. Sands Bedwin, Bobbachy Bahawder,"[7] and an &c. which the reader may fill at his pleasure through a dozen close lines of small type.

And in her commerce with the great our dear friend showed the same frankness which distinguished her transactions with the lowly in station. On one occasion, when out at a very fine house, Rebecca was (perhaps rather ostentatiously) holding a conversation in the French language with a celebrated tenor singer of that nation, while the Lady Grizzel Macbeth looked over her shoulder scowling at the pair.

"How very well you speak French," Lady Grizzel said, who herself spoke the tongue in an Edinburgh accent most remarkable to hear.

"I ought to know it," Becky modestly said, casting down her eyes. "I taught it in a school, and my mother was a Frenchwoman."

Lady Grizzel was won by her humility, and was mollified towards the little woman. She deplored the fatal levelling tendencies of the age, which admitted persons of all classes into the society of their superiors: but her ladyship owned, that this one at least was well behaved and never forgot her place in life. She was a very good woman: good to the poor: stupid, blameless, unsuspicious.—It is not her ladyship's fault that she fancies herself better than you and me. The skirts of her ancestors' garments have been kissed for centuries: it is a thousand years, they say, since the tartans of the head of the family were embraced by the defunct Duncan's lords, and councillors, when the great ancestor of the House became King of Scotland.

Lady Steyne, after the music scene, succumbed before Becky, and perhaps was not disinclined to her. The younger ladies of the House of Gaunt were also compelled into submission. Once or twice they set people at her, but they failed. The brilliant Lady Stunnington tried a passage of arms with her, but was routed with great slaughter by the intrepid little Becky. When attacked sometimes, Becky had a knack of adopting a demure *ingénue* air, under which she was most dangerous. She said the wickedest things with the most simple unaffected air

4. Interpreter.
5. By this time Pitt is actually Sir Pitt.
6. Most of the names in this paragraph derive from varieties of cheese.
7. Sands Bedwin (Bedouin?) may be based on James J. Morier (d. 1849), author of *Hajji Baba* (1824), whom Thackeray met in October 1847. Bobbachy Bahawder or "Male Cook Brave Warrior" is a name Thackeray invented in "The Tremendous Adventures of Major Gahagan" (1838).

when in this mood, and would take care artlessly to apologise for her blunders, so that all the world should know that she had made them.

Mr. Wagg, the celebrated wit, and a led captain and trencher-man of my Lord Steyne, was caused by the ladies to charge her; and the worthy fellow, leering at his patronesses, and giving them a wink, as much as to say, "Now look out for sport,"—one evening began an assault upon Becky, who was unsuspiciously eating her dinner. The little woman, attacked on a sudden, but never without arms, lighted up in an instant, parried and reposted with a home-thrust, which made Wagg's face tingle with shame; then she returned to her soup with the most perfect calm and a quiet smile on her face. Wagg's great patron, who gave him dinners and lent him a little money sometimes, and whose election, newspaper, and other jobs Wagg did, gave the luckless fellow such a savage glance with the eyes as almost made him sink under the table and burst into tears. He looked piteously at my lord, who never spoke to him during dinner, and at the ladies, who disowned him. At last Becky herself took compassion upon him, and tried to engage him in talk. He was not asked to dinner again for six weeks; and Fiche,[8] my lord's confidential man, to whom Wagg naturally paid a good deal of court, was instructed to tell him that if he ever dared to say a rude thing to Mrs. Crawley again, or make her the butt of his stupid jokes, Milor would put every one of his notes of hand into his lawyer's hands, and sell him up without mercy. Wagg wept before Fiche, and implored his dear friend to intercede for him. He wrote a poem in favour of Mrs. R. C., which appeared in the very next number of the "Harumscarum Magazine," which he conducted. He implored her good will at parties where he met her. He cringed and coaxed Rawdon at the club. He was allowed to come back to Gaunt House after a while. Becky was always good to him, always amused, never angry.

His lordship's vizier and chief confidential servant (with a seat in parliament and at the dinner table), Mr. Wenham, was much more prudent in his behaviour and opinions than Mr. Wagg. However much he might be disposed to hate all parvenus (Mr. Wenham himself was a staunch old True Blue Tory, and his father a small coal-merchant in the north of England), this aide-de-camp of the Marquis never showed any sort of hostility to the new favourite; but pursued her with stealthy kindnesses, and a sly and deferential politeness, which somehow made Becky more uneasy than other people's overt hostilities.

How the Crawleys got the money which was spent upon the entertainments with which they treated the polite world, was a mystery which gave rise to some conversation at the time, and probably added zest to these little festivities. Some persons averred that Sir Pitt Crawley gave his brother a handsome allowance: if he did, Becky's power over the baronet must have been extraordinary indeed, and his character greatly changed in his advanced age. Other parties hinted that it was Becky's habit to levy contributions on all her husband's friends: going to this one in tears with an account that there was an execu-

8. The name means index or filing card.

tion in the house; falling on her knees to that one, and declaring that the whole family must go to gaol or commit suicide unless such and such a bill could be paid. Lord Southdown, it was said, had been induced to give many hundreds through these pathetic representations. Young Feltham, of the —th Dragoons (and son of the firm of Tiler and Feltham, hatters and army accoutrement makers), and whom the Crawleys introduced into fashionable life, was also cited as one of Becky's victims in the pecuniary way. People declared that she got money from various simply disposed persons, under pretence of getting them confidential appointments under government. Who knows what stories were or were not told of our dear and innocent friend? Certain it is, that if she had had all the money which she was said to have begged or borrowed or stolen, she might have capitalised and been honest for life, whereas,—but this is advancing matters.

The truth is, that by economy and good management—by a sparing use of ready money and by paying scarcely anybody,—people can manage, for a time at least, to make a great show with very little means: and it is our belief that Becky's much-talked-of parties, which were not, after all was said, very numerous, cost this lady very little more than the wax candles which lighted the walls. Stillbrook and Queen's Crawley supplied her with game and fruit in abundance. Lord Steyne's cellars were at her disposal, and that excellent nobleman's famous cooks presided over her little kitchen, or sent by my lord's order the rarest delicacies from their own. I protest it is quite shameful in the world to abuse a simple creature, as people of her time abused Becky, and I warn the public against believing one-tenth of the stories against her. If every person is to be banished from society who runs into debt and cannot pay—if we are to be peering into everybody's private life, speculating upon their income, and cutting them if we don't approve of their expenditure—why, what a howling wilderness and intolerable dwelling Vanity Fair would be. Every man's hand would be against his neighbour in this case, my dear Sir, and the benefits of civilisation would be done away with. We should be quarrelling, abusing, avoiding one another. Our houses would become caverns: and we should go in rags because we cared for nobody. Rents would go down. Parties wouldn't be given any more. All the tradesmen of the town would be bankrupt. Wine, wax-lights, comestibles, rouge, crinoline-petticoats, diamonds, wigs, Louis-Quatorze-gimcracks,[9] and old china, park hacks and splendid high-stepping carriage horses—all the delights of life, I say,—would go to the deuce, if people did but act upon their silly principles, and avoid those whom they dislike and abuse. Whereas, by a little charity and mutual forbearance, things are made to go on pleasantly enough: we may abuse a man as much as we like, and call him the greatest rascal unhung—but do we wish to hang him therefore? No. We shake hands when we meet. If his cook is good we forgive him, and go and dine with him; and we expect he will do the same by us. Thus trade flourishes—civilisation advances: peace is kept; new dresses are wanted for new assemblies every week; and the last year's

9. Souvenirs or objects of seventeenth-century France; Louis XIV died in 1715.

vintage of Lafitte[1] will remunerate the honest proprietor who reared it.

At the time whereof we are writing, though the Great George was on the throne and ladies wore *gigots*[2] and large combs like tortoise-shell shovels in their hair, instead of the simple sleeves and lovely wreaths which are actually in fashion, the manners of the very polite world were not, I take it, essentially different from those of the present day: and their amusements pretty similar. To us, from outside gazing over the policemen's shoulders at the bewildering beauties as they pass into Court or ball, they may seem beings of unearthly splendour, and in the enjoyment of an exquisite happiness by us unattainable. It is to console some of these dissatisfied beings, that we are narrating our dear Becky's struggles, and triumphs, and disappointments, of all of which, indeed, as is the case with all persons of merit, she had her share.

At this time the amiable amusement of acting charades had come among us from France: and was considerably in vogue in this country, enabling the many ladies amongst us who had beauty to display their charms, and the fewer number who had cleverness, to exhibit their wit. My Lord Steyne was incited by Becky, who perhaps believed herself endowed with both the above qualifications, to give an entertainment at Gaunt House, which should include some of these little dramas—and we must take leave to introduce the reader to this brilliant *réunion,* and, with a melancholy welcome too, for it will be among the very last of the fashionable entertainments to which it will be our fortune to conduct him.

A portion of that splendid room, the picture-gallery of Gaunt House, was arranged as the charade theatre. It had been so used when George III. was king;[3] and a picture of the Marquis of Gaunt is still extant, with his hair in powder and a pink ribbon, in a Roman shape, as it was called, enacting the part of Cato in Mr. Addison's tragedy of that name, performed before their Royal Highnesses the Prince of Wales, the Bishop of Osnaburgh, and Prince William Henry,[4] then children like the actor. One or two of the old properties were drawn out of the garrets, where they had lain ever since, and furbished up anew for the present festivities.

Young Bedwin Sands, then an elegant dandy and Eastern traveller, was manager of the revels. An Eastern traveller was somebody in those days, and the adventurous Bedwin, who had published his quarto, and passed some months under the tents in the desert, was a personage of no small importance.—In his volume there were several pictures of Sands in various oriental costumes; and he travelled about with a black attendant of most unprepossessing appearance, just like another Brian de Bois Guilbert.[5] Bedwin, his costumes, and

1. Château Lafitte wine.
2. Leg-of-mutton sleeves.
3. 1760–1820.
4. Joseph Addison's *Cato* (1713). George, prince of Wales; his brother Frederick (1763–1837) was made bishop of Osnaburg at age one by his father, who as elector of Hanover had the power of appointment; his second brother William Henry (1765–1837) became King William IV in 1830. The performance is supposed to have taken place in the 1770s.
5. Villanous Templar in Sir Walter Scott's *Ivanhoe* (1819).

black man, were hailed at Gaunt House as very valuable acquisitions.

He led off the first charade. A Turkish officer with an immense plume of feathers (the Janizzaries[6] were supposed to be still in existence, and the tarboosh[7] had not as yet displaced the ancient and majestic head-dress of the true believers) was seen couched on a divan, and making believe to puff at a narghile,[8] in which, however, for the sake of the ladies, only a fragrant pastille[9] was allowed to smoke. The Turkish dignitary yawns and expresses signs of weariness and idleness. He claps his hands and Mesrour[1] the Nubian appears, with bare arms, bangles, yataghans,[2] and every eastern ornament—gaunt, tall, and hideous. He makes a salaam before my lord the Aga.[3]

A thrill of terror and delight runs through the assembly. The ladies whisper to one another. The black slave was given to Sands Bedwin by an Egyptian Pasha in exchange for three dozen of Maraschino.[4] He has sown up ever so many odalisques[5] in sacks and tilted them into the Nile.

"Bid the slave-merchant enter," says the Turkish voluptuary, with a wave of his hand. Mesrour conducts the slave-merchant into my lord's presence: he brings a veiled female with him. He removes her veil. A thrill of applause bursts through the house. It is Mrs. Winkworth (she was a Miss Absolom)[6] with the beautiful eyes and hair. She is in a gorgeous oriental costume; the black braided locks are twined with innumerable jewels; her dress is covered over with gold piastres.[7] The odious Mahometan expresses himself charmed by her beauty. She falls down on her knees, and entreats him to restore her to the mountains where she was born, and where her Circassian lover is still deploring the absence of his Zuleikah.[8] No entreaties will move the obdurate Hassan. He laughs at the notion of the Circassian bridegroom. Zuleikah covers her face with her hands, and drops down in an attitude of the most beautiful despair. There seems to be no hope for her, when—when the Kislar Aga appears.

The Kislar Aga brings a letter from the Sultan. Hassan receives and places on his head the dread firman. A ghastly terror seizes him, while on the negro's face (it is Mesrour again in another costume) appears a ghastly joy. "Mercy! mercy!" cries the Pasha;[9] while the Kislar Aga, grinning horribly, pulls out—*a bow-string*.

The curtain draws just as he is going to use that awful weapon. Hassan from within bawls out, "First two syllables"[1]—and Mrs. Raw-

6. Turkish guards.
7. Red, fez-like head cap with tassel.
8. Hookah, water-cooled smoking pipe.
9. Aromatic paste, perfume.
1. Name of executioner in *Arabian Nights*.
2. Long curved knives.
3. Ottoman officer or master (a key to the charade).
4. Three dozen bottles of cherry liqueur.
5. Slaves and concubines of a harem.
6. Her maiden name indicates she was Jewish.
7. Turkish coins.
8. Circassian: from the Russian Caucasus. Zuleikah: from Byron's *The Bride of Abydos* (1813), a generic name for romantically beautiful Oriental women.
9. Hassan appears in *The Arabian Nights* and Oriental works by Thomas Moore, Sir Walter Scott, and Lord Byron. Firman: a sultan's edict. Pasha: commander.
1. "Aga" (for Ottoman officer).

don Crawley, who is going to act in the charade, comes forward and compliments Mrs. Winkworth on the admirable taste and beauty of her costume.

The second part of the charade takes place. It is still an eastern scene. Hassan, in another dress, is in an attitude by Zuleikah, who is perfectly reconciled to him. The Kislar Aga has become a peaceful black slave. It is sunrise on the desert, and the Turks turn their heads eastward and bow to the sand. As there are no dromedaries at hand, the band facetiously plays "The Camels are coming."[2] An enormous Egyptian head figures in the scene. It is a musical one,—and, to the surprise of the oriental travellers, sings a comic song, composed by Mr. Wagg. The eastern voyagers go off dancing, like Papageno and the Moorish King, in "The Magic Flute." "Last two syllables" roars the head.[3]

The last act opens. It is a Grecian tent this time. A tall and stalwart man reposes on a couch there. Above him hang his helmet and shield. There is no need for them now. Ilium is down. Iphigenia is slain. Cassandra[4] is a prisoner in his outer halls. The king of men (it is Colonel Crawley, who, indeed, has no notion about the sack of Ilium or the conquest of Cassandra), the anax andrôn[5] is asleep in his chamber at Argos. A lamp casts the broad shadow of the sleeping warrior flickering on the wall—the sword and shield of Troy glitter in its light. The band plays the awful music of Don Juan, before the statue enters.[6]

Ægisthus[7] steals in pale and on tiptoe. What is that ghastly face looking out balefully after him from behind the arras? He raises his dagger to strike the sleeper, who turns in his bed, and opens his broad chest as if for the blow. He cannot strike the noble slumbering chieftain. Clytemnestra glides swiftly into the room like an apparition—her arms are bare and white,—her tawny hair floats down her shoulders,—her face is deadly pale,—and her eyes are lighted up with a smile so ghastly, that people quake as they look at her.

A tremor ran through the room. "Good God!" somebody said, "it's Mrs. Rawdon Crawley."

Scornfully she snatches the dagger out of Ægisthus's hand, and advances to the bed. You see it shining over her head in the glimmer of the lamp, and—and the lamp goes out, with a groan, and all is dark.

The darkness and the scene frightened people. Rebecca performed the part so well, and with such ghastly truth, that the spectators were all dumb, until, with a burst, all the lamps of the hall blazed

2. Robert Burns' "The Campbells Are Coming."
3. Papageno and Monostatos, comic characters in Mozart's 1791 opera. The singing head is of Memnon, Egyptian who died at Troy and whose gigantic statue legendarily emitted musical sounds each morning when first struck by sunlight. Last two syllables are "Memnon."
4. Iphigenia: Agamemnon's daughter, whom he sacrificed. Cassandra: Agamemnon's Trojan slave, whose ability to foretell the future was combined with the curse that no one would believe her.
5. King of men, Homer's tag for Agamemnon in *The Iliad*.
6. In Mozart's *Don Giovanni* (1787), the music heard before the statue of the Commendatore comes to take Giovanni to hell.
7. While Agamemnon was fighting at Troy, his wife, Clytemnestra, took a lover, Ægisthus; on his return, they murdered Agamemnon in his sleep.

out again, when everybody began to shout applause. "Brava! brava!" old Steyne's strident voice was heard roaring over all the rest. "By —, she'd do it too," he said between his teeth. The performers were called by the whole house, which sounded with cries of "Manager! Clytemnestra!" AGAMEMNON[8] could not be got to show in his classical tunic, but stood in the back ground with Ægisthus and others of the performers of the little play. Mr. Bedwin Sands led on Zuleikah and Clytemnestra. A great personage insisted upon being presented to the charming Clytemnestra. "Heigh ha? Run him through the body. Marry somebody else, hay?" was the apposite remark made by his Royal Highness.

"Mrs. Rawdon Crawley was quite killing in the part," said Lord Steyne. Becky laughed; gay, and saucy looking, and swept the prettiest little curtsey ever seen.

Servants brought in salvers covered with numerous cool dainties, and the performers disappeared, to get ready for the second charade-tableau.

The three syllables of this charade were to be depicted in pantomime, and the performance took place in the following wise:—

First syllable. Colonel Rawdon Crawley, C.B., with a slouched hat and a staff, a great coat, and a lantern borrowed from the stables, passed across the stage bawling out, as if warning the inhabitants of the hour. In the lower window are seen two bagmen playing apparently at the game of cribbage, over which they yawn much. To them enters one looking like Boots,[9] (the Honourable G. Ringwood,) which character the young gentleman performed to perfection, and divests them of their lowering covering; and presently Chambermaid (the Right Honourable Lord Southdown) with two candlesticks, and a warming-pan. She ascends to the upper apartment, and warms the bed. She uses the warming-pan as a weapon wherewith she wards off the attention of the bagmen. She exits. They put on their night-caps, and pull down the blinds. Boots comes out and closes the shutters of the ground-floor chamber. You hear him bolting and chaining the door within. All the lights go out. The music plays *Dormez, dormez chers Amours*. A voice from behind the curtain says, "First syllable."[1]

Second syllable. The lamps are lighted up all of a sudden. The music plays the old air from John of Paris, *Ah quel plaisir d'être en voyage*.[2] It is the same scene. Between the first and second floors of the house represented, you behold a sign on which the Steyne arms are painted. All the bells are ringing all over the house. In the lower apartment you see a man with a long slip of paper presenting it to another, who shakes his fist, threatens and vows that it is monstrous. "Ostler, bring round my gig," cries another at the door. He chucks Chambermaid (the Right Honourable Lord Southdown) under the

8. First printing printed this word in normal type: Agamemnon
9. Bagmen: salesmen. Boots: boot black, shoe shiner.
1. Sleep, sleep, dear loves. Popular musical romance by Amédée de Beauplan, pseudonym of Amédée Rousseau (1790–1853) (Tillotson). The first syllable is "night."
2. Oh, what pleasure it is to travel. From *Jean de Paris* (1812), by François-Adrien Boëldieu (Tillotson).

The Triumph of Clytemnestra

chin; she seems to deplore his absence, as Calypso did that of that other eminent traveller Ulysses.[3] Boots (the Honourable G. Ringwood) passes with a wooden box, containing silver flagons, and cries "Pots" with such exquisite humour and naturalness, that the whole house rings with applause, and a bouquet is thrown to him. Crack, crack, crack, go the whips. Landlord, chambermaid, waiter rush to the door; but just as some distinguished guest is arriving, the curtains close, and the invisible theatrical manager cries out "Second syllable."[4]

"I think it must be 'Hotel,'" says Captain Grigg of the Life Guards; there is a general laugh at the Captain's cleverness. He is not very far from the mark.

While the third syllable is in preparation, the band begins a nautical medley—All in the Downs, Cease Rude Boreas, Rule Britannia, In the Bay of Biscay O[5]—some maritime event is about to take place. A bell is heard ringing as the curtain draws aside. "Now, gents., for the shore!" a voice exclaims. People take leave of each other. They point anxiously as if towards the clouds, which are represented by a dark curtain, and they nod their heads in fear. Lady Squeams (the Right Honourable Lord Southdown), her lap-dog, her bags, reticules, and husband sit down, and cling hold of some ropes. It is evidently a ship.

The Captain (Colonel Crawley, C.B.), with a cocked hat and a telescope, comes in, holding his hat on his head, and looks out; his coat tails fly about as if in the wind. When he leaves go of his hat to use his telescope, his hat flies off, with immense applause. It is blowing fresh. The music rises and whistles louder and louder; the mariners go across the stage staggering, as if the ship was in severe motion. The Steward (the Honourable G. Ringwood) passes reeling by, holding six basins. He puts one rapidly by Lord Squeams—Lady Squeams giving a pinch to her dog, which begins to howl piteously, puts her pocket-handkerchief to her face, and rushes away as for the cabin. The music rises up to the wildest pitch of stormy excitement, and the third syllable[6] is concluded.

There was a little ballet, Le Rossignol,[7] in which Montessu and Noblet used to be famous in those days, and which Mr. Wagg transferred to the English stage as an opera, putting his verse, of which he was a skilful writer, to the pretty airs of the ballet. It was dressed in old French costume, and little Lord Southdown now appeared admirably attired in the disguise of an old woman hobbling about the stage with a faultless crooked stick.

3. In *The Odyssey* Ulysses is detained for years on Calypso's island and then mourned when he is gone.
4. "Inn," or "In(n)."
5. "All in the downs the fleet was moor'd," titled "Black-Eyed Susan" (R. Leveridge); "Cease, rude Boreas, blust'ring railer," or "The Storm"; "Rule Britannia" (T. A. Arne, words by J. Thomson); "The Bay of Biscay" (J. Davy) (Harden).
6. "Gale."
7. The Nightingale. L. S. Lebrun's one-act opera *Le Rossignol* (1816), in which Lise Noblet and Pauline Montessu, as members of the Paris Opéra company, would have appeared. A translation by Edward James Loder was performed at the Princess Theatre in London a year before this was written.

Trills of melody were heard behind the scenes, and gurgling from a sweet pasteboard cottage covered with roses and trellis work. "Philomèle, Philomèle,"[8] cries the old woman, and Philomèle comes out.

More applause—it is Mrs. Rawdon Crawley in powder and patches, the most *ravissante*[9] little Marquise in the world.

She comes in laughing, humming, and frisks about the stage with all the innocence of theatrical youth—she makes a curtsey. Mamma says "Why, child, you are always laughing and singing," and away she goes, with—

THE ROSE UPON MY BALCONY.[1]

The rose upon my balcony the morning air perfuming,
Was leafless all the winter time and pining for the spring;
You ask me why her breath is sweet and why her cheek is blooming,
It is because the sun is out and birds begin to sing.

The nightingale, whose melody is through the greenwood ringing,
Was silent when the boughs were bare and winds were blowing keen:
And if, Mamma, you ask of me the reason of his singing;
It is because the sun is out and all the leaves are green.

8. Philomèle, in myth, was transformed into a nightingale.
9. Ravishingly beautiful.
1. By Thackeray, reprinted in *Ballads* (1855).

Thus each performs his part, Mamma, the birds have found their voices,
The blowing rose a flush, Mamma, her bonny cheek to dye;
And there's sunshine in my heart, Mamma, which wakens and rejoices,
And so I sing and blush, Mamma, and that's the reason why.

During the intervals of the stanzas of this ditty, the good-natured personage addressed as mamma by the singer, and whose large whiskers appeared under her cap, seemed very anxious to exhibit her maternal affection by embracing the innocent creature who performed the daughter's part. Every caress was received with loud acclamations of laughter by the sympathising audience. At its conclusion (while the music was performing a symphony as if ever so many birds were warbling) the whole house was unanimous for an *encore:* and applause and bouquets without end were showered upon the NIGHTINGALE of the evening. Lord Steyne's voice of applause was loudest of all. Becky, the nightingale, took the flowers which he threw to her, and pressed them to her heart with the air of a consummate comedian. Lord Steyne was frantic with delight. His guests' enthusiasm harmonised with his own. Where was the beautiful black-eyed Houri whose appearance in the first charade had caused such delight. She was twice as handsome as Becky, but the brilliancy of the latter had quite eclipsed her. All voices were for her. Stephens, Caradori, Ronzi de Begnis,[2] people compared her to one or the other, and agreed with good reason, very likely, that had she been an actress none on the stage could have surpassed her. She had reached her culmination: her voice rose trilling and bright over the storm of applause: and soared as high and joyful as her triumph. There was a ball after the dramatic entertainments, and everybody pressed round Becky as the great point of attraction of the evening. The Royal Personage declared with an oath, that she was perfection, and engaged her again and again in conversation. Little Becky's soul swelled with pride and delight at these honours; she saw fortune, fame, fashion before her. Lord Steyne was her slave; followed her everywhere, and scarcely spoke to any one in the room beside; and paid her the most marked compliments and attention. She still appeared in her Marquise costume, and danced a minuet with Monsieur de Truffigny, Monsieur Le Duc de la Jabotière's attaché; and the Duke, who had all the traditions of the ancient court, pronounced that Madame Crawley was worthy to have been a pupil of Vestris,[3] or to have figured at Versailles. Only a feeling of dignity, the gout, and the strongest sense of duty and personal sacrifice, prevented his Excellency from dancing with her himself; and he declared in public, that a lady who could talk and dance like Mrs. Rawdon, was fit to be ambassadress at any court in Europe. He was only consoled when he heard that she was half a Frenchwoman by birth. "None but a compatriot," his Excellency declared, "could have performed that majestic dance in such a way."

2. Catherine Stephens (1794–1882), noted ballad singer, became countess of Essex; Maria Caradori-Allan (1800–65), Italian operatic singer, came to London in 1822; Ronzi de Begnis (1800–53) was an Italian operatic singer. All were noted for their beauty and honorable reputations.
3. Maria Auguste Vestris (1760–1842), famous dancer and ballet teacher at the Paris Opéra.

Then she figured in a waltz with Monsieur de Klingenspohr, the Prince of Peterwaradin's cousin and attaché. The delighted Prince, having less *retenue*[4] than his French diplomatic colleague, insisted upon taking a turn with the charming creature, and twirled round the ball-room with her, scattering the diamond out of his boot-tassels and hussar jacket until his highness was fairly out of breath. Papoosh Pasha himself would have liked to dance with her if that amusement had been the custom of his country. The company made a circle round her, and applauded as wildly as if she had been a Noblet or a Taglioni.[5] Everybody was in ecstacy; and Becky too, you may be sure. She passed by Lady Stunnington with a look of scorn. She patronised Lady Gaunt and her astonished and mortified sister-in-law—she *écraséd*[6] all rival charmers. As for poor Mrs. Winkworth, and her long hair and great eyes, which had made such an effect at the commencement of the evening; where was she now? Nowhere in the race. She might tear her long hair and cry her great eyes out; but there was not a person to heed or to deplore the discomfiture.

The greatest triumph of all was at supper time. She was placed at the grand exclusive table with his Royal Highness the exalted personage before mentioned, and the rest of the great guests. She was served on gold plate. She might have had pearls melted into her champagne if she liked—another Cleopatra;[7] and the potentate of Peterwaradin would have given half the brilliants off his jacket for a kind glance from those dazzling eyes. Jabotière wrote home about her to his government. The ladies at the other tables, who supped off mere silver, and marked Lord Steyne's constant attention to her, vowed it was a monstrous infatuation, a gross insult to ladies of rank. If sarcasm could have killed, Lady Stunnington would have slain her on the spot.

Rawdon Crawley was scared at these triumphs. They seemed to separate his wife farther than ever from him somehow. He thought with a feeling very like pain how immeasurably she was his superior.

When the hour of departure came, a crowd of young men followed her to her carriage, for which the people without bawled, the cry being caught up by the link-men[8] who were stationed outside the tall gates of Gaunt House, congratulating each person who issued from the gate and hoping his Lordship had enjoyed this noble party.

Mrs. Rawdon Crawley's carriage, coming up to the gate after due shouting, rattled into the illuminated court-yard, and drove up to the covered way. Rawdon put his wife into the carriage, which drove off. Mr. Wenham had proposed to him to walk home, and offered the Colonel the refreshment of a cigar.

They lighted their cigars by the lamp of one of the many link-boys outside, and Rawdon walked on with his friend Wenham. Two

4. Caution.
5. Lise Noblet, of the Paris Opéra. Maria Taglioni, who danced from 1827 to her retirement in 1847, was a favorite of Thackeray's, figuring in his works from *Floré et Zephyr* (1837) to *The Newcomes* (1854–55).
6. Crushed.
7. At a banquet for Antony, Cleopatra desolved a pearl in acid and drank it, saying, "My draught to Antony shall exceed in value the whole banquet."
8. Men who, for a fee, carried torches lighting the way through unlighted London.

Colonel Crawley is wanted

persons separated from the crowd and followed the two gentlemen; and when they had walked down Gaunt Square a few score of paces, one of the men came up, and touching Rawdon on the shoulder, said, "Beg your pardon, Colonel, I vish to speak to you most particular." The gentleman's acquaintance gave a loud whistle as the latter spoke, at which signal a cab came clattering up from those stationed at the gate of Gaunt House—and the aide-de-camp ran round and placed himself in front of Colonel Crawley.

That gallant officer at once knew what had befallen him. He was in the hands of the bailiffs. He started back, falling against the man who had first touched him.

"We're three on us—it's no use bolting," the man behind said.

"It's you, Moss, is it?" said the Colonel, who appeared to know his interlocutor. "How much is it?"

"Only a small thing," whispered Mr. Moss, of Cursitor Street, Chancery Lane, and assistant officer to the Sheriff of Middlesex[9]—"One hundred and sixty-six, six and eightpence, at the suit of Mr. Nathan."

"Lend me a hundred, Wenham, for God's sake," poor Rawdon said—"I've got seventy at home."

"I've not got ten pounds in the world," said poor Mr. Wenham—"Good night, my dear fellow."

"Good night," said Rawdon ruefully. And Wenham walked away—and Rawdon Crawley finished his cigar as the cab drove under Temple Bar.[1]

9. Bailiffs arrested debtors, keeping them temporarily in a spunging house so they could arrange payment and avoid debtors' prison. Moss' house is probably based on Sloman's spunging house, which was actually in Cursitor Street. Wenham was Lord Steyne's "vizier and chief confidential servant."

1. The gateway formerly standing near the Royal Court of Justice where the Strand becomes Fleet Street near the end of Chancery Lane, from which Cursitor Street leads and where Moss has his spunging house. Rawdon had intended a walk of a few blocks from Gaunt Square (a fictional locale in May Fair, possibly Berkeley Square) to his house in Curzon Street.

## *Chapter LII.*

### IN WHICH LORD STEYNE SHOWS HIMSELF IN A MOST AMIABLE LIGHT.

WHEN[1] Lord Steyne was benevolently disposed, he did nothing by halves, and his kindness towards the Crawley family did the greatest honour to his benevolent discrimination. His lordship extended his good-will to little Rawdon: he pointed out to the boy's parents the necessity of sending him to a public school; that he was of an age now when emulation, the first principles of the Latin language, pugilistic exercises, and the society of his fellow-boys would be of the greatest benefit to the boy. His father objected that he was not rich enough to send the child to a good public school; his mother, that Briggs was a capital mistress for him, and had brought him on (as indeed was the fact) famously in English, the Latin rudiments, and in general learning: but all these objections disappeared before the generous perseverance of the Marquis of Steyne. His lordship was one of the governors of that famous old collegiate institution called the Whitefriars. It had been a Cistercian Convent[2] in old days, when the Smithfield, which is contiguous to it, was a tournament ground. Obstinate heretics used to be brought thither convenient for burning hard by. Harry VIII., the Defender of the Faith, seized upon the monastery and its possessions, and hanged and tortured some of the monks who could not accommodate themselves to the pace of his reform. Finally, a great merchant bought the house and land adjoining, in which, and with the help of other wealthy endowments of land and money, he established a famous foundation hospital for old men and children. An extern school grew round the old almost monastic foundation, which subsists still with its middle-age costume and usages: and all Cistercians pray that it may long flourish.

Of this famous house, some of the greatest noblemen, prelates, and dignitaries in England are governors: and as the boys are very comfortably lodged, fed, and educated, and subsequently inducted to good scholarships at the University and livings in the Church, many

1. Initial illustration is of Alnaschar in the *Arabian Nights,* who in a dream of splendor spurns the vizier's daughter with his foot, accidentally overturning his glassware, by which he had hoped to gain his fortune.
2. The following description applies more or less to Thackeray's old school, Charterhouse, formerly a Carthusian monastery, appropriated to other uses in Henry VIII's time, and established by Thomas Sutton as a school for boys and nursing home for old men in 1611.

little gentlemen are devoted to the ecclesiastical profession from their tenderest years, and there is considerable emulation to procure nominations for the foundations. It was originally intended for the sons of poor and deserving clerics and laics; but many of the noble governors of the Institution, with an enlarged and rather capricious benevolence, selected all sorts of objects for their bounty. To get an education for nothing, and a future livelihood and profession assured, was so excellent a scheme, that some of the richest people did not disdain it; and not only great men's relations, but great men themselves, sent their sons to profit by the chance—Right Rev. Prelates sent their own kinsmen or the sons of their clergy, while, on the other hand, some great noblemen did not disdain to patronise the children of their confidential servants,—so that a lad entering this establishment had every variety of youthful society wherewith to mingle.

Rawdon Crawley, though the only book which he studied was the Racing Calendar, and though his chief recollections of polite learning were connected with the floggings which he received at Eton in his early youth, had that decent and honest reverence for classical learning which all English gentlemen feel, and was glad to think that his son was to have a provision for life, perhaps, and a certain opportunity of becoming a scholar. And although his boy was his chief solace and companion, and endeared to him by a thousand small ties, about which he did not care to speak to his wife, who had all along shown the utmost indifference to their son, yet Rawdon agreed at once to part with him, and to give up his own greatest comfort and benefit for the sake of the welfare of the little lad. He did not know how fond he was of the child until it became necessary to let him go away. When he was gone, he felt more sad and downcast than he cared to own—far sadder than the boy himself, who was happy enough to enter a new career, and find companions of his own age. Becky burst out laughing once or twice, when the Colonel, in his clumsy, incoherent way, tried to express his sentimental sorrows at the boy's departure. The poor fellow felt that his dearest pleasure and closest friend was taken from him. He looked often and wistfully at the little vacant bed in his dressing-room, where the child used to sleep. He missed him sadly of mornings, and tried in vain to walk in the Park without him. He did not know how solitary he was until little Rawdon was gone. He liked the people who were fond of him; and would go and sit for long hours with his good-natured sister Lady Jane, and talk to her about the virtues, and good looks, and hundred good qualities of the child.

Young Rawdon's aunt, we have said, was very fond of him, as was her little girl, who wept copiously when the time for her cousin's departure came. The elder Rawdon was thankful for the fondness of mother and daughter. The very best and honestest feelings of the man came out in these artless outpourings of paternal feeling in which he indulged in their presence, and encouraged by their sympathy. He secured not only Lady Jane's kindness, but her sincere regard, by the feelings which he manifested, and which he could not show to his own wife. The two kinswomen met as seldom as possible. Becky laughed bitterly at Jane's feelings and softness; the other's kindly and gentle nature could not but revolt at her sister's callous behaviour.

It estranged Rawdon from his wife more than he knew or acknowledged to himself. She did not care for the estrangement. Indeed, she did not miss him or anybody. She looked upon him as her errand-man and humble slave. He might be ever so depressed or sulky, and she did not mark his demeanour, or only treated it with a sneer. She was busy thinking about her position or her pleasures or her advancement in society; she ought to have held a great place in it, that is certain.

It was honest Briggs who made up the little kit for the boy which he was to take to school. Molly, the housemaid, blubbered in the passage when he went away—Molly kind and faithful in spite of a long arrear of unpaid wages. Mrs. Becky could not let her husband have the carriage to take the boy to school. Take the horses into the City!—such a thing was never heard of. Let a cab be brought. She did not offer to kiss him when he went: nor did the child propose to embrace her: but gave a kiss to old Briggs, (whom, in general, he was very shy of caressing,) and consoled her by pointing out that he was to come home on Saturdays, when she would have the benefit of seeing him. As the cab rolled towards the City, Becky's carriage rattled off to the Park. She was chattering and laughing with a score of young dandies by the Serpentine, as the father and son entered at the old gates of the school—where Rawdon left the child, and came away with a sadder purer feeling in his heart than perhaps that poor battered fellow had ever known since he himself came out of the nursery.

He walked all the way home very dismally, and dined alone with Briggs. He was very kind to her, and grateful for her love and watchfulness over the boy. His conscience smote him that he had borrowed Briggs's money and aided in deceiving her. They talked about little Rawdon a long time, for Becky only came home to dress and go out to dinner—And then he went off uneasily to drink tea with Lady Jane, and tell her of what had happened, and how little Rawdon went off like a trump, and how he was to wear a gown and little knee-breeches, and how young Blackball, Jack Blackball's son, of the old regiment, had taken him in charge and promised to be kind to him.

In the course of a week, young Blackball had constituted little Rawdon his fag,[3] shoe-black, and breakfast toaster; initiated him into the mysteries of the Latin Grammar, and thrashed him three or four times; but not severely. The little chap's good-natured honest face won his way for him. He only got that degree of beating which was, no doubt, good for him; and as for blacking shoes, toasting bread, and fagging in general, were these offices not deemed to be necessary parts of every young English gentleman's education?

Our business does not lie with the second generation and Master Rawdon's life at school, otherwise the present tale might be carried to any indefinite length. The Colonel went to see his son a short time afterwards, and found the lad sufficiently well and happy, grinning and laughing in his little black gown and little breeches.

3. Underclassman required to serve menially an upperclassman.

His father sagaciously tipped Blackball, his master, a sovereign, and secured that young gentleman's good will towards his fag. As a *protégé* of the great Lord Steyne, the nephew of a County member, and son of a Colonel and C.B., whose name appeared in some of the most fashionable parties in the *Morning Post,* perhaps the school authorities were disposed not to look unkindly on the child. He had plenty of pocket-money, which he spent in treating his comrades royally to raspberry tarts, and he was often allowed to come home on Saturdays to his father, who always made a jubilee of that day. When free, Rawdon would take him to the play, or send him thither with the footman; and on Sundays he went to church with Briggs and Lady Jane and his cousins. Rawdon marvelled over his stories about school, and fights, and fagging. Before long, he knew the names of all the masters and the principal boys as well as little Rawdon himself. He invited little Rawdon's crony from school, and made both the children sick with pastry, and oysters, and porter after the play. He tried to look knowing over the Latin grammar when little Rawdon showed him what part of that work he was "in." "Stick to it, my boy," he said to him with much gravity, "there's nothing like a good classical education! nothing!"

Becky's contempt for her husband grew greater every day,—"Do what you like,—dine where you please,—go and have ginger-beer and saw-dust at Astley's,[4] or psalm-singing with Lady Jane,—only don't expect *me* to busy myself with the boy. I have your interests to attend to, as you can't attend to them yourself. I should like to know where you would have been now, and in what sort of a position in society, if I had not looked after you?" Indeed, nobody wanted poor old Rawdon at the parties whither Becky used to go. She was often asked without him now. She talked about great people as if she had the fee-simple[5] of May Fair; and when the Court went into mourning, she always wore black.

Little Rawdon being disposed of, Lord Steyne, who took such a parental interest in the affairs of this amiable poor family, thought that their expenses might be very advantageously curtailed by the departure of Miss Briggs; and that Becky was quite clever enough to take the management of her own house. It has been narrated in a former Chapter, how the benevolent nobleman had given his *protégé* money to pay off her little debt to Miss Briggs, who however still remained behind with her friends: whence my lord came to the painful conclusion that Mrs. Crawley had made some other use of the money confided to her than that for which her generous patron had given the loan. However, Lord Steyne was not so rude as to impart his suspicions upon this head to Mrs. Becky, whose feelings might be hurt by any controversy on the money-question, and who might have a thousand painful reasons for disposing otherwise of his lordship's generous loan. But he determined to satisfy himself of the real state of the case: and instituted the necessary inquiries in a most cautious and delicate manner.

In the first place he took an early opportunity of pumping Miss Briggs. That was not a difficult operation. A very little encouragement would set that worthy woman to talk volubly, and pour out all within her. And one day when Mrs. Rawdon had gone out to drive (as Mr. Fiche, his lordship's confidential servant, easily learned at the livery stables where the Crawleys kept their carriage and horses, or rather, where the livery-man kept a carriage and horses for Mr. and Mrs. Crawley)—my lord dropped in upon the Curzon Street house—asked Briggs for a cup of coffee—told her that he had good accounts of the little boy at school—and in five minutes found out from her that Mrs. Rawdon had given her nothing except a black silk gown, for which Miss Briggs was immensely grateful.

He laughed within himself at this artless story. For the truth is, our dear friend Rebecca had given him a most circumstantial narration of Briggs's delight at receiving her money—eleven hundred and twenty-five pounds—and in what securities she had invested it: and what a pang Becky herself felt in being obliged to pay away such a delightful sum of money. "Who knows," the dear woman may have thought within herself, "perhaps he may give me a little more?" My lord, however, made no such proposal to the little schemer—very likely thinking that he had been sufficiently generous already.

4. An amphitheater for exhibitions and large public entertainments.
5. Outright ownership.

He had the curiosity, then, to ask Miss Briggs about the state of her private affairs—and she told his lordship candidly what her position was—how Miss Crawley had left her a legacy—how her relatives had had part of it—how Colonel Crawley had put out another portion, for which she had the best security and interest—and how Mr. and Mrs. Rawdon had kindly busied themselves with Sir Pitt, who was to dispose of the remainder most advantageously for her, when he had time. My lord asked how much the Colonel had already invested for her, and Miss Briggs at once and truly told him that the sum was six hundred and odd pounds.

But as soon as she had told her story, the voluble Briggs repented of her frankness, and besought my lord not to tell Mr. Crawley of the confessions which she had made. "The Colonel was so kind—Mr. Crawley might be offended and pay back the money, for which she could get no such good interest anywhere else." Lord Steyne, laughing, promised he never would divulge their conversation, and when he and Miss Briggs parted he laughed still more.

"What an accomplished little devil it is!" thought he. "What a splendid actress and manager! She had almost got a second supply out of me the other day, with her coaxing ways. She beats all the women I have ever seen in the course of all my well-spent life. They are babies compared to her. I am a green-horn myself, and a fool in her hands—an old fool. She is unsurpassable in lies." His lordship's admiration for Becky rose immeasurably at this proof of her cleverness. Getting the money was nothing—but getting double the sum she wanted, and paying nobody—it was a magnificent stroke. And Crawley, my lord thought—Crawley is not such a fool as he looks and seems. He has managed the matter cleverly enough on his side. Nobody would ever have supposed from his face and demeanour that he knew anything about this money business; and yet he put her up to it, and has spent the money, no doubt. In this opinion my lord, we know, was mistaken; but it influenced a good deal his behaviour towards Colonel Crawley, whom he began to treat with even less than that semblance of respect which he had formerly shown towards that gentleman. It never entered into the head of Mrs. Crawley's patron that the little lady might be making a purse for herself; and, perhaps, if the truth must be told, he judged of Colonel Crawley by his experience of other husbands, whom he had known in the course of the long and well-spent life, which had made him acquainted with a great deal of the weakness of mankind. My lord had bought so many men during his life, that he was surely to be pardoned for supposing that he had found the price of this one.

He taxed Becky upon the point on the very first occasion when he met her alone, and he complimented her, good-humouredly, on her cleverness in getting more than the money which she required. Becky was only a little taken aback. It was not the habit of this dear creature to tell falsehoods, except when necessity compelled, but in these great emergencies it was her practice to lie very freely; and in an instant she was ready with another neat plausible circumstantial story which she administered to her patron. The previous statement which she had made to him was a falsehood—a wicked falsehood: she owned it; but who had made her tell it? "Ah, my Lord," she said, "you don't know all I have to suffer and bear in silence: you see me gay and happy before you—you little know what I have to endure when there is no protector near me. It was my husband, by threats and the most savage treatment, forced me to ask for that sum about which I deceived you. It was he, who, foreseeing that questions might be asked regarding the disposal of the money, forced me to account for it as I did. He took the money. He told me he had paid Miss Briggs; I did not want, I did not dare to doubt him. Pardon the wrong which a desperate man is forced to commit, and pity a miserable, miserable woman." She burst into tears as she spoke. Persecuted virtue never looked more bewitchingly wretched.

They had a long conversation, driving round and round the Regent's Park in Mrs. Crawley's carriage together, a conversation of which it is not necessary to repeat the details: but the upshot of it was, that, when Becky came home, she flew to her dear Briggs with a smiling face, and announced that she had some very good news for her. Lord Steyne had acted in the noblest and most generous manner. He was always thinking how and when he could do good. Now that little Rawdon was gone to school, a dear companion and friend was no longer necessary to her. She was grieved beyond measure to part with Briggs; but her means required that she should practise every retrenchment, and her sorrow was mitigated by the idea that her dear Briggs would be far better provided for by her generous patron than in her humble home. Mrs. Pilkington, the housekeeper at Gauntly Hall, was growing exceedingly old, feeble, and rheumatic: she was not equal to the work of superintending that vast mansion, and must be on the look out for a successor. It was a splendid position. The family did not go to Gauntly once in two years. At other times the housekeeper was the mistress of the magnificent mansion—had four covers daily for her table; was visited by the clergy and the most respectable people of the county—was the lady of Gauntly, in fact; and the two last housekeepers before Mrs. Pilkington had married rectors of Gauntly: but Mrs. P. could not, being the aunt of the present Rector. The place was not to be hers yet; but she might go down on a visit to Mrs. Pilkington, and see whether she would like to succeed her.

What words can paint the extatic gratitude of Briggs! All she stipulated for was that little Rawdon should be allowed to come down and see her at the Hall. Becky promised this—any thing. She ran up to her husband when he came home, and told him the joyful news. Rawdon was glad, deuced glad; the weight was off his conscience about poor Briggs's money. She was provided for, at any rate, but—but his mind was disquiet. He did not seem to be all right somehow. He told little Southdown what Lord Steyne had done, and the young man eyed Crawley with an air which surprised the latter.

He told Lady Jane of this second proof of Steyne's bounty, and she, too, looked odd and alarmed; so did Sir Pitt. "She is too clever and—and gay to be allowed to go from party to party without a companion," both said. "You must go with her, Rawdon, wherever she goes, and you *must* have somebody with her—one of the girls from

Queen's Crawley, perhaps, though they were rather giddy guardians for her."

Somebody Becky should have. But in the meanwhile it was clear that honest Briggs must not lose her chance of settlement for life; and so she and her bags were packed, and she set off on her journey. And so two of Rawdon's out-sentinels were in the hands of the enemy.

Sir Pitt went and expostulated with his sister-in-law upon the subject of the dismissal of Briggs, and other matters of delicate family interest. In vain she pointed out to him how necessary was the protection of Lord Steyne for her poor husband; how cruel it would be on their part to deprive Briggs of the position offered to her. Cajolements, coaxings, smiles, tears could not satisfy Sir Pitt, and he had something very like a quarrel with his once admired Becky. He spoke of the honour of the family: the unsullied reputation of the Crawleys; expressed himself in indignant tones about her receiving those young Frenchmen—those wild young men of fashion, my Lord Steyne himself, whose carriage was always at her door, who passed hours daily in her company, and whose constant presence made the world talk about her. As the head of the house he implored her to be more prudent. Society was already speaking lightly of her. Lord Steyne, though a nobleman of the greatest station and talents, was a man whose attentions would compromise any woman; he besought, he implored, he commanded his sister-in-law to be watchful in her intercourse with that nobleman.

Becky promised anything and everything Pitt wanted; but Lord Steyne came to her house as often as ever, and Sir Pitt's anger increased. I wonder was Lady Jane angry or pleased that her husband at last found fault with his favourite Rebecca? Lord Steyne's visits continuing, his own ceased; and his wife was for refusing all further intercourse with that nobleman, and declining the invitation to the Charade-night which the Marchioness sent to her; but Sir Pitt thought it was necessary to accept it, as his Royal Highness would be there.

Although he went to the party in question, Sir Pitt quitted it very early, and his wife, too, was very glad to come away. Becky hardly so much as spoke to him or noticed her sister-in-law. Pitt Crawley declared her behaviour was monstrously indecorous, reprobated in strong terms the habit of play-acting and fancy dressing, as highly unbecoming a British female; and after the charades were over, took his brother Rawdon severely to task for appearing himself, and allowing his wife to join in such improper exhibitions.

Rawdon said she should not join in any more such amusements, but indeed, and perhaps from hints from his elder brother and sister, he had already become a very watchful and exemplary domestic character. He left off his clubs and billiards. He never left home. He took Becky out to drive: he went laboriously with her to all her parties. Whenever my Lord Steyne called, he was sure to find the Colonel. And when Becky proposed to go out without her husband, or received invitations for herself, he peremptorily ordered her to refuse them; and there was that in the gentleman's manner which enforced obedience. Little Becky, to do her justice, was charmed with Rawdon's gallantry. If he was surly, she never was. Whether friends were present or absent, she had always a kind smile for him, and was attentive to his pleasure and comfort. It was the early days of their marriage over again: the same good humour, *prévenances,*[6] merriment, and artless confidence and regard. "How much pleasanter it is," she would say, "to have you by my side in the carriage than that foolish old Briggs! Let us always go on so, dear Rawdon. How nice it would be, and how happy we should always be, if we had but the money!" He fell asleep after dinner in his chair; he did not see the face opposite to him, haggard, weary, and terrible; it lighted up with fresh candid smiles when he woke. It kissed him gaily. He wondered that he had ever had suspicions. No, he never had suspicions; all those dumb doubts and surly misgivings which had been gathering on his mind were mere idle jealousies. She was fond of him; she always had been. As for her shining in society it was no fault of hers; she was formed to shine there. Was there any woman who could talk, or sing, or do anything like her? If she would but like the boy! Rawdon thought. But the mother and son never could be brought together.

And it was while Rawdon's mind was agitated with these doubts and perplexities that the incident occurred which was mentioned in the last Chapter; and the unfortunate Colonel found himself a prisoner away from home.

## *Chapter LIII.*

### A RESCUE AND A CATASTROPHE.

RIEND RAWDON drove on then to Mr. Moss's mansion in Cursitor Street, and was duly inducted into that dismal place of hospitality. Morning was breaking over the cheerful house-tops of Chancery Lane as the rattling cab woke up the echoes there, and a[1] little pink-eyed Jew-boy with a head as ruddy as the rising morn let the party into the house, and Rawdon was welcomed to the ground-floor apartments by Mr. Moss, his travelling

6. Kindnesses.
1. Revised edition reads: there. A

companion and host, who cheerfully asked him if he would like a glass of something warm after his drive.

The Colonel was not so depressed as some mortals would be, who, quitting a palace and a *placens uxor,*[2] find themselves barred into a spunging-house, for, if the truth must be told, he had been a lodger at Mr. Moss's establishment once or twice before. We have not thought it necessary in the previous course of this narrative to mention these trivial little domestic incidents: but the reader may be assured that they can't unfrequently occur in the life of a man who lives on nothing a-year.

Upon his first visit to Mr. Moss, the Colonel, then a bachelor, had been liberated by the generosity of his Aunt; on the second mishap, little Becky, with the greatest spirit and kindness, had borrowed a sum of money from Lord Southdown, and had coaxed her husband's creditor (who was her shawl, velvet-gown, lace pocket-handkerchief, trinket, and gim-crack purveyor, indeed) to take a portion of the sum claimed, and Rawdon's promissory note for the remainder: so on both these occasions the capture and release had been conducted with the utmost gallantry on all sides, and Moss and the Colonel were therefore on the very best of terms.

"You'll find your old bed, Colonel, and everything comfortable," that gentleman said, "as I may honestly say. You may be pretty sure its kep aired, and by the best of company, too. It was slep in the night afore last by the Honorable Capting Famish, of the Fiftieth Dragoons, whose Mar took him out, after a fortnight, jest to punish him, she said. But, Law bless you, I promise you, he punished my champagne, and had a party ere every night—reglar tip-top swells, down from the clubs and the West End—Capting Ragg, the Honourable Deuceace, who lives in the Temple, and some fellers as knows a good glass of wine, I warrant you. I've got a Doctor of Diwinity up stairs, five gents in the Coffee-room, and Mrs. Moss has a tably-dy-hoty[3] at half-past five, and a little cards or music afterwards, when we shall be most happy to see you."

"I'll ring, when I want anything," said Rawdon, and went quietly to his bed-room. He was an old soldier, we have said, and not to be disturbed by any little shocks of fate. A weaker man would have sent off a letter to his wife on the instant of his capture. "But what is the use of disturbing her night's rest?" thought Rawdon. "She won't know whether I am in my room or not. It will be time enough to write to her when she has had her sleep out, and I have had mine. It's only a hundred-and-seventy, and the deuce is in it if we can't raise that." And so, thinking about little Rawdon (whom he would not like to[4] know that he was in such a queer place), the Colonel turned into the bed lately occupied by Captain Famish, and fell asleep. It was ten o'clock when he woke up, and the ruddy-headed youth brought him, with conscious pride, a fine silver dressing-case, wherewith he might perform the operation of shaving. Indeed Mr. Moss's house, though somewhat dirty, was splendid throughout. There were dirty trays,

2. Charming wife. Horace, *Odes* II.xiv 21–22.
3. *Table d'hôte*, fixed-price meal.
4. Revised edition reads: not have

and wine-coolers *en permanence* on the side-board, huge dirty gilt cornices, with dingy yellow satin hangings to the barred windows which looked into Cursitor Street—vast and dirty gilt picture-frames surrounding pieces sporting and sacred, all of which works were by the greatest masters; and fetched the greatest prices, too, in the bill transactions, in the course of which they were sold and bought over and over again. The Colonel's breakfast was served to him in the same dingy and gorgeous plated ware. Miss Moss, a dark-eyed maid in curl papers, appeared with the teapot, and, smiling, asked the Colonel how he had slep? and she brought him in the *Morning Post,* with the names of all the great people who had figured at Lord Steyne's entertainment the night before. It contained a brilliant account of the festivities, and of the beautiful and accomplished Mrs. Rawdon Crawley's admirable personifications.

After a lively chat with this lady (who sate on the edge of the breakfast table in an easy attitude displaying the drapery of her stocking and an ex-white satin shoe, which was down at heel), Colonel Crawley called for pens and ink, and paper; and being asked how many sheets, chose one which was brought to him between Miss Moss's own finger and thumb. Many a sheet had that dark-eyed damsel brought in; many a poor fellow had scrawled and blotted hurried lines of entreaty, and paced up and down that awful room until his messenger brought back the reply. Poor men always use messengers instead of the post. Who has not had their letters, with the wafers wet, and the announcement that a person is waiting in the hall?

Now on the score of his application, Rawdon had not many misgivings. "Dear Becky," Rawdon wrote, "*I hope you slept well.* Don't be *frightened* if I don't bring you in your *coffy.* Last night as I was coming home smoaking, I met with an *accadent.* I was *nabbed* by Moss of Cursitor Street—from whose *gilt and splendid parler* I write this—the same that had me this time two years. Miss Moss brought in my tea—she is grown very *fat,* and as usual, had *her stockens down at heal.*

"It's Nathan's business—a hundred-and-fifty—with costs, hundred-and-seventy. Please send me my desk and some *cloths*—I'm in pumps and a white tye (something like Miss M.'s stockings)—I've seventy in it. And as soon as you get this, Drive to Nathan's—offer him seventy-five down, and ask *him to renew*—say I'll take wine[5]—we may as well have some dinner sherry; but not *picturs,* they're too dear.

"If he won't stand it. Take my ticker and such of your things as you can *spare,* and send them to Balls[6]—we must, of coarse, have the sum to-night. It won't do to let it stand over, as to-morrow's Sunday; the beds here are not very *clean,* and there may be other things out against me—I'm glad it an't Rawdon's Saturday for coming home. God bless you.

"Yours in haste,<br>R. C.

"P.S. Make haste and come."

5. An offer to continue purchasing wine from his creditor.
6. Pawnbroker; the characteristic sign of pawnshops was three balls.

This letter, sealed with a wafer, was dispatched by one of the messengers who are always hanging about Mr. Moss's establishment; and Rawdon, having seen him depart, went out in the court-yard, and smoked his cigar with a tolerably easy mind—in spite of the bars over head; for Mr. Moss's court-yard is railed in like a cage, lest the gentlemen who are boarding with him should take a fancy to escape from his hospitality.

Three hours, he calculated, would be the utmost time required, before Becky should arrive and open his prison doors: and he passed these pretty cheerfully in smoking, in reading the paper, and in the Coffee-room with an acquaintance, Captain Walker, who happened to be there, and with whom he cut for sixpences for some hours, with pretty equal luck on either side.

But the day passed away and no messenger returned,—no Becky. Mr. Moss's tably-de-hoty was served at the appointed hour of half-past five, when such of the gentlemen lodging in the house as could afford to pay for the banquet, came and partook of it in the splendid front parlour before described, and with which Mr. Crawley's temporary lodging communicated, when Miss M., (Miss Hem, as her papa called her,) appeared without the curl-papers of the morning, and Mrs. Hem did the honours of a prime boiled leg of mutton and turnips, of which the Colonel ate with a very faint appetite. Asked whether he would "stand" a bottle of champagne for the company, he consented, and the ladies drank to his 'ealth, and Mr. Moss, in the most polite manner "looked towards him."

In the midst of this repast however, the door-bell was heard,—young Moss of the ruddy hair, rose up with the keys and answered the summons, and coming back, told the Colonel that the messenger had returned with a bag, a desk and a letter, which he gave him. "No ceramony, Colonel, I beg," said Mrs. Moss with a wave of her hand, and he opened the letter rather tremulously.—It was a beautiful letter, highly scented, on a pink paper, and with a light green seal.

*"Mon pauvre cher petit,"*[7] (Mrs. Crawley wrote). "I could not sleep *one wink* for thinking of what had become of *my odious old monstre:* and only got to rest in the morning after sending for Mr. Blench (for I was in a fever), who gave me a composing draught and left orders with Finette that I should be disturbed *on no account.* So that my poor old man's messenger, who had *bien mauvaise mine* Finette says, and *sentoit le Genièvre,*[8] remained in the hall for some hours waiting my bell. You may fancy my state when I read your poor dear old ill-spelt letter.

"Ill as I was, I instantly called for the carriage, and as soon as I was dressed (though I couldn't drink a drop of chocolate—I assure you I couldn't without my *monstre* to bring it to me), I drove *ventre à terre*[9] to Nathan's. I saw him—I wept—I cried—I fell at his odious

7. My poor little dear.
8. An ugly look and smelled of gin.
9. Top speed; literally, belly to the ground.

knees. Nothing would mollify the horrid man. He would have all the money, he said, or keep my poor monstre in prison. I drove home with the intention of paying that *triste visite chez mon oncle,*[1] (when every trinket I have should be at your disposal though they would not fetch a hundred pounds, for some, you know, are with *ce cher oncle* already,) and found Milor there with the Bulgarian old sheep-faced monster, who had come to compliment me upon last night's performances. Paddington came in, too, drawling and lisping and twiddling his hair; so did Champignac, and his chef—everybody with *foison*[2] of compliments and pretty speeches—plaguing poor me, who longed to be rid of them, and was thinking *every moment of the time* of *mon pauvre prisonnier.*[3]

"When they were gone, I went down on my knees to Milor; told him we were going to pawn everything, and begged and prayed him to give me two hundred pounds. He pish'd and psha'd in a fury—told me not to be such a fool as to pawn—and said he would see whether he could lend me the money. At last he went away, promising that he would send it me in the morning: when I will bring it to my poor old monster with a kiss from his affectionate

"Becky."

"I am writing in bed. Oh I have such a headache and such a heartache!"

When Rawdon read over this letter, he turned so red and looked so savage, that the company at the table d'hote easily perceived that bad news had reached him. All his suspicions, which he had been trying to banish, returned upon him. She could not even go out and sell her trinkets to free him. She could laugh and talk about compliments paid to her, whilst he was in prison. Who had put him there? Wenham had walked with him. Was there . . . . He could hardly bear to think of what he suspected. Leaving the room hurriedly, he ran into his own—opened his desk, wrote two hurried lines, which he directed to Sir Pitt or Lady Crawley, and bade the messenger carry them at once to Gaunt Street, bidding him to take a cab, and promising him a guinea if he was back in an hour.

In the note he besought his dear brother and sister, for the sake of God; for the sake of his dear child and his honour; to come to him and relieve him from his difficulty. He was in prison: he wanted a hundred pounds to set him free—he entreated them to come to him.

He went back to the dining-room after dispatching his messenger, and called for more wine. He laughed and talked with a strange boisterousness, as the people thought. Sometimes he laughed madly at his own fears, and went on drinking for an hour; listening all the while for the carriage which was to bring his fate back.

At the expiration of that time, wheels were heard whirling up to the gate—the young Janitor went out with his gate-keys. It was a lady whom he let in at the bailiff's door.

1. Sad visit to my uncle (i.e., the pawnbroker).
2. Plenty.
3. My poor prisoner.

"Colonel Crawley," she said, trembling very much. He, with a knowing look, locked the outer door upon her—then unlocked and opened the inner one, and calling out, "Colonel, you're wanted," led her into the back parlour, which he occupied.

Rawdon came in from the dining-parlour where all those people were carousing, into his back room; a flare of coarse light following him into the apartment where the lady stood, still very nervous.

"It is I, Rawdon," she said, in a timid voice, which she strove to render cheerful. "It is Jane." Rawdon was quite overcome by that kind voice and presence. He ran up to her—caught her in his arms—gasped out some inarticulate words of thanks, and fairly sobbed on her shoulder. She did not know the cause of his emotion.

The bills of Mr. Moss were quickly settled, perhaps to the disappointment of that gentleman, who had counted on having the Colonel as his guest over Sunday at least; and Jane, with beaming smiles and happiness in her eyes, carried away Rawdon from the bailiff's house, and they went homewards in the cab in which she had hastened to his release. "Pitt was gone to a parliamentary dinner," she said, "when Rawdon's note came, and so, dear Rawdon, I—I came myself;" and she put her kind hand in his. Perhaps it was well for Rawdon Crawley that Pitt was away at that dinner. Rawdon thanked his sister a hundred times, and with an ardour of gratitude which touched and almost alarmed that soft-hearted woman. "Oh," said he, in his rude, artless way, "you—you don't know how I'm changed since I've known you, and—and little Rawdy. I—I'd like to change somehow. You see I want—I want—to be—."—He did not finish the sentence, but she could interpret it. And that night after he left her, and as she sate by her own little boy's bed, she prayed humbly for that poor wayworn sinner.

Rawdon left her and walked home rapidly. It was nine o'clock at night. He ran across the streets, and the great squares of Vanity Fair, and at length came up breathless opposite his own house. He started back and fell against the railings, trembling as he looked up. The drawing-room windows were blazing with light. She had said that she was in bed and ill. He stood there for some time, the light from the rooms on his pale face.

He took out his door-key and let himself into the house. He could hear laughter in the upper rooms. He was in the ball-dress in which he had been captured the night before. He went silently up the stairs; leaning against the bannisters at the stair-head.—Nobody was stirring in the house besides—all the servants had been sent away. Rawdon heard laughter within—laughter and singing. Becky was singing a snatch of the song of the night before; a hoarse voice shouted "Brava, Brava;"—it was Lord Steyne's.

Rawdon opened the door and went in. A little table with a dinner was laid out—and wine and plate. Steyne was hanging over the sofa on which Becky sate. The wretched woman was in a brilliant full toilette, her arms and all her fingers sparkling with bracelets and rings; and the brilliants on her breast which Steyne had given her. He had her hand in his, and was bowing over it to kiss it, when Becky started up with a faint scream as she caught sight of Rawdon's white face. At the next instant she tried a smile, a horrid smile, as if to welcome her husband: and Steyne rose up, grinding his teeth, pale, and with fury in his looks.

He, too, attempted a laugh—and came forward holding out his hand. "What, come back! How d'ye do, Crawley?" he said, the nerves of his mouth twitching as he tried to grin at the intruder.

There was that in Rawdon's face which caused Becky to fling herself before him. "I am innocent, Rawdon," she said; "before God, I am innocent." She clung hold of his coat, of his hands; her own were all covered with serpents,[4] and rings, and baubles. "I am innocent.—Say I am innocent," she said to Lord Steyne.

He thought a trap had been laid for him, and was as furious with the wife as with the husband. "You innocent! Damn you," he screamed out. "You innocent! Why every trinket you have on your body is paid for by me. I have given you thousands of pounds which this fellow has spent, and for which he has sold you. Innocent, by ——! You're as innocent as your mother, the ballet-girl, and your husband the bully. Don't think to frighten me as you have done others. Make way, sir, and let me pass;" and Lord Steyne seized up his hat, and, with flame in his eyes, and looking his enemy fiercely in the face, marched upon him, never for a moment doubting that the other would give way.

But Rawdon Crawley springing out, seized him by the neck-cloth, until Steyne, almost strangled, writhed, and bent under his arm.

4. Bracelets.

"You lie, you dog!" said Rawdon. "You lie, you coward and villain!" And he struck the Peer twice over the face with his open hand, and flung him bleeding to the ground. It was all done before Rebecca could interpose. She stood there trembling before him. She admired her husband, strong, brave, and victorious.

"Come here," he said.—She came up at once.

"Take off those things."—She began, trembling, pulling the jewels from her arms, and the rings from her shaking fingers, and held them all in a heap, quivering and looking up at him. "Throw them down," he said, and she dropped them. He tore the diamond ornament out of her breast, and flung it at Lord Steyne. It cut him on his bald forehead. Steyne wore the scar to his dying day.

"Come up stairs," Rawdon said to his wife. "Don't kill me, Rawdon," she said. He laughed savagely.—"I want to see if that man lies about the money as he has about me. Has he given you any?"

"No," said Rebecca, "that is——"

"Give me your keys," Rawdon answered, and they went out together.

Rebecca gave him all the keys but one: and she was in hopes that he would not have remarked the absence of that. It belonged to the little desk which Amelia had given her in early days, and which she kept in a secret place. But Rawdon flung open boxes and wardrobes, throwing the multifarious trumpery of their contents here and there, and at last he found the desk. The woman was forced to open it. It contained papers, love-letters many years old—all sorts of small trinkets and woman's memoranda. And it contained a pocket-book with bank notes. Some of these were dated ten years back, too, and one was quite a fresh one—a note for a thousand pounds which Lord Steyne had given her.

"Did he give you this?" Rawdon said.

"Yes;" Rebecca answered.

"I'll send it to him to-day," Rawdon said (for day had dawned again, and many hours had passed in this search), "and I will pay Briggs, who was kind to the boy, and some of the debts. You will let me know where I shall send the rest to you. You might have spared me a hundred pounds, Becky, out of all this—I have always shared with you."

"I am innocent," said Becky. And he left her without another word.

What were her thoughts when he left her? She remained for hours after he was gone, the sunshine pouring into the room, and Rebecca sitting alone on the bed's edge. The drawers were all opened and their contents scattered about,—dresses and feathers, scarfs and trinkets, a heap of tumbled vanities lying in a wreck. Her hair was falling over her shoulders; her gown was torn where Rawdon had wrenched the brilliants out of it. She heard him go down stairs a few minutes after he left her, and the door slamming and closing on him. She knew he would never come back. He was gone for ever. Would he kill himself?—she thought—not until after he had met Lord Steyne. She thought of her long past life, and all the dismal incidents of it. Ah, how dreary it seemed, how miserable, lonely and profitless! Should she take laudanum,[5] and end it, too—have done with all hopes, schemes, debts, and triumphs? The French maid found her in this position—sitting in the midst of her miserable ruins with clasped hands and dry eyes. The woman was her accomplice and in Steyne's pay. "Mon Dieu, Madame, what has happened?" she asked.

What *had* happened? Was she guilty or not? She said not; but who could tell what was truth which came from those lips; or if that corrupt heart was in this case pure? All her lies and her schemes, all her selfishness and her wiles, all her wit and genius had come to this bankruptcy. The woman closed the curtains, and with some entreaty and show of kindness, persuaded her mistress to lie down on the bed. Then she went below and gathered up the trinkets which had been lying on the floor since Rebecca dropped them there at her husband's orders, and Lord Steyne went away.

*Number 16* *Apr. 1848*

## *Chapter LIV.*

### SUNDAY AFTER THE BATTLE.

HE mansion of Sir Pitt Crawley in Great Gaunt Street, was just beginning to dress itself for the day, as Rawdon, in his evening costume, which he had now worn two days, passed by the scared female who was scouring the steps, and entered into his brother's study. Lady Jane in her morning-gown, was up and above stairs in the nursery, superintending the toilettes of her children, and listening to the morning prayers which the little creatures performed at her knee. Every morning she and they performed this duty privately, and before the public ceremonial at which Sir Pitt presided, and at which all the people of the household were expected to assemble. Rawdon sate down in the study before the baronet's table, set out with the orderly blue books and the letters, the neatly docketted bills and symmetrical pamphlets; the locked account-books, desks, and dispatch boxes, the Bible, the *Quarterly Review,*[1] and the *Court Guide,* which all stood as if on parade awaiting

5. Alcohol and opium sedative known to be fatal in overdose.
1. The Tory answer to the Whigs' *Edinburgh Quarterly*.

Sir Pitt's Study-Chair

the inspection of their chief.

A book of family sermons, one of which Sir Pitt was in the habit of administering to his family on Sunday mornings, lay ready on the study table, and awaiting his judicious selection. And by the sermon-book was the *Observer* newspaper,[2] damp and neatly folded, and for Sir Pitt's own private use. His gentleman alone took the opportunity of perusing the newspaper before he laid it by his master's desk. Before he had brought it into the study that morning, he had read in the journal a flaming account of "Festivities at Gaunt House," with the names of all the distinguished personages invited by the Marquis of Steyne to meet his Royal Highness. Having made comments upon this entertainment to the housekeeper and her niece as they were taking early tea and hot-buttered toast in the former lady's apartment, and wondered how the Rawding Crawleys could git on, the valet had damped and folded the paper once more, so that it looked quite fresh and innocent against the arrival of the master or the house.

Poor Rawdon took up the paper and began to try and read it until his brother should arrive. But the print fell blank upon his eyes; and he did not know in the least what he was reading. The Government news and appointments, (which Sir Pitt as a public man was bound to peruse, otherwise he would by no means permit the introduction of Sunday papers into his household,) the theatrical criticisms, the fight[3] for a hundred pounds a-side between the Barking Butcher and the Tutbury Pet, the Gaunt House chronicle itself, which contained a most complimentary though guarded account of the famous charades of which Mrs. Becky had been the heroine—all these passed as in a haze before Rawdon, as he sat waiting the arrival of the chief of the family.

Punctually, as the shrill-toned bell of the black marble study clock began to chime nine, Sir Pitt made his appearance, fresh, neat, smugly shaved, with a waxy clean face, and stiff shirt collar, his scanty hair combed and oiled, trimming his nails as he descended the stairs majestically, in a starched cravat and a gray flannel dressing-gown,—a real old English gentleman, in a word,—a model of neatness and every propriety. He started when he saw poor Rawdon in his study in tumbled clothes, with blood-shot eyes, and his hair over his face. He thought his brother was not sober, and had been out all night on some orgy. "Good Gracious, Rawdon," he said, with a blank face, "what brings you here at this time of the morning? Why ain't you at home?"

"Home," said Rawdon, with a wild laugh. "Don't be frightened, Pitt. I'm not drunk. Shut the door; I want to speak to you."

Pitt closed the door and came up to the table, where he sate down in the other arm chair,—that one placed for the reception of the steward, agent, or confidential visitor who came to transact business with the baronet,—and trimmed his nails more vehemently than ever.

"Pitt, it's all over with me," the Colonel said, after a pause. "I'm done."

2. The leading Sunday paper in London.
3. Boxing prize fight.

"I always said it would come to this," the Baronet cried, peevishly, and beating a tune[4] with his clean-trimmed nails. "I warned you a thousand times. I can't help you any more. Every shilling of my money is tied up. Even the hundred pounds that Jane took you last night were promised to my lawyer to-morrow morning; and the want of it will put me to great inconvenience. I don't mean to say that I won't assist you ultimately. But as for paying your creditors in full, I might as well hope to pay the National Debt. It is madness, sheer madness, to think of such a thing. You must come to a compromise. It's a painful thing for the family; but everybody does it. There was George Kitely, Lord Ragland's son, went through the Court last week, and was what they call white-washed, I believe. Lord Ragland would not pay a shilling for him, and——"

"It's not money I want," Rawdon broke in. "I'm not come to you about myself. Never mind what happens to me——"

"What is the matter, then?" said Pitt, somewhat relieved.

"It's the boy," said Rawdon, in a husky voice. "I want you to promise me that you will take charge of him when I'm gone. That dear good wife of yours has always been good to him; and he's fonder of her than he is of his . . .—Damn it. Look here, Pitt—you know that I was to have had Miss Crawley's money. I wasn't brought up like a younger brother: but was always encouraged to be extravagant and kep idle. But for this I might have been quite a different man. I didn't do my duty with the regiment so bad. You know how I was thrown over about the money, and who got it."

"After the sacrifices I have made, and the manner in which I have stood by you, I think this sort of reproach is useless," Sir Pitt said. "Your marriage was your own doing, not mine."

"That's over now," said Rawdon.—"That's over now." And the words were wrenched from him with a groan, which made his brother start.

"Good God! is she dead?" Sir Pitt said, with a voice of genuine alarm and commiseration.

"I wish *I* was," Rawdon replied. "If it wasn't for little Rawdon I'd have cut my throat this morning—and that damned villain's too."

Sir Pitt instantly guessed the truth, and surmised that Lord Steyne was the person whose life Rawdon wished to take. The Colonel told his senior briefly, and in broken accents, the circumstances of the case. "It was a regular plan between that scoundrel and her," he said. "The bailiffs were put upon me: I was taken as I was going out of his house: when I wrote to her for money, she said she was ill in bed, and put me off to another day. And when I got home I found her in diamonds and sitting with that villain alone." He then went on to describe hurriedly the personal conflict with Lord Steyne. To an affair of that nature, of course, he said, there was but one issue: and after his conference with his brother, he was going away to make the necessary arrangements for the meeting which must ensue. "And as it may end fatally for me," Rawdon said with a broken voice, "and as the boy has no mother, I must leave him to you and Jane, Pitt—only it will be a comfort to me if you will promise me to be his friend."

4. First printing reads: tattoo

The elder brother was much affected, and shook Rawdon's hand with a cordiality seldom exhibited by him. Rawdon passed his hand over his shaggy eyebrows. "Thank you brother," said he. "I know I can trust your word."

"I will, upon my honour," the Baronet said. And thus, and almost mutely, this bargain was struck between them.

Then Rawdon took out of his pocket the little pocket-book which he had discovered in Becky's desk: and from which he drew a bundle of the notes which it contained. "Here's six hundred," he said—"you didn't know I was so rich. I want you to give the money to Briggs, who lent it to us—and who was so kind to the boy—and I've always felt ashamed of having taken the poor old woman's money. And here's some more—I've only kept back a few pounds—which Becky may as well have, to get on with." As he spoke he took hold of the other notes to give to his brother: but his hands shook, and he was so agitated that the pocket-book fell from him, and out of it the thousand pound note which had been the last of the unlucky Becky's winnings.

Pitt stooped and picked them up, amazed at so much wealth. "Not that," Rawdon said—"I hope to put a bullet into the man whom that belongs to." He had thought to himself, it would be a fine revenge to wrap a ball in the note, and kill Steyne with it.

After this colloquy the brothers once more shook hands and parted. Lady Jane had heard of the Colonel's arrival, and was waiting for her husband in the adjoining dining-room, with female instinct, auguring evil. The door of the dining-room happened to be left open, and the lady of course was issuing from it as the two brothers passed out of the study. She held out her hand to Rawdon, and said she was glad he was come to breakfast; though she could perceive, by his haggard unshorn face, and the dark looks of her husband, that there was very little question of breakfast between them. Rawdon muttered some excuses about an engagement, squeezing hard the timid little hand which his sister-in-law reached out to him. Her imploring eyes could read nothing but calamity in his face; but he went away without another word. Nor did Sir Pitt vouchsafe her any explanation. The children came up to salute him, and he kissed them in his usual frigid manner. The mother took both of them close to herself, and held a hand of each of them as they knelt down to prayers, which Sir Pitt read to them, and to the servants in their Sunday suits or liveries, ranged upon chairs on the other side of the hissing tea-urn. Breakfast was so late that day, in consequence of the delays which had occurred, that the church-bells began to ring whilst they were sitting over their meal: and Lady Jane was too ill, she said, to go to church, though her thoughts had been entirely astray during the period of family devotion.

Rawdon Crawley meanwhile hurried on from Great Gaunt Street, and knocking at the great bronze Medusa's head which stands on the portal of Gaunt House, brought out the purple Silenus[5] in a red and silver waistcoat, who acts as porter of that palace. The man was scared

5. Medusa's head: door knocker in the shape of Medusa, the gorgon with snakes for hair. Silenus: drunken satyr.

also by the Colonel's dishevelled appearance, and barred the way as if afraid that the other was going to force it. But Colonel Crawley only took out a card and enjoined him particularly to send it in to Lord Steyne, and to mark the address written on it, and say that Colonel Crawley would be all day after one o'clock at the Regent Club in St. James's Street—not at home. The fat red-faced man looked after him with astonishment as he strode away; so did the people in their Sunday clothes who were out so early; the charity boys with shining faces, the green-grocer lolling at his door, and the publican shutting his shutters in the sunshine, against service commenced. The people joked at the cabstand about his appearance, as he took a carriage there, and told the driver to take[6] him to Knightsbridge Barracks.

All the bells were jangling and tolling as he reached that place. He might have seen his old acquaintance Amelia on her way from Brompton to Russell Square had he been looking out. Troops of schools were on their march to church, the shiny pavement and outsides of coaches in the suburbs were thronged with people out upon their Sunday pleasure; but the Colonel was much too busy to take any heed of these phenomena, and, arriving at Knightsbridge, speedily made his way up to the room of his old friend and comrade Captain

6. Revised edition reads: drive

Macmurdo, who Crawley found, to his satisfaction, was in barracks.

Captain Macmurdo, a veteran officer and Waterloo man, greatly liked by his regiment, in which want of money alone prevented him from attaining the highest ranks, was enjoying the forenoon calmly in bed. He had been at a fast supper-party, given the night before by Captain the Honourable George Cinqbars, at his house in Brompton Square, to several young men of the regiment, and a number of ladies of the corps de ballet, and old Mac, who was at home with people of all ages and ranks, and consorted with generals, dog-fanciers, opera-dancers, bruisers, and every kind of person, in a word, was resting himself after the night's labours, and, not being on duty, was in bed.

His room was hung round with boxing, sporting, and dancing pictures, presented to him by comrades as they retired from the regiment, and married and settled into quiet life. And as he was now nearly fifty years of age, twenty-four of which he had passed in the corps, he had a singular museum. He was one of the best shots in England, and, for a heavy man, one of the best riders; indeed, he and Crawley had been rivals when the latter was in the army. To be brief, Mr. Macmurdo was lying in bed, reading in *Bell's Life* an account of that very fight between the Tutbury Pet and the Barking Butcher, which has been before mentioned—a venerable bristly warrior, with a little close-shaved grey head, with a silk nightcap, a red face and nose, and a great dyed moustache.

When Rawdon told the Captain he wanted a friend, the latter knew perfectly well on what duty of friendship he was called to act, and indeed had conducted scores of affairs for his acquaintances with the greatest prudence and skill. His Royal Highness the late lamented Commander-in-Chief[7] had had the greatest regard for Macmurdo on this account; and he was the common refuge of gentlemen in trouble.

"What's the row about, Crawley, my boy?" said the old warrior. "No more gambling business, hay, like that when we shot Captain Marker?"

"It's about—about my wife," Crawley answered, casting down his eyes and turning very red.

The other gave a whistle. "I always said she'd throw you over," he began:—indeed there were bets in the regiment and at the clubs regarding the probable fate of Colonel Crawley, so lightly was his wife's character esteemed by his comrades and the world:—but seeing the savage look with which Rawdon answered the expression of this opinion, Macmurdo did not think fit to enlarge upon it further.

"Is there no way out of it, old boy?" the Captain continued in a grave tone. "Is it only suspicion, you know, or—or what is it? Any letters? Can't you keep it quiet? Best not make any noise about a thing of that sort if you can help it." "Think of his only finding her out now," the Captain thought to himself, and remembered a hundred particular conversations at the mess-table, in which Mrs. Crawley's reputation had been torn to shreds.

7. George IV's brother, Frederick Augustus, duke of York and commander-in-chief of British forces from 1793 till his death in 1827, had famously fought a duel in 1789 in which he refused to return fire.

"There's no way but one out of it," Rawdon replied—"and there's only a way out of it for one of us, Mac—do you understand? I was put out of the way: arrested: I found 'em alone together. I told him he was a liar and a coward, and knocked him down and thrashed him."

"Serve him right," Macmurdo said. "Who is it?"

Rawdon answered it was Lord Steyne.

"The deuce! a Marquis! they said he—that is, they said you ——"

"What the devil do you mean?" roared out Rawdon; "do you mean that you ever heard a fellow doubt about my wife, and didn't tell me, Mac?"

"The world's very censorious, old boy," the other replied. "What the deuce was the good of my telling you what any tom-fools talked about?"

"It was damned unfriendly, Mac," said Rawdon, quite overcome; and, covering his face with his hands, he gave way to an emotion, the sight of which caused the tough old campaigner opposite him to wince with sympathy. "Hold up, old boy," he said; "great man or not, we'll put a bullet in him, damn him. As for women, they're all so."

"You don't know how fond I was of that one," Rawdon said, half inarticulately. "Damme, I followed her like a footman. I gave up everything I had to her. I'm a beggar because I would marry her. By Jove, Sir, I've pawned my own watch in order to get her anything she fancied: and she—she's been making a purse for herself all the time, and grudged me a hundred pound to get me out of quod." He then fiercely and incoherently, and with an agitation under which his counsellor had never before seen him labour, told Macmurdo the circumstances of the story. His adviser caught at some stray hints in it.

"She may be innocent, after all," he said. "She says so. Steyne has been a hundred times alone with her in the house before."

"It may be so," Rawdon answered, sadly: "but this don't look very innocent:" and he showed the Captain the thousand pound note which he had found in Becky's pocket-book. "This is what he gave her, Mac: and she kep it unknown to me: and with this money in the house, she refused to stand by me when I was locked up." The Captain could not but own that the secreting of the money had a very ugly look.

Whilst they were engaged in their conference, Rawdon dispatched Captain Macmurdo's servant to Curzon Street, with an order to the domestic there to give up a bag of clothes of which the Colonel had great need. And during the man's absence, and with great labour and a Johnson's Dictionary, which stood them in much stead, Rawdon and his second composed a letter, which the latter was to send to Lord Steyne. Captain Macmurdo had the honour of waiting upon the Marquis of Steyne, on the part of Colonel Rawdon Crawley, and begged to intimate that he was empowered by the Colonel to make any arrangements for the meeting which, he had no doubt, it was his Lordship's intention to demand, and which the circumstances of the morning had rendered inevitable. Captain Macmurdo begged Lord Steyne, in the most polite manner, to appoint a friend, with whom he (Captain M'M.) might communicate, and desired that the meeting might take place with as little delay as possible.

In a postscript the Captain stated that he had in his possession a bank-note for a large amount, which Colonel Crawley had reason to suppose was the property of the Marquis of Steyne. And he was anxious, on the Colonel's behalf, to give up the note to its owner.

By the time this note was composed, the Captain's servant returned from his mission to Colonel Crawley's house in Curzon Street, but without the carpet-bag and portmanteau, for which he had been sent: and with a very puzzled and odd face.

"They won't a give 'em up," said the man; "there's a regular shinty in the house; and everything at sixes and sevens. The landlord's come in and took possession. The servants was a drinkin up in the drawing-room. They said—they said you had a gone off with the plate, Colonel"—the man added after a pause:—"One of the servants is off already. And Simpson, the man as was very noisy and drunk indeed, says nothing shall go out of the house until his wages is paid up."

The account of this little revolution in May Fair, astonished and gave a little gaiety to an otherwise very *triste*[8] conversation. The two officers laughed at Rawdon's discomfiture.

"I'm glad the little'un isn't at home," Rawdon said biting his nails. "You remember him, Mac, don't you in the Riding School. How he sat the kicker[9] to be sure: didn't he?"

"That he did, old boy," said the good-natured Captain.

Little Rawdon was then sitting, one of fifty gown-boys in the Chapel of Whitefriars School: thinking, not about the sermon, but about going home next Saturday, when his father would certainly tip him, and perhaps would take him to the play.

"He's a regular trump that boy," the father went on, still musing about his son. "I say, Mac, if anything goes wrong—if I drop—I should like you to—to go and see him you know: and say that I was—very fond of him and that. And—dash it—old chap, give him these gold sleeve-buttons: it's all I've got." He covered his face with his black hands: over which the tears rolled and made furrows of white. Mr. Macmurdo had also occasion to take off his silk night cap and rub it across his eyes.

"Go down and order some breakfast," he said to his man in a loud cheerful voice—"What'll you have, Crawley? Some devilled kidneys and a herring let's say—And, Clay, lay out some dressing things for the Colonel: we were always pretty much of a size, Rawdon, my boy, and neither of us ride so light as we did when we first entered the Corps—" With which, and leaving the Colonel to dress himself, Macmurdo turned round towards the wall, and resumed the perusal of *Bell's Life;* until such time as his friend's toilette was complete and he was at liberty to commence his own.

This, as he was about to meet a Lord, Captain Macmurdo performed with particular care. He waxed his mustachios into a state of brilliant polish, and put on a tight cravat and a trim buff waistcoat:

8. Sad.
9. Horse.

so that all the young officers in the mess room, whither Crawley had preceded his friend, complimented Mac on his appearance at breakfast and asked if he was going to be married that Sunday?

## *Chapter LV.*

### IN WHICH THE SAME SUBJECT IS PURSUED.

BECKY did not rally from the state of stupor and confusion in which the events of the previous night had plunged her intrepid spirit, until the bells of the Curzon Street Chapels were ringing for afternoon service, and rising from her bed she began to ply her own bell, in order to summon the French maid who had left her some hours before.

Mrs. Rawdon Crawley rang many times in vain; and though, on the last occasion, she rang with such vehemence as to pull down the bell-rope, Mademoiselle Fifine did not make her appearance,—no, not though her mistress, in a great pet, and with the bell-rope in her hand, came out to the landing-place with her hair over her shoulders, and screamed out repeatedly for her attendant.

The truth is, she had quitted the premises for many hours, and upon that permission which is called French leave[1] among us. After picking up the trinkets in the drawing-room, Mademoiselle had ascended to her own apartments, packed and corded her own boxes there, tripped out and called a cab for herself, brought down her trunks with her own hand, and without ever so much as asking the aid of any of the other servants, who would probably have refused it, as they hated her cordially, and without wishing any one of them good-bye, had made her exit from Curzon Street.

The game, in her opinion, was over in that little domestic establishment. Fifine went off in a cab, as we have known more exalted persons of her nation to do under similar circumstances:[2] but, more provident or lucky than these, she secured not only her own property, but some of her mistress's (if indeed that lady could be said to have any property at all)—and not only carried off the trinkets be-

1. Without notice.
2. Such as Louis Philippe, who fled Paris in the month this installment was written, but also like Charles X, who fled in 1830, Louis XVIII, in 1815, and Louis XVI, in 1792.

fore alluded to, and some favourite dresses on which she had long kept her eye, but four richly gilt Louis Quatorze candlesticks, six gilt Albums, Keepsakes, and Books of Beauty,[3] a gold enamelled snuff-box which had once belonged to Madame du Barri,[4] and the sweetest little inkstand and mother-of-pearl blotting-book, which Becky used when she composed her charming little pink notes, had vanished from the premises in Curzon Street together with Mademoiselle Fifine, and all the silver laid on the table for the little *festin*[5] which Rawdon interrupted. The plated ware Mademoiselle left behind her as too cumbrous probably, for which reason, no doubt, she also left the fire irons, the chimney-glasses, and the rosewood cottage piano.

A lady very like her subsequently kept a milliner's shop in the Rue du Helder at Paris,[6] where she lived with great credit and enjoyed the patronage of my Lord Steyne. This person always spoke of England as of the most treacherous country in the world, and stated to her young pupils that she had been *affreusement volé*[7] by natives of that island. It was no doubt compassion for her misfortunes which induced the Marquis of Steyne to be so very kind to Madame de Saint Amaranthe. May she flourish as she deserves,—she appears no more in our quarter of Vanity Fair.

Hearing a buzz and a stir below, and indignant at the impudence of those servants who would not answer her summons, Mrs. Crawley flung her morning robe round her, and descended majestically to the drawing-room, whence the noise proceeded.

The cook was there with blackened face, seated on the beautiful chintz sofa by the side of Mrs. Raggles, to whom she was administering Maraschino. The page with the sugar-loaf buttons, who carried about Becky's pink notes, and jumped about her little carriage with such alacrity, was now engaged putting his fingers into a cream dish; the footman was talking to Raggles, who had a face full of perplexity and woe—and yet, though the door was open, and Becky had been screaming a half dozen of times a few feet off, not one of her attendants had obeyed her call. "Have a little drop, do'ee now Mrs. Raggles," the cook was saying as Becky entered, the white cashmere dressing gown flouncing around her.

"Simpson! Trotter!" the mistress of the house cried in great wrath. "How dare you stay here when you heard me call? How dare you sit down in my presence? Where's my maid?" The page withdrew his fingers from his mouth with a momentary terror: but the cook took off a glass of Maraschino, of which Mrs. Raggles had had enough, staring at Becky over the little gilt glass as she drained its contents. The liquor appeared to give the odious rebel courage.

"*Your* sofy, indeed!" Mrs. Cook said. "I'm a settin' on Mrs. Raggles's sofy. Don't you stir, Mrs. Raggles, Mum. I'm a settin' on Mr. and Mrs. Raggles's sofy, which they bought with honest money, and very dear

3. Highly decorated anthologies of poems, stories, and illustrations usually published around Christmastime as gifts.
4. Marie Jeanne Bécu, mistress of Louis XV.
5. Feast.
6. Off the Boulevard des Italiens, indicating that she had done well with her booty.
7. Fearfully robbed.

it cost 'em, too. And I'm thinkin' if I set here until I'm paid my wages, I shall set a precious long time, Mrs. Raggles; and set I will, too—ha! ha!" and with this she filled herself another glass of the liquor, and drank it with a more hideously satirical air.

"Trotter! Simpson! turn that drunken wretch out," screamed Mrs. Crawley.

"I shawn't," said Trotter the footman; "turn out yourself. Pay our selleries, and turn me out too. *We'll* go fast enough."

"Are you all here to insult me?" cried Becky in a fury; "when Colonel Crawley comes home I'll—"

At this the servants burst into a hoarse haw-haw, in which, however, Raggles, who still kept a most melancholy countenance, did not join. "He ain't a coming back," Mr. Trotter resumed. "He sent for his things, and I wouldn' let 'em go, although Mr. Raggles would: and I don't b'lieve he's no more a Colonel than I am. He's hoff: and I suppose you're a goin' after him. You're no better than swindlers, both on you. Don't be a bullyin' *me*. I won't stand it. Pay us our selleries, I say. Pay us our selleries." It was evident, from Mr. Trotter's flushed countenance and defective intonation, that he, too, had had recourse to vinous stimulus.

"Mr. Raggles," said Becky, in a passion of vexation, "you will not surely let me be insulted by that drunken man?" "Hold your noise, Trotter; do now," said Simpson the page. He was affected by his mistress's deplorable situation, and succeeded in preventing an outrageous denial of the epithet 'drunken' on the footman's part.

"O Mam," said Raggles, "I never thought to live to see this year day. I've known the Crawley family ever since I was born. I lived butler with Miss Crawley for thirty years; and I little thought one of that family was a goin' to ruing me—yes, ruing me"—said the poor fellow with tears in his eyes. "Har you a goin' to pay me? You've lived in this ouse four year. You've 'ad my substance: my plate and linning. You ho me a milk and butter bill of two undred pound, you must ave noo laid heggs for your homlets, and cream for your spanil dog."

"She didn't care what her own flesh and blood had," interposed the cook. "Many's the time, he'd have starved but for me."

"He's a charaty boy now, Cooky," said Mr. Trotter, with a drunken "ha! ha!"—and honest Raggles continued, in a lamentable tone, an enumeration of his griefs. All he said was true. Becky and her husband had ruined him. He had bills coming due next week and no means to meet them. He would be sold up and turned out of his shop and his house, because he had trusted to the Crawley family. His tears and lamentations made Becky more peevish than ever.

"You all seem to be against me," she said, bitterly. "What do you want? I can't pay you on Sunday. Come back to-morrow and I'll pay you everything. I thought Colonel Crawley had settled with you. He will to-morrow. I declare to you upon my honour that he left home this morning with fifteen hundred pounds in his pocket-book. He has left me nothing. Apply to him. Give me a bonnet and shawl and let me go out and find him. There was a difference between us this morning. You all seem to know it. I promise you upon my word that you shall all be paid. He has got a good appointment. Let me go out and find him."

This audacious statement caused Raggles and the other personages present to look at one another with a wild surprise, and with it Rebecca left them. She went up stairs and dressed herself this time without the aid of her French maid. She went into Rawdon's room, and there saw that a trunk and bag were packed ready for removal, with a pencil direction that they should be given when called for; then she went into the Frenchwoman's garret; everything was clean, and all the drawers emptied there. She bethought herself of the trinkets which had been left on the ground, and felt certain that the woman had fled. "Good Heavens! was ever such ill luck as mine?" she said; "to be so near, and to lose all. Is it all too late? No; there was one chance more."

She dressed herself, and went away unmolested this time, but alone. It was four o'clock. She went swiftly down the streets (she had no money to pay for a carriage), and never stopped until she came to Sir Pitt Crawley's door, in Great Gaunt Street. Where was Lady Jane Crawley? She was at church. Becky was not sorry. Sir Pitt was in his study, and had given orders not to be disturbed—she must see him—she slipped by the sentinel in livery at once, and was in Sir Pitt's room before the astonished Baronet had even laid down the paper.

He turned red and started back from her with a look of great alarm and horror.

"Do not look so," she said. "I am not guilty, Pitt, dear Pitt; you were my friend once. Before God, I am not guilty. I seem so. Everything is against me. And O! at such a moment! just when all my hopes were about to be realised: just when happiness was in store for us."

"Is this true, what I see in the paper, then?" Sir Pitt said—a paragraph in which had greatly surprised him.

"It is true. Lord Steyne told me on Friday night, the night of that fatal ball. He has been promised an appointment any time these six months. Mr. Martyr, the Colonial Secretary, told him yesterday that it was made out. That unlucky arrest ensued; that horrible meeting. I was only guilty of too much devotedness to Rawdon's service. I have received Lord Steyne alone a hundred times before. I confess I had money of which Rawdon knew nothing. Don't you know how careless he is of it, and could I dare to confide it to him?" And so she went on with a perfectly connected story, which she poured into the ears of her perplexed kinsman.

It was to the following effect. Becky owned, and with perfect frankness, but deep contrition, that having remarked Lord Steyne's partiality for her (at the mention of which Pitt blushed), and being secure of her own virtue, she had determined to turn the great peer's attachment to the advantage of herself and her family. "I looked for a peerage for you, Pitt," she said, (the brother-in-law again turned red). "We have talked about it. Your genius and Lord Steyne's interest made it more than probable, had not this dreadful calamity come to put an end to all our hopes. But, first, I own that it was my object to rescue my dear husband,—him whom I love in spite of all his ill usage and suspicions of me,—to remove him from the poverty and ruin which was impending over us. I saw Lord Steyne's partiality for me," she said, casting down her eyes. "I own that I did everything in my power to make myself pleasing to him, and as far as an honest woman may, to secure his—his esteem. It was only on Friday morning that the news arrived of the death of the Governor of Coventry Island,[8] and my Lord instantly secured the appointment for my dear husband. It was intended as a surprise for him,—he was to see it in the papers to-day. Even after that horrid arrest took place (the expenses of which Lord Steyne generously said he would settle, so that I was in a manner prevented from coming to my husband's assistance), my Lord was laughing with me, and saying that my dearest Rawdon would be consoled when he read of his appointment in the paper, in that shocking spun—bailiff's house. And then—then he came home. His suspicions were excited,—the dreadful scene took place between my Lord and my cruel, cruel Rawdon,—and, O my God, what will happen next? Pitt, dear Pitt! pity me, and reconcile us!" And as she spoke she flung herself down on her knees, and bursting into tears, seized hold of Pitt's hand, which she kissed passionately.

It was in this very attitude that Lady Jane, who, returning from church, ran to her husband's room directly she heard Mrs. Rawdon Crawley was closeted there, found the Baronet and his sister-in-law.

"I am surprised that woman has the audacity to enter this house,"

8. There is no such place, but "to be sent to Coventry" is an old saying of obscure origins meaning to be shunned or ostracized socially.

Lady Jane said, trembling in every limb, and turning quite pale. (Her ladyship had sent out her maid directly after breakfast, who had communicated with Raggles and Rawdon Crawley's household, who had told her all, and a great deal more than they knew, of that story, and many others besides). "How dare Mrs. Crawley to enter the house of—of an honest family?"

Sir Pitt started back, amazed at his wife's display of vigour. Becky still kept her kneeling posture, and clung to Sir Pitt's hand.

"Tell her that she does not know all. Tell her that I am innocent, dear Pitt," she whimpered out.

"Upon my word, my love, I think you do Mrs. Crawley injustice," Sir Pitt said; at which speech Rebecca was vastly relieved. "Indeed I believe her to be——"

"To be what?" cried out Lady Jane, her clear voice thrilling, and her heart beating violently as she spoke. "To be a wicked woman—a heartless mother, a false wife? She never loved her dear little boy, who used to fly here and tell me of her cruelty to him. She never came into a family but she strove to bring misery with her, and to weaken the most sacred affections with her wicked flattery and falsehoods. She has deceived her husband, as she has deceived everybody; her soul is black with vanity, worldliness, and all sorts of crime. I tremble when I touch her. I keep my children out of her sight. I—"

"Lady Jane!" cried Sir Pitt, starting up, "this is really language——"

"I have been a true and faithful wife to you, Sir Pitt," Lady Jane continued, intrepidly; "I have kept my marriage vow as I made it to God, and have been obedient and gentle as a wife should. But righteous obedience has its limits, and I declare that I will not bear that—that woman again under my roof: if she enters it, I and my children will leave it. She is not worthy to sit down with Christian people. You—you must choose, Sir, between her and me;" and with this my Lady swept out of the room, fluttering with her own audacity, and leaving Rebecca and Sir Pitt not a little astonished at it.

As for Becky, she was not hurt; nay, she was pleased. "It was the diamond-clasp you gave me," she said to Sir Pitt, reaching him out her hand; and before she left him (for which event you may be sure my Lady Jane was looking out from her dressing-room window in the upper story) the Baronet had promised to go and seek out his brother, and endeavour to bring about a reconciliation.

Rawdon found some of the young fellows of the regiment seated in the mess-room at breakfast, and was induced without much difficulty to partake of that meal, and of the devilled legs of fowls and soda-water with which these young gentlemen fortified themselves. Then they had a conversation befitting the day and their time of life: about the next pigeon-match[9] at Battersea, with relative bets upon Ross and Osbaldiston: about Mademoiselle Ariane of the French Opera, and who had left her, and how she was consoled by Panther Carr; and about the fight between the Butcher and the Pet, and the prob-

9. Shooting pigeons released from traps.

abilities that it was a cross.[1] Young Tandyman, a hero of seventeen, laboriously endeavouring to get up a pair of mustachios, had seen the fight, and spoke in the most scientific manner about the battle, and the condition of the men. It was he who had driven the Butcher on to the ground in his drag, and passed the whole of the previous night with him. Had there not been foul play he must have won it. All the old files of the Ring were in it: and Tandyman wouldn't pay; no, dammy, he wouldn't pay.—It was but a year since the young Cornet, now so knowing a hand in Cribb's parlour,[2] had a still lingering liking for toffy, and used to be birched at Eton.

So they went on talking about dancers, fights, drinking, demireps,[3] until Macmurdo came down and joined the boys and the conversation. He did not appear to think that any especial reverence was due to their boyhood;[4] the old fellow cut in with stories, to the full as choice as any the youngest rake present had to tell;—nor did his own gray hairs, nor their smooth faces detain him. Old Mac was famous for his good stories. He was not exactly a lady's man; that is, men asked him to dine rather at the houses of their mistresses than of their mothers. There can scarcely be a life lower, perhaps, than his; but he was quite contented with it, such as it was, and led it in perfect good nature, simplicity, and modesty of demeanour.

By the time Mac had finished a copious breakfast, most of the others had concluded their meal. Young Lord Varinas was smoking an immense Meerschaum pipe, while Captain Hugues was employed with a cigar: that violent little devil Tandyman, with his little bull-terrier between his legs, was tossing for shillings with all his might (that fellow was always at some game or other) against Captain Deuceace: and Mac and Rawdon walked off to the Club, neither, of course, having given any hint of the business which was occupying their minds. Both, on the other hand, had joined pretty gaily in the conversation; as, why should they interrupt it? Feasting, drinking, ribaldry, laughter, go on alongside of all sorts of other occupations in Vanity Fair,—the crowds were pouring out of church as Rawdon and his friend passed down Saint James's Street and entered into their Club.

The old bucks and habitués, who ordinarily stand gaping and grinning out of the great front window of the Club, had not arrived at their posts as yet,—the newspaper-room was almost empty. One man was present whom Rawdon did not know; another to whom he owed a little score for whist, and whom, in consequence, he did not care to meet; a third was reading the *Royalist* (a periodical famous for its scandal and its attachment to Church and King) Sunday paper at the table, and, looking up at Crawley with some interest, said, "Crawley, I congratulate you."

1. Horatio Ross (1801–86) and George Osbaldiston (1787–1866) were sportsmen. Ariane is untraced, as are the boxers, Barker Butcher and Tutbury Pet. A crossed fight was a fixed fight.
2. Cribb's was a common name for pubs and inns, named for Tom Cribb, the boxing champion.
3. Persons (women) of questionable reputation.
4. An allusion to Juvenal's *Satires*: "maxima debetur puero reverentia" (the greatest respect is due to a child), a quotation repeated by Thackeray in Latin in *The Newcomes*.

"What do you mean?" said the Colonel.

"It's in the *Observer* and the *Royalist* too," said Mr. Smith.

"What?" Rawdon cried, turning very red. He thought that the affair with Lord Steyne was already in the public prints. Smith looked up wondering and smiling at the agitation which the Colonel exhibited as he took up the paper, and trembling, began to read.

Mr. Smith and Mr. Brown (the gentleman with whom Rawdon had the outstanding whist account) had been talking about the Colonel just before he came in.

"It is come just in the nick of time," said Smith. "I suppose Crawley had not a shilling in the world."

"It's a wind that blows everybody good," Mr. Brown said. "He can't go away without paying me a pony[5] he owes me."

"What's the salary?" asked Smith.

"Two or three thousand," answered the other. "But the climate's so infernal, they don't enjoy it long. Liverseege died after eighteen months of it: and the man before went off in six weeks, I hear."

"Some people say his brother is a very clever man. I always found him a d—— bore," Smith ejaculated. "He must have good interest, though. He must have got the Colonel the place."

"*He!*" said Brown, with a sneer—"Pooh.—It was Lord Steyne got it."

"How do you mean?"

"A virtuous woman is a crown to her husband,"[6] answered the other, enigmatically, and went to read his papers.

Rawdon, for his part, read in the *Royalist* the following astonishing paragraph:—

"GOVERNORSHIP OF COVENTRY ISLAND.—H.M.S. Yellowjack, Commander Jaunders, has brought letters and papers from Coventry Island. H.E. Sir Thomas Liverseege had fallen a victim to the prevailing fever at Swamptown. His loss is deeply felt in the flourishing colony. We hear that the Governorship has been offered to Colonel Rawdon Crawley, C.B., a distinguished Waterloo officer. We need not only men of acknowledged bravery, but men of administrative talents to superintend the affairs of our colonies; and we have no doubt that the gentleman selected by the Colonial Office to fill the lamented vacancy which has occurred at Coventry Island is admirably calculated for the post which he is about to occupy."

"Coventry Island! where was it? who had appointed him to the government? You must take me out as your secretary, old boy," Captain Macmurdo said laughing; and as Crawley and his friend sat wondering and perplexed over the announcement, the Club waiter brought in to the Colonel a card, on which the name of Mr. Wenham was engraved, who begged to see Colonel Crawley.

The Colonel and his aide-de-camp went out to meet the gentleman, rightly conjecturing that he was an emissary of Lord Steyne. "How d'ye do, Crawley? I am glad to see you," said Mr. Wenham,

5. Twenty-five pounds.
6. Quoted from Proverbs 12.4; the other half of the verse adds, "but she that maketh ashamed is a rottenness in his bones."

with a bland smile, and grasping Crawley's hand with great cordiality.

"You come, I suppose, from——"

"Exactly," said Mr. Wenham.

"Then this is my friend Captain Macmurdo of the Life Guards Green."

"Delighted to know Captain Macmurdo, I'm sure," Mr. Wenham said, and tendered another smile and shake of the hand to the second, as he had done to the principal. Mac put out one finger, armed with a buckskin glove, and made a very frigid bow to Mr. Wenham over his tight cravat. He was, perhaps, discontented at being put in communication with a *pékin,*[7] and thought that Lord Steyne should have sent him a Colonel at the very least.

"As Macmurdo acts for me, and knows what I mean," Crawley said, "I had better retire and leave you together."

"Of course," said Macmurdo.

"By no means, my dear Colonel," Mr. Wenham said; "the interview which I had the honour of requesting was with you personally, though the company of Captain Macmurdo cannot fail to be also most pleasing. In fact, Captain, I hope that our conversation will lead to none but the most agreeable results, very different from those which my friend Colonel Crawley appears to anticipate."

"Humph!" said Captain Macmurdo.—Behanged to these civilians, he thought to himself, they are always for arranging and speechifying. Mr. Wenham took a chair which was not offered to him—took a paper from his pocket, and resumed—

"You have seen this gratifying announcement in the papers this morning, Colonel? Government has secured a most valuable servant, and you, if you accept office, as I presume you will, an excellent appointment. Three thousand a-year, delightful climate, excellent government-house, all your own way in the Colony, and a certain promotion. I congratulate you with all my heart. I presume you know, gentlemen, to whom my friend is indebted for this piece of patronage?"

"Hanged, if I know," the Captain said: his principal turned very red.

"To one of the most generous and kindest men in the world, as he is one of the greatest—to my excellent friend, the Marquis of Steyne."

"I'll see him d—— before I take his place," growled out Rawdon.

"You are irritated against my noble friend," Mr. Wenham calmly resumed: "and now, in the name of common sense and justice, tell me why?"

"*Why?*" cried Rawdon in surprise.

"Why? Dammy!" said the Captain, ringing his stick on the ground.

"Dammy, indeed," said Mr. Wenham, with the most agreeable smile; "still, look at the matter as a man of the world—as an honest man, and see if you have not been in the wrong. You come home from a journey, and find—what?—my Lord Steyne supping at your house in Curzon Street with Mrs. Crawley. Is the circumstance strange or novel? Has he not been a hundred times before

7. Derogatory slang for "civilian."

in the same position? Upon my honour and word as a gentleman," (Mr. Wenham here put his hand on his waistcoat with a parliamentary air,) "I declare I think that your suspicions are monstrous and utterly unfounded, and that they injure an honourable gentleman who has proved his good will towards you by a thousand benefactions—and a most spotless and innocent lady."

"You don't mean to say that—that Crawley's mistaken?" said Mr. Macmurdo.

"I believe that Mrs. Crawley is as innocent as my wife, Mrs. Wenham," Mr. Wenham said, with great energy. "I believe that, misled by an infernal jealousy, my friend here strikes a blow against not only an infirm and old man of high station, his constant friend and benefactor, but against his wife, his own dearest honour, his son's future reputation, and his own prospects in life.

"I will tell you what happened," Mr. Wenham continued with great solemnity; "I was sent for this morning by my Lord Steyne, and found him in a pitiable state, as, I need hardly inform Colonel Crawley, any man of age and infirmity would be after a personal conflict with a man of your strength. I say to your face; it was a cruel advantage you took of that strength, Colonel Crawley. It was not only the body of my noble and excellent friend which was wounded—his heart, Sir, was bleeding. A man whom he had loaded with benefits and regarded with affection, had subjected him to the foulest indignity. What was this very appointment, which appears in the journals of to-day, but a proof of his kindness to you? When I saw his Lordship this morning I found him in a state pitiable indeed to see; and as anxious as you are to revenge the outrage committed upon him, by blood. You know he has given his proofs, I presume, Colonel Crawley?"

"He has plenty of pluck," said the Colonel. "Nobody ever said he hadn't."

"His first order to me was to write a letter of challenge, and to carry it to Colonel Crawley. One or other of you, he said, must not survive the outrage of last night."

Crawley nodded. "You're coming to the point, Wenham," he said.

"I tried my utmost to calm Lord Steyne. Good God! Sir, I said, how I regret that Mrs. Wenham and myself had not accepted Mrs. Crawley's invitation to sup with her!"

"She asked you to sup with her?" Captain Macmurdo said.

"After the Opera. Here's the note of invitation—stop—no, this is another paper—I thought I had it, but it's of no consequence, and I pledge you my word of honour as a gentleman[8] to the fact. If we had come—and it was only one of Mrs. Wenham's headaches which prevented us—she suffers under them a good deal, especially in the spring—if we had come, and you had returned home, there would have been no quarrel, no insult, no suspicion—and so it is positively because my poor wife has a headache that you are to bring death down upon two men of honour, and plunge two of the most excellent and ancient families in the kingdom into disgrace and sorrow."

8. Revised edition omits: of honour as a gentleman

Mr. Macmurdo looked at his principal with the air of a man profoundly puzzled: and Rawdon felt with a kind of rage that his prey was escaping him. He did not believe a word of the story, and yet, how discredit or disprove it?

Mr. Wenham continued with the same fluent oratory, which in his place in parliament he had so often practised—"I sate for an hour or more by Lord Steyne's bedside, beseeching, imploring Lord Steyne to forego his intention of demanding a meeting. I pointed out to him that the circumstances were after all suspicious—they were suspicious. I acknowledge it, any man in your position might have been taken in—I said that a man furious with jealousy is to all intents and purposes a madman, and should be as such regarded—that a duel between you must lead to the disgrace of all parties concerned—that a man of his Lordship's exalted station had no right in these days, when the most atrocious revolutionary principles, and the most dangerous levelling doctrines are preached among the vulgar, to create a public scandal; and that, however innocent, the common people would insist that he was guilty. In fine, I implored him not to send the challenge."

"I don't believe one word of the whole story," said Rawdon, grinding his teeth. "I believe it a damned[9] lie, and that you're in it, Mr. Wenham. If the challenge don't come from him, by Jove it shall come from me."

Mr. Wenham turned deadly pale at this savage interruption of the Colonel, and looked towards the door.

But he found a champion in Captain Macmurdo. That gentleman rose up with an oath, and rebuked Rawdon for his language. "You put the affair into my hands, and you shall act as I think fit, by Jove, and not as you do. You have no right to insult Mr. Wenham with this sort of language; and dammy, Mr. Wenham, you deserve an apology. And as for a challenge to Lord Steyne, you may get somebody else to carry it, I won't. If my lord, after being thrashed, chooses to sit still, dammy let him. And as for the affair with—with Mrs. Crawley, my belief is, there's nothing proved at all: that your wife's innocent, as innocent as Mr. Wenham says she is: and at any rate, that you would be a d— fool not to take the place and hold your tongue."

"Captain Macmurdo, you speak like a man of sense," Mr. Wenham cried out, immensely relieved—"I forget any words that Colonel Crawley has used in the irritation of the moment."

"I thought you would," Rawdon said, with a sneer.

"Shut your mouth, you old stoopid," the Captain said, good-naturedly. "Mr. Wenham ain't a fighting man; and quite right, too."

"This matter, in my belief," the Steyne emissary cried, "ought to be buried in the most profound oblivion. A word concerning it should never pass these doors. I speak in the interest of my friend, as well as of Colonel Crawley, who persists in considering me his enemy."

"I suppose Lord Steyne won't talk about it very much," said Captain Macmurdo; "and I don't see why our side should. The affair ain't a very pretty one, any way you take it; and the less said about it

9. Revised edition reads: d——

the better. It's you are thrashed, and not us; and if you are satisfied, why, I think, we should be."

Mr. Wenham took his hat, upon this, and Captain Macmurdo following him to the door, shut it upon himself and Lord Steyne's agent, leaving Rawdon chafing within. When the two were on the other side, Macmurdo looked hard at the other ambassador, and with an expression of anything but respect on his round jolly face.

"You don't stick at a trifle, Mr. Wenham," he said.

"You flatter me, Captain Macmurdo," answered the other, with a smile. "Upon my honour and conscience, now, Mrs. Crawley did ask us to sup after the Opera."

"Of course; and Mrs. Wenham had one of her headaches. I say, I've got a thousand-pound note here, which I will give you if you will give me a receipt, please; and I will put the note up in an envelope for Lord Steyne. My man shan't fight him. But we had rather not take his money."

"It was all a mistake,—all a mistake, my dear Sir," the other said, with the utmost innocence of manner; and was bowed down the Club steps by Captain Macmurdo, just as Sir Pitt Crawley ascended them. There was a slight acquaintance between these two gentlemen; and the Captain, going back with the Baronet to the room where the latter's brother was, told Sir Pitt, in confidence, that he had made the affair all right between Lord Steyne and the Colonel.

Sir Pitt was well pleased, of course, at this intelligence; and congratulated his brother warmly upon the peaceful issue of the affair, making appropriate moral remarks upon the evils of duelling, and the unsatisfactory nature of that sort of settlement of disputes.

And after this preface, he tried with all his eloquence to effect a reconciliation between Rawdon and his wife. He recapitulated the statements which Becky had made, pointed out the probabilities of their truth, and asserted his own firm belief in her innocence.

But Rawdon would not hear of it. "She has kep money concealed from me these ten years," he said. "She swore, last night only, she had none from Steyne. She knew it was all up, directly I found it. If she's not guilty, Pitt, she's as bad as guilty; and I'll never see her again,—never." His head sank down on his chest as he spoke the words; and he looked quite broken and sad.

"Poor old boy," Macmurdo said, shaking his head.

Rawdon Crawley resisted for some time the idea of taking the place which had been procured for him by so odious a patron: and was also for removing the boy from the school where Lord Steyne's interest had placed him. He was induced, however, to acquiesce in these benefits by the entreaties of his brother and Macmurdo: but mainly by the latter pointing out to him what a fury Steyne would be in, to think that his enemy's fortune was made through his means.

When the Marquis of Steyne came abroad after his accident, the Colonial Secretary bowed up to him and congratulated himself and the Service upon having made so excellent an appointment. These congratulations were received with a degree of gratitude which may be imagined on the part of Lord Steyne.

The secret of the *rencontre* between him and Colonel Crawley was buried in the profoundest oblivion, as Wenham said; that is by the seconds and the principals. But before that evening was over it was talked of at fifty dinner-tables in Vanity Fair. Little Cackleby himself went to seven evening parties, and told the story with comments and emendations at each place. How Mrs. Washington White revelled in it! The Bishopess of Ealing was shocked beyond expression: the Bishop went and wrote his name down in the visiting-book at Gaunt House that very day. Little Southdown was sorry: so you may be sure was his sister Lady Jane, very sorry. Lady Southdown[1] wrote it off to her other daughter at the Cape of Good Hope. It was town-talk for at least three days, and was only kept out of the newspapers by the exertions of Mr. Wagg, acting upon a hint from Mr. Wenham.

The bailiffs and brokers seized upon poor Raggles in Curzon Street, and the late fair tenant of that poor little mansion was in the meanwhile—where? Who cared? Who asked after a day or two? Was she guilty or not? We all know how charitable the world is, and how the verdict of Vanity Fair goes when there is a doubt. Some people said she had gone to Naples in pursuit of Lord Steyne; whilst others averred that his Lordship quitted that city, and fled to Palermo on hearing of Becky's arrival; some said she was living in Bierstadt, and had become a *dame d'honneur*[2] to the Queen of Bulgaria; some that she was at Boulogne; and others, at a boarding-house at Cheltenham.

Rawdon made her a tolerable annuity; and we may be sure that she was a woman who could make a little money go a great way, as the saying is. He would have paid his debts on leaving England, could he have got any Insurance Office to take his life; but the climate of Coventry Island was so bad that he could borrow no money on the strength of his annuity. He remitted, however, to his brother punctually, and wrote to his little boy regularly every mail. He kept Macmurdo in cigars; and sent over quantities of shells, cayenne pepper, hot pickles, guava[3] jelly, and colonial produce to Lady Jane. He sent his brother home the *Swamp Town Gazette*, in which the new Governor was praised with immense enthusiasm; whereas, the *Swamp Town Sentinel*, whose wife was not asked to Government House, declared that his Excellency was a tyrant, compared to whom Nero[4] was an enlightened philanthropist. Little Rawdon used to like to get the papers and read about his Excellency.

His mother never made any movement to see the child. He went home to his aunt for Sundays and holidays; he soon knew every bird's nest about Queen's Crawley, and rode out with Sir Huddleston's hounds, which he admired so on his first well-remembered visit to Hampshire.

1. First printing reads: Macbeth
2. Maid of honor.
3. West Indian and South American fruit.
4. Roman emperor (54–69 A.D.) alleged to have burned Rome for an amusement.

## *Chapter LVI.*

### GEORGY IS MADE A GENTLEMAN.

EORGY OSBORNE[1] was now fairly established in his grandfather's mansion in Russell Square: occupant of his father's room in the house, and heir-apparent of all the splendours there. The good looks, gallant bearing, and gentlemanlike appearance of the boy won the grandsire's heart for him. Mr. Osborne was as proud of him as ever he had been of the elder George.

The child had many more luxuries and indulgencies than had been awarded to his father. Osborne's commerce had prospered greatly of late years. His wealth and importance in the City had very much increased. He had been glad enough in former days to put the elder George to a good private school; and a commission in the army for his son had been a source of no small pride to him: for little George and his future prospects the old man looked much higher. He would make a gentleman of the little chap, was Mr. Osborne's constant saying regarding little Georgy. He saw him in his mind's eye, a collegian, a parliament-man,—a Baronet, perhaps. The old man thought he would die contented if he could see his grandson in a fair way to such honours. He would have none but a tip-top college man to educate him,—none of your quacks and pretenders,—no, no. A few years before, he used to be savage, and inveigh against all parsons, scholars, and the like,—declaring that they were a pack of humbugs, and quacks, that weren't fit to get their living but by grinding Latin and Greek, and a set of supercilious dogs, that pretended to look down upon British merchants and gentlemen, who could buy up half a hundred of 'em. He would mourn now, in a very solemn manner, that his own education had been neglected, and repeatedly point out, in pompous orations[2] to Georgy, the necessity and excellence of classical acquirements.

When they met at dinner the grandsire used to ask the lad what he had been reading during the day, and was greatly interested at the report the boy gave of his own studies: pretending to understand little George when he spoke regarding them. He made a hundred blunders, and showed his ignorance many a time. It did not increase the respect which the child had for his senior. A quick brain and a better

1. Posed in the initial vignette as George IV in coronation robes.
2. First printing reads: in his pompous manner

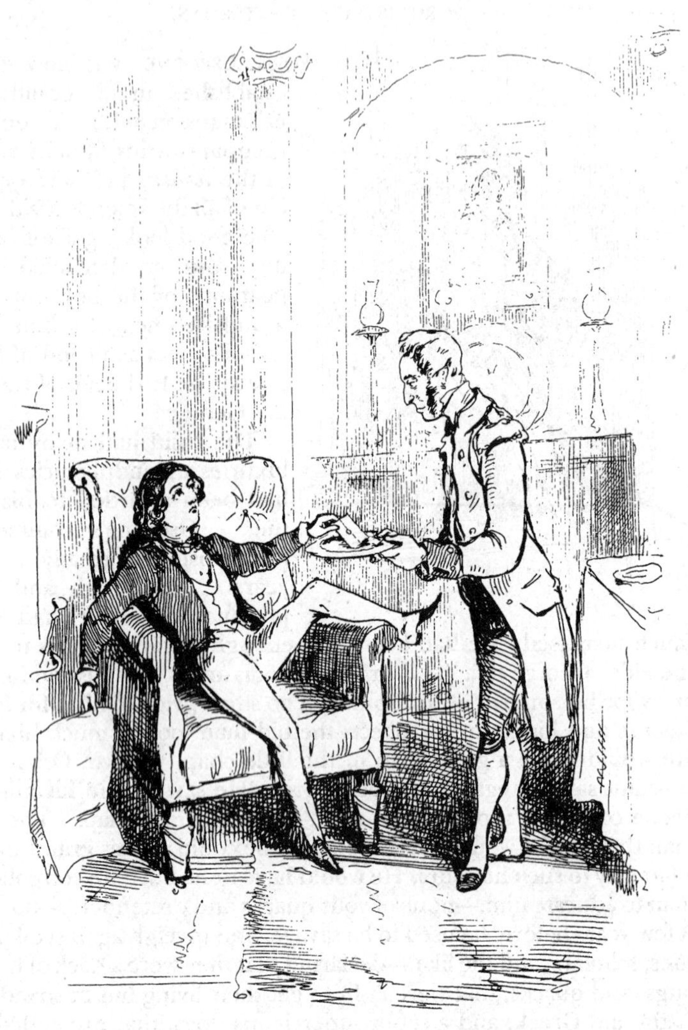

Georgy a Gentleman

education elsewhere showed the boy very soon that his grandsire was a dullard: and he began accordingly to command him and to look down upon him; for his previous education, humble and contracted as it had been, had made a much better gentleman of Georgy than any plans of his grandfather could make him. He had been brought up by a kind, weak, and tender woman, who had no pride about anything, but about him, and whose heart was so pure and whose bearing was so meek and humble, that she could not but needs be a true lady. She busied herself in gentle offices and quiet duties; if she never said brilliant things, she never spoke or thought unkind ones: guileless and artless, loving and pure, indeed how could our poor little Amelia be other than a real gentlewoman?

Young Georgy lorded over this soft and yielding nature: and the contrast of its simplicity and delicacy with the coarse pomposity of the dull old man with whom he next came in contact, made him lord over the latter too. If he had been a Prince Royal he could not have been better brought up to think well of himself.

Whilst his mother was yearning after him at home, and I do believe every hour of the day, and during most hours of the sad lonely nights, thinking of him, this young gentleman had a number of pleasures and consolations administered to him, which made him for his part bear the separation from Amelia very easily. Little boys who cry when they are going to school—cry because they are going to a very uncomfortable place. It is only a very few who weep from sheer affection. When you think that the eyes of your childhood dried at the sight of a piece of gingerbread, and that a plum-cake was a compensation for the agony of parting with your mamma and sisters; O my friend and brother, you need not be too confident of your own fine feelings.

Well, then, Master George Osborne had every comfort and luxury that a wealthy and lavish old grandfather thought fit to provide. The coachman was instructed to purchase for him the handsomest pony which could be bought for money; and on this George was taught to ride, first at a riding-school, whence, after he had performed satisfactorily without stirrups, and over the leaping-bar, he was conducted through the New Road[3] to Regent's Park, and then to Hyde Park, where he rode in state with Martin the coachman behind him. Old Osborne, who took matters more easily in the City now, where he left his affairs to his junior partners, would often ride out with Miss O. in the same fashionable direction. As little Georgy came cantering up with his dandyfied air, and his heels down, his grandfather would nudge the lad's aunt, and say, "Look, Miss O." And he would laugh, and his face would grow red with pleasure, as he nodded out of the window to the boy, as the groom saluted the carriage, and the footman saluted Master George. Here too his aunt, Mrs. Frederic Bullock, (whose chariot might daily be seen in the Ring, with bullocks *or*[4] emblazoned on the panels and harness, and three pasty-faced little Bullocks, covered with cockades and feathers, staring from the

3. Called New Road until 1857, it is the present Marylebone Road, from Paddington to Islington.
4. Heraldic gold bullocks.

windows,)—Mrs. Frederic Bullock, I say, flung glances of the bitterest hatred at the little upstart as he rode by with his hand on his side and his hat on one ear, as proud as a lord.

Though he was scarcely eleven years of age, Master George wore straps and the most beautiful little boots like a man. He had gilt spurs, and a gold-headed whip, and a fine pin in his handkerchief; and the neatest little kid gloves which Lamb's Conduit Street could furnish. His mother had given him a couple of neck-cloths, and carefully hemmed and made some little shirts for him; but when her Samuel[5] came to see the widow, they were replaced by much finer linen. He had little jewelled buttons in the lawn shirt-fronts. Her humble presents had been put aside—I believe Miss Osborne had given them to the coachman's boy. Amelia tried to think she was pleased at the change. Indeed, she was happy and charmed to see the boy looking so beautiful.

She had had a little black profile of him done for a shilling; and this was hung up by the side of another portrait over her bed. One day the boy came on his accustomed visit, galloping down the little street at Brompton, and bringing, as usual, all the inhabitants to the windows to admire his splendour, and with great eagerness, and a look of triumph in his face, he pulled a case out of his great-coat—(it was a natty white great-coat, with a cape and a velvet collar)—pulled out a red morocco case, which he gave her.

"I bought it with my own money, Mamma," he said. "I thought you'd like it."

Amelia opened the case, and giving a little cry of delighted affection, seized the boy and embraced him a hundred times. It was a miniature of himself, very prettily done (though not half handsome

5. First edition erroneously reads "Eli"—the name of the priest to whose service Samuel was dedicated (I Samuel 1–2).

enough, we may be sure, the widow thought). His grandfather had wished to have a picture of him by an artist whose works, exhibited in a shop-window, in Southampton Row, had caught the old gentleman's eyes; and George, who had plenty of money, bethought him of asking the painter how much a copy of the little portrait would cost, saying that[6] he would pay for it out of his own money, and that he wanted to give it to his mother.[7] The pleased painter executed the copy for a small price; and old Osborne himself, when he heard of the incident, growled out his satisfaction, and gave the boy twice as many sovereigns as he paid for the miniature.

But what was the grandfather's pleasure compared to Amelia's extacy? That proof of the boy's affection charmed her so, that she thought no child in the world was like her's for goodness. For long weeks after, the thought of his love made her happy. She slept better with the picture under her pillow; and how many many times did she kiss it, and weep and pray over it! A small kindness from those she loved made that timid heart grateful. Since her parting with George she had had no such joy and consolation.

At his new home Master George ruled like a lord: at dinner he invited the ladies to drink wine with the utmost coolness, and took off his champaigne in a way which charmed his old grandfather. "Look at him," the old man would say, nudging his neighbour with a delighted purple face, "did you ever see such a chap? Lord, Lord! he'll be ordering a dressing-case next, and razors to shave with; I'm blest if he won't."

The antics of the lad did not, however, delight Mr. Osborne's friends so much as they pleased the old gentleman. It gave Mr. Justice Coffin no pleasure to hear Georgy cut into the conversation and spoil his stories. Colonel Fogey was not interested in seeing the little boy half tipsy. Mr. Serjeant Toffy's lady felt no particular gratitude when, with a twist of his elbow, he tilted a glass of port-wine over her yellow satin, and laughed at the disaster: nor was she better pleased, although old Osborne was highly delighted, when Georgy "wopped" her third boy (a young gentleman a year older than Georgy, and by chance home for the holidays from Dr. Tickleus's at Ealing School) in Russell Square. George's grandfather gave the boy a couple of sovereigns for that feat, and promised to reward him further for every boy above his own size and age whom he wopped in a similar manner. It is difficult to say what good the old man saw in these combats; he had a vague notion that quarreling made boys hardy, and that tyranny was a useful accomplishment for them to learn. English youth have been so educated time out of mind, and we have hundreds of thousands of apologists and admirers of injustice, misery, and brutality, as perpetrated among children.

Flushed with praise and victory over Master Toffy, George wished naturally to pursue his conquests further, and one day as he was strutting about in prodigiously dandified new clothes, near St. Pancras,[8]

6. First printing reads: cost, as to his mother, saying
7. First printing reads: to her.
8. A working-class neighborhood.

and a young baker's boy made sarcastic comments upon his appearance, the youthful patrician pulled off his dandy jacket with great spirit, and giving it in charge to the friend who accompanied him (Master Todd, of Great Coram Street, Russell Square, son of the junior partner of the house of Osborne and Co.)—George tried to wop the little baker. But the chances of war were unfavourable this time, and the little baker wopped Georgy: who came home with a rueful black eye and all his fine shirt frill dabbled with the claret drawn from his own little nose. He told his grandfather that he had been in combat with a giant; and frightened his poor mother at Brompton with long, and by no means authentic, accounts of the battle.

This young Todd, of Coram Street, Russell Square, was Master George's great friend and admirer. They both had a taste for painting theatrical characters; for hard bake and raspberry tarts; for sliding and skating in the Regent's Park and the Serpentine, when the weather permitted; for going to the play, whither they were often conducted, by Mr. Osborne's orders, by Rowson, Master George's appointed body-servant; with whom they sate in great comfort in the pit.

In the company of this gentleman they visited all the principal theatres of the metropolis—knew the names of all the actors from Drury

Lane to Sadler's Wells;[9] and performed, indeed, many of the plays to the Todd family and their youthful friends, with West's famous characters, on their pasteboard theatre.[1] Rowson, the footman, who was of a generous disposition, would not unfrequently, when in cash, treat his young master to oysters after the play, and to a glass of rum-shrub for a night-cap. We may be pretty certain that Mr. Rowson profited in his turn, by his young master's liberality and gratitude for the pleasures to which the footman inducted him.

A famous tailor from the West End of the town,—Mr. Osborne would have none of your City or Holborn bunglers he said, for the boy (though a City tailor was good enough for *him*),—was summoned to ornament little George's person, and was told to spare no expense in so doing. So, Mr. Woolsey of Conduit-street, gave a loose to his imagination, and sent the child home fancy trousers, fancy waistcoats, and fancy jackets enough to furnish a school of little dandies. Georgy had little white waistcoats for evening parties and little cut velvet waistcoats for dinners, and a dear little darling shawl dressing-gown, for all the world like a little man. He dressed for dinner every day, "like a regular West End Swell," as his grandfather remarked: one of the domestics was affected to his especial service, attended him at his toilette, answered his bell, and brought him his letters always on a silver tray.

Georgy, after breakfast, would sit in the arm-chair in the dining-room, and read the "Morning Post," just like a grown-up man. "How he *du* dam and swear," the servants would cry, delighted at his precocity. Those who remembered the Captain his father, declared Master George was his Pa every inch of him. He made the house lively by his activity, his imperiousness, his scolding, and his good nature.

George's education was confided to a neighbouring scholar and private pedagogue who "prepared young noblemen and gentlemen for the Universities, the senate, and the learned professions: whose system did not embrace the degrading corporal severities, still practised at the ancient places of education, and in whose family the pupils would find the elegancies of refined society and the confidence and affection of a home." It was in this way that the Reverend Lawrence Veal of Hart Street, Bloomsbury, and domestic Chaplain to the Earl of Bareacres, strove with Mrs. Veal his wife to entice pupils.

By thus advertising and pushing sedulously, the domestic Chaplain and his Lady generally succeeded in having one or two scholars by them: who paid a high figure: and were thought to be in uncommonly comfortable quarters. There was a large West Indian, whom nobody came to see, with a mahogany complexion, a woolly head, and an exceedingly dandified appearance: there was another hulking boy of three-and-twenty whose education had been neglected, and whom Mr. and Mrs. Veal were to introduce into the polite world: there were two sons of Colonel Bangles of the East India Company's Service: these four sate down to dinner at Mrs. Veal's genteel board, when Georgy was introduced to her establishment.

9. Drury Lane Theatre at Covent Garden, central London; Sadler's Wells Theatre off the Islinton Road, north London.
1. William West (1796–1888) created toy theaters (Harden).

Georgy was, like some dozen other pupils, only a day boy: he arrived in the morning under the guardianship of his friend Mr. Rowson, and if it was fine, would ride away in the afternoon on his pony, followed by the groom. The wealth of his grandfather was reported in the school to be prodigious. The Rev. Mr. Veal used to compliment Georgy upon it personally, warning him that he was destined for a high station; that it became him to prepare, by sedulity and docility in youth, for the lofty duties to which he would be called in mature age; that obedience in the child was the best preparation for command in the man; and that he therefore begged George would not bring toffy into the school, and ruin the health of the Masters Bangles, who had everything they wanted at the elegant and abundant table of Mrs. Veal.

With respect to learning, "the Curriculum," as Mr. Veal loved to call it, was of prodigious extent: and the young gentlemen in Hart Street might learn a something of every known science. The Rev. Mr. Veal had an orrery,[2] an electrifying machine, a turning lathe, a theatre (in the wash-house), a chemical apparatus, and, what he called a select library of all the works of the best authors of ancient and modern times and languages. He took the boys to the British Museum, and descanted upon the antiquities and the specimens of natural history there, so that audiences would gather round him as he spoke, and all Bloomsbury highly admired him as a prodigiously well informed man. And whenever he spoke (which he did almost always), he took care to produce the very finest and longest words of which the vocabulary gave him the use; rightly judging, that it was as cheap to employ a handsome, large, and sonorous epithet, as to use a little stingy one.

Thus he would say to George in school, "I observed on my return home from taking the indulgence of an evening's scientific conversation with my excellent friend Doctor Bulders—a true archæologian, gentlemen, a true archæologian—that the windows of your venerated grandfather's almost princely mansion in Russell Square were illuminated as if for the purposes of festivity. Am I right in my conjecture, that Mr. Osborne entertained a society of chosen spirits round his sumptuous board last night?"

Little Georgy, who had considerable humour, and used to mimic Mr. Veal to his face with great spirit and dexterity, would reply, that Mr. V. was quite correct in his surmise.

"Then those friends who had the honour of partaking of Mr. Osborne's hospitality, gentlemen, had no reason, I will lay any wager, to complain of their repast. I myself have been more than once so favoured. (By the way, Master Osborne, you came a little late this morning, and have been a defaulter in this respect more than once.) I myself, I say, gentlemen, humble as I am, have been found not unworthy to share Mr. Osborne's elegant hospitality. And though I have feasted with the great and noble of the world—for I presume that I may call my excellent friend and patron, the Right Honourable George Earl of Bareacres, as one of the number—yet I assure you that

2. Clock-driven mechanism representing the solar system.

the board of the British merchant was to the full as richly served, and his reception as gratifying and noble. 'Mr. Bluck, Sir, we will resume, if you please, that passage of Eutropius, which was interrupted by the late arrival of Master Osborne.'"

To this great man George's education was for some time entrusted. Amelia was bewildered by his phrases, but thought him a prodigy of learning. That poor widow made friends with[3] Mrs. Veal, for reasons of her own. She liked to be in the house, and see Georgy coming to school there. She liked to be asked to Mrs. Veal's *conversazioni,*[4] which took place once a month (as you were informed on pink cards, with *AΘHNH*[5] engraved on them), and where the Professor welcomed his pupils and their friends to weak tea and scientific conversation. Poor little Amelia never missed one of these entertainments, and thought them delicious so long as she might have Georgy sitting by her. And she would walk from Brompton in any weather, and embrace Mrs. Veal with tearful gratitude for the delightful evening she had passed, when, the company having retired and Georgy gone off with Mr. Rowson his attendant, poor Mrs. Osborne put on her cloaks and her shawls preparatory to walking home.

As for the learning which Georgy imbibed under this voluble master of a hundred sciences, to judge from the weekly reports which the lad took home to his grandfather, his progress was remarkable. The names of a score or more of desirable branches of knowledge were printed on a table, and the pupil's progress in each was marked by the professor. In Greek Georgy was pronounced aristos, in Latin optimus, in French *très bien,*[6] and so forth; and everybody had prizes for everything at the end of the year. Even Mr. Swartz, the woolly-headed young gentleman, and half-brother to the Honourable Mrs. Mac Mull, and Mr. Bluck, the neglected young pupil of three-and-twenty from the agricultural districts, and that idle young scapegrace of a Master Todd before mentioned, received little eighteen-penny books, with "Athene" engraved in them, and a pompous Latin inscription from the Professor to his young friends.

The family of this Master Todd were hangers-on of the house of Osborne. The old gentleman had advanced Todd from being a clerk to be a junior partner in his establishment.

Mr. Osborne was the godfather of young Master Todd (who in subsequent life wrote Mr. Osborne Todd on his cards, and became a man of decided fashion) while Miss Osborne had accompanied Miss Maria Todd to the font, and gave her *protegée* a prayer-book, a collection of tracts, a volume of very low church[7] poetry, or some such memento of her goodness every year. Miss O. drove the Todds out in her carriage now and then: when they were ill her footman, in large plush smalls and waistcoat, brought jellies and delicacies from Russell Square to Coram Street. Coram Street trembled and looked up to Russell Square indeed; and Mrs. Todd, who had a pretty hand

3. Revised edition reads: of
4. Conversations, relatively formal assemblies for intellectual discussion.
5. Athene: Greek goddess of wisdom.
6. Best, best, and very good, respectively.
7. Evangelical, enthusiast branch of the Church of England, opposed to the papal tendencies of the high church.

at cutting out paper trimmings for haunches of mutton, and could make flowers, ducks, &c., out of turnips and carrots in a very creditable manner, would go to "the Square," as it was called, and assist in the preparations incident to a great dinner, without even so much as thinking of sitting down to the banquet. If any guest failed at the eleventh hour, Todd was asked to dine. Mrs. Todd and Maria came across in the evening, slipped in with a muffled knock, and were in the drawing-room by the time Miss Osborne and the ladies under her convoy reached that apartment; and ready to fire off duets and sing until the gentlemen came up. Poor Maria Todd; poor young lady! How she had to work and thrum at these duets and sonatas in the Street, before they appeared in public in the Square!

Thus it seemed to be decreed by fate, that Georgy was to domineer over everybody with whom he came in contact, and that friends, relatives, and domestics were all to bow the knee before the little fellow. It must be owned that he accommodated himself very willingly to this arrangement. Most people do so. And Georgy liked to play the part of master, and perhaps had a natural aptitude for it.

In Russell Square everybody was afraid of Mr. Osborne, and Mr. Osborne was afraid of Georgy. The boy's dashing manners, and offhand rattle about books and learning, his likeness to his father, (dead unreconciled in Brussels yonder,) awed the old gentleman, and gave the young boy the mastery. The old man would start at some hereditary feature or tone unconsciously used by the little lad, and fancy that George's father was again before him. He tried by indulgence to the grandson to make up for harshness to the elder George. People were surprised at his gentleness to the boy. He growled and swore at Miss Osborne as usual: and would smile when George came down late for breakfast.

Miss Osborne, George's aunt, was a faded[8] old spinster, broken down by more than forty years of dullness and coarse usage. It was easy for a lad of spirit to master *her.* And whenever George wanted anything from her, from the jam-pots in her cupboards, to the cracked and dry old colours in her paint-box (the old paint-box which she had had when she was a pupil of Mr. Smee, and was still almost young and blooming), Georgy took possession of the object of his desire, which obtained, he took no further notice of his aunt.

For his friends and cronies, he had a pompous old schoolmaster, who flattered him, and a toady, his senior, whom he could thrash. It was dear Mrs. Todd's delight to leave him with her youngest daughter, Rosa Jemima, a darling child of eight years old. The little pair looked so well together, she would say (but not to the folks in 'the Square,' we may be sure),—"Who knows what might happen? Don't they make a pretty little couple?" the fond mother thought.

The broken-spirited, old, maternal grandfather was likewise subject to the little tyrant. He could not help respecting a lad who had such fine clothes, and rode with a groom behind him. Georgy, on his side, was in the constant habit of hearing coarse abuse and vulgar satire levied at John Sedley, by his pitiless old enemy, Mr. Osborne.

8. First printing reads: miserable

Osborne used to call the other the old pauper, the old coal-man, the old bankrupt, and by many other such names of brutal contumely. How was little George to respect a man so prostrate? A few months after he was with his paternal grandfather, Mrs. Sedley died. There had been little love between her and the child. He did not care to show much grief. He came down to visit his mother in a fine new suit of mourning, and was very angry that he could not go to a play upon which he had set his heart.

The illness of that old lady had been the occupation and perhaps the safeguard of Amelia. What do men know about women's martyrdoms? We should go mad had we to endure the hundredth part of those daily pains which are meekly borne by many women. Ceaseless slavery meeting with no reward; constant gentleness and kindness met by cruelty as constant; love, labour, patience, watchfulness, without even so much as the acknowledgment of a good word; all this, how many of them have to bear in quiet, and appear abroad with cheerful faces as if they felt nothing. Tender slaves that they are, they must needs be hypocrites and weak.

From her chair Amelia's mother had taken to her bed, which she had never left: and from which Mrs. Osborne herself was never absent except when she ran to see George. The old lady grudged her even those rare visits: she, who had been a kind, smiling, good-natured mother once, in the days of her prosperity, but whom poverty and infirmities had broken down. Her illness or estrangement did not affect Amelia. They rather enabled her to support the other calamity under which she was suffering, and from the thoughts of which she was kept by the ceaseless calls of the invalid. Amelia bore her harshness quite gently: smoothed the uneasy pillow; was always ready with a soft answer to the watchful, querulous voice; soothed the sufferer with words of hope, such as her pious simple heart could best feel and utter, and closed the eyes that had once looked so tenderly upon her.

Then all her time and tenderness were devoted to the consolation and comfort of the bereaved old father, who was stunned by the blow which had befallen him, and stood utterly alone in the world. His wife, his honour, his fortune, everything he loved best had fallen away from him. There was only Amelia to stand by and support with her gentle arms the tottering, heart-broken, old man. We are not going to write the history: it would be too dreary and stupid. I can see Vanity Fair yawning over it: *d'avance.*[9]

One day as the young gentlemen were assembled in the study at the Rev. Mr. Veal's, and the domestic chaplain to the Right Honourable the Earl of Bareacres was spouting away as usual—a smart carriage drove up to the door decorated with the statue of Athene, and two gentlemen stepped out. The young Masters Bangles rushed to the window, with a vague notion that their father might have arrived from Bombay. The great hulking scholar of three-and-twenty, who was crying secretly over a passage of Eutropius, flattened his ne-

9. In advance.

glected nose against the panes, and looked at the drag, as the *laquais de place*[1] sprang from the box and let out the persons in the carriage.

"It's a fat one and a thin one," Mr. Bluck said, as a thundering knock came to the door.

Everybody was interested, from the domestic chaplain himself, who hoped he saw the fathers of some future pupils, down to Master Georgy, glad of any pretext for laying his book down.

The boy in the shabby livery, with the faded copper-buttons, who always thrust himself into the tight coat to open the door, came into the study and said, "Two gentlemen want to see Master Osborne." The Professor had had a trifling altercation in the morning with that young gentleman, owing to a difference about the introduction of crackers in school-time; but his face resumed its habitual expression of bland courtesy, as he said, "Master Osborne, I give you full permission to go and see your carriage friends,—to whom I beg you to convey the respectful compliments of myself and Mrs. Veal."

Georgy went into the reception-room, and saw two strangers, whom he looked at with his head up, in his usual haughty manner. One was fat, with mustachios, and the other was lean and long, in a blue frock-coat, with a brown face, and a grizzled head.

"My God, how like he is!" said the long gentleman, with a start. "Can you guess who we are, George?"

The boy's face flushed up, as it did usually when he was moved, and his eyes brightened. "I don't know the other," he said, "but I should think you must be Major Dobbin."

Indeed it was our old friend. His voice trembled with pleasure as he greeted the boy, and taking both the other's hands in his own, drew the lad to him.

"Your mother has talked to you about me—has she?" he said.

"That she has," Georgy answered, "hundreds and hundreds of times."

1. Footmen.

*Number 17* *May 1848*

## *Chapter LVII.*

### EOTHEN.[1]

It was one of the many causes for personal pride with which old Osborne chose to recreate himself, that Sedley, his ancient rival, enemy, and benefactor, was in his last days so utterly defeated and humiliated, as to be forced to accept pecuniary obligations at the hands of the man who had most injured and insulted him. The successful man of the world cursed the old pauper, and relieved him from time to time. As he furnished George with money for his mother, he gave the boy to understand by hints, delivered in his brutal, coarse way, that George's maternal grandfather was but a wretched old bankrupt and dependant, and that John Sedley might thank the man to whom he already owed ever so much money, for the aid which his generosity now chose to administer. George carried the pompous supplies to his mother and the shattered old widower whom it was now the main business of her life to tend and comfort. The little fellow patronised the feeble and disappointed old man.

It may have shown a want of "proper pride" in Amelia that she chose to accept these money benefits at the hands of her father's enemy. But proper pride and this poor lady had never had much acquaintance together. A disposition naturally simple and demanding protection; a long course of poverty and humility, of daily privations, and hard words, of kind offices and no returns, had been her lot ever since womanhood almost, or since her luckless marriage with George Osborne. You who see your betters, bearing up under this shame every day, meekly suffering under the slights of fortune, gentle and unpitied, poor, and rather despised for their poverty, do you ever step down from your prosperity and wash the feet of these poor wearied beggars? The very thought of them is odious and low. "There must be classes—there must be rich and poor," Dives says, smacking his claret—(it is well if he even sends the broken meat out to Lazarus sitting under the window). Very true; but think how mysterious and often unaccountable it is—that lottery of life which gives to this man the purple and fine linen, and sends to the other rags for garments and dogs for comforters.

1. Dawn; also the title of Alexander Kinglake's book, alluded to in chapter LI.

So I must own, that without much repining, on the contrary with something akin to gratitude, Amelia took the crumbs that her father-in-law let drop now and then and with them fed her own parent. Directly she understood it to be her duty, it was this young woman's nature (ladies, she is but thirty still, and we choose to call her a young woman even at that age)—it was, I say, her nature to sacrifice herself and to fling all that she had at the feet of the beloved object. During what long thankless nights had she worked out her fingers for little Georgy whilst at home with her; what buffets, scorns, privations, poverties had she endured for father and mother! And in the midst of all these solitary resignations and unseen sacrifices, she did not respect herself any more than the world respected her; but I believe thought in her heart that she was a poor-spirited, despicable little creature, whose luck in life was only too good for her merits. O you poor women! O you poor secret martyrs and victims, whose life is a torture, who are stretched on racks in your bedrooms, and who lay your heads down on the block daily at the drawing-room table; every man who watches your pains, or peers into those dark places where the torture is administered to you, must pity you—and—and thank God that he has a beard. I recollect seeing, years ago, at the prison for idiots and madmen at Bicêtre, near Paris, a poor wretch bent down under the bondage of his imprisonment and his personal infirmity, to whom one of our party gave a halfpennyworth of snuff in a *cornet* or "screw" of paper. The kindness was too much for the poor epileptic creature. He cried in an anguish of delight and gratitude: if anybody gave you and me a thousand a-year, or saved our lives, we could not be so affected. And so, if you properly tyrannise over a woman, you will find a halfp'orth of kindness act upon her, and bring tears into her eyes, as though you were an angel benefiting her.

Some such boons as these were the best which Fortune allotted to poor little Amelia. Her life, begun not unprosperously, had come down to this—to a mean prison and a long, ignoble bondage. Little George visited her captivity sometimes, and consoled it with feeble gleams of encouragement. Russell Square was the boundary of her prison: she might walk thither occasionally, but was always back to sleep in her cell at night; to perform cheerless duties; to watch by thankless sick-beds; to suffer the harassment and tyranny of querulous disappointed old age. How many thousands of people are there, women for the most part, who are doomed to endure this long slavery?—who are hospital-nurses without wages,—sisters of Charity, if you like, without the romance and the sentiment of sacrifice,—who strive, fast, watch, and suffer, unpitied; and fade away ignobly and unknown. The hidden and awful Wisdom which apportions the destinies of mankind is pleased so to humiliate and cast down the tender, good, and wise; and to set up the selfish, the foolish, or the wicked. Oh, be humble, my brother, in your prosperity! Be gentle with those who are less lucky, if not more deserving. Think, what right have you to be scornful, whose virtue is a deficiency of temptation, whose success may be a chance, whose rank may be an ancestor's accident, whose prosperity is very likely a satire.

They buried Amelia's mother at the church-yard at Brompton;

upon just such a rainy, dark day, as Amelia recollected when first she had been there to marry George. Her little boy sate by her side in pompous new sables.[2] She remembered the old pew-woman and clerk. Her thoughts were away in other times as the parson read. But that she held George's hand in her own, perhaps she would have liked to change places with . . . Then, as usual, she felt ashamed of her selfish thoughts, and prayed inwardly to be strengthened to do her duty.

So she determined with all her might and strength to try and make her old father happy. She slaved, toiled, patched and mended, sang and played backgammon, read out the newspaper, cooked dishes for old Sedley, walked him out sedulously into Kensington Gardens or the Brompton Lanes, listened to his stories with untiring smiles and affectionate hypocrisy, or sate musing by his side and communing with her own thoughts and reminiscences, as the old man, feeble and querulous, sunned himself on the garden benches and prattled about his wrongs or his sorrows. What sad, unsatisfactory thoughts those of the widow were! The children running up and down the slopes and broad paths in the gardens, reminded her of George who was taken from her: the first George was taken from her: her selfish, guilty love, in both instances, had been rebuked and bitterly chastised. She strove to think it was right that she should be so punished. She was such a miserable wicked sinner. She was quite alone in the world.

I know that the account of this kind of solitary imprisonment is insufferably tedious, unless there is some cheerful or humorous incident to enliven it,—a tender gaoler, for instance, or a waggish commandant of the fortress, or a mouse to come out and play about Latude's beard and whiskers, or a subterranean passage under the castle, dug by Trenck with his nails and a toothpick:[3] the historian has no such enlivening incident to relate in the narrative of Amelia's captivity. Fancy her, if you please, during this period, very sad, but always ready to smile when spoken to; in a very mean, poor, not to say vulgar position of life; singing songs, making puddings, playing cards, mending stockings, for her old father's benefit. So, never mind, whether she be a heroine or no; or you and I, however old, scolding, and bankrupt;—may we have in our last days a kind soft shoulder on which to lean, and a gentle hand to soothe our gouty old pillows.

Old Sedley grew very fond of his daughter after his wife's death; and Amelia had her consolation in doing her duty by the old man.

But we are not going to leave these two people long in such a low and ungenteel station of life. Better days, as far as worldly prosperity went, were in store for both. Perhaps the ingenious reader has guessed who was the stout gentleman who called upon Georgy at his school in company with our old friend Major Dobbin. It was another old acquaintance returned to England, and at a time when his presence was likely to be of great comfort to his relatives there.

2. Mourning clothes.
3. Jean Henri Latude (1725–1805) and Friedrich von der Trenck (1726–94) spent much of their lives in and out of jails, frequently escaping; both wrote popular memoirs.

Major Dobbin having easily succeeded in getting leave from his good-natured commandant to proceed to Madras, and thence probably to Europe, on urgent private affairs, never ceased travelling night and day until he reached his journey's end, and had directed his march with such celerity, that he arrived at Madras in a high fever. His servants who accompanied him, brought him to the house of the friend with whom he had resolved to stay until his departure for Europe in a state of delirium; and it was thought for many many days that he would never travel farther than the burying-ground of the church of St. George's, where the troops should fire a salvo over his grave, and where many a gallant officer lies far away from his home.

Here as the poor fellow lay tossing in his fever, the people who watched him might have heard him raving about Amelia. The idea that he should never see her again depressed him in his lucid hours. He thought his last day was come; and he made his solemn preparations for departure: setting his affairs in this world in order, and leaving the little property of which he was possessed to those whom he most desired to benefit. The friend in whose house he was located witnessed his testament. He desired to be buried with a little brown hair-chain which he wore round his neck, and which, if the truth must be known, he had got from Amelia's maid at Brussels, when the young widow's hair was cut off, during the fever which prostrated her after the death of George Osborne on the plateau of Mount St. John.

He recovered, rallied, relapsed again, having undergone such a process of blood-letting and calomel as showed the strength of his original constitution. He was almost a skeleton when they put him on board the Ramchunder, East Indiaman, Captain Bragg, from Calcutta touching at Madras; and so weak and prostrate, that his friend who had tended him through his illness, prophesied that the honest Major would never survive the voyage, and that he would pass some morning, shrouded in flag and hammock, over the ship's side, and carrying down to the sea with him, the relic that he wore at his heart. But whether it was the sea air, or the hope which sprang up in him afresh, from the day that the ship spread her canvass and stood out of the roads towards *home,* our friend began to amend, and he was quite well (though as gaunt as a greyhound) before they reached the Cape. "Kirk will be disappointed of his majority this time," he said with a smile: "he will expect to find himself gazetted by the time the regiment reaches home." For it must be premised that while the Major was lying ill at Madras, having made such a prodigious haste to go thither, the gallant —th which had passed many years abroad, which after its return from the West Indies had been baulked of its stay at home by the Waterloo campaign, and had been ordered from Flanders to India, had received orders home; and the Major might have accompanied his comrades, had he chosen to wait for their arrival at Madras.

Perhaps he was not inclined to put himself in his exhausted state again under the guardianship of Glorvina. "I think Miss O'Dowd would have done for me," he said, laughingly, to a fellow-passenger, "if we had had her on board, and when she had sunk me, she would have fallen upon you, depend upon it, and carried you in as a prize to Southampton, Jos, my boy."

For indeed it was no other than our stout friend who was also a passenger on board the Ramchunder. He had passed ten years in Bengal.—Constant dinners, tiffins, pale ale and claret, the prodigious labours of cutcherry, and the refreshment of brandy-pawnee which he was forced to take there,[4] had their effect upon Waterloo Sedley. A voyage to Europe was pronounced necessary for him—and having served his full time in India, and had fine appointments which had enabled him to lay by a considerable sum of money, he was free to come home and stay with a good pension, or to return and resume that rank in his service to which his seniority and his vast talents entitled him.

He was rather thinner than when we last saw him, but had gained in majesty and solemnity of demeanour. He had resumed the moustachios to which his services at Waterloo entitled him, and swaggered about on deck in a magnificent velvet cap with a gold band, and a profuse ornamentation of pins and jewellery about his person. He took breakfast in his cabin, and dressed as solemnly to appear on the quarter-deck, as if he was going to turn out for Bond Street, or the Course at Calcutta. He brought a native servant with him, who was his valet and pipe-bearer; and who wore the Sedley crest in silver on his turban. That oriental menial had a wretched life under the tyranny of Jos Sedley. Jos was as vain of his person as a woman, and took as long a time at his toilette as any fading beauty. The youngsters among the passengers, Young Chaffers of the 150th, and poor little Ricketts, coming home after his third fever, used to draw out Sedley at the cuddy-table, and make him tell prodigious stories about himself and his exploits against tigers and Napoleon. He was great when he visited the Emperor's tomb at Longwood,[5] when to these gentlemen and the young officers of the ship, Major Dobbin not being by, he described the whole Battle of Waterloo, and all but announced that Napoleon never would have gone to Saint Helena at all but for him, Jos Sedley.

After leaving St. Helena he became very generous, disposing of a great quantity of ship stores, claret, preserved meats, and great casks packed with soda-water, brought out for his private delectation. There were no ladies on board; the Major gave the pas of precedency to the civilian, so that he was the first dignitary at table; and treated by Captain Bragg, and the officers of the Ramchunder, with the respect which his rank warranted. He disappeared rather in a panic during a two-days' gale, in which he had the portholes of his cabin battened down; and remained in his cot reading the "Washerwoman of Finchley Common," left on board the Ramchunder by the Right Honourable the Lady Emily Hornblower, wife of the Rev. Silas Hornblower, then on their passage out to the Cape, where the Reverend gentleman was a missionary; but, for common reading, he had brought a stock of novels and plays which he lent to the rest of

4. Cutcherry: court or administrative office work. Brandy-pawnee: brandy and water.
5. Napoleon's temporary grave at his final home, Longwood, on St. Helena. He was reburied in Paris in 1840.

the ship, and rendered himself agreeable to all by his kindness and condescension.

Many and many a night, as the ship was cutting through the roaring dark sea, the moon and stars shining over head, and the bell singing out the watch, Mr. Sedley and the Major would sit on the quarter-deck of the vessel talking about home, as the Major smoked his cheroot, and the civilian puffed at the hookah[6] which his servant prepared for him.

In these conversations it was wonderful with what perseverance and ingenuity Major Dobbin would manage to bring the talk round to the subject of Amelia and her little boy. Jos, a little testy about his father's misfortunes and unceremonious applications to him, was soothed down by the Major, who pointed out the elder's ill fortunes and old age. He would not perhaps like to live with the old couple: whose ways and hours might not agree with those of a younger man, accustomed to different society, (Jos bowed at this compliment): but, the Major pointed out, how advantageous it would be for Jos Sedley

6. Cheroot: short, squared-off cigar. Hookah: water-cooled smoking pipe.

to have a house of his own in London, and not a mere bachelor's establishment as before; how his sister Amelia would be the very person to preside over it; how elegant, how gentle she was, and of what refined good manners. He recounted stories of the success which Mrs. George Osborne had had in former days at Brussels, and in London, where she was much admired by people of very great fashion: and he then hinted how becoming it would be for Jos to send Georgy to a good school and make a man of him; for his mother and her parents would be sure to spoil him. In a word this artful Major made the civilian promise to take charge of Amelia and her unprotected child. He did not know as yet what events had happened in the little Sedley family; and how death had removed the mother, and riches had carried off George from Amelia. But the fact is that every day and always, this love-smitten and middle-aged gentleman was thinking about Mrs. Osborne, and his whole heart was bent upon doing her good. He coaxed, wheedled, cajoled, and complimented Jos Sedley with a perseverance and cordiality of which he was not aware himself, very likely: but some men who have unmarried sisters or daughters even, may remember how uncommonly agreeable gentlemen are to the male relations when they are courting the females; and perhaps this rogue of a Dobbin was urged by a similar hypocrisy.

The truth is, when Major Dobbin came on board the Ramchunder, very sick, and for the three days she lay in the Madras Roads, he did not begin to rally, nor did even the appearance and recognition of his old acquaintance, Mr. Sedley, on board much cheer him, until after a conversation which they had one day, as the Major was laid languidly on the deck. He said then he thought he was doomed; he had left a little something to his godson in his will; and he trusted Mrs. Osborne would remember him kindly, and be happy in the marriage she was about to make. "Married? not the least," Jos answered; "he had heard from her; she made no mention of the marriage, and by the way, it was curious, she wrote to say that Major Dobbin was going to be married, and hoped that *he* would be happy." What were the dates of Sedley's letters from Europe? The civilian fetched them. They were two months later than the Major's; and the ship's surgeon congratulated himself upon the treatment adopted by him towards his new patient, who had been consigned to ship-board by the Madras practitioner with very small hopes indeed; for, from that day, the very day that he changed the draught, Major Dobbin began to mend. And thus it was that deserving officer, Captain Kirk, was disappointed of his majority.

After they passed St. Helena, Major Dobbin's gaiety and strength was such as to astonish all his fellow-passengers. He larked with the midshipmen, played single-stick[7] with the mates, ran up the shrouds like a boy, sang a comic song one night to the amusement of the whole party assembled over their grog after supper, and rendered himself so gay, lively, and amiable, that even Captain Bragg, who thought there was nothing in his passenger, and considered he was a poor-spirited feller at first, was constrained to own that the Major was a reserved but well-informed and meritorious officer. "He ain't got

7. Fenced with sticks with hand guards.

distangy[8] manners, dammy," Bragg observed to his first mate; "he wouldn't do at Government House, Roper, where his Lordship and Lady William[9] was as kind to me, and shook hands with me before the whole company, and asking me at dinner to take beer with him before the Commander-in-Chief himself; he ain't got manners, but there's something about him—." In which opinion[1] Captain Bragg showed that he possessed discrimination as a man, as well as ability as a commander.

But a calm taking place when the Ramchunder was within ten days' sail of England, Dobbin became so impatient and ill-humoured as to surprise those comrades who had before admired his vivacity and good temper. He did not recover until the breeze sprang up again, and was in a highly excited state when the pilot came on board. Good God, how his heart beat as the two friendly spires of Southampton[2] came in sight!

## *Chapter LVIII.*

### OUR FRIEND THE MAJOR.

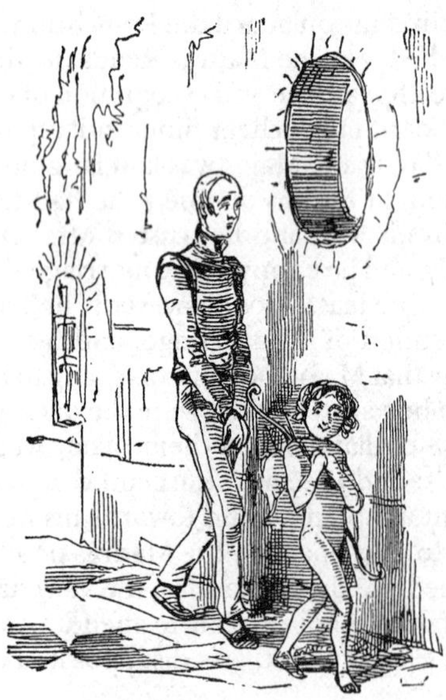

UR[1] Major had rendered himself so popular on board the Ramchunder, that when he and Mr. Sedley descended into the welcome shore-boat which was to take them from the ship, the whole crew, men and officers, the great Captain Bragg himself leading off, gave three cheers for Major Dobbin, who blushed very much, and ducked his head in token of thanks. Jos who very likely thought the cheers were for himself, took off his gold-laced cap and waved it majestically to his friends, and they were pulled to shore and landed with great dignity at the pier, whence they proceeded to the Royal George Hotel.

Although the sight of that magnificent round of beef, and the silver tankard suggestive of real British home-brewed ale and porter, which perennially greet the eyes of the traveller returning

8. *Distingué*, distinguished.
9. Lord William Cavendish Bentinck, governor-general of Bengal (1823–33) and of India (1833–35).
1. Revised edition reads: And thus
2. Cathedral towers in the south coast seaport.
1. Initial illustration: Dobbin and Cupid.

from foreign parts, who enters the coffee-room of the George, are so invigorating and delightful, that a man entering such a comfortable snug homely English inn, might well like to stop some days there, yet Dobbin began to talk about a post-chaise[2] instantly, and was no sooner at Southampton than he wished to be on the road to London. Jos, however, would not hear of moving that evening. Why was he to pass a night in a post-chaise instead of a great large undulating downy featherbed which was there ready to replace the horrid little narrow crib in which the portly Bengal gentleman had been confined during the voyage? He could not think of moving till his baggage was cleared, or of travelling until he could do so with his chillum.[3] So the Major was forced to wait over that night, and dispatched a letter to his family announcing his arrival; entreating from Jos a promise to write to his own friends. Jos promised, but didn't keep his promise. The Captain, the surgeon, and one or two passengers came and dined with our two gentlemen at the inn: Jos exerting himself in a sumptuous way in ordering the dinner: and promising to go to town the next day with the Major. The landlord said it did his eyes good to see Mr. Sedley take off his first pint of porter. If I had time and dared to enter into digressions, I would write a chapter about that first pint of porter drunk upon English ground. Ah, how good it is! It is worth while to leave home for a year, just to enjoy that one draught.

Major Dobbin made his appearance the next morning very neatly shaved and dressed, according to his wont. Indeed, it was so early in the morning, that nobody was up in the house except that wonderful Boots of an inn who never seems to want sleep: and the Major could hear the snores of the various inmates of the house roaring through the corridors as he creaked about in those dim passages. Then the sleepless Boots went shirking round from door to door, gathering up at each the Bluchers, Wellingtons, Oxonians,[4] which stood outside. Then Jos's native servant arose and began to get ready his master's ponderous dressing apparatus, and prepare his hookah: then the maid servants got up, and meeting the dark man in the passages shrieked and mistook him for the devil. He and Dobbin stumbled over their pails in the passages as they were scouring the decks of the Royal George. When the first unshorn waiter appeared and unbarred the door of the inn, the Major thought that the time for departure was arrived, and ordered a post-chaise to be fetched instantly, that they might set off.

He then directed his steps to Mr. Sedley's room, and opened the curtains of the great large family bed wherein Mr. Jos was snoring. "Come, up! Sedley," the Major said, "it's time to be off; the chaise will be at the door in half an hour."

Jos growled from under the counterpane to know what the time was; but when he at last extorted from the blushing Major (who never told fibs, however much they might be to his advantage) what was the

2. Hired carriage and horses, as opposed to public transportation.
3. Hookah.
4. Bluchers: low-top boots named for the Prussian general in the Napoleonic wars. Wellingtons: knee boots named for the duke of Wellington. Oxonians: button-top shoes.

real hour of the morning, he broke out into a volley of bad language, which we will not repeat here, but by which he gave Dobbin to understand that he would jeopardy his soul if he got up at that moment, that the Major might go and be hanged, that he would not travel with Dobbin, and that it was most unkind and ungentlemanlike to disturb a man out of his sleep in that way: on which the discomfited Major was obliged to retreat, leaving Jos to resume his interrupted slumbers.

The chaise came up presently, and the Major would wait no longer.

If he had been an English nobleman travelling on a pleasure tour; or a newspaper courier, bearing dispatches, (government messages are generally carried much more quietly) he could not have travelled more quickly. The post boys wondered at the fees he flung amongst them. How happy and green the country looked as the chaise whirled rapidly from mile-stone to mile-stone, through neat country towns where landlords came out to welcome him with smiles and bows; by pretty road-side inns, where the signs hung on the elms, and horses and waggoners were drinking under the chequered shadow of the trees; by old halls and parks; rustic hamlets clustered round ancient grey churches—and through the charming friendly English landscape. Is there any in the world like it? To a traveller returning home it looks so kind—it seems to shake hands with you as you pass through it.—Well, Major Dobbin passed over all this from Southampton to London, and without noting much beyond the mile-stones along the road.—You see he was so eager to see his parents at Camberwell.

He grudged the time lost between Piccadilly and his old haunt at the Slaughters',[5] whither he drove faithfully. Long[6] years had passed since he saw it last, since he and George, as young men, had enjoyed many a feast, and held many a revel there. He had now passed into the stage of old-fellow-hood. His hair was grizzled, and many a passion and feeling of his youth had grown grey in that interval. There, however, stood the old waiter at the door in the same greasy black suit, with the same double chin and flaccid face, with the same huge bunch of seals at his fob, rattling his money in his pockets as before, and receiving the Major as if he had gone away only a week ago. "Put the Major's things in twenty-three, that's his room," John said, exhibiting not the least surprise. "Roast fowl for your dinner I suppose. You ain't got married? They said you was married—the Scotch surgeon of your's was here. No, it was Captain Humby of the thirty-third, as was quartered with the —th in Injee. Like any warm water? What do you come in a chay for, ain't the coach good enough?" And with this, the faithful waiter, who knew and remembered every officer who used the house, and with whom ten years were but as yesterday, led the way up to Dobbin's old room, where stood the great moreen bed, and the shabby carpet, a thought more dingy, and all the old black furniture covered with faded chintz, just as the Major recollected them in his youth.

5. Coffee house and inn. See chapter XIII.
6. First printing reads: Ten

He remembered George pacing up and down the room, and biting his nails, and swearing that the Governor must come round, and that if he didn't, he didn't care a straw, on the day before he was married. He could fancy him walking in, banging the door of Dobbin's room, and his own hard by—

"You ain't got young," John said, calmly surveying his friend of former days.

Dobbin laughed. "Ten years and a fever don't make a man young, John," he said. "It is you that are always young:—No, you are always old."

"What became of Captain Osborne's widow," John said. "Fine young fellow that. Lord how he used to spend his money. He never came back after that day he was married from here. He owes me three pound at this minute. Look here, I have it in my book. April 10, 1815, Captain Osborne: £3. I wonder whether his father would pay me," and so saying, John of the Slaughters' pulled out the very morocco pocket-book in which he had noted his loan to the Captain, upon a greasy faded page still extant, with many other scrawled memoranda regarding the bygone frequenters of the house.

Having inducted his customer into the room, John retired with perfect calmness; and Major Dobbin, not without a blush and a grin at his own absurdity, chose out of his kit the very smartest and most becoming civil costume he possessed, and laughed at his own tanned face and grey hair as he surveyed them in the dreary little toilet-glass on the dressing table.

"I'm glad old John didn't forget me," he thought. "She'll know me, too, I hope." And he sallied out of the inn, bending his steps once more in the direction of Brompton.

Every minute incident of his last meeting with Amelia was present to the constant man's mind as he walked towards her house. The arch and the Achilles statue[7] were up since he had last been in Piccadilly; a hundred changes had occurred which his eye and mind vaguely noted. He began to tremble as he walked up the lane from Brompton, that well remembered lane leading to the street where she lived. Was she going to be married or not? If he were to meet her with the little boy—Good God, what should he do? He saw a woman coming to him with a child of five years old—was that she? He began to shake at the mere possibility. When he came up to the row of houses, at last, where she lived, and to the gate, he caught hold of it and paused. He might have heard the thumping of his own heart. "May God Almighty bless her, whatever has happened," he thought to himself. "Psha! she may be gone from here," he said, and went in through the gate.

The window of the parlour which she used to occupy was open, and there were no inmates in the room. The Major thought he recognised the piano though, with the picture over it, as it used to be in former days, and his perturbations were renewed. Mr. Clapp's brass

7. The Burton arch opposite Apsley House, Wellington's home, was built in 1825; the Achilles statue, also in Wellington's honor, was erected in 1822. Dobbin is walking by in 1827, a year before the erection of the Pimlico arch. See "*Vanity Fair* and the London Skyline" in this volume.

plate was still on the door; at the knocker of which Dobbin performed a summons.

A buxom-looking lass of sixteen, with bright eyes and purple cheeks, came to answer the knock, and looked hard at the Major as he leant back against the little porch.

He was as pale as a ghost, and could hardly falter out the words—"Does Mrs. Osborne live here?"

She looked him hard in the face for a moment—and then turning white too—said "Lord bless me—it's Major Dobbin." She held out both her hands shaking—"Don't you remember me?" she said, "I used to call you Major Sugarplums." On which, and I believe it was for the first time that he ever so conducted himself in his life, the Major took the girl in his arms and kissed her. She began to laugh and cry hysterically, and calling out "Ma, Pa!" with all her voice, brought up those worthy people, who had already been surveying the Major from the casement of the ornamental kitchen, and were astonished to find their daughter in the little passage in the embrace of a great tall man in a blue frock coat and white duck trowsers.

"I'm an old friend," he said—not without blushing though. "Don't you remember me, Mrs. Clapp, and those good cakes you used to make for tea?—Don't you recollect me, Clapp? I'm George's godfather, and just come back from India!" A great shaking of hands ensued—Mrs. Clapp was greatly affected and delighted; she called upon heaven to interpose a vast many times in that passage.

The landlord and landlady of the house led the worthy Major into the Sedleys' room (whereof he remembered every single article of furniture, from the old brass ornamented piano, once a natty little instrument, Stothard maker,[8] to the screens and the alabaster miniature-tombstone, in the midst of which ticked Mr. Sedley's gold watch), and there as he sat down in the lodger's vacant arm-chair, the father, the mother, and the daughter, with a thousand ejaculatory breaks in the narrative, informed Major Dobbin of what we know already, but of particulars in Amelia's history of which he was not aware—namely, of Mrs. Sedley's death, of George's reconcilement with his grandfather Osborne, of the way in which the widow took on at leaving him, and of other particulars of her life. Twice or thrice he was going to ask about the marriage-question, but his heart failed him. He did not care to lay it bare to these people. Finally, he was informed that Mrs. O. was gone to walk with her Pa in Kensington Gardens,[9] whither she always went with the old gentleman (who was very weak and peevish now, and led her a sad life, though she behaved to him like an angel, to be sure,) of a fine afternoon after dinner.

"I'm very much pressed for time," the Major said, "and have business to-night of importance. I should like to see Mrs. Osborne tho'. Suppose Miss Polly would come with me and show me the way."

8. The piano, purchased at Broadwood's for thirty-five guineas and sold to Dobbin at the Sedley auction for twenty-five (see chapter XVII), was probably made by Stodart, a large London piano design and manufacturing firm, founded in 1775 by Robert Stodart, formerly an apprentice at Broadwood, and carried on by his son William Stodart. It is not known if Stodart pianos were actually available from Broadwood's.

9. West of Hyde Park and north of Brompton, where the Sedleys now lived.

Miss Polly was charmed and astonished at this proposal. She knew the way. She would show Major Dobbin. She had often been with Mr. Sedley when Mrs. O. was gone—was gone Russell Square way: and knew the bench where he liked to sit. She bounced away to her apartment, and appeared presently in her best bonnet and her mamma's yellow shawl and large pebble[1] brooch, of which she assumed the loan in order to make herself a worthy companion for the Major.

That officer, then in his blue frock-coat and buckskin gloves, gave the young lady his arm, and they walked away very gaily. He was glad to have a friend at hand for the scene which he dreaded somehow. He asked a thousand more questions from his companion about Amelia: his kind heart grieved to think that she should have had to part with her son. How did she bear it? Did she see him often? Was Mr. Sedley pretty comfortable now in a worldly point of view? Polly answered all these questions of Major Sugarplums to the very best of her power.

And in the midst of their walk an incident occurred which, though very simple in its nature, was productive of the greatest delight to Major Dobbin. A pale young man with feeble whiskers and a stiff white neckcloth came walking down the lane, *en sandwich:*—having a lady, that is, on each arm. One was a tall and commanding middle-aged female, with features and a complexion similar to those of the clergyman of the Church of England by whose side she marched, and the other a stunted little woman with a dark face, ornamented by a fine new bonnet and white ribbons, and in a smart pelisse with a rich gold watch in the midst of her person. The gentleman, pinioned as he was by these two ladies, carried further a parasol, shawl, and basket, so that his arms were entirely engaged, and of course he was unable to touch his hat in acknowledgment of the curtsey with which Miss Mary Clapp greeted him.

He meekly bowed his head in reply to her salutation, which the two ladies returned in a patronising air, and at the same time looking severely at the individual in the blue coat and bamboo cane, who accompanied Miss Polly.

"Who's that," asked the Major, amused by the group, and after he had made way for the three to pass up the lane. Mary looked at him rather roguishly.

"That is our curate, the Reverend Mr. Binney, (a twitch from Major Dobbin,) and his sister Miss B. Lord bless us, how she did use to worret us at Sunday-school; and the other lady, the little one with a cast in her eye, and the handsome watch, is Mrs. Binney—Miss Grits that was; her Pa was a grocer, and kept the Little Original Gold Tea Pot in Kensington Gravel Pits. They were married last month, and are just come back from Margate. She's five thousand pound to her fortune; but her and Miss B., who made the match, have quarrelled already."

If the Major had twitched before, he started now, and slapped the bamboo on the ground with an emphasis which made Miss Clapp cry, "Law," and laugh too. He stood for a moment silent with open mouth looking after the retreating young couple, while Miss Mary told their history; but he did not hear beyond the announcement

1. Agate.

of the reverend gentleman's marriage; his head was swimming with felicity. After this rencontre he began to walk double quick towards the place of his destination; and yet they were too soon (for he was in a great tremor at the idea of a meeting for which he had been longing any time these ten years)—through the Brompton lanes, and entering at the little old portal in Kensington Garden wall.

"There they are," said Miss Polly, and she felt him again start back on her arm. She was a confidante at once of the whole business. She knew the story as well as if she had read it in one of her favourite novel-books—"Fatherless Fanny," or the "Scottish Chiefs."[2]

"Suppose you were to run on and tell her," the Major said. Polly ran forward, her yellow shawl streaming in the breeze.

Old Sedley was seated on a bench, his handkerchief placed over his knees, prattling away according to his wont, with some old story about old times, to which Amelia had listened, and awarded a patient smile many a time before. She could of late think of her own affairs, and smile or make other marks of recognition of her father's stories, scarcely hearing a word of the old man's tales. As Mary came bouncing along, and Amelia caught sight of her, she started up from her bench. Her first thought was, that something had happened to Georgy; but the sight of the messenger's eager and happy face dissipated that fear in the timorous mother's bosom.

"News! News!" cried the emissary of Major Dobbin. "He's come! He's come!"

"Who is come?" said Emmy, still thinking of her son.

"Look there," answered Miss Clapp, turning round and pointing; in which direction Amelia looking, saw Dobbin's lean figure and long shadow stalking across the grass. Amelia started in her turn, blushed up, and, of course, began to cry. At all this simple little creature's fêtes, the *grandes eaux*[3] were accustomed to play.

He looked at her—oh, how fondly—as she came running towards him, her hands before her, ready to give them to him. She wasn't changed. She was a little pale: a little stouter in figure. Her eyes were the same, the kind trustful eyes. There were scarce three lines of silver in her soft brown hair. She gave him both her hands as she looked up flushing and smiling through her tears into his honest homely face. He took the two little hands between his two, and held them there. He was speechless for a moment. Why did he not take her in his arms, and swear that he would never leave her? She must have yielded: she could not but have obeyed him.

"I—I've another arrival to announce," he said, after a pause.

"Mrs. Dobbin?" Amelia said, making a movement back—Why didn't he speak?

"No," he said, letting her hands go: "Who has told you those lies?—I mean, your brother Jos came in the same ship with me, and is come home to make you all happy."

2. *Fatherless Fanny; or A Young Lady's First Entrance into Life Being the Memoirs of a Little Mendicant and Her Benefactors* (1819); *The Scottish Chiefs* (1810), by Jane Porter—both frequently reprinted and available at bookshops when *Vanity Fair* was published.

3. Great waters, playful reference to the water fountains at Versailles (and their imitations at Pumpernickel, in chapter LXIII), which were made to spout on special occasions.

A meeting

"Papa, papa!" Emmy cried out, "here are news! My brother is in England. He is come to take care of you.—Here is Major Dobbin."

Mr. Sedley started up, shaking a great deal, and gathering up his thoughts. Then he stepped forward and made an old-fashioned bow to the Major, whom he called Mr. Dobbin, and hoped his worthy father, Sir William, was quite well. He proposed to call upon Sir William, who had done him the honour of a visit a short time ago. Sir William had not called upon the old gentleman for eight years—it was that visit he was thinking of returning.

"He is very much shaken," Emmy whispered, as Dobbin went up and cordially shook hands with the old man.

Although he had such particular business in London that evening, the Major consented to forego it upon Mr. Sedley's invitation to him to come home and partake of tea. Amelia put her arm under that of her young friend with the yellow shawl, and headed the party on their return homewards, so that Mr. Sedley fell to Dobbin's share. The old man walked very slowly, and told a number of ancient histories about himself and his poor Bessy, his former prosperity, and his bankruptcy. His thoughts, as is usual with failing old men, were quite in former times. The past,[4] with the exception of the one catastrophe which he felt, he knew little about. The Major was glad to let him talk on. His eyes were fixed upon the figure in front of him—the dear little figure always present to his imagination and in his prayers, and visiting his dreams wakeful or slumbering.

Amelia was very happy, smiling, and active all that evening; performing her duties as hostess of the little entertainment with the utmost grace and propriety, as Dobbin thought. His eyes followed her about as they sate in the twilight. How many a time had he longed for that moment, and thought of her far away under hot winds and in weary marches, gentle and happy, kindly ministering to the wants of old age, and decorating poverty with sweet submission—as he saw her now. I do not say that his taste was the highest or that it is the duty of great intellects to be content with a bread-and-butter paradise, such as sufficed our simple old friend; but his desires were of this sort whether for good or bad; and, with Amelia to help him, he was as ready to drink as many cups of tea as Doctor Johnson.

Amelia seeing this propensity, laughingly encouraged it; and looked exceedingly roguish as she administered to him cup after cup. It is true she did not know that the Major had had no dinner, and that the cloth was laid for him at the Slaughters', and a plate laid thereon to mark that the table was retained, in that very box in which the Major and George had sate many a time carousing, when she was a child just come home from Miss Pinkerton's school.

The first thing Mrs. Osborne showed the Major was Georgy's miniature, for which she ran up stairs on her arrival at home. It was not half handsome enough of course for the boy, but wasn't it noble of him to think of bringing it to his mother? Whilst her papa was awake she did not talk much about Georgy. To hear about Mr.

4. Some later, nonauthoritative editions read "The present" which may be preferable. The catastrophe in the past was the bankruptcy; in the present, it was the recent death of his wife.

Osborne and Russell Square was not agreeable to the old man, who very likely was unconscious that he had been living for some months past mainly on the bounty of his richer rival; and lost his temper if allusion was made to the other.

Dobbin told him all, and a little more perhaps than all, that had happened on board the Ramchunder; and exaggerated Jos's benevolent dispositions towards his father, and resolution to make him comfortable in his old days. The truth is that during the voyage the Major had impressed this duty most strongly upon his fellow-passenger and extorted promises from him that he would take charge of his sister and her child. He soothed Jos's irritation with regard to the bills which the old gentleman had drawn upon him, gave a laughing account of his own sufferings on the same score, and of the famous consignment of wine with which the old man had favoured him: and brought Mr. Jos, who was by no means an ill-natured person when well pleased and moderately flattered, to a very good state of feeling regarding his relatives in Europe.

And in fine I am ashamed to say that the Major stretched the truth so far as to tell old Mr. Sedley that it was mainly a desire to see his parent which brought Jos once more to Europe.

At his accustomed hour Mr. Sedley began to dose in his chair, and then it was Amelia's opportunity to commence her conversation which she did with great eagerness;—it related exclusively to Georgy. She did not talk at all about her own sufferings at breaking from him, for indeed this worthy woman, though she was half-killed by the separation from the child, yet thought it was very wicked in her to repine at losing him; but everything concerning him, his virtues, talents, and prospects, she poured out. She described his angelic beauty; narrated a hundred instances of his generosity and greatness of mind whilst living with her: how a Royal Duchess had stopped and admired him in Kensington Gardens; how splendidly he was cared for now, and how he had a groom and a pony; what quickness and cleverness he had, and what a prodigiously well-read and delightful person the Reverend Lawrence Veal was, George's master. "He knows *everything,*" Amelia said. "He has the most delightful parties. You who are so learned yourself, and have read so much, and are so clever and accomplished—don't shake your head and say no—*He* always used to say you were—you will be charmed with Mr. Veal's parties. The last Tuesday in every month. He says there is no place in the bar or the senate that Georgy may not aspire to. Look here," and she went to the piano-drawer and drew out a theme of Georgy's composition. This great effort of genius, which is still in the possession of George's mother, is as follows:

*On Selfishness.*—Of all the vices which degrade the human character, Selfishness is the most odious and contemptible. An undue love of Self leads to the most monstrous crimes; and occasions the greatest misfortunes both in *States and Families.* As a selfish man will impoverish his family and often bring them to ruin: so a selfish king brings ruin on his people and often plunges them into war.

Example: The selfishness of Achilles, as remarked by the poet

Homer, occasioned a thousand woes to the Greeks—*μυρί 'Αχαιôις ἄλγε' ἔθηκε*—(Hom. Il. A. 2).[5] The selfishness of the late Napoleon Bonaparte occasioned innumerable wars in Europe, and caused him to perish, himself, in a miserable island—that of Saint Helena in the Atlantic Ocean.

We see by these examples that we are not to consult our own interest and ambition, but that we are to consider the interests of others as well as our own.

GEORGE S. OSBORNE.

*Athenè House,* 24 *April,* 1827.

"Think of him writing such a hand, and quoting Greek too, at his age," the delighted mother said. "O William," she added, holding out her hand to the Major—"what a treasure Heaven has given me in that boy! He is the comfort of my life—and he is the image of—of him that's gone!"

"Ought I to be angry with her for being faithful to him?" William thought. "Ought I to be jealous of my friend in the grave, or hurt that such a heart as Amelia's can love only once and for ever? Oh, George, George, how little you knew the prize you had, though." This sentiment passed rapidly through William's mind, as he was holding Amelia's hand, whilst the handkerchief was veiling her eyes.

"Dear friend," she said, pressing the hand which held hers, "How good, how kind you always have been to me! See! Papa is stirring. You will go and see Georgy to-morrow, won't you?"

"Not to-morrow," said poor old Dobbin. "I have business." He did not like to own that he had not as yet been to his parents and his dear sister Anne—a remissness for which I am sure every well-regulated person will blame the Major. And presently he took his leave, leaving his address behind him for Jos, against the latter's arrival. And so the first day was over, and he had seen her.

When he got back to the Slaughters', the roast fowl was of course cold, in which condition he ate it for supper. And knowing what early hours his family kept, and that it would be needless to disturb their slumbers at so late an hour, it is on record, that Major Dobbin treated himself to half-price at the Haymarket Theatre[6] that evening, where let us hope he enjoyed himself.

5. Muri Achaiois alge etheke: caused the Achaians many woes.
6. After 8:00 P.M. tickets were half price.

## *Chapter LIX.*

### THE OLD PIANO.

THE[1] Major's visit left old John Sedley in a great state of agitation and excitement. His daughter could not induce him to settle down to his customary occupations or amusements that night. He passed the evening fumbling amongst his boxes and desks, untying his papers with trembling hands, and sorting and arranging them against Jos's arrival. He had them in the greatest order—his tapes and his files, his receipts, and his letters with lawyers and correspondents; the documents relative to the Wine Project (which failed from a most unaccountable accident, after commencing with the most splendid prospects), the Coal Project (which only a want of capital prevented from becoming the most successful scheme ever put before the public), the Patent Saw-mills and Sawdust Consolidation Project, &c. &c.—All night, until a very late hour, he passed in the preparation of these documents, trembling about from one room to another, with a quivering candle and shaky hands.—Here's the wine papers, here's the sawdust, here's the coals; here's my letters to Calcutta and Madras, and replies from Major Dobbin, C. B., and Mr. Joseph Sedley to the same. "He shall find no irregularity about *me,* Emmy," the old gentleman said.

Emmy smiled. "I don't think Jos will care about seeing those papers, Papa," she said.

"You don't know anything about business, my dear," answered the sire, shaking his head with an important air. And it must be confessed, that on this point Emmy was very ignorant, and that is a pity, some people are so knowing. All these twopenny documents arranged on a side table, old Sedley covered them carefully over with a clean bandanna handkerchief, (one out of Major Dobbin's lot,) and enjoined the maid and landlady of the house, in the most solemn way, not to disturb those papers, which were arranged for the arrival of Mr. Joseph Sedley the next morning, "Mr. Joseph Sedley of the Honourable East India Company's Bengal Civil Service."

Amelia found him up very early the next morning, more eager, more hectic, and more shaky than ever. "I didn't sleep much, Emmy,

1. Initial illustration: see the last sentence of the chapter.

my dear," he said. "I was thinking of my poor Bessy. I wish she was alive, to ride in Jos's carriage once again. She kept her own, and became it very well." And his eyes filled with tears, which trickled down his furrowed old face. Amelia wiped them away, and smilingly kissed

him, and tied the old man's neckcloth in a smart bow, and put his brooch into his best shirt frill, in which, in his Sunday suit of mourning, he sat from six o'clock in the morning awaiting the arrival of his son.

However[2] when the postman made his appearance, the little party were put out of suspense, by the receipt of a letter from Jos to his sister, who announced, that he felt a little fatigued after his voyage, and should not be able to move on that day, but that he would leave Southampton early the next morning, and be with his father and mother at evening. Amelia as she read out the letter to her father, paused over the latter word; her brother, it was clear, did not know what had happened in the family. Nor could he: for the fact is that though the Major rightly suspected that his travelling companion never would be got into motion in so short a space as twenty-four hours, and would find some excuse for delaying, yet Dobbin had not

2. This and the next paragraph were misplaced eleven paragraphs later (following the paragraph ending "before she went to sleep") in all editions until the late 1950s, when Thackeray's biographer, Gordon Ray, pointed out the error. Thackeray remarked in a letter, "One or 2 people have found out how careless the last no of V.F. is" (*Letters* II.383).

written to Jos to inform him of the calamity which had befallen the Sedley family: being occupied in talking with Amelia until long after post-hour.

The same morning brought Major Dobbin a letter to the Slaughters' Coffee House from his friend at Southampton; begging dear Dob to excuse Jos for being in a rage when awakened the day before (he had a confounded head-ache, and was just in his first sleep), and entreating Dob to engage comfortable rooms at the Slaughters' for Mr. Sedley and his servants. The Major had become necessary to Jos during the voyage. He was attached to him, and hung upon him. The other passengers were away to London. Young Ricketts and little Chaffers went away on the coach that day—Ricketts on the box, and taking the reins from Botley; the Doctor was off to his family at Portsea; Bragg gone to town to his co-partners; and the first mate busy in the unloading of the Ramchunder. Mr. Jos was very lonely at Southampton, and got the landlord of the George to take a glass of wine with him that day; at the very hour at which Major Dobbin was seated at the table of his father, Sir William, where his sister found out (for it was impossible for the Major to tell fibs) that he had been to see Mrs. George Osborne.

There are some splendid tailors' shops in the High Street of Southampton, in the fine plate-glass windows of which hung gorgeous waistcoats of all sorts, of silk and velvet, and gold and crimson, and pictures of the last new fashions in which those wonderful gentlemen with quizzing glasses, and holding on to little boys with the exceeding large eyes and curly hair, ogle ladies in riding habits prancing by the Statue of Achilles at Apsley House.[3] Jos, although provided with some of the most splendid vests that Calcutta could furnish, thought he could not go to town until he was supplied with one or two of these garments, and selected a crimson satin, embroidered with gold butterflies, and a black and red velvet tartan with white stripes and a rolling collar, with which, and a rich blue satin stock and a gold pin, consisting of a five-barred gate with a horseman in pink enamel jumping over it, he thought he might make his entry into London with some dignity. For Jos's former shyness and blundering blushing timidity had given way to a more candid and courageous self-assertion of his worth. "I don't care about owning it," Waterloo Sedley would say to his friends, "I am a dressy man:" and though rather uneasy if the ladies looked at him at the Government House balls, and though he blushed and turned away alarmed under their glances, it was chiefly from a dread lest they should make love to him, that he avoided them, being averse to marriage altogether. But there was no such swell in Calcutta as Waterloo Sedley, I have heard say: and he had the handsomest turn-out, gave the best bachelor dinners, and had the finest plate in the whole place.

To make these waistcoats for a man of his size and dignity took at least a day, part of which he employed in hiring a servant to wait upon him and his native; and in instructing the agent who cleared his

3. See chapters XXII and LVIII.

baggage, his boxes, his books, which he never read; his chests of mangoes, chutney, and currie-powders; his shawls for presents to people whom he didn't know as yet; and the rest of his *Persicos apparatus.*[4]

At length, he drove leisurely to London on the third day, and in the new waistcoat. The native, with chattering teeth, shuddering in a shawl on the box by the side of the new European servant, Jos puffing his pipe at intervals within, and looking so majestic, that little boys cried Hooray, and many people thought he must be a Governor-General. *He,* I promise, did not decline the obsequious invitation of the landlords to alight and refresh himself in the neat country towns. Having partaken of a copious breakfast, with fish, and rice, and hard eggs, at Southampton, he had so far rallied at Winchester as to think a glass of sherry necessary. At Alton he stepped out of the carriage, at his servant's request, and imbibed some of the ale for which the place is famous. At Farnham he stopped to view the Bishop's Castle,[5] and to partake of a light dinner of stewed eels, veal cutlets, and French beans, with a bottle of claret. He was cold over Bagshot Heath, where the native chattered more and more, and Jos Sahib[6] took some brandy-and-water; in fact, when he drove into town, he was as full of wine, beer, meat, pickles, cherry-brandy, and tobacco, as the steward's cabin of a steam-packet. It was evening when his carriage thundered up to the little door in Brompton, whither the affectionate fellow drove first, and before hying to the apartments secured for him by Mr. Dobbin at the Slaughters'.

All the faces in the street were in the windows; the little maid-servant flew to the wicket-gate, the Mesdames Clapp looked out from the casement of the ornamented kitchen; Emmy, in a great flutter, was in the passage among the hats and coats, and old Sedley in the parlour inside, shaking all over. Jos descended from the post-chaise and down the creaking swaying steps in awful state, supported by the new valet from Southampton and the shuddering native,[7] whose brown face was now livid with cold, and of the colour of a turkey's gizzard. He created an immense sensation in the passage presently, where Mrs. and Miss Clapp, coming perhaps to listen at the parlour door, found Loll Jewab shaking upon the hall-bench under the coats, moaning in a strange piteous way, and showing his yellow eyeballs and white teeth.

For, you see, we have adroitly shut the door upon the meeting between Jos and the old father, and the poor little gentle sister inside. The old man was very much affected: so, of course, was his daughter: nor was Jos without feeling. In that long absence of ten years, the most selfish will think about home and early ties. Distance sanctifies both. Long brooding over those lost pleasures exaggerates their charm and sweetness. Jos was unaffectedly glad to see and shake the hand of his father, between whom and himself there had been a coolness—glad to see his little sister, whom he remembered so pretty

4. Oriental luxury: "Persicos odi, puer, apparatus" (I despise Oriental luxury, my boy), Horace, *Odes* I.xxxviii.1.
5. A twelfth-to-seventeenth-century castle, home of the bishop of Winchester.
6. Indian term of respect for the British.
7. Hookahbadar, in the illustration of this passage, means servant in charge of the hookah.

Mr. Jos's Hookahbadar

and smiling, and pained at the alteration which time, grief, and misfortune had made in the shattered old man. Emmy had come out to the door in her black clothes and whispered to him of her mother's death, and not to speak of it to their father. There was no need of this caution, for the elder Sedley himself began immediately to speak of the event, and prattled about it, and wept over it plenteously. It shocked the Indian not a little, and made him think of himself less than the poor fellow was accustomed to do.

The result of the interview must have been very satisfactory, for when Jos had reascended his post-chaise, and had driven away to his hotel, Emmy embraced her father tenderly, appealing to him with an air of triumph, and asking the old man whether she did not always say that her brother had a good heart?

Indeed, Joseph Sedley, affected by the humble position in which he found his relations, and in the expansiveness and overflowing of heart occasioned by the first meeting, declared that they should never suffer want or discomfort any more, that he was at home for some time at any rate, during which his house and everything he had should be theirs; and that Amelia would look very pretty at the head of his table—until she would accept one of her own.

She shook her head sadly, and had, as usual, recourse to the waterworks. She knew what he meant. She and her young confidante, Miss Mary, had talked over the matter most fully, the very night of the Major's visit; beyond which time the impetuous Polly could not refrain from talking of the discovery which she had made, and describing the start and tremor of joy by which Major Dobbin betrayed himself when Mr. Binney passed with his bride, and the Major learned that he had no longer a rival to fear. "Didn't you see how he shook all over when you asked if he was married, and he said, 'Who told you those lies?' O Ma'am," Polly said, "he never kept his eyes off you; and I'm sure he's grown grey a-thinking of you."

But Amelia, looking up at her bed, over which hung the portraits of her husband and son, told her young *protegée,* never, never, to speak on that subject again; that Major Dobbin had been her husband's dearest friend, and her own and George's most kind and affectionate guardian; that she loved him as a brother—but that a woman who had been married to such an angel as that, and she pointed to the wall, could never think of any other union. Poor Polly sighed: she thought what she should do if young Mr. Tomkins, at the Surgery, who always looked at her so at church, and who, by those mere aggressive glances had put her timorous little heart into such a flutter that she was ready to surrender at once,—what she should do if he were to die? She knew he was consumptive, his cheeks were so red, and he was so uncommon thin in the waist.

Not that Emmy, being made aware of the honest Major's passion, rebuffed him in any way, or felt displeased with him. Such an attachment from so true and loyal a gentleman could make no woman angry. Desdemona was not angry with Cassio,[8] though there is very

8. In *Othello* Cassio pays court to Desdemona, seeking reinstatement as Othello's lieutenant, not, as falsely accused by Iago, to seduce her.

little doubt she saw the Lieutenant's partiality for her (and I for my part believe that many more things took place in that sad affair than the worthy Moorish officer ever knew of); why, Miranda was even very kind to Caliban,[9] and we may be pretty sure for the same reason. Not that she would encourage him in the least,—the poor uncouth monster—of course not. No more would Emmy by any means encourage her admirer, the Major. She would give him that friendly regard, which so much excellence and fidelity merited; she would treat him with perfect cordiality and frankness until he made his proposals; and *then* it would be time enough for her to speak, and to put an end to hopes which never could be realised.

She slept, therefore, very soundly that evening, after the conversation with Miss Polly, and was more than ordinarily happy, in spite of Jos's delaying. "I am glad he is not going to marry that Miss O'Dowd," she thought. "Colonel O'Dowd never could have a sister fit for such an accomplished man as Major William." Who was there amongst her little circle, who would make him a good wife? Not Miss Binney, she was too old and ill-tempered; Miss Osborne?—too old too. Little Polly was too young. Mrs. Osborne could not find anybody to suit the Major before she went to sleep.

Jos was so comfortably situated in Saint Martin's Lane, he could enjoy his hookah there with such perfect ease, and could swagger down to the theatres, when minded, so agreeably, that, perhaps, he would have remained altogether at the Slaughters' had not his friend, the Major, been at his elbow. That gentleman would not let the Bengalee rest until he had executed his promise of having a home for Amelia and his father. Jos was a soft fellow in anybody's hands; Dobbin most active in anybody's concerns but his own; the civilian was, therefore, an easy victim to the guileless arts of this good-natured diplomatist, and was ready to do, to purchase, hire, or relinquish whatever his friend thought fit. Loll Jewab, of whom the boys about Saint Martin's Lane used to make cruel fun whenever he showed his dusky countenance in the street, was sent back to Calcutta in the Lady Kicklebury East Indiaman, in which Sir William Dobbin had a share; having previously taught Jos's European the art of preparing curries, pilaws, and pipes. It was a matter of great delight and occupation to Jos to superintend the building of a smart chariot, which he and the Major ordered in the neighbouring Long Acre: and a pair of handsome horses were jobbed, with which Jos drove about in state in the Park, or to call upon his Indian friends. Amelia was not seldom by his side on these excursions, when also Major Dobbin would be seen in the back seat of the carriage. At other times Old Sedley and his daughter took advantage of it: and Miss Clapp, who frequently accompanied her friend, had great pleasure in being recognised as she sate in the carriage, dressed in the famous yellow shawl, by the young gentleman at the surgery, whose face might commonly be seen over the window-blinds as she passed.

9. In *The Tempest* the deformed, semihuman Caliban makes uncouth love, hardly distinguishable from rape, to Prospero's daughter Miranda.

Shortly after Jos's first appearance at Brompton, a dismal scene, indeed, took place at that humble cottage, at which the Sedleys had passed the last ten years of their life. Jos's carriage (the temporary one, not the chariot under construction) arrived one day and carried off old Sedley and his daughter—to return no more. The tears that were shed by the landlady and the landlady's daughter at that event were as genuine tears of sorrow as any that have been outpoured in the course of this history. In their long acquaintanceship and intimacy they could not recall a[1] harsh word that had been uttered by Amelia. She had been all sweetness and kindness, always thankful, always gentle, even when Mrs. Clapp lost her own temper, and pressed for the rent. When the kind creature was going away for good and all, the landlady reproached herself bitterly for ever having used a rough expression to her—how she wept, as they stuck up with wafers on the window, a paper notifying that the little rooms so long occupied were to let! They never would have such lodgers again, that was quite clear. After-life proved the truth of this melancholy prophecy: and Mrs. Clapp revenged herself for the deterioration of mankind by levying the most savage contributions upon the tea-caddies and legs of mutton of her *locataires*.[2] Most of them scolded and grumbled; some of them did not pay: none of them stayed. The landlady might well regret those old, old friends, who had left her.

As for Miss Mary, her sorrow at Amelia's departure was such as I shall not attempt to depict. From childhood upwards she had been with her daily, and had attached herself so passionately to that dear good lady, that when the grand barouche came to carry her off into splendour, she fainted in the arms of her friend, who was indeed scarcely less affected than the good-natured girl. Amelia loved her like a daughter. During eleven years the girl had been her constant friend and associate. The separation was a very painful one indeed to her. But it was of course arranged that Mary was to come and stay often at the grand new house whither Mrs. Osborne was going; and where Mary was sure she would never be so happy as she had been in their humble cot as Miss Clapp called it in the language of the novels which she loved.

Let us hope she was wrong in her judgment. Poor Emmy's days of happiness had been very few in that humble cot. A gloomy Fate had oppressed her there. She never liked to come back to the house after she had left it, or to face the landlady who had tyrannised over her when ill-humoured and unpaid; or when pleased had treated her with a coarse familiarity scarcely less odious. Her servility and fulsome compliments when Emmy was in prosperity were not more to that lady's liking. She cast about notes of admiration all over the new house, extolling every article of furniture or ornament; she fingered Mrs. Osborne's dresses, and calculated their price. Nothing could be too good for that sweet lady, she vowed and protested. But in the vulgar sycophant who now paid court to her, Emmy always remembered the coarse tyrant who had made her miserable many a time;

1. First printing reads: an
2. Lodgers.

to whom she had been forced to put up petitions for time, when the rent was overdue; who cried out at her extravagance if she bought delicacies for her ailing mother or father; who had seen her humble and trampled upon her.

Nobody ever heard of these griefs, which had been part of our poor little woman's lot in life. She kept them secret from her father, whose improvidence was the cause of much of her misery. She had to bear all the blame of his misdoings, and indeed was so utterly gentle and humble as to be made by nature for a victim.

I hope she is not to suffer much more of that hard usage. And, as in all griefs, there is said to be some consolation, I may mention that poor Mary, when left at her friend's departure in a hysterical condition, was placed under the medical treatment of the young fellow from the surgery, under whose care she rallied after a short period. Emmy, when she went away from Brompton, endowed Mary with every article of furniture that the house contained: only taking away her pictures (the two pictures over the bed) and her piano—that little old piano which had now passed into a plaintive jingling old age, but which she loved for reasons of her own. She was a child when first she played on it: and her parents gave it her. It had been given to her again since, as the reader may remember, when her father's house was gone to ruin, and the instrument was recovered out of the wreck.

Major Dobbin was exceedingly pleased when, as he was superintending the arrangements of Jos's new house, which the Major insisted should be very handsome and comfortable; the cart arrived from Brompton, bringing the trunks and band-boxes of the emigrants from that village, and with them the old piano. Amelia would have it up in her sitting-room, a neat little apartment on the second floor, adjoining her father's chamber: and where the old gentleman sate commonly of evenings.

When the men appeared then bearing this old music-box, and Amelia gave orders that it should be placed in the chamber aforesaid, Dobbin was quite elated. "I'm glad you've kept it," he said in a very sentimental manner. "I was afraid you didn't care about it."

"I value it more than anything I have in the world," said Amelia.

"*Do* you, Amelia?" cried the Major. The fact was, as he had bought it himself, though he never said anything about it, it never entered into his head to suppose that Emmy should think anybody else was the purchaser, and as a matter of course, he fancied that she knew the gift came from him. "Do you, Amelia?" he said; and the question, the great question of all, was trembling on his lips, when Emmy replied—

"Can I do otherwise?—did not *he* give it me?"

"I did not know," said poor old Dob, and his countenance fell.

Emmy did not note the circumstance at the time, nor take immediate heed of the very dismal expression which honest Dobbin's countenance assumed; but she thought of it afterwards. And then it struck her, with inexpressible pain and mortification too, that it was William who was the giver of the piano; and not George, as she had fancied. It was not George's gift; the only one which she had received from her lover, as she thought—the thing she had cherished beyond all others—her dearest relic and prize. She had spoken to it about George; played his favourite airs upon it; sate for long evening hours, touching, to the best of her simple art, melancholy harmonies on the keys, and weeping over them in silence. It was not George's relic. It was valueless now. The next time that old Sedley asked her to play, she said it was shockingly out of tune, that she had a headache, that she couldn't play.

Then, according to her custom, she rebuked herself for her pettishness and ingratitude, and determined to make a reparation to honest William for the slight she had not expressed to him, but had felt for his piano. A few days afterwards, as they were seated in the drawing-room, where Jos had fallen asleep with great comfort after dinner, Amelia said with rather a faltering voice to Major Dobbin,—

"I have to beg your pardon for something."

"About what?" said he.

"About—about that little square piano. I never thanked you for it when you gave it me; many, many years ago, before I was married. I thought somebody else had given it. Thank you, William." She held out her hand; but the poor little woman's heart was bleeding; and as for her eyes, of course they were at their work.

But William could hold no more. "Amelia, Amelia," he said, "I did buy it for you. I loved you then as I do now. I must tell you. I think I loved you from the first minute that I saw you, when George brought me to your house, to show me the Amelia whom he was engaged to. You were but a girl, in white, with large ringlets; you came down singing—do you remember?—and we went to Vauxhall. Since then I have thought of but one woman in the world, and that was you. I think there is no hour of the day has passed for twelve years that I haven't thought of you. I came to tell you this before I went to India, but you did not care, and I hadn't the heart to speak. You did not care whether I stayed or went."

"I was very ungrateful," Amelia said.

"No; only indifferent," Dobbin continued, desperately. "I have nothing to make a woman to be otherwise. I know what you are feeling now. You are hurt in your heart at that discovery about the piano; and that it came from me and not from George. I forgot, or I should never have spoken of it so. It is for me to ask your pardon for being a fool for a moment, and thinking that years of constancy and devotion might have pleaded with you."

"It is you who are cruel now," Amelia said with some spirit. "George is my husband, here and in heaven. How could I love any other but him? I am his now as when you first saw me, dear William. It was he who told me how good and generous you were, and who taught me to love you as a brother. Have you not been everything to me and my boy? Our dearest, truest, kindest, friend and protector? Had you come a few months sooner perhaps you might have spared me that—that dreadful parting. O, it nearly killed me, William—but you didn't come, though I wished and prayed for you to come, and they took him too away from me. Isn't he a noble boy, William? Be his friend still and mine"—and here her voice broke, and she hid her face on his shoulder.

The Major folded his arms round her, holding her to him as if she was a child, and kissed her head. "I will not change, dear Amelia," he said. "I ask for no more than your love. I think I would not have it otherwise. Only let me stay near you, and see you often."

"Yes, often," Amelia said. And so William was at liberty to look and long: as the poor boy at school who has no money may sigh after the contents of the tart-woman's tray.

## *Chapter LX.*

### RETURNS TO THE GENTEEL WORLD.

OOD fortune now begins to smile upon Amelia. We are glad to get her out of that low sphere in which she has been creeping hitherto, and introduce her into a polite circle; not so grand and refined as that in which our other female friend, Mrs. Becky, has appeared, but still having no small pretensions to gentility and fashion. Jos's friends were all from the three presidencies,[1] and his new house was in the comfortable Anglo-Indian district of which Moira Place is the centre. Minto Square, Great Clive Street, Warren Street, Hastings Street, Ochterlony Place, Plassy Square, Assaye Terrace,[2] ("Gardens" was a felicitous word not applied to stucco houses with asphalte terraces in front, so early as 1827)—who does not know these respectable abodes of the retired Indian aristocracy, and the quarter which Mr. Wenham calls the Black Hole,[3] in a word? Jos's position

1. The three administrative units into which all India was divided under the East India Company; i.e., Jos's friends were from all over India and all from India.
2. Only Warren Street is real; all these names evoke persons, places, and events in British Indian history. The second earl of Moira, the first earl of Minto, and Warren Hastings were governor-generals; Lord Clive was a governor of Bengal; Sir David Ochterlony, a British general in Nepal; and celebrated British military victories took place at Plassy and Assaye.
3. Regardless of the inaccuracy of the accounts, the Black Hole of Calcutta is remembered as the infamous place of confinement where many British prisoners died in one night in 1746.

in life was not grand enough to entitle him to a house in Moira Place, where none can live but retired Members of Council,[4] and partners of Indian firms (who break after having settled a hundred thousand pounds on their wives, and retire into comparative penury to a country place and four thousand a year): he engaged a comfortable house of a second or third-rate order in Gillespie Street,[5] purchasing the carpets, costly mirrors, and handsome and appropriate planned furniture by Seddons,[6] from the assignees of Mr. Scape, lately admitted partner into the great Calcutta House of Fogle, Fake, and Cracksman,[7] in which poor Scape had embarked seventy thousand pounds, the earnings of a long and honourable life, taking Fake's place, who retired to a princely Park in Sussex, (the Fogles have been long out of the firm, and Sir Horace Fogle is about to be raised to the peerage as Baron Bandanna)—admitted, I say, partner into the great agency house of Fogle and Fake two years before it failed for a million, and plunged half the Indian public into misery and ruin.

Scape, ruined, honest, and broken-hearted at sixty-five years of age, went out to Calcutta to wind up the affairs of the house. Walter Scape was withdrawn from Eton, and put into a merchant's house. Florence Scape, Fanny Scape, and their mother faded away to Boulogne, and will be heard of no more. To be brief, Jos stepped in and bought their carpets and sideboards, and admired himself in the mirrors which had reflected their kind handsome faces. The Scape tradesmen, all honourably paid, left their cards, and were eager to supply the new household. The large men in white waistcoats, who waited at Scape's dinners, green-grocers, bank-porters, and milkmen in their private capacity, left their addresses, and ingratiated themselves with the butler. Mr. Chummy, the chimney-purifier, who had swep the last three families, tried to coax the butler and the boy under him, whose duty it was to go out covered with buttons and with stripes down his trowsers, for the protection of Mrs. Amelia whenever she chose to walk abroad.

It was a modest establishment. The butler was Jos's valet also, and never was more drunk than a butler in a small family should be who has a proper regard for his master's wine. Emmy was supplied with a maid, grown on Sir William Dobbin's suburban estate: a good girl, whose kindness and humility disarmed Mrs. Osborne, who was at first terrified at the idea of having a servant to wait upon herself, who did not in the least know how to use one, and who always spoke to domestics with the most reverential politeness. But this maid was very useful in the family, in dexterously tending old Mr. Sedley, who kept almost entirely to his own quarter of the house, and never mixed in any of the gay doings which took place there.

Numbers of people came to see Mrs. Osborne. Lady Dobbin and daughters were delighted at her change of fortune, and waited upon

4. Administrative Council of the East India Company.
5. Another invented name, probably after Brigadier General Robert Rollo Gillespie, who served in India with panache from 1806 to 1814.
6. George Seddons and his descendants were cabinetmakers at No. 150 Aldersgate from 1750 to 1836.
7. Assignees handle the disbursement of a bankrupt's estate; a fogle is a pickpocket; a fake is a forger; a cracksman is a burglar.

her. Miss Osborne from Russell Square came in her grand chariot with the flaming hammercloth[8] emblazoned with the Leeds arms. Jos was reported to be immensely rich. Old Osborne had no objection that Georgy should inherit his uncle's property as well as his own. "Damn it, we will make a man of the feller," he said; "and I'll see him in Parliament before I die. *You* may go and see his mother, Miss O., though I'll never set eyes on her:" and Miss Osborne came. Emmy, you may be sure, was very glad to see her, and so be brought nearer to George. That young fellow was allowed to come much more frequently than before to visit his mother. He dined once or twice a week in Gillespie Street, and bullied the servants and his relations there, just as he did in Russell Square.

He was always respectful to Major Dobbin, however, and more modest in his demeanour when that gentleman was present. He was a clever lad, and afraid of the Major. George could not help admiring his friend's simplicity, his good-humour, his various learning quietly imparted, his general love of truth and justice. He had met no such man as yet in the course of his experience, and he had an instinctive liking for a gentleman. He hung fondly by his god-father's side; and it was his delight to walk in the Parks and hear Dobbin talk. William told George about his father, about India and Waterloo, about everything but himself. When George was more than usually pert and conceited, the Major made jokes at him, which Mrs. Osborne thought very cruel. One day, taking him to the play, and the boy declining to go into the pit because it was vulgar, the Major took him to the boxes, left him there, and went down himself to the pit. He had not been seated there very long, before he felt an arm thrust under his, and a dandy little hand in a kid-glove squeezing his arm. George had seen the absurdity of his ways, and come down from the upper region. A tender laugh of benevolence lighted up old Dobbin's face and eyes as he looked at the repentant little prodigal. He loved the boy, as he did everything that belonged to Amelia. How charmed she was when she heard of this instance of George's goodness! Her eyes looked more kindly on Dobbin than they ever had done. She blushed, he thought, after looking at him so.

Georgy never tired of his praises of the Major to his mother. "I like him, Mamma, because he knows such lots of things; and he ain't like old Veal, who is always bragging and using such long words, don't you know? The chaps call him 'Longtail' at school. I gave him the name; ain't it capital? But Dob reads Latin like English, and French and that; and when we go out together he tells me stories about my Papa, and never about himself; though I heard Colonel Buckler, at Grandpapa's, say that he was one of the bravest officers in the army, and had distinguished himself ever so much. Grandpapa was quite surprised, and said '*That* feller! why, I didn't think he could say Bo to a goose'—but *I* know he could, couldn't he Mamma?"

Emmy laughed: she thought it was very likely the Major could do thus much.

8. Driver's seat-cover.

If there was a sincere liking between George and the Major, it must be confessed that between the boy and his uncle no great love existed. George had got a way of blowing out his cheeks, and putting his hands in his waistcoat pockets, and saying, "God bless my soul, you don't say so," so exactly after the fashion of old Jos, that it was impossible to restrain from laughter. The servants would explode at dinner if the lad, asking for something which wasn't at table, put on that countenance and used that favourite phrase. Even Dobbin would shoot out a sudden peal at the boy's mimicry. If George did not mimic his uncle to his face, it was only by Dobbin's rebukes and Amelia's terrified entreaties that the little scapegrace was induced to resist. And the worthy civilian being haunted by a dim consciousness that the lad thought him an ass, and was inclined to turn him into ridicule, used to be extremely timorous and, of course, doubly pompous and dignified in the presence of Master Georgy. When it was announced that the young gentleman was expected in Gillespie Street to dine with his mother, Mr. Jos commonly found that he had an engagement at the Club. Perhaps nobody was much grieved at his absence. On those days Mr. Sedley would commonly be induced to come out from his place of refuge in the upper storeys; and there would be a small family party, whereof Major Dobbin pretty generally formed one. He was the *ami de la maison*;[9] old Sedley's friend, Emmy's friend, Georgy's friend, Jos's counsel and adviser. "He might almost as well be at Madras for anything *we* see of him," Miss Ann Dobbin remarked, at Camberwell. Ah! Miss Ann, did it not strike you that it was not *you* whom the Major wanted to marry?

Joseph Sedley then led a life of dignified otiosity such as became a person of his eminence. His very first point, of course, was to become a member of the Oriental Club: where he spent his mornings in the company of his brother Indians, where he dined, or whence he brought home men to dine.

Amelia had to receive and entertain these gentlemen and their ladies. From these she heard how soon Smith would be in Council, how many lacs[1] Jones had brought home with him: how Thomson's House in London had refused the bills drawn by Thomson, Kibobjee and Co., the Bombay House, and how it was thought the Calcutta House must go too: how very imprudent, to say the least of it, Mrs. Brown's conduct (wife of Brown of the Ahmednuggar Irregulars)[2] had been with young Swankey of the Body Guard, sitting up with him on deck until all hours, and losing themselves as they were riding out at the Cape: how Mrs. Hardyman had had out her thirteen sisters, daughters of a country curate, the Rev. Felix Rabbits, and married eleven of them, seven high up in the service: how Hornby was wild because his wife would stay in Europe, and Trotter was appointed Collector at Ummerapoora. This and similar talk took place, at the grand dinners all round. They had the same conversation; the same

9. Friend of the family.
1. A lakh is 100,000 rupees.
2. Though the Irregulars were probably a fictional unit, invented by Thackeray first in *The Tremendous Adventures of Major Gahagan* (1837), Ahmednuggar is the real name of a fort captured by Arthur Wellesley, later duke of Wellington, in 1803.

silver dishes; the same saddles of mutton, boiled turkeys, and entrées. Politics set in a short time after dessert, when the ladies retired up stairs and talked about their complaints and their children.

*Mutato nomine,*[3] it is all the same. Don't the barristers' wives talk about Circuit?—don't the soldiers' ladies gossip about the Regiment? —don't the clergymen's ladies discourse about Sunday Schools, and who takes whose duty?—don't the very greatest ladies of all talk about that small clique of persons to whom they belong, and why shall our Indian friends not have their own conversation?—only I admit it is slow for the laymen whose fate it sometimes is to sit by and listen.

Before long Emmy had a visiting-book, and was driving about regularly in a carriage, calling upon Lady Bludyer (wife of Major-General Sir Roger Bludyer, K.C.B., Bengal Army); Lady Huff, wife of Sir G. Huff, Bombay ditto; Mrs. Pice, the lady of Pice the Director, &c. We are not long in using ourselves to changes in life. That carriage came round to Gillespie Street every day: that buttony boy sprang up and down from the box with Emmy's and Jos's visiting cards; at stated hours Emmy and the carriage went for Jos to the Club, and took him an airing; or, putting old Sedley into the vehicle, she drove the old man round the Regent's Park. The lady's-maid and the chariot, the visiting-book and the buttony page, became soon as familiar to Amelia as the humble routine of Brompton. She accommodated herself to one as to the other. If Fate had ordained that she should be a duchess, she would even have done that duty too. She was voted, in Jos's female society, rather a pleasing young person—not much in her, but pleasing, and that sort of thing.

The men, as usual, liked her artless kindness and simple refined demeanour. The gallant young Indian dandies at home on furlough—immense dandies these—chained and moustached—driving in tearing cabs, the pillars of the theatres, living at West End Hotels,—nevertheless admired Mrs. Osborne, liked to bow to her carriage in the Park, and to be admitted to have the honour of paying her a morning visit. Swankey of the Body Guard himself, that dangerous youth, and the greatest buck of all the Indian army now on leave, was one day discovered by Major Dobbin *tête-à-tête* with Amelia, and describing the sport of pig-sticking to her with great humour and eloquence: and he spoke afterwards of a d—d king's officer that's always hanging about the house—a long, thin, queer-looking oldish fellow—a dry fellow though, that took the shine out of a man in the talking line.

Had the Major possessed a little more personal vanity he would have been jealous of so dangerous a young buck, as that fascinating Bengal Captain. But Dobbin was of too simple and generous a nature to have any doubts about Amelia. He was glad that the young men should pay her respect; and that others should admire her. Ever since her womanhood almost, had she not been persecuted and undervalued? It pleased him to see how kindness brought out her good qualities, and how her spirits gently rose with her prosperity. Any person who appreciated her paid a compliment to the Major's good

3. Change the name: "Change the name and the tale is told of thee." Horace, *Satires* I.i.69–70.

judgment—that is, if a man may be said to have good judgment who is under the influence of Love's delusion.

After Jos went to Court, which we may be sure he did as a loyal subject of his Sovereign (showing himself in his full court suit at the Club, whither Dobbin came to fetch him in a very shabby old uniform,) he who had always been a staunch Loyalist and admirer of George IV., became such a tremendous Tory and pillar of the State, that he was for having Amelia to go to a drawing-room, too. He somehow had worked himself up to believe that he was implicated in the maintenance of the public welfare, and that the Sovereign would not be happy unless Jos Sedley and his family appeared to rally round him at Saint James's.

Emmy laughed. "Shall I wear the family diamonds, Jos?" she said.

"I wish you would let me buy you some," thought the Major. "I should like to see any that were too good for you."

## *Chapter LXI.*

### IN WHICH TWO LIGHTS ARE PUT OUT.

HERE came a day when the round of decorous pleasures and solemn gaieties in which Mr. Jos Sedley's family indulged, was interrupted by an event which happens in most houses. As you ascend the staircase of your house from the drawing towards the bed-room floors, you may have remarked a little arch in the wall right before you, which at once gives light to the stair which leads from the second story to the third (where the nursery and servants' chambers commonly are) and serves for another purpose of utility, of which the undertaker's men can give you a notion. They rest the coffins upon that arch, or pass them through it so as not to disturb in any unseemly manner the cold tenant slumbering within the black arch.[1]

That second-floor arch in a London house, looking up and down the well of the staircase, and commanding the main thoroughfare by which the inhabitants are passing; by which cook lurks down before daylight to scour her pots and pans in the kitchen; by which young master stealthily ascends, having left his boots in the hall, and let himself in after dawn from a jolly night at the Club; down which miss comes rustling in fresh ribbons and spreading muslins, brilliant and beautiful, and prepared for conquest and the ball; or master Tommy slides, preferring the bannisters for a mode of conveyance, and disdaining danger and the stair; down which the mother is fondly carried smiling in her strong husband's arms, as he steps steadily step by

1. Several editors, objecting that "black arch" is nonsense, print "black ark" or terminate the sentence after "within." It could be argued that "black arch" refers to the coffin or to death itself and echoes "little arch" a few lines previous. All arguments are conjectural.

step, and followed by the monthly nurse, on the day when the medical man has pronounced that the charming patient may go down stairs; up which John lurks to bed, yawning with a sputtering tallow candle, and to gather up before sunrise the boots which are awaiting him in the passages;—that stair, up or down which babies are carried, old people are helped, guests are marshalled to the ball, the parson walks to the christening, the doctor to the sick room, and the undertaker's men to the upper floor—what a memento of Life, Death, and Vanity it is—that arch and stair—if you choose to consider it, and sit on the landing, looking up and down the well! The doctor will come up to us too for the last time there, my friend in motley. The nurse will look in at the curtains, and you take no notice—and then she will fling open the windows for a little, and let in the air. Then they will pull down all the front blinds of the house and live in the back rooms—then they will send for the lawyer and other men in black, &c.—Your comedy and mine will have been played then, and we shall be removed, O how far, from the trumpets, and the shouting, and the posture-making. If we are gentlefolks they will put hatchments over our late domicile, with gilt cherubim, and mottoes stating that there is "Quiet in Heaven." Your son will new furnish the house, or perhaps let it, and go into a more modern quarter; your name will be among the "Members Deceased," in the lists of your clubs next year. However much you may be mourned, your widow will like to have her weeds neatly made—the cook will send or come up to ask about dinner—the survivors will soon bear to look at your picture over the mantel-piece, which will presently be deposed from the place of honour, to make way for the portrait of the son who reigns.

Which of the dead are most tenderly and passionately deplored? Those who love the survivors the least, I believe. The death of a child occasions a passion of grief and frantic tears, such as your end, brother reader, will never inspire. The death of an infant which scarce knew you, which a week's absence from you would have caused to forget you, will strike you down more than the loss of your closest friend, or your first-born son—a man grown like yourself, with children of his own. We may be harsh and stern with Judah and Simeon—our love and pity gushes out for Benjamin, the little one.[2] And if you are old, as some reader of this may be or shall be—old and rich, or old and poor—you may one day be thinking for yourself—"These people are very good round about me; but they won't grieve too much when I am gone. I am very rich, and they want my inheritance—or very poor, and they are tired of supporting me."

The period of mourning for Mrs. Sedley's death was only just concluded, and Jos scarcely had had time to cast off his black and appear in the splendid waistcoats which he loved, when it became evident to those about Mr. Sedley, that another event was at hand, and that the old man was about to go seek for his wife in the dark land whither

2. Jacob's famous partiality for Joseph and Benjamin, sons of his favorite wife, Rachel, was resented by the eleven older brothers, including Judah and Simeon, who sold Joseph into slavery and forced Jacob to give up Benjamin in exchange for food during famine. Genesis 37 and 43.

she had preceded him. "The state of my father's health," Jos Sedley solemnly remarked at the Club, "prevents me from giving my *large* parties this season: but if you will come in quietly at half-past six, Chutney, my boy, and take a homely dinner with one or two of the old set—I shall be always glad to see you." So Jos and his acquaintances dined and drank their claret among themselves in silence; whilst the sands of life were running out in the old man's glass up stairs. The velvet-footed butler brought them their wine; and they composed themselves to a rubber after dinner: at which Major Dobbin would sometimes come and take a hand: and Mrs. Osborne would occasionally descend, when her patient above was settled for the night, and had commenced one of those lightly troubled slumbers which visit the pillow of old age.

The old man clung to his daughter during this sickness. He would take his broths and medicines from scarcely any other hand. To tend him became almost the sole business of her life. Her bed was placed close by the door which opened into his chamber, and she was alive at the slightest noise or disturbance from the couch of the querulous invalid. Though, to do him justice, he lay awake many an hour, silent and without stirring, unwilling to awaken his kind and vigilant nurse.

He loved his daughter with more fondness now, perhaps, than ever he had done since the days of her childhood. In the discharge of gentle offices and kind filial duties, this simple creature shone most especially. "She walks into the room as silently as a sunbeam," Mr. Dobbin thought, as he saw her passing in and out from her father's room: a cheerful sweetness lighting up her face as she moved to and fro, graceful and noiseless. When women are brooding over their children, or busied in a sick room, who has not seen in their faces those sweet angelic beams of love and pity?

A secret feud of some years' standing was thus healed: and with a tacit reconciliation. In these last hours and touched by her love and goodness, the old man forgot all his grief against her, and wrongs which he and his wife had many a long night debated: how she had given up everything for her boy: how she was careless of her parents in their old age and misfortune, and only thought of the child: how absurdly and foolishly, impiously indeed, she took on, when George was removed from her. Old Sedley forgot these charges as he was making up his last account, and did justice to the gentle and uncomplaining little martyr. One night when she stole into his room, she found him awake, when the broken old man made his confession. "O, Emmy, I've been thinking we were very unkind and unjust to you," he said, and put out his cold and feeble hand to her. She knelt down and prayed by his bedside, as he did too, having still hold of her hand. When our turn comes, friend, may we have such company in our prayers.

Perhaps as he was lying awake then, his life may have passed before him—his early hopeful struggles, his manly successes and prosperity, his downfal in his declining years, and his present helpless condition—no chance of revenge against Fortune, which had had the better of him—neither name nor money to bequeath—a spent-out,

bootless life of defeat and disappointment, and the end here! Which, I wonder, brother reader, is the better lot, to die prosperous and famous, or poor and disappointed? To have, and to be forced to yield; or to sink out of life, having played and lost the game? That must be a strange feeling, when a day of our life comes and we say, "*To-morrow,* success or failure won't matter much: and the sun will rise, and all the myriads of mankind go to their work or their pleasure as usual, but I shall be out of the turmoil."

So there came one morning and sunrise, when all the world got up and set about its various works and pleasures, with the exception of Old John Sedley, who was not to fight with fortune, or to hope or scheme any more: but to go and take up a quiet and utterly unknown residence in a churchyard at Brompton by the side of his old wife.

Major Dobbin, Jos, and Georgy followed his remains to the grave, in a black cloth coach. Jos came on purpose from the Star and Garter at Richmond, whither he retreated after the deplorable event. He did not care to remain in the house, with the—under the circumstances, you understand. But Emmy staid and did her duty as usual. She was bowed down by no especial grief, and rather solemn than sorrowful. She prayed that her own end might be as calm and painless, and thought with trust and reverence of the words which she had heard from her father during his illness, indicative of his faith, his resignation, and his future hope.

Yes, I think that will be the better ending of the two, after all. Suppose you are particularly rich and well to do, and say on that last day, "I am very rich; I am tolerably well known; I have lived all my life in the best society, and, thank Heaven, come of a most respectable family. I have served my King and country with honour. I was in Parliament for several years, where, I may say, my speeches were listened to, and pretty well received. I don't owe any man a shilling: on the contrary, I lent my old college friend, Jack Lazarus, fifty pounds, for which my executors will not press him. I leave my daughters with ten thousand pounds a-piece—very good portions for girls: I bequeath my plate and furniture, my house in Baker Street, with a handsome jointure, to my widow for her life; and my landed property, besides money in the funds, and my cellar of well-selected wine in Baker Street, to my son. I leave twenty pound a-year to my valet; and I defy any man after I am gone to find anything against my character." Or suppose, on the other hand, your swan sings quite a different sort of dirge, and you say, "I am a poor, blighted, disappointed old fellow, and have made an utter failure through life. I was not endowed either with brains or with good fortune: and confess that I have committed a hundred mistakes and blunders. I own to having forgotten my duty many a time. I can't pay what I owe. On my last bed I lie utterly helpless and humble; and I pray forgiveness for my weakness, and throw myself with a contrite heart, at the feet of the Divine Mercy." Which of these two speeches, think you, would be the best oration for your own funeral? old Sedley made the last; and in that humble frame of mind, and holding by the hand of his daughter, life and disappointment and vanity sank away from under him.

"You see," said old Osborne to George, "what comes of merit and industry, and judicious speculations, and that. Look at me and my banker's account. Look at your poor grandfather, Sedley, and his failure. And yet he was a better man than I was, this day twenty years—a better man I should say, by ten thousand pound."

Beyond these people and Mr. Clapp's family, who came over from Brompton to pay a visit of condolence, not a single soul alive ever cared a penny piece about old John Sedley, or remembered the existence of such a person.

When old Osborne first heard from his friend Colonel Buckler (as little Georgy has already informed us) how distinguished an officer Major Dobbin was, he exhibited a great deal of scornful incredulity, and expressed his surprise how ever such a feller as that should possess either brains or reputation. But he heard of the Major's fame from various members of his society. Sir William Dobbin had a great opinion of his son, and narrated many stories illustrative of the Major's learning, valour, and estimation in the world's opinion. Finally, his name appeared in the lists of one or two great parties of the nobility; and this circumstance had a prodigious effect upon the old aristocrat of Russell Square.

The Major's position, as guardian to Georgy, whose possession had been ceded to his grandfather, rendered some meetings between the two gentlemen inevitable; and it was in one of these that old Osborne, a keen man of business, looking into the Major's accounts with his ward and the boy's mother, got a hint which staggered him very much, and at once pained and pleased him, that it was out of William Dobbin's own pocket that a part of the fund had been supplied upon which the poor widow and the child had subsisted.

When pressed upon the point, Dobbin, who could not tell lies, blushed and stammered a good deal, and finally confessed. "The marriage," he said, (at which his interlocutor's face grew dark,) "was very much my doing. I thought my poor friend had gone so far, that retreat from his engagement would have been dishonour to him, and death to Mrs. Osborne; and I could do no less, when she was left without resources, than give what money I could spare to maintain her."

"Major D.," Mr. Osborne said, looking hard at him, and turning very red too—"You did me a great injury; but give me leave to tell you, Sir, you are an honest feller. There's my hand, Sir, though I little thought that my flesh and blood was a living on you—" and the pair shook hands, with great confusion on Major Dobbin's part, thus found out in his act of charitable hypocrisy.

He strove to soften the old man, and reconcile him towards his son's memory. "He was such a noble fellow," he said, "that all of us loved him, and would have done anything for him. I, as a young man in those days, was flattered beyond measure by his preference for me; and was more pleased to be seen in his company than in that of the Commander-in-Chief. I never saw his equal for pluck and daring, and all the qualities of a soldier;" and Dobbin told the old father as many stories as he could remember regarding the gallantry and achievements of his son. "And Georgy is so like him," the Major added.

"He's so like him that he makes me tremble sometimes," the grandfather said.

On one or two evenings the Major came to dine with Mr. Osborne, (it was during the time of the sickness of Mr. Sedley,) and as the two sate together in the evening after dinner all their talk was about the departed hero. The father boasted about him according to his wont, glorifying himself in recounting his son's feats and gallantry, but his mood was at any rate better and more charitable than that in which he had been disposed until now to regard the poor fellow; and the Christian heart of the kind Major was pleased at these symptoms of returning peace and good will. On the second evening old Osborne called Dobbin, William, just as he used to do at the time when Dobbin and George were boys together: and the honest gentleman was pleased[3] by that mark of reconciliation.

On the next day at breakfast when Miss Osborne, with the asperity of her age and character, ventured to make some remark reflecting slightingly upon the Major's appearance or behaviour—the master of the house interrupted her. "You'd have been glad enough to git him for yourself Miss O. But them grapes are sour.[4] Ha! Ha! Major William is a fine feller."

"That he is, Grandpapa," said Georgy, approvingly: and going up close to the old gentleman he took a hold of his large grey whiskers, and laughed in his face good-humouredly and kissed him. And he

3. First printing reads: affected
4. In Aesop's fable, the fox declares unattainable grapes sour and undesirable.

told the story at night to his mother: who fully agreed with the boy. "Indeed he is," she said. "Your dear father always said so. He is one of the best and most upright of men." Dobbin happened to drop in very soon after this conversation, which made Amelia blush perhaps; and the young scapegrace increased the confusion by telling Dobbin the other part of the story. "I say Dob," he said, "there's such an uncommon nice girl wants to marry you. She's plenty of tin: she wears a front:[5] and she scolds the servants from morning till night."

"Who is it?" asked Dobbin.

"It's aunt O," the boy answered, "Grandpapa said so. And I say, Dob, how prime it would be to have you for my uncle." Old Sedley's quavering voice from the next room at this moment weakly called for Amelia and the laughing ended.

That old Osborne's mind was changing was pretty clear. He asked George about his uncle sometimes, and laughed at the boy's imitation of the way in which Jos said "God-bless-my-soul" and gobbled his soup. Then he said, "It's not respectful, Sir, of you younkers to be imitating of your relations. Miss O, when you go out a-driving today, leave my card upon Mr. Sedley, do you hear. There's no quarrel betwigst me and him anyhow."

The card was returned, and Jos and the Major were asked to dinner,—to a dinner the most splendid and stupid that perhaps ever Mr. Osborne gave; every inch of the family plate was exhibited, and the best company was asked. Mr. Sedley took down Miss O. to dinner, and she was very gracious to him; whereas she hardly spoke to the Major, who sate apart from her, and by the side of Mr. Osborne, very timid. Jos said, with great solemnity, it was the best clear turtle soup he had ever tasted in his life; and asked Mr. Osborne where he got his Madeira?

"It is some of Sedley's wine," whispered the butler to his master. "I've had it a long time, and paid a good figure for it, too," Mr. Osborne said aloud to his guest; and then whispered to his right-hand neighbour how he had got it "at the old chap's sale."

More than once he asked the Major about—about Mrs. George Osborne—a theme on which the Major could be very eloquent when he chose. He told Mr. Osborne of her sufferings—of her passionate attachment to her husband, whose memory she worshipped still,—of the tender and dutiful manner in which she had supported her parents, and given up her boy, when it seemed to her her duty to do so. "You don't know what she endured, Sir," said honest Dobbin, with a tremor in his voice; "and I hope and trust you will be reconciled to her. If she took your son away from you, she gave hers to you; and however much you loved your George, depend on it, she loved hers ten times more."

"By God, you are a good feller, Sir," was all Mr. Osborne said. It had never struck him that the widow would feel any pain at parting with the boy, or that his having a fine fortune could grieve her. A reconciliation was announced as speedy and inevitable; and Amelia's

5. Tin: money. Front: hairpiece.

heart already began to beat at the notion of the awful meeting with George's father.

It was never, however, destined to take place. Old Sedley's lingering illness and death supervened, after which a meeting was for some time impossible. That catastrophe and other events may have worked upon Mr. Osborne. He was much shaken of late, and aged, and his mind was working inwardly. He had sent for his lawyers, and probably changed something in his will. The medical man who looked in, pronounced him shaky, agitated, and talked of a little blood, and the sea-side; but he took neither of these remedies.

One day when he should have come down to breakfast, his servant missing him, went into his dressing-room, and found him lying at the foot of the dressing-table in a fit. Miss Osborne was apprised; the doctors were sent for: Georgy stopped away from school: the bleeders and cuppers came. Osborne partially regained cognizance; but never could speak again, though he tried dreadfully once or twice, and in four days he died. The doctors went down; the undertaker's men went up the stairs; and all the shutters were shut towards the garden in Russell Square. Bullock rushed from the city in a hurry. "How much money had he left to that boy?—not half, surely? Surely share and share alike between the three?" It was an agitating moment.

What was it that poor old man had tried once or twice in vain to say? I hope it was that he wanted to see Amelia, and be reconciled before he left the world to the dear and faithful wife of his son: it was most likely that; for his will showed that the hatred which he had so long cherished had gone out of his heart.

They found in the pocket of his dressing-gown the letter with the great red seal, which George had written him from Waterloo. He had looked at the other papers too, relative to his son, for the key of the box in which he kept them was also in his pocket, and it was found the seals and envelopes had been broken—very likely on the night before the seizure—when the butler had taken him tea into his study, and found him reading in the great red family bible.

When the will was opened, it was found that half the property was left to George, and the remainder between the two sisters. Mr. Bullock to continue, for their joint benefit, the affairs of the commercial house, or to go out, as he thought fit. An annuity of five hundred pounds, chargeable on George's property, was left to his mother, 'the widow of my beloved son George Osborne,' who was to resume the guardianship of the boy.

'Major William Dobbin, my beloved son's friend,' was appointed executor; 'and as out of his kindness and bounty, and with his own private funds, he maintained my grandson, and my son's widow, when they were otherwise without means of support,' (the testator went on to say) 'I hereby thank him heartily, for his love and regard for them; and beseech him to accept such a sum as may be sufficient to purchase his commission as a Lieutenant-Colonel, or to be disposed of in any way he may think fit.'

When Amelia heard that her father-in-law was reconciled to her, her heart melted, and she was grateful for the fortune left to her. But when she heard how Georgy was restored to her, and knew how and by whom, and how it was William's bounty that supported her in poverty, how it was William who gave her her husband and her son—O, then she sank on her knees, and prayed for blessings on that constant and kind heart: she bowed down and humbled herself, and kissed the feet, as it were, of that beautiful and generous affection.

And gratitude was all that she had to pay back for such admirable devotion and benefits—only gratitude! If she thought of any other return, the image of George stood up out of the grave, and said, "You are mine, and mine only, now and for ever."

William knew her feelings: had he not passed his whole life in divining them?

When the nature of Mr. Osborne's will became known to the world, it was edifying to remark how Mrs. George Osborne rose in the estimation of the people forming her circle of acquaintance. The servants of Jos's establishment, who used to question her humble orders, and say they would "ask Master," whether or not they could obey, never thought now of that sort of appeal. The cook forgot to sneer at her shabby old gowns (which, indeed, were quite eclipsed by that lady's finery when she was dressed to go to church of a Sunday evening), the others no longer grumbled at the sound of her bell, or delayed to answer that summons. The coachman, who grumbled that his osses should be brought out, and his carriage made into an ospital for that old feller and Mrs. O., drove her with the utmost alacrity now, and trembling lest he should be superseded by Mr. Osborne's coachman, asked "what them there Russell Square coachmen knew about town, and whether *they* was fit to sit on a box before a lady?" Jos's friends, male and female, suddenly became interested about Emmy, and cards of condolence multiplied on her hall table. Jos himself, who had looked on her as a good-natured harmless pauper, to whom it was his duty to give victuals and shelter, paid her and the rich little boy, his nephew, the greatest respect—was anxious that she should have change and amusement after her troubles and trials, "poor dear girl"—and began to appear at the breakfast-table, and most particularly to ask how she would like to dispose of the day.

In her capacity of guardian to Georgy, she, with the consent of the Major, her fellow-trustee, begged Miss Osborne to live in the Russell Square house as long as ever she chose to dwell there; but that lady, with thanks, declared that she never could think of remaining alone in that melancholy mansion, and departed in deep mourning, to Cheltenham, with a couple of her old domestics. The rest were liberally paid and dismissed; the faithful old butler, whom Mrs. Osborne proposed to retain, resigning and preferring to invest his savings in a public-house, where, let us hope, he was not unprosperous. Miss Osborne not choosing to live in Russell Square, Mrs. Osborne also, after consultation, declined to occupy the gloomy old mansion there. The house was dismantled; the rich furniture and effects, the awful chandeliers and dreary blank mirrors packed away and hidden, the rich rosewood drawing-room suite was muffled in straw, the carpets were rolled up and corded, the small select library of well-bound books was stowed into two wine chests, and the whole paraphernalia rolled away in several enormous vans to the Pantechnicon,[6] where they were to lie until Georgy's majority. And the great heavy dark plate-chests went off to Messrs. Stumpy and Rowdy, to lie in the cellars of those eminent bankers until the same period should arrive.

One day Emmy with George in her hand and clad in deep sables went to visit the deserted mansion which she had not entered since she was a girl. The place in front was littered with straw where the vans had been laden and rolled off. They went into the great blank rooms, the walls of which bore the marks where the pictures and mirrors had hung. Then they went up the great blank stone-staircases into the upper rooms, into that where grandpapa died, as George said in a whisper, and then higher still into George's own room. The boy was still clinging by her side, but she thought of another besides him. She knew that it had been his father's room as well as his own.

She went up to one of the open windows (one of those at which she used to gaze with a sick heart when the child was first taken from her) and thence as she looked out she could see over the trees of Russell Square, the old house in which she herself was born, and where she had passed so many happy days of sacred youth. They all came back to her, the pleasant holidays, the kind faces, the careless, joyful past times; and the long pains and trials that had since cast her down. She thought of these and of the man who had been her constant protector, her good genius, her sole benefactor, her tender and generous friend.

"Look here, mother," said Georgy, "here's a G. O. scratched on the glass with a diamond; I never saw it before, *I* never did it."

"It was your father's room long long before you were born, George," she said, and she blushed as she kissed the boy.

She was very silent as they drove back to Richmond where they had taken a temporary house: where the smiling lawyers used to come bustling over to see her (and we may be sure noted the visit in the bill): and where of course there was a room for Major Dobbin too, who rode over frequently, having much business to transact in behalf of his little ward.

Georgy at this time was removed from Mr. Veal's on an unlimited holiday, and that gentleman was engaged to prepare an inscription for a fine marble slab, to be placed up in the Foundling under the monument of Captain George Osborne.

The female Bullock, aunt of Georgy, although despoiled by that little monster of one-half of the sum which she expected from her father, nevertheless showed her charitableness of spirit by being reconciled to the mother and the boy. Roehampton is not far from Richmond, and one day the chariot, with the golden Bullocks emblazoned on the panels, and the flaccid children within, drove to Amelia's house at Richmond; and the Bullock family made an irruption into the garden, where Amelia was reading a book, Jos was in an arbour placidly dipping strawberries into wine, and the Major in

6. A two-acre, fireproof warehouse established in 1830 in Motcomb Street. (It burned in 1874.)

one of his Indian jackets was giving a back to Georgy, who chose to jump over him. He went over his head, and bounded into the little advance of Bullocks, with immense black bows in their hats, and huge black sashes, accompanying their mourning mamma.

"He is just of the age for Rosa," the fond parent thought, and glanced towards that dear child, an unwholesome little Miss of seven years of age.

"Rosa, go and kiss your dear cousin," Mrs. Frederic said. "Don't you know me, George?—I am your aunt."

"*I* know you well enough," George said; "but I don't like kissing, please;" and he retreated from the obedient caresses of his cousin.

"Take me to your dear mamma, you droll child," Mrs. Frederic said; and those ladies accordingly met, after an absence of more than fifteen years. During Emmy's cares and poverty the other had never once thought about coming to see her; but now that she was decently prosperous in the world, her sister-in-law came to her as a matter of course.

So did numbers more. Our old friend, Miss Swartz, and her husband came thundering over from Hampton Court, with flaming yellow liveries, and was as impetuously fond of Amelia as ever. Swartz would have liked her always if she could have seen her. One must do her that justice. But, *que voulez vous?*[7]—in this vast town one has not the time to go and seek one's friends; if they drop out of the rank they disappear, and we march on without them. Who is ever missed in Vanity Fair?

But so, in a word, and before the period of grief for Mr. Osborne's death had subsided, Emmy found herself in the centre of a very genteel circle indeed; the members of which could not conceive that anybody belonging to it was not very lucky. There was scarce one of the ladies that hadn't a relation a peer, though the husband might be a drysalter[8] in the City. Some of the ladies were very blue and well informed; reading Mrs. Somerville, and frequenting the Royal Institution; others were severe and Evangelical, and held by Exeter Hall.[9] Emmy, it must be owned, found herself entirely at a loss in the midst of their clavers,[1] and suffered wofully on the one or two occasions in which she was compelled to accept Mrs. Frederic Bullock's hospitalities. That lady persisted in patronising her, and determined most graciously to form her. She found Amelia's milliners for her, and regulated her household and her manners. She drove over constantly from Roehampton, and entertained her friend with faint fashionable fiddlefaddle and feeble Court slipslop. Jos liked to hear it, but the Major used to go off growling at the appearance of this woman, with her twopenny gentility. He went to sleep under Frederic Bullock's

7. What do you expect?
8. Dried- and salted-goods dealer.
9. Mary Somerville (1780–1872), a member of the Royal Society, was just beginning a distinguished career as science writer and lecturer. The Royal Institution, founded in Albemarle Street in 1799, was the site of regular lectures on science and technology. Exeter Hall opened in 1831 in the Strand for religious and scientific meetings; at a Temperance Society meeting held there in 1840, it was discovered that the cellars were rented to a wine merchant.
1. Chatterings.

bald head, after dinner, at one of the banker's best parties, (Fred was still anxious that the balance of the Osborne property should be transferred from Stumpy and Rowdy's to them,) and whilst Amelia, who did not know Latin, or who wrote the last crack article in the Edinburgh,[2] and did not in the least deplore, or otherwise, Mr. Peel's late extraordinary tergiversation in the fatal Catholic Relief Bill,[3] sate dumb amongst the ladies in the grand drawing-room, looking out upon velvet lawns, trim gravel walks, and glistening hot-houses.

"She seems good-natured but insipid," said Mrs. Rowdy; "that Major seems to be particularly *épris*."[4]

"She wants *ton* sadly," said Mrs. Hollyock. "My dear creature, you never will be able to form her."

"She is dreadfully ignorant or indifferent," said Mrs. Glowry, with a voice as if from the grave, and a sad shake of the head and turban—"I asked her if she thought that it was in 1836, according to Mr. Jowls, or in 1839, according to Mr. Wapshot, that the Pope was to fall: and she said—'Poor Pope! I hope not—What has he done?'"[5]

"She is my brother's widow, my dear friends," Mrs. Frederic replied, "and as such I think we're all bound to give her every attention and instruction on entering into the world. You may fancy there can be no *mercenary* motives[6] in those whose *disappointments* are well known."

"That poor dear Mrs. Bullock," said Rowdy to Hollyock, as they drove away together—"she is always scheming and managing. She wants Mrs. Osborne's account to be taken from our house to hers—and the way in which she coaxes that boy, and makes him sit by that blear-eyed little Rosa, is perfectly ridiculous."

"I wish Glowry was choked with her Man of Sin and her Battle of Armageddon,"[7] cried the other; and the carriage rolled away over Putney Bridge.

But this sort of society was too cruelly genteel for Emmy: and all jumped for joy when a foreign tour was proposed.

2. Articles in the *Edinburgh Review,* established in 1802 as a Whig quarterly, were all anonymous.
3. In 1829 Catholic emancipation became law under a government led by the duke of Wellington. Sir Robert Peel, in the cabinet at the time, abandoned his previous objections and supported the change.
4. Infatuated.
5. Amelia has confused the pope with someone named Pope, probably Alexander Pope (1763–1835), a painter and actor who had recently come into prominence in London. It is not likely that she meant the other Alexander, the poet, who died in 1744. Predictions of the fall of the pope, like predictions of the end of the world, were frequent.
6. Revised edition reads: motive
7. Evangelical tracts; Armageddon is the scene of the end-of-the-world battle predicted in Revelation 16.16.

## *Chapter LXII.*

### AM RHEIN.[1]

THE above every-day events had occurred, and a few weeks had passed, when, on one fine morning, Parliament being over, the summer advanced, and all the good company in London about to quit that city for their annual tour in search of pleasure or health, the Batavier steamboat left the Tower-stairs laden with a goodly company of English fugitives. The quarter-deck awnings were up, and the benches and gangways crowded with scores of rosy children, bustling nursemaids, ladies in the prettiest pink bonnets and summer dresses, gentlemen in travelling caps and linen jackets, whose mustachios had just begun to sprout for the ensuing tour; and stout trim old veterans with starched neckcloths and neat-brushed hats, such as have invaded Europe any time since the conclusion of the war, and carry the national Goddem[2] into every city of the Continent. The congregation of hat-boxes, and Bramah desks,[3] and dressing-cases was prodigious. There were jaunty young Cambridge-men travelling with their tutor, and going for a reading excursion to Nonnenwerth or Königswinter:[4] there were Irish gentlemen, with the most dashing whiskers and jewellery, talking about horses incessantly, and prodigiously polite to the young ladies on board, whom, on the contrary, the Cambridge lads and their pale-faced tutor avoided with maiden coyness: there were old Pall Mall loungers bound for Ems and Wiesbaden,[5] and a course of waters to clear off the dinners of the season, and a little roulette and *trente-et-quarante*[6] to keep the excitement going: there was old Methuselah, who had married his young wife, with Captain Papillon[7] of the Guards holding her parasol and guide-books: there was young May who was carrying off his bride on a pleasure tour, (Mrs. Winter that was, and who had been at school with May's grandmother;) there was Sir John and my Lady with a dozen children, and corresponding nursemaids; and the great

1. On the Rhine.
2. On the Continent, Englishmen were often referred to by their most frequent oath.
3. Portable writing desk by Joseph Bramah (1748–1814), cabinetmaker and inventor.
4. Towns on the Rhine near Bonn.
5. Spa towns further up the river.
6. Card game also known as *rouge et noir*.
7. The name means "butterfly."

grandee Bareacres family that sate by themselves near the wheel, stared at everybody, and spoke to no one. Their carriages, emblazoned with coronets, and heaped with shining imperials, were on the foredeck; locked in with a dozen more such vehicles: it was difficult to pass in and out amongst them: and the poor inmates of the fore-cabin had scarcely any space for locomotion. These consisted of a few magnificently attired gentlemen from Houndsditch,[8] who brought their own provisions, and could have bought half the gay people in the grand saloon; a few honest fellows with mustachios and portfolios, who set to sketching before they had been half-an-hour on board; one or two French *femmes de chambre* who began to be dreadfully ill by the time the boat had passed Greenwich;[9] a groom or two who lounged in the neighbourhood of the horse-boxes under their charge, or leaned over the side by the paddle-wheels, and talked about who was good for the Leger, and what they stood to win or lose for the Goodwood cup.[1]

All the couriers, when they had done plunging about the ship, and had settled their various masters in the cabins or on the deck, congregated together and began to chatter and smoke; the Hebrew gentlemen joining them and looking at the carriages. There was Sir John's great carriage that would hold thirteen people; my Lord Methuselah's carriage, my Lord Bareacres' chariot, britska, and fourgon,[2] that anybody might pay for who liked. It was a wonder how my Lord got the ready money to pay for the expenses of the journey. The Hebrew gentlemen knew how he got it. They knew what money his Lordship had in his pocket at that instant, and what interest he paid for it, and who gave it him. Finally there was a very neat, handsome travelling carriage, about which the gentlemen speculated.

*"A qui cette voiture là?"*[3] said one gentleman-courier with a large morocco money-bag and ear-rings, to another with ear-rings and a large morocco money-bag.

*"C'est à Kirsch je bense—je l'ai vu toute à l'heure—qui brenoit des sangviches dans la voiture,"*[4] said the courier in a fine German French.

Kirsch emerging presently from the neighbourhood of the hold where he had been bellowing instructions intermingled with polyglot oaths to the ship's men engaged in secreting the passengers' luggage, came to give an account of himself to his brother interpreters. He informed them that the carriage belonged to a Nabab from Calcutta and Jamaica, enormously rich, and with whom he was engaged to travel; and at this moment a young gentleman who had been warned off the bridge between the paddle-boxes, and who had dropped thence on to the roof of Lord Methuselah's carriage, from which he had made his way over other carriages and imperials until he had clambered on to his own, descended thence and through the

8. The "old clothes district" in east London; hence, Jewish merchants.
9. I.e., while still in the river.
1. Horse races: the St. Leger at Doncaster, in September, and the Goodwood Cup at Goodwood near Chichester, in July.
2. Bareacres has a closed carriage, an open carriage, and a baggage wagon.
3. Whose carriage is this?
4. It is Kirsch's I think—I saw him a while ago—taking sandwiches to the carriage.

window into the body of the carriage to the applause of the couriers looking on.

*"Nous allons avoir une belle traversée,*[5] Monsieur George," said the courier with a grin, as he lifted his gold-laced cap.

"D— your French," said the young gentleman, "where's the biscuits, ay?"[6] Whereupon, Kirsch answered him in the English language or in such an imitation of it as he could command,—for though he was familiar with all languages, Mr. Kirsch was not acquainted with a single one and spoke all with indifferent volubility and incorrectness.

The imperious young gentleman who gobbled the biscuits, (and indeed it was time to refresh himself, for he had breakfasted at Richmond full three hours before,) was our young friend George Osborne. Uncle Jos and his mamma were on the quarter deck with a gentleman of whom they used to see a good deal, and the four were about to make a summer tour.

Jos was seated at that moment on deck under the awning, and

5. We shall have a fine crossing.
6. Revised edition reads: eh?"

pretty nearly opposite to the Earl of Bareacres and his family, whose proceedings absorbed the Bengalee almost entirely. Both the noble couple looked rather younger than in the eventful year '15, when Jos remembered to have seen them at Brussels (indeed he always gave out in India that he was intimately acquainted with them). Lady Carabas's[7] hair which was then dark was now a beautiful golden auburn, whereas Lord Carabas's whiskers, formerly red, were at present of a rich black with purple and green reflections in the light. But changed as they were, the movements of the noble pair occupied Jos's mind entirely. The presence of a lord fascinated him, and he could look at nothing else.

"Those people seem to interest you a good deal," said Dobbin, laughing and watching him. Amelia too laughed. She was in a straw bonnet with black ribbons, and otherwise dressed in mourning: but the little bustle and holiday of the journey pleased and excited her, and she looked particularly happy.

"What a heavenly day," Emmy said, and added, with great originality, "I hope we shall have a calm passage."

Jos waved his hand, scornfully glancing at the same time under his eyelids at the great folks opposite. "If you had made the voyages *we* have," he said, "you wouldn't much care about the weather." But nevertheless, traveller as he was, he passed the night direfully sick in his carriage, where his courier tended him with brandy-and-water and every luxury.

In due time this happy party landed at the quays of Rotterdam, whence they were transported by another steamer to the city of Cologne. Here the carriage and the family took to the shore, and Jos was not a little gratified to see his arrival announced in the Cologne newspapers as 'Herr Graf Lord von Sedley nebst Begleitung aus London.'[8] He had his court dress with him: he had insisted that Dobbin should bring his regimental paraphernalia: he announced that it was his intention to be presented at some foreign Courts, and pay his respects to the Sovereigns of the countries which he honoured with a visit.

Wherever the party stopped, and an opportunity was offered, Mr. Jos left his own card and the Major's upon "Our Minister." It was with great difficulty that he could be restrained from putting on his cocked hat and tights to wait upon the English consul at the Free City of Judenstadt, when that hospitable functionary asked our travellers to dinner. He kept a journal of his voyage, and noted elaborately the defects or excellencies of the various inns at which he put up, and of the wines and dishes of which he partook.

As for Emmy, she was very happy and pleased. Dobbin used to carry about for her her stool and sketch-book, and admired the drawings of the good-natured little artist, as they never had been admired before. She sate upon steamers' decks and drew crags and cas-

7. A character in Perrault's *Puss in Boots* and in a song by Béranger (1816). Le marquis de Carabas was a fossilized old aristocrat who took credit for everyone else's success. Apparently an alert, but not literate, compositor of the revised edition, noticing that the name here refers to the earl of Bareacres and his lady, "corrected" the text to read "Lady Bareacres'" and in the next line "Lord Bareacres'". It is not likely that Thackeray made this change.

8. Count Lord von Sedley and his party from London.

A fine Summer Evening

tles, or she mounted upon donkeys and ascended to ancient robber-towers, attended by her two aides-de-camp, Georgy and Dobbin. She laughed, and the Major did too, at his droll figure on donkey-back, with his long legs touching the ground. He was the interpreter for the party, having a good military knowledge of the German language; and he and the delighted George fought the campaigns of the Rhine and the Palatinate:[9] in the course of a few weeks, and by assiduously conversing with Herr Kirsch on the box of the carriage, Georgy made prodigious advance in the knowledge of High Dutch, and could talk to hotel waiters and postillions in a way that charmed his mother, and amused his guardian.

Mr. Jos did not much engage in the afternoon excursions of his fellow-travellers. He slept a good deal after dinner, or basked in the arbours of the pleasant inn-gardens. Pleasant Rhine gardens! Fair scenes of peace and sunshine—noble purple mountains, whose crests are reflected in the magnificent stream—who has ever seen you, that has not a grateful memory of those scenes of friendly repose and beauty? To lay down the pen, and even to think of that beautiful Rhineland makes one happy. At this time of summer evening, the cows are trooping down from the hills, lowing and with their bells tinkling, to the old town, with its old moats, and gates, and spires, and chestnut-trees, with long blue shadows stretching over the grass; the sky and the river below flame in crimson and gold; and the moon is already out, looking pale towards the sunset. The sun sinks behind the great castle-crested mountains, the night falls suddenly, the river grows darker and darker, lights quiver in it from the windows in the old ramparts, and twinkle peacefully in the villages under the hills on the opposite shore.

So Jos used to go to sleep a good deal with his bandanna over his face and be very comfortable, and read all the English news, and every word of Galignani's admirable newspaper, (may the blessings of all Englishmen who have ever been abroad rest on the founders and proprietors of that piratical print!)[1] and whether he woke or slept his friends did not very much miss him. Yes, they were very happy. They went to the Opera often of evenings—to those snug, unassuming, dear old operas in the German towns, where the noblesse sits and cries, and knits stockings on the one side, over against the bourgeoisie on the other; and His Transparency[2] the Duke and his Transparent family, all very fat and good-natured, come and occupy the great box in the middle; and the pit is full of the most elegant slim-waisted officers with straw-coloured mustachios, and twopence a-day on full pay. Here it was that Emmy found her delight, and was introduced for the first time to the wonders of Mozart and Cimarosa.[3] The Major's musical taste has been before alluded to, and his performances on the flute commended. But perhaps the chief pleasure

9. The Rhine-Pfalz district, once ruled by a count palatine of the Holy Roman Empire.
1. Galignani was a Paris publisher, for whom Thackeray may have worked in early days, whose English language books and newspapers catered to the English on the Continent. Their pages were filled with material cribbed from English publications, as there were no international copyright agreements at the time.
2. Probably a play on the German word for "Excellency" or "Highness": *Durchlaucht. Durch* means "through"; *durchsichtig* is German for "transparent."
3. Domenico Cimarosa (1749–1801), Italian composer of comic operas whose name was often linked with Mozart's.

he had in these operas was in watching Emmy's rapture while listening to them. A new world of love and beauty broke upon her when she was introduced to those divine compositions: this lady had the keenest and finest sensibility, and how could she be indifferent when she heard Mozart? The tender parts of "Don Juan" awakened in her raptures so exquisite that she would ask herself when she went to say her prayers of a night, whether it was not wicked to feel so much delight as that with which "Vedrai Carino" and "Batti Batti" filled her gentle little bosom?[4] But the Major, whom she consulted upon this head, as her theological adviser (and who himself had a pious and reverent soul), said that for his part, every beauty of art or nature made him thankful as well as happy; and that the pleasure to be had in listening to fine music, as in looking at the stars in the sky, or at a beautiful landscape or picture, was a benefit for which we might thank Heaven as sincerely as for any other worldly blessing. And in reply to some faint objections of Mrs. Amelia's (taken from certain theological works like the "Washerwoman of Finchley Common" and others of that school, with which Mrs. Osborne had been furnished during her life at Brompton) he told her an Eastern fable of the Owl who thought that the sunshine was unbearable for the eyes, and that the Nightingale was a most overrated bird. "It is one's nature to sing and the other's to hoot," he said, laughing, "and with such a sweet voice as you have yourself, you must belong to the Bulbul faction."

I like to dwell upon this period of her life, and to think that she was cheerful and happy. You see she has not had too much of that sort of existence as yet, and has not fallen in the way of means to educate her tastes or her intelligence. She has been domineered over hitherto by vulgar intellects. It is the lot of many a woman. And as every one of the dear sex is the rival of the rest of her kind, timidity passes for folly in their charitable judgments; and gentleness for dulness; and silence—which is but timid denial of the unwelcome assertion of ruling folks, and tacit protestantism—above all, finds no mercy at the hands of the female Inquisition. Thus, my dear and civilised reader, if you and I were to find ourselves this evening in a society of greengrocers, let us say; it is probable that our conversation would not be brilliant; if, on the other hand, a greengrocer should find himself at your refined and polite teatable, where everybody was saying witty things, and everybody of fashion and repute tearing her friends to pieces in the most delightful manner, it is possible that the stranger would not be very talkative, and by no means interesting or interested.

And it must be remembered, that this poor lady had never met a gentleman in her life until this present moment. Perhaps these are rarer personages than some of us think for. Which of us can point out many such in his circle—men whose aims are generous, whose truth is constant, and not only constant in its kind but elevated in its degree; whose want of meanness makes them simple: who can look the world honestly in the face with an equal manly sympathy for the great and the small? We all know a hundred whose coats are

4. "You'll see, my darling" and "Beat me, beat me" are arias sung by Zerlina in Mozart's *Don Giovanni*.

very well made, and a score who have excellent manners, and one or two happy beings who are what they call, in the inner circles, and have shot into the very centre and bull's eye of the fashion; but of gentlemen how many? Let us take a little scrap of paper and each make out his list.

My friend the Major I write, without any doubt, in mine. He had very long legs, a yellow face, and a slight lisp, which at first was rather ridiculous. But his thoughts were just, his brains were fairly good, his life was honest and pure, and his heart warm and humble. He certainly had very large hands and feet, which the two George Osbornes used to caricature and laugh at; and their jeers and laughter perhaps led poor little Emmy astray as to his worth. But have we not all been misled about our heroes, and changed our opinions a hundred times? Emmy, in this happy time, found that hers underwent a very great change in respect of the merits of the Major.

Perhaps it was the happiest time of both their lives indeed, if they did but know it—and who does? Which of us can point out and say that was the culmination—that was the summit of human joy? But at all events, this couple were very decently contented and enjoyed as pleasant a summer tour as any pair that left England that year. Georgy was always present at the play, but it was the Major who put Emmy's shawl on after the entertainment; and in the walks and excursions the young lad would be on a-head, and up a tower-stair or a tree, whilst the soberer couple were below, the Major smoking his cigar with great placidity and constancy, whilst Emmy sketched the site or the ruin. It was on this very tour that I, the present writer of a history of which every word is true, had the pleasure to see them first, and to make their acquaintance.

It was at the little comfortable Grand Ducal[5] town of Pumpernickel (that very place where Sir Pitt Crawley had been so distinguished as an *attaché;* but that was in early early days, and before the news of the battle of Austerlitz[6] sent all the English diplomatists in Germany to the right about) that I first saw Colonel Dobbin and his party. They had arrived with the carriage and courier at the Erbprinz Hotel, the best of the town, and the whole party dined at the *table d'hôte*. Everybody remarked the majesty of Jos, and the knowing way in which he sipped, or rather sucked, the Johannisberger,[7] which he ordered for dinner. The little boy, too, we observed, had a famous appetite, and consumed schinken, and braten, and kartoffeln,[8] and cranberry jam, and salad, and pudding, and roast fowls, and sweetmeats, with a gallantry that did honour to his nation. After about fifteen dishes, he concluded the repast with dessert, some of which he even carried out of doors; for some young gentlemen at table, amused with his coolness and gallant free and easy manner, induced him to pocket a handful of macaroons, which he discussed on his way to the theatre, whither everybody went in the cheery social little German place. The lady in black, the boy's mamma, laughed and blushed, and looked

5. Revised edition reads: comfortable ducal
6. Napolean defeated the Russo-Austrian army there in 1805.
7. A Rhine wine.
8. Ham and roast and potatoes.

exceedingly pleased and shy as the dinner went on, and at the various feats and instances of *espièglerie*[9] on the part of her son. The Colonel—for so he became very soon afterwards—I remember joked the boy with a great deal of grave fun, pointing out dishes which he *hadn't* tried, and entreating him not to baulk his appetite, but to have a second supply of this or that.

It was what they call a *gast-rolle*[1] night at the Royal Grand Ducal Pumpernickelisch Hof,—or Court theatre; and Madame Schroeder Devrient, then in the bloom of her beauty and genius, performed the part of the heroine in the wonderful opera of "Fidelio."[2] From our places in the stalls we could see our four friends of the *table d'hôte,* in the loge which Schwendler of the Erbprinz kept for his best guests: and I could not help remarking the effect which the magnificent actress and music produced upon Mrs. Osborne, for so we had heard the stout gentleman in the mustachios call her. During the astonishing Chorus of the Prisoners[3] over which the delightful voice of the actress rose and soared in the most ravishing harmony, her face[4] wore such an expression of wonder and delight that it struck even little Fipps, the *blasé* attaché, who drawled out, as he fixed his glass upon her, "Gayd, it really does one good to see a woman caypable of that stayt of excaytement." And in the Prison Scene where Fidelio, rushing to her husband, cries "Nichts nichts mein Florestan," she fairly lost herself and covered her face with her handkerchief.[5] Every woman in the house was snivelling at the time: but I suppose it was because it was predestined that I was to write this particular lady's memoirs that I remarked her.

The next day they gave another piece of Beethoven: "Die Schlacht bei Vittoria."[6] Malbrook is introduced at the beginning of the performance, as indicative of the brisk advance of the French Army. Then come drums, trumpets, thunder of artillery, and groans of the dying, and at last in a grand triumphant[7] swell, "God save the King" is performed.

There may have been a score of Englishmen in the house, but at the burst of that beloved and well-known music, every one of them, we young fellows in the stalls, Sir John and Lady Bullminster (who had taken a house at Pumpernickel for the education of their nine children), the fat gentleman with the mustachios, the long Major in white duck trowsers, and the lady with the little boy upon whom he was so sweet; even Kirsch, the courier in the gallery, stood bolt upright in their places, and proclaimed themselves to be members of

9. Mischief.
1. Role played by a guest artist.
2. Wilhelmine Schroeder (1801–60), wife of Ludwig Devrient, played Leonora, who dresses as a man (Fidelio), in order to see her husband (Florestan) in prison in Beethoven's *Fidelio* (1805). Thackeray spent six months in Weimar in 1830–31, when he saw Madame Devrient in the performance Amelia supposedly saw in Pumpernickel.
3. End of Act I.
4. Revised edition reads: harmony, the English lady's face
5. Florestan, released from prison, asks his wife what she has done for him. She replies, "Nothing, nothing, my Florestan."
6. "The Battle of Vittoria," also known as "Wellington's Victory," is about Malbrook or Malbouk (thought by some to be a mispronunciation of Marlborough), who is a warrior. Napoleon is said to have hummed the title song, "Malbrouk s'en va-t-en guerre," each time he rode off to battle.
7. Revised edition reads: triumphal

the dear old British nation. As for Tapeworm, the Secretary of Legation,[8] he rose up in his box and bowed and simpered, as if he would represent the whole empire. Tapeworm was nephew and heir of old Marshal Tiptoff, who has been introduced in this story as General Tiptoff, just before Waterloo, who was Colonel of the —th regiment in which Major Dobbin served, and who died in this year full of honours, and of an aspic of plovers' eggs; when the regiment was graciously given by his Majesty to Colonel Sir Michael O'Dowd, K.C.B., who had commanded it in many glorious fields.

Tapeworm must have met with Colonel Dobbin at the house of the Colonel's Colonel, the Marshal, for he recognised him on this night at the theatre; and with the utmost condescension, his Majesty's minister came over from his own box, and publicly shook hands with his new-found friend.

"Look at that infernal sly boots of a Tapeworm," Fipps whispered, examining his Chief from the stalls. "Wherever there's a pretty woman he always twists himself in." And I wonder what were diplomatists made for but for that?

"Have I the honour of addressing myself to Mrs. Dobbin," asked

the Secretary, with a most insinuating grin.

Georgy burst out laughing, and said "By Jove, that *is* a good

8. Revised edition erroneously alters this to "the Chargé de'Affaires," but that is Macabau, not Tapeworm, as is made clear later.

'un."—Emmy and the Major blushed: we saw them from the stalls.

"This lady is Mrs. George Osborne," said the Major, "and this is her brother, Mr. Sedley, a distinguished officer of the Bengal Civil Service: permit me to introduce him to your lordship."

My lord nearly sent Jos off his legs, with the most fascinating smile. "Are you going to stop in Pumpernickel," he said. "It is a dull place: but we want some nice people, and we would try and make it *so* agreeable to you. Mr.—Ahum—Mrs.—Oho. I shall do myself the honour of calling upon you to-morrow at your inn."—And he went away with a Parthian grin and glance, which he thought must finish Mrs. Osborne completely.

The performance over, the young fellows lounged about the lobbies, and we saw the society take its departure. The Duchess Dowager went off in her jingling old coach, attended by two faithful and withered old maids of honour, and a little snuffy spindle-shanked gentleman in waiting, in a brown jasey[9] and a green coat covered with orders—of which the star and the grand yellow cordon[1] of the order of Saint Michael of Pumpernickel was most conspicuous. The drums rolled, the guards saluted, and the old carriage drove away.

Then came his Transparency the Duke and Transparent family, with his great officers of state and household. He bowed serenely to everybody. And amid the saluting of the guards, and the flaring of the torches of the running footmen, clad in scarlet, the Transparent carriages drove away to the old Ducal Schloss,[2] with its towers and pinnacles standing on the Schlossberg. Everybody in Pumpernickel knew everybody. No sooner was a foreigner seen there, than the Minister of Foreign Affairs, or some other great or small officer of state, went round to the Erbprinz, and found out the name of the new arrivals.

We watched them, too, out of the theatre. Tapeworm had just walked off, enveloped in his cloak, with which his gigantic chasseur[3] was always in attendance, and looking as much as possible like Don Juan. The Prime Minister's lady had just squeezed herself into her sedan, and her daughter, the charming Ida, had put on her calash and clogs: when the English party came out, the boy yawning drearily, the Major taking great pains in keeping the shawl over Mrs. Osborne's head, and Mr. Sedley looking grand, with a crush opera-hat[4] on one side of his head, and his hand in the stomach of a voluminous white waistcoat. We took off our hats to our acquaintances of the *table d'hôte*, and the lady, in return, presented us with a little smile and a curtsey, for which everybody might be thankful.

The carriage from the inn, under the superintendence of the bustling Mr. Kirsch, was in waiting to convey the party; but the fat man said he would walk, and smoke his cigar on his way homewards; so the other three, with nods and smiles to us, went without Mr. Sedley, Kirsch, with the cigar-case, following in his master's wake.

9. Worsted-wool wig.
1. Ribbon.
2. Castle.
3. Footman.
4. Collapsible top hat.

We all walked together, and talked to the stout gentleman about the *agréments*[5] of the place. It was very agreeable for the English. There were shooting-parties and battues;[6] there was a plenty of balls and entertainments at the hospitable Court; the society was generally good; the theatre excellent, and the living cheap.

"And our Minister seems a most delightful and affable person," our new friend said. "With such a representative, and—and a good medical man, I can fancy the place to be most eligible. Good night, gentlemen." And Jos creaked up the stairs to bedward, followed by Kirsch with a flambeau.[7] We rather hoped that nice-looking woman would be induced to stay some time in the town.

## *Chapter LXIII.*

### IN WHICH WE MEET AN OLD ACQUAINTANCE.

SUCH[1] polite behaviour as that of Lord Tapeworm did not fail to have the most favourable effect upon Mr. Sedley's mind, and the very next morning, at breakfast, he pronounced his opinion that Pumpernickel was the pleasantest little place of any which they[2] had visited on their tour. Jos's motives and artifices were not very difficult of comprehension: and Dobbin laughed in his sleeve, like a hypocrite as he was, when he found by the knowing air of the Civilian and the off-hand manner in which the latter talked about Tapeworm Castle, and the other members of the family, that Jos had been up already in the morning, consulting his travelling Peerage. Yes, he had seen the Right Honourable the Earl of Bagwig, his lordship's father; he was sure he had, he had met him at—at the Levee—didn't Dob remember? and when the Diplomatist called on the party, faithful to his promise, Jos received him with such a salute and honours as were seldom accorded to the little Envoy. He winked at Kirsch on his Excellency's arrival, and that emissary instructed beforehand, went out and superintended an entertainment of cold meats, jellies, and other delicacies, brought in

5. Comforts, amenities.
6. Hunts.
7. Torch.
1. Initial illustration: Becky as sorceress, perhaps Circe, who turned Ulysses' men to swine.
2. Revised edition reads: he

upon trays, and of which Mr. Jos absolutely insisted that his noble guest should partake.

Tapeworm, so long as he could have an opportunity of admiring the bright eyes of Mrs. Osborne (whose freshness of complexion bore daylight remarkably well) was not ill pleased to accept any invitation to stay in Mr. Sedley's lodgings; he put one or two dexterous questions to him about India and the dancing-girls there; asked Amelia about that beautiful boy who had been with her, and complimented the astonished little woman upon the prodigious sensation which she had made in the house; and tried to fascinate Dobbin by talking of the late war, and the exploits of the Pumpernickel contingent under the command of the Hereditary Prince, now Duke of Pumpernickel.

Lord Tapeworm inherited no little portion of the family gallantry, and it was his happy belief, that almost every woman upon whom he himself cast friendly eyes, was in love with him. He left Emmy under the persuasion that she was slain by his wit and attractions, and went home to his lodgings to write a pretty little note to her. She was not fascinated; only puzzled by his grinning, his simpering, his scented cambric handkerchief, and his high-heeled lacquered boots. She did not understand one half the compliments which he paid; she had never, in her small experience of mankind, met a professional ladies' man as yet, and looked upon my lord as something curious rather than pleasant; and if she did not admire, certainly wondered at him. Jos, on the contrary, was delighted. "How very affable his Lordship is," he said; "How very kind of his Lordship to say he would send his medical man! Kirsch, you will carry our cards to the Count de Schlüsselback directly: the Major and I will have the greatest pleasure in paying our respects at Court as soon as possible. Put out my uniform, Kirsch,—both our uniforms. It is a mark of politeness which every English gentleman ought to show to the countries which he visits, to pay his respects to the sovereigns of those countries as to the representatives of his own."

When Tapeworm's doctor came, Doctor von Glauber, Body Physician to H.S.H. the Duke, he speedily convinced Jos that the Pumpernickel mineral springs and the Doctor's particular treatment would infallibly restore the Bengalee to youth and slimness. "Dere came here last year," he said, "Sheneral Bulkeley, an English Sheneral, tvice so pic as you, Sir. I sent him back qvite tin after tree months, and he danced vid Baroness Glauber at the end of two."

Jos's mind was made up, the springs, the doctor, the Court, and the Chargé d'Affaires[3] convinced him, and he proposed to spend the autumn in these delightful quarters.—And punctual to his word, on the next day the Chargé d'Affaires presented Jos and the Major to Victor Aurelius XVII., being conducted to their audience with that sovereign by the Count de Schlüsselback, Marshal of the Court.

They were straightway invited to dinner at Court, and their intention of staying in the town being announced, the politest ladies of the whole town instantly called upon Mrs. Osborne; and as not one of these, however poor they might be, was under the rank of a Baroness, Jos's delight was beyond expression. He wrote off to Chutney at the

3. Diplomatic representative serving as ambassador.

Club to say that the Service was highly appreciated in Germany, that he was going to show his friend, the Count de Schlüsselback, how to stick a pig in the Indian fashion, and that his august friends, the Duke and Duchess, were everything that was kind and civil.

Emmy, too, was presented to the august family, and as mourning is not admitted in Court on certain days, she appeared in a pink crape dress, with a diamond ornament in the corsage, presented to her by her brother, and she looked so pretty in this costume that the Duke and Court (putting out of the question the Major, who had scarcely ever seen her before in an evening dress, and vowed that she did not look five-and-twenty) all admired her excessively.

In this dress she walked a Polonaise[4] with Major Dobbin at a Court-ball, in which easy dance Mr. Jos had the honour of leading out the Countess of Schlüsselback, an old lady with a hump back, but with sixteen good quarters of nobility,[5] and related to half the royal houses of Germany.

Pumpernickel stands in the midst of a happy valley, through which sparkles—to mingle with the Rhine somewhere, but I have not the map at hand to say exactly at what point—the fertilising stream of the Pump. In some places the river is big enough to support a ferry-boat, in others to turn a mill; in Pumpernickel itself, the last Transparency but three, the great and renowned Victor Aurelius XIV., built a magnificent bridge, on which his own statue rises, surrounded by water-nymphs and emblems of victory, peace and plenty; he has his foot on the neck of a prostrate Turk—history says he engaged and ran a Janissary through the body at the relief of Vienna by Sobieski,—but, quite undisturbed by the agonies of that prostrate Mahometan, who writhes at his feet in the most ghastly manner—the Prince smiles blandly, and points with his truncheon in the direction of the Aurelius Platz, where he began to erect a new palace that would have been the wonder of his age, had the great-souled Prince but funds to complete it.[6] But the completion of Monplaisir (*Monblaisir* the honest German folks call it)[7] was stopped for lack of ready money, and it and its park and garden are now in rather a faded condition, and not more than ten times big enough to accommodate the Court of the reigning Sovereign.

The gardens were arranged to emulate those of Versailles, and amidst the terraces and groves there are some huge allegorical waterworks still, which spout and froth stupendously upon fête-days, and frighten one with their enormous aquatic insurrections. There is the Trophonius' cave in which, by some artifice, the leaden Tritons are made not only to spout water, but to play the most dreadful

4. A very slow dance.
5. Each of the four quarters of her heraldic shield was itself quartered, indicating an advanced degree of nobility.
6. Victor Aurelius, like his statue, his park, and his town of Pumpernickel, are a fiction. He is named for a Roman historian. John Sobieski was king of Poland from 1674 to 1696, and defeated the Turks at Vienna in 1683.
7. The palace's name, Monplaisir, means "my pleasure." Monblaisir suggests "my bubble"; *blase* means "bubble" and *bläser*, "blower."

Jos performs a Polonaise

groans out of their lead conchs[8]—there is the Nymph-bath and the Niagara cataract, which the people of the neighbourhood admire beyond expression, when they come to the yearly fair at the opening of the Chamber, or to the fêtes with which the happy little nation still celebrates the birth-days and marriage-days of its princely governors.

Then from all the towns of the Duchy which stretches for nearly ten miles,—from Bolkum, which lies on its western frontier bidding defiance to Prussia, from Grogwitz where the Prince has a hunting-lodge, and where his dominions are separated by the Pump river from those of the neighbouring Prince of Potzenthal; from all the little villages, which besides these three great cities, dot over the happy Principality—from the farms and the mills along the Pump, come troops of people in red petticoats and velvet head-dresses, or with three-cornered hats and pipes in their mouths, who flock to the Residenz and share in the pleasures of the fair and the festivities there. Then the theatre is open for nothing, then the waters of Monblaisir begin to play (it is lucky that there is company to behold them for one would be afraid to see them alone)—then there come mountebanks and riding troops (the way in which his Transparency was fascinated by one of the horse-riders, is well known, and it is believed that *La Petite Vivandière,*[9] as she was called, was a spy in the French interest), and the delighted people are permitted to march through room after room of the Grand Ducal palace, and admire the slippery floor, the rich hangings, and the spittoons at the doors of all the innumerable chambers. There is one Pavilion at Monblaisir which Aurelius Victor XV. had arranged—a great Prince but too fond of pleasure—and which I am told is a perfect wonder of licentious elegance. It is painted with the story of Bacchus and Ariadne,[1] and the table works in and out of the room by means of a windlass so that the company was served without any intervention of domestics. But the place was shut up by Barbara, Aurelius XV.'s widow, a severe and devout Princess of the House of Bolkum and Regent of the Duchy during her son's glorious minority, and after the death of her husband, cut off in the pride of his pleasures.

The theatre of Pumpernickel is known and famous in that quarter of Germany. It languished a little when the present Duke in his youth insisted upon having his own operas played there, and it is said one day, in a fury from his place in the orchestra, when he attended a rehearsal, broke a bassoon on the head of the Chapel Master, who was conducting, and led too slow; and during which time the Duchess Sophia wrote domestic comedies which must have been very dreary to witness. But the Prince executes his music in private now, and the Duchess only gives away her plays to the foreigners of distinction who visit her kind little Court.

It is conducted with no small comfort and splendour. When there are balls, though there may be four hundred people at supper, there

8. Trophonius was a Greek oracle into whose cave suppliants were dragged, assaulted by howling, shrieks, and bellowings, and then unceremoniously ejected.
9. Little provisions-vender.
1. Ariadne, daughter of the king of Crete, was abandoned by Theseus on Naxos and consoled by Bacchus, who married her.

is a servant in scarlet and lace to attend upon every four, and every one is served on silver. There are festivals and entertainments going continually on; and the Duke has his chamberlains and equerries,[2] and the Duchess her mistress of the wardrobe and ladies of honour just like any other and more potent potentates.

The Constitution is or was a moderate despotism, tempered by a Chamber that might or might not be elected. I never certainly could hear of its sitting in my time at Pumpernickel. The Prime Minister had lodgings in a second floor; and the Foreign Secretary occupied the comfortable lodgings over Zwieback's Conditorey.[3] The army consisted of a magnificent band that also did duty on the stage, where it was quite pleasant to see the worthy fellows marching in Turkish dresses with rouge on and wooden scimetars, or as Roman warriors with ophicleides[4] and trombones,—to see them again, I say, at night, after one had listened to them all the morning in the Aurelius Platz, where they performed opposite the Café where we breakfasted. Besides the band, there was a rich and numerous staff of officers, and, I believe, a few men. Besides the regular sentries, three or four men, habited as hussars, used to do duty at the Palace, but I never saw them on horseback, and *au fait,*[5] what was the use of cavalry in a time of profound peace?—and whither the deuce should the hussars ride?

Everybody—everybody that was noble of course, for as for the Bourgeois we could not quite be expected to take notice of *them*—visited his neighbour. H. E. Madame de Burst received once a week, H. E. Madame de Schnurrbart[6] had her night—the theatre was open twice a week, the Court graciously received once, so that a man's life might in fact be a perfect round of pleasure in the unpretending Pumpernickel way.

That there were feuds in the place, no one can deny. Politics ran very high at Pumpernickel, and parties were very bitter. There was the Strumpff faction and the Lederlung party, the one supported by our Envoy and the other by the French Chargé d'Affaires, M. de Macabau.[7] Indeed it sufficed for our Minister to stand up for Madame Strumpff, who was clearly the greatest singer of the two, and had three more notes in her voice than Madame Lederlung her rival—it sufficed, I say, for our Minister to advance *any* opinion to have it instantly contradicted by the French diplomatist.

Everybody in the town was ranged in one or other of these factions. The Lederlung was a prettyish little creature certainly, and her voice, (what there was of it,) was very sweet, and there is no doubt that the Strumpff was not in her first youth and beauty, and certainly too stout; when she came on in the last scene of the *Sonnambula*[8] for instance in her night-chemise with a lamp in her hand,

2. House managers and stable masters.
3. Pastry shop, named for a dry biscuit.
4. Large brass horn with keys.
5. In any case.
6. Her Highness Burst (brush) and Her Highness Schnurrbart (mustache).
7. Strumpff: stocking. Lederlung: leather lung. Macabau: a type of snuff.
8. In *The Sleepwalker,* 1831 opera by Vincenzo Bellini (1801–35), the heroine, Amina, walks a plank over a millstream to join Elvino, her betrothed.

and had to go out of the window, and pass over the plank of the mill, it was all she could do to squeeze out of the window, and the plank used to bend and creak again under her weight—but how she poured out the finale of the opera! and with what a burst of feeling she rushed into Elvino's arms—almost fit to smother him! Whereas the little Lederlung—but a truce to this gossip—the fact is, that these two women were the two flags of the French and the English party at Pumpernickel, and the society was divided in its allegiance to those two great nations.

We had on our side the Home Minister, the Master of the Horse, the Duke's Private Secretary, and the Prince's Tutor: whereas of the French party were the Foreign Minister, the Commander-in-chief's Lady, who had served under Napoleon, and the Hof-Marschall and his wife, who was glad enough to get the fashions from Paris, and always had them and her caps by M. de Macabau's courier. The Secretary of his Chancery was little Grignac, a young fellow, as malicious as Satan, and who made caricatures of Tapeworm in all the albums of the place.

Their head-quarters and table d'hôte were established at the Pariser Hof, another[9] inn of the town; and though, of course, these gentlemen were obliged to be civil in public, yet they cut at each other with epigrams that were as sharp as razors, as I have seen a couple of wrestlers in Devonshire, lashing at each other's shins, and never showing their agony upon a muscle of their faces. Neither Tapeworm nor Macabau ever sent home a despatch to his government, without a most savage series of attacks upon his rival. For instance, on our side we would write, "The interests of Great Britain in this place, and throughout the whole of Germany, are perilled by the continuance in office of the present French envoy; this man is of a character so infamous that he will stick at no falsehood, or hesitate at no crime, to attain his ends. He poisons the mind of the Court against the English minister, represents the conduct of Great Britain in the most odious and atrocious light, and is unhappily backed by a minister whose ignorance and necessities are as notorious as his influence is fatal." On their side they would say, "M. de Tapeworm continues his system of stupid insular arrogance and vulgar falsehood against the greatest nation in the world. Yesterday he was heard to speak lightly of Her Royal Highness Madame the Duchess of Berri: on a former occasion he insulted the heroic Duke of Angoulême, and dared to insinuate that H.R.H. the Duke of Orleans was conspiring against the august throne of the lilies.[1] His gold is prodigated in every direction which his stupid menaces fail to frighten. By one and the other, he has won over creatures of the Court here,—and, in fine, Pumpernickel will not be quiet, Germany tranquil, France respected, or Europe

9. Weimar, the original for Pumpernickel, had two inns, the Erprinz and the Elefant. In the fictional Pumpernickel, Jos's hotel is the Erbprinz and Becky's is the Elephant; Tapeworm's hotel, the Pariser Hof, therefore, is "another" hotel. First printing reads: at the Elephant, the other ] Second printing reads: at the Pariser Hof, the other

1. The duchess of Berri, Marie Caroline (1798–1870), was niece by marriage to Charles X, last Bourbon king of France and father of Louis Antoine de Bourbon, Duc d'Angoulême. Charles X abdicated in 1830 and was succeeded not by his son but by the duke of Orléans, who reigned as Louis-Philippe and who replaced the Bourbon lilies with the tricolored flag. In short, Tapeworm was telling the truth.

content, until this poisonous viper be crushed under heel:" and so on. When one side or the other had written any particularly spicy despatch, news of it was sure to slip out.

Before the winter was far advanced it is actually on record that Emmy took a night and received company with great propriety and modesty. She had a French master who complimented her upon the purity of her accent and her facility of learning; the fact is she had learned long ago, and grounded herself subsequently in the grammar so as to be able to teach it to George; and Madame Strumpff came to give her lessons in singing, which she performed so well and with such a true voice that the Major's windows, who had lodgings opposite under the Prime Minister, were always open to hear the lesson. Some of the German ladies, who are very sentimental and simple in their tastes, fell in love with her and began to call her *du*[2] at once. These are trivial details, but they relate to happy times. The Major made himself George's tutor, and read Cæsar[3] and mathematics with him, and they had a German master and rode out of evenings by the side of Emmy's carriage—she was always too timid, and made a dreadful outcry at the slightest disturbance on horseback. So she drove about with one of her dear German friends, and Jos asleep on the back-seat of the barouche.

He was becoming very sweet upon the Gräfinn Fanny de Butterbrod, a very gentle tender-hearted and unassuming young creature, a Canoness and Countess in her own right,[4] but with scarcely ten pounds per year to her fortune, and Fanny for her part declared that to be Amelia's sister was the greatest delight that heaven could bestow on her, and Jos might have put a Countess's shield and coronet by the side of his own arms on his carriage and forks; when—when events occurred, and those grand fêtes given upon the marriage of the Hereditary Prince of Pumpernickel with the lovely Princess Amelia of Humbourg-Schlippenschloppen took place.

At this festival the magnificence displayed was such as had not been known in the little German place since the days of the prodigal Victor XIV. All the neighbouring Princes, Princesses, and Grandees were invited to the feast. Beds rose to half-a-crown per night in Pumpernickel, and the army was exhausted in providing guards of honour for the Highnesses, Serenities, and Excellencies, who arrived from all quarters. The Princess was married by proxy, at her father's residence, by the Count de Schlüsselback. Snuff-boxes were given away in profusion (as we learned from the Court-jeweller, who sold and afterwards bought them again), and bushels of the Order of Saint Michael of Pumpernickel were sent to the nobles of the Court, while hampers of the cordons and decorations of the Wheel of St. Catherine of Schlippenschloppen were brought to ours. The French envoy got both. "He is covered with ribbons like a prize cart-horse," Tapeworm said, who was not allowed by the rules of his service to take any decorations: "Let him have the cordons; but with whom is the vic-

2. Familiar form of address reserved for intimates.
3. Julius Cæsar's *Commentaries* was a standard Latin school text.
4. Gräfinn de Butterbrod: countess of Buttered Bread. A canoness is a lay sister not under permanent vows.

tory?" The fact is, it was a triumph of British diplomacy: the French party having proposed and tried their utmost to carry a marriage with a Princess of the house of Potztausend-Donnerwetter, whom, as a matter of course, we opposed.

Everybody was asked to the fêtes of the marriage. Garlands and triumphal arches were hung across the road to welcome the young bride. The great Saint Michael's Fountain ran with uncommonly sour wine, while that in the Artillery Place frothed with beer. The great waters played; and poles were put up in the park and gardens for the happy peasantry, which they might climb at their leisure, carrying off watches, silver forks, prize sausages hung with pink ribbon, &c., at the top. Georgy got one, wrenching it off, having swarmed up the pole to the delight of the spectators, and sliding down with the rapidity of a fall of water. But it was for the glory's sake merely. The boy gave the sausage to a peasant, who had very nearly seized it, and stood at the foot of the mast, blubbering, because he was unsuccessful.

At the French Chancellerie they had six more lampions in their illumination than our's had; but our transparency, which represented the young Couple advancing, and Discord flying away, with the most ludicrous likeness to the French ambassador, beat the French picture hollow; and I have no doubt got Tapeworm the advancement and the Cross of the Bath, which he subsequently attained.

Crowds of foreigners arrived for the fêtes: and of English of course. Besides the Court balls, public balls were given at the Town Hall and the Redoute, and in the former place there was a room for *trente-et-quarante* and *roulette* established, for the week of the festivities only, and by one of the great German companies from Ems or Aix-la-Chapelle.[5] The officers or inhabitants of the town were not allowed to play at these games, but strangers, peasants, ladies were admitted, and anyone who chose to lose or win money.

That little scapegrace Georgy Osborne amongst others, whose pockets were always full of dollars, and whose relations were away at the grand festival of the Court, came to the Stadthaus' ball in company of his uncle's courier, Mr. Kirsch, and having only peeped into a play-room at Baden Baden when he hung on Dobbin's arm, and where, of course, he was not permitted to gamble, came eagerly to this part of the entertainment, and hankered round the tables where the croupiers and the punters were at work. Women were playing; they were masked, some of them; this license was allowed in these wild times of carnival.

A woman with light hair, in a low dress, by no means so fresh as it had been, and with a black mask on, through the eyelets of which her eyes twinkled strangely, was seated at one of the roulette-tables with a card and a pin, and a couple of florins before her. As the croupier called out the colour and number, she pricked on the card with great care and regularity, and only ventured her money on the colours after the red or black had come up a certain number of times. It was strange to look at her.

5. Gambling tables were run by professionals imported from spa towns for the occasion.

But in spite of her care and assiduity she guessed wrong, and the last two florins followed each other under the croupier's rake, as he cried out with his inexorable voice, the winning colour and number. She gave a sigh, a shrug with her shoulders, which were already too much out of her gown, and dashing the pin through the card on to the table, sat thrumming it for a while. Then she looked round her, and saw Georgy's honest face staring at the scene. The little scamp! what business had he to be there?

When she saw the boy, at whose face she looked hard through her shining eyes and mask, she said, *"Monsieur n'est pas joueur."*[6]

*"Non, Madame,"* said the boy: but she must have known, from his accent of what country he was, for she answered him with a slight foreign tone. "You have nevare played—will you do me a littl' favor?"

"What is it?" said Georgy, blushing again. Mr. Kirsch was at work for his part at the *rouge et noir,* and did not see his young master.

"Play this for me, if you please, put it on any number, any number." And she took from her bosom a purse, and out of it a gold piece, the only coin there, and she put it into George's hand. The boy laughed, and did as he was bid.

It came up the number[7] sure enough. There is a power that arranges that, they say, for beginners.

"Thank you," said she, pulling the money towards her; "thank you. What is your name?"

"My name's Osborne," said Georgy, and was fingering in his own pockets for dollars, and just about to make a trial, when the Major, in his uniform, and Jos, *en Marquis,*[8] from the Court ball, made their appearance. Other people finding the entertainment stupid, and preferring the fun at the Stadthaus, had quitted the Palace ball earlier; but it is probable the Major and Jos had gone home and found the boy's absence, for the former instantly went up to him, and taking him by the shoulder, pulled him briskly back from the place of temptation. Then, looking round the room, he saw Kirsch employed as we have said, and going up to him, asked how he dared to bring Mr. George to such a place.

*"Laissez-moi tranquille,"* said Mr. Kirsch, very much excited by play and wine. *"Il faut s'amuser, parbleu. Je ne suis pas au service de Monsieur."*[9]

Seeing his condition the Major did not choose to argue with the man; but contented himself with drawing away George, and asking Jos if he would come away. He was standing close by the lady in the mask, who was playing with pretty good luck now; and looking on much interested at the game.

"Hadn't you better come, Jos," the Major said, "with George and me?"

"I'll stop and go home with that rascal, Kirsch," Jos said; and for the same reason of modesty, which he thought ought to be preserved

6. Sir, you are not a player?
7. Revised edition reads: The number came up
8. Dressed as a marquis.
9. Leave me alone. One must enjoy himself, by God. I'm not in your service.

before the boy, Dobbin did not care to remonstrate with Jos, but left him and walked home with Georgy.

"Did you play?" asked the Major, when they were out, and on their way home.

The boy said "No."

"Give me your word of honour as a gentleman, that you never will."

"Why?" said the boy: "It seems very good fun." And, in a very eloquent and impressive manner, the Major showed him why he shouldn't, and would have enforced his precepts by the example of Georgy's own father, had he liked to say anything that should reflect on the other's memory. When he had housed him he went to bed, and saw his light, in the little room outside of Amelia's, presently disappear. Amelia's followed half an hour afterwards. I don't know what made the Major note it so accurately.

Jos, however, remained behind over the play-table; he was no gambler, but not averse to the little excitement of the sport now and then; and he had some Napoleons chinking in the embroidered pockets of his court waistcoat. He put down one over the fair shoulder of the little gambler before him, and they won. She made a little movement to make room for him by her side, and just took the skirt of her gown from a vacant chair there.

"Come and give me good luck," she said, still in a foreign accent, quite different from that frank and perfectly English "Thank you," with which she had saluted Georgy's *coup* in her favour. The portly gentleman, looking round to see that nobody of rank observed him, sat down; he muttered—"Ah, really, well now, God bless my soul. I'm very fortunate; I'm sure to give you good fortune,"—and other words of compliment and confusion.

"Do you play much?" the foreign mask said.

"I put a Nap or two down," said Jos, with a superb air, flinging down a gold piece.

"Yes; ay nap after dinner," said the mask, archly. But Jos looking frightened, she continued, in her pretty French accent, "You do not play to win. No more do I. I play to forget, but I cannot. I cannot forget old times, Monsieur. Your little nephew is the image of his father; and you—you are not changed—but yes, you are. Every body changes every body forgets; nobody has ay heart."

"Good Ged, who is it?" asked Jos in a flutter.

"Can't you guess, Joseph Sedley?" said the little woman, in a sad voice, and undoing her mask, she looked at him. "You have forgotten me."

"Good Heavens! Mrs. Crawley!" gasped out Jos.

"Rebecca," said the other, putting her hand on his; but she followed the game still, all the time she was looking at him.

"I am stopping at the Elephant," she continued. "Ask for Madame de Raudon. I saw my dear Amelia to-day; how pretty she looked, and how happy! So do you! Everybody but me, who am wretched, Joseph Sedley." And she put her money over from the red to the black, as if by a chance movement of her hand, and while she was wiping her eyes with a pocket-handkerchief fringed with torn lace.

The red came up again, and she lost the whole of that stake. "Come away," she said. "Come with me a little—we are old friends, are we not, dear Mr. Sedley?"

And Mr. Kirsch having lost all his money by this time, followed his master out into the moonlight, where the illuminations were winking out, and the transparency over our mission was scarcely visible.

*Number 19/20* *July 1848*

## *Chapter LXIV.*

### A VAGABOND CHAPTER.

WE[1] must pass over a part of Mrs. Rebecca Crawley's biography with that lightness and delicacy which the world demands—the moral world, that has, perhaps, no particular objection to vice, but an insuperable repugnance to hearing vice called by its proper name. There are things we do and know perfectly well in Vanity Fair, though we never speak them: as the Ahrimanians[2] worship the devil, but don't mention him: and a polite public will no more bear to read an authentic description of vice than a truly-refined English or American female will permit the word breeches to be pronounced in her chaste hearing. And yet, Madam, both are walking the world before our faces every day, without much shocking us. If you were to blush every time they went by, what complexions you would have! It is only when their naughty names are called out that your modesty has any occasion to show alarm or sense of outrage, and it has been the wish of the present writer, all through this story, deferentially to submit to the fashion at present prevailing, and only to hint at the existence of wickedness in a light, easy, and agreeable manner, so that nobody's fine feelings may be offended. I defy any one to say that our Becky, who has certainly some vices, has not been presented to the public in a perfectly genteel and inoffensive manner. In describing this syren, singing and smiling, coaxing and cajoling, the author, with modest pride, asks his readers all round, has he once forgotten the laws of politeness, and showed the monster's hideous tail above water? No! Those who like may peep down under waves that are pretty transparent, and

1. Initial vignette of Becky as Napoleon gazing at England from the French coast. The pose was made famous by Benjamin Robert Haydon, who painted multiple versions of *Napoleon Musing at St. Helena* (1831– ).
2. Worshippers of Ahriman, angel of darkness, in Zoroastrian religion.

see it writhing and twirling, diabolically hideous and slimy, flapping amongst bones, or curling round corpses; but above the water-line, I ask, has not everything been proper, agreeable, and decorous, and has any the most squeamish immoralist in Vanity Fair a right to cry fie? When, however, the syren disappears and dives below, down among the dead men, the water of course grows turbid over her, and it is labour lost to look into it ever so curiously. They look pretty enough when they sit upon a rock, twanging their harps and combing their hair, and sing, and beckon to you to come and hold the looking-glass; but when they sink into their native element, depend on it those mermaids are about no good, and we had best not examine the fiendish marine cannibals, revelling and feasting on their wretched pickled victims. And so, when Becky is out of the way, be sure that she is not particularly well employed, and that the less that is said about her doings is in fact the better.

If we were to give a full account of her proceedings during a couple of years that followed after the Curzon Street catastrophe, there might be some reason for people to say this book was improper. The actions of very vain, heartless, pleasure-seeking people are very often improper (as are many of yours, my friend with the grave face and spotless reputation;—but that is merely by the way); and what are those of a woman without faith—or love—or character? And I am inclined to think that there was a period in Mrs. Becky's life, when she was seized, not by remorse, but by a kind of despair, and absolutely neglected her person, and did not even care for her reputation.

This *abattement*[3] and degradation did not take place all at once: it was brought about by degrees, after her calamity, and after many struggles to keep up—as a man who goes overboard hangs on to a spar whilst any hope is left, and then flings it away and goes down, when he finds that struggling is in vain.

She lingered about London whilst her husband was making preparations for his departure to his seat of government: and it is believed made more than one attempt to see her brother-in-law, Sir Pitt Crawley, and to work upon his feelings which she had almost enlisted in her favour. As Sir Pitt and Mr. Wenham were walking down to the House of Commons, the latter spied Mrs. Rawdon in a black veil, and lurking near the palace of the legislature. She sneaked away when her eyes met those of Wenham, and indeed never succeeded in her designs upon the Baronet.

Probably Lady Jane interposed. I have heard that she quite astonished her husband by the spirit which she exhibited in this quarrel, and her determination to disown Mrs. Becky. Of her own movement, she invited Rawdon to come and stop in Gaunt Street until his departure for Coventry Island, knowing that with him for a guard Mrs. Becky would not try to force her door: and she looked curiously at the superscriptions of all the letters which arrived for Sir Pitt, lest he and his sister-in-law should be corresponding. Not but that Rebecca could have written had she a mind: but she did not try to see or to

3. Despondency.

write to Pitt at his own house, and after one or two attempts consented to his demand that the correspondence regarding her conjugal differences should be carried on by lawyers only.

The fact was, that Pitt's mind had been poisoned against her. A short time after Lord Steyne's accident Wenham had been with the Baronet; and given him such a biography of Mrs. Becky as had astonished the member for Queen's Crawley. He knew everything regarding her: who her father was; in what year her mother danced at the Opera; what had been her previous history, and what her conduct during her married life:—as I have no doubt that the greater part of the story was false and dictated by interested malevolence, it shall not be repeated here. But Becky was left with a sad sad reputation in the esteem of a country gentleman and relative who had been once rather partial to her.

The revenues of the Governor of Coventry Island are not large. A part of them was set aside by his Excellency for the payment of certain outstanding debts and liabilities;[4] the charges incident to[5] his high situation required considerable expense; finally, it was found that he could not spare to his wife more than three hundred pounds a year, which he proposed to pay to her on an undertaking that she would never trouble him. Otherwise: scandal, separation, Doctors' Commons[6] would ensue. But it was Mr. Wenham's business, Lord Steyne's business, Rawdon's, everybody's—to get her out of the country, and hush up a most disagreeable affair.

She was probably so much occupied in arranging these affairs of business with her husband's lawyers, that she forgot to take any step whatever about her son, the little Rawdon, and did not even once propose to go and see him. That young gentleman was consigned to the entire guardianship of his aunt and uncle, the former of whom had always possessed a great share of the child's affection. His mamma wrote him a neat letter from Boulogne when she quitted England, in which she requested him to mind his book, and said she was going to take a Continental tour, during which she would have the pleasure of writing to him again. But she never did for a year afterwards, and not, indeed, until Sir Pitt's only boy, always sickly, died of hooping-cough and measles;—then Rawdon's mamma wrote the most affectionate composition to her darling son, who was made heir of Queen's Crawley by this accident, and drawn more closely than ever to the kind lady, whose tender heart had already adopted him. Rawdon Crawley, then grown a tall, fine lad, blushed when he got the letter. "Oh Aunt Jane, you are my mother!" he said; "and not—and not that one." But he wrote back a kind and respectful letter to Mrs. Rebecca, then living at a boarding-house at Florence.—But we are advancing matters.

Our darling Becky's first flight was not very far. She perched upon the French coast at Boulogne, that refuge of so much exiled English

4. At the end of chapter LV, we were told that no insurance office would insure Rawdon's life. First printing reads: certain debts and the insurance of his life;
5. Revised edition reads: on
6. Doctors of civil law, lawyers pleading cases in ecclesiastical courts through which divorce cases were handled.

innocence; and there lived in rather a genteel, widowed manner, with a *femme de chambre* and a couple of rooms, at an hotel. She dined at the *table d'hôte,* where people thought her very pleasant, and where she entertained her neighbours by stories of her brother, Sir Pitt, and her great London acquaintance; talking that easy, fashionable slipslop, which has so much effect upon certain folks of small breeding. She passed with many of them for a person of importance; she gave little tea-parties in her private room, and shared in the innocent amusements of the place,—in sea-bathing, and in jaunts in open carriages, in strolls on the sands, and in visits to the play. Mrs. Burjoice, the printer's lady, who was boarding with her family at the hotel for the summer, and to whom her Burjoice came of a Saturday and Sunday, voted her charming; until that little rogue of a Burjoice began to pay her too much attention. But there was nothing in the story, only that Becky was always affable, easy, and good-natured—and with men especially.

Numbers of people were going abroad as usual at the end of the season, and Becky had plenty of opportunities of finding out by the behaviour of her acquaintances of the great London world the opinion of "society" as regarded her conduct. One day it was Lady Partlet and her daughters whom Becky confronted as she was walking modestly on Boulogne pier, the cliffs of Albion shining in the distance across the deep blue sea. Lady Partlet marshalled all her daughters round her with a sweep of her parasol, and retreated from the pier darting savage glances at poor little Becky who stood alone there.

On another day the packet came in. It had been blowing fresh, and it always suited Becky's humour to see the droll woe-begone faces of the people as they emerged from the boat. Lady Slingstone happened to be on board this day. Her ladyship had been exceedingly ill in her carriage, and was greatly exhausted and scarcely fit to walk up the plank from the ship to the pier. But all her energies rallied the instant she saw Becky smiling roguishly under a pink bonnet: and giving her a glance of scorn, such as would have shrivelled up most women, she walked into the Custom House quite unsupported. Becky only laughed: but I don't think she liked it. She felt she was alone, quite alone; and the far-off shining cliffs of England were impassable to her.

The behaviour of the men had undergone too I don't know what change. Grinstone showed his teeth and laughed in her face with a familiarity that was not pleasant. Little Bob Suckling, who was cap in hand to her three months before, and would walk a mile in the rain to see for her carriage in the line at Gaunt House, was talking to Fitzoof of the Guards (Lord Heehaw's son) one day upon the jetty, as Becky took her walk there. Little Bobby nodded to her over his shoulder without moving his hat, and continued his conversation with the heir of Heehaw. Tom Raikes[7] tried to walk into her sitting-room at the inn with a cigar in his mouth; but she closed the door upon him and would have locked it only that his fingers were

7. A well-known dandy who spent 1833–41 on the Continent avoiding his financial obligations in England.

inside. She began to feel that she was very lonely indeed. "If *he'd* been here," she said, "those cowards would never have dared to insult me." She thought about "him" with great sadness, and perhaps longing—about his honest, stupid, constant kindness and fidelity: his never-ceasing obedience; his good humour; his bravery and courage. Very likely she cried, for she was particularly lively, and had put on a little extra rouge when she came down to dinner.

She rouged regularly now: and—and her maid got Cognac for her besides that which was charged in the hotel bill.

Perhaps the insults of the men were not, however, so intolerable to her as the sympathy of certain women. Mrs. Crackenbury and Mrs. Washington White passed through Boulogne on their way to Switzerland. (The party were protected by Colonel Horner,[8] young Beaumoris, and of course old Crackenbury, and Mrs. White's little girl.) *They* did not avoid her. They giggled, cackled, tattled, condoled, consoled, and patronised her until they drove her almost wild with rage. To be patronised by *them!* she thought, as they went away simpering after kissing her. And she heard Beaumoris's laugh ringing on the stair, and knew quite well how to interpret his hilarity.

It was after this visit that Becky, who had paid her weekly bills, Becky who had made herself agreeable to every body in the house, who smiled at the landlady, called the waiters "Monsieur," and paid the chambermaids in politeness and apologies, what far more than compensated for a little niggardliness in point of money (of which Becky never was free), that Becky, we say, received a notice to quit from the landlord, who had been told by some one that she was quite an unfit person to have at his hotel, where English ladies would not sit down with her. And she was forced to fly into lodgings, of which the dullness and solitude were most wearisome to her.

Still she held up, in spite of these rebuffs, and tried to make a character for herself, and conquer scandal. She went to church very regularly, and sang louder than anybody there. She took up the cause of the widows of the shipwrecked fishermen, and gave work and drawings for the Quashyboo Mission; she subscribed to the Assembly, and *wouldn't* waltz. In a word, she did everything that was respectable, and that is why we dwell upon this part of her career with more fondness than upon subsequent parts of her history, which are not so pleasant. She saw people avoiding her, and still laboriously smiled upon them; you never could suppose from her countenance what pangs of humiliation she might be enduring inwardly.

Her history was after all a mystery. Parties were divided about her. Some people, who took the trouble to busy themselves in the matter, said that she was the criminal; whilst others vowed that she was as innocent as a lamb, and that her odious husband was in fault. She won over a good many by bursting into tears about her boy, and exhibiting the most frantic grief when his name was mentioned, or she saw anybody like him. She gained good Mrs. Alderney's heart in that way, who was rather the Queen of British Boulogne, and gave

8. First printing reads: Hornby,

the most dinners and balls of all the residents there, by weeping when Master Alderney came from Doctor Swishtail's academy to pass his holidays with his mother. "He and her Rawdon were of the same age, and *so* like," Becky said, in a voice choking with agony; whereas there was five years' difference between the boys' ages, and no more likeness between them than between my respected reader and his humble servant. Wenham, when he was going abroad, on his way to Kissingen[9] to join Lord Steyne, enlightened Mrs. Alderney on this point, and told her how he was much more able to describe little Rawdon than his mamma, who notoriously hated him, and never saw him; how he was thirteen years old, while little Alderney was but nine; fair, while the other darling was dark,—in a word, caused the lady in question to repent of her good humour.

Whenever Becky made a little circle for herself with incredible toils and labour, somebody came and swept it down rudely, and she had all her work to begin over again. It was very hard: very hard: lonely, and disheartening.

There was Mrs. Newbright, who took her up for some time, attracted by the sweetness of her singing at church, and by her proper views upon serious subjects, concerning which in former days, at Queen's Crawley, Mrs. Becky had had a good deal of instruction.—Well, she not only took tracts, but she read them. She worked flannel petticoats for the Quashyboos—cotton night-caps for the Cocoanut Indians—painted handscreens for the conversion of the Pope and the Jews—sate under Mr. Rowls, on Wednesdays, Mr. Huggleton on Thursdays, attended two Sunday services at church, besides Mr. Bawler, the Darbyite,[1] in the evening, and all in vain. Mrs. Newbright had occasion to correspond with the Countess of Southdown about the Warmingpan Fund for the Feejee Islanders (for the management of which admirable charity both these ladies formed part of a female committee), and having mentioned her "sweet friend," Mrs. Rawdon Crawley, the Dowager Countess wrote back such a letter regarding Becky, with such particulars, hints, facts, falsehoods, and general comminations, that intimacy between Mrs. Newbright and Mrs. Crawley ceased forthwith: and all the serious world of Tours, where this misfortune took place, immediately parted company with the reprobate. Those who know the English Colonies abroad know that we carry with us our pride, pills, prejudices, Harvey-sauces, cayenne-peppers, and other Lares,[2] making a little Britain wherever we settle down.

From one colony to another Becky fled uneasily. From Boulogne to Dieppe, from Dieppe to Caen, from Caen to Tours—trying with all her might to be respectable, and alas! always found out some day or other, and pecked out of the cage by the real daws.[3]

Mrs. Hook Eagles took her up at one of these places:—a woman without a blemish in her character, and a house in Portman-square.

9. Spa town in Bavaria.
1. John Darby founded the Plymouth Brethren, a dissenting evangelical sect, in 1831.
2. Harvey-sauces: apple sauce. Lares: household gods.
3. Crows.

She was staying at the hotel at Dieppe, whither Becky fled, and they made each other's acquaintance first at sea, where they were swimming together, and subsequently at the *table d'hôte* of the hotel. Mrs. Eagles had heard,—who indeed had not?—some of the scandal of the Steyne affair; but after a conversation with Becky, she pronounced that Mrs. Crawley was an angel, her husband a ruffian, Lord Steyne an unprincipled wretch, as everybody knew, and the whole case against Mrs. Crawley, an infamous and wicked conspiracy of that rascal Wenham. "If you were a man of any spirit, Mr. Eagles, you would box the wretch's ears the next time you see him at the Club," she said to her husband. But Eagles was only a quiet old gentleman, husband to Mrs. Eagles, with a taste for geology, and not tall enough to reach anybody's ears.

The Eagles then patronised Mrs. Rawdon, took her to live with her at her own house at Paris, quarrelled with the ambassador's wife because she would not receive her *protégée,* and did all that lay in woman's power to keep Becky straight in the paths of virtue and good repute.

Becky was very respectable and orderly at first, but the life of humdrum virtue grew utterly tedious to her before long. It was the same routine every day, the same dullness and comfort, the same drive over the same stupid Bois de Boulogne, the same company of an evening, the same Blair's Sermon of a Sunday night—the same opera always being acted over and over again: Becky was dying of weariness, when, luckily for her, young Mr. Eagles came from Cambridge, and his mother, seeing the impression which her little friend made upon him, straightway gave Becky warning.

Then she tried keeping house with a female friend; then the double *ménage*[4] began to quarrel and get into debt. Then she determined upon a boarding-house existence, and lived for some time at that famous mansion kept by Madame de Saint Amour, in the Rue Royale, at Paris, where she began exercising her graces and fascinations upon the shabby dandies and fly-blown beauties who frequented her landlady's *salons.* Becky loved society, and, indeed, could no more exist without it than an opium-eater without his dram, and she was happy enough at the period of her boarding-house life. "The women here are as amusing as those in May-fair," she told an old London friend who met her—"only, their dresses are not quite so fresh. The men wear cleaned gloves, and are sad rogues, certainly, but they are not worse than Jack This, and Tom That. The mistress of the house is a little vulgar, but I don't think she is so vulgar as Lady ——" and here she named the name of a great leader of fashion that I would die rather than reveal. In fact, when you saw Madame de Saint Amour's rooms lighted up of a night, men with *plaques* and *cordons*[5] at the *écarté* tables, and the women at a little distance, you might fancy yourself for a while in good society, and that Madame was a real Countess. Many people did so fancy: and Becky was for a while one of the most dashing ladies of the Countess's *salons.*

4. Household.
5. Medals and ribbons.

But it is probable that her old creditors of 1815 found her out and caused her to leave Paris, for the poor little woman was forced to fly from the city rather suddenly; and went thence to Brussels.

How well she remembered the place! She grinned as she looked up at the little *entresol*[6] which she had occupied, and thought of the Bareacres family, bawling for horses and flight, as their carriage stood in the *porte-cochère*[7] of the hotel. She went to Waterloo and to Laeken, where George Osborne's monument much struck her. She made a little sketch of it. "That poor Cupid!" she said; "how dreadfully he was in love with me, and what a fool he was! I wonder whether little Emmy is alive. It was a good little creature: and that fat brother of her's. I have his funny fat picture still among my papers. They were kind simple people."

At Brussels Becky arrived, recommended by Madame de Saint Amour to her friend, Madame la Comtesse de Borodino, widow of Napoleon's General, the famous Count de Borodino, who was left with no resource by the deceased hero but that of a *table-d'hôte* and an *écarté* table. Second-rate dandies and *roués,* widow-ladies who always have a law-suit, and very simple English folks, who fancy they see "Continental society" at these houses, put down their money, or ate their meals, at Madame de Borodino's tables. At the *table-d'hôte* the gallant[8] young fellows treated the company round to champagne,[9] rode out with the women, or hired horses on country excursions, clubbed money[1] to take boxes at the play or the Opera, betted over the fair shoulders of the ladies at the *écarté* tables, and wrote home to their parents, in Devonshire, about their felicitous introduction to foreign society.

Here, as at Paris, Becky was a boarding-house queen: and ruled in select *pensions*. She never refused the champagne, or the bouquets, or the drives into the country, or the private boxes; but what she preferred was the *écarté* at night,—and she played audaciously. First she played only for a little, then for five-franc pieces, then for Napoleons, then for notes: then she would not be able to pay her month's *pension:* then she borrowed from the young gentlemen: then she got into cash again, and bullied Madame de Borodino, whom she had coaxed and wheedled before: then she was playing for ten sous at a time, and in a dire state of poverty: then her quarter's allowance would come in, and she would pay off Madame de Borodino's score: and would once more take the cards against Monsieur de Rossignol, or the Chevalier de Raff.[2]

When Becky left Brussels, the sad truth is, that she owed three months' *pension* to Madame de Borodino, of which fact, and of the gambling, and of the drinking, and of the going down on her knees to the Reverend Mr. Muff, Ministre Anglican, and borrowing money of him, and of her coaxing and flirting with Milor Noodle, son of Sir

6. Mezzanine.
7. Carriage gate.
8. Revised edition reads: tables. The gallant
9. Revised edition reads: champagne at the *table-d'-hôte,*
1. Pooled their money.
2. Rossignol: picklock. Raff: low-class, rubbish.

Noodle, pupil of the Rev. Mr. Muff, whom she used to take into her private room, and of whom she won large sums at *écarté*—of which fact, I say, and of a hundred of her other knaveries, the Countess de Borodino informs every English person who stops at her establishment, and announces that Madame Rawdon was no better than a *vipère*.[3]

So our little wanderer went about setting up her tent in various cities of Europe, as restless as Ulysses or Bampfylde Moore Carew.[4] Her taste for disrespectability grew more and more remarkable. She became a perfect Bohemian ere long, herding with people whom it would make your hair stand on end to meet.

There is no town of any mark in Europe but it has its little colony of English raffs—men whose names Mr. Hemp the officer reads out periodically at the Sheriffs' Court—young gentlemen of very good family often, only that the latter disowns them; frequenters of billiard-rooms and estaminets,[5] patrons of foreign races and gaming-tables. They people the debtors' prisons—they drink and swagger—they fight and brawl—they run away without paying—they have duels

3. Viper.
4. Ulysses' return home took ten years; Carew, "King of the Gypsies," published his *Life and Adventures* in 1788.
5. Cafés with liquor.

with French and German officers—they cheat Mr. Spooney at *écarté*—they get the money, and drive off to Baden in magnificent britzkas—they try their infallible martingale,[6] and lurk about the tables with empty pockets, shabby bullies, penniless bucks, until they can swindle a Jew banker with a sham bill of exchange,[7] or find another Mr. Spooney to rob. The alternations of splendour and misery which these people undergo are very queer to view. Their life must be one of great excitement. Becky—must it be owned?—took to this life, and took to it not unkindly. She went about from town to town among these Bohemians. The lucky Mrs. Rawdon was known at every play-table in Germany. She and Madame de Cruchecassée[8] kept house at Florence together. It is said she was ordered out of Munich; and my friend Mr. Frederic Pigeon avers that it was at her house at Lausanne that he was hocussed at supper and lost eight hundred pounds to Major Loder and the Honourable Mr. Deuceace.[9] We are bound, you see, to give some account of Becky's biography; but of this part, the less, perhaps, that is said the better.

They say, that when Mrs. Crawley was particularly down on her luck, she gave concerts and lessons in music here and there. There was a Madame de Raudon, who certainly had a *matinée musicale*[1] at Wildbad, accompanied by Herr Spoff, premier pianist to the Hospodar of Wallachia,[2] and my little friend Mr. Eaves, who knew every body, and had travelled everywhere, always used to declare that he was at Strasburg in the year 1830, when a certain Madame Rebecque made her appearance in the opera of the *Dame Blanche,*[3] giving occasion to a furious row in the theatre there. She was hissed off the stage by the audience, partly from her own incompetency, but chiefly from the ill-advised sympathy of some persons in the *parquet,*[4] (where the officers of the garrison had their admissions); and Eaves was certain that the unfortunate *débutante* in question was no other than Mrs. Rawdon Crawley.

She was, in fact, no better than a vagabond upon this earth. When she got her money she gambled; when she had gambled it she was put to shifts to live; who knows how or by what means she succeeded? It is said that she once was seen at St. Petersburgh, but was summarily dismissed from that capital by the police, so that there cannot be any possibility of truth in the report that she was a Russian spy at Töplitz[5] and Vienna afterwards. I have even been informed, that at Paris she discovered a relation of her own, no less a person than her maternal grandmother, who was not by any means a Montmorenci, but a hideous old box-opener at a theatre on the Boulevards. The meeting between them, of which other persons, as it is hinted elsewhere, seem

6. Doubling the bet after every loss so that one win will recoup all.
7. Promissory note.
8. The name means "broken pitcher" and connotes a twit.
9. The names Pigeon, Loder, and Deuceace suggest dupe, dice loader, and card shark.
1. Afternoon musical gathering.
2. Governor of Wallachia, now in Romania.
3. 1825 opera by François-Adrien Boïldieu.
4. Pit.
5. Spa town in Austria.

to have been acquainted, must have been a very affecting interview. The present historian can give no certain details regarding the event.

It happened at Rome once, that Mrs. de Rawdon's half-year's salary had just been paid into the principal banker's there, and, as every body who had a balance of above five hundred scudi[6] was invited to the balls which this prince of merchants gave during the winter, Becky had the honour of a card, and appeared at one of the Prince and Princess Polonia's splendid evening entertainments. The Princess was of the family of Pompili, lineally descended from the second king of Rome, and Egeria of the house of Olympus,[7] while the Prince's grandfather, Alessandro Polonia, sold wash-balls,[8] essences, tobacco, and pocket-handkerchiefs, ran errands for gentlemen, and lent money in a small way. All the great company in Rome thronged to his saloons—Princes, Dukes, Ambassadors, artists, fiddlers, monsignori, young bears with their leaders[9]—every rank and condition of man. His halls blazed with light and magnificence; were resplendent with gilt frames, (containing pictures) and dubious antiques; and the enormous gilt crown and arms of the princely owner, a gold mushroom on a crimson field (the colour of the pocket-handkerchiefs which he sold), and the silver fountain of the Pompili family shone all over the roof, doors, and panels of the house, and over the grand velvet baldaquins[1] prepared to receive Popes and Emperors.

So Becky, who had arrived in the diligence from Florence, and was lodged at an inn in a very modest way, got a card for Prince Polonia's entertainment, and her maid dressed her with unusual care, and she went to this fine ball leaning on the arm of Major Loder, with whom she happened to be travelling at the time; (the same man who shot Prince Ravioli at Naples the next year, and was caned by Sir John Buckskin for carrying four kings in his hat besides those which he used in playing at *écarté,*)—and this pair went into the rooms together, and Becky saw a number of old faces which she remembered in happier days, when she was not innocent, but not found out. Major Loder knew a great number of foreigners, keen-looking whiskered men with dirty striped ribbons in their button-holes, and a very small display of linen; but his own countrymen, it might be remarked, eschewed the Major. Becky, too, knew some ladies here and there—French widows, dubious Italian countesses, whose husbands had treated them ill—faugh—what shall we say, we who have moved among some of the finest company of Vanity Fair, of this refuse and sediment of rascals? If we play, let it be with clean cards, and not with this dirty pack. But every man who has formed one of the innumerable army of travellers has seen these marauding irregulars hanging on, like Nym and Pistol, to the main force; wearing the king's colours, and boasting of his commission, but pillaging for themselves, and occasionally gibbeted by the road-side.[2]

6. Italian coin worth about four shillings; i.e., a balance above one hundred pounds.
7. Pompilius Numa, legendary king of Rome, and Egeria, his goddess adviser and alleged wife.
8. Soap.
9. Young men on tour with their tutors.
1. Canopies.
2. Corporal Nym and Lieutenant Pistol, braggart pilfering associates of Falstaff in Shake-

Well, she was hanging on the arm of Major Loder, and they went through the rooms together, and drank a great quantity of champagne at the buffet, where the people, and especially the Major's irregular corps, struggled furiously for refreshments, of which when

the pair had had enough, they pushed on until they reached the Duchess's own pink velvet saloon, at the end of the suite of apartments (where the statue of the Venus is, and the great Venice looking-glasses, framed in silver,) and where the princely family were entertaining their most distinguished guests at a round table at supper. It was just such a little select banquet as that of which Becky recollected that she had partaken at Lord Steyne's—and there he sat at Polonia's table, and she saw him.

The scar cut by the diamond on his white, bald, shining forehead, made a burning red mark; his red whiskers were dyed of a purple hue, which made his pale face look still paler. He wore his collar and orders, his blue ribbon and garter. He was a greater prince than any there, though there was a reigning duke and a royal highness, with their princesses, and near his lordship[3] was seated the beautiful Countess of Belladonna, née de Glandier, whose husband (the Count Paolo della Belladonna) so well known for his brilliant entomological[4] collections, had been long absent on a mission to the Emperor of Morocco.

When Becky beheld that familiar and illustrious face, how vulgar

speare's *Henry V, The Merry Wives of Windsor,* and *Henry IV*, Parts 1 and 2. Nym was gibbeted (hanged).

3. First printing reads: and at his lordship's side
4. Insect, butterfly.

all of a sudden did Major Loder appear to her, and how that odious Captain Rook[5] did smell of tobacco! In one instant she reassumed[6] her fine-ladyship, and tried to look and feel as if she was in May Fair once more. "That woman looks stupid and ill-humoured," she thought; "I am sure she can't amuse him. No, he must be bored by her—he never was by me." A hundred such touching hopes, fears, and memories palpitated in her little heart, as she looked with her brightest eyes (the rouge which she wore up to her eyelids made them twinkle) towards the great nobleman. Of a Star and Garter night Lord Steyne used also to put on his grandest manner, and to look and speak like a great prince, as he was. Becky admired him smiling sumptuously, easy, lofty, and stately. Ah, *bon Dieu,* what a pleasant companion he was, what a brilliant wit, what a rich fund of talk, what a grand manner!—and she had exchanged this for Major Loder, reeking of cigars and brandy-and-water, and Captain Rook with his horse-jockey jokes and prize-ring slang, and their like. "I wonder whether he will know me," she thought. Lord Steyne was talking and laughing with a great and illustrious lady at his side, when he looked up and saw Becky.

She was all over in a flutter as their eyes met, and she put on the very best smile she could muster, and dropped him a little, timid, imploring curtsey. He stared aghast at her for a minute, as Macbeth might on beholding Banquo's sudden appearance at his ball-supper;[7] and remained looking at her with open mouth, when that horrid Major Loder pulled her away.

"Come away into the supper-room, Mrs. R.," was that gentleman's remark; "seeing these[8] nobs grubbing away has made me peckish too. Let's go and try the old governor's champagne." Becky thought the Major had had a great deal too much already.

The day after she went to walk on the Pincian Hill—the Hyde Park of the Roman idlers—possibly in hopes to have another sight of Lord Steyne. But she met another acquaintance there: it was Mr. Fiche,[9] his lordship's confidential man, who came up nodding to her rather familiarly, and putting a finger to his hat. "I knew that Madame was here," he said; "I followed her from her hotel. I have some advice to give Madame."

"From the Marquis of Steyne?" Becky asked, resuming as much of her dignity as she could muster, and not a little agitated by hope and expectation.

"No," said the valet; "it is from me. Rome is very unwholesome."

"Not at this season, Monsieur Fiche,—not till after Easter."

"I tell Madame it is unwholesome now. There is always malaria for some people. That cursed marsh wind kills many at all seasons. Look, Madame Crawley, you were always *bon enfant,* and I have an

5. The name denotes both a large crow or raven and a swindler.
6. Revised edition reads: resumed
7. Having had Banquo murdered, Macbeth blanched at the appearance of Banquo's ghost in Shakespeare's *Macbeth,* III.iv.
8. Revised edition reads: those
9. First printing reads "Fenouil," which means "fennel," a spice. The second printing changed the name to "Fiche," which was his name in chapter LI.

interest in you, *parole d'honneur.*[1] Be warned. Go away from Rome, I tell you—or you will be ill and die."

Becky laughed, though in rage and fury. "What! assassinate poor little me?" she said. "How romantic. Does my lord carry bravos for couriers, and stilettos in the fourgons?[2] Bah! I will stay, if but to plague him. I have those who will defend me whilst I am here."

It was Monsieur Fiche's turn to laugh now. "Defend you," he said, "and who? The Major, the Captain, any one of those gambling men whom Madame sees, would take her life for a hundred louis. We know things about Major Loder (he is no more a Major than I am my Lord the Marquis) which would send him to the galleys or worse. We know everything, and have friends everywhere. We know whom you saw at Paris, and what relations you found there. Yes, Madame may stare, but we do. How[3] was it that no minister on the Continent would receive Madame? She has offended somebody: who never forgives—whose rage redoubled when he saw you. He was like a madman last night when he came home. Madame de Belladonna made him a scene about you, and fired off in one of her furies."

"O, it was Madame de Belladonna, was it?" Becky said, relieved a little, for the information she had just got had scared her.

"No—she does not matter—she is always jealous. I tell you it was Monseigneur. You did wrong to show yourself to him. And if you stay here you will repent it. Mark my words. Go. Here is my lord's carriage"—and seizing Becky's arm, he rushed down an alley of the garden as Lord Steyne's barouche, blazing with heraldic devices, came whirling along the avenue, borne by the almost priceless horses, and bearing Madame de Belladonna lolling on the cushions, dark, sulky, and blooming, a King Charles[4] in her lap, a white parasol swaying over her head, and old Steyne stretched at her side with a livid face and ghastly eyes. Hate, or anger, or desire, caused them to brighten now and then still; but ordinarily, they gave no light, and seemed tired of looking out on a world of which almost all the pleasure and all the best beauty had palled upon the worn-out wicked old man.

"Monseigneur has never recovered the shock of that night, never," Monsieur Fiche whispered to Mrs. Crawley as the carriage flashed by, and she peeped out at it from behind the shrubs that hid her. "That was a consolation at any rate," Becky thought.

Whether my lord really had murderous intentions towards Mrs. Becky, as Monsieur Fiche said—(since Monseigneur's death he has returned to his native country, where he lives much respected, and has purchased from his Prince the title of Baron Ficci),[5]—and the factotum objected to have to do with assassination; or whether he simply had a commission to frighten Mrs. Crawley out of a city where his lordship proposed to pass the winter, and the sight of her would be eminently disagreeable to the great nobleman, is a point which

1. *Bon enfant*: good kid. *Parole d'honneur*: word of honor.
2. Baggage wagons.
3. Revised edition reads: And how
4. Spaniel.
5. First printing reads: Finelli

has never been ascertained: but the threat had its effect upon the little woman, and she sought no more to intrude herself upon the presence of her old patron.

Everybody knows the melancholy end of that nobleman, which befel at Naples two months after the French Revolution of 1830:[6] when the Most Honourable George Gustavus, Marquis of Steyne, Earl of Gaunt and of Gaunt Castle, in the Peerage of Ireland, Viscount Hellborough, Baron Pitchley and Grillsby, a Knight of the Most Noble Order of the Garter, of the Golden Fleece of Spain, of the Russian Order of Saint Nicholas of the First Class, of the Turkish Order of the Crescent, First Lord of the Powder Closet and Groom of the Back Stairs, Colonel of the Gaunt or Regent's Own Regiment of Militia, a Trustee of the British Museum, an elder Brother of the Trinity House, a Governor of the Whitefriars, and D.C.L.,[7]—died, after a series of fits, brought on, as the papers said, by the shock occasioned to his lordship's sensibilities by the downfall of the ancient French monarchy.

An eloquent catalogue appeared in a weekly print, describing his virtues, his magnificence, his talents, and his good actions. His sensibility, his attachment to the illustrious House of Bourbon, with which he claimed an alliance, were such that he could not survive the misfortunes of his august kinsmen. His body was buried at Naples, and his heart—that heart which always beat with every generous and noble emotion—was brought back to Castle Gaunt in a silver urn. "In him," Mr. Wagg said, "the poor and the Fine Arts have lost a beneficent patron, society one of its most brilliant ornaments, and England one of her loftiest patriots and statesmen," &c., &c.

His will was a good deal disputed, and an attempt was made to force from Madame de Belladonna the celebrated jewel called the "Jew's-eye" diamond, which his lordship always wore on his forefinger, and which it was said that she removed from it after his lamented demise. But his confidential friend and attendant, Monsieur Fiche, proved that the ring had been presented to the said Madame de Belladonna two days before the marquis's death; as were the bank notes, jewels, Neapolitan and French bonds, &c., found in his lordship's secretaire, and claimed by his heirs, from that injured woman.

6. Charles X, last of the Bourbon kings, abdicated in 1830, to be replaced by Louis-Philippe (Philippe Égalité), the citizen king.

7. Trinity House: society devoted to the promotion of safety at sea. Whitefriars: school modeled on Charterhouse. D.C.L.: doctor of civil law. The first printing reads "Grey Friars", the second printing, "White Friars"; but previously in the book, it has always been referred to as "Whitefriars".

*Chapter LXV.*

FULL OF BUSINESS AND PLEASURE.

THE[1] day after the meeting at the play-table, Jos had himself arrayed with unusual care and splendour, and without thinking it necessary to say a word to any member of his family regarding the occurrences of the previous night, or asking for their company in his walk, he sallied forth at an early hour, and was presently seen making inquiries at the door of the Elephant Hotel. In consequence of the *fêtes* the house was full of company, the tables in the street were already surrounded by persons smoking and drinking the national small-beer, the public rooms were in a cloud of smoke, and Mr. Jos having, in his pompous way, and with his clumsy German, made inquiries for the person of whom he was in search, was directed to the very top of the house, above the first-floor rooms where some travelling pedlars had lived, and were exhibiting their jewellery and brocades; above the second-floor apartments occupied by the *état major*[2] of the gambling firm; above the third-floor rooms, tenanted by the band of renowned Bohemian vaulters and tumblers; and so on to the little cabins of the roof, where, among students, bag-men, small tradesmen, and country-folks, come in for the festival, Becky had found a little nest;—as dirty a little refuge as ever beauty lay hid in.

Becky liked the life. She was at home with everybody in the place, pedlars, punters, tumblers, students and all. She was of a wild, roving nature, inherited from father and mother, who were both Bohemians, by taste and circumstance; if a lord was not by, she would talk to his courier with the greatest pleasure; the din, the stir, the drink, the smoke, the tattle of the Hebrew pedlars, the solemn braggart ways of the poor tumblers; the *sournois*[3] talk of the gambling-table officials; the songs and swagger of the students and the general buzz and hum of the place had pleased and tickled the little woman, even when her luck was down and she had not wherewithal to pay her bill. How pleasant was all this bustle to her now that her purse was full of the money, which little Georgy[4] had won for her the night before.

1. Initial vignette shows Jos as Falstaff bewitched by Becky as Doll Tearsheet.
2. Headquarters.
3. Sly.
4. MS reads: now, that she had plenty of money in her purse which <she> ↑little Georgy↓

Jos[5] came creaking and puffing up the final[6] stairs and was speechless when he got to the landing and began to wipe his face and then to look for No. 92 the room where he was directed to seek for the person he wanted—the door of the opposite chamber, No. 90, was open and a student in jack-boots and a dirty schlafrock[7] was lying on the bed smoking a long pipe whilst another student in long yellow hair and a braided coat exceeding

smart and dirty too was actually on his knees at No. 92, bawling through the keyholes supplications to the person within.

"Go away," said a well known voice, which made Jos thrill, "I expect somebody; I expect my grandpapa. He mustn't see you there."

"Angel Engländerinn!" bellowed the kneeling[8] student with the whitey-brown[9] ringlets and the large finger-ring, "do take compassion upon us. Make an appointment. Dine with me and Fritz[1] at

5. All printed editions have "As Jos", which resulted from the original compositor's failure to note that "As" was canceled in the manuscript.
6. The word "final" is interlined in the MS.
7. Nightshirt.
8. The word "kneeling" is interlined in the MS.
9. MS reads: <yellow> ↑whitey-brown↓
1. First printing reads: Fitz

the Inn in the Park. We will have roast pheasants and porter, plum-pudding and French wine, we shall die if you don't."

"That we will," said the young nobleman on the bed—and this colloquy Jos overheard, though he did not comprehend it for the reason that he had never studied the language in which it was carried on.

*"Newmero kattervang dooze, si vous plait,"*[2] Jos said in his grandest manner, when he was able to speak.

*"Quater fang tooce!"*[3] said the student, starting up, and he bounced into his own room, where he locked the door, and where Jos heard him laughing with his comrade on the bed.

The gentleman from Bengal was standing disconcerted by this incident when the door of the 92 opened of itself, and Becky's little head peeped out full of archness and mischief. She lighted on Jos. "It's you," she said, coming out. "How I have been waiting for you! Stop! not yet—in one minute you shall come in." In that instant she put a rouge-pot, a brandy bottle, and a plate of broken meat into the bed, gave one smooth to her hair, and finally let in her visitor.

She had, by way of morning robe, a pink domino,[4] a trifle faded and soiled, and marked here and there with pomatum; but her arms shone out from the loose sleeves of the dress very white and fair, and it was tied round her little waist, so as not ill to set off the trim little figure of the wearer. She led Jos by the hand into her garret. "Come in," she said. "Come, and talk to me. Sit yonder on the chair;" and she gave the civilian's hand a little squeeze, and laughingly placed him upon it. As for herself, she placed herself on the bed—not on the bottle and plate, you may be sure—on which Jos might have reposed, had he chosen that seat; and so there she sate and talked with her old admirer.

"How little years have changed you," she said, with a look of tender interest. "I should have known you anywhere; what a comfort it is amongst strangers to see once more the frank honest face of an old friend!"

The frank honest face, to tell the truth, at this moment bore any expression but one of openness and honesty: it was, on the contrary, much perturbed and puzzled in look. Jos was surveying the queer little apartment in which he found his old flame. One of her gowns hung over the bed, another depending from a hook of the door: her bonnet obscured half the looking-glass, on which, too, lay the prettiest little pair of bronze boots; a French novel was on the table by the bed side, with a candle, not of wax. Becky had[5] thought of popping that into the bed too, but she only put in the little paper night-cap, with which she had put the candle out on going to sleep.

"I should have known you anywhere," she continued; "a woman never forgets some things. And you were the first man I ever—I ever saw."

2. Anglicized French: Number 92, if you please.
3. Heavily germanized French: 92.
4. Cloak with a hood, partly concealing the face.
5. Revised edition omits: had

"Was I, really?" said Jos. "God bless my soul, you—you don't say so."

"When I came with your sister from Chiswick, I was scarcely more than a child," Becky said. "How is that dear love? Oh, her husband was a sad wicked man, and of course, it was of me that the poor dear was jealous. As if I cared about him, heigho: when there was somebody—but no—don't let us talk of old times;" and she passed her handkerchief with the tattered lace across her eyelids.

"Is not this a strange place," she continued, "for a woman, who has lived in a very different world too, to be found in? I have had so many griefs and wrongs, Joseph Sedley, I have been made to suffer so cruelly, that I am almost made mad sometimes. I can't stay still in any place, but wander about always restless and unhappy. All my friends have been false to me—all. There is no such thing as an honest man in the world. I was the truest wife that ever lived, though I married my husband out of pique, because somebody else—but never mind that. I was true, and he trampled upon me, and deserted me. I was the fondest mother. I had but one child, one darling, one hope, one joy, which I held to my heart with a mother's affection, which was my life, my prayer, my—my blessing; and they—they tore it from me—tore it from me;" and she put her hand to her heart with a passionate gesture of despair, burying her face for a moment on the bed.

The brandy-bottle inside clinked up against the plate which held the cold sausage. Both were moved, no doubt, by the exhibition of so much grief. Max and Fritz were at the door listening with wonder to Mrs. Becky's sobs and cries. Jos, too, was a good deal frightened and affected at seeing his old flame in this condition. And she began, forthwith, to tell her story—a tale so neat, simple, and artless, that it was quite evident from hearing her, that if ever there was a white-robed angel escaped from heaven to be subject to the infernal machinations and villany of fiends here below, that spotless being—that miserable unsullied martyr—was present on the bed before Jos—on the bed, sitting on the brandy-bottle.

They had a very long, amicable, and confidential talk there; in the course of which, Jos Sedley was somehow made aware (but in a manner that did not in the least scare or offend him) that Becky's heart had first learned to beat at his enchanting presence: that George Osborne had certainly paid an unjustifiable court to *her,* which might account for Amelia's jealousy, and their little rupture; but that Becky never gave the least encouragement to the unfortunate officer, and that she had never ceased to think about Jos from the very first day she had seen him, though, of course, her duties as a married woman were paramount—duties which she had always preserved, and would, to her dying day, or until the proverbially bad climate in which Colonel Crawley was living, should release her from a yoke which his cruelty had rendered odious to her.

Jos went away, convinced that she was the most virtuous, as she was one of the most fascinating of women, and revolving in his mind all sorts of benevolent schemes for her welfare. Her persecutions ought to be ended: she ought to return to the society of which she was an ornament. He would see what ought to be done. She must quit that place, and take a quiet lodging. Amelia must come and see her, and befriend her. He would go and settle about it, and consult with the Major. She wept tears of heartfelt gratitude as she parted from him, and pressed his hand as the gallant stout gentleman stooped down to kiss her's.

So Becky bowed Jos out of her little garret with as much grace as if it was a palace of which she did the honours; and that heavy gentleman having disappeared down the stairs, Max and Fritz came out of their hole, pipe in mouth, and she amused herself by mimicking Jos to them as she munched her cold bread and sausage and took draughts of her favourite brandy-and-water.

Jos walked over to Dobbin's lodgings with great solemnity, and there imparted to him the affecting history with which he had just been made acquainted, without, however, mentioning the play-business of the night before. And the two gentlemen were laying their heads together, and consulting as to the best means of being useful to Mrs. Becky, while she was finishing her interrupted *déjeûner à la fourchette*.[6]

How was it that she had come to that little town? How was it that she had no friends and was wandering about alone? Little boys at school are taught in their earliest Latin book, that the path of Avernus is very easy of descent.[7] Let us skip over the interval in the history of her downward progress. She was not worse now than she had been in the days of her prosperity, only a little down on her luck.

As for Mrs. Amelia, she was a woman of such a soft and foolish disposition, that when she heard of anybody unhappy, her heart straightway melted towards the sufferer; and as she had never thought or done anything mortally guilty herself, she had not that abhorrence for wickedness which distinguishes moralists much more knowing. If she spoiled everybody who came near her with kindness and compliments,—if she begged pardon of all her servants for troubling them to answer the bell,—if she apologised to a shop-boy who showed her a piece of silk, or made a curtsey to a street-sweeper, with a complimentary remark upon the elegant state of his crossing—and she was almost capable of every one of these follies—the notion that an old acquaintance was miserable was sure to soften her heart; nor would she hear of anybody's being deservedly unhappy. A world under such legislation as her's, would not be a very orderly place of abode; but there are not many women, at least not of the rulers, who are of her sort. This lady, I believe, would have abolished all gaols, punishments, handcuffs, whippings, poverty, sickness, hunger, in the world; and was such a mean-spirited creature, that—we are obliged to confess it—she could even forget a mortal injury.

When the Major heard from Jos of the sentimental adventure which had just befallen the latter, he was not, it must be confessed,[8] nearly as much interested as the gentleman from Bengal. On the contrary, his excitement was quite the reverse from a pleasurable one;

6. Literally, breakfast with a fork; i.e., not a continental breakfast, but one with meat.
7. "The path to the underworld is easy . . . but to withdraw one's steps and make a way out to the upper air, that is the task, that is the labor." Vergil, *The Aeneid* VI.126–29.
8. Revised edition reads: owned,

he made use of a brief but improper expression regarding a poor woman in distress, saying, in fact,—"the little minx, has she come to light again?" He never had had the slightest liking for her, but, on the contrary, had[9] heartily mistrusted her from the very first moment when her green eyes had looked at, and turned away from, his own.

"That little devil brings mischief wherever she goes," the Major said, disrespectfully. "Who knows what sort of life she has been leading; and what business has she here abroad and alone? Don't tell me about persecutors and enemies; an honest woman always has friends, and never is separated from her family. Why has she left her husband? He may have been disreputable and wicked, as you say. He always was. I remember the confounded blackleg, and the way in which he used to cheat and hoodwink poor George. Wasn't there a scandal about their separation? I think I heard something," cried out Major Dobbin, who did not care much about gossip; and whom Jos tried in vain to convince that Mrs. Becky was in all respects a most injured and virtuous female.

"Well, well; let's ask Mrs. George," said that arch-diplomatist of a Major. "Only let us go and consult *her*. I suppose you will allow that *she* is a good judge at any rate, and knows what is right in such matters."

"Hm! Emmy is very well," said Jos, who did not happen to be in love with his sister.

"Very well? by Gad, Sir, she's the finest lady I ever met in my life," bounced out the Major. "I say at once, let us go and ask her if this woman ought to be visited or not—I will be content with her verdict." Now this odious, artful rogue of a Major was thinking in his own mind that he was sure of his case. Emmy, he remembered, was at one time cruelly and deservedly jealous of Rebecca, never mentioned her name but with a shrinking and terror—a jealous woman never forgives, thought Dobbin: and so the pair went across the street to Mrs. George's house, where she was contentedly warbling at a music-lesson with Madame Strumpff.

When that lady took her leave, Jos opened the business with his usual pomp of words. "Amelia, my dear," said he, "I have just had the most extraordinary—yes—God bless my soul! the most extraordinary adventure—an old friend—yes, a most interesting old friend of yours, and I may say in old times, has just arrived here, and I should like you to see her."

"Her!" said Amelia, "who is it? Major Dobbin, if you please not to break my scissars." The Major was twirling them round by the little chain from which they sometimes hung to their lady's waist, and was thereby endangering his own eye.

"It is a woman whom I dislike very much," said the Major, doggedly; "and whom you have no cause to love."

"It is Rebecca, I'm sure it is Rebecca," Amelia said blushing, and being very much agitated.

"You are right; you always are," Dobbin answered. Brussels, Waterloo, old, old times, griefs, pangs, remembrances, rushed back into

9. Revised edition reads: her; but had

Amelia's gentle heart, and caused a cruel agitation there.

"Don't let me see her," Emmy continued. "I couldn't see her."

"I told you so," Dobbin said to Jos.

"She is very unhappy, and—and that sort of thing," Jos urged. "She is very poor and unprotected: and has been ill—exceedingly ill—and that scoundrel of a husband has deserted her."

"Ah!" said Amelia.

"She hasn't a friend in the world," Jos went on, not undexterously; "and she said she thought she might trust in you. She's so miserable, Emmy. She has been almost mad with grief. Her story quite affected me:—'pon my word and honour, it did—never was such a cruel persecution borne so angelically, I may say. Her family has been most cruel to her."

"Poor creature!" Amelia said.

"And if she can get no friend, she says she thinks she'll die," Jos proceeded, in a low tremulous voice.—"God bless my soul! do you know that she tried to kill herself? She carries laudanum with her—I saw the bottle in her room—such a miserable little room—at a third-rate house, the Elephant, up in the roof at the top of all. I went there."

This did not seem to affect Emmy. She even smiled a little. Perhaps she figured Jos to herself panting up the stair.

"She's beside herself with grief," he resumed. "The agonies that woman has endured are quite frightful to hear of. She had a little boy, of the same age as Georgy."

"Yes, yes, I think I remember," Emmy remarked. "Well?"

"The most beautiful child ever seen," Jos said, who was very fat, and easily moved, and had been touched by the story Becky told; "a perfect angel, who adored his mother. The ruffians tore him shrieking out of her arms, and have never allowed him to see her."

"Dear Joseph," Emmy cried out, starting up at once, "let us go and see her this minute." And she ran into her adjoining bed-chamber, tied on her bonnet in a flutter, came out with her shawl on her arm, and ordered Dobbin to follow.

He went and put her shawl—it was a white Cashmere, consigned to her by the Major himself from India—over her shoulders. He saw there was nothing for it but to obey; and she put her hand into his arm, and they went away.

"It is number 92, up four pair of stairs," Jos said, perhaps not very willing to ascend the steps again; but he placed himself in the window of his drawing-room, which commands the place on which the Elephant stands, and saw the pair marching through the market.

It was as well that Becky saw them too from her garret; for she and the two students were chattering and laughing there; they had been joking about the appearance of Becky's grandpapa—whose arrival and departure they had witnessed—but she had time to dismiss them, and have her little room clear before the landlord of the Elephant, who knew that Mrs. Osborne was a great favourite at the Serene Court, and respected her accordingly, led the way up the stairs to the roof-story, encouraging Miladi and the Herr Major as they achieved the ascent.

"Gracious lady, gracious lady!" said the landlord, knocking at Becky's door; he had called her Madame the day before, and was by no means courteous to her.

"Who is it?" Becky said, putting out her head, and she gave a little scream. There stood Emmy in a tremble, and Dobbin, the tall Major, with his cane.

He stood still watching, and very much interested at the scene; but Emmy sprang forward with open arms towards Rebecca, and forgave her at that moment, and embraced her and kissed her with all her heart. Ah, poor wretch, when was your lip pressed before by such pure kisses?

## *Chapter LXVI.*

### AMANTIUM IRÆ.[1]

RANKNESS and kindness like[2] Amelia's were likely to touch even such a hardened little reprobate as Becky. She returned Emmy's caresses and kind speeches with something very like gratitude, and an emotion that,[3] if it was not lasting, for a moment was almost genuine. That was a lucky stroke of her's about the child "torn from her arms shrieking." It was by that harrowing misfortune that Becky had won her friend back, and it was one of the very first points, we may be certain, upon which our poor simple little Emmy began to talk to her new found acquaintance.

"And so they took your darling child from you," our simpleton cried out. "Oh, Rebecca, my poor dear suffering friend, I know what it is to lose a boy, and to feel for those who have lost one. But please Heaven your's will be restored to you, as a merciful, merciful Providence has brought me back mine."

"The child, my child? Oh, yes, my agonies were frightful," Becky owned, not perhaps without a twinge of conscience. It jarred upon

1. "The lover's quarrel [is the renewal of love]." Terence, *Andria*.
2. First printing reads: such as
3. Revised edition reads: which,

her, to be obliged to commence instantly to tell lies in reply to so much confidence and simplicity. But that is the misfortune of beginning with this kind of forgery. When one fib becomes due as it were, you must forge another to take up the old acceptance, and so the stock of your lies in circulation inevitably multiplies, and the danger of detection increases every day.

"My agonies," Becky continued, "were terrible (I hope she won't sit down on the bottle) when they took him away from me; I thought I should die; but I fortunately had a brain fever, during which my doctor gave me up, and—and I recovered, and—and here I am poor and friendless."

"How old is he?" Emmy asked.

"Eleven," said Becky.

"Eleven!" cried the other. "Why, he was born the same year with Georgy, who is—"

"I know, I know," Becky cried out, who had in fact quite forgotten all about little Rawdon's age. "Grief has made me forget so many things, dearest Amelia. I am very much changed: half wild sometimes. He was eleven when they took him away from me. Bless his sweet face; I have never seen it again."

"Was he fair or dark?" went on that absurd little Emmy. "Show me his hair."

Becky almost laughed at her simplicity. "Not to-day, love,—some other time, when my trunks arrive from Leipsic, whence I came to this place,—and a little drawing of him, which I made in happy days."

"Poor Becky, poor Becky!" said Emmy. "How thankful, how thankful I ought to be!" (though I doubt whether that practice of piety inculcated upon us by our womankind in early youth, namely to be thankful because we are better off than somebody else, be a very rational religious exercise;) and then she began to think as usual, how her son was the handsomest, the best, and the cleverest boy in the whole world.

"You will see my Georgy," was the best thing Emmy could think of to console Becky. If anything could make her comfortable that would.

And so the two women continued talking for an hour or more, during which Becky had the opportunity of giving her new friend a full and complete version of her private history. She showed how her marriage with Rawdon Crawley had always been viewed by the family with feelings of the utmost hostility; how her sister-in-law (an artful woman) had poisoned her husband's mind against her; how he had formed odious connexions, which had estranged his affections from her; how she had borne everything—poverty, neglect, coldness from the being whom she most loved—and all for the sake of her child; how, finally, and by the most flagrant outrage, she had been driven into demanding a separation from her husband, when the wretch did not scruple to ask that she should sacrifice her own fair fame so that he might procure advancement through the means of a very great and powerful but unprincipled man—the Marquis of Steyne, indeed. The atrocious monster!

This part of her eventful history Becky gave with the utmost feminine delicacy, and the most indignant virtue. Forced to fly her husband's roof by this insult, the coward had pursued his revenge, by taking her child from her. And thus Becky said she was a wanderer, poor, unprotected, friendless, and wretched.

Emmy received this story, which was told at some length, as those persons who are acquainted with her character may imagine that she would. She quivered with indignation at the account of the conduct of the miserable Rawdon and the unprincipled Steyne. Her eyes made notes of admiration for every one of the sentences in which Becky described the persecutions of her aristocratic relatives, and the falling away of her husband. (Becky did not abuse him. She spoke rather in sorrow than in anger. She had loved him only too fondly: and was he not the father of her boy?) And as for the separation-scene from the child, while Becky was reciting it, Emmy retired altogether behind her pocket handkerchief, so that the consummate little tragedian must have been charmed to see the effect which her performance produced on her audience.

Whilst the ladies were carrying on their conversation, Amelia's constant escort, the Major, who, of course, did not wish to interrupt their conference, and finding[4] himself rather tired of creaking about the narrow stair passage of which the roof brushed the nap from his hat, descended to the ground-floor of the house and into the great room common to all the frequenters of the Elephant, out of which the stair led. This apartment is always in a fume of smoke, and liberally sprinkled with beer. On a dirty table stand scores of corresponding brass-candlesticks with tallow candles for the lodgers, whose keys hang up in rows over the candles. Emmy had passed blushing through the room anon, where all sorts of people were collected; Tyrolese glove-sellers and Danubian linen-merchants, with their packs; students recruiting themselves with butterbrods and meat; idlers, playing cards or dominoes on the sloppy, beery tables; tumblers refreshing during the cessation of their performances;—in a word, all the *fumum* and *strepitus* of a German inn in fair time.[5] The waiter brought the Major a mug of beer, as a matter of course; and he took out a cigar, and amused himself with that pernicious vegetable and a newspaper until his charge should come down to claim him.

Max and Fritz came presently down stairs, their caps on one side, their spurs jingling, their pipes splendid with coats-of-arms and full-blown tassels; and they hung up the key of No. 90 on the board, and called for the ration of butterbrod and beer. The pair sate down by the Major, and fell into a conversation of which he could not help hearing somewhat. It was mainly about "Fuchs" and "Philister,"[6] and duels and drinking-bouts at the neighbouring University of Schoppenhausen, from which renowned seat of learning they had just come in the Eilwagen,[7] with Becky, as it appeared, by their side, and in order to be present at the bridal fêtes at Pumpernickel.

4. Revised edition reads: found
5. Allusion to "The smoke [*fumum*] and riches and din [*strepitus*] of Rome." Horace, *Odes*.
6. Literally, fox and philistine, but referring to gownsmen and townsmen.
7. Express coach.

"The little Engländerinn seems to be *en bays de gonnoissance,*"[8] said Max, who knew the French language, to Fritz, his comrade. "After the fat grandfather went away, there came a pretty little compatriot. I heard them chattering and whimpering together in the little woman's chamber."

"We must take the tickets for her concert," Fritz said. "Hast thou any money, Max?"

"Bah," said the other, "the concert is a concert *in nubibus.*[9] Hans said that she advertised one at Leipsic: and the Burschen[1] took many tickets. But she went off without singing. She said in the coach yesterday that her pianist had fallen ill at Dresden. She cannot sing, it is my belief: her voice is as cracked as thine, O thou beer-soaking Renowner!"

"It is cracked; *I* heard her trying out of her window a schrecklich English ballad, called 'De Rose upon de Balgony.'"

"Saufen und singen go not together,"[2] observed Fritz with the red nose, who evidently preferred the former amusement. "No, thou shalt take none of her tickets. She won money at the *trente* and *quarante* last night. I saw her: she made a little English boy play for her.

We will spend thy money there or at the theatre, or we will treat her to French wine or Cognac in the Aurelius Garden, but the tickets we will not buy. What sayest thou? Yet, another mug of beer?" and one and another successively having buried their blond whiskers in the

8. Germanized French: among friends.
9. In the clouds, i.e., imaginary.
1. Fellows.
2. Schrecklich: terrible. "The Rose upon the Balcony": see chapter LI. "Saufen und singen": boozing and singing.

mawkish draught, curled them and swaggered off into the fair.

The Major, who had seen the key of number 90 put up on its hook, and had heard the conversation of the two young university bloods, was not at a loss to understand that their talk related to Becky. "The little devil is at her old tricks," he thought, and he smiled as he recalled old days, when he had witnessed the desperate flirtation with Jos, and the ludicrous end of that adventure. He and George had often laughed over it subsequently, and until a few weeks after George's marriage, when he also was caught in the little Circe's toils, and had an understanding with her which his comrade certainly suspected, but preferred to ignore.[3] William was too much hurt or ashamed to ask to fathom that disgraceful mystery, although once, and evidently with remorse on his mind, George had alluded to it. It was on the morning of Waterloo as the young men stood together in front of their line, surveying the black masses of Frenchmen who crowned the opposite heights, and as the rain was coming down, "I have been mixing in a foolish intrigue with a woman," George said. "I am glad we were marched away. If I drop, I hope Emmy will never know of that business. I wish to God it had never been begun!" And William was pleased to think, and had more than once soothed poor George's widow with the narrative, that Osborne, after quitting his wife, and after the action of Quatre Bras, on the first day, spoke gravely and affectionately to his comrade of his father and his wife. On these facts, too, William had insisted very strongly in his conversations with the elder Osborne: and had thus been the means of reconciling the old gentleman to his son's memory, just at the close of the elder man's life.

"And so this devil is still going on with her intrigues," thought William. "I wish she were a hundred miles from here. She brings mischief wherever she goes." And he was pursuing these forebodings and this uncomfortable train of thought, with his head between his hands, and the "Pumpernickel Gazette" of last week unread under his nose, when somebody tapped his shoulder with a parasol, and he looked up and saw Mrs. Amelia.

This woman had a way of tyrannising over Major Dobbin (for the weakest of all people will domineer over somebody), and she ordered him about, and patted him, and made him fetch and carry just as if he was a great Newfoundland dog. He liked, so to speak, to jump into the water if she said "High, Dobbin!" and to trot behind her with her reticule in his mouth. This history has been written to very little purpose if the reader has not perceived that the Major was a spooney.

"Why did you not wait for me, Sir, to escort me downstairs?" she said, giving a little toss of her head, and a most sarcastic curtsey.

"I couldn't stand up in the passage," he answered, with a comical deprecatory look; and, delighted to give her his arm, and to take her out of the horrid smoky place, he would have walked off without even so much as remembering the waiter, had not the young fellow

3. Circe, in *The Odyssey,* turned Ulysses' men into pigs. First printing reads: when he seemed to be caught in the little Circe's toils too, and had an understanding with her which his comrade might have suspected, but preferred to ignore.

run after him and stopped him on the threshold of the Elephant to make him pay for the beer which he had not consumed. Emmy laughed: she called him a naughty man, who wanted to run away in debt; and, in fact, made some jokes suitable to the occasion and the small-beer. She was in high spirits and good humour, and tripped across the market-place very briskly. She wanted to see Jos that instant. The Major laughed at the impetuous affection Mrs. Amelia exhibited; for, in truth, it was not very often that she wanted her brother "that instant."

They found the Civilian in his saloon on the first floor; he had been pacing the room, and biting his nails, and looking over the market-place towards the Elephant a hundred times at least during the past hour, whilst Emmy was closeted with her friend in the garret, and the Major was beating the tattoo on the sloppy tables of the public room below, and he was, on his side too, very anxious to see Mrs. Osborne.

"Well?" said he.

"The poor dear creature, how she has suffered!" Emmy said.

"God bless my soul, yes," Jos said, wagging his head, so that his cheeks quivered like jellies.

"She may have Payne's room; who can go up stairs," Emmy continued. Payne was a staid English maid and personal attendant upon Mrs. Osborne, to whom the courier, as in duty bound, paid court, and whom Georgy used to "lark" dreadfully with accounts of German robbers and ghosts. She passed her time chiefly in grumbling, in ordering about her mistress, and in stating her intention to return the next morning to her native village of Clapham. "She may have Payne's room," Emmy said.

"Why, you don't mean to say you are going to have that woman into the *house?*" bounced out the Major, jumping up.

"Of course we are," said Amelia in the most innocent way in the world. "Don't be angry, and break the furniture, Major Dobbin. Of course we are going to have her here."

"Of course, my dear," Jos said.

"The poor creature, after all her sufferings," Emmy continued: "her horrid banker broken and run away: her husband—wicked wretch—having deserted her and taken her child away from her (here she doubled her two little fists and held them in a most menacing attitude before her, so that the Major was charmed to see such a dauntless virago), the poor dear thing! quite alone and absolutely forced to give lessons in singing to get her bread—and not have her here!"

"Take lessons, my dear Mrs. George," cried the Major, "but don't have her in the house. I implore you don't."

"Pooh," said Jos.

"You who are always good and kind: always used to be at any rate: I'm astonished at you, Major William," Amelia cried. "Why, what is the moment to help her but when she is so miserable? Now is the time to be of service to her. The oldest friend I ever had, and not—"

"She was not always your friend, Amelia," the Major said, for he was quite angry. This allusion was too much for Emmy, who looking the Major almost fiercely in the face, said "For shame, Major Dobbin!"

and, after having fired this shot, she walked out of the room with a most majestic air, and shut her own door briskly on herself and her outraged dignity.

"To allude to *that!*" she said, when the door was closed. "Oh it was cruel of him to remind me of it," and she looked up at George's picture, which hung there as usual, with the portrait of the boy underneath. "It was cruel of him. If I had forgiven it, ought he to have spoken? No. And it is from his own lips that I know how wicked and groundless my jealousy was; and that you were pure,—Oh yes, you were pure, my saint in heaven!"

She paced the room trembling and indignant. She went and leaned on the chest of drawers over which the picture hung, and gazed and gazed at it. Its eyes seemed to look down on her with a reproach that deepened as she looked. The early dear, dear memories of that brief prime of love rushed back upon her. The wound which years had scarcely cicatrised bled afresh, and oh, how bitterly! She could not bear the reproaches of the husband there before her. It couldn't be. Never, never.

Poor Dobbin; poor old William! That unlucky word had undone the work of many a year—the long laborious edifice of a life of love and constancy—raised too upon what secret and hidden foundations, wherein lay buried passions, uncounted struggles, unknown sacrifices—a little word was spoken, and down fell the fair palace of hope—one word, and away flew the bird which he had been trying all his life to lure!

William, though he saw by Amelia's looks that a great crisis had come, nevertheless continued to implore Sedley, in the most energetic terms, to beware of Rebecca: and he eagerly, almost frantically, adjured Jos not to receive her. He besought Jos[4] to inquire at least regarding her: told him how he had heard that she was in the company of gamblers and people of ill repute: pointed out what evil she had done in former days: how she and Crawley had misled poor George into ruin: how she was now parted from her husband, by her own confession, and, perhaps, for good reason. What a dangerous companion she would be for his sister, who knew nothing of the affairs of the world! William implored Jos, with all the eloquence which he could bring to bear, and a great deal more energy than this quiet gentleman was ordinarily in the habit of showing, to keep Rebecca out of his household.

Had he been less violent, or more dexterous, he might have succeeded in his supplications to Jos; but the Civilian was not a little jealous of the airs of superiority which the Major constantly exhibited towards him, as he fancied (indeed, he had imparted his opinions to Mr. Kirsch, the courier, whose bills Major Dobbin checked on this journey, and who sided with his master), and he began a blustering speech about his competency to defend his own honour, his

4. First printing reads "besought Jos eagerly" and the second printing reads "besought Mr. Sedley"—the exigency of making a change in stereotyped plates is that a replacement must be of approximately the same length. This correction (made, probably, to avoid the repetition of "eagerly" from the previous line) would probably have, under other circumstances, consisted merely of deleting "eagerly" because Jos is not elsewhere referred to as Mr. Sedley.

desire not to have his affairs meddled with, his intention, in fine, to rebel against the Major, when the colloquy—rather a long and stormy one—was put an end to in the simplest way possible, namely, by the arrival of Mrs. Becky, with a porter from the Elephant Hotel, in charge of her very meagre baggage.

She greeted her host with affectionate respect, and made a shrinking, but amicable, salutation to Major Dobbin, who, as her instinct assured her at once, was her enemy, and had been speaking against her; and the bustle and clatter consequent upon her arrival brought Amelia out of her room, who[5] went up and embraced her guest with the greatest warmth, and took no notice of the Major, except to fling him an angry look—the most unjust and scornful glance that had perhaps ever appeared in that poor little woman's face since she was born. But she had private reasons of her own, and was bent upon being angry with him. And Dobbin, indignant at the injustice, not at the defeat, went off, making her a bow quite as haughty as the killing curtsey with which the little woman chose to bid him farewell.

He being gone, Emmy was particularly lively and affectionate to Rebecca, and bustled about the apartments and installed her guest in her room with an eagerness and activity seldom exhibited by our placid little friend. But when an act of injustice is to be done, especially by weak people, it is best that it should be done quickly; and Emmy thought she was displaying a great deal of firmness and proper feeling and veneration for the late Captain Osborne in her present behaviour.

Georgy came in from the fêtes for dinner-time, and found four covers laid as usual; but one of the places was occupied by a lady, instead of by Major Dobbin. "Hullo! where's Dob?" the young gentleman asked, with his usual simplicity of language. "Major Dobbin is dining out, I suppose," his mother said; and, drawing the boy to her, kissed him a great deal, and put his hair off his forehead, and introduced him to Mrs. Crawley. "This is my boy, Rebecca," Mrs. Osborne said—as much as to say—can the world produce anything like that? Becky looked at him with rapture, and pressed his hand fondly. "Dear boy!" she said—"he is just like my——" Emotion choked her further utterance; but Amelia understood, as well as if she had spoken, that Becky was thinking of her own blessed child. However, the company of her friend consoled Mrs. Crawley, and she ate a very good dinner.

During the repast, she had occasion to speak several times, when Georgy eyed her and listened to her. At the dessert Emmy was gone out to superintend further domestic arrangements: Jos was in his great chair dozing over Galignani: Georgy and the new arrival sat close to each other: he had continued to look at her knowingly more than once, and at last he laid down the nut-crackers.

"I say," said Georgy.

"What do you say?" Becky said, laughing.

"You're the lady I saw in the mask at the Rouge et Noir."

5. Revised edition reads: room. Emmy

"Hush! you little sly creature," Becky said, taking up his hand and kissing it. "Your uncle was there too, and mamma mustn't know."

"Oh no—not by no means," answered the little fellow.

"You see we are quite good friends already," Becky said to Emmy, who now re-entered; and it must be owned that Mrs. Osborne had introduced a most judicious and amiable companion into her house.

William, in a state of great indignation, though still unaware of all the treason that was in store for him, walked about the town wildly until he fell upon the Secretary of Legation, Tapeworm, who invited him to dinner. As they were discussing that meal, he took occasion to ask the Secretary whether he knew anything about a certain Mrs. Rawdon Crawley, who had, he believed, made some noise in London; and then Tapeworm, who of course knew all the London gossip, and was besides a relative of Lady Gaunt, poured out into the astonished Major's ears such a history about Becky and her husband as astonished the querist, and supplied all the points of this narrative, for it was at that very table years ago that the present writer had the pleasure of hearing the tale. Tufto, Steyne, the Crawleys, and their history—everything connected with Becky and her previous life passed under the record of the bitter diplomatist. He knew everything and a great deal besides, about all the world;—in a word, he made the most astounding revelations to the simple-hearted Major. When Dobbin said that Mrs. Osborne and Mr. Sedley had taken her into their house, he[6] burst into a peal of laughter which shocked the Major, and asked if they had not better send into the prison, and take in one or two of the gentlemen in shaved heads and yellow jackets, who swept the streets of Pumpernickel, chained in pairs, to board and lodge, and act as tutor to that little scapegrace Georgy.

This information astonished and horrified the Major not a little. It had been agreed in the morning (before meeting with Rebecca) that Amelia should go to the Court ball that night. There[7] would be the place to[8] tell her. The Major went home and dressed himself in his uniform, and repaired to Court, in hopes to see Mrs. Osborne. She never came. When he returned to his lodgings all the lights in the Sedley tenement were put out. He could not see her till the morning. I don't know what sort of a night's rest he had with this frightful secret in bed with him.

At the earliest convenient hour in the morning he sent his servant across the way with a note, saying, that he wished very particularly to speak with her. A message came back to say, that Mrs. Osborne was exceedingly unwell, and was keeping her room.

She, too, had been awake all that night. She had been thinking of a thing which had agitated her mind a hundred times before. A hundred times on the point of yielding, she had shrunk back from a sacrifice which she felt was too much for her. She couldn't, in spite of his love and constancy, and her own acknowledged regard, respect, and gratitude. What are benefits, what is constancy, or merit? One

6. Revised edition reads: Tapeworm
7. Revised edition reads: That
8. Revised edition reads: place where he should

curl of a girl's ringlet, one hair of a whisker, will turn the scale against them all in a minute. They did not weigh with Emmy more than with other women. She had tried them; wanted to make them pass; could not; and the pitiless little woman had found a pretext, and determined to be free.

When at length, in the afternoon, the Major gained admission to Amelia, instead of the cordial and affectionate greeting to which he had been accustomed now for many a long day, he received the salutation of a curtsey, and of a little gloved hand, retracted the moment after it was accorded to him.

Rebecca, too, was in the room, and advanced to meet him with a smile and an extended hand. Dobbin drew back rather confusedly. "I—I beg your pardon, Ma'am," he said; "but I am bound to tell you that it is not as your friend that I am come here now."

"Pooh! damn; don't let us have this sort of thing!" Jos cried out, alarmed, and anxious to get rid of a scene.

"I wonder what Major Dobbin has to say against Rebecca?" Amelia said in a low, clear voice with a slight quiver in it, and a very determined look about the eyes.

"I will *not* have this sort of thing in my house," Jos again interposed. "I say I will not have it: and Dobbin, I beg, Sir, you'll stop it." And he looked round trembling and turning very red, and gave a great puff, and made for his door.

"Dear friend!" Rebecca said with angelic sweetness, "do hear what Major Dobbin has to say against me."

"I will *not* hear it, I say," squeaked out Jos at the top of his voice, and, gathering up his dressing-gown, was[9] gone.

"We are only two women," Amelia said. "You can speak now, Sir."

"This manner towards me is one which scarcely becomes you, Amelia," the Major answered haughtily; "nor I believe am I guilty of habitual harshness to women. It is not a pleasure to me to do the duty which I am come to do."

"Pray proceed with it quickly, if you please, Major Dobbin," said Amelia, who was more and more in a pet. The expression of Dobbin's face, as she spoke in this imperious manner, was not pleasant.

"I came to say—and as you stay, Mrs. Crawley, I must say it in your presence—that I think you—you ought not to form a member of the family of my friends. A lady who is separated from her husband, who travels not under her own name, who frequents public gaming-tables—"

"It was to the ball I went," cried out Becky.

"—is not a fit companion for Mrs. Osborne and her son," Dobbin went on: "and I may add that there are people here who know you, and who profess to know that regarding your conduct about which I don't even wish to speak before—before Mrs. Osborne."

"Your's is a very modest and convenient sort of calumny, Major Dobbin," Rebecca said. "You leave me under the weight of an accusation which, after all, is unsaid. What is it? Is it unfaithfulness to my husband? I scorn it, and defy anybody to prove it—I defy you,

9. Revised edition reads: he was

I say. My honour is as untouched as that of the bitterest enemy who ever maligned me. Is it of being poor, forsaken, wretched, that you accuse me? Yes, I am guilty of those faults, and punished for them every day. Let me go, Emmy. It is only to suppose that I have not met you, and I am no worse to-day than I was yesterday. It is only to suppose that the night is over and the poor wanderer is on her way. Don't you remember the song we used to sing in old, dear old days?[1] I have been wandering ever since then—a poor castaway, scorned for being miserable, and insulted because I am alone. Let me go: my stay here interferes with the plans of this gentleman."

"Indeed it does, Madam," said the Major. "If I have any authority in this house—"

"Authority, none!" broke out Amelia. "Rebecca, you stay with me. *I* won't desert you, because you have been persecuted, or insult you, because—because Major Dobbin chooses to do so. Come away, dear." And the two women made towards their door.

William opened it. As they were going out, however, he took Amelia's hand, and said—"Will you stay a moment and speak to me?"

"He wishes to speak to you away from me," said Becky, looking like a martyr. Amelia griped her hand in reply.

"Upon my honour it is not about you that I am going to speak," Dobbin said. "Come back, Amelia," and she came. Dobbin bowed to Mrs. Crawley, as he shut the door upon her. Amelia looked at him, leaning against the glass: her face and her lips were quite white.

"I was confused when I spoke just now," the Major said, after a pause; "and I misused the word authority."

"You did," said Amelia, with her teeth chattering.

"At least I have claims to be heard," Dobbin continued.

"It is generous to remind me of our obligations to you," the woman answered.

"The claims I mean, are those left me by George's father," William said.

"Yes, and you insulted his memory. You did yesterday. You know you did. And I will never forgive you. Never!" said Amelia. She shot out each little sentence in a tremor of anger and emotion.

"You don't mean that, Amelia?" William said, sadly. "You don't mean that these words, uttered in a hurried moment, are to weigh against a whole life's devotion. I think that George's memory has not been injured by the way in which I have dealt with it, and if we are come to bandying reproaches, I at least merit none from his widow and the mother of his son. Reflect, afterwards when—when you are at leisure, and your conscience will withdraw this accusation. It does even now." Amelia held down her head.

"It is not that speech of yesterday," he continued, "which moves you. That is but the pretext, Amelia, or I have loved you and watched you for fifteen years in vain. Have I not learned in that time to read all your feelings, and look into your thoughts? I know what your heart is capable of: it can cling faithfully to a recollection, and cherish

1. Possibly "Bleak and barren was the moor," which Becky sang in chapter IV, and which includes the line "Heaven pity all poor wanderers lone!"

a fancy; but it can't feel such an attachment as mine deserves to mate with, and such as I would have won from a woman more generous than you. No, you are not worthy of the love which I have devoted to you. I knew all along that the prize I had set my life on was not worth the winning; that I was a fool, with fond fancies, too, bartering away my all of truth and ardour against your little feeble remnant of love. I will bargain no more: I withdraw. I find no fault with you. You are very good-natured, and have done your best; but you couldn't—you couldn't reach up to the height of the attachment which I bore you, and which a loftier soul than yours might have been proud to share. Good bye, Amelia! I have watched your struggle. Let it end. We are both weary of it."

Amelia stood scared and silent as William thus suddenly broke the chain by which she held him, and declared his independence and superiority. He had placed himself at her feet so long that the poor little woman had been accustomed to trample upon him. She didn't wish to marry him, but she wished to keep him. She wished to give him nothing, but that he should give her all. It is a bargain not unfrequently levied in love.

William's sally had quite broken and cast her down. *Her* assault was long since over and beaten back.

"Am I to understand then,—that you are going—away,—William?" she said.

He gave a sad laugh. "I went once before," he said, "and came back after twelve years. We were young then, Amelia. Good-bye. I have spent enough of my life at this play."

Whilst they had been talking, the door into Mrs. Osborne's room had opened ever so little; indeed, Becky had kept a hold of the handle, and had turned it on the instant when Dobbin quitted it; and she heard every word of the conversation that had passed between these two. "What a noble heart that man has," she thought, "and how shamefully that woman plays with it." She admired Dobbin; she bore him no rancour for the part he had taken against her. It was an open move in the game, and played fairly. "Ah!" she thought, "if I could have had such a husband as that—a man with a heart and brains too! I would not have minded his large feet;"—and, running into her room, she absolutely bethought herself of something, and wrote him a note, beseeching him to stop for a few days—not to think of going—and that she could serve him with A.

The parting was over. Once more poor William walked to the door and was gone; and the little widow, the author of all this work, had her will, and had won her victory, and was left to enjoy it as she best might. Let the ladies envy her triumph.

At the romantic hour of dinner Mr. Georgy made his appearance, and again remarked the absence of "Old Dob." The meal was eaten in silence by the party; Jos's appetite not being diminished, but Emmy taking nothing at all.

After the meal, Georgy was lolling in the cushions of the old window, a large window, with three sides of glass abutting from the gable, and commanding on one side the Market Place, where the Elephant is, and in front the opposite side of "Goswell Street over the way," like the immortal casement of Mr. Pickwick,—Georgy, I say, was lolling in this window,[2] his mother being busy hard by, when he remarked symptoms of movement at the Major's house on the other side of the street.

"Hullo!" said he, "there's Dob's trap—they are bringing it out of the court-yard." The "trap" in question was a carriage which the Major had bought for six pounds sterling, and about which they used to rally him a good deal.

Emmy gave a little start but said nothing.

"Hullo!" Georgy continued, "there's Francis coming out with the portmanteaus, and Kunz, the one-eyed postilion, coming down the market with three schimmels.[3] Look at his boots and yellow jacket,—ain't he a rum one? Why—they're putting the horses to Dob's carriage. Is he going anywhere?"

"Yes," said Emmy; "he is going on a journey."

"Going a journey; and when is he coming back?"

"He is—not coming back," answered Emmy.

"Not coming back!" cried out Georgy, jumping up. "Stay here, Sir," roared out Jos. "Stay, Georgy," said his mother, with a very sad face. The boy stopped; kicked about the room; jumped up and down from the window-seat with his knees, and showed every symptom of uneasiness and curiosity.

The horses were put to. The baggage was strapped on. Francis came out with his master's sword, and[4] cane, and umbrella tied up together, and laid them in the well, and his desk and old tin cocked-hat case, which he placed under the seat. Francis brought out the stained old blue cloak lined with red camlet,[5] which had wrapped the owner up any time these fifteen years, and had *manchen Sturm erlebt,*[6] as a favourite song of those days said. It had been new for the campaign of Waterloo, and had covered George and William after the night of Quatre Bras.

Old Burcke, the landlord of the lodgings came out, then Francis, with more packages—final packages—then Major William;—Burcke wanted to kiss him. The Major was adored by all people with whom he had to do. It was with difficulty he could escape from this demonstration of attachment.

"By Jove, I *will* go!" screamed out George. "Give him this," said Becky, quite interested, and put a paper into the boy's hand. He had rushed down the stairs and flung across the street in a minute—the yellow postilion was cracking his whip gently.

William had got into the carriage, released from the embraces of his landlord. George bounded in afterwards and flung his arms round the Major's neck (as they saw from the window), and began asking him multiplied questions. Then he felt in his waistcoat-pocket

2. Pickwick lodged with Mrs. Bardwell in Goswell Street in Charles Dickens' *Pickwick Papers* (1837). Revised edition omits: and in front the opposite side of "Goswell Street over the way," like the immortal casement of Mr. Pickwick,—Georgy, I say, was lolling in this window,
3. White horses.
4. Revised edition omits: and
5. Fabric blended of cotton, wool, linen, and sometimes camel or angora goat hair.
6. "Weathered many a storm"; from the *Mantellied* or coat song in Karl von Holtei's drama *Lenore* (1828).

and gave him a note. William seized at it rather eagerly, he opened it trembling, but instantly his countenance changed, and he tore the paper in two and dropped it out of the carriage. He kissed Georgy on the head, and the boy got out, doubling his fists into his eyes, and with the aid of Francis. He lingered with his hand on the panel. Fort Schwager![7] The yellow postilion cracked his whip prodigiously, up sprang Francis to the box, away went the schimmels, and Dobbin with his head on his breast. He never looked up as they passed under Amelia's window: and Georgy, left alone in the street, burst out crying in the face of all the crowd.

Emmy's maid heard him howling again during the night, and brought him some preserved apricots to console him. She mingled her lamentations with his. All the poor, all the humble, all honest folks, all good men who knew him, loved that kind-hearted and simple gentleman.

As for Emmy, had she not done her duty? She had her picture of George for a consolation.

## *Chapter LXVII.*

### WHICH CONTAINS BIRTHS, MARRIAGES, AND DEATHS.

WHATEVER Becky's private plan might be by which Dobbin's true love was to be crowned with success, the little woman thought that the secret might keep, and indeed, being by no means so much interested about anybody's welfare as about her own, she had a great number of things pertaining to herself to consider, and which concerned her a great deal more than Major Dobbin's happiness in this life.

She found herself suddenly and unexpectedly in snug comfortable quarters: surrounded by friends, kindness, and good-natured simple people, such as she had not met with for many a long day; and, wanderer as she was by force and inclination, there were moments when rest was pleasant to her; as the most hardened Arab that ever careered across the Desert over the hump of a dromedary, likes to repose sometimes under the date-trees by

7. Onward, postilion!

the water; or to come into the cities, walk in the bazaars, refresh himself in the baths, and say his prayers in the Mosques, before he goes out again marauding. Jos's tents and pilau were pleasant to this little Ishmaelite.[1] She picketted her steed, hung up her weapons, and warmed herself comfortably by his fire. The halt in that roving, restless life, was inexpressibly soothing and pleasant to her.

So, pleased herself, she tried with all her might to please everybody, and we know that she was eminent and successful as a practitioner in the art of giving pleasure. As for Jos, even in that little interview in the garret at the Elephant Inn, she had found means to win back a great deal of his good will. In the course of a week, the civilian was her sworn slave and frantic admirer. He didn't go to sleep after dinner, as his custom was, in the much less lively society of Amelia. He drove out with her[2] in his open carriage. He asked little parties and invented festivities to do her honour. Tapeworm, the Secretary of Legation, who had abused her so cruelly, came to dine with Jos, and then came every day to pay his respects to Becky. Poor Emmy, who was never very talkative, and more glum and silent than ever after Dobbin's departure, was quite forgotten when this superior genius made her appearance. The French Minister was as much charmed with her as his English rival. The German ladies, never particularly squeamish as regards morals, especially in English people, were delighted with the cleverness and wit of Mrs. Osborne's charming friend; and though she did not ask to go to Court, yet the most august and Transparent Personages there heard of her fascinations, and were quite curious to know her. When it became known that she was noble, of an ancient English family, that her husband was a Colonel of the Guard, Excellenz and Governor of an island, only separated from his lady by one of those trifling differences which are of little account in a country where "Werther" is still read, and the "Wahlverwandtschaften" of Goethe is considered an edifying moral book;[3] nobody thought of refusing to receive her in the very highest society of the little Duchy, and the ladies were even more ready to call her *du,* and to swear eternal friendship for her, than they had been to bestow the same inestimable benefits upon Amelia. Love and Liberty are interpreted by those simple Germans in a way which honest folks in Yorkshire and Somersetshire little understand, and a lady might, in some philosophic and civilised towns, be divorced ever so many times from her respective husbands, and keep her character in society. Jos's house never was so pleasant, since he had a house of his own, as Rebecca caused it to be. She sung, she played, she laughed, she talked in two or three languages, she brought every body to the house, and she made Jos believe that it was his own great social tal-

1. Pilau: spicy oriental dish of rice and meat. Ishmael was the outcast son of Abraham and Hagar doomed to be ever a wanderer. Though it seems too early to refer to Becky as Jos's, the revised edition reads: his little Ishmaelite.
2. Revised edition reads: Becky
3. *The Sorrows of Young Werther* (1774), which made Goethe famous, is about a young man's impossible love for a married woman. *Elective Affinities* (1809) explores the attractions and possibilities of extramarital love. Though both books were objectionable by Victorian norms, both were translated and reprinted frequently in England throughout the century.

ents and wit which gathered the great[4] society of the place round about him.

As for Emmy, who found herself not in the least mistress of her own house, except when the bills were to be paid, Becky soon discovered the way to soothe and please her. She talked to her perpetually about Major Dobbin sent about his business, and made no scruple of declaring her admiration for that excellent, high-minded gentleman, and of telling Emmy that she had behaved most cruelly regarding him. Emmy defended her conduct, and showed that it was dictated only by the purest religious principles; that a woman once, &c., and to such an angel as him whom she had had the good fortune to marry, was married for ever; but she had no objection to hear the Major praised as much as ever Becky chose to praise him; and indeed brought the conversation round to the Dobbin subject a score of times every day.

Means were easily found to win the favour of Georgy and the servants. Amelia's maid, it has been said, was heart and soul in favour of the generous Major. Having at first disliked Becky for being the means of dismissing him from the presence of her mistress, she was reconciled to Mrs. Crawley subsequently, because the latter became William's most ardent admirer and champion. And in these mighty conclaves in which the two ladies indulged after their parties, and while Miss Payne was "brushing their 'airs," as she called the yellow locks of the one, and the soft brown tresses of the other, this girl always put in her word for that dear good gentleman Major Dobbin. Her advocacy did not make Amelia angry any more than Rebecca's admiration of him. She made George write to him constantly, and persisted in sending Mamma's kind love in a postscript. And as she looked at her husband's portrait of nights, it no longer reproached her—perhaps she reproached it, now William was gone.

Emmy was not very happy after her heroic sacrifice. She was very *distraite*,[5] nervous, silent, and ill to please. The family had never known her so peevish. She grew pale and ill. She used to try and sing certain songs, ("Einsam bin ich nicht alleine," was one of them; that tender love-song of Weber's,[6] which, in old-fashioned days, young ladies, and when you were scarcely born, showed that those who lived before you knew too how to love and to sing);—certain songs, I say, to which the Major was partial; and as she warbled them in the twilight in the drawing-room, she would break off in the midst of the song, and walk into her neighbouring apartment, and there, no doubt, take refuge in the miniature of her husband.

Some books still subsisted, after Dobbin's departure, with his name written in them; a German Dictionary, for instance, with "William Dobbin, —th Reg.," in the fly-leaf; a guide-book with his initials, and one or two other volumes which belonged to the Major. Emmy cleared these away, and put them on the drawers, where she placed her work-box, her desk, her Bible, and Prayer-book, under the pictures of the two Georges. And the Major, on going away, having

4. Revised edition omits: great
5. Absentminded.
6. "Though alone, I am not lonely," from Carl Maria von Weber's opera *Preciosa* (1821).

left his gloves behind him, it is a fact that Georgy, rummaging his mother's desk sometime afterwards, found the gloves neatly folded up, and put away in what they call the secret drawers of the desk.

Not caring for society, and moping there a great deal, Emmy's chief pleasure in the summer evenings was to take long walks with Georgy (during which Rebecca was left to the society of Mr. Joseph), and then the mother and son used to talk about the Major in a way which even made the boy smile. She told him that she thought Major William was the best man in all the world; the gentlest and the kindest, the bravest, and the humblest. Over and over again, she told him how they owed everything which they possessed in the world to that kind friend's benevolent care of them; how he had befriended them all through their poverty and misfortunes; watched over them when nobody cared for them; how all his comrades admired him though he never spoke of his own gallant actions; how Georgy's father trusted him beyond all other men, and had been constantly befriended by the good William. "Why, when your Papa was a little boy," she said, "he often told me that it was William who defended him against a tyrant at the school where they were; and their friendship never ceased from that day until the last, when your dear father fell."

"Did Dobbin kill the man who killed Papa?" Georgy said. "I'm sure he did, or he would if he could have caught him; wouldn't he, Mother? When I'm in the army, won't I hate the French?—that's all."

In such colloquies the mother and the child passed a great deal of their time together. The artless woman had made a confidant of the boy. He was as much William's friend as everybody[7] else who knew him well.

By the way, Mrs. Becky, not to be behind-hand in sentiment, had got a miniature too hanging up in her room, to the surprise and amusement of most people, and the delight of the original, who was no other than our friend Jos. On her first coming to favour the Sedleys with a visit, the little woman, who had arrived with a remarkably small shabby kit, was perhaps ashamed of the meanness of her trunks and band-boxes, and often spoke with great respect about her baggage left behind at Leipsic, which she must have from that city. When a traveller talks to you perpetually about the splendour of his luggage, which he does not happen to have with him; my son, beware of that traveller! He is, ten to one, an impostor.

Neither Jos nor Emmy knew this important maxim. It seemed to them of no consequence whether Becky had a quantity of very fine clothes in invisible trunks; but as her present supply was exceedingly shabby, Emmy supplied her out of her own stores, or took her to the best milliner in the town, and there fitted her out. It was no more torn collars now, I promise you, and faded silks trailing off at the shoulder. Becky changed her habits with her situation in life—the rouge-pot was suspended—another excitement to which she had accustomed herself was also put aside, or at least only indulged in in

7. Revised edition reads: was everybody

privacy; as when she was prevailed on by Jos of a summer evening, Emmy and the boy being absent on their walks, to take a little spirit-and-water. But if she did not indulge—the courier did: that rascal Kirsch could not be kept from the bottle; nor could he tell how much he took when he applied to it. He was sometimes surprised himself at the way in which Mr. Sedley's Cognac diminished. Well, well; this is a painful subject. Becky did not very likely indulge so much as she used before she entered a decorous family.

At last the much-bragged-about boxes arrived from Leipsic;—three of them not by any means large or splendid;—nor did Becky appear to take out any sort of dresses or ornaments from the boxes when they did arrive. But out of one, which contained a mass of her papers (it was that very box which Rawdon Crawley had ransacked in his furious hunt for Becky's concealed money), she took a picture with great glee, which she pinned up in her room, and to which she introduced Jos. It was the portrait of a gentleman in pencil, his face having the advantage of being painted up in pink. He was riding on an elephant away from some cocoa-nut trees, and a pagoda: it was an Eastern scene.

"God bless my soul, it is my portrait," Jos cried out. It was he indeed, blooming in youth and beauty, in a nankeen jacket of the cut of 1804. It was the old picture that used to hang up in Russell Square.

"I bought it," said Becky, in a voice trembling with emotion; "I went to see if I could be of any use to my kind friends. I have never parted with that picture—I never will."

"Won't you?" Jos cried, with a look of unutterable rapture and satisfaction. "Did you really now value it for my sake?"

"You know I did, well enough," said Becky; "but why speak,—why think,—why look back? It is too late now!"

That evening's conversation was delicious, for Jos. Emmy only came in to go to bed very tired and unwell. Jos and his fair guest had a charming *tête-à-tête* and his sister could hear, as she lay awake in her adjoining chamber, Rebecca singing over to Jos the old songs of 1815. He did not sleep, for a wonder, that night, any more than Amelia.

It was June, and, by consequence, high season in London; Jos, who read the incomparable "Galignani" (the exile's best friend) through every day, used to favour the ladies with extracts from his paper during their breakfast. Every week in this paper there is a full account of military movements, in which Jos, as a man who had seen service,[8] was especially interested. On one occasion he read out—"Arrival of the —th regiment.—Gravesend, June 20.—The Ramchunder, East Indiaman, came into the river this morning, having on board 14 officers, and 132 rank and file of this gallant corps. They have been absent from England 14 years, having been embarked the year after Waterloo, in which glorious conflict they took an active part, and having subsequently distinguished themselves in the Burmese war. The veteran colonel, Sir Michael O'Dowd, K.C.B.,

8. For details of Jos's service, see chapters XXXI–XXXII.

with his lady and sister, landed here yesterday, with Captains Posky, Stubble, Macraw, Malony; Lieutenants Smith, Jones, Thompson, F. Thomson; Ensigns Hicks and Grady; the band on the pier playing the national anthem, and the crowd loudly cheering the gallant veterans as they went into Wayte's hotel, where a sumptuous banquet was provided for the defenders of Old England. During the repast, which we need not say was served up in Wayte's best style, the cheering continued so enthusiastically, that Lady O'Dowd and the Colonel came forward to the balcony, and drank the healths of their fellow-countrymen in a bumper of Wayte's best claret."

On a second occasion Jos read a brief announcement—Major Dobbin had joined the —th regiment at Chatham; and subsequently he promulgated accounts of the presentations at the Drawing-room, of Colonel Sir Michael O'Dowd, K.C.B., Lady O'Dowd (by Mrs. Molloy Malony of Ballymalony), and Miss Glorvina O'Dowd (by Lady O'Dowd). Almost directly after this, Dobbin's name appeared among the Lieutenant-Colonels: for old Marshal Tiptoff had died during the passage of the —th from Madras, and the Sovereign was pleased to advance Colonel Sir Michael O'Dowd to the rank of Major-General on his return to England, with an intimation that he should be Colonel of the distinguished regiment which he had so long commanded.

Amelia had been made aware of some of these movements. The correspondence between George and his guardian had not ceased by any means: William had even written once or twice to her since his departure, but in a manner so unconstrainedly cold, that the poor woman felt now in her turn that she had lost her power over him, and that, as he had said, he was free. He had left her, and she was wretched. The memory of his almost countless services, and lofty and affectionate regard, now presented itself to her, and rebuked her day and night. She brooded over those recollections according to her wont; saw the purity and beauty of the affection with which she had trifled, and reproached herself for having flung away such a treasure.

It was gone indeed. William had spent it all out. He loved her no more, he thought, as he had loved her. He never could again. That sort of regard, which he had proffered to her for so many faithful years, can't be flung down and shattered, and mended so as to show no scars. The little heedless tyrant had so destroyed it. No, William thought again and again, "It was myself I deluded, and persisted in cajoling: had she been worthy of the love I gave her, she would have returned it long ago. It was a fond mistake. Isn't the whole course of life made up of such? and suppose I had won her, should I not have been disenchanted the day after my victory? Why pine, or be ashamed of my defeat?" The more he thought of this long passage of his life, the more clearly he saw his deception. "I'll go into harness again," he said, "and do my duty in that state of life in which it has pleased Heaven to place me. I will see that the buttons of the recruits are properly bright, and that the serjeants make no mistakes in their accounts. I will dine at mess, and listen to the Scotch surgeon telling his stories. When I am old and broke, I will go on half-pay, and my old sisters shall scold me. I have 'geliebet and gelebet' as the girl in *Wallenstein* says.[9] I am done.—Pay the bills, and get me a cigar: find out what there is at the play to-night, Francis; to-morrow we cross by the 'Batavier.'" He made the above speech, whereof Francis only heard the last two lines, pacing up and down the Boompjes at Rotterdam.[1] The "Batavier" was lying in the basin. He could see the place on the quarter-deck, where he and Emmy had sate on the happy voyage out. What had that little Mrs. Crawley to say to him? Psha! to-morrow we will put to sea, and return to England, home, and duty!

After June all the little Court Society of Pumpernickel used to separate, according to the German plan, and make for a hundred watering-places, where they drank at the wells; rode upon donkeys; gambled at the *redoutes*,[2] if they had money and a mind; rushed with hundreds of their kind, to gormandise at the *tables d'hôte;* and idled away the summer. The English diplomatists went off to Toeplitz and Kissingen, their French rivals shut up their *chancellerie* and whisked away to their darling Boulevard de Gand.[3] The Transparent reigning family took, too, to the waters, or retired to their hunting-lodges. Everybody went away having any pretensions to politeness, and, of course, with them, Doctor von Glauber, the Court Doctor, and his Baroness. The seasons for the baths were the most productive periods of the Doctor's practice—he united business with pleasure, and his chief place of resort was Ostend, which is much frequented by Germans, and where the Doctor treated himself and his spouse to what he called a "dib" in the sea.

His interesting patient, Jos, was a regular milch cow to the Doctor, and he easily persuaded the civilian, both for his own health's sake and that of his charming sister, which was really very much shattered, to pass the summer at that hideous seaport town. Emmy did not care where she went much. Georgy jumped at the idea of a move. As for Becky, she came as a matter of course in the fourth place inside of the fine barouche Mr. Jos had bought: the two domestics being on the box in front. She might have some misgivings about the friends whom she should meet there,[4] and who might be likely to tell ugly stories—but, bah! she was strong enough to hold her own. She had cast such an anchor in Jos now as would require a strong storm to shake. That incident of the picture had finished him. Becky took down her elephant, and put it into the little box which she had had from Amelia ever so many years ago. Emmy also came off with her Lares,—her two pictures,—and the party, finally, were lodged in an exceedingly dear and uncomfortable house at Ostend.

9. Loved and lived. Thekla's song in Friedrich Schiller's play *The Piccolomini*, III.7 (second part of his *Wallenstein* trilogy): "I have enjoyed earthly happiness; I have lived and loved."
1. Batavier: ship named for the Dutch island of Batavia. Boompjes: Dutch for "little trees," a section of the Rotterdam harbor lined with small linden trees.
2. Assembly halls.
3. In Paris near the Opéra, now called the Boulevard des Italiens.
4. Revised edition reads: at Ostend,

There Amelia began to take baths, and get what good she could from them, and though scores of people of Becky's acquaintance passed her and cut her, yet Mrs. Osborne, who walked about with her, and who knew nobody, was not aware of the treatment experienced by the friend whom she had chosen so judiciously as a companion; indeed, Becky never thought fit to tell her what was passing under her innocent eyes.

Some of Mrs. Rawdon Crawley's acquaintances, however, acknowledged her readily enough,—perhaps more readily than she would have desired. Among these were Major Loder (unattached), and Captain Rook (late of the Rifles), who might be seen any day on the Dyke, smoking and staring at the women, and who speedily got an introduction to the hospitable board and select circle of Mr. Joseph Sedley. In fact, they would take no denial; they burst into the house whether Becky was at home or not, walked into Mrs. Osborne's drawing-room, which they perfumed with their coats and mustachios, called Jos "Old buck," and invaded his dinner-table, and laughed and drank for long hours there.

"What can they mean?" asked Georgy, who did not like these gentlemen. "I heard the Major say to Mrs. Crawley yesterday, 'No, no, Becky, you shan't keep the old buck to yourself. We must have the bones in, or, dammy, I'll split.'[5] What could the Major mean, Ma?"[6]

"Major! don't call *him* Major!" Emmy said. "I'm sure I can't tell what he meant." His presence and that of his friend inspired the little lady with intolerable terror and aversion. They paid her tipsy compliments; they leered at her over the dinner-table. And the Captain made her advances that filled her with sickening dismay, nor would she ever see him unless she had George by her side.

Rebecca, also,[7] to do her justice, never would let either of these men remain alone with Amelia; the Major was disengaged too, and swore he would be the winner of her. A couple of ruffians were fighting for this innocent creature, gambling for her at her own table; and though she was not aware of the rascals' designs upon her, yet she felt a horror and uneasiness in their presence, and longed to fly.

She besought, she entreated Jos to come home.[8] Not he. He was slow of movement, tied to his Doctor, and perhaps to some other leading-strings. At least Becky was not anxious to go to England.

At last she took a great resolution—made the great plunge. She wrote off a letter to a friend whom she had on the other side of the water; a letter about which she did not speak a word to anybody, which she carried herself to the post under her shawl, nor was any remark made about it; only that she looked very much flushed and agitated when Georgy met her; and she kissed him and hung over him a great deal that night. She did not come out of her room after

5. Though "bones" is slang for dice, Loder and Rook want to help Becky pick Jos's bones. To split is to reveal the game.
6. Revised edition reads: Mamma?"
7. Revised edition omits: also,
8. Revised edition reads: Jos to go home. "Come home" suggests "take me home," in a way not conveyed by "go home," which suggests "and leave me here."

her return from her walk. Becky thought it was Major Loder and the Captain who frightened her.

"She mustn't[9] stop here," Becky reasoned with herself. "She must go away, the silly little fool. She is still whimpering after that gaby[1] of a husband—dead, (and served right!) these fifteen years. She shan't marry either of these men. It's too bad of Loder. No; she shall marry the bamboo-cane, I'll settle it this very night."

So Becky took a cup of tea to Amelia in her private apartment, and found that lady in the company of her miniatures, and in a most melancholy and nervous condition. She laid down the cup of tea.

"Thank you," said Amelia.

"Listen to me, Amelia," said Becky, marching up and down the room before the other, and surveying her with a sort of contemptuous kindness. "I want to talk to you. You must go away from here and from the impertinences of these men. I won't have you harassed by them; and they will insult you if you stay. I tell you they are rascals; men fit to send to the hulks. Never mind how I know them. I know everybody. Jos can't protect you, he is too fat and[2] weak, and wants a protector himself. You are no more fit to live in the world than a baby in arms. You must marry, or you and your precious boy will go to ruin. You must have a husband, you fool; and one of the best gentlemen I ever saw has offered you a hundred times, and you have rejected him, you silly, heartless, ungrateful little creature!"

"I tried—I tried my best, indeed I did, Rebecca," said Amelia, deprecatingly, "but I couldn't forget—;" and she finished the sentence by looking up at the portrait.

"Couldn't forget *him!*" cried out Becky, "that selfish humbug, that low-bred cockney-dandy, that padded booby, who had neither wit, nor manners, nor heart, and was no more to be compared to your friend with the bamboo-cane than you are to Queen Elizabeth. Why, the man was weary of you, and would have jilted you, but that Dobbin forced him to keep his word. He owned it to me. He never cared for you. He used to sneer about you to me, time after time; and made love to me the week after he married you."

"It's false! It's false! Rebecca," cried out Amelia, starting up.

"Look there, you fool," Becky said, still with provoking good humour, and taking a little paper out of her belt, she opened it and flung it into Emmy's lap. "You know his hand-writing. He wrote that to me—wanted me to run away with him—gave it me under your nose, the day before he was shot—and served him right!" Becky repeated.

Emmy did not hear her; she was looking at the letter. It was that which George had put into the bouquet and given to Becky on the night of the Duchess of Richmond's ball. It was as she said: the foolish young man had asked her to fly.

Emmy's head sank down, and for almost the last time in which she shall be called upon to weep in this history, she commenced that work. Her head fell to her bosom, and her hands went up to her eyes;

9. Revised edition reads: musn't
1. Simpleton.
2. Revised edition omits: fat and

The letter before Waterloo

and there for awhile, she gave way to her emotions, as Becky stood on and regarded her. Who shall analyse those tears, and say whether they were sweet or bitter? Was she most grieved, because the idol of her life was tumbled down and shivered at her feet, or indignant that her love had been so despised, or glad because the barrier was removed which modesty had placed between her and a new, a real affection? "There is nothing to forbid me now," she thought. "I may love him with all my heart now. O, I will, I will, if he will but let me, and forgive me." I believe it was this feeling rushed over all the others which agitated that gentle little bosom.

Indeed, she did not cry so much as Becky expected—the other soothed and kissed her—a rare mark of sympathy with Mrs. Becky. She treated Emmy like a child, and patted her head. "And now let us get pen and ink, and write to him to come this minute," she said.

"I—I wrote to him this morning," Emmy said, blushing exceedingly.

Becky screamed with laughter—*"Un biglietto,"* she sang out with Rosina, *"eccolo qua!"*[3]—the whole house echoed with her shrill singing.

Two mornings after this little scene, although the day was rainy and gusty, and Amelia had had an exceedingly wakeful night, listening to the wind roaring, and pitying all travellers by land and by water,[4] yet she got up early, and insisted upon taking a walk on the Dyke with Georgy; and there she paced as the rain beat into her face, and she looked out westward across the dark sea line, and over the swollen billows which came tumbling and frothing to the shore. Neither spoke much, except now and then, when the boy said a few words to his timid companion, indicative of sympathy and protection.

"I hope he won't cross in such weather," Emmy said.

"I bet ten to one he does," the boy answered. "Look, mother, there's the smoke of the steamer." It was that signal, sure enough.

But though the steamer was under weigh, he might not be on board; he might not have got the letter; he might not choose to come.—A hundred fears poured one over the other into the little heart, as fast as the waves on to the Dyke.

The boat followed the smoke into sight. Georgy had a dandy telescope, and got the vessel under view in the most skilful manner. And he made appropriate nautical comments upon the manner of the approach of the steamer as she came nearer and nearer, dipping and rising in the water. The signal of an English steamer in sight went fluttering up to the mast on the pier. I dare say Mrs. Amelia's heart was in a similar flutter.

Emmy tried to look through the telescope over George's shoulder, but she could make nothing of it. She only saw a black eclipse[5]

3. In Rossini's opera *The Barber of Seville* (1816), Figaro encourages Rosina to write a letter to her suitor, but she already has: "A letter; here it is."
4. Echo of the Litany in *The Book of Common Prayer*: "That it may please thee to preserve all that travel by land or by water."
5. Though "ellipse" has been suggested as a proper emendation here, "eclipse" suggests that the telescope, for Amelia, merely obscured all vision, an ordinary experience with novice users.

bobbing up and down before her eyes.

George took the glass again and raked the vessel. "How she does pitch!" he said. "There goes a wave slap over her bows. There's only two people on deck besides the steersman. There's a man lying down, and a—chap in a—cloak with a—Hooray!—It's Dob by Jingo!" He clapped to the telescope and flung his arms round his mother. As for that lady: let us say what she did in the words of a favourite poet—*Δακρυσεν γελασασα*.[6] She was sure it was William. It could be no other. What she had said about hoping that he would not come was all hypocrisy. Of course he would come: what could he do else but come? She knew he would come.

The ship came swiftly nearer and nearer. As they went in to meet her at the landing-place at the Quay, Emmy's knees trembled so that she scarcely could run. She would have liked to kneel down and say her prayers of thanks there. Oh, she thought, she would be all her life saying them!

It was such a bad day that as the vessel came alongside of the Quay there were no idlers abroad; scarcely even a commissioner on the look-out for the few passengers in the steamer. That young scapegrace George had fled too: and as the gentleman in the old cloak lined with red stuff stepped on to the shore, there was scarcely any one present to see what took place, which was briefly this:

A lady in a dripping white bonnet and shawl, with her two little hands out before her, went up to him, and in the next minute she had altogether disappeared under the folds of the old cloak, and was kissing one of his hands with all her might; whilst the other, I suppose, was engaged in holding her to his heart (which her head just about reached) and in preventing her from tumbling down. She was murmuring something about—forgive—dear William—dear, dear, dearest friend—kiss, kiss, kiss, and so forth—and in fact went on under the cloak in an absurd manner.

When Emmy emerged from it, she still kept tight hold of one of William's hands, and looked up in his face. It was full of sadness and tender love and pity. She understood its reproach, and hung down her head.

"It was time you sent for me, dear Amelia," he said.

"You will never go again, William."

"No, never," he answered: and pressed the dear little soul once more to his heart.

As they issued out of the Custom-house precincts, Georgy broke out on them, with his telescope up to his eye, and a loud laugh of welcome; he danced round the couple, and performed many facetious antics as he led them up to the house. Jos wasn't up yet; Becky not visible (though she looked at them through the blinds). Georgy ran off to see about breakfast. Emmy, whose shawl and bonnet were off in the passage in the hands of Mrs. Payne, now went to undo the clasp of William's cloak, and—we will, if you please, go with George, and look after breakfast for the Colonel. The vessel is in port. He

6. *Dakyroen gelasasa*: smiling through her tears. Andromache parting from Hector, in Homer's *Iliad*, VI.484.

has got the prize he has been trying for all his life. The bird has come in at last. There it is with its head on his shoulder, billing and cooing close up to his heart, with soft outstretched fluttering wings. This is what he has asked for every day and hour for eighteen years. This is what he pined after. Here it is—the summit, the end—the last page of the third volume. Good-bye, Colonel—God bless you, honest William!—Farewell, dear Amelia—Grow green again, tender little parasite, round the rugged old oak to which you cling!

---

Perhaps it was compunction towards the kind and simple creature, who had been the first in life to defend her, perhaps it was a dislike to all such sentimental scenes,—but Rebecca, satisfied with her part in the transaction, never presented herself before Colonel Dobbin and the lady whom he married. "Particular business," she said, took her to Bruges, whither she went; and only Georgy and his uncle were present at the marriage ceremony. When it was over, and Georgy had rejoined his parents, Mrs. Becky returned (just for a few days) to comfort the solitary bachelor Joseph Sedley. He preferred a continental life, he said, and declined to join in housekeeping with his sister and her husband.

Emmy was very glad in her heart to think that she had written to her husband before she read or knew of that letter of George's. "I knew it all along," William said; "but could I use that weapon against the poor fellow's memory? It was that which made me suffer so when you——"

"Never speak of that day again," Emmy cried out, so contrite and humble, that William turned off the conversation, by his account of Glorvina and dear old Peggy O'Dowd, with whom he was sitting when the letter of recall reached him. "If you hadn't sent for me," he added with a laugh, "who knows what Glorvina's name might be now?"

At present it is Glorvina Posky (now Mrs. Major Posky), she took him on the death of his first wife; having resolved never to marry out of the regiment. Lady O'Dowd is also so attached to it that, she says, if anything were to happen to Mick, bedad she'd come back and marry some of 'em. But the Major-General is quite well, and lives in great splendour at O'Dowdstown, with a pack of beagles, and (with the exception of perhaps their neighbour, Hoggarty of Castle Hoggarty) he is the first man of his county. Her Ladyship still dances jigs, and insisted on standing up to the Master of the Horse at the Lord Lieutenant's last ball. Both she and Glorvina declared that Dobbin had used the latter *sheamfully*, but Posky falling in, Glorvina was consoled, and a beautiful turban from Paris appeased the wrath of Lady O'Dowd.

When Colonel Dobbin quitted the service, which he did immediately after his marriage, he rented a pretty little country place in Hampshire, not far from Queen's Crawley, where, after the passing of the Reform Bill, Sir Pitt and his family constantly resided now. All idea of a Peerage was out of the question, the baronet's two seats in

Parliament being lost.[7] He was both out of pocket and out of spirits by that catastrophe, failed in his health, and prophesied the speedy ruin of the Empire.

Lady Jane and Mrs. Dobbin became great friends—there was a perpetual crossing of pony-chaises between the Hall and the Evergreens, the Colonel's place (rented of his friend Major Ponto, who was abroad with his family). Her Ladyship was godmother to Mrs. Dobbin's child, which bore her name, and was christened by the Rev. James Crawley, who succeeded his father in the living: and a pretty close friendship subsisted between the two lads, George and Rawdon, who hunted and shot together in the vacations, were both entered of the same College at Cambridge, and quarrelled with each other about Lady Jane's daughter, with whom they were both, of course, in love. A match between George and that young lady was long a favourite scheme of both the matrons, though I have heard that Miss Crawley herself inclined towards her cousin.

Mrs. Rawdon Crawley's name was never mentioned by either family. There were reasons why all should be silent regarding her. For wherever Mr. Joseph Sedley went, she travelled likewise; and that infatuated man seemed to be entirely her slave. The Colonel's lawyers informed him that his brother-in-law had effected a heavy insurance upon his life, whence it was probable that he had been raising money to discharge debts. He procured prolonged leave of absence from the East India House, and indeed his infirmities were daily increasing.

On hearing the news about the insurance, Amelia, in a good deal of alarm, entreated her husband to go to Brussels, where Jos then was, and inquire into the state of his affairs. The Colonel quitted home with reluctance (for he was deeply immersed in his "History of the Punjaub," which still occupies him, and much alarmed about his little daughter, whom he idolizes, and who was just recovering from the chicken-pox), and went to Brussels and found Jos living at one of the enormous hotels in that city. Mrs. Crawley, who had her carriage, gave entertainments, and lived in a very genteel manner, occupied another suite of apartments in the same hotel.

The Colonel, of course, did not desire to see that lady, or even think proper to notify his arrival at Brussels, except privately to Jos by a message through his valet. Jos begged the Colonel to come and see him that night, when Mrs. Crawley would be at a *soirée,* and when they could meet *alone.* He found his brother-in-law in a condition of pitiable infirmity; and dreadfully afraid of Rebecca, though eager in his praises of her. She tended him through a series of unheard-of illnesses, with a fidelity most admirable. She had been a daughter to him. "But—but—oh for God's sake, do come and live near me, and—and—see me sometimes," whimpered out the unfortunate man.

The Colonel's brow darkened at this. "We can't, Jos," he said. "Considering the circumstances, Amelia can't visit you."

"I swear to you—I swear to you on the Bible," gasped out Joseph, wanting to kiss the book, "that she is as innocent as a child, as spotless as your own wife."

7. The Reform Bill of 1832 redistributed parliamentary representation and abolished rotten boroughs.

Becky's second appearance in the character of Clytemnestra

"It may be so," said the Colonel, gloomily; "but Emmy can't come to you. Be a man, Jos: break off this disreputable connexion. Come home to your family. We hear your affairs are involved."

"Involved!" cried Jos. "Who has told such calumnies? All my money is placed out most advantageously. Mrs. Crawley—that is—I mean,—it is laid out to the best interest."

"You are not in debt then? Why did you insure your life?"

"I thought—a little present to her—in case anything happened; and you know my health is so delicate—common gratitude you know—and I intend to leave all my money to you—and I can spare it out of my income, indeed I can," cried out William's weak brother-in-law.

The Colonel besought Jos to fly at once—to go back to India, whither Mrs. Crawley could not follow him; to do anything to break off a connexion which might have the most fatal consequences to him.

Jos clasped his hands, and cried,—"He would go back to India. He would do anything: only he must have time: they mustn't[8] say anything to Mrs. Crawley:—she'd—she'd kill me if she knew it. You don't know what a terrible woman she is," the poor wretch said.

"Then, why not come away with me?" said Dobbin in reply; but Jos had not the courage. "He would see Dobbin again in the morning; he must on no account say that he had been there. He must go now. Becky might come in." And Dobbin quitted him full of forebodings.

He never saw Jos more. Three months afterwards Joseph Sedley died at Aix-la-Chapelle. It was found that all his property had been muddled away in speculations, and was represented by valueless shares in different bubble companies. All his available assets were the two thousand pounds for which his life was insured, and which were left equally between his beloved "sister Amelia, wife of, &c., and his friend and invaluable attendant during sickness, Rebecca, wife of Lieutenant-Colonel Rawdon Crawley, C.B.," who was appointed administratrix.

The solicitor of the Insurance Company swore it was the blackest case that ever had come before him; talked of sending a commission to Aix to examine into the death, and the Company refused payment of the policy. But Mrs., or Lady Crawley, as she styled herself, came to town at once (attended with her solicitors, Messrs. Burke, Thurtell, and Hayes, of Thavies Inn,)[9] and dared the Company to refuse the payment. They invited examination, they declared[1] that she was the object of an infamous conspiracy, which had been pursuing her all through life, and triumphed finally. The money was paid, and her character established, but Colonel Dobbin sent back his share of the legacy to the Insurance Office, and rigidly declined to hold any communion[2] with Rebecca.

8. Revised edition reads: musn't
9. The firm's name echoes those of William Burke (1792–1829), supplier of corpses for medical study, John Turtell (1794–1824), murderer, and Catherine Hayes (1690–1726), husband killer and main character in Thackeray's first novel, *Catherine*. Thavies Inn is a real Inn of Chancery, though its name is appropriately suggestive.
1. First printing reads: payment: invited examination: declared
2. Revised edition reads: communication

Virtue rewarded. A booth in Vanity Fair

She never was Lady Crawley, though she continued so to call herself. His Excellency Colonel Rawdon Crawley died of yellow fever at Coventry Island, most deeply beloved and deplored, and six weeks before the demise of his brother, Sir Pitt. The estate consequently devolved upon the present Sir Rawdon Crawley, Bart.

He, too, has declined to see his mother, to whom he makes a liberal allowance; and who, besides, appears to be very wealthy. The Baronet lives entirely at Queen's Crawley, with Lady Jane and her daughter; whilst Rebecca, Lady Crawley, chiefly hangs about Bath and Cheltenham, where a very strong party of excellent people consider her to be a most injured woman. She has her enemies. Who has not? Her life is her answer to them. She busies herself in works of piety. She goes to church, and never without a footman. Her name is in all the Charity Lists. The Destitute Orange-girl, the Neglected Washerwoman, the Distressed Muffin-man,[3] find in her a fast and generous friend. She is always having stalls at Fancy Fairs for the benefit of these hapless beings. Emmy, her children, and the Colonel, coming to London some time back, found themselves suddenly before her at one of these fairs. She cast down her eyes demurely and smiled as they started away from her; Emmy skurrying off on the arm of George, (now grown a dashing young gentleman,) and the Colonel seizing up his little Janey, of whom he is fonder than of anything in the world—fonder even than of his "History of the Punjaub."

"Fonder than he is of me," Emmy thinks, with a sigh. But he never said a word to Amelia that was not kind and gentle; or thought of a want of hers that he did not try to gratify.

Ah! *Vanitas Vanitatum!*[4] Which of us is happy in this world? Which of us has his desire? or, having it, is satisfied?—Come children, let us shut up the box and the puppets, for our play is played out.

3. Stock characters in the tracts formerly passed out by Lady Jane's mother.
4. Vanity of vanities, the refrain of Ecclesiastes.

"Vauxhall," chapter VI, was originally chapter V, following directly after a somewhat shorter chapter IV. When first set in type, this original configuration extended to the middle of what would have been page 35 of a first installment that had to be only 32 pages. Eventually the first installment was made up entirely of chapters I through IV: woodcut illustrations were added, extending the text two full pages; and a paragraph was added near the beginning of chapter IV, and the last page and a half of that chapter was also added.

"Vauxhall" was rewritten to become what it is in the reading text of this edition. We now have the original manuscript, with, of course, alterations made by Thackeray in the course of composition. We also have a copied over and revised manuscript in Thackeray's hand, with a few fragments of proof pasted in. The pasted-in proofs are from a corrected stage of proofs for the original typesetting, which was subsequently aborted. Thackeray made a few alterations on the proof fragments, which he pasted into his new manuscript for the chapter.

The Norton text of the chapter was constructed by retaining the punctuation and spelling of the original manuscript for those parts of the text that remained essentially unchanged. Where Thackeray supplied wholely new manuscript prose, the punctuation and spelling were taken from the new manuscript. Alterations penned onto the proofs were also adopted. The Norton text thus contains the most revised substantive readings but retains the most authoritative punctuation and spelling.

The passages printed below represent the substantive original passages later revised by Thackeray.

¶1 *Instead of:* I know that the tune which I am piping is a very mild one,—(although there are some terrific chapters coming presently)—and must beg the good-natured reader to remember that we are only discoursing at present about a stock-broker's family

*The original manuscript reads:* The reader I know is growing very weary of these little mean unromantic details about a vulgar stock broker's family

¶1 *Instead of:* The argument stands thus—Osborne in love with Amelia has asked an old friend to dinner and to Vauxhall—Jos Sedley is in love with Rebecca. Will he marry her? That is the great subject now in hand. ¶We might have treated this subject in the genteel or in the romantic or in the facetious manner. Suppose we had laid the scene in Grosvenor Square with the very same adventures—would not some people have listened? Suppose we had shown how Lord Joseph Sedley fell in love

*The manuscript reads:* If we had but laid the scene in Grosvenor Square and described how Lord Joseph Sedley fell in love

¶2 *Instead of:* father; or

*The manuscript reads:* father: there would have been some excuse for indulging in these ample though trivial details. If

¶3 *Instead of:* No soul braved that tempest—the watchmen shrank into their boxes whither the searching rain followed them—where the crashing thunderbolt fell and destroyed them—one had so been slain opposite The Foundling—a scorched gaberdine a shivered lantern a staff rent in twain by the flash were all that remained of stout Will Steadfast. A

*The manuscript reads:* Fourteen men had already been stricken down as though on tented field by these strange weapons of the storm!—A

¶3 *Instead of:* Row—and whither? But the whirlwind

*The manuscript reads:* Row—a child of the Foundling hospital having occasion to leave his bed at night had been swept away—and whither? ask the annals of Lamb's conduit—but the whirl wind

¶8 *Instead of:* rose-water style—The Marquis of Osborne has just dispatched his *petit tigre* with a *billet doux* to the Ladye Amelia. ¶The dear creature has received it from the hands of her *femme de chambre,* Mademoiselle Anastasie. ¶Dear Marquis! What amiable politeness! His lordship's note contains the wished for invitation to Devonshire House! ¶"Who

*The manuscript reads:* impassioned style and in stead of the night at Vauxhall (to wh. place of entertainment any body might go who paid three shillings) The fête at Devonshire House might form the subject of this present chapter. The characters should be made to speak in the real genteel fashionable polyglot Londonderry-Trollope style (no where is the language of fashion more carefully diversified than in the works of the above named authors)—and by way of giving to the work the real undoubted air of fashion, well known characters of the aristocracy should be introduced to keep company with the fictitious heroes of the romance. As for instance ¶Who

¶19 *Instead of:* Thus you see, ladies, how this story *might* have been written, if the author had but a mind—for to tell the truth he is just as familiar with Newgate as with the palaces of our revered aristocracy, and has seen the outside of both. But as I don't understand the language or manners of the Rookery, nor that polyglot conversation which according to the fashionable novelists is spoken by the leaders of *ton*—we must if you please preserve our middle course modestly amidst those scenes and personages with which we are most familiar. In a word this chapter about Vauxhall

*The manuscript reads:* Thus we see how this present romance *might* have been written, and how the public curiosity might have been roused. For it has an appetite for the unknown our gracious public. Situated, as it is between Saint Giles's and Saint James's, it loves to hear stories of them more than of itself. It has never been hanged before Newgate any more than it has danced at the Queens ball. Hence accounts either of the prison or the palace are the most welcome to it: and a novel wh. should be made to bring those two buildings together, and wh. should pass abruptly from the Queens bowers to Bow Street and vice versâ—such a novel as the famous French Mysterès de Paris for instance would be sure of acquiring great success, and creating a general sympathy. But we must take our story as we find it—in the neighbourhood of common life not in the extreme heights and depths of it, and as another famous

French novelist, the great Victor Hugo in his book of travels on the Rhine devotes 2 pages of his account of the city of Cologne, to enumerating of the sights wh. he did *not* see in that town. We have dared to imitate that great authority of romance, and show what we *could* have done with this romance—only that it was necessary to do otherwise. ¶In a word this Chapter about Vauxhall,

¶19 *Instead of:* Are not there little chapters in every body's life, that seem to be nothing and yet affect all the rest of the history? ¶Let us then step into the coach with the Russell Square party and be off to the Gardens. There is barely room between Jos and Miss Sharp who are on the front seat—Mr. Osborne sitting bodkin opposite between Captain Dobbin and Amelia. ¶Every soul in the coach agreed that on that night Jos would propose to make Rebecca Sharp Mrs. Sedley. The parents at home had acquiesced in the arrangement: though between ourselves,
*The manuscript reads:* ¶Did you ever in the old old days, drink rack punch at Vauxhall? Rack punch was one of the great causes of all and singular the events wh. are about to be narrated in this history—a vulgar humble cause if you please, but the great events of life hang on such, and there is no reason after all why rack punch should not be made an agent in a novel of every day life just as much as arsenic or a pocket pistol the conclusion of a tragedy. ¶Well then. The fated day came on wh. the party to Vauxhall was really to take place, no thunder storm intervened this time, and the four young people in Mr. Sedleys coach were set down at the gates of 'the Royal property,' and no doubt welcomed by Mr. Simpson there. ¶But four or five days had elapsed between the tea party in the former chapter & the Vauxhall trip: four or five days during almost every one of wh. Mr. Jos Sedley had paid a visit to Russell Square, so that it became evident to every person in the establishment that he had some very particular attraction in the house. ¶It certainly was not his mother or his sister—nor could it be his respectable father. Between ourselves

¶21 *Instead of:* It's no affair of mine." ¶Amelia on the other hand, as became a young woman of her prudence and temperament was quite enthusiastic for the match. Once or twice Jos had been on the point of saying something very important to her, to which she was most willing to lend an ear, but the fat fellow could not be brought to unbosom himself of his great secret, and very much to his sister's disappointment he only rid himself of a large sigh and turned away. ¶This mystery served to keep Amelia's gentle bosom in a perpetual flutter of excitement. If
*The manuscript reads:* ¶In fact it was visible to all the world that Jos was in love with Miss Rebecca. He had been discovered holding her skein of silk (for finishing the green purse mentioned previously) he had driven her and his sister to the Park, and even to Richmond—his mother being of these parties of pleasure and giving them as it were her sanction. Once or twice he had been on the point of saying something very important to Amelia; to the wh. that young person was very willing to lend an ear but the fat fellow could not be brought to unbosom himself of his great secret, and

very much to his sister's disappointment he only rid himself of a large sigh, and turned away. ¶This state of things, this love manifest though unconfessed, this chance of establishing in the world her dear sweet darling Rebecca, this necessity of pretending to know nothing of the matter in her conversations with Miss Sharp, produced a delightful state of excitement in the gentle bosom of Amelia Sedley. What good-natured young lass is there whom the idea of a friend's marriage does not set in a flutter?. Amelia was charmed beyond measure, if

¶27 *Instead of:* Such was the state of affairs as the carriage crossed Westminster bridge. ¶The party was landed at the Royal Gardens in due time. As the majestic Jos stepped out of the creaking vehicle the crowd gave a cheer for the fat gentleman, who blushed and looked very big and mighty, as he walked away with Rebecca under his arm. George, of course, took charge of Amelia. She looked as happy as a rose-tree in sunshine. ¶"I say, Dobbin," says George, "just look to the shawls and things there's a good fellow." And so while he paired off with Miss Sedley: and Jos squeezed through the gate into the Gardens with Rebecca at his side: honest Dobbin contented himself by giving an arm to the shawls and by paying at the door for the whole party. ¶He walked very modestly behind them. He was not willing to spoil sport. About Rebecca and Jos he did not care a fig. But he thought Amelia worthy even of the brilliant George Osborne and as he saw that good looking couple, threading the walks to the girl's delight and wonder, he watched her artless happiness with a sort of fatherly pleasure. Perhaps he felt that he would have liked to have something on his own arm besides a shawl; (the people laughed at seeing the gawky young officer carrying this female burthen) but William Dobbin was very little addicted to selfish calculation at all: and so long as his friend was enjoying himself; how should he be discontented? And the truth is that of all the delights of the Gardens—of

*The manuscript reads:* Although the gardens of Vauxhall have passed away as much as the gardens of Babylon, yet there is no need to describe what our young people saw on their visit to the first mentioned of these two places of splendid entertainment. Fond memory has not forgotten as yet all the delights and wonders of the Royal Gardens,

*In that same passage, the revised manuscript originally read:* Westminster Bridge. <Captain Dob> 'Keep clear of Jos & Amelia's little friend' Osborne whispered to Captain Dobbin— ¶Yes & of George & Amelia I suppose thought poor Dobbin to himself—and <as he saw her take> so he contented himself by paying at the door for the whole party while Jos squeezed through the gate ¶So while George

¶30 *Instead of:* place—Captain William Dobbin did not take the slightest notice. ¶He carried about Amelia's white cashmere shawl, and having attended under the gilt cockle-shell while Mrs. Salmon performed the Battle of Borodino (a savage cantata against the Corsican Upstart, who had lately met with his Russian reverses)—Mr. Dobbin tried to hum it as he walked away, and found he was humming—the tune which Amelia Sedley sang on the stairs as she came down to dinner. ¶He burst out laughing at himself; for the truth is he could sing no better than an owl.

*The manuscript reads:* ămusements of the place. Peace be with him. His Ghost may wander about now in the Ghost of a royal property where the spirit of Madame Sacqui is still dancing on the apparition of a tight rope, and the old departed ham-cutters are carving slices scarcely more visionary than those wh. in life they supplied.

¶38 *Instead of:* Captain Dobbin had some thoughts of joining the party at supper: as in truth he found the Vauxhall amusement not particularly lively—but he paraded twice before the box where the now united couples were met and nobody took any notice of him. Covers were laid for four. The mated pairs were prattling away quite happily, and Dobbin knew he was as clean forgotten as if he had never existed in this world. ¶'I should only be *de trop,*' said the Captain looking at them rather wistfully. 'I'd best go and talk to the hermit'—and so he strolled off out of the hum of men, and noise and clatter of the banquet, into the dark walk at the end of which lived that well-known pasteboard Solitary. It wasn't very good fun for Dobbin—and indeed to be alone at Vauxhall, I have found from my own experience to be one of the most dismal sports ever entered into by a bachelor. ¶The two couples were perfectly happy then in their box: where the most delightful and intimate conversation took place. Jos was in his glory ordering about the waiters with great majesty. He made

*The manuscript reads:* At supper when the four of course met together, the most delightful and intimate conversation took place. Jos made

¶40 *Instead of:* rack punch: every body had rack punch at Vauxhall. "Waiter, Rack Punch." ¶That bowl of rack punch was the cause of all this history. And why not a bowl of rack punch as well as any other cause? Was not a bowl of Prussic acid the cause of fair Rosamond's retiring from the world? Was not a bowl of wine the cause of the demise of Alexander the Great, or at least does not Dr. Lempriere say so?—so did this bowl of rack punch influence the fates of all the principal characters in this Novel without a hero, which we are now relating. It influenced their life although most of them did not taste a drop of it.

*The manuscript reads: rack-punch.*—that very bowl wh. was the cause of all this history.

¶48 *Instead of:* hint Captain Dobbin

*The manuscript reads:* hint Captain Tawney

¶48 *Instead of:* Mr. Jos Sedley

*The manuscript reads:* this fat Bacchanalian

¶49 *Instead of:* George Osborne conducted the girls home in safety: and when the door was closed upon them and as he walked across Russell Square laughed so as to astonish the watchman. Amelia looked very ruefully at her friend as they went up stairs, and kissed her, and went to bed without any more talking.

*The manuscript lacks this paragraph.*

Another major change took place in this chapter in 1853 for the revised "Cheap Edition."

¶2 *Instead of the two half pages mocking Newgate and Silverfork fiction from* "Fancy this chapter having been headed THE NIGHT ATTACK" *through* "In a word, this chapter about Vauxhall would have been so exceedingly short but for the above little disquisition, that it scarcely would have deserved"

*The 1853 revision reads:* But my readers must hope for no such romance, only a homely story, and must be content with a chapter about Vauxhall, which is so short that it scarce deserves

# BACKGROUNDS AND CONTEXTS

# Composition and Production

## WILLIAM MAKEPEACE THACKERAY

### Selected Letters†

*To Mrs. Carmichael-Smyth, July 2, 1847*

* * *

Of course you are quite right about Vanity Fair and Amelia being selfish—it is mentioned in this very number.[1] My object is not to make a perfect character or anything like it. Dont you see how odious all the people are in the book (with exception of Dobbin)—behind whom all there lies a dark moral I hope. What I want is to make a set of people living without God in the world[2] (only that is a cant phrase) greedy pompous mean perfectly self-satisfied for the most part and at ease about their superior virtue. Dobbin & poor Briggs are the only 2 people with real humility as yet. Amelia's is to come, when her scoundrel of a husband is well dead with a ball in his odious bowels; when she has had sufferings, a child, and a religion[3]—But she has at present a quality above most people whizz: LOVE—by w[h] she shall be saved. Save me, save me too O my God and Father, cleanse my heart and teach me my duty.

I wasn't going to write in this way when I began. But these thoughts pursue me plentifully. Will they ever come to a good end? I should doubt God who gave them if I doubted that.

* * *

*To the Duke of Devonshire, May 1, 1848*

Kensington: May 1, 1848.

My Lord Duke,—Mrs. Rawdon Crawley, whom I saw last week, and whom I informed of your Grace's desire to have her portrait, was good enough to permit me to copy a little drawing made of her "in happier days," she said with a sigh, by Smee, the Royal Academician.

Mrs. Crawley now lives in a small but very pretty little house in Belgravia, and is conspicuous for her numerous charities, which always get into the newspapers, and her unaffected piety. Many of the

† From *The Letters and Private Papers of William Makepeace Thackeray*, ed. Gordon N. Ray, 4 vols. (Cambridge: Harvard University Press, 1945–46), II: 309, 375–77, 384. Reprinted by permission.

1. VII for July, chapters 23 to 25. For the passage to which Thackeray refers, see p. 245.
2. *Ephesians*, 2, 12. Compare the celebrated paragraph in Newman's *Apologia pro Vita Sua* (ed. Wilfrid Ward, Oxford, 1913, pp. 334–335), which turns upon the same phrase.
3. Amelia's husband dies in chapter 32 (number IX), her child is born in chapter 35 (X), and her severest sufferings occur in chapters 46 and 50 (XIII and XIV).

most exalted and spotless of her own sex visit her, and are of opinion that she is a *most injured woman.* There is no *sort of truth* in the stories regarding Mrs. Crawley and the late Lord Steyne. The licentious character of that nobleman alone gave rise to reports from which, alas! the most spotless life and reputation cannot always defend themselves. The present Sir Rawdon Crawley (who succeeded his late uncle, Sir Pitt, 1832; Sir Pitt died on the passing of the Reform Bill) does not see his mother, and his undutifulness is a cause of the deepest grief to that admirable lady. "If it were not for *higher things,*" she says, how could she have borne up against the world's calumny, a wicked husband's cruelty and falseness, and the thanklessness (sharper than a serpent's tooth) of an adored child?[4] But she has been preserved, mercifully preserved, to bear all these griefs, and awaits her reward *elsewhere.* The italics are Mrs. Crawley's own.

She took the style and title of Lady Crawley for some time after Sir Pitt's death in 1832; but it turned out that Colonel Crawley, Governor of Coventry Island, had died of fever three months before his brother, whereupon Mrs. Rawdon was obliged to lay down the title which she had prematurely assumed.

The late Jos. Sedley, Esq., of the Bengal Civil Service, left her two lakhs of rupees, on the interest of which the widow lives in the practices of piety and benevolence before mentioned. She has lost what little good looks she once possessed, and wears false hair and teeth (the latter give her rather a ghastly look when she smiles), and—for a pious woman—is the best-crinolined lady in Knightsbridge district.

Colonel and Mrs. W. Dobbin live in Hampshire, near Sir R. Crawley; Lady Jane was godmother to their little girl, and the ladies are exceedingly attached to each other. The Colonel's *History of the Punjaub* is looked for with much anxiety in some circles.

Captain and Lt.-Colonel G. Sedley-Osborne (he wishes, he says, to be distinguished from some other branches of the Osborne family, and is descended by the mother's side from Sir Charles Sedley) is, I need not say, well, for I saw him in a most richly embroidered cambric pink shirt with diamond studs, bowing to your Grace at the last party at Devonshire House. He is in Parliament; but the property left him by his Grandfather has, I hear, been a good deal overrated.

He was very sweet upon Miss Crawley, Sir Pitt's daughter, who married her cousin, the present Baronet, and a good deal cut up when he was refused. He is not, however, a man to be permanently cast down by sentimental disappointments. His chief cause of annoyance at the present moment is that he is growing bald, but his whiskers are still without a gray hair and the finest in London.

I think these are the latest particulars relating to a number of persons about whom your Grace was good enough to express some interest. I am very glad to be enabled to give this information, and am—

Your Grace's very much obliged servant,
W. M. Thackeray.

4. *King Lear,* I, ii, 311–312. Lady Kicklebury's pleasant variation on these lines will be remembered: "Shakespeare was very right in stating how much sharper than a thankless tooth it is to have a serpent child" (*Works,* IX, 207).

P.S.—Lady O'Dowd is at O'Dowdstown arming. She has just sent in a letter of adhesion to the Lord-Lieutenant, which has been acknowledged by his Excellency's private secretary, Mr. Corry Connellan. Miss Glorvina O'Dowd is thinking of coming up to the Castle to marry the last-named gentleman.

P.S.2.—The India mail just arrived announces the utter ruin of the Union Bank of Calcutta, in which all Mrs. Crawley's money was. Will Fate never cease to persecute that suffering saint?

* * *

*To Miss Smith, June 6, 1848*

13 Young St. Kensington.
June 6. 1848.

Boney runnin away like anythink

Ah, dear Miss Smith! I shale be outatown on Sunday the 18th: and I never dine out on that day because it is the Hannawersary of the death of ~~Cat~~ my dear friend Captain George Osborne of the —th Regiment.

Yours always W M T.

Captin Dobbin

Sofers

Pore duvvle!

Captin Hosbin ded a bulliet through his Art.

# ANNE THACKERAY RITCHIE

## [Introduction to *Vanity Fair*]†

* * *

Once more he writes on the 2nd July, 1848: " 'Vanity Fair' is this instant done, and I have worked so hard, that I can hardly hold a pen and say God bless my dearest old mother. I had not time even to listen to the awful cannonading in your town. Thank God! you are going to leave it. . . . I am very pleased to have done, very melancholy and beat"; and then he goes on to speak of his hope that he may not feel too much elation from the praise he gets; and so once more sends his blessing to his mother.

Even now after a lifetime, when generations of readers have succeeded those who first read and praised "Vanity Fair," that moment seems almost present again as one looks at the old letter on its half-sheet of paper, and realises what it must have been to the mother who read the letter, and to my father who wrote it. Now and again, in all the troubles and changes of life, I think he must have realised, as only a few can do, the consciousness of repose, of well-earned rest after effort, the immense happiness of good work achieved, the satisfaction of sympathy, and recognition coming after the years in which he had laboured, alone and *in silence* as it were, and without any great success. And though it was with the same cheerful humour that he wrote on, whether with success or without it, looking the world honestly and trustfully in the face, yet when people came at last with cordial words of appreciation and praise, it made him glad: and when material difficulties were smoothed away for him and his, he enjoyed it to the full.

"Vanity Fair" was dedicated to Mr. Procter, who had been so good to my father when he was in great trouble. There is a passage in a letter to Mrs. Brookfield from W. M. T. saying, "Old Dilke of the *Athenæum* vows that Procter and his wife between them wrote 'Jane Eyre,' and when I protest ignorance says, Pooh! you know very well who wrote it." . . . The second edition of "Jane Eyre" came out with a dedication to my father. "I wonder whether it can be true (that the Procters wrote 'Jane Eyre')," he says. "It is just possible, and then, what a singular circumstance the crossfire of the two dedications."

My brother-in-law had some of the early MS. of "Vanity Fair." It was curious to compare it with that of "Esmond," for instance, which flows on straight and with scarcely an alteration. The early chapters of "Vanity Fair" are, on the contrary, altered and re-written with many erasures and with sentences turned in many different ways.

We get a sidelight upon "Vanity Fair," when writing to Mrs. Brookfield from Brussels in 1848 her correspondent says: "I am going today to the Hotel de la Terrasse where Becky used to be, and I shall pass by Captain Osborne's lodgings where I recollect meeting him

† From *Centenary Biographical Edition of the Works of William Makepeace Thackeray* (London: Smith, Elder, 1910), 2:37–42.

and his little wife—who has married again, somebody told me—but it is always the way with those grandes passions—Mrs. Dobbins or some such name she is now; always an overrated woman I thought. How curious it is, I believe perfectly in all these people and feel quite an interest in the inn in which they lived."

* * *

In "Appleton's Journal," which appeared long ago, there is an article by Mr. J. E. Cooke, which was called "An hour with Thackeray," during which hour the writer asked my father whether he ever dictated. The answer was that the whole of "Esmond" was dictated and a great part of "Pendennis." The talk then turned on "Vanity Fair." "As you speak of Becky Sharp, Mr. Thackeray," said Mr. Cooke, "there is one mystery about her which I should like to have cleared up. Nearly at the end of the book there is a picture of Jos Sedley seated, a sick old man in his chamber, and behind the curtain glaring and ghastly is Becky grasping a dagger. Beneath the picture is the single word 'Clytemnestra.' "

"Yes."

"Did Becky kill him, Mr. Thackeray?"

He smoked meditatively as if he was endeavouring to arrive at the solution of some problem, and then with a slow smile dawning on his face, replied, "I do not know."

## GORDON RAY

# [Originals]†

* * *

The broadening and deepening of Thackeray's powers can best be illustrated by examining the relation between three prominent figures in *Vanity Fair* and their background in Thackeray's life. A study of these test cases will show how Thackeray's personal loyalties shaped the moral convictions about which *Vanity Fair* is organized. It will reveal as well that his sympathetic emotional involvement with certain of his characters, though in some respects a dangerous and distorting practice, was an integral factor in his new-found ability to penetrate to the profounder levels of personality.

* * * In portraying Amelia Thackeray drew on his recollections of Isabella Shawe during his years of courtship and marriage. Upon completing *Vanity Fair* Thackeray told Mrs. Brookfield that she and Mrs. Carmichael-Smyth had also counted for something in the creation of Amelia;[1] but he retracted this statement in another letter to her written three months later. "After all," he then remarked, "I see

† Reprinted by permission of the publishers from *The Buried Life* by Gordon N. Ray (Cambridge: Harvard University Press, 1950), 30–37. Copyright © 1952 by the President and Fellows of Harvard College.

1. "You know you are only a piece of Amelia—My mother is another half: my poor little wife *y est pour beaucoup*" (*The Letters and Private Papers of William Makepeace Thackeray*, ed. Gordon N. Ray, 4 vols. [Cambridge University Press, 1945–46], II, 394).

on reading over my books, that the woman I have been perpetually describing is not you nor my mother but that poor little wife of mine, who now does not care 2d. for anything but her dinner and her glass of porter."[2]

Amelia is presented as a small, shy, defenceless girl who makes her appeal primarily to the protective instinct of the men who admire her. She has the pure mind, the even temper, the warm heart that Thackeray had found in Isabella;[3] but she also shares the deficiencies of Thackeray's wife. Her mental horizon is narrowly limited; she has hardly any interests outside her family and friends. Her amusements are to play and sing at her piano and to gossip. Immersed in the small concerns of domestic life, she is equally unable to take the place in society that George Osborne expects her to occupy and to share the intellectual interests of Dobbin. On most subjects she feels rather than thinks. She is easily stirred emotionally—almost any disappointment reduces her to tears—, and she is a confirmed self-deceiver, never able to see people as they are, always allowing her picture of them to be blurred by her feelings. In sum, she is simple, weak, and ill-equipped for the battle of life.

Now, everyone would admit that there are many such women; no one would deny that Thackeray's insight into the type is comprehensive and profound, omitting none of the essential traits of "the kind, fresh, smiling, artless, tender little domestic goddess, whom men are inclined to worship."[4] Amelia is a complete person, all of whose thoughts and actions are described without suppression or distortion. It was Thackeray's new conception of the novelist's responsibility that enabled him to achieve this portrait. It was this same conception, however, that occasioned the great difficulty that every reader of *Vanity Fair* feels in accepting Thackeray's picture of Amelia, the nature of his commentary about her.

Throughout nine-tenths of his novel Thackeray is himself the blindest worshipper of this domestic goddess. Does Amelia show herself to be empty, silly, and vain? Thackeray asserts that these are the very attributes which he prizes in women. Does she display shallowness and ignorance? Thackeray exults in these deficiencies, holding that women should properly keep aloof from the weightier issues of life. The reader thinks of Fielding's heroine after whom Thackeray christened Amelia—of the self-reliance, the sturdiness, the *serviceableness*, in a word, that she combines with the softer qualities that make her namesake in *Vanity Fair* attractive—and wonders at Thackeray's seeming perverseness.

Knowing from whom Thackeray drew Amelia, we have the key to this discrepancy between text and commentary. Thackeray shows towards the heroine of his novel the same cherishing and tender affection that he had felt for her original in his own life. Hence the fond and indulgent language that he uses about her. On her first appearance she is presented as "one of the best and dearest creatures that

2. *Letters*, II, 440.
3. See *Letters*, I, 321.
4. W. M. Thackeray, *Works*, 17 vols. (London: Oxford University Press, 1908), XI, 131–132 [115].

ever lived."[5] When she offers to kiss her brother, who has brought her a nosegay, Thackeray observes, "I think for a kiss from such a dear creature as Amelia, I would purchase all Mr. Lee's conservatories out of hand."[6] An account of her neglect by George Osborne is followed by a passage of pitying commentary. "Poor little tender heart!" Thackeray begins; "and so it goes on hoping and beating, and longing and trusting."[7] When Amelia's destiny is about to be decided by the Waterloo campaign, Thackeray cannot forbear to inquire: "is it not hard that the fateful rush of the great Imperial struggle can't take place without affecting a poor little harmless girl of eighteen, who is occupied in billing and cooing, or working muslin collars in Russell Square? You, too, kindly, homely flower!"[8]

Inevitably Thackeray drew directly in some passages of Amelia's history upon episodes of his tragic experience with Isabella. His conduct on these occasions sometimes seemed to him in retrospect inadequate and imperceptive. Not surprisingly his fictional reproduction of them is overstrained and excessive. Knowing what Thackeray had been through, one wonders chiefly at the relative sureness of his control. One thinks of Newman's words in his *Apologia pro Vita Sua* before he begins to rehearse the critical events of his Anglican history: "as to that calm contemplation of the past, in itself so desirable, who can afford to be leisurely and deliberate, while he practises on himself a cruel operation, the ripping up of old griefs, and the venturing again upon the 'infandum dolorem' of years, in which the stars of this lower heaven were one by one going out?"[9]

Two examples must suffice of Thackeray's transposition of episodes from his intimate experience to fiction. In describing George Osborne's neglect of Amelia after their marriage and the pain and distress that his disregard causes her, Thackeray was mindful of his own negligence towards Isabella and the degree to which it was responsible for the sad termination of his married life. One accordingly notes in his account of Amelia's sufferings and George's occasional fits of remorse a shrillness, almost a hysteria, quite foreign to Thackeray's usual manner. Consider first a passage in which Thackeray tells of Amelia's visit to her parents' home not long after her marriage, but at a time when she had already been made aware of the careless indifference with which her husband was for the most part to treat her:

> She looked at the little white bed which had been hers a few days before, and thought she would like to sleep in it that night, and wake, as formerly, with her mother smiling over her in the morning. . . . Dear little white bed! how many a long night had she wept on its pillow! How she had despaired and hoped to die there; and now were not all her wishes accomplished, and the lover of whom she had despaired her own for ever? . . . She went and knelt down by the bedside; and there this wounded and

5. *Works*, XI, 881. In the 1864 edition the phrase is altered to "a dear little creature" (p. 7) [5].
6. *Works*, XI, 84 [35].
7. *Works*, XI, 134 [118].
8. *Works*, XI, 211 [178].
9. Ed. Wilfrid Ward (London, 1913), pp. 191–192.

> timorous, but gentle and loving soul, sought for consolation, where as yet, it must be owned, our little girl had but seldom looked for it. Love had been her faith hitherto; and the sad, bleeding, disappointed heart began to feel the want of another consoler.[1]

This is Amelia's (and Isabella's) side of the picture. Elsewhere we are given George Osborne's, which is Thackeray's to a certain extent as well. George has returned to Amelia early in the morning after the Duchess of Richmond's ball:

> By the pale night-lamp he could see her sweet, pale face—the purple eyelids were fringed and closed, and one round arm, smooth and white, lay outside of the coverlet. Good God! how pure she was; how gentle, how tender, and how friendless! and he, how selfish, brutal, and black with crime! Heart-stained, and shame-stricken, he stood at the bed's foot, and looked at the sleeping girl. How dared he—who was he, to pray for one so spotless! God bless her! God bless her! He came to the bedside, and looked at the hand, the little soft hand, lying asleep; and he bent over the pillow noiselessly towards the gentle pale face.
>
> Two fair arms closed tenderly round his neck as he stooped down. 'I am awake, George,' the poor child said, with a sob fit to break the little heart that nestled so closely by his own.[2]

In the ensuing chapters of *Vanity Fair*, where Amelia's sanity seems threatened for a time by the trials that she undergoes, Thackeray drew on his memories of Isabella in August and September, 1840. Dobbin's impressions of Amelia at the time of George's departure for Waterloo may be referred quite specifically to Thackeray's recollections, sharpened and clarified by what afterwards occurred, of Isabella's hysterical despondency at the prospect of being separated from him, when he left for his short tour of Belgium just before her malady declared itself:

> Dobbin . . . got sight of Amelia's face once more. But what a face it was! So white, so wild and despair-stricken, that the remembrance of it haunted him afterwards like a crime, and the sight smote him with inexpressible pangs of longing and pity.
>
> She was wrapped in a white morning dress, her hair falling on her shoulders, and her large eyes fixed and without light. By way of helping on the preparations for the departure, and showing that she too could be useful at a moment so critical, this poor soul had taken up a sash of George's from the drawers whereon it lay, and followed him to and fro with the sash in her hand, looking on mutely as his packing proceeded. She came out and stood, leaning at the wall, holding this sash against her bosom, from which the heavy net of crimson dropped like a large stain of blood. Our gentle-hearted captain felt a guilty shock as he looked at her. 'Good God,' thought he, 'and is it grief like this I dared to pry into?' And there was no help: no means to soothe and comfort this helpless, speechless misery. He stood for a mo-

1. *Works*, XI, 320–321 [262].
2. *Works*, XI, 360 [292–93].

> ment and looked at her, powerless and torn with pity, as a parent regards an infant in pain.[3]

It seems for a time as if the shock of George's departure will be enough in itself to unsettle Amelia's mind. Even Becky is subdued by the state in which she finds her friend:

> 'Are you come to fetch him from me?' she [Amelia] continued in a wilder tone. 'He was here, but is gone now. There on that very sofa he sat. Don't touch it. We sat and talked there. I was on his knee, and my arms were round his neck, and we said, "Our Father." Yes, he was here: and they came and took him away, but he promised me to come back.'
>
> 'He will come back, my dear,' said Rebecca, touched in spite of herself.
>
> 'Look,' said Amelia, 'this is his sash—isn't it a pretty colour?' and she took up the fringe and kissed it. She had tied it round her waist at some part of the day. She had forgotten her anger, her jealousy, and the very presence of her rival seemingly. For she walked silently and almost with a smile on her face, towards the bed, and began to smooth down George's pillow.
>
> Rebecca walked, too, silently away. 'How is Amelia?' asked Jos, who still held his position in the chair.
>
> 'There should be somebody with her,' said Rebecca. 'I think she is very unwell': and she went away with a very grave face.[4]

During many months Amelia's recovery is in doubt; but Thackeray is kinder to her than destiny was to Isabella, and she is permitted to retain her sanity.

Henceforth, perhaps he does not identify Amelia with Isabella so closely as in the earlier part of his novel. But it is only as *Vanity Fair* draws to a close that Thackeray's attitude towards his heroine changes substantially. He originally intended to show her redeemed by her trials from the faults that he had excused but not concealed.

> Dobbin and poor Briggs are the only 2 people with real humility as yet, [he wrote after the first third of the novel was completed]. Amelia's is to come, when her scoundrel of a husband is well dead with a ball in his odious bowels; when she has had sufferings, a child, and a religion.[5]

But this intended rehabilitation did not take place. In the final double number of *Vanity Fair* Thackeray regards Amelia with none of the forbearance that he had hitherto displayed towards her. Perhaps the mature woman in her middle thirties who rejects Dobbin on his return from India no longer brought Isabella to Thackeray's mind.[6] In any event, he does not defend Amelia when Dobbin, exacerbated by long ill-usage, turns on her at last.

3. *Works*, XI, 371–372 [300–1].
4. *Works*, XI, 383 [310].
5. *Letters*, II, 309.
6. One is reminded of the very different pictures that Dickens drew of the young Maria Beadnell as Dora in *David Copperfield* and of the middle-aged Maria Beadnell as Flora Finching in *Little Dorrit*. There is considerable evidence, it should be noted, that Thackeray modelled the Amelia of *Vanity Fair*'s later chapters upon Mrs. Brookfield quite as much as upon Isabella. In the early months of 1848 Thackeray was not yet profoundly attached to Mrs. Brookfield, since his intimacy with her was just beginning. See *Letters*, II, 394–395, 684.

> No, you are not worthy of the love which I have devoted to you [Dobbin tells her]. I knew all along that the prize I had set my life on was not worth the winning; that I was a fool, with fond fancies, too, bartering away my all of truth and ardour against your little feeble remnant of love. I will bargain no more: I withdraw. I find no fault with you. You are very good-natured, and have done your best; but you couldn't—you couldn't reach up to the height of the attachment which I bore you, and which a loftier soul than yours might have been proud to share.[7]

Thackeray offers no mitigation of his searching and severe analysis; and the reader is left with the impression that like Dobbin he has weighed Amelia and found her wanting. It is true that he marries her to Dobbin,[8] but this development is hardly presented as Dobbin's crowning felicity. "If I had made Amelia a higher order of woman," Thackeray explained to Robert Bell, "there would have been no vanity in Dobbin's falling in love with her, whereas the impression at present is that he is a fool for his pains that he has married a silly little thing and in fact has found out his error rather a sweet and tender one however, *quia multum amavit.*"[9] Thus Amelia too is made to illustrate the theme of Thackeray's book: "Which of us is happy in this world? Which of us has his desire? or, having it, is satisfied?"[1]

Apart from these final chapters of *Vanity Fair,* however, every reader of the novel is conscious of the discrepancy between what Amelia says and does and the opinion that Thackeray entertains of her. We have seen how this incongruity had its origin in the emotional allegiance that Thackeray felt towards Amelia because of his identification of her with his wife. The question remains whether it seriously impairs her success as a character. From the first Thackeray's favoritism irritated readers into protest. Miss Rigby wrote contemptuously in the *Quarterly Review* of "the little dolt Amelia," all of whose "philoprogenitive idolatries do not touch us like one fond instinct of 'stupid Rawdon.' "[2] The *Athenæum*'s critic noted that "Even the heroine Amelia—with whom the writer seems to have been somewhat enamoured (a feeling of which he is likely to have the monopoly)—is thoroughly selfish as well as silly."[3] And the *Spectator,* reproving Thackeray for his praise of Amelia, found her conduct "rather mawkish than interesting."[4] But for the most part Victorian readers were gratified by Thackeray's open partisanship. It assured them, and the assurance was welcome in so mocking and misanthropic a book as they

7. *Works,* XI, 852–853 [670].
8. He perhaps yielded to pressure from his readers in this matter. "Mrs. Liddell one day said, 'Oh, Mr. Thackeray, you must let Dobbin marry Amelia.' 'Well,' he replied, 'he shall; and when he has got her, he will not find her worth having.' " (*Letters,* II, 642). George Eliot's comment concerning Trollope's *Sir Harry Hotspur of Humblethwaite* applies equally to the conclusion of Thackeray's history of Dobbin and Amelia: "Men are very fond of glorifying that sort of dog-like attachment," she wrote (J. W. Cross, *George Eliot's Life as Related in her Letters and Journals,* 3 vols. [Edinburgh: W. Blackwoods, 1885], III, 128). "It is one thing to love because you falsely imagine goodness,—that belongs to the finest natures,—and another to go on loving when you have found out your mistake."
9. *Letters,* II, 423.
1. *Works,* XI, 878 [688].
2. "*Vanity Fair*—and *Jane Eyre,*" *Quarterly Review* LXXXIV (December, 1848), 159–160 [763].
3. "*Vanity Fair,*" *Athenæum,* 12 August 1848, p. 795.
4. "*Vanity Fair,*" *Spectator,* 22 July 1848, p. 709.

found *Vanity Fair* to be, that Thackeray (like Disraeli some years later) was after all "on the side of the angels."

As the nineteenth century drew to a close, and the Victorian heroine (of whom Amelia had come to be regarded as the great prototype and exemplar) fell into disfavor, critics friendly to Thackeray but anxious to bring his books into harmony with the new age hit on a curious theory. Assuming that so intelligent a writer must have shared their own opinions, they interpreted his praise of Amelia as ironical. So Charles Whibley assures us that "Amelia, a very Niobe of tears, is drawn with a cold contempt, and I am not certain that she is not as savage a piece of satire as Becky herself."[5] Similarly the writer of a centenary article on Thackeray in the *Fortnightly Review* holds that Amelia is "A satire on the conventional theory of feminine virtue which prevailed sixty years ago. She is the traditional good woman of the poets and novelists reduced to an absurdity."[6] More recently Miss Elizabeth Drew has advanced a somewhat different account of Thackeray's intentions with regard to Amelia, also designed to palliate his offences against modern taste.

> It is impossible as we read Thackeray [she contends in a paragraph already quoted in part] not to be convinced that he had the greatest contempt for the opinion of his day as to what made a 'good woman.' . . . We feel Thackeray himself to have envisaged very clearly the truth of the position [between Dobbin and Amelia]—indeed it is proved that he does so by Dobbin's final outburst, where he declares her to be a mere self-deceiver in her idiotic fidelity to the memory of her worthless young husband, and to be quite unworthy of the love he has devoted to her. But this declaration comes too late, and is hopelessly weakened by Thackeray having kept us in the dark throughout the book as to his real opinion, and having time upon time insisted that Amelia is the perfect type of sweet selfless womanhood. This is what his age wanted to think, and that is what he feels he must give them.[7]

These attempts at benevolent exegesis are interesting chiefly as illustrations of the ease with which critics otherwise well-equipped may come a cropper because of their deficiency in historical sense. The disparity between Amelia's character and Thackeray's commentary upon it cannot be explained away, though it can be accounted for. But should this discrepancy greatly trouble the modern reader? It is not as if Thackeray had allowed his partisanship to blur the lines of his portrait. He tells the truth about Amelia, even when he praises her most outrageously. It is the sharp fidelity with which he reports her words and actions, indeed, that arouses his reader to so acute a sense of dissatisfaction with his comments upon them. Thackeray rightly claims in his preface to *Vanity Fair* that "the Amelia doll . . . has . . . been carved and dressed with the greatest care by the artist."[8] His new-found human sympathy enabled him to cut beneath the sur-

5. A statement in the introduction to the interesting edition of *Vanity Fair* published by Chivers at Bath in 1919. Whibley had been equally positive in *William Makepeace Thackeray* (London, 1903), p. 96. "There is little doubt," he wrote, "that Thackeray despised Amelia."
6. "Mrs. Rawdon Crawley," *Fortnightly Review* XCV (June, 1911), 1022.
7. *The Enjoyment of Literature* (New York, 1933), pp. 118–119.
8. *Works*, XI, 2.

face to the deeper levels of personality in drawing Amelia's portrait, to proceed much further in the detailed analysis of character than he had in any of the figures of his earlier fiction. Need we be too severe in judging the occasional excesses of sentiment into which he is led? Perhaps we should do better to apply to Amelia Henry James's words concerning the most appealing of his heroines, Isabel Archer: "she would be an easy victim of scientific criticism if she were not intended to awaken on the reader's part an impulse more tender."[9]

## EDGAR F. HARDEN

# The Discipline and Significance of Form in *Vanity Fair*†

Almost all critics of *Vanity Fair* have assumed that Thackeray's novel had no very carefully worked out structure and have been content to make rather general comments on the form of the novel: it was loosely improvised along the line of a contrast between Becky and Amelia. J. Y. T. Greig, for example, believes that Thackeray not only lacked Fielding's ability to work out a highly detailed plot but also suffered from the additional handicap of being forced to compose hurriedly for monthly serialization. To Greig, "*Vanity Fair* is unified and shapely up to and including the episodes of Brussels and the Battle of Waterloo: for although it contains two heroines, the adventures and sufferings of the one are causally related to the adventures and sufferings of the other. It becomes unified and shapely again after Chapter xliii (Pumpernickel), and for the same reason. But in between—roughly 300 pages—the plot of the first and last sections of the book is suspended, and the unity of the novel disappears."[1]

These statements raise a number of issues that invite special comment. In the first place, a causal relationship between the adventures and sufferings of Becky and those of Amelia is almost totally nonexistent prior to the reunion of the married couples in Brighton (Chapter xxii).[2] Up to that point, the adventures of the two girls had led them to Russell Square and agreeable hours with Jos and George, but after that, the sole causal relationship had occurred when Amelia's position as George's fiancée caused him snobbishly to prevent Becky's entering the family by marrying Jos; George's deliberate attempt to embarrass the suffering Vauxhall carouser on the morning after (p. 62) [59–60] caused Jos's headlong flight to Cheltenham (Chapter vi). Between Chapters vi and xxv, there is no causal connection whatever

9. *The Portrait of a Lady.*

† Reprinted by permission of the Modern Language Association of America from *PMLA* 82 (1967): 530–41.

1. J. Y. T. Greig, *Thackeray: A Reconsideration* (London and New York, 1950), p. 106. See also such appraisals as Anthony Trollope, *Thackeray* (New York and London, 1902), p. 96; Charles Whibley, *William Makepeace Thackeray* (Edinburgh and London, 1903), pp. 91–92; George Saintsbury, *A Consideration of Thackeray* (London, 1931), p. 166; and John W. Dodds, *Thackeray: A Critical Portrait* (New York, 1963), p. 110.

2. All citations are taken from *Vanity Fair*, ed. Geoffrey and Kathleen Tillotson (Boston, 1963). [Page references in brackets are to this Norton Critical Edition.]

between the two plots. Furthermore, though Becky's later success in gaining entry to the household of Jos and Amelia indeed isolates Amelia (Chapter lxvi) and places her in jeopardy (Chapter lxvii), there are few other effects; Thackeray is at pains to show that Amelia wrote the crucial letter to Dobbin before Becky urged her to do so and produced George's note [679–80].

Indeed, there is no necessity for an intimate causal relationship between the two plots of any novel, especially this one. The thematic significance of *Vanity Fair* depends not on any such causal relationship but on parallels among the lives of its characters. The novel's structure shows careful planning and an intricate linking of details. Furthermore, such phenomena as the exigencies of serial publication and Thackeray's tardiness, which critics like Greig so easily assume to be causes of poor artistry, require further study and interpretation. Almost alone among critics of Thackeray, Mrs. Tillotson has argued that "the serial novel, serially written, is . . . really the less likely to be loose and rambling."[3] While acknowledging that Thackeray's continuing journalistic efforts required considerable time, and remembering that his labors for each monthly part included the creation of drawings for two steel engravings and a number of woodcuts, one might also suggest that Thackeray's frequent struggles at the end of the month can justly be seen not simply as the result of indolence and the cause of poor workmanship, but perhaps equally as evidence of agonizing efforts to write a well-ordered serial novel.

Since we have little surviving evidence of Thackeray's practices in composing *Vanity Fair*, except for the manuscript in the Morgan Library that preserves twelve of the first thirteen chapters, we must turn to the printed text and study it primarily as a serial publication. When we do, we discover evidence that revises our opinion of Thackeray's method and permits a deeper awareness of the relationship between theme and structure in *Vanity Fair*. So far, the two chief studies of unity in Thackeray have been by Geoffrey Tillotson and Myron Taube. Tillotson believes that although none of Thackeray's novels reveals the wonders of plot construction found in *Tom Jones*, "Thackeray had it in him to have made a big intricate unity."[4] In writing *Vanity Fair*, Thackeray very possibly had no more than a sketch of the general plot, which he fleshed out as he went along (hence, for example, the repeated postponement of Waterloo), but as Gordon Ray has shown, he did know his direction long in advance.[5] The question then becomes one of method: exactly how did he go about organizing the novel?

Tillotson asserts that in Thackeray's novels the reader finds "continuity" (p. 20), a oneness of subject, form, and manner, while Taube explains[6] that *Vanity Fair* abandons the traditional unity of plot and instead finds coherence in a new principle: the contrast of characters and their actions. Each monthly number concentrates on revealing

3. K. Tillotson, *Novels of the Eighteen-Forties* (Oxford, 1956), pp. 239–240.
4. G. Tillotson, *Thackeray the Novelist* (London, 1963), p. 12.
5. *Thackeray: The Uses of Adversity* (New York, 1955), pp. 406–409, 499.
6. Myron Taube, "Contrast as a Principle of Structure in *Vanity Fair*," *NCF*, XVIII (1963), 119–135.

the characters and does so by providing us with a complete set of contrasts. Except for the misleading assertion that the contrasts come "complete" (p. 131) in each number, these statements are true, though they still leave the novel with only an intermittent regularity. Taube has emphasized the pairings *within* individual numbers, but further examination of the work leads to a more radical discovery. Although it has been claimed that Thackeray's novel lacks the kind of design that keeps the reader aware of its overall unity,[7] the fundamental argument of this paper is the exact reverse. *Vanity Fair* has a thorough-going pattern that specifically pairs and groups successive installments, carefully linking one serial part to another with multiple and rhythmic connections. As the original subtitle implies, sketch is matched with sketch, portrait with portrait, and action with action.

We do not know exactly when Thackeray began planning or writing *Vanity Fair*; we can merely observe that the surviving fragment of text in the Morgan manuscript appears to have been started by early 1845, about two years prior to the beginning of serial publication. Some time before 8 May 1845 a portion of the novel had been submitted to Henry Colburn with inconclusive results, but Thackeray had found a publisher by January 1846; the novel's appearance was subsequently deferred from May of that year until January 1847. The point is that after the original period of incubation Thackeray had a considerable length of time for further thought, during which he found a new principle of design. Although Thackeray's manuscript in the Morgan Library shows numerous revisions, one stands out: the writing and insertion of Chapter v, "Dobbin of Ours," into an older version of the text. This addition was crucial, for thereby Thackeray committed himself to the pattern of the novel as we now have it.[8] Chapter v makes a vital connection with Chapter i and so begins the symmetrical arrangement of monthly parts that represents Thackeray's most interesting contribution to the form of the serial novel. The outline (see Appendix) indicates this structure. Though the schema has a cumulative weight, such an extreme condensation of materials limits the conclusiveness of the arguments. The outline, therefore, is intended to serve as a guide through the complicated detail; its implications will be discussed below.

The parallel structure of the first two numbers has been recognized, though not in a sufficiently exact way. Professor and Mrs. Tillotson, for example, offer thematic justification for Chapter v and briefly explain how the structure of the new number recalls that of its predecessor by balancing Swishtail's against Miss Pinkerton's and showing how the schoolboy relations and snobberies extend into the adult world (p. xix). One might add that the prominent mock-heroic tone[9] also enforces the parallelism between the two chapters, as does the satire on English schools and school life. Yet there are also a number of specific parallels that provoke comparison and contrast.

7. G. Tillotson, *Thackeray the Novelist*, p. 49.
8. For a summary of the evidence covering this two-year period, see Ray, *Thackeray: The Uses of Adversity*, pp. 384–387, 494–495, and *Vanity Fair*, pp. xvii–xxi, xxvii–xxix.
9. For a discussion of the mock-heroic tone and its function in these two chapters and later, see my article "The Fields of Mars in *Vanity Fair*," *Tennessee Studies in Literature*, x (1965), 123–132.

In Chapter i, Amelia's character and popularity contrast with Becky's character and unpopularity; the same antithesis exists in Chapter v between Cuff and Dobbin. Therefore, in comparing the two underdogs, we see the pointed difference between Becky and Dobbin, which is further developed in these two chapters and later. In Chapter i, when Miss Pinkerton is bidding farewell to Amelia, Becky enters and disrupts the parting; in Chapter v, when Cuff is beating George, Dobbin intervenes to defend the victim. The first climax in Chapter i consists of a battle between Becky and her mock-heroic opponent, Miss Pinkerton; the Dobbin-Cuff engagement obviously recalls that incident, not only by being another battle, but because both Becky and Dobbin are struggling against domineering bullies after having had an indecisive encounter with their rivals previously. Becky's "little battle" (p. 16) [7] with Miss Pinkerton is fought for baser motives, of course, and with crueller weapons. She gains her objective—freedom—and then insults Miss Pinkerton amusingly but also gratuitously, snobbishly, and with malice.

This characterization of Becky is reinforced in the second climax and its parallels: after Becky sweepingly rejects Miss Jemima's generous if simple-minded present of the dictionary, events in Chapter v twice serve to contrast with her gesture. Cuff magnanimously offers assistance to Dobbin, who blushingly accepts it; as an indirect result, Dobbin receives a prize-book in Becky's "mother-tongue" (p. 19) [10] and generously responds by giving a tuck-out for the whole school (p. 51) [45]. The only section[1] of either chapter that does not fit into a joint pattern is the ending of Chapter v (pp. 52–54) [46–48], which carries forward from the conclusion of the first number the movement towards Vauxhall. The final important fact to observe, however, is that Thackeray has begun a practice he will repeat: a suspension of chronological development allows him not only to offer information retrospectively but to present material in a sequence parallel to that of an earlier number. Almost the whole of Chapter v manifests this practice.

The middle of the first number, Chapters ii and iii, might be entitled "The Opening of the Campaign Against Joseph Sedley"; its counterpart, Chapter vi, relates the close of that campaign. We begin with two coach rides, one to Russell Square and one to Vauxhall, and then slip into two retrospective sections: the narrator's unfavorable account of Becky's past (pp. 20–24) [11–16], including her attempts on the Reverend Mr. Crisp, and, in Chapter vi, a survey of foolishly favorable attitudes towards a match between Becky and Jos (pp. 55–56) [52–53]. After arriving in Russell Square and touring the Sedley house, Amelia gives Becky presents and important information about Jos's financial and bachelor status; the section ends as Becky silently vows to catch Jos (p. 25) [17]. After the arrival at Vauxhall in Chapter vi, Becky also goes on a tour, this time with Amelia's brother through

1. I use the term "section" in referring to those portions of each chapter that are marked off by a break in the text. Ch. v, for example, has 4 sections: pp. 38–40, 40–43, 43–46, and 46–48. The latter is one of the relatively few sections that has no counterpart in a paired number. Though Ch. i has only 2 sections, it offers parallels to the 3 sections of Ch. v, just as the 3 chapters of No. 2 pair off with the 4 chapters of No. 1.

the gardens; though Becky encourages Jos all she can, here it is his intention that remains unspoken (p. 60) [55], and so her vow of Chapter ii remains unfulfilled. The ironic point of this comic pairing seems clear: his blundering is a match for her cunning.

In Chapter iii, Mr. Sedley's mocking of Jos's appearance seriously alarms the timid dandy, but when in Chapter vi George more selfishly and elaborately makes fun of Jos's behavior, the effect is even more unsettling. Mr. Sedley's action, though coarse, contrasts favorably with George's conduct, for the young man's motives are as snobbish and pompous as anything in the behavior of his victim. George's mimicry, of course, rasps on the tender nerves of the bacchanalian, who is not mollified as in Chapter iii, but left alone to ponder on his ludicrousness. Consequently, while Becky could quickly recover from the embarrassments of curry and chili (pp. 30–31) [22–23], Jos finds the aftereffects of rack-punch and mockery more agonizing and enduring: he stays in bed all day and dares not return to Russell Square (pp. 63–64) [59–62]. Therefore, while Chapter iii ends with only a temporary setback for Becky, who fruitlessly awaits the timid Jos in the drawing-room upstairs, Chapter vi comes to a climax as Amelia watches George approach her father's house while Becky looks out in vain for Jos. In place of the tip-toeing Jos departing from Russell Square in Chapter iii, we have Jos's note announcing his departure from London without calling again; it is then Becky who must leave Russell Square permanently.

The concluding chapter of Number Two ironically establishes Sir Pitt Crawley and, to a lesser degree, his younger son as counterparts to Mr. Sedley and Jos. In Chapter iv, Jos had arrived at Russell Square to begin a new, if limited, series of adventures with Becky; Chapter vii begins as Becky arrives in Great Gaunt Street for an introduction to a new and considerable series of experiences. The analogies are all comically inverted: here the place at a prosperous table of the coarsely jesting Mr. Sedley, whose notion of placating his victim consists of offering him excellent champagne (pp. 34–35) [27], is taken by the coarsely jesting Sir Pitt, offering Becky a drop of beer, demanding his pint for carrying her baggage, and finally apportioning out the penurious fare of tripe and onion (pp. 70–71) [69–70].

The thunderstorm which keeps the young people indoors in Chapter iv leads to a cheerful evening at Russell Square, as Jos entertains Becky with long stories about India (pp. 38–39) [29] amid the festive accompaniments of music and refreshments, while in Chapter vii Becky spends a much more quiet evening in the dark house on Great Gaunt Street, though she finds entertainment in listening to Sir Pitt's extended confidences (p. 71) [71]. The two numbers end as Jos fails to propose while bound in Becky's green silk skein but prepares himself for Vauxhall by vowing to "pop the question" (p. 44) [36] there; in Chapter vii, after the failure of her campaign against Jos, Becky looks toward a new quarry and prepares for Queen's Crawley by choosing to dream of Rawdon (p. 72) [72]. Apparently a short passage was needed to fill out the second number, since the lament for things past has no counterpart in Number One. Thackeray makes his addition relevant by casting the passage in a melancholy tone and adopting his characteristic point of view, the retrospective vision, which culminates here in the cry: *ubi sunt?* Just as the Gardens in which Jos prepared for an imaginary future with Becky have now passed away, so too the evanescence of Becky's conveyance, as she moves towards her insubstantial future, has been revealed by time.

After indicating his novel's structure by this obvious pairing of the first two monthly numbers, Thackeray went on to elaborate his technique, grouping most of the numbers together in pairs and gathering the rest, on two occasions, into units of three. Unlike most subsequent readers, his original audience did not have the disadvantage of reading an edition that ignored the novel's division into serial parts. Consequently, Thackeray could count on some recognition of *Vanity Fair*'s structure. For the less observant reader, he added overt cross-references between the grouped numbers.

One such obvious link connecting Numbers Three, Four, and Five can be found at the end of Chapters viii, xii, and xv, where the narrator comments on his own role. In Number Three, he asks us to recognize the difference between him and his characters so that we may be fully aware of his moral purpose: "to combat and expose" (p. 81) [84] folly and evil while approving goodness. In Number Four, we are requested to observe the distinction between selfishness and idolatry. While "shift, self, and poverty" (p. 112) [121] instruct Becky and find their emblem in the orange blossoms of mercenary attachments (p. 113) [121], and while Amelia is guilty of an extravagant hero-worship, yet if we understand the superiority of the warm-hearted excess over the coldly calculating one, we can adequately sympathize with Amelia's love for George and value "this blind devotion" (p. 114) [122], for it is directed towards another human being instead of solely tnowards one's self. At this point the narrator reminds us of his omniscience and his ability to play a dual part, but he renounces the betraying role of Iachimo for the approving role of Moonshine, since Amelia's love reflects faith, beauty, and innocence (p. 114) [122], in contrast to the "Faithless, Hopeless, Charityless" (p. 81) [84] rogues of Chapters viii, xii, and—as we are about to see—xv.

In the corresponding portion of Number Five, the narrator explicitly recalls this passage while talking about Becky: "If, a few pages back, the present writer claimed the privilege of peeping into Miss Amelia Sedley's bed-room, and understanding with the omniscience of the novelist all the gentle pains and passions which were tossing upon that innocent pillow, why should he not declare himself to be Rebecca's confidante too, master of her secrets, and seal-keeper of that young woman's conscience?" (p. 148) [158]. Now, however, he goes on to expose rather than sympathize and approve. Moreover, by recalling the earlier passage, itself connected to the one at the end of Chapter viii, in effect he asks us to compare the three of them and to notice how he applies the original purpose (Chapter viii) to approve behavior in Chapter xii and to undermine it in Chapter xv. Amelia, we are told in Chapter xii, has "not a well-regulated mind" (p. 114) [122]; instead of acting in a well-regulated and, by implication, selfish way, she manifests the genuine feeling that makes selfish, patterned behavior seem empty and worthless. As a result of this tripartite structure, we can now, in Chapter xv, understand those passages fully, for we again see the desire to serve one's self by worldly attachment; this time Becky manifests it and the ironic narrator calls such a desire the wish of a "properly regulated mind" (p. 148) [158]. When Becky regrets that she had to decline such "a piece of marvellous good fortune" (p. 148) [158] as marriage to Sir Pitt, we see the orange-blossom mentality at work again. Only, this time, instead of sympathizing with its opposite, the narrator emphasizes the shortcomings of selfishness. Becky's hasty choice of the impecunious Rawdon when she might have had the baronet clearly reveals how the calculations of human beings are inevitably limited by the incalculable. Therefore, we are placed in a position to evaluate, as Becky cannot in her eager greed, the improbability of her hope for Rawdon's future and for Miss Crawley's money (pp. 149–150) [158–59].

Another example of the narrator's openly calling attention to a parallelism of successive monthly units occurs in Numbers Twelve and Thirteen. The subject is a series of contrasts between the Osborne and Sedley households. Chapter xlii opens with pictures of Osborne's tyranny and unhappiness (pp. 411–412) [424], while Chapter xlvi shows us Sedley's dependency and unhappiness (pp. 443–444) [457]. Fred Bullock's mercenary behavior (p. 412) [424] is set off by Clapp's faithful attachment (p. 444) [458], and Maria's coldness to her father (pp. 413–414) [425–26] by Amelia's devotion to her son (pp. 444–446) [458–59]. We then shift to a completely overt parallelism as the narrator recalls Jane Osborne's "awful existence" (p. 414) [427], caused especially by her father's continuing estrangement from young George and his growing rage at his other grandchildren: "We have seen how one of George's grandfathers . . . , in his easy chair in Russell Square, daily grew more violent and moody, and how his daughter, with her fine carriage, and her fine horses, and her name on half the public charity lists of the town, was a lonely, miserable, persecuted old maid" (p. 446) [459]. Now, however, Osborne is about to relent towards George, and so towards Jane. The purpose of the narrator's cross-reference, therefore, is to remind us of what prompts Osborne's brooding tyranny and to highlight its reversal: Jane sees young George and tells Osborne (p. 417) [429] at the end of Number Twelve, while at the end of Number Thirteen, Osborne himself sees the boy (p. 447) [460] and Amelia comes to believe that young George's future is properly with his wealthy grandfather (p. 450) [463]. To understand one number fully, we have to retain a consciousness of its paired predecessor.

We are assisted in doing so by Thackeray's illustrations as well as by his text. In Numbers Six and Seven, for example, the growth and diminution of George's devotion to Amelia is governed primarily by the presence of other women, as the engraving of Miss Swartz (p. 200) [211] and that of the "Family Party at Brighton" (p. 235) [244] remind us. Likewise in Number Sixteen, to epitomize young George's life in Osborne's house and to emphasize the epistolary connection to Numbers Fourteen and Fifteen, Thackeray provides an engraving

(p. 544) [568] that depicts the young sybarite taking up a letter from a tray being held out to him. In Numbers Seventeen and Eighteen the happy reunion of Dobbin and Amelia, captured in part by a steel engraving (p. 564) [583], is matched and developed by their happiness together in Germany, with its engraving, "A fine Summer Evening" (p. 599) [619].

As we make these connections between numbers, we discover that the effects produced by Thackeray's technique are infinitely varied. At one point, for example, the eighth and ninth numbers focus on a series of contrasts between individual characters: Amelia's wifely incompetence (p. 248) [258] and Mrs. O'Dowd's capable preparations (pp. 282–284) [293–95]; Amelia's melancholy response to marriage (p. 251) [261–62] and Rawdon's joyous one (p. 284) [295]; and finally, George's collection and then dispersal of his inheritance (p. 254) [262–63] versus Rawdon's presentation of his effects to Becky and her calculation of their worth (pp. 286–288) [296–99]. This series ends with a widening of scope: morning approaches as the transports load for departure to Belgium (p. 260) [270–71], and it arrives as the regiment marches off to war (p. 290) [301]. At another point, we find the most famous use of pairing: to produce the effect of shocking contrast of events. Number Eight ends with dawn, as the city awakes (p. 281) [293], and the first major section of the novel is brought to a close with the last (revised) words of Number Nine: "Darkness came down on the field and city: and Amelia was praying for George, who was lying on his face, dead, with a bullet through his heart" (p. 315) [326]. Thackeray also uses parallels for the purpose of alternating contrasts and comparisons, as he does in connecting Numbers Three, Four, and Five. Pitt's ambition (Chapter ix) establishes a value with which we contrast Amelia's love (Chapter xiii) and compare the selfish ambitions of Becky and Mrs. Bute (Chapter xvi). Sir Pitt's prosperity (pp. 85–86) [88–90] then finds lateral counterparts in Osborne's dominance (pp. 120–122) [129–34] and, ironically, in Miss Crawley's hysteria and Sir Pitt's impotent rage when they discover the identity of Becky's husband (pp. 157–158) [168–69].

The development of action may also occur laterally and produce rhythmic sequences. After the new Sir Pitt's familial letter to Rawdon (pp. 397–398) [408–9] and his check for little Rawdon (p. 429) [442], we note Becky's delight at the first acknowledgment (p. 399) [410] and then compare her use of the second, which reveals more clearly how financially "unsafe" (p. 429) [442] her position is. We observe a worsening also in a succeeding parallel: in Chapter xl, Becky frees herself from her husband's company and attention by securing a "house-dog" (p. 400) [412], Briggs; in Chapter xliv, the servants have come to believe her guilty of using that liberty to establish an adulterous relationship with Steyne (p. 432) [444]. The two visits of Becky and Rawdon to Queen's Crawley continue the pattern: in Chapter xli, Becky conciliates both Sir Pitt and Lady Jane (pp. 405–407) [415–17], but she is not so successful with Lady Jane (p. 439) [452] on her next visit (Chapter xlv). In Chapters xx and xxiv, Dobbin arranges George's marriage in the former (pp. 186–187) [198–202] and tells

Osborne about it in the corresponding portion of the latter (pp. 218–221) [230]. Whereas George's vanity is flattered by Amelia's love (p. 187) [196], his father's vanity is first flattered by the false expectation of surrender and then balked by the news of George's marriage (p. 221) [228]. In addition, Sedley's senile anger and empty prohibition (pp. 191–193) [202] find their more extreme and effective counterparts in Osborne's violent rage and alteration of his will (pp. 221–226) [230–34]. Even their facial appearances suggest each other: Sedley's ghastly expression at hitting Osborne a blow (p. 193) [202] and Osborne's "strange look" at having dealt with George (p. 226) [236].

One should note especially that the novelist could accomplish this parallelism only by distorting the narrative sequence, and that such a distortion suggests the strength of Thackeray's wish to achieve symmetry and rhythmic progression of the narrative. Instead of ending Number Six with, say, a condensed version of Chapter xxiii culminating in the avenging thunderclap at the door (p. 217) [226], Thackeray chooses to end it by shifting to Brighton. Consequently, Chapters xxiii and xxiv, which deal with Dobbin's efforts in London and parallel the structure of Chapters xix and xx, constitute a flashback. Admittedly, several additional reasons may be offered to explain this particular distortion, the most plausible of which seems to be that Thackeray had already decided on the conclusion of Number Seven and therefore wished to end Number Six with mention of the move towards Belgium; repeated evidence also makes clear, however, that doubling back appears at such times and is conducted in such a way as to preserve and take advantage of the structural pattern outlined in this essay.

At one point the narrator calls attention to his maneuver and emphasizes its plausibility: "Our history is destined in this chapter to go backwards and forwards in a very irresolute manner seemingly, and having conducted our story to to-morrow presently, we shall immediately again have occasion to step back to yesterday, so that the whole of the tale may get a hearing" (p. 234) [246]. Insofar as this narrative retrospection is a comic "disorder," however, it is a disorder related to the war—in fact, caused by the war:

> Although all the little incidents must be heard, yet they must be put off when the great events make their appearance; and surely such a circumstance as that which brought Dobbin to Brighton, viz. the ordering out of the Guards and the line to Belgium, and the mustering of the allied armies in that country under the command of his Grace the Duke of Wellington—such a dignified circumstance as that, I say, was entitled to the *pas* over all minor occurrences whereof this history is composed mainly, and hence a little trifling disarrangement and disorder was excusable and becoming. (p. 236) [246]

The narrative disorder is only seeming, of course, and has its various effects. Amid the comedy we already have an ironic foreshadowing: when we come to observe the disarrangement and disorder caused by the war, they will be neither "excusable," "becoming," nor, ultimately, "trifling," but they and not the "dignified" circumstances will, as usual, constitute the novel's subject matter and interest. Consequently, in terms of the narrative structure, "dignified" circumstances and the events of men's little peacetime pursuits each take their appropriate place; as the mocking tone of the passage indicates, though the former may ostensibly take precedence, the latter will comment on them and reduce their significance at last, as we shall see at the end of Number Seven, for example. The climax of Number Seven balances and undercuts the "dignified circumstance" which concludes Number Six, for the news of the army being ordered to Belgium finds its ironic structural equivalent in the news of money which sends Becky and Rawdon to London. The mixture of discomfiture and amusement, success and failure, which we see at the end of this portion of the novel suggests also what the war will bring to all these characters, and such appears to be the passage's ultimate purpose.

Looking at *Vanity Fair* from a more distant standpoint, we can see nine blocks of material that fall into groups of four and five, the demarcation coming after the battle of Waterloo. The first block begins with the departure from Chiswick Mall and the opening of the campaign against Jos (Number One); it concludes with the close of the campaign against him and with Becky's subsequent departure from London (Number Two). Block Two commences as Becky establishes herself with Sir Pitt (Number Three) and concludes as Amelia is accepted by George (Number Five). Unsuccessful efforts to conciliate Miss Crawley begin and close the third block, while the fourth moves from England to Waterloo. In short, the first portion of the novel rises to a climax in its middle, which is found in the unique block of three numbers. Actually we find a double climax: first comes the revelation that Becky has a husband; then Number Five, the center of these nine numbers, reveals his identity and triumphantly concludes with Amelia's success in getting a husband, thereby preparing for the climax of Number Nine when she loses him.

This larger movement, first toward the success represented by marriage and then away from it to complete separation, is reversed in the last five-ninths of the novel, and in terms of an elaborate counterrhythm. This time there is a central block and it consists of the only other unit comprising three numbers; moreover, the symmetry is utterly precise, for the climax occurs in the middle number of the central block, Number Fifteen, when Becky's marriage is permanently disrupted. This event is thus the negative counterpart of Block Two's climax. The novel's concluding movement then develops Amelia's success, as she now finds her second husband. Here is the positive counterpart of Amelia's loss of George at the end of Block Four (Number Nine). Since Becky began the pattern of rejections in Chapter i, it remains in Chapter lxvii only for Dobbin and Amelia to reject her.[2] In an overall as well as closely detailed sense, therefore, *Vanity*

2. Contrast the admiring but inaccurate description by Lord David Cecil in *Early Victorian Novelists* (London, 1934), p. 80.

*Fair* shows thorough "unity" and "shapeliness," to adopt the terms and values of Greig and others critical of Thackeray's craftsmanship.

Thackeray never again organized a novel quite so elaborately, and his subsequent works themselves suggest reasons why. Perhaps after mastering the exacting compositional requirements of a novel published in parts, he found the intricacy of *Vanity Fair*'s pattern too demanding; it is certain, however, that the particular method of this work is not nearly so appropriate for his later serial novels because they do not offer the contrasts produced by a continuous double plot. Though his next serial, *Pendennis* (1848–50), is also a novel without a "hero," it does have one main character and it follows his adventures with a single-mindedness absent from *Vanity Fair.* The same is true in varying degrees of *The Newcomes* (1853–55), each half of *The Virginians* (1857–59), and the late shorter works: *Lovel the Widower* (1860), *Philip* (1861–62), and *Denis Duval* (1864), all three of which appeared in the looser confines of a periodical. We can still see traces of the lateral pattern in *Pendennis,* but not in *The Newcomes* nor in any work written after *Henry Esmond* (1852). *Esmond,* of course, reverts to the older kind of plot mastered by Fielding and remains independent of the demands made by publication in parts; as a regression in this sense, it helps mark a permanent change in Thackeray's writing habits.

Instead, then, of developing an elaborate plot in *Vanity Fair,* Thackeray offers us two loose plots with highly articulated connections. The functions of such a pattern seem apparent. A writer still making the transition from journalism to novel-writing and beginning an ambitious attempt to construct a full, twenty-layered work—according to the standards set by Dickens[3]—apparently needed the restraints imposed by this new form. Although Thackeray had previously written fiction for serialization, he had now to deal with the immense difference between writing for periodical publication in a magazine and for serialization in separate monthly numbers; the difference, in a word, is uniformity in length. As a glance at *Fraser's Magazine* will show, none of Thackeray's fiction before *Vanity Fair* had appeared in equal installments. For example, the installments of *Catherine* (1839–40) varied between 9 and 18 pages, those of *A Shabby Genteel Story* (1840), between 12 and 16, those of *The Great Hoggarty Diamond* (1841), between 11 and 20, and those of *Barry Lyndon* (1844), between 12 and 20 pages. Even in *Barry Lyndon,* the work which offers closest parallel as an extended novel, where his apparent goal was one sheet of 16 pages, he achieved that length only five times out of 11, missing on the other occasions by one, three, four, four, two, and two pages. Such inconsistency by one contributor, of course, did not much matter to a magazine editor, who needed only to produce an issue of 126 pages, whatever the length of its individual pieces might be.

But the writer of a novel whose parts each had to fill 32 pages, a length doubling the former chance of error, now had to be exactly

3. See K. Tillotson, *Novels of the Eighteen-Forties,* p. 29, and John Butt and K. Tillotson, *Dickens at Work* (London, 1963), p. 14.

right. If he ran slightly short, he could use woodcuts or a tailpiece to fill up space, but he could not run too short or print a text that ran over. The procedure Thackeray chose enabled him to "time" his installments, for he had a repetitive sequence. The pattern, however, permitted the novelist considerable latitude. One of its most important functions was to provide useful guidelines for fresh achievement, since the material of one number furnished the basis for its counterpart. The writer had his pattern; he could then work out the major analogies, expanding and supplementing them as he saw fit and as imagination suggested.

Its most immediate usefulness was to the writer himself, but because paired numbers had the same internal rhythm, he could not only "time" installments while writing them but also expect his audience consciously and unconsciously to make the same lateral connections —even across a month's time, since the number was the unit of memory, and especially because he so obviously paired the first two numbers and made overt cross-references between subsequent groups. Although the physical form of almost all editions puts the reader at a disadvantage by failing to indicate *Vanity Fair*'s part-structure, if he is aware of the serial parts he can appreciate their important function, for besides providing considerable artistic discipline, the pattern of juxtaposition itself reveals the novel's meaning: the thematic effect of detailed parallelism between two or three monthly numbers emerges as the latter regularly recalls and comments on the former, and so provides a comment on itself. More broadly, the structure emphasizes that, in spite of the differences in men and their lives, all the inhabitants of Vanity Fair are ultimately circumscribed by an inescapable pattern of sameness that epitomizes their most fundamental significance.

## APPENDIX

| Number One | Number Two |
|---|---|
| i | v |
| education at Miss Pinkerton's | education at Dr. Swishtail's |
| Amelia's popularity; Becky's unpopularity | Cuff's popularity; Dobbin's unpopularity |
| Miss P's parting with Amelia; Becky enters | Cuff beating George; Dobbin intervenes |
| battle between Miss P and Becky | battle between Cuff and Dobbin |
| Miss Jemima kindly gives dictionary; Becky tosses it back | {Cuff is magnanimous; Dobbin accepts help<br>Dobbin receives prize-book; gives tuckout for school |
| ii | vi |
| coach ride to Russell Square | coach ride to Vauxhall |
| retrospect: narrator's unfavorable account of Becky's past | retrospect: various favorable views of Becky's and Jos's future together |
| Amelia and Becky tour house; Becky vows to catch Jos | Jos and Becky tour Vauxhall; Jos fails to propose |
| iii | |
| Mr. Sedley mocks Jos's appearance; Jos alarmed | George mocks Jos's behavior; Jos alarmed |
| Becky overcome by curry and chili, but rallies | Jos remains in bed, overcome; fails to call |
| Becky awaits Jos, who leaves Russell Square | B awaits Jos, whose note announces departure from London |
| iv | vii |
| Jos arrives at Russell Square | Becky arrives at Great Gaunt Street |
| Mr. Sedley coarsely jesting; offer of champagne | Sir P coarsely jesting; offer of beer; reqnest for beer |
| a cheerful evening at Russell Square | a quiet evening in gloomy Great Gaunt Street |
| Jos prepares for Vauxhall: vows to propose to Becky | B prepares for Q's Crawley: chooses to dream of Rawdon |

| Number Three | Number Four | Number Five |
|---|---|---|
| viii | xii | xv |
| Becky settles at Queen's Crawley | Amelia rejected by fashionable ladies | Becky offered protection at QC by Sir P |
| B's amusement and satire re Crawleys | Amelia's timidity and hero-worship | Becky's affected modesty re Crawleys |
| | | |
| ix | xiii | xvi |
| Sir Pitt dominant | George dominant | Becky dominant |
| Pitt protects Lady Crawley | Dobbin helps Amelia | Miss Crawley offers Becky protection |
| Pitt's ambition | Amelia's love | Becky's ambition; Mrs. Bute's ambition |
| Sir Pitt's prosperity | Osborne's dominance | Miss C's hysteria; Sir P's impotent rage |
| Miss Crawley's monetary security and hence dignity | Amelia's doubts, caused by Osborne's mercenary suspicions | Rawdon's monetary doubts; B's confidence |
| | | |
| x | | xvii |
| Becky makes secure her position at Queen's Crawley | George succeeds in getting money from Osborne | dispersal of Sedley's effects; Dobbin vs. Becky & Rawdon |
| Rawdon's fortunes vs. Pitt's | George's fortunes vs. Sedley's | R's & B's fortunes vs. Mrs. Bute's |
| | | |
| xi | xiv | xviii |
| Mrs. Bute sees threat in Becky's arrival at Queen's Crawley | Briggs displaced by Becky's arrival in Park Lane | Europe threatened by Napoleon's landing at Cannes |
| Mrs. Bute promotes Rawdon's interest in Becky | Becky captivates Rawdon, who sees Mrs. Bute's efforts | Osborne brutally rejects Sedley and Amelia |
| B promised as match for father & son | Sir P proposes to B; she already married to son | George proposes to Amelia |

| Number Six | Number Seven |
|---|---|
| xix | xxiii |
| Mrs. Bute takes command in Park Lane | Dobbin becomes George's economic plenipotentiary in London |
| Mrs. Bute greedily searches out details of Becky's past | Dobbin charitably details virtues of George & Amelia |
| Becky & Rawdon appeal to Miss Crawley in the Park | the chidren pay court to the one with the penny |
| | |
| xx | xxiv |
| Dobbin arranges George's marriage | Dobbin tells Osborne of George's marriage |
| George's vanity flattered by Amelia's love | Osborne's vanity flattered by expectation of surrender; balked by George's marriage |
| Sedley's senile anger; his *pro forma* prohibition | Osborne's violent rage; he changes will |
| George respects Amelia as the only lady in O's circle | Dobbin is the most respected officer in the regiment |
| | |
| xxi | xxv |
| Osborne fawns over Miss Swartz | Dobbin attempts to entertain Amelia |
| Osborne orders George to secure Miss Swartz | letter announcing George is cut off |
| George collects money from Chopper | Becky tells Rawdon to collect from George |
| Geo taken by Amelia's society, offended by Miss Swartz's | George prefers Becky's society to Amelia's |
| George's picture of himself as a noble man of honor | George's picture of himself as a thoughtful husband |
| George's oath to marry Amelia | Amelia's vow to go to Belgium with George |
| | |
| xxii | |
| Osborne's expectations of victory remain unfulfilled | Mrs. Bute's reign unexpectedly ends |
| George & Amelia married | Becky & Briggs reconciled |
| Jos's pose deludes him | Becky's letter deludes her |
| Becky makes up with George | Miss Crawley accepts call from Rawdon |
| news of army ordered to Belgium | news of money sends Becky & Rawdon to London |

| Number Eight | Number Nine |
|---|---|
| xxvi | xxx |
| hotel in Cavendish Square; Amelia timid & ignorant | O'Dowd's quarters; Mrs. O'D capably serving her husband |
| effect of marriage on Amelia: melancholy | effect of marriage on Rawdon: happiness |
| George collects his inheritance & begins its dispersal | Rawdon gives his effects to Becky; she totals her valuables |
| | |
| xxvii | |
| George, Amelia, & Jos join the regiment | Dobbin entrusts Amelia to Jos |
| Mrs. O'Dowd in command | Amelia helpless |
| morning: transports loading for Belgium | morning: regiment marches off to war |
| | |
| xxviii | xxxi |
| Jos gallantly agrees to escort Amelia abroad | Jos in command at Brussels |
| Jos gets Belgian servant; Belgian love of commerce | Isidor's servile greed |
| Brussels: a perpetual military festival | Brussels: rumors of the war |
| Becky arrives with Tufto; Amelia saddened | Becky prepares for retreat with Jos; Amelia hostile |
| | |
| xxix | |
| Becky's brilliance at opera subdues Amelia & Mrs. O'D | Mrs. O'D replies to B's neglect of Amelia |
| | |
| | xxxii |
| George's idea of himself as woman-killer | Van Cutsum's idea of self as warrior; Jos's as military man |
| Becky triumphs over Amelia at ball; accepts Geo's note | B triumphs over Bareacres, rejects note; offers Jos horses |
| George exultant, gambles frantically & wins | Jos frantic, pays immensely |
| news that army will march; George returns to quarters | news of allied victory at Quatre Bras; Jos remains |
| George prepares for departure | sound of cannon; Jos flees |
| dawn: the city awakes | night: George dead |

| Number Ten | Number Eleven |
|---|---|
| xxxiii | xxxvi |
| news of Rawdon's promotion | news of Rawdon's quitting Guards & selling out of army |
| Becky amuses Miss Crawley with letter from Continent | Becky captivates Parisian society |
| behavior of Sir Pitt begets scandal | Rawdon's gambling begets unfortunate reputation |
| Pitt cultivates Miss Crawley | Becky deals with Rawdon's creditors |
| | |
| xxxiv | xxxvii |
| Pitt & Lady Jane establish themselves with Miss C | Becky & Rawdon establish themselves with Raggles |
| Lady Jane artlessly succeeds with Miss Crawley | B's flippancy in vogue among a certain class in London |
| Pitt's difficulties: Jim as rival; Pitt prevails | Becky's difficulties; Rawdon's threats; Becky prevails |
| B's success in Paris capped by birth of son & heir | B looks to success in London; sees poss. death of y. Pitt |
| Pitt marries & becomes Miss Crawley's heir | Pitt inherits Miss C's money; B & R ingratiate themselves |
| Pitt dominated by aunt & mother-in-law | R as Mrs. C's husband; to be replaced by Steyne & companion |
| | |
| xxxv | |
| George beloved & unforgiven by father | y. Rawdon neglected by mother; doted on by father |
| the past: Osborne visits Belgium | the future: y. George meets y. Rawdon |
| | |
| | xxxviii |
| Osborne's rigid imperviousness | Sedley's tottering delusions |
| Osborne's jealous rejection of Amelia and unborn child | Amelia's jealous quarrel with mother over y. George |
| Dobbin's devotion | Dobbin's devotion |
| y. George is Amelia's life; Dobbin shut out | y. George is Amelia's life; Dobbin shut out |

| Number Twelve | Number Thirteen |
|---|---|
| xxxix | xliii |
| Mrs. Bute's hypocrisy | Lady O'Dowd's tyranny & kindness |
| Pitt & Lady Jane visit QC; Sir Pitt gives her pearls | Glorvina besieges Dobbin; she gets pink dress |
| Sir Pitt's dotage; Ribbons' delusions | Dobbin's indifference; Glorvina's delusions |
| Mrs. Bute takes command on evening of Sir Pitt's stroke | Dobbin requests leave on news of Amelia's engagement |
| xl | xliv |
| Pitt assumes control of Queen's Crawley | Becky is general-in-chief in Great Gaunt St. |
| new Sir Pitt's letter to Rawdon | Sir Pitt's check for y. Rawdon |
| Becky's delight at acknowledgment | Becky's delight at acknowledgment |
| Becky's dismissal of y. Rawdon | Becky's repudiation of y. Rawdon |
| Becky secures Briggs as moral sheep dog | servants pronounce Becky guilty of adultery |
| xli | |
| Becky & Rawdon visit Queen's Crawley | Becky & Rawdon visit Queen's Crawley |
| | xlv |
| Becky conciliates Sir Pitt and Lady Jane | Becky pleases Sir Pitt but not Lady Jane |
| Jane gives banknote for y. R; Sir P promises education | Sir Pitt gives Rawdon £ 100 |
| Sir PCs look forward to seeing R Crawleys in London | R visits Jane; Sir P visits B; women keep apart |
| xlii | xlvi |
| Osborne's tyranny and unhappiness | Sedley's dependence and unhappiness |
| Bullock's mercenary behavior | Clapp's faithful attachment |
| Maria's coldness to Osborne | Amelia's devotion to y. George |
| Jane's miserable life vs. Maria's | Jane's miserable life vs. Maria's |
| Osborne ends Jane's relations with Smee | Osborne accepts Jane's relation with y. George |
| Jane sees y. George & tells Osborne | Osborne sees y. Geo; A believes his future is with O |

| Number Fourteen | Number Fifteen | Number Sixteen |
|---|---|---|
| xlvii | li | liv |
| Gaunt House & its back door | Gaunt House & doors it opens for Becky | G. Gaunt St: R enters Sir P's house |
| "natural" oppositions in Steyne family | B overcomes inevitable social opposition | Mac believes B guilty; seeks reconciliation |
| madness of George Gaunt; presentiment haunts Steyne | charades: death, illicit love; illusion & precarious triumphs | news about revolution of servants in Mayfair |
| xlviii | lii | lv |
| B triumphant: presented to King | Steyne triumphs: gets place for y. R | B insulted; partly quells rebellion |
| Becky asks Steyne for money to give Briggs & gets it | Steyne amused to discover B's deception but removes Briggs | Wenham asserts Steyne's innocence; Mac accepts but returns money |
| Raggles paid; B puts away rest of money for herself | Rawdon becomes attentive to B & stifles doubts | Raggles bankrupt; Rawdon goes off to Coventry |
| xlix | liii | lvi |
| Steyne orders invitation to Gaunt House written for Becky & Rawdon | Rawdon writes to Becky from spunging-house | y. George fully established in Osborne's house; receives ltrs on silver tray |
| Becky ignored by the women; pitied & helped by Steyne's wife | Rawdon ignored by Becky; pitied & helped by Sir Pitt's wife | y. George toadied to by schoolmaster & Osborne |
| l | | |
| Amelia breaks down re y. Geo under hysterical mother & imprudent father | Becky's pose re Steyne breaks down in front of Rawdon | Amelia bears up under querulous mother & tottering father |
| Amelia gives up son; y. George delighted | Rawdon leaves Becky; she in state of shock | Dobbin arrives at school with Jos; y. George delighted |

| Number Seventeen | Number Eighteen |
|---|---|
| lvii | lxi |
| lottery of life giving different fates | second-floor arch: inevitability of a common fate |
| death of Mrs. Sedley | death of Sedley |
| Dobbin sick but recovers | Osborne dies |
| Jos flattered by D into caring for Amelia & y. George | Jos takes interest in Amelia after inheritance |
| Dobbin delighted at arriving in England | everyone delighted at departing for Continent |
| | |
| lviii | lxii |
| disembarkation: Dobbin's journey to London | embarkation: journey to Rotterdam |
| Dobbin dresses up to see Amelia | Jos brings court suit for presentations |
| Dobbin & Amelia happily reunited | Dobbin & Amelia happy together |
| Amelia taken in by y. George | Amelia educated to see Dobbin's merits |
| | |
| lix | lxiii |
| Jos detained at Southampton | Jos decides to stay in Pumpernickel |
| Jos conducted to reunion with Sedley | Jos conducted to audience with Victor Aurelius XVIII |
| Amelia rejects idea of marriage with Dobbin | Amelia walks a polonaise with Dobbin |
| Dobbin prompts Jos to estabish a fine house | vanity prompts Victor Aurelius XIV to build Monplaisir |
| | |
| lx | |
| Amelia gets visiting book, page, maid, chariot | Becky alone, tattered, losing money |
| Jos goes to court; Amelia stays home | Jos goes gambling & meets Becky |

| Number Nineteen | Number Twenty |
| --- | --- |
| lxiv | lxvi |
| Becky dispiritedly neglects herself & reputation | Becky feelingly narrates her misfortunes to Amelia |
| Becky gains entrances but is rejected | Amelia decides to accept Becky; Dobbin urges rejection |
| Becky rejected by Steyne; leaves Rome | Amelia refuses to reject Becky; Dobbin breaks away |
| lxv | lxvii |
| Becky attracts Jos | Becky attracts Jos |
| Dobbin dubious about Becky | Becky becomes supporter of Dobbin |
| reunion between Becky & Amelia | reunion between Dobbin & Amelia |

# GEOFFREY TILLOTSON

## [Philosophy and Narrative Technique]†

* * *

One of the ways Dickens and Thackeray differ as narrators is in the role they assign to people subsidiary to principals. While Thackeray is narrating, as distinct from commenting, he never takes his eyes off his principals, which means that subsidiaries are introduced only when they concern them. Subsidiaries exist in their hundreds, and yet are numbered. What they contribute would be evidence in a court of law. Such a role may be assigned to subsidiaries by Dickens, or it may not—he does not seem to mind. In . . . *Nicholas Nickleby* the genial nod of a word or two was devoted to anybody who happened to catch his eye while he imagined the likely scene as the coach was preparing to set out. The *likely* scene—Dickens is thinking of *any* such scene. The itinerant newsman had nothing to do with Nicholas; Dickens takes his eyes off Nicholas in order to describe him. The newsman was a wheel revolving in adjacent space, whereas in Thackeray any wheel mentioned, however small, would have cogged in with whatever other wheels were turning. Take as a fair sample of Thackeray's method a comparable passage from Chapter vii of *Vanity Fair*, where the orphan Becky Sharp is taking up her post as governess in the household of Sir Pitt Crawley:

> John, the groom, who had driven the carriage alone, did not care to descend to ring the bell; and so prayed a passing milk-boy to perform that office for him. When the bell was rung, a head appeared between the interstices of the dining-room shutters, and the door was opened by a man in drab breeches and gaiters, with a dirty old coat, a foul old neckcloth lashed round his bristly neck, a shining bald head, a leering red face, a pair of twinkling grey eyes, and a mouth perpetually on the grin.
>
> 'This Sir Pitt Crawley's?' says John, from the box.
>
> 'Ees,' says the man at the door with a nod.
>
> 'Hand down these 'ere trunks then,' said John.
>
> 'Hand 'n down yourself,' said the porter.
>
> 'Don't you see I can't leave my hosses? Come, bear a hand, my fine feller, and Miss will give you some beer,' said John, with a horse-laugh, for he was no longer respectful to Miss Sharp, as her connexion with the family was broken off, and as she had given nothing to the servants on coming away.

The principals here are Becky and Sir Pitt (whom she quite understandably mistakes for the porter), and the other people get a look in because they are vitally connected with the principals. John is necessary to Becky because she and her baggage could not have arrived on the scene without his agency, and his enlisting the services of the milk-boy is necessary because Becky does not rate a carriage fully manned and John is in sole charge of it.

† Reprinted from *A View of Victorian Literature* by Geoffrey Tillotson (Oxford: Clarendon Press, 1978), 156–85, by permission of Oxford University Press © Oxford University Press 1978.

Throughout the narrative part of his fiction Thackeray exercises economy. While narrating he is saying that the people whose story he has chosen to tell are all in all to him till that story is told, whatever their general importance or non-importance. His exclusive concentration on them is the return he makes to them for their being so kind as to have provided him with a story. Intervening between stretches of narrative are the stretches of commentary. They have themselves received much comment from critics: at this point I note only their function as a relaxation. They accord with the narrator's right to relax his strenuous concentration on the story, a right no sensitive reader will dispute. The relaxation, however, as far as people go, is of the busman's holiday sort. The economy exercised in the narrative is itself carried over into the commentary, since no one of the many personages introduced into it lacks the credentials of those who figure in the narrative proper. There is no credit for Thackeray in this, economy being inevitable when the only reason for bringing people into the commentary at all is as illustration. Credit is conspicuously due, however (and was especially in the nineteenth century), when economy is exercised in the narration. To provide it was to be brought into collision with that widely applied contemporary principle making for multitudinousness. In the eighteenth century there had been much interest in 'plenitude', the divine principle by which the world was furnished with a complete range of things, but things in the nineteenth century seemed denser still, the scientists now bringing so many more of them into significance. Moreover, people in the nineteenth century—those at least in the upper of the 'Two Nations'—had many more things in their personal possession. Their lives were crowded with bric-à-brac and larger furniture as never before. Dickens and Browning, to name the two chief rejoicers in this density, honour as much of it in their writings as they can. Some other writers, Thackeray and Emily Brontë being the most noteworthy, prefer to exercise the right to select strictly. The extraordinary thing is that, exercising this right, Thackeray represents multitudinousness so adequately, simply by dint of writing so much. And yet things are introduced only as they serve the vital purposes of narrative or commentary. Keeping his eye steadily on people meant that things are mentioned only as people intimately attach themselves to them. He never relaxed hold of his principle by taking time off to paint a scene for its own sake, which meant forgoing the exercise of a power much indulged at the time, and which he himself possessed in abundance —as we know from the descriptions supplied in his travel books. Thackeray's novels are like the fir trees on the hillside, vital with trunks, stems, and needles before they receive all the glittering additions Dickens liked to hang on them, out of pure perpetual Christmas spirit. Dickens will describe anything that happens to belong to a scene, Thackeray only what intimately concerns the people in it.

Economy over wide stretches—practicable only for a writer of strong intellect, which it is not customary to claim for Thackeray—is evinced over the whole of his writings. If he selects economically it is according to a principle. He is a conscious critic at the same time as a rapt creator, the critic in him directing the creation, giving it, as it were, a spine. Whatever else he is doing, he is making a point, sometimes a point in favour of a reform. The title-pages of the novels announce a theme, or at least an intellectual interest: *Vanity Fair. A Novel Without a Hero; The History of Pendennis. His Fortunes and Misfortunes, His Friends and His Greatest Enemy,* that greatest enemy being himself; that of *Philip* is related to the parable of the Good Samaritan—*The Adventures of Philip, on his way through the world, shewing who robbed him, who helped him, and who passed him by. The Book of Snobs* is built on a single idea. When a description is called for in the novels it is called for because the account of one or more human beings will not be complete without it: the description itself, however, has its theme: here is the Newcomes' family home at Clapham:

> It was a serious paradise. As you entered at the gate, gravity fell on you; and decorum wrapped you in a garment of starch. The butcher-boy who galloped his horse and cart madly about the adjoining lanes and common, whistled wild melodies (caught up in abominable play-house galleries), and joked with a hundred cookmaids, on passing that lodge fell into an undertaker's pace, and delivered his joints and sweetbreads silently at the servant's entrance. The rooks in the elms cawed sermons at morning and evening; the peacocks walked demurely on the terraces; the guineafowls looked more quaker-like than those savoury birds usually do. The lodge-keeper was serious, and a clerk at a neighbouring chapel. The pastors who entered at that gate, and greeted his comely wife and children, fed the little lambkins with tracts. The head-gardener was a Scotch Calvinist, after the strictest order, only occupying himself with the melons and pines provisionally, and until the end of the world, which event he could prove by infallible calculations, was to come off in two or three years at farthest.[1]

Thackeray's intellect made him a fighter. The first half of the huge amount of his writings was a battlefield with occasional lulls in the fighting. If, in his later work, which includes all the novels after *Vanity Fair,* he was less combative, that was not only because combativeness cannot readily make the organizing principle of the long novel, but because his campaign had been a success. Partly, or largely, because of him, other great novelists—Trollope, Mrs. Gaskell, the Brontës, George Eliot, Reade, Meredith—wrote with due regard for what he called 'truth'. Indeed, it was the promoting of this principle that made him the prime reformer of mid-century fiction. Where it had erred and strayed, he conspicuously helped to bring it back on to the right path. He belonged to the same school as Marryat, Harriet Martineau, and Surtees. They all wrote, as Jane Austen and Maria Edgeworth had, about what they could vouch for, as it were in a court of law. This is how, they say, we have noticed ordinary men and women behaving, and what by observation we have adduced as to their moral character, moral character being the prime interest of a novelist. They achieved what they called 'truth' by the use of their eyes and any other of the senses—including their common sense!—that were called for.

1. Ch. ii. 'Serious' was a recognized term in the Evangelical vocabulary.

In adopting this principle they were opposing the 'idealism' popular at the time. The most that could be allowed idealism by a novelist was allowed by George Eliot: 'Art', she said in a letter, 'must be either real and concrete, or ideal and eclectic. Both are good and true in their way, but my stories are of the former kind.'[2] We all practise a certain amount of idealism as we exist from day to day. At certain times we see things flatteringly—after a good meal, for instance, or when we are in love. The idealists, of whom Bulwer Lytton was the chief, were for writing as if they were always slightly intoxicated or head over heels in love. People when actually in those states may sometimes write, but they seldom read, and accordingly readers expect the sobriety they almost always get from writers who are great. Thackeray, more wholly than Dickens, wanted to see and write as if sober. He believed with Horace that 'fictions meant to please should be as like actuality as possible';[3] he believed that novelists should take to heart what Carlyle had said in praise of Burns, that 'he does not write from hearsay, but from sight and experience';[4] that, as Ruskin said, 'the greatest thing a human soul ever does in this world is to *see* something and to tell what it *saw* in a plain way';[5] that the writer should take 'human faces', again to quote Ruskin, 'as God made them'; should work as Balzac did, and ignore Joubert's remark that 'Fiction has no business to exist unless it is more beautiful than reality'.[6] He believed that novelists, or anybody else for that matter, should ignore German philosophers, who, like Kant, were for finding an ideal world under or within the actual world; should dissociate themselves from what Ruskin called 'Purist Idealism', which 'results from unwillingness of pure and tender minds to contemplate evil', and of which his illustration was Fra Angelico;[7] and that instead they should proceed as the painters Thackeray himself commended, who 'do not generally attempt what is called the highest species of art, and content themselves with depicting nature as they find her, and trusting to the poetry and charms of the scenes which they copy, rather than to their own powers of invention, and [of] representing ideal beauty'.[8] Many powerful statements were made on this burning question, one of the most remarkable being this comment on George Sand's 'transcendentalism':

> a term which we take to mean the science of proving that everything is something else, rejecting Bishop Butler's contrary axiom that 'everything is the thing it is, and not another thing'. Persons who profess an especial enlightenment come naturally to assimilate whatever they admire to something in themselves; the object contemplated is not so much on its own account as for advancing a cause; it is not studied for its simple merits, but as proving some point peculiar to the observer. By some magic process of transformation it loses its identity, and only subscribes

2. *George Eliot Letters,* II. 362 (12 June 1857).
3. *Ars Poetica,* 338.
4. *Edinburgh Review* (Dec. 1828).
5. *Modern Painters,* 5 vols. (London: Smith, Elder, 1843–60), vol. III, Ch. xvi.
6. Quoted in Matthew Arnold's 'Joubert', *Essays in Criticism* (1865).
7. *Modern Painters,* vol. III, Ch. vi.
8. *Morning Chronicle* (29 Apr. 1844; *Contributions to the Morning Chronicle,* ed. G. N. Ray, 1955, p. 27).

> to his fancies and ideas. . . . And yet all the while there need not have been any real proper appreciation at all, for the mind has been too full of itself for the humble learner's part.[9]

Florence Nightingale herself could not forgo a hit at the idealists in her *Notes on Nursing* (1859):

> In writings of fiction, whether novels or biographies, these death-beds are generally depicted as almost seraphic in lucidity of intelligence. Sadly large has been my experience in death-beds, and I can only say that I have seldom or never seen such. Indifference, excepting with regard to bodily suffering, or to some duty the dying man desired to perform, is the far more usual state.

Thackeray was prominently on the side of such realists, believing that a novelist writes, as a scientist does, about what he has found for himself, his imagination existing to create a world as nearly indistinguishable from the actual one as possible. In his preface to *Pendennis* he made his prime principle clear: 'this person writing strives to tell the truth. If there is not that, there is nothing.' The compliment Thackeray must have prized most comes quietly in a review of *Vanity Fair* by Forster: the personages of the novel 'are drawn from actual life, not from books and fancy'. It was the compliment paid to the great scientists, who, like Thackeray, ignored books and fancy except as things to confirm, modify, or contradict from their own experience of men and things.

* * *

Having a philosophy consciously held meant that Thackeray was never inside the narrative. This apartness affected the account he gave of his personages. For him Carlyle's behest to see for yourself had peculiar cogency. He liked to restrict his material to what the eye can see, and what the mind can infer from the sight without losing hold of it. Aristotle had noted the evidence of character afforded by the body, and Bacon had particularly noted that 'a number of subtle persons, whose eyes do dwell upon the faces and functions of men, well know the advantage' of observing those 'lineaments of the body [that] disclose the disposition and inclination of the mind'. If human beings, then novelists. Thackeray, writing his novels, was looking not at human beings but at their counterparts in his imagination. Yet more than most novelists he restricted himself to the role of the 'subtle persons' remarked by Bacon. His eyes were supplemented by his ears. Introducing *The Virginians* he remarks: 'I have drawn the figures as I fancied they were; set down conversations as I think I might have heard them.' This testimony assumes that the novelist's eyes and ears are those of Everyman—which brings us back to the problem about what we see and what a genius makes of what he sees. Whatever the participation of Thackeray's genius in the record of what he sees and hears, the result as it strikes the reader resembles what he himself experiences. What he sees and hears is all weighed.

Reviewers were divided as to whether or not his method led to

9. Anne Mozley, in *Bentley's Quarterly Review* (1860).

representing people completely. Writing in 1848, when *Vanity Fair* was before him, Abraham Hayward in the *Edinburgh* declared: 'He can skim the surface, and he can penetrate to the core'. It is noticeable, however, that those who think his province to be mainly 'surface' are the idealists. The eloquent W. C. Roscoe can speak for them:

> Man is his study; but man the social animal, man considered with reference to the experiences, the aims, the affections, that find their field in his intercourse with his fellow-man: never man the individual soul. He never penetrates into the interior, secret, *real* life that every man leads in isolation from his fellows, that chamber of being open only upwards to heaven and downwards to hell. He is wise to abstain; he does well to hold the ground where his pre-eminence is unapproached,—to be true to his own genius. But this genius is of a lower order than the other.[1]

Such criticism is obtuse, being true only if we cannot read, as Hayward could, the signs that imply the core, without describing it. It is true that the core is usually that of ordinary people, whom Thackeray deliberately preferred to write of, and who would not themselves lay claim to the possession of much core. And it is also true, even of these ordinary people, that Thackeray deliberately refrains from prying into the most private secrets—again in accordance with his philosophy, which demanded of him reverence towards the naked human heart. When we have allowed for these two things we may well have as much implied as even the greatest analysts provide. If he deprecated a describing of those dark places, this did not mean that he did not know what they contained. Thackeray represents mankind profoundly; I find a Shakespearian depth in his simplicities. When Becky concludes, after making her monetary calculations, that if Rawdon should be killed at Waterloo she can 'look her [widow's] weeds steadily in the face', when a 'sexual jealousy' is discovered in the mother as her son meditates marriage, when Laura Bell, during Pen's neglect of her or worse, practises the piano for long spells—those things and a thousand more tally with our own reading of life. The famous instance, however, is provided by *Esmond*, of which George Eliot reported in a letter to a friend: ' "Esmond" is the most uncomfortable book you can imagine. You remember, Cara, how you disliked [George Sand's] "François le Champi". Well, the story of Esmond is just the same. The hero is in love with the daughter all through the book, and marries the mother at the end.'[2] Forster thought the marriage 'incredible'.[3] Mrs. Oliphant called it 'monstrous': 'our most sacred sentiments are outraged, and our best prejudices shocked by the leading feature of this tale'.[4] Nevertheless, George Brimley, in his review in the *Spectator*, felt himself equal to demonstrating its psychological truth, as 'a complex feeling, in which filial affection and an unconscious passion are curiously blended,' and shows how Thackeray turns the difficulty into triumph, with

1. *National Review* (1856).
2. *The George Eliot Letters*, ed. Gordon S. Haight, 9 vols. (New Haven: Yale University Press, 1954–78), II. 67.
3. *Examiner* (6 Nov. 1852).
4. *Blackwood's* (Jan. 1855).

'beauties which a safer ambition would not have dared to attempt'.[5] And the last words are Saintsbury's: 'there is . . . nothing for it but to confess that it is very shocking—and excessively human'.[6]

The personages he imagines are mainly ordinary. When he goes back in time, and brings in the great people whom his more ordinary people come up against, he reduces their greatness. He might have acknowledged that the idea of the heroic was proving useful for Carlyle in his campaign to bring out the best in ordinary people, but he found no use in it himself. The idea smacked too much of idealism. As Trollope said of him: 'The heroic . . . appeared contemptible to him, as being untrue'.[7] In his *Second Funeral of Napoleon* Thackeray had given a brilliant account of the ceremonies in Paris, which *The Times* objected to as irreverent, and to which Thackeray replied: 'O, you thundering old *Times*! Napoleon's funeral was a humbug, and your constant reader said so. The people engaged in it were humbugs, and this your Michael Angelo hinted at. There may be irreverence in this, and the process of humbug-hunting may end rather awkwardly for some people.'[8] It is significant that the sub-title of *Vanity Fair* is 'A Novel without a Hero' and when he himself writes a historical novel in *Esmond* he produced what Trollope hailed as 'the first truthful historical novel'. After *Esmond* came *The Virginians* as sequel, with, finally, a dip into French history in *Denis Duval*. Nor does any of it degrade the term 'historical', Thackeray being as close a student of the past as Carlyle. The only serious criticism brought up against its factual truthfulness pertains to his picture of the Old Pretender, which is held to malign an upright and honourable man. Thackeray's truthfulness may here have been the victim of political and religious prejudice. Usually, however, he had no difficulty in giving an authentic humanity to his historical personages.

Action as well as personages is kept at a distance. We are made aware of it as lying outside the narrator, sometimes no farther than at the tip of his pen, but sometimes as far away as the sun and moon. Thackeray saw the world represented in his novels as spectacle rather than as an arena in which the author and his personages interlock. He felt that Charlotte Brontë was too much embroiled in the moments as they came. He himself is not embroiled. He judges, if that is not too harsh a term, thinks about, comments on the moments, even when they are of the exciting kind. He is sometimes so detached that he notices the motion of the heavens above the card-tables. He is so much aware of what lies around the action that he can describe himself as a showman working his puppets. He shows us himself keeping pace with the implications of what is taking place in his imagination.

His distance from the narrative is furthest when narrative gives place to commentary, extended sometimes to the length of a long paragraph. It has been this extended commentary that has led critics

5. *Essays*, ed. W. G. Clark (Cambridge: Macmillan, 1860), p. 258.
6. Introduction in the *Works of William Makepeace Thackeray*, 17 vols. (London: Oxford University Press, 1908), xiv, pp. xii–xiii.
7. *Thackeray* (London: Macmillan, 1879), p. 91.
8. 'On Men and Pictures', *Fraser's* (July 1841).

to allege breaks in the continuity. To think so, however, is to have failed to respond duly to the nature of Thackeray's particular kind of narrative. That kind is never pure, or rather it is more impure than narrative need be. Attended to closely, pure narrative does not exist, simply because whatever is written has a writer whose existence is noticed in the very choice of the words, the style being the man. Thackeray's narrative, however, while having this authorial existence inevitably noticeable in it, has also a more tangible sign of it. To existence is joined participation. I have said that he keeps the narrative at a distance, and the most continuous means of his doing so lies in the constant bestowing of epithets denoting comment, appraisal, sometimes judgement. A favourite epithet is 'little', which evinces his function as showman of puppets. Because of the constant comment, appraisal, judgement, conveyed in epithets of this sort, the narrative already includes criticism before narrative gives place to comment at paragraph length.

The very prose of his novels witnesses to his philosophy in being the prose we should all write if we could—unassuming, easy, comfortable, elegant, making the fewest demands on the reader, as limpid when its sense is profound as when not. One of his reviewers noted that he makes his personages speak as ordinary people speak every hour of their lives, and for his own prose he takes theirs, and gives it a supple continuity. The result has always been admired; his prose is the most distinguished in the whole range of our fiction. Its distinction, however, is in making us receive its art as completely natural. It has many marks of the colloquial. Thackeray likes to end a sentence with 'though' or 'very likely', and write such a one as 'And a very good thing too', or 'And so they went on in *Arcadia* itself, *really*', or '. . . as far away as Clive's almost'. It is a style without fuss. Its deadly remarks are said quietly. The almost unnoticeable way in which he makes tremendous statements reminds one of Dryden's praise for the kind of satirist who cuts off a man's head and leaves the body standing in its place.

His philosophy also led him to reject the well-made plot. The kind he preferred were those that dispensed with what he called 'tricks of art', and so he helped to revolutionize the concept of the novel form. We give him full credit for this only when we see how strong was the contemporary addiction to the plot so elaborately contrived as to collide sometimes or often with the improbable. We get an idea of this addiction when we discover that the publisher's reader complained of deficiency of plot in Trollope's *Barchester Towers*, and that Clough, praising *The Newcomes*, admits that 'there is certainly no story nor very much anything' in it.[9] Clough's remark is particularly illuminating—he must have felt that *The Newcomes* was so lifelike as to be vaguely confusing and intangible to a novel-reader. Thackeray subscribed to Hazlitt's desideratum that the story-teller should 'invent according to nature', and would have applauded Zola's remark that a well-made plot is the sort of work expected of 'women and children'. It was not

9. Letter of 3 Mar. 1854 (*The Correspondence of Arthur Hugh Clough*, ed. F. L. Mulhauser, II. 478). Writing from Cambridge, Mass., Clough could hardly have read further than Ch. xvi.

a 'man's job'. He would also have applauded Trollope's view that plot was 'the most insignificant part of a tale'[1] because, as Reade put it, 'in my experience a complete plot rarely exists except in a drama or story'. Life itself having no plots, novels should not. In the obituary published in *Fraser's,* Thackeray is represented as himself laughing at the way he ended *Philip*: the old coach is made to upset and the lost will to come to light among the debris, which 'discovery' sends 'the necessary fortune . . . in the right direction'. He rejected the ingenious plot from conviction. It was not an instance of sour grapes. Structural ingenuity exists brilliantly in the ten tales that make up *Punch's Prize Novelists,* and one of the best critics of the shapely *Barry Lyndon* is Fitzjames Stephen, who remarks that 'the story is as natural and easy as if it were true'. Thackeray's kind of plots prompted Roscoe to invent a phrase that was later modified into the technical term, a 'slice of life'—he says that Thackeray 'cuts a square out of life, just as much as he wants, and sends it to [his publishers] Bradbury and Evans'.

## PETER L. SHILLINGSBURG

# The "Trade" of Literature†

In his own day Thackeray's satiric view of the romantic ideals of his profession made him appear weak, ambivalent, his own worst enemy. And that view, with a hefty boost from Trollope, has carried over into the image of Thackeray as an undisciplined craftsman, leading more than one critic to characterize him as a "careless putter forth" or hasty or even lazy improviser.[1] And this unflattering view extends to the image of Thackeray the businessman or, as he implied with characteristic deflation, tradesman.

The word *tradesman* in Victorian England denoted, as it still to some extent does, an outlook and a rank in life that were incompatible with imagination and beauty, which were central to the concept of artist, poet, or even novelist. One equates tradesman in Victorian England with Mr. Pumblechook in *Great Expectations* and Mr. Polly in H. G. Wells's *History of Mr. Polly* or, on a higher economic—though not sensibility—scale, Mr. Freeman in John Fowles's *French Lieutenant's Woman,* whose industrial and commercial sensibilities are impervious to art. But Thackeray was a practical man who had learned, from more than one penniless crisis, the reality of writing for money. That reality was a fact to be honestly acknowledged. If authorship had certain high ideals, it included, on the other hand, the mundane practical details of the trade of writing. By using the loaded word *trade* for the artist, Thackeray undercut both the social snobbery and the mystical trappings of *artist,* which some writers cultivated.

1. *Autobiography,* (London: Blackwoods, 1883), Ch. vii.

† From *Pegasus in Harness: Victorian Publishing and W. M. Thackeray* (Charlottesville, Va: University Press of Virginia, 1992), 26–32. Reprinted by permission.

1. The phrase comes from George Saintsbury's Introduction to *Pendennis* (London: Oxford Univ. Press, [1908]), in which he also called Thackeray a shrewd reviser.

The social snobbery probably was an unconscious outgrowth, rather than a desired aim, of earlier proponents of the mystical view. The Victorian version of that view derived at least in part from the notions of poet or artist promulgated by Wordsworth in the preface to *Lyrical Ballads*, where the poet's sensibilities above the common run of men is claimed, and by Shelley's "Defense of Poesie," where the poet's position as an unacknowledged legislator of the world is proclaimed. But perhaps the strongest impetus to view the writer's calling in a special light with special capabilities and privileges was Thomas Carlyle's portrayal of the "Man of Letters" in *On Heroes, Hero Worship, and the Heroic in History*. Thackeray's early send-ups of Dr. Lardner and Sir Edward Bulwer Lytton as pompous snobs playing off their roles as artists in social settings is an indication of his suspicion of the role. As a practicing writer, he turned to the trade rather than the calling in order to deflate the aggrandized view.

Thackeray became, in fact, an able and a reliable businessman who expected publishers and illustrators to fulfill their commitments with equal promptness. To his publishers, Bradbury and Evans, Thackeray wrote in May 1854 to complain of Richard Doyle, the illustrator Thackeray himself had chosen for *The Newcomes*: "However much I may regard Doyle as a friend it is clear that as men of business we cannot allow our property to suffer by his continual procrastination. The original agreement with Doyle, made between Bradbury myself & him was that the blocks & plates for the ensuing month should always be supplied by Doyle on the 15th of the month current. I have now written to him, to say that I shall hold him to his agreement & that if by the 15 June the plates & blocks of No 10 of the Newcomes are not in your hands I shall employ another designer" (NLS) [National Library of Scotland]. It would have been the height of arrogance and insensitivity for Trollope's Thackeray to require promptness and commitment from another man—holding Doyle to standards too rigid for himself. But Trollope's Thackeray was a fiction. The real Thackeray was a reliable professional masked by a public image. The popular concept of a harried Thackeray dashing off the last lines of the monthly number for the printer just in the nick of time is a romantic misunderstanding of serial publication.

In thirty years of professional writing, Thackeray failed to meet only three deadlines that seriously affected a publisher. Only one of these commitments lay within his power to fulfill. The October 1844 installment of *Barry Lyndon* was delayed one month for lack of copy, and even then there were mitigating circumstances. He mailed off the October installment on 23 September from Smyrna while on his Eastern tour (recounted in *From Cornhill to Grand Cairo*), and it arrived too late in London for the October number of the magazine. He finished the book on 3 November.[2] In September 1848 he became so ill he had to suspend the writing and publishing of the monthly numbers of *Pendennis* for three months, and in August 1859 he was too ill to write a complete final double number for *The Virginians*, providing

2. Gordon N. Ray, *Thackeray: The Uses of Adversity* (New York: McGraw-Hill, 1955), p. 343; *The Letters and Private Papers of William Makepeace Thackeray*, ed. Gordon N. Ray, 4 vols. (Cambridge: Harvard University Press, 1945–46), 2:153–54, 156.

instead a one-part number 23 and a one-part final number in September.

Thackeray's sense of the business requirements of authorship was hard won. Though he had earned his livelihood by journalism for ten years when he began *Vanity Fair,* he was in 1846 still very much a petitioner appealing to the largess of the proprietors of *Punch* and other publishers, and he was dependent on their valuation of the goods he brought for sale. But by 1854 the author of *The Newcomes* saw himself as coproprietor with the publisher. The change is dramatic, and the composition, production, and financial success of *Vanity Fair* mark the watershed of Thackeray's career as a businessman, transforming him from the investor/gambler, the writer waiting upon publishers with his goods, into the propertied tradesman who built himself a debt-free mansion at 2 Palace Green, Kensington.

Five chapters of *Vanity Fair* were written by early spring 1846. Thackeray announced to his mother that serial publication would begin on 1 May, and in March or April the first five chapters were set in type.[3] Production problems immediately became apparent: when the corrected galleys were paged, it was discovered that the fourth chapter reached page 28 and the fifth chapter extended to the middle of page 35. Serial publication, however, required exactly thirty-two pages, no more and no less. The first of May passed with no publication. The type for chapters 1–5 was knocked down and redistributed to the typecases, while Thackeray eked out his living with "The Snobs of England" and "Novels by Eminent Hands"—contributions to *Punch* lasting beyond the publication of the revised initial number of *Vanity Fair* in January 1847.

What Thackeray learned during the eight-month delay in the publication of *Vanity Fair* can only be surmised from the regularity of his serial numbers from 1 January 1847 to the end of his life (except in the fall of 1848 and August 1859 when illness, not lassitude, prevented the professional fulfillment of his commitments to the public). The process he worked out was fairly simple but has only recently been understood by scholars. Except when he wrote *The Newcomes,* a few numbers of *Philip,* and *Denis Duval,* Thackeray never completed a monthly installment before the month it was due at the print shop. His contract for *Vanity Fair*—written and signed, curiously enough, on 25 January 1847 as the second installment was being printed—specifies that he was to submit copy by the fifteenth of each month. According to his letters, however, often on about the twenty-fifth of the month he would write that he had "just ended his number." Such statements, along with his frequent self-accusations of procrastination and the picture of the sleeping printer's devil waiting at the door, combine to give the superficial and false impression of a writer who could not meet his contracted deadlines. In fact, the process was a smooth, if hectic, coordination of writing, typesetting, proofreading, correcting, and printing responsibilities.

3. The manuscript with imbedded fragments of proofs from the first typesetting is in the Pierpont Morgan Library [New York]. The discovery of the nature of those proof fragments was first revealed in the *Thackeray Newsletter,* nos. 6 and 7 (1977), and expanded in the Textual Introduction to my edition of *Vanity Fair* (New York: Garland, 1989).

The reason Thackeray "ended" his numbers on the twenty-fifth or so is that serial publication does not lend itself to the submission of a finished manuscript on the fifteenth. The first time Thackeray tried that, his installment would have occupied either twenty-eight or thirty-five pages had it been published. Instead, he would submit about three-quarters of an installment to the printer—probably by the twentieth or earlier—to be set in type. With as many as five compositors working on a single installment (their names are on the manuscripts), typesetting twenty to thirty pages could be completed in a day or less. The printer's devil would then carry proofs to Thackeray, who corrected them and measured them with a string corresponding in length to a page of the printed book.[4] Arriving at a fairly accurate estimate of the amount of text still required to fill the number, he would revise and augment or cut as necessary. A printer's boy or the mails would then return the corrected and augmented proof to the printshop. Second proofs with page headings and page numbers embedded would be ready in another day or so, making it possible for Thackeray to read proofs and make final adjustments in length by the twenty-fifth or twenty-sixth of the month. The printers and binders then usually had about five days to get an installment ready for distribution by the last day of the month.

This coordination of production effort lends itself to the concept of writing as a trade. The artist's fancy is not free; the grinding schedule of production curtailed the craftsman's time and forced his energies in ways which Thackeray is on record as both appreciating and lamenting. The conditions of serial novel writing were not very different from newspaper journalism or the scheduled inches of letterpress Thackeray was responsible for in *Punch.* Novel writers of Thackeray's standing today may have a fellowship or an advance from the publisher and a full year or eighteen months to write the novel. Not so Thackeray. Yet the pressure was invigorating; he lived, talked, ate, slept his fiction up until deadline time. Thackeray's enthusiasm for the invigorating aspect of the engines of journalism shows in George Warrington's praises of it in *Pendennis*:

> There she is—the great engine—she never sleeps. She has her ambassadors in every quarter of the world—her couriers upon every road. Her officers march along with armies, and her envoys walk into statesmen's cabinets. They are ubiquitous. Yonder journal has an agent, at this minute, giving bribes at Madrid; and another inspecting the price of potatoes in Covent Garden. Look! here comes the Foreign Express galloping in. They will be able to give news to Downing Street tomorrow: funds will rise or fall, fortunes be made or lost; Lord B. will get up, and, holding the paper in his hand, and seeing the noble marquis in his place, will make a great speech; and—and Mr. Doolan will be called away from his supper at the Back Kitchen; for he is foreign sub-

4. Thackeray explained the measurement in a letter to Doyle, 5 June 1854, *Letters* 3:372. Alternatively, Thackeray could have counted words as is indicated in his October 1854 letter to Mark Lemon explaining why he would no longer work for *Punch* at the new rates they proposed, "A page of Newcomes contains 47 lines of 56 letters = 2612 letters. 4 pages = 10448" (photocopy supplied by William Baker).

editor, and sees the mail on the newspaper sheet before he goes to his own.[5]

The mock-heroic tone of the adjective "ubiquitous," of the exclamation "Look!", and of the juxtaposition of bribes in Madrid with the price of potatoes in Covent Garden introduces a faint distrust of the enthusiasm but does not belie the excitement Warrington feels for the press. The positive part of the passage echoes the spirit of historic significance that prompted the 1832 pressmen's parades in London, complete with a working press carried in a cart producing ink-wet pamphlets on freedom of the press for the crowd. But Warrington's detachment, echoing Thackeray's own, balances the sentiment with the dash and the pun on Mr. Doolan's mundane diurnal oscillation between the printed sheets and his bed sheets. The double view suggests that the situation is too complex to be captured by one feeling or one attitude. That same sleepless engine is also the inexorable, insatiable engine which fed on the writer and caused the haste and the drain of energy which sapped the health of more men than just Thackeray.

Thackeray's sense of the economic realities of publishing was acute—won at the price of two failed literary magazines and years of journalistic hand-to-mouth work. His image of Pegasus drawing a wagon and his unaristocratic equation of the literary profession with the trades are of a piece with his mockery of inflated self-importance in any calling in life. These self-deprecatory remarks cannot be taken to mean more than they do—that literary men must work hard, must meet their deadlines, must accept the consequences of the responses of publishers as merchandisers and readers as the market for art: they must write what will be published and purchased. Thackeray's remarks on his profession do not mean that he held it in low regard or that he had no sense of the dignity of literature. For Thackeray the dignity of the profession lay in the integrity of presenting the world he knew as he saw it—including the business of authorship. In a letter to John Forster he indicated what humbug he thought lay at the root of attempts to assert the dignity of literature by any other means: "I don't believe in the Guild of Literature I dont believe in the Theatrical Scheme; I think *that* is against the dignity of our profession,—but you are honest and clever men and free to your opinion (thank you for nothing say you) well, believe that mine's loyally entertained too."[6] Thackeray was saying that the artist cannot with honesty or true dignity hide behind cant about a high calling.

Thackeray's position is neither starry-eyed or simpleminded. He knew the plight of many literary men who could be said to want the dignity of a bare living; his purse was frequently open to them.[7] With similar honesty he acknowledged the ambiguity of good and evil, a

5. William Makepeace Thackeray, *The History of Pendennis*, ed. Peter L. Shillingsburg (New York: Garland, 1991), 1:308.
6. It appears that this letter may not have been sent; the original is with Smith's correspondence from Thackeray (NLS), who may have been content with showing it to his publisher.
7. This seems particularly true in his days as editor of the *Cornhill* when, perhaps because his "brother authors" knew his ship had come in, they wrote asking for various kinds of help. One letter from Thackeray with a draft for £10 remains among George Smith's papers (NLS), for Smith intercepted and effectively canceled that bit of Thackeray's generosity.

view which more positive men took to reveal weakness. Nor is his position uncomplicatedly open and without subtlety of its own. A chapter of Thackeray's life remains to be written by someone who can see beyond or beneath the surface and untangle the remark in John Chapman's diary for 14 June 1851: "I find that his religious views are perfectly free, but he does not mean to lessen his popularity by fully avowing them, he said he had debated the question with himself whether he was called upon to martyrise himself for the sake of his views and concluded in the negative. His chief object seems to be the making of money. He will go to America for that purpose. He impresses me as much abler than the lecture I heard, but I fear his success is spoiling him."[8]

Thackeray's net worth when he died unexpectedly on 23 December 1863, at age fifty-three, attests for our material age his business success. His house was sold for £10,000. His furniture and personal effects sold for £2,000; his wine for £400. His copyrights brought his daughters £5,000. A total of about £18,000—one thousand more than his father had left him.

It is difficult to understand in modern terms the meaning of £18,000 or of an annual income of £2,000 to £4,000, which Thackeray was making in the last six or seven years of his life. An exchange rate does not help much because buying power changes as goods and services go up or come down. According to an article on the Royal Literary Fund in the *Smithsonian Magazine* (May 1985), London postmen made £50 a year in 1839. Of Anthony Trollope, John Sutherland has said, "With a bit of scrimping £250 was a tolerable annual salary."[9] Another source claims that £250 was the minimum required to be a gentleman. By such meaningless standards the man who wrote a chapter of *Vanity Fair* called "How to Live on Nothing a Year" was twelve times a gentleman.

8. Manuscript diary, Beinecke [New Haven, Conn.]. Chapman had met Thackeray after one of his lectures on Richard Steele two days earlier, at which time Thackeray expressed an interest in purchasing "at the 'trade price' some of my 'atheistic' publications." In his 14 June meeting at Chapman's, Thackeray declined an invitation to write a review of "Modern Novelists for the Westminster Review" because he could get more for his prose elsewhere and because he thought himself unprepared to do such an article. He also "complained of the rivalry and partizanship which is being fostered, I think chiefly Fo(r)ster'd, in respect to him and Dickens by foolish friends." Though Thackeray suggested that Charlotte Brontë write the proposed article, Mary Ann Evans objected, and George Lewes finally agreed to do it.

9. Fred Strebigh, "Keeping the Hacks and Geniuses Out of Debtors Prison," *Smithsonian* (May 1985), p. 126; Sutherland, *Victorian Novelists and Publishers,* (Chicago: University of Chicago Press, 1976), p. 16. See also Robert Patten's interesting worry with this question in *Charles Dickens and His Publishers* (Oxford: Clarendon Press, 1978), p. 3. R. V. Jackson's "The Structure of Pay in Nineteenth-Century Britain," *Economic History Review,* 2d ser., 40 (1987): 563, notes a variety of "nominal annual earnings in skilled service occupations" for 1851 within the civil service: schoolmasters £81 a year, clergy £167, surgeons and doctors £200, and as top pay for solicitors and barristers £1,837.

# Reception

## ROBERT A. COLBY

### [Reception Summary]†

* * *

It is sometimes assumed that Thackeray was unknown to the reading public at the time when *Vanity Fair* was published. Such is the impression given by Henry Kingsley, Thackeray's younger fellow novelist, who recalled in an obituary tribute that *Vanity Fair* "took the world by surprise. Its appearance was a kind of era in the lives of men whose ages were at the time four or five years of twenty; and for aught we know in the lives of men older and wiser."[1] However, there is evidence that Thackeray was familiar to readers, both in his own name and in his literary disguises, at the time when his great novel emerged. "We were perfectly aware that Mr. Thackeray had of old assumed the jester's habit, in order the more unrestrainedly to indulge the privilege of speaking the truth," wrote Elizabeth Rigby in her famous *Quarterly Review* critique, adding, however, "but still we were little prepared for the keen observations, the deep wisdom, and the consummate art which he has interwoven in the slight texture and whimsical pattern of *Vanity Fair*."[2] Robert Stephen Rintoul, the editor of the *Spectator*, reviewing *Vanity Fair*, considered it the latest manifestation of qualities exhibited in Thackeray's earlier works: ". . . his keen perception of the weaknesses, vanities, and humbugs of society, the felicitous point with which he displays or the pungent good nature with which he exposes them, and the easy, close, and pregnant diction in which he clothes his perceptions . . . ," though this latest work seemed to him to exhibit "a depth and at times a pathos which we do not remember to have met with in Mr. Thackeray's previous writings. . . ."[3] *The Western Times*, one of those quoted in Number 13 of *Vanity Fair*, referred to its author familiarly as "Thack the Snobkiller."[4] In America the reviewer for the *Knickerbocker Magazine*, obvi-

† From "Historical Introduction," *Vanity Fair* (New York: Garland, 1989), 632–37. Reprinted by permission.

1. "Thackeray," *Macmillan's Magazine*, 9 (February, 1864), 356.
2. "*Vanity Fair* and *Jane Eyre*," *Quarterly Review*, 84 (December, 1848), 153.
3. *Spectator*, 21 (July 22, 1848), 709–10.
4. January, 1848 (last of the advertisements).

ously no stranger to Thackeray's work, spoke of *Vanity Fair* as "the best we have seen from his pen."[5]

Amidst the eulogies, *Vanity Fair* had its denigrators, like Harriet Martineau who condemned it as "a raking up of dirt and rotten eggs,"[6] and Archbishop Whately who likened it somewhat murkily to "a dinner with, for top dish a roasted fox, stuffed with tobacco and basted with train oil. . . ."[7] "Does everybody like that clever, unbelieving, disagreeable book?" queried the prolific Scottish novelist and critic Mrs. Oliphant.[8] Actually most of the literary fraternity of the time whose opinions are on record liked it, if for a variety of reasons. Carlyle, at first repelled by its cynicism and preferring the geniality of *Dombey and Son,* in time found "more reality" in Thackeray than in Dickens.[9] The actor Macready detected "more of the mark of the educated man" in Thackeray than in his chief rival, "a very extraordinary and wise book; most entertaining; to me, who will think, and feel, and look truth in the face, most instructive."[1] The snob appeal is reflected also in a sentence from Abraham Hayward's famous and influential review: "In a word, the book is the work of a gentleman, which is one great merit; and not the work of a fine (or would-be fine) gentleman, which is another." (Hayward undoubtedly wrote these words with a glance at the Silver-Forks that Thackeray had parodied in "Lords and Liveries" and other Punch Prize Novels.) To Elizabeth Rigby the great virtue of *Vanity Fair* lay in its appearing not to be a novel, but a "literal photograph of the manners and habits of the nineteenth century, thrown on to paper by the light of a powerful mind." The writer Robert Bell, in a review for *Fraser's Magazine* that especially pleased Thackeray, declared that "few writers have displayed within the compass of a single story more fertility of invention, or a more accurate knowledge of life." To George Henry Lewes *Vanity Fair* was "one of the most remarkable works of modern fiction."[2]

To Thackeray's contemporaries, from the evidence of reviews, *Vanity Fair* appears not to have been something new in his work so much as a carrying forward of his familiar line with wider sweep and deeper tone. It definitely established him as a writer of stature; it also eventually became his most popular and enduring novel. Nevertheless it was slow in catching on with the public; as Thackeray complained in a letter to Edward FitzGerald, "It does everything but pay."[3] A hint as to why is provided here and there in pronouncements by two or

5. *Knickerbocker,* 32 (September, 1848). In "Thackeray's Journalism: Apprenticeship for Writer and Reader," *Victorian Newsletter,* No. 57 (Spring, 1980), 23–27, Elizabeth Segel contends that Thackeray was not so unknown to the reading public at the time when *Vanity Fair* came out as is commonly supposed, pointing out that in fact his various literary disguises prepared readers for the idiosyncratic manner of its narration.
6. Unpublished letter to Helen Martineau, n.d., Manchester College, Oxford University; quoted in R. K. Webb, *Harriet Martineau* (New York: Columbia University Press, 1960), p. 38.
7. Letter to Nassau Senior, January 12, 1853, *Life and Correspondence of Archbishop Whately,* ed. Jane Whatley, 2 vols. (London: Longmans, Green, 1866), II, 264.
8. "Mr. Thackeray and His Novels," *Blackwood's Magazine,* 77 (January, 1855), 89.
9. Sir Charles Gavan Duffy, *Conversations with Carlyle* (New York: Scribner's, 1892), p. 76.
1. *The Diaries of William Charles Macready, 1833–1851,* ed. William Toynbee, 2 vols. (New York: G. Putnam's Sons, 1912), II, 418 (Entry for January 31, 1849).
2. *Edinburgh Review,* January, 1848, p. 50; *Quarterly Review,* December, 1848, p. 86; *Fraser's Magazine,* September, 1848, p. 333; *Athenæum,* August 12, 1848, p. 794.
3. March–May, 1848, *Letters,* II, 365.

three early reviewers who judged the novel piecemeal while it was coming out in monthly numbers. David Masson, on the basis of numbers 1–3 (ending with Chapter 11, "Arcadian Simplicity," centering on the Crawley family), praised the ease and grace with which the story was told, but indicated that its very quietness did not destine it for popularity. Masson considered the promise of "terrific chapters coming presently" in Chapter 6 as credible as the alleged likeness of the author to the figure on the cover.[4] By the time that Henry Fothergill Chorley got around to reviewing it for the *Athenaeum*, the story had advanced to its seventh number (ending with Chapter 25, "In Which All the Principal Personages Think Fit to Leave Brighton"). Chorley was generally impressed with the author's wit, but noted that these sketches are of "mean persons" rather than of "English society" as a whole. "Should 'Vanity Fair' fail to take a fast and permanent hold of the public," he conjectured, "it will be the fault of the preference on the author's part for the unpleasing (a thing totally distinct from Cynicism or the apotheosis of Deformity) and not because he fails in force of portraiture and in probability of dialogue, or in truth to the by-way and back-stairs and kennel life of this Valley of Tears!" Furthermore, Chorley warned the author to "beware of banter" and admonished him that "a gallery filled with Dutch studies by Maas and Brouwer and Jan Steen and Ostade makes a monotonous show. . . ."[5] Although he concluded that "we wait with more than ordinary curiosity for the 'reckoning' of 'Vanity Fair,' " we do not know how Chorley received the Bareacres and Lord Steyne or the Pumpernickel episodes, which should have satisfied his desire for "English society."

On the other hand, Abraham Hayward, who reviewed *Vanity Fair* through its eleventh number (ending with Chapter 38, "A Family in a Very Small Way"), was favorably disposed towards it from the outset. "The great charm of this work is its entire freedom from mannerism and affectation both in style and sentiment," Hayward wrote, praising Thackeray further for "the confiding frankness with which the reader is addressed,—the thoroughbred carelessness with which the author permits the thoughts and feelings suggested by the situations to flow in their natural channel. . . ." This casualness and leisurely pace which turned some ordinary readers away was a source of pleasure to Hayward. Also, the lack of excitement that others complained of was to Hayward one of the supreme merits of *Vanity Fair*. "[Thackeray's] effects are uniformly the effects of sound and wholesome legitimate art; and we need hardly add that we are never harrowed up with the physical horrors of the Eugène Sue school in his writings, or that

4. "Popular Serial Literature," *North British Review*, 7 (May, 1847), 120. Among works reviewed along with *Vanity Fair* were Dickens's *Dealings with the Firm of Dombey and Son* and *The Battle of Life*, Albert Smith's *Adventures of Christopher Tadpole* and Gilbert à Beckett's *Comic History of England* (which like *Vanity Fair* had its genesis in *Punch*). All of these writers were likened to Scheherezade in that they live only so long as they have a story to tell. "Alas!" concludes the reviewer, "the ocean to which most of them are tending is not of immortality, but of oblivion."

5. *Athenæum*, July 24, 1847, pp. 785–86. Chorley quoted at length as an example of Thackeray's powerful writing the episode near the end of Chapter 24 where old Osborne takes down the family Bible and obliterates George's name from it. He added: "The critic would be justified in being stringent if not severe with a novelist who could write the foregoing passage yet fail to produce a complete work of high order."

there are no melodramatic villains to be found in them." (Actually Thackeray had planned to translate *The Mysteries of Paris* some years before, and mentioned Sue in passages of the manuscript of *Vanity Fair* that were subsequently deleted. The various hints in the published novel of hidden "mysteries" in the past of Becky and other characters are veiled allusions to this project.) Hayward appears to have been the only one of the reviewers of the uncompleted novel to assume that Thackeray was still uncertain as to the fate of his characters. Comparing his position to that of the readers of *Clarissa* who interceded with Richardson to save the heroine from a tragic end, Hayward presumes to advise Thackeray to have Rawdon appointed to a consulship on the coast of Africa. As we know, Hayward was not actually far off from Thackeray's eventual disposition of Rawdon, except for his thinking of it as "an appropriate punishment for Becky, for she would be deprived of profligate peers to flirt with and tradesmen to cheat."[6] He did prove prescient in his prediction that Amelia would marry Dobbin—especially shrewd at this juncture of the narrative where Dobbin's engagement to Glorvina O'Dowd in India is just announced.

Twentieth-century criticism has discovered how much of what Trollope called the "elbow grease" of forethought went into *Vanity Fair* both in its overall structure and in the linking of its original parts by analogy and contrast.[7] Unfortunately for his future reputation, some of Thackeray's contemporaries associated part publication with looseness and carelessness, and this stigma clung to *Vanity Fair* even when it was issued in book form. Robert Stephen Rintoul, one of the most fervent of Thackeray's admirers, thought nevertheless that *Vanity Fair* was "considered as a whole . . . rather a succession of connected scenes and characters than a well-constructed story. Both incidents and persons belong more to the sketch than the finished picture. Either from natural bias or long habits of composition, Mr. Thackeray seems to have looked at life by bits rather than as a whole."[8] The reviewer for the *Dublin University Magazine* (actually its editor at the time, John Francis Waller) concluded that *Vanity Fair* "bears upon its pages the indelible impress of a genius so original and so striking that it must at once lift its author into a high position among the writers of his age and country," but in the body of his review he had characterized it as a series of brilliant sketches "with a description of the effect which the combinations of fortune produce upon each of the *dramatis personae*, rather than any deep analysis of the passions or feelings of the human heart."[9] Waller detected signs of what he thought was month-by-month *composition* (not merely publication), in particular with the transformation of Rawdon Crawley from profligate to respectable gentleman, deviations from the original conceptions of characters. George Henry Lewes thought Thackeray's parodies of the genteel, facetious, and romantic manners of novel writing in

6. *Edinburgh Review*, January, 1848, p. 60.
7. See in particular, Edgar F. Harden's article "The Discipline and Significance of Form in *Vanity Fair*," *PMLA* 82 (December, 1967), 530–41 [710–30].
8. *Spectator*, July 22, 1848, p. 710.
9. *Dublin University Magazine*, October, 1848, pp. 446–47.

Chapter 6 "impertinent," and a lapse "into his old magazine manner."[1] Thackeray of course dropped these parodies in the revised book edition of 1853, possibly in response to such criticism. The change of the subtitle from "Pen and Pencil *Sketches* . . . ," redolent of Thackeray's early 'magazinery,' to "A *Novel* without a Hero" may have been intended by Thackeray as an indication that this was a unified, connected work, but if so, some of the reviewers missed the point.

A culling of reviews throughout Thackeray's career testifies that readers of his generation were impressed and dazzled by *Vanity Fair*, but in time esteemed *Pendennis*, *Henry Esmond*, and *The Newcomes* more. It is an oddity of Thackeray's literary reputation that in his own age his prestige should have been secured by the novels after *Vanity Fair*, whereas to ours he survives mainly through his first popular success. We, it seems, are attracted to the very qualities that disturbed Thackeray's contemporaries—impersonality, cynicism, tough-mindedness. Indeed, its coruscating wit, ingenuity, and vivacious style continue to make *Vanity Fair* the most immediately attractive of Thackeray's novels to the general reader. It is also true that, moving and appealing as are the later novels, Thackeray never again created a character with the magnetism of Becky Sharp (although Beatrix Esmond comes close). "We were fully alive to that lady's faults; indeed she did not take any vast trouble to conceal them," recalled Henry Kingsley at age thirty-seven about his impressions of twenty years back, "but in spite of this she simply gave a whisk of her yellow hair, and an ogle with her green eyes, took us by the nose, and led us wheresoever she would. And did ever woman lead men such a dance as she led us?"[2] It is interesting to see readers then as now coming to Becky's defense. While disturbed by the lack of a strong moral impression in the novel as a whole, Miss Rigby had nothing but praise for the characterization of Becky, even absolving her from any blame in Jos's death, suggesting that it was caused by imprudent eating and drinking in India.[3] John Francis Waller, for another, was pleased that Becky was left unpunished, commending Thackeray for being too sophisticated and worldly to follow the beaten track by bringing his heroine to retribution.[4]

* * *

## [ABRAHAM HAYWARD]

## Thackeray's Writings†

In forming our general estimate of this writer, we wish to be understood as referring principally, if not exclusively, to 'Vanity Fair' (a novel in monthly parts), though still unfinished; so immeasurably su-

1. *Athenæum*, August 12, 1848, p. 794.
2. *Macmillan's Magazine*, February, 1864, p. 356.
3. *Quarterly Review*, December, 1848, p. 86.
4. *Dublin University Magazine*, October, 1848, p. 459.

† From the *Edinburgh Review* 87 (January 1848): 50–51, 53.

perior, in our opinion, is this to every other known production of his pen. The great charm of this work is its entire freedom from mannerism and affectation both in style and sentiment,—the confiding frankness with which the reader is addressed,—the thoroughbred carelessness with which the author permits the thoughts and feelings suggested by the situations to flow in their natural channel, as if conscious that nothing mean or unworthy, nothing requiring to be shaded, gilded, or dressed up in company attire, could fall from him. In a word, the book is the work of a gentleman, which is one great merit; and not the work of a fine (or would-be fine) gentleman, which is another. Then, again, he never exhausts, elaborates, or insists too much upon anything; he drops his finest remarks and happiest illustrations as Buckingham dropped his pearls, and leaves them to be picked up and appreciated as chance may bring a discriminating observer to the spot. His effects are uniformly the effects of sound wholesome legitimate art; and we need hardly add that we are never harrowed up with physical horrors of the Eugene Sue school in his writings, or that there are no melodramatic villains to be found in them. One touch of nature makes the whole world kin, and here are touches of nature by the dozen. His pathos (though not so deep as Mr. Dickens') is exquisite; the more so, perhaps, because he seems to struggle against it, and to be half ashamed of being caught in the melting mood: but the attempt to be caustic, satirical, ironical, or philosophical, on such occasions, is uniformly vain; and again and again have we found reason to admire how an originally fine and kind nature remains essentially free from worldliness, and, in the highest pride of intellect, pays homage to the heart.

'Vanity Fair' was certainly meant for a satire: the follies, foibles and weaknesses (if not vices) of the world we live in, were to be shown up in it, and we can hardly be expected to learn philanthropy from the contemplation of them. Yet the author's real creed is evidently expressed in these few short sentences:

'The world is a looking-glass, and gives forth to every man the reflection of his own face. Frown at it, and it will in turn look sourly upon you; laugh at it and with it, and it is a jolly kind companion; and so let all young persons take their choice.'

But this theory of life does not lead Mr. Thackeray to the conclusion that virtue is invariably its own reward, nor prevent him from thinking that the relative positions held by great and small, prosperous and unprosperous, in social estimation, might sometimes be advantageously reversed.

* * *

We heartily rejoice that Mr. Thackeray has kept his science and political economy (if he has any) for some other emergency, and given us a plain old-fashioned love-story, which any genuine novel reader of the old school may honestly, plentifully, and conscientiously cry over.

We fear a novel reader must be literally of the old school to enter fully into the humour of the work; for the scene is laid when George the Fourth was (not king, but) regent; the most stirring period is the Waterloo year, 1815; and the dress, manner, modes of thought, amusements, &c. &c. are supposed to be in keeping. The war fever was at its height: Napoleon was regarded as an actual monster: the belief that one Englishman could beat two Frenchmen, and ought to do it whenever he had an opportunity, was universal, (perhaps beneficially so, for 'those can conquer who believe they can'): the stage coach was the only mode of travelling for the commonalty: gentlemen occasionally attended prize-fights: top-boots and hessians were the common wear: black neckcloths were confined to the military; and tight integuments for the nether man were held indispensable; so much so, indeed, that when some rash innovators attempted to introduce trousers at Almack's, the indignant patronesses instantly posted up a notification, that, 'in future, no gentleman would on any account be admitted without breeches.'[1]

# CHARLOTTE BRONTË

## Selected Letters†

### *To W. S. Williams, March 29, 1848*

* * *

You mention Thackeray and the last number of *Vanity Fair*. The more I read Thackeray's works the more certain I am that he stands alone—alone in his sagacity, alone in his truth, alone in his feeling (his feeling, though he makes no noise about it, is about the most genuine that ever lived on a printed page), alone in his power, alone in his simplicity, alone in his self-control. Thackeray is a Titan, so strong that he can afford to perform with calm the most herculean feats; there is the charm and majesty of repose in his greatest efforts; *he* borrows nothing from fever, his is never the energy of delirium—his energy is sane energy, deliberate energy, thoughtful energy. The last number of *Vanity Fair* proves this peculiarly. Forcible, exciting in its force, still more impressive than exciting, carrying on the interest of the narrative in a flow, deep, full, resistless, it is still quiet—as quiet as reflection, as quiet as memory; and to me there are parts of it that sound as solemn as an oracle. Thackeray is never borne away by his own ardour—he has it under control. His genius obeys him—it is his servant, it works no fantastic changes at its own wild will, it must still achieve the task which reason and sense assign it, and none other. Thackeray is unique. I *can* say no more, I *will* say no less.—Believe me, yours sincerely,

C. BELL.

### *To W. S. Williams, August 14, 1848*

I have already told you, I believe, that I regard Mr. Thackeray as the first of modern masters, and as the legitimate high priest of Truth;

1. This fact, curiously enough, is forgotten in the woodcuts, old Sedley, Mr. Chopper, Rawdon Crawley, &c. &c., being represented in trousers.

† From Clement Shorter, ed., *The Brontës: Life and Letters* (London: Hodder and Stoughton, 1908), 405, 445.

I study him accordingly with reverence. He, I see, keeps the mermaid's tail below water, and only hints at the dead men's bones and noxious slime amidst which it wriggles; *but,* his hint is more vivid than other men's elaborate explanations, and never is his satire whetted to so keen an edge as when with quiet mocking irony he modestly recommends to the approbation of the public his own exemplary discretion and forbearance. The world begins to know Thackeray rather better than it did two years or even a year ago, but as yet it only half knows him. His mind seems to me a fabric as simple and unpretending as it is deep-founded and enduring—there is no meretricious ornament to attract or fix a superficial glance; his great distinction of the genuine is one that can only be fully appreciated with time. There is something, a sort of 'still profound,' revealed in the concluding part of *Vanity Fair* which the discernment of one generation will not suffice to fathom. A hundred years hence, if he only lives to do justice to himself, he will be better known than he is now. A hundred years hence, some thoughtful critic, standing and looking down on the deep waters, will see shining through them the pearl without price of a purely original mind—such a mind as the Bulwers, etc., his contemporaries have *not,*—not acquirements gained from study, but the thing that came into the world with him—his inherent genius: the thing that made him, I doubt not, different as a child from other children, that caused him, perhaps, peculiar griefs and struggles in life, and that now makes him as a writer unlike other writers. Excuse me for recurring to this theme, I do not wish to bore you.

## WILLIAM MAKEPEACE THACKERAY

## Letter to George Henry Lewes, March 6, 1848†

13 Young St. Kensington.
6 March. 1848
My dear Sir

I have just read your notice in the Chronicle[1] (I conclude it is a friend who has penned it) and am much affected by the friend-

† Letter to G. H. Lewes, 6 March 1848 reprinted from *Letters and Private Papers of William Makepeace Thackeray* ed. Gordon N. Ray, 4 vols. (Cambridge: Harvard University Press, 1945–46), 2: 353–54. Reprinted by permission.

1. An article ostensibly on *The Book of Snobs* which develops into a general survey of Thackeray's work. Though Lewes deals chiefly in praise, he finds reason for protest in Thackeray's books. He complains that the world is not so corrupt as Thackeray would have us believe; "in *Vanity Fair,* his greatest work, how little there is to love! The people are all scamps, scoundrels, or humbugs." Lewes takes particular exception to a "detestable passage" in chapter 41 of the novel (*Biographical Edition of the Works of William Makepeace Thackeray,* 13 vols. [London: Smith, Elder, 1898–99], I, 407–408) [422], "wherein after allowing Becky, with dramatic propriety, to sophisticate with herself to the effect that it is only her poverty which makes her vicious, [Thackeray] adds from himself this remark:—'And who knows but Rebecca was right in her speculations—and that it was only a question of money and fortune which made the difference between her and an honest woman? If you take temptations into account, who is to say that he is better than his neighbour? A comfortable career of prosperity, if it does not make people honest, at least keeps them so. An alderman coming from a turtle feast will not step out of his carriage to steal a leg of mutton; *but put him to starve, and see if he will not purloin a loaf.*' Was it carelessness, or deep misanthropy, distorting an otherwise clear judgment, which allowed such a remark to fall? What, in the face of starving thousands, men who literally die for want of bread, yet who prefer death to stealing, shall it be said that honesty is only the virtue of abundance!" (*Morning Chronicle,* March 6)

liness of the sympathy, and by the kindness of the reproof of the critic.

That passage w^h you quote bears very hardly upon the poor alderman certainly: but I don't mean that the man deprived of turtle would as a consequence steal bread: only that he in the possession of luxuries and riding through life respectably in a gig, should be very chary of despising poor Lazarus on foot, & look very humbly and leniently upon the faults of his less fortunate brethren—If Becky had had 5000 a year I have no doubt in my mind that she would have been respectable; increased her fortune advanced her family in the world: laid up treasures for herself in the shape of 3 per cents, social position, reputation &c—like Louis Philippe let us say, or like many a person highly & comfortably placed in the world not guilty of many wrongs of commission, satisfied with himself, never doubting of his merit, and decorously angry at the errors of less lucky men. What satire is so awful as Lead us not into temptation? What is the gospel and life of our Lord (excuse me for mentioning it) but a tremendous Protest against pride and self-righteousness? God forgive us all, I pray, and deliver us from evil.

I am quite aware of the dismal roguery w^h goes all through the Vanity Fair story—and God forbid that the world should be like it altogether: though I fear it is more like it than we like to own. But my object is to make every body engaged, engaged in the pursuit of Vanity and I must carry my story through in this dreary minor key, with only occasional hints here & there of better things—of better things w^h it does not become me to preach.

I never scarcely write letters to critics and beg you to excuse me for sending you this. It is only because I have just laid down the paper, and am much moved by the sincere goodwill of my critic.

very faithfully yours
W M Thackeray.

# [GEORGE HENRY LEWES]

## Review†

* * *

For some years Mr. Thackeray has been a marked man in letters, —but known rather as an amusing sketcher than as a serious artist. Light playful contributions to periodical literature, and two amusing books of travel, were insufficient to make a reputation; but a reputation he must now be held to have established by his 'Vanity Fair.' It is his greatest effort and his greatest success. The strength which lay within him he has here put forth for the first time. The work before us retains traces of the writer's old fault—a fault fostered no doubt by the carelessness and impromptu proper to serial publication—viz. a sort of indifference to the serious claims of literature, a cavalier impertinence of manner as if he were playing with

† *Athenæum,* August 12, 1848, pp. 794–97.

his subject. Nothing could be more impertinent, for instance, than Mr. Thackeray's second number,—in which he relapsed into his old magazine manner, and postponed the continuation of his narrative to imitations of some of his contemporary writers of fiction. Fit subjects for ridicule such writers may be—but the ridicule is misplaced in the work which Mr. Thackeray had in hand, considered as a work of Art. In the same number he becomes suddenly aware of the discrepancy between the costume of the period in which he has laid his scene and the costume in which he has depicted the characters in his pictorial illustrations. All he does on the discovery is to notify the fact in a note, and flippantly pretend that the real costume was too hideous for his purpose. He has been guilty, however, of the same confusion of periods throughout the work. Sometimes we are in the early part of the present century—at others we are palpably in 1848. Writing from month to month encourages such laches; but for the sake of such a reputation as Mr. Thackeray has now arrived at, it will be well that he should be more upon his guard.

The style of 'Vanity Fair' is winning, easy, masculine, felicitous, and humorous. Its pleasant pages are nowhere distorted by rant. The author indulges in no sentimentalities—inflicts no fine writing on his readers. Trusting to the force of truth and humour, he is the *quietest* of contemporary writers,—a merit worth noting in a literary age which has a tendency to mistake spasm for force. The book has abundant faults of its own,—and we shall presently notice some of them; but they are not the faults most current in our literature. The writer is quite free from theatricality. No glare from the foot-lights is thrown upon human nature, exaggerating and distorting it. He is guiltless too—let us be thankful for such a boon in the sense here intended —of a "purpose." Unfettered by political or social theories, his views of men and classes are not cramped. The rich in his pages are not necessarily vicious—the poor not as a consequence of their poverty virtuous and high-minded. Again—many jesters take advantage of their cap and bells, and adopt as their motto, "Ridentem dicere *falsum* quid vetat." Under the plea that laughter is not a serious thing, and what is laughingly spoken is not to be critically judged, they have sacrificed truth to their joke. No advocate of any cause, however, should be more scrupulously watched than he who laughing teaches. Against the dogmas of the politician, philosopher, or theologian the reader is on his defence. These "come in such a questionable shape" that we *must* examine them. Their seriousness alarms us. We scrutinize proofs and combat conclusions. But the jester is privileged. He throws us off our guard by the smile of his approach, and insinuates conviction by the bribery of laughter. The laughter passes, but the error may remain. It has gained admittance into our unsuspecting minds,—and is left there unsuspected.

It is a much-disputed question, whether or not ridicule be a test of truth? To us the question appears answered by saying that if the ridicule be developed *ab intra* from the argument—not thrown on it *ab extra*—it is a test. If a wit descries the latent absurdity grinning under a moral mask, and exposes it, he has confuted the argument; if he himself grins and makes faces *at* the mask, he may excite laughter but has not carried confutation. A famous illustration of the former method is the reply made to that philosopher who argued, with a sort of seductive plausibility, that the emotion inspired in the heart of man by the sight of woman's bosom is owing to association of ideas —to his dim remembrance of having drawn his first nourishment from that sacred source. "If," said the wit who saw—or believed he saw—a fallacy lurking under the suggestion, "a child brought up by hand were to see a wooden spoon, he would in that case experience the same emotions!"—It is one of Thackeray's peculiar excellencies that he almost always ridicules *ab intra.* An absurdity is stated by him in the quietest and gravest manner, as if he were himself a believer in it like others, and—enforced by such means of self-accumulation as leave it to unmitigated contempt. His irony of this kind is perfect,—but it is a weapon which he uses far too exclusively. He has shown himself, as we have said, a satirist—but not an artist. With himself we exclaim, "O brother wearers of motley! are there not moments when one grows sick of grinning and tumbling and the jingling of bells?" There is nothing so sad as a constant smile. Laughter becomes wearisome when too much prolonged,—for it is then a sort of blasphemy against the divine beauty which is in life. Mr. Thackeray grows serious and pathetic at times—but almost as if he were ashamed of it, like a man caught in tears at the theatre.—It is one weakness of the satirist that he is commonly afraid of the ridicule of others!

We have said that Mr. Thackeray is a satirist, not an artist:—and from that characteristic may be deduced many of his deficiencies. For instance, the reader of 'Vanity Fair' will have observed that we have in it nothing but scenes and sketches—only glimpses, not views. There is constant succession of description, but no developement of story. The passions are taken at their culminating point, not exhibited in the process of growth; the incidents are seldom transacted before our eyes, but each is taken as a *fait accompli.* Nor is there anything like proportion kept. The writer opens a chapter, and his pen runs on easily, fed by a full and observant mind,—but recording the suggestions of the moment rather than building up the various portions of an edifice already planned and in which each part has its due significance.

Mr. Thackeray is deficient, too, in passion:—a deficiency that sits lightly on a satirist, but is serious in a writer of fiction. He has no command over this quality—apparently but little knowledge of it. The curtain of the tragedy of life has seldom risen before him—or he has looked on its representations with an incurious eye. Altogether, one may say that Mr. Thackeray has not very curiously or patiently observed moral phenomena. Life he has seen both at home and abroad, and he has reflected on what he has seen. We feel that he is painting after Nature: and this conviction it is which makes his work so delightful. Nothing is permanently interesting but truth.

As a consequence of Mr. Thackeray's satirical tendency may be noted the prodigality of vice and folly to be found in his pages—and which affords no true representation of human nature, but only the exaggeration of a feature. It has been made a serious reproach against this writer that he has arrived at such a pitch of misanthropy or doubt as to think, with Chamfort, that an honest man is a variety of the human species. It is not the first time that this great defect of art has been conspicuous in the writings of Mr. Thackeray. The 'Snob Papers,' undertaken to expose the folly of a class, gradually expanded under the writer's satiric heat till they found snobbery every *where* and marked every *body* for a snob. Good instincts and impulses came under the ridicule which should have branded a folly or a vice—and long ere the 'Papers' came to a close all feeling of sincerity was gone. The author who began with a moral was content at last to get a laugh—and ruined his moral by laughing in holy places. So with this book. The writer began, no doubt, with the wholesome intention of lashing the vices and follies of Vanity Fair in a more restrictive sense—regarded as one of the social phases: but gradually *all* the districts of society are swept into his Vanity Fair—and there is *nothing good in it.* This is false and unwholesome teaching. What a mass of scoundrels, blacklegs, fools, and humbugs Mr. Thackeray has crowded together. There is scarcely a good or estimable person in the book and as little of affection as of virtue. Even the heroine Amelia—with whom the writer seems to have been somewhat enamoured (a feeling of which he is likely to have the monopoly)—is thoroughly selfish as well as silly. The one fine exception is Major Dobbin—a sketch not unworthy of the hand that drew 'My Uncle Toby.'

As we have said, Mr. Thackeray's humour is peculiarly his own. He never frames and glazes an idea. The simplest words and in the simplest manner are used to bring out his meaning; and everything seems to flow from him as water from a rock. We may add that when he chooses to be pathetic, a quality of the same kind gives wonderful effect to his pathos. How beautiful is the scene in which Amelia has resolved at length to part from her child!—[Pages 493.14–494.22; 495.3up–496.36 in this Norton Critical Edition.]

The character of Becky is amongst the finest creations of modern fiction. She is perfectly unlike any other clever, heartless woman yet drawn. With great art, she is made rather selfish than wicked—though the excess of the selfishness rises to the force and has the effect of wickedness. Profound immorality is made to seem consistent with unfailing good humour. Becky has neither affections, nor passions, nor principles. She uses men as chessmen—and is not checkmated at last. It is very strange that the reader has a sort of liking for her in spite of his better knowledge. The fact is, the author has contrived in a surprising way to represent not only Becky's *mind* but her *manner.* We are in some sort under her spell,—as Rawdon was. To us she is almost as lively, entertaining and good-humoured as she was to those amongst whom she lived. Like Lord Steyne, we may see through her yet covet her society. Her equability of temper is a nice touch:—it belongs to the physiology of such a character. They who have no affections and no principles can be wounded only in their self-love, and may obtain the character of being good-tempered at the cheapest possible cost. The consistency of this remarkable character is maintained to the last. How full yet brief—graphic and suggestive—is the microscopic view of her life after her separation from her husband! —[Pages 639.2up–642.3up in this Norton Critical Edition.]

Next in point of skill to that of Becky is the portrait of Rawdon Crawley—the heavy, stupid, gentlemanly dragoon and blackleg so completely subjugated by his clever little wife. His affection for his child quite whitewashes him. The reader forgets the blackleg in the father. It is worthy of note with what consummate truth this heavy dragoon is made to feel his insignificance by the side of his clever little wife, but how completely paralyzed the adroit little woman is when she stands guilty before her husband:—how silently she obeys him who has hitherto obeyed her,—how she feels that her arts are powerless against his passion. Brute strength long led by mental cunning here reasserts its empire and is undisputed. The whole scene is most masterly.

Joe Sedley is rather a failure:—nor is he consistently drawn. We are introduced to him as a man painfully shy, nervous, and stupid; but as the story proceeds he drops his shyness, and retains only the gluttony and stupidity of his former self. Meant as a decidedly *comic* character, he creates but little mirth.—George Osborne, the vain and foolish young officer, is capitally drawn. Lord Steyne is one of those *telling* exaggerations which make people exclaim, "How true!" when their acquaintance with lords is confined to fashionable novels. Though overdone, however, it is an exaggeration by a master; and the descriptions of Gaunt House and its inmates transcend all previous efforts in that style. Old Miss Crawley is capital. Her selfishness, her sagacity, her terrors in ill health, her triumph over the meanness which surrounds her and which she laughs at and profits by, are vividly presented, yet by the simplest strokes. Here is a sentence pregnant with meaning and very characteristic of the author:—"Picture to yourself, oh fair young reader, a worldly, selfish, graceless, thankless, religionless old woman, writhing in pain and fear, and *without her wig*! Picture her to yourself, and ere you be old learn to love and pray!"

Mrs. O'Dowd must not be forgotten. The gallant woman has won the hearts of her regiment,—and of all her readers. How true, homely, affectionate, and wise is the description of her packing up the Major's traps and preparing his coffee for him on the eve of Waterloo!

The vividness with which the whole of the scenes at Brussels stand out before the eye is marvellous when we reflect that the author is not describing the scenes which he himself witnessed, but only painting after the descriptions of others. They imply a fine faculty for historical romance. Nor is it only in this more elaborate painting that Mr. Thackeray has exhibited a constant mastery in the present book. The instances are abundant of meaning conveyed and intensified by a single line of illustration. Take only one, where Amelia reads over George's letters.—

"She read them over—as if she did not know them by heart already: but she could not part with them. That effort was too much for her; she placed them back in her bosom again—*as you have seen a woman nurse a child that is dead.*"

Our extracts, though sparing, will suffice to warrant the terms in which we have spoken of 'Vanity Fair.' Its great excellence, however, cannot be tested by extracts. The charm of the work *pervades* it—and is not gathered up into separate "bits." Knowledge of life, good humoured satire, penetration into motive, power of characterization, and great truthfulness are qualities in fiction as rare as they are admirable; and no work that has been published for many years past can claim these qualities so largely as 'Vanity Fair.'

## [ROBERT BELL]

## Review†

Every periodical has its white days and ambrosial memories. We have ours, and the great indigo book before us reminds us of one of them. *Fraser's Magazine* was the nursery-bed in which Michael Angelo Titmarsh quickened. Out of the 'Yellow-Plush Correspondence' grew the Jeameses and the Perkinses, the Crawleys, Dobbins, and Sharps. Transplanted into more open ground, Michael Angelo expanded with increased luxuriance; more salt was laid at the roots of his humour, which fattened and flourished accordingly.

But he is the same Michael Angelo still. The same characteristics may be traced throughout; the same quality of subtle observation, penetrating rarely below the epidermis, but taking up all the small vessels with microscopic vision; the same grotesque exaggeration, with truth at the bottom; the same constitutional instinct for seizing on the ridiculous aspect of things, for turning the 'seamy side' of society outwards, and for exposing false pretensions and the genteel ambition of *parvenus.* The task to which the natural bent of Michael Angelo's genius leads him is a disagreeable one, and often distressingly painful; but he never seems to be aware of that fact. He dissects his victims with a smile; and performs the cruellest of operations on their self-love with a pleasantry which looks provokingly very like good-nature. The peculiarities and eccentricities of matter and manner with which he started are here as trenchant as ever. No author ever advanced so far in reputation without advancing further in novelty of enterprise. He has never gone out of himself from the beginning, or out of the subjects over which he possesses so complete a mastery. He has never broken new pastures, but only taken a wider and more thoughtful survey of the old. Yet such are the inexhaustible resources of the soil, and such the skill with which he works them, that we are never conscious of the slightest sense of monotony. All is fresh, versatile, and original.

The follies, vices, and meannesses of society are the game hunted down by Mr. Thackeray. He keeps almost exclusively amongst the middle-classes; not the fashionable circles, but the people who ape them. The distinction is important, since it gives him a larger scope with less restriction. It is by this standard he must be tested. We must

† *Fraser's Magazine* 38 (September 1848), 320–22.

always keep in mind that his *Vanity Fair* is not the Vanity Fair of the upper ranks, where a certain equanimity of breeding absorbs all crudenesses and angularities of character, but the Vanity Fair of the vulgar great, who have no breeding at all. Into this picture all sorts of portraits are freely admissible. There is nothing too base or too low to be huddled up in a corner of the canvass. The most improbable combinations, the most absurd contrasts, are not out of place in this miscellaneous *mélange.* The life that is here painted is not that of high comedy, but of satiric farce; and it is the business of the artist to shew you all its deformities, its cringing affectations, its paltry pride, its despicable finery, its lying, treachery, and penury of soul in the broadest light. Starting from this point, and with this clear understanding, we shall be the better able to comprehend and estimate the nature of the entertainment prepared for us.

The people who fill up the motley scenes of *Vanity Fair,* with two or three exceptions, are as vicious and odious as a clever condensation of the vilest qualities can make them. The women are especially detestable. Cunning, low pride, selfishness, envy, malice, and all uncharitableness, are scattered amongst them with impartial liberality. It does not enter into the design of *Vanity Fair* to qualify these bitter ingredients with a little sweetness now and then; to shew the close neighbourhood of the vices and the virtues as it lies on the map of the human heart, that mixture of good and evil, of weakness and strength, which, in infinitely varied proportions, constitutes the compound individual. The parts here are all patented for set functions, and no lapse into their opposites ever compromises the integrity of the *rôle.* There is some reason in this. The special section of society painted in this book resembles, in more particulars than mere debauchery of life, the conduct of a masquerade where a character is put on as a disguise, and played out with the best skill of the actor, until drunkenness or the death-bed betrays his secret. It is a lie from first to last; and no class of people in the world stand in such need of consistency as liars. We must not quarrel with Mr. Thackeray, then, for not giving Rebecca Sharp an occasional touch of remorse or tenderness, for not suffering paternal Osborne to undergo a twitch of misgiving, and for bringing together a company of fools and rogues who cannot muster up amongst them a single grain of sincerity or good-feeling. He knows his sitters well, and has drawn them to the life. *Vanity Fair* is a movable wardrobe, without hearts or understandings beneath. But there still remains the question—important to all Art that addresses itself to the laudable business of scourging the foibles and criminalities of mankind—Is there any den of vice so utterly depraved, any round of intercourse so utterly hollow and deceitful, that there is not some redeeming feature lurking somewhere, under rags or tinsel?

This revolting reflex of society is literally true enough. But it does not shew us the whole truth. Are there not women, even in *Vanity Fair,* capable of nobler things than are here set down for them? Are they all schemers or *intrigantes,* world-wise, shuffling, perfidious, empty-headed? With the exception of poor Amelia, whose pale lustre shines out so gently in the midst of these harpies, there is scarcely a woman in *Vanity Fair* from whom we should not shrink in private life as from a contagion. And poor Amelia goes but a short way to purify the foul atmosphere. The author has given her a heart, but no understanding. If he has made her patient and good, loving, trusting, enduring, he has also made her a fool. Her meekness under suffering, her innocent faith in the evils which she lacks sagacity to penetrate, constantly excite our pity; but the helpless weakness of her character forces the sentiment to the verge of that feeling to which pity is said to be akin.

We touch upon this obvious defect in this remarkable work because it lies upon the surface, and must not only challenge general observation, but is not unlikely to draw down in some quarters indiscriminating censure. Over-good people will be apt to shudder at a story so full of petty vices and grovelling passions. They will be afraid to trust it in the hands of young ladies and gentlemen, lest the unredeemed wickedness of its pictures should corrupt their morals, and send them into the world shut up in a crust of selfishness and suspicion. But this sort of apprehension, natural enough in its way, is manifestly founded upon a false and superficial estimate of the tendency of the work. Beneath the sneers and cynicism of *Vanity Fair* there is an important moral, which the large population of novel-readers, who skim hastily over the pages of a book, are almost sure to miss, although they are the very people of all the world to whom practically it ought to be most useful. The vices painted in this book lie about us as 'thick as leaves in Vallambrosa.' We tread amongst them every day of our lives. Mr. Thackeray exposes them for the benefit of mankind. He shews them plainly in all their hideousness. He warns us off the infected spots. It is not enough to say that he never makes them tempting or successful, although he exhibits the attractions by which they sometimes prosper, and even goes so far as to give us a glimpse of the uneasy triumphs they sometimes achieve (more repulsive than the most ignominious failures); but that he produces upon the whole such a view of the egotism, faithlessness, and low depravities of the society he depicts, as to force us to look into the depths of a loathsome truth which the best of us are willing enough to evade, if we can. No doubt we pant for a little clear air in this pestiferous region; we feel oppressed by the weight of these loaded vapours, this stifling malaria. But who objects to Hogarth's 'Gin Lane' that it discloses a scene which offends his taste and shocks his sensibility? The moralist often effects the largest amount of good when he assails the nerves and faltering judgment of people who want the courage to follow out his labours to their final issues.

The defect is not in the moral of *Vanity Fair,* but in the artistical management of the subject. More light and air would have rendered it more agreeable and more healthy. The author's genius takes him off too much in the direction of satire. He has so quick an instinct for the ridiculous, that he finds it out even in the most pathetic passages. He cannot call up a tear without dashing it off with a sarcasm. Yet his power of creating emotion is equal to his wit, although he seems to have less confidence in it, or to have an inferior relish for the use of it. Hence the book, with a great capacity for tenderer and graver things, excels in keen ridicule, and grotesque caricature, and irresistible exaggerations of all sorts of social follies and delinquencies. The universal traits and general truths which he scatters about are accidental, not elementary; his men and women are expressly denizens of Russell Square and Park Lane; he keeps close to his text throughout; his heads are portraits, not passions; he describes less the philosophy of human action than the contrasts and collisions of a conventional world; and he seizes upon the small details which make up the whole business of the kind of life he paints with a minuteness, precision, and certainty, and throws them out with a sharpness of outline and depth of colour rarely if ever equalled. The sustaining power with which these influential trivialities are carried through a narrative of extraordinary length, and the tact with which they are selected and accumulated, display a knowledge of the 'frets and stops' of familiar experience, and an artistical faculty which will present as salient attractions to future readers as to ourselves. Alas! there will always be a Vanity Fair in this world, of which this crafty book will be recognised as the faithful image.

* * *

# WILLIAM MAKEPEACE THACKERAY

## Letter to Robert Bell, September 3, 1848†

Sunday, Septr. 3rd
My dear Bell

Although I have made a rule to myself never to thank critics yet I like to break it continually, and especially in the present instance for what I hope is the excellent article in Fraser.[1] It seems to me very just in most points as regards the author: some he questions as usual—If I had put in more fresh air as you call it my object would have been defeated—It is to indicate, in cheerful terms, that we are for the most part an abominably foolish and selfish people "desperately wicked" and all eager after vanities. Everybody is you see in that book,—for instance if I had made Amelia a higher order of woman there would have been no vanity in Dobbins falling in love with her, whereas the

† Letter to Robert Bell, 3 September 1848, reprinted from *Letters and Private Papers of William Makepeace Thackeray* ed. Gordon N. Ray, 4 vols. (Cambridge University Press, 1945–46), 2: 423–25. Reprinted by permission. Bell (1800–1867) [was] a journalist and miscellaneous writer whose most memorable enterprise was an annotated edition of the English poets in twenty-four volumes (1854–1857). He was long a close friend of Thackeray, near whom he was buried (at his own desire) in Kensal Green Cemetery.

1. Bell writes in his generally admiring review (*Fraser's Magazine*, September, 1848, pp. 320–323) [758]: "Over-good people will be apt to shudder at a story so full of petty vices and grovelling passions. They will be afraid to trust it in the hands of young ladies and gentlemen, lest the unredeemed wickedness of its pictures should corrupt their morals, and send them into the world shut up in a crust of selfishness and suspicion." "The people who fill up the motley scenes of *Vanity Fair*, with two or three exceptions, are as vicious and odious as a clever condensation of the vilest qualities can make them. . . . And poor Amelia goes but a short way to purify the foul atmosphere." But on the whole he justifies Thackeray as a moralist who portrays vices for "the benefit of mankind."

impression at present is that he is a fool for his pains that he has married a silly little thing and in fact has found out his error rather a sweet and tender one however, *quia multum amavit* I want to leave everybody dissatisfied and unhappy at the end of the story—we ought all to be with our own and all other stories. Good God dont I see (in that may-be cracked and warped looking glass in which I am always looking) my own weaknesses wickednesses lusts follies shortcomings? in company let us hope with better qualities about which we will pretermit discourse. We must lift up our voices about these and howl to a congregation of fools: so much at least has been my endeavour. You have all of you taken my misanthropy to task—I wish I could myself: but take the world by a certain standard (you know what I mean) and who dares talk of having any virtue at all? For instance Forster says After a scene with Blifil, the air is cleared by a laugh of Tom Jones[2] —Why Tom Jones in my holding is as big a rogue as Blifil. Before God he is—I mean the man is selfish according to his nature as Blifil according to his. In fact I've a strong impression that we are most of us not fit for—never mind.

Pathos I hold should be very occasional indeed in humourous works and indicated rather than expressed or expressed very rarely. In the passage where Amelia is represented as trying to separate herself from the boy—She goes upstairs and leaves him with his aunt 'as that poor Lady Jane Grey tried the axe that was to separate her slender life'[3] I say that is a fine image whoever wrote it (& I came on it quite by surprize in a review the other day) that is greatly pathetic I think: it leaves you to make your own sad pictures—We shouldn't do much more than that I think in comic books—In a story written in the pathetic key it would be different & then the comedy perhaps should be occasional. Some day—but a truce to egotistical twaddle. It seems to me such a time ago that V F was written that one may talk of it as of some body elses performance. My dear Bell I am very thankful for your friendliness & pleased to have your good opinion.

Faithfully yours
W. M. Thackeray.

2. Though Forster calls *Vanity Fair* "one of the most original works of real genius that has of late been given to the world," he devotes a good part of his article in *The Examiner* to what he terms Thackeray's "grave defect": "If Thackeray falls short of Fielding, much of whose peculiar power and more of whose manner he has inherited or studiously acquired, it is because an equal amount of large cordiality has not raised him entirely above the region of sneering, into that of simple uncontaminated human affection. . . . It cannot be denied that it is in those characters where great natural talents and energy are combined with unredeemed depravity that the author puts forth his full powers, and that in the management and contemplation of them he seems absolutely to revel. . . . We feel that the atmosphere of the work is overloaded with these exhalations of human folly and wickedness. We gasp for a more liberal alternation of refreshing breezes of unsophisticated honesty. Fielding, after he has administered a sufficient dose of Blifil's choke-damp, purifies the air by a hearty laugh from Tom Jones. But the stifling ingredients are administered by Mr. Thackeray to excess, without the necessary relief." (*Examiner,* July 22, 1848, p. 468)

3. Chapter 50 (*Biographical Edition of the Works of William Makepeace Thackeray,* 13 vols. [London: Smith, Elder, 1898–99], I, 484) [pp. 495–96 in this Norton Critical Edition].

# CHARLOTTE BRONTË

## Preface to the Second Edition of *Jane Eyre*†

* * *

There is a man in our own days whose words are not framed to tickle delicate ears: who, to my thinking, comes before the great ones of society, much as the son of Imlah came before the throned Kings of Judah and Israel; and who speaks truth as deep, with a power as prophet-like and as vital—a mien as dauntless and as daring. Is the satirist of *Vanity Fair* admired in high places? I cannot tell; but I think if some of those amongst whom he hurls the Greek fire of his sarcasm, and over whom he flashes the levin-brand of his denunciation, were to take his warnings in time—they or their seed might yet escape a fatal Ramoth-Gilead.

Why have I alluded to this man? I have alluded to him, Reader, because I think I see in him an intellect profounder and more unique than his contemporaries have yet recognised; because I regard him as the first social regenerator of the day—as the very master of that working corps who would restore to rectitude the warped system of things; because I think no commentator on his writings has yet found the comparison that suits him, the terms which rightly characterise his talent. They say he is like Fielding: they talk of his wit, humour, comic powers. He resembles Fielding as an eagle does a vulture: Fielding could stoop on carrion, but Thackeray never does. His wit is bright, his humour attractive, but both bear the same relation to his serious genius, that the mere lambent sheet-lightning playing under the edge of the summer-cloud, does to the electric death-spark hid in its womb. Finally, I have alluded to Mr. Thackeray, because to him—if he will accept the tribute of a total stranger—I have dedicated this second edition of *Jane Eyre.*

Currer Bell.
*Dec. 21st, 1847.*

# [ELIZABETH RIGBY]

## Review†

We must discuss 'Vanity Fair' first, which, much as we were entitled to expect from its author's pen, has fairly taken us by surprise. We were perfectly aware that Mr. Thackeray had of old assumed the jester's habit, in order the more unrestrainedly to indulge the privilege of speaking the truth;—we had traced his clever progress through 'Fraser's Magazine' and the ever-improving pages of 'Punch'—which wonder of the time has been infinitely obliged to him—but still we were little prepared for the keen observation, the deep wisdom, and the consummate art which he has interwoven in the slight texture

† Edited by Jane Jack and Margaret Smith (Oxford: Clarendon Press, 1969).
† *Quarterly Review* 84 (December 1848), 155–62.

and whimsical pattern of Vanity Fair. Everybody, it is to be supposed, has read the volume by this time; and even for those who have not, it is not necessary to describe the order of the story. It is not a novel, in the common acceptation of the word, with a plot purposely contrived to bring about certain scenes, and develop certain characters, but simply a history of those average sufferings, pleasures, penalties, and rewards to which various classes of mankind gravitate as naturally and certainly in this world as the sparks fly upward. It is only the same game of life which every player sooner or later makes for himself—were he to have a hundred chances, and shuffle the cards of circumstance every time. It is only the same busy, involved drama which may be seen at any time by any one, who is not engrossed with the magnified minutiæ of his own petty part, but with composed curiosity looks on to the stage where his fellow men and women are the actors; and that not even heightened by the conventional colouring which Madame de Staël philosophically declares that fiction always wants in order to make up for its not being truth. Indeed, so far from taking any advantage of this novelist's license, Mr. Thackeray has hardly availed himself of the natural average of remarkable events that really do occur in this life. The battle of Waterloo, it is true, is introduced; but, as far as regards the story, it brings about only one death and one bankruptcy, which might either of them have happened in a hundred other ways. Otherwise the tale runs on, with little exception, in that humdrum course of daily monotony, out of which some people coin materials to act, and others excuses to doze, just as their dispositions may be.

It is this reality which is at once the charm and the misery here. With all these unpretending materials it is one of the most amusing, but also one of the most distressing books we have read for many a long year. We almost long for a little exaggeration and improbability to relieve us of that sense of dead truthfulness which weighs down our hearts, not for the Amelias and Georges of the story, but for poor kindred human nature. In one light this truthfulness is even an objection. With few exceptions the personages are too like our everyday selves and neighbours to draw any distinct moral from. We cannot see our way clearly. Palliations of the bad and disappointments in the good are perpetually obstructing our judgment, by bringing what should decide it too close to that common standard of experience in which our only rule of opinion is charity. For it is only in fictitious characters which are highly coloured for one definite object, or in notorious personages viewed from a distance, that the course of the true moral can be seen to run straight—once bring the individual with his life and circumstances closely before you, and it is lost to the mental eye in the thousand pleas and witnesses, unseen and unheard before, which rise up to overshadow it. And what are all these personages in Vanity Fair but feigned names for our own beloved friends and acquaintances, seen under such a puzzling cross-light of good in evil, and evil in good, of sins and sinnings against, of little to be praised virtues, and much to be excused vices, that we cannot presume to moralise upon them—not even to judge them,—content to exclaim sorrowfully with the old prophet, 'Alas! my brother!' Every actor on the crowded stage of Vanity Fair represents some type of that perverse mixture of humanity in which there is ever something not wholly to approve or to condemn. There is the desperate devotion of a fond heart to a false object, which we cannot respect; there is the vain, weak man, half good and half bad, who is more despicable in our eyes than the decided villain. There are the irretrievably wretched education, and the unquenchably manly instincts, both contending in the confirmed *roué*, which melt us to the tenderest pity. There is the selfishness and self-will which the possessor of great wealth and fawning relations can hardly avoid. There is the vanity and fear of the world, which assist mysteriously with pious principles in keeping a man respectable; there are combinations of this kind of every imaginable human form and colour, redeemed but feebly by the steady excellence of an awkward man, and the genuine heart of a vulgar woman, till we feel inclined to tax Mr. Thackeray with an under estimate of our nature, forgetting that Madame de Staël is right after all, and that without a little conventional rouge no human complexion can stand the stage-lights of fiction.

But if these performers give us pain, we are not ashamed to own, as we are speaking openly, that the chief actress herself gives us none at all. For there is of course a principal pilgrim in Vanity Fair, as much as in its emblematical original, Bunyan's 'Progress;' only unfortunately this one is travelling the wrong way. And we say 'unfortunately' merely by way of courtesy, for in reality we care little about the matter. No, Becky—our hearts neither bleed for you, nor cry out against you. You are wonderfully clever, and amusing, and accomplished, and intelligent, and the Soho *ateliers* were not the best nurseries for a moral training; and you were married early in life to a regular blackleg, and you have had to live upon your wits ever since, which is not an improving sort of maintenance; and there is much to be said for and against; but still you are not one of us, and there is an end to our sympathies and censures. People who allow their feelings to be lacerated by such a character and career as yours, are doing both you and themselves great injustice. No author could have openly introduced a near connexion of Satan's into the best London society, nor would the moral end intended have been answered by it; but really and honestly, considering Becky in her human character, we know of none which so thoroughly satisfies our highest *beau idéal* of feminine wickedness, with so slight a shock to our feelings and proprieties. It is very dreadful, doubtless, that Becky neither loved the husband who loved her, nor the child of her own flesh and blood, nor indeed any body but herself; but, as far as she is concerned, we cannot pretend to be scandalized—for how could she without a heart? It is very shocking of course that she committed all sorts of dirty tricks, and jockeyed her neighbours, and never cared what she trampled under foot if it happened to obstruct her step; but how could she be expected to do otherwise without a conscience? The poor little woman was most tryingly placed; she came into the world without the customary letters of credit upon those two great bankers of humanity, 'Heart and Conscience,' and it was no fault of hers if they dishonoured all her bills. All she could do in this dilemma was to establish the firmest connexion with the inferior commercial branches of 'Sense and Tact,' who secretly do much business in the name of the head concern, and with whom her 'fine frontal development' gave her unlimited credit. She saw that selfishness was the metal which the stamp of heart was suborned to pass; that hypocrisy was the homage that vice rendered to virtue; that honesty was, at all events, acted, because it was the best policy; and so she practised the arts of selfishness and hypocrisy like anybody else in Vanity Fair, only with this difference, that she brought them to their highest possible pitch of perfection. For why is it that, looking round in this world, we find plenty of characters to compare with her up to a certain pitch, but none which reach her actual standard? Why is it that, speaking of this friend or that, we say in the tender mercies of our hearts, 'No, she is not *quite* so bad as Becky?' We fear not only because she has more heart and conscience, but also because she has less cleverness.

No; let us give Becky her due. There is enough in this world of ours, as we all know, to provoke a saint, far more a poor little devil like her. She had none of those fellow-feelings which make us wondrous kind. She saw people around her cowards in vice, and simpletons in virtue, and she had no patience with either, for she was as little the one as the other herself. She saw women who loved their husbands and yet teazed them, and ruining their children although they doated upon them, and she sneered at their utter inconsistency. Wickedness or goodness, unless coupled with strength, were alike worthless to her. That weakness which is the blessed pledge of our humanity, was to her only the despicable badge of our imperfection. She thought, it might be, of her master's words, 'Fallen cherub! to be weak is to be miserable!' and wondered how we could be such fools as first to sin and then to be sorry. Becky's light was defective, but she acted up to it. Her goodness goes as far as good temper, and her principles as far as shrewd sense, and we may thank her consistency for showing us what they are both worth.

It is another thing to pretend to settle whether such a character be *primâ facie* impossible, though devotion to the better sex might well demand the assertion. There are mysteries of iniquity, under the semblance of man and woman, read of in history, or met with in the unchronicled sufferings of private life, which would almost make us believe that the powers of Darkness occasionally made use of this earth for a Foundling Hospital, and sent their imps to us, already provided with a return-ticket. We shall not decide on the lawfulness or otherwise of any attempt to depict such importations; we can only rest perfectly satisfied that, granting the author's premises, it is impossible to imagine them carried out with more felicitous skill and more exquisite consistency than in the heroine of 'Vanity Fair.' At all events, the infernal regions have no reason to be ashamed of little Becky, nor the ladies either: she has, at least, all the cleverness of the sex.

The great charm, therefore, and comfort of Becky is, that we may study her without any compunctions. The misery of this life is not the evil that we see, but the good and the evil which are so inextricably twisted together. It is that perpetual memento ever meeting one—

'How in this vile world below
Noblest things find vilest using,'

that is so very distressing to those who have hearts as well as eyes. But Becky relieves them of all this pain—at least in her own person. Pity would be thrown away upon one who has not heart enough for it to ache even for herself. Becky is perfectly happy, as all must be who excel in what they love best. Her life is one exertion of successful power. Shame never visits her, for ''Tis conscience that makes cowards of us all'—and she has none. She realizes that *ne plus ultra* of sublunary comfort which it was reserved for a Frenchman to define —the blessed combination of '*le bon estomac et le mauvais coeur.*' for Becky adds to her other good qualities that of an excellent digestion.

Upon the whole, we are not afraid to own that we rather enjoy her *ignis fatuus* course, dragging the weak and the vain and the selfish, through mud and mire, after her, and acting all parts, from the modest rushlight to the gracious star, just as it suits her. Clever little imp that she is! What exquisite tact she shows!—what unflagging good humour!—what ready self-possession! Becky never disappoints us; she never even makes us tremble. We know that her answer will come exactly suiting her one particular object, and frequently three or four more in prospect. What respect, too, she has for those decencies which more virtuous, but more stupid humanity, often disdains! What detection of all that is false and mean! What instinct for all that is true and great! She is her master's true pupil in that: she knows what is really divine as well as he, and bows before it. She honours Dobbin in spite of his big feet; she respects her husband more than ever she did before, perhaps for the first time, at the very moment when he is stripping not only her jewels, but name, honour, and comfort off her.

We are not so sure either whether we are justified in calling hers '*le mauvais coeur.*' Becky does not pursue any one vindictively; she never does gratuitous mischief. The fountain is more dry than poisoned. She is even generous—when she can afford it. Witness that burst of plain speaking in Dobbin's favour to the little dolt Amelia, for which we forgive her many a sin. 'Tis true she wanted to get rid of her; but let that pass. Becky was a thrifty dame, and liked to despatch two birds with one stone. And she was honest, too, after a fashion. The part of wife she acts at first as well, and better than most; but as for that of mother, there she fails from the beginning. She knew that maternal love was no business of hers—that a fine frontal development could give her no help there—and puts so little spirit into her imitation that no one could be taken in for a moment. She felt that that bill, of all others, would be sure to be dishonoured, and it went against her conscience—we mean her sense—to send it in.

In short, the only respect in which Becky's course gives us pain is when it locks itself into that of another, and more genuine child of this earth. No one can regret those being entangled in her nets whose vanity and meanness of spirit alone led them into its meshes—such are rightly served: but we do grudge her that real sacred thing called *love,* even of a Rawdon Crawley, who has more of that self-forgetting, all-purifying feeling for his little evil spirit than many a better man has for a good woman. We do grudge Becky *a heart*, though it belong only to a swindler. Poor, sinned against, vile, degraded, but still true-hearted Rawdon!—you stand next in our affections and sympathies to honest Dobbin himself. It was the instinct of a good nature which made the Major feel that the stamp of the Evil One was upon Becky; and it was the stupidity of a good nature which made the Colonel never suspect it. He was a cheat, a black-leg, an unprincipled dog; but still 'Rawdon *is* a man, and be hanged to him,' as the Rector says. We follow him through the illustrations, which are, in many instances, a delightful enhancement to the text—as he stands there, with his gentle eyelid, coarse moustache, and foolish chin, bringing up Becky's coffee-cup with a kind of dumb fidelity; or looking down at little Rawdon with a more than paternal tenderness. All Amelia's philoprogenitive idolatries do not touch us like one fond instinct of 'stupid Rawdon.'

Dobbin sheds a halo over all the long-necked, loose-jointed, Scotch-looking gentlemen of our acquaintance. Flat feet and flap ears seem henceforth incompatible with evil. He reminds us of one of the sweetest creations that have appeared from any modern pen—that plain, awkward, loveable 'Long Walter,' in Lady Georgina Fullerton's beautiful novel of 'Grantley Manor.' Like him, too, in his proper self-respect; for Dobbin—lumbering, heavy, shy, and absurdly over-modest as the ugly fellow is—is yet true to himself. At one time he seems to be sinking into the mere abject dangler after Amelia; but he breaks his chains like a man, and resumes them again like a man, too, although half disenchanted of his amiable delusion.

But to return for a moment to Becky. The only criticism we would offer is one which the author has almost disarmed by making her mother a Frenchwoman. The construction of this little clever monster is diabolically French. Such a *lusus naturæ* as a woman without a heart and conscience would, in England, be a mere brutal savage, and poison half a village. France is the land for the real Syren, with the woman's face and the dragon's claws. The genus of Pigeon and Laffarge claims her for its own—only that our heroine takes a far higher class by not requiring the vulgar matter of fact of crime to develop her full powers. It is an affront to Becky's tactics to believe that she could ever be reduced to so low a resource, or, that if she were, anybody would find it out. We, therefore, cannot sufficiently applaud the extreme discretion with which Mr. Thackeray has hinted at the possibly assistant circumstances of Joseph Sedley's dissolution. A less delicacy of handling would have marred the harmony of the whole design. Such a casualty as that suggested to our imagination was not intended for the light net of Vanity Fair to draw on shore; it would have torn it to pieces. Besides it is not wanted. Poor little Becky is bad enough to satisfy the most ardent student of 'good books.' Wickedness, beyond a certain pitch, gives no increase of gratification even to the sternest moralist; and one of Mr. Thackeray's excellences is the sparing quantity he consumes. The whole *use*, too, of the work—that of generously measuring one another by this standard—is lost, the moment you convict Becky of a capital crime. Who can, with any face, liken a dear friend to a murderess? Whereas now there are no little symptoms of fascinating ruthlessness, graceful ingratitude, or ladylike selfishness, observable among our charming acquaintance, that we may not immediately detect to an inch, and more effectually intimidate by the simple application of the Becky gauge than by the most vehement use of all ten commandments. Thanks to Mr. Thackeray, the world is now provided with an *idea*, which, if we mistake not, will be the skeleton in the corner of every ball-room and boudoir for a long time to come. Let us leave it intact in its unique point and freshness—a Becky, and nothing more. We should, therefore, advise our readers to cut out that picture of our heroine's 'Second Appearance as Clytemnestra,' which casts so uncomfortable a glare over the latter part of the volume, and, disregarding all hints and inuendoes, simply to let the changes and chances of this mortal life have due weight in their minds. Jos had been much in India. His was a bad life; he ate and drank most imprudently, and his digestion was not to be compared with Becky's. No respectable office would have ensured 'Waterloo Sedley.'

'Vanity Fair' is pre-eminently a novel of the day—not in the vulgar sense, of which there are too many, but as a literal photograph of the manners and habits of the nineteenth century, thrown on to paper by the light of a powerful mind; and one also of the most artistic effect. Mr. Thackeray has a peculiar adroitness in leading on the fancy, or rather memory of his reader from one set of circumstances to another by the seeming chances and coincidences of common life, as an artist leads the spectator's eye through the subject of his picture by a skilful repetition of colour. This is why it is impossible to quote from his book with any justice to it. The whole growth of the narrative is so matted and interwoven together with tendril-like links and bindings, that there is no detaching a flower with sufficient length of stalk to exhibit it to advantage. There is that mutual dependence in his characters which is the first requisite in painting every-day life: no one is stuck on a separate pedestal—no one is sitting for his portrait. There may be one exception—we mean Sir Pitt Crawley, senior: it is possible, nay, we hardly doubt, that this baronet was closer drawn from individual life than anybody else in the book; but granting that fact, the animal was so unique an exception, that we wonder so shrewd an artist could stick him into a gallery so full of our familiars. The scenes in Germany, we can believe, will seem to many readers of an English book hardly less extravagantly absurd—grossly and gratuitously overdrawn; but the initiated will value them as containing some of the keenest strokes of truth and humour that 'Vanity Fair' exhibits, and not enjoy them the less for being at our neighbour's expense. For the thorough appreciation of the chief character they are quite indispensable too. The whole course of the work may be viewed as the *Wander-Jahre* of a far cleverer female *Wilhelm Meister.* We have watched her in the ups-and-downs of life—among the humble, the fashionable, the great, and the pious—and found her ever new, yet ever the same; but still Becky among the students was requisite to complete the full measure of our admiration.

* * *

# Contexts

## A PRETTY FELLOW

### Wanted a Governess, on Handsome Terms†

We lately met with the subjoined advertisement in a morning newspaper:—

Governess.—A comfortable home, *but without salary*, is offered to any lady wishing for a situation as GOVERNESS in *a gentleman's family*, residing in the country, to instruct two little girls *in music, drawing and English; a thorough knowledge of the French language is required.* Direct to A. B.—*Times, 27 June.*

An advertisement long enough fully to suit A. B.'s purpose would, we know, have cost that economical "gentleman" too much. We perceive, clearly, that A. B. is one of those nice persons who love to divest the flint of its integuments; and out of very pity for the poor creature, we will ask, free of expense, the following questions of any lady desirous of his "comfortable home."

How few slices of bread, with how little butter upon each, will she be content with for breakfast? Can she drink her tea without sugar; or if not, what would be her smallest number of knobs? Will she engage not to want ham should there be any on the table at that meal? Will she, though ever so hungry, always abstain from lunch? Will she promise never to take fish or soup at dinner, to ask only once for meat, decline taking wine when invited to do so before company, and altogether eschew malt liquor? Can she agree to dispense with supper before going to bed, notwithstanding she may feel faint for the want of it? Can she sleep in a garret upon a straw mattress, without curtains; and how few blankets will she need to cover her? Will she find herself in all requisites for her toilet, including soap, unless she is prepared to put up with common yellow?

And now, having asked these questions for A. B., we will ask a few more of him. Pray, does he give his cook and housemaid any wages? If so, does he consider their menial services more valuable than the instruction of his children? What, according to his ideas, is the equivalent, by weight, in victuals, to "music, drawing, and English," with "a thorough knowledge of the French language?" Does he regard a governess as a horse, that he would work her like one, and on terms corresponding to keep and stabling? And lastly, on what principle or pretence does he presume to call his family "a *gentleman's*?" Answer that, A. B.! Answer that!

† *Punch,* July 12, 1845, p. 25.

# MARIA EDGEWORTH

## Female Accomplishments, Etc.†

Parents who do not think that they have leisure, or feel that they have capacity, to take the entire direction of their children's education upon themselves, will trust this important office to a governess. The inquiry concerning the value of female accomplishments, has been purposely entered into before we could speak of the choice of a governess, because the estimation in which these are held will very much determine parents in their choice.

If what has been said of the probability of a decline in the public taste for what are usually called accomplishments; of their little utility to the happiness of families and individuals; of the waste of time, and waste of the higher powers of the mind in acquiring them; if what has been observed on any of these points is allowed to be just, we shall have little difficulty in pursuing the same principles farther. In the choice of a governess we should not then consider her fashionable accomplishments as her best recommendations; these will be only secondary objects. We shall examine, with more anxiety, whether she possess a sound, discriminating, and enlarged understanding: whether her mind be free from prejudice; whether she has steadiness of temper to pursue her own plans; and, above all, whether she has that species of integrity which will justify a parent in trusting a child to her care. We shall attend to her conversation and observe her manners, with scrupulous minuteness. Children are *imitative animals,* and they are peculiarly disposed to imitate the language, manners, and gestures, of those with whom they live, and to whom they look up with admiration. In female education, too much care cannot be taken to form all those habits in morals and in manners which are distinguishing characteristics of amiable women. These habits must be acquired early, or they will never appear easy or graceful; they will necessarily be formed by those who see none but good models.

We have already pointed out the absolute necessity of union among all those who are concerned in a child's education. A governess must either rule or obey, decidedly. If she do not agree with the child's parents in opinion, she must either know how to convince them by argument, or she must with strict integrity conform her practice to their theories. There are few parents who will choose to give up the entire care of their children to any governess; therefore, there will probably be some points in which a difference of opinion will arise. A sensible woman will never submit to be treated, as governesses are in some families, like the servant who was asked by his master what business he had to think: nor will a woman of sense or temper insist upon her opinions without producing her reasons. She will thus ensure the respect and the confidence of enlightened parents.

It is surely the interest of parents to treat the person who educates their children with that perfect equality and kindness which will conciliate her affection, and which will at the same time preserve her

† From *Practical Education* (New York: Harper and Brothers, 1835), 395–400.

influence and authority over her pupils. And it is with pleasure we observe, that the style of behaviour to governesses, in wellbred families, is much changed within these few years. A governess is no longer treated as an upper servant, or as an intermediate being between a servant and a gentlewoman: she is now treated as the friend and companion of the family; and she must, consequently, have warm and permanent interest in its prosperity: she becomes attached to her pupils from gratitude to their parents, from sympathy, from generosity, as well as from the strict sense of duty.

* * *

# KATHLEEN TILLOTSON

## [Propriety and the Novel]†

'They are a little broad, but she may read anything now she's married, you know.'

Mr. Brooke, in George Eliot's *Middlemarch*, ch. xxx.

The novelist of the eighteen-forties was, then, allowed more licence for sentimental pathos than accords with modern taste; we generally assume him, however, to have been much more restricted in other respects. The death-bed might be public, but not the marriage-bed. But before I consider how far the novelists were seriously hampered by considerations of 'propriety' in this sense, a warning is necessary against the popular foreshortening of the Victorian age, against confusing the eighteen-forties with the sixties, seventies, or eighties, or on the other hand with the strictness of Evangelicals in the early years of the century. It is too commonly supposed that Bowdler was a Victorian. He was, in fact, a contemporary of Shelley. He is also too commonly seen as a mere censor, whereas he was rather a popularizer. Many Victorian children met their Shakespeare first in Bowdler's edition,[1] and were not ungrateful. A tribute from an unexpected quarter is Swinburne's:

> More nauseous and more foolish cant was never chattered than that which would deride the memory or depreciate the merits of Bowdler. No man ever did better service to Shakespeare than the man who made it possible to put him into the hands of intelligent and imaginative children. . . .[2]

Bowdler's expurgations were indeed moderate in comparison with those of some of his predecessors. In 1806 the Rev. James Plumptre had altered the second line of 'Under the Greenwood Tree' to

> Who loves to work with me.[3]

† Reprinted from *Novels of the Eighteen-Forties* (Oxford: Clarendon Press, 1954), 54–58, 68–73, by permission of Oxford University Press. 

1. The complete edition was first published in 1818, the sixth edition in 1831.
2. 'Social Verse', 1891 (*Studies in Prose and Poetry*, 1894, pp. 98–99); quoted in G. Lafourcade, *La Jeunesse de Swinburne* (Paris, 1928), i. 68.
3. In *A Collection of Songs . . . selected and revised* (3 vols., 1806–8), i. 170. M. J. Quinlan, *Victorian Prelude* (New York, 1941), pp. 229–37, gives an account of Plumptre's expurgations [work *for* lie].

Such absurdities reappear in the eighteen-sixties, and novelists who were writing then as well as in the eighteen-forties serve to mark the change. It is in *Our Mutual Friend* that Dickens introduces Mr. Podsnap, with his abhorrence of anything that might bring a blush to the cheek of the young person. Podsnappery in all its fulness is a phenomenon of the sixties, and is probably related to the rise of the shilling magazines which extended the family reading of fiction still further. A surviving Victorian has said that,

> the (largely imaginary) prudery and reticence of the Victorians is chiefly due to this habit of family reading. It would take a tough father to read some modern novels aloud to his children.[4]

One of those new shilling magazines, the *Cornhill*, rejected a story by Trollope,[5] and the editor responsible was, of all people, Thackeray. Trollope protested in vain against this 'squeamishness', reminding Thackeray of precedents, some very recent—Effie Deans, Beatrix Esmond, Jane Eyre, and Hetty Sorrel—and added:

> I could think of no pure English novelist, pure up to the Cornhill standard, except Dickens; but then I remembered Oliver Twist and blushed for what my mother and sister read in that very fie-fie story.[6]

But Thackeray remained firm—this was a new magazine and his business was to get and keep subscribers. The interesting point for us is that Trollope, a sensitive chronicler of manners, is noting a change. A change perhaps also in the attitude to Dickens, for it was also in the sixties that a headmistress escorted her girls out of the hall where Dickens was giving a reading from *Martin Chuzzlewit*; they left at the point where Mr. Pecksniff calls on Mrs. Gamp, and is mistaken by the neighbours for an expectant father. Presumably for the sake of the same young persons, Keene's illustrations to *Mrs. Caudle's Curtain Lectures* avoided the bedroom setting.[7] A reviewer of *Tom Brown at Oxford* remonstrated with the author for making his hero carry a girl who had broken her ankle: 'If this be muscular Christianity, the less we have of it the better.'[8] Ten years later Thackeray's successor, Leslie Stephen, begged Hardy to treat seduction 'in a gingerly fashion' in *Far from the Madding Crowd* and also cautioned him on *The Hand of Ethelberta*: 'Remember the country parson's daughters. *I* have always to remember them!'[9] Suppose we remember, in contrast, three country parson's daughters of a generation earlier; the Brontë sisters read, and wrote, as they pleased. Of the later age there are abundant examples from life—some within living memory—of prohibitions to daughters, who might not read the third volume of *The Mill on the*

4. E. E. Kellett, in *Early Victorian England* (1934), ii. 48 n.
5. 'Mrs. General Talboys', published in *Tales of all Countries*, second series (1863).
6. *Letters and Private Papers of William Makepeace Thackeray*, ed. Gordon N. Ray, 4 vols. (Cambridge: Harvard University Press, 1945–46), iv. 207.
7. This new edition, a 'Christmas Book' of 1865, is noticed with amusement in the *Saturday Review* (2 December 1865), p. 712.
8. *Athenæum* (30 November 1861), p. 72. Compare Hardy's enforced introduction of a wheelbarrow in the scene where Angel Clare carries the milkmaids in the serial version of *Tess*.
9. Hardy's recollections, in F. W. Maitland, *Life and Letters of Leslie Stephen* (1906), pp. 274–6.

*Floss*, or any of *Jane Eyre*,[1] until marriage or middle-age, whichever came first. The apparent assumption was, in the words of Mrs. Lynn Linton (writing as an old lady in 1898), that 'knowledge of vice should come gradually in advancing age'[2]—the immediate instance of 'vice' in the manuscript novel criticized was the hero's squeezing the heroine's 'ungloved hand' in a hansom cab. Against this tyranny of the Young Person arise the famous protests of the eighties and nineties in the critical articles of Hardy, Henry James, and George Moore. It was in that period, too, that Samuel Butler gleefully recorded Festing Jones's *bon mot*, that Canon Ainger 'is the kind of man who is capable of bringing out an expurgated edition of Wordsworth'.[3]

But it is an error to refer this attitude back into the eighteen-forties. There were then—as far as my knowledge goes—no similar instances of squeamish editors, and fewer protests from readers and critics. One, indeed, speaks strongly but vaguely:

> Almost any serial will give hints enough to an acute boy, [and] . . . guide him to the door with the red lamp.[4]

Perhaps the earliest general outcry[5] against a novel on grounds of propriety came in 1853 against Mrs. Gaskell's *Ruth*, in which a Dissenting parson helps a seduced girl to pass herself off as a widow.[6] The 'burnings' of Froude's *Shadows of the Clouds* in 1847 by his father the Archdeacon and of *The Nemesis of Faith* in 1849 by the Sub-Rector of Exeter College seem to have been rather from disapproval of religious heterodoxy than of sexual impropriety. Contemporary reviewers of *Jane Eyre* did not suggest its unsuitability for young girls. Almost the only attack on its morality came in the well-known review in the *Quarterly*, which appeared over a year after the novel was published, and was probably designed to counteract the general applause.[7]

* * *

The kind of freedom sought by Thackeray and his method of attaining it is different. Bagehot's definition of the difference can be accepted in the main; it has to be remembered that he wrote in 1858, when the awareness of limitations was already growing stronger:

> No one can read Mr. Thackeray's writings without feeling that he is perpetually treading as close as he dare to the borderline that separates the world which may be described in books from

1. From many instances I choose one; Elizabeth Malleson (a lady of progressive views and a friend of George Eliot) read *Jane Eyre* aloud to her children some time in the eighties, 'entirely omitting Rochester's mad wife, and so skillfully that we noticed nothing amiss with the plot!' (*Elizabeth Malleson, 1828–1916*, privately printed, 1926, p. 90).
2. G. S. Layard, *Mrs. Lynn Linton* (1901), p. 228.
3. *Further Extracts from the Note-Books* (1934), p. 304.
4. 'Advice to an Intending Serialist' (mainly aimed at Dickens, but presumably not in this respect), in *Blackwood's* (November 1846), p. 595.
5. Wilkie Collins's second novel *Basil* (1852), the story of a youth trapped into a private, unconsummated marriage, was, he reports, 'condemned off-hand by a certain class of readers, as an outrage on their sense of propriety' (Dedication of revised edition, 1862).
6. There were more favourable than unfavourable reviews, but one library withdrew the book from circulation and at least two fathers of families burnt the last volume. See Mrs. Gaskell's letters as quoted in E. Haldane, *Elizabeth Gaskell and her Friends* (1931), and the survey in A. B. Hopkins, *Elizabeth Gaskell: Her Life and Work* (1952), ch. vii.
7. Review by Elizabeth Rigby, excerpts of which are included above as they relate to *Vanity Fair*.

> the world which it is prohibited so to describe. No one knows better than this accomplished artist where that line is, and how curious are its windings and turns. The charge against him is that he knows it but too well; that with an anxious care and a wistful eye he is ever approximating to its edge, and hinting with subtle art how thoroughly he is familiar with, and how interesting he could make the interdicted region on the other side. He never violates a single conventional rule; but at the same time the shadow of the immorality that is not seen is scarcely ever wanting to his delineation of the society that is seen. Everyone may perceive what is passing in his fancy. Mr. Dickens is chargeable with no such defect; he does not seem to feel the temptation. By what we may fairly call an instinctive purity of genius, he not only observes the conventional rules, but makes excursions into topics which no other novelist could safely handle, and, by a felicitous instinct, deprives them of all impropriety. No other writer could have managed the humour of Mrs. Gamp without becoming unendurable.[8]

But does Thackeray feel even the constraint implied by the phrase 'wistful eye'? Does he not rather make play at his readers' expense with his awareness of the winding line, and, ingenious in circumvention, nevertheless say all he needs to? That was at least the view of more than one contemporary: 'his hint', says Charlotte Brontë,

> is more vivid than other men's elaborate explanations, and never is his satire whetted to so keen an edge as when with quiet mocking irony he modestly recommends to the approbation of the public his own exemplary discretion and forbearance.[9]

The passage she had in mind is given particular emphasis by its position at the beginning of the concluding double number of *Vanity Fair*: the eye here is surely not 'wistful':

> . . . it has been the wish of the present writer, all through this story, deferentially to submit to the fashion at present prevailing, and only to hint at the existence of wickedness in a light, easy, and agreeable manner, so that nobody's fine feelings may be offended. I defy anyone to say that our Becky, who has certainly some vices, has not been presented to the public in a perfectly genteel and inoffensive manner. In describing this syren, singing and smiling, coaxing and cajoling, has he once forgotten the laws of politeness, and showed the monster's hideous tail above water? No! Those who like may peep down under waves that are pretty transparent, and see it writhing and curling, diabolically hideous and slimy, flapping amongst bones, or curling round corpses; but above the waterline, I ask, has not everything been proper, agreeable, and decorous, and has any the most squeamish immoralist in Vanity Fair a right to cry fie? When, however, the syren disappears and dives below, down among the dead men, the water of course grows turbid over her, and it is labour lost to look into it ever so curiously. They look pretty enough when they sit upon a rock, twanging their harps and combing their hair, and sing,

8. Walter Bagehot, *Literary Studies*, 2 vols. (London: Dutton, 1911), ii. 187–8.
9. Letter to W. H. Williams, 14 August 1848; *The Brontës: Their Lives, Friendships, and Correspondence*, 4 vols. (Oxford: Shakespeare Head, 1932), ii. 244.

> and beckon to you to come and hold the looking-glass; but when they sink into their native element, depend upon it those mermaids are about no good, and we had best not examine the fiendish marine cannibals, revelling and feasting on their wretched pickled victims. And so, when Becky is out of the way, be sure that she is not particularly well employed, and that the less that is said about her doings is in fact the better.[1]

By means of this artful imagery, Thackeray makes Becky's goings-on sufficiently clear. The reader who wants further hints may gather them from a considerable number of details scattered over the book, and the uncertainty as to particulars has its own verisimilitude. Thackeray has lost nothing by his half-observance of propriety. A more direct treatment would have put the emphasis wrong. Becky's master-passion is for money and power; what precisely she paid for them is not important—and we know enough of her to be sure that the price would be as low as possible. Thackeray, proceeding by means of suggestions, found it easier to do so because of the period and place in which his action lay (the last years of George IV, the post-war London of the eighteen-twenties), a time associated with licence and one that many of his readers remembered for themselves. No one who reads *Vanity Fair* carefully would dream of calling it a squeamish novel. Thackeray does more than avoid squeamishness on his own part; he exploits it as it exists on the part of many of his readers. It is turned against themselves, and very openly. The passage quoted above continues:

> If we were to give a full account of her proceedings during a couple of years that followed after the Curzon Street catastrophe, there might be some reason for people to say this book was improper. The actions of very vain, artless, pleasure-seeking people are very often improper (as are many of yours, my friend with the grave face and spotless reputation;—but that is merely by the way); and what are those of a woman without faith—or love—or character?

But sometimes skill in circumvention was not enough; Thackeray had to challenge his readers' limited preconceptions about the novel:

> Since the writer of *Tom Jones* was buried, no writer of fiction among us has been permitted to depict to his utmost power a MAN.

Some of the subscribers to *Pendennis*, he says in the Preface, left him because he described a young man 'affected by temptation'; but he had not made concessions to them.

> A little more frankness than is customary has been attempted in this story. . . . If truth is not always pleasant, at any rate truth is best.

This passage, which refers of course to the Fanny Bolton episode, has sometimes been misunderstood, as if Thackeray were in fact making concessions by showing Pendennis as in the end resisting temptation.

1. Ch. lxiv.

This, however, is in character; Arthur Pendennis is not Tom Jones, but a sentimental well-intentioned young man of the eighteen-thirties. The pressure of the time is seen, if at all, in Thackeray's initial choice of such a hero. And the doubt as to how far he will go, combined with the anxious suspicions of his mother, adds to both narrative suspense and moral interest.

The point at which possessive affection shades into jealousy held a fascination for Thackeray, and here perhaps is found a more insidious undermining of convention. First in Amelia, and then in Helen Pendennis, the sacred emotion of mother-love is tentatively explored, and its seamier side ambiguously indicated; and in his next novel, *Esmond*, Thackeray went far enough to disturb many of his readers. Such words as 'uneasiness' and 'sinister' recur in criticisms of the novel;[2] Charlotte Brontë, Thackeray's ardent admirer, was 'grieved and exasperated' by Lady Castlewood's jealousy;[3] and George Eliot probably voiced a common response when she wrote:

> 'Esmond' is the most uncomfortable book you can imagine. You remember how you disliked 'François le Champi'. Well, the story of 'Esmond' is just the same. The hero is in love with the daughter all through the book, and marries the mother at the end.[4]

It is 'uncomfortable' because the reader (and this includes the modern reader) is led on in innocence, supposing Lady Castlewood's feelings to be purely maternal when in fact they are otherwise. One could not feel safe with such an author; he held the keys of what Carlyle called 'the Bluebeard Chambers of the heart'.

* * *

# JOAN STEVENS

## *Vanity Fair* and the London Skyline†

The London reader who picked up from his bookstall in January 1847 the first Number of the new monthly-part novel, *Vanity Fair*, would at once recognise the scene in the design on its yellow paper cover. The picture is a half-page woodcut, set above the title and sub-title, *Vanity Fair: Pen and Pencil Sketches of English Society*. The name of the author, W. M. Thackeray, given in big type beneath, would not perhaps be familiar, but would soon be identified from the rubric which follows,

> Author of "The Irish Sketch Book:" "Journey from Cornhill to Grand Cairo:" of "Jeames's Diary" and the "Snob Papers" in "Punch:" &c. &c.

He was, to readers of 1847, that indefatigable artist and journalist-of-all-work, Michael Angelo Titmarsh, also variously known as Gahagan,

2. See for example *Fraser's* (December 1852), pp. 622–33.
3. Letter to George Smith, 14 February 1852; *S.H.B.* iii. 314–15.
4. Letter to the Brays, 22 October 1852; J. W. Cross, *George Eliot's Life as Related in Her Letters and Journals*, 3 vols. (Edinburgh and London: W. Blackwoods, 1885), ch. v.

† *Costerus*, ns II (1974), 13–41. Reprinted by permission of Editions Rodopi BV.

Yellowplush, Ikey Solomons, Fitzboodle, W.M.T., Our Fat Contributor, and, of course, Jeames De la Pluche and Mr Snob. The *Punch* connection is further stressed by the information given below, "Published at the Punch Office, 85, Fleet Street." Everybody knew *Punch.*

Everybody, almost, would know also the setting of the scene in the woodcut. Associated as it is with the title, *Vanity Fair,* it points to and identifies the world of the novel, locating it for contemporary readers positively as "here" and "now," in London, and in the 1840's.

Unhappily, when the novel was issued in book form at the end of its 19-month run in July 1848, this cover design was not reproduced. The other illustrations (totalling one hundred and ninety) were included, the book being made up from existing sheets and reprints, but a new vignette replaced the cover design on the title page which was supplied with the final double issue of Numbers XIX–XX. The design and sub-title on the yellow part-issue covers were lost to view. Only of recent years have some paperback editions brought them once more to the attention of readers. Even those who today can look at the design, however, may well fail fully to appreciate its relevance to Thackeray's purpose.

Examine it carefully. We see a group of figures in clown costumes, one of them elevated on a tub with his left hand raised in an oratorical flourish of some kind. Behind the figures is a screen of trees, and behind that on the skyline stand two monuments. The one on our right, towards which perhaps the clown-orator is gesticulating, is an equestrian figure riding in bold caricature across an enormous triumphal arch. The one on our left is a single figure standing on his head on the top of a tall column.

Look first at the personages in the foreground. On our left, there is a scraggy old man in what may be a mortar board, spectacles perched on a big nose, with a stick in his hand. Behind him two outline figures in fools-caps are engaged in eager gossip. Nearest to us, from left to right, there are: a child with a wide paper hat and a wooden sword; a mother seated nursing a child, both in "long-eared" caps; and a painted circus clown who sits with his chin in his hands gazing vacantly at the speaker. Behind him to our right are a profile clown figure in a shovel hat, a smock-frocked figure in a fools-cap, and a silly flirting couple. From behind the tub, two more silly faces gape at us from under their eared caps. The speaker himself wears clown's costume, with the ruff, the smock, the full sleeves, the pantaloons, and the fools-cap. A jug stands beside him on the tub, containing liquid no doubt to keep his voice in trim. This is the "moralist, who is holding forth on the cover," in the dry authorial comment of Chapter viii (Number III, March 1847).

> But my kind reader will please to remember, that these histories in their gaudy yellow covers have 'Vanity Fair' for a title, and that Vanity Fair is a very vain, wicked, foolish place, full of all sorts of humbugs and falseness and pretensions. And while the moralist, who is holding forth on the cover (an accurate portrait of your humble servant), professes to wear neither gown nor bands, but only the very same long-eared livery in which his congregation is arrayed: yet, look you, one is bound to speak the truth as far as

one knows it, whether one mounts a cap and bells or a shovel-hat.[1]

The relevance of this little circle of figures to the concerns of *Vanity Fair* has never been in doubt, but the deliberate emphasis which Thackeray gives to the conception by reiterated illustration throughout the novel may well be unknown to readers of today's editions. Clowns reappear in the woodcuts for the chapter initials, maintaining inside the monthly issue the visual metaphor offered outside it on the "gaudy yellow covers." The child with the wooden sword reappears first, in the initial cut for Chapter v (Number II), in mimic warfare with another small boy on a wooden horse: he is, I believe, Dobbin. Thackeray with his clown's mask removed and held in his hand sits crosslegged facing us in the well-known sketch originally set as the tailpiece to Chapter ix (Number III). A clown with a coronet surmounting his fools-cap stands on his tub in a circle of sycophants in the initial design for Chapter x (Number III). A figure in motley bows to Napoleon in the initial for Chapter xviii (Number V). Another balances the initial on his nose in the design for Chapter xxxvii (Number XI). A clown in a wide hat is perched on stilts in the initial for Chapter xxvii (Number VIII). In the unusually large initial cut for Chapter xl (Number XII), a trio of clowns advances towards the reader with the "proper stealthy and tragical demeanour" of mourners' mutes, holding furled black banners in their hands, their caps and bodies wreathed in crape, in funerary tribute to that honorable deceased baronet, Sir Pitt Crawley. Queen's Crawley, with its "tall chimneys and gables of the style of Queen Bess" can be seen behind them.[2] Other clown designs appear in the initials for Chapters xlii (Number XII), xlvi (Number XIII), and xlix (Number XIV), while in the final issue, Numbers XIX–XX, the clown-moralist himself appears in the vignette for the volume title page. Thus, with a total of eleven designs added to the nineteen repetitions on the covers, the monthly reader of 1847–48 was in no danger of forgetting the basic attitudes of the narrator.

But *whereabouts* is the scene of clownish tub-thumping supposed to take place? The reader of the time, as I have said, would recognise the setting at once. As onlooker, he finds himself standing in Hyde Park at Hyde Park Corner, not far within the gates, looking East. On his right he sees the "Great Wellington Statue" (see Figure 1), that "hideous equestrian monster" whose erection was the most controversial public event for Londoners in the immediately preceding months of 1846, while on his left is a tall memorial column. This could be either that of the Duke of York in Carlton Gardens, by the Mall, or that of Nelson, a little further off in Trafalgar Square. Since Thackeray stands the figure on the column on its head, we are at liberty to identify the monument as belonging to either. Somewhere just behind the preacher, but screened from sight by the trees of those days, is Apsley House, the residence of the Duke of Wellington.

1. *Vanity Fair*, ed. Geoffrey and Kathleen Tillotson (Boston: Riverside, 1963), p. 80 [83]. Subsequent references are to this edition, which indicates the part-issue text and Number divisions. [Page references in brackets are to this Norton Critical Edition.]
2. *VF*, pp. 76, 404, 407–408 [78, 416, 420].

Figure 1. The Wellington Statue, "taken from the archway of the Hyde-Park screen, next Apsley House." *Illustrated London News*, 21 November 1846, p. 329. From a copy in the Alexander Turnbull Library, Wellington, New Zealand.

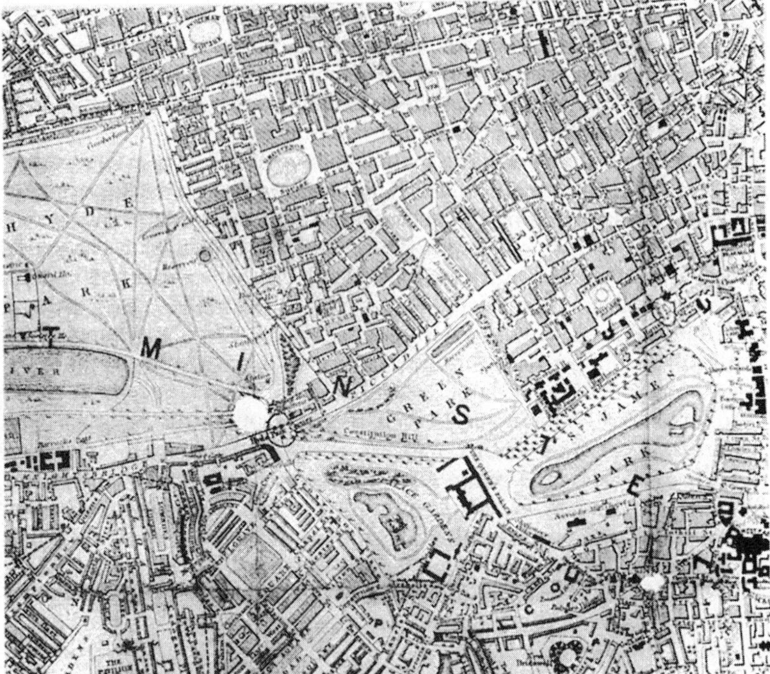

Figure 2. The West End from "Map of London and Its Vicinity," in *The Pictorial Handbook of London* (London: Bohn, 1854).

Thackeray's woodcut, that is, offers the reader a view that leads him into the story area of the novel, both geographically and socially (see Figure 2). We are in Hyde Park, where so many of the characters are to ride, drive or stroll, and not far from the Knightsbridge Barracks where Rawdon Crawley is serving in the Life Guards. Just beyond the trees lie Park Lane where Miss Crawley has a "snug little house," May Fair where Becky will reside at No. 201 Curzon Street, and the "old brick palace" of the Court of St. James, where, at the height of her career, Lord Steyne will present Becky to the "Star of Brunswick."[3] Clubland, too, lies just over there, where Rawdon fleeces Southdown at Wattier's and The Cocoa Tree. On the skyline, the pretentions of national and military glory, imaged in bronze statuary, are indicated and satirized. The clown's gesture seems, moreover, to draw our attention particularly to the equestrian Duke on his triumphal Arch. This, then, is the time, the place, the "English Society" of *Vanity Fair.*

In the years 1841–46 Thackeray was closely involved with the affairs of this London world. As Titmarsh, he contributed regularly to *Fraser's Magazine, The Morning Chronicle, The Pictorial Times,* etc., speaking out both seriously and as a humourist on painting, sculpture, book illustration, and literature. As a *Punch* man, he was a close follower of both politics and City affairs; he attended the Wednesday policy din-

3. *VF,* pp. 93, 361, 460 [97, 372, 475]. But cf. p. 488 [504], where Becky's number in Curzon Street seems to be 101, not 201. The identification of Vanity Fair with May Fair is clearer when the contemporary spelling of the latter is noted as given here.

ners at which the big cartoons were planned, and was the inspiration of one of Leech's happiest hits in these, "The Mrs Caudle of the House of Lords" (9 August 1845)[4]; he himself proposed four cartoons, contributed dozens of items ranging from two-line jests to two-column occasional articles, wrote a number of regular series, and provided hundreds of drawings. "Jeames's Diary" appeared at intervals from 1845 to 1850 while "The Snobs of England" was a major weekly attraction from 28 February 1846 to 27 February 1847. It was as "one of the principal contributors of *Punch*," that Kate Perry met him at the Ship Inn at Brighton in October or November 1846, when he was revising the opening chapters of *Vanity Fair*.[5]

Among the controversies into which *Punch* men threw themselves gleefully in those years, none sparked off so constant a fire of jokes as that about Wyatt's statue of the Duke of Wellington, which came to a climax in September 1846. This affair, one of the greatest fine art disputes of the century, had a long history, much of it relating to Hyde Park Corner. Although the Corner was the western entry to the Cities of Westminster and London, it was before the 1820's neither courtly nor metropolitan. The visitor approaching along Knightsbridge had the old St. George's Hospital on his right, and the Park on his left behind a notorious old wall with a shabby little gateway. Next he came to a stand of oil lamps at the turnpike gates, then to Apsley House on his left and Green Park on his right, with Piccadilly ahead of him (see Figure 3).

The whole approach was replanned in the 1820's. Decimus Burton designed a tripartite arched screen for the entrance to Hyde Park, the old wall was replaced by light iron railings, the oil lamps and turnpike were removed in 1825, and the Hospital was rebuilt in 1829. Apsley House, which had become the property of the Duke of Wellington in 1820, was remodelled in 1828, with a new facing of Bath stone replacing the original red brick. A corinthian portico and a banqueting hall added to its Ducal dignity. Its front was enclosed by a bronzed palisade, to match the nearby elaborate entrance to the Park.

In those days Green Park came to its apex at the top of Constitution Hill just across the roadway from Hyde Park. In order to give unity and some sense of relationship to the two entrances, Burton designed for Green Park a triumphal Arch to stand opposite his tripartite screen. On this Arch, built in 1825, it had been intended to set up a statue in a quadriga, looking out to the front and over the open ground of Hyde Park, in the antique memorial tradition. This final touch was not added, however, and Burton's Arch remained untenanted.

When, therefore, some twenty years after Waterloo, there were renewed proposals for monuments to the achievements of its hero, eyes were turned towards this vacancy. In August 1836, Matthew Wyatt's pig-tailed equestrian statue of George III was set up in Cockspur

4. M. H. Spielmann, *The Hitherto Unidentified Contributions of W. M. Thackeray to Punch* (New York: Harper, 1899), pp. 9–11.
5. *Letters and Private Papers*, ed. G. N. Ray (Cambridge: Harvard University Press, 1945), 1, cxxv–vi.

Figure 3. Hyde Park Corner in 1820. Edward Walford, *Old and New London* (1878) IV, 283.

Street, amid considerable controversy: the firm of Bankers whose windows looked out on it lost their lawsuit of protest, and drew their blinds ostentatiously down on the day of the unveiling. One Mr Simpson of the City Court of Common Council was inspired to suggest that the Duke of Wellington should be honoured by a similar equestrian statue, to be erected in the City of London. In the event, Chantrey, not Wyatt, was selected as sculptor for this statue, which was placed in front of the rebuilt Royal Exchange in 1844. Meanwhile, the indefatigable Simpson began to urge the propriety of having a statue of the Duke in the West End as well as in the City. A committee was formed, and money amounting in the end to £35,000 was raised, Wyatt this time being chosen as the artist. In May 1838, the Committee resolved "that the summit of the triumphal Arch at the entrance to Green Park, on Constitution Hill, going out of Piccadilly, would . . . be an appropriate situation on which to place such Equestrian Statue, provided her Majesty the Queen's permission can be obtained for that purpose."

The Queen agreed, and in spite of Burton's protests, preparations began. Among the most vigorous promoters of the scheme was Sir Frederick Trench, then well known as an advocate for the improvement of the Thames Embankment. But there were plenty of voices raised in opposition. In particular, a wooden model erected on the Arch in 1838 resulted in bitter recriminations between Burton, Wyatt, Trench, and the Committee. Although the decision was taken, the question of the site continued to be a matter of hot controversy, even in Parliament. Yet what could seem more suitable than the Green Park Arch? The Duke would be able to look at himself, giant size in bronze, out of his front windows, while the empty Arch would have an adequately heroic tenant. Hyde Park Corner was moreover already a place of Wellington associations, not only because of Apsley House, but because of the "Achilles" statue just inside the Park, by the Serpentine road. This, too, the Duke could see from Apsley House, but from its back windows. The "Achilles" is a bronze figure by Westmacott, cast from cannon taken in Wellington's wars, and erected in the Duke's honour in 1822 by the women of England. Known jocularly therefore as "The Ladies' Trophy," it represents a naked Roman athlete, 20 feet high, with a figleaf, a flyaway cloak, a shield, a sword, and a laurel wreath. A modern commentator has called it the "archetype of that strange, characteristically English amalgam of the heroic, the portentous, and the absurd in our public statuary."[6]

The Achilles, too, had roused violent controversy. His nakedness seemed inappropriate, to say the least. However, there he stood, thirty-three tons of everlasting bronze, on his mound in the southeast corner of the Park. Those who so earnestly promoted the crowning of Burton's Arch just over the way with a Duke in full costume may have felt that something was needed as a counterpoise[7] (see Figure 4).

6. David Piper, *The Companion Guide to London* (New York: Harper and Row, 1965), p. 165.
7. George Cruickshank's coloured cartoon, "Ladies buy your Leaf" (1822), satirises the difficulty. It shows the lower half of the statue, with an emphatic fig-leaf; a girl gesticulating before the plinth is obviously in the middle of a strip-tease act, while a group of fashionable old crones look on in eager horror.

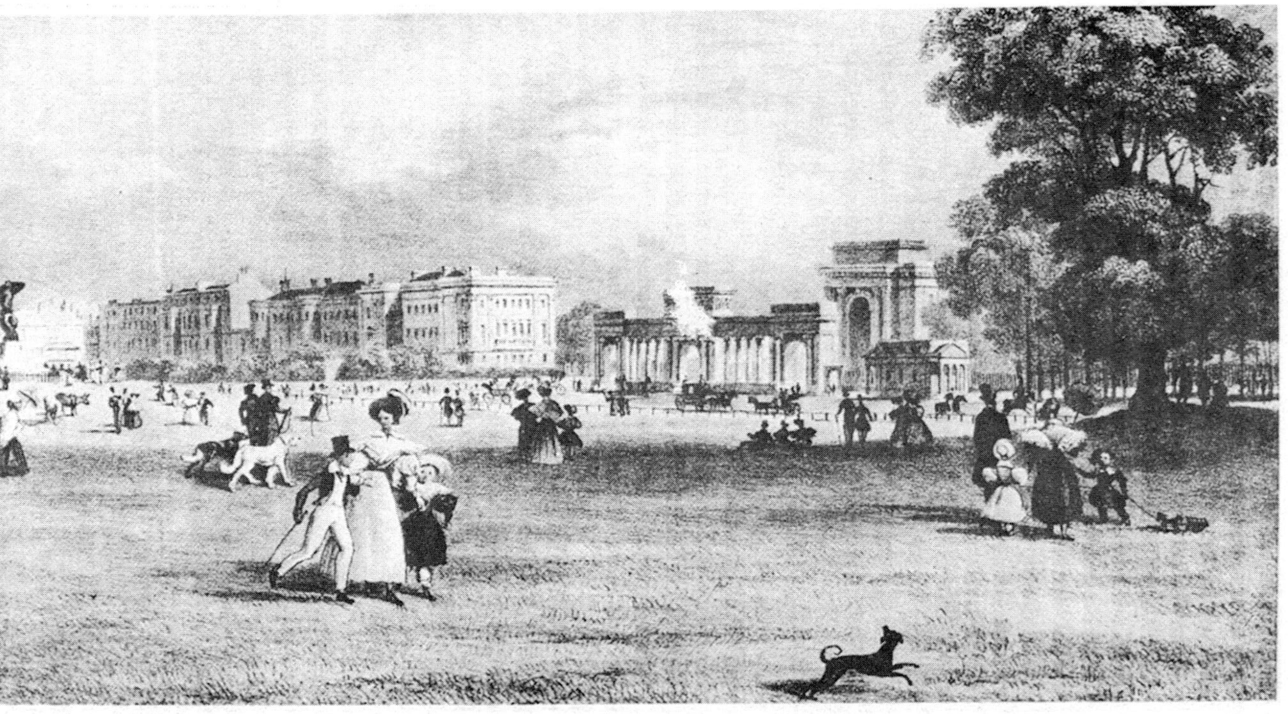

Figure 4. Hyde Park, looking towards Apsley House, showing the new Grand Entrance from Piccadilly. T. M. Baynes, del., G. Hallmandel, sculp., 1845. Crace Collection. By courtesy British Museum.

Wyatt spent several years on the model of the Duke's Statue. Then the casting began, while the disagreements grew hotter. Statistics, perhaps, will give some idea why. The Statue represents the Duke riding his horse Copenhagen, as at Waterloo. It weighs 60 tons, and is nearly 30 feet high. The horse measures 26 feet from nose to tail, is over 22 feet round the girth, and has 6 feet of head. "Such is the bulk of the horse that eight persons have dined within one half of it" remarked an awestruck *Illustrated London News* (11 July 1846). The Duke, with markedly Roman nose, and wearing his customary short cloak, rides stiffly with his right hand pointing a baton between his horse's ears. Burton's Arch is 67 feet high, and there was to be a 10 foot plinth above that, so that the total height from the ground to the top of the Duke's cocked hat would be over 100 feet.

Argument raged about all aspects of this monster. Would the Arch support it? What was the Duke pointing at? Where was he going? Riding sideways across the Arch, he would get nowhere, whereas the intended quadriga would at least have been setting off for Hyde Park. Why put him up so high, where no one could see him? This last objection was also made about Nelson, whose invisibility on his pillar in Trafalgar Square was already the joke of London.

As the final date for the elevation of the Duke grew near, the agitation increased. The committee, yielding to pressure, proposed that the Statue be hoisted up for a three week trial, to let the public judge the issue.

Parliament agreed, to the wrath of the *Times*, which mockingly suggested (10 August 1846) that a book be kept at the Arch "for passers by to rush in and write down the emotions with which they happen to be seized." The *Illustrated London News* gave the Statue elaborate coverage, with pictures of it in Wyatt's foundry in Harrow-Road, on 11 July and again on 15 August, when "many hundreds of the nobility and gentry" had been by invitation to see it.

Removal Day, Tuesday, 29 September 1846, must have been a memorable occasion. The streets were thronged with "well-dressed persons," the sun shone, the house tops were crowded, a "brilliant assemblage of beauty, rank, and fashion" gathered at vantage points, while the Queen and a host of the nobility waited at the windows of Apsley House. Indeed, so reminiscent is the whole stuffy pageant of some of the goings on in *Vanity Fair* that direct quotation from the *Illustrated London News* is called for to give the flavour of the experience. Among the "very numerous circle of fashionables" whom the *News* names as often as possible, the Hereditary Grand Duke of Mecklenburg Strelitz would seem to have crossed straight over the water from Thackeray's Pumpernickel, while the Committee "The Duke of Rutland, the Marquis of Londonderry, the Earl of Cardigan, Adjutant-General Sir F. Trench, Sir John Macdonald, Mr. John Wilson Croker, and Mr. Simpson" are constantly mentioned.

A "detachment of the detective force," appropriately in charge of Inspector Schacknell, was "in attendance." Wyatt's foundry was unroofed to get the Duke out, one hundred Fusilier Guards hauling him to the 20 ton "car" on which he was to travel. Twenty-nine horses, "supplied by Mr. Goding, the brewer," three abreast and crowned with laurel, were yoked up and driven by "ten sturdy draymen, one wearing upon his breast a Waterloo medal." As the clock of Paddington Church struck twelve, the "cortège" set out "amid loud and continued cheering." The colossus then jerked on its way in a procession led by the Life Guards, the Fusilier Guards, and a trumpeter, with one hundred Fusiliers massed behind and hanging on to guide ropes "in case of necessity." The bands of the Fusilier Guards, the Grenadier Guards and the Coldstream Guards supplied music, including, alternately, *God Save the Queen* and *See the Conquering Hero Comes.* All eyes "were centred upon the Statue . . . the shouts and enthusiasm of the people bespoke their grateful triumph." The *News* was at this point quite overcome by its feelings. "Rome never thronged round the triumphal car of Consul or Praetor more joyously, than London thronged on Tuesday round the twenty-nine stalwart dray horses that slowly and solemnly drew the great effigy of the Great Captain of the Age to its aerial pedestal on Constitution hill.

> They bear him on majestically near,
> Great Goding's horses, strong as Goding's beer.
> How gloriously the brazen image glows!
> Firm is his look as when he faced our foes.
> And eagle-like is curl'd his Roman nose."

An enterprising spectator "made several interesting pictures of the scene by his Daguerrotype process." The carriage shaft broke twice, and once the wheels locked "against a post in the centre of the crossing of Oxford-street and the Edgeware-road." By 1:30 p.m. the Statue was opposite Apsley House, where the crowds were thickest. Within the Ducal residence, "a distinguished party" was assembled to "witness the installation of this tribute to the prowess of the noble proprietor," amongst whom the *News* listed, not only of course the Queen, but once more "their Royal Highnesses the Hereditary Grand Duke and Grand Duchess of Mecklenburg Strelitz," a variety of other Royal Highnesses, one Serene Highness, a sprinkling of Princesses, several Counts, Earls and Viscounts, a few plain gentlemen, and finally, by way of chorus, the little litany given above of "the following members of the Committee," "The Duke of . . . x, y, z, . . . Mr. Simpson, etc."

Next day, Wednesday, forty-four riggers from the Woolwich Dockyard began the hoist, a matter of some technical difficulty. It took all day, till after moonrise; by Thursday afternoon the Statue was bolted into place, "destined, we trust," concluded the *News,* "for centuries, to commemorate the bravery of the British Hero; the skill of the British Artist; and the gratitude of the British Nation."[8] Indeed, as the *Times* remarked that day (2 October), it seemed unlikely that, whatever the public verdict, the Statue would be taken down again, since "possession is nine points of the law" (see Figure 5).

When the trial period was up in November, the still smouldering controversy broke out again. If the Duke was not to stay on the Arch, where was he to go? The Lord Mayor consulted the Royal Academy;

8. *Illustrated London News,* 3 October 1846, pp. 213–214, 216–218, 224.

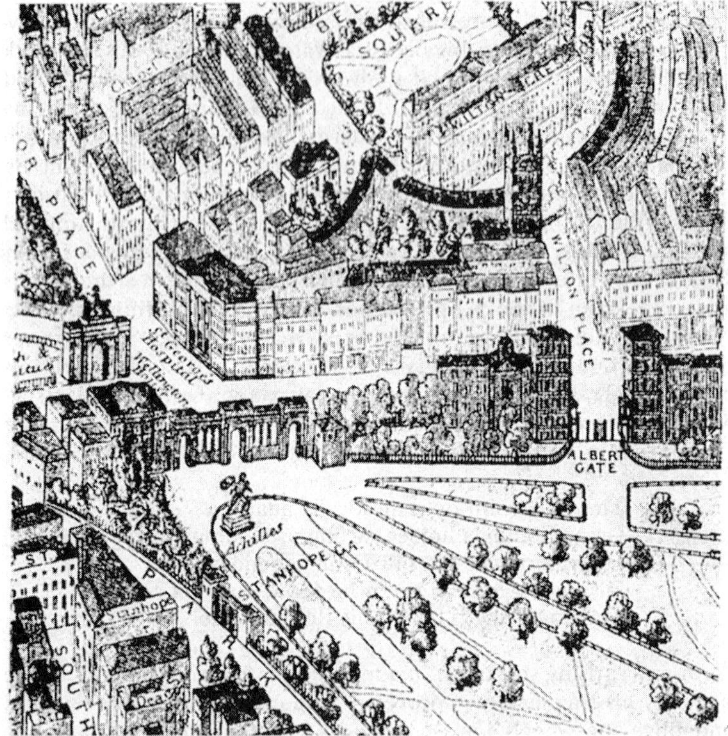


Figure 5. Hyde Park Corner from *A Balloon View of London, as seen from the North* (London: Appleyard and Hetting, 1851).

wags had made various suggestions, including the Eddystone Lighthouse, and Carlton Gardens between the Athenaeum and the United Service Clubs, where Wellington would be able to turn his back on York. The general opinion was that one should let erected statues stand, and that above all the artistic experts were not to be trusted. Had it not been so-called experts who had "stuck up" the Nelson column only three years before?

All this was, of course, wonderful copy for *Punch.* Jesting at Wellington statues had begun in 1844, with Chantrey's rider outside the Royal Exchange. Other monuments that amused *Punch* included York, and Wyatt's previous effort, the pigtailed George III in Cockspur Street. The invisible Nelson was of course a constant butt.

In the second half of 1846, however, just when Thackeray was revising *Vanity Fair,* Wyatt's second "equestrian monster" became *Punch*'s staple jest, good for several taunts in every issue. Indeed it bulks so large as a topic that Doyle included it among the items sketched in his title page to the July-December volume (XI), where it adorns the top right-hand corner, competing for attention with the state of Ireland, Free Trade, Peel, and the Corn Laws.[9]

The onslaught began on 13 June, with issue number 257, which devoted the weekly cartoon to "The Proposed Statue of the Iron

9. See Joan Stevens, "A Roundabout Ride," *Victorian Studies,* 13 (Sept. 1969), pp. 57–58.

Duke." In the same issue, there was an article on absurd London statues: Nelson, "tied by the leg" in Trafalgar Square; York, "perhaps placed where he would like to have been in his own lifetime, quite above the reach of all annoyances" (creditors); and now Wellington, "riding to posterity along the park railings." On 25 July, the news of the dinner party inside the horse led *Punch* to remark that the Duke "will certainly beat all other statues hollow," and to suggest that he could be let for lodgings, "the situation is exceedingly airy, the prospect delightful. . . . The Duke's head is still vacant." Or perhaps the Duke could "hold the Waterloo Banquets . . . inside his own statue"?[1] On 1 August, a picture shows the "colossal monster" crashing through the Arch; on 8 August, alternative sites are proposed. On 22 August, it is suggested that the Corner should be given symmetry by the erection of a second colossus, an Equestrian Punch, on Burton's other archway, the triple screen to Hyde Park (p. 78). By 29 August, when the trial period had been mooted, *Punch* is suggesting that "every article thrown at the horse" be "considered as one hostile vote" (p. 88), and deploring the nation's reliance on those "remarkably competent persons who settled the proportions of the Nelson monument and the costume of Mr. Wyatt's George III" (p. 91). On 5 September, there is comic verse, "The Committee is met, the mould is set, the Duke is cast today" (p. 103). On 12 September, *Punch* produced an illustrated parody, "This is the Duke that Trench built," and an "Inauguration Ode" (pp. 107, 112).

These issues of *Punch* are of course those in which *Snobs* is appearing, sometimes, as on page 91 for 29 August, on the same page as a Wellington joke. It is not therefore surprising that Thackeray glances at the affair in a minor *Snob* paper, "What's come to the Clubs," on 19 September. This little known piece is a letter by "Captain Alured Mogyns" (see *Snobs* Chapter vii), who complains of the stoppage in Piccadilly and the disorganisation of the Clubs. "Snooks," the "Polyanthus," the "Horse Marine," are all in chaos. Only the "Megatherium" is open, and that is useless, because there in the Library reading the paper aloud is "that infernal bore Sir John Roarer." Thackeray sketches the dreary room, in which Sir John is sitting beneath a picture of the Statue. The "business of importance" which has brought Mogyns up to London, is, obviously, the forthcoming installation.

By the date of the next issue, Saturday, 26 September, the great moving day is near, and *Punch* references increase: The Statue will cause an eclipse, it will jam the traffic; the horses lent by the City brewer "are accustomed to carrying barrels, and will find nothing strange to them in being compelled to drag the greatest butt in London" (p. 34); the Duke will be able to see his country's tribute "out of his front windows, which he can now enjoy only from his back ones, in the contemplation of the ACHILLES." *Punch* "never saw any absurdity," he declares, "that promised to bring him in so much" (p. 131).

On 3 October, a mock item from the Gazette records the transfer,

1. *Punch*, 11 (July–December 1846), p. 41. Subsequent page references to *Punch* incorporated in the text are to this volume.

"MILITARY MOVEMENTS. FIELD MARSHALL THE DUKE OF WELLINGTON, from Mr Wyatt's Studio, to the top of the arch at Hyde Park Corner" (p. 141).

The next week, 10 October, *Punch* presents a scene from *Don Giovanni,* with Trench as the Don and Punch as Leporello: "Hyde Park Corner, moonlight . . . How cleverly we've rooked 'em/And raised the Iron *Duke* to an *Arch-dukedom.*" Will he descend from his perch, or stay "*in Statu quo*"? (p. 145). Even the *Times* noticed this jest.[2]

On the next page is a double spread on "the progress of the Statue," in subtle mockery of the manner of the *News*; the invalids mustered on the roof of the Hospital "looked like patients on a monument," the Duke's cloak was "a capital design for getting rid of artistical difficulties" and so on (pp. 145–147). There are eleven other items in this same issue. One of them notes that for the price the Duke is very "dear to his country," another that if the Statue must be moved, it should be put beside Achilles, since that personage already has his hand outstretched and "might be employed holding the DUKE's horse" (pp. 158, 159).

The issue for 17 October keeps the pot boiling with four items, of which the best is *A Sad Look-Out.* "As the Duke of Wellington was looking the other day out of Apsley House, and saw the Achilles on one side of him and the Monster Statue on the other, he was heard to sing, in a voice of the utmost feeling—'How happy could I be with neither' " (p. 163).

On 24 October, there are four references, on 31 October, three, on 7 November, two, on 14 November, four. Here the fun takes another turn. If the statue is to come down again, what can be done with it? On the 21st, *Punch* suggested that it was already "engaged at Astley's to appear in a grand new Equestrian Christmas Pantomime, to be called 'The Statues of London' " (p. 215), an idea that also occurred to the *Illustrated London News,* which unlike *Punch* thought the idea of removal silly. Suppose the Statue could be turned into a show? ". . . people would pay eagerly to see it, especially in the country, where they have heard so much about it," and "benevolent brewers" could always be found to "horse it from one town to another."[3] The issue of *Punch* for 21 November devoted the weekly cartoon to the affair, Leech drawing a scene in Green Park in which the Queen and Prince Albert speak to Punch about it. Behind them on the skyline we see both the Achilles and the Equestrian Monster.

Right up to the end of 1846 the jokes continue: "use it as a breakwater," put it on top of Buckingham Palace, which "wants height," and so on (pp. 240, 251). But the Statue remained on Burton's Arch until 1883, when the Corner was once more reconstructed (see Figures 6 and 7). Opportunity was then taken to remove it to a deserted heath at Aldershot, under revived *Punch* mockery.[4] In its stead, another equestrian statue of the Duke, by Boehm, was set up opposite Apsley House. The Arch was finally crowned in 1912 with its long-

2. *The Times,* 4 November 1846, p. 4.
3. *News,* 28 November 1846, p. 346.
4. *Punch,* 84 (1883), p. 76; 85 (1883), p. 3.

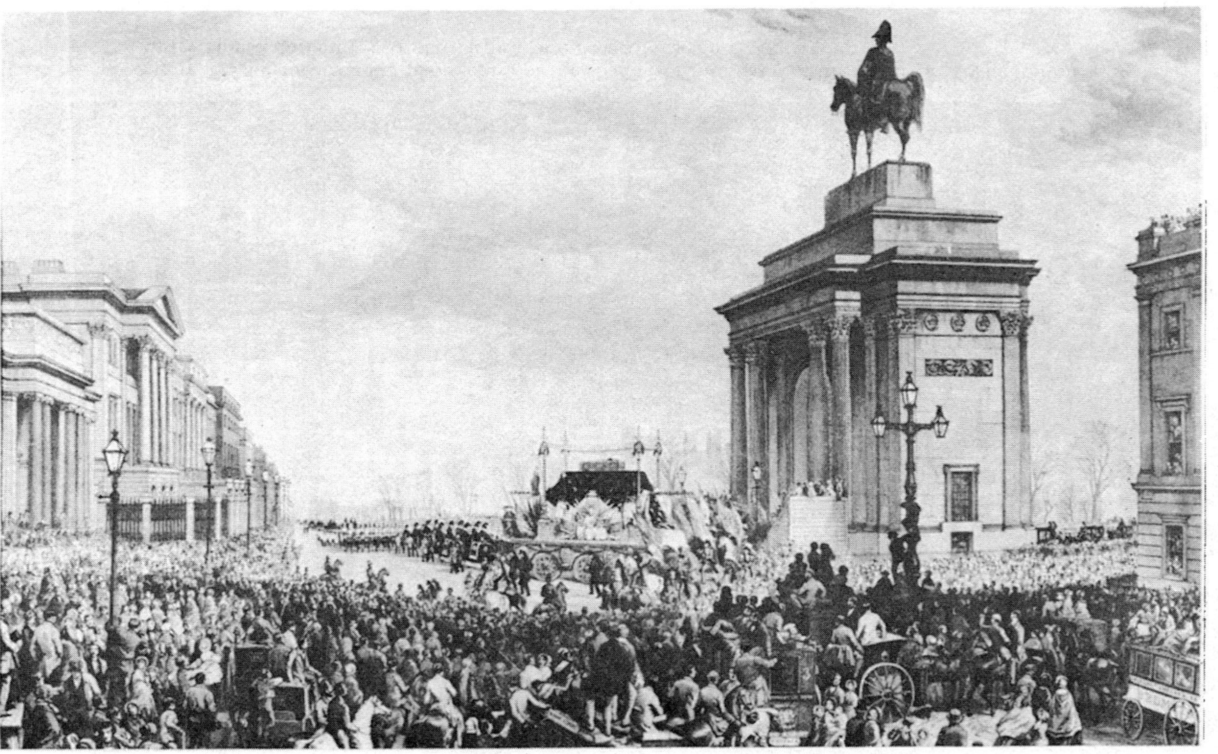

Figure 6. The Funeral Procession of the Duke of Wellington. Lithograph 1852, by T. Picken from a painting by Lewis Hague. By courtesy Victoria and Albert Museum.

Figure 7. Late 19th century photograph of the shadow of the statue of the Duke of Wellington on Apsley House. By courtesy of the Victoria and Albert Museum.

awaited quadriga, and now serves to hide the ventilators of the Hyde Park Corner underpass.

Throughout this controversy, Thackeray was a committed *Punch* man. He crossed swords with Trench in the *Morning Chronicle,* too, on 5 October, saying that "only the worst could be expected from the guardian genius of the Bronze Horse." Let Trench be proud, if he could, of "the Wellington enormity," which was "an abominable waste of bronze."[5]

This, then, is the story of the Great Wellington Statue. The climax of the affair falls in those very months, September to November 1846, when Thackeray was revising the opening chapters of *Vanity Fair.* The novel had been accepted, presumably by Bradbury and Evans, in January 1846, when at least the first Number, Chapters i–iv, must have been drafted.[6] In March, Thackeray wrote: " 'The Novel without a hero' begins to come out on the first of May," but there was more delay, due partly, according to the Tillotsons, to revisions and reconsiderations. At last, under the title *Vanity Fair,* Bradbury and Evans advertised the novel in *Punch* on 28 November, and more fully as *Vanity Fair: Pen and Pencil Sketches of English Society* in the December Number of *Dombey and Son,* and elsewhere. "Sometime between March and November, then," conclude the Tillotsons, " 'the Novel without a Hero' had found its title." As recalled by Kate Perry, "He told me some time afterwards that after ransacking his brain for a name for his novel, it came upon him unawares, in the middle of the night, as if a voice had whispered, 'Vanity Fair'."[7]

The moment of this revelation cannot be precisely dated, but came during Thackeray's visit to the Ship Inn at Brighton in October or early November 1846. The finding of the title crystallised his ideas, and led to numerous revisions of the draft of Numbers I and II (Chapters i–iv, v–vii). The close study of the MS made by the Tillotsons leads them to conclude that, apart from the well known references to "Vanity Fair" in Chapters viii and ix, "the most obvious and far-reaching of his additions and revisions . . . is the introduction of Dobbin in Chapters v and vi. . . . Thackeray may not even have thought of Dobbin until he came to revise."

In October, then, or early November, just at the climax of the affair of the Bronze Horse, the spirits whispered to Thackeray his brilliant title. He tried it out, combined with the original "Novel without a Hero" subtitle, in a pencilled outline of a cover design; this was reproduced by Anne Thackeray in *The Orphan of Pimlico* in 1876. It shows below the title two little heralds waving a banner bearing the sub-title, against the skyline of the City of London, indicated by the outline of St. Paul's and a couple of church spires.[8]

The spirits that gave Thackeray his final title *Vanity Fair,* however, obviously went further and imaged for him his final design for the cover, in which the West End and its military monuments replace the

5. *Contributions to the Morning Chronicle,* ed. G. N. Ray (Urbana: Illinois University Press, 1955), pp. 187–192.
6. *VF,* pp. xvii–xxvii.
7. *Letters,* I, cxxvi.
8. This sketch is reproduced in the Biographical Edition of the *Works* (London: Smith, Elder, 1898), vol. I, p. xxviii.

City and its churches as the background. Though he returned to his first idea for the subtitle, "Novel without a Hero," on the volume title page, Thackeray abandoned for good his sketch of the skyline of the City. It is possible that the planning of Leech's cartoon for 21 November at the regular *Punch* dinner the week before gave Thackeray the idea for a design with a setting in Hyde Park. Certainly nothing could so well underline for readers in January 1847 the contemporary relevance of the book. Nominally, of course, the story begins "while the present century was in its teens," with rich and accurate historical detail; nevertheless Thackeray constantly through his commentary brings the moral application into his own period, an effect markedly reinforced by his illustrations, in which the characters are in "modern dress." With the straight face of the jester Thackeray explains his reasons for this policy at the end of Chapter vi. "I have not the heart," he says, "to disfigure my heroes and heroines by costumes so hideous" as those of the beginning of the century, and so he has "on the contrary, engaged a model of rank dressed according to the present fashion."[9] The subtlety of this is lost on the twentieth century reader, for whom all the costumes are alike "historical."

This modern dress, added to the presence every month on the "gaudy yellow covers" of the West End skyline as it was in late 1846, makes the contemporary quality of Thackeray's satire still more unmistakable.

The small boy with the wooden sword, identifiable as Dobbin, appears both in the cover design and in the initial for the chapter of his introduction (v), further evidence that text and illustrations were revised together. As for the figure standing on its head on the column to the left of the skyline, this may be York, who was Commander-in-

9. *VF*, p. 65 [63–64].

Chief at the time of the story.[1] Although York is still remembered best for the nursery song in which "he had ten thousand men," and "marched them up a hill so high / And marched them down again," Thackeray seems to have respected him as a brave enough soldier. The real target of the mockery is, as with Wellington, the humbug of the national tribute, not the man himself. Or is this columnar midget not York, but Nelson? From the viewer's stance in Hyde Park, either column would be in that position, though York's is nearer. He stands 13 feet high, on a column of 124 feet, Nelson stands 17 feet high, on a column of 167 feet; both were landmarks in those days. But it is towards "the Wellington enormity" that the preaching clown makes his gesture.

Thackeray's cover design has, however, another function besides that of asserting the novel's contemporary relevance. The caricatured rider on his Arch is the Duke of Wellington, victor of Waterloo, that battle which is the preoccupation, the hinge, of the story. Everything that happens between the "sunshiny day" in June when Becky and Amelia leave Chiswick Mall, and that other day in June 1815 when George Osborne lies on the battlefield with a bullet through his heart, is coloured for the reader with the irony of foreknowledge. This irony is an integral part of the tone of the novel, of its sense of *Vanitas Vanitatum.* And when Waterloo is over, at the end of Number IX, its consequences reverberate throughout the rest of the story.

While this ironic foreknowledge is a constant presence, it strengthens to a climax of tone in certain key passages, of which that in Chapter xxii is the best instance (Number XI, for June 1847). Thackeray is telling of George's wedding day, but juxtaposing in a type of cinematic montage the present of the reader with the present of the characters, so that every stroke in the description carries a double significance.[2] He chooses for his image of time and mutability that very spot at Hyde Park Corner to which his cover design draws attention, in the certainty that his readers will register the full force of the allusions.

In the preceding chapters Thackeray has been shading in our apprehension of what lies ahead. In Chapter xviii, "our surprised story . . . finds itself . . . hanging on to the skirts of history" as Napoleon landed "in the month of March, Anno Domini 1815 . . . and Louis XVIII fled, and all Europe was in alarm, and the funds fell, and good old John Sedley was ruined." In consequence of this, Amelia would have lost George but for Dobbin's interference. Their story in the following chapters, xviii–xxii (Numbers V and VI for May and June), is insistently presented against the swift movement of historical events, with a quickening sense of doom that brings us to "one gusty raw day at the end of April" (the 25th, in fact),[3] when Dobbin meets

1. *VF,* pp. 123, 523 [132, 541].
2. Cf. *VF,* pp. xxxiii–xxxiv, ". . . it is characteristic of his general method in depicting the past to make use especially of what has recently been revived or extended into the present, appealing to his readers' sense of change and continuity." I am indebted to Professor Tillotson here for drawing my attention to Chapter xxii.
3. *VF,* p. 379 [391].

George at the old Slaughter's Coffee-House in Saint Martin's Lane, and drives off with him down to Fulham to his wedding.

Then we have this passage:

> And the carriage drove on, taking the road down Piccadilly, where Apsley House and St. George's Hospital wore red jackets still; where there were oil-lamps, where Achilles was not yet born; nor the Pimlico arch raised; nor the hideous equestrian monster which pervades it and the neighbourhood; and so they drove down by Brompton to a certain chapel near the Fulham road there.[4]

The part-issue reader of 1847 met this with instant comprehension. Every item has a Wellingtonian ring, and is an indication of what was, in 1815, the future. To recapitulate, Apsley House, built about 1770 in red brick, became the property of the Duke in 1820 and in 1828 was remodelled in grey Bath stone. St. George's Hospital opposite, also originally in red brick, was rebuilt in plain stone in 1829. The Achilles statue was erected in 1822, and in 1825 the oil lamps and the Kensington turnpike were removed. Burton's Arch was built in 1825; the "hideous equestrian monster" was hoisted on top of it, as we have seen, in 1846.

George Osborne, however, drives past the Corner as it was in April 1815 (see Figure 3), unconscious of the changes that will come, changes that will celebrate the battle in which he will be killed, six weeks beyond the present narrative moment. For Thackeray's 1847 readers, these details were masterstrokes of irony, given not only immediate force by the controversy of 1846, but recurring resonance throughout the novel by the repetition of the cover design.

Nor does Thackeray leave matters here. When in Chapter lviii he begins to complete the circle of Amelia's story with Dobbin's return from India, he carefully retraces the steps of this wedding journey, using place (as in *Esmond*) to make us vividly aware of the passage of time. Slaughter's Coffee-House and the greasy waiter have not changed, but everything else has. "The arch and the Achilles statue were up since he [Dobbin] had last been in Piccadilly," and "a hundred other changes had occurred which his eye and mind vaguely noted."[5]

At this point, moreover, Thackeray once more provides specific dates for his story: the waiter has an old bill of George's, "April 10, 1815, Captain Osborne: 3£," George's essay is dated 24 April, 1827; 1827 is also picked out for mention in a parenthesis about the "comfortable Anglo-Indian district" to which Jos moves his father and sister.

In the same area of the story, too, Thackeray introduces other references to Napoleon, Wellington, and the consequent changes at Hyde Park Corner. George's essay mentions both Achilles (the hero, not the Statue) and "the late Napoleon Bonaparte."[6] Alluring advertisements that tempt Waterloo Sedley into the tailors' shops of South-

4. *VF*, p. 206 [216].
5. *VF*, p. 560 [579].
6. *VF*, pp. 567, 578 [586, 597].

ampton feature gorgeously waistcoated gentlemen who "ogle ladies in riding habits prancing by the Statue of Achilles at Apsley House."[7] Finally, the return of Dobbin, Amelia and Jos to Brussels completes the cycle. Becky's re-entry into their lives is marked by the chapter initial of Chapter lxiv, in which she is shown as Napoleon gazing across the dividing English Channel. It is with devices such as these that Thackeray contrives that our consciousness of Waterloo shall colour the entire novel.

To the end of his life, Thackeray found amusement in the statues of London. They appear frequently in references and drawings. One delightful reference is that in "Small Beer Chronicle" (*Roundabout Papers*, July 1861):

> Those poor people in brass, on pedestals, hectoring about Trafalgar Square and that neighbourhood, don't you think many of them—apart even from the ridiculous execution—cut rather a ridiculous figure, and that we are too eager to set up our ordinaire heroism and talent for port? A Duke of Wellington or two I will grant, though even of these idols a moderate supply will be sufficient. Some years ago a famous and witty French critic [Janin] was in London, with whom I walked the streets. I am ashamed to say that I informed him . . . that all the statues he saw represented the Duke of Wellington. That on the arch opposite Apsley House? the duke in a cloak, and cocked-hat, on horseback. That behind Apsley House in an airy fig-leaf costume? the duke again. That in Cockspur Street? the duke with a pigtail—and so on. I showed him an army of dukes . . .
>
> I say again that ordinaire should not give itself port airs, and that an honest ordinaire would blush to be found swaggering so. I am sure if you could consult the Duke of York, who is impaled on his column between the two clubs, and ask his late Royal Highness whether he thought he ought to remain there, he would say no. A brave, worthy man, not a braggart or boaster, to be put upon that heroic perch must be painful to him. . . .[8]

The cover design of *Vanity Fair*, as has been noted, is not always included in any illustrations reproduced today in the ordinary editions of the novel. As an artist, Thackeray had learned in his *Punch* years to make his satirical points with pencil as well as with pen, reinforcing his words with his sketch. The public who saw Bradbury and Evans's advertisement in late 1846 of a "New Work by Michael Angelo Titmarsh" would be expecting something that functioned on both levels, and would have greeted the woodcut on the cover with the delight born of amused recognition. It is one of the clues, not only to the setting and the central event of the novel, but to its narrative tone and its pointed relevance to "English Society" at the time.

7. *VF*, p. 570 [589]. See also note 7 [on p. 784] above.
8. W. M. Thackeray, *Works*, 17 vols. (London: Oxford University Press, 1908), XVII, 512–513.

## ROBERT A. COLBY

# [Victor Cousin and the Foundation for an "Edifice of Humanity"]†

* * *

Thackeray regarded himself as a historian, but, to judge from his favorite reading, the forms of history that interested him most were "private history" and "secret history," works of reflection that helped men and women understand their own natures. "The condition of reflection is memory; and the condition of memory is time," wrote the philosopher-educator Victor Cousin in his *Cours de l'histoire de la philosophie*, the book that young Thackeray was "absorbed by" in the reading room of the Palais Royal in Paris, according to his daughter. Thackeray's own remark at the time is laconic, but enthusiastic: "Read Cousin's History of Philosophy . . . am much pleased with Cousin his style & his spirit. The excitement of metaphysics must equal almost that of gambling."[1] This was tribute indeed from a young man about town whose own gambling fever was transferred to the "rooks and pigeons" of his early magazine stories such as Bob Stubbs, Jack Attwood, Algernon Deuceace, and Sam Titmarsh, and for whom the casino wheel and the gaming table attained emblematic significance as prominent as the stage, the masquerade and the ballroom in his "chronicles of fate's surprises." Thackeray came to Cousin in his maturity, and, despite a paucity of references to him in his writing, there is reason to believe that this philosopher was the most significant of all the early influences in the shaping of his mental attitude and in providing a frame of reference for his novels. Thackeray himself invites such conjecture by the words with which his diary entry ends: ". . . I found myself giving utterance to a great number of fine speeches & imagining many wild theories w[h] I found it impossible to express on paper."

* * * Among the entries in [Thackeray's] diary for this period is a sentence from Cousin's lecture on Descartes's *Discourse on Method:* * * * "To doubt is to believe; for to doubt is to think. Does he who doubts believe that he doubts, or does he doubt whether he doubt or not? If he doubt whether he doubt or not, he destroys his own skepticism; and if he believes that he doubts, he destroys it again."[2] The theme of this lecture is brought out in the sentence

† Reprinted from *Thackeray's Canvass of Humanity: An Author and His Public* (Columbus: Ohio State University Press, 1979), 27–34, 51–52, by permission. 

1. Diary, 22 August 1832, *Letters and Private Papers of William Makepeace Thackeray*, ed. Gordon N. Ray, 4 vols. (Cambridge: Cambridge University Press, 1945–46), 1:225.
2. Diary, 22 August 1831, *Letters*, 1:225–26. The quoted passage is from lecture 5 of the *Cours de l'histoire*, in Victor Cousin, *Introduction to the History of Philosophy*, trans. Henning Gotfried Linberg (Boston: Hilliard, Gray, Little, & Wilkins, 1832), p. 138.

   Some years later Thackeray echoed this passage in reviewing a book on David Hume, "a sceptic and utter worldling, a man entirely without imagination. . . . His life is consistent at least, and he is the same from sixteen to sixty, insensible to a future seemingly, and untroubled by conscience or remorse, or doubt even about his doubts" (review of J. H. Burton's *Life and Correspondence of David Hume, Morning Chronicle*, 23 March 1846; reprinted in *William Makepeace Thackeray: Contributions to the Morning Chronicle*, ed. Gordon N. Ray [London and Urbana: University of Illinois Press, 1966], pp. 113–14).

immediately preceding the one Thackeray copied out, which reads in translation: "What is said of doubt, what Descartes has demonstrated in regard to doubt, applies with greater force to the idea of nothingness." Cousin's teachings, we can gather, have a bearing on Thackeray's own lifelong struggle against cynicism and skepticism—most explicitly dramatized in *Pendennis,* his most personal novel. Other aspects of Cousin's thought too are reflected in his writing.

* * *

Victor Cousin's reputation was kept alive after his death in 1867 by a circle of faithful disciples, but it has hardly outlasted his century. In ours there has been a tendency to downgrade him. He "was not a great philosopher, as is clear from any of his philosophical writings," asserts a modern student. "His language was rhetorical, his thought was naively and pompously idealistic, and his general attitude overbearing."[3] But the very affirmative nature of his thought, deplored by this critic, and the fervor with which it was expressed, account for Cousin's appeal to the impressionable youth of Thackeray's generation. His first biographer called him "*Restaurateur De La Philosophie Spiritualiste Au XIX Siècle,*" indicative of his importance in the history of ideas.[4] Cousin at first called his philosophy "the new idealism," signifying his reaction against the materialist tendency of the schools that had preceded him, the *sensualistes* (notably Condillac) of the Enlightenment, and the rationalist circle known as the *idéologues* in vogue during the Napoleonic period. It is true, however, that Cousin was not an original philosopher, his contribution to thought being rather as a historian and synthesizer of philosophies. *Eclecticism,* the overall term he early applied to his system as a whole, puts the emphasis where he wished it, on the process of inquiry itself, rather than on specific doctrines, on aim and purpose, rather than on content. For Cousin the very freedom from absolutism gave philosophy its preeminent position among humane studies. "After having . . . proclaimed the supremacy of philosophy, we hasten to add that it is essentially tolerant," he concluded his introductory lecture. "In fact philosophy is the understanding and the explanation of all things. Of what, then, aside from error and crime, can it be the enemy?"[5]

Cousin's "metaphysics" apparently attracted Thackeray by its comprehensiveness and its attitude of general tolerance, what Cousin called "universal sympathy." For Cousin the primary function of the philosopher in the modern world was to reconcile conflicting posi-

3. Frederic Will, *Flumen Historicum: Victor Cousin's Aesthetic and Its Sources* (Chapel Hill: University of North Carolina Press, 1965), p. 1. Will concedes that Cousin's teachings "played a large role in the formation of the Romantic temperament in France," but attributes it to "the post-revolutionary drought of ideas, and . . . the impoverishment of French philosophy at this time." Donald G. Charlton contends to the contrary: "Posterity has indeed been harsh—too harsh . . . in its judgment of Cousin and his school. . . . His achievements in philosophy are well known, but underrated" ("Victor Cousin and the French Romantics," *French Studies* 17 [October 1963], p. 312).
4. J. Barthélemy Saint-Hilaire, dedication to *M. Victor Cousin, Sa vie et sa correspondance,* 3 vols. (Paris, 1895). The third volume includes a valuable topic index.
5. Lecture 1, pp. 26–27 (Wight trans.). Cousin's thought combines elements of Plato, Descartes, Leibniz, Locke, Kant, Hegel, and (under the influence of his teacher and later colleague Royer-Collard) the Scottish common sense school. Frederic Will traces his aesthetic thought back to the "mythological eclecticism" of the Alexandrians (*Flumen Historicum,* p. 28).

tions. As an eclectic he taught "that every system contains a part of the truth; that all systems taken together contain the whole truth, that there is no need to discover truth, only to unite its scattered fragments."[6] Thackeray himself was praised in his time for just this disinterested frame of mind. According to one of his admirers, he "offends no one by the vehemence of his opinions, nor by dogmatism of manner . . . [he] is not a man to create partizans, he espouses no 'cause': has no party." Another characterized his mind as a "hospitable brain . . . tolerant of contradictions." Cousin taught that "each system is true by what it affirms and false by what it denies." Thackeray's most recent biographer, Gordon Ray, in summing up his accomplishment, has written: "In his comprehensive and impartial appraisal of English life, Thackeray praised what was good, while he attacked what was bad," a succinct enough statement of the eclectic position.[7]

We can understand too why Thackeray, with his introspective temperament, responded to the "philosophie spiritualiste" of Cousin. "The study of consciousness is the study of human nature," concludes the lecture on Descartes that Thackeray quoted in his diary. In "restoring" the mind to the primacy from which the "sensualists" had dislodged it, Cousin employed a term that was novel at the time: "Man is a universe in miniature; *psychology* [*la psychologie*] is universal science concentrated. Psychology contains and reflects everything, both that which is of God and that which is of the world—under the precise and determinate angle of consciousness; everything is brought within a narrow compass, but everything is there."[8] In his intuitive way Thackeray became a practitioner of this "universal science." He wrote once in a letter to an editor that he enjoyed the exercise of "the humorous *ego*," a less exact term than Cousin's "precise and determinate angle of consciousness," but indicating the pleasure he took in the play of mind over what Cousin called "that which is of the world," and which Thackeray referred to simply as "society in general."[9] What Cousin referred to as "that which is of God" also figures in Thackeray's fictional universe. In *Pendennis* he clearly dissociates himself from the law student Paley to whom "All was dark outside his reading lamp," so that "Love, and Nature, and Art (which is the expression of our praise and sense of the beautiful world of God) were shut out from him" (chap. 29). He is more in accord with Cousin, who affirmed in his lecture "The Idea of Philosophy" that "Philosophy does not cut from art its divine wings, but follows it in its flight, measures its reach and aim, Sister of Religion, it draws, from an intimate connection with her, powerful inspirations."[1]

Although he conceived of the mind as a microcosm, Cousin saw it as bounded by man's limitations. He distinguished between the

6. Jules Simon, *Victor Cousin,* trans. Melville S. Anderson and Edward Playfair Anderson (Chicago: A. C. McClurg, 1988), pp. 55–56.
7. George Henry Lewes, review of *The Book of Snobs, Morning Chronicle,* 6 March 1848, p. 3; [Richard Simpson], "Thackeray," *Home and Foreign Review* 4 (April 1864):405 (author identification provided by *The Wellesley Index,* vol. 1); Gordon N. Ray, *William Makepeace Thackeray: The Uses of Adversity,* (New York: McGraw-Hill, 1955), p. 418.
8. Lecture 5, p. 147 (Linberg); italics mine.
9. 6 April 1845 to Thomas Longman, editor of the *Edinburgh Review, Letters,* 2:190–91.
1. Lecture 1, p. 27 (Wight).

"spontaneous reason" that we all share and the "reflective reason" unique to each individual. The "spontaneous reason" when it operates grasps the nature of reality in a flash of insight, but it is inhibited by the "reflective reason," which "considers the elements of thought successively and not all at once . . . [and] considers each, for a moment at least, in a state of isolation."[2] In one of his addresses to the reader in *Pendennis,* Thackeray describes this solipsistic condition: "O philosophic reader . . . a distinct universe walks about under your hat and under mine—all things in nature are different to each—the woman we look at has not the same features, the dish we eat from has not the same taste to the one and the other—you and I are but a pair of infinite isolations, with some fellow-islands a little more or less near to us?"[3] (chap. 16). The very wrapper design that confronted the first readers of *Pendennis,* showing the hero with chin in hand, puzzled and pondering, torn between the domestic virtues and evil spirits, can be interpreted as an emblem of the "reflective reason" beset with doubts and prone to error.

Because of their limited perspective and their state of isolation, "Men are scarcely ever more than halves and quarters of men; who, unable to understand, accuse each other," Cousin declares in a succeeding lecture. The philosopher, according to Cousin's ideal, transcends these limitations through his capacity to identify himself with all mankind by means of "universal sympathy": "And, do you know the means, gentlemen, by which you may arrive at this tolerance, or rather at this universal sympathy [Cousin addresses his students]? You can arrive at it on one condition only; and that is, that you yourselves get rid of every exclusive prepossession; that you embrace all the elements of thought, and thus reconstruct the whole edifice of humanity in your own minds." This accomplished, Cousin continues: ". . . whosoever of your fellow creatures may present himself to you, and whatever may be the exclusive idea that prepossesses him . . . will not be wanting to you; you will therefore, in him, pardon humanity; for you will comprehend it . . . because you will possess it entirely. This is the only remedy against the malady of fanaticism; which, whatever be its object, proceeds from nothing but the prepossession of the mind by one object exclusively, whilst we are ignorant of, and despise every other."[4]

Arthur Pendennis, in the course of one of his debates with his friend and fellow law student George Warrington, has his say on what Cousin denounced as "the malady of fanaticism": " 'Make a faith or dogma absolute, and persecution becomes a logical consequence;

2. Lecture 6, p. 176 (Linberg).
3. In one of his literary essays, Thackeray wrote with reference to artists: "Is not individuality the great charm of most works of art? Let any two painters make a picture of the same landscape, and the performance of each will differ of course. The distance appears purple to one pair of eyes which is gray to the other's, one man's fields are brown and his neighbour's green, one insists upon a particular feature and details it, while his comrade slurs it over. . . . Every man has a manner of painting, or seeing, or thinking of his own; and lucky it is for us too, for in this manner of every one's work is a new one, and books are fresh and agreeable, though written upon subjects however stale" ("The Rhine, by Victor Hugo," *Foreign Quarterly Review,* April 1842, p. 80; *New Sketch Book: Essays Collected from the Foreign Quarterly Review,* ed. Robert S. Garnett [London: Alston Rivers, 1906], pp. 8–9). The book under review was Hugo's *Le Rhin, lettres à un ami.*
4. Lecture 7, pp. 198–200 (Linberg).

and Dominic burns a Jew, or Calvin an Arian, or Nero a Christian, or Elizabeth or Mary a Papist or Protestant; or their father both or either, according to his humour; and acting without any pangs of remorse,—but on the contrary, with strict notions of duty fulfilled. Make dogma absolute, and to inflict or to suffer death becomes easy and necessary' " (chap. 61).

To make dogma absolute is, of course, just what Victor Cousin opposes. "I hope that those youths, who for some time will frequent this lecture room, will there contract different habits," he urged in his lecture entitled "Reflection—the Element of Error," that they will "learn to understand that, as every error should be treated with profound indulgence, and that all those halves of men that we constantly meet with around us, are, nevertheless, fragments of humanity, and that in them, we should still respect that truth and that humanity of which they participate." Arthur Pendennis has taken heed: " 'You call me a sceptic because I acknowledge what *is*,' " continues his colloquy with Warrington; " 'and in acknowledging that, be it linnet or lark, or priest or parson; be it, I mean, any single one of the infinite varieties of the creatures of God . . . I say that the study and acknowledgement of that variety amongst men especially increases our respect and wonder for the Creator, Commander, and Ordainer of all these minds so different, and yet so united' " (chap. 61).

The "profound indulgence" toward error that Victor Cousin preached called for an eclectic attitude toward men's opinions as well as toward systems of thought. "The truth, friend! . . . where is the truth?" exclaims Arthur Pendennis in another of his philosophic moods. "Show it me. That is the question between us. I see it on both sides. I see it on the Conservative side of the House, and amongst the Radicals, and even on ministerial benches. . . . If the truth is with all these, why should I take side with any one of them?" (chap. 61). Henry Esmond too is eclectic, on matters both spiritual and temporal:

> In the course of his reading (which was neither pursued with that seriousness or that devout mind which such a study requires), the youth found himself at the end of one month, a Papist, and was about to proclaim his faith; the next month a Protestant, with Chillingworth; and the third a sceptic, with Hobbes and Bayle.
>
> . . . Harry brought his family Tory politics to college with him, to which he must add a dangerous admiration for Oliver Cromwell, whose side or King James's by turns, he often chose to take in the disputes which the young gentlemen used to hold in each other's rooms, where they debated the state of the nation, crowned and deposed kings, and toasted past and present heroes or beauties in flagons of college ale.[5]

Along with his open-mindedness, Henry, it might be added, displays an unusual disposition to "pardon humanity":

> I look into my heart and think that I am as good as my Lord Mayor, and know I am as bad as Tyburn Jack. Give me a chain

5. *Henry Esmond*, bk. 1, chap. 10.

> and red gown and a pudding before me, and I could play the part of Alderman very well, and sentence Jack after dinner. Starve me, keep me from books and honest people, educate me to love dice, gin, and pleasure, and put me in Hounslow Heath, with a purse before me and I will take it. "And I shall be deservedly hanged," say you, wishing to put an end to this prosing. I don't say no. I can't but accept the world as I find it, including a rope's end, as long as it is in fashion.[6]

The classical motto *Homo sum; humani nihil a me alienum puto* was invoked by Victor Cousin as the theme of his message of tolerance, the very same motto quoted by Thackeray in one of his early articles on popular literature.[7] Certainly no man was alien to Thackeray as a novelist. His vast gallery of characters, taking in criminals, gamblers, miscreants of various sorts, demireps, the more respectable classes of shopkeepers, professionals, and just ordinary citizens, all the way up to the gentry and the aristocracy, indeed scales the entire "edifice of humanity" from its subbasement to its summit.

* * *

In trying to pin down [Thackeray's] protean nature, contemporaries of Thackeray used such phrases as "crystal of many facets" and "a strange effervescence of . . . widely differing elements."[8] His friend George Henry Lewes spoke of him as a "Janus bifrons" with a "predominating tendency to antithesis."[9] All of these come close to "the harmony of contrarieties" that Victor Cousin defined as the task of the moral philosopher and one that Thackeray clearly set for himself. Eclecticism is the term that seems best to describe Thackeray's myriad-mindedness, his adroit, nimble, mercurial disposition, "the variety, the changeableness, the power of rapid transformation which is to be found only in the highest intelligences . . . by turns humorous, contemptuous, tender," as one of his fellow novelists put it.[1] His peripatetic spirit, his tendency to view life through a series of sliding lenses, his simulation of a wide range of moods from melancholy to jocularity, his wide empathy, all fall into place as his means of appropriating to himself "entire humanity." Thackeray's moral relativism, an attitude that some have attributed to indifference or pococurantism on his part, is more properly interpreted as part of his eclectic outlook, his attempt to illuminate man's confusion out of the cumulated wisdom and folly of the ages, to aid humanity, in Cousin's words, "from incomplete view to incomplete view . . . to arrive at a

6. Ibid., opening of bk. 1.
7. "Horae Catnachianae," *Fraser's Magazine*, April 1839, p. 424.
8. Simpson, "Thackeray," p. 405; "Thackeray's Place in English Literature," *Spectator*, 2 January 1864, p. 9.
9. George Henry Lewes, "Pendennis," *Leader*, 21 December 1850, p. 929. Raymond Las Vergnas entitles one chapter of his study "Le dualisme thackerayan. Ses multiples aspects," and organizes his analysis of Thackeray's mind about a series of resolved "Contradictions" (*W. M. Thackeray, l'homme—lepenser—le romancier* [Paris: Librarie Champion, 1932], pp. 52–70).
1. Mrs. Oliphant, "Mr. Thackeray's Sketches," *Blackwood's Magazine* 119 (February 1876): 235. In her monograph Barbara Hardy describes him, particularly in relation to *Vanity Fair*, as "an *eclectic* figure, itself a virtuoso performance, shifting roles with the mercurial adaptability of an Elizabethan character-actor . . ." (*The Exposure of Luxury: Radical Themes in Thackeray* [London: Peter Owen, 1972], p. 72; italics mine).

complete view of itself and of all its substantial elements."[2] Furthermore, what another of his fellow writers called his "literary chameleon" nature indicates that with books too he was eclectic and highly adaptable. One of Thackeray's admirers went so far to see even in Thackeray's notorious gift for parody evidence of his sympathetic faculty at work, his desire to see the "soul" beneath a work of art, and to "reembody" it in his own.[3] Certainly he learned much from fellow writers, even those he lampooned, showing a remarkable ability, as will appear in later chapters, to extract precious metal from crude ore. That "knowledge of human nature so wide and comprehensive in its nature that it seems unrivalled in the annals of fiction"[4] for which he was praised in the last century was the distillation of a lifetime of self-education spent "with men as well as with books," as one of his first guides, Isaac Watts, advised. But it is evident that from his early years he displayed his special predilection for self-study and confessional writing, curiosity about the vagaries of behavior (those studies known in his time as "mental and moral science"), and a tolerant understanding of human foibles, and that he was further directed in his youth toward the study of man in his social milieu, viewed against the panoramic background of cultural history. Upon this intellectual base he erected, out of his extensive experience—artistic, theatrical, journalistic, literary—the "edifice of humanity" that emerges from his novels.

2. Lecture 6, p. 190 (Linberg). Cousin's influence on Thackeray did not extend to the political sphere. Various essays that he contributed to the *National Standard* from May 1833 to the end of January 1834 as editor and correspondent indicate that he did not share Cousin's admiration for Louis Philippe or his enthusiasm for the Charter of 1830 (*La Charte*) that later inspired the Chartist movement in England. Later, as Paris correspondent for the *Constitutional*, he continuously denounced the July Monarchy for its hypocrisy and tyranny. See *Mr. Thackeray's Writings for the "National Standard" and "Constitutional,"* (London: W. T. Spencer, 1899), passim.
3. George Augustus Sala, *Things I Have Seen and People I Have Known*, 2 vols. (London: Cassell & Co., 1894), 1:9; Simpson, "Thackeray," pp. 477–78.
4. Charles L. Eastlake, as quoted in James Grant Wilson, *Thackeray in the United States*, 2 vols. (London: Smith, Elder, 1904), vol. 1, verso of dedication page.

# CRITICISM

# WILLIAM C. BROWNELL

## William Makepeace Thackeray†

* * *

The question is, after all, mainly one of technic. When Thackeray is reproached with "bad art" for intruding upon his scene, the reproach is chiefly the recommendation of a different technic. And each man's technic is his own, and that of a master may be accepted as possessing some inner principle of propriety which any suggested improvement would compromise. But it may also be said that for the novel on a large scale, the novel as Thackeray understood and produced it, Thackeray's technic has certain clear advantages. In order to deal with life powerfully, persuasively, and successfully, the direct method is in some respects superior to the detached. It is a commonplace in painting that the scale of subject and the kind of effect sought legitimately dictate technic; and the contention, once common among academic painters, for the same treatment of subordinate spaces and objects as that given to the salient ones, to the end that you might enjoy the result one way in the mass and then another way in the detail, has perhaps ceased to be widely held. A miniature demands a unified treatment, whereas even the intrusive "Doge Praying" of a Venetian canvas is not too great a strain on the imaginative appreciation of the beholder. And, similarly, the famous "short story," the writing of which *has* become "a finer art" since the day of "The Kickleburys on the Rhine," demands a treatment appropriate to its episodic or microcosmic character which the novel does not. And among its requisites is, very likely,—beyond all question, when one considers the personal force of most practitioners of the art,—the attitude of reserve and detachment in the writer. But Thackeray wrote novels. He was not one of the "Little Masters." He could do Dutch painting with the most adept of the cherry-stone carvers, on occasion, but he never lost sight of relations and atmosphere, and for these—in which the sense of reality resides—a freer technic is salutary.

Now the one reason for insisting on "objectivity" in art is that it is often the condition of illusion—the illusion of reality in virtue of which art is art and not itself reality, the mere material of art. If Thackeray's "subjectivity" destroyed illusion it would indeed be inartistic. The notable thing about it is that it deepens illusion. The reality of his "happy, harmless fable-land" is wonderfully enhanced by the atmosphere with which his moralizing enfolds it, and at the same time the magic quality of this medium itself enforces our sense that it *is* fable-land, and enables us to savor *as* illusion the illusion of its art. Nothing could establish the edifice of his imaginative fiction on so sound a basis as those confidences with the reader—subtly inspired by his governing passion for truth—in which he is constantly

† From *Victorian Prose Masters* (New York: Scribner's, 1901), 7–10, 15–18, 41–43.

protesting that it is fiction after all. The artistic service of this element of his fiction is aptly indicated by such a contrast as that furnished by Maupassant—a master of objective technic if there ever was one. When Maupassant exchanges the short story, in which his touch and his attainment are perfection, for a larger canvas his atmosphere evaporates. Mr. James says of "Une Vie" that if its subject had been the existence of an English lady, "the air of verisimilitude would have demanded that she should have been placed in a denser medium." He would have her surrounded with more figures, with more of the "miscellaneous *remplissage* of life." The suggestion is that of the practitioner, and in harmony with Mr. James's impersonal practice; and, aside from the point about the nationality of the heroine, which is not very apposite, it is very just. Mr. James would have successfully condensed the medium by the "miscellaneous *remplissage* of life." But there is also the short cut to verisimilitude of a technic with more color, more personal feeling—the technic that provides a medium of sensible density by attuning the reader to the rhythm of the subject, and establishes between them a mutuality of relationship, the technic of Thackeray.

And it is to be observed that this atmosphere, which exists to such serviceable artistic ends in Thackeray's fiction, exists invariably *as* atmosphere. It accentuates the impression of verisimilitude, and constitutes in itself an element of magical artistic charm; but it is not used constructively in either character or composition. The reticulation of personal comment that rests so lightly and decoratively on the fabric of his story, all the imaginative connotation, so to say, philosophical and sentimental, of his novels, has but an auxiliary function and plays no structural part. It is not used to fill out the substance and round the outlines of his personages, who exist quite independently of it. It serves, on the contrary, to detach them from the background, to detach them from their creator himself. It is absolutely true that Thackeray's "subjectivity" in this way subtly increases the objectivity of his creations. They are in this way definitely "exteriorized." In this way we get the most vivid, the most realizing sense of them as independent existences; and in this way we get Thackeray too.

* * *

Thackeray's practice is not perhaps to be recommended, and critics who have the art of fiction at heart cannot do better than to insist on the value of the detached attitude in the author. But any view of Thackeray is an imperfect one which does not perceive that he is a notable exception to the rule wisely enough prescribing this attitude in general. His personal force and charm take him quite outside of its operation. The perfection with which the artist and the satirist are united—or rather fused—in him almost entitles his novels to classification as a different *genre.* At least, in order to consider them profitably it is necessary to take into account in far greater degree than in other instances the man himself as well as his works. A correct synthesis is reached most directly in his case by regarding his works mainly as manifestations of the genius that unifies them. Even critics who think it bad art for an author to obtrude his personality must admit that the evil is lessened in proportion to the interest of the personality so obtruded. As to the interest of Thackeray's, there is likely to be no contention. It is one of the most marked in letters. When one considers his personal force, the notion of confining its direct expression to pure dissertation appears grotesque. To the true Thackerayan, of course—like Dr. John Brown, Mr. Herman Merivale, or Mr. William B. Reed—no price is too great to pay for any of its manifestations. It has as much charm as power, and is infinitely gracious and winning. It provides an atmosphere of its own in which his characters live and move, and to which they owe no small portion of their attractiveness—in virtue of which, indeed, they constitute an organic community by themselves. If he is their "showman," he certainly shows them off to advantage, and he himself is not the least interesting figure of the show. The spectacle gains immensely from his association with the company. How he thinks and feels in the presence of the drama they are enacting immensely extends the range of our interest. Conceive "The Newcomes" without the presence of Thackeray upon the stage—minus the view it gives us of the working of its author's mind, the glimpses of his philosophy, the touches of his feeling. The result would be like that of eliminating the commentary which Colonel Henry Esmond interweaves with his autobiography. Well, but Esmond is one of the characters of the book, and his prosings are therefore pertinent, says Taine. So is Arthur Pendennis, Esq., the putative author of "The Newcomes." But Pendennis is the thinnest of whimsical disguises for the real author, and the half-hearted attempt to continue him and Laura as characters is purely playful. True, they *are* needless sops to the critical Cerberus, and, aside from adding pleasantly to the machinery of the story, they really serve to show how legitimately the reader who is not a pedant may enjoy the personality of Thackeray apart from as well as with any artistic expedients of the sort.

In a more definite and apposite way, therefore, than is true of a personality that produces works of a more impersonal order, Thackeray's own nature becomes the most interesting and important subject to consider in connection with his works. He was above all else a lover of truth. The love of truth was with him, indeed, less a sentiment than a passion. It absorbed his mind and inspired its activity. To the moral temperament thus attested falsehood of all kinds seemed the one thing in the universe worth the evocation of militant energy. The exposure of sham enlisted all his artistic faculty. He pursued it with the most searching subtlety ever devoted to a definite artistic aim in all his books. The villain of all his stories is the hypocrite. Some of them—"Barry Lyndon," "The Tremendous Adventures of Major Gahagan," "The Book of Snobs"—are concerned with pretence alone, the pretence that eludes the detection of others and that which deceives the pretender himself. "The Book of Snobs" is an amazing series of variations on this single theme—hardly robust enough in itself to have avoided flatness and failure, in the course of such elaboration, by a writer less "possessed" by it. This at least is what saves its perennial interest for other readers than those familiar with the particular society it satirizes, for other than English readers, that is to say. "You must not judge hastily or vulgarly of snobs; to do so shows that you are yourself a snob. I myself have been taken for one." These statements are for all nationalities.

* * *

Whatever judgment of Thackeray's art and substance proves final, there is no doubt that the contemporary verdict of his style will stand. "Thackeray is not, I think, a great writer," Matthew Arnold observed, but at any rate his style is that of one. What a great writer is, in his view, Arnold has formulated in his remark that "the problem is to express new and profound ideas in a perfectly sound and classical style," and his refusal to recognize in Addison a writer of the first rank is based on "the commonplace of his ideas." It is idly possible to call Thackeray's ideas commonplace, but his style is at all events perfectly sound and classical. It is not the style of Burke, whom Arnold calls "our greatest English prose-writer"—probably because, together with his incomparable style, Burke's distinction is, as he says, that he saturates politics with thought. It is, however, far more perfectly sound and classical. Burke's elevation does not wholly save his style from that tincture of rhetoric which is the vice of English style in general—that rhetorical color which is so clearly marked in the contentious special pleading of Macaulay, in the exaltation of Carlyle, in the rhapsody of Ruskin, in the periodic stateliness of Gibbon, and even in the dignity of Jeremy Taylor. Thackeray's is as destitute of this element as Swift's or Addison's, with which, of course, it is rather to be compared. Rhetoric means the obvious ordering of language with a view to effect—when it does not spring from the elementary desire simply to relieve one's mind; and the great merit of the Queen Anne writers—from whom Thackeray derives—is their freedom from this element of artistic mediocrity. It is to this turn for elegance rather than rhetoric—as unfortunate perhaps in its poetry as beneficial in its prose—that the Queen Anne age owes its epithet Augustan. Thackeray is undoubtedly to be classed with the world's elegant writers—the writers of whom Virgil may stand as the type and exemplar, the writers who demand and require cultivation in the reader in order to be understood and enjoyed. "Nobody in our day wrote, I should say, with such perfection of style," Carlyle affirmed, and, as Thackeray observes of Gibbon's praise of Fielding, "there can be no gainsaying the sentence of this great judge," in such a matter. His taste is sure. In this respect some of his writing is like a page of Plato. One may feel shortcomings, but at its best it is without faults. The vulgarian can see that it is flawless, lacking as it may be in the glitter or the rhythm that excites his imagination and quickens his pulse.

* * *

# DAVID CECIL

## [A Criticism of Life]†

* * *

Ten minutes' steady reading is enough to teach one that Thackeray's novels are living works of art, not dead period pieces. But they have not the triumphant independence of time which characterizes those of Dickens. They are more occupied with the ephemeral customs and concerns of the age in which they were written; one has to understand something of these customs and concerns if one is fully to appreciate their point. This involves more trouble than you and I, dear reader, like often to take; so that on Thackeray's pages, grain by fine grain, the dust begins to settle.

But it is a pity, for we should enjoy him. Thackeray is a great novelist, and a very original one. In his own time he was always being compared to Dickens, and he has been ever since. But no comparison could be more inept; they belong to two entirely different species of writer. Of course, they have the common characteristics of their common school and period. Their moral values are much the same, the moral values, sterling, domestic, unspiritual of the Victorian middle class for which they both wrote. They both admire simple, kindly, reliable, unintellectual men; simple, modest, gentle, unintellectual women. And considered in its literary aspect the work of both is work in the English tradition, with its accompanying merits and defects. But in all that makes their work memorable they are unlike each other: the nature of their inspiration is wholly different. They have a different range.

Not that they wrote about different people. Thackeray's characters are contemporary English people; and though they are higher in the social scale than Dickens', they are predominantly middle-class. But they are regarded from a different angle. Dickens is interested in individuality. His great figures live in virtue of the characteristics in which they differ from their fellows. Thackeray's are equally alive; but they live in virtue of the characteristics they share. Nor are these, as with Scott, say, the common characteristics of a group. Thackeray is interested not in the variety, but in the species; not in men, but in man.

This does not mean his range is larger than that of Dickens or Scott; in some ways, indeed, it is more limited. But it is not limited as theirs is to types of human character, but to certain aspects of human character as a whole. Certain motives and qualities universally present in man stir Thackeray's imagination; it is in so far as it deals with these qualities and motives that his writing is creative. His range is determined by the range of human activities involving these motives and interests.

This range is hard to define completely in a phrase. The shortest

† Reprinted with the permission of Macmillan Publishing Company from *Early Victorian Novelists* (New York: Bobbs-Merrill, 1934), 77–80, 83–84, 86–96, 98–107, 114–116. 

way of doing it is to say it covers all the aspects of human nature implied in the titles of his two most characteristic books, *Vanity Fair* and *The Book of Snobs.* That sounds a hostile view of human nature, but it is not so. Thackeray liked people, and for the most part he thought them well-intentioned. But he also saw very clearly that they were all in some degree weak and vain, self-absorbed and self-deceived. And he had a power unparalleled among novelists for detecting these qualities in their various degrees and manifestations. His out-and-out climbers and snobs and egotists are the most profoundly studied in English literature. And he can discern equally well the slight streak of sentimental self-indulgence in a maternal affection like that of Mrs. Pendennis: of self-important vanity in a persevering ambition like young Sir Pitt Crawley's; of self-distrustful egotism in the excesses of a young man like George Osborne; of innocent self-deception in the unworldliness of Colonel Newcome; of sentimental self-deception in the submissive love of Amelia Sedley. It is not a comfortable talent. At moments the reader feels as if he can hardly bear to look, as one victim after another is laid on the operating table, one after another petty shame, petty arrogance, petty subterfuge, is exposed to the light of day by Thackeray's neat unrelenting scalpel. All the same it is the fountain of his achievement, the instrument of his creative imagination; it is by its means that he makes his characters alive. Amelia Sedley saying farewell to George on his departure for Waterloo would be merely the conventional figure of a desolate wife, were it not for the insight with which Thackeray has seized on her characteristic ineffectiveness at a moment of crisis.

* * *

[Thackeray's] detective power, though it is the source of [his] achievement, is not its whole secret. In itself it merely shows he was an acute observer. And observation, however imaginative, is not enough to create that self-dependent, self-consistent world which is the special mark of the great novelist. How far he can do this depends on the use he makes of his observation.

Now its ignorances and vanities, its self-deceptions and self-absorptions, are far from making up the whole of human nature. But they are, it must be repeated, universal to it. They appear in some degree or other in every age, country, sex and character; moreover, there is not a human thought or activity in which they do not take some share; nothing anyone does or thinks, good, bad or indifferent, is without some strand of human egotism interwoven into its texture. It is Thackeray's first and characteristic achievement that by isolating and exhibiting these motives in all their ubiquitous and tortuous manifestations through the labyrinth of human conduct, he imposes a new unity and order on that chaotic human life which is the material of his art. This is the way his creative imagination expresses itself; this is how he makes his world. It is a world as individual as that of Dickens, but its individuality is not given to it by the peculiar idiosyncrasy of its landscape and atmosphere and inhabitants, but by its moral structure. Dickens, of course, founds his picture on reality; but its glory comes from the fact that it is not at all like it; Mr. Pecksniff,

Mrs. Gamp, Mr. Micawber are unlike anyone we ever met; our hearts go out to Dickens for introducing us to such unique and enchanting strangers. But the interest of Lady Kew and Rawdon Crawley and Major Pendennis is that they are exactly like people we have met. "Oh," we exclaim with delighted recognition, as Thackeray discovers for us a characteristic trait, "how like Mr. So-and-So, how like oneself, how like human nature!"

Only Thackeray's books have not the heterogeneous incoherence of real human nature. *His* creative power shows itself, not in transforming the facts he has observed about life, but in arranging them. Dickens' imagination is a distorting glass turning to grotesque comedy or grotesque terror the world that it reflects; Thackeray's is a kaleidoscope, shaking the colored fragments of his observation into a symmetrical order, round the center of a common canon of conduct. "How does Mr. Smith deceive himself?" he asks. "Is Mrs. Brown an egotist? What pathetic vanity made Mr. Robinson commit that crime? What is the secret self-satisfaction that persuades Mr. Jones to his altruistic activities?" always he asks these questions, and in the perspective of a single moral vision, chaos assumes order and proportion.

* * *

Thackeray is the first novelist to do what Tolstoy and Proust were to do more elaborately—use the novel to express a conscious, considered criticism of life. He has generalized from the particular instances of his observation to present his reader with a systematic philosophy of human nature.

It was a great innovation—his unique precious contribution to the development of the novel. And of course it gives his books a force unshared by any, however full of genius, that deal merely with particulars. It may be a narrow view—Thackeray's was—but even a narrow view of so big a subject is something pretty big; only a creative imagination of a high power could work on so large a scale; choose for its ground so huge an area of experience, assimilate to its own color so different and varied a mass of facts. And the impression it makes on the reader is proportionately formidable. Here is no mere picture of Tom or Dick or Harry, he feels; here is a coherent and considered view of that common man of whom Tom and Dick and Harry are only individual examples. This is how Thackeray looked on his life, this is how I could look on my life if I chose. And he is in consequence stirred to a more serious response than could be raised in him by the record of a mere particular instance.

Nor was this the only new effect to which Thackeray's innovation gave him access. Effects of time, for instance. In Dickens and Fielding, concentrated as we are on the fortunes of individuals, we live in the present, sometimes looking forward in anxiety, never looking back. But in Thackeray, looking on the individuals as we do only as representatives of a common humanity, we stand farther away and are cognizant of the general curve of life, of the flight of time and change, of decay and renewal. The inevitable influence of years on character, wearing down love, slackening ambition, making faint memory itself, appears in Thackeray's pages for the first time in the English novel. We see Esmond pass from childhood to youth, from youth to middle age, we watch his love for Beatrix wax, wane, and finally give place to that for Lady Castlewood. Tom Jones is eternally young, and so far as his limited notion of constancy allows eternally constant to the lady of his serious preference.

The effects of time, indeed, are the occasion of some of Thackeray's most characteristic triumphs. He had a special sensibility to the relics of the past; what more poignant emblems are there of man's transitoriness and vanity? Old pictures, old toys, old letters with their yellowing paper and browning ink, the ridiculous, charming poems of the eighteen-year-old, the ball-dress once so fresh and modish, now grotesque in its antiquated fripperies, George Osborne's room opened after years to show a half-finished scrawl on the writing-table, a pair of spurs, their gilt dusty now, left on the mantelpiece, a schoolboy's cap, a carnival favor; these things never fail to touch him to a sort of poetry; the faded, ironical, plaintive poetry, so sad and yet so mellow, of memory. Indeed, Thackeray's books are like memories, memories of an old man looking back, disillusioned but not embittered by experience, in the calm summer twilight of his days.

Finally, his vision enabled him to impose an organic unity on the chaos of the large-scale English novel. Outwardly his stories seem just like Fielding's or Dickens', a heterogeneous mass of people and incidents artificially united by their association with a central figure. Fielding and Dickens want to bring in a great variety of people with no intrinsic connection with each other, so they connect them by making them all part of the adventures of Tom Jones or Nicholas Nickleby; their books are a series of pictures wholly different save for one figure coming into all of them. But in Thackeray the variety is the subject; for all its manifestations are different illustrations of those laws of human conduct which it is his object to portray. Pendennis or Clive Newcome is there, to give the particular point of vantage through which we survey these laws at work, and in consequence Thackeray's books suffer from none of that irrelevancy and division of interest which we find in everything Dickens or Scott ever wrote. His best characters do not play secondary rôles in the story like Mrs. Gamp or Dandy Dinmont: each has its necessary contribution to make toward the total impression.

* * *

In his masterpiece, *Vanity Fair*, he breaks with the convention altogether. This is Thackeray's second great claim to fame. For his new matter, he did in *Vanity Fair* invent a new and absolutely original form, a form supremely adapted to suit his intricate subject. His contemporaries hardly seemed to realize this; nor has it been completely realized since. There are enough of the old formulas left in *Vanity Fair* to make people speak of it as if it were a Victorian novel of the orthodox type, an inchoate mass of incident and character clustering round a conventional, virtuous heroine, Amelia Sedley, who, after passing through many vicissitudes, finally achieves happiness in marriage. But a glance at Thackeray's title should have shown them they were wrong. For one thing it is not called "Amelia Sedley," but *Vanity Fair*; the center of the book, that is, is not to be found in any one figure. And secondly it is called a "Novel without a Hero." Now this does not just mean that it has a heroine instead; it means that there is no character through whose eyes we are supposed to survey the rest of the story and with whose point of view we are meant wholly to sympathize. For here, that panorama of life which is the subject of all Thackeray's books is openly the subject; here, writing about Vanity Fair, he calls his book *Vanity Fair.* And it is the salient fact about *Vanity Fair,* in Thackeray's view, that it admits no heroes. To be heroic is to dominate circumstance; in the Vanity Fair of Thackeray's imagination everyone is the slave of circumstance. To exhibit this he has devised his original structure; a structure that so far from being loose and illogical is of an almost operatic symmetry.

To illustrate the universal character of the laws controlling Vanity Fair Thackeray shows us them as exhibited in the careers of two characters. That of the first, Becky Sharp, beginning low, describes a curve reaching its highest point in the middle of the book and then descending low again, at the end rises to a middle position. That of the other, Amelia, follows a contrary curve—just at the moment when Becky is at her highest Amelia is at her lowest, and then, as Becky descends, once more rises. Long separated, they meet again in the last chapters to settle down in life at an equal and middle station.

The characters of the two girls are designed to illustrate the laws controlling Vanity Fair as forcibly as possible. And in order to reveal how universally these laws work, they are of strongly contrasted types.

Amelia is an amiable character, simple, modest and unselfish. But, says Thackeray, in Vanity Fair such virtue always involves as a corollary a certain weakness. Amelia is foolish, feeble and self-deceived. She spends a large part of her youth in a devotion, genuine enough to begin with, later merely a sentimental indulgence in her emotions, to a man unworthy of her. For him she rejects a true lover; though she is ultimately persuaded to marry this lover, it is only, ironically enough, through the chance caprice of the woman for whom her first love had rejected her. Nor is she wholly saved from punishment of her error. By the time he marries her, her true lover has learned to see her as she is.

Becky, the second "heroine," is not weak and self-deceived; she is a "bad" character, a wolf not a lamb, artful, bold and unscrupulous. But she, no more than Amelia, can escape the laws governing the city of her nativity. By nature a Bohemian, she is beguiled, by the false glitter surrounding the conventional rank and fashion which are the vulgar and predominant idols of Vanity Fair, to spend time and energy in trying to attain them. She succeeds, but she is not satisfied. Nor is she able to maintain her success. She is too selfish to treat the husband, who is necessary to her position, with the minimum of consideration necessary to keep him. She sinks to the underworld of society. But her eyes are not opened; and the rest of her life is spent in attempting to retrieve herself, so far successfully that we see her last as a charitable dowager, a pattern of respectability, a final flamboyant example of the deceptiveness of outward appearances in Vanity Fair.

* * *

The structural scheme of *Vanity Fair* is Thackeray's greatest technical achievement, and the structural originality which conceived it his greatest technical talent. But he was by nature a virtuoso, and he had several others. Thackeray's subjects, involving as they do an enormous number of heterogeneous characters and diverse incidents and generally more than one plot going on at the same time, present difficult problems to the writer. He must be able to keep the reader interested in several different characters and different worlds at the same time: yet he must not linger too long over any one of them, the reader must not have time to forget about one group while he is reading about the other. While if the book is to be a work of art at all it must maintain some sort of unity of tone. Thackeray solves these problems. No one has ever been better at manipulating a huge mass of material. He can make his effects so quickly: indicate a situation, draw a scene in few words; he had that unteachable gift for dialogue which can make a character reveal itself in its lightest phrase.

* * *

He evolved a method of telling the story which joins the fragments together. Fielding had inaugurated the device by which the author tells the story openly in his own first person, interrupting the action from time to time to comment on what is taking place; but Fielding had confined his comments to certain sections of the book designed for the purpose; Thackeray extends this method. He tells us the story as he might tell it if he was sitting talking to us in his armchair; it is thus easy for him to cover a great deal of ground; he does not need a set theater, he acts the parts himself, and when his point is made he can shift the scene without any further assistance than he can supply with his own voice. This method not only makes it easy for him to control his material, to move his puppets about, but it also helps him to solve his artistic problem, to impose a unity of tone on a heterogeneous subject matter. Over the surface of the whole book is spread equally the tone of Thackeray's personality. However varied the vicissitudes through which the story moves, it is told us by the same voice, with the same tricks of speech; however different the characters and scenes he is drawing, they bear the signature of Thackeray's style of draughtsmanship.

And it is a highly individual style. Thackeray's creative imagination is most impressively apparent in the moral order he imposes on experience, but it shows itself in another way too, in his way of presenting his story. His actual method of describing scene and character is, to steal a phrase from the art critics, a "stylized" method. Unlike Dickens his achievement lies in its truth to recognizeable reality, but like Dickens he is not a realist. He does not attempt to reproduce with a photographic accuracy all the facts, important and unimportant, that make up the surface of any scene—like Zola, say. He sedulously selects from them those he thinks the most significant. And even these he does not present with the unemphasized plainness of Trollope. In the visible as much as in the moral world he accentuates the traits which in his view give his model its individuality, heightens the lights, darkens the shadows.

* * *

The second distinguishing mark of Thackeray's method of presentation is the mood in which he writes. Told as they are openly in his person, the scenes of the story are inevitably steeped in the mood with which he regarded life in general and them in particular. Of course, this is true of all novels if they are any good at all. The novel is not a record of facts objectively observed, like a scientific text-book, but of facts seen subjectively through the temperament of the writer. But in a novelist like Defoe, say, this temperament can only be traced indirectly by the facts he selects and the proportion in which he selects them: apparently, at any rate, we are given nothing but the actual facts as though we were present at the scene he is describing. In Thackeray, however, we are never present at the event, we are present in Thackeray's room as he tells us about it afterward. And in consequence we are conscious of a double emotion, that of its actors and, more predominantly, that of Thackeray observing them. The plain positive colors of the drama are refracted through the painted glass of Thackeray's mood. We see Sir Pitt Crawley's death, for instance, partly as a matter for grief as it seemed to Sir Pitt, partly as a matter for congratulation as it seemed to his heir, but predominantly as a matter for sardonic irony as it seemed to Thackeray.

For irony is the keynote of Thackeray's attitude. Indeed no other was possible to one watching the little victims of "Vanity Fair" at play all heedless of their fate: Thackeray can be dramatic and pathetic and comic and didactic: but pathos, drama, comedy and preaching alike are streaked with the same irony. Captain Costigan is the sort of character Dickens often drew, a jolly, drunken old reprobate. But Dickens would have made him a figure of pure humor: we should have laughed at the things he said because they were funny; in Thackeray we laugh at them for the ironical way in which they expose their speaker. Lady Castlewood's love for her daughter's suitor is a subject that might have attracted Stendhal, but Stendhal would have been concerned to analyze her passion; Thackeray to bring out the ironical situation in which it involves her. If Thackeray is out to expose, the irony is bitter: if to illustrate those domestic affections which he thought the most amiable of human impulses, it is almost dissolved in sentiment. But it is always present—always we are sensible of the unique, Thackerayan irony, owing something sentimental in it to Sterne, something virile to Fielding, but essentially unlike either, warm, lazy, powerful, the irony of the elderly, experienced man surveying from his armchair in the evening of his days his long memories of "Vanity Fair."

His very choice of words is dictated by it. And this brings us to his last distinguishing talent, his style. Thackeray's style is of a piece with the rest of his work. It seems negligent enough, full of colloquialisms and digressions and exclamations and abrupt transitions. But in reality it is a highly conscious affair—with its negligence beautifully adapted to express his prevailing slippered reminiscent mood. Its most colloquial expressions are picked, its easiest rhythms calculated, every chapter, every paragraph works up from a chosen and effective opening to a final telling sentence. And it reaps the reward of its conscientiousness. Its apparent ease makes it flexible enough to cover without awkwardness all the vast variety of mood and incident which Thackeray's subject matter entails, and to pass naturally from one to the other. The writing never, as in the novels of many conscious artists, gets between us and the subject. Most novelists with a deliberate style tend to be a little stiff; Mr. George Moore, for instance, petrifies all emotions equally in the chiseled marble of his sentences. But Thackeray can soar and drop and brood and perorate and weep and laugh with equal ease. His style is at home and as much itself whether broadly laughing at Jos Sedley or glowing to romantic eloquence over the beauty of Beatrix.

For it is eloquent. It has the precision and felicity of the real stylist, the vigilant sense of words that makes the most trifling page living and significant and pleasing. A writer without a style like Trollope is interesting when he is writing about something interesting, flat when he is writing about something flat; his inspiration shows itself only in his matter. But a writer whose inspiration is actually in his style is never wholly flat; nor is Thackeray. And it is style that enables him to do what Trollope could never do, rise to an effect of beauty; the sunset serenity as of a long and stormy day coming to a tranquil end, windless air, fading mellow sky, in which he steeps the last two pages of *Vanity Fair*, that sad passionate meditation over old friends, old days, gone forever, which stirs within him as he contemplates Pendennis' University days, Esmond, home after seven years, watching the candle-light catch Lady Castlewood's fair head as she prays in the unfrequented cathedral, above all Beatrix Esmond descending the stairs in the first flush of her incomparable beauty.

* * *

Yet for all his accomplishment Thackeray is not the most successful Victorian novelist. He is as open to criticism as Dickens, and more damaging criticism. For one thing he is among the writers, like Tennyson, whose executive talent was on a greater scale than his creative inspiration. He can conceive huge structural schemes, but only muster up a sparse band of ideas for them to carry. He can manipulate masses of material, but the masses are all masses of the same thing. Further, though man's vanity and helplessness reveal themselves in every aspect of his life, they are far from being the only things that reveal themselves. And Thackeray thought they were. Nothing can appear on his pages without it has been sifted through the sieve of his moral canon: and some of the largest chunks of human experience do not get through such a sieve at all. There is a large area of experience to which a moral test does not apply; adventure, for instance, romance, mystery, pure humor; these elements of experience have provided the subject matter of a large proportion of the world's best literature; and of some or all of them the other Victorian novelists, Dickens and the Brontës, were full. Even as a moral canon, Thackeray's is a limited one. As we have seen, it admits of no heroic characters; it has no bearing on those larger, subtler problems that face the characters of George Eliot. Dorothea Brooke, thirsting to dedicate herself to a great cause, but unable to find such a cause in the provincial society of Middlemarch; Lydgate, torn between his duty to that scientific research which is his high vocation and the claims of his selfish wife; the order Thackeray imposed so lucidly on life gave no room for such problems. His plots turn on the struggle between selfishness, worldly, self-indulgent or vain, and instinctive honesty, kindness and humility. And they turn on nothing else at all.

Nor is his world so big as it appears at first sight. One is apt to get an impression that a writer who uses a large and crowded canvas commands a greater variety of characters than one who paints on a small scale. But this is not necessarily true; Jane Austen paints on the smallest scale of any novelist of the first order, but she has a very large range of character: for she never repeats her personages. Her virtuous heroines, Anne Elliot, Fanny Price, are not variations on the same theme, they are intrinsically different from each other. But Thackeray, concerned again and again with the same situation and the same motives, repeats his characters again and again. *His* virtuous heroines, Amelia Sedley, Helen Pendennis, Lady Castlewood, are the same people in different costumes. And not his virtuous heroines alone: all his chief characters can be grouped into a few categories. Mrs. Bute Crawley is Mrs. Mackenzie married to a clergyman; how, were they not labeled by different names, should we distinguish the religious hypocrisy of Lady Bareacres from that of Mrs. Hobson Newcome? Each gentle virtuous heroine, Amelia, Helen and Rachel Castlewood, has her heartless, artful Becky or Blanche or Beatrix as counterpart. Again and again the same object of satire is brought up for our scorn, the underbred young man out to cut a dash in society, and ashamed of his humble origin, the hypocrisy of well-to-do evangelicals, the lion-huntress, the decayed beauty. Thackeray's army is a stage army; only put up your opera-glasses and—shadowed by different helmets, led under different banners—you meet the same faces.

Thackeray, too, like all Victorian novelists, is a very uncertain craftsman. In spite of his virtuosity, there were some branches of his craft he never fully mastered or was too lazy to trouble about if he did. In his more conventionally ordered books his hold on structure is very slack; he does not bother to weave the different strands of his theme together, loose ends dangle in the air; no careful revision has cut out the tufts of unnecessary material that have accumulated during the hurry of first writing. And he is almost always too long. With the mellowness of old age he has all its garrulity. He repeats himself. He underlines a point already printed glaringly red; he will bring in five illustrations of a point if anything too obvious on its first appearance. And after that he pauses to point its moral. Thackeray's armchair method brings with its advantages some terrible dangers; he cannot mention that a character is cheated of twopence without stepping forward and explaining to us that things are not always what they seem, that many apparent sheep are really wolves in sheep's clothing, that the love of money is a great temptation, and a hundred other such unheard-of and astonishing truisms; and he repeats them again and again and again. Dickens can be cheap, Trollope can be flat: Thackeray can be worse, Thackeray can be a bore.

It is a distressing fault, but not a fatal one. Tediousness and over-emphasis are faults of presentation; and though faults of presentation may conceal a writer's merits they do not diminish them. The grave accusation that can be brought against Thackeray is that he sometimes errs in conception; and that, where his genius should have shown itself most triumphant, in his conception of character. That insight into human infirmity which is the actuating impulse of his imagination sometimes fails him, that moral order which it was his brilliant achievement to impose on experience, suddenly breaks down. This happens especially when the plot of his story brings him up against an incident involving the delicate question of sexual irregularity. *Pendennis*, for instance, is avowedly an attempt to portray in its true colors the life of a healthy young man susceptible to passion and not more self-controlled than other young men. It is surely improbable that such a character should maintain himself till the age of twenty-nine, in a state of virginity. But he does; and this in spite of considerable temptations to the contrary. Again, Thackeray's "bad" women, Beatrix, Blanche Amory, are, as far as we can gather from their actions, women of pleasure, hard-hearted, but of a fiery sensual temperament. Yet Thackeray represents them as cold as stones, never betraying by word or gesture a glimpse of the animal which is so strong within them.

But it is not only when he ought to be dealing with their sexual weaknesses that Thackeray's grasp on his characters slackens. It can be as surprisingly uncertain when describing characters with no sexual weaknesses at all, his respectable people, above all his respectable women. He is not uncertain about their actual respectability. Indeed he is never more long-winded than when extolling his heroines' virtues. Only when at last he does leave off praising them to depict them in action, his mood seems to change. With ruthless penetration he exposes the meanness and vanity which underlie much of their seeming goodness, so that the reader is left doubtful what he should think of them—is he to believe the praise or the facts?

* * *

It is one of *Vanity Fair*'s many claims to be his masterpiece that, in it, he does not falsify virtue. Amelia, though much the same type as Mrs. Pendennis, is not represented as wholly admirable; and Dobbin, who is so represented, is an honest man genuinely deserving of our respect. But, even in *Vanity Fair* the pressure of his period forced Thackeray to compromise his integrity. Becky, if she is to provide ironical contrast to Amelia, ought to be treated with perfect justice. We should feel her, bad as she is, to possess some virtues denied to Amelia. And so she does, as her character was originally conceived. But Thackeray has not had the nerve to carry out his conception. He seems to fear that he will make us like her so much that we forgive her faults. And thus, in order to restore a moral balance, he endows her with bad qualities foreign to her nature. Fear, conscious or unconscious, of public opinion, has made him run a flaw through his most striking character, and in doing so destroy the consistency of his most brilliantly conceived book.

The truth is—and it is the first truth to be realized in arriving at any estimate of Thackeray's achievement—that he was born in the wrong period. He is the only important Victorian novelist who was. No doubt an age of stricter critical standards would have improved the books of Dickens and Charlotte Brontë; their plots would have been better constructed, their characters truer to actual life. But these would only have been negative improvements; they would not have increased their positive value. For this positive value arises, not from good construction or realistic verisimilitude, but from imaginative force. And for the development of imaginative force no age could have provided more favorable conditions than the Victorian. Thackeray's strength, on the other hand, lies not in imaginative force, but in his power of construction and his insight into the processes of human nature. Moreover, it needs for its full expression an atmosphere of moral tolerance. His genius, in fact, and his age, were always pulling him different ways. And he yielded to the age.

He can hardly be blamed. Only eccentric, unsociable geniuses—Blake, Emily Brontë—can pursue their chosen paths, unaffected by the temper of the time in which they live. And Thackeray's was eminently a sociable genius. None the less, his weakness was disastrous to him. For it meant that he fell into the greatest fault to which an artist is liable, he was false to his central creative inspiration. Dickens writes badly if he writes about the French Revolution or the aristocracy; for they are outside his range. But once he is within it, once he is writing about fantastic London, he never fails. His genius soars up, strong and true, to its perfect fulfillment.

Thackeray never does so fulfill himself. Deliberate artist as he was, he never wrote outside his range; but at its very center, in his keenest penetration of human infirmity, his hand, hampered by the pressure of his period, will sometimes falter, fumble, swerve aside. With the consequence that his achievement, in spite of all its originality, all its technical brilliance, is ultimately—and judged by the very highest standards—dissatisfying. In the midst of Thackeray's subtlest melody, his richest passage of orchestration, there jars on our ears, faintly, a false note.

# G. ARMOUR CRAIG

## On the Style of *Vanity Fair*†

. . . there is still a very material difference of opinion as to the real nature and character of the Measure of Value in this country. My first question, therefore, is, what constitutes this Measure of Value? What is the signification of that word 'a Pound'?

Speech of Sir Robert Peel on the Bank Charter Acts (6 May 1844)

Perhaps I might be a heroine still, but I shall never be a good woman, I know.

Mrs. Gaskell, *Wives and Daughters* (1866)

"Among all our novelists his style is the purest, as to my ears it is also the most harmonious. Sometimes it is disfigured by a slight touch of affectation, by little conceits which smell of the oil;—but the language is always lucid." The judgment is Anthony Trollope's and the lucidity he praises is Thackeray's: "The reader, without labour, knows what he means, and knows all that he means."[1] The judgment has been shared by many, perhaps even by Thackeray himself, for he was vigilant in detecting "fine writing" or "claptraps" in the work of others,[2] and for himself he insisted that "this person writing strives to tell the truth. If there is not that, there is nothing."[3] Yet some reconciling is necessary, for the truth is not always lucid and lucidity may not always be quite true.

There is at any rate a passage in chapter 42 of *Vanity Fair*[4] for Trollope's judgment of which the modern reader—at least this reader—would give a good deal. It describes the life of Jane Osborne keeping house for her father: her sister is now the fashionable Mrs. Frederick Bullock, her brother, disowned by their father for his marriage to Amelia Sedley, has been killed at Waterloo, and Jane now lives in idle spinsterhood in the great glum house in Russell Square.

> It was an awful existence. She had to get up of black winter's mornings to make breakfast for her scowling old father, who would have turned the whole house out of doors if his tea had not been ready at half-past eight. She remained silent opposite to him, listening to the urn hissing, and sitting in tremor while the parent read his paper, and consumed his accustomed portion of muffins and tea. At half-past nine he rose and went to the City, and she was almost free till dinner-time, to make visitations in the kitchen and to scold the servants: to drive abroad and descend upon the tradesmen, who were prodigiously re-

† From Harold C. Martin, ed., *Style in Prose Fiction* (New York: Columbia University Press, 1959), 87–92, 97–103, 105–6, 108–13. 

1. *An Autobiography*, ed. by Frederick Page (London, 1950), p. 244.
2. See, e.g., his review of "A New Spirit Of The Age," *Works—The Oxford Thackeray*, ed. by George Saintsbury (17 vols.; London, 1908), VI, 424; or some advice on "fine writing" in *The Letters and Private Papers of William Makepeace Thackeray*, ed. by Gordon N. Ray (4 vols.; Cambridge, Mass., 1945), II, 192.
3. Preface to *Pendennis*.
4. References are to the Modern Library College Editions reprint (New York, 1950), which is based on the edition of 1864. [Page references in brackets are to this Norton Critical Edition.]

> spectful: to leave her cards and her papa's at the great glum respectable houses of their City friends; or to sit alone in the large drawing-room, expecting visitors; and working at a huge piece of worsted by the fire, on the sopha, hard by the great Iphigenia clock, which ticked and tolled with mournful loudness in the dreary room. The great glass over the mantle-piece, faced by the other great console glass at the opposite end of the room, increased and multiplied between them the brown holland bag in which the chandelier hung; until you saw these brown holland bags fading away in endless perspectives, and this apartment of Miss Osborne's seemed the centre of a system of drawing-rooms. When she removed the cordovan leather from the grand piano, and ventured to play a few notes on it, it sounded with a mournful sadness, startling the dismal echoes of the house. (pp. 441–42) [427]

Thackeray's prose is seldom better than this. The passage comes from a paragraph that comments on the difference between Jane Osborne's life and that of her sister: "One can fancy the pangs" with which Jane regularly read about Mrs. Frederick Bullock in the "Morning Post," particularly the account of her presentation at the Drawing-room. The reader, characteristically, is invited to supply from his own observation the sort of vulgar envy that feeds upon accounts of "Fashionable Reunions" in the newspaper and to look down on Jane Osborne's suffering as no more than the deprivation of the snobbish pleasures of elegant society. The passage begins, then, easily enough: "It was an awful existence." And "awful" is at first simply a colloquial affectation. It becomes something more, however, as we move into the account of Jane's routine and ascend from the tremors of the breakfast table to the solitude of the drawing room with its covered chandelier "fading away in endless perspectives": the conversational pitch turns momentarily solemn with the vision of "this apartment of Miss Osborne's" as "the centre of a system of drawing-rooms"—including perhaps even that most august of all such apartments where her sister has been received. It would be hard to find this an example of the "little conceits which smell of the oil," for even here Thackeray does not lose his customary confidential hold upon the reader. The vision is kept close to us by his usual resource: the opposing mirrors "increased and multiplied between them the brown holland bag in which the chandelier hung; until *you* saw these brown holland bags fading away in endless perspectives." The "you" is no doubt as unobtrusive as an idiom. But it is not inconsistent with Thackeray's constant and fluent address to his reader, an address at its best as easy as idiom. In this very short passage Thackeray has moved from an example of the snobbery he loved to detect to a memorable symbol of the society in which snobbery flourishes. It is a society of endless perspectives, a system of drawing rooms whose center is everywhere, whose circumference is nowhere.

But is this what Thackeray meant? And is it the "all" that he meant? Certainly the symbol is not characteristic—it is indeed unique in *Vanity Fair.* Usually, or at any rate perhaps too often, Thackeray renders the barren routines of high life in mock genealogies or in the kind of mildly allegorical guest list that follows this passage. We are told that twice a month the solitary dinners of Mr. and Miss Osborne are shared with "Old Dr. Gulp and his lady from Bloomsbury Square, . . . old Mr. Frowser the attorney, . . . old Colonel Livermore, . . . old Serjeant Toffy, . . . sometimes old Sir Thomas Coffin." *Vanity Fair,* we recall, began as "Pen and Pencil Sketches of English Society," as an extension of *The Book of Snobs.* Yet Thackeray seems to have felt the need of some larger, more inclusive presiding idea. In the early stages of writing the first few numbers he "ransacked" his brain for another title, and "Vanity Fair," he said, came to him suddenly in the middle of the night.[5] It seems to have summed up for him a position from which he could confidently go on with his "Novel without a Hero," but a position of course very different from John Bunyan's. The original Vanity Fair as described by Evangelist is the dwelling place of abominations. But it is after all only one more obstacle on the road to the Celestial City, and all such obstacles are rewards in disguise. "He that shall die there," says Evangelist, "although his death will be unnatural, and his pain perhaps great, he will yet have the better of his fellow." While there are some unnatural and painful deaths in Thackeray's Fair, there seems to be no act of resistance or sacrifice by which anyone can get the better of anyone else, and the irony of the title has no doubt been lively in the minds of many readers. But Evangelist lays down a more poignantly ironical prescription: "he that will go to the [Celestial] City, and yet not go through this Town [where Vanity Fair is kept], *must* needs *go out of the World.*"[6] If there is no Celestial City beyond Thackeray's Fair, and if there is no hero determined to fight on to a heavenly peak, it is even more certain that none of Thackeray's characters shall go out of this world. On every page of *Vanity Fair* we find description, exposure, comment, from a position much less elevated and secure than that of an evangelist, yet one from which we do see into an "all" as large as a whole society.

* * *

Every reader of *Vanity Fair* remembers the "discovery scene" of chapter 53—the scene in which Becky suffers exposure and isolation after her husband and Lord Steyne violently clash. And every student of the novel knows that this scene is a battleground upon which the judgments of a number of Thackeray's critics have collided. Rawdon, having been freed from the spunging house, hurries "across the streets and the great squares of Vanity Fair," and bursts in upon his wife and Lord Steyne in something less than *flagrante delicto* though ready for embarrassment. [Quotation from p. 533 in this Norton Critical Edition.]

The theatricality of the passage—Becky's clinging and quivering, the serpents and baubles on her hands, Rawdon's springing out and his terse manifesto, the flame in the eyes of the wicked nobleman and the lifelong scar on his head—all such features suggest that the creator of Punch's Prize novelists is once again engaged in something

5. Gordon N. Ray, *Thackeray: The Uses of Adversity: 1811–1846* (New York, 1955), pp. 384–85.
6. *The Pilgrim's Progress* . . . , ed. by Edmund Venables, rev. by Mabel Peacock (Oxford, 1925), pp. 82 ff.

like parody.[7] On the other hand it has been asserted that far from a joke, the scene "is the chief ganglion of the tale; and the discharge of energy from Rawdon's fist [*sic*] is the reward and consolation of the reader."[8] The most extensive criticism of the scene finds it unprepared for and conveyed by a dramatic technique foreign to Thackeray's genius,[9] but this judgment has in turn been disposed of by another critic who finds Thackeray's usual stamp upon it and some other felicities as well. He suggests that one of these is the way in which "Steyne wore the scar" echoes "Steyne wore the star."[1] By the same sort of reasoning we might infer from "He tore the diamond ornament out of her breast" that Becky's heart is surpassing hard; and certainly Thackeray tells us that the battle takes the heart out of her. But the one touch upon which Thackeray himself is known to have commented is Becky's response to the sudden burst of energy from Rawdon: "She stood there trembling before him. She admired her husband, strong, brave, and victorious." Of this observation Thackeray is reported to have said that it was a touch of genius,[2] and it does consort well with his special genius in the rest of the book.

For although the battle seems to be the expression of outraged honor, it is a collision that misses its main issue and prize. As the resistless masses meet, Becky stands off to one side, and although her admiration is unacceptable or even unknown to Rawdon, and although we are told that her life seems so "miserable, lonely, and profitless" after Rawdon has silently departed that she even thinks of suicide, there is still a profound irrelevance in this violent scene. Becky's maid comes upon her in her dejection and asks the question that is in every reader's mind: "*Mon Dieu,* madame, what has happened?" And the "person writing" concludes this crucial chapter with an enlargement of the same question:

> What *had* happened? Was she guilty or not? She said not; but who could tell what was truth which came from those lips; or if that corrupt heart was in this case pure? All her lies and her schemes, all her selfishness and her wiles, all her wit and her genius had come to this bankruptcy. (p. 556) [535]

Becky lies down, the maid goes to the drawing room to gather up the pile of trinkets, and the chapter ends. If Thackeray has not risen to a cruel joke on those readers who find consolation and reward in the discharge of energy from Rawdon, he has at least interrupted their satisfaction.

Lord Steyne's meaning of "guilty"—"He thought a trap had been laid for him" by Becky and Rawdon—is of course quite false, though it corroborates the characterization of Steyne as one experienced in

7. As has been suggested by Kathleen Tillotson, *Novels of the Eighteen-Forties* (Oxford, 1954), pp. 233–34.
8. Robert Louis Stevenson, "A Gossip on Romance," *Memories and Portraits* (New York, 1910), p. 239 (Vol. 17 of the biographical Edition of the *Works*). Stevenson's judgment is endorsed by Professor Ray in *Uses of Adversity*, p. 410.
9. Percy Lubbock, *The Craft of Fiction* (London, 1954), pp. 101 ff. Lubbock's argument has been criticized by Professor Ray (*Uses of Adversity*, pp. 409–10) and by Geoffrey Tillotson, *Thackeray the Novelist* (Cambridge, 1954), pp. 82 ff.
1. G. Tillotson, *Thackeray the Novelist*, p. 84.
2. See Ray, *Uses of Adversity*, p. 500, n. 19; and *Letters and Private Papers*, II, 352*n*.

double-dealing. "Guilty" from Rawdon's point of view of course means, as he tells Pitt next day, that "it was a regular plan between that scoundrel and her" to get him out of the way (chap. 54, p. 559) [538]. And Thackeray goes to as great lengths to make it impossible for us to know that this interpretation is true as he does to conceal the timing and motives of Becky's marriage. To see the entangling and displacing of any clear answer, we need only ask "guilty of what?" The usual answer is of course "guilty of adultery" (or guilty of getting ready for it),[3] and Thackeray's silence is commonly attributed to his awareness of the "squeamishness" of his public. Indeed he himself lends real authority to this account of the matter. In 1840, writing on Fielding, he complains that the world no longer tolerates real satire. "The same vice exists now, only we don't speak about it; the same things are done, but we don't call them by their names."[4] And in *Vanity Fair* he complains that he must be silent about some events in Becky's later career because he must satisfy "the moral world, that has, perhaps, no particular objection to vice, but an insuperable repugnance to hearing vice called by its proper name" (chap. 64, p. 671) [637]. There may well be evidence in Thackeray's personal history to suggest in addition that he was, perhaps even before the separation from his mad wife, evasive and unclear on the subject of sexual behavior. But however complicated the tensions of Thackeray's own emotional experience, and however rigid the scruples of his audience, the answer to the questions with which he comments on this most important episode cannot be a single "name" or possess any "proper name." For he has led us here, however uneasily, with mingled attitudes of parody and outrage, to a startling though incomplete vision of a new social world, a vision exactly proportioned to the irrelevance of the violence we have witnessed.

The words of the passage that command our moral response are precisely those that most nearly approach parody: Becky responds to a nameless "that" in Rawdon's face by exclaiming "I am innocent." If the reader trained in melodrama scoffs at the response and turns Becky into a consummate villain, he will have some trouble getting through the rest of the novel, and it is likely that he will long since have become exasperated with Thackeray's tone, his silences and implications. The same is true, moreover, of the sentimental reader who throws down the volume and declares that Becky has been monstrously wronged and victimized by wicked men in a bad world. But the reader who says, in effect, "it is impossible to tell whether or of what she is guilty" is exactly in the difficult position of one who accepts Thackeray's narrative as it is given. And what such a reader sees from this position must fill him with wonder if not dismay. For he sees that while he wants to answer these questions, he cannot do so, and he can only conclude that he is looking at a situation before which his moral vocabulary is irrelevant. Becky in her isolation has finally gone out of this world, and it will take a new casuistry to bring her back. Thackeray uses some strong moral words in his comment, it is true: "who could tell what was truth which came from those lips;

3. See, e.g., Ray, *Uses of Adversity*, p. 502, n. 14.
4. *Works*, III, 385.

or if that corrupt heart was in this case pure?" But while we know that Becky has lied heartily to Steyne, and to his hearty admiration, we cannot know that she is lying to Rawdon when she insists on her innocence. Whatever corruption we may have seen, the question this time is in earnest. The qualities named in the final statement, and especially by its last word, tell us where we are: "All her lies and her schemes, all her selfishness and her wiles, all her wit and her genius had come to this bankruptcy." For these are the terms not so much of moral as of financial enterprise, and "this bankruptcy" is the real touch of genius in the passage. Thackeray's questions and his comment express neither indignation nor sympathy. Rather, they bring before us the terrible irresolution of a society in which market values and moral values are discontinuous and separate. And Thackeray will not—he can not—support us as we revolt from such a spectacle.

* * *

The first mention of the "guilt" or "innocence" of Becky's relations to Lord Steyne comes in a passage about the "awful kitchen inquisition" of the servants of Vanity Fair. We are told that Raggles, the retired butler of Miss Crawley, who owns the house in Curzon Street where Becky and Rawdon live well on nothing a year, is ruined by his extension of credit to them. But he is the victim of something more than the simple excess of liabilities over assets. The "*Vehmgericht* of the servants'-hall" early pronounces Becky guilty:

> And I shame to say, she would not have got credit had they not believed her to be guilty. It was the sight of the Marquis of Steyne's carriage-lamps at her door, contemplated by Raggles, burning in the blackness of midnight, "that kep him up," as he afterwards said; that, even more than Rebecca's arts and coaxings. (chap. 44, pp. 461–62) [445]

The question of guilt here is quite subordinate to the question of credit, and Raggles is ruined not because he is right about Becky's guilt but because he believes in a strict correlation between Becky's moral and financial status. The last of Raggles is seen at the drunken party of the servants on the morning after the battle; our last glimpse of him is not as he suffers in ruin but as he looks at his fellows "with a wild surprise" upon hearing from Becky that Rawdon "has got a good appointment" (chap. 55, p. 565) [547]. It is no wonder that Thackeray should have said in a letter to his mother written during the very month when the "discovery scene" appeared,

> I cant find the end of the question between property and labour. We want something almost equal to a Divine Person to settle it. I mean if there is ever to be an elucidation of the mystery it is to be solved by a preacher of such novelty and authority, as will awaken and convince mankind—but O how and when?[5]

* * *

In *Vanity Fair* at any rate Becky's bankruptcy offers no clearer connection between villainy—or goodness—and loss of credit than does the situation of Old John Sedley that Osborne so ruthlessly catego-

5. *Letters and Private Papers*, II, 356.

rizes. The thoroughness with which Thackeray has covered his tracks suggests that no single transaction, not even payment by adultery, is at issue here. The kind of credit upon which the Crawleys lived so well in London and Paris is beyond the power of any act or value to overtake, for it is the social version of that system in which the perpetual promise to pay is taken for the perpetual fact of payment. "The truth is, when we say of a gentleman that he lives well on nothing a year, we use the word 'nothing' to signify something unknown" (chap. 36, p. 374) [363]. It may be that Rawdon and Becky are "wicked," but their wickedness will not account for their credit as they pursue the fashionable life. Just as the war that so mysteriously yet inevitably ruined John Sedley was, as Thackeray tells us, a lucky accident interrupting the endless double- and triple-dealing among nations (chap. 28, pp. 279–80) [277], so for Becky an accident interrupts the double-dealing and counter double-dealing of the scramble for social power. The perspectives here are indeed almost endless; they are certainly beyond the limits of innocence or guilt. Even Rawdon, who experiences something like conversion or reform as Becky's career reaches its height, is not quite secure. His one assertion to Becky after the battle is an ironic fulfillment of Steyne's accusation: "You might have spared me a hundred pounds, Becky, out of all this—I have always shared with you" (chap. 53, p. 556) [534].[6] And the last words he speaks in the novel are as ambiguous as any question from the narrator:

> "She has kep money concealed from me these ten years," he said. "She swore, last night only, she had none from Steyne. She knew it was all up, directly I found it. If she's not guilty, Pitt, she's as bad as guilty, and I'll never see her again, never." (chap. 55, p. 579) [555]

It is hardly possible to find the outrage of manly honor in these exactly struck last words. The distinction between "guilty" and "as bad as guilty" would be the final viciousness if it were not the final irrelevance.

But, again, is this what Thackeray means, and is it the *all* that he means? We can believe so only by acknowledging that the easy confidence between reader and writer promised at the beginning has been renounced, for we are here outside the domain of laziness, benevolence, or sarcasm. If the renunciation were the deliberate act of a supreme ironist who turns and rends us for our naive acceptance of his confidential detachment, Thackeray would indeed have created a masterpiece. But in the crucial scene and in portions of the chapters that lead to it Thackeray has exposed us to violent emotions that no politeness can conceal. The enmity between Little Rawdy and Lord Steyne, for example, is an extension of Becky's neglect of her child that erupts into physical violence: Becky boxes his ears for listening to her on the stairs as she entertains Lord Steyne (chap. 44, p. 460) [444]. The child indeed makes his first speaking appearance in the same chapter as that in which Lord Steyne also first appears, grinning "hideously, his little eyes leering towards Rebecca" (chap. 37, p. 389)

6. For a quite different interpretation, see Tillotson, *Novels of the Eighteen-Forties*, pp. 248, 251.

[377]. The juxtaposition is emphasized when little Rawdon is apostrophized:

> O thou poor lonely little benighted boy! Mother is the name for God in the lips and hearts of little children; and here was one who was worshipping a stone. (p. 392) [380]

The appeal is no mere instance of competing with the creator of little Paul Dombey, as everyone who has read Thackeray's letters to his own mother will know. It is an appeal similar to many others in the narrative of Amelia, although there Thackeray is more characteristically reticent. When Amelia and her mother are reunited after her marriage, though Thackeray begins by referring to "How the floodgates were opened," he adds, "Let us respect Amelia and her mamma whispering and whimpering and laughing and crying in the parlour and the twilight." And when Amelia retreats to meditate in "the little room" with its "little white bed" in her old home, Thackeray desists:

> Have we a right to repeat or to overhear her prayers? These, brother, are secrets, and out of the domain of Vanity Fair, in which our story lies. (chap. 26, pp. 262, 264) [259, 262]

Even—especially—if we construe this scene and its secrets as an expression of Amelia's first awareness that she is to be a mother herself, it still involves relationships and sentiments outside the "domain" that Thackeray so thoroughly explored. It is a domain bounded by the "politeness" invoked in that early address to the reader in which the narrator promises "to love and shake by the hand" his "good and kindly" characters, "to laugh confidentially in the reader's sleeve" at the "silly" ones, but "to abuse in the strongest terms that politeness admits of" all those who are "wicked and heartless" (chap. 8, p. 79) [84]. Such terms of abuse for the wicked and love for the good are for the most part so polite that we accept them with all the detachment guaranteed by the Manager of the Performance. But the limits of this detachment—its very bankruptcy—can be shown only as we glimpse the howling wilderness outside, where the secrets of private feelings are violently confused with public forces of huge and mysterious dimensions, and where there is neither lucidity nor truth.

What Thackeray does then exhibit within the domain of the Fair is the impossibility of self-knowledge and, in the fullest sense, dramatic change. The most intimate experiences of the self, whether in prayer or in love, in disappointment or in outrage, must be kept outside. Becky's "I am innocent" is no more an articulation of the truth than it is the lucid exposure of a lie. But to put us where we cannot know "What *had* happened" and to face us with the bewildering irrelevance of our polite detachment, Thackeray was driven to an extreme that no style of his could control. He could not be clear without being untruthful, and he could not be truthful without being obscure. He tried to recover himself, it is true, in the subsequent chapters by returning to the conception of Becky that most saves his book. The most interesting feature of her characterization is not that she begins from the ambiguous social position of the orphan and governess—" 'I don't trust them governesses, Pinner,' says the Sedley housekeeper with enormous assurance, 'they're neither one thing nor t'other. They give themselves the hairs and hupstarts of ladies, and their wages is no better than you nor me' " (chap. 6, p. 60) [63]. Thackeray is concerned with much more than the favorite Victorian example of social mobility. The greater truth about Becky is that she is a mimic, that she trades on the difference between fantasy and society, between the role and the fact. But the truth of endless mimicry is much too large for the domain of the lucid. It is larger than any drawing room, park, or square of Vanity Fair, and it could be forced in only by an act of violence that darkened lucidity and concealed truth. The casuistry upon which *Vanity Fair* rests is unique, and the responses of many thousands of readers for a hundred years to this much-read book must constitute one of the most erratic subterranean currents of our moral history.

# JOHN LOOFBOUROW

## Neo-Classical Conventions†

When in *Vanity Fair* Thackeray fused his early, satiric expressive conventions into an integral narrative form, a new kind of novel was in the making. In earlier fiction, content, form, and style were separate elements; they could be considered individually as subjects in their own right. But in Thackeray's major novels, as in the work of many modern writers, these aspects of fiction are inseparable and the language itself is a creative element. The difference is like the familiar contrast between classic and romantic art.

The classic-romantic antithesis involves a fairly clear distinction between two ways of envisioning the form-style-content relationship—ways that may conveniently be called "illustration" and "expression." In classical or "illustrative" art, it is the writer's subject that is of primary importance; style is only a means of communicating, form a way of organizing, content. The classicist begins by defining his subject; then he selects an appropriate style and plans an effective presentation. In romantic or "expressive" art, the writer's style is part of the content of his work; his words create meaning, and patterns develop in the process—the method is thought of as a continuous act of expression. The antithesis is figurative—in practice no writer can begin without words or continue without a plan. But the disparity implies dissimilar creative methods and the results are as different as Proust from Fielding. So, in the classical, illustrative tradition, Horace's *Ars Poetica* defines style as decorous exposition (*locum teneant sortita decentum*), form as appropriate presentation (*sibi covenientia finge*), and both form and style merely as instruments for conveying rational content (*verbaque provisam rem non invita sequentur*).[1] The

† From *Thackeray and the Form of Fiction* (Princeton: Princeton University Press, 1964), 73–74, 83, 89. © 1964 by Princeton University Press. Reprinted by permision of Princeton University Press.

1. Horace, *Ars Poetica* (Loeb Classical Library Edition), ll. 92, 119, 311.

proto-romantic Longinus, however, considers the expressive medium to be synonymous with the artistic concept ("the expressiveness of the word is the essence of art").[2]

English fiction before Thackeray was in the illustrative tradition. Eighteenth-century writers—Defoe, Smollett, Fielding—equated the novel's subject with rational content; for these novelists, form was identical with plot, an effective arrangement of the narrative materials; and style was an expository or decorative means of communication rather than a creative medium. If Richardson's structures were less controlled, his style less apposite, it was due to technical insufficiency rather than artistic originality, and Sterne is the exception, as he is to all literary rules. Long after the content of the nineteenth-century novel had become "romantic," the illustrative method continued to control the writing of English fiction; the development of new narrative methods does not date from the break between the early romantic poets and the neoclassical tradition. The technique of the novel remained basically unchanged from Fielding to Thackeray.

* * *

In *Vanity Fair*, expressive realization of emotional event is the novel's effective drama, as in the satirical mating of Dobbin and Amelia. *Vanity Fair*'s dramatic "form" depends on allusive continuities—sequences of sentiment and romance—rather than on plot progressions; and these expressive sequences, their entries, their reversals, and their exits, can be graphically visualized in terms of the novel's time-span in such a way as to represent the narrative structure that readers commonly feel in the novel:

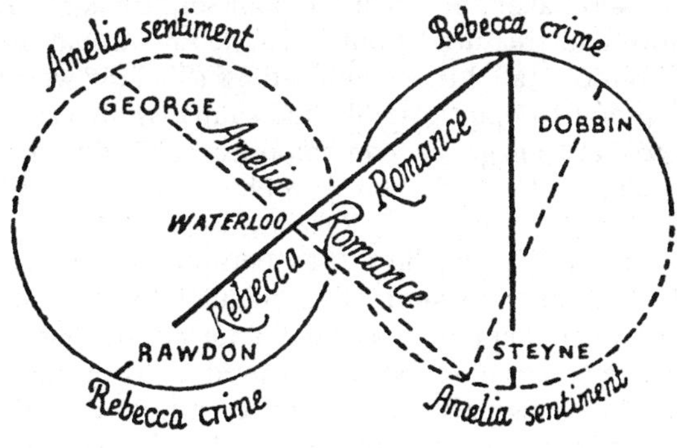


1″ = 265 pp.

These patterns, evolved from expressive continuities, correspond more closely to effective form in *Vanity Fair* than analyses of literal event. The novel's opening scenes are filled with subtle discriminations in fashionable sin and sentiment—Amelia's "*Sehnsucht nach der Liebe*," Rebecca's "Charming Alnaschar visions." At the first intimation of the heroines' future marriages, the arcs of fashionable parody are intersected by opposing tangents of chivalric satire—Amelia's "little tender heart . . . beating, and longing and trusting" to George,

2. Longinus, *Peri Huspos*, l. 3.

Becky's "barbed shaft" quivering in Rawdon's "dull hide."[3] Waterloo, the satiric paradigm of knightly combat, is *Vanity Fair*'s expressive center—a sentimental-chivalric crux: the novel's opposing tangents of romance—Amelia's amorous grail-motifs, Rebecca's magic metaphors—intersect; the heroines' hostilities qualify Amelia's agony, imaged in the blood-red laceration of George's military sash; and Rebecca's victorious visit to her prostrate rival combines picaresque parody (Becky's exploits) with sentimental satire (Amelia's animosity). After the battle, chivalric oppositions are reversed. Rebecca's magical success approaches satirical apotheosis; Amelia's masochism reaches its nadir in the ironies of maternal sacrifice. As Dobbin returns, Amelia's romantic reprieve spans Rebecca's farcical disaster with Steyne; the swift descent of the glittering rogue is crossed by the amorous dove's ascending flight—and the final sequences are suffused with the satirical sentimentality that opened the novel.

*Vanity Fair*'s expressive form is a vast metaphor, an extended figure filled with typifications. If the novel is named from *The Pilgrim's Progress,* its allegory begins in Bunyan's "Town . . . wherein should be sold . . . Lusts, Pleasures, and Delights of all sorts"[4]—"Yes, this is Vanity Fair," the novel's prologue announces, "eating and drinking, making love and jilting . . . not a moral place certainly; nor a merry one, though very noisy." As Thackeray's actors begin to suffer, their subjective world becomes a dramatic scene, and the novel's symbolic psychology revives the *Psychomachia*'s generic image of inner strife—a *bellum intestinum* that C. S. Lewis calls "the root of all allegory":[5] "The combat, which we describe in a sentence or two, lasted for many weeks in poor Amelia's heart . . . one by one the outworks of the little citadel were taken, in which the poor soul passionately guarded her only love and treasure."[6] But if Thackeray's initial metaphor is borrowed from Bunyan, his personifications ("behind whom all there lies a dark moral I hope"),[7] unlike the simple symbolism of *The Pilgrim's Progress,* are images of contemporary subjective complexities. Amelia is Love, but delusive love; Dobbin's Faith and Charity are colored by George's Hypocrisy; Rebecca, a moral reprobate, is also a type of Fun and Truth, the artist's persona personified. Thackeray's "Love" becomes an ambivalent quality when the novel's semi-Shakespearian commentary mocks the amorous ingenue. ("Perhaps some beloved female subscriber has arrayed an ass in the splendour and glory of her imagination . . . and used him as the brilliant fairy Titania did a certain weaver at Athens.")[8] "Of course you are quite right," Thackeray remarks in a letter, "about Vanity Fair and Amelia being selfish. . . . My object is not to make a perfect character or

3. *The Works of William Makepeace Thackeray,* 13 vols. (Biographical Edition) (New York: Harper and Brothers, 1898–99), I, ch. 4, p. 30 [32]; ch. 3, p. 18 [20]; ch. 12, p. 103 [118]; ch. 14, p. 124 [142]. [Page numbers in brackets are to this Norton Critical Edition.]
4. John Bunyan, *The Pilgrim's Progress,* ed. James Blanton Wharey (Oxford: Clarendon Press, 1928), 94.
5. C. S. Lewis, *The Allegory of Love* (London: Oxford University Press, 1936), p. 68.
6. *Works* I, ch. 50, p. 481 [492].
7. *The Letters and Private Papers of William Makepeace Thackeray,* ed. Gordon N. Ray, 4 vols., (Cambridge: Harvard University Press, 1945–46), II, 309.
8. *Works* I, (ch. 13, p. 112 [128]).

anything like it."[9] In certain satirical perspectives the ambiguity is intensified—as when Amelia's pathetic poses are ironically reflected in Rebecca's insincerities. Allegory becomes a comic anti-masque when Amelia and Rebecca are beatified—when Amelia's thoughts, "as if they were angels," try "to peep into the barracks where George was"—"the gates were shut, and the sentry allowed no one to pass; so that the poor little white-robed angel could not hear the songs those young fellows were roaring over the whisky-punch."[1]—and when Rebecca, the students' "Angel Engländerin," sobs out her simulated sufferings at Baden: "it was quite evident from hearing her, that if ever there was a white-robed angel escaped from heaven to be subject to the infernal machinations and villainy of fiends here below, that spotless being—that miserable unsullied martyr, was present on the bed before Jos—on the bed, sitting on the brandy-bottle."[2]

*Vanity Fair*'s recension of the allegory of emotional experience is the beginning of a new kind of fiction that includes such disparate exponents as Meredith, Firbank, and Virginia Woolf; it prepares a medium for such a development as *To the Lighthouse*, where drama is interior, experience subjective, fantasy fused with reality in the symbolism of World War I, as it is at Waterloo in *Vanity Fair*. But, unlike Thackeray, Virginia Woolf forces her war-metaphor to function as an objective as well as an emotional event, sacrificing the imaginative suspension of disbelief that is achieved by Thackeray's displacement of literal incident; the symbolic pattern that is sustained in *Vanity Fair* is discredited in *To the Lighthouse* by the intrusion of the realities it symbolizes.

If *Vanity Fair*'s expressive method revived the techniques and typifications of Sidney, Spenser, and *The Pilgrim's Progress*, its content, like Wagner's orchestration, was a radical polyphony. "I think I see in him an intellect profounder and more unique than his contemporaries have yet recognised," Charlotte Brontë wrote. Thackeray's ability to "scrutinise and expose" seemed to her "prophet-like"—"No commentator on his writings has yet found," she insisted, "the terms which rightly characterise his talent."[3]

An aspect of this insight was Thackeray's expressive representation of psychological relativity ("after looking into a microscope how infinite littleness even is"). The glittering allusive tangents of his prose reflected a sustained ambivalent logic—a recognition of the range of possible relationships: "O philosophic reader . . . a distinct universe walks about under your hat and mine—all things are different to each—the woman we look at has not the same features, the dish we eat from has not the same taste to the one and the other—you and I are but a pair of infinite isolations, with some fellow-islands a little more or less near to us."[4] In *Vanity Fair*, perceptions like these fuse bits of human anomaly and fragments of shattered idealisms into ec-

9. *Letters* II, 309 (July 2, 1847, to Mrs. Carmichael Smyth).
1. *Works* I, ch. 13, p. 111 [127].
2. Ibid., ch. 65, p. 642 [655].
3. Charlotte Brontë, *Jane Eyre* (preface to the second edition).
4. *Works* II, ch. 15, p. 143 [3].

centric images of psychological truth. "In the passage where Amelia is represented as trying to separate herself from the boy," Thackeray wrote to the critic for *Fraser's Magazine*, " 'as that poor Lady Jane Grey tried the axe that was to separate her slender life' I say that is a fine image whoever wrote it . . . it leaves you to make your own sad pictures."[5] In this sequence, the mother's suffering is mirrored in images that reflect the whole range of her sentimental neurosis—her personified denial of reality and defeat by truth, her chivalric fetishism, her amorous idolatry. The episode is conceived in several dimensions—the mother's possessiveness, her jealousy of the boy's aunt, her obsessive image of George, the child's ironic indifference—"terror is haunting her . . . George's picture and dearest memory. . . . The child must go from her—to others—to forget her. Her heart and her treasure—her joy, hope, love, worship—her God, almost! . . . The mother had not been so well pleased, perhaps, had the rival been better looking . . . preparing him for the change . . . He was longing for it."[6]

Amelia's compulsive fantasies—"her God, almost!"—anticipating religious ironies in the novel's final love-scene, discredit the Victorian image of romantic maternity; and the allegory of Vanity Fair is largely concerned with revealing such emotional compulsions in the elements of accepted conventions. George Henry Lewes, who could accept George Eliot's ambiguities, found Thackeray's too unpleasant ("in *Vanity Fair* . . . how little there is to love") and protested the inclusion of that "detestable passage," rephrased in the prologue to *Esmond*, "wherein [the author] adds from himself this remark:—'And who knows but Rebecca was right in her speculations—and that it was only a question of money and fortune which made the difference between her and an honest woman? . . . An alderman . . . will not step out of his carriage to steal . . . *but put him to starve, and see if he will not purloin a loaf.*' [Lewes' italics] Was it carelessness, or deep misanthropy, distorting an otherwise clear judgment, which allowed such a remark to fall?"[7]

The passage is not personal observation; it is commentary—the rigorous recognition of the relativity of human values that typifies the novel's method. In *Vanity Fair*, the Commentator is a dimension of dissent—"I wonder is it because men are cowards in heart that they admire bravery so much"? " 'Was Rebecca guilty or not?' The Vehmgericht of the servants' hall had pronounced against her"[8]—and, instead of solving dilemmas, asks questions unanswered in the silence at the end: "Ah! *Vanitas, Vanitatum!* which of us is happy in this world? Which of us has his desire? or, having it, is satisfied?" To the *Times'* critic, Thackeray wrote "I want to leave everybody dissatisfied and unhappy at the end"—an image of reality "in that may-be cracked and warped looking glass in which I am always looking."[9]

* * *

5. *Letters* II, 424 (September 3, 1848, to Robert Bell).
6. *Works* I, ch. 50, pp. 480–85 [492].
7. G. H. Lewes, *Morning Chronicle*, March 6, 1848.
8. *Works* I, ch. 30, p. 285 [301]; ch. 44, p. 432 [445].
9. *Letters* II, 423–24.

# PETER K. GARRETT†

## [Dialogic Form]

For Thackeray it might be appropriate to begin with his endings, which tend to dramatize not the inclusive power of narrative but its arbitrariness and inadequacy. Contemplating the New Palace of Westminster, Thackeray "declared he saw no reason why it stopped; it ended nowhere, and might just as well have gone on to Chelsea."[1] Some contemporary critics perceived the same formal problem in Thackeray's own works: "His conception of a story . . . is incomplete. There is no reason why he should begin where he does, no reason why he should end at all."[2] Modern readers are more likely to praise the realism of such "incompleteness,"[3] but this revaluation of what is perceived as formal looseness fails to confront the more general problem of form in Thackeray. We shall be concerned at several points with moments in his novels that blur the outlines of narrative form: uncertain or multiple beginnings, displaced or muffled climaxes, inconclusive or ironically conventional endings; but these are only more dramatic instances of the way forms ranging from conventions of social behavior to underlying conceptual structures of thought are continually placed in question by Thackeray's fiction.

Thackeray and Dickens share a strong sense of conventional patterns, types, and forms, but Dickens' symbolic imagination tends to work through inherited forms like the mystery plot, intensifying and reinterpreting them, while Thackeray works against them, resisting their arbitrariness and attempting to displace and discredit them in his effort to reveal a truth they obscure.

* * *

*Vanity Fair* is a less intimate novel than Thackeray's later works. It does not ask us to become so closely and continuously involved in its characters' experiences as we do in those of Pendennis, Henry Esmond, or Clive and Ethel Newcome. Of all Thackeray's novels it best exemplifies that "panoramic method" which he represented for Percy Lubbock,[4] the detached, broad survey of space and time that refuses to be confined to a single perspective or line of development, and of all his novels it most fully exploits the compositional possibilities of multiple narrative. In such a work there would seem to be little direct application for those preliminary notions of experience and its mediations we have derived from *Pendennis.* But in turning back to *Vanity Fair* we can recognize not only the same pattern of

† From *The Victorian Multiplot Novel: Studies in Dialogical Form* by Peter K. Garrett (New Haven: Yale University Press, 1980), 95–96, 104–110. Reprinted by permission of the author.

1. Gordon N. Ray, *Thackeray: The Age of Wisdom* (New York: McGraw-Hill, 1958), p. 331.
2. W. C. Roscoe, in *National Review,* January 1856, reprinted in *Thackeray: The Critical Heritage,* ed. Geoffrey Tillotson and Donald Hawes (London: Routledge, 1968), p. 271. Tillotson considers Roscoe the best of Thackeray's Victorian critics. [See, however, Tillotson's rejection of Roscoe, p. 731 above. Ed.] See also R. S. Rintoul on the arbitrariness of the ending of *Pendennis, Spectator,* 21 (July 22, 1848), pp. 99–100.
3. For example, Geoffrey Tillotson, who praises "the bufferless endings of the novels. . . . Thackeray designed them to be loose so that they represent life more truthfully." *Thackeray the Novelist* (Cambridge: Cambridge University Press, 1954), p. 173.
4. *The Craft of Fiction* (1921; rpt. New York: Viking, 1957), pp. 93–109.

relationship between the narrator and his narrative but the same terms for representing it. Consider the late, minor scene which occurs during the excursion to Pumpernickel, where, the narrator informs us, "I first saw Colonel Dobbin and his party" at the table d'hôte of the Erbprinz Hotel. Later that evening, he sees them again:

> It was what they call a *gast-rolle* night at the Royal Grand Ducal Pumpernickelisch Hof,—or Court theatre: and Madame Schroeder Devrient, then in the bloom of her beauty and genius, performed the part of the heroine in the wonderful opera of Fidelio. From our places in the stalls we could see our four friends of the *table d'hôte*, in the loge which Schwendler of the Erbprinz kept for his best guests: and I could not help remarking the effect which the magnificent actress and music produced upon Mrs. Osborne, for so we had heard the stout gentleman in the mustachios call her. During the astonishing Chorus of the Prisoners over which the delightful voice of the actress rose and soared in the most ravishing harmony, the English lady's face wore such an expression of wonder and delight that it struck even little Fipps, the *blasé* attaché, who drawled out, as he fixed his glass upon her, "Gayd, it really does one good to see a woman caypable of that stayt of excaytement." And in the Prison Scene where Fidelio, rushing to her husband, cries "Nichts nichts mein Florestan," she fairly lost herself and covered her face with her handkerchief. Every woman in the house was snivelling at the time: but I suppose it was because it was predestined that I was to write this particular lady's memoirs, that I remarked her. (62)[5]

The immediate function of the scene is to illustrate this stage of Amelia's experience: "I like to dwell on this period of her life," the narrator has just explained, "and to think that she was cheerful and happy," and he goes on to remark of both Amelia and Dobbin, "perhaps it was the happiest time of both their lives indeed, if they did but know it—and who does? Which of us can point out and say that was the culmination—that was the summit of human joy?" The ability to perceive such a pattern is of course developed only in retrospect, but here Thackeray characteristically superimposes that more distant, superior vision on the immediate moment. This undramatic episode is the actual "culmination" for this couple, not, as required by conventional form, their later, tearful reunion on the pier at Ostend: "Here it is," the narrator ironically exclaims, "the summit, the end —the last page of the third volume" (67).

Amelia and Dobbin's idyll at Pumpernickel is thus set in the context of their previous trials and subsequent anticlimax, and it is here that "Thackeray" first encounters his characters and learns their story: "It was on this very tour that I, the present writer of a history of which every word is true, had the pleasure to see them first, and to make their acquaintance." The scene at the theatre, he affirms only half-jokingly, is thus located at the origin of the entire narrative,

5. [The numbers in parentheses in this essay are chapter numbers. Garrett did not identify his source text.]

and we recognize that its pattern of doubled response is an emblem of mediated feeling, in which Amelia becomes the surrogate for more detached observers like the narrator.

If we consider the relation between Amelia and the writer of her "memoirs" which is presented here as the "original" relation between the narrator and characters of *Vanity Fair,* we postulate a narrative whose figures function first of all as registers of experience, instruments for establishing a characteristic relation to the world. This is admittedly an unfamiliar way of describing *Vanity Fair.* It seems more easily applicable to a novel by Henry James, where the characters' inner lives are much more fully developed and there is less discrepancy between their level of consciousness and the narrator's. But the paradox of a narrative which aims to recreate experience that is never directly available is, as our brief consideration of *Pendennis* has suggested, a major constituent of Thackeray's fiction. In *Vanity Fair,* where his irony more clearly reflects on his own authorial activity, we can explore that paradox further. At this point, let us simply note the implications of the theatre scene, which stresses the process of mediation and subordinates the questions of moral judgment that usually preoccupy critical discussion of the novel. We can return to the way the characters register experience after examining the novel's narrative perspectives and developmental structure.

The account of "Thackeray" as a friend of the characters and witness to their experiences is, of course, only one of many authorial images in *Vanity Fair* and stands opposed to the figure of the showman who manipulates his puppets while subjecting them to a constant stream of commentary. Thackeray's shifting narrative stances serve the rhetorical purpose of controlling distance, but they also cast an ironic perspective on the act of narration itself, exposing the problematic process of mediation which conditions all knowledge and evaluation of the fictional world. The possibility of a multiple narrative rests, as we have seen in Dickens, on the convention of narrative omniscience, which permits the shift of focus between concurrent actions. Thackeray frequently exploits this power, as in the famous juxtaposition which concludes chapter 32: "Darkness came down on the field and city: and Amelia was praying for George, who was lying on his face, dead, with a bullet through his heart." The repeated presentation of simultaneous actions creates an awareness that any given event or sequence is only part of a larger pattern and creates an expectation that it will be correlated with others, an expectation on which the narrator can in turn play: "In the autumn evenings (when Rebecca was flaunting at Paris, the gayest among the gay conquerors there, and our Amelia, our dear wounded Amelia, ah! where was she?) Lady Jane would be sitting in Miss Crawley's drawing-room singing sweetly to her" (34).

Yet for all the novel's heavy reliance on this convention, the narrator repeatedly reminds us that it *is* a convention ("novelists have the privilege of knowing everything" [3]) and that his ability to reveal the separate, hidden lives of his characters depends on the assumption of a fictive role:

> I know where [Amelia] kept that packet she had—and can steal in and out of her chamber like Iachimo—like Iachimo? No—that is a bad part. I will only act Moonshine, and peep harmless into the bed where faith and beauty and innocence lie dreaming. (12)

> If, a few pages back, the present writer claimed the privilege of peeping into Miss Amelia Sedley's bed-room, and understanding with the omniscience of the novelist all the gentle pains and passions which were tossing upon that innocent pillow, why should he not declare himself to be Rebecca's confidante too, master of her secrets, and seal-keeper of that young woman's conscience? (15)

Furthermore, the claim to omniscience may just as easily be withdrawn, leaving the narrator uncertain ("My belief is . . ." [16]) or unable to decide on the correct version: "But who can tell you the real truth of the matter?" (2). Later, lacking entrée to the aristocratic world of Gaunt House, he must rely on the reports of "little Tom Eaves" (47), and eventually we are told that much of the novel has been derived from Tapeworm, the Secretary of Legation at Pumpernickel, "who of course knew all the London gossip, and was besides a relative of Lady Gaunt," and who, in response to Dobbin's questions, "poured out into the astonished Major's ears such a history about Becky and her husband as astonished the querist, and supplied all the points of this narrative, for it was at that very table years ago that the present writer had the pleasure of hearing the tale" (66).

The doubtful authenticity of such information is matched by the doubtful authority of the narrator as moral commentator. The general moral perspective imposed by the title is enforced by numerous reflections on the vanity of the world and its distorted values, and "Thackeray" appears to strengthen his criticism by disowning any moral superiority, admitting his own implication in these errors: he is the preacher in cap and bells addressing his "brother wearers of motley." But the more he tries to define his position in relation to his story and audience, the more deeply compromised he becomes:

> I have heard a brother of the story-telling trade, at Naples, preaching to a pack of good-for-nothing honest lazy fellows by the sea-shore, work himself up into such a rage and passion with some of his villains whose wicked deeds he was describing and inventing, that the audience could not resist it, and they and the poet together would burst out into a roar of oaths and execrations against the fictitious monster of the tale, so that the hat went round, and the bajocchi tumbled into it, in the midst of a perfect storm of sympathy.
>
> At the little Paris theatres, on the other hand, you will not only hear the people yelling out, "*Ah gredin! Ah monstre!*" and cursing the tyrant of the play from the boxes; but the actors themselves positively refuse to play the wicked parts, such as those of *infâmes Anglais,* brutal Cossacks, and what not, and prefer to appear at a smaller salary, in their real characters as loyal Frenchmen. I set the two stories one against the other, so that you may see that it is not from mere mercenary motives that the present performer

> is desirous to show up and trounce his villains; but because he has a sincere hatred of them, which he cannot keep down, and which must find a vent in suitable abuse and bad language.
>
> I warn my "kyind friends," then, that I am going to tell a story of harrowing villany and complicated—but, as I trust, intensely interesting—crime. My rascals are no milk-and-water rascals, I promise you. When we come to the proper places we won't spare fine language—No, no!. . . .
>
> And, as we bring our characters forward, I will ask leave, as a man and a brother, not only to introduce them, but occasionally to step down from the platform, and talk about them: if they are good and kindly, to love them and shake them by the hand; if they are silly, to laugh at them confidentially in the reader's sleeve: if they are wicked and heartless, to abuse them in the strongest terms which politeness admits of.
>
> Otherwise you might fancy it was I who was sneering at the practice of devotion, which Miss Sharp finds so ridiculous; that it was I who laughed good-humouredly at the reeling old Silenus of a baronet—whereas the laughter comes from one who has no reverence except for prosperity, and no eye for anything beyond success. Such people there are living and flourishing in the world—Faithless, Hopeless, Charityless: let us have at them, dear friends, with might and main. Some there are, and very successful too, mere quacks and fools: and it was to combat and expose such as those, no doubt, that Laughter was made. (8)

The two juxtaposed stories hardly demonstrate the narrator's high motives or moral rectitude. Instead, emerging from a confusion of fictive and "real characters," of commercial and religious values, the claim of "sincere hatred" for vice seems no less an assumed role than the expression at other points of cynical worldly wisdom, where " 'I' is . . . introduced to personify the world in general" (36). Irony infects every moral stance the narrator and his audience may adopt, whether he offers them the pleasures of righteous condemnation ("let us have at them") or of tolerant acquiescence: "It is all vanity, to be sure, but who will not own to liking a little of it?" (51).

As a result, every comment or interpretation which the narrator introduces can exert only conditional authority. His formulations raise but cannot resolve the novel's issues; they must be tested against the implications of the narrative as a whole. A brief example, in which Thackeray again sets two stories "one against the other" may be found in chapter 61, "In Which Two Light Are Put Out," presenting the deaths of the two old merchants, Sedley and Osborne. The chapter opens with the well-known meditation on the "second-floor arch," in which that detail of Victorian domestic architecture becomes "a memento of Life, Death, and Vanity," and these general reflections on the common fate soon modulate into more pointed remarks (with glances at the story of Dives and Lazarus) on the best state of mind and worldly condition in which to meet death: "Which, I wonder, brother reader, is the better lot, to die prosperous and famous, or poor and disappointed?" Sedley exemplifies the latter; having become reconciled to his daughter during his final illness, the old bankrupt dies a humble penitent.

The shift of focus to his prosperous enemy Osborne strengthens our expectation that the narrative will now fulfill the illustration of the narrator's general moral contrast:

> "You see," said old Osborne to George, "what comes of merit and industry, and judicious speculations, and that. Look at me and my banker's account. Look at your poor grandfather, Sedley, and his failure. And yet he was a better man than I was, this day twenty years—a better man I should say by ten thousand pound."

But in the following account of Osborne's last days, the simple opposition breaks down. He comes to recognize the virtues of Dobbin, whom he has scorned and avoided since George's marriage, and becomes reconciled with him: " 'Major D.,' Mr. Osborne said, looking hard at him, and turning very red too—'You did me a great injury [inducing George to marry Amelia]; but give me leave to tell you, you are an honest feller. There's my hand, sir.' " Through Dobbin's advocacy, he also becomes reconciled with Amelia and leaves her an annuity in his will. As this old tyrant softens and attempts to make restitution at the end, his story becomes more parallel than opposed to Sedley's. In this complication of the schematic opposition which the narrator has formulated we may find an effect of "realism" (life does not conform to abstract patterns), or we may see instead the substitution of one pattern for another, stressing our common humanity instead of separating sheep and goats. We may even consider this shift in purely formal terms as the modification of illustrative functions by plot functions, since Osborne's will not only provides for Amelia's independence but informs her of her great debt to Dobbin. In any case, the episode shows how the significance of Thackeray's narrative emerges only from the play of all its elements against each other, and it also illustrates the tendency which most often directs that play, the decomposition of stylized antitheses.

We can observe this process not only on the scale of circumscribed episodes but in the developmental structure of the entire novel, which is also, of course, essentially composed of two stories set against each other, the careers of Amelia and Becky. By this doubling Thackeray made *Vanity Fair* "A Novel without a Hero," not only in its ironic refusal to embody moral ideals (Pendennis, as his biographer repeatedly reminds us, is also "not a hero" in this sense), but more fundamentally in its lack of a center. Its meaning is produced by the relation between its narrative lines, and that relation is always changing, like the narrator's shifting roles and stances. The absence of a single compositional center or perspective thrusts the problem of formal and thematic coherence into unusual prominence, so that the question of whether and how the separate narratives are to be connected becomes an active concern for the reader as well as the author.

* * *

# RICHARD BARICKMAN, SUSAN MACDONALD, AND MYRA STARK

## [Politics of Sexuality]†

* * *

*Vanity Fair* makes it clear that the characters' basic psychological natures are inseparable from the corrupt social world they inhabit. There is no cloister from vulgarity here, no way after the crass sensuality of old Sir Pitt, the sneering brutality of the Marquis of Steyne, and the unwitting collaboration of even the sensitive and generous Dobbin with the prevailing forces of the sexual marketplace, to make any valid distinction between refinement and vulgarity. That Vanity Fair is primarily a place where sexual wares are sold—either openly as Old Osborne attempts to do in his lust to secure the money of Miss Swartz or more subtly as Becky does in her various intrigues—becomes abundantly clear in the novel. The pursuit of money, place, security, power always comes down, in the novel's development of plot and theme, to fundamental sexual issues.

The detached, reflective consciousness, which husbands its emotions and lets them play only over the secure and restricted field of remembered experience, making a gentle erotic disillusionment a means of furthering illusions, simply has no place in this novel. The one figure who attempts to live in this mode, Dobbin, is first made to subserve the interests of his antithesis, George Osborne, and then literally exiled from the novel's main action. And even Dobbin's moment of real power and insight in the novel—like Rawdon Crawley's—comes when he sees the shoddiness of the woman he has idolized. By that point the novel has fully exposed the spuriousness of the masculine ideals that have created the modes in which both Amelia and Becky operate, so that the real shoddiness is in the ideals themselves, not in the women who embody them.

The world *Vanity Fair* reveals is defined by its social operations. The privacy of self-reflection can be fruitful only as a defensive measure or an effort to prepare for some pending social conflict; real self-knowledge can never be gained. Sustained states of reflection rather than action are regularly described as metaphoric death or paralysis; this is true for Amelia's self-lacerating agonies of rejected love, for Dobbin's more stoic suffering, for Jane Osborne's submission to her father, for the ruined Sedley's broodings on his misfortune, and for Old Osborne's bitter grief at the banishment and death of his son. The novel comes close to suggesting that acute consciousness, in the social world that is the novel's subject, can only be a weakness. The only sort that works to advantage is Becky's sort, an intelligence deliberately limited to self-serving stratagems in the sexual battle that defines the society's preoccupations.

Because the novel's male characters are so overpowered by their

† From *Corrupt Relations: Dickens, Thackeray, Trollope, Collins, and the Victorian Sexual System* (New York: Columbia University Press, 1982), 173–93. 

conscious and unconscious emotional lives (emotions that invariably center on sexual role and sexual power), only female characters can exercise the kind of calculating intelligence that Becky supremely exhibits. This inversion of the traditional stereotype is exemplified by a host of seemingly ill-sorted male characters: Old Osborne, Steyne, Old Sir Pitt, Bute Crawley, George Osborne, Dobbin, Jos Sedley, by every important male character in the novel. While Becky is unsurpassed in her control over her emotional life, she does have some female counterparts: Mrs. Bute Crawley, Miss Crawley, Lady Jane Crawley, and even Miss Pinkerton. Ironically, though, this greater feminine power over emotions comes about through a severing of personal desires from pragmatic intelligence. It starts by relinquishing the hope of sexual fulfillment and the urge for direct control over personal circumstances that the male characters still seek. It implicitly acknowledges and accepts the role of an inferior, a flatterer, a servant to the desires of men. Becky as a child performing before her father and his Bohemian friends, learning to be on stage at all times, succeeding through cynical mimicry of the social world about her, learns a valuable lesson: the one lesson that allows a woman in the novel to keep some independent power to herself. As much as Esther Summerson, though, Becky gains power through relinquishing personal desires and a search for personal identity.

What sustains Becky, for a long while at least, is the exuberance of her own spirit, her ability to take the vicious sexual game as, nevertheless, a game to be played for all it is worth. She pushes a dependent's, a caterer's, and flatterer's power about as far as it can be pushed. To sustain the game she must move from man to man, eluding the efforts of each one to confine her. And so the young Reverend Crisp (briefly) replaces her father in her first effort to become the puppeteer rather than the puppet; he is replaced by Jos Sedley, then Rawdon (and his father), George, Major Tufto, the Marquis of Styne, and a series of male escorts in the gambling centers of Europe.

She overplays her game with Steyne, as she must overplay it with someone eventually. The inevitability of her defeat is not the result of her greed or arrogance but is built into the game; sooner or later she must submit to the real power that underlies the sexual appearances that she manipulates so adroitly. However little satisfaction this ultimate power brings to the patriarchal figures like Steyne and Osborne who chiefly wield it in the novel, it is theirs to exercise. So Becky must either submit to Steyne's desires—and the desire for sadistic power is stronger than his physical lust, as his treatment of the women in his own family makes clear—or she must move on. Not only is she weary of such a profitless game by this point, near despair at times, the narrator tells us, but she sees no place to go if she refuses Steyne. In terms of the conscious desires she has for social position, for security, even for respectability, he has the power to make her a social outcast even as he has the power to force his wife and daughter-in-law and mother to invite her to Gaunt House. Her "rescue" from this dilemma ironically will plunge her into a still more despairing and openly sordid round of the same sordid game. And, in another irony, the rescue comes through a momentary resurgence of a stereotypic masculine display of physical courage and outraged sexual honor that seems almost wholesome by comparison with the masculine modes of behavior that dominate *Vanity Fair.*

As A. E. Dyson has said of the celebrated question of Becky's guilt or innocence in the Steyne affair: "What Thackeray comes near to suggesting, like Bunyan before him, is that a society based upon privilege and money is rotten in some fundamental sense. The very concepts of Christian morality become, in such a context, an evasion; an attempt to visit upon the underprivileged and unprotected the sins which more properly belong to the society at large." G. Armour Craig agrees substantially with this assessment: the reader's "moral vocabulary is irrelevant" because the novel presents "a society in which market values and moral values are discontinuous and separate."[1]

Dyson and Craig, like most other critics of *Vanity Fair,* recognize that the social world of the novel is not a "sector" of society like the isolated military, political, literary, academic, and variously genteel circles that appear in Thackeray's other novels. It is emblematic of the entire culture, as the allusions to Bunyan and *Ecclesiastes* imply, and the narrator's sweeping condemnations make explicit. The novel is primarily concerned with people who are scrabbling to gain money and status because they epitomize the forces that are taking over the culture. The ruin of Raggles, the former butler of Lady Crawley, by the Rawdon Crawleys' practice of living on nothing a year is an emblem of this spread of corruption. At the other end of the class spectrum, the Marquis of Steyne is himself drawn into Becky's world and overpowered by it for all his personal and class presumptions. The precariously genteel world of Becky, Rawdon, the Sedleys, and the Osbornes holds the novel's focus because it is the unstable center of change; it subjects the traditional values of the whole culture to a crucial test.

Yet the fundamental rottenness that is exposed, the fundamental values that are tested, are not primarily matters of class privilege or the depredations of a market economy but issues of sexual values and sexual abuses. Dyson is quite right that "Becky *belongs* to Vanity Fair, both as its true reflection, and as its victim; for both of which reasons, she very resoundingly serves it right."[2] But shrewd as this observation is, it does not go far enough. What Becky epitomizes, above all, is the workings of the sexual marketplace. Her power and her methods are based upon her sexuality; her intelligence, resourceful imagination, exuberance, courage, and persistence are all subordinated to sexual pursuits.

As Becky gains more of the externals which are the object of her conscious desires—material luxury, status, the fashionable diversions of balls and suppers, even the appearance of respectability—she becomes less and less satisfied. They are not really what she is after:

1. A. E. Dyson, "*Vanity Fair*: An Irony Against Heroes," in *The Crazy Fabric: Essays in Irony* (London: Macmillan, 1965), p. 85; G. Armour Craig, "On the Style of *Vanity Fair,*" in *Style in Prose Fiction: English Institute Essays,* ed. Harold C. Martin (New York: Columbia University Press, 1958), p. 66.
2. Dyson, "*Vanity Fair,*" p. 81.

> the poor woman herself was yawning in spirit. "I wish I were out of it," she said to herself. "I would rather be a parson's wife, and teach a Sunday school than this; or a sergeant's lady, and ride in the regimental waggon; or, O how much gayer it would be to wear spangles and trousers, and dance before a booth at a fair."
> (II, xvi, 189) [503–4][3]

Becky, of course, would soon grow bored with any of those roles, any roles the society allows her to play; she is no more committed to these idle fantasies than she is to the idea that she could be happy in a country estate with £5,000 a year.

But the passage reveals something essential about her desires and the reasons they are inevitably frustrated, for all her tone of idle whimsy. Becky cannot conceive a life for herself apart from a man, and in a social role subordinate to him. She has danced to men's desires since she was a child ("she had never been a girl, she said; she had been a woman since she was eight years old"; I, ii, 14 [12]); she will do so until she dies. As the novel pursues the implications of her career, she becomes more and more haggard until finally "there [is] a period in Mrs. Becky's life, when she [is] seized, not by remorse, but by a kind of despair" (II, xxix, 365 [638]). In the last pose she assumes in the novel, she has retreated from explicit sexual encounters to the female stereotype that forms the life of Rachel Esmond and Helen Pendennis, the pious lady of charitable works.

It is surely significant that Thackeray has founded his exposure of social corruption on the careers of two women. As they move toward opposite extremes, Becky and Amelia establish the limits for women's experience in *Vanity Fair.* And, more than this, they set the terms for the whole novel. Their careers dominate plot and thematic development in a way that is unique in Thackeray's fiction, for female or male characters.[4] Through the symbolic opposition of the careers of Becky and Amelia, Thackeray exposes a crisis common to all the various social practices and personal relations in the novel.

It is understandable that many readers have taken money, materialism—or the mechanism for the rapid spread of materialism, a credit economy—as the central target of *Vanity Fair*'s satire. Money is what Becky thinks she is after, certainly what she hoards; money disputes precipitate the break between George and his father; money causes the Sedleys to lose their whole world of social relations; and money gives Jos whatever status he has. But in all the major economic dealings of the novel, sexual forces are the real determinants of the action and the deepest source of characters' motivation.

The chief representative of brutal economic power in the novel, that self-made man who has made himself into a virtual Mammon, demonstrates the way that sexual conflicts fuel all apparent economic conflicts. We never see Osborne on the Stock Exchange; all his dealings come down to one project, his effort to buy a wife for George. His attempt to bribe George into marrying Miss Swartz, his default

3. [*The Works of Thackeray* (Centenary Biographical Edition), 23 vols. (London: Smith, Elder, 1910–11). Page numbers in brackets are to this Norton Critical Edition.]
4. John Loofbourow discusses (and graphs) this dominance of the plot by the two heroines in *Thackeray and the Form of Fiction* (Princeton: Princeton University Press, 1964), pp. 80–84.

on the marriage contract with the Sedleys, and finally his disinheriting of George are all consequences of this initial project. Even his effort to buy gentility for his son, through schooling and an army commission, is part of a struggle to force his patriarchal will on the entire family. (The blatantly symbolic ornamental clock, depicting the sacrifice of Iphigenia by Agamemnon, that ticks away in the Osborne dining room suits the crassness and violence of Osborne's desires; and it stresses just how much his character is involved in the sacrifice of women to his own desires, first his wife, then Amelia, then Miss Swartz, then his daughter, and finally Amelia again, as he uses his money to blackmail her into giving up Georgy to him.) None of these transactions fulfills his desires though; he is psychologically memorable for his scenes of rage and smouldering violence, both expressing the frustration of desire.

Osborne becomes part of an analogical set in the novel, a group of raging, frustrated old men that includes Sir Pitt, Steyne, and Major Tufto and thus incorporates the novel's chief patriarchs. Their economic power and social status, their own arrogant assumptions that they can dispose of the lives of others at will, are all frustrated by their inability to achieve their sexual desires. Sexual desires encompass, in this novel's searching view of an essentially modern society, the desire to control a son's or daughter's sexual life and the desire to humiliate a wife as well as the more obvious lusts of a Sir Pitt.

In a virtual fusion of Sir Pitt and Old Osborne, the novel produces a third imperious and frustrated patriarch, Lord Steyne. The characterization of Steyne reveals how multiple sexual forces inform what at first seems to be simple lechery. Steyne's sadistic intimidation of his wife and daughters-in-law, in a scene unmatched for brutality in the novel, reveals a desire for power that is regularly expressed through control and humiliation of women:

> "Who are you to give orders here? [he says to Lady Gaunt] You have no money. You've got no brains. You were here to have children, and you have not had any. Gaunt's tired of you; and George's wife is the only person in the family who doesn't wish you were dead. Gaunt would marry again if you were." . . . "You may strike me if you like, sir, or hit any cruel blow," Lady Gaunt said. To see his wife and daughter suffering always put his Lordship into a good humour.
>
> "My sweet Blanche," he said, "I am a gentleman, and never lay my hand upon a woman, save in the way of kindness."
>
> . . . "As for Mrs. Crawley's character, I shan't demean myself or that most spotless and perfectly irreproachable lady, by even hinting that it requires a defence. You will be pleased to receive her with the utmost cordiality, as you will receive all persons whom I present in this house. . . . Who is the master of it? and what is it? This Temple of Virtue belongs to me. And if I invite all Newgate or all Bedlam here, by —— they shall be welcome."
>
> After this vigorous allocution, to one of which Lord Steyne treated his "Hareem" whenever symptoms of insubordination appeared in his household, the crest-fallen women had nothing for it but to obey.
>
> (II, xiv, 164–65) [484-85]

Though Lord Steyne's relations with Becky are broken off by Rawdon's assault, there is little doubt that they could, and in all probability would, deteriorate to this sort of contemptuous torment once he tired of her. Just as we are shown Old Osborne directing the impotent rage of a whole futile life toward his son and daughter, so Steyne, when he encounters Becky years after his humiliating failure to impose his will upon her, gapes at her "with a livid face and ghastly eyes" and threatens to have her murdered. Steyne has been duped by Becky, his lust unfulfilled and his money taken; he has been insulted and struck by Rawdon; and has been forced to back away from a duel. Virtually all the masculine powers and prerogatives Steyne prides himself on—control of money, shrewd wit, a cynical manipulation of women for his own pleasure, courage, pride, honor—are overthrown in this encounter. When we see him for the next and last time after this episode, he is a ghastly ruin: "Hate, or anger, or desire, caused [his eyes] to brighten now and then still; but ordinarily they gave no light, and seemed tired of looking out on a world of which almost all the pleasure and all the best beauty had palled upon the worn-out wicked old man" (II, xxix, 381) [650].

Steyne is also haunted, like Osborne, by a horrible image of his son that threatens him in a way he cannot defend himself against. Osborne's bitter, raging anguish results from George's death, which seals forever his father's guilt at banishing him, and perhaps even more from his failure to force his will upon George. Steyne is haunted by his son's madness, the result of a hereditary illness that might attack Steyne himself. Both situations come about through sexual corruption that has nothing to do with simple lust. Osborne's effort to force a moneyed wife on George and the inbreeding which has produced the stain of madness in the house of Gaunt both suggest far more insidious and pervasive corruptions of patriarchal power than the sexual cravings of old Sir Pitt. After the horrible examples of Steyne and Osborne, Sir Pitt seems relatively decent. At least he neglects his wife rather than sadistically tormenting her; his lust is open and he pays his mistresses for it openly; and he is a scandal to the world rather than an honored aristocrat or merchant prince.

The only important father in the novel who does not quite fit this group is Sedley, the only one who does not attempt to force his will upon his family, to determine sexual roles and relations. (For all his cruel tormenting of Jos for his girth, vanity, and "feminine" traits, Sedley is quite willing to let him live as he likes, marry whom he wants: "Why not she as well as another, Mrs. Sedley? The girl's a white face at any rate. *I* don't care who marries him. Let Joe please himself"; I, iv, 35 [29]). The racism is ugly, and Sedley surely bears some responsibility for Jos' grotesque substitution of food for sex and the fear of masculine sexual roles which it suggests. But Sedley has the most decent relations with his family of any man in the novel, except Dobbin. And the Sedleys have the only marriage in the novel that is not, sooner or later, a failure. Sedley's economic ruin is a symbolic, if not exactly a logical, consequence of this distinction (though the easy, trusting, essentially nonaggressive relationship he has with his wife, son, and daughter may have some bearing on his inability to survive in the rapacious economic world of the novel).

In sharp contrast to the later novels' discursive presentation of multiple careers, Osborne and Steyne are not seen engaged in the economic and political activities that supposedly underlie their social power. The exercise and the frustration of their power in the novel almost totally involve sexual dealings, and these center on the buying, selling, and emotional abuse of women. Lévi-Strauss' theory that social organization began with the exchange of women by men may be an inaccurate, or at least an untestable, hypothesis; like Freud's theory of the primal horde, it may be an extrapolation backwards of an insight into contemporary culture. But it does describe a dominant pattern in sexual relations in Western culture, flourishing in Victorian England and scarcely altered today.[5] As *Vanity Fair* abundantly demonstrates, the deferential attitudes toward women, the sentimental idealization of women, the protective masculine displays toward women are wholesale hypocrisies. As in *Martin Chuzzlewit,* disputes over the possession of women underlie nearly all the dealings between men in the novel. The abuses are so systemic that the most self-sacrificing of Dobbin's transactions on Amelia's behalf have something of the taint.

All the characters' motives and pursuits cannot be collapsed into one pattern of sexual desire, insecurity, hostility, and frustration. The pursuit of money, social status, military glory, and so forth have a reality in themselves that resists such programmatic assimilation. One of Thackeray's most brilliant and convincing dramatic effects, in fact, is to present the mixed and often sporadic motives that determine his characters' behavior. Yet the novel insists on the multitude of ways that sexuality so informs the other manifest business of *Vanity Fair* that it becomes an inseparable element of every other preoccupation. Thus sexual fraud is a major element in every other kind of fraud in the novel.

We have seen how the overbearing patriarchal figures of the novel are drawn into the prevailing sexual pattern through their own obsessions; their desire to dominate the barter of women is its own undoing, leaving them in frenzies of impotent rage. But the character whom the narrator holds up as the novel's one instance of a true gentleman also illustrates the prevailing masculine dilemma. Dobbin loses interest in his military career just as he has lost his one friend (through disillusion about George's character even before George's death) because he has set his heart on the hopeless pursuit of Amelia.

Dobbin is the most admirable character in the novel, by traditional moral norms and by the standards of a traditional masculine sexual ethic (epitomized by Austen's George Knightley); he is also the most frustrated character in the book. He has neither the protective illusions about himself that even Jos Sedley can rebuild after every hu-

5. For a very interesting application of Lévi-Strauss' theories about the exchange of women to the nineteenth-century novel, see Tony Tanner, *Adultery in the Novel: Contract and Transgression* (Baltimore: Johns Hopkins Press, 1979), pp. 79–87.

miliation, nor the temporary accomplishment of provisional goals that sustains most of the characters. Dobbin acts, but only in the interests of others. In *Vanity Fair* this ethic, based upon secularized Christian precepts and older, more general ideals of friendship, can only intensify hypocrisy and viciousness and the destruction of the self; for the people and the system it serves are so caught up in corrupt practices that furthering their interests is furthering corruption. This is fully exemplified in the marriage of Amelia and George that Dobbin arranges. Dobbin's supposed virtue, like Becky's supposed vice, is thus nearly nullified by its consequences in the world at large.

Dobbin's folly is underscored by the narrator from the beginning and is finally brought home even to Dobbin himself. His dependence on a woman is thoroughly incapacitating, through its own sentimental distortions and not through Amelia's flaws. His own false sentimentality blinds him to the weakness, inanity, and self-mortifying devotion intrinsic to the stereotypic feminine virtues that Amelia incarnates. The presentation of his situation is not tinctured with the excessive narrative pathos of *Esmond* and *Pendennis* that washes over and obliterates the fundamental errors in the sexual attitudes of their heroes. As a result Dobbin is not only a more balanced character but a more admirable one. His generosity and decency are made more attractive because the narrator is not always there to camouflage his limitations. We are likely to value his real virtues all the more, as we are the virtues of Becky, because we have been shown the destructive sexual forces they must necessarily struggle against.

*Vanity Fair* also avoids the obsessive, though often disguised, preoccupation with the sentimentally erotic relation of son and mother that subverts the development of character and theme in Thackeray's late novels. There is no saintly self-sacrificing mother, to start with. Instead we are presented with the refreshingly ordinary and worldly Mrs. Sedley, the thoroughly abject and demoralized Lady Crawley, and so on. George's mother has died long before the narrative begins; Dobbin's is kept out of the direct narrative. This not only allows a clearer focus on the fathers who struggle to dominate the world and the patriarchal system that is corrupted by its victimization of women; it also allows Thackeray to avoid entrapment in the complex of emotions that clearly dominated his own personal life and frustrated some of the finest potential developments in his late fiction.

Amelia does become a self-abnegating mother, of course, so much so that the narrator describes her existence as "a maternal caress." But the destructive effects of her development, on Georgy, on her parents, and on Amelia herself, are so thoroughly exposed by the novel that she becomes a parody of the ideal that incapacitates *Esmond* and *Pendennis.* The parody is unmistakable when the narrator describes her as an agonized Hannah relinquishing her Samuel. Her Samuel is as selfish and as snobbish as they come in *Vanity Fair,* and he is delivered up to Mammon, the money power of Old Osborne, not to God. The response of a contemporary reader of the novel,

Mrs. Jameson, was shrewd: "No woman resents Rebecca . . . but every woman resents his selfish and inane Amelia."[6]

The demolition of stereotypes about sexual relations in the family, in courtship and marriage, and in society at large accompanies the novel's focus on Becky Sharp. She eventually succumbs to the power of the traditional stereotypes, and we are led to see how they have shaped her course all along. But she is, like Emma Woodhouse and Catherine Earnshaw, a woman who acts not just to achieve her own personal aims but to give the world about her coherence, purpose, and energy. She is in this sense the chief actor in *Vanity Fair,* as well as its most accomplished performer of manipulative and deceptive rituals.

Becky's goals and her modes of operation are, however, essentially no different from those of the world about her; they are merely pursued with a remarkable wit, energy, resourcefulness, and dramatic skill. It is not that the world cannot live up to her expectations but that she lives down to the standards of the world. If this saves her from the arrogance of Emma and Catherine, it also prevents her from participating in an effort like theirs to reshape the world to a finer ideal of human existence.

Becky is certainly in many senses the heroine, as she is the chief projection of the author—the creator of dramatic scenes and a brilliant satirist. But she, like the novel at large, serves to scuttle the very idea that personal heroism is possible in such a thoroughly corrupt social world. Both she and Dobbin, antitheses in most ways, demonstrate that even a moderately decent life is nearly impossible in the scrabble for money, security, and status that characterizes the surface life of this society.

Though Becky has unusual intelligence, a robust spirit, and a remarkable ability to mimic and manipulate social mannerisms, her whole career is based on her sexual attractiveness. Without her youth, her figure, her status as both a licit and illicit object of male desires, she would have remained a governess. However she turns the stereotypic notions against themselves, however she exposes the fatuous bravado and sentimentality of a vicious sexual world, she has no other conceptions of what life is or might be than the very stereotypes she so adroitly uses to her advantage. The advantage is only temporary, and it is ultimately not only unsatisfying but degrading. The degradation that matters most is not Becky's soiled social reputation in the novel's closing European episodes but the degradation of her spirit. A fashionable world whose arbiters of decorum are figures like the Marquis of Steyne has lost all right, all ability to make distinctions.

The novel's own traditional moral norms, represented by Dobbin and by one set of impulses in an ambivalent narrator, are rendered irrelevant to Becky. The supposedly sordid Becky, so distasteful to Dobbin and so unfit, in his opinion, to associate with Amelia, provides the one resurgence of vitality and humor in the increasingly despondent, bitter mood of the novel's close. This is the wonderful scene

6. Quoted by J. W. Dodds, *Thackeray: A Critical Portrait* (London: Oxford University Press, 1941), p. 130. Kathleen Tillotson quotes Dodds (*Novels of the Eighteen-Forties* [Oxford: Clarendon Press, 1954], p. 47), and adds that Thackeray's mother made similar comments.

that returns us to the opening episodes of the novel, where Becky courts Jos once more while the brandy bottle, rouge pot, and plate with scraps of a meal on it—all of which she has shoved under the bedspread in hasty preparation for her visitor—clink away merrily in counterpoint to the arts she once more exercises over Jos. Although this scene already contrasts sharply, to Becky's advantage, with the increasingly somber and even pompous moral tone of Dobbin, with his dog-like devotion to Amelia, the narrator enlarges Becky's virtues much more than this:

> Becky liked the life. She was at home with everybody in the place, pedlars, punters, tumblers, students and all. She was of a wild, roving nature, inherited from father and mother, who were both Bohemians, by taste and circumstance; if a lord was not by, she would talk to his courier with the greatest pleasure; the din, the stir, the drink, the smoke, the tattle of the Hebrew pedlars, the solemn, braggart ways of the poor tumblers, the *sournois* talk of the gambling-table officials, the songs and swagger of the students, and the general buzz and hum of the place had pleased and tickled the little woman, even when her luck was down, and she had not wherewithal to pay her bill. How pleasant was all the bustle to her now that her purse was full of the money which little Georgy had won for her the night before!
>
> (II, xxx, 385) [652]

If Becky enjoys this sort of world, so did Chaucer and Shakespeare. Becky might well sigh with one of her great progenitors, "It tikleth me about myn herte roote . . . That I have had my world as in my time." For she does experience exuberantly, and reveal to us, much more of the world than any other character in the novel. In this passage the narrative presents a sector of the world that might well leaven the sterile hypocrisies of the fashionable society that excludes Becky, and the more subtle hypocrisies of the moral world of Dobbin and Amelia. It is, of course, still inevitably a world of pretensions and self-serving, but it is rich, varied, bustling; it includes all who come to it, even when they can't pay their bills, rather than excluding them like the would-be genteel world that has been the novel's primary subject. Clearly it is more attractive in every way than the viciousness of Gaunt House and the self-absorbed, timorous, inbred little house where Amelia lived with her parents and Georgy. Dobbin makes a great deal of Becky's abuse of little Georgy when she has him gamble for her. But the narrative analogies, though not the narrator himself, are pointedly there to undercut Dobbin's moral censure. Becky induces Georgy to gamble; Amelia sold him to his grandfather, whose riches can only further Georgy's progress in the ways of Vanity Fair.

The novel's plot is brilliantly contrived to reinforce this point. Becky returns Dobbin's enmity by acting to fulfill his desires. When she exposes George Osborne's true sexual nature to Amelia, Becky does the one thing that can make Amelia accept Dobbin's offer of marriage. Ironically, the necessary proof, the note that George wrote her, is the result of the very sexual wiles that both Amelia and Dobbin piously condemn. Once again the moral and sentimental world is made the beneficiary of the sordid sexual world that it alternately ignores and disdains but that shapes it at every turn.

When Dobbin has just openly condemned Becky to Amelia in Becky's presence and has tried to prevent any contact between them, the narrator gives us her reflections: " 'What a noble heart that man has,' she thought, 'and how shamefully that woman plays with it.' She admired Dobbin; she bore him no rancour for the part he had taken against her. It was an open move in the game, and played fairly" (II, xxxi, 409) [670]. Becky's generosity will seem surprising only if we have failed to recognize that she has been, together with Dobbin and Rawdon, one of the very few characters in the novel who has consistently acted with generosity and good humor (when such behavior did not directly conflict with her self-serving plans, of course). Her metaphor of life as a game is a much more accurate reflection of the world both she and Dobbin inhabit, and a much surer guide to conduct in it, than Dobbin's sentimental idealizations and moral norms. It is, in fact, the metaphor Dobbin himself uses during his one moment of real lucidity and creative strength, when he declares his intention to leave Amelia: "I have spent enough of my life at this play" (II, xxxi, 409) [670].

The novel does not make this the single, final perspective on Becky, of course. There is no single comprehensive resolution of any of the contradictions in the world the narrator describes or in his own ambivalent attitudes toward it. But the narrator's urge to condemn Becky and all the disturbing things she represents exposes its own strains increasingly in the novel, so that the most lurid description of her vices also appears in the final episodes:

> it has been the wish of the present writer, all through this story, deferentially to submit to the fashion at present prevailing, and only to hint at the existence of wickedness in a light, easy, and agreeable manner, so that nobody's fine feelings may be offended. . . . In describing this Siren [Becky], singing and smiling, coaxing and cajoling, the author, with modest pride, asks his readers all round, has he once forgotten the laws of politeness, and showed the monster's hideous tail above water? No! Those who like may peep down under waves that are pretty transparent, and see it writhing and twirling, diabolically hideous and slimy, flapping amongst bones, or curling round corpses; but above the water-line, I ask, has not everything been proper, agreeable, and decorous, and has any the most squeamish immoralist in Vanity Fair a right to cry fie?
>
> (II, xxix, 364–65) [637–38]

The satire here is obviously directed at the hypocrisy of that sort of reader whose squeamishness is actually a cover for unacknowledged voyeuristic and sadistic urges—the "squeamish immoralist."

The real emotional excesses on the part of the narrator do not appear in passages like this where he contemplates Becky, but in passages where he revels in the self-lacerating torments of little Amelia ("O you poor secret martyrs and victims, whose life is a torture, who are stretched on racks in your bedrooms . . . [E]very man who . . .

peers into those dark places where the torture is administered to you, must pity you. . . ."; II, xxii, 275–76 [570]). This is scarcely less lurid than the passage on Becky, but here the narrator is an excited participant, as voyeuristic as any of his readers.

The qualities of temperament that make Becky so compelling and so attractive must either struggle for sporadic and usually fleeting expression (her generosity toward Dobbin, her genuine fondness for Rawdon, her realization that he is "worth twenty George Osbornes") or they must subserve the warped sexual values that control the whole society's behavior. It is to her credit that she exposes the system's corruption even as she uses it to her own advantage and even when she succumbs to its power over her. This is the real nature of her rebellion: persistent mockery of the only world she knows, a mockery that allies her with the satiric narrator.[7]

Arnold Kettle has written of her rebellion:

> Only two courses are open to her, the passive one of acquiescence to subjugation or the active one of independent rebellion. . . . And so she uses consciously and systematically all the men's weapons plus her one natural material asset, her sex, to storm the men's world. And the consequence is of course morally degrading and she is a bad woman all right. But she gains our sympathy nevertheless—not our approving admiration, but our human fellow-feeling—just as Heathcliff does, and she too gains it not in spite but because of her rebellion.[8]

We would qualify this fine perception a little: Becky's sexual assets, her power to gain what she thinks she wants and to expose what the whole society is after, are highly artificial—not natural—products of a deeply divided patriarchal society, and they operate most profoundly in a psychological and spiritual, not a material, context. Her rebellion can only reveal what is wrong with the world even as it ensnares her more and more tightly in corruption. The despair that settles increasingly over her own spirit shows how futile for her own life are the services she performs for the reader's enlightenment.

Kettle is absolutely right about Becky's basic appeal, however. She does not exercise the traditional feminine charms over the reader, neither the charm of open seduction nor the more furtive erotic appeal of coy innocence. Her attraction is based upon rebellion against a system that subjugates the oppressors as well as the victims, and it arouses a *human* fellow-feeling—the only way that the novel can escape the stereotypes that crush its characters. Her chief weapon is ridicule, forcing the snobs and hypocrites, the self-righteous and the vicious, to see themselves, for a moment, as they are.

As a consequence of a thoroughly disoriented sexual world, none of the main characters in the novel is able to pursue a "normal" sexual career. Amelia, Dobbin, and Jos are all kept in a condition of enforced celibacy and frustrated erotic desires. Becky uses her marriage as a means to gain the social advancement she wants, first as a

7. As a number of critics have noted, Becky's satiric evaluations of the people about her frequently agree with the narrator's own evaluations. She becomes a direct satiric persona in her letters to Amelia.
8. Arnold Kettle, *An Introduction to the English Novel* (London: Hutchinson, 1951), p. 20.

front for a virtual gambling house and then as a cover for sexual adventurism. Though Becky has the physical desires most of the characters repress or sublimate (the narrator suggests that her relationship with Rawdon is physically satisfying to both) she destroys the marriage by using her sexual attractiveness as a stratagem to gain money and status. In the world of Vanity Fair, as Becky knows best, female sexuality can retain some measure of independence only by delaying or denying the desires it arouses; personal sexual satisfaction is at best an expendable luxury. Women who attempt some direct fulfillment of direct physical desires must accept the victim's role, as Amelia illustrates. Women who retain some control over their lives all work outside the standard erotic expectations: Miss Crawley, Mrs. Bute Crawley, Miss Pinkerton, and so forth.

George Osborne is the only character who follows, until his early death, a fairly standard sexual career; and it serves as a satire of romantic norms. The first stage is submission to family arrangements for marriage, whose chief criterion is social status. In the second stage he is ready to submit to his father's will, to abandon Amelia if not to marry Miss Swartz, until Dobbin shames him into momentary romantic heroism. Even this heroism is disastrous—not because it fails but because it succeeds: because there is no firm love or commitment to sustain George's impulse, and because Amelia's love is founded on romantic illusions, the marriage is doomed whether he lives or dies. (In fact its life is prolonged far beyond all likelihood by his death, as Amelia enshrines his spurious virtues in her memory.) The point is made by the plot, which has him on the verge of an adulterous relationship with Becky as the summons to Waterloo occurs.

George's strong sensual desires appear only in this adulterous context. This is typical of the novel, where the rare expressions of direct physical sexuality always occur in a context of deception and betrayal. It is also typical that the affair is not consummated. Because sexual roles and rituals are so warped and inadequate, sexual desires are manifested in frustration, not fulfillment. Although *Vanity Fair* displays the swaggering of rakes and the seductive enticements of both demure and brazen coquettes, this display is as phony as every other social pretense. What we remember, what the novel creates most vividly, are scenes of erotic impasse and erotic failure: George defying his father's effort to force Miss Swartz upon him, in ugly racist terms ("Marry that mulatto woman? . . . I don't like the colour, sir. Ask the black that sweeps opposite Fleet Market, sir. *I'm* not going to marry a Hottentot Venus" (I, xxi, 225) [214]; Emily deserted in her funereal marriage bed, "nursing the corpse of love"; Sir Pitt, Major Tufto, and Lord Steyne maddened by balked desire; Rawdon outraged at Becky's infidelity; Dobbin self-martyred by his hopeless love for Amelia; Jane Osborne sacrificed to her father's tyranny and, even more, to a sexual system that condemns her to a life of grim celibacy.

The frustration of the conscious sexual desires of the characters and the pressures of unconscious sexual conflicts work together to *transform* the characters into stereotypes. They become, in the course of the narrative, the puppets that the narrator initially describes them as; but the force that controls them is not the manipulation of an arbitrary authorial presence but the "unseen hand" (to borrow Adam Smith's phrase) of the society's sexual economy. George is transformed into a paragon of martial and marital virtue by Amelia's imagination; Amelia narrows her own life to the faithful widow and selfless mother; Dobbin becomes the rejected but faithful lover who suffers in silence; Rawdon Crawley—for all the real nobility of his action—plays the part of the gallant hero defending his wife's honor against the wicked aristocrat; Mr. Sedley shrinks to the ruined merchant harping on the injustice he has suffered, almost a humour character. All the young characters, but Becky in particular, begin with richer possibilities than the world can accommodate. The exterior roles that society forces on them become interiorized. They are subdued to what they work in. And their mannerisms, habits of mind, and ideas about their motives become more habitual, until we have Amelia the "tender little parasite" clinging to Dobbin the "rugged old oak," and then the narrator puts his puppets away and shuts up the box.

Stereotypes have this impact because the novel insists on their predominant power in the struggling social milieu it takes as the epitome of Victorian society. The complexity of the characters persists, but it is more and more repressed from their consciousness and from other characters' attitudes toward them. The complexity reveals itself in unconscious, symbolic behavior that the novel discloses through a brilliant rendering of the nuances of dramatic action and its interconnection of related scenes through symbolic analogy. Thackeray's well-known idea that character is static is yet another way of stressing the tremendous power of social conditioning. In Thackeray's bleak but persuasive view, only a very few people manage to turn the quirks of their behavior into a unique personality. The persistent delusion in the later fiction that characters like Esmond and Warrington *might have been* something great except for the tragic force of circumstances is already in *Vanity Fair* exposed to the most cynical scrutiny.

The narrator of *Vanity Fair* makes the stuff of stereotypes into a provocative means of unsettling and enlightening the reader, working to achieve more directly what the plot, symbolic configurations, and dramatic action achieve implicitly. The narrator does not attempt to turn contradictions into comprehensive resolutions that are themselves stereotypic or even platitudinous—as too often happens in Thackeray's later fiction. Contradictions, festering emotions, and the deforming nature of stereotypes are thrust before us by the extreme form in which they are cast and by their juxtaposition with contradictory stereotypes:

> The illness of that old lady [Mrs. Sedley] had been the occupation and perhaps the safeguard of Amelia. What do men know about women's martyrdoms? We should go mad had we to endure the hundredth part of those daily pains which are meekly borne by many women. Ceaseless slavery meeting with no reward; constant gentleness and kindness met by cruelty as constant . . . all this, how many of them have to bear in quiet, and appear abroad with cheerful faces as if they felt nothing. Tender slaves that they are, they must needs be hypocrites and weak.
>
> (II, xxi, 271) [567]

The male narrator presumes to tell us what men don't know about women. Amelia's attack on her mother for dosing George with patent medicines (Amelia accuses her of poisoning Georgy) is hardly the expression of "constant gentleness"; it causes a rift between them that is never joined. But even apart from these ironies developed through the dramatic context, the passage reveals contradictory attitudes toward women through its own substance and its own rhetoric. Somehow the enormous strength of women (not as the strength of ten but of a hundred men) and their meekness, gentleness, and kindness become weakness and hypocrisy by the end of the passage. And, of course, the passage evades, and makes its evasion obvious, the question of who is responsible for the "martyrdom" the narrator tries to simultaneously lament and praise—surely not dying old ladies. The simple categories of traditional sentimental pathos and traditional antifeminist patronization cannot contain the character of Amelia or the responses of the narrator to her; but the passage does imply how much the two stereotypic attitudes have in common.

This sort of juxtaposition of contradictory attitudes within the narrative appears regularly through the novel. The narrator's generalization about "that secret talking and conspiring which form the delight of female life" is almost sure to be followed or preceded by a comment that does not qualify but contradicts it. In this case, it is the narrator's revelation that "that young whiskered prig, Lieutenant Osborne" has been secretly conspiring against Becky by warning Rawdon to be on guard against her (I, xiv, 171–72) [150].

The narrator of *Vanity Fair* is certainly caught up in contradictions but not in the confusion or even incoherence that obscures and limits the later novels. The blatantly contradictory views have disturbed readers from the time *Vanity Fair* appeared because they call attention to their own inconsistencies. The narrator "encapsulates" absolute statements about the sexual world (women are made, by instinct, either to scheme or to love; men are as vain as women about their personal appearance) that *rhetorically* treat the world as if it were a stable and consistent thing. These comments take a momentary foothold in words but they are continually contradicted by the dramatic and symbolic substance of the novel. Was Lady Crawley made to scheme or to love? How vain is Dobbin about his personal appearance? What we see in nearly every instance when the narrator smugly delivers an absolute judgment is an effort transparently born of the failure of all traditional categories to encompass the complexity that the novel describes. Winslow Rogers has complained that "no event in a Thackeray novel can have a stable meaning; no character can be finally known."[9] But this is surely one of the most profound insights that Thackeray had about Victorian culture. Many critics who find Thackeray's methods disturbing seem to be asking, through discussion of aesthetic issues, for a more reassuring view of the modern world than Thackeray can be expected to give.

9. Winslow Rogers, "Thackeray's Self-Consciousness," in *The Worlds of Victorian Fiction*, edited by Jerome H. Buckley, Harvard English Studies, vol. 6. (Cambridge: Harvard University Press, 1975), p. 151.

# INA FERRIS

## The Narrator of *Vanity Fair*†

* * *

In the Preface to *Pendennis* Thackeray defined a novel as "a sort of confidential talk between writer and reader," and some readers of *Vanity Fair* have complained that there is rather too much of this talk in the novel. Certainly, the narrator dominates to a degree unusual even in Victorian fiction. Furthermore, his voice is puzzling as well as intrusive, playing now the fool, now the preacher, now the man of the world, now the man of sentiment. His age changes and he never seems to be quite sure about his marital status. Suddenly he appears in Pumpernickel where he meets the characters. Whereas other Victorian narrators (like those of George Eliot, for instance) reassure and guide the reader, Thackeray's slippery character keeps us off-balance and uncertain. And that is the whole point. Through the narrator Thackeray turns reading from a passive into an active process, so furthering his campaign for realism by bringing closer together the experience of reading and the experience of living.[1]

Thackeray's narrator is distinguished by his conversational, personal tone. Dickens usually assumes a public, oratorical voice; George Eliot creates a detached analyst; and even Fielding (whom Thackeray occasionally resembles) adopts a more impersonal role. But the informal style of *Vanity Fair* puts us in a more private, familiar world where the narrator can respond to his characters and to his hypothetical reader in a more casual and intimate fashion. Thackeray presents his narrator in the prologue as Manager of the Performance, and in one of the novel's more formal moments the narrator asks leave "as a man and a brother" not only to introduce his characters but "to step down from the platform, and talk about them" (ch. 8). The novel as a whole takes place down here, away from the platform with its implied superiority and detachment. The effect of the narrator's highly personal tone, as Juliet McMaster has pointed out, is to make the reader react personally both to the narrator and to the characters; and this in turn animates the fiction. The narrator's fallible commentary provokes our own response to the characters. By so responding, we endow them with a life resembling that of real people and turn their world into one "that has somehow overlapped with [our] own."[2]

This overlapping is also managed more directly by the frequent breaking of dramatic illusion when the narrator moves out of the fictional world into the world of the reader. After introducing the rich Miss Crawley, for example, he proceeds to generalize: "What a dignity it gives an old lady, that balance at the banker's!" To ensure

† Excerpted with permission of Twayne Publishers, an imprint of Macmillan Publishing Company from *William Makepeace Thackeray* by Ina Ferris (Boston: Twayne, 1983), 34–35. 

1. Wolfgang Iser analyzes the active role of the reader in *Vanity Fair* in *The Implied Reader* (Baltimore, 1974), pp. 101–20.
2. Juliet M. McMaster, *Thackeray: The Major Novels* (Toronto, 1971), p. 1. See Chapter 1 for an extended analysis of the function of the narrator.

recognition of the relevance of this irony to actuality, he involves the reader, creating an elaborate hypothesis about "your" life: "Your wife" and "your little girls" work busily to please the wealthy relative. "You yourself, dear sir, forget to go to sleep after dinner. . . . Is it so, or is it not so? I appeal to the middle classes." Characteristically, the narrator himself is not immune: "Ah, gracious powers! I wish you would send me an old aunt" (ch. 9). Moments like these break down the barrier between fiction and life, asserting a parallel between the narrative and our own lives. Fiction is no longer another reality but a way back to this one, provoking self-confrontation. *Vanity Fair* thus continues and refines the technique developed in *Catherine* of puncturing complacency and of making the reader as much the subject of the fiction as the characters. Its ever-changing narrative roles demand constant alertness, trapping the reader into a response only to reveal its inadequacy. "*Vanity Fair*," A. E. Dyson has written, "is surely one of the world's most devious novels."[3] And so it is. But it is also oddly straightforward in its fusing of technique and theme. In a novel about the vanity of the world all wear the fool's garb of motley shown on the original cover: narrator, characters, reader.

* * *

## CATHERINE PETERS

## [Didacticism]†

* * *

By developing the strategy, already familiar from his earlier work, of using highly individual, even idiosyncratic, narrative voices, [Thackeray] separated the author or, rather, what Wayne Booth has christened 'the implied author'[1] from the narrator. The latter becomes a character in his own right, though a confusingly self-contradictory one, existing in an artistic no man's land, somewhere between the reader and the characters in the story. Thackeray himself points to this separation of 'author' and narrator in the preface 'Before the Curtain' written for the 1848 edition, where he makes a distinction between the 'Author' of the work and the 'Manager of the Performance'. But he also refers in the preface to the 'man with a reflective turn of mind' who walks through the Fair as an observer, and to 'poor Tom Fool', who is clearly the same person who looks at his distorted image in the frontispiece. The confusion this creates in the reader's mind—who *is* the narrator, the reliable and omniscient voice who will tell us the story and also what to think about it?—is quite deliberate. His lifelong fascination with the theatre, and the relationship

3. A. E. Dyson, "Thackeray: An Irony Against Heroes," in his *The Crazy Fabric* (London: Macmillan, 1965), p. 76.

† From *Thackeray's Universe: Shifting Worlds of Imagination and Reality* (New York: Oxford University Press; and London: Faber and Faber Ltd, 1987), 150–51. 

1. Wayne Booth, *The Rhetoric of Fiction* (Chicago: University of Chicago Press, 1961), pp. 71–77.

between illusion and reality, already present as early as *Flore et Zephyr*, emerges once more in the unnamed but ever-present cast of characters who surround the 'real' characters of the story of *Vanity Fair*. These are, in fact, all different faces of the 'Manager of the Performance', who is an actor-manager of the old school, a true pro who is a bewildering quick-change artist. He can appear to hold one opinion with sincere conviction at one moment, and at the next add another twist to his argument which brings it crashing to the ground. Sometimes his views coincide with those of the 'author', sometimes not.

With this acrobatic harlequin performance going on in the foreground, the story, and the characters in it, appear to gain in solidity by contrast, so that when the 'Manager' describes them as puppets, and claims that it is he who manipulates them for our entertainment, we react indignantly. Ever since the novel first appeared, critics have gone to the lengths of claiming that we know more about his characters than Thackeray does, or that he 'lies' about them, or that he has somehow lost control of his own book: 'The Art of Novels *is* to represent Nature: to convey as strongly as possible the sentiment of reality . . .'[2] Thackeray wrote, objecting to the grotesque and theatrical in Dickens's early novels. In *Vanity Fair* he takes care to make those elements the property of the narrator, and not of the characters.

The meaning that *Vanity Fair* has held for most readers is contained in the narrative's insistence that there are no inviolable standards of good and evil available in this world. Not all the book's readers have approved of this: Harriet Martineau, who much admired *Esmond*, was not alone in being unable to read *Vanity Fair* 'from the moral disgust it occasions'.[3] Good not only does not triumph over evil, except in the most marginal and limited ways, it is apparent that it cannot. Becky, an adulteress and murderess, is not assigned any terrible fate at the end of the novel, nor is one projected for her outside the book. Writing to the Duke of Devonshire, who had inquired about the futures of his characters, Thackeray assigned Becky 'a small but very pretty little house in Belgravia' and a circle of respectable friends who consider her 'a *most injured woman*'.[4] Becky's punishment is no more than the boredom and weariness that she feels after each successive triumph, which may not seem to differ materially from the boredom and weariness that Dobbin feels at the end of his story. It is hard to imagine this being permitted in the moral universe of any other English nineteenth-century novel. We may even feel that Becky, with her energy and inventiveness, and her capacity to accept the down-turns of fortune with good humour, comes off best after all, since even the least ambiguous spokesmen for the 'humblemindedness' Thackeray admired—Dobbin and Lady Jane Sheepshanks—do not obtain happiness through behaving correctly. It is the moment of rebellion in each, Dobbin's when he rounds at last on Amelia, and Lady Jane

2. *The Letters and Private Papers of William Makepeace Thackeray*, 4 vols. (Cambridge: Harvard University Press, 1945–46), II, p. 772.
3. Harriet Martineau, *Autobiography* (London: Smith, Elder, 1877), p. 376.
4. *Letters*, II, p. 375.

when she refuses to have any more to do with Becky, that the reader admires. Yet those rebellions, though they do produce results, do not bring happiness either. Though *Vanity Fair* is, in its own distinctive way, an exemplary and didactic novel, it does not convey its message through simple cause and effect exposition.

* * *

## JAMES PHELAN

# *Vanity Fair*: Listening as a Rhetorician—and a Feminist†

### *Some Functions of the Showman's Multiple Voices*

In order to understand the functions of the showman's voices, we need a fuller explanation of the context in which they are heard. Broadly defined, Thackeray's purpose in the narrative is to expose the condition of universal vanity he describes in the final paragraph: "Ah! *Vanitas Vanitatem!* Which of us is happy in this world? Which of us has his desire? or, having it, is satisfied?"[1] To achieve this purpose, Thackeray invents his dramatized male narrator and has him tell the story of the progress of two very different women through a society that consistently reflects and reveals the ineradicable but multifarious vanity of its inhabitants. This story is frequently (though not ubiquitously) linked with gender issues: Not only does the male narrator comment on the careers of the women, but those careers themselves expose the patriarchal structures as well as the vanity of society. Again speaking schematically, we can see that Thackeray takes his two female characters, places them in the same setting but in different circumstances in the opening chapters, then sends them off in different directions so that he might conduct a relatively comprehensive survey of nineteenth-century society; he then brings them back together at the end of the narrative as a way to achieve closure.

He uses Amelia to explore the workings of vanity in the private sphere—the realm of the home and the heart—and he uses Becky to explore those workings in the public sphere—the realm of social climbing and social status. In keeping with his overriding thematic purpose, Thackeray uses Amelia and Becky, first, as a means to expose the vanity of others and, second, as exemplars of certain vain behaviors. In the case of Becky, the procedure works effectively and straightforwardly. He gives her a temporary license to succeed in her vain pursuits by playing upon the greater vanity of others, and then, once she has exposed that vanity in creatures ranging from Miss Pinkerton to Lord Steyne, he takes the license away and emphasizes what has

† From *Out of Bounds: Male Writers and Gender(ed) Criticism*, ed. Laura Claridge and Elizabeth Langland (Amherst: University of Massachusetts Press, 1990), 136–47. 

1. William Makepeace Thackeray, *Vanity Fair: A Novel without a Hero* (Boston: Houghton Mifflin, 1963), 666 [688]; hereafter cited in text by page number. The novel was first published serially in 1847–48 and in book form in 1848. [Page references in brackets are to this Norton Critical Edition.]

never been far from the foreground of the narrative: Becky's own vanity-driven life. In the case of Amelia, however, the situation is more complex. He uses her constancy, love, and dependence on George first as a way to expose the vanity of George and those like him; later, Thackeray tries to expose the negative side of these very same qualities as he shows how they ultimately destroy Dobbin's love for her—and thus the chance for happiness for them both.

Although the stories of Becky and Amelia have clear beginnings, middles, and ends, although the characters move from an initial situation to a final one, the principle controlling the linking of episodes is, for the most part, an additive rather than an integrative one. That is, unlike a novel by Jane Austen in which the significance of each episode derives from its consequences for and interaction with later episodes, *Vanity Fair* is built upon episodes that typically derive their significance from their contribution to the overriding theme of ubiquitous vanity.[2] One consequence of this broad design is that it allows Thackeray to vary the way in which he treats his characters. Sometimes they appear to be autonomous beings for whom he wants us to feel deeply, sometimes obvious artificial devices for making his thematic points, and sometimes largely incidental to the showman's disquisitions about the workings of society.

One consequence of this fluctuation is that it allows the showman great freedom in his use and selection of voice. He can move from intimacy to distance, from formality to informality, from treating the characters as puppets to treating them as people, provided that the movement remains in the service of the thematic end. Indeed, because of the additive structure and the length of the whole narrative it is almost incumbent upon Thackeray to take full advantage of that freedom and make the narrator's performance one source of our sustained interest in the narrative.[3] The performances I will focus on here are, though not fully representative, illustrative of many other transactions that go on between Thackeray and his audience. As this way of talking about the narrative performances indicates, I see the showman as Thackeray's mouthpiece; the only distance between author and narrator is created by the author's knowledge that the narrator is created. On this reading, the showman is the knowing source of the numerous ironies of the narrative discourse. Thackeray, in other words, does not communicate to his audience behind the showman's back but rather uses the protean showman as the orchestrator of virtually all the narrative's effects. It is of course impossible to do justice in a single essay to the range of effects Thackeray achieves through his use of voice; I focus here on two passages that represent

2. There are exceptions of course. Sometimes episodes cluster together into larger incidents that make the thematic point—most noteworthy here is the mininarrative surrounding the end of Becky's intrigue with Lord Steyne. And, given the device of following the same cast of characters, Thackeray can, as the narrative progresses, return to material that he has used earlier and give it some new uses. He does this recycling most obviously at the end of the narrative when Becky shows Amelia the letter George wrote her before Waterloo and when Becky reattaches herself to Jos. For a somewhat different account of the pattern of the whole, see Mark H. Burch, " 'The world is a looking-glass': *Vanity Fair* as Satire," *Genre* 15 (1982): 265–79.

3. This point in a sense builds upon the case that Juliet McMaster has made for the importance of the showman's commentary in her thoughtful study, *Thackeray: The Major Novels* (Toronto: University of Toronto Press, 1971).

the extremes of his attitude toward the patriarchal elements of Vanity Fair.[4]

In chapter 3 the showman comments upon Becky's interest in Jos Sedley:

> If Miss Rebecca Sharp had determined in her heart upon making the conquest of this big beau, I don't think, ladies, we have any right to blame her; for though the task of husband-hunting is generally, and with becoming modesty, entrusted by young persons to their mammas, recollect that Miss Sharp had no kind parent to arrange these delicate matters for her, and that if she did not get a husband for herself, there was no one else in the wide world who would take the trouble off her hands. What causes young people to "come out," but the noble ambition of matrimony? What sends them trooping to watering-places? What keeps them dancing till five o'clock in the morning through a whole mortal season? What causes them to labour at piano-forte sonatas, and to learn four songs from a fashionable master at a guinea a lesson, and to play the harp if they have handsome arms and neat elbows, and to wear Lincoln Green toxophilite hats and feathers, but that they may bring down some "desirable" young man with those killing bows and arrow of theirs? What causes respectable parents to take up their carpets, set their houses topsy-turvy, and spend a fifth of their year's income in ball suppers and iced champagne? Is it sheer love of their species, and an unadulterated wish to see young people happy and dancing? Psha! they want to marry their daughters; and, as honest Mrs. Sedley has, in the depths of her kind heart, already arranged a score of little schemes for the settlement of her Amelia, so also had our beloved but unprotected Rebecca determined to do her very best to secure the husband, who was even more necessary for her than for her friend. (28) [19–20]

The showman speaks here—for the most part—in the sociolect of the genteel upper middle class. He is someone who knows and feels comfortable in the social circuit of that class: the well-informed gentleman speaking politely but firmly—and with a certain air of superiority—to a group of women from the class. His diction is generally formal, but he will occasionally drop the register to something more familiar—"mammas" or "take the trouble off her hands." Furthermore, the genteel and formal qualities of the voice are reinforced by the parallel structure of the rhetorical questions and their well-chosen concreteness—"four songs from a fashionable master at a guinea a lesson." In adopting his air of knowing gentility, the showman also positions himself at a considerable distance from Becky. He calls her "Miss Rebecca Sharp" at the outset, and even later when he speaks of her as "our beloved but unprotected Rebecca," his sym-

4. For some worthwhile studies of Thackeray's technique along lines different from the ones I am developing here, see Geoffrey Tillotson, *Thackeray the Novelist* (Cambridge: Cambridge University Press, 1954); John Loofbourow, *Thackeray and the Form of Fiction* (Princeton, NJ: Princeton University Press, 1964); James Wheatley, *Patterns in Thackeray's Fiction* (Middletown, CT: Wesleyan University Press, 1967); Ina Ferris, *William Makepeace Thackeray* (New York: Twayne, 1983); S. K. Sinha, *Thackeray: A Study in Technique*, Salzburg Studies in English Literature 86 (Salzburg: Institut für Anglistik and Amerikanistik, 1979); and Elaine Scarry, "Enemy and Father: Comic Equilibrium in No. 14 of *Vanity Fair*," *Journal of Narrative Technique* 10 (1980): 145–55.

pathy does not overpower the distance. As a result of the genteel stance and the cool distance from Becky, the voice appears to be considering her as a "case," one that he is finally sympathetic to but one that he is interested in as much for what it generally illustrates.

Within this general sociolect, there are significant modulations—so significant, in fact, that even as we read we come to see the dominant voice as a pretense, one that the showman puts on to expose the limitations of the values associated with it. The showman's strategy is twofold: He occasionally lets a certain aggressive element enter the genteel voice; and, more dramatically, he temporarily shifts to a voice that is critical of the dominant one and then lets this voice invade and subvert the dominant. One major consequence of this strategy is that while making his apologia for Becky the showman offers a powerful indictment of courtship behavior in this male-controlled society.

The showman adopts the genteel voice right away, but in the second half of the first sentence the voice momentarily drops into a different, franker register as the showman mentions "the task of husband-hunting." The phrase not only calls to mind the image of the social circuit as a jungle where women are the predators, men the prey, but also insists on the hunt as work rather than sport. Although the showman quickly readopts his genteel voice, everything he says in the rest of the sentence is now double-voiced, undermined by the candid, antigenteel voice of the earlier phrase.

When the genteel voice calls the business of the hunt "delicate matters," we register not only the discrepancy between this description and "the task of husband-hunting" and the corresponding conflict between the values associated with each but also the showman's privileging of the antigenteel voice: His reference to "the task of husband-hunting" makes the phrase "delicate matters" an ironic euphemism. When the showman modulates his voice in a different way by moving from the formal tone of the genteel voice to an informal and affectionate one with his reference to "mammas," the earlier presence of the frank, antigenteel voice strongly ironizes the new modulation—and, indeed, the whole clause in which it appears. When the showman tells us that "the task of husband-hunting is generally, and with becoming modesty, entrusted by young persons to their mammas," we recognize the disparity between the image of the hunt and the alleged modesty of those in the hunting party. Moreover, we infer that the "young persons" have no choice about "entrusting" the hunt to their "mammas": The mammas manage, whether the daughters entrust them to or not, as we learn more directly later when we are told that "Mrs. Sedley has . . . arranged a score of little schemes for the settlement of her Amelia." We see, in short, that the real predators are those that by another name we call "mammas." This realization in turn adds another layer of irony to the phrase a "kind parent to arrange these delicate matters."

The initial reference to husband hunting as a "task" is echoed in the aggressive note that repeatedly creeps into the showman's use of the genteel voice: "What *sends them trooping* to watering-places?" "What *keeps* them dancing . . . ?" "What *causes them to labour* . . . ?" (It is worth noting here, if only in passing, that the grammar of the passage suggests that "them" refers to "young people" but "young people" actually means "young women.") "What *causes respectable parents to take up their carpets, set their houses topsy-turvy, and spend a fifth of their year's income* . . . ?" (Italics mine.) The aggressive note is given more emphasis toward the end of this series of questions, when the showman slides very smoothly from the genteel voice to the franker, antigenteel one of the first sentence. His reference to the young people wearing "Lincoln Green toxophilite hats and feathers" is parallel to the previous phrases about their learning musical instruments. But once the topic of archery is introduced through this description of their clothes, the showman quickly appropriates the earlier hunting metaphor: What keeps them doing all these things "but that they may bring down some 'desirable' young man with those killing bows and arrows of theirs?" The result is that the showman strongly reinforces the subversion of the social values implied in the dominant voice: These genteel "young persons" and their "mammas" are no better than prisoners of their patriarchally imposed task, the purpose of which no one has even mentioned yet—nor has anyone apparently given any thought to what happens once the hunter has bagged her game. In other words, as the passage proceeds, it implies that the mammas and their daughters are no less prey than the young men: They are driven to their "task" by the values of the patriarchal society that insist that a woman must be married and married as "well" as she can.

The critique of "courtship" in the Fair reaches its high point in the final sentences of this passage as the showman turns to answer his own questions about the motives for the behavior he describes. His interjection, "Psha!," followed by the direct assertion "they want to marry their daughters," marks the entrance into the passage of a third voice—a more honest, more direct voice than the genteel one that has been speaking so far. With this third voice, the showman is overtly setting himself above his genteel audience to reject their pretense and speak a truth that they also know but don't usually admit. This shift then sets up the final statement as an apologia for Becky's behavior, one that is convincing according to the values associated both with the genteel language he once again adopts—"so also had our beloved but unprotected Rebecca determined to do her very best to secure the husband"—and, significantly, with the new superior voice—"who was even more necessary for her than for her friend."

Because the new voice is clearly superior to the dominant one and because it is not ironized the way that the genteel one is (note all the undercutting in the description of "honest Mrs. Sedley" and her "schemes"), the apologia has real force. Yes, what Becky is doing is no different from what every other woman in this jungle does; yes, precisely because she has "no kind parents," a husband is more necessary for her than for Amelia. Yet the presence of the earlier subversion of the dominant voice and its values complicates this apologia. The case for Becky works only in terms of the values that we have been made to question by the earlier interaction between the voices; the case does not recognize how the very role that Becky "justifiably" adopts (i.e., mamma's role) has been exposed as itself constrained by patriarchy, as itself something to be lamented rather than celebrated. Consequently, by the light of the values associated with the frankest voice of the passage, the apologia is unconvincing. In this sense, then, the superior voice of the last few sentences of the passage is itself undercut; though it drops the pretenses of the genteel voice, it does not question the basic assumptions and values of the upper-middle-class social circuit, assumptions and values that reinforce the power of the patriarchy even as they have negative consequences for both women and men.

### *Evaluating the Showman's Voices*

The interaction between this superior voice and the earlier, antigenteel one highlights an important effect of the passage that is characteristic of Thackeray's position throughout the novel. By insisting on both the limitations of and the constraints on Becky's behavior, the showman offers a critique without offering an alternative. The power of the Fair is such that virtually no one can get outside it. The corollary of this point has been well illustrated by the rhetorical analysis of the passage: The power of the patriarchy is also often such that no one can get outside it. It seems fair to conclude—at least tentatively—that Thackeray's analysis of Vanity Fair is in part a critique of the patriarchy, and a critique which comes through a voice that is clearly identified as male. Let me now probe that tentativeness, by looking first at some other elements of the chosen passage and then at the novel more generally.

The very positioning of the male voice in relation to the "ladies" addressed in the passage raises a question about the thoroughness of the critique, about whether the rhetorical setup of the passage works against the message conveyed through the modulation of the voices. Note, first, that the address to "ladies" is made in the showman's genteel voice, the one that is most undercut in the whole passage. As that voice takes on and reflects the values of the genteel society, it takes on the assumption that the man can tell the "ladies" the truth about their behavior. When we see that this voice doesn't have the truth, this assumption is itself called into question. In that respect, the narrator-audience relationship reinforces rather than undercuts the message conveyed through the voices.

The passage, to be sure, does not suggest that the "ladies" see the full critique; instead, it presupposes that they will agree with the superior voice of the final sentences. But that presupposition does not make the rhetorical setup one in which we participate in an easy putdown of the ladies. Instead, it suggests that the "ladies" of genteel society, like Becky, the mammas, and the superior male voice, are caught in the trap of patriarchy. The rhetorical setup would offer the reader an uncomfortable position if it presupposed some assumption by Thackeray, as orchestrator of the play of voices, that men could see the full critique but women couldn't. The passage offers no evidence of such an assumption. Thus Thackeray's critique of courtship has strong affinities with one we might make from a feminist perspective.

Nevertheless, I think that the analysis so far indicates not only Thackeray's considerable virtuosity in the manipulation of voice but also a potentially negative—or at least rhetorically risky—side to that virtuosity. The complex interplay of voices and their effects leads us back to their source, to what we might call the metavoice of the showman. In addition to the qualities of wit, intelligence, learning, and a willingness to criticize, the showman's virtuosity here leaves him and us outside the fray, complimenting him and ourselves on our superior knowledge as we look down upon the Fair and those caught in it. Although there are places in the narrative when the showman indicates that he too can't escape the traps of vanity, his frequently displayed penchant for one-upmanship at the expense of his characters and his addressed audiences sometimes makes us uncomfortable. We feel that we're asked to participate in the metavoice's smugness or snideness or superciliousness.[5] This feature of the metavoice obviously has consequences for any evaluation of it, but this feature has an especially noteworthy role in a feminist evaluation.

When we look at the novel more broadly than we have so far, we soon see that the showman is hardly Jane Eyre's brother under the skin. His most obvious limitations are that he does not follow consistently through on his insights into patriarchy's shaping of women's behavior and that he sometimes reveals his own complicity with the patriarchy, thus inviting the reader to join in that complicity. Many instances could be cited to make these points, especially his ambivalent treatment of Amelia, but perhaps the clearest evidence is in the famous passage in chapter 64 describing Becky as "syren."

> I defy any one to say that our Becky, who has certainly some vices, has not been presented to the public in a perfectly genteel and inoffensive manner. In describing this syren, singing and smiling, coaxing and cajoling, the author, with modest pride, asks his readers all around, has he once forgotten the laws of politeness, and showed the monster's hideous tail above water? No! Those who like may peep down under waves that are pretty transparent, and see it writhing and twirling, diabolically hideous and slimy, flapping amongst bones, or curling round corpses; but above the water line, I ask, has not everything been proper, agreeable, and decorous, and has any the most squeamish immoralist in Vanity Fair a right to cry fie? When, however, the syren disappears and dives below, down among the dead men, the water of course grows turbid over her, and it is labour lost to look into it ever so curiously. They look pretty enough when they sit upon a rock, twanging their harps and combing their hair, and sing, and beckon to you to come and hold the looking-glass; but when they sink into their native element, depend on

5. In *A Rhetoric of Irony* (Chicago: University of Chicago Press, 1974), Wayne Booth has persuasively argued that all irony involves victims—or at least potential victims: those people who don't get it. The difference between Thackeray's ironic one-upmanship and, say, Austen's ironic treatment of Mrs. Bennet is that Austen's narrator, unlike the showman, never gives us ironic commentary about Mrs. Bennet that also announces her own superiority. Indeed, although Austen's narrator frequently speaks ironically, she rarely gives direct ironic commentary in her own voice about any character but instead uses the irony to establish norms that can themselves ironically undercut a character's speech (quoted or reported) or behavior. She is not showing off at the character's expense the way Thackeray sometimes appears to do.

> it those mermaids are about no good, and we had best not examine the fiendish marine cannibals, revelling and feasting on their wretched pickled victims. And so, when Becky is out of the way, be sure that she is not particularly well employed, and that the less that is said about her doings is in fact the better. (617) [637–38]

The interplay among voices is characteristically complex here, as the showman gives the very picture he is praising himself for having suppressed. He uses a refined, almost prissy voice to praise himself for his decorum, and then, when talking about what he has not done, he adopts a melodramatic one that likes to dwell on the seamier side of things. The alternation between these voices is clear and striking throughout but perhaps nowhere more so than when it occurs within the same sentence: "has he once forgotten the laws of politeness, and showed the monster's hideous tail above water?" The hierarchy established between the voices brings the snideness of the showman's metavoice into play. The melodramatic voice is privileged here: The chief effect of the passage is to convey the showman's clear condemnation of Becky as a hideous female creature.[6] The refined voice acts as a cover under which the showman asserts that Becky is ugly, fiendish, and murderous. Thackeray's early understanding of how Becky's behavior can be seen as shaped and constrained by the patriarchy seems to have vanished. Instead, the showman enjoys himself at Becky's expense and asks us to do the same as he links her with a whole group of creatures whose evil derives in part from their femaleness and especially from their female sexuality.

In linking Becky this way, the showman is not only performing an all too familiar sexist maneuver but asking his readers to enjoy the cleverness of his performance. We are left in the position of either joining him in his perpetuation of the values of the patriarchy or repudiating the performance, clever and skillful though it is. From the feminist perspective, the choice is simple, and our evaluation of Thackeray and the book as a whole must be very mixed indeed.

At the same time, Thackeray's sliding away from a feminist perspective on his female characters can be approached from a different direction, one that privileges the rhetorical perspective. If Thackeray has the perspective sometime, why doesn't he have it all the time? Or, to put the question another way, are there good—or at least plausible—reasons, within the working of the narrative itself, why he would turn away from the insights yielded by that perspective?

If we consider the narrative as a whole once again, then the lack of consistency in the critique of the patriarchy can be seen in a different light. Thackeray is a moralist as well as a social analyst, and he insists on locating some instances of vanity and its related sins—as well as its opposite virtues—in individuals themselves: Consider his treatment of Jos Sedley on the one side and of Dobbin (for most of

6. G. Armour Craig, "On the Style of *Vanity Fair*," in *Style in Prose Fiction*, ed. Harold Martin (New York: Columbia University Press, 1959), 87–113, argues that in many cases the narrator's coyness about Becky's guilt, e.g., in her relationship with Lord Steyne, adds to the complexity of the issue. McMaster, *Thackeray*, makes a similar point. As will become clear, I do not think the coyness works that way in this passage.

the narrative) on the other. Since his aim is to show the multifarious and ubiquitous operations of vanity, then sometimes he uses Becky and Amelia as instruments for exposing vanity in others or in the structures governing the society, and at other times as exemplars of certain manifestations of the problem. If Thackeray used his female protagonists only as instruments of exposure, then his critique of patriarchy would be stronger and more consistent, but his demonstration of the omnipresent workings of vanity would be weakened.

In other words, our evaluation is complicated here by our awareness of Thackeray's purpose. It is one thing to fault him for failing to be consistent in his exposure of patriarchy if such exposure is his purpose, quite another to fault him for that when the accomplishment of a different purpose makes the inconsistency almost necessary. In the first case, we would be meeting him on ground that he has staked out for himself; in the second, we are insisting that he occupy our ground. The first case is unproblematic, the second more intriguing. We can, I think, still fault him: From the feminist perspective, his very purpose is questionable, because his attempt to locate vanity in Becky and Amelia is tantamount to blaming the victim. But our awareness that we are making him occupy our ground should also, I think, give him a chance to talk back. Why are you so convinced that these women are only victims? Is not your concern with the patriarchy as a social institution itself too limited, one that does not sufficiently consider—as my book does—the ways in which certain women manipulate it for their own vain or otherwise unworthy ends?

These questions from a hypothetical Thackeray yielded by our rhetorical understanding of the book can of course be answered from the feminist perspective; for example, the manipulation can itself be seen as the only possible alternative they have. Indeed, one might project Becky herself into a twentieth-century feminist perspective and listen to her voice evaluate Thackeray's treatment of her and Amelia. These answers in turn would create further response from our hypothetical Thackeray, who in the presence of Becky could employ his skill at modulating voices to make his case. Exactly where such a dialogue would end will no doubt vary from reader to reader, according to how strongly each believes in certain key matters such as the influence of social organization on individual behavior. The larger point for my purposes here is that the rhetorical and feminist perspectives usefully complicate our responses to Thackeray's achievement with voice and with the narrative as a whole. Despite the limitations I have pointed to—indeed, to some extent because of them—*Vanity Fair* offers a rich encounter to any rhetorician who tries to listen to it as a feminist.

# Chronology

| | | |
|---|---|---|
| 1811 | July 18 | Born in Calcutta |
| 1815 | Sept. 13 | Death of his father, Richmond Thackeray |
| 1817 | June 15 | Arrives in England from India; attends boarding school |
| 1819 | | Thackeray's mother returns to England as Mrs. Carmichael-Smyth |
| 1822–28 | | Attends Charterhouse School in London |
| 1825 | | Carmichael-Smyths move to Devon |
| 1829–30 | | Attends Trinity College, Cambridge |
| 1830 | June | Leaves Cambridge, having lost £1,500 gambling |
| | July–Mar. '31 | In Germany |
| 1831 | June | Enters Middle Temple to study law |
| 1833 | | Engages in bill discounting; becomes part owner and Paris correspondent for *The National Standard*; studies art in Paris; loses fortune through failure of Indian bank |
| 1834 | | Failure of *The National Standard* |
| 1835 | | Continues art studies |
| 1836 | | *Flore et Zéphyr* published; marries Isabella Shawe; begins publishing in *The Constitutional* |
| 1837 | Mar. | Moves to London |
| | June 9 | Birth of Anne Isabella Thackeray (later Lady Ritchie) |
| | July | *The Constitutional* fails |
| | Nov. | Begins *The Yellowplush Papers* |
| 1838 | May | Begins *Catherine* in *Fraser's Magazine* |
| | July 9 | Jane born |
| 1839 | Mar. 14 | Jane dies |
| 1840 | May 27 | Harriet Marian born (later Mrs. Leslie Stephen) |
| | June | Begins *A Shabby Genteel Story* in *Fraser's* |
| | July | *The Paris Sketch Book* published |
| | Sept. | Wife Isabella's insanity recognized |
| 1841 | Jan. | *The Second Funeral of Napoleon* published |
| | Sept. | Begins *The Great Hoggarty Diamond* in *Fraser's* |
| 1842 | June | Begins contributions to *Punch Magazine* |
| | July–Nov. | In Ireland writing travel book |
| 1843 | | *The Irish Sketch-Book* published |

| | | |
|---|---|---|
| 1844 | Jan. | Begins *Barry Lyndon* in *Fraser's* |
| | Aug–Nov. | Tours Mediterranean |
| 1845 | May | Manuscript of beginning of *Novel without a Hero* submitted to Colburn, who rejects it |
| 1846 | Jan. | *Notes of a Journey from Cornhill to Grand Cairo* published |
| | Mar. | Begins *The Book of Snobs* in *Punch* |
| | April | First number of *Novel without a Hero* set in type, then abandoned |
| | Autumn | Adopts *Vanity Fair* as title and revises first number |
| | Dec. | *Mrs. Perkins's Ball* published |
| 1847 | Jan. | Begins publication of *Vanity Fair* |
| | June | Quarrels with John Forster |
| | Dec. | *Our Street* published |
| 1848 | June | Completes *Vanity Fair* |
| | Aug. | Begins *Pendennis* |
| | Nov. | First number of *Pendennis* published |
| | Dec. | *Dr. Birch and His Young Friends* published |
| 1949 | Sept. | Serious illness interrupts all work for three months |
| | Dec. | *Rebecca and Rowena* published |
| 1850 | Jan. | "Dignity of literature" controversy with John Forster |
| | Nov. | *Pendennis* finished |
| | Dec. | Begins work on *English Humourists* lectures; *The Kickleburys on the Rhine* published |
| 1851 | | Lectures in London, Cambridge, Oxford, and Scotland |
| | Aug. | Begins *Henry Esmond* |
| | Dec. | Resigns from *Punch* over political differences |
| 1852 | | Lectures in London, Manchester, Liverpool, and Scotland |
| | Oct. | *Henry Esmond* published |
| | Oct. | Begins five-month lecture tour in America; visits New York, Boston, Providence, Philadelphia, Baltimore, Washington, Richmond, Savannah, and Charleston |
| 1853 | April | Returns to England, travels on Continent |
| | July | Begins *The Newcomes* |
| | Oct. | First number of *The Newcomes* published |
| | Nov.–Mar. '54 | Travels on Continent, especially Rome and Naples |
| 1854 | Jan. | Begins *The Rose and the Ring* |
| | Dec. | *The Rose and the Ring* published |
| 1855 | July | Final number of *The Newcomes* published |
| | Aug. | Begins *The Four Georges* lectures |
| | Oct.–April '56 | Lecture tour of America |
| 1856 | July | Briefly begins *The Virginians* |

| | | |
|---|---|---|
| | Nov.–May '57 | Lectures on four Georges in England and Scotland |
| 1857 | May | Begins again on *The Virginians* |
| | July | Fails in bid for seat in Parliament |
| | Nov. | First number of *The Virginians* published |
| 1858 | June–Mar. '59 | Controversy with Edmond Yates over the "Garrick Club affair" |
| 1859 | Aug. | Agrees to edit a new magazine to be called *The Cornhill Magazine* |
| | Sept. | Completes *The Virginians* |
| 1860 | Jan. | First number of *The Cornhill Magazine* published, containing the first of *Lovel the Widower* and *Roundabout Papers* |
| | Mar. | Buys his final home at 2 Palace Green, Kensington |
| 1861 | Jan. | First number of *The Adventures of Philip* published in *The Cornhill* |
| 1862 | Mar. | Resigns as editor of *The Cornhill* |
| | July | Completes *The Adventures of Philip* |
| 1863 | May | Begins *Denis Duval* |
| | Nov. | Final *Roundabout Paper* published |
| | Dec. 24 | Thackeray dies |
| | Dec. 29 | Buried in Kensal Green Cemetery |

# Selected Bibliography

Within each section the arrangement is chronological. This list excludes items excerpted in Backgrounds and Criticism.


**Editions:**

Thackeray, William Makepeace. *Vanity Fair.* Edited by Peter Shillingsburg with historical introduction by Robert Colby and note on illustrations by Nicholas Pickwoad. New York: Garland, 1989.

**Letters:**

*The Letters and Private Papers of William Makepeace Thackeray.* Edited by Gordon N. Ray. 4 vols. Cambridge, Mass: Harvard University Press, 1944.

A supplement in 2 volumes, edited by Edgar F. Harden, is projected. New York: Garland.

**Bibliography, Primary:**

Melville, Lewis [pseud.]. *William Makepeace Thackeray: A Biography, Including Hitherto Uncollected Letters and Speeches and a Bibliography of 1,300 Items.* 2 vols. London: John Lane, 1910.

Van Duzer, Henry S. *A Thackeray Library.* 1919. Reprint, New York: Kennikat Press, 1965.

**Bibliography, Secondary:**

Flamm, Dudley. *Thackeray's Critics.* Chapel Hill: University of North Carolina Press, 1967 (with a checklist of nineteenth-century criticism).

Olmsted, John C. *Thackeray and His Twentieth-Century Critics: An Annotated Bibliography, 1900–1975.* New York: Garland, 1977.

Goldfarb, Sheldon. *William Makepeace Thackeray: An Annotated Bibliography, 1976–1987.* New York: Garland, 1989.

**Biography:**

Tillotson, Geoffrey. *Thackeray the Novelist.* Cambridge: Cambridge University Press, 1954. Reprint, London: Methuen, 1963.

Ray, Gordon N. *Thackeray: The Uses of Adversity.* New York: McGraw-Hill, 1955.

——. *Thackeray: The Age of Wisdom.* New York: McGraw-Hill, 1958.

Forster, Margaret. *Memoirs of a Victorian Gentleman.* London: Martin Secker and Warburg, 1978.

Monsarrat, Ann. *An Uneasy Victorian: Thackeray the Man, 1811–1863.* New York: Dodd, Mead, 1980.

**Backgrounds, Reception, and Criticism:**

Masson, David. "Popular Serial Literature." *North British Review* 7 (May 1847).

[Chorley, Henry F.] Review. *Athenaeum* (July 24, 1847).

[Anon.] Review. *Times* (July 10, 1848).

[Forster, John.] Review. *Examiner* (July 22, 1848).

[Rintoul, Robert S.] Review. *Spectator* 21 (July 22, 1848).

[Anon.] "A Contrast." *Bentley's Miscellany* 24 (September 1848).

B[risted], C[harles] A. Review. *American (Whig) Review* 8 (October 1848).

[Anon.] "Contemporary Authors—Mr. Thackeray." *Dublin University Magazine* 32 (October 1848).

[Anon.] "Two English Novelists: Dickens and Thackeray." *Dublin Review,* NS 16 (April 1871): 315–50.

Trollope, Anthony. *Thackeray.* London: Macmillian, 1879.

Stevens, Leslie. "The Writings of W. M. Thackeray." Introduction to *Works of William Makepeace Thackeray,* deluxe edition. 24: 305–67. London: Smith, Elder, 1879.

Howells, William Dean. *My Literary Passions,* 97–103. New York: Harper, 1895.

Cross, Wilbur L. "The Return to Realism." In *Development of the English Novel,* 196–211. New York: Macmillan, 1899.

Chesterton, G. K. *Thackeray.* London: G. Bell, 1909.

Saintsbury, George. Introductions to the Oxford edition of Thackeray's Works, 17 vols. (London: Oxford University Press, 1917). Reprint in *A Consideration of Thackeray* (London: Oxford University Press, 1931).

Lubbock, Percy. *The Craft of Fiction,* Chapter 7. London: Jonathan Cape, 1921.

Dodds, John. *Thackeray: A Critical Portrait.* New York: Oxford University Press, 1941.

Greig, J. Y. T. *Thackeray: A Reconsideration.* London: Oxford University Press, 1950.

Brown, E. K. *Rhythm in the Novel*, 3–30. Toronto: University of Toronto Press, 1950.

Ray, Gordon N. "One Version of the Novelist's Responsibility." *Essays by Divers Hands* 25 (1950): 87–101.

Van Ghent, Dorothy. *The English Novel: Form and Function*, 139–52. New York: Holt, Rinehart and Winston, 1953.

Lester, John. "Thackeray's Narrative Technique." *PMLA* 69 (1954): 392–409.

Johnson, E. D. H. "*Vanity Fair* and *Amelia*: Thackeray in the Perspective of the Eighteenth Century." *Modern Philology* 59 (1961): 100–13.

Harden, Edgar F. "The Function of Mock-Heroic Satire in *Vanity Fair*." *Anglia* 84 (1966): 178–95.

Hannah, Donald. " 'The Author's Own Candles': The Significance of the Illustrations to *Vanity Fair*." In *Renaissance and Modern Essays Presented to Vivian de Soal Pinto in Celebration of His Seventieth Birthday*, edited by G. R. Hibbard, 119–27. London: Routledge and Kegan Paul, 1966.

Blodgett, Harriet. "Necessary Presence: The Rhetoric of the Narrator in *Vanity Fair*." *Nineteenth Century Fiction* 22 (1967): 211–23.

Priestley, F. E. L. Introduction to *Vanity Fair*. New York: Odyssey, 1969.

Knoepflmacher, U. C. "*Vanity Fair*: The Bitterness of Retrospection." In *Laughter and Despair: Readings in Ten Novels*, 50–83. Berkeley and Los Angeles: University of California Press, 1971.

Mauskopf, Charles. "Thackeray's Concept of the Novel." *Philological Quarterly* 50 (1971): 239–52.

McMaster, Juliet. *Thackeray: The Major Novels*. Toronto: University of Toronto Press, 1971.

Hardy, Barbara. *The Exposure of Luxury: Radical Themes in Thackeray*. London: Peter Owen, 1972.

Sutherland, John. "A Date for the Early Composition of *Vanity Fair*." *English Studies* 53 (1972): 47–52.

Monod, Sylvère. " 'Brother Wearers of Motley.' " *Essays and Studies*, NS 26 (1973): 66–82.

Sutherland, John. "The Expanding Narrative of *Vanity Fair*." *Journal of Narrative Technique* 3 (1973): 149–69.

Iser, Wolfgang. "The Reader as a Component Part of the Realistic Novel: Esthetic Effects in Thackeray's *Vanity Fair*." In *The Implied Reader: Patterns of Communication in Prose Fiction from Bunyan to Beckett*. Baltimore: Johns Hopkins University Press, 1974.

Sutherland, John. *Thackeray at Work*. London: Athlone Press, 1974.

Lougy, Robert E. "Fiction and Satire: The Warped Looking Glass in *Vanity Fair*." *PMLA* 90 (1975): 256–69.

Sheets, Robin Ann. "Art and Artistry in *Vanity Fair*." *ELH* 42 (1975): 420–32.

Gneiting, Teona Tone. "The Pencil's Role in Vanity Fair." *Huntington Library Quarterly* 39 (1976): 171–202.

McMaster, Juliet. "Thackeray's Things: Time's Local Habitation." In *The Victorian Experience: The Novelists*, edited by Richard A. Levine, 49–86. Athens: Ohio University Press, 1976.

Véga-Ritter, Max. "Women under Judgment in *Vanity Fair*." *Cahiers Victoriens ed Edouardiens* 3 (1976): 7–23.

Williamson, Jerry W. "Thackeray's Mirror." *Tennessee Studies in Literature* 22 (1977): 133–53.

Harden, Edgar F. *The Emergence of Thackeray's Serial Fiction*. Athens: University of Georgia Press, 1979.

DiBattista, Maria. "The Triumph of Clytemnestra: The Charades in *Vanity Fair*." *PMLA* 95 (1980): 827–37.

Polhemus, Robert M. *Comic Faith: The Great Tradition from Austen to Joyce*. Chicago: University of Chicago Press, 1980.

Scarry, Elaine. "Enemy and Father: Comic Equilibrium in Number Fourteen of *Vanity Fair*." *Journal of Narrative Technique* 10 (1980): 145–55.

Bledsoe, Robert T. "*Vanity Fair* and Singing." *Studies in the Novel* 13 (1981): 51–63.

Musselwhite, David. "Notes on a Journey to Vanity Fair." *Literature and History* 7 (1981): 62–90. Reprinted in *Partings Welded Together: Politics and Desire in the Nineteenth-Century English Novel*. London: Methuen, 1987.

Fisher, Judith. "Siren and Artist: Contradiction in Thackeray's Aesthetic Ideal." *Nineteenth-Century Fiction* 39 (1985): 392–419.

Simon, Richard Keller. "*Vanity Fair*: The History of Comedy." In *The Labyrinth of the Comic*, 117–37. Tallahassee: Florida State University Press, 1985.

Dalski, H. M. "Strategies in *Vanity Fair*." In *Unities: Studies in the English Novel*. Athens: University of Georgia Press, 1985.

MacKay, Carol H. *Soliloquy in Nineteenth-Century Fiction*. London: Macmillan, 1987.

Prawer, Siegbert S. *Israel at Vanity Fair: Jews and Judaism in the Writings of W. M. Thackeray*. Leiden and New York: E. Brill, 1992.